by Irving Wallace

Fiction

THE PLOT
THE MAN
THE THREE SIRENS
THE PRIZE
THE CHAPMAN REPORT
THE SINS OF PHILIP FLEMING

Nonfiction

THE SUNDAY GENTLEMAN
THE TWENTY-SEVENTH WIFE
THE FABULOUS SHOWMAN
THE SQUARE PEGS
THE FABULOUS ORIGINALS

THE
PLOT

a novel by

IRVING
WALLACE

SIMON AND SCHUSTER
New York

SECOND PRINTING

LIBRARY OF CONGRESS CATALOG CARD NUMBER: 67-16723
MANUFACTURED IN THE UNITED STATES OF AMERICA
AMERICAN BOOK—STRATFORD PRESS, NEW YORK

To
Three Loves plus One
Sylvia
David
Amy
&
Paris

'Tis time to fear when tyrants seem to kiss.
—SHAKESPEARE, 1608

Be patient, my soul: thou hath suffered
worse than this.
—HOMER, *c*.800 B.C.

I

H E STARED AHEAD, WAITING.
They were late.

He was tempted to divert his gaze from Houston Street to the grassy knoll sloping from the railroad bridge on his right, to see if the other one waited, too. But he knew that he did not dare the distraction.

Kneeling at the sixth-floor corner window, safely shielded from the doorway behind him by the semicircle of piled cardboard cartons stamped BOOKS, facing the lower portion of the window that had been raised halfway, he rested his gloved left hand on his thigh and his naked right hand on the wooden stock of the bolt-action rifle that leaned against the three stacked cartons beside him.

He concentrated on the ribbon of thoroughfare below. They were almost five minutes late now. Nerveless, unmoved, unmoving, he continued to wait.

And then in the near distance, he saw them. The procession of the motorcade came into view as it turned off Main Street onto Houston. Silently, he counted. First, the motorcycles. Second, the pilot car. Third, another phalanx of motorcycles. Fourth, the lead car. Fifth, the 1961 Lincoln limousine, the open limousine minus the plastic bubble-top, with its four occupants in the rear barely distinguishable.

His eyes narrowed and held on the Lincoln limousine alone as it moved slowly north on Houston Street toward the Texas School Book Depository and eventually the Triple Underpass.

Watching, he saw the limousine, its chrome gleaming in the sun, reach the intersection of Houston Street and Elm Street, and then begin its slow turn into Elm, which curved southwest at a slight downgrade past him toward the Triple Underpass and the Freeway.

His eyes caught the dial of the large steel wristwatch above his gloved hand. The time was 12:30.

Unhurriedly, using both hands, he picked up the 7.65 bolt-action Mauser, adjusted the cheap wooden stock against his shoulder, rested the barrel firmly upon the uppermost tilted carton, poked the rifle through the bottom half of the window, and braced a knee beneath the sixth-story window ledge.

Calmly he placed his right eye behind the four-power telescopic sight attached to the barrel.

At once the radiator of the Lincoln limousine spread wide and clear to his aiming eye. Shifting his rifle slightly upward and to the left, he caught and focused upon the occupants of the open rear of the car, their heads and shoulders appearing almost life-size in his magnifier. Gently he shifted the rifle scope again, so that the intersection of the cross hairs in the glass fastened upon the brown-haired young head, tracked that head in the circle, and then he knew that he had it.

Unexpectedly the head was gone, blocked out by the heavy foliage of an oak tree. Then for a fleeting moment the head was visible through the leaves and branches. For an instant it was hidden a second time, and suddenly the limousine emerged into the clear, and the head, caught again in his scope, was unobstructed.

His forefinger tugged at the trigger.

There was a loud clap in his ear.

As he threw the bolt open to eject the empty cartridge case, he heard the second shot, and he knew it was not an echo.

Pigeons, in a frightened flurry, were noisily flapping off their perches and taking wing above him. Undistracted, his eye stayed at the telescopic sight, where the brown-haired head remained frozen in his scope, but now a hand had gone to the throat.

He pulled the trigger again. There was the clap in his ear once more, followed by a distant fourth explosion, no echo of his own shot. With a reflex motion he threw the bolt, reloading the chamber.

Relentlessly his glass-reinforced eye followed the receding target. The head, its skull partially torn away, began to lurch forward and then to the left. Hastily he pulled the trigger one last time, but this shot, he knew, had missed, for the head had left the view of his magnifying scope too soon.

Coolly he drew the rifle back into the room. He glanced at the bridge above the underpass, where at least a dozen terrified people were milling, scattering, and then his gaze went to the grassy knoll where more frightened people seemed to be scrambling away.

He rose slowly and backed against his fortress of cartons. Carefully, yet swiftly, efficiently, he found his handkerchief. Then holding the Mauser in his gloved hand, he wiped down the barrel, the knob of the bolt, the trigger and its housing, the wooden stock. Forcing his handkerchief into a suit-coat pocket, still holding the rifle in his gloved hand, he dusted his trouser knee with his bare hand and smoothed his wrinkled suit.

Quickly, now, he left the carton barricade and crossed the storage room. If there had been no mistake or miscalculation, the sixth-floor corridor would be empty. The warehouseman, the shipping wrapper, the clerk who filled orders, were all just below, on the fifth floor, eating lunch as they watched the motorcade. There would be only one person arriving on this floor shortly. That had been arranged.

He hesitated at the door, peered at his wristwatch. One minute and thirty-five seconds had passed. There was still time enough.

Confidently he stepped into the corridor. As he had expected, it was empty.

With caution, but without haste, he walked up the corridor, the rifle still gripped in his gloved left hand, held vertically close to his body. Near the landing of the sixth-floor staircase, there were rows of boxes. He went to them, lowered the Mauser between two of the rows, and, with his shoe, pushed the weapon out of view.

Behind him he heard the grinding of the east elevator, then the jolting sound of its stop. Falling back slightly, he looked down the corridor.

The elevator door was opening. A slight figure, that of a young man holding a clipboard with attached invoices for book orders, appeared in the hall. He studied the man. There was no mistake. The man was Lee Harvey Oswald.

The moment Oswald disappeared into the room that he himself had just left, he would be free.

After that, there would not be any time to lose. In those seconds when Oswald saw the arrangement of the cartons at the window and the empty cartridge shells on the floor, and heard the chaos outside six floors beneath the open window, he would dimly comprehend, would realize his own position and how he had been used. Oswald would be out of that room fast.

He watched Oswald start for the room. He watched until Oswald disappeared inside it.

Then, instantly, he abandoned his position next to the cartons in the corridor and rushed to the west freight elevator, pushed the wall button, waited for the car, and entered it. He took it down to the fifth floor and left it. Going rapidly, he headed for the staircase and speedily he descended to the fourth floor. There, on the landing, he halted. He could hear footsteps of persons scrambling up toward him. Casting about for the vestibule, he found it and quickly ducked inside. Seconds later he caught a glimpse of two breathless men, one in the uniform of the Dallas police, the other in ordinary dress, hurrying past to continue their climb. The moment that they were out of sight, he left the vestibule and resumed his steady descent to the first floor.

Arriving on the ground floor below, he consulted his watch one last time. Three minutes and ten seconds had passed. There would be activity at the front entrance of the building. But the rear would yet be unobserved and unguarded.

He went out the rear exit. There was no one to stop him.

What had been plotted in Vienna, thirty months before this month and this day, had finally been successfully achieved in the faraway alien place called Dallas. The deed was done. Already it was history. The future would be better for it. And best of all, the logical killer would be found, would be convicted, and so the case would be closed forever. All of them were beyond suspicion, and all of them were safe. . . .

Or so the assassins of an American President reasoned on the afternoon of November 22, 1963, and in the months and years to follow.

But they were wrong.

For I am here to write that "he" is known and "they" are known, that their evil international conspiracy and horrendous political crime are known, fully known, to this reporter, after years of relentless sleuthing and research.

Like Zola's *J'accuse* against the conspirators who used the innocent Captain Dreyfus to protect the true author of the *bordereau,* and the true betrayers of France, this documented brief is my accusation against, and exposé of, the conspirators who used the innocent Oswald to mask their roles in the most infamous assassination of the twentieth century.

Before the bar of history, Truth, like murder, Will Out. And so, the world shall hear the Truth, at last. . . .

*A*nd so, the world shall hear the Truth, at last.

Jay Thomas Doyle's puffy hands remained at rest on the keyboard of his Swiss portable typewriter as he contemplated the last sentence he had written.

It was powerful enough to cap the opening section of his book, a

12

provocative sentence that would surely bring a million readers excitedly into the heart of his sensational story. Yet, perhaps, as things stood, it promised too much. Considering the one piece of evidence that he still lacked, the categorical and authoritative ring of that sentence might invite a subsequent letdown and a reaction of antagonism from his book's next reader—and that might be fatal.

Thoughtfully, Jay Thomas Doyle weighed the possibility of modifying the last sentence, in fact, the last paragraphs, and instinctively he knew that what he had just finished typing must stand as it had been written.

The approval of the next reader of his manuscript, perhaps his last reader for better or for worse, was too crucial to Doyle's life and future to risk losing because of equivocation and moderation in his narrative. Better, by far, to chance promising everything and deliver only half, than to promise half and default entirely. His next reader had been lured here to Vienna by great expectations. Any other bait would have failed to catch him.

In less than two hours, this next reader, Sydney Ormsby, head of Ormsby Books, a subsidiary of Ormsby Press Enterprises, Ltd., of London, would be sitting across from him at dinner, reading the pages he had written and rewritten, and now rewritten at least a tenth time, during these years. There had been too many rejections and failures before. This was the last Main Chance. The very fact that instead of going directly to Paris Sydney Ormsby had come to Vienna first, merely to read Doyle's chapter and his detailed outline, meant that the publisher's interest was keen. There must be no disappointing him. At the moment that he picked up the first page, he must become engrossed.

As to the ending of the exposé, if it did not live up to its beginning, no matter. Ormsby would have been gripped through it until then, and there would be time enough to discuss what yet was possible. He might regale Ormsby with an old Edgar Wallace anecdote. Wallace had published a serial, and at the end of the exciting opening installment the hero had been trapped in a deep well, snared, lost, with no possibility of escape, and hundreds of thousands of British readers had held their collective breath for the opening of the second installment and the solution. When the second installment had appeared, it began, blithely, "Once out of the well . . ."

Yes, Doyle decided, he would let stand what he had written, unaltered by timidity or conservatism.

He yanked the page out of the typewriter, slipped it behind the other four pages he had just rewritten and retyped, and clipped them to the thirty-page outline of the remainder of the book. Pushing his huge bulk, imprisoned in the modernistic chair, away from the table that held his portable typewriter, Doyle clumsily backed into the footboard of his bed, and there was a clatter of dishes from the tray on the bed behind him.

With a shoatish grunt, Doyle turned his chair to examine with relief and affection the abundant tray of tantalizing food that Room Service had delivered from the kitchen a half hour ago, and that he had neglected in his absorption with work. It was this, the products of the Hotel Imperial's kitchen, this and the fact that the management remembered his days of glory with the same awed respect that they still conferred upon the reign of Emperor Franz Joseph, that brought Doyle back to the Imperial on each visit to Vienna and overcame his aversion to the hostel's disquietingly contemporary rooms.

His single and bath, like most of the other 154 rooms, contradicted the traditional ambience of the old Austrian city and the needs of his own person. The furniture, functional and reminiscent of Swedish modern, like the colors and lighting, was too bright, too jarring, and the lines of the chairs, divan, tables were too geometrical, too angular, for one of his soft, fleshy rotundity. Friends, the few that were left, described him (as they had described an eminent journalist predecessor) as one who dressed like, and resembled, an unmade bed.

Except when shaving—an act that seemed as time-consuming as trying to mow an African veldt—Doyle avoided mirrors. He was tired of their rebuke, tired of the infinite recession of hairline moving up toward the sparse thin hair struggling to survive on top of his cranial desert, tired of the oxlike eyes and rubicund bulbous nose wedged between bulging cheeks, tired of the contour of two chins that now had a chin of their own, tired of his hamlike arms and the protuberant belly that hung over his belt. At forty-five, and at this morning's reckoning 240 pounds on the scale, he was the victim, he knew, of countless gastronomical orgies in countless temples of alimentary seduction like La Scala, The Four Seasons, Mirabelle, Lapérouse, La Réserve, Tre Scalini.

Not many years ago, in the time of his fame, in the time of those duchesses and actresses and Hazel, he had been stocky and attractive. But failure had brought him down to his avocation, gastronomy, and continuing failure had eventually reduced him from gourmet to glutton, and so he was no longer stocky and attractive. He was, no corroborating mirror needed, fat and repulsive. He was a man still, but doubled and redoubled. He envied those lost even to alcohol or lust. At least their weaknesses were serious. His weakness was low comedy. Yet he was helpless, and if he disliked the rooms in the Hotel Imperial, he was in one of them without complaint because here was the incomparable kitchen, a kitchen which was not new Vienna but old Vienna, and which catered to a civilized people on the Danube who ate five meals a day, and which rendered him helpless.

There was the waiting tray on his bed, meant for the day's fourth repast, the *Jause,* the afternoon snack. Doyle's porcine eyes caressed the platters. There was the heaping plate of Bauernschmaus, and next to the sausages, sauerkraut, dumplings, there was the still-warm coffee, and next to that the generous portion of Guglhupf mit Schlag, the treasure of rich pound cake buried under a mountain of whipped cream.

Accompanying his action with an asthmatic wheeze, Jay Thomas Doyle removed the typewriter from the table, and replaced it with the tray holding his *Jause,* and then he succumbed, each mouthful and swallow punctuated by a purr of ecstasy. As he ate, his tension abated, and he complacently examined the title page of his manuscript: *The Conspirators Who Killed Kennedy . . . The Sensational Factually Documented Exposé* by Jay Thomas Doyle. He began to turn the familiar pages and to proofread them. Once again, unfailingly, the manuscript renewed his spirits, just as, when he had been a youngster and impatient with school in November, he had been renewed by the knowledge that there would always be Christmas in December.

Presently the five pages were read and finished. And so, too, the Bauernschmaus and Guglhupf mit Schlag were finished. And Jay Thomas Doyle, his dulled palate and distended stomach still ravenous, felt revived and almost ready to sit across from the all-important Sydney Ormsby at an elegant dinner table in the Hotel Sacher restaurant, awaiting the decision.

Belching softly, Doyle struggled to his feet and thumped across the lavender carpet to the divan where his mobile file, a scuffed brown briefcase, lay open against the throw pillows. He had meant to insert the manuscript in the handsome fiber folder in readiness for Ormsby, and then to dress for dinner, but his traveling clock on the chiffonier told him that there was an hour and twenty minutes until his appointment.

Although, without further food to sustain him, it would be a distressing, nervous-making gap of time, he reminded himself that it could be a useful time. By concentrating, he might be able to review his entire book outline and detect any trivial flaws that had escaped the critical scrutiny of so many previous publishers who had stupidly declined his earlier drafts. Also, he realized, a rereading of his revised chapter notes would refresh his memory and better arm him to turn aside any of Ormsby's challenges.

Settling into the uncomfortable divan, spreading out on its resisting cushion, Doyle placed the manuscript beside him, turned to the briefcase, finally located and extracted a manila folder labeled CORRESPONDENCE.

Opening it, he found the carbon copy of his clever letter to Sydney Ormsby, written some weeks ago from Munich, introducing himself with modest but effective understatement ("Besides remembering me for my three topical books on conflicts around the world, you may remember me as the author of the daily column 'Inside and Straight,' which was syndicated to 509 newspapers in the United States and Great Britain, with a readership estimated at 16,000,000"). His letter then advised Ormsby that he had given up the column to return to books, especially one book, a sensational and factual exposé ("which I am at last ready to present to a publisher, a book requiring a publisher with the power and facilities to communicate it to as wide an audience as possible, and my friends in high places have assured me that Ormsby Press Enterprises, Ltd., is just such a publisher"). Then, in three hard-hitting, pithy paragraphs, Doyle had dangled the bait, and added that he would be pleased to meet with Ormsby in Vienna, his next stop, or was free to fly to London, if necessary, to submit his manuscript and discuss it.

Clipped to his carbon copy was Sydney Ormsby's reply, typed on the finest rag paper, grandly embossed "Ormsby Press Enterprises, Ltd., Book Publishing Division, Red Lion Square, London, W.C.1" and "Office of the Managing Director." Hopeful as Doyle had been, the promptness of Sydney Ormsby's response, its unqualified enthusiasm and accommodation, had taken him by surprise.

Ormsby had written that he was fully aware of Doyle's reputation as a journalist, and indeed he and his brother, Sir Austin Ormsby, were admirers of Doyle's prose and followed his daily column avidly. (The last had disconcerted Doyle briefly, since for two years he'd had no column to be followed "avidly," but he attributed the inaccuracy to fervor and to the fact that his columns had been so memorable that they still seemed, to Constant Readers, quite current and alive.) Ormsby and his staff, Ormsby had written, were unanimous in their opinion that Doyle's exposé on the Kennedy assassination, so long hoped for, so long needed after so many previous volumes of mere speculation, could become one of the most widely read books of the twentieth century. If Doyle was, as he had indicated, prepared to allow Ormsby to see the manuscript outline on an exclusive basis, Ormsby was prepared, upon reading the outline, to offer the best contract possible for worldwide rights, accompanied by a generous cash advance that would give Doyle the freedom needed to complete his opus. While Ormsby would not be in London in the next weeks—he was accompanying his brother, Sir Austin, to the Five-Power Summit Conference in Paris, to which his brother was a delegate, since he himself had business engagements in that city—he would be delighted to change his immediate plans and fly directly to Vienna to dine with Doyle the evening of Saturday, June 14, to discuss the project and conclude the formality of a contract. Would Doyle cable confirming date?

Optimism restored, almost manic with excitement, Doyle had cabled immediately, setting the dinner appointment for seven-thirty in the evening, on June 14, at the Hotel Sacher in Vienna.

Now, upon rereading it, Doyle could see that Ormsby's letter was more than promising. It was, in effect, a contract, or as nearly a contract as a letter could be, and once the formal contract was signed tonight, and the advance payment put in his hands, Doyle's future and inevitable success were guaranteed. For the first time, in all the years since he had undertaken his project, he would have sufficient funds to free himself of restrictive bread-and-butter hackwork, have the funds to go to Moscow and remain there as long as necessary (no matter how costly) to see Hazel Smith and win her favor once more, and if necessary pay her off, and then return to New York with the documentation that would enable him to complete his thunderous best seller.

In a warm glow, thinking of all this, Doyle allowed his fingers to riffle through the stack of letters beneath Ormsby's letter, the buttered rejections from shortsighted American publishers who had not seen the potential of his project, or rather had not believed in it. All of them had been anesthetized by the *Report of the President's Commission on the Assassination of President Kennedy,* and therefore regarded his outline as "farfetched" when, indeed, as he knew and as Hazel knew, it was the Warren Report that was the fable, a quick and easy sop to assuage the guilty conscience of an uneasy American citizenry.

Fortunately—oh, why had he not seen this before, and gone to an English publisher earlier?—Sydney Ormsby, steeped in British tradition, raised on the probability and logic that conspiracy figured in most assassinations of public figures (raised on the planned murders of Thomas à Becket, Edward V and his brother, Sir Thomas Overbury, Colonel Rainsborough, Lord Cavendish, educated in violent intrigues and intriguers like the Rye House Plot, the Gowrie Conspiracy, Guy

Fawkes and the Gunpowder Plot, Sir Roger Casement), would appreciate the likelihood that a conspiracy had arranged President Kennedy's death.

Yes, the British publishers possessed the historical conditioning to accept his book, just as their European neighbors (whose heritage included the conspiratorial liquidations of Henri IV, Rasputin, King Alexander, Foreign Minister Barthou, Archduke Francis Ferdinand, Chancellor Dollfuss, Trotsky, and whose knowledge included a familiarity with Balkan murder societies like IMRO and the Black Hand and the Croatian Ustaša, and political cabals as varied as the Soviet MKVD and KGB and the Nazi Gestapo, all their roots going deep into ancient times to the Ides of March) would accept his evidence and his book. Only in idiot America, milk-fed, hayseed America, would people point a finger at John Wilkes Booth and call him a loner, and forget that Arnold, O'Laughlin, Herold, Atzerodt, Payne, Spangler, Mudd, the Surratts were his conspirators. Only in America would they forget the motivation behind Collazo and Torresola, also conspirators, as they had tried to shoot their way into Blair House to cut down a President. Only in America would citizens close their eyes and ears to the Old World's old-fashioned, ugly word, *conspiracy,* and quickly dispose of the assassination of President Kennedy, a national crime, their crime, by accepting the judgment of a seven-man commission: that the killer, who had played a lone hand, was neurotic, antisocial, and not externally motivated. Thank God, Doyle thought, that he had finally had the sense to approach someone in publishing with intelligence and wisdom.

These reflections continued to hearten Jay Thomas Doyle. In little more than an hour he would confront a publisher who was receptive to his thesis. As important, he would confront a publisher who was—or whose older brother was—a Croesus of communications, no hole-in-the-wall, frayed-cuff, pence-pinching printer in Grub Street or on the fringes of Fleet Street, but a publisher whose empire and largess could match those of Lord Beaverbrook, Cecil Harmsworth King, Lord Kemsley, Roy Thomson, Lord Rothermere. Doyle wondered: Would the request for a $20,000 advance seem too niggardly, as if he were undervaluing his great exposé? Or would $30,000 *and* expenses sound better, just right? He would see, he would judge his man, and he would decide.

With a start, he realized that he still held the open CORRESPONDENCE file in his lap, and that the letters of rejection from American publishers had sent his mind wandering. There was, he saw, one sheaf of letters left, his own carbon copies, really, and these, too, were in a sense rejections.

There were forty or fifty in all, some letters consisting of many pages, some merely notes, and the first had been dated six years before the last one, and they were uniformly addressed to "My Dear Hazel."

Skimming his letters to Hazel, Doyle squirmed as he again recognized their change in tone. The early letters had been romantic, even loving. The middle letters had been hurt, aggrieved, and equated friendship with business. The last letters and notes—and Doyle reddened as he scanned them—had been desperate, abject, pleading, begging, pitiful. Most had been addressed to "Miss Hazel Smith, c/o Atlas News Association" in Moscow. But when he had seen her by-line originate from other places, numerous letters had been addressed to Belgrade, Athens, Istanbul, Calcutta, Hong Kong, always places beyond his physical reach if not that of his pen. All of his letters, like a stuck needle in a phonograph record, played on two notes—their old relationship, and his need of irrefutable evidence proving her sketchy story about a Kennedy conspiracy, told him in Vienna so long ago.

The correspondence with Hazel was unique in only one respect. It was one-way. It contained copies of his letters to her. It contained not a single letter from Hazel to him, not one, not a letter, not a note, not a word. Nor, as he had complained in several of his letters, had she ever been in her office in Moscow when he had expended large sums to telephone her long-distance from New York, London, Paris. Nor had she ever acknowledged the messages that he had left with her associates in the Moscow news service bureau.

To a stranger, Doyle knew, it would appear that he had been addressing himself to a nonexistent person. But Hazel's corporeal existence had been verified daily by the newspapers. Every morning, in these past years, the slug—"by Hazel Smith, ANA special correspondent"—had taunted him. Sometimes his bitterness and anger were directed at the woman who held the key to his future. More often his fury was directed at himself for his callow insensitivity in his handling of her in the past, and his neglect of her when it had most mattered to her. In his masochistic moods, a familiar fragment of poetic chastisement often floated across his mind. Once he had even troubled to look it up. It was from William Congreve's *The Mourning Bride,* and the correct quotation, although he was no happier for knowing it, had been "Heav'n has no rage, like love to hatred turn'd,/Nor Hell a fury, like a woman scorn'd."

True, she had given herself to him, a compliant if bony virgin from Wisconsin. He had been her first love and lover. She had offered herself totally, without reservation, and for over two years he had taken her, and when he had had enough—or rather, when he had had better prospects (or so he had thought)—he had ruthlessly discarded her. The reasonable Doyle accepted her "rage" and "fury" afterwards, as reasonably normal and reasonably just. What he had never been able to understand was the stamina and endurance of her "rage" and "fury" toward him. Years had passed, and apparently they had neither healed nor mellowed her anger. Years had altered their worldly positions, for, no denying it, she was now the success and the celebrity, and he was now the once-successful and the formerly celebrated Jay Thomas Doyle. Now that he needed her, and had gone to her stripped of pride, it amazed him that she had shown no pity.

Yet he had never ceased to believe in the infallible magnetism of his presence. No letter, he had recently decided, no telephone call, could really touch her. Only a personal confrontation, face to face, might restore their old relationship. She had loved him once, and she would love him again. And even if time had so hardened her, there was another approach. For she had grown up in poverty, and struggled, and had always respected the fact that security was synonymous with money. Doyle's openhandedness with money, his lavish spending, had always unnerved her in that other time. No matter what her success now, ANA could not pay her enough to make her invulnerable to a huge cash offer (thank you, Mr. Ormsby). In either case it would work. For love or money, he would have all of Hazel's secret, the information that she had once tried to give him—but had never given him completely because he had ridiculed her—about President Kennedy's assassination, some thirty months before it had actually taken place.

With a sigh that became another wheeze, Doyle closed the CORRESPONDENCE file and returned it to his briefcase. Then, searching between the leather dividers, he found the handsome fiber folder, removed it, and snapped his manuscript into it.

He considered the manuscript lovingly. He was tempted to scan it one more time before turning it over to Ormsby's judgment. It was an indulgence, he knew. He had read and reread it so often, rewritten it so many times, that it was practically committed to memory. Yet, with his last work on it, it was as polished as the Sancy diamond, and he was eager once more to enjoy the reflection from its riches. He looked at the clock. Fifty minutes. Time enough for a hasty perusal, and to change suits and be off with minutes to spare.

But then there was the persistent hollow in his stomach that had to be filled. Heaving himself off the divan, Doyle marched toward the bed and the bountiful tray, forgetting that Lucullus had already sacked it. Dismayed at its emptiness, he wondered if there was time to send down for two more orders of Guglhupf mit Schlag, but then knew that there

20

was not. Frustrated, he began to tramp around the room in anguish, gnawed by hunger pangs, feeling feeble and gaunt, as his jiggling belly joined in his grief. Suddenly, he swerved and made an elephantine charge at his bulging leather suitcase, tore it open, and dug inside, beneath the pajamas, shorts, shirts, socks, for the emergency rations he kept against famine. His groping fingers found the carton of chocolate bars, and then the tin of cashew nuts. His hand encircled the tin and dragged it out through the hodge-podge of apparel.

Perspiring from the effort, Doyle mopped his brow and the top of his pate, then broke off the opener, and shakily unwound the metal strip around the can. Tossing the lid of the can and the oily circle of paper that covered the nuts into the wastebasket, he hurried back to the divan and dropped heavily beside his portfolio. Clawing into the cashews, he excavated a fistful and threw them into his mouth. Crunching and grinding and swallowing, he felt the muscles beneath the folds of his neck untensing at last. With his free hand he brought the fiber folder to his lap, opened it, enjoyed the title page once more, quickly flipped through the first chapter with the five pages he had just retyped. Then, folder in one hand, another fistful of cashews in the other, he began to review hastily his dynamic yet classic prose, a narrative of high adventure and ultimate tragedy that exceeded in drama the best of Euripides.

Masticating the cashews, Doyle began to read his detailed outline for Chapter Two, trying to see it through the eyes of a British publisher like Sydney Ormsby:

This book had its beginnings, even though I did not know it at the time, in Vienna during early June of 1961. A new American President, a vigorous and exciting young Chief Executive, John F. Kennedy, was scheduled to arrive in Vienna for his first official meeting with Nikita S. Khrushchev, Premier of Soviet Russia. As a widely syndicated columnist, then, I naturally was on hand in Vienna, one of 1,400 journalists from every corner of the earth who had converged on the old-fashioned Austrian city of Lehár and Strauss and Franz Joseph, of the Blue Danube and the Ringstrasse and the Prater, to cover this electric Big Two conference, which was to last forty-eight hours. It was during the latter eighteen of those forty-eight hours that I stumbled upon an international conspiracy so daring and shocking in its purpose and implications as to defy credulity. It was in Vienna on June 3, 1961, that I learned that there was a sinister plot, organized by a small group of Cominform conspirators (whether acting officially or unofficially, whether of Russian or Soviet satellite origin, I cannot say), a plot to assassinate John F. Kennedy, either at the Schönbrunn Palace outside Vienna or en route to the Schwechat Airport outside Vienna.

It was late in the afternoon of President Kennedy's first day in Vienna, after his initial conference with Premier Khrushchev in the suburban two-story villa that is the United States Embassy, and before Austrian President Adolf Schärf's dinner for the two leaders in the Great Gallery of Maria Theresa's Schönbrunn Palace, that I first heard of the conspiracy against President Kennedy's life.

Correspondents assigned to cover the conference, and lesser delegates and ministers assigned to lay the groundwork for the meetings, Russians as well as Americans, had arrived in Vienna several days before the Big Two themselves had appeared. Since reporters respect no frontiers—the fourth estate is, in a sense, one world—the American and Russian journalists mixed freely and comfortably together, as did some of the American and Russian delegates, and the vodka and gin flowed, and brief friendships were quickly established in the days before President Kennedy arrived by jet plane from Washington, D.C., via Paris, and Premier Khrushchev arrived by train from Moscow.

It was after three or four days of this friendly mingling between Russian and American reporters and delegates that a longtime friend of mine—a little-known American writer, an attractive young lady whom I knew to be intensely accurate—breathlessly sought me out at the Hotel Imperial. She was in possession of what she called "the greatest news scoop in modern times."

Through interminable hours of heavy drinking, she had become very close to a minor Russian delegate, yet one important enough to be on Premier Khrushchev's advisory staff, and she had become his confidante, and endless glasses of vodka had loosened his tongue. He had hinted to her that he had been approached by a certain group of his Communist colleagues to join them in the liquidation of the one they thought was obstructing Russia's future, to join in a plot to assassinate President Kennedy either that evening or the following day in Vienna. He had backed away from the conspiracy. But it was clear to him that the assassination would take place, if not in Vienna, then elsewhere in the near future, and he deplored it.

My friend felt that she did not possess the journalistic stature to file such a story, but she felt that I did possess such stature, and that if the story came from me it would be accepted and published—and not only would it be a momentous newsbeat, but it would certainly prevent the conspirators from making their assassination attempt.

Because I was loath to file so sensational a story without stronger evidence, because I suspected the story had been leaked to my friend as a trick to discredit our democratic journalist corps, I declined to accept the story as true and refused to write and file it.

When President Kennedy attended the Schönbrunn Palace dinner and left unharmed, when he went to Mass at St. Stephen's Cathedral the following day and met with Khrushchev at the three-story Soviet Embassy shortly after, and emerged from both places unharmed, when he left by jet for London the next morning still unharmed, I felt that my skepticism had been well-founded. Obviously, my innocent female friend had been taken in by a transparent Russian trick. I dismissed this nonsense from my mind.

That was June of 1961.

And then, it was November of 1963—and at Parkland Memorial Hospital in Dallas, President Kennedy, a bullet hole in his throat, a great gaping wound in the right rear of his skull, lay dying, and shortly afterwards the White House assistant press secretary announced his death by an assassin's bullets to the entire stunned world.

The Dallas police, the FBI, and eventually the President's Commission on the Assassination of President Kennedy, with Chief Justice Earl Warren as chairman, announced that the killing had been done by one man, unaffiliated with any political group. That man, they stated, was Lee Harvey Oswald. But my memory went back to a late afternoon in Vienna, thirty months before Dallas, and then I *knew* that the assassination had not been committed by Oswald. I *knew* that it had been committed not merely by another, but by others, by a company of international conspirators. And so I undertook my long, difficult, hazardous hunt, my search for the missing half of the story that had been partially revealed to me in Vienna in 1961. . . .

Jay Thomas Doyle lowered the manuscript to his lap as he reflected on the candor and veracity of his written words, so disarmingly simple and so filled with good purpose, when the real truth of it, or rather the whole truth of it—so inexplicably complex and so cluttered by his personal selfishness and vanity—still lay hidden deep in his mind and conscience, unrevealed in the surface words.

Remembering the whole truth, the secret, private truth most men cannot face seeing in themselves or, facing it, cannot divulge to others—he gradually reconstructed (as a reality of the present that he must live with) what had actually happened in the Vienna of 1961.

Reliving it, he remembered that he was received in the Austrian capital with the ceremony and respect once accorded Hapsburg princes. He was a Big Name then, really big and he was treated as one with absolute authority. He perceived that among his journalistic con-

23

temporaries there were those more erudite, more clever, more wise than himself, yet they were merely philosophers of the fourth estate while he was an emperor, because he had legions to support him. His legions were formed by his vast and loyal reading public, the millions who followed his column and believed his every word. When Doyle issued his daily edicts, lively, dramatic, firsthand reports and opinions on the world's trouble spots—Korea, Algeria, Vietnam, India, Communist China, Mississippi—his followers believed him, hailed him, and their massive plebeian chorus was heard in high places in Washington, D.C., as well as abroad. As a result, the private-key elevator to the sacrosanct seventh floor of the Department of State, and the guarded doors to the Oval Office of the White House, were always wide-open to him. Every President from Eisenhower to Earnshaw had been his friend.

Until that time in Vienna of 1961, and, well, perhaps for a little more than two years after, Doyle had worked alone. Rival news bureaus sent teams of reporters to cover an event. Doyle was a team unto himself. So much in favor was he that he often did not deign to seek information. Story leads came to *him,* and were transformed by his mediocre but showman's intelligence into daily columns under the standing head "Inside and Straight," and thereafter they became mass opinion and sometimes national policy.

As emperor, he needed diversions, rewards beyond money. He wanted the best of food, the most venerable wine, the most sought-after women. The food and wine were always there, but in those days he took them in relative moderation, took them as a gastronome not as a glutton. And the women were there, too, only the most choice, the ones who met his high standards, and although he desired them all, he took them sparingly. Because of his exalted station he was wary of the glittering, easy women. He did not want to be dragged from eminence to a common bed, another "name" conquered by breasty amoral gossips, a vulnerable bedmate trapped in the pillows by so many dangerous Clytemnestras.

Yet that was not his dominant fear of the glittering, easy women. His dominant fear, the one that inhibited him from enjoying the final pleasure he needed, was that he did not want to be used. Instead, he wanted to use. He did not want to be invaded, to be forced to compromise with another, to be made to surrender a portion of his sovereignty to any single overpowering spoiled female. In short, he did not want a royal equal. He wanted a devoted subject. He did not wish a relationship. He wished an accommodating vassal.

And so, for the final diversion, he peered down from his position of eminence, and what he found was Miss Hazel Smith, of Baraboo,

Wisconsin, a cub reporter on the staff of the Atlas News Association and freshly arrived in New York.

Recollecting their early months, Doyle saw Hazel as naïve, pliable, sweet, unformed, and ambitious only at the minimum self-preservation level. Lonely for male companionship, for male warmth, for belonging to someone, she was struck dumb with reverence for, and instantly overwhelmed by, the attention of an emperor. With her submission, Doyle had found his perfect female vassal.

She was anything but beautiful. Her nest of unchic, carroty hair, her close-set eyes and lantern jaw, her flat breasts and splayed hips, her straight legs, were anything but a decorative delight. Certainly, with her shiny face devoid of makeup, her unpolished nails, her masculine gait, and practical shoes, she was not a choice hostess to showcase at gatherings of the great. Doyle's devotion to her often surprised him, he who would reject a plush restaurant for its unesthetic lighting, a dinner jacket for a single seam wrinkle, a Béarnaise sauce for its slight excess of vinegar. Yet he liked her, because she was comfortable, because she was undemanding, because she was whatever he wanted her to be, because she was there. These were the virtues, and there were others. Hazel gave him attentiveness undivided, respect unqualified, and, above all, sexual love uncomplicated by previous experience and undiluted by conflicting interests.

But then, after a year and a half, hardly aware that it was happening, Doyle began to resent her and became ashamed of his affair. He had risen higher and higher, and she had not risen at all, and he was not concerned with the possibility that his own overbearing personality and neurotic boundaries might have arrested her potential growth. He was tiring of her, he began to realize, not because she did not please him in private but because she had become a faint embarrassment to him in their infrequent appearances in public. Her shopgirl plainness lessened his esteem of himself and his good taste when he returned to her after some society ball or exclusive reception at which he had been a star among guest lists culled from the Social Register.

At such times he found himself examining her and re-evaluating her with hard, spoiled eyes. Returning to his Park Avenue apartment, after a penthouse or town house dinner party, where well-bred young women with glossy upswept hair, décolleté beaded gowns, finishing-school accents, the latest flowering of old family trees, had fawned upon him, it became increasingly difficult to desire or feel amorous toward a mistress who did her own hair in plastic curlers, whose stubby fingers were forever stained from changing typewriter ribbons, who wore bargain-basement housecoats, whose accent was harsh Midwestern, and who was too serious about the eleven o'clock news broadcast ever to be gay and frivolous and flirtatious in the late evening.

Comparisons were odious, he knew, yet he could not put them aside. Also, he knew that making a comparison between those who were to the manor born and one who had never had their advantages was unfair, snobbish and somehow demeaned him, who had grown to fame out of the muck and blood and lice of Korea and who had become the Voice of the People. Looking for an answer to his problem, he even reread Dreiser's *An American Tragedy* in paperback, remembering that although Dreiser's hero, Clyde Griffiths, yearned for social position—which Doyle already possessed—his involvement with his mistress, a factory employee, created for him the same conflict that Doyle was enduring and suffering because of Hazel. Dreiser had resolved his hero's problem by having him murder his poor mistress. Doyle decided that this melodrama could hardly be applied to his own life. Dreiser had merely succeeded in making him feel guilty about his attitude toward Hazel, so Doyle threw the book away and put it out of his mind.

But he could not put his determination to be free of Hazel out of his mind. Or rather, his mind, with a will of its own, a life of its own, prejudices of its own, constantly oppressed and dominated his soft and sentimental heart.

His shrewd mind said: Doyle, enjoy those other women, your equals, while you can. They are your kind of women and you deserve them. They are lovely, gracious women in whom you can take pride, the products of the oldest American and English families, of stately mansions, of debutante balls, of Vassar, of the Sorbonne; the products of exacting tutors who have schooled them in manners, in art appreciation, in conversation, in riding to the hounds, in dance, in flawless French, in the ability to wear clothes from Dior and Balenciaga.

His relentless mind said: Doyle, you have had enough of Hazel Smith, your inferior; drop her while you can. She is not your kind, and you have done enough for her, been good enough to her, shown her worlds she would otherwise never have known. Let her be. She will make her way, find herself a proper husband who is the manager of a shoe store, or an accountant, or a dentist, and she will live in Far Rockaway or Jersey City with four runny-nosed children who take piano lessons, and she will have the bridge club every Wednesday and be the happier for it. Don't weaken, Doyle. Sentimentality is fine for your column, but don't let it ruin your life. Look at her, look at Hazel—"poor Hazel"—a shallow, plain, gauche creature unprepared to share your future, an average girl with no potential, a familiar

26

product of scared and clumpy Russian immigrant parents ("green-horns"), who came to Wisconsin from Narevka and Vilna early in the century by way of Ellis Island; Gary, Indiana; Chicago, Illinois; the product of a rundown and peeling wooden house with a broken plank in the porch floor and weeds and dandelions in the front lawn; the product of family reunions attended by aunts always named Yetta or Gertrude or Rose, of American Legion fund-raising carnivals and hayrides and the high school in Baraboo (where she changed her name to the easily spelled Smith), of two years in a teachers college near Oshkosh and a year as a Hearst stringer in Racine; the product of an unfortunate environment that limited her table manners to raising her pinky when spooning soup, her linguistic range to Russian acquired from her immigrant parents (no, no, Doyle, *that* kind of Russian will never do, never), her wardrobe to shiny black (black, Doyle) under-things and rayon-crepe dresses purchased by mail order from Sears, Roebuck and Co. (and more lately, Doyle, from Klein's and, big step, Ohrbach's).

His teasing mind said: Really, Doyle, listen to your mind—unless you're out of it.

And so, after two years, he listened.

Just before the Vienna conference, he had decided that she was an impossible mate for him. The price he paid for her dependency upon him, her undemanding companionship, was too high, considering his social loss due to her presence. His news syndicate wanted him to cover President Kennedy's visits with de Gaulle in Paris, with Khrushchev in Vienna, with Macmillan in London, and he seized upon this journey abroad as the perfect opportunity to break away from Hazel. Because he hated finality, he rationalized that after the break, if ever he needed her, she would be around somewhere. He simply did not want her around when he did not need her.

He had already, for some months, shown his annoyance and irritation with her fawning oppressive love. Now he converted his bad temper from transient erratic moods to permanent domestic policy. He was always difficult in her presence, mean and difficult, surly and neglectful, raking her with criticism, being contradictory and sarcastic, allowing her no area of right and good, constantly parading before her his encounters with beautiful, witty, sophisticated women, and even disappearing from the apartment for days on end with no explanation upon his return. Deliberately, too, he "forgot" her birthday and their ridiculous anniversaries.

And yet she took it and did not fight back. Except for occasionally biting her lip, or brushing a hand over her eyes, she betrayed no emotion. It was as if some maiden aunt had once told her that men were that way and you had to endure it, ride it out, and all would eventually be well. She deflected his provocation and absorbed his punishment without offering retaliation. She would give him no cue for a climactic scene. She was steadfast in her stoicism, and it maddened him, and he knew that he would finally have to do what he abhorred most. He would have to tell her it was over.

Three days before leaving for Vienna, reinforced by four Scotches and a mental review of their incompatibility, he provoked the showdown in their apartment kitchen.

"Hazel, listen, there's something important—we've got to talk—we can't go on like this."

They did not talk, but he did, a half hour of monologue filled with pseudo-psychoanalytic cant, egocentricity, self-pity, inflated grievances, phony unselfish concern, and the sum total of it, his decision: "It's not just me I'm thinking of, Hazel, it's you, too. For your sake as well as mine, let's take a little rest from one another. While I'm gone, you'll have more time for your job, and—new friends. You can find a place of your own. I'll lend you some money if you need it, don't worry about that. But you've got to start thinking ahead. This being on your own, it'll give you a different perspective, revitalize you, believe me. You'll thank me one day, you can bet. Okay, that's it. All right?"

She had not interrupted, had not spoken once. And she did not speak when he was done. His question hung there between them, the trap for an answer that would lead to a fight and a clean angry honest break. But she did not answer. No fight. No scene. Yet she was hurt. No hiding that either. She showed her hurt in her moist eyes, quivering lips, pale disbelief. She started past him toward the bedroom, but he followed her with his unanswered question. "All right?" She paused, stared at him. "If you say so," she said, and she went into the bedroom. And that was that.

She had moved out of the apartment, leaving it neat and clean, by the time he returned from his office the following afternoon. The day after that he joined the White House press corps on the jet plane for Paris, feeling liberated and carefree and with only the slightest residue of shame and guilt (which drinks, poker, French food, and the assignment would soon wash away, he was certain). He found his seat on the plane, cast about for familiar faces, and suddenly his heart seemed to stop and he gasped audibly. Across the aisle, one row back, calmly reading a magazine, was Hazel Smith.

His shock turned to fury. She was shadowing him like a bad conscience. She was badgering him. She was—she was—this was an invasion of privacy. He fell upon her. What in the hell was she doing here? She was wide-eyed and ingenuous. What was *he* doing here? She was here for the very same reason that he was here. She was on an assignment to cover the Kennedys abroad. ANA needed someone to handle the woman's angle, and their regular female correspondent was down with a virus infection, and so they'd given her this wonderful opportunity, her first foreign assignment. What was he so upset about? She had no intention of haunting him. There was bigger game for her now, a chance to prove herself. Hadn't he told her that she would have the time to devote to her career? Well, that's what she was doing, just what he thought she should be doing. She had expected he would be pleased for her, congratulate her, wish her well. They were friends still, weren't they?

With mounting irritation, he conceded that they were friends still, of course, and what she did was her own damn business, and, yes, good luck. But he just wanted to remind her that he would be busy, very busy, in Paris, Vienna, and London.

The smile never left her face. Oh, she of all people knew how important he was, the demands made on him. She could promise him she'd be occupied enough on her own and would not get in his hair. She arched her eyebrows at him, and said almost mockingly, "All right?" He remembered. "Yeah," he said, "as long as you say so." Exactly what troubled him, when he returned to his seat, he could not define. It was only after their takeoff that he knew. Three days ago he had broken off with a girl. And now, by what magic he could not understand, he had just encountered a woman. It was reason enough to distrust her, and fear her, even more.

During the three days in Paris, Doyle saw Hazel Smith only twice, once at a press briefing in the theater inside Annex C of the United States Embassy in the Faubourg St.-Honoré, and again at the Quai d'Orsay where she was awaiting Mrs. Kennedy's descent from the royal suite. He was grimly pleased that she was not tagging after him, bothering him, playing on his pity. Yet, unaccountably, he was annoyed by her self-sufficiency. It pleased him to work so hard in Paris —he got off several excellent columns comparing Kennedy and de Gaulle—and it pleased him to find elegant Frenchwomen so impressed by his reputation and so accessible.

The last evening, he escorted the magnificent, well-bred daughter of a wealthy French ambassador to dinner at Le Petit Bedon in the Rue Pergolèse. His eyes feasted on her more than on the cuisine. Her aristocratic young profile, her flashing diamond earrings setting off her brunette, bell-shaped coiffure, her smooth small breasts, her minute waist, her sleek flanks barely concealed by the translucent silk cocktail dress—all of this contradicted her Catholic Bourbon containment and poise. She brought out the best in Doyle, and he was happy. This was more like it. This was what he had wanted. He studied her heavy lids, pouting red lips, long fingers on the gold cigarette holder, and he wondered.

But after dinner the suspense was brief. She invited him back to her Oriental apartment in the Avenue Foch. She offered him considerable champagne. Then she matter-of-factly offered him herself. The ease of it surprised him, but the promise of her giving stimulated him wildly. And finally there she was, disrobed, and there he was, undressed, and then there they were together. And then it was over, and when it was over he knew that it had been disappointing. She had been as remote and ungiving as a piece of classical statuary in the Louvre. She had been more an Illusion than a Woman.

Later, sauntering back to his suite in the Hotel George-V, Doyle realized that the high point of the evening had been the filet of sautéed veal, done with butter, mushrooms, shallots, sherry, Gruyère cheese, all wrapped in the folds of a thin crêpe, served as his dinner entrée. The French ambassador's exquisite daughter, wrapped in the folds of a thin silk dress, had offered less sensual pleasure than the warm filet. In fact—and this disconcerted him—she had offered less than the inelegant daughter of Russian immigrant parents in Wisconsin, far less.

Confused, he wondered about the other rewards of success that he might now possess. Was their promise illusory too? Well, he would find out. Anyway, there was a certain satisfaction in knowing that one had slept with a descendant of Bourbon royalty. The scented nude body might not linger long in memory. But the conquest of the Name would remain forever. There was something to be said for that. Yes, he decided, he had made the right decision about Hazel. If only she would leave him alone, here and in Vienna.

To prevent becoming involved with Hazel, Doyle avoided the regular press plane and took a commercial jet to Vienna. Arriving at the Schwechat Airport several days before President Kennedy was expected, Doyle felt more relaxed than ever as he was driven past the Danube, the water brackish and more brown than blue, past the baroque Gothic landmarks of the old town at the center of the inner Ring, until he was deposited before the Hotel Imperial at Kärntnerring 16.

Ordering the uniformed doorman to take care of his bags, Doyle left the veiny blue marble pillars and marble-fronted canopy of the hotel entrance, and as usual found himself bowed through the modern glass doors onto the sweeping red carpet of the lobby, where the manager, assistant manager, and concierge awaited him. It was heady and pleasing, and more than ever Doyle was enchanted by the possibilities of his new freedom and future, which would begin in this gracious place.

He had no desire to work. He was caught up in Vienna's mood of *Schlamperei*—the mood of leaving things undone—and after granting a few interviews, contacting some local friends, he devoted himself to pleasure. Usually with a pretty girl or woman on his arm—always the daughter or flirtatious wife of an Austrian Hapsburg or an Austrian millionaire, including one vivacious Esterhazy in her thirties—he listened to Strauss waltzes in Stadtpark, rode the Riesenrad and the five-schilling Liliputbahn (the largest ferris wheel and tiniest train he had ever ridden) in the Wurstelprater, and attended a football game which the Wonderteam lost. Above all, he ate, with discrimination and with good companions, in the candlelight of the Drei Husaren, in the lofty Hochhaus overlooking the city, in the charming relic that was Schöner's and at the very table at which Lehár had once dined. This was the Vienna he loved, the Alt Wien of Gluck, Haydn, Mozart, Schubert, the Vienna that honored these but lacked the patience to name a street for or erect a monument to its own Sigmund Freud. In fact, Doyle bestirred himself to write an amusing column about this paradox.

Then, suddenly, Vienna became the city of *The Third Man*, not "The Merry Widow Waltz." For Nikita Khrushchev had arrived, and a day later John F. Kennedy, and the Big Two conference was under way. Good-bye, *Schlamperei*. Things were getting done. The atmosphere became charged with talk about Laos, international control of nuclear testing, the continuing problem of Berlin, and the threat of Red China's growing power. There was time for only one moment of levity, and that was when Kennedy touched two star-shaped medals adorning Khrushchev's barrel chest and inquired what they signified. Khrushchev explained proudly that they were both Lenin Peace Medals, to which Kennedy remarked wryly, "I hope you keep them."

Before the conference had begun, Doyle was aware, from catching a single glimpse of her, that Hazel Smith was in the city. Beyond that, she did not cross his path. But once the Big Two meetings were under way, Doyle found Hazel more in evidence, always serious, always concentrating on her pencil and note pad, and always trying to be fiercely independent. Except an occasion when he saw her chatting easily with several Russian delegates, she was alone. He tried not to feel sorry for her, but he was. Several times he caught her observing him, to her embarrassment, and he suspected that she was still pathetically hopeful that she would win him back. Twice he blessed her with hurried tidbits of information and advice, for which she was excessively appreciative. Otherwise, to remind her that nothing had changed, he firmly ignored her. And then, on their fifth or sixth day in Vienna, Kennedy's last day, Doyle began to realize that Hazel was not around. He wondered about her absence and was briefly curious, and then he forgot about her.

But suddenly, late in the afternoon of that day, out of the blue, as it were—quite astonishingly, all things considered—Hazel appeared at his Hotel Imperial suite, flushed and breathless and bursting with a tremendous secret. Although he was dressing for cocktails and the opera (it would be the Esterhazy countess tonight, and it would be easy), Doyle was forced to receive Hazel because he could not be rude to this lonely girl in this strange city and because, finally, she whispered that she had an earthshaking "scoop," a word that made him wince and that he had not heard used since the era of early talking pictures.

Shutting the door, he found her quivering, in extreme agitation, in the middle of his drawing room. He did not ask her to sit down. In fact, as he would recollect long after, they had stood facing each other through the entire conversation.

"Okay, Hazel, what is it?" he demanded.

"Jay, I—I've never come across anything like this before. It's the biggest story in our time. It's tremendous. I had to tell you. You won't mind my being here, once I tell you."

Since Doyle had always been skeptical of the sensitivity of her untrained nose for news, he was automatically wary of what Hazel might regard as "the biggest story in our time," but he would be polite. "Okay, Hazel, get it off your chest. Who, what, why, when, and where?"

"President Kennedy—they're going to assassinate President Kennedy!"

His eyebrows had gone up. His voice remained cool. "Who is *they?*"

"A small group of Russian and satellite Communists. They're going to kill him."

"Who says so—besides you?"

"It's—I—I can't—" She faltered, and then composed herself. "An unimpeachable source."

"Not good enough. You know better, Hazel."

"I swear it's true."

"Still not good enough, sweetie. I can get you big stories from the

32

bartender downstairs or a waitress at Demel's or some senile muttonchop-whiskered driver of a carriage in the Hauptallee—but who'll believe it? Now you're kicking off with a wild one, a Communist conspiracy against Kennedy—"

"To murder him here. That's the truth, Jay."

"All right, a plot to kill Kennedy right here. That's big—agreed. Nothing bigger would be possible for the wires and our Government. But you're not writing blind items in a gossip column. You're in the business of news, and news spells fact—fact, sweetie, nothing less. Now where'd you get your story? If you haven't got a solid source, or can't reveal it, you've got nothing. *Who*, Hazel?"

She swallowed hard, and she burst forth: "A—a Russian official—a Soviet delegate—he—he told me—honest to God, he told me straight."

For a fleeting second Doyle was impressed, curious, and then, recovering, skeptical once more. "Why in the hell should he tell you a thing like that? His head could be chopped off. Look, Hazel, I don't—"

"Jay, wait, listen to me, let me explain. I'd better explain the whole thing."

And then she began, and she went on and on, words tumbling over one another.

She'd never been away from home, from her country, so far away, alone, she was saying. She did not know a single one of the other famous American foreign correspondents on the Presidential junket, and it was hard to become friends with them because they did not want to know her or did not take her seriously or were too occupied with their work and personal pleasures. Anyway, the first night in Vienna, about to return to her room in the Bristol Hotel, she had decided that she desperately wanted to be among people, and so she detoured into the hotel bar, where she found a couple of American correspondents drinking with their Russian counterparts, all men and all fairly intoxicated. One of the Americans, who had been standoffish on the plane and in Paris, but was in his cups and free of his earlier reserve, recognized her and beckoned her to his table. He invited her to join him and his friends, because they needed a live American woman around to prove to the Russians that American women were not, as the Russians contended, unfeminine and of the same gender as American men. Her host was too thick-tongued and bleary to remember her name, or the names of the Russians around him, and so Hazel introduced herself to the Russians and they, very well-mannered, introduced themselves to her, and she accepted their challenge about the femininity of American women and sat down to drink and debate with them.

33

Well, Hazel continued, after a while the Americans had had enough, and excused themselves and staggered off to bed. Hazel found herself alone with a half-dozen Russians, and she meant to leave, too, but when the Communist correspondents learned that she spoke fluent Russian, they were intrigued and wouldn't let her go, insisting upon another round of drinks. During the next hour, one by one, the Russian correspondents excused themselves to get some sleep. When there were two left with her, and one started to leave, she came to her feet and said good night—but the one who remained asked her to stay for a last drink. He had been the quietest, the nicest, and he appeared so eager for her company that she consented. Without the others, with just the two of them, and their fourth vodkas before them, the talk became more personal. Hazel's Soviet friend revealed that he was not a journalist but a diplomat, one of the lesser delegates with the Russian party, one of several assigned to help Premier Khrushchev's press secretary, Mikhail Kharlamov, with background data so that he could properly brief the press at the Hofburg palace.

Now, Hazel told Doyle, it was her turn to be intrigued. She had wanted to know more about her Russian companion and so they talked on, and the fourth drink became a fifth, and then when her new friend asked her to go out on the town with him, she agreed, and they drove in his dark-gray Moskvich compact from place to place—drinking in the Eden-Bar, the Kaiser-Bar, drinking and dancing in the Flaker-Bar—and they became very good friends, very good.

Her Russian friend was busy the next day, and so was she, but when evening came, there he was with the Moskvich, waiting to take her out, and they'd driven outside the city, to an inn near the chapel of the Carmelite nuns that stood on the site of the bedroom where Archduke Rudolf of Hapsburg and his mistress, Maria Vetsera, had committed suicide. From the Mayerling inn they went on to a restaurant in a resort hotel, the Tulbinger Kogel Berghotel, in the Vienna Woods. It turned out that her Soviet delegate friend was as lonely as she was, and as desperate for companionship, so far from home, and although he spoke good English, it was wonderful for him to find a foreign female who could speak flawless Russian. And so they got on great, drinking, dancing, exchanging confidences.

And it continued the third night, and part of yesterday, and all last night, and this morning, and he had become—well, quite attached to her—and they'd had some gay and crazy times together, always winding up—well—sort of plastered—well, not really, but pretty high with all that drinking.

Anyway, said Hazel, the point was that her gentleman friend had become sort of dependent upon her and he trusted her as if she were

34

one of his own people, in fact more, actually. And last night, well, he'd been sort of preoccupied and troubled, but after a whole night of drinking he'd got kind of foolishly sentimental about her—it wasn't important to go into that—except somewhere along the way, being sentimental and his tongue loosened by liquor, he began to confide in her very intimately. Suddenly she was hearing things she couldn't believe she had heard, but he repeated them quite a few times. What he was telling her was why he had been so troubled the night before. He had been cautiously approached by an old school friend, now on the staff of a Russian newspaper—*Izvestia* or one of the *Pravdas,* she could not remember which—anyway he had been approached about joining with a group of unnamed international Communist officials who were fanatic in their belief that Kennedy stood in their country's way, and would be increasingly dangerous in the future, and that therefore Kennedy must be liquidated immediately, and if that were not possible, then the deed must be done in the near future.

Unable to believe her ears, Hazel questioned her friend as best she could. He kept repeating what he had said, that there was this foolish conspiracy aimed at Kennedy, and he was against it and had refused to have any part of it, for he saw no gain from it. Anyway, the whole thing disturbed him, because the headstrong conspirators could create a real mess in the world by their act, and because he himself was endangered by having been given this knowledge of a conspiracy and having refused to participate. Containing her horror, wanting to know the details of the conspiracy, Hazel questioned her friend further, but by then, exhausted and drunk, he had fallen off to sleep.

"Afterwards, when I saw him sober, I was afraid to bring it up again," Hazel said. "In broad daylight he seemed to have forgotten what he'd told me, and I thought it wouldn't be wise to remind him. I knew I was on to something tremendous, but I didn't know what to do with it until I thought of you, Jay. I tried to get away from my friend all day, but I couldn't. Luckily, an hour ago he was called to the Russian Embassy, and the second I was free, I came right here to tell you. So there you have it, everything that I know, and much as I hate double-crossing a nice guy, a really sincere, decent guy, I decided it is more important to protect our President and future peace by announcing this horrible plot to the world. Don't you agree, Jay?"

Doyle had listened carefully, his head swarming with conflicting reactions, and now that she had finished her story, he knew that his final judgment would depend upon her answer to one question. "Hazel, you haven't told me everything that you know. There is one thing missing."

"What's that?"

"His name."

She seemed startled. "Oh—I—I can't tell that."

"Do you know his name?"

"Of course!"

"Then why won't you tell it?"

"Because it wouldn't be fair—I mean, it wouldn't be right." She paused, bewildered. "A reporter doesn't have to reveal her source."

"Not usually, but in this case you must."

"No, I can't." Her firmness surprised him. "It's not important," she added.

"Hazel, it's the only thing that is important."

"No."

"I see."

And he did see. She'd been picked up by this drunken Russian bum, delegate or no, but a drunken phony or provocateur—she'd have been too simple to perceive that, too eager for any man since she had been dropped by him—and she had probably let this vodka swiller take her to bed, not once, but day and night, and she'd got this little fable from him, either as her two dollars on the table or for more sinister reasons. No, of course Hazel the Great wouldn't give the name if the Russian Orlov or Potemkin had been or still was her lover.

Or, on the other hand, maybe she couldn't give the name because her Russian delegate friend was nonexistent. Quite possibly this crude fiction was a trick of hers, a warped means of wreaking vengeance on Doyle himself, by getting him to swallow it, spew it to the world, and thus be exposed for an unreliable fool and finally ruined. But then he doubted that, knowing Hazel as well as he did. Whether she had invented the embarrassing "scoop" or it had been planted on her, she was here with it now, using it to seduce him once more and win him back. Yes, he was sure that was it. She had picked up this nonsense, or created it, and had brought it to her former lover as a family cat brings a dead bird and drops it on the doormat, expecting the rewards of praise and love.

"Hazel," he found himself saying, "you're a naïve and gullible child to believe that garbage. Either you've been taken in or you're trying to take me in."

She stared at him with disbelief. "What do you mean?"

"Okay, I'll tell you what I mean. Let's say there is this Russian friend of yours and he is a delegate to the conference, which I doubt. Okay, so he has a little fun with you—you know what I mean—"

Her lips were quivering. "No, I don't know what you mean."

"Never mind. So he realizes he's got this simple little girl reporter, who doesn't know a damn thing about politics or Russian methods,

36

and he knows she'll believe anything, and she's from this great big American news service in great big dumb America. So he puts on the lonely and sincere act, the nice and cozy act, so that she trusts him. Then, pretending to be a little loaded, he lets slip this fat and fancy top secret. And then he sits back and waits for her to run wildly off and write it hysterically and send it out, flash, stop presses, and the minute the sensational mythical story is out, he has the Soviet press secretary challenge us for proof, and charge us, once again, with warmongering, troublemaking, and hit out at the irresponsibility of the capitalistic, imperialistic press."

"Oh, Jay, no—"

"Let me finish. Little Hazel has her big beat. And since she believes it, she can get a lot of credit, a lot of success mileage out of it, but she figures there is something better she can get. She can bring it to Jay Doyle and give it to him, to prove she's the best girl in the world for him, because look what she's done for him—greater love hath no woman—and with this she's shown she still loves him and he should be indebted to her. Or maybe little Hazel has something else in mind. Maybe she knows the silly story is a lie, maybe she even invented it, but she brings it to good old Jay, knowing he can't use it without the source, but thus proving to him she is still true-blue and he'd better not forget it. Or—no, hold it, sweetie, you just hear me out—maybe little Hazel is more devious than I think, and she tells herself she's going to invent this story, and invent a source, and bring it to good old Jay, get him to jump, get him to go whooping out on a limb in print, and then the limb'll be cut and good old Jay, the bastard who let little Hazel down, will have a great big fall, and Hazel will have her revenge. I don't know which or what, but whatever your motive, love or revenge, your whole childish ruse is so transparent as to be laughable. Now, that's what I think."

Her face was immobile and ashen, and only her lips moved. "Is that what you think?"

"Yes, because if it were true and such a hot story, why didn't you file it with ANA under your by-line and become a great big heroine?"

"Because I'm 'little Hazel,' " she said quietly. "Because I'm nobody, and even ANA would be nervous about a big one like this coming from me my first time out. I came here to—to give it to you because it's true and your name would assure its credence and veracity—and, knowing the CIA wouldn't treat me seriously right now, I wanted to have it exposed in public—to save our President. And, all right, I came to you because you were the only one I knew and because when I walked through that door, I thought I still loved you—"

Doyle threw back his head with a laugh of triumph. "At last," he

37

said, grinning. "Why didn't you say so in the first place? So that's what your little fairy tale comes to, a cute piece of fiction to bring us back together? That's it, isn't it, sweetie? Well, listen to me, honey—no, thanks, I'm not buying, not that way. Now I've had just about enough, so why don't we call it quits, and thanks for the memory, and you take off and go back to your Russian Hans Christian Andersen—and just let me change for the opera, because I've got somebody coming by any minute—an authentic Esterhazy countess, if you want to know—and it could be embarrassing. Okay, baby? I think we understand each other now."

She stood, very straight, rigid, staring steadily at him, and finally she spoke. "I'm just looking at you this way because it's like seeing you clearly for the first time. You know what I'm seeing? I'm seeing what you really are. You're an ignorant, conceited, stupid fathead. And worse, you're a goddam son of a bitch. I never want to see you again in my life—never again, never!"

With that she spun away, ran to the door, and slammed out of his suite—and he never saw her again, not once in all the years from that day in Vienna to the present.

And now, sitting here in Vienna once more, so long after, in a single room and not a suite, looking back on what had happened and what had been, he conceded that Hazel had been right all down the line. He *had* been an ignorant, conceited fathead. He *had* been a goddam son of a bitch. Worst of all, he *had* been monumentally stupid.

On the late night of November 22, 1963, while he was turning off his television set, the full impact of Hazel's rightness and his wrongness had hit him. But not until nine months later, after the appearance of the Warren Commission Report, had his obsession to right the wrong been born.

With a wrench and a wheeze, rattling the almost empty can of cashews and pouring the last few nuts into his hand, he escaped unhappy memory and returned to the more hopeful reality of the present moment.

Chewing the cashews, he stared down at the glorious manuscript open on his capacious lap. These beautiful pages would serve to rectify his past asininity, his blindness in not appreciating Hazel's old love, his blindness in not accepting her gift of love that might have prevented the assassination of Kennedy, his blindness in laughing away what would have been the greatest story of his career. But he had labored hard to make up for his blunder. There was hope now. As long as his manuscript was alive, there was hope. And a triumph tonight would halt his steadily sliding decline from eminence into anonymity.

Mindful of the approaching meeting with Sydney Ormsby, he quickly lifted the manuscript from his lap and hastily resumed reading the outline of the remaining chapters. It was all there, he could see, and it was powerful and sound. Many men, in many lands, after the appearance of the Warren Report, had attempted to discredit it and had been branded crackpots for their dissent. This, he perceived, was because governments and the public preferred the peace of crimes solved and cases closed, which made them feel safer, easier, and permitted them to go on with the immediate business of life. And where the disturbers of peace had failed was in their ability to produce any incontrovertible proof beyond circumstantial evidence and theory. But the manuscript in Doyle's hands, once completed, could not be turned aside. It would not be theory constructed on flimsy conjecture but solid proof, a concrete edifice based on newly discovered fact—and it would offer governments and the public an alternate solution, which they could accept and substitute for the Warren Commission's erroneous one.

To clear away the underbrush of myth, so that truth might be seen plainly by everyone, Doyle had summarized the findings of the Warren Commission, and then gone on to show the weaknesses in the Commission's report, the unlikeliness of Lee Harvey Oswald as lone assassin, and the available evidence that dramatically built to a totally different version of the murder and conclusively pointed to a conspiracy.

Now, Doyle began to reread his concise and fair summary of the Warren Commission Report, the straw man he would quickly topple. The Commission had said that President Kennedy had been killed, and Governor Connally wounded, by three shots fired from a Mannlicher-Carcano rifle, Model 91/38, caliber 6.5 mm., bearing the identifying number C2766 and the legend MADE ITALY, and equipped with a cheap telescopic sight. All three shots had been fired from the sixth-floor window at the southeast corner of the Texas School Book Depository. There were the empty cartridge cases on the sixth floor to prove the shots had been three, there were witnesses who had seen a rifle in the sixth-floor window, there were physicians and experts to verify that the shots had been fired from behind the President.

The Commission had then decided that Lee Harvey Oswald had been the lone assassin. He had been on the sixth floor at the time of the killing. He had owned a Mannlicher-Carcano 6.5 rifle, later found hidden between cartons on the sixth floor. He had carried a paper bag, large enough to hold a rifle, into the Depository the morning of the assassination. "Based on testimony of the experts . . . the Commission has concluded that a rifleman of Lee Harvey Oswald's capabilities could have fired the shots from the rifle used in the assassination within the elapsed time of the shooting." Seven months earlier Oswald had tried to shoot down Major General Walker, "thereby demonstrating his disposition to take human life." Shortly after the assassination, Oswald, confronted by police officer Tippit, had killed the policeman with a revolver, and then resisted arrest. Once captured, Oswald had not been subjected to physical coercion by police. He had been offered legal assistance and had rejected it at the time.

A little more than two days after Oswald's arrest, while being transferred to the county jail, Oswald had been murdered by Jack Ruby. There was no evidence to back up the rumor that Ruby had been assisted by the Dallas Police Department in eliminating Oswald. There was no evidence that Oswald and Ruby had known one another. Despite the fact that Oswald had ended his two-and-a-half-year stay in the Soviet Union in 1962 and brought home to Texas a Russian bride, Marina, despite his visits to the Russian and Cuban embassies in Mexico City in 1963, despite his affiliations with left-wing political groups, there had been no factual evidence that Oswald was employed, persuaded, or encouraged by a foreign government to assassinate President Kennedy.

Doyle studied his quotation from the Warren Commission Report on the possibility of an American conspiracy. "In its entire investigation the Commission has found no evidence of conspiracy, subversion, or disloyalty to the U.S. Government by any Federal, State, or local official."

Since the Commission had concluded that Oswald had committed the crime on his own, it tried to explain his motivation for the assassination. Oswald had been unstable. He was hostile to all authority. He was unable to enter into meaningful relationships with people. He was committed to his own versions of Marxism and Communism, and he was antagonistic toward the United States. Having consistently failed in his many undertakings, he was determined to find a place in history. Ergo: He had achieved his first success, no matter how infamous, by killing a President of the United States.

Wetting his dry lips, Doyle hastily skimmed through his ringing challenge to the Warren Commission and its acceptance of Oswald's guilt. Hastily turning his manuscript pages, as he reread his case, Doyle's satisfaction with his part-time labor of years grew.

Despite the Warren Commission's desperate dredging for a motive for Oswald's alleged crime, Doyle made it clear that Oswald had no known motive at all for killing Kennedy. Oswald had told a public gathering he was not a Communist. He had told the American Civil

40

Liberties Union he resented the anti-Semitic and anti-Catholic remarks made at an ultra-rightist meeting headed by General Walker. And just before the assassination he had stated that the United States was more progressive than Russia in the area of civil rights, and he had warmly praised President Kennedy for his championing of civil rights.

Then Doyle went on to stress that Oswald could not have planned to assassinate Kennedy from the Depository window, because when Oswald obtained the job in the Depository, the President's route had not been announced, and the motorcade's final route past the Depository was a detour Oswald could hardly have known about. As to carrying a rifle into the Depository, a witness, Mrs. Linnie Mae Randle, had said that Oswald's bag was less than two feet long, whereas the rifle measured over three feet. Shortly after police officer Weitzman—who sold rifles in his spare time—found the assassin's rifle on the sixth floor, he had sworn that it was a 7.65 Mauser, and described it in detail, and District Attorney Wade also announced that the assassin's weapon was a German Mauser. Yet, at the moment the Dallas police learned that Oswald owned an Italian Mannlicher-Carcano 6.5 rifle, they switched their story and suddenly a clearly marked German Mauser became a clearly marked Italian carbine. And, as Doyle wrote, there were no legible fingerprints or palm prints belonging to Oswald on his Italian rifle, and no powder burns on his face.

The question of Oswald's marksmanship, Doyle had known from the start, was a crucial one, and he made the most of it in his manuscript. The Commission had concluded that Oswald was using a twenty-three-year-old inferior Italian weapon with a cheap scope, which he had purchased secondhand for a little less than twenty dollars (and with which he had never practiced, according to his landlady). Yet he had been enough of a crack shot to fire three bullets in five seconds at a moving target from about 100 yards' distance, and of the six persons in the target vehicle, he had hit only the two persons of interest to an assassin. However, an Olympic rifle champion using a Mannlicher-Carcano rifle could not duplicate Oswald's alleged feat, finding a bolt-action too slow. And to add to that, there was evidence that Oswald was anything but an outstanding marksman, that he had in fact been a poor marksman. After three years in the Marines, where the minimum acceptable shooting score was 190, he had been able to score only 212, whereas 95 per cent of the trainees did better early in their first year.

Much of the case for Oswald's guilt was built on the presumption that three shots, and only three, had been fired into the Presidential limousine, and all from one direction—from behind the President. Yet Governor Connally had insisted that he had not been hit by a bullet that had first passed through the President, although he must have been wounded by one of the bullets that hit Kennedy, if there was only one assassin. Furthermore, Dr. Perry of Parkland Hospital had stated that the bullet in question had been of "low velocity," thereby supporting Governor Connally's contention that it could not have had the power to penetrate his body also.

The truth was that originally most persons at the scene of the assassination, Governor Connally among them, thought there had been as many as a half-dozen shots fired. But the police, perhaps because they realized the Mannlicher-Carcano rifle's limitations, had firmly settled for three shots, insisting that they had come from the Depository. Still, numerous creditable witnesses persisted in the belief that they had heard from four to six shots, and some of these witnesses, including a Secret Service agent, said that there were enough shots so that some were bunched together.

Doyle had pointed out that this was of great significance. For, if there were four to six shots, and some were bunched together, the volley could not have been fired by one man using a relatively slow bolt-action rifle. Such a series of rapid-fire shots would have required at least two assassins. Based on this evidence, Doyle had concluded that there was a total of five shots, fired by two assassins working in tandem. One was shooting from the Depository behind Kennedy, the other shooting from the grassy knoll or from the wooden fence above the knoll or from the concrete wall along the railroad bridge atop the Triple Underpass, all of which were situated in front of Kennedy. Two bullets smashed into Kennedy, two hit Connally, and a fifth missed and was found by a police officer in the grass nearby.

Yes, Doyle charged in his manuscript, there had been two assassins, although the Warren Commission had curiously ignored most of this impressive evidence. According to the original statement of three of the physicians at the Parkland Hospital, the President's throat wound was an entry wound. This meant that someone in front of Kennedy, aiming toward the approaching limousine, had fired straight at him from the grassy knoll or the overpass. Only Kennedy's fatal skull wound had come from behind him, from the Depository building. There were a great number of on-the-spot witnesses to attest to a second assassin firing head-on at the President. There was Mary Woodward, who heard the actual rifle shots from the grassy knoll; there was S. M. Holland, who heard four shots and then saw puffs of smoke from the knoll; there was Lee E. Bowers, Jr., and also a Washington, D.C., reporter, who saw a motorcycle policeman plunge purposefully toward the knoll and quickly scramble up the embankment, until diverted by the other shots from the Depository behind; there was the eyewitness who observed someone running down the knoll to the Triple Underpass beneath; there was Mrs. Jean Hill, who saw a man in a hat and long brown overcoat racing for the train tracks; there was the railroad yardman who told police that he believed the shots had come from near the wooden fence atop the incline, and who saw somebody throw something into the bushes; there was James Tague, a spectator to the motorcade, who was wounded in the cheek by the fragment of a bullet that had been fired from the knoll north of Elm Street and which had ricocheted off the street pavement. There were all of these to support the theory of an accomplice for the assassin in the Depository.

Jay Doyle, absorbed in contemplating his manuscript, nodded in contented agreement with himself. His case, demolishing the overeager, superficial prejudgment of the Warren Commission, slowly, inexorably, cleared the way for public acceptance of his evidence of an international conspiracy. Smiling with grim satisfaction, Doyle felt the consolidation of his confidence in the power of his argument, one that would overwhelm Sydney Ormsby. Then, scanning the remainder of his outline, Doyle realized that if Ormsby was not convinced by what had already been written, he would be convinced by the summing up, the relentless, accusing question marks that peppered the closing chapters. These questions, Doyle was positive, would make Ormsby see that the assassination had been, until now, a modern historical mystery unsolved, and that Doyle was deserving of an enormous cash advance, which would enable him to proceed to the final solution, to which Hazel Smith in Moscow held the key.

With nervous pleasure, his chubby fingers drumming on the empty cashew tin, Jay Doyle reviewed his telling questions about the assassination. Why did Lee Harvey Oswald get his visa to enter the Soviet Union so quickly—why, when most applicants had to wait a week or two, did Oswald receive his visa in a single day? Why was Oswald given special privileges inside Russia? Why was he able to take a Russian wife out of the Soviet Union and to the United States (ordinarily very difficult) with such ease? Why did Oswald receive money, from a source not known, while he was unemployed in the United States? Why was Oswald said to have tried out an automobile on a Dallas car lot when he did not know how to drive? Why did a gunsmith in Irving, Texas, claim that for a customer who called himself Oswald he had mounted a telescopic lens on a rifle, using three screws to mount the scope, when the scope on Oswald's actual rifle had been mounted with only two screws? Why was Oswald, so well-known to the FBI, not watched the day before and the day of the assassination? Why did Oswald, who the police and FBI insisted was a crack marksman well able to murder a victim who was 100 yards away and a moving target, fail to shoot down General Walker, who was a stationary target only yards away from him? Why were the Dallas police not interested in the empty cigarette package found in the sixth-floor stock room of the Depository, especially since the accused Oswald did not smoke? Why did Oswald's wife, Marina, confirm that her husband's rifle was missing, and then later claim that she had never known he owned a rifle? Why did Oswald, immediately following the assassination, bother to go home and pick up a jacket, if he was really guilty and eager to escape the police? Why, when Oswald reached his boardinghouse after the assassination, did a police car pull up before his house and honk for him, but then drive off without him? Why did Oswald seem to be heading for Jack Ruby's apartment after the killing? Why were authorities so certain that Oswald and Ruby had never met when they lived within two blocks of one another and had post-office boxes almost next to each other? Why did police officer Tippit, before leaving his squad car to confront Oswald, chat with him so casually and easily?

Reviewing these familiar questions, as fascinated as ever by their implications, Jay Doyle could not resist engaging in more literary narcissism. Why was the behavior of the experienced Dallas police force, after the assassination, so disoriented, inconsistent, and baffling? Why did some members of the Dallas police force repeatedly misrepresent or conceal certain evidence, and publicly claim to possess other evidence that they were never able to produce? Why did Sheriff Decker issue an alert to the police five minutes before a single shot was fired? Why did neither the police nor the FBI cover the rear exit of the Depository until twenty minutes after the assassination, and why did they not follow through on the statement of a witness, Worrell, who saw a man leave the rear exit and run away? Why, as Bertrand Russell demanded to know, was Oswald's description as the murderer of Officer Tippit broadcast over the Dallas police radio at 12:43, when Tippit was not shot until after one o'clock? Why did the Dallas police settle on Oswald's guilt so fast, and why did they not bother to hunt for possible accomplices along the motorcade route or bother to check airports and train and bus depots for fleeing suspects? Why, after two days of interrogating Oswald, were the Dallas Chief of Police and the FBI unable to furnish a single record or scribbled note of the questions and Oswald's answers? Why were the medical notes made during the autopsy performed on the President's corpse at Bethesda Hospital destroyed? Why were 580 files of the Warren Commission records classified as secret, and not shown to the public or to investigators like Doyle himself?

These were questions that Doyle had put to paper, and there were many more. Perhaps some were important and some were not applicable, Doyle saw, but all of them were mysterious and hence deserved thorough investigations which had never been made. Why was the secondary witness to the murder of Officer Tippit, an auto dealer named Warren Reynolds, himself murderously attacked in his office not long after Kennedy's death? Why had his attacker's girl friend, Betty MacDonald, who had worked for Jack Ruby as a striptease dancer, and later been jailed for a minor cause, finally committed suicide in her cell? Why had thirteen persons who testified before the Warren Commission, or who had some connection with the tragedy in Dallas, as Texas editor Penn Jones, Jr., pointed out, died of murder, suicide, accident and other unnatural causes within two years after the assassination? Why was Jack Ruby allowed into the Police Department basement at the exact time Oswald was to be brought through there for transfer to the county jail, when even Secret Service agents had to display credentials to enter the basement? Why was Marina Oswald's sudden prosperity, after the killings, not investigated by the Warren Commission? Why was her business manager, who was said to have known Ruby, introduced to her by the FBI? Why was Marina's story, the only source for evidence that her husband had once tried to assassinate General Walker, accepted without further question or corroboration?

Why and why and why?

Based on his personal researches and investigations, Doyle knew that many other persons, like himself, wondered about the answers and had their suspicions. Some had come to definite conclusions. Léo Sauvage, the American correspondent for the respected *Le Figaro* of Paris, had written that "it is logically untenable, legally indefensible, and morally unacceptable to assert that Lee Harvey Oswald was the assassin of President Kennedy." This dissenting judgment, Doyle knew, like so many others, had been based on unanswered questions alone. For Doyle and the world, questions were not enough. One had to have answers—the one big answer, really—and in the world that lay outside the conspiracy Doyle knew that only two persons on earth had the answers—the one big answer, actually. There was Hazel Smith, of course, and there was himself. The two of them, alone, knew that as early as 1961 an international Communist conspiracy was in the making and in 1963 it had been carried off successfully. The conspirators, needing a smoke screen, had worked on Oswald, had cleverly set him up as dupe and scapegoat, had created a series of circumstances that would incriminate him and make his arrest inevitable. Then the conspirators had committed the carefully planned crime themselves and left Oswald holding the gun bag, so to speak. Once Oswald had been arrested, and killed (by accident or plan, Doyle did not know which), the real assassins were safe with their secret. They had miscalculated on only two counts: the frailty of all secrets, and the persistence of a journalist of the caliber of Jay Thomas Doyle.

Squatting on the divan, Doyle had fallen into a state of complete joyous reverie. In his waking dream he visualized his beautifully bound published book. He visualized the worldwide sensation it would create. He saw it as one of those rare books that become earthquakes, upending the minds of men and altering their outlooks forever. It would jolt American complacency, his book would, and kindle the fire of justice in men's hearts, as had Thomas Paine's *Common Sense,* Henry Thoreau's *Civil Disobedience,* Harriet Beecher Stowe's *Uncle Tom's Cabin,* Upton Sinclair's *The Jungle,* and Sinclair Lewis's *Main Street.* And because of its political revelation, it might shake the world as strongly as had Karl Marx's *Das Kapital* and Adolf Hitler's *Mein Kampf,* although in a different way. And with its publication, in a single stroke, Doyle would lift himself from the abyss where has-beens dwell to the highest reach and ultimate pinnacle of success, his wealth and influence restored, his name immortalized.

Doyle realized that an earthly hammering was disturbing his sweet silent daydreaming, and abruptly his mind stumbled down and back into the here and now. He listened. The sharp knocking on his hotel door had resumed. Laying the precious manuscript aside, Doyle heaved himself to his feet, and then, wondering, he waddled to the door and pulled it open.

A beardless young bellboy, in a natty bright uniform like that of a cadet, stood in the doorway, offering Doyle a silver tray on which lay a solitary envelope. Digging into his pocket for the tip, Doyle produced a handful of Austrian coins, sorted out five schilling pieces, and handed them to the grateful boy as he accepted the envelope.

Closing the door, studying the thin plain envelope marked "For Mr. J. T. Doyle" and "Deliver by hand," he was apprehensive. Could it be from Sydney Ormsby, canceling their dinner? Could Ormsby have run into a fellow publisher from America who had told him that Doyle's manuscript was improbable and oft-rejected? Or had Ormsby received an urgent call to go on to Paris or return to London, and could he be sending a message postponing their meeting indefinitely?

Breathing heavily, nasally, Doyle ripped the envelope open and unfolded the two pages inside, and instantly his breathing came easier. The first page was a brief note from the manager of Demel's, one of the world's foremost confectioners, apologizing for the delay but enclosing the recipe that Doyle had requested for inclusion in his new cookbook. The second page contained the neatly typed recipe for Topfenpalatschinken, a sweet pancake dessert that was stuffed with a toothsome cottage-cheese mixture. The reading of the recipe had a Pavlovian effect on Doyle. His mouth watered. And then he hated himself for this, this weakness, and for how that damn recipe symbolized his present station in life.

Angrily he made his way back to the divan, trying to avoid looking at his manuscript, *The Conspirators Who Killed Kennedy,* as he went directly to his bulging briefcase. Searching the back of it, he tugged out the thick manila folder, as overstuffed as he himself, with its tab reading NOTES AND RECIPES FOR COOKBOOK. Opening the folder, he tried to avoid the title page but could not, and so had to read again, *The Old World's Best New Recipes—by Jay Thomas Doyle.*

Quickly Doyle flipped through the English and French recipes and notes on restaurants already collected, and reached the Austrian section, into which he shoved the Demel's dessert recipe. He was about to close the manila folder when a page slipped out. Lifting it from the divan, Doyle saw that it was his epigraph for the cookbook. It read: "The discovery of a new dish does more for human happiness than the discovery of a new star," and, typed beneath the quotation, the source, Brillat-Savarin. Blushing at the frivolity of it, and at his degradation in having committed himself to the project, Doyle shoved the offending page back into the folder and jammed the folder as far back in his briefcase as he could.

Standing there motionless before the divan, he was filled with intense hatred for the cookbook and with complete self-loathing. He could not imagine how he had ever descended to this, but in reality he knew.

His syndicated column had been at its height when, in fatigues and combat boots, he had been able to cover violent events first-hand—the police action in Korea, the Hungarian revolt several years later, the Algerian convulsion in 1960, the blockade of Cuba, the early part of the Vietnam conflict—and to report colorfully on them and to philosophize about their importance for Everyman. But as small conflicts in unpronounceable areas replaced actual wars, and as these conflicts began to repeat themselves monotonously, the reading public, despite the entreaties of the Department of State, began to identify with them less and less, lost interest and became bored, and so, too, had they gradually become bored with Doyle's column. As he lost newspapers and readership, Doyle began to eat compulsively, and then quite naturally, not only as a diversion for his readers but because eating had become his main interest, he began to write occasional pieces about the food and restaurants in exotic places. When finally he lost his column, there were still loyal magazine editors who remembered his most recent writings about food and assigned him articles to write on gastronomy. Then, recently, a book publisher had suggested the cookbook, offering a reasonable cash advance and a travel-expense account, and Doyle, still smarting from the rejections of his assassination manuscript, had succumbed to the cookbook project and the cash advance.

A little short of a month ago he had arrived in Europe to eat, to write about his culinary experiences, and to earn enough for his immediate self-support and his eventual Moscow trip. But frustration had turned him into a glutton, ever indulging his digestive tract, ever living beyond his expense account and his means. By now he knew that while the dreadful cookbook would keep him alive, it would not bring him one inch closer to Hazel and the solution of his magnum opus.

It was shameful, he knew, that one as talented as himself, who had told the world of the recapture of Seoul, who had interviewed General MacArthur after President Truman had relieved him of his Far East command, who had dissected the Puerto Rican nationalists after they had turned their guns loose in the House of Representatives, who had marched with Fidel Castro in the take-over of Cuba, and fought with guerrillas in Laos, it was shameful that he was reduced to hacking out monstrously calorific recipes to include in a gift book for overweight housewives. It distressed him that the renowned standing head of his column "Inside and Straight," once read and admired by Presidents, would soon be cheapened by its appearance on the jacket of a cookbook. He did not belong here in Vienna this week, consorting with pompous *Herr Obers* and beefy chefs in steaming kitchens of overexpensive restaurants. He belonged, this moment, in Paris, there consorting with statesmen and interviewing the Ministers and Heads of State of Soviet Russia, Great Britain, France, the United States, and the People's Republic of China, who were assembling in the magnificent Palais Rose to save the world or see its ending, now that intractable China was in possession of the devastating neutron bomb.

On the verge of sinking into a depressive mood, Doyle was rescued and lifted upward by the remembrance of what he had almost forgotten —that a savior named Sydney Ormsby had come to this city to join with him in a common cause. By midnight tonight Doyle would have bountiful support for his crusade, would be able to abandon the damned cookbook and return the advance payment for it, and with his new ally's riches be able to go forward to ultimate victory and greatness. Remembering Ormsby, Doyle was reminded that he had forgotten the hour completely. He looked at his travel clock. There were only twenty minutes left before his appointment. He must not affront a patron by being tardy, and this fear galvanized him into action.

Quickly Doyle stripped down to his plaid shorts. Then, rushing into the bathroom, he took up his electric razor, removed the shadows from the vast expanses of his moon face, washed it, dried it, wet his hair, combed, doused himself with lotion and cologne. In the wardrobe he found a crisp monogrammed Italian shirt, and once he had it on, he examined his three pressed suits. The first, he decided, had the rubbed shine that reflected failure, and he returned it to the hanger. The second, his favorite, had, here and there, the faint but permanent stains of food on the coat front and upper trousers, the sartorial scars of countless engagements with vinegar-and-olive-oil dressings, demiglace, mayonnaise, Béarnaise sauce, marinades, Worcestershire, that no cleaner could remove. Reluctantly Doyle returned this suit, also, to its hanger. One garment remained, the custom-made suit tailored in Rome for his appearance at the Zurich Parley four years ago. It was fresh and spotless because he had outgrown it and wore it infrequently. It would fit him like a scuba diver's wet suit and cause him much discomfort, providing no room for his stomach to expand during dinner, but it would make him appear prosperous and independent. There was no choice. He must sacrifice his comfort for this protective armor.

When he was ready, the relentless hands of the clock conceded him nine minutes to rendezvous. Taking up the folder that held his manuscript, slipping it into a wafer-thin imitation-leather portfolio, Doyle hastened out of the room.

Once outside the hotel, standing splendid but constricted beneath the canopy of the Imperial, he decided that the distance to the Hotel Sacher restaurant was short enough to make it on foot within the time left him. Waving off a taxi, he proceeded up the broad Kärtnerring, appreciating the promisingly warm and soothing night air. When he reached Vienna's main thoroughfare, Kärtnerstrasse, he turned right, joining the crowds waiting for the light to change, then going with them. In short fast strides, hardly aware of the massive dark pile of the State Opera House that filled a square block across the way, ignoring the lure of the shops—except for the distracting aroma of hot sausages and onion that came from one tiny Gastwirtschaft, which teased after him briefly—Doyle reached the corner unhindered. Swinging left, he darted between taxis and bicycles with the grace of a dancing bear to the opposite side of the busy Kärtnerstrasse. Presently, gasping for oxygen, he slowed past the outdoor café terrace and arrived at 4 Philharmonikerstrasse, the canopied entrance leading into the shabbily regal three-story hostelry of the Hapsburgs, the Hotel Sacher, and its restaurant inside.

Pausing to pull himself together, then gripping his portfolio as tightly as if it contained a winning lottery ticket, Jay Doyle entered the hotel lobby and continued to the restaurant anteroom with its gallery of photographs autographed by Romberg, Lehár, the Duke of Windsor, and countless uniformed hussars.

He was pleased when the captain recognized him immediately and greeted him with *"Willkommen, Herr Doyle."*

"Guten Abend," Doyle replied in his self-conscious German. Like so many old-time opera bassos, whose only knowledge of foreign languages was confined to memorized lyrics, Doyle was ill at ease with German, French, Italian, except where they related to special dishes and drinks, and then his use of these languages and his accent were confident and unfaltering.

Pleased that he was known from his two previous visits to Sacher's when he had interviewed the restaurant's management and its chefs for his cookbook, and sampled the *haute cuisine* (at a generous discount), he reverted to English. "I'm expecting an important guest, the English publisher, Mr. Sydney Ormsby," said Doyle. "I hope he hasn't arrived before me."

"No, not yet, Herr Doyle. But I promise you, everything will be perfection. May I show you to your table?"

"I guess so. I'll wait for him there."

Following the captain through the long, narrow, red-carpeted and red-draped Marmorsaal dining room, sparkling with its circular chandeliers and its silver service and white damask tablecloths, sedate yet lively with its wealthy tourists and well-dressed Viennese couples (the old intimacy of another day still in the air, a day when archdukes met their mistresses from the opera ballet in this room), Doyle felt reassured that he had selected the best setting for his appointment.

Seated at a table beside the marble wall, his precious portfolio propped next to him, he refused a drink, fiddled with his napkin, half listening to the lulling soft music, his eyes constantly on the dining room entrance. Briefly his attention roamed to a young, attractive, pert Austrian brunette, being affectionate to her companion, an obviously affluent older man, and briefly Doyle suffered an aching nostalgia for his own affluent past. When he turned away and looked ahead, he realized that the captain was approaching, nodding, closely followed by a surprisingly short young man, with the young-old face of a jockey, who was fingering his drooping incongruous mustache and swinging an umbrella cane.

With a mammoth effort, Doyle slid sideways off his chair and swiftly rose to his feet.

"Your guest is here, Herr Doyle," the captain was saying.

"Good—good to meet you, Mr. Ormsby," Doyle said, grabbing the publisher's delicate hand with its ornate crested ring in his own plump paw. "I'm so glad you could make it."

"Delighted, absolutely delighted, Mr. Doyle," said Sydney Ormsby in a voice that was thin and shrill, his accent clipped and Mayfair.

Since the captain still hovered, Doyle completed the amenities. Awkwardly indicating his guest, he said to the Sacher captain, *"Ich erlaube mir Herrn Ormsby vorzustellen."* The captain took Ormsby's limp hand, pumped it once, twice, half bowed and retreated. Somewhat lamely Doyle explained, "I thought he should meet you. Never can tell when you'll want a reservation. Or have you been to Vienna before?"

"Never, Mr. Doyle. I'm afraid that this is my first and my bloody last visit."

"Oh, I'm sorry. Is anything wrong?"

"I'll be only too pleased to tell you. Mind if we sit down?"

Disconcerted by Ormsby's displeasure with Vienna, Doyle waited for his guest to sit and then himself squeezed behind the table. Equally disconcerting, Doyle decided, was the unexpectedness of his guest's physical appearance. For Doyle, people were categorized as recognizable stereotypes, which had made his simple columns once so acceptable to simple readers. For Doyle, the word royalist evoked Emperor Franz Joseph, the word industrialist evoked Zaharoff, the word chemist evoked Pasteur. And so, hearing "publishing giant," he had expected Hearst, no less. What he had first seen, instead, was the caricature of an Eton schoolboy, who came no higher than his own shoulders, and what he saw now was a seemingly callow, somewhat pimply, somebody's brother who was impeccably repulsive.

After a third glance, Doyle had Sydney Ormsby, busy propping up his umbrella cane, whole: sand-colored slick hair combed sideways, tiny ferret eyes, thin pointed nose, wide pink ears, a straggling full ginger mustache sometimes hiding the small yellow teeth, and an adenoidal, oddly pornographic smile that tried to become a grin but graduated only to a smirk. Yet position and wealth were evident in the accessories: the blazing Cartier jeweled tiepin, the Au Vieux Cadran enameled wristwatch, the chambray shirt and silk kerchief poking out of the charcoal silk Savile Row suit. The accessories did not modify Ormsby's physical unattractiveness. Desperately Doyle tried to believe that this young man was more than he appeared to be, because Doyle *had* to believe that he was more, because after all his guest *had* been enthusiastic about Doyle's great book idea and had come this far to serve as Doyle's patron.

With a start, Doyle became aware that the *Ober,* the headwaiter, was bending over Ormsby, and that Ormsby was ordering a double whisky-and-water without ice.

Immediately, Doyle asserted his hosthood. "Mr. Ormsby, if you don't mind, if I may suggest—the dishes are so very delicious here—I guarantee you have a treat in store—but Sacher's cooking requires an absolutely unspoiled, discerning palate, and the harshness of whisky could, well, interfere with your appreciation of the dinner. I hope you don't mind my saying this, but political specialist though I am, my avocation and one affectation is gastronomy."

"I don't mind. Thanks for the advice."

"If you wish to drink, I'd suggest a Viennese beer, say a glass of Schwechtar."

Sydney Ormsby looked up at the waiter. "I'll have the double Scotch."

Heart sinking, Doyle ordered a bottle of Schwechtar.

"Now, m'dear chap," said Ormsby as he faced Doyle, "you wanted to know why this is my first and last visit to Vienna? Well, I'll be only too glad to tell you. You know what I've found out in five hours here today? This beastly provincial village has no women, not a goddam one, and it has no night life at all after ten o'clock, I'm told. They roll up the bloody sidewalks at ten, as you Americans say."

"If by 'women' you mean pretty women, Vienna has its fair share."

"Oh, yes? Where? All I saw today were some bloated *Hausfrauen* and some dowdy shop clerks reeking of garlic, and secretaries with thick legs."

"Well, of course, you've got to look around—"

"Forgive the funk, m'dear chap, but I haven't the time to look around. Anyway, I can judge a city in an hour. Either they are there, shaking it in your face, or they are not there at all. There is nothing here, Mr. Doyle, nothing."

"You're right about the night life, of course. Some may be found for tourists, but generally it's nonexistent. I guess there's no market for it. After five hearty meals your average Viennese is ready for nothing more active than television or sleep, which amount to the same thing."

The waiter had brought the drinks, and Sydney Ormsby snatched at his and lifted the glass in a toast. "Here's to Paris then—where the action is."

Doyle lifted his beer glass, smiling weakly, and drank a little as he watched Ormsby down half his Scotch.

"Matter of fact," Ormsby was saying, "I didn't plan to join my brother until tomorrow, but if we can conclude our business this evening, and I see no reason why we can't, I may take a midnight plane out of here, or even an earlier one."

For the first time since meeting his publisher, Doyle's heart tripped with pleasure. Ormsby's optimism about concluding their business "this evening" sounded the exact note that Doyle had hoped to hear. Dinner or no dinner, Doyle determined to pursue the business at hand without delay. But before he could follow through, two small cards intruded between Ormsby and himself. The dinner menus had been offered.

Meaning to brush the menus aside and suggest another round of drinks, since drinks seemed more likely to establish a congenial atmosphere of receptivity in Ormsby than food might, Doyle was halted by Ormsby's high-pitched announcement, "Good Lord, I am hungry. Didn't realize how much until this moment. If you've no objections, suppose we order?" Instantly Doyle surrendered business to his guest's sudden famine.

Ormsby was scanning the menu. Then he muttered through his mustache, "Reads like Whitaker's *Almanack*. I don't have the patience. Any suggestions?"

Doyle relaxed. Here he was on solid ground. "As a matter of fact, I've had considerable experience with Viennese cooking. While their national cuisine doesn't have the artfulness and variety of the French, I do believe you'll find Sacher's kitchen exceptional."

"Good, good," said Ormsby, drumming his fingers on the table. "But food. I'm hungry."

"Yes, of course. For an appetizer I'd recommend Butterteigpaste-tchen mit Geflügelragout—that spells creamed chicken in a patty shell —it dissolves in your—"

"Skip the appetizer."

"Then a soup. Let us say Rindsuppe mit Leberknödel, that's a liver dumpling in beef consommé—"

"If you say so, that is it. Now, the main course—"

"I'd suggest the specialty of the house—Tafelspitz—"

"What in the devil's that?"

"Well, it's boiled beef really, but—"

"Forget it. I've had boiled beef in London until it comes out of my ears."

"But, Mr. Ormsby, this is not quite the same as your English boiled

53

beef. There are countless slices of beef, and Sacher's Tafelspitz is the magnificent brisket portion. I would suggest you—"

"Mr. Doyle, forgive me, but Tafelwhatever is out."

Doyle, who had begun to perspire at the brow, shrugged good-naturedly. "In that case, I'd suggest Wiener Schnitzel—that is a veal cutlet fried—"

"Mr. Doyle, I know what Wiener Schnitzel is. Good. That'll do it."

"And for a dessert, of course, it'll be the pastry that made Sacher's famous—"

"Don't tell me. Let me guess. Sachertorte." Ormsby grinned maliciously. "I hate it."

"Hate it?" Doyle was taken aback. "But this is the original—chocolate cake, chocolate icing, apricot jam—Sacher first invented it for Prince Metternich, when the Prince—"

"Have they got stewed fruit?"

"Ah, Gemisches Kompott—definitely."

"Stewed fruit, then. I don't like to overeat when I'm about to discuss business. And make it another whisky."

With a wheeze, Doyle summoned the headwaiter. Somewhat embarrassed, he ordered for Ormsby. About to order for himself, he hesitated, inhibited by the publisher's remark about overeating. Hunger pangs, as well as the temptress menu, weakened him, and he cursed himself for not having taken one of his yellow appetite-depressant pills. Anguished, he compromised, avoiding the appetizers, requesting a small bowl of soup instead of a large one, confining himself to a normal portion of Tafelspitz instead of a giant portion, and then defiantly insisting upon Sachertorte and coffee.

When the sommelier materialized, Ormsby was disinterested and left it to Doyle to determine the selection of wine. After nervous consideration of the list, Doyle rejected the Heuriger vintages as too new, and settled for a safe, expensive old Rotwein.

Returning his attention to Ormsby, Doyle found the publisher inspecting him. "You're quite the trencherman, Mr. Doyle."

Doyle wanted to deny it, but then he knew that he could not deny his bloated face or protruding belly. "Well," he began with forced cheer, "as some Viennese philosopher once put it—all men have a sentence of death passed on them at birth, and then they have the sentence indefinitely suspended, so their only sensible behavior is to emulate a condemned man, that is, 'hope for the best and have a good meal.' "

Ormsby grinned. "A bit gloomy but I'll go along with it, if you substitute 'a good woman' for 'a good meal' and add to it—that is, if I may include business with pleasure—'and enjoy a good book.' " Ormsby drained his Scotch glass, then winked. "That's why I came all the way here, old chap, to find myself a good book."

Doyle glowed. His guest's earlier edginess had been dulled by the whisky. Ormsby even seemed likable now. Doyle waited for the consommé, crackers, and rolls to be set before them, and then he said, "You've come to the right place, Mr. Ormsby. This book is the product of years—years of detective work—"

"Evidently, from your letter. It should be a remarkable exposé." He had a spoonful of soup, and without looking up he said, "I'm honored you came to us. I assume no other publisher has seen the outline."

Doyle would not permit his voice to betray him. He said evenly, "Oh no, I wouldn't let it out of my hands until it was ready. When I knew it was ready, I wrote you first."

"You'll never regret your choice. It so happens"—he dug into his inner coat pocket and produced a fuchsia-colored pamphlet—"we specialize in political works." He handed the pamphlet to Doyle. "This might interest you. Our fall announcement catalogue. You'll find a preponderance of political books, important current histories and biographies, many by noted statesmen. Of course, you know that my brother, Sir Austin, is in the Prime Minister's Cabinet—in fact, arriving in Paris with the P.M. tomorrow for the Summit on Monday— and, no need hiding it, my brother's position naturally attracts many important political figures and authors to our house. Have a look."

"Thank you," said Doyle, happy to be considered once more as the equal of important political figures and authors.

Finishing his soup, Doyle turned the pages of the fall nonfiction announcement catalogue. There was the usual number of English books on weather, bird-watching, great country houses, cricket, Byzantine painting, Germany, early clocks, steam locomotives, World War I, the Great Fire, Victoria, both Lawrences, Islamic culture, and rose gardens—but there were also, Doyle noted, autobiographies and personal adventures of international political leaders, journalists, explorers, espionage agents.

Doyle was impressed and eager to be among them. He passed the catalogue back to Ormsby, who was ravishing the Wiener Schnitzel. "I'd be proud to be on a list like that," Doyle said.

"Let's have you on the list as soon as possible," said Ormsby between mouthfuls. He glanced at his wristwatch. "I daresay it's not too soon to get on with our business. With decent luck, we should be able to conclude it within the hour. Then I can trundle off to Paris tonight, and you can dash to your typewriter and finish up the book. What do you say to that?"

Eating his delicious Tafelspitz, Doyle was reluctant to spoil the joy of it by having to worry about Ormsby's reactions to the manuscript during dinner. Moreover, he disliked having the manuscript compete with the Wiener Schnitzel. Yet he was eager for the final triumph. "Whatever you think best, Mr. Ormsby."

"You have the manuscript. I have the contract. I think it best that I read the manuscript straightaway. Only a formality, you know, but still—" He paused. "It's not too long, is it?"

"Oh, no, no," said Doyle quickly, pulling open the zipper of his portfolio and extracting the folder containing the chapter and outline. "A half hour should do it." He tried to keep his hand from trembling as he handed the manuscript across the table to Ormsby. "I—I'm sure you'll like it."

"No fear, old boy." He fondled the folder, then opened it and pressed it on the table beside his remnant of Wiener Schnitzel. "If you don't mind keeping busy with the boiled beef, I'll just concentrate on our book."

Doyle's throat was dry. "Never mind about me. You—you read."

Immediately Sydney Ormsby began to read, and Doyle pretended nonchalance and complete devotion to his Tafelspitz, which somehow had turned tasteless and did nothing to sate the clutching hunger in his stomach.

With elaborate care Doyle fussed over the beef, accompanying each slice with a fresh crusty roll. His forehead was wet, and his throat constricted as he forced down the last piece of beef, following it with one more roll and a swallow of wine. Head bent over his empty plate, he stole a look at his juror across the table. Ormsby had turned four pages and was on the fifth, and following Ormsby's small eyes as they darted from margin to margin, Doyle could almost remember and recite, word for word, what the publisher was reading. Fascinated, almost hypnotized, Doyle watched Ormsby, whose eyes were fastened on the pages. Doyle's right hand absently fumbled for the basket of rolls, felt inside it, found no rolls left, and pulled back. Shame suffused Doyle. He had consumed *all* the rolls. Should he send for more? No, that might distract Ormsby. His own traitorous, insatiable stomach begged to be filled. Silently Doyle tried to quiet it with every side dish, every crumb left on the table. He wondered if he could survive his angry stomach's demands. Should he order more Tafelspitz? No, it would disturb Ormsby's reading.

Suddenly Ormsby looked up, tongue sucked between his teeth. "Cracking good chapter, that first one. Real jolter, a brute. Jolly good.

Can't wait to press on." Sipping his wine, he turned the page and started reading the outline.

Doyle had sagged with relief, and now he sat beaming foolishly at the admirable Ormsby. Before his gaze Ormsby had been transformed. He was Ormsby the Wise, Ormsby the Handsome, Pericles and Apollo in one. Doyle watched another page turn, then another, and he searched Ormsby's face, seeking a sign, any sign, an eyebrow movement, a blink, an exhalation, any reaction of continuing approval. But the peerless publishing face was an inanimate mask.

Doyle could not endure another second of this suspense. He leaned forward, whispering, "Please excuse me, I've got to visit the men's room." It was as if the absorbed Ormsby had not heard him. Trying to pull in his stomach so as not to jar the table, Doyle wriggled out of his chair, stood up, and walked away from the excruciating testing ground.

Once inside the lavatory, he had no idea why he was there except that he had said he was going there. He moved aimlessly about, stopped before a washbasin, washed and soaped his hands and face, dried them, consulted his watch. This had consumed five minutes. In twenty minutes Ormsby would be through. Doyle could not bring himself to return to the decisive battlefield. Then his stomach, crying out for anesthesia, gave him guidance.

Swiftly Doyle left the lavatory, and passing the captain, he murmured that he wanted some air before the Sachertorte. Once outside, Doyle turned left and almost trotted to Kärntnerstrasse. There he sought and located the old-fashioned café he had remembered. Pushing inside, he found a chair at the marble table between the jukebox and the espresso machine. Ignoring the newspapers that the waiter brought him, Doyle explained that he was in great haste, and would like to order whatever was hot and ready. Told that the Rindsgulyas was prepared, Doyle nodded, and requested a double order.

In less than a minute the mound of beef goulash lay before him. He flung himself at it with the enthusiasm of a barbarian attacking a vestal virgin. He ate steadily, hardly chewing, hardly thinking, chomping and swallowing as his fork rose and fell in perpetual motion. In ten minutes the plate had been devastated. Belching, Doyle paid his bill, came unsteadily to his feet, and intoxicated and topheavy with food, he staggered out of the café and headed back to Sacher's.

Inside the hotel restaurant once more, his agitated nerves smothered under goulash, he made his way to the table, flexing his plump writing hand, the one that would sign the contract. Ormsby was there, absently finishing the stewed fruit, the manuscript open beside him. The publisher looked up curiously as Doyle moored himself behind the table.

"Sorry to be so long," he said.

57

Ormsby nibbled at a slice of pear but said nothing.

Doyle swallowed and indicated the manuscript. "Have you—have you finished it yet?"

"I don't know."

Puzzled, Doyle asked, "You don't know?"

"I don't know if I've finished. The last page seems to be missing. Where is it?"

Filled with consternation, Doyle grabbed for the open manuscript and stared at the page to which it was opened, and then stared at the publisher. "But this *is* the last page," said Doyle. "It's right here. You've read it."

"You mean, that's all of it? M'dear chap, you're not having me on—?"

Doyle's face twitched beyond control. "I don't know what you mean. The whole thing is here—"

Sydney Ormsby's features had hardened. "My good fellow, if that's the whole of it, then you've brought me to this miserable village under false pretenses. What you have there might be suitable, with sufficient revisions, for a juvenile series we publish called 'Young People's Fairy Tales From Many Lands.' Because that's all your bloody manuscript amounts to, as it stands, a goddam fairy tale. Your letter promised me a fully documented exposé, and because of your word and reputation, I went to considerable expenditure of both money and time to fly out of my way to see your bloody masterpiece. Instead—well—what is it in fact? A stack of warmed-over, rehashed, twice-told innuendos and deductions about faults in the Warren Commission Report, leading up to the claim that Oswald was not the culprit."

"But he wasn't—he wasn't!" Doyle cried out. Then aware that he had attracted the attention of other diners, he tried to lower his voice. "Oswald wasn't guilty. It was an out-and-out Communist conspiracy. You read the first chapter and the outline. I heard the truth firsthand, right here in this city in 1961—and it's authentic. I heard about the plan to kill Kennedy, and he *was* killed—"

Ormsby's tone was full of shrill contempt. "Your President was assassinated by one man, one psychotic screwball. There is not a shred of proof in your book that anyone else did it or that it was a conspiracy. What you fell for was the silly gossip of some deranged female—"

Doyle was reduced to beggary. "Mr. Ormsby, listen," he pleaded, "I swear it's all fact, it's—"

"It's worthless rot, it's nothing," said Ormsby with anger. "If it's fact, then what is the name of the woman who passed it on to you, and what is the name of her highly placed Russian informant, and what are the names of the conspirators who planned to kill your President? Where is that kind of fact, and where are the affidavits and documentation to back it up?"

As Ormsby reached for his umbrella cane, Doyle tried desperately to stay him. "But, Mr. Ormsby, can't you see? I mean, can't you see it's possible for me to get what you want, all the names, affidavits, everything that you require? If I just have a contract with a sufficient advance to—to buy me time to get to the right people, to pay them off—that's all I need. There's enough in the manuscript to justify a contract and to give me a chance—"

Sydney Ormsby was on his feet. "M'dear chap, Ormsby Press Enterprises, Limited, is not a charitable institution. We do not dole out guineas and pounds to alchemists to encourage their insane schemes. We are in the business of supporting real authors who write real books, not obsessed fanatics."

Listening to him speak, Doyle could see how incredibly unattractive Ormsby was, after all, and who it was in ancient Rome that Ormsby resembled. The twenty-third Emperor of Rome had been Elagabalus, a sadistic, detestable, effeminate fourteen-year-old who used eye shadow, and rouge on his cheeks, and kept a burly male slave beside him for his mate. Definitely Elagabalus, that tiny and dainty painted creature who never wore the same robe twice, that shrill and gaudy hysteric who used his power to murder helpless children and who celebrated by having sycophants served feasts of pheasant eggs, beans covered with pearl dust, tongues of larks, heels of camels, and who, when his time came, was dragged kicking and screaming from his hideout in a latrine, and then butchered and cast into the Tiber.

Doyle looked up at Ormsby with disbelief that he was Ormsby and not Elagabalus, and that he had not been butchered and cast into the Danube.

As from a distance, Doyle could hear the shrill Mayfair voice. "I'm sure I need not thank you for the price of the dinner, Doyle, considering what you really owe me for the expense of this wild goose chase and what you owe me for trying to bring you back to your senses. Good night."

Alone, at last, Jay Thomas Doyle sat too numbed to think.

His bursting stomach groaned. Automatically, he sought to soothe it. He ate his Sachertorte. He drank his coffee. He ordered and ate another basket of rolls, another Sachertorte, and he gulped down two more cups of coffee. When he felt ready to faint, he croaked out, *"Zahlen, bitte,"* and the *Ober* came at once with the silver platter bearing the bill.

Glassily, Doyle examined each item, and shuddered at the total of

59

the check. Had he obtained the contract and cash advance from Elagabalus, as he had expected, the bill would have been reasonable enough. Although it would further deplete his budget in any case, it could have been regarded as a successful investment in his immediate future, a future which would have brought him much more money. But in his present condition, with no future except the damn cookbook, this bill represented a serious outlay.

Doyle coughed, and said to the puzzled headwaiter, "May I see the captain?"

The headwaiter hesitated. "If there is anything wrong—any mistake, sir—?"

"Let me see the captain."

Uneasily Doyle waited, wondering if his pose should be offended arrogance or sorrowful wheedling. By the time the worried captain appeared, Doyle had decided upon offended wheedling.

He held up the bill. "Herr Captain—"

"Yes, Herr Doyle?"

"—there seems to have been a slight error, and omission. You—you've neglected my twenty per cent discount."

"Discount?" The captain had taken the bill but did not look at it. "I do not understand?"

This was embarrassing, and Doyle found it difficult to go on, but every penny counted now. When a man was down and out, anything—begging, borrowing, stealing from prideful better days—was justified. "I—I only mean, the times I was here before, you gave me a twenty per cent discount automatically. I mean—you understood that my dinners were to your best interests in terms of future promotion, publicity. I'm giving Sacher's a good deal of space in my cookbook, and the book will be widely circulated. I—"

He stopped, shamefaced, because he could detect that the captain's professional respect had been replaced by personal scorn. They were no longer guest and servant, but equals haggling like fishwives in the marketplace. "I could refer this to the management, sir, but I doubt if you would receive an answer other than the one I give. The policy of most first-class restaurants in Austria is to cooperate with those of the visiting press, but only up to a point. You have been our dinner guest twice in a week, and we saw fit to show our appreciation. However, it is unusual that on a third visit a guest would expect—"

Humiliation had colored Doyle's puffy face, and he sought to retain a last vestige of dignity through invoking justice. "As you wish, Captain," he said, "but it seemed to me only fair that since I intended to do so much for you, you should continue to be cooperative. The

60

money itself is of no interest to me. It is a matter of principle. However, if you don't see fit to cooperate, we'll forget it."

The captain had been pretending to study the bill. When his head lifted, his features had resumed their servile politeness, but his tone of voice could not fully conceal his contempt. "Very well, Herr Doyle. We will stretch our policy this one time. Let us compromise. Let us say that the discount shall be ten per cent."

With a pencil the captain adjusted the bill and dropped it on the table. After according Doyle a stiff bow, he departed.

Doyle, counting out his schilling bank notes, knew that this had been only a shabby victory for his soul. Rising from the table and waddling away, he was oblivious to the fact that there was no one, not even the captain, to wish him good evening. Because for no one had it been a good evening.

Outdoors, the air, despite a drop in temperature, did not refresh Doyle. It was one of those black nights of the mind and heart when a human being could not see ahead. He walked blindly along Kärtnerstrasse, as if in a desolate community divested of all life but his own.

It surprised him when he had reached the neon brightness of the Hotel Imperial. He had no idea how he had been propelled there. Briefly he was again conscious of his bodily existence. Physically his compulsive gluttony had debilitated him, and breathing was difficult, and his stomach and legs ached. Mentally he was in the lowest depths of despair that he had ever known. His manuscript of the conspiracy and assassination had as much chance of seeing publication as the Book of Jasher or any other of the lost books of the Bible. His hopes for the final solution had vanished, because, considering his financial situation, Moscow was now on Mars. There was nothing left except the cookbook, which would allow him to eat himself to death, but it was an oblivion he now despised because of its slowness.

He entered the hotel lobby, went to the concierge's desk, and accepted his room key and the morning's international edition of the New York *Herald Tribune*. (He, like most old Paris hands, persisted in calling the newspaper by its former name, loyally refusing to acknowledge the Washington *Post* in the masthead.)

Out of habit, and not interest, since the world held no attractions for him, he unfolded the newspaper and automatically scanned the front page as he crossed the lobby to the elevators. The lead story told him that the ministers of the five powers had arrived in Paris, in advance of their leaders, and were meeting in the Quai d'Orsay to lay out an agenda for Monday's first Summit conference. Another story told him of preparations at Orly for the arrival of the President of the United

61

States and his staff that afternoon, and of plans for receiving the Prime Minister of Great Britain on Sunday morning, and the Premier of Soviet Russia and the Chairman of the Chinese Communist Party on Sunday afternoon. The headlines near the bottom of the page referred to a dock strike in New York, the opening of the fashion shows by the foremost French couturiers in two days, and the arrival of the retired former President of the United States, Emmett A. Earnshaw, in London to receive some honor or other from the British-American Friendship Society.

It was all as remote and unrelated to Doyle's life, these people, these events, as if he were reading the Boston *Gazette* of June 14, 1777.

Turning the front page and folding it back, he entered the elevator and gave the operator his floor number. As the elevator doors closed and entombed him, Doyle's gaze fell disinterestedly on the third page of the international edition of the *Herald Tribune,* and then he blinked, but ceased blinking as his eyes widened with astonishment.

There, out of the mass of newspaper print, was the long-elusive, familiar female face staring up at him. And then, beneath the face, the bold caption thundering at him:

HAZEL SMITH, ANA'S STAR CORRESPONDENT, IN PARIS TO COVER SUMMIT.

ANA has summoned its leading correspondents from around the globe to guarantee readers the fullest coverage of the most momentous international conference in history. Among these is the celebrated Hazel Smith, veteran of ANA's Moscow Bureau, who arrived in Paris yesterday to give readers close-ups of the colorful personalities surrounding the Summit. Enjoy Hazel Smith's feature stories daily, beginning with her first one datelined Paris today (see column 8).

His eyes almost out of their sockets, Doyle's head jerked, forcing them to the right-hand column. Yes, it was true. There was the by-line, "By Hazel Smith." There was the dateline, "PARIS, JUNE 14 (ANA)." There was her lead:

Everyone's second city, the City of Light, is brighter than ever today because the shining promise of peace on earth is in the air. Shortly after landing at Orly yesterday, I dined lavishly in Maxim's with several wives of Russian delegates, whom I had known in Moscow. They were unanimous in their belief that Premier Alexander Talansky and the entire USSR delegation are determined to cast their lot with the West in the conviction that this will guarantee nuclear disarmament and future peace. Ever since Communist China tested its first neutron bomb and displayed its first intercontinental ballistic missile, the Russians have leaned West, knowing that the New China could not go it alone and would have to submit to joining a peaceful community of nations in disarmament. And so the Russian wives were celebrating, and in Maxim's their talk was not of politics but of feminine fashion and haute couture and the designs of Yves St.-Laurent, Marc Bohan, Balenciaga, Givenchy, and Legrande, who will have their collections shown concurrently with the opening of the Summit Conference. Also—"

Doyle felt a hand touch his arm, and he looked up, startled.

It was the elevator boy saying, "Your floor, sir."

Doyle realized that the elevator doors had been open some time at his floor. Dazed, he once more peered down at the newspaper in his hand, at the insert cut of Hazel Smith (solemn, and suddenly beautiful), at her by-line (friendly as an RSVP).

His mind, so deadened by the evening's defeat, had leaped back to life, reeling and dancing with excitement.

Hazel Smith in Paris! For the first time in all these years, Hazel Smith within his reach!

In the wink of a second, his hopes, his dreams of glory, were restored. Suddenly everything, anything, was possible.

"Take me down to the lobby," he ordered the elevator boy.

"The lobby?"

"Fast!"

The frightened operator whirled to punch his buttons, and metal doors closed, and the elevator began its descent. As it dropped, Doyle's spirits soared as if freed of ballast. Good God. Praise God, he thought, he would be saved yet. He needed no cash advances. He needed no Moscow. He needed no one, he needed nothing, except Hazel, and she had emerged from hiding, she was at hand, almost underfoot. He need not appeal to her purse, only to her heart. All women had hearts, and all women's hearts were frail and forgiving. He would be attractive for her. He would diet, crash-diet, lose twenty pounds in a week. He would be young and attentive again. He would love her. He *did* love her; he loved her more these moments than he had ever loved anyone in his life.

"The lobby, sir," the boy was saying.

Jay Thomas Doyle crumpled his newspaper under his arm and rushed across the red carpet to the concierge, who was waiting for him. Tugging his money clasp out of his pocket, Doyle peeled off three 100-schilling notes and shoved them into the bewildered concierge's hand.

"For you," Doyle said. "Now here's what I want you to do for me. Get me on the first jet plane leaving for Paris tonight—*tonight,* you understand? I've got to be at a Paris conference by morning."

"You mean the Summit, Herr Doyle?"

"In a way, yes, I suppose you could call it that," said Doyle. "I'll be upstairs packing. Do your best."

Then humming and wheezing happily, swinging his leather portfolio, Jay Doyle headed back to the elevator to prepare for his Summit.

As his audience applauded his last remarks, former President of the United States Emmett A. Earnshaw paused, smiled warmly and reached for the tumbler of water set on the lectern beside him. Taking a swallow of water to ease his hoarse throat, Earnshaw stood nodding his acknowledgment on the dais of the Dorchester Hotel ballroom in London, enjoying almost the first public appreciation he had received in many months.

Rocking slightly on his heels, Earnshaw did not want to interrupt the clapping hands. It was wonderful to be approved of, and wanted by someone somewhere. Clearly, even after three years out of the White House, he was still honored here, by a civilized and good people who dwelt an ocean away from his home. Warmly conscious of the Stars and Stripes and the Union Jack draped behind him, the row of dignitaries that included his sponsors, Sir Austin Ormsby and Lord Eric Blenkinsop, seated behind him, and happily conscious of the long tables crowded with 400 members of the British-American Friendship Society stretching before him, ex-President Earnshaw's self-esteem was briefly restored.

The applause was waning. He decided that he'd better not spoil a good thing by excessive oratory. Earlier in the day, in Buckingham Palace, Great Britain's reigning monarch had bestowed upon him the K.B.E., which made him an honorary Knight Commander of the Order of the British Empire. This evening the award ceremony had been celebrated. And now, for twenty-five minutes, in his homey, unpretentious style (which spiteful political detractors had called "his circumloquacious style"), he had reminisced about his cordial relations with British Prime Ministers, whether Labor or Conservative, about the rich heritage the United States had received from its Motherland, about the necessity for the two nations to continue to stand as one, as models of democracy, free enterprise, civilization for those nations who must soon be brought into the Free World.

All of this had been spoken, unrehearsed, from a single page of notes. This lack of a prepared text was one of Earnshaw's few conceits. He liked to think that he refused to write out his speeches

64

because prepared texts made words stilted, devoid of the human touch, as if echoing the clatter of a typewriter instead of the beat of a heart. He refused to admit that he disliked prepared speeches because he disliked the strain of organizing his thoughts and the struggle to phrase those thoughts creatively, which speech-writing entailed.

He glanced at his cryptic notes through the tortoise-shell spectacles now low on the bridge of his nose, made up his mind to skip the next suggested headings and instead go directly to the conclusion. Removing his spectacles, folding them into the breast pocket of his dinner jacket, he surveyed the hushed Dorchester ballroom.

"My good friends," he resumed, his native Western accent softened by his years in the Eastern states and by the mellowness of sixty-six years, "my very good friends and hosts, let me say that your kindness, your hospitality, as well as the Order of the British Empire and the honorary title which your Monarch has seen fit to bestow upon me, and which your Foreign Secretary, Sir Austin Ormsby, has spoken of this evening, have all made this night a memorable one for a public servant now in the autumn of his career. I cannot thank you enough. I mean it. At home I have often spoken of the ideal of good old-fashioned Americanism. Here, in London, I am sure that you understand I meant nothing chauvinistic or provincial by such remarks. By Americanism I meant morality and decency in the way men treat one another, and I've always known this Great Tree of Freedom had its first kernel and roots in English soil. Tonight we are met here on the eve of a momentous five-power meeting, a meeting at which the foremost powers of the world are meeting—are gathered to—uh—to meet—in the Palais Rose of Paris. Your Prime Minister leaves for that crucial Summit tonight. Our President is already there. They represent our belief in the possible future still to be shaped. That future? What is it? You know, we once had a Secretary of State named John Foster Dulles. Yes. And—uh—when I was President, my right-hand aide and assistant, Mr. Simon Madlock, God bless his memory, was an admirer of Dulles as was I. And how often Madlock used to quote to me the words from Dulles' last public paper, and these are the words I quote to you tonight: 'I was brought up in the belief that this nation of ours was not merely a self-serving society but founded with a mission to help build a world where liberty and justice would prevail.' "

For a moment Earnshaw inhaled, paused, and then quickly, lest there be premature applause, he concluded:

"Our leaders and statesmen have gone to Paris and they will not leave until their goals, which embody our ideals, your ideals and mine, America's and Great Britain's alike, do prevail throughout this planet

65

of ours. Therefore, in the name of liberty and justice for every man individually, and all mankind collectively, do I accept your Order of the British Empire with overwhelming gratefulness and pride. Thank you, my friends, and good night."

Once again, as he now expected, ex-President Emmett A. Earnshaw was embraced by enthusiastic and deafening applause. Taking up his page of notes, touching his badge and star of the Order, he acknowledged the accolade to his worth with a modest half-bow, a half-smile, then backed off, and erect and brisk, despite his years, he returned to his empty place. Accepting Lord Blenkinsop's congratulatory handshake, he settled his long frame into the chair.

As His Lordship reached the lectern to make his closing remarks, Earnshaw continued to bask in the continuing ovation. Feeling the light cool touch of feminine fingers on his clasped hands, he twisted his head to find his niece Carol, her plain Dutch face wreathed in a proud smile, leaning toward him.

"You were wonderful, Uncle Emmett," she whispered.

He winked and squeezed her hand. He was relieved that she, the only one close to him now, who had recently seen so much that was displeasing happen to him, had been witness to this occasion. Briefly his eyes held on her, enjoying her as if she were his own daughter, which she practically had been for half her nineteen years. She was sweet and more pretty than plain, he thought, with her taffy hair and short bob, upturned nose, freckled face, rosy mouth, and she looked rather smart and grown up in the silk organza dress made for this event. The slight neckline exposed her slim throat, which was set off by the three strands of pearls that his Isabel had willed to her. Oddly, Carol resembled him, Earnshaw decided, more than she did her own father, his younger brother, so long dead. Once again he squeezed her hand, and then released it.

Shifting in his chair, Earnshaw turned away from Carol to thank his friend, Sir Austin Ormsby, seated on the other side. But to his surprise, Sir Austin's back was to him, neck craning toward someone, a hotel manager apparently, who was beckoning him urgently. Already Sir Austin had slipped out of his place, and then, bent low so as not to distract the audience from the master of ceremonies' concluding address, he was leaving the platform. Only mildly curious, Earnshaw observed Sir Austin as the hotel manager whispered into his ear, and he saw his aristocratic British host nod, nod again, and then hastily yet quietly start for the waiters' exit behind the platform.

Earnshaw politely gave his attention to the speaker, Lord Blenkinsop, who resembled G. K. Chesterton from the rear (Chesterton

66

had been one of Earnshaw's favorite detective story writers, recommended to him by Simon Madlock for the Father Brown stories). His Lordship, having extolled the former President as a worthy holder of the K.B.E., now launched into Earnshaw's contributions, along with England's contributions, to the pioneering nuclear disarmament schemes that were on the agenda of the forthcoming Summit in Paris.

Impatient with His Lordship's digression into politics, for politics had come to bore Earnshaw more and more in recent years, Earnshaw let his attention drift from the speaker to the audience. There were too many faces, a forest without trees, and he gave up trying to identify any that he might know. He studied the blue drapes on the walls enclosing the vast ballroom, then fastened on the mammoth circular inverted light in the ceiling above that had been referred to as "the dome." Mesmerized by its concave brightness, Earnshaw found his thoughts turning inward, to the recent past so poorly illuminated.

He supposed it had started going badly for him in the next to last year of his Administration, the year that produced the only black mark, minor though it had been, against his good years in office. That was when the defection at the Zurich Parley had occurred, and when his trusted right-hand man and confidant, Simon Madlock, had suddenly died of a heart attack shortly afterward. Of course, there had still been his wife Isabel, so solid and reassuring, and there had been Carol, although she had been too young to be more than a slight diversion for his troubled mind.

In his last year in the Oval Office he had wanted nothing more than to be liberated from thinking and decision-making and tiresome politics. And when the White House physician, Admiral Oates, had detected the not yet significant heart murmur and high blood pressure and advised him to go easy, he had seized upon this as a warning to retire.

Despite the anguished protests of party leaders, Earnshaw had refused to run again, promising to throw the weight of his goodwill with the electorate behind his colorless but able Vice-President. Earnshaw had predicted an easy victory for his hand-picked successor. But in the savage election contest that followed, enchanted by his prospects and plans for the easy life of retirement, and increasingly helpless since Madlock's death, Earnshaw had not campaigned for his candidate with the intensity or devotion that he had intended. The opposition party's candidate had won, less on the irritating pledge that he would awaken the nation from its Earnshawed stupor and abdication of responsibility in a world ringed by nuclear threats than on the simple fact that Earnshaw could not invest his own candidate with his own personality.

The opposition candidate, a cold, tough product of a science-oriented clique, had become President of the United States, and after three years was President still and now making a big showy circus of his attendance at the Summit in Paris.

Even though discomfited by this rejection of his personal choice by the electorate, and his resultant alienation from committeemen in his party, Earnshaw had not really minded. Retirement, at least the first year of it, had been all that he had dreamed it would be, at least as long as Isabel was beside him and the public's mass face beamed upon him and worshiped him. He and Isabel had exercised their option on the sprawling fifteen-room old Spanish-style house outside Rancho Santa Fe, south of Los Angeles and near the Pacific Ocean, and they had remodeled it, as well as the modest stable.

Other Presidents, he knew, had failed to find the leisure they had anticipated, after their retirement from the White House. It had surprised General Eisenhower how little time there had been for golf, and how much political work was still demanded of him, in retirement. Eisenhower had been constantly occupied, during long hours of long days, with party leaders, with White House consultations, with receiving foreign envoys and delegations of visitors, with writing books when not replying to endless letters. Truman had been equally busy, and the Truman Library had often been almost as demanding of his time and energy as had been his duties as Chief Executive during his years in the White House.

In Earnshaw's first twelve months of total freedom he had managed to keep his freedom total. He read the polls and knew that he was loved. He noticed his weekly mountain of mail and knew that he was respected. But he allowed Isabel and Carol to reply to his mail in his name. He avoided political party contacts, except for a handful of old card-playing cronies. His appearances on television were few and of short duration, and were usually restricted to patriotic occasions. He visited Washington only for official funerals. He had left visiting dignitaries to the Department of State and the smart-aleck in the White House. He devoted himself completely to bridge, poker, chess, to billiards on the magnificent antique table that Isabel had installed, to mystery stories that were not too long and complicated and that were in large typefaces. And, for half of each warm day outdoors, he gave time to his wonderful rose gardens, his three riding horses, his fishing schooner in the nearby bay. And then it ended.

He could never be certain afterward whether his peace and pleasure had ended with Isabel's unexpected death in the beginning of his second year of retirement, or with his slow realization that the opposi-

68

tion party in power was chipping away at his reputation. He had slowly awakened to the fact that he was losing the cushion of love he had always taken for granted and depended upon, that affection which came from the very real but quite faceless electorate out there, out there somewhere. Isabel's death, at sixty-one, had been too sudden. One evening she was there, with the hot roast, the television programs they watched, the hair curlers and plump smile and yawning pillow talk. The next morning she was not there. She had left him, to await their reunion at another time in another place. It had been terrible, that void, and neither the outpouring of public remembrance and sympathy nor the temporary return of old friends had filled the void, and not even dear Carol, then seventeen and only on the brink of understanding, had filled its emptiness.

Somehow, after the mourning, Earnshaw had tried to fill the void by keeping himself unmindful of its existence. Gradually the card games were resumed, and the fishing trips, and the garden was improved and the stable enlarged, but it had been no good. The rewards of retirement had gone stale.

Then one day, he did not know what day, he did not know when or how, the void had been filled, filled by Time, he suspected. He had found himself conscious and alive again, as an entity, as an ex-President and a personage. And he had not liked what he found of himself in the teeming, moving, progressing world. He had possessed an ally in Carol, and she was closer, more intelligent, more meaningful in her burgeoning maturity. But, to his surprise, he had not had his vast public any longer, he had not kept their interest, let alone their respect, and he had perceived dimly that the only pleasure of his late years would be to keep his pages intact in the future histories of his beloved America, but the sure promise of pages (plural) was diminishing to a page, a half-page, a footnote, and he had hated it.

He could not discern, at first, how it had happened, or was happening. In his early resentment he had blamed the President in power, the opposition party, and the press that they now coddled and controlled, for his fall from favor. He had condemned them for cleverly constructing the slide that would bring him down into final oblivion. Their motive, he had thought, was political: to reduce his effectiveness in future elections. The reporters, the journalists, had been another matter, actually. Their business was news, living news, and Earnshaw, as an amiable hermit, was no longer news except when he was ill-used in the handouts of his political enemies. The new historians and political scientists, with their pretentious half-baked evaluations and analyses of his personality and administration, were understandable, too. These clever ones throve on Presidents who were involved in conflict, domestic or foreign. The reactions of such Presidents to crisis were studied and praised, but in superficially examining Earnshaw's term, his critics had found a good, easy Chief Executive in a good, easy time, an era of little internal stress and devoid of international strife. And so they had downgraded him as if avoiding trouble and playing caretaker to peace were a weakness and a sin.

But inescapably Earnshaw's private accusations had swung from others to himself. Could the blame for his diminished position lie in some personal failure, after all? Quite possibly, he had decided. His strength, his power, his future in history, had always rested in the hands of the dependable public. They had elevated him to their highest office and supported him in the Executive Mansion because they respected and admired him as authority and hero. And after he had retired, they remained his worshiping family because they knew that he was still there, a living oracle, a voice of wisdom to sort out their own confusion, answer their questions, relieve their tensions, give assurance to their hopes. Yes, after his retirement they had been there for him—but then, he had come to understand, he had not been there for them to lean upon. They had needed him, and he had ignored them, left them to the cold one in the White House. In their eyes he had abdicated his place to satisfy his own selfish requirements. It was as if a beloved and respected parent, with many children who had long leaned upon him, had suddenly taken off to dwell hedonistically in isolation on some distant island, unmindful of his brood's needs and problems, refusing to answer their phone calls or their letters or see them in person. Like that French banker who had abandoned his family to gratify his own selfish need to paint in Tahiti.

Earnshaw had turned away from his public when they needed him, and when he had turned back, later, it should not have surprised him that they were no longer there. And without this massive public, who would never permit a usurper to replace him in their esteem (as long as he did not fail or betray them), Earnshaw was the head of a family without a family. And without his relations he was helpless before the advance of political enemies bent on destroying him. Yet in a last desperation move, more than a year ago, he had sought to fight back. In his way, as best he could, he had issued a call for his clan to rally around him. Somehow he had clung to the belief that the old charm, the old magic, would work as it had always worked. He had been shocked when his call was not heard. It had been as if his public thought that he had ceased to exist, that the pleading voice had been only the whisper of a ghost—or worse, as if the pleading voice had been heard, clearly heard, but was no longer heeded. It was as though his behavior outside of office had only confirmed the opinions of those who insisted it resembled his behavior in office, and now he was discredited, a hero of clay from head to foot.

Yet there had been those, here and there, who heard his call. His old friends in England, for example, who had announced this honor and invited him to accept it. While he was preparing for London, some faith in his old magic had been momentarily restored. When he was at his peak, even in retirement, columnists had always enjoyed speculating upon his appeal. And Isabel, with Carol's assistance, had enjoyed filling scrapbook after scrapbook with these analyses. The formula for his magic, the press had believed, consisted of many elements—his unaffected speech, his simple wisdom (uncorrupted by intellectuals, whom he distrusted), his relaxed style, and above all his benign countenance and attractive physical appearance. Even his worst enemies had conceded that Earnshaw's looks were his greatest asset, which no intelligent argument could overcome at the ballot box.

While Earnshaw had never liked this business about his looks, he had reconsidered it before leaving for his small English triumph. His outer aspect, currently, differed little from what it had been when he left the White House three years ago. He was still, as he had been in favored days, tall and unbent, and he retained the winning ungainliness of the country lawyer he had once been (people tended to forget that he had also been a corporation lawyer in an Eastern metropolis). He possessed still his full shock of gray hair, peaked bushy eyebrows, cheerful blue eyes, pug nose, broad happy mouth, dimpled cheek, cleft chin, all drawn on a long, frank, grandfatherly face, all (except the nose) quite like Uncle Sam with the beard removed.

While Earnshaw wore his custom-tailored wool suits easily, they did not appear as expensive and fashionable as they were, because of his gangling height, slight potbelly, long arms and big reddish hands, and his jerky, bobbing gait. When he entered a room, everyone in it expected that he was bringing them presents, for he seemed so *good,* so pleased, so twinkling, chuckling, glad-handing, happy. When he was on a plane, other passengers felt easier, as if knowing nothing could happen to them. Too, one felt safer, truly, with a man who could misquote from Mark Twain, George Ade, P. T. Barnum, Ring Lardner, Clarence Darrow, Vachel Lindsay, S. S. Van Dine, and who could not even pronounce Thorstein Veblen, René Descartes, Franz Boas, Carl Jung, Fyodor Dostoevski, Percy Bysshe Shelley, Rufus Choate, than with a hundred supercilious know-it-alls who knew everything except how to get people to elect them to office.

Earnshaw's magic was no secret from anyone, not really. Instinctively he liked people, and as a result they liked him. Earnshaw's philosophy was no secret either. The world was inhabited by two kinds of men—the good ones and the bad ones. The good ones liked America and Earnshaw. The bad ones were bad not because they were cruel or ignorant or tyrannical, but because they did not like America or Earnshaw. Well, any darn fool could understand that now. If someone was around, or came along, who didn't like your country or didn't like you, well, you weren't going to think very highly of him, were you?

Reviewing the past reviews of himself, even the worst by "the *Fraudian* headshrinkers of the press who try to put every public figure on the couch of their columns," as Simon Madlock had once so cleverly punned it, Earnshaw was certain that he had not changed a bit since his heyday. If the elements that had made him popular not long ago still existed in his person, then his popularity could be regained. Perhaps the Order of the British Empire would remind the public of an old love.

Suddenly, far off as he was in retrospection, Earnshaw heard his own name resound in his ears, and he dropped his gaze from the blazing dome on which it had been fixed, and by a great effort of will he swiveled his mind's eye from the past to the present, and then he sat straight.

The portly peer at the lectern had concluded his tribute and was pointing toward him, and 400 dinner guests throughout the ballroom were noisily on their feet applauding and cheering him once more, and above the din he could hear Carol's excited cry, "Oh, how marvelous, Uncle Emmett!"

Earnshaw bounded to his feet, went forward with his old ebullience, linking his arm in His Lordship's arm, murmuring his thanks, then waving and waving to his English public out there.

And then all the lights were brighter, and the applause had ended, and there were the indistinct sounds of groups conversing below, moving their chairs, shuffling toward the gold-trimmed glass doors of the regal entrance that would take them out into Park Lane where their cars would be waiting in the summer night's fog.

Earnshaw tried to reach his niece, but he found himself surrounded by both beefy and ascetic English faces, and he was occupied while strange hands pumped his own and strange voices congratulated him, and for fleeting seconds he enjoyed the emotions of Election Night over again. Presently, when he reached the edge of the platform, he came upon a happy Carol waiting, ignoring attentive swains to be with him. As he spoke his last appreciations for the evening and began to take leave of the festivities, he realized the immensity of his exhaustion. His shoulders and back ached; his arms felt leaden and his legs

72

knobby and ancient. It had been a long trip from California to London. It had been an endless day of sights and events, which he had not resisted because this was Carol's first trip abroad. It had been an evening of pressure, this evening of his comeback, and now that it was over, a success, he was weary to the marrow of his bones. He wanted only the privacy of his suite, shoes off, cigar, one brandy, and the softness of bed and sleep, since tomorrow he and Carol must awaken early to catch the cruise ship for Norway, Sweden and Denmark.

Turning down the numerous impromptu invitations to drinks, to supper, to nightclubs—and Carol loyally declining them with him—Earnshaw clumped down the wooden stairs to the ballroom floor. The hotel manager, an assistant, and two Secret Service men were waiting to escort him to his suite. Gratefully he had started toward them, when a constraining hand gripped his elbow. Turning his head sharply, he found Sir Austin Ormsby next to him.

A movement of Sir Austin's eyes signaled him to come to one side for something private. Tired but anxious to be agreeable, Earnshaw followed Sir Austin to the nearest empty table.

"Well, Austin," Earnshaw began, "I can't tell you how pleased—"

"Emmett, I must see you privately in your rooms at once. There is a pressing matter I must discuss with you."

Earnshaw grimaced good-naturedly. "Can't it wait, Austin? I've been looking forward to a little time alone with you. But I thought you might join me at early breakfast, before Carol and I leave. Right now, I don't mind telling you, I'm suffering from too much of a good thing—too much of your hospitality and too much of too many birthdays. Isn't it something we can put off until morning?"

Sir Austin's countenance, for one so well-bred, reflected a surprising absence of consideration. There was a single-minded determination in his features. "Emmett, I do suggest you make a little time for me now. A matter has just come up, a matter of utmost urgency to you and your welfare. It can't be put off until morning."

Earnshaw's weariness was instantly pushed aside by curiosity shaded with anxiety. "What's so urgent it can't be put off until tomorrow?"

"You may want to change your plans. It may not be feasible for you to go on to Scandinavia tomorrow."

"Look here, Austin, what in the devil is this all about?"

"It concerns your reputation, Emmett, and it could be serious. I doubt if it would be wise to discuss it further here."

Earnshaw nodded. "Very well. I'll expect you upstairs in—let's say in fifteen minutes."

"I'll be there," Sir Austin said grimly.

Troubled, Earnshaw quickly rejoined Carol and the protective Prae torians, making sure to press a smile onto his face so that there would be no questions from his niece.

After leaving the Dorchester ballroom, they proceeded through the broad luxurious lobby. Grateful that Carol had engaged their escorts in conversation, Earnshaw tried to evaluate Sir Austin's ominous words. Concentrating, he was hardly aware of the hotel guests and visitors, two rows deep in the lobby, eagerly trying to catch a glimpse of him. To a spattering of applause, Earnshaw kept his reluctant smile firm, and waved, as he tried to sort out his thoughts once more. He tried to imagine what kind of "matter of utmost urgency," one involving his "reputation," one "serious" enough to make him cancel his trip to Scandinavia, Sir Austin could wish to speak to him about.

Earnshaw's personal life had always been one of restraint, moderation, good sense. No blemish of scandal or potential scandal marred it. Equally spotless had been the record of his term as President. There had been, of course, the minor scandal of the Varney defection to Communist China during the Zurich Parley, an event oversensationalized by the opposition press. But at his own insistence, that had been aired openly in a Congressional hearing, and the Executive Branch had been held blameless, and after young Brennan's resignation the whole matter had been properly dismissed by the public.

Beyond that there had been nothing else. True, since he had been out of office, and especially in recent months, there had been mounting criticisms of his Administration. Yet none of his critics dared even hint at anything dishonest or improper in Earnshaw's conduct as President. Their carpings usually added up to the same estimate—that Earnshaw had been unimaginative, indecisive, overly conservative, and lacking in initiative and leadership. This criticism always bewildered him more than angered him. Imagine being attacked for an unspectacular term in office, he would think, as if stability were a crime. It is those other ones, he would think, the innovators, agitators, gamblers with human life—like the pinheads who had the ear of his successor, with their airy untried ideas—who should be charged with unpatriotic behavior for treating their countrymen as so many guinea pigs. But certainly his own theory of government—doing nothing, when nothing need be done—had been neither faulty nor grounds for scandal.

Yet apparently there was something wrong that threatened his reputation, and Earnshaw could not be less than apprehensive, since the carrier of the bad tidings (if such they were) was Sir Austin Ormsby, a trustworthy millionaire, a reliable Cabinet Minister, a staunch Tory, not given to repeating irresponsible gossip.

74

"Why suddenly so gloomy, Uncle Emmett?"

Startled, Earnshaw realized that Carol was addressing him, and that they stood before the green elevators off the lobby entrance.

Earnshaw sought his smile. "Not gloomy a bit, my dear. Perhaps a little tired. You'd think I was in my sixties or something."

He heard the hotel manager say, "The lift, Mr. Earnshaw."

Earnshaw touched his niece's arm. "Here we go." He thanked the manager and his assistant, and entered the elevator, quickly followed by Carol and the two young Secret Service agents.

"Eighth floor," he said to the elderly uniformed operator.

The ancient bobbed his head to the closing doors. "Oh yes, I know, sir."

When they emerged on the eighth floor, Earnshaw led the way up the soft patterned maroon carpet. As they moved between the bright electric candles encased in brass-trimmed boxes bracketed to the corridor walls, Earnshaw listened to Carol chattering with the agents behind him, yet all he could hear, still, was Sir Austin's disturbed voice. Perhaps, Earnshaw thought, for all of the Englishman's sensibility, he had become overly concerned about a matter that would prove to be of relative unimportance.

At the second intersecting corridor Earnshaw turned right and halted abruptly before the door bearing the lettering HARLEQUIN AND TERRACE SUITES. He waited impatiently for Carol to finish her conversation with the agents, so he could quickly shake hands and thank both of them for their attentiveness.

The taller of the Secret Service agents, opening the door for him, said with evident sincerity, "The assignment has been a pleasure for us, Mr. President. If anything should come up, we'll be here."

Earnshaw went through the doorway and started the steep ascent of the staircase, pausing only once to lean against the gold-and-black metal railing to catch his breath and reassure his niece that he was fine. At the landing, where the door's lettering heralded what lay behind it as the TERRACE SUITE, Earnshaw rang the bell. Almost immediately the door was opened.

The diminutive cockney valet, head inclined respectfully, welcomed them. "Good evening, Your Honor. I trust it went well, sir."

"Just perfect, Thatcher, thank you," said Earnshaw. He turned to bring Carol into the suite ahead of him; then, in the guest foyer, he stopped to say, "Thatcher, I'm expecting a visitor shortly—Sir Austin Ormsby—in about ten minutes or so. You can let him in, get us some drinks, and that'll do it for tonight. If I need you later, I'll buzz."

"Yes, sir."

Undoing his bow tie, Earnshaw entered the spacious, luxuriously furnished sitting room, saw Carol disappear into her bedroom ahead, allowed Thatcher to help him off with his dinner jacket and take it to the closet, and watched the valet close himself into the kitchen. Letting down his suspenders, slowly unbuttoning his starched shirt, Earnshaw found himself at the French doors leading to the terrace. The heavy drapes, of a floral print interwoven with Chinese figures, had been only partially drawn. Through the French doors, Earnshaw could see, behind the mist, the Union Jack hanging limply from the flagpole on the terrace, and then, beyond the terrace wall, barely visible in the night, the outlines of the treetops in Hyde Park.

In the daytime the pastoral view, so British, was soothing. Tonight it showed him little and offered nothing to calm his apprehension.

Pivoting away, he crossed the room to the small hall and went into the master bedroom. His matched luggage stood in a neat row beside the window desk, already packed by the valet and maid for his departure tomorrow, except for one suitcase that sat open on the canopied bed. The assembled luggage increased his apprehension. Sir Austin had warned him that it might not be feasible to go to Scandinavia tomorrow—whatever in the devil that was supposed to mean.

Determined to put the minor mystery out of his mind, to cease speculating upon it, Earnshaw hastened into the bathroom to wash and revive himself. But even as he removed his shirt and doused his hot face with cold water, his thoughts willfully returned to his imminent meeting and to Sir Austin Ormsby himself.

Earnshaw had first met Sir Austin Ormsby fifteen years before, just after Austin had inherited his father's press empire and well before he would earn himself knighthood through his political activities. Earnshaw had taken temporary leave of a lucrative private law practice to go into politics, and had arrived in London as an earlier President's special ambassador to treat with the British, French, and West Germans over a grave trade dispute. His London stay had lasted six months, and although Earnshaw was well acquainted with many prominent members of the French and German missions, through his legal work in international corporate law, he had found himself spending most of his spare time with Sir Austin.

Looking back, it had made no sense, for he and the young Englishman (who had become a self-appointed social host to many of the foreign visitors because of his company's enormous investments on the Continent) had so little in common. In that year Earnshaw had been fifty-one years old, and Sir Austin merely twenty-five. Earnshaw had been married for ages, and Sir Austin had been a confirmed bachelor.

Above all, their backgrounds had been completely different, and as a consequence, their personalities and tastes had been disparate. Earnshaw had been then, as he was to this day, an easygoing, folksy, grassroots American, unpolished, frank, simple in habits, opinions, tastes. Sir Austin had been then, as he was still (only more so now), an aristocrat in all but the technical sense of the word, for if his family had not evolved through Burke's Peerage, it had always been a mainstay of Burke's Landed Gentry.

While Earnshaw's conversations with Sir Austin then, and in their occasional meetings in England and America since, had never been intimate, they had provided Earnshaw with a certain amount of information about the wealthy younger man. Sir Austin had naturally gone to Eton, where the masters felt that he possessed great promise, and he had naturally gone on to Oxford. He had wanted to enter Christ Church, to be one of the "Christ Church Bloodies," but a muscular parental arm had entered him in Balliol, to become another Macmillan or, at least, a Toynbee. As an undergraduate he had wanted Engineering, but had again been firmly advised to read History.

In Oxford, to his father's distress, Sir Austin had undergone an identity crisis, rebelled against parental authority, and become part of a company of idealistic liberals. His father, in what had amounted to a postal snort, had found and underlined and sent him a newspaper cutting that described Sir Austin's new companions. "Frail men with earnest, luminous eyes, wearing heavy tweed suits and voluminous colored ties; mostly tubercular, pipe-smokers, courteous, little given to mirth, ethically Christian." It had gone on like that, and since it had been signed by someone with the improbable name of Muggeridge, Sir Austin had been merely amused and had not taken the description or his parent's sarcastic disapproval seriously.

But once he was out of Oxford, and brought into the family firm, Sir Austin's incipient liberalism had collapsed under the weight of righteous Toryism, tradition, Money-Is-Power, and Power-Demands-Responsibility-and-Duty. In the brief time that he had been heir apparent to his father's empire, and after he had become the heir, Sir Austin had gradually, then completely, reverted to the aristocratic Englishman that a hundred ancestors had intended him to be, and he had unwaveringly remained that person to this very day.

The collage of Sir Austin past and Sir Austin present merged into a single unified portrait in Earnshaw's mind. The bits and pieces that made the whole consisted of a princely, urbane, suave country gentleman and minister to the throne. Sir Austin was tasteful, fastidious, complex, affecting a fatigued Edwardian manner. His eyes were hooded, his nose thinly hooked, his small mustache slicked, his chin undershot. A brilliant public speaker, with a style largely supercilious, ironic, self-deprecating, witty, learned, he had made his debut in the Chamber of the House of Commons demolishing "the Right Honorable Gentleman" of the Opposition and had brought a clamorous ovation from the Strangers' Gallery. Sir Austin believed in Pageantry, Continuity, Decency, Lord Melbourne, Press Freedom, and The Ruling Class. The family estate in Surrey, built after Arbury Hall, had been remodeled from early Tudor to neo-Gothic, although the wrought-iron gates designed by Sir Christopher Wren had remained untouched. Sir Austin had his hunting dogs, his black Daimler, his membership in the Athenaeum and the Travellers, his town house in Hyde Park Gate, and lately he had enjoyed two more baubles. One had been the green scrambler telephone installed for all Cabinet Ministers. The other had been, after thirty-nine ascetic years of bachelorhood, his first wife, the former Fleur Grearson, twenty-nine-year-old daughter of a real-estate millionaire. Earnshaw, meeting her for the first time on this visit, had not been sure about Lady Fleur. She had seemed too mannered, too poised, too perfect, and this had made Earnshaw uncomfortable, and her conversation about the arts had been too specialized for him to understand or enjoy. Sir Austin's most persistent irritant, as Earnshaw remembered it, had been his younger brother Sydney, who had attended Bristol University (not quite Oxbridge), and whose social life seemed to be devoted to drinking and gambling at White's and making lewd remarks to chambermaids. Earnshaw had been relieved last night, for Carol's sake as well as his own, to know that Sydney was out of the city.

Recollecting this now, Earnshaw emerged from the bathroom into his bedroom and changed into a sport shirt, gray slacks, and the silk smoking jacket that Isabel had bought for him the year before her death. Knotting the belt of the smoking jacket, Earnshaw concluded that he and Sir Austin, although so contrasting in every way, had become friends from the start—not real friends but, rather, friendly companions or acquaintances—because he had wanted to know a typical upper-class Englishman who was sturdy and dependable, and because Sir Austin had wanted a more agreeable, permissive father image. And although they now had even less in common than in the past, they remained distant friends because Sir Austin was pleased to know a former President of the United States and because Earnshaw was simply a creature of habit.

Hearing footsteps in the sitting room, Earnshaw located a cigar and went into the room for his confrontation with Sir Austin. Instead he found Carol, who had exchanged her evening gown for a matching pink sweater and slacks, fiddling with the large television set in the wall above the yellow armchair.

She was surprised to see him. "Uncle Emmett, I thought you were in bed. You ought to be, you know, after a day like this and all the excitement this evening. It was glorious. I was so proud of you."

"I'd like to be in bed," he said, "but—" The television had come on, and he said, "Carol, do you mind looking at the set in your bedroom? I'm staying up only because I have some business to discuss with Sir Austin. He'll be here in a minute."

"Of course, I don't mind," she said cheerfully, moving to the set and turning it off. "Must you see him tonight?"

"I'm afraid so."

"I just hate to see you get too tired." She had started for the bedroom, then stopped and kissed him on the cheek. "I'd rather eavesdrop on you two than watch television," she said. "Sir Austin fascinates me."

"This is private business, Carol. Nothing that would interest you."

"I was only joking, Uncle Emmett. But I meant that about Sir Austin."

"Oh yes, he's interesting enough. Very bright. The youngest one, I believe, in the Prime Minister's Cabinet. Yes, he's got a lot ahead, no question—"

"I don't mean *him* per se. I just mean, well, the way he must have been embarrassed during the Paddy Jameson affair, and just wasn't shook up a bit—I mean, you listen to him, look at him, and it's like it literally never happened. Of course, the one I'm really interested in is his kid brother—you know, Sydney Ormsby—that was my only disappointment last night, that Sydney wasn't there. I could have lived off that for months back home."

"I'm just as happy Sydney wasn't there. He's stupid and quite irresponsible. He'd have ruined the evening."

"Not for me, Uncle Emmett," Carol insisted. "I've been reading about the Paddy Jameson affair since I was sixteen." Then she added teasingly, "After all, anyone who could get involved with a beautiful girl like Medora Hart, and upset the Government, and get away with it, can't be all bad."

Earnshaw squinted at his niece through his first puff of blue cigar smoke. "I haven't the faintest idea what you're talking about—"

"Sir Austin's younger brother and Medora Hart."

"Medora who?"

Carol was blinking at him. "You mean you don't remember?"

79

"Carol, please—remember what?"

"The Paddy Jameson affair three years ago. Paddy Jameson was a tennis bum and a procurer—"

Earnshaw frowned. "Now, where did you pick that word up?"

"Uncle Emmett, my God, I'm not still in gym bloomers. Anyway, this Jameson had a half-dozen gorgeous girls, I mean young girls, nice ones, and he was a go-between to help these girls meet high-class men who wanted to meet beautiful young women—important men who wanted women—and Medora Hart, you should see pictures of her, she was one of these party girls—and one of her men was Sydney Ormsby—and then it blew sky-high, a fantastic scandal—oh, you must remember—it was ten times more exciting than the old Profumo affair."

Earnshaw was utterly bewildered. "Profumo affair? Now, what in the devil was that?"

Carol slapped her forehead with her palm and pretended to collapse. "Oh, Uncle Emmett, my God, if someone could hear you! Really, you should read something besides the political stories and editorials in the papers. You don't know what you're missing."

"If you're giving me a sample of what I'm missing," said Earnshaw dryly, "I'll pass, thank you."

"But I mean, you've been seeing Sir Austin Ormsby all this time and you don't know about what really goes on. Now you sit down and let me—"

The doorbell sounded once, twice, and Earnshaw put his finger to his lips, and Carol choked down her words, nodding. The valet came hurriedly through the sitting room.

Carol made a mock grimace of distress. "Okay, Uncle Emmett, I get television, and you get the real thing." She pecked a kiss at him again. "Remind me to tell you the whole story on the way to Oslo. Don't stay up too late. See you at breakfast. I'll be packed."

She ran off to her bedroom. As her door closed, Earnshaw spun around to find Thatcher ushering Sir Austin Ormsby into the sitting room.

As the valet took Sir Austin's hat, topcoat, and umbrella back to the foyer, Earnshaw shook his friend's hand. "It was a wonderful evening, Austin. I owe it all to you."

Sir Austin nervously patted his hair and small mustache, and then the lace ruffles of his dress shirt, and said without smiling, "My dear friend, it was less than you deserve."

Heartened, Earnshaw said, "I'm having a brandy. What'll it be for you, Austin?"

Sir Austin glanced at the valet. "Short gin-and-tonic."

Earnshaw led the way across the room to the two silken green armchairs flanking the black marble fireplace. He waited for Sir Austin to settle into one chair, then himself sat on the edge of the other, one slippered foot propped on the velvet footstool, as if to show that he had no concern about this meeting. Behind Sir Austin the valet had unlocked the dummy bookshelves, fronted with the glued-on leather spines of classics like Lord Chesterfield's *Letters* and Fielding's *Tom Jones,* and disclosed a liquor cabinet. Waiting for the valet to prepare the drinks, Earnshaw sought to fill the time before they were alone.

"That was quite an evening last night," he said. "My niece hasn't stopped talking about the dinner at the Mirabelle, and the nightclub we went to later—"

"The Colony. I'm glad she was pleased. Not my sort of thing, really, but Fleur thought it just right for a young lady on her first evening in London."

"I'm sorry your bride couldn't make it tonight."

"Well, Fleur isn't much for politics, you know, but in this case she was stricken that she could not attend. She's really terribly impressed by you, Emmett. But she had that damn charity exhibit at the Tate. She was one of the sponsoring committee—"

"Golly Moses, I don't mind. I merely meant I'd like to have become better acquainted with her." His thoughts went to the conversation with Carol before Sir Austin's arrival, and he said, "My niece was quite awed by your wife. She asked about your brother, also—missed him, since he's made such a hit in publishing, and she's a journalism major in college."

Sir Austin wrinkled his patrician nose. "As between us, tell her no loss. Sydney has his points, but one of them is not discussing literature with journalism majors. Matter of fact, though, I've got him a bit more serious about his responsibilities in publishing. He's in Vienna now on a book matter, and after that he's to join me in Paris. I must say, Paris seems to be attracting everyone for different reasons right now. I have the sticky Summit business, of course. And Fleur thinks the fashion openings have been moved up early just for her. And Sydney—well—a great number of the publishers on the Continent will be there, hounding delegates for books, and I've ordered Sydney to be among them."

He paused to accept his gin-and-tonic from the valet. Earnshaw took the brandy snifter and nodded. "Thank you, Thatcher. This'll do it. Good night."

He puffed on his cigar, laid it in a tray, and took a sip of brandy, listening for the kitchen door to close. When he heard it and knew that

Sir Austin and he had privacy at last, he peered at his English friend inquiringly.

Sir Austin had set down his drink and pushed himself forward from the soft ease of the armchair. "I don't want to hold you up any longer, Emmett, and I do believe you'll want some time to think after you've heard what I have to report. You don't mind if I plunge right into it?"

Earnshaw's curiosity by now consumed him. "Plunge ahead," he said.

Sir Austin stared at the carpet a moment, then murmured, "Not quite certain where to begin." He raised his head. "Let me begin with a question, and after that I'll go on. How well do you know Dr. Dietrich von Goerlitz?"

It was the name that Earnshaw had least expected to hear in the hushed privacy of his ninth-floor Dorchester suite, and his long face did not hide his surprise. "Goerlitz?" he repeated. "How well do I know him?" He was really asking this of himself, and he considered the question. As a prominent corporation attorney, before his political career had begun, Earnshaw had met and dealt with Dr. Dietrich von Goerlitz on numerous occasions, in Washington, D.C., as well as in the vast offices of the Goerlitz Industriebau in Frankfurt-am-Main. Several times in those days he had even been received at dinner in the eighty-room stone ancestral castle, Villa Morgen, a dozen kilometers outside Frankfurt, a castle built by the Goerlitz family before the Franco-Prussian War. Since Earnshaw's clients, industrial giants themselves, shared many international patents and licenses with Goerlitz, his meetings with the gruff German had been necessities. The meetings had always made Earnshaw uncomfortable because Goerlitz was humorless and his conversation devoid of small talk. He would discuss coal, steel, mining machinery, electrical plants, nuclear generators, cargo ships, jet airplanes, all of which he manufactured, with intense passion, or speak of his rivals in West Germany, like Alfried Krupp von Bohlen of Essen, with harsh anger. Yet Earnshaw had always got on with him because Goerlitz was a tycoon of quick and firm decisions and a man of his word.

After Earnshaw had gone into politics, he had seen less of Goerlitz. And after the Spelvin Steel case investigation which had been aired on national television (when Earnshaw's gentle homespun style, contrasted to the snide legalistics of the Attorney General's staff, had catapulted him into public favor and won him the Presidential nomination, and eventually the occupancy of the White House), he had not seen Goerlitz at all. Occasionally the German's name had come up

82

during Cabinet meetings, and several times Simon Madlock had mentioned him in passing, but there had been no more personal contact between the industrialist and himself.

Now Earnshaw realized that Sir Austin had asked him a question and was waiting for his answer. "Forgive me," said Earnshaw. "I was trying to remember. I find that more and more, as I grow older, when someone inquires about something or someone in my past, and I have to go back to remember, I become lost in the past. All right. You wanted to know how well I know, or knew, Dr. Dietrich von Goerlitz. I don't think anyone was ever really close to him, if you want my guess. Maybe his children—a son, and two or three married daughters —but I doubt if even they knew him well. Uh—I'd say he and I had a fairly friendly business relationship. Of course, that was some time before I became President."

"But after you became President, Emmett? How was it then?"

Earnshaw hesitated. "Well, of course, for a while there it would have been improper to—to maintain any relationship. As I recollect, he was not tried at Nuremberg as a war criminal for lack of substantial evidence. Later, perhaps a dozen years later, before the West German statute of limitations ran out, your people turned up evidence, and Goerlitz and some lesser German Nazis were tried by another International Military Tribunal reconvened in Munich, and Goerlitz was found guilty of—what was it?—using slave labor, I think, and plundering occupied nations in the Second World War—although there was some question about that. Then he was tossed into prison—I forget how long—"

"The sentence was twenty years," said Sir Austin. "I believe he had served less than one quarter of the sentence when the Russians pressed for a pardon, and it was granted, and his factories and holdings were returned to him."

"Yes, I do remember. He made an astonishing comeback. I read somewhere recently that he has exceeded Krupp in production and sales."

"The Minister for Overseas Development was telling me only the other day that Goerlitz is matching Krupp in building contracts in the underdeveloped countries, especially India, and he's taken the lead in dealings and sales with the Communist bloc on the Continent, and especially in Red China. You did say you haven't seen him recently?"

Earnshaw shook his head. "No, I've been out of things, Austin. I was still in the White House when Goerlitz was released, but there was no reason to renew our old relationship. Of course, some of our people were in touch with him, as they were with all international industrial-

83

ists. I think my aide, Simon Madlock, did see him in Frankfurt on one trip."

"When was that?"

"Oh, I'm not sure. Nothing of consequence. I think—well, it might have been four or five years ago." Earnshaw paused, and regarded his English friend with curiosity. "Austin, I don't think I understand this discussion of Goerlitz. It seems irrelevant. You said that you wanted to speak to me about a highly personal and urgent matter. You indicated that it might have to do with my—my good name. I can't see what that old German has to do with my life. He's been out of it for years."

Sir Austin stared at the footstool between them, and, without looking up, he said, "Emmett, I'm afraid Dr. Dietrich von Goerlitz is back in your life. Very much so. In a rather nasty way, too."

Earnshaw sat stiffly on the edge of his armchair, puzzled and worried. There was a constriction in his chest, a terror of the unknown which he felt but could not fathom. "What do you mean, Austin? What are you trying to say?"

Sir Austin came forward in his armchair, so that his bony knees almost touched the footstool. He licked at his mustache before he spoke. "Dr. Dietrich von Goerlitz is an old man now, and I'm told he's physically on the decline. He must be in his seventies. He's had everything money and power can buy. What is there left for an old man who has no interests outside his business empire? One thing only. To set his past in order, set the record straight, prepare an apologia for the future. Remember, he had one bitter period in his life. He was imprisoned as a war criminal, and he's always claimed it was unjust. Very well. One thing left. Settle old scores. That's the final indulgence for an angry old man with wealth and power." Sir Austin hesitated, but at last addressed Earnshaw directly. "Goerlitz has written his memoirs in German, Emmett. He's put every bloody thing into them, from his memory, from journals, from correspondence, from business files. I'm told they are shockingly frank, brutally so, and every word, every disclosure, every sensational revelation is fully supported by photostats of documents that he intends to publish with his narrative. Emmett, I'm afraid you are in those memoirs, an entire chapter's worth."

"Me?" Earnshaw's disbelief was instantaneous and sincere. "What on earth could Goerlitz possibly write about me?"

Sir Austin rubbed his right knee nervously and contemplated the footstool. "I detest going on with this, Emmett—"

"You go right on and tell me what he wrote."

"I'm afraid, for your sake, I must. In his memoirs Goerlitz writes that you were the most indecisive President in American history, and

84

therefore the most irresponsible and the weakest. He writes that you refused to come to grips with any crisis, that you were unable to make up your mind at any time, that you had no interest in your office and its duties, and that therefore you delegated all decisions and authority to your subordinates, especially to Simon Madlock. And because of your disinterest, and Madlock's Messianic unrealism, you played into Red China's hands—you gave China the neutron bomb through Professor Varney's defection at Zurich and you gave China other critical materials that enabled her to build up her rocketry arsenal—and as a result you, primarily, and Madlock, secondarily, are responsible for Red China's full emergence as a nuclear world power. Then he writes—"

Earnshaw's cheeks were crimson with anger. "It's a damned lie!" he blurted, voice shaking. "It's a ridiculous, malicious, Nazi-madman lie, and if old Goerlitz actually wrote that and dares publish it, I'll have him in court immediately for libel and defamation. I've had my share of criticism and insult, the usual prattling political nonsense, but this kind of vengeful and extreme character assassination exceeds any license of free speech. How dare he make such accusations without a bit of evidence? As a former attorney, let alone former President of the United States, I'm telling you—"

With a pained expression Sir Austin had lifted a hand to interrupt. "Emmett—Emmett—of course, I don't blame you for being outraged—you have every right—but, Emmett, he has photographs of documents and letters, two of them signed by you, the rest by Madlock in your name, ordering certain nuclear materials from Goerlitz Industriebau, to be paid for out of secret government defense funds, and ordering these materials consigned through Goerlitz to Red China on a long-term credit basis."

Still flushed, trembling, Earnshaw snapped, "That's insane! Even if it were true, by what logic would we have given Communist China such materials through a German intermediary?"

"According to Goerlitz, your adviser, Madlock, believed fervently, almost mystically, that Red China could be brought to our side, to peace, by gestures of goodwill, by help and guidance, by employing a sort of Marshall Plan policy. Fearing it might be unpopular, Madlock took certain initial steps on his own. He arranged for Goerlitz to send off to China the machinery for synthetic textile factories and cotton mills, he ordered shipments of tools, trucks, tractors, *and* he instigated the sending of various materials for nuclear reactors intended for medical and agricultural use, even though the reactors could be converted to the production of fissionable fuel for ultimate employment in aggression. I repeat, Madlock appeared to take these steps on his own initiative, apparently with your wholehearted support and with—"

"My support?" Earnshaw exploded. "Does Goerlitz think I was a stupid fool? Does he think I'd work behind my own country's back? Or that an intelligent, trustworthy public servant like Madlock would? I tell you, Goerlitz has become a senile lunatic."

"Well—" Sir Austin began doubtfully.

Disturbed by the other's dubiousness, Earnshaw suddenly demanded, "Where are those documents with my signature that Goerlitz has? You give me his book and the so-called evidence, and I'll expose his falsehoods and forgeries at once, right here, this minute."

He saw that Sir Austin was trying to soothe him, but Earnshaw would not be calmed down. Yet when Sir Austin spoke, he tried to listen.

"I don't have a full manuscript copy of the Goerlitz memoirs yet," Sir Austin said. "No one has. But those of us in publishing have our literary spies. The competition for major books is so great that Sydney and I maintain representatives in most Western capitals, and these representatives are well paid to learn, by whatever means, what important books are being prepared or completed, and to acquire an advance look at these works. I don't mind saying that some bribery is involved. In any event, our man in Munich went down to Frankfurt to help in preparations for the annual Frankfurt Book Fair. There he ran into Goerlitz's German publisher and learned that the publisher had in his possession—only temporarily—since it was to be turned over to a French literary agent—the final-draft manuscript of the memoirs. For a not inconsiderable sum our man was able to borrow these memoirs for a single evening. He found them electrifying, and was up an entire night writing a sketchy synopsis of them and making Minox copies of some of the documentation. His express package, announcing his coup and urging that Sydney and I purchase this tremendous work for publication, arrived earlier this evening. I had only to glance at what he had sent to know that the book will have international repercussions—and, along the way, will unfairly damage your own reputation beyond repair. In fact, in his attack upon you, Goerlitz even had the gall to disparage me, as a friend of yours. Dreadful stuff. I knew that we would have no part of the scurrilous book—but others, less ethical than ourselves, will snatch it up and publish it in every nation in the world. My real duty was clear. You were my friend. You were maligned. You must be told of this, and thus forewarned, you would be forearmed."

Earnshaw wanted his brandy desperately, but he knew that his hand would not be steady. His cheeks were hot and his lungs parched. "You mean, Austin, you really give this—this thing by Goerlitz—credence?"

"Emmett, I'm at a loss. I can only tell you what I've read and seen."

"Where is it, that stuff your man sent you? Do you have it on you?"

"Yes."

"Let me see it, please."

Sir Austin's hand had already gone to the pocket of his dinner jacket. He tugged out a folded envelope, straightened it, and removed what appeared to be four or five sheets of paper. "The synopsis," he said, "and a sampling of the documentation attached."

Earnshaw took the sheets, pushed himself to his feet, and circled to the desk for his spare reading glasses. Hooking them on, he stood beside the desk and read the synopsis of the Goerlitz memoirs in silence. When he was done, he examined the photocopies. Two were reproductions of the last pages of official White House documents, plainly orders for goods from the Goerlitz Industriebau to be shipped to Albania and thence to Shanghai. Both of these last pages were signed by Emmett A. Earnshaw, President of the United States.

After a while, dazed, he slowly shambled toward Sir Austin, aware that his English friend was watching him closely, and he prodded the velvet footstool toward the fireplace and sat down on it. He wanted to dispatch his mind back through a corridor of memory, but it would not move because the corridor was dark. Looking at the signed documents again with unseeing eyes, he wanted to protest that these signatures had been forged, but he knew in his heart that they were his own, they were authentic, they were his autographs.

"Yes," he said at last, "those are my signatures." He dropped the papers on the chair he had vacated and he swung back to Sir Austin. "I—I can't remember signing them. Certainly this is not the sort of thing I would sign. But evidently I did, unless it is the most adroit forgery on earth, which I doubt."

"There must be some explanation," said Sir Austin softly. "You read in the synopsis—Goerlitz charges that you had abdicated the Presidency to your adviser—let him go off on his own in foreign affairs—and that either he persuaded you to come along on Chinese loans or deceived you into signing these orders."

"No." He thought about Simon Madlock, then added, "He never tried to persuade me on any subject about which I was reluctant to be persuaded. And he—he never deceived me."

"But, Emmett—"

87

"Only one possibility comes to mind. There were so many papers to sign in those days, and sometimes I was so sick of it, that I signed whatever was placed before me. I plead guilty to—to that—to disinterest in detail. But not in important matters. On vital decisions I always had the problems screened, evaluated first, and had Simon brief me—but I don't recall any briefing on this business, except that we had kicked around our views on Red China, how to handle the Chinese—yes—and while not in the same context, Simon had mentioned Goerlitz—or—or maybe it *was* in relation to this and I wasn't attentive, and maybe he had assumed that I was agreeable and so he went ahead—and that might be how I signed this with hundreds of other papers." He shook his head. "I don't know." Absently he reached for his brandy and drank.

"Well, there it is," Sir Austin said quietly. "You know you are innocent, and I know you are, but there it is on paper, and once it is out in a bound book, out for the world to see, you will be undeservedly damaged. You'll have no legal case against Goerlitz. You can't enjoin publication of the book or demand a retraction. You can only make explanations to the press. As a publisher, I can tell you that won't be enough. Your political enemies at home will seize upon this to cover their own sins, make you the scapegoat responsible, in large part, for China's being a nuclear threat and for any difficulties arising at this Summit meeting. You must be ready for that, Emmett."

He nodded wearily, his mind unable to concentrate. He wanted extra minds to supplant his own poor mind, Isabel's or Simon Madlock's, but he was alone. "Yes," he said finally, "I can see what will happen. I dread it. I dread it more than anything that's come up in years. But I don't know what I can do."

"You can stop it," Sir Austin said firmly. "You can stop it from being published." He jumped to his feet and stood over Earnshaw. "That is the only course you can follow. You have no other choice. None."

Earnshaw was confused. "I—I don't understand."

Sir Austin had walked to the center of the sitting room. Suddenly he wheeled around. "Dr. Dietrich von Goerlitz is in Paris. He arrived in Paris this morning. He's at the Ritz Hotel. He is going to be in Paris a week and a half. I have my pipelines, you know, both as Foreign Secretary and as a publisher, and this I've learned. Goerlitz is in Paris for two reasons—first, to meet with some of the Chinese Communist delegates, to sign final contracts with them for a nuclear reactor plant and a prefabricated city that his engineers are going to construct for the Chinese, a complex for peaceful uses of nuclear energy, that sort of thing—and second, instead of waiting for the Frankfurt Book Fair, he

88

is going to turn his memoirs over to a French literary agent, who will negotiate international publication rights with foreign publishers gathering in Paris. You must prevent the release of the memoirs in their present form, Emmett. This you *must* do."

Earnshaw rocked on the footstool and finished the last of his brandy. "I want to prevent it," he said helplessly. "But I don't know how."

"By canceling your trip to Scandinavia and going to Paris instead. By going to Goerlitz and having it out with him, man to man—you are old friends, after all—give him your explanation, the other half of the truth, and persuade him to modify or drop that chapter about you. I know you can succeed in doing this. You have a relationship with him. You have enormous prestige. And—let's be perfectly honest, Emmett —you have great natural charm, and when you wish to, you can melt steel into liquid. It's the one sensible solution left you, Emmett. Paris."

"I—I don't know."

"You can't equivocate about this. If you care one iota about your future, your place in history, you must go. I know your situation in America, what the opposition has tried to do to you. But you've started to overcome them. Your Library. Your autobiography. Your coming here to receive the Order of the British Empire. All the right steps, in the right direction. But all wasted if you falter now. However, once you've seen Goerlitz in Paris—"

Earnshaw interrupted. "Surely, Austin, as a Government Minister, you can see the impropriety of it. The elected President of the United States is in Paris, representing every American as he convenes with the world powers. To have a former President arrive, uninvited, unannounced, a former President who once advocated different policies, might be inhibiting to him, certainly a terrible embarrassment. And it could be—could be embarrassing for me—"

"I understand. Still, there are times when we must ignore protocol and even personal feelings. You could slip in quietly, stay a day or two, see Goerlitz privately, slip right out again, and resume your Scandinavian jaunt."

"It wouldn't be easy," Earnshaw protested. "The President would have to know that I was there, underfoot. The press would know. I can't tell you how I'd hate that. You—you don't entirely understand the background."

He fumbled for his used cigar. Then, beginning to light it, he saw Sir Austin shrug and walk to the liquor cabinet for another gin-and-tonic. Miserably puffing at his soggy cigar, Earnshaw tried to examine the protocol barriers that stood between him and such a Paris visit.

Then he realized, in honesty, that it was not protocol that made him resist the suggestion of Paris, but rather his deep resentment of the incumbent President of the United States. Pursuing this resentment, he fastened on one incident that had occurred about four weeks ago. Before that incident one of the President's staff, one of the few who had been held over from Earnshaw's own term in office, "happened" to be in the vicinity of Rancho Santa Fe and had called upon him. Casually the President's aide had leaked out the privileged information that the Chief Justice of the Supreme Court, due to mounting infirmities, would resign by autumn. The President was casting about for an American of stature to fill the expected vacancy. It had been an obvious "feeler." Although Earnshaw had concurred as to the importance of the high seat on the highest bench in the United States, he had been otherwise noncommittal. When the unofficial emissary had departed, Earnshaw felt that the emissary would report to his leader that the ex-President was receptive.

Earnshaw had not known how receptive he really was, disliking as he did the responsibilities of decision that every Chief Justice must assume, yet being attracted by the honor of such an appointment and by the fact that such a role might revive him in the public eye.

Four weeks ago, there had come the telephone summons inviting him to call upon the President at the White House. Such courtesies had been rare in recent years, and Earnshaw agreed without hesitation to see the President. At first he had thought that the President wished to see him to tender him the seat on the bench. Later he had decided that this would be premature, and another reason for the White House invitation had suggested itself. The Five-Power Summit Conference in Paris was forthcoming. American public opinion was divided, mostly along party lines, on whether to trust the People's Republic of China in any international disarmament agreement. Aware of this, the Peking delegates would appear in Paris feeling assured that the American imperialists, being divided in their feelings, would more readily make compromises and concessions. Therefore, the President had invited the elder statesman from the opposition party in order to offer him a position on the American delegation to the Summit. With a former President and a current President seated side-by-side at the bargaining table, America would present a solid, unshakable front at the Summit, and Chinese arrogance and rigidity would be reduced to reasonableness. This had been the sense of it to Earnshaw, and the chance to serve again, help his country, restore his name, had excited him. He had flown to Washington in high spirits.

To his surprise and gratification, his return to the capital city had been widely covered by the press. Once inside the Oval Office of the

West Wing, he had felt not nostalgia but the stimulation of being in the center of power (such as he had not felt when he himself had been the occupant of Hoban's elliptic room). The Rose Garden, visible through the French doors to his left, had been in full bloom, and through the windows behind the incumbent President's desk he had been able to see that the white birches planted during his own term had grown considerably.

Best of all, the President, usually remote and formal, had been almost affable. Disarmed by his hospitable reception, Earnshaw had been relaxed and loquacious. They had discussed many matters, mostly of little consequence. When the President had begun to discuss a recent case tried before the Supreme Court, Earnshaw had waited with wonder. But the President had made no mention of the forthcoming vacancy on the bench, and Earnshaw, while a trifle surprised, had not been disappointed, for it had been too early for that.

When the incumbent President had at last come to the subject of the Summit conference, Earnshaw eagerly awaited the invitation. The President had gone into the agenda, the obstacles that must be overcome if a nuclear disarmament agreement among the five powers was to be achieved, and then he had said that the American delegation would need all the wisdom available to make this critical meeting a success. With this in mind, he had brought the former President here to sound him out on his views on several of the disarmament schemes and on the trustworthiness of the ruling Communist Chinese hierarchy.

Enthusiastically and at great length, out of his knowledge and experience, Earnshaw had discoursed on these grave matters. But gradually, and then certainly, after ten minutes, Earnshaw had realized that the restless President was hardly listening to him, was, in fact, rudely inattentive. The moment that Earnshaw had finished, the President had stood up, briskly thanked him, and buzzed for the photographers to be sent into the Oval Office.

It was then, posing beside his successor in the midst of the carnival of cameras and exploitation, that the truth behind this confrontation had struck Earnshaw. He had not been invited to the White House to receive an appointment as a delegate to the Summit. It had not even been mentioned, as the Supreme Court vacancy had not been mentioned. He had not been brought here to offer advice to the one who must represent their beloved country in a Summit that would determine the future of man on this planet. He had been brought here to be *used*—politically manipulated—brought here merely to pose for the photographers, to give the partisan President a bipartisan, Great-White-Father-of-all-Americans look before he went to Paris.

Leaving the Oval Office, Earnshaw had never felt more rejected and angry, and the humiliation of the incident rankled still in his memory.

Now, in this London hotel suite, conscious of Sir Austin Ormsby settling in the chair across from him, Earnshaw was forced to shake his head vigorously. "No, Austin, I doubt if I could go to Paris while the President is there at the same time. There are circumstances that you— you are not aware of."

"If it has something to do with your pride, Emmett," the Foreign Secretary said shrewdly, "I'd suggest you put pride aside. You'd be less wounded right now than you will be in the near future if you permit that chapter to remain in Goerlitz's memoirs. How your successor feels about you, or you feel about him, is simply of no account at this time. All that matters is Goerlitz and how he feels—"

"Well, yes, I suppose that's it, after all," Earnshaw conceded. And then he understood fully that his deepest hidden resistance to Paris was not the presence of the incumbent Chief Executive but the presence of the German industrialist. Earnshaw realized that he had been evading his real fear, and he determined to speak forthrightly of it. "I must be as honest as possible with you, Austin. Otherwise my reluctance to try to save myself may make no sense to you. You see, if my fate is in the hands of Dr. Dietrich von Goerlitz, then I don't think I can save myself. The whole Paris detour would be a foolhardy waste of time."

"What are you saying?"

"I'm saying that Goerlitz would have every reason not to cooperate with me in any way. His view of it would be that I had refused to help him in a moment of need, and now, shoe on the other foot, he'd have no reason to help me. Goerlitz has an unsentimental barter mentality. He'd trade favors. That he might do. But I have no favors to exchange. You see, when they finally indicted him as a war criminal, on some flaky evidence—questionable evidence in terms of his personal partici- pation in the Nazi cause—well, Goerlitz was desperate for character references, that is, from personages of standing. He appealed to me privately, in two communications, asking that I speak up for him at the trial, by affidavit or as a witness, to affirm to the best of my knowledge that he had never been an active Nazi. Well, dammit, Austin, I was being considered for President, and I couldn't make up my mind about helping him. I wasn't sure if he had been a Nazi or not. And—well, I wasn't sure how my standing up beside him would affect my candidacy. I kept debating it in my mind, and before I could decide, well, the trial was over and he was found guilty and sentenced. I guess I—uh—I never got back to him, and I'd say, just from his tone in his memoirs, he's never forgotten that. And there's more, Austin. After a while, Goerlitz's attorney approached our Government to instigate pardon proceedings. I was in the White House then. And you know, I couldn't decide, and so Goerlitz's attorney gave up waiting for me and turned to the Russians. And for their own reasons, to utilize Goerlitz's industrial genius, the Russians agreed that he should be pardoned, and they put on pressure and he was pardoned. Well, there you are, and I won't say I'm proud of my equivocating, but those are the facts. Now, how do you think Goerlitz will feel about seeing me in Paris and—and giving me a hand?"

Sir Austin contemplated the highball glass that he had been twisting in his fingers. "I think he'll be tough, hard as nails, but I think he'll give in."

"You do?"

Sir Austin looked up. "Yes, I do. All right, you are one of the people he hates. He's put them all down, myself included, and got all the venom out of his system. That's done. Now you come to him, and, in a manner of speaking, you humble yourself before him. You bare your soul. You admit to your mistakes. In effect, you concede his present power over you. This gives him a sort of divinity. Alexander Pope, you know: 'To err is human, to forgive divine.' This has got to soften the old Prussian, Emmett. And then you explain the facts behind those documents he wants to publish, how they do not represent the entire truth of your personal behavior in the Presidency or your policy as President, and how they would be misinterpreted. That would give him a new view of the whole chapter. I'd wager he would revise and modify the chapter, perhaps drop it altogether."

"You're persuasive, Austin. You make it seem almost possible."

"I think it is possible." Sir Austin stood up. "And even if it seems impossible, I'd urge you to try. No man on earth can afford a low blow like this against his reputation. You must make every effort to defend yourself, as if your very survival is at stake."

Earnshaw ground his cigar butt into the glass tray. He rose to his feet, smiling wanly at his English friend. "Well, I don't know if there's enough left of me to be worth defending. I don't know if it's worth going to Paris to face a humiliation and a defeat—if I wouldn't be better off to go on to Scandinavia and then creep back to California and let happen what may. History determines its own flow. I'm not sure any individual can change that flow."

"At least consider what I've suggested."

Earnshaw smiled again and placed his arm around his friend's shoulder. "Oh yes, you can be sure I'll consider it. I'll sleep on it." He began to lead Sir Austin to the foyer. "You've taken enough of your time trying to save an old man, and believe me, you don't know how grateful I am." He took down Sir Austin's hat and topcoat and found his umbrella and handed them to him.

At the door Sir Austin said, "Fleur and I aren't leaving for Paris until ten in the morning. If we're going to see you there, let me know at the Foreign Office, or let my secretary know your plans if I've gone, and we'll make all the arrangements for you."

"Very kind of you, Austin, but there's no hiding a trip like this. It's got to come into the open. If I go to Paris, I'll contact our own Embassy. Otherwise, well, again my thanks, and you'll have a postcard from Oslo or Stockholm. Good night."

After closing the door, Earnshaw wandered back into the sitting room, feeling achy and infirm. A single word rattled inside his skull and would not cease tormenting him. The one enemy word that had brought him down.

Indecision.

To his original physical weariness had been added emotional exhaustion. His mind was too weak to bear the weight of further thought that might force the rattling of indecision to a halt. The sweet oblivion of sleep would not come fast enough to rescue his mind. In moments like this, so alone with himself, he often sought another. But there was no one left, except Carol. So he sought her company, even if briefly.

He hobbled into the hallway, past the kitchen, then tiptoed across the ornate dining room to her bedroom door. There was no sound of television. Gently he turned the knob and opened her door. The room was dark, but the light from behind him faintly illuminated part of her green bed, and he could make out the mound of blanket and her head pressed into the pillow that was propped against the high headboard. He studied her, so peaceful in sleep, and envied her, and thanked the good Lord for the blessing of her companionship.

Closing her bedroom door, he trudged back through the dining room, finally turning into his own master bedroom. As he removed the open suitcase from the canopied bed, his temples throbbed. The word *indecision* continued to bang and bump tauntingly inside his skull, and he knew that he could arrest it only by admitting other words into his head and sorting these words into regimented thought.

With effort he tried to reason out his dilemma, and although the endeavor was a strain, it was less painful than trying to keep his mind a vacuum. Slowly, as he changed into his blue cotton pajamas, he reviewed something that Sir Austin Ormsby had mentioned, something about his reputation being once more on the ascendency. Sir Austin had cited the publication of Earnshaw's autobiography, the opening of his Presidential Library, and tonight's Order of the British Empire.

At this gloomy midnight hour Earnshaw possessed a harsher view, and a more honest one, of the revival of his reputation. He had been disinterested in the autobiography of his Presidential years from the start. He had allowed his staff to assemble the material, organize it, and even set it in a narrative form, with the assistance of a onetime White House correspondent. Positive that his public was his monument, Earnshaw had done little more than dictate some added material for the book, some corrections and inserts, and at the last moment he had merely scanned the whole of it before its delivery to the publisher. By the time that it was on press, when the reality of his dwindling position in American life had begun to be evident to him, he had hoped more and more that the autobiography would restore him to his rightful place. But secretly he had worried about the book, for his uninvolvement had allowed it to become a mere compendium of colorless facts, data, reports, a bloodless volume utterly unrepresentative of his real personality, his warmth, his humor, his homey point of view.

His fears had not been misplaced. Upon its appearance, the autobiography had been derided by reviewers and critics for its shallowness and dullness. And of the 100,000 copies in print, it was evident after returns that only 16,500 had been sold, and the rest were this day being remaindered at one-sixth the original price in countless bargain basements.

The Earnshaw Presidential Library, in San Diego, had interested him more. His initial neglect of it, his leaving its construction and stocking to other hands, had been supplanted at the last moment by a determination to make this depository of the records of his term in office the equal of the Franklin D. Roosevelt Library in Hyde Park, the Truman Library in Independence, the Eisenhower Library in Abilene, the Kennedy Library in Cambridge, the Johnson Library in Austin. Personally he had invited national figures to the opening, and many of them had come. And as he had guided them through the halls and stacks, it had come as a surprise to him how limited was the corpus of his collection, how bland and lacking in interest were the materials, and how little he had ever created or committed to paper. Still, the dedication ceremonies had been heartening, and he had had high hopes. But once the festivities were ended and the library was thrown open to the public, it had shocked him how few visitors came to see his papers. There had been a trickle of tourists, of course, but almost no students, and no scholars at all.

This rejection had been followed by yet one more. A silly thing, really, yet a significant one. Annually, the leading national opinion poll had listed the twenty most admired living Americans, and for a half-dozen years Emmett A. Earnshaw had led the names on that poll. But two years ago he had dropped from first place to fourth in popularity, and last year he had sunk to tenth, and this year, only short weeks ago, he had plummeted down to twentieth.

And this Order of the British Empire tonight, what did it mean, actually? That he had been a friend of the English, and that now the English honored the remembrance of him with a bauble. But who in his own, his native land would be impressed or even care? The attention of the American public would be focused not on London but on an active leader in Paris, fighting a real fight for their welfare and the nation's future.

Sir Austin had exaggerated the revival of Earnshaw's reputation. There had been no revival, because there was no reputation left to revive. Goerlitz's chapter in the memoirs was being aimed at a nonexistent target. Why attempt to blunt an arrow that could strike at nothing but thin air?

Depressed, Earnshaw secured the bottom button of his pajama top, stuck his feet into his slippers, and made his way into the sitting room. Automatically he gravitated toward the liquor cabinet. For the first time in years he wanted a second brandy before bedtime.

Pouring his brandy, he leaned against the wall, drinking it, feeling the heat of it in his throat and chest, and trying to warm himself into dwelling on better times. The happier past eluded him, as the shining White House years eluded him. All that remained fixed in his mind was a summary, in some young smart-aleck historian's book, of the style of Earnshaw's Presidency. The historian had summarized it by repeating that hackneyed anecdote of the French Revolution. A citizen of the revolution had been dining at the window table of a Paris restaurant with a foreign visitor. Suddenly, through the window, he had seen a great mob of Frenchmen rushing past, and instantly the French citizen had leaped to his feet and excused himself. "I must catch up with that mob," he had said apologetically. "I am their leader."

Earnshaw swallowed the last of the brandy, returned to his bed, turned down the lamp, and crawled under the covers.

As he lay there, warmed and dizzied by his two drinks, near sleep, painful memories departed, leaving only the rattling haunting of the one word.

Unaccountably, a stray remembered incident of his past returned to mind. The year after he had left the White House and the newly elected President had entered it, there had been the annual ribald Gridiron Dinner given by the Washington press corps, and there had been a quip from the stage which had not found its way into print but which had

96

become an underground joke and had finally reached his ear. Some comedian had said that Earnshaw's nickname now was The Ex, standing for Ex-President, but that even when he'd been in the White House as President there were those who called him The Ex.

Hilarity.

And in that instant of sleepy recollection the taunting word rattling in his skull was trapped, smothered, dead.

Decision.

The Ex in the White House. It had been cruel, and that it still mattered to him meant that there was something left of him that mattered and must be preserved. His life, the judgments passed upon it, were not his to offer up willfully and suicidally to nothingness. His life was other lives, the meaning of his beloved parents, his Isabel, his Simon, his Carol, his bridge companions, the 16,500 who had bought his book, the Midwestern tourists who visited his Library, the countless numbers who had once made him the American they admired the most.

Decision.

He owed so much to so many. He owed himself so much. He must not allow a spiteful German's vicious misrepresentations to hammer the last nail into the coffin that would bury him far from history's Pantheon.

He would rise at dawn. He would notify the United States Embassy in London of his change of itinerary. He would wake Carol early and tell her that he had special business in Paris, and that she would like Paris more than the Scandinavian capitals. He would take a jet—no, not a jet, no flying, doctor's orders—he would take the Golden Arrow to Paris, and take a suite at the Lancaster, and have it out with Goerlitz, and retain some shred of mortality if not immortality.

Life had been kind to him, and he had cheated on Life, because he had never done as much with it as he had been capable of doing or as much with it as he had expected to do. But he would make up for it, yes, do this for yesterday's Isabel, tomorrow's Carol, and for all the voters and Electoral College members who had once put their lives in his hands.

Decision.

He would be The Ex for Ex-President, not The Ex for Extinction. No, never would he pull a blanket of earth over his head if he could help it and if the Lord helped him. Only a bed blanket over his head, soft blanket, so there would be morning not mourning.

He yawned, and felt better, and then he tried to sleep. . . .

It was enervating, on a hot Saturday morning like this, rehearsing the new numbers, especially when she had not completely made up her mind that she would extend her engagement at Chez 88-40-88.

Listening to the beat of the jazzed-up French recording of the classic old American minstrel song blaring through the amplifier above the stage, Medora Hart tapped one thonged sandal on the polished dance floor and waited for her cue. The heat seeping into the almost empty nightclub from the pavements of Juan-les-Pins was stifling, and Medora Hart wished that she was climbing down into the cool water of the Provençal hotel beach or, better yet, was strolling in the chill morning air of London's East End from her mother's flat to the grocer's.

Fleetingly she remembered how many of Paddy's girls had become his girls because they dreamed of the Riviera, the Côte d'Azur, and—crikey!—if they only knew how she hated it. You can have it, girls, she thought, you can have every yacht off Villefranche, every swimming pool in Cap d'Antibes, every casino from Juan-les-Pins here to Monte Carlo, and I'll throw in the Croisette, too—you can have it all for just one smell of Billingsgate, one glimpse of Soho, one stroll across Blackfriars Bridge.

The tinny recording was louder, the beat faster, and as she anticipated her cue, Medora Hart automatically snapped her fingers, hunched and weaved her shoulders in the professionally sexy all-with-it way, and took a step to the microphone. Catching the musical cue, and in her half-singing, half-reciting, partially intimate, slightly girlish voice, she sang out with forced frenzy (although under wraps, it being a rehearsal, it being so profanely hot):

> De Camptown ladies sing this song,
> Doo-dah! Doo-dah!
> De Camptown race track five miles long,
> Oh! Doo-dah Day!

From the corner of an eye she could see that the only other occupants of the nightclub, stocky old Jouvet, the proprietor, and jittery young Mauclair, the director, were watching and listening, and now Mauclair, standing behind the proprietor, was bending down to whisper to him.

Disregarding them, addressing the number to the empty tables and upturned chairs before her, Medora Hart continued:

98

I come down dah wid my hat caved in,
Doo-dah! Doo-dah!
I go back home wid a pocket full of tin,
Oh! Doo-dah Day!

She went on until the recording stopped and decided that, incongruous as it was to render the American Negro song in her theatrical English accent, it was lively enough, noisy and swinging enough, for the highly charged atmosphere of the late show. That was the hour when Chez 88-40-88 was always overflowing, full of smoke and chatter, the American and German tourists drunk and the bearded Belgian boys finally getting their hands under the short skirts of their French girl friends.

Breaking off, she took the throat of the microphone and said matter-of-factly, "That should warm them up, Monsieur Jouvet. Then I thought you could bring the lights down, put a soft yellow spot on me, and let the band go into 'That Old Black Magic.' I prefer it to 'Les Flonflons du Bal,' slower beat, easier to handle. I'd wear the new cocktail ensemble I picked up in Cannes, there's enough of it to take off and bring me to the end of the reprise. Something like this—"

Humming the song briefly, she began to pantomime her projected striptease. "Sing-sing, then off with the white gloves and slow unbuttoning and off with the sequined jacket," she intoned. "Then sing-sing, a little pirouetting dance around the floor, right up along the tables, so they can see the blouse, high front but nearly backless and the skirt flares beautifully, so they'll get a tidbit of my thighs and bottom. Then back to the mike. Sing-sing while I undo the blouse and pull it off. Next, unbutton and unzip the chiffon skirt. Step out of it. Then I'd shake out of the half-slip, next unhook the garter belt and get rid of my stockings. Now only music, no vocal, maybe humming or whistling, a few phrases, I'd circle around the customers' tables—maybe a little banter instead of humming, whatever you think—and all the while fumbling with the nylon bra, the skin-tone one, then return to this point, and off with the bra, give them the breasts and some kind of squirming dance for a chorus, then, picking up the lyrics, I'd turn my back or maybe you can start revolving the color wheel in front of the spot, and off come my pants, flesh briefs I think, and that leaves me with only the gold necklace and the gold patch, which is *au naturel* enough. After that, maybe glide to the center of the floor, full spot, then arms up high, legs wide apart, head thrown back, hair loose, eyes closed, do a kind of undulating, ravished, pain-and-ecstasy dance, all in one place, nothing moving but my body, kind of black magic of sex, and as the number ends, I'd burst forward, go down on my knees, head arched way back, and you cut the lights and I get off."

She had become so entranced by her oral choreography, her creativity, that she failed to realize she had been addressing no one but the microphone and herself.

Enthusiastically she turned to Jouvet and Mauclair, asking, "What do you think? I think it can be effective. I'm tired of all the crazy, tricky stuff."

Mauclair, who had drawn up a chair beside Jouvet and was engaging him in low and intense conversation, had not been paying attention to her. And the proprietor, listening to his director and automatically nodding his approval to her, had been almost as inattentive.

Irritated at the energy she had expended on two blocks of wood, she pressed her mouth to the microphone and demanded loudly, "Well, do you agree with me or not?"

The proprietor's face, a warted pickle, was instantly alert. *"Très bien,* Medora. What next?" But simultaneously, caught by something the director was saying, he had turned away from Medora once more.

"Next," she said, hands on her hips, "you can both *aller vous faire foutre!* And for me, next, I'm going to the W.C. And if you bother me, I'll flush you both down the loo!"

She started across the barren dance floor, as haughtily as possible for a child-woman so long advertised as the Continent's sex goddess. Passing the two loutish Frenchmen, she heard them arguing about francs, and the union, and the General Labor Confederation, and she continued on to the front of the club. In the club's entryway, so close to the street, the heat assailed her, and she felt spent and drained of energy. Removing several coins from her belt pocket, she went to the Coke machine, and the minute that she had the ice-cold bottle and had begun to drink from it, she felt slightly better, slightly.

Inexplicably let down, listless, she entered the ladies' room, snapped on the lights, took another swallow of Coke and set the bottle on a chair. Twisting the faucet marked FROID, she placed her wrists under the stream of water, having heard that this cooled the body quickly. Then she applied water to her damp forehead, and behind her ears and neck, and traced the wetness across her chest and down between her breasts. Finding a clean towel, she dried herself, and while doing so, she studied her reflection in the wide mirror above the basin.

Studying mirrors was one of Medora Hart's favorite preoccupations. Rarely did she pass a mirror without halting to consider pensively what was shown in it, to hold interior dialogues with that image, to philosophize and psychologize over that image, to wonder about the ingredients of that image that had cast her so high up in the world and had then sent her tumbling so far down, so far down that now she teetered on the brink of Hell.

She stared at the upper half of the five feet four inches of herself in the mirror, and the self that was captured in the polished glass stared back at her. Tossing the towel aside, she backed off diagonally the width of the tiled bathroom floor until she could see herself almost full length. Her sun-blanched flaxen hair, tied in a mane, fell below her shoulder blades. Her shining brow was unmarked, although she was already twenty-one years old, and her huge, frank, gray-green eyes were clear, although her suitors and lovers liked to tell her they looked at once experience-old and little-girl-lost, which she had learned to translate as really meaning that they promised free giving and promiscuity.

Her delicate small nose, she had long decided, gave her part of that innocent girlish aspect. The mouth was another matter. The cherry-colored full lips, shaped in a pout, seemed sulky and full of teasing sensuality, in contradiction to the innocence of the nose and smooth cheeks and dainty ears.

The expensive St.-Tropez costume, she knew, was perfect for her near-perfect body. The short V-necked loose blouse draped down across her bosom hung straight from the firm points of her breasts, and since she'd worn no brassiere this morning and the blouse was nearly transparent, the large circles of her nipples and the shadowy outline of her high abundant bosom were plainly visible. Her tanned midriff, set off by the white above and below, was bare today. A wide leather belt, buckled below the slash of her navel, held the skintight stretch pants in place. She marveled at the way the pants were molded along her thighs, buttocks, shapely legs, so that every contour was her own and every movement of a muscle could be seen.

This was all she had, she thought, this voluptuous, falsely promising face and body. Her measurements, some men's magazine had said, were as much her identity as her name. Hello, Medora Hart. Hello, 38-22-36. Hello, Medora—38 or whoever you are, anymore.

Then she thought, Jouvet, you old swine, you've had a bargain and you ought to pay salary by the inch. Jouvet had named his profitable nightclub Chez 88-40-88, meaning that no girl who appeared in his shows would ever have a bust measurement less than 88 centimeters, a waist less than 40 centimeters, hips less than 88 centimeters, meaning 35-16-35 in inches, meaning Medora was not only qualified, but superqualified.

She had been pleased by the one in the mirror, for she had seen there her inheritance, education, pound value in the marketplace, and as long as that was there, she was safe from the ultimate degradation. With this much going for her, she could be an independent entertainer, read it any way. Without all this she could be only a whore.

She had enjoyed totting up her bank balance and almost felt better, but moving back to the washbasin, seeing herself again in the horrible mirror, she was immediately depressed and on real and familiar grounds once more. For the last glance at the mirror had done her in. Four years ago, in her senseless glory, she had looked like this, and three years ago, during the scandal, she had looked like this, and now, at twenty-one, she still looked like this. Suddenly it would be three more years of exile, and then six, and then you were old, when so many others were young, and you had nothing, no home, no family, no money, no career, nothing, except street corners which were for nothing.

She took up the Coke and sitting against the basin, her back to the mirror, she drank and wondered what she should do—immediately, and the day after immediately.

There were three straws offered and she must draw one. Not any one of them would solve her real problem, but two would continue to solve the problem of day-to-day subhuman existence, not living but surviving. She needed money because she spent too much since it sometimes seemed there was nothing to save for. Yet, she needed money for her mother, for her pitiable little sister (yet not so little, forgetting that Cynthia had grown older in the last three years and must be sixteen even though her mind was chained to seven or eight). She needed money for a solicitor to take her case and a barrister to fight her persecution (and there was a famous one, a flabby, gross, odious one, at Eden Roc, there always was a barrister, and this one a Q.C., and he would "look into it," but of course there would be a fee, and in lieu of a substantial down payment of cash, he would be receptive to other favors, but—crikey, no thank you, not with that one!—and so it would have to be cash). Finally, once she'd won her case and been permitted to go back legally to where she came from, she needed money to undertake what she'd wanted from the start, her training as a beautician, so that she'd have a career that was proper and respectable until she could find a young man who was proper and respectable and who no longer remembered the Paddy Jameson affair. Je-sus, how she hated Ormsby, not that impotent ass Sydney with his fancy polka-dot drawers, but her real Judas, Sir Austin, that conniving poseur, that bloody, cheating, lying toad, Je-sus, if people only knew the truth . . . but then here she was, becoming overwrought again, hot on the inside as well as the outside, and it was no use, as it was never any use, because you couldn't hit what was out of reach and impregnable, like a mouse trying to tear apart a lion.

With an immense effort made possible by three years of daily effort-building, Medora banished Sir Austin from her mind, and that left the immediate problem, which was always the same immediate problem, which was always immediate money for immediate survival.

So, three straws to choose from, with the choice and draw to be made quickly.

The first straw to grasp was Chez 88-40-88. She had been booked into this Juan-les-Pins cabaret for eight weeks as the featured attraction, the scandalous English playgirl who offered songs and *"la danse sexy."* There had been good houses when she opened off-season, but recently, with the tourist influx into the Riviera, her raucous audiences had been overflowing. Her eight-week engagement had ended with the final show last night. She had four weeks free until her next booking in San Remo, which was to be followed by a stand in Genoa. But then, a week ago, a tearful Jouvet had come to her waving a telegram. His next featured attraction, an emaciated Montmartre female sparrow, who was to succeed Medora and make a singing debut tomorrow night, had fallen ill in Marseille and canceled her engagement.

In desperation, the proprietor had pleaded with Medora to forgo her four-week vacation and continue her appearance in Juan-les-Pins. If she extended her stay by four weeks, and saved him and the club, he would raise her weekly salary by twenty per cent. He would announce that she had been held over by popular demand, and she could retain most of her old material, if she substituted three or four new numbers for old ones so that Jouvet could advertise that she was presenting a *new* show. This would bring back customers who had already seen her, and attract newly arrived tourists from Cannes, Nice, and Juan-les-Pins itself.

Although she was tired of working, the promise of a raise in salary had interested Medora. She had told Jouvet that she would consider it and give him his decision by tonight. Then, considering the extended booking, not knowing whether she would accept it or not, she had, in a desultory way, to fend off boredom mostly, worked out several new numbers for her act. When Jouvet had telephoned her early this morning, she had sleepily told him that she had not yet made up her mind, but if he and the director would meet her at the cabaret around ten, she would run through some fresh material. After that, she would see.

The second straw to grasp was the Club Lautrec in Paris. No sooner had she hung up on Jouvet than a wire had been delivered to her room from Alphonse Michaud, the extravagant, attractive, successful (she had seen a picture-spread on him in *Paris Match* last month) owner of the vast and booming Club Lautrec off the Champs-Élysées. Michaud had stated that in a conversation with Medora's booking agent he had learned she was available for four weeks beginning Sunday. Although his show, "The World Comes to Gay Paree," featured its standard dancers, The Troupe, who, Medora knew, rivaled the Lido's Bluebell Girls in fame, and although his show was fully booked with renowned specialty artists, Michaud wanted one more, and the one he wanted was Medora Hart.

His flattering telegram explained that he had followed her successes in the capitals and resorts of Europe, that he now regarded her as a premier attraction of international reputation, and that four weeks of her time would guarantee the prosperity of his show. He had been advised of her salary, but for this brief engagement he was prepared to offer her fifty per cent more plus her transportation to Paris and from Paris to her next engagement, and all her expenses for room and board while in Paris.

The impact of the telegram had, at first, excited Medora. During her shower her mind had been full of it. She had never played in anything as big and well-known as the Club Lautrec. She had never before been offered the kind of money that Michaud was offering her. Even though the Club Lautrec was an enormous flesh factory, gaudy and brassy, anything but class, it did attract the top level of tourists and everybody who was somebody went there, sooner or later, at least once. For Medora, it would be a marvelous showcase and, somehow, a step upward. To what and where this step upward, she did not know, as she never knew, but it sounded good.

Yet Michaud's telegram puzzled her. For three years since the scandal and her banishment, like that Wandering Jew, she had dragged herself around the mainland of Europe with her baggage of a body, appearing in small clubs in big cities, and big clubs in small cities (like Juan-les-Pins), but at no time had a big club in a big city ever offered her its stage. She had had no illusions about this. She had not been sold for her ability to sing or dance, for she had never been more than an amateur at this, although lately she had acquired more stage presence. She had been sold, really, as a dirty book is sold, something immoral and scandalous and forbidden. She was a body hired directly from the secret plush bedrooms of the wealthy and aristocratic to be displayed to the peasantry at last—come one, come all, and see the sex creature enjoyed by your betters, the naked body that almost brought down a government. She was a titillation, she knew (from having read about it), an attraction to the thousands, the millions, who must indulge their lewd dreams and fantasies secondhand. She was this. She was not an entertainer. The big shows in the big cities wanted entertainers, and so they had never wanted Medora Hart. Now, overnight, the Club Lautrec in Paris wanted Medora Hart. It was puzzling.

But during her Continental breakfast on the balcony outside her spacious double room on the third floor of the Provençal, what was puzzling her was quickly solved by the ringing telephone. The long-distance call was from her booking agent in Munich. He had just returned to his office from Paris. Had Medora received a telegram from M. Michaud of the fabulous Club Lautrec? She had. Was not the sum offered impressive? It was. Was not this the major opportunity of her career? Possibly, maybe. What did she mean by that? She meant (now wondering and suspicious) that she was confused by the offer. She had never been wanted by a club so grand as the Lautrec—and yes, yes, she was sure her agent had done a magnificent selling job, as always, but he had never brought her anything on this scale before, and she was curious as to how it had happened this time.

Her agent, who was an effective agent because he was insensitive and treated clients as pieces of beef hung in a butcher shop, was proud to tell her what had transpired with Michaud. During their meeting in the Club Lautrec, Michaud had complained that he had no stellar attraction with special appeal for the thousands of extraordinary, free-spending delegates and their wives and staffs who were crowding into Paris to attend the two-week Summit conference. Like the Lido and Crazy Horse and Moulin Rouge, Michaud was presenting a lively but routine show. Since cabaret competition was fierce, he would give anything to obtain one unusual act that might have special international magnetism for the Americans, English, Germans, even the Russians and Chinese, who were arriving in Paris. Then the agent had announced that he had just such an attraction, and that she happened to be available, and that her name—of course, Michaud would know her name, *everyone* knew her name—was Medora Hart. And Michaud had slapped his thighs, and excitedly agreed that this was exactly the attraction to seduce every foreigner in Paris for the Summit, and he was ready to contract for the admirable lady.

That was the whole story, her agent had said, and was it not wonderful? For Medora, heart sinking, it was considerably less than wonderful. In fact, it was hateful. The agent was going on. Would she wire her acceptance of the offer to Michaud at once? In a dead voice, she said she did not know. Did not know? Well (white lie), she'd half committed herself to stay on in Juan-les-Pins, and it wouldn't be easy to get out of it. Her agent began to argue, and Medora squirmed and was feminine and vague, and at last, in disgust, the agent had said she must inform Michaud one way or the other today. But, he warned her, if she turned the offer down, she would always regret it, always. If she said yes, it would mean a new life for her.

On her tray the coffee had become cold, and she had sat staring out across the pines in the park below, at the gleaming blue Mediterranean beyond, and she had known that she did not want the kind of new life the Club Lautrec and Paris might give her.

On the balcony of the Provençal hotel a few hours ago, as in the ladies' room of the Chez 88-40-88 this moment, she understood what troubled her about the Club Lautrec offer. A success there would not give her anything she really wanted, and it might give her everything she did not want. For what she wanted above all, far more important than the day-to-day money, was some means of overcoming Sir Austin Ormsby, so that he would be forced to capitulate and allow her to return home to London. If she could become prominent enough, and therefore powerful enough as a Name, to enlist other powerful people on her side, and with this alliance and strength overcome Sir Austin, a success would be meaningful. But such a success she could not have, not in the Club Lautrec, not anywhere, because she did not have the talent for a success that would bring her prestige. The only success she could hope for, in showing herself at the Club Lautrec, would be to excite and attract once again the so-called highest type of lechers and bring them to her bed. The push of her appearance, her appearance itself, would bring them running, the rich playboys and industrialists, the powerful ministers of many governments, and for a night with her naked body they would give her money, jewels, furs—everything except the only thing she desired: help to get home again. They would come to her, and use her, and pay her off with the only kind of remuneration they understood, and then they would leave her. They would go back to their homes and leave her as she had been, homeless and lost, a stranger exiled in a foreign land, only not quite as she had been, for she would be even more sullied and degraded and devoid of self-respect than before.

That was what she hated about the capital cities, and Paris was the worst of all for one like herself. She knew, because three years ago she had begun her exile in Paris and made her show-business debut in Paris, and it had been rotten, finally. Oh, there was so much about Paris that she would have loved if only she'd been left alone, the quiet Left Bank hotel near the Seine, the kiosk with the Byrrh sign on the corner, the crooked little cobbled streets off St.-Germain-des-Prés, the fresh-smelling greenness of the Luxembourg Gardens with children's sailboats in the basin, the Guignol fun in the Bois, the poached mussels in that cozy bistro on the Rue des Écoles. But then there was the night

Paris of the stifling smoke-filled cabarets, the powdered-skin flesh smells of the audience, and when you were alone on the stage, it was beastly, hateful. You were up there shedding your decency, revealing your naked parts, and the panting voyeurs were down there with their hot minds, unblinking bright eyes, parted dry lips, nervous fingers and knees, and it came at you, put you down, violated you, like you were the victim of a gang rape. And when it was done, it was not over, because then came the flowers and cards and the gentlemen themselves, the rich, the famous, the sex acrobats, the jaded hunting for some new charge. They came with their propositions, their promises and tedious lovemaking and inevitable disrespect, and left you on countless rumpled beds, while they returned to their comfortable wives and homes and businesses. For them, as the Westerns on the telly used to put it, another notch in their pistols, a stag conquest, a conversation piece. For you, aching thighs, loathing heart, some bloody bauble on the table.

That was the Paris she remembered and abominated, and by comparison those days had been relatively good because she had worked in a little-known cheap club on the Left Bank, frequented by relatively decent clerks and lorry drivers, and only when it was known to the wealthier classes that it was *she* (with the Jameson affair still in the papers) did it become bad, and from this she had finally fled. Now, if she returned to Paris, spotlighted in one of its greatest show palaces, audiences dominated by sophisticated males of every nationality on the prowl, it would be worse, far worse. The pressure would be relentless, and she would give in, let go and give, because in the end you were worn down, too weary to resist, and besides, since you were lonely anyway, going nowhere anyway, saving yourself for nothing, you gave in and gave in and gave in and didn't give a damn—until later.

At least here in Juan-les-Pins it was a little better. Only the older male tourists were troublesome. Most of the rest of them were boys, younger, cleaner, healthier, and to those kids she was a contemporary but a little too old and well-known, and to them the Jameson affair was ancient history, and her nudity was no nuder than any on the streets and beaches, and they didn't need her because there were so many girls everywhere anyway, and it was all so easy and natural—and this made her life here a bit easier, a bit more natural, than it could ever be in Paris. No, Paris, for whatever its false inducements, was the second choice.

But there was yet a third straw to grasp, and that was not to work in Juan-les-Pins, not to work in Paris, but rather simply not to work at all, anywhere. She needed a vacation, four weeks of nothing, no hours, no costumes, no music, no audiences, just nothing. This might be the best solution in the world for her.

Instantly she knew that was a lie. Calling four weeks of leisure a vacation was like calling death a vacation. She would worry about emptying The Piggy, her leather-encased savings bank, which had pitifully little money in it anyway. Worse, she would have too much time to brood, to measure her helplessness, her lack of future, and she had long ago used up ways to fill free time. She had tired of gambling, water-skiing, motorboat chuting, and so the only sports would be excessive drinking, immoderate dosages of Nembutal, and drunken daydreams about what had been and what might have been and should she kill Sir Austin Ormsby before she killed herself. A vacation could only be a vacuum that revived every aspect of her exile.

Once, browsing in a bookstore somewhere, in Deauville—or was it Frankfurt?—she had seen some English books, and one was about celebrated exiles, and in the front of the book was a quotation from somebody named Ovid or Ibid, one of those names you always see and never remember, but she'd never forgotten the quotation, because she had memorized it: *Exilium mors est.* Later she let some young language professor, who reeked of beer, pet her breasts in return for the translation. The translation was: *Exile is death.*

Her exile was not only the most unjust but the longest in history because—when you figured it out—she'd been banished from England when she was eighteen, and now she was twenty-one, and three years out of twenty-one was one-seventh of her whole life, and not even Ovid or Ibid, she would wager, had been exiled that many filthy years. Exile is death. True. Vacation is death. True. The four-week vacation was the last straw, and the one she would not cling to. And Paris wasn't any straw to cling to, either. And as for Juan-les-Pins, she was sick of it.

Depressed, she realized that she was still in the ladies' room and that the Coke bottle in her hand was empty. She kicked open the door, dropped the empty bottle beside the vending machine, and considered a second Coke.

Suddenly hearing her name, she wheeled around, and it was Jouvet approaching, mopping his face. *"Ah, chérie—voilà—*I worried—"

"Well, look who's here," she said crossly. "I didn't think you knew I still existed."

Jouvet's hands went to his head as he shook it in profound apology. "Your forgiveness a thousand times, but that idiot director with his new ideas wants to make this the Folies, and it was imperative I explain to him I am not a millionaire. But Medora, *chérie,* you must

108

believe Jouvet—despite that idiot dinning in my ear, my other ear was for you, and my eyes and heart. Your new numbers were exquisite. Accepted! Do you have more you wish to show me?"

"Not now. I'm not in the mood."

"No matter. With you it is not important. It is only important that you rehearse with the girls tomorrow afternoon, and even if it is not the smoothest, no one will mind, and you can open tomorrow night. *Voilà,* we go to my office. I have the contract."

She shrugged her shoulders. "I don't know." Wearily she moved into the cabaret dining room, and as she traversed the dance floor, Jouvet pursued her.

"But, *chérie,* please—"

"I haven't made my mind up yet." She found her floppy white hat atop her straw bag. "Give me time to think."

Jouvet quivered with agitation. "But time—time is what matters—time is money—time is the show. I must know at once—to prepare handbills—the new sign in front—to know if it is you, or the stupid team from Monte Carlo. Medora, I plead, it must be you, and you must say yes now."

She was adjusting the hat on her head. "This minute I cannot say yes, I won't say no, I can only say maybe. I have to be by myself, and think it through. I'll let you know by morning—by tonight, if I can—but by morning for sure."

"By early morning the latest," Jouvet implored. He covered her hands with his, paternally. "Time, Medora, time is important."

"Not to me," she said. With that, she picked up her straw bag and started for the exit.

Once outside, in the Avenue Maréchal Joffre, she took her oversized white-rimmed sunglasses from her bag and slipped them on. Sauntering to the Avenue Guy de Maupassant, she felt the dry heat scald her arms and bare midriff but she enjoyed it. The sun felt cleansing and restored her to purposeful life.

As she walked along the avenue to the main square, the town seemed uninhabited, her own, and she liked it best this way. With nightfall Juan-les-Pins would become a raucous, noisy, uncouth carnival for the young, the jazz *Américain* from the caves and the crazy cyclist doing his tricks before Le Crystal café and the swarming unwashed adolescents, and there would be the crush of foreign cars, but at the noon hour it was lazy and quiet and private.

Approaching the square, she reconsidered grasping straw three, the four-week do-nothing vacation here. In her rented Mercedes-Benz sports car, she could visit similar isolated resorts nearby, enjoy the peace of Beaulieu, wonderful despite the pebble beach, or luxuriate on the sun wharf at La Napoule, relaxing despite the highway above it. There were islands of escape here, really, and the Riviera could be more than the restless, tourist-crowded beaches and bars in St.-Tropez or Cannes or Monte Carlo. She had not been to Cannes in weeks, and then only to savor Mama's dish of l'osso-buco in La Mère Besson, the restaurant two blocks behind La Croisette. Too, and this best of all, she could drive into the unspoiled hills above the Riviera, wander through the ancient, precariously perched villages rimming the Vallée du Loup. Or go more frequently to St.-Paul and sit quietly in Nardeau's villa, watching him paint, and then read until she dozed, and share a thick pot of bouillabaisse, sharp with garlic, with Nardeau and his wife and his mistress and talk late into the night, without self-consciousness, about the meaning of life and the wonders of life. She realized that she had not seen Nardeau in a month and that she missed him deeply, not for his genius but for his peasant honesty and his true friendship.

She found herself standing in the square, before the unoccupied chairs of the Crystal café, loving Juan-les-Pins at this bright, silent hour. She squinted into the café, considering an ice cream, answered the friendly wave of a waiter, then decided that she must return to her hotel room and compose a telegram to Paris and a letter to London.

She waited for a station wagon and a Maserati to pass, then leisurely crossed the street to the corner *librairie*. A few French youngsters were inside browsing among the books and there was a couple listening to an American phonograph record. At last she turned from the entrance to the outdoor newsstand with its racks of foreign periodicals and newspapers. She realized that she had had such an active and troubled interior life the past week that she had neglected her reading. She pulled out the latest *News of the World* and a week-old issue of the *Sunday Times* of London, which she bought only for the rotogravure section. Quickly, she went into the shop, paid for the newspapers, and departed.

She proceeded up the Boulevard Baudouin, between the municipal park to her left and Gould Park to her right. As she neared the hotel, where the Boulevard Baudouin became Boulevard du Littoral, a faint cooling sea breeze came up from the beach through the heavy pines and curled around her face and waist, and she wondered if she should change and go directly down to the Provençal hotel beach. She decided that Michaud's telegram must be answered promptly with a firm but tactful telegram of her own.

During a gap in the traffic, she hastened to the beach entrance of the

Provençal and hurried inside, where the temperature drop was so sudden that goose pimples formed on her arms. The kiosk and stylish dress shop were closed for lunch. Obtaining her key at the small desk, she waited for the lift and took it to her floor.

Entering her grand, airy corner room—she liked space, especially at night before the first Nembutal had taken hold, so she could wander around and around until she was tired or drugged—Medora was pleased to see that the maids had already been in. The room was spotless, the breakfast tray gone from the balcony, and the double bed neatly done up. Medora hated disheveled beds in late mornings or early afternoons. They were monuments to all her failings, reminders and rebukes of so many nights of her past, evoking memories of a weak, apologetic father with whisky on his breath, one who had never been around when you needed him but one whom you still vaguely remembered with love, resentment, and regret.

Removing the floppy hat, she tossed it on the bed, located a gold pencil in her bag, then closed the bag and dropped it, along with her sunglasses, next to the hat. Kicking off her sandals, she sat down at the glass-topped, ivory-colored table in the center of the room, opened a drawer holding hotel stationery and telegram blanks, twisted her pencil for more lead, and finally, elbows on the cool table, chin resting in her cupped hands, she tried to think what she should say in her telegram to the owner of the Club Lautrec in Paris.

She would decline, of course—because of exhaustion and the need of a holiday, she would tell him. Yet she should not emphasize exhaustion too much because, as her survival instinct warned, it might be used against her, a question mark if Michaud ever considered her in the future, and she needed him. Perhaps it would be better to state that she had already committed herself to an extended stay in the Juan-les-Pins show. It would imply that, since she was being held over, she was popular, much in demand. And she might add how sincerely grateful she was for the offer, how long she had desired to appear in the Club Lautrec, and possibly a booking could be arranged at a future date.

In her heart she knew that there would be no future date, no second chance in Paris, unless she went there now and made it big now. She was being summoned only because of an unusual circumstance—the influx of English and Americans at the Summit conference, all of whom knew of her scandal, and because she was especially exploitable for that audience in this time—but if judging her on merit alone, the important clubs would ignore her in the future as they had done in the past.

She tried a quick rough draft of the telegram, not wanting it to be wordy since it was a telegram and she had been raised to be frugal about telegrams, and the result was not only clumsy but curt. It made her too busy, too much in demand, and it would only make a sophisticate like Michaud laugh. Also, she was saying that she was committed to an extended appearance at Chez 88-40-88, and what if she did not go through with it, took her vacation instead, and Michaud found out the lie? No good, no good. She must find a foolproof means of turning him down, while keeping him interested in her.

She attempted an even hastier second draft of the telegram, and stopped midway through because it was a jumble, as was her mind, because she was awkward with words. Impatiently she tore it up, gazed out the corner window at the green treetops and the velvety sea in the distance. She was too tired and distraught to organize such a vital telegram. She would do it later, she decided. After all, she had no performance tonight and nothing but time. She would go down to the quiet beach and rest in the sun. This rarely failed to ease her mind. Afterwards, clearheaded, she would get the wire off to Paris.

But before the beach, there was the letter she owed her mother, always sent with a funny drawing at the bottom for her retarded sister. The mother letter was easy. She wrote three times a week—telephoning only on holidays, which she hated to do because it made her so horribly homesick—and there was little to put in each new letter, and the letter was really only a memorandum to prove that she was alive, and that, as her mother would write in her crabbed hand, where there is life there is hope. Like hell, Mum.

Hastily, in the ornate calligraphy she had long affected, as artificial but by now as automatic as the genteel soft theatrical West End accent she had also affected, she began her letter with "Sat., June 14" under the blue imprint of the stationery that read "Le Provençal . . . Juan-les-Pins," which made her salutation, "Dear Mummy," seem even more ridiculous.

She wrote of the wonderful reception that she had enjoyed in her closing numbers at Chez 88-40-88. She wrote that everyone wanted to book her, including one of the best cabarets in Paris, but that she would consider all that later, because now she just wanted to rest for four weeks and maybe work on a fresh approach to her act. She was going to spend much of her month off investigating, once more, the possibilities of returning home. She was saving her money again, even though living continued to be costly on the Continent. She was meeting with a famous barrister staying at Cap d'Antibes, who thought that there were loopholes in the charge the Ormsbys had raised against her, and that besides there were legal possibilities of getting around any law. Of course, the barrister was expensive (she did not tell his entire fee, because she had promised her mother no more of that), but whatever fee he wanted to handle her case would be well worth it, just to get home again, to be with Mum and Cynthia again. On this note of false optimism, she concluded her regular letter, signing it "Yr loving daughter, Me," and added a row of X's, and the sketch of an evilly grinning cat (which somehow reminded her of Sydney Ormsby) with an arrow pointing to it and the caption in block letters, "For dear Cynthy, a Persian cat I'll buy you one day. Lovingly, Me."

By now too tired to address the envelope—she'd do that and the telegram later, and take them down to the concierge—she left the letter on the table and prepared to change for the beach. She removed her short shift of a blouse, unzipped the stretch pants and rolled them down her thighs and legs and, holding on to the back of a chair, pulled them off. It was like taking off adhesive tape. Then, once she had stepped out of the pink nylon panties, she was naked and feeling as natural and liberated as any nudist on the île du Levant.

Moving to the bag on her bed, proud that no part of her anatomy, except the breasts, jiggled or shimmied, that her body was firm and taut after so many twenty-one years, she sought a cigarette and lit it. Smoking, she went to the armoire at the far end of the room, opened the third drawer, which was filled with bikinis, examined and discarded two sets but kept the third, the briefest of the lot, which was nearly as weightless as a handkerchief. She settled for this particular white bikini not because its brevity and thin cotton would attract and excite (Heaven forbid, and anyway the beach was always empty at midday, with the hotel guests dining on the terrace mostly out of sight), but because it allowed more of her flesh to be exposed to the sun and would thus even out her tan. She was always trying for a total tan, because when she did her striptease act, she disliked exposing the two narrow white lines that the bikinis left, that defied body makeup, and that seemed (in an indoor nightclub) obscene because of the way they accentuated her breast points and her private parts.

With practiced ease she tied on the wisp of bra and bikini bottom, then padded on bare feet to the full-length bathroom mirror to see if they were fastened decently. The white band of bra was a problem as usual, because of the size of her bosom. When she pulled it up slightly to cover the embarrassing exposure of the top half-moons of her brown nipples, this raised the bottom of the bra, revealing the underpart of her breasts, but that wasn't so bad because that was only tanned flesh. As for the bikini bottom, a tiny triangle of clinging cotton caught between her thighs and stopping three inches below her navel, held secure by strings tied at her hips, it was properly adjusted and no problem. She liked the way the two bits of white accentuated her small supple waist and the rolling bronzed curves of her body.

Quickly she untied her mane of flaxen hair, allowed the hair to fall loose below her shoulders, and then she doused herself with cologne, slipped her feet into Italian beach shoes, and went back to the bedroom. She took down a light mesh pullover sweater and tugged it on, went to the bed for her white-rimmed sunglasses and straw bag, separated the rotogravure section from the rest of the bulky *Sunday Times,* stuffed it in her bag, and, ready at last, she departed for the lift and two hours on the sand.

Downstairs, and once more on the other side of the Boulevard du Littoral, Medora entered the wooded park, walking along the dirt path between the shading pines. Emerging from the path into the glaring sunlight, crossing the cement walk that led both to the Provençal dining terrace overlooking the water ahead and to the stone stairs leading to the beach below, she chose the stairs. One glimpse of the terrace told her that the luncheon crowd was being fed, which promised her a vacant beach of her own.

Relieved, she descended the steps and followed the cement walk under the overhang, around the corner post, to her blue locker door, and opened it. Leaving her beach shoes inside, yanking off her mesh sweater, folding it and placing it on the shelf, she extracted the *Sunday Times* magazine supplement, cigarettes, and lighter from her bag, and left the bag beside her sweater. Closing the door, she stepped down into the soft warm yellow sand and headed for her regular place in the second row from the back. The attendant had finished driving the pole of the umbrella into a new spot, so that it would not come between her body and the blinding disk of sun, and when she reached him, he had already shaken out her beach pad and turned it over.

"*Voilà,* Mademoiselle Hart. Call when the sun is too much and I will move the umbrella."

Absently nodding her thanks, she surveyed the square of beach, a grove of open umbrellas and empty pads, and was grateful she could be alone. Lifting her sunglasses, she could see that the Mediterranean was its deepest cobalt blue, undisturbed by swimmers or bathers or waves, except for the small wake behind two brown youngsters paddling a pontoon-boat. Even the voices from the dining terrace could not be heard. It was idyllic.

Placing her paraphernalia on the tiny table beside her pad, Medora squirted the sunburn lotion into one hand and slowly rubbed it deep into her cheeks, neck, chest, and the bulges of her bosom above and below the ribbon of bikini bra. She had begun to rub lotion across her stomach when she was startled by a babble of voices and uncouth laughter.

She straightened, and saw three couples coming down the stone steps and gathering around the beach attendant. From their pasty white complexions, she could tell they were new ones. They had just arrived, and they were ordering pads, and several of them were loud. Their words and accents carried, and at once Medora's spirits sagged. They were English visitors, not the best, business and commerical Englishmen away from Liverpool and London at last and here to make a time of it. Their voices, the old nostalgic street voices, disconcerted Medora, making her feel homesick and uncomfortable. There were very few English tourists in Juan-les-Pins now, and Medora had expected no more on this beach until the bank holiday, but here they were engulfing her private beach already, and their presence unsettled her.

Sighing, she resumed with the sunburn lotion. She was nearly done, having just taken off her sunglasses to touch up the area below her eyes, when she heard them approaching. Her head came up as the invaders, led by the attendant, abruptly turned off to the row in front, but one of them, a curly-haired man in his thirties, an albino almost, lingered to admire her nudity. He was beaming his compliment when suddenly his brow furrowed, his grin froze, and he chased off after his male companions.

Turning her back to them, Medora knew what to expect. The only question was whether she would overhear it or not. She would hear it, of course. Unrepressed excitement, of course.

"Nigel, Nigel, have a look. Isn't that—blimey, I'll bet ten bob it is, am I right?—isn't that Medora Hart? You know, the Jameson girl?"

"You're dreaming. Where?"

"Shhh. Over there."

Brazenly, anger controlled and defiant, she turned to face the voices and give them their bloody ten bob's worth of the Jameson girl.

"Cor! I'll be damned!" she heard one exclaim, and as she turned her back to them once more and slipped on her sunglasses, she could hear their silence, feel their beastly bulging eyes on her nude back. Then came their faint whisperings to the women, and the little gurgles and gigglings of sensation. Their first day, their whole damn holiday, was made, and her day, like countless older days, was horribly ruined.

She wanted to stalk off, but she would not give those holier-than-thou's the satisfaction, and so she was trapped. Well, at least she wouldn't give them any more free looks. If they wanted to see the Jameson girl naked, they could bloody well pay for it in some damn club.

She lowered herself to the pad, out of their sight, and lay on her back, wriggling once or twice to make herself comfortable, and then, still on her back, arms straight at her sides, legs outstretched, she let the sun beat down on her, hoping it would consume and cremate her and let her be freed forever from this bloody travail of anti-suicide that was called staying alive.

But after a while, as she lay there inert, allowing the sun to caress and gently knead her tight muscles, her anger melted into tiny pools of remembrances, and the ones up ahead with their Peeping Tom uncleanliness and gaucherie had dissolved in the welcomed blaze from above.

And so all that remained, at last, as it always had, was the Jameson girl.

Isn't that Medora Hart, the Jameson girl? You bet your tight little arse it is, Nigel, old boy.

It always came back to her like this, some cue, some fragments of searing recollection, some fighting to beat them away and leave her free, but then there were too many fragments closing in on her and her fists were helpless, and rather than fight any more she would lie back and surrender to all of them, to all the experiences of the past, and let memory have its way until it had used her and been sated and left her a wretched lump curled in self-pity and whimpering helplessness.

The Jameson girl met the Jameson man just after her seventeenth birthday. A few months before, increasingly aware that she would never raise the money for beautician's school by trying to save from her shopgirl's salary, and increasingly aware that her maturing face and body had commercial value, she had answered the advertisement of a nightclub in Soho off Piccadilly Circus. The nightclub was interviewing applicants for "the lucrative" position of cigarette girl, "must be young, pretty, shapely, well-mannered, of amiable disposition." Without her mother's knowledge Medora applied, and although a line of candidates a half-block long stood outside the cabaret, she was hired two minutes after the manager saw her and the rest were sent home. Her income, nine pounds a week in salary, five pounds a week in tips, staggered her. She would soon be richer than a princess.

The only uncomfortable aspect of the new position was the attire that she was expected to wear. The costume consisted of a top hat, a sateen vest cut daringly low and leaving her midriff exposed, an abbreviated skirt that was slit hip high, with long sheer black silk stockings drawn up beneath, and a pair of high-heeled pumps. Outside of her bedroom she had never revealed so much of her adolescent figure. But the money was really super, the gem-studded cigarette tray made it seem less immoral, the management did not require that she sit with customers, and so, excitedly informing her mother that she had become a model for an advertising photographer whose main eccentricity was a preference for working evenings and whose main account was an exclusive milliner in George Street, she began the job.

Although located in the heart of raffish and exotic Soho, on Old Compton Street, the club in which Medora Hart made her public debut was considered one of London's better cabarets. It was not as large as Murray's or the Bal Tabarin. It was similar to, if somewhat more crowded than, the Gargoyle or Eve. If Medora's judgment, based on the women's gowns and the men's accents and tips, was accurate, the clientele represented wealth and the Establishment. What amazed her most, as she passed among these male sophisticates night after night, was the attention that she received. Even though the gorgeous, sleek, tall showgirls and chorines on the stage were in a permanent state of undress, the majority of male eyes followed Medora when she meandered among the tables and the stands holding silver champagne buckets. After several months, her head turned by compliments (accepted) and requests for her telephone number (declined), she began to feel jealous of the competition on the stage. Childishly determined not to lose her own audience, she went to the cabaret's management to suggest a new costume of her own design, one consisting of a beaded brassiere instead of the sateen vest and of a pair of tights, scantier and more form-fitting than those she had been wearing, without the abbreviated skirt. The management complied, and added a raise in salary to her growing income from tips, and with the extra money Medora secretly started to take private afternoon lessons in diction, etiquette, and dancing.

After that, and after her seventeenth birthday, she began to date selectively. There were the impressive veteran juvenile lead of a drawing-room comedy playing in Shaftesbury Avenue, the elderly owner of three department stores, an Indian prince who was a graduate student at Cambridge, and she had lost not only her virginity on the first occasion, but her naïveté on the ensuing two occasions, in quick, confusing, unecstatic bouts. Although grateful to be grown up and have expensive gifts lavished upon her, she wondered what the romance surrounding sex was all about. While some of her sudden affluence had gone into new furnishings for her mother's flat, and new therapists for her sister, most of it had been spent on clothes and accessories (professional necessities, she now believed). Her dream of becoming a beautician with a chain of shops still persisted, but her savings for her training course had not materially increased. Anyway, it was rather pleasant, all the attention and admiration and being wanted.

Then, one night, after closing, there was Paddy Jameson.

Two of the chorines had been invited to a late supper party in

Mayfair, and they had specifically been asked to bring Medora along, too. Their host, a regular at the club (whom Medora had never met or noticed), would be waiting at the stage door to escort them. Because of the hour, Medora hesitated, but when the chorines insisted that it was to be only a little after-the-theater party, attended by nobility and millionaires and several renowned journalists, an elegant gathering in good taste, Medora's curiosity as well as ambition made her accept the invitation.

The car outside the stage door was a Rolls-Royce Silver Shadow, and their host was Paddy Jameson, who was introduced to Medora as the "famous decorator," but Medora had never heard of him. The catered supper was served in Jameson's richly furnished two-story flat in Chester Place. And, indeed, among Jameson's sixteen guests, mostly male, there were names familiar to Medora through her reading of the newspapers. Of the half-dozen females at the party, Medora was the most striking, and the one most attended by gentlemanly admirers.

For Medora this was a new social plateau, and its possibilities stimulated her. Recently she had started drinking, but only moderately. That night, made heady by her surroundings, she had considerably exceeded previous limitations on her alcoholic intake. By four in the morning she was quite drunk, and Paddy Jameson, until then flitting here and there playing the amusing host, had been inattentive. While other guests spoke highly of his wit and creative genius, Medora was unable to discern the reason for such lavish praise. To her bleary eyes, Paddy Jameson appeared no more than an amiable lightweight with his neat toupee, his sallow fish-face riddled by acne scars, his foppish clothes and effeminate gestures and slurred wicked, gossipy anecdotes. But at four in the morning he became devoted at last and interesting, and as the guests made their elaborate farewells and drifted off, he promised Medora he would personally escort her to her home. By five o'clock the last of the guests had long since disappeared, and there were she and Paddy on the Sheraton sofa, so cozy, she comfortable in his arms, heavy-lidded and thick-tongued and weak.

Of course, it was too late to take her home, and she agreed, being agreeable to anything as long as it would allow her to lie down. He helped her to the bedroom, and undressed her, and took her to his precious Queen Anne bed, and he made love to her, and it was good, really good.

At noon, waking and somewhat sobered, she found him waiting with Bloody Marys. Protesting, grimacing, she accepted one, which cleared her head for the second one, which made her feel fine. After that he removed his robe, and it surprised her that he was naked and startled her that she was naked, too. She resisted his endearments and petting briefly, then unable to withstand his touch, she resigned herself to another bout of copulation. It was tremendous, really. She had never been so completely and shamefully aroused, and had never imagined that she could be made to behave as she had. His perversions and his lovemaking were concentrated on pleasing her, on giving her pleasure (which no man ever had), and the sensation had been memorable.

After that, she became Paddy Jameson's girl. She was helplessly drawn to him, an addict of his giving, unable to resist the mind-expanding drug of excitation. Her instincts and two medical books had told her that he was probably a practicing homosexual and, driven by the guilt of this and in an effort to deny his deviation, he sought to dominate women by pleasing them and thereby making them dependent upon him. But after several months, Medora realized her analysis had been incomplete and that there had been a more practical motive in his design.

Paddy had been buying her exquisite dresses and accessories, and escorting her to the poshest parties, and presenting her as his hostess at gatherings of his own, and no one less than a baronet or an authentic millionaire was ever present. And then one night, at some eccentric lord's stately house near Runnymede, she drank heavily knowing that it was safe with Paddy nearby, and after midnight she had been unable to locate Paddy and found herself alone with the cadaverous lord of the manor, who wanted only to care for her and protect her. Drunkenly angered by Paddy's abandonment, dazed by His Lordship's promises, exhausted by the whole damn business—besides, what difference, what was there to lose?—she stayed the night, and the weekend as well, and you know, it hadn't been half bad, in fact, rather smashing, not having to give or commit yourself, enduring a few minutes' romp in bed in return for the magnificent pleasures of living beyond your means in a castle on an estate, liveried servants, everything—and, waiting for you on the seat of the chauffeured Bentley going back to London, a box containing a sable jacket and a box containing a solid gold bracelet.

So that was it, finally, and eight more months of it to come, before the scandal exploded. Her situation became clear to her soon enough. Her man, Paddy Jameson, was not her man alone but a man with five other Medoras dwelling in various sections of the city, five others who were young, beautiful, ambitious, and whose physical endowments equaled if not surpassed her own. Paddy Jameson's avocation was society decorator, but his vocation was procurer. On the one hand, he was an intimate of great and important men; on the other hand, he was a libertine who scouted for attractive, relatively unused girls, won them, trained them, and quietly passed them on to his wealthy male circle. He employed his mistresses with discretion. They were neither courtesans nor prostitutes. They were merely free and independent party girls and girl friends. There was no overt professionalism at all. Not one of the girls ever received a direct fee for services rendered. Like any woman who had been kind, she received gifts, and sometimes these took the form of cash.

As for Paddy Jameson, in those months, Medora had never been able to solve the mystery of what there was in it for him. It was evident that he had never accepted monetary payment for performing as a go-between and agent. Perhaps, Medora once speculated, he did it to please the rich, so he could enjoy their society. Or perhaps, by acting for them in this way, he was given special interior decorating commissions. Yet the last was doubtful, for Medora had never observed him using his time other than on the tennis court, in the swimming pool, at social gatherings—or in bed.

In the eight months that followed, she saw less and less of Paddy. At his behest she resigned from her position as cigarette girl at the cabaret. He assisted her in locating and furnishing a lovely and luxurious service flat within a short walk of Marble Arch, one in which she could receive the most distinguished gentlemen callers. As for Paddy, instead of his former daily visits, he gradually settled into dropping in on her once a week. Only on the occasions when he had to appease her jealousy and anger did he come more than once a week and remain overnight. She saw him frequently, of course, at the wild weekend parties in the country, and often he was with one of the other girls, but she did not mind.

Those had been crazy, wonderful months, really. Through Paddy she had taken up with only five lovers—well, six actually, if you counted the last one. Four had been well-known Government officials, two of these highly placed. In eight months, living as a lady of leisure, in refined splendor, Medora had been showered with gifts of diamonds, gowns, mink coats, antiques, a motorcar, sets of Wedgwood bone china, a charge arrangement at Harrods, and nearly £10,000 in cash, except in the end she had been unable to account for £9,000 of it.

On only one occasion had the whole business been distasteful. She had complained to Paddy that with the way things were, she could not hold on to money. He suggested that the best way to hold on to money was simply to earn more of it. Did she wish to earn more? Well, she wouldn't mind, she told him, as long as it did not involve real promiscuity. He vowed to keep an eye open for her, and then, one evening, he escorted her to a sprawling ancestral mansion not many miles past Hampton Court. The host was a duke and a Cabinet Minister, and there were perhaps two dozen guests. The party had seemed rather routine at the outset, until Medora realized with shock that the young serving girls, wearing abbreviated apron skirts, were stark naked beneath their aprons. There had been heavy drinking, and reefers for those who wanted them, and gradually the older men and younger girls were undressing one another, and Paddy went along and laughingly teased Medora into joining the fun, although her shock had heightened. After that, the evening became a nightmare for her—two nude girls whipping His Grace, who was prone on the bear rug, five guests performing a disgusting sex circus in the middle of the living room to general hilarity, other guests lining up for peeks through a one-way mirror to see (themselves being unseen) an unsuspecting pair coupling in the master bedroom. Refusing to participate, Medora hid herself, then dressed and fled back to London.

The following day, Paddy came by early, making light of the nightmare evening, remarking that he had only wanted to have Medora witness a real live orgy. She spoke her mind, and he quickly agreed that she had too much reserve and class for that type of thing—but slyly added that young ladies who had participated received gifts twice as generous as any Medora had ever known. Nevertheless, Medora was not interested, and she was never again invited to attend an orgy.

The last of the ones that Paddy introduced her to was that dapper buck-toothed Charlie, Sydney Ormsby, young and silly and panting with passion. His family was enormously wealthy and influential, and he had an income above and beyond the stipend he received as a minor member of British Intelligence. His was a desk job politically obtained for him by his family in an effort to straighten him out, a job for which he was ill-suited and which he chafed to leave. Although he was sex-obsessed, Medora found him an ineffectual rabbit and hardly troublesome at all. He inspired the one bon mot of her career, repeated to Paddy: "The only thing Sydney can screw up properly is his courage." Sydney heaped expensive gifts upon her and spoke glowingly of their future, and briefly Medora was caught up in the possibilities of making an advantageous marriage.

Then, suddenly, in their fourth week, for the very first time, Sydney Ormsby did not keep an appointment. He did not appear that night, or the following night, or any night ever again. Incredulous at such strange and uncharacteristic behavior, Medora tried to reach Paddy the next morning, and the morning after, and every day for a week, and Paddy, too, seemed to have disappeared from the face of the earth.

Then, at last, it had all been explained to her, and a frightened Medora Hart was mystified no longer.

The headlines were bigger, blacker, more provocative and threatening than they had been in the John Profumo-Christine Keeler-Stephen Ward affair of her childhood. Fleet Street was on a Roman holiday. Parliament was in a turmoil. The Establishment trembled. England held its collective breath.

Paddy Jameson had been quietly arrested by a detective chief inspector and a detective sergeant, at the instigation of the Security Service, and had been brought before a Marylebone magistrate, and had been indicted for trial at the Old Bailey on five vice charges.

Quaking with fear, Medora read and reread the charges and tried to understand how they might affect her. One charge, based on the Sexual Offences Act, was that Paddy Jameson had conspired to procure "several young ladies," unnamed, to engage in unlawful sexual intercourse, and had supplied them with "goods and services" to encourage them to indulge in prostitution. Another charge had been that Paddy had engaged in blackmail against wealthy, prominent male acquaintances, to whom he had previously supplied young ladies of easy virtue. Yet another charge, in bold-faced type, accused Paddy of employing his party girls—"immoral tarts," one newspaper called them—to acquire information from those of their lovers who were in the Government, some of this information being secret and classified, and which information Paddy in turn sold to the press and to friends he had in three foreign embassies.

Medora Hart somehow thought, whenever her activities passed through the amoral filter of her conscience, that Paddy and his girls and she herself were performing naturally in a perfectly acceptable, somewhat known, entirely legal, if permissive way. In the very few times that she had been apprehensive, wondering whether the activity was contrary to the law, she had put her fears aside, assuming that Paddy knew everybody who counted, and what could be done and not be done, and that, anyway, they were all of them above the law since their lovers were, in a sense, the law itself. Yet, apparently, now the police and the press decreed otherwise, and the scandal was shaking the foundations of Great Britain and being emblazoned across a thousand front pages, in hundreds of tongues, around the entire globe. She was stricken less by what appeared to be misconduct on her part than by the danger of being humiliated and punished for doing what she had not known was wrong.

Considering Paddy's notable and illustrious patrons, Medora could not conceive how their private behavior had been revealed to the slobbering masses. But as lurid newspaper edition supplanted lurid newspaper edition, the truth came into the open. Paddy Jameson had been a victim of his own weakness, unknown to her, and his weakness had been gambling. He had fallen deeply into debt, and his life had been threatened by a gang of Soho boys. Unable to obtain personal loans from his friends for a large enough amount, he had clumsily attempted to blackmail the crusty old duke, the one out near Hampton Court, the host of the orgies, and Paddy had miscalculated His Grace's temper. Infuriated by a young man's blackmail, and too old to care about his already tarnished career, the duke had gone to Scotland Yard, turned over the evidence of blackmail, and told all he had seen and all in which he had been a participant. This confession had led the investigators to an alcoholic newspaper columnist who had bought Paddy's tidbits and secondhand bed talk and transformed them, without names and with much use of the words "rumor" and "alleged," into print. Since his Catholic conscience, and liver and gout had recently been nagging him, the newspaperman added substantially more and racier information to His Grace's confession.

And so the scandal was loosed and out—at least, some of it was out. Paddy himself, when interrogated at the Yard, pretended rage, claimed persecution, defended his good name, and admitted to nothing. Paddy's flat, the police had expected, would be the depository of enough evidence to convict him, but its drawers and desks and safe offered them only fastidious respectability, Bond Street apparel, birthday cards from relatives, insurance policies, bills from the corner chemist. Obviously, someone, with more of a stake in Jameson's future than a mere loss of friendship, had visited the flat first. The police departed empty-handed.

The disappointment of the officers of the Yard and the Security Service did not trouble or long deter the public prosecutor. He already possessed enough to proceed. Two of Paddy's girls were located and arrested. Four members of Paddy's illustrious clientele were located and interrogated and retained as Crown witnesses. There were hints of others, other girls, other patrons, but the public prosecutor did not worry, certain that some would come forward voluntarily and the rest would be flushed out by the sensational headlines and the ominous police statements in the daily press.

For an entire week Medora kept herself to her service flat, maintaining liaison with the outer world through the newspapers that her loyal, overpaid, backward Jamaican housekeeper brought to her. Two and three times daily Medora combed each fresh edition, with the same caution and dread that the elderly feel when they turn to each day's obituary notices. So far her name had not been mentioned in print. The two of Paddy's girls under arrest had not known her name, and of the three remaining at large only one knew her name, address, and something of her history. As to those of Paddy's clients who were being assembled for testimony, not one had been her client. So far, safe. But safe from what, she was unable to understand. The case against Paddy was strong. But the case against Paddy's girls was not clearly set forth—only references to "prostitution," which were, to Medora, utterly ridiculous.

Her fear, a throwback to childhood's fear of suffering hellfire for immorality, she could only attribute to the public prosecutor's thundering pronouncements about corruption and sin, his latest pronouncement having drawn upon a predecessor, the one who had prosecuted Stephen Ward during the Profumo affair and who had said, "We have come in this case to the depths of lechery and depravity." The tone reminded Medora not of Lord Chief Justice Jeffreys but of the Reverend Davidson. She did not fear justice but rather sanctimonious hypocrisy. Miss Sadie Thompson's contemptuous hatred had been in her mind: "You men! You filthy, dirty pigs! You're all the same, all of you." And then, thinking of this, Medora would be afraid.

For Medora, in her seclusion, the second week of the scandal proved to be the most suspenseful and trying. The second week began promisingly. Preparations for the trial were under way. The prosecution admitted, with sniffing dismay, that no new girls had been turned up, but they were still seeking Paddy's male acquaintances. For Medora, faint hope. Then new editions, later stories, vaguely alarming, soon sinister. Several of Paddy's acquaintances had been traced, had agreed to cooperate with the police, were being questioned in secrecy today. For Medora, fainter hope, but hope still, not despair. Compulsively, she ate her sweets, and between newspaper editions she listened to the wireless, and she waited, hopefully waited. No news, her mother used to say, was good news, luv.

Then overnight, with the first front page of the new morning, with the vacuous face staring up at her, all hope was shattered.

The headline read:

ORMSBY NAMED IN JAMESON AFFAIR!

The subheadline read:

NEW WITNESS REVEALS INTELLIGENCE DEPT. OFFICER,
BROTHER OF MILLIONAIRE M.P., SEEN AT
PADDY'S ORGIES.

Her wide eyes raced down the column for her name. It was not there. Exhaling her relief, she began to read the story from the start. One of the latest witnesses had given the police a half-dozen names of influential persons that he had recently met during a brief cocktail visit to Paddy Jameson's flat. Among these, he had recalled, was Mr. Sydney Ormsby, attached to British Intelligence, and the younger brother of the rising politician, Sir Austin Ormsby, Member of Parliament and head of Ormsby Press Enterprises, Ltd. The younger Ormsby had, on that occasion, been accompanied by a pretty blond girl in her twenties. The witness did not know her name. However, young Ormsby had seemed to be quite familiar with her and apparently was on the best of terms with Paddy Jameson. The newspaper story concluded with the fact that Mr. Sydney Ormsby was being summoned by the police for questioning.

Huddled in her service flat, forgoing sweets for gin-and-tonic, Medora fatalistically surrendered to the inevitable. She waited for the officers of the law. Yet, throughout the day, no one came to her door. She waited for the late evening newspapers, and when they appeared she was almost limp with relief, as if a last-minute reprieve had rescued her from the gallows. There was a news photograph of Sydney arriving for the interrogation, smirking and confident. There was a portrait of Sir Austin, bearing a caption to the effect that the M.P. "stood steadfastly behind his allegedly errant brother." Then there was the report of the interrogation: Sydney Ormsby had flatly contradicted the testimony of the witness who claimed to have seen him in Paddy Jameson's flat. Sydney had sworn that while he did have a nodding acquaintance with the defendant, he had never once been inside Jameson's flat. Even more firmly he had sworn that, at least to the best of his knowledge, he had never met a so-called Jameson girl, let alone enjoy the favors of any of them. It had surprised him, he added, to learn that the mild, well-bred Jameson had actually been a procurer.

As she read this, Medora's relief was leavened by amusement at Sydney's audacity. Sydney had brazened out a lie, she knew, had maybe even committed outright perjury, but he had convinced his inquisitors that he was blameless and uninvolved. Somehow she felt safer after this, because if someone in Sydney Ormsby's position could dare such a denial under oath, and come off with it, then she need have no alarm for herself. For the first time, she possessed the comforting feeling that her anonymity would continue to be preserved.

That night, having washed her hair and done it up in curlers, she felt optimistic enough to ignore the wireless for once and to give the late hours over to an old American film spectacle about the romantic South that was being presented on the telly. Sipping a Grand Marnier, relaxed on her ruffled divan, she was fully absorbed in the gracious plantation set among the magnolias, and the brooding master caught between two women, when suddenly a shrill piercing sound startled her, sent a chill through her, and made her sit upright.

The doorbell had rung. And three short, sharp raps followed it.

Fumbling for her robe, heart thudding, she realized that what she had dreaded most was finally happening. She was having a caller. The police, she had often read, always came at midnight, when your resistance was low.

Pressing herself against the door, she asked tremulously, "Who is it?"

The voice was almost inaudible. "A friend. Please let me in."

Distrustful, but fearful of opposing the law, she hastily unlatched the door and opened it.

At first she did not recognize him and then, from her obsessive reading of the newspapers, she did. She was face to face with The Brother. He stood there, aristocratic, contained, scrutinizing her with shrewd eyes, and then he said somewhat wearily, "Miss Hart, I presume? I am Austin Ormsby. If you are alone, I would suggest that you allow me inside."

In the living room he glanced about, then slowly walked through the flat, and returned. He refused to remove his topcoat and he rejected the offer of a drink, but instead planted himself in the armchair, umbrella between his legs, and motioned her to the divan opposite him. She obeyed instantly, and waited for what was to happen.

Although his voice was unhurried, he said at once that time was short and that he must come directly to the point of his visit. Of course, as she might imagine, the visit concerned his younger brother, Sydney, and Medora herself. Yes, yes, despite the press, he knew the truth of his brother's relationship with her and with Paddy Jameson. It was most unfortunate, for everyone involved, but there it was and they must be realistic and make the best of a bad thing. But before proceeding further, a preliminary question.

"Miss Hart, has the inspector of the police been by today?"

"No—no one," she said breathlessly.

"Good," he said, his face reflecting no satisfaction. "Then we still have time."

He would explain quickly, and without burdensome detail, and she must accept his word for all that he would say. With that, he went on. He had reason to believe that both she and his brother were in imminent danger. In his position he had access to certain reliable sources of information. He had learned, not more than two hours ago, that the police investigators were on to a lead that might ultimately, and seriously, involve Miss Hart and Sydney in the shoddy Jameson affair. Through a go-between the police were in contact with a third one of

Jameson's girls, and this young lady was prepared to come forward with a full confession, but only if the law would guarantee to drop charges of prostitution against her. A compromise was this moment being discussed through the go-between.

"A compromise will be effected," Sir Austin said, "and when it is, this girl will emerge from hiding and will reveal the names of every one of you who have been represented by Jameson, and she will name all of your male friends as well. If this happens, as I am led to believe that it will shortly, your name will be made public, Miss Hart, and so will my brother's again, and it distresses me to think of what will become of both of you."

Tears filled Medora's eyes, and Sir Austin made a perfunctory effort to calm her. When she regained her composure, hc said that he must inform her of the worst of it before undertaking to tell her the best of it. Waiting prayerfully for the best of it, Medora stiffened to hear the worst of it.

If Medora should be found by the police and forced to stand in the witness box for the Crown, against the accused, Paddy Jameson, her testimony under oath would be ruinous not only to Jameson but to Sydney and to herself. A young woman, Sir Austin sermonized, has no greater asset than her public reputation. Once there is a blot on her fair name, she is ruined for life. An appearance in court would damage Medora Hart beyond repair. Moreover, if the Crown could prove that Jameson engaged or sold his girls as prostitutes, then after his trial and conviction each of his young ladies could be tried, under the Sexual Offences Act, for prostitution. This action might be difficult for the Government to sustain, but it was a possibility not to be lightly regarded, and it could mean a jail sentence for Medora Hart.

His own brother would suffer, Sir Austin admitted, but to a lesser degree. Once Medora was made to confess to her affair with him, Sydney, in turn, would be forced to acknowledge it, and to stand witness against Jameson in the near future and against Medora at a later date. While this kind of scandal was rarely as damaging to a male as to a female, Sir Austin explained in a somewhat pretentiously paternal tone, still it would do harm to Sydney's future career, and, worse, it would unfairly embarrass Sir Austin himself and the entire Ormsby family. Did Medora fully understand all the consequences that would result from her detention and exposure in the Old Bailey?

Medora fully understood; and, by now controlled, she also understood that The Brother had been giving her the most of it and Sydney the least of it.

"You forgot one thing about my testimony," she said bravely. "It would land Sydney smack in prison for perjury. He swore to the police he'd never had anything to do with any of us, but he had, and I'd be the second one made to say it."

Sir Austin studied her with new respect, and he nodded gravely. "Yes, Miss Hart, I daresay that might be a possibility. It would depend on whether my brother made his denial this morning under oath. There is a legal question there that is debatable. But yes, that would remain a possibility. In any event, and you must believe me, it is not for Sydney alone that I am here tonight, but to protect you as well."

The worst of it had been horrifying, and Medora's composure had begun to disintegrate. Thinking of her prospects, she was no longer able to conceal her agitation. "What can be done?" she asked with anguish.

"What can be done by us? Everything. What can be done by the police? Nothing, Miss Hart, nothing—as long as you are not here to cooperate with them."

"But I am here!"

"Today, yes. But tomorrow—it is my hope, and my advice, that tomorrow you will be far from here, out of the reach of the law and the scandal."

"You mean run away?"

"Run away, Miss Hart? Not at all. What would you be running away from if you were to leave England for the Continent tomorrow? You would be merely another young lady, with an income, seeking a change of climate and enjoying a long-desired holiday. As of now— and for the next twenty-four hours, I trust—you are a free citizen of a free land, at liberty to go where you wish and to do as you please within the limits of the law. If you choose to vacation in France, there is no reason why you cannot do so. Legally you have as yet no connection with the Jameson case, and so you are of no interest to the police. If, however, while you happened to be on the Continent, outside British jurisdiction, it should turn out you were wanted as a witness in England, you would be safe to ignore a summons. You would be within your rights, I assure you, and there would be no effort at extradition. The Crown will have witnesses enough. The trial would consequently go on and end without you. And once Jameson is convicted and sentenced, the affair will be forgotten, and you will be forgotten, and after a lovely holiday of three or four months, you would be free to return to London, your reputation unimpaired, your freedom unfettered, your future before you."

"And Sydney, he'd get off, too?"

"He would not be involved. The unsubstantiated evidence that he had consorted with one of Mr. Jameson's girls? Who is there to prove it? Indeed, where is the girl?"

"I see."

"Do you? Very well. I am prepared to finance your holiday on the Continent until the trial is over and it is perfectly safe for you to return. The only condition is that you must leave no later than tomorrow."

While Medora had not been deceived by Sir Austin's solicitude—she had been perfectly aware that his sole concern was to protect the Ormsby family name—she realized that whatever course served his self-interest also served her own. She nodded. "All right. I'll do whatever you tell me."

"Clever girl."

Immediately he replaced paternal regard with a solicitor's questions. Did she have a passport? Yes, she had obtained one about six months ago to spend a weekend in Deauville with a friend. Could she shut down the flat and pack at once? Yes, easily, if she paid the van and storage people in advance and retained her housekeeper to undertake the task of packing after she had gone. Were there any papers, correspondence, diaries, photographs, receipts, cuttings, notes in the flat that would be self-incriminating and so should be destroyed? Nothing. Everything like that had already been destroyed. Did she have any money of her own? No, not really, unless she pawned her furs and jewels. Would she mind taking these valuables abroad? Oh, she would take them anyway. Did she have any urgent personal matters to settle before departing? Well, she'd have to see her mother and sister, drop by the bank, pack what she'd need on the Continent, arrange about the van and storage, and give up the flat.

"Do it all by late tomorrow morning," Sir Austin said emphatically as he rose to his feet. "I'll look in at noon with your plane tickets, sufficient allowance in currency to take care of all your needs for three months, and an address where you can reach me in an emergency. Be prepared to leave London Airport at two o'clock tomorrow afternoon. You'll land at Orly Airport outside Paris. Do not forget your passport."

"But I *can* be back in London in three months and it'll be safe?"

"Three months, four at the most. I promise you."

"Thank God."

"Then it is arranged. Remember this. Speak to no one outside your immediate relatives. Make no telephone calls and accept none from this moment on."

"One more thing. In Europe—Paris—what if someone recognizes me?"

"No harm done. Simply keep your lips sealed, and certainly stay out of sight as much as possible until the trial is over. Good night, Miss Hart, and good luck to both of us."

To her amazement, it had all gone off without an incident. She left London and arrived in Paris as anonymously as any shopgirl on her way to a fortnight of fun.

Sir Austin's warning and assistance had come in the nick of time. Two days later, in the air editions of the London newspapers and in the international edition of the New York *Herald Tribune,* Medora Hart found herself the celebrated "mystery party-girl" of the Jameson affair. The third of Jameson's gay tarts had given herself up, turned Crown's evidence, and named three other girls, one of them being Medora, and named a dozen lovers of these girls, one of them being Sydney Ormsby.

Despite the fact that the English Channel stood between her and the scandal, Medora continued to be apprehensive about her personal safety. When the police learned that she had left the country for some unknown destination abroad, she had expected hounds to come baying after her. But there were no statements in the press that she was being sought as a witness, and no authorities of the law, either English or French, who appeared at her Left Bank hotel to make inquiries. Feeling safer, she began to relax and enjoy her new celebrity in print.

Because Medora had been the youngest and most appealing of Paddy's harem, because several of her men had been among the most illustrious names cited, and, above all, because she had seemingly vanished into thin air, she had been made into the most glamorous of the participants by the fiction writers of Fleet Street and the American wire services. At first it frightened her, but soon she came to relish it, except for the difficulties of writing denials and explanations to her mother, who had been bombarding her with hysterical letters sent care of Cook's in Paris.

Six weeks after her flight to Paris, the long-awaited trial got under way in the majestic courtroom of the historic Old Bailey. From her hideout Medora followed every word reported on the trial with curious detachment. It was as if she were viewing on television an entertainment featuring players she had never known. There were, indeed, marvelous strangers: the High Court Justice with his nylon wig and billowing black gown; the prosecution's counsel with his hatchet features and knifing sarcasm; the defense counsel with his chubby bland sweetness and Church of England background. There were also the ones that she had known, but hardly knew now, speaking lines she seemed never to have heard before and mentioning acts that fascinated and shocked her. There they were, the victims, cornered: Paddy

Jameson, the defendant, stuttering, shrill, dismayingly unamusing; the five girls, prosecution witnesses, overdressed, ashamed or defiant, posturing, defensive, self-pitying, determinedly respectable; the parade of males, England's best, the ruling class, laconic, surprised, tricked, irritated, angry Paddy-victims.

The legal festival went on and on, a smash hit, provocative reviews, standing room only. There was the mention of Sydney Ormsby's name by two witnesses, one shown to be malicious, the other possibly unreliable. Sydney's name but no Sydney, for there existed no solid evidence that he had known Paddy Jameson or one of Jameson's girls—since the only conceivable material witness who might accuse him was missing, was unavailable to the prosecution. And throughout the trial it was the elusive Medora Hart, constantly mentioned, who was becoming the star.

She gloried in the attention, and read with fascination the serialized biographies of her life and times and loves in *The People* and the *News of the World,* the widely circulated newspapers that had always been her favorite reading. She reveled in her notoriety, which had some distinction, some naughty-Cinderella quality about it, and she did not understand her fame or infamy at all—until it was explained to her by a psychologist-journalist in *The Observer,* who could have picked, Medora thought, better photographs of her from the old ones in her mother's album. According to the psychologist-journalist, the cast of characters involved in the scandal appeared captivating, colorful, exotic, when you saw them from afar or only read of their adventures. Paddy seemed a dashing gay Casanova and his girls seemed like so many fun-loving Nell Gwyns, and grudgingly you either admired or envied them for daring to defy convention and rebel against the straitlaced mores of society, for being unlicensed and above and beyond ordinary man's laws. But that was when you observed them from a distance, themselves indistinct but the image of them and of their behavior rather something to covet secretly. For these were of a class that made you restless with your own life, so limited, so anxiety-ridden, so repressed, so awfully dull, and you would look at these women and men and know you were missing too much that was a part of life, and that you would live and you would die and never once enjoy such audacious experiences.

But then, suddenly, the members of the cast of characters were no longer to be seen from afar. They were right before you, right under your nose, dragged by the scruffs of the necks, defrocked of dignity and independence and privacy, and they were made to stand up within the four walls of a people's room, within the confines of a witness box, and be tried for their misdeeds. And up close they were less attractive, no Casanovas, no Nell Gwyns, but small drifting people, blemished, warped, misshapen, nasty, common, as viewed publicly by Justice's clear eye looking through Freud's relentless magnifying glass. You could see that they were not gay or cheerfully amoral, this clique of pleasure seekers, only lonely and lost and weak and afraid, self-destructive in their sexual aberrations, perversions, loveless givings and takings. Up close they were pathetic, they were tawdry, they were cheaply depraved, the petty thieves of normality and the frightened fugitives of life. The men were incapable of natural intercourse with healthy women. The girls were no better than ten-bob knocks behind the officers' mess.

Only one member of the cast of characters in the Jameson affair had not disappointed her public, the psychologist-journalist wrote, and this one was Miss Medora Hart, and she had succeeded where her friends had failed only because she was not there to be seen in the flesh, close up, for what she really was, a tart like the rest of Paddy's girls. It was because the disenchanted public still wanted its illusions that they had seized upon Medora Hart, romanticized her background, her beauty, her character, her indulgences, her immorality. Medora Hart alone would remain the single romantic figure of the trial, a desirable sex goddess, because, as ever, distance made hearts grow fonder. The only possible analogy was courtship and marriage. When you desired a mate but could not have her, when she was remote and inaccessible, you worshiped and loved her with abiding passion and imagined her as being able to dispense unspeakable delights, such as you imagined were offered by Helen of Troy or Cleopatra. But once she was brought close, yours in legal marriage, attained, possessed, brought down, divested of mystery and marvel, once she had become familiar and habitual, all foolish romanticism ended. Up close, the woman who seemed a goddess from afar became the tiresome, gossipy, bedraggled accountant of your income and caretaker of your snotty children. Medora Hart would remain the solitary authentic sex goddess of the miserable Jameson affair only as long as she kept her distance.

This was bewildering to Medora, this analysis of her celebrity read in the confines of her Paris hideout, and it bothered her, all that mean junk about Paddy and the girls and what they had been forced to do because that's the way life was and that's the way untutored and hungry young girls like herself were corrupted by older men who had power and riches.

But soon there was more to read, and by now, bored with her anonymity and inactivity, eager to be free to reap the rewards of her fresh fame and return home, Medora impatiently waited for the trial to end and finally it was over and done with, judgment made, sentence passed, implacable justice served. Poor Paddy. Of the five criminal charges on which he had been tried, there were three, all concerned with his role in promoting prostitution, on which he had been found not guilty; but on the remaining two, both concerned with his efforts at blackmail and his attempts to sell to foreign embassies the Government secrets he had acquired through his girls, he had been found guilty. He had been sentenced to twenty years' imprisonment.

This was unhappy news, this cruel persecution of Paddy, but Medora's distress was quickly alleviated by happy news for herself. The prosecution had decided that, since it had failed to convince the jurors that Jameson had been a procurer, it was not in possession of enough firsthand evidence to convict Jameson's five party girls who were present, and Miss Hart, *in absentia,* of prostitution. Moreover, the public weal would not be served by extending the scandal through another series of sensational trials. And so the prosecution announced that it was dropping charges against the Jameson girls, the missing Medora Hart included, and that the Jameson affair was, once and for all time, closed.

For Medora, in Paris, the thrilling proclamation of freedom was greeted with the excitement of an adolescent on birthday morning, on the last day of school, on social debut. For her the wearying travail was ended, and just in time. It was almost three months since she had fled London, and in recent weeks the enforced hiding had become almost unendurable. Also, her allowance from Sir Austin Ormsby had almost run out. There was less than £150 in francs in her hotel safe-deposit box downstairs. There was but one formality left to her before homecoming. She must write to Sir Austin Ormsby, at the box number he had given her, to inform him of her intention so she could be positively assured that the prosecutor's public statement had been no ruse and that she was, as were the other Jameson girls, absolutely safe. Ecstatically she telephoned her mother long-distance to ask her to prepare her old room, and take some of her furnishings out of storage, and be ready to welcome her home. And then with great care, no reference to the trial, of course, she wrote a guarded letter to Sir Austin in care of his London post-office box and sent it off.

After purchasing her plane ticket back to London, and while impatiently waiting for Sir Austin's green light, she shopped for gifts for the family and neighborhood friends in the Rue de Rivoli and in the Faubourg St.-Honoré. A week passed, and there was no reply from Sir Austin. This worried her. They had not once dared exchange correspondence after she had left London, and somehow she had expected him to respond gratefully by return airmail to her first letter, in celebration of their mutual triumph. Yet nothing had come in the post. Then, on the tenth day of freedom and waiting, a letter in a familiar hand arrived—familiar because it had been penned in her own hand. It was her own letter to Sir Austin, returned to her, the envelope coldly stamped by the post office RETURN TO SENDER.

Upset, she placed the same letter in a fresh envelope, addressing this one to Sir Austin at the offices of his newspaper publishing firm, and she waited two days, five days, seven. Distraught, she wrote him three letters at the same time, addressing them to his business, to his country manor, and to Westminster Palace, all of them airmail and *exprès*. Not one was acknowledged. Frenzied by the frustration of it, as well as by her dangerously low funds, she sent Sir Austin one telegram, then a second. And these were not acknowledged. Now her hysterical anxiety gave way to anger—it was like the selfishness of a man you loved who, finished with you, simply turned over and went to sleep—and she determined to do what would have been unthinkable earlier. She telephoned Sir Austin at Ormsby Press Enterprises, Ltd., in London, and reached his secretary, and told the woman that she must speak to Sir Austin personally on a matter of urgency, and she gave her name, and she waited, self-assured once more. After a long interval the secretary returned and said simply, "Sorry to have kept you, miss, but Sir Austin is unavailable." In a temper, she demanded to know when he would be available. The secretary coolly replied, "I'm afraid I can't say, miss. Sorry," and hung up in her ear. Infuriated by the effrontery of the beast for not even pretending to be out of the city, she telephoned Sir Austin twice the following day, but apparently a warning about her calls had been sent down to the switchboard, for she got no further than the company operator who merely said, "Sir Austin is unavailable today."

With effort, that night, Medora contained her bad temper and tried to reason out why Sir Austin Ormsby was refusing to speak to her or even acknowledge her existence. Only one logical answer existed: Considering his position, he was afraid to have any contact with her or own up to knowing her. It was unfair, but at least it made sense. At once she realized that she was overvaluing the necessity of any good word from Sir Austin. At this point, to be positively realistic, she had no need of him. Their lives had crossed briefly in a moment of bad crisis. He had helped her. She had helped him. The crisis was no more for either of them. Their relationship had ended, because the awful trial was over. The danger to herself was nonexistent. She was truly on her own. The air was free.

The next morning aboard a Caravelle jetliner, her heart singing, Medora flew from Paris back to her beloved London.

The same afternoon, six hours later, tearful and in a state of near collapse, Medora flew from London back to Paris.

Returned to Orly, still in a daze, she directed her luggage to be placed in a taxi and ordered the taxi to take her to the British Embassy. In thirty minutes she was deposited at 35 Faubourg St.-Honoré. After tipping the driver to stand by with her luggage, she hastened into the horrid old building. The receptionist, bewildered by Medora's incoherence, directed her to an office on the ground floor, and the gentleman there sent her to another office, and the lady there made several interoffice telephone calls and at last guided Medora to the young consular official, who was the one to see about her special problem.

The young consular official, a brash and cheeky boy from Manchester, tried to be attentive and serious as he ogled her bosom throughout her recital. Desperately attempting to calm herself, to be lucid, Medora poured out details of the morning's shocking events at London Airport. She was a British citizen because she was included on her father's naturalization papers, and she had been returning home from her holiday with her perfectly good British passport, but when she routinely displayed it to the uniformed immigration man, he had got as far as her name, suddenly stopped, studied her face and the photograph in the passport, and said, "You are Miss Medora Hart?" She had confirmed her identity. The immigration officer had said, "Will you have a seat, Miss Hart? Please excuse me. There is something here I must check."

Bureaucratic red tape, she had thought, and waited twenty minutes, with mounting annoyance, until the immigration man returned carrying not only her passport but a manila folder. Reluctantly, like a physician disclosing the discovery of a fatal disease to a patient, he had told her that due to special circumstances she could not be admitted to England at this time, at least not until her citizenship status had been fully investigated and reviewed. She had treated this news as a sadistic joke. But then, it had been the truth, the incredible, monstrous truth. She was being temporarily banned from her own homeland. She was Alice, and he was the Mad Hatter, and one of them was insane.

Her protests, her demands for an explanation, her outrage, hastily brought a second immigration official to the aid of his colleague. Together, they had tried to clarify her position. Medora's long-dead father had migrated from Hungary to England and become a naturalized citizen, but a very recent investigation had revealed that his application had what might be called "misrepresentations" in it, and so the legality of his naturalization was being questioned. The entire matter was up before the Secretary of State for the Home Office and his advisory committee, and eventually it would be judged, but, for the time being, the letter of the law must be observed. Members of his family were technically aliens, as he had been, and because of this circumstance, as well as the fact that Medora had been born in Budapest when her parents once visited their relatives there, she could not be permitted to re-enter England from abroad, at least not until the matter was settled. Since the citizenship case was pending, Miss Hart would be permitted, for the time, to retain her British passport—with a special restrictive stamp inside it—for use abroad, and she would have the status of a British protected person, but she would not be permitted to enter any part of the United Kingdom unless a favorable decision on her father's certificate of naturalization was eventually rendered.

In relating this to the British consular official in Paris, she could hardly recall what had happened to her next at London Airport. Dimly she recollected that she had begun to rail and shout at the immigration officers, call them bloody lunatics, perverts, Nazis, anything obscene that had sprung to her mind. She had shrieked that she was as British as any of them, that this country was her home and no one was going to keep her from her home—and then she had tried to make a run for it. One of the immigration officers, and an airport guard, had caught her, held her, and she had beat at them and cursed them, and ranted about a plot against her, an illegal plot by filthy Government officials who were trying to convict her without trial a second time because they didn't succeed the first time, and they were afraid of her.

At the climax of the scene she had broken down and had been half dragged, half carried past a crowd of fascinated bystanders to a private room, and there she had fallen into a fit of sobbing. The immigration officer who had stayed with her, and a bobby the airport had summoned, had both been kindly, and someone had brought smelling salts and someone else had brought tea, and a third someone had brought forms to fill out, and a short time later she had been led to a plane about to take off for Paris. Weakened and defeated, she had pleaded with them to tell her what she should do, and she had been told to keep in regular touch with the British Embassy in Paris, or British Embassies wherever she might be, and word on the disposition of her case would reach her presently.

"And here I am," she said to the consular official.

"Ummm, yes. Well, Miss Hart, let me see what more I can find out."

He stepped into an adjoining records room, rummaged through the file drawers, and eventually he left for his superior's office. She nervously smoked three cigarettes before he returned with a yellow sheet of paper.

"Yes," he said, "you are definitely on the list."

"What list?" she almost shouted.

He looked up, as if surprised that she did not know. "Undesirable aliens," he said matter-of-factly. "It's rather routine, you know. When an alien's or a naturalized citizen's name comes up, for any reason—crime, scandal, whatever it may be—his background is automatically investigated. This procedure was followed in your case, and a misstatement in your father's naturalization certificate was discovered. This made you, well, technically, temporarily, an alien, worse luck. If you are declared a permanent alien, then under the latest revised code—well, we need to go into the definition—"

"You go into it. I want to know."

"Yes. Well. Questionable moral character, that would be one thing that could bar an alien who wanted to apply for citizenship."

She sat stone still. Questionable moral character. Then that was it. Her suspicion, put down for hours, was now confirmed. This was not the wretched Home Office. This was Sir Austin Ormsby's doing. He had packed her off not for three months but forever. No wonder that he had never been in touch with her. No wonder that he had not answered her letters, wires, telephone calls. For him, she had no more existence, she was—how did the French put it?—*ci-devant*. He was powerful. A brief phone call to the right ministry—all one club, you know, and we must keep Britain pure, you know, keep the young and our homes uncorrupted—one phone call and the machinery turned. A loophole was found. If there had been none, one would have been invented. Likely, this one had been invented. Now, she was out of his life. She would remain out of it for the rest of their days on earth. She would never be there, in England, a source of potential scandal to the Ormsby family. If only she could get to him, butcher knife in hand, the filthy, rotten bastard.

"I'm sorry," she heard the consular boy say, staring at her bust once more. "I'm afraid all you can do is keep in touch with me weekly. Often these matters take time."

"Time? How much time?"

"They can drag along for weeks, months, sometimes even years."

She wanted to say—sometimes forever, this purgatory—but she felt weak again and remained silent.

"Of course, I—I could try to expedite the decision. You know, a memorandum. I'd like to be of help."

She got up. "Thanks, I'd appreciate anything."

He caught up her handbag, and relinquished it to her reluctantly at the door. "I—I've read about you, you know. Rather favorable press, I thought. All on your side." He hesitated. "If you're alone here, ever need company, a little cheering up, well, I'm alone, too, and I know my way around. Perhaps we could have an evening."

To shut the door, or leave it ajar? She detested the gauche young fool. She compromised. "I'll be busy awhile, but I'll keep in touch. I'll let you know."

Bastards, all of them.

She went back to the small hotel where she found that her room had not yet been occupied, and so she moved into it again. Throughout that night she sat on the sofa in a comatose state, too beaten to think, too ill to eat, lost. After a few whiskies, and the coming of dawn, she went to sleep.

She awakened in a rage against Sir Austin Ormsby, with only one crimson thought—to revenge herself upon him. She possessed a club, she knew: the truth about what had really happened to her, the truth about how the great Sir Austin had come crawling in the night to beg her to get out of the country, to subvert the law, making her an accessory to his crime in order to protect his brother and his bloody family name. Oh, now, wouldn't that look pretty in big black newspaper headlines!

Driven by the need for retribution, she plunged into the city of Paris on her holy crusade. A wild, uncontrolled, savage two weeks of making the rounds of the English and American press bureaus in Paris. She went to the assistant editor of the New York *Herald Tribune,* to the bureau chiefs of Reuters, Associated Press, United Press International, Atlas News Association, *The Times* of London, *The New York Times, The Observer,* a half-dozen others, and everywhere she was royally received as a celebrity and was heard out. She disclosed the truth about Sir Austin Ormsby to one and all, at first telling her story with cold factuality, in later versions coloring and exaggerating it more and more. And everywhere, she found great interest, and sincere sympathy—and, finally, rejection. The reactions were everywhere the same. Proof was needed, documentation was required. Did she have anything about this from Sir Austin in writing? She had nothing, nothing but what was in her own memory, and the value of her own word. How clever he had been to leave her with so little. Unfortunately, her word was not enough, anywhere. A revelation like this, without absolute proof, could bring on a libel suit, a defamation suit, from Sir Austin. No, it was impossible, although everywhere they were eager to do interviews with

Medora, glossing over the Ormsby incident, of course. She had no patience for interviews. She wanted only to see the truth about Sir Austin in print.

The rejections had not impaired her determination to continue the crusade. There were a dozen French newspapers, and she started after them. And once more she found the same initial interest, reduced finally to sympathy, rejection—and invitations to dinner. The crusade had failed. Again, she had lost. Sir Austin had won.

Then, overnight, the desire for vengeance was pushed aside by a greater necessity, the need for survival. The Judas money from Sir Austin had long since been spent. Her jewels and furs had been sold, and the money from them had wasted away. Now she was naked to the world and afraid. Two choices were open to her: to commit suicide or become a whore. But suddenly, neither choice was necessary. One of the French dailies that she had visited decided that it would like to help her prepare her autobiography, a by-lined story of her lurid life—sans Sir Austin, of course—and it would pay her well for the serialization rights. She did not even pretend to consider it. She accepted the offer at once.

Medora had hoped to save something from this money for a solicitor whom her mother might retain to investigate her banishment from England. But somehow, there was nothing to save. After paying her mother's bills, and her own in Paris, there was hardly a franc left. By the time the third installment of her autobiography appeared, and was being discussed not only in France but in England and over the Continent as well, Medora was broke and living on credit. Her desperation was greater than ever. But the autobiography had revived her name, and she was constantly being invited to dinner parties in Paris. She detested these parties, because she knew that she was being invited only as a fortune-teller or a newly arrived musician might be invited, to amuse and entertain jaded guests by her novelty. Still, she accepted the invitations because they provided her with free meals. She never imagined that they might also provide her with a career, but, to her amazement, one such party at a private flat off the Place du Trocadéro did exactly that.

A theatrical agent from Munich, who had representatives in cities throughout Europe, became intrigued by her at the dinner party. Her autobiography, he told her, was the talk of salons and cafés in every European capital. It was a pity, he said, to waste all that priceless publicity. She did not fully comprehend what he meant when he described the serialization of her life story as publicity. What he meant, he explained patiently, was if she were in the entertainment field, she could reap the rewards of such a buildup. But she was not an entertainer, she said, and then added she wished that she were. The agent seized upon this admission. Was she interested? Was she free? Would she consider performing in public? She responded with absolute candor. She would consider anything that would help her survive. She was broke.

"But what could I possibly do?" she asked. "I've had no training as an actress or anything else."

"I could book you into a hundred nightclubs tomorrow."

"Doing what? Tell me that."

"Can you carry a tune?"

"A little. I've never had a lesson, but I have an ear."

"Can you dance?"

"Not really, not the way you mean."

He stepped back and studied her from head to toe. It was obvious to her that there was no lechery involved in his examination. His eyes, and his tone of voice, were clinical. "You've got a remarkable figure, you know."

"I know."

"Would you mind using it?"

"I'm not interested in that sort of thing," she said sharply.

"No, no—I mean, would you mind exposing it professionally? A song, a faked dance, a partial striptease?"

"Who'd pay good money for that?"

"For that alone? Not many. But for that, plus your greatest asset? Thousands would pay happily."

"My greatest asset?" she said warily. "What is that?"

"The simple fact that you were *the* Jameson girl. . . . There you have it, young lady. What do you say?"

"I say—when do we begin?"

They began a week later in that smoky cabaret on the Left Bank, and then he kept her moving and moving and moving, and in her three years of painful exile she had never stopped. And what had started out so lonely, so long ago, the tortuous journey that had taken her not one centimeter closer to home, had now brought her once more, as it had every previous summer, to a burning afternoon on the sands of the Provençal beach in Juan-les-Pins.

She lay quietly on her white pad, opening her eyes behind her tinted glasses to the present in an effort to obliterate the past, but knowing full well that the past was woven into the fabric of the present and that she must live with it every day of her life. Blinking through her sunglasses at the incandescent sun, she realized how scorched her midriff and thighs felt. Raising her arm, she squinted at her wristwatch. She realized that she had been replaying her song, the dirge, for fifty minutes. If she did not remove herself from the sun at once, she would be roasted alive.

She lifted herself to her elbows, and remembering the wretched English tourists who had started the whole miserable playback, she peered ahead. They were gone, with their pasty white skins, thank the Lord. She sat up. The beach was still relatively empty, and as best she could make out, the terrace lunch crowd had also thinned or disappeared.

The beach attendant was approaching. "The umbrella, I can move it now, Mademoiselle Hart? If not, you will perhaps suffer tonight."

She jumped to her feet. "No, thanks. I've had enough for today. I'd better have a spot of lunch."

Stretching, she became aware that a string of the bikini bottom had loosened, and hastily she secured the knot. After checking to see if her bikini top was in place, she took the magazine supplement of the *Sunday Times,* returned to the locker, slipped her bare feet into the beach sandals, snatched up her handbag, and started for the outdoor terrace.

Ascending the stone stairs to the walk above, she turned right, quickly went down a second set of stairs, past the glass showcases with their prepared desserts and salads, and onto the wooden deck that stretched over the water.

She had meant to relax at a metal table, beneath the shade of an umbrella, and there eat and read, but as she started for a table, she slowed. At least three of the tables were occupied by numerous tourist-type hotel guests, mostly men, mainly American, English, German, and a few native French. Abruptly, she halted. Her entrance, as usual, had brought conversation to a stop at two of the tables; chairs were being wrenched around, and all male eyes were leering at her. That instant, she regretted the brevity of the bikini, and she prayed that she had knotted the string tightly. She felt their eyes on her nakedness, and she stared back at them, unsmiling, quickly pivoted away, and strode to the shaded outdoor bar.

Propping herself on a stool, her back to the slobbering monsters, she determined to ignore them. But she could feel their bloodshot eyes on her bare shoulder blades, spine, buttocks.

Her friend, the kindly, happily married French bartender, materialized at once, greeting her and waiting.

"I'm not too hungry, Jean," she said. "Tell you what. Make it salade niçoise. And a glass of wine. I think Tavel."

"Ah, Mademoiselle Hart, the prepared salade niçoise is depleted. The vultures descended and poof—gone. But if you will wait—five minutes, no more—Madame will mix a fresh one for you."

"Of course, Jean. But the Tavel anyway. I'm parched."

When the pink wine arrived, she tried it, and it was delicious. Spoiling it somewhat were the occasional lewd phrases that floated up from behind her, someone recounting a dirty joke about a nude woman, followed by an obscene chorus of laughter. Again the silence, and the groping and touching of the eyes, and she was tempted to stand up, tear off her bikini and yell at them, All right, you bloody bastards, here it is, now what have you got?

In truth, what would they have? What would they see that was different from what they had seen hundreds of times before? You could buy it from any streetwalker or from any five-franc art magazine. It was the same old thing, same nude breasts, torso, vaginal mound, thighs, legs, buttocks. Yet what men went through to observe, and imagine possessing, these anatomical parts of hers, as if they would be different, the wonders of the world. Once, long ago, she had been proud of her individual parts, her naked body whole, because it had brought her favors and fun. But now she resented her body because it divested her of privacy and peace, and reduced most civilized men to packs of dirty animals, who came panting after the body, to see it, feel it, knead it, invade it. There they were behind her, violating her decency, all knowing her past and all so sure it could be done again. Secondhand goods, you know. Cheap. Easy. At least here, with some of their wives around, they couldn't proposition her—but they had done so, and they would do so again, when their wives were out having their hair fixed in town or were off shopping in Cannes. With the exception of a scattered handful of older men, mature ones like Nardeau, there was not one with whom she could have a relationship that transcended bed and body.

But then, sipping her Tavel, she decided that it was not her body that she should blame for her hellish existence, but primarily Sir Austin Ormsby. It was he who had decreed her exile, and it was her solitary exile that had exposed her to this unremitting insult and humiliation. No one on earth could fully realize what it was like to be publicly disgraced and forced into exile, except someone who had endured the experience.

She remembered the time, late last summer, when she had been appearing in a small club on the Lido, across from Venice. An English film executive, who had come up from his office in Rome, had made her acquaintance and offered her the use of his cabana on the Excelsior beach. One afternoon he had pointed out an attractive middle-aged man strolling along the water's edge, a self-absorbed, aloof figure of an American in T-shirt and denim slacks. That man, her companion had told her, was none other than Matthew Brennan, the one who had been suspected some years before of being a traitor, and who had been forced to resign from the U.S. Department of State. "I wonder what it's like," her companion had mused, "being in exile like that?" Her own reaction had fascinated her, the flip-flop of it, and had remained with her ever since. The moment that she had heard Brennan characterized as "traitor," she had regarded him unsympathetically, but the moment that she had heard the word "exile" applied to him, she had felt immediate sympathy. She had watched his slouching lonely figure recede along the Italian beach, and her heart had reached out in kinship toward another who, like herself, had been ill-used and driven off to a desert island. A loser, she had thought, and then she had thought, It takes one to know one.

The salade niçoise was before her. She took up her fork and picked at it. She had no appetite, but eating was something to do. She buttered a crust of French bread, nibbled at it, nibbled again at her salad, then sighing, put down the bread, and pulled the *Sunday Times* magazine supplement from under her handbag.

Slowly eating, she opened the smooth, thick rotogravure section and began to turn the pages, and to her dismay she saw that the entire issue was a special one devoted to the Five-Power Summit Conference in Paris. Politics was as mystifying and stultifying to her as were the allegory and language of *The Faerie Queene*—"When foggy mistes or cloudy tempests have/The faithfull light of that faire lampe yblent"— she had once tried to fathom that to please one of her men, some bearded creep bent on improving her—crikey!—and the layouts and captions given over to the United States President, to Russian Premier Talansky, to the Red Chinese Chairman Kuo Shu-tung, to meaningless words like "clean bomb" and "on-site inspections" and "demilitarization" were just as senseless.

About to throw the disappointing supplement aside, she realized that she had reached a full-page picture of the British Prime Minister, flanked by members of his Cabinet, in the act of departing from No. 10 Downing Street, and there in the blurry photograph, behind the Prime Minister was the Foreign Secretary, none other, the one she hated in her waking and sleeping dreams. The directions in the parenthesis of the caption, after Sir Austin's name, told her to turn to pages 36–44. She flipped the pages of the supplement to 36, and there a stylized heading read: AMONG GREAT BRITAIN'S BEST, SIR AUSTIN ORMSBY, ALL-

IMPORTANT DELEGATE TO THE SUMMIT, HERE SEEN AT WORK AND AT PLAY.

The photographs of Sir Austin with the inner cabinet in Downing Street, Sir Austin with open attaché case on his lap in his official Humber, Sir Austin in Whitehall—these only depressed her. She had seen enough photographs of that filthy hypocrite in his different seats of power, and they did no more than remind her of her own helplessness against so formidable an opponent. She lingered longer over the caption. In a week, she read, the Foreign Secretary would be in Paris, to bring his diplomatic skills to bear against the unpredictable Chinese Communist delegation. In a week Sir Austin would be in Paris, and then it occurred to her that her supplement was one week old, and so a week had passed, and tomorrow was another Sunday and Sir Austin would be in Paris tomorrow.

She stared at her salad and thought: tomorrow in Paris. He would be in a country where she was accepted, not banished; within reach, an hour and a half by jet plane from Nice, or overnight by Train Bleu from the Juan-les-Pins depot. The possibility of confronting him was tempting. She fantasied it, remembering some lurid, sentimental feature story in a French magazine about others who had done it—who? —yes, the young girl from Caen, Charlotte Corday, and the mighty Marat in his bath, and she had been admitted to see him, and had plunged a dagger into his heart. Medora tried to visualize herself in Paris cornering Sir Austin, the two of them alone, and her threatening to murder him unless he wrote and signed a document allowing her to return home, and his immediate fear and compliance. But the biting salt of an anchovy on her tongue brought her back to the Provençal beach and made her realize the futility of her daydream. Sir Austin was too prominent to be reached by a nobody. And even were she to reach him, she possessed no weapon (as Corday had had her lie and her dagger) with which to intimidate him into abject surrender. It was a hopeless dream. If you bargained, you had to have strength. Her arsenal was empty.

In despair, discarding her fork for the glass of Tavel, Medora turned another page, revealing her tormentor at play, and finally her tormentor's recent bride, new wife, Her Ladyship, the twenty-nine-year-old Fleur Ormsby, with the hounds on the rolling green meadows of the country place, with the ancient groom at their stables, with the bishop's wife at tea, with her personal maid studying her latest wardrobe designed for the Summit, with her most recent still life on the easel in her skylighted studio—and with her fabulous collection of Picassos, Braques, Giacomettis, Nardeaus in the background.

Medora hated her, too. The waxen, supercilious, haughty, moneyed, upper-class features, the chignon with not a single strand of hair out of place, the linen Legrande sheath hanging faultlessly. Not really good breasts, Medora thought, and rather thick ankles. She read the caption. While Sir Austin fenced with world ministers at the Quai d'Orsay and the Palais Rose, Her Ladyship would grace and enhance the social whirl surrounding the Summit, and she would make an indelible mark because of her beauty, wit, manners, and cosmopolitan background. ("For the evolution of a Social Queen, see next pages.")

Reluctantly Medora flipped to the next pages: Fleur's wealthy antecedents, the Grearson family. Fleur at five on a pony. Fleur at ten with her governess. Fleur at fifteen in a private school near Lucerne. Fleur at eighteen at the Sorbonne, and Fleur at nineteen traveling about France. Caption: "In her formative years, Fleur Grearson turned her back on the Beaufort Hunt and the debutante routine and kited off to the Continent. Accompanied by girls of her own class, and driving a red Ferrari roadster, she traveled the Continent, rounding out her formal education with firsthand forays into the world of art. 'As a student abroad, I was shy and inhibited,' recalls Her Ladyship today, 'yet so eager was I to taste of the wells of creativity that I brought myself to meet and interview authors like Sartre, and painters like Nardeau, who was especially generous of his time.' "

Resentful over the fact that her enemy had once shared Nardeau, Medora moved her eyes from the caption to a portrait of Fleur Grearson, taken in a studio in Cannes by a renowned Swiss photographer, when she was nineteen. Medora stared at the full-length reproduction of a girl with all the advantages, and had to concede—no flat breasts or thick ankles here—that she had possessed a lovely face, that is, if you liked such features: high cheek bones, rosebud mouth, swan's neck.

Medora wondered what Nardeau had thought of her. He had never mentioned meeting her. Of course, that had been a decade ago and she had not yet become the darling of the Sunday supplements, although her appearance at nineteen differed little from her appearance today at twenty-nine. Besides, Nardeau had met so many women, or girls, of so many nationalities. Still, you'd think—and that moment Medora's eyes widened, and she bent down over the photograph of the nineteen-year-old Fleur Ormsby, inspecting it anew with a growing chill of discovery and excitement.

Medora gave her memory freedom to range from this face, back to another, then to this face again, and Medora realized that she was shivering at the enormity of what she had just detected in the Sunday supplement before her, because of what she had disinterred from her recent past. It couldn't be—it was impossible, she told herself, trying to check her mind; yet there could be no doubt. As her eyes darted from picture to picture of the willowy young Fleur, she knew that her memory was not deceiving her.

Suddenly, she was positive.

She set down her glass of Tavel with a thump, clutching the open supplement and trying to sift out the full meaning of her incredible find. If it were true—but it was true, but if it was really, really true, why, she had her Corday weapon. Not merely for petty vengeance. That, too, but there was more, She had the weapon with which she could slash free from the imprisonment of exile, liberate herself, go home again. Absolutely no question about it.

One person possessed the key to unshackle her, emancipate her: Nardeau.

And Nardeau was her friend.

She felt the blood in her temples, the beating of her heart, the intoxication of recovered hope.

Hastily folding the Sunday supplement, she shoved it into her handbag and called out to Jean, "Pay you tomorrow! I've got to dash!"

The male heads had lecherously swiveled toward her as she leaped off the counter stool, her white bikini bottom precariously loosened. She didn't care. She was armed against them now, all the Sir Austins— well, almost, almost. She heard Jean cry out after her, "But the salade—"

"I'm late for an appointment," she called back over her shoulder, and found herself smiling and thinking to herself, yes, late, three years late, as she rushed down to the beach.

In the locker, she drew on her mesh pullover, did her lips, combed her long flaxen hair. Then, grabbing her handbag, she half ran and half skipped along the cement walk, up the stone steps, and through the pine-wooded park. Bursting out of the park, she scurried across the Boulevard du Littoral, veered to the left of the hotel's beach entrance, and hastily climbed up the front driveway to the lobby doors. Approaching the uniformed doorman, she shouted, "Émile, get me my motorcar, please!"

In seconds she was off, spinning her Mercedes coupé out of the Provençal hotel driveway. In short minutes she had raced past Cap d'Antibes and taken the Route Nationale 7 toward Nice, oblivious of the unattractive camping sites along the way. At the dividing of the highway she bore left, watching for the sign that gave the kilometers to Cagnes-sur-Mer. When she saw it, she kept an eye out for the first turnoff, and reaching this, she swung left up into the hilly hinterland, leaving the coastline and Mediterranean behind.

She gunned the Mercedes along sweeping curves, going too fast, she knew, yet eager to reach her destination. Even though unremittingly conscious of the magazine supplement stuffed in her handbag on the leather seat beside her, conscious of the two faces of Fleur Grearson Ormsby, conscious of what Nardeau alone could do for her, she tried to keep them all out of her mind. She would not permit herself to think of the implications of her discovery. It meant simply too much, the last hope of normal life left, and she feared that examining it, pro and con, would dim the shining brilliance of hope.

Until now, nearing La Colle-sur-Loup, she had been steering the coupé by instinct, as blind to her surroundings as if she were roaring through an endless, colorless tunnel. It was remarkable what anxiety and obsession could block out, for this was her favorite drive, so much better than the noisy glittering crowded resort elegance of the streets along the Mediterranean coast. On every occasion when she had taken this drive to Nardeau's pink villa during the last three years, she had never failed to escape exhaustion and tension briefly. She had always loved to wave to the vineyard laborers and farmers, with their ready sunburned smiles, to look across the smooth green valleys and espy tiny distant villages fortified by ancient ramparts, still waiting for Moslem pirates and barbaric Huns with their spears and cutlasses, and tolerating, instead, tourists in shorts with their offensive cameras.

Circling upward and upward, Medora was fleetingly aware, more by smell than sight, of a passage through rows of formal pleached limes, and of terraced banks covered with jasmine, wild white freesias, spicy geraniums, roses, and of the dusty soft evergreen foliage of countless olive trees. She was nearly there, she knew, and slowing, she rolled into the village of St.-Paul. Braking to a bouncing halt before the arch leading into the Auberge Colombe d'Or, she honked her horn three times and peered through her open car window. She could see a portion of the leafy outdoor terrace of the restaurant, the guests having wine at tables, a cluster of doves, a small boy in leather shorts throwing darts. She honked again, and a puzzled waiter appeared.

"Monsieur, excusez-moi," she called out in her execrable French, "but I am seeking Nardeau. Is he at lunch?"

"Nardeau? Non, mademoiselle!"

"Merci!"

She wondered if, by chance, he might be shopping in one of the cubicles off the ancient stone street of St.-Paul proper, or having a bowl of bouillabaisse at a table in the café across from the twelfth-century church. She squinted into her rearview mirror, saw inter-mingled natives and tourists passing in and out of the fortified hill town, but no one resembling Nardeau. She had no patience to park and search for him. Consulting her wristwatch, she decided that he most likely would be in the villa, possibly working, even though it was Saturday.

She shifted to forward gear and fell in behind the traffic until it opened up, and then she rapidly began to pass the cars of sightseers as she ascended the climbing highway north toward La Fondation Maeght. After two kilometers, the cracked ruin of the obscene cement blockhouse the German Nazis had built during their occupation came into view, and after that the dirt road, and Medora turned the Mercedes left for the short, steep, bumpy climb to the villa.

As ever, the suddenness and the size of the two-story pink villa surprised her. She skidded to a halt in the parking area before the garage, took up her handbag, and hastened across the flagstone court-yard to the sheltering awning over the entrance. She wondered if Nardeau was asleep in the vine-covered, second-story turret, or dozing on the roof of the sunny rotunda which stood between the house and his studio and overlooked his two-acre fruit orchard and his thirty-foot swimming pool, or if, indeed, he was deep at work in the vast unkempt studio which, together with his storerooms, took up an entire wing of the villa.

Momentarily, at the heavy wooden door set on wrought-iron hinges, she hesitated. Perhaps she should have telephoned first. But no, he was a friend, he knew her past, her entire travail, and in this crucial time, when he could save her if anyone could, he would receive her at any hour and unannounced.

Ignoring the decorative bronze knocker, Medora pressed firmly on the doorbell.

Waiting, Medora wondered which of the artist's two women would respond: Mme. Nardeau, his second wife, wed to him fifteen years, with her increasing corpulence and fading prettiness, always abject, tolerant, unobtrusive, concerned only with their gangling son and the kitchen? Or Signe Andersson, the painter's statuesque, intellectual, multilingual, candid young Swedish model and mistress of the past two years?

There was the clack of footsteps on the hardwood floor inside, and the door opened, and there, tall and sinuous in a low-cut silk blouse and short pleated skirt, ashen hair sleek and bunned, bare-legged, was Signe Andersson.

"Medora!" Signe cried with sincere delight. "What a nice surprise."

148

And then, in Swedish, which she used only to confuse close friends, she demanded, *"Hur star det till?"*

Her arms were open, and Medora went into them, and they hugged one another. "If you asked how I am, I'm fine—never better."

They were in the entrance hall, and Signe, closing the door with one hand, held Medora off with the other, searching her face. "You are beautiful as always. Maybe you can use more sleep. I think you have much on your mind."

"I always have, Signe," Medora said with a wan smile. "Especially today." As the Swedish model led her into the living room, Medora again marveled that one whose flawless complexion was never touched by the sun could look so healthy, so much a creature of the outdoors. "I've never seen you more radiant, Signe."

"Ah, but I have Nardeau."

"How is he? Is he here?"

"At work. Always at work now. I go to sleep, and he is not yet there. I wake up, and he is already gone." She stopped at the opening to the rotunda, lifted her hand to the slight breeze, then smiled at Medora. "But I understand. After all, his sixtieth-year Retrospective Exhibit is to begin in Paris next week, and—"

"I'd completely forgotten. Of course. I read about it."

"—and while he refuses to attend—he says it is not a publicity Cirque d'Hiver for him to perform in the center ring—he has pride that it must be the best. So every day, one more picture to touch up, alter, always something. I am taking the last of them to Paris in a few days." She gestured toward the rotunda. "Tea, Medora?"

"No, thank you. I rather want to see him. A personal matter, but urgent. I can wait until he's finished."

"Finished? He is never finished. He would not want you to wait. If we kept you, he would be furious." She had taken Medora by the arm, and started her into the rotunda.

Medora protested. "I'm afraid to interrupt—"

"I am afraid not to. I am one who cannot interrupt. Madame is another who cannot. His son cannot. But you—ah, always he is speaking of you, with affection, with worry—Medora, his pet. . . . Let us put our heads in the studio and see."

They had crossed the cool tiled rotunda and entered a narrow passageway of the villa. As she followed the Swedish girl, Medora nostalgically recalled the familiar walk. How often she had made it during her first summer on the Riviera, when for several months she had been Nardeau's favorite model. Now, remembering that time, relating something that had happened then to the Sunday supplement that had captured Fleur Ormsby in her handbag, she began to have doubts about her discovery. Maybe memory had deceived her, or maybe wish had altered memory in an effort to serve her desperation and despair.

At the door to the studio, the door with Nardeau's carving of a grotesque basilisk—"Self-portrait," Nardeau liked to call it—Signe stopped, listened, tentatively knocked. There was no reply. She shrugged, softly opened the door, peeked inside, then silently signaled to Medora. She entered, and Medora followed.

In the very center of the enormous atelier, Nardeau, his bare back to them, the vertebrae of his spine showing as he bent his glistening bald head toward the easel, dabbed his brush at the vivid Montmartre scene, with its bold contrasts of light and dark, that he was painting.

Signe tiptoed forward, waited for the brush to leave the canvas. When it did, she whispered, *"Psst, cher ami. Monsieur Nardeau est-il visible?"* Then, in English, she said more loudly, "Lover, there is a friend here to see you."

Nardeau's head bobbed acknowledgment, without turning, and a movement of his palette indicated the only piece of usable furniture in the studio, an oversized sofa to the left of his easel. Pleased, Signe propelled Medora toward the sofa, after which she quickly slipped out of the room.

Nervously Medora settled on the sofa, knowing that Nardeau had not yet seen her. Already his brush had returned to the oil painting. Once again she enjoyed her favorite studio—the pieces of sculpture standing on the floor and on the stained tables, one an immense and wise fish, another a rugged peasant's head; the piles of stretched, unframed brilliant canvases, some abstract, most expressionistic, sensuous nudes of Signe, portraits of his son, Riviera landscapes, views of Montmartre in the spring, harlequins, or the streets of Lyon where he had been born. Across the studio was the doorway to Nardeau's kitchenette, tiny office, and storage rooms. Near the door stood a heating unit with a stovepipe rising along the whitewashed wall. Everywhere, the broad barred windows. Above, the skylight, with the afternoon's sun filtering through.

She gave her attention once more to Nardeau, squatting on a low crude stool, transported to the Paris of his past on the easel. She loved her friend with his shining hairless skull, his sunken eyes, sometimes brooding, sometimes piercing, his broad pugilist's nose, his wide mouth and square jaw. While only five feet seven, he seemed even shorter because of his stubbiness, his hairy barrel-chest, his abnormally muscular legs. At sixty he was incredibly spry—vigorous really, virile—and none of the naked and uninhibited Riviera girls would refer to him, as they contemptuously referred to the flabby winking aging male tourists, as one of *les croulants*—the crumbling ones.

Art dealers and critics considered Nardeau, now that his fame matched the fame of Picasso and Giacometti, as the personification of ego—insulting, cantankerous, erratic, irascible, a terror, a one-man plague. But those who knew him well, Medora for example, knew that much of this behavior was a defense against the locusts of business, who were the dealers, and the bloodsuckers of creativity, who were the critics. Where no defensive stance was required, Nardeau was possessed of a nature hospitable enough to embrace those he respected or adored, and for these permanent boarders he had only humor, warmth, helping hands. If one could love a friend, Medora loved this genius.

Relaxed, more hopeful about her quest, Medora kicked off her beach shoes, brought her bare legs up off the floor and hugged her knees, snugly watching him.

Apparently the sound of her shoes plopping to the floor had distracted him. Pausing with his wet brush in midair, he slowly turned in the direction of the sound, and then he saw her and the wide mouth curled into a great grin of pleasure.

"Maydor!" he boomed, instantly setting his brush down, wiping his hands on his jeans, and springing to his feet. "Maydor, *poupoule!* Why did that Nordic bitch not say it was you?"

Nardeau rushed to her before she could untangle and rise, and his powerful arms encircled her, lifting her into the air, swinging her around. Then, kissing her cheeks, he lowered her back onto the sofa.

"*Poupoule,*" he rasped with genuine delight, "I have missed you, always meaning to telephone, but always busy." He sank down into the sofa, pointing his finger at the easel. "Damn tyrant, that one. I do not know why I fuss so over that Retrospective Exhibit. What do I care? I am Nardeau, no more, no less, and another show is meaningless."

"But it's your anniversary show, Nardeau. That is important."

"Not important, but the commercial celebrants force one to look backward, explore the past. You know that canvas up there. I've retouched it a dozen times in the year. It is the exterior of the bateau lavoir at 13 Rue Ravignan up in Montmartre. It is like a piece of my younger heart torn out and put on canvas. You are too young to know of it. Even the street address is now changed to Place Émile-Goudeau. But long ago all the rising artists, Picasso for one, and the poets, and street peddlers, bums, laundresses lived in that crazy room. I came to it later, and I was a boy and stimulated, and somehow I try to find those months once more in oil, for my exhibit. . . . Enough. You are still at that club in Juan showing your pretty breasts, making old men young for an hour?"

"I finished my engagement last night. I have four weeks off."

He was studying her narrowly, and she felt uneasy under his penetrating gaze. Impulsively he reached for her hand and took it. "Maydor," he said gruffly, *"quelle mouche t'a piqué?"* Whenever he spoke intimately to a dear one, Medora knew, he lapsed into the argot of street French.

"Actually, nothing's eating me, Nardeau, except the usual."

"You keep trying? You have no luck?"

She suddenly squeezed his hand hard and sat up straight. "No luck, no hope, nothing—until today," she said intently. "Today everything is possible—it depends—it depends on—on how much you can help me."

"Maydor, *poupoule,* for you I will do anything, you know that is true."

"Oh, I pray you can help. Let me show you." She brought her handbag to her lap, tugged free the Sunday supplement still folded to the layout of Fleur Ormsby in her youth, and she opened it, flattened it, and handed it to the mystified artist. She pointed to the picture in the supplement. "That's Sir Austin Ormsby's recent bride shown as she looked when she was much younger. Read what it says. It says she was traveling around France and she met you. Look at her face again, Nardeau. Does it mean anything? Do you recognize her?"

He blinked at the photograph, held the supplement up high, then sideways, then directly before him again. Slowly he shook his head. "I am afraid not, Maydor."

"Think hard, please. She's twenty-nine years old now. She was nineteen then. That's only ten years ago."

"No, the face is not familiar." He lifted his shoulders in apology. "Ten years, Maydor. There have been many women." Medora's disappointment was so complete that Nardeau, forehead wrinkled, immediately inquired, "Why is it of importance that I recognize this one?"

"I'll tell you, and maybe I'm just crazy mad and bothering you, but you know how I snatch at anything. I've never had a chance against Sir Austin Ormsby. He's been too big, and today he's even bigger, in the Cabinet, and arriving in Paris tomorrow with the British Prime Minister for the Summit conference."

"Yes, I was reading of it in *Le Figaro* at breakfast. I saw his name and thought of you."

"Sir Austin was always a bachelor, but less than a year ago he married this society girl. A real lady, it says here, all the graces, manners, wealthy background, a perfect Cabinet Minister's wife. Well, what chance has a nobody like me got against them, those spotless people, those perfect ones? But I've never forgotten Sir Austin's big weakness. That's his worry about the family name. Not just his name, but the family name. Look how he hustled me out of England before the trial, to protect his idiot brother, only because his brother has his name. Look how he's kept me in exile, still to protect the family name. All right. Now he's got himself a wife, someone even closer than his brother, and his family name has become her name. Now, what if her name, what she is or was, proved not to be as spotless as he thought? What if there were a bad thing in her past that would cast doubts on her lily-white reputation and reflect on him, embarrass him? And what if I found it out? For the first time I'd have a weapon, and he would be vulnerable to it, wouldn't he? I could force him to deal with me, withdraw that immigration ruling against me, force him to let me go home again—in return for preserving his perfect wife's perfect reputation."

"Maydor, this is clear. But you speak in circles. Be direct. Where am I in your plot?"

"Three years ago, when I was modeling for you—one afternoon when we finished early—I wanted to see the other nudes you had painted, the ones of young women. Remember?"

"I think so—voilà, exact, I remember! I brought them out, and we had wine, and made up amusing titles for each oil."

"Yes, Nardeau, that was the time," she said excitedly. "Now listen," she went on feverishly, "because apparently the faces of some of those nude models remained stuck in my mind. A couple of hours ago I remembered one. A full-length nude of a young English girl who'd posed for you—on some kind of furry rug on the floor, if I remember —on her back—all of her stark naked—with a sort of bower of flowers around her. I asked you—I think I did at the time—who she was, because she was quite something, and the pose was rather daring, and you said she was a wild English kid who came around pestering you—worshiped you—a strange, reckless girl from some rich family— and to get rid of her you'd slept with her, so she could put that in her diary maybe, and you painted several pictures of her—two or three heads, I think you said, and this nude as a present, only she was afraid to take it home, the nude, so she left it." Medora caught her breath. "Well, when I saw that picture layout of Fleur Ormsby in the supplement today, and read that as a young girl she'd called on you, click— crikey, it went click—something clicked, Nardeau. Then I *knew,* I felt sure of it. The face in the supplement, Fleur Ormsby's face, was the face of that nude you'd once showed me, the nude of the wild English girl you'd slept with. One and the same, I could swear. So I dashed right up here to be sure I was right." She halted, searching Nardeau's thoughtful face, then begging, "Oh, darling, you do remember, don't you? Try to remember, please try!"

He had closed his eyes and leaned forward, elbows on his knees, lost in thought.

Suddenly his eyes opened, and he was smiling. "I remember, Maydor." He nodded. "I remember the nude you speak of, and how I characterized the model, yes. But, in honesty, I do not remember if the nude is the same as your Fleur Ormsby in the supplement."

Medora grabbed his bare arm. "Let's find out. Do you still have that nude, Nardeau?"

He laughed. "If I had it three years ago, I have it still." He stood up. "You know how I hoard my girls. Come, *poupoule,* let us see, once and for all."

Anxiously she trailed after him as he crossed the studio, went through the kitchenette, the office, through the first small storage room into the larger rear room. He had turned on the yellow overhead light, making visible open wooden compartments on each of the four walls.

"My wife has them classified by periods," he muttered, "so I can never find what I want. Ten years ago, you say?" Crouching, he began pulling out unframed canvases, glancing at them, returning them to their places. Crablike, he moved to the next compartment, again withdrawing and returning paintings. At the third compartment he dragged out two canvases, pushed them back, sorted through several more, then suddenly yanked forth an oil, perhaps two feet high, four feet long, and exclaimed, *"Voilà!"*

Medora held her breath as he brought it to her, angling it toward the yellow bulb overhead and blowing at the thin film of dust.

Medora stared at the reclining nude, so like Manet's *Olympia* except that the inbred haughty English face was younger and bolder, the breasts smaller, the hips narrower, the legs longer, the whole of it more shameless and wanton than *Olympia.*

"That's it," Medora gasped. She placed the Sunday supplement up alongside it. "Look, Nardeau—"

He cocked his head to see what she saw, and at last his sparkling eyes met her own. "The same girl," he said.

Medora's eyes were directed to the canvas again. She was smiling wickedly. "The lady is a tramp—like any of us," she said softly. "Or perhaps I should say—Her Ladyship was a tramp."

Nardeau studied the figure on the canvas with admiration. "I remember it all now. Not tramp, Maydor, but—what is your word—trollop, yes? It was her best position, the only time she was not affected or tiresome, and from my experience of women, this one was, in those days, rarely affected or tiresome."

"Oh, Nardeau, I can't tell you—"

"Wait. We must be certain." Returning the Sunday supplement to Medora, carrying the canvas, he hastened on stumpy legs out of the storage room, through the next, to his messy acajou Directoire writing table in the office. There he turned the canvas around, examined the back of it, and found what he wanted. "I date everything," he said, and propping the canvas against the table, he reached up to the shelf overhead and ran his forefinger across the spines of a series of worn logbooks that were kept clamped together by bookends on the unpainted wooden shelf. He jerked one free, brought it down, and moved to the chair at his desk before leafing through it.

"What is that?" Medora wanted to know.

"My record of paintings—each with the date of completion, a description of the subject or model . . . *attends,* Maydor." His finger traveled down the page, stopped, and he looked up. "It is here. See. 'Mlle. Fleur Grearson—London, England—Sorbonne—oil titled *Nude in the Garden.' "* He appeared puzzled. "Fleur, yes. But Grearson?"

"Her maiden name!" Medora exclaimed. "She *was* a Grearson, it's in all the papers, and after she married Sir Austin, she became an Ormsby."

"*Bien,* you are right, and now all is verified. It is what you wanted." His brow contracted once more. "But what is it you really hope for from this?"

"Nardeau, I was trying to explain before—can't you see?—it's my weapon, the one chance to use something to force Sir Austin to lift the ban against me and let me go home to Mum."

"Yes, I see. How do you propose to do this?"

She was standing over him, trembling with the urgency of her need and opportunity. "Please, Nardeau, you must lend this nude of Fleur to me, for only a week, no more. Just let me use it. I'd thought of asking you for a photograph of it, but that wouldn't be real, not half as effective. The actual oil is what's needed. I'll go to Paris with it, and I'll somehow arrange for Sir Austin to learn that I have it so he'll come to see me—and the painting. Once he *sees* it, sees *this,* he'll give me anything on earth I want."

"Maydor, what if he denies that this is his wife?"

"How can he? It *is* his wife, and if I threaten him that I'll have it reproduced in the papers, everyone'll know it is his wife. Besides, there's your logbook—"

Nardeau was on his feet. "No, that I cannot do, my pet. You know I am unafraid of the Ormsbys or anyone alive. But I could never reveal a model, identify her, under such circumstances. It would not be ethical."

"I'm sorry—I didn't mean that—all I need is the painting, really. Sir Austin'll *know*. He'll be so scared of a scandal in the same newspapers that ruined me that he'll give in right away. I'm absolutely certain of it. I'll show it to him, and once I have my entry permit from him, I'll guarantee him it'll never be shown in public again, and I'll return it to you."

Nardeau smiled. "He'll want the painting, Maydor."

She was suddenly dismayed. "You think so?"

"When you barter, you must give in order to get. When he hands you your entry permit, you will have to hand him the nude, so that he can destroy it forever."

"Oh, damn, I never thought of that. Maybe it'll have to be a photograph, after all, except if I handed him a photograph to destroy, he'd know it wasn't enough, because copies might exist . . . Nardeau, it's simply got to be the original oil! Let me buy it from you. Any price. I'll pay you out of my salary, every week I'll pay you on it, I promise."

He was frowning, and he seemed angry. "You think so little of me, young lady? You value our friendship so cheaply that you think you can buy my part of it? I am disappointed."

Her face had fallen, and tears were welling. "I'm sorry, I really am. I meant no—" She stopped abruptly, bewildered, as she saw that his leathery countenance had crinkled into a broad smile.

He laughed, shaking his head. "Foolish, foolish baby, you do not know yet when Nardeau teases you. Of course you can have the stupid oil. But not to buy. It is yours as a gift, all yours, not a gift of friendship but a gift of a weapon to fight the evil ones. Understood? Now take it and go."

With a sob of relief, Medora fell upon him, embracing him, kissing his forehead and cheeks and lips. "I can't tell you what you've done for me—"

Grunting, he freed himself of her. "I can tell you what you're doing to me." He eyed her with mock lust. "I should have taken you to bed when I had the chance."

"Anytime, you sweet dear lecher," she sang out, picking up the painting. "But it'll have to be in London, because that's where I intend to be."

He walked with her into the studio, where she recovered her shoes, and then he said, "But first, Paris. When do you go?"

"Tonight. I've got to phone a nightclub there that wants me to appear. I'll do their show while waiting for Sir Austin to come crawling. And he'll come crawling, believe me." She lifted the painting up high. "This is one chippy that'll open his eyes."

At the door she felt Nardeau's grip on her arm. She was surprised at the concern in his features.

"Maydor," he said slowly, "I am a man of the world, and of many years, so heed my warning. You must be careful, very careful. Your little white blackmail the Lord will shut one eye to, but I will not shut my eyes without reminding you that it is a dangerous game you will play. You are baiting and taunting supreme omnipotent people, and omnipotent people do not live by the same laws the world has. They are not used to losing, to surrendering to one little girl who is alone. You will think of this?"

She laughed gayly and kissed his grizzled cheek. "I am not one little girl alone," she said, patting the top of the canvas oil. "I have an ally now, an ally more deadly than the whole Ormsby family put together. How many big powers were to be at the Summit? Five?" She opened the door. "Now there will be six!"

THEY HAD SLEPT LATE this Saturday morning, and now he lay alone, fully awake at last, listening to the sounds of Venice.

The sounds, muffled by the rusty metal shutters latched over double windows to keep his bedroom darkened and cool, were blended into one harmonious echo, yet from his experience of three years of listening, he was able to distinguish and sort out each individual chord.

Hands behind his head on the pillow, Matthew Brennan listened. There was the constant tread of women's low-heeled pumps and men's heavier walking shoes, tapping and shuffling across the worn stone arch, from which one could see the Bridge of Sighs through the shadows of the narrow canal. There was the coughing of the powerful engine of the CIGA *motoscafo* as it waited in the water at the side entrance of the Danieli Royal Excelsior Hotel, the launch about to ferry two dozen hotel guests to the sibling Excelsior Palace Hotel on the Lido island beach twelve minutes away across the open stretch of water. There were the business shouts of the eccentric and proud gondoliers grouped before their graceful, high-prowed gondolas in front of the ducal palace on the Ponte della Paglia. There was the bumping of an incoming *vaporetto*, as the water taxi's wooden beams hit the floating platform of the crowded San Zaccaria station. There was the steady lapping of the water in the lagoon of the Grand Canal, artificial waves born of the milling and churning of gondolas, motorboats, passenger ferries (or natural waves produced by a long-desired breeze), against the stone pavement of the Riva degli Schiavoni, the thoroughfare that separated the ground-floor entrance and lobby of the Danieli Hotel from the lagoon beyond.

In short, there was Venice alive beneath his late-morning bedroom.

Matt Brennan's attention had isolated one sound, held to it. The slapping and sloshing of water. Gradually the one sound became two, and involuntarily, idiotically (since he was, for the time, alone), he found himself smiling. For the second sound, more lovely even than the first, came from beyond the opposite side of his bed, from his bathroom where Lisa (incredibly once, correctly and formally, Elizabeth) had gone ten or fifteen minutes earlier to take her hand shower in the bathtub.

Now, hearing only the faint but distinct musical splashing of the water on her flesh, he felt more than visualized the pleasure of her body.

For the first time since he had known her, it had been two weeks, for the first time with any woman since the beginning of his black death of despair, it had been three years, actually four, he had made love twice in a night. They had gone to bed at midnight, knowing the occasion, and in each other's arms, whispering, caressing, mutually hungering at last, they had joined their bodies into a single bliss. Then, hours later, he had felt the warm palm of her hand on his naked arm. He had turned, and she had come into his arms, clutching him frantically, and he had understood her fear and need, and his own as well. In this frantic embrace they both had known what the day would bring, and they had wanted the night to be forever. This time, more than any other, they had made love without restraint, silently, with uncontrolled passion—and finally, minds and bodies spent, they had slept on and on, prolonging the night and cheating the day.

But now, the day was here, already old, as he was again old. The pleasure of her began to recede from his mind as the sounds of her splashing became inaudible, and he could hear only the lapping of the lagoon, the waters that would, in short hours, carry her motorboat to the waiting train that would take her out of his life.

Because of the past four years, disenchanted and finally embittered by life, Matt Brennan had ceased to believe in miracles. Not that he had ever actually believed in miracles, being a rationalist, but somehow he had always endorsed the remark of an eighteenth-century French noblewoman who, when asked if she believed in ghosts, had retorted, "No. But I am afraid of them." Yet the entrance of Lisa Collins into his life had been a true miracle.

He had been dead, if this could be said of a person who still breathed: dead brain, dead eyes, dead heart, dead hopes. Then Lisa had appeared, and touched him in some supernatural way, and even though he had been too distrustful to believe anyone could reanimate a corpse, this young, vivacious, vibrant girl had briefly ignited within him the spark of life. She had revived him sufficiently for him to feel that he was somewhat more than a zombi if somewhat less than a human being, and that total resurrection might be possible one day.

But during an afternoon recently, momentarily isolated from Lisa's magnificent sorcery, aware that he must make a hard decision quickly, he re-examined the realities of his future while sitting in his Mechitar monk's cell, his improvised office and study, on the quiet tiny island of San Lazzaro degli Armeni. The heady interval had passed. Brennan had returned himself to the remorseless truth at last, and he had concluded that no sorcery could give him back to life.

Brooding over his desk in the austere cell, Brennan had realized that this was no place to hang a lie and accept it for truth. Here, within these plain, flat walls, only facts could be considered without mockery. Four years had not changed the facts.

Four years earlier Brennan had been a bright-young-man-going-places, and no colleague in the Department of State, in Washington, D.C., had possessed better prospects. He had been economist, diplomat, expert in the field of nuclear disarmament, respected by the Secretary of State, President Earnshaw, by the President's aide, Simon Madlock. He had been husband, father, the delight of every hostess on the Potomac. He had been all of this and more to others, perhaps less than this to himself, but on the basis of his record there was reason enough to select him for a key role at the Zurich Parley.

That was where the debacle had occurred. Zurich. The unexpected, the unthinkable, had happened, and overnight he had been reduced from potential hero to obvious villain. In the neat ledger of public government, every serious debit must be balanced by entering the name of one who might have incurred it. A scapegoat was wanted after Zurich, not one too important or well-known, nor yet one too lowly or obscure. Brennan's measurements had been right. And so he had been made to fit the crime. Four years ago a standing Congressional committee, unjudicial custodians of public welfare performing their public relations job on television, had tried him, judged him, savagely torn off his epaulets of high standing, removed his ornaments of achievement, and turned him loose branded unofficial traitor and official leper.

Unofficial traitor had been what rankled most, for there had been no official proof of treason. The American Government and citizenry, in a hurry, in a time of things condensed, synopsized, digested, miniaturized, in a time of yes or no, true or false, black or white, had no patience with shadings.

A defendant on trial was guilty or not guilty, one or the other. The wise old Scottish verdict of "Not proven," therefore acquitted, had been meaningless in a yes-or-no culture. In the hearings that had become an illegal trial, the burden of proof had been placed on the computer-selected scapegoat. Could the scapegoat prove that he had not been responsible for Professor Arthur Varney's shocking defection to Red China? Yes, he could prove it, because there had been a decent delegate from the Soviet Union, Nikolai Rostov, working side by side with American delegates, with Brennan himself, who had been witness to the defection and could attest to Brennan's absolute innocence. Rostov? Yes, sir, Rostov. Very well, could the scapegoat produce Rostov? No, he could not; he had tried but he could not. Rostov had disappeared somewhere inside Russia, in Moscow or Siberia or somewhere. Ah, so there was nothing but the scapegoat's own word? No, nothing but his own word.

Not proven. Yet, to the American Government and its citizenry, proof enough. Guilty. Not legally guilty, but so judged by a kangaroo court and mob rule. And thus Matthew Brennan's good name had been lynched, and what had been left for him to live with in the world of his fellows was a nameless dangling corpse, one dangling somewhere between Alger Hiss and J. Robert Oppenheimer.

And no matter how far he had shouted, there had been no Nikolai Rostov to come to his aid, to cut him down, to free him and restore his good name. And so he had done what he could, untied himself from the gallows but not from the noose, and he had removed himself from the world of his jeering fellow countrymen and for three years had remained in hiding, an outcast without respect, without career, without wife and children, without future, without warmth or love.

And then Lisa had foolishly come to treat him as a man to be respected, a person with a future, and to remind him that warmth and love were still possible. He had resisted her until, helplessly, then eagerly, he had succumbed to her fantasy. But he had succumbed only briefly, because after a short interval, pressed by the need to make a decision, he had been able to sit in his monastic cell and realize that he could not re-enter her world of the living. He had been able to see that any effort to follow her capricious footsteps would bring disaster down upon both of them, and she deserved a better fate. He had told her so, and she would not accept his reasoning. Nevertheless, he had kept on telling her, and finally she had realized his mind was made up, and last night she had loved him with the passion of insane, breast-beating, uncontrolled mourning.

Now, lying on his Hotel Danieli bed, he mourned, too, and he dreaded what was left of the day ahead, the realities to be faced, the end of Elizabeth Collins—how odd to revert to their first formal self-introductions—and the end of his relationship with his son. He had almost forgotten it, the impending reunion and confrontation with his son, Stefani's son now, who must have arrived in Venice by this time—well, to be faced, the end of that relationship, too, the farewell to fatherhood and to the last living carrier of his once good name.

He heard the air conditioning come on, which meant that it was becoming warm outside, and he considered getting out of bed. But he could hear the hand shower again in use, and so there was no need to hurry his last hours with Lisa.

He propped himself up on the rumpled bed and found a cigarette. Smoking, he tried to reject the day ahead and replace it with another, better day. He sought not an old day of long ago but a younger day from the recent past. There was such a day, of course. It was the first of the last fourteen days, so shining and glorious. Considering it, he smoked, and half smiling at the memory of a miracle he would never have believed possible, he plucked that day from the fresh past, and he lived it once more.

He had met her, the first time, in a camera shop located in the Piazza San Marco. It was a shop that he frequently visited, not for photographic supplies (he had no interest in taking pictures or memorializing his Venice years in any manner), but to gossip with his old friend, the robust Armenian proprietor, or to bring him a message or package from one of the Mechitar fathers on the nearby island of San Lazzaro, one of the world's three remaining Armenian educational centers.

The camera shop was crowded with German tourists this particular noon, and Brennan squeezed in between customers at the glass counter, handed his package to the Italian adolescent at the cash register, and was about to leave when his attention was arrested by the uncommonly attractive American girl beside him.

She had finished stuffing some newly purchased film into her large purse, and looked up to speak to the proprietor again. "Sir, could you tell me where—?"

161

The Armenian proprietor's back was already to her, and he was volubly engaged with his German tourist customers. The girl smiled helplessly as she turned and almost bumped into Brennan. She shrugged good-naturedly and said to him, as she might address thin air, "Oh well, I just wanted to find out about the main shopping street, but maybe one of the pigeons will know." Then, as if uncertain of Brennan's knowledge of English, she smiled once more, this time apologetically, and headed for the door.

Brennan watched her go. She was wearing a cool sleeveless silk print, fashionable but sensible, and the dress was short enough to set off her long slim nylon-sheathed legs. She was special, he thought, and the accent had been reminiscent of New England. She was standing outside, statuesque and alone in the shaded arcade, as poised as Rizzo's *Eve* in the Doge's Palace, yet plainly not knowing which way to turn in this island city cut into 120 jigsaw parts. It was not Brennan's habit to play Good Samaritan with tourists, especially American tourists, and these last years he had had little interest in pretty American girls, yet he found himself moving outside, going directly to her.

"Pardon me," he heard himself saying. She turned quickly, dark eyes widening, as he went on. "Did I overhear you asking about the main street?"

"Oh, you're an American. I wasn't sure in there. Yes, I'd hoped to do some gift-shopping. But it's all so confusing——"

Recalling his first day in Venice three years before, he was sympathetic. "I know. Well, look, if you stroll under the arcades around this rectangle of the Piazza, you'll find some excellent shops. Depends on what you want, of course. Linen, jewelry, leather goods, there's something of everything, good and bad. But the main shopping street is straight ahead." He pointed across the broad Piazza, with its milling tourists, gamboling children, dense clusters of pecking pigeons, and he said, "You see the clock tower there—right there in the eastern corner?"

"Yes," she said hesitantly.

He tried to be patient. "The tower with the two giant figures of Moors on top, and the bronze bell, and the huge clock with Roman numerals and signs of the zodiac?"

"That weird clock. I couldn't believe it when I saw it last night."

"Well, right beneath is an archway. It leads you into a narrow twisting street, the Merceria, and you simply follow it and you'll find everything you want."

She nodded. "I think I tried it last night. I was trying to find the Rialto. I kept making the wrong turn, taking the wrong bridge. I've never seen so many bridges."

"Four hundred."

"Really? Well, I guess they're all in the—what?—yes, Merceria. Everywhere I turned, I wound up against a blank wall. I'd ask some Venetian, and he'd spin me around and point just like you did, and say, *'Sempre diretto'*—the concierge at the Gritti Palace told me that means 'Thataway'—and so I'd go thataway, and in ten seconds flat I'd be lost again." She lifted her purse higher. "But you've given me courage. I thank you. I'll try again."

Before she could leave, there was the clanging of bells, and the mechanical Moors astride the clock tower were stiffly moving, swinging their hammers at the big bell to signal the arrival of midday, and hordes of fluttering pigeons were aloft, winging, dipping, rising in a circle above the Piazza San Marco, faking fright and putting on their daily show for the spectators.

"Wow," she said, impressed, and then she turned back to Brennan, and added with a tinge of regret, "I've taken up enough of your time. Thank you so much. I'd better start my shopping."

"Too late," Brennan said. "I'd forgotten it was almost noon. Most of the shops will be closed for a couple hours."

"Oh, no," she groaned. "Now I won't get anything done. And I've got to leave in the morning."

"Don't leave in the morning. Give Venice another day."

"I wish I could. I like it more than I thought I would—I mean, what little I've seen. But I've got an itinerary."

"Business or pleasure?"

"Well, a sixteen-day vacation, sort of. Then back to work. I'm in the fashion business and I've got to cover the collections in Paris. I've never been to Europe before, so I had a quick sight-seeing tour laid out for me. I took a fast look at Rome—hot—then Florence—lovely, but the noise—then here, and from here to Milan, Nice, Cannes—let me see, Geneva, Zurich—I missed one or two other places—then Paris and the openings. Everyone said a day and a half would be enough for Venice."

"It isn't."

She showed surprise. "It isn't? You sound as if you live here."

"I do."

For the first time she looked at him carefully, and with interest. "I never imagined any—any Americans lived in this city permanently. Everyone says it's a tourist trap. Are you an artist or expatriate or something like that?"

"I suppose something like that." He could not understand what encouraged him to do what he did next. Was it his boredom, his persistent ennui, his desire to be rid of another endless day? Or was it a newly born, flickering desire to remain in contact with one so vital, bright, alive, and learn if such a one could transmit a breath of life into him? Or was it a need, so long denied, to enjoy briefly beauty more animate than the marble splendor of Venice?

Throughout their conversation he had been appraising her. She was tall. Judging her against his height of five feet eleven, she was easily five feet seven, he had decided. Physically her strongest asset was a remarkable figure, broad shoulders, lissomely curved body, slim shapely legs. Her brunette hair was arranged with curls brushed forward onto her cheeks, and her face, with dark direct eyes, Grecian nose, overgenerous mouth, gave her an appearance of girlish buoyancy superimposed upon sensual maturity.

As he spoke, Brennan was conscious of the fact that he had not examined a female so closely in years. "Look," he was saying, "since you have so little time here, you might do best to spend the two hours of the siesta seeing some of the sights you'll want to see—the Basilica, over there, for one thing—until the shops open. But if you have nothing else to do, and you'd like to get off your feet, maybe you wouldn't mind joining a middle-aged-old fellow American in a cup of tea in the café?"

"Freely translated—is that an invitation?"

"It is."

"I accept," she said cheerfully. "Heavens, I thought you'd never invite me."

Holding her elbow lightly, he directed her down the steps into the sunny Piazza. "I'm shy," he said. "I've been out of human contact. Would you like lunch somewhere?"

"Any of the cafés here. I'm not hungry."

"Right over there, then. Florian's. It's the oldest. Opened in 1720. It was Lord Byron's hangout a hundred years later." They had arrived at the seven rows of round cream-colored wicker chairs, most of the rows exposed to the midday sun. "Would you prefer to sit in the sun or the shade?"

"Wherever it's more comfortable. The shade."

He led her between the rows, to where the rim of shade fell on the last of the tables lined before the old arcade pillars. He remained standing while she set her purse on the extra chair. After they sat down, she coolly faced him. "For purposes of identification," she said, "I have a mole on my chin, a beauty mark next to my navel, and I'm known to men who take me out to dine the first time as Miss Elizabeth Collins, fugitive from Bridgeport, Connecticut, currently a resident of Manhattan."

Awkwardly she extended her hand. Amused, he took the long tapering fingers lightly, replying, "I'm honored, Miss Collins." He hesitated ever so briefly, and then he uttered it: "I'm Matthew Brennan." He waited. No flicker of recognition crossed her face, and his relief was instantaneous. "But I'd prefer Matt," he said. "Or am I going too fast, Elizabeth?"

"Let's shift into first. Elizabeth is for my driver's license, maiden aunts, and married buyers who try to date me. For anyone else, across a crowded Piazza, I'm diminutive—Lisa."

Fourteen days ago, almost to the hour, that was the beginning.

It had been an enchanted day, wondrous and seemingly devoid of hours, that one. Sitting in Florian's, they had whiskies, then he ordered frittata al prosciutto for himself, and she preferred to have whatever he was having, and then he ordered a bottle of Fuiggi, and caffè for each of them. Treat or no treat, she insisted upon sharing the 4,000-lire bill, and, as insistently, he refused to accept the money.

For two persons just met, they had too much to discuss in a mere afternoon. Initially the conversation was impersonal. She inquired about starred sights noted in her guidebook, and he, who had almost forgotten their historic fascination, told her what he could of each, as colorfully as possible. When she quoted from her guidebook the consternation of Robert Benchley, the humorist, upon arriving in Venice, and his desperate cable to a friend—"Streets full of water. Please advise."—Brennan laughed, and tried to explain this crazy island of 177 canals, an island halved by the principal S-shaped Grand Canal, which snaked two miles through the city. He spoke of the immortal couples who had come to Venice to make love in palaces and hotels along the Canal, Byron and his married Countess Guiccioli, D'Annunzio and his Duse, de Musset and his George Sand (although he had fallen ill shortly after arriving, and Sand had taken up with his physician).

She asked him about the Piazza San Marco, and he told her that Ruskin, like Napoleon before him, had called it "the most beautiful room in Europe." There beside them was the soaring needle of the Campanile, the bell tower begun in 912, which had buckled and collapsed without killing a soul in 1902, and was restored a decade later with the original bell, Venice's oldest, once more hanging in its belfry. There, behind it, the golden basilica of St. Mark, a rainbow of mosaics, guarded on high by four Hellenic gilded bronze horses stolen from Constantinople by marauding Venetians, and from Venice by Bonaparte's soldiers, and the comings and goings of these horses always signaled the downfall of an empire. There were, before them, the countless gray pigeons of the Piazza, ridiculously waddling, ridiculously fattened from the maize thrown them by three quarters of a million tourists annually, and twice a day, by municipal decree, they were also fed by the city at the expense of the natives.

"Nothing is like it," Brennan told Lisa, "nothing equal to it, not a second Venice in the world. That's not me speaking. That's Elizabeth Barrett Browning." Everyone who was anyone in history, he told her, had been here where they sat, and most had agreed with Mrs. Browning, and these included Goethe and Proust, Dickens and Long-fellow, Shelley and Stendhal, Wagner and Whistler. Of the great cities on earth that he had seen, Brennan told her, Venice alone looked as it had looked two or three centuries ago. "Sometimes, sitting here, I imagine Lord Byron descending some heavenly staircase to return to Venice for one night," Brennan said. "Except for thinking that the inhabitants are in masquerade, he might return to Florian's and sit here just as he did in 1819, or ride a horse on the Lido beach, and not suspect that a thing had changed."

Carried away, Brennan went on. He was sorry for people who came abroad yet never visited Venice, warned off by fastidious and antiseptic friends who insisted that the stink of the canals on hot nights and the carnival of tourism were not to be endured. "Poor fools," added Brennan, "it's like refusing an affair with Madame du Barry because it was rumored that sometimes she might have bad breath."

Even more, Brennan went on, he resented the beautiful, empty guidebooks, because they stressed the doges, the Madonnas, the Titians, the gondolas, and missed the essence of the real Venice. "You can't get it in a day or two, or a week or two, but maybe you could in a year or two. The essence of Venice is its lack of pressure on its visitors. If you stay here, there is no place to go, nothing to do, except relax and learn that relaxation can be fulfillment. There's not an auto to rush off in, a taxi or bus to catch, in the entire city. There's not even a bicycle. What you *can* do is walk, and you can breathe, you can sit, you can think or dream, without being oppressed by the obligations of accomplishing, competing, progressing. I suppose that's not for most people. Maybe it's not for you, Lisa. But it is for me."

She replied quietly, "It could be for me, too, Matt. Though not if I were by myself. I'd have to be with someone who—well—thinks the way you think, and the way I do underneath."

And so they had come to themselves, at last.

Embarrassed by his long discourse and his enthusiasm, both things uncharacteristic of him in recent years, and by his flash of self-revelation, he temporized. "Of course, holing up like this is for your elders. You're much too young. You've got too much to do and see."

"I'm glad you brought that up," she said seriously. "When we met, you spoke of yourself as 'middle-aged-old.' You're not that old. Anything but. And forgive me, but I'm not a child. I'm twenty-two."

"You could be my daughter, almost. I'm thirty-seven, soon thirty-eight. I'm old enough to give advice, and you're young enough to take it. So take it now. Avoid depressing and decrepit men like myself."

"What's bothering you? Why such a fix on age?" He was tempted to tell her, but he held his tongue, and Lisa went on. "I've been out with plenty of boys in their twenties. Maybe I'm a case for Freud, but I find them tiresome. I've never had one-tenth as good a time with any of them as I've been having with you. Does that frighten you?"

He smiled wearily, yet was pleased. "It's not me, Lisa, it's Venice."

"Oh, you *are* difficult," she said in mock exasperation.

He knew that he was. He always was, these days. Yet he was feeling better than he had felt for almost as long as he could remember. He was not ready to free her yet, and least of all was he ready to discuss his own difficult self. That would certainly drive her off. A defensive holding operation was wanted. "I'm sorry," he said, "and I'm going to become even more difficult, because I'm going to pry. I'm curious about a twenty-two-year-old who feels older than young. You mentioned being in the fashion business. You mentioned Bridgeport and Manhattan. I'm interested in what came between. Do you mind?"

She did not mind. She was thoughtful awhile, bemused, drinking her Fuiggi water, accepting a cigarette for her filtered holder, and smoking companionably while he smoked. There was really little to tell him, she said, because she hadn't done much, and he would probably find her life dull and boring. She relaxed in the wicker chair, crossing her long sheathed legs, throwing her head back in profile to gaze up at the cloudless sky roof of the Piazza. His eyes had gone from her lips down to her exposed knees and the slender legs, and he decided that he would never find anything about her dull and boring. He felt excited by her presence, no longer lethargic, and the day had become curiously suspenseful.

Elizabeth Collins had been born in Eugene, Oregon—"some people are, you know," she had said—but she had grown up and attended high school in Bridgeport, where both her parents still lived, her father a dentist and her mother a hypochondriac. At the University of Connecticut, in Storrs, she had been popular on campus, had been elected Homecoming Queen, and had enjoyed seeing her picture in the newspapers. A promoter of one of those perennial beauty contests had enjoyed seeing her picture, too, and, overcoming the technicality of nonresidence, had arranged for her to compete, in evening gown and in

167

two-piece swimming suit, for the title of Miss New York City. She had been judged the runner-up, which meant no contract for public appearances, only a plaque and more photographs in the newspapers. But as a result, because of her height, her symmetry, her bust which was just right at a size thirty-four, her lank boniness ("I was 117 pounds then, and my shoulder blades and ribs showed, which was considered chic, though I think I look better at 124, right now," she said), she was offered a job by an advertising agency to pose in scanty underthings for photographers.

She had left college, despite her mother's hysteria and high blood pressure, to move to New York City and to work modeling underpinnings, as the fashion trade called undergarments. But she found that it embarrassed her to see herself in the advertisements, stretched out in a sheer nightgown or bra and panty girdle, and in her spare time she had sought something more proper. The second model agency she visited had taken her on, and soon this had led to a better-paying and more secure job as a model for a fashion salon, the House of Fernald, on Seventh Avenue. "I was great in chiffons, but best in one of those svelte décolleté black dresses, a strand of baroque pearls, elbow-length white gloves, a fur. Really, Matt, you must see me like that one day."

But modeling the collections, whether in the Grand Ballroom of the Waldorf Astoria Hotel or in the Crystal Room of the Beverly Hills Hotel, was exhausting, uninspiring work, and promised no future, except becoming some wealthy businessman's kept woman. Poking around the fashion house, Lisa had found herself growing fascinated by design. To a natural creativity she added the practical knowledge she'd acquired from showing clothes, and she began to ask questions, store away answers, play at designing during evenings in her apartment. One day she got up the courage to show her employer, Fernald, several of her crude originals. He had been immediately impressed, adapted one or two of her sketches, and encouraged her to do more designing on his time. Even more impressed by what she had subsequently produced, he had entered her in the Parsons School of Design, only to withdraw her after a short time so that she would not be spoiled by conformity, and he had promoted her from fashion model to designer's assistant. She had drawn, draped, pinned, cut, and last year she had been graduated to full-time designer and become a member of The Fashion Group, Inc.

Her meteoric rise had been fantastic for a girl of twenty-two. And the tiara of success had resulted in an assignment, her first, to cover the collections of the French couturiers in Paris. Then, because she had not seen Europe, and because a vacation was long due her, she had been permitted two and a half weeks abroad, on her own, before joining up with the firm's buyers in Paris.

"And here I am," she said. "Why did you let me carry on like that? I told you it would be dull."

"It's all fascinating," he said.

"It's all unfair," she said. "Now you know about me, and I still don't know a thing about you."

He had dreaded the inevitable moment of turnabout. He had anticipated her complaint, had tried to imagine what he could possibly tell her except the truth, yet he was reluctant to reveal himself and end their meeting. He tried to rationalize deceit. She had really told him little about herself except some interesting but tame facts. He need tell her nothing except some facts—but his facts, no matter how few, would be considerably more revealing, and they would shock her or, at very least, dismay her. And then it would be over, this sweet meeting of strangers in the Piazza San Marco, each so new and unmarked for the other, until one was forced to disclose the mean scars and ugliness concealed beneath the garments of superficial chatter.

"Cat got your tongue, Mr. Brennan?"

"I was just thinking of what I could tell you."

"Well, don't tell me you're not interesting."

He tried to smile. "I'm interesting enough to a lot of people. But so is a cadaver to a dissecting surgeon."

"Now, what does that mean?"

"It means that sometimes it's better not to know all about another person."

Her brow contracted. "I don't agree. When two people are together, and one disrobes, well, the other should, too. Otherwise it's indecent. When I give the truth, I like the truth back. What do I know about you? You've been in Venice for a long time. You love Venice. You don't love yourself, or you pretend not to. You're literate and educated. You pick up stray American girls and you intrigue them—and then what, Matt? How did you come here? I must know. From the beginning."

He nodded in resigned surrender, stared awhile at two pigeons waddling between the tables, and then, in a reticent monotone tinged with his usual cynicism, self-mockery, detachment, he told her what he could tell her.

His parents had both been Philadelphia Main Line. His maternal grandfather had been the family mint. His father had devoted his life to preserving the inherited fortune. He himself had wanted a more challenging career, and after his older brother, Elia, whom he idolized,

169

had been killed in Korea, Matt had known what that career would be. He would dedicate himself to politics, the hard politics of peace. At Georgetown his major had been economics. But his secondary specialty had been political science. In summary, his goal had been that of becoming an expert in the field of nuclear disarmament.

Brennan had been a research economist at the Rand Corporation in California, and at the same time he had been active in a half-dozen peace movements and organizations. Then, because he had been considered solid, feet-on-the-ground, knowledgeable, dedicated, but practical, he had been appointed President of the Schweitzer World Peace Fund. From time to time this work had brought him into contact with the White House and the Department of State, and at last he had been sworn in as a United States delegate to the United Nations. After President Earnshaw's inauguration, Brennan's record had come to the attention of Earnshaw's powerful aide, Simon Madlock, who had mentioned him to the Secretary of State, who in turn had recommended him to the Director of the United States Arms Control and Disarmament Agency. Brennan had then been appointed to the staff of 180 in the Agency which advised America's peace negotiators.

As an expert in developing national security through arms control, Matthew Brennan had achieved a lifelong ambition. No more was he a mere propaganda voice in overidealistic, ineffectual, peace committees. Now, as an adviser and negotiator on the staff of a government agency that reported to the Secretary of State, and to the President himself, Brennan had become a force—a minor force, but a force nevertheless —in promoting international nuclear disarmament.

He had been assigned to numerous disarmament meetings and conferences abroad—Warsaw, Bonn, Paris, Geneva—and then, four years and one month ago, at the recommendation of Simon Madlock, he had been named to participate in the most important peace meeting of all, the Zurich Parley—the most important because representatives of the People's Republic of China had attended it so eagerly. The Swiss meeting had been a stalemate and a failure, and it had produced not international disarmament but international discord and fear, for as a result of Zurich, the Red Chinese had acquired the neutron bomb. And the repercussions had shattered Matthew Brennan's career and his life.

There it was, and here he was, stripped and exposed again. The afternoon's idyll was ended. He hated to look up from the table and see her face.

At last, after a strained silence, he looked up. He was surprised at the concentration in her face as she busied herself with lighting a cigarette.

"Well," he said, "now you know."

She turned to him. "I never knew you were such a big shot. I could blush for the way I bothered you with my silly prattle."

"But I'm not—" He paused, confused. "Lisa, did you understand everything I told you?"

"Of course. I could recite it word for word back to you."

"I mean, about the trouble I got into?"

"Everyone gets into trouble."

"Lisa, you don't remember reading about me?"

"I'm ashamed. I hate to seem so stupid. I guess I never was terribly interested in politics. I mean before this."

"But certainly you—you've heard of the Varney defection, the scandal, the Dexter committee hearings?"

"It rings a bell, vaguely. Those were—were those the witch-hunters or something?"

He sat back and considered this new insight into her. She did not know who he was, or how he had been disgraced. Gradually it became understandable. He had nothing else in his life but the scandal. He had lived it and relived it through the months and years, magnified it because of his own hurt ego, until it crowded out everything else of life. But other people had no need to dwell on one episode like this. Their lives were filled with other episodes, newer, fresher, more contemporary. Of course. What was a total sum in his mind was a fraction in the minds of others. Besides, this girl was only twenty-two years old. She had been no more than eighteen during his trouble, probably as self-centered as any adolescent, serious and frivolous by turn, apolitical, concerned with happiness, advancement, and Life with that big young L. For her, at that time, his headlines would have been subordinate to the latest football scores, fashion crazes, want ads.

Still, he must let her know.

"Lisa, listen. The Joint Committee on Internal Security held a series of hearings. The members decided that I had once been a leftist, was still soft on Communism, a bleeding heart who wanted peace at any price. They decided that I had encouraged one of our key nuclear physicists to go over to Red China because I felt that this would strengthen China and preserve the delicate balance between war and peace. They could not prove it, but nevertheless that was their belief. As a result I lost my security clearance, and I was asked to resign from the Government agency, and I resigned. I was branded a traitor. Not legally, but a traitor none the less. And that's what I've been considered ever since. You are too young to remember. But ask your father, he'll know."

She was solemn. "If I were to ask anyone, I'd prefer to ask you, Matt."

"You'd prefer to ask me?"

"Yes. If you were guilty, that is. Frankly, whatever you say wouldn't make any difference in how I felt about you, one way or the other. But if it makes you feel better—okay, I'll ask it—were you guilty?"

"No, Lisa, I was not guilty."

"Then that's all I want to hear of that." She paused, briefly thoughtful, and looked at him once more. "However, there is something I'd like to know, unless you consider it too personal. Are you married?"

"I was."

"I'm sorry."

"I was married until the hearings began. The day they were over, she walked out."

"Maybe it's not for me to say, but that doesn't sound very loyal."

"No, but perfectly understandable, at least to me. I suppose these breakups always begin a good deal earlier. In any case, I know ours did. Looking back, I can see that Steffi and I were breaking up from the day we were married. We were married too young. I didn't turn out to be the man she needed. I was too introspective, too intellectual, too withdrawn for her. I suppose, in her eyes, I lacked toughness, aggressiveness, ambition, so with the hearings—well, when I came out weak and suspect, the humiliation was more than she could bear. She got the divorce, as well as full custody of the children, and so good-bye. She's remarried now."

"Her leaving you when she did, that must have been a bad blow."

"There had been so many, it could only be a lesser one. To be honest, I don't regret losing her, or losing the eighteen years with her that went down the drain. I only regret being separated from my son and daughter. But it's just as well. What could I have done with them?" He moved in his chair restlessly, settled back and regarded Lisa with his half smile. "Had enough, young lady?"

She ignored his question. "Matt, how do you get along in Venice?"

He had determined to keep his tone light from this moment on. He hated people who perpetually whined and indulged in self-pity. If he regarded himself as all but anatomically dead, he felt that this should be his secret. Since he chose to remain on earth and walk among men, he felt a responsibility toward the community of men. He would wear some caul of human dignity. And so, these years, he had tried to do this. Only, too often, his attempt did not work very well. His wit remained, but it was corroded by cynicism and bitterness. His candor, one of his better traits, was frequently blunted by the evasiveness and uncertainty of noncommitment. His intellect and learning, once pleas-

172

ant attributes, were occasionally warped by prejudices spawned by his sufferings. His lucidity, long-admired, was sometimes muddled by his inner confusion. His wry, self-deprecating asides, a diplomatic asset, were more and more poisoned by a will for self-destruction.

Yet he tried, even when it did not matter, and he determined to try now, when somehow it did matter. He had gone too far in revealing the piteous and complaining part of his martyrdom. He determined to show her that he was more. What had she asked? Yes. Matt, how do you get along in Venice?

"Well," he said with a cheerful inflection, "depends on what you mean. Do you mean financially? My father left a trust in my name. It's more than adequate. No man should be without one. Or do you mean vocationally? In the beginning I tried to get myself restored to Government. Some gall, eh? Then I tried to obtain a position in the States, social service work, teaching, busboy, anything useful. No luck. Maybe they could see I was inept. An ex-diplomat isn't much good at anything else. Then I traveled, destination unknown. Since settling here, I've tried my hand at writing. No go. Didn't know enough words. Besides, Hemingway slept here first, in your very hotel, in fact. I thought of becoming a doge and starting a small war so I could make use of my old peace-negotiating skills. But no one around here feels like fighting, and me least of all. Lately I've been spending my afternoons on a little island out in the basin, an outpost for Armenian fathers who took a fancy to me—it's called San Lazzaro—if you were staying longer I'd insist you see it—and I've been studying Eastern languages there. Actually, an opportunity for a job with a shady import-export firm in Genoa has come up, and since their dealings are in the Near East, a few even in the Far East, a couple of usable languages would be an advantage. I don't know if I'll be ready before the job is filled. But no matter. At least I'll know Arabic and Hebrew. So there you are, dear Lisa, that's how I get along."

"I really meant—how you get along emotionally?"

Everything, he thought, came down to Freudian patter, at last. He shrugged. "I hide. I brood. I hum college songs. I cherish my hobby— collecting grievances. I've mounted a beautiful collection. Also, when I feel daring—Casanova was a Venetian, you know—I collect inquisitive and pretty fashion designers with a penchant for older men."

She laughed, suddenly vivacious, and said, "I like the last. That sounds promising, although I apologize for being too inquisitive. It only means I'm interested in you." She lifted her dress an inch higher above her knee. "I hope I qualify for your collection."

"You qualify—" he said, but before he could continue with the flirtatious talk, there was the resounding interruption of hammering on the big bronze bell above the clock tower. Startled, he glanced up at the moving Moors, then squinted down at his wristwatch. "Unbelievable, Lisa, but I've kept you here three solid hours. If you want to get any shopping done—"

"Shopping? Did I want to shop? I completely forgot about that." Retrieving her purse, she said, "Frankly, it's been more fun talking to you. I can't remember when I've enjoyed myself more." She uncrossed her knees and put them together primly, swinging around to face him squarely. "I thank you, sir. I've taken up enough of your time."

He refused to recognize any parting, and remained casually slumped, one arm hooked over the back of his café chair. "If you're worried about time, it's my most plentiful asset, Lisa. It's something of which I have nothing else but. And all of it is yours, if you half meant what you said. I'd enjoy helping you shop, or taking you sightseeing, or doing whatever you like."

"You wouldn't mind?" she asked anxiously.

He signaled the waiter. "Just try to get away, and see what happens."

Leaving Florian's, he tendered her his arm theatrically, and quickly she linked her arm in his, and they strolled across the Piazza, zigzagging among the gobbling pigeons, the crouching amateur photographers, the running children spraying their kernels of corn over the square, the clusters of gawking tourists in shorts, slacks, cotton dresses, chorusing their superlatives in a Babel of tongues.

They were never apart that day and evening. They window-shopped in the shadowy Merceria and on the massive Rialto Bridge. They explored quaint squares, lolled on unexpected tiny bridges, and studied a Madonna in a niche. They sat at the foot of one of the granite columns in the Piazzetta, sunning themselves and watching the aged ganzers draw gondolas to the quayside with their poles, and both of them were mesmerized by the silhouette of the Church of San Giorgio Maggiore etched against the soft blue sky across San Marco Basin.

Late in the afternoon they were back in the Piazza, drawn to the old woman behind her seed stand, who was still shaking her metal can filled with maize, and they bought two bags, and laughed and laughed while pigeons lighted on their hands and in their hair, pecking for their meal of corn. They found yellow straw chairs, behind yellow tables imprinted MARTINI, at Quadri's outdoor café, and they drank their cocktails and held hands as they listened to the romantic music played by the orchestra on the elevated platform nearby.

Later, they strolled back toward the Rialto, and he led her down a small dark side-street to where the Albergo Ristorante al Graspo da Ua stood. Inside, at their corner table, they had scampi, and then

Valpolicella, that good red wine, and then tagliatelle serenissima and another wine, and then charcoal-broiled filetto di bue and more wine. Sometimes they talked, but mostly they were silent, and either way, they felt very close.

They had learned more of each other, and it had been personal and important. Brennan had spoken of his former wife, and of a brief unsatisfactory affair with a secretary so long ago, and of his infrequent sexual experiences with Italian women. Lisa, in turn, had recalled the boy she'd slept with in college, to find out what it was like, and once knowing, she'd decided she would wait to be married. She had spoken of going to New York, of the brash newspaperman who interviewed her for a feature story on fashion models, of dating him and sleeping with him for a short time because she had been lonely, but disliking him really, and vowing nevermore until she was married, or at least until she was deeply in love, truly in love, if such a thing ever happened to her.

Somehow, before midnight, they again found themselves in Florian's on the Piazza San Marco, with the square almost deserted, or so it seemed, and the music sweet and low, and the dots of light making it all unreal and a fairyland.

They had finished their second round of cognacs, and Brennan had been considering a third, when suddenly he faced her, releasing her hand. "It's late if you have to leave tomorrow," he said. "I'll see you back to the Gritti."

She stared at him a long time, unblinking, unmoving, and then she said, carefully so that the words would not slur, "Mr. Brennan, sir, tell me why you haven't made a pass at me."

He hesitated. "I suppose I care for you too much to take a chance of spoiling it. I didn't think you'd want to be bothered by a man almost twice your age. And I—I didn't want another rejection."

She continued to stare at him. "How could you think I'd reject you?" She covered his hand with her own. "As for your age, my age, that's for me to decide, Matt. What would you say if I were to tell you that I love you?"

He met her intense gaze with momentary silence. Then he said, "I wouldn't know what to say—except—perhaps—to tell you it made me happy, and—well—to tell you I feel exactly the same way."

She nodded, withdrew her hand, took up her purse, and looked at him again. "I don't want to go back to the Gritti. I want to go to your hotel, Matt." She paused. "Have I shocked you?"

"You—you've made me feel the way I haven't felt in years—young, and hopeful, and in love—in love, Lisa, and alive."

They walked, arms about each other's waists, past the Campanile, past the columns and vaulted windows of the Doge's Palace, over the small bridge, and into the Hotel Danieli. He took his key from the night concierge, and they ascended the red-carpeted steps to the first floor, turned into a narrow passageway, and went up a second staircase to his door.

Neither of them had spoken a word until they were inside his bedroom. Then, breathless, she came into his arms, and as he held her, kissing her hair, her brow, her closed eyelids, he heard her whisper, "I love you."

That was the first day, and the first night of their oneness, and that was the beginning.

Vividly remembering it as he sat on his bed on this, the fourteenth day, he was reluctant to take leave of the happier time that had come before. He ground out the butt of his cigarette, absently drew a fresh one from his pack and lighted it, found it harsh before breakfast, but continued to puff steadily as his mind groped to bring back the wonder of the days with Lisa Collins that had followed their first day together. The days from the past two weeks that he was able to restore were more difficult to separate and relive than had been that first day. There were undated experiences, and isolated snatches of conversation, but for the most these ran together and became a revival of feelings and emotions.

At first there were the places of their shared pleasures, and as one day merged into another, Venice was new to him again. They were in the vast Great Council Chamber of the Doge's Palace, the Palazzo Ducale, staring up at the largest painting in the world, Tintoretto's *Paradise,* covering the back wall. They were in the noisy vegetable market of the Rialto, then in San Giacomo, the oldest church in Venice, translating the Latin inscription, "May the law of the merchants around the temple be fair, the weights just, the contracts honest." They were on the cushions of an elegant gondola at night, gliding along the Grand Canal, as the gondolier's song brought their lips together. They were at a table in the Hotel Danieli's roof restaurant, at night, enjoying their cannelloni alla ligure, their piccata di vitello, their coppa Danieli dessert with its ice cream, fruit, and spun sugar, and they were lost in the enchantment of the twinkling crisscrossing of slow-motion lights on the lagoon below. They were wandering, hand in hand, amid the rustic houses and green fields of Torcello, and spending leisurely hours in Brennan's monastery office on San Lazzaro, and sunning in the sand before his cabana on the Excelsior Lido beach.

In the two weeks past, he had entered into Lisa's world, a world of youth and fashion, a world of precosity and enthusiasm, but mostly a world that hummed and sang with the promise of life ahead. Lisa's world was a whirling kaleidoscope of orange nylon stretch pants and empire bodices and pleated pink skirts and sheer chartreuse peignoirs and plaid shirtwaist dresses, and knit boleros with purple jeans, and gingham shirts with white twill slacks, and dramatic capes and chinchilla jackets and camel's-hair sport coats and brown tweed suits and beaded evening dresses and charm bracelets and alligator bags and alligator shoes. Lisa's world was a pinwheel of knit pullovers with wispy bikini bottoms, and transparent nude-colored nylon bras and lace-trimmed half-slips and sapphire pendants and strands of pearls and custom-made hairpieces and carmine lipstick and seductive perfume. Lisa's world was an animated Brueghel of bicycling and tennis and skiing and surfing and moonlight and jazz records and hamburgers with thick milk shakes and doughnuts and strawberry shortcake and sweet Alexanders and rum-with-anything and sit-ups and bending-and-touching-the-toes and running fast and laughing easily. Lisa's world was a fresh-air heaven that banished tranquilizers and sleeping capsules and energy pills and psychologists and psychoanalysts and old cracked dreams, a heaven that admitted within its realm immediate wisdom and naïveté and anything-is-possible and no-one-can-be-all-bad and spontaneity and High Hopes.

It was a world of abundant todays and infinite tomorrows and so few pasts. It was a special twenty-two-year-old world. It was Lisa's own world. As a stranger to it, Brennan had entered it briefly, been swept up by it briefly, almost believing that he could belong.

It was pleasurable, but it was not easy, at least not for one from an older and devastated planet. Sometimes her exuberance, more often her newness to life, inhibited Brennan. To Lisa, he knew, events, people, usages of his planet, which he had considered modern and contemporary and had grown up with, were ancient or antique. To Lisa, he knew, the Second World War and the Korean action were as unreal as the Revolutionary War; propeller-driven aircraft and early jets were as ridiculous as Montgolfier's balloons; F.D.R. and J.F.K. were as far away as Abe Lincoln; the use of ether by a surgeon's aide was as primitive as the incantations of a witch doctor; step-ins were as funny as bloomers. And Elvis who? Presley? Who was he?

Wanting to be young enough for her, he would guard his speech. Time and time again he would catch himself on the verge of making a reference from his own past, that might emphasize that he was already grown when she was still in her infancy. He found himself omitting the proper names of those who had peopled his past, a President, a statesman, an actress, an athlete, so that these would not date him in her eyes. But not every allusion to his years could be avoided. Once, when he had to tell her of his children, he found it hard to admit that he had a son just graduated from prep school who would be enrolled in college in the fall. He worried that she would calculate their respective ages and realize that she was closer to his son's than to his own, and after that she would have to admit that their relationship was quite absurd. But then, having told her about Ted, his son, he was pleased at how quickly and automatically she allied herself with his own wise years and regarded his son as "a youngster."

She was, he decided, remarkable. Apparently, any sensitivity about the gap of years that separated them was largely his own. Apparently, if she was aware of their differences, she was ready to blame them not on their calendar ages but on their experiences with life, her own life having been relatively sheltered, superficial, lacking in conflict as opposed to his life which had been public, engaged, and savagely damaged.

Yet, no matter. More often than not he could ignore the physical facts. In Lisa's world he was alive and hopeful again. For the first time in years he disliked the waste of sleep and looked forward to companionship with another. He resumed his exercises. He refurbished his wardrobe. He remembered his haircut. He used colognes. He tried to be as erect in posture and vigorous in movement as the young males who visited Venice. He wished that he were more attractive, and wondered what there was about his relic self that pleased her. He had not appraised the external appearance he presented to the world in years, but these days, recollecting fragments of a feature story about him that had been published in the English press two years ago, less, he became conscious of how he looked.

His aspect was that of a benevolent but disenchanted hawk. His shock of dark hair was graying ever so slightly, and a forelock hung over the scowl lines pressed into his tan brow. His angular face had become gaunt, making his brown eyes more deep-set than they used to be, making his straight nose too prominent, making his chin line excessively sharp. Where once his visage had been that of the well-bred gentleman in a shirt advertisement, it had recently acquired a tight thinness and seaminess that made it appear older than its years. Where once the face had been keen, questing, assured, it had been altered to look aloof, remote, sardonically amused. Once, he recalled, his clothes, bearing, physique had been neat, trim, firm. Of late, pre-Lisa, he had become casual, slouching, almost sloppy, and his walk had become lethargic and aimless. In every way, he had surrendered to hopelessness and had ceased trying. His mind, as well as his body, had become soft and flabby. And desperately, he wished that he had met Lisa, as she was now, ten years before, as he was then.

Several times, sunning on a mat before their awninged cabana on the Lido beach, he watched her come out of the water, an Aphrodite rising from the Adriatic, and when she approached, her smooth, taut flesh dripping, he covered himself with a towel or turned on his stomach to try to hide the first gray hairs on his chest, the slight bulge of his belly, the wrinkles and veins of ill-usage and bad times. He rarely fooled her. Lisa startled him with her perception and the directness that grew from it. Once, after lunch on the beach and two drinks, she said with nice exasperation, "Matt, will you please stop trying to hold your stomach in. I love you the way you are. I don't give a damn if you take a hundred pills or entered college the year I was born or if you're only a little bit younger than my parents or if you can't climb steps without panting or if you're only allowed to play doubles. I love you just this way, no other way, and please, please don't Freud us out of existence with any idiotic father-image nonsense. Now, come on, take me back to the Danieli. I want to show you how much I need you."

The nights were the best of their times. In his bed, the blanket thrown back, with only the light of the moon coming through the windows, lying there holding her, caressing her, observing her closed eyes, her parted lips, hearing her breathing against his shoulder, her incoherent murmurings, he would close his own eyes and his ears, and possess her, at last mindless, at last fully alive. In those delicious and wild minutes he was as twenty-two as she was, or she was as old as he was, or they were of no age countable. At the height of those minutes, the memories of Zurich, of Rostov, of Madlock, of the Congressional investigators, of Stefani, of the children, of the photographers and newspapermen and pointing tourists, of deadness, were obliterated. Then no longer was he alien to humanity, but one who belonged and who had the capacity to give and receive pleasure, one who wanted to survive because he had found a reason for living, and if tonight was possible, then tomorrow could be a day of infinite possibility.

She always slept quickly, easily, without remembered dreams. He liked to kiss her eyelids, her soft open lips, her throat hollow, then lie back in one of her outstretched arms, for a while observing her closed eyes, the curve of her nose, the smiling lips. Then, on his back, he would stare into the rays of moonlight, knowing that he was in love and unafraid (except of death) and eager to go on and on. And then, at last, he would slowly sink into sleep, his body satisfied and his mind at peace. But with morning, and the sounds of Venice drifting up from below, he would gradually become conscious of his real position, of the hostile universe beyond this bed and this island, and his mind would become apprehensive and uneasy, and his body tense.

It had been that way last night, before sleeping, and this morning, upon awakening.

The gift of two weeks had not been a gift, after all, but a loan, time borrowed, hope borrowed, and now it was the fourteenth and final day, and the time could not be extended and the hope must be forfeited.

He listened. She was no longer showering. He swung off the bed, dropped his cold cigarette butt into a tray, hitched up his pajama bottoms, and went barefoot to the bottle of Fuiggi water on the table. He poured a glassful. The water felt tepid, but welcome on his dry lips and inside his parched mouth.

In the open doorway to the bathroom, he paused to consider Lisa and enjoy her. She was wearing only a thin lace brassiere and brief pink panties, and she was a perfectly symmetrical picture of femininity as she leaned against the washbasin, head close to the mirror, concentrating on darkening her eyebrows with an eyebrow pencil.

Without looking at him, she said, "You're up, darling. I thought you'd fallen asleep again."

"I've been up all the time," he said, entering the bathroom.

He came behind her and gently kissed the back of her neck, so that involuntarily she squeezed her neck muscles and contracted her shoulders, and she gradually exhaled. She studied him in the mirror. "I love you, darling."

He stroked one bare shoulder. "I love you more, Lisa."

"I bet." She held the eyebrow pencil poised before her brow. "What would you like to do today?"

She knew what day it was then, he thought, and she'd been thinking about it. "Whatever you'd like to do. Let's start with breakfast. Maybe in the Piazza."

"Good." She resumed with her makeup.

He drew the soggy shower curtain across the tub, untied his pajama trousers and let them drop. With one foot he flipped them into the air, caught them, and hung them over his pajama top on the bathroom hook.

He realized that she had stopped again and was watching him in the mirror. He was tempted to suck in his stomach, but he did not bother.

"You're handsome," she said, seriously.

"You're beautiful," he replied, "if somewhat overdressed."

"Silly."

Gingerly he climbed into the wet bathtub, and behind the curtain he took up the hand shower and started the spray. It was warm, and he began adjusting it. He wanted colder water to dash on futile dreams.

180

He heard her: "Matt, what were you doing in there this past hour?"

"Just thinking."

"Of what?"

"Of you."

"Oh, sure. If you were, you wouldn't let me leave Venice alone."

There it was, the beginning of the litany to a special death in Venice. "Honey, to quote myself, if this is meant to be, if we are meant to be, it'll all work out, some way, somehow, in due time." Then, to prevent any more of this, he turned up the shower spray full blast.

Twenty minutes later, shaved, refreshed, dressed in a seersucker sport jacket, open-collar sport shirt, and gray linen slacks, he found her at the window, the metal shutters open. She was moodily staring out at the campanile and dome that crowned the island of San Giorgio Maggiore—Boschini's jewel set in crystal—across the shimmering lagoon.

"How can anyone leave this?" she said quietly, almost to herself.

He was determined to divert her mood. "It doesn't have a chance against you." He turned her around and held her off. She was wearing a pale blue wool-jersey chemise. Sleeveless and low-necked, it revealed her shoulders and unadorned throat.

"What a lovely dress. I don't remember seeing it before."

"I was saving it for an occasion. I guess this is an occasion. The color matches my mood." Then, seeing his gravity, she slipped her arm into his and forced a smile. "Sorry, forgive the vapors, Matt. I'm no good before breakfast. Take me to the pigeons."

Hastily, they left the room, went downstairs in step, and passed through the busy lobby corridor, cordially waving to the head concierge, who was an ally of all lovers of love and Venice.

Emerging into the sunlight of the Riva degli Schiavoni, they both turned away from the sudden glare to grope for their sunglasses. Lisa looked up at the red front of the Hotel Danieli, at the crimson awnings over the miniature white balconies, and she said, "It was a palace once, wasn't it?"

"Yes. Named after Doge Dandalo. He helped supply the Fourth Crusade with men."

"I wish he'd help my crusade with one man." Turning her back to the hotel and with determined practicality, she said, "Don't let me forget my suitcase, Matt."

"The concierge is sending it over to the Gritti by porter."

"Oh. Then this is it. Okay. Let's eat."

They traversed the bridge, hearing the noon cannon go off behind the Doge's Palace, and strolled along the waterfront promenade, brushing against a curling breeze. Circling between the two granite columns of the Piazzetta, pushing through dense crowds, they attained the shaded area between the San Marco arcade and the towering Campanile, and without pausing, quite naturally, they headed for the Café Florian.

Seated at their outdoor table, they picked at their light breakfasts in silence. When this had happened two days ago, Lisa had wondered how they, unlike most other couples, could spend such protracted periods without conversation. Brennan had meant to say to her then, "Well, perhaps because we have less to talk about than other people, Lisa. We have only the past and the present. We don't have the future." He had not said it, because it had an overly sentimental ring to his ear, and besides, it simply was not his style. And he did not say it now, whether she wondered about their silences or not.

But after the late breakfast, and their first good cigarettes, they were once more in a mood to talk. He had forgotten her schedule of activity in Paris, and he asked her about that. Her New York fashion associates from the House of Fernald would be arriving at the Plaza-Athénée tomorrow, and she would be there to meet and confer with them. On Monday the new fall showings of the French couturiers would begin, with their accompanying cocktail parties, and she would be on the merry-go-round for two weeks. A month ago this promise of excitement had filled her every waking hour. Now the promise was an empty one, and the prospect of being alone in New York was hateful. What would Matt do after she left?

He did not dare tell her the truth, since he foresaw that his relapse into the old pit of despair would be deeper. He could not allow her to feel that their encounter had been futile. And so he acted out the role of the inspired swain. He would, he told her, be more ambitious, more determined about conquering those new languages and pursuing the position with the import-export firm in Genoa. And simultaneously, motivated by her, he would make another effort to clear his name. He would, he promised, vigorously renew his search for Nikolai Rostov and the evidence that would be proof of his loyalty. If he succeeded— well, Lisa would hear from him.

It had rung false, his playlet, and he knew it and knew that she knew it, but both submitted to acceptance of the pretense of a future together. Seeking safer ground, he changed the subject.

"What time does the Simplon Orient leave tonight?" he asked.

"Eight-thirty."

"Well, that means you'd better start for the depot about seven-thirty. Are you packed?"

"I haven't seen my room in days. I'm sure it's a complete mess."

"Then you'll need a couple of hours for that." He consulted his wristwatch. "It's two-fifteen. I should get you back to the Gritti by five-fifteen, no later. Well, Lisa, we have three hours. My house is your house, as the Spaniards put it. What do you say?"

"Not Venice," she said. "Not today." For several moments she was lost in thought. At last she considered him with a wistful half-smile, which she had unconsciously borrowed from him, and which replaced the buoyancy of her former smile. "Maybe the beach, Matt. Would you like that? Just sun and air and water."

"Perfect. Let's go."

They started back to the Danieli to take the hotel *motoscafo* to the Excelsior Palace across the way, but then Lisa decided that it would be more fun to travel—as she liked to describe it—"peasant." They continued on to the San Zaccaria station, and when the *vaporetto* arrived, they stepped aboard and located a free wooden bench next to the railing.

The water bus chugged and wallowed across the lagoon, and after two stops the ancient boat overflowed with camera-laden tourists and chattering Italians with their rambunctious, squalling offspring. A half hour later they reached the bobbing station behind the Casino, and with the dozens of others, they disembarked on the island of the Lido. Hand in hand they climbed from the dock to the street, and breathless, they strode along the Lungomare Marconi, halting only once under the cool arcade so that Lisa could admire silk prints in the show window of the Emilio Pucci dress shop.

Presently, inside the Excelsior Palace Hotel, where the concierges and management personnel on either side greeted Signor Brennan as one of them, they hastened through the immense lobby and out onto the open-air terrace. Seen like this from above, the rows of colorful tented cabanas stretched out like the wings of a giant bird that had settled over the yellow sand. Before them, the blue-green expanse of the Adriatic lay like a luxurious carpet, leading to mysterious and exotic lands that hid beyond the indelible border of the distant horizon.

They descended the broad hotel staircase to the beach, and strolled along the narrow walk behind the cabanas, ignoring the diners still at lunch in the dim recesses of the outdoor beach restaurant. They hastened past plump Italian girls in ruffled bikinis, and elderly Italian businessmen in jock swim trunks. Then, at the rear of Cabana 67, they stepped off into the sand and trudged to the front of their tent. While Lisa went inside to change, Brennan ordered towels and two Camparis. After that, he waited in the sand, his drawn face lifted to the sun, absorbing its heat, wishing the solar disk could drain him of the accumulated poison of so many years, wishing it could give him youth and a fresh start.

When Lisa emerged, and he saw her, his heart ached. In her two-piece, low-backed navy blue swimsuit, the bra held in place by thin bands around her neck and ribs, the side-slit bottoms buttoned up each hip, she was tall and as graceful as a goddess. But no, not a goddess, he thought, watching the feline movements of her muscles beneath the smooth flesh as she removed sunglasses, watch, and beach sandals. The silky texture of her skin, he imagined, was similar to that of Phryne of Thespiae, the courtesan so admired by all Athenians and at last possessed by Praxiteles. Like Phryne, his Lisa of Venice was essentially modest, both in her public appearances and in private love-making (for like Phryne, his Lisa would make love only in darkness). But then, just as Phryne had appeared annually at the Eleusinian festival, stripping off her robes in the portico of the temple to walk in nudity to the sea and pay homage to the gods, his Lisa now walked in nudity (at least in his eyes) to the sea to celebrate the last of their summer's love.

He wanted her for eternity, and under the spell of love he was tempted to cry out for her not to leave, to forsake all others and remain with him in Venice forever, and he knew that she would happily do so, just as he knew that in the end, in the years ahead, it would be ruinous to their love.

"See you in the water, Matt," she called, her features again vivacious and alive.

"See you in a minute," he replied.

Briefly he watched her lope through the sand. With a sigh he turned away, entering the darkness of the cabana, again alone, the spell broken. He had survived his weakness but was left with only regret.

After that it was, at least for the time that they were in the mild sea, great fun. He waded far out before the water reached his armpits. He swam in strong overhand strokes to meet her, and they gamboled in the water, racing each other to the jetty, then wrestling, then kissing beneath the sea. They trapped a floating striped ball, and played catch, and then they swam again.

Finally, exhausted, they returned to the cabana and slumped in their beach chairs, drying in the blaze of sun, as they sipped their Camparis.

It was Lisa who sat up first. "Matt, how much time do we have left?"

He found his watch in a shoe. "Better than an hour."

"Let's go to San Lazzaro. That's what I'd most like to remember."

They dressed hurriedly, and within fifteen minutes they had crossed through the underground corridors of the hotel, come out on the rear wharf, and hired a private motorboat to take them to his island.

They sat at the back of the low-slung motorboat so that they could enjoy the spray and the wind. As the boat's sharp prow cut through the waters of the lagoon, Lisa lay back in Brennan's arm, nestled close to him, and she pressed even closer when the waves of a passing craft made their own craft bounce and roll.

When they had covered about a third of the distance from the Lido to Venice, Brennan peered ahead and was able to define the tiny island of San Lazzaro, his island, his special refuge, but then not his alone. Another Western expatriate, driven from his homeland by scandal just as Brennan had been driven, had discovered the virtues of San Lazzaro a century and a half before him. "A small island situated in the midst of a tranquil lake," Lord Byron had noted, and, from Venice, had written to his friend Moore, "In the mornings I go over in my gondola to hobble Armenian with the friars of the Convent of St. Lazarus."

Actually, it was Lord Byron who had guided Brennan to this island hideout. Like so many men who were thinkers, not doers, Brennan had always been fascinated by literate men of action, intellectuals like himself who also possessed the traits of daring and boldness, and had preferred personal adventure to armchair adventure.

Byron's reckless activities had always enchanted Brennan, just as the lives of Sir Richard Burton (the subject of one of his own favorite college term papers), François Villon, and Giacomo Casanova had always intrigued him. In fact, it had been their mutual interest in the intellectual and creator as man of action that had drawn Brennan and Nikolai Rostov into an even closer friendship at the Zurich Parley.

Rostov had been Brennan's counterpart on the staff of the Russian delegation. Both had been students of peace, experts on disarmament, and both had fought (Rostov especially well, since his training had included intensive courses on the Far East) to convince the Communist delegates from the People's Republic of China that their nation must be prepared to junk its hard-earned nuclear arsenal totally if it was to enjoy membership in a peaceful world community of nations.

During many of their evenings together, as if to escape the grim and frustrating afternoon diplomatic discussions about pacifism, Brennan and Rostov had sat for hours in the Cabaret Voltaire or the Bierrestaurant Kropf evaluating the madcap and daredevil lives of their historical favorites. In fact, Rostov's interest in, if not his knowledge of, Lord Byron and Sir Richard Burton was greater than Brennan's, for Rostov's avocation was collecting rare books and manuscripts, and his collection on Burton, an Orientalist like himself, was substantial. It had unsettled Brennan, upon his first visit to the San Lazzaro library, to find a rare set of Sir Richard Burton's books—some of them erotic volumes, all of them autographed by Burton—the collection the gift of a millionaire Egyptian. It had unsettled Brennan because he had arrived on this isolated Armenian isle as a result, he then suspected, of Rostov's treachery (or, at the very least, Rostov's inhuman desertion of their friendship). And the first hosts on this island had been the shades of Byron and Burton, the very ghosts who had introduced Brennan to Rostov in a city on the neutral island of Switzerland.

Resenting the intrusion of Rostov upon the memory of his island, and on this day, Brennan pushed the Russian from his mind and devoted himself to San Lazzaro, unsullied and his own. Watching the small campanile, the monastery, the waterfront garden loom in his vision, he held Lisa close and he tried to remember.

After the Congressional hearing, the divorce, the joblessness, the disgrace, the despair of righteous wrath, he had fled to Europe. He had wandered without purpose, until in Venice, feeling less oppressed than anywhere else, he had stayed on, meaning to remain only three weeks or three months, yet somehow remaining three years. Perusing the history of the quaint city, he had had his reunion with Lord Byron, and unexpectedly had learned of the poet's association with San Lazzaro. And so, for want of anything better to do, Brennan had paid a visit to the Armenian island.

For him it had been love at first sight. The groves of olive trees and rows of cypresses, the quiet and contentment of the out-of-the-way haven, had enchanted him and permanently won his troubled mind and heart. Above all, his appreciation of the unobtrusive, kindly, yet urbane and worldly Mechitar fathers and the lay brothers had been reciprocated. They welcomed his intellect and understood his agony. Based on mutual esteem, their fraternity became a lasting one.

From the abbot himself, after a few months, had come the invitation for Brennan to make San Lazzaro his home away from home, and to accept the privileges of an upstairs office for his studies, a room from which could be seen the distant needle of the Campanile of San Marco. With alacrity Brennan had accepted the invitation. In the years since, although living in Venice, he had spent most of his afternoons on San Lazzaro, sometimes working, more often brooding about his fate.

Suddenly he realized that Lisa had moved out of the circle of his arm. "Here we are," she said.

He rose, waited for the pilot to secure the motorboat to the wharf, and then he helped Lisa out of the boat and asked the pilot to stand by.

In the serene garden overlooking the lagoon, Lisa squeezed his hand. "I'm glad we came," she said.

For a full minute Brennan stood silent, inhaling the fresh air with its fragrance unique to San Lazzaro—a combination of scents that came from the green lagoon water, the rose petals, the cypress trees—and he studied the cool monastery walls. Two and a half centuries ago, he remembered, San Lazzaro had been a flat, uninhabited tract of land that lay in the lagoon between the Doge's principal island and the Lido island. It had held no interest for Venetians. When the Turkish armies swept across Armenia in 1715, the Abbot Peter Mechitar, leader of a sect of fathers whose religion was Roman Catholic but whose church rites were Oriental, fled with his followers to independent Venice. There they were given asylum, and soon they were given the deserted tract that was San Lazzaro. On this private island Mechitar established a Little Armenia with Venetian overtones, building a monastery, a chapel, a school, a library, and installing a printing press, creating on the barren tract one of the last surviving centers for Armenian scholarship and a miniature utopia for those with a contemplative bent.

Where Brennan stood now with Lisa, Lord Byron had often stood following his arrival on the island in the autumn of 1816. "By way of divertissement," Byron had written Moore, "I am studying daily, at an Armenian monastery, the Armenian language. I found that my mind wanted something craggy to break upon. . . ." Regularly, Byron had toiled in the library of the monastery, but at last found the language "obdurate" with a "Waterloo of an alphabet." And in the end what this island had given the poet, Brennan realized, was what it had provided for Brennan himself, a brief respite from the turbulence of the hostile world outside.

Taking Lisa by the arm, Brennan led her into the monastery, and along the refreshing cloistered walk from which, between the columns, they could see the cassocked friars in the verdant and colorful garden court. For a half hour they retraced old steps, uninterrupted by the discreet monks. They paused in the chapel, looked in on the multilingual printing room, and examined Canova's plaster cast of L'Aiglon. Climbing upstairs, they wandered through the museum, grinning back at the grinning Egyptian mummy, and trying to read the letter from Longfellow. They lingered in Byron's library, once more inspecting the Armenian grammar on which His Lordship had collaborated. Following this, they visited Brennan's cubicle nearby, holding hands before his desk filled with pencils, yellow legal-sized pads, and dictionaries of Eastern languages.

Presently they sat together on a bench beside a cedar of Lebanon in the garden of the central building. A tall, clean-shaven father, carrying a breviary and a bouquet of roses, passed them, and benignly greeted both Brennan and Lisa by name, and prudently went his way.

Lisa's eyes followed the father. She turned back to Brennan. "What must they think of me always here with you? Those poor virtuous monks, watching us kiss or hold hands."

"They think you're a young niece, young and incestuous."

"Oh, Matt, really!"

"They're highly sophisticated, tolerant of man's foibles and weaknesses. Look how they accepted me, despite my public record. And now they accept us both. They are wise enough to know that God's charity also embraces sinners. They overlooked Byron's private life when he came here. It was the juiciest gossip in the cafés of the Piazza. Did you know that, at the very time Byron was working here, he was having an affair with another man's wife in Venice?"

"You're teasing me."

"It's a fact. You'll find a play-by-play account in many of his letters to friends. There was, as Byron put it, 'a Merchant of Venice' who had a twenty-two-year-old wife named Marianna—"

"Twenty-two? Now I know you're teasing."

"I swear. How did he describe her? Let me see if I can remember. Yes—'She has the large, black, oriental eyes, with that peculiar expression' that was too much for Byron. Let me see, yes—'Her features are regular, rather aquiline, mouth small, skin clear and soft, with a kind of hectic color'—I love that 'hectic color'—and 'her hair is of the dark gloss, curl, and color of Lady J' and something about her figure, yes—'light and pretty.' An early version of you, Lisa."

"Thank you."

"So while Signor Segati, the cuckolded merchant, worked, his wife played. Byron became her *cavalier servente,* and Marianna became his *amorosa.* And the good Holy Fathers on San Lazzaro knew it and did not mind." Absently Brennan plucked a blade of grass and smoothed it between his fingers. "Those were romantic times."

"Is it different now?"

He stared at her. "No—I suppose not, Lisa."

Meeting his gaze frankly, she said, "Why do we have to end it, Matt? If you really love me—"

"You know I love you."

"Then come home with me. All that disgrace of yours—the messy business—it's old hat, forgotten by everyone but you. We can make a fresh start—"

"It's not forgotten, Lisa. It's been revived by that Summit conference in Paris. Just the other day—I didn't bother to tell you—there was a roundup feature in the Rome *Daily American*—a wire story published everywhere—and there was my name, the whole messy business, as you call it, not forgotten but revived—a complete calendar of the events leading to Red China's getting the neutron bomb and rocketry, and menacing peace, and leading to this Summit—and among the events listed was our Government's irresponsible assignment of a leftist and poor security risk, namely Matthew Brennan, to go to Zurich where he encouraged one of our foremost nuclear physicists, Professor Varney, to defect to China and help the so-called enemy build that neutron bomb. And you say it's forgotten, Lisa?"

"But, Matt—"

"Let me work this out in my own way," he said brusquely, and then he stood up. "Come, I've got to get you back."

Fifteen minutes later, having been transported by their motorboat across the San Marco Basin and up a short distance of the Grand Canal, they docked before the Gritti Palace Hotel. San Lazzaro had already receded into a dim dream.

He saw her to the lobby entrance. "I'll say good-bye here, Lisa."

Resigned, she merely nodded.

"I—I've got to be at the hotel when my son comes by."

She touched his sleeve. "I'm sorry to be difficult. Of course, you must. I know meeting him must be on your mind, too. I wish I could help you with that."

"I'll manage somehow."

She was reluctant to leave him. "Will he be unsociable?"

"Ted?" He shrugged. "I can't say. Seventeen is a tough age to handle at best. I don't know how angry he is with me, or how he regards me now. I haven't seen him in a long time. And I don't write much any more, because his answers are always short and, well, rather stiff, you know, duty letters." He forced his half-smile. "It may be, at worst, a bit awkward. But it's rather important to me. Don't you worry about it."

"I worry about *you*," she said. Then she added, "You don't have to rush the meeting with your son to see me off. I'll understand. Just call me in Paris, and—and write sometimes."

"Ted and I are having an early dinner, and it may be a very quick one. If it is, I'll be here by seven-thirty to take you to the station. If I can't get away, well, I'll call you in Paris tomorrow."

She leaned forward, kissed him on the lips. Eyes filling, she whispered. "I'll love you forever." With that, she turned and disappeared into the hotel.

Matt Brennan stood there feeling lost and depressed, and at last he slowly returned to the waiting motorboat and ordered the pilot to take him to the Danieli.

Once in the Danieli lobby, he had started for the staircase when he remembered that he did not have his key. Returning to the concierge's desk, he held out his hand for his key, and received with it a folded slip of paper.

As he moved to the staircase, he opened the slip of paper. It was a telephone message: "Mr. Shepperd called at approx. 17:00. He will be waiting at the Hotel de la Gare Germania. The number is 26489."

For a moment, his mind still on Lisa, he was unable to place the unfamiliar name. Shepperd? Did he know anyone named—and at once it struck him, and he felt a constriction in his chest. It was a name he had seen twice before, above his son's return address on letters mailed from Boston. Shepperd was Steffi's new husband, and Ted's stepfather.

Resentment suffocated him as he climbed the staircase. Ted was still his son, his legal son, his only son born of his flesh and blood. His son was Ted Brennan, no other. Yet recently, and now again, the boy had been rebellious enough, insensitive and cruel enough, to pass himself off as Ted Shepperd to his own father.

This was the mark of Steffi, Brennan thought, and his anger abated. Most likely it was not Ted who was ashamed of his real name, but Steffi alone who had dictated the change. Was she capable, still, of such malice? Or—another thought—was she protecting their son with this new surname, trying to give him an easier time in college, to save him from the burden of explaining and hating the name of Brennan?

In any case, it was a bad prelude to this crucial reunion, he decided, entering his room. He turned up the lights, half expecting that Lisa would be waiting to console him, but Lisa was not there. He paced restlessly, thinking about the son named Shepperd, whom he was soon to meet. The boy had been hurt by the notoriety surrounding the family, Brennan knew, but he had been only thirteen, not quite fourteen, and certainly the separation and divorce had hurt him more, at least at the time. While Steffi had remarried, and yes, Shepperded his son and his little girl into the respectable home and life of a Boston widower and physician, Brennan had fled abroad. He knew that he had, in a sense, forfeited his children.

He had been back to the United States only twice in these past three years, both times on job prospects that did not develop favorably, and both times, briefly, he had seen his son, as well as his daughter Tracy, who were brought by a governess, to New York for a single day. The last time he had seen Ted was—well, it must have been a year and a half ago, and the little girl Tracy, suffering a cold, had been kept busy in his hotel room with numerous gifts, while he and Ted had spent the chilly afternoon at a baseball game. The boy had been uncomfortable, and so had he, but they had retained enough of their old father-and-son relationship to save the afternoon, which had been filled with home runs, hot dogs, Ted's stories about his high school experiences and favorite television serials, and Brennan's own colored accounts of his adventures in Italy. It had not been too bad, actually quite good, but after all, Ted had been merely a callow fifteen and Shepperd still a stranger to him, and his father had appeared more as a fascinating wanderer than a fleeing traitor. Now, at college age, it was Ted Shepperd, because now the identity thing was everything, and now, at last, Ted *knew*.

The letter in Brennan's box, three weeks ago, had been unexpected. It had contained three paragraphs, which were stylistically restrained and formal. Ted had graduated from prep school in the upper tenth of his class. He had been accepted by Yale and would enter there in the fall. He had thanked his father for the gold Swiss watch and check. Mother's graduation gift had been a trip to Europe for six weeks. Ted and two friends would be in Venice on June fourteenth for one day. "If you are there, I would leave time to see you."

Brennan had written his son at once, a long, enthusiastic letter, congratulating him on his graduation, on his acceptance by Yale. He had suggested sites and cities that Ted and his friends might be interested in visiting during their trip. And yes, of course, Venice, definitely yes, he would be in Venice, eager to see his son. "Let's plan on having dinner together, Ted. I look forward to it."

And now Ted Shepperd had arrived.

Brennan felt weakened by the day past and the day ahead. The last of Lisa had been manfully faced. Now the last of Ted, or perhaps a new start with Ted, must be faced.

With effort Brennan went to the bed, sat down and lifted the receiver. He requested that the operator get him 26489. Nervously he waited, heard the buzzing, heard the female voice at the other end say, "Hotel de la Gare Germania." He asked for Mr. Ted Shepperd, and again he waited.

The male voice was low, cautious, and unfamiliar. Was this Ted or one of his friends?

"Hello," said Brennan, "is Ted there?" No concessions to Shepperd now, he had decided.

"This is Ted." The voice had become strained.

"Welcome to Venice, son. This is your father."

There was the briefest pause. "Hi, how are you?"

"Wonderful to hear your voice, and to have you here. When did you get in?"

"Uh—last night—we parked the car outside the city, and took one of those crazy boats."

"Have you had a chance to look around?"

"Yes. We got up early and spent the whole day walking. I think we covered nearly everything."

"I hope you liked it. Perhaps I can show you and your friends something you may have missed? When are you leaving?"

"Well, very early in the morning."

"I wish I could persuade you to stay a day or two longer. Not only because I'd love to spend more time with you, but because there's really a lot to do here."

"Thanks. I'm afraid we've got to push on. We want to give some extra time to Florence and Rome, and go to Capri. I think we've about had Venice."

"I'm sorry," Brennan said. "But I know you have your plans. We're set for dinner, aren't we?"

"Yes."

"Any preferences? Any restaurants you've read about?"

"No."

"Will your friends be joining us?"

"No. I—uh—it'll be just me. They're eating with a couple of American girls we bumped into this morning in St. Mark's."

"Will you be free after dinner?"

There was a pause, and then Ted spoke, voice catching in his throat. "Uh—actually—there are three of those American girls—they're on a tour, and they've shaken the tour for the night—so, I sort of promised to catch up with them."

"Good. I'm glad you're getting some action." Brennan realized that his hand on the receiver was clammy. "Okay, I suggest we dine early, so you'll have plenty of time left. There are any number of good restaurants here. Let me think." Actually, he had given it some thought earlier. "I think I have just the place. Ever hear of Harry's Bar?"

"Of course. Hemingway."

"That's right, that's the one. Marvelous atmosphere. About the best food in Europe. You'll like it. Should we make it Harry's?"

"Whatever you say."

"It's Harry's by a unanimous vote. Where's your hotel?"

"Across from the railroad station."

"I'll get a motorboat and pick you up in twenty minutes."

192

"That's not necessary," Ted said quickly. "I can meet you where we're eating."

"You're sure you can find it?"

"I'll find it all right."

"It's at the end of the Calle Vallaresso, going to the Canal. On the corner. You can take a *vaporetto*."

"Yes."

"Shall we say around six o'clock?"

"I'll be there. I'll leave now."

"Okay. Meet you in front of the entrance."

Hanging up, Brennan realized that his moist hands were trembling. He wanted to see his son, wanted to speak to him, yet at this moment he would have given anything if the boy had not come to Venice. The reunion would be more strained than he had anticipated. The boy was definitely hostile, offering nothing, no interest in him, in them, no warmth, only forced respect. How hastily Ted had rejected the idea of being picked up. Was it because he dreaded being alone with his father, because of shame of him or resentment toward him, and therefore he had automatically narrowed filial duty down to a meeting in a public place?

Instinctively Brennan was relieved that the dinner would be of short duration, and that Ted was otherwise occupied afterwards—if there really were those American girls. But thinking about it, Brennan suddenly wished that he and Ted might have more time, much more time, so that he could know his son again and his son could know him. He wanted Ted to understand him fully, now that the boy had reached an age for understanding. He wanted Ted to know the truth, not the Steffi-truth or the newspaper-truth, but the real truth, so that Ted could leave Venice with real regard for his father and forever after observe the fifth Commandment.

But now it was too late.

Then, remembering that Ted would already be on his way, Brennan took up the telephone and called down to the concierge. He asked the concierge to ring up Harry's Bar, speak to the proprietor personally, and explain to him that Brennan and his son would arrive there for dinner very shortly, and that they'd prefer one of the two corner tables downstairs, or else one at the far end of the room.

After that, Brennan quickly exchanged his sport shirt for a solid blue button-down shirt and a narrow dark-blue knit tie. Yanking on his tweed jacket, making sure that his wallet was in place, he hastened out of his room and down the hotel corridor and lobby.

In long strides Brennan went past the Piazzetta, continued on along the Canal past the novelty stalls before the Gardinetti, past the comic-opera air terminal, elbowing his way through the traffic being disgorged from ferries at the San Marco station. Reaching the corner, hesitant, wanting to turn back, he broke his stride and faltered, but finally he willed himself to turn the corner.

Ted was there, leaning against the wall beside the entrance, hands stuck in his pockets, as he observed the stream of foot traffic.

As yet unseen, Brennan was able to take a careful look at his son, and what he saw startled him, and gave him hope and commitment. Those forty-eight chromosomes of eighteen years ago had been faithful, Brennan could see. The boy was, like it or not, his father's son. This was Matt himself at seventeen, with hair the same color, although Ted's was close-cropped, with the same gaunt, serious countenance, although occupied by several adolescent pimples, and the same skinny slouching sharp-boned frame. And now, by coincidence or by heredity, the fresh drip-dry shirt with the button-down collar, narrow knit tie, tweed sport coat.

Spirits lifting, Brennan advanced toward his son. "Glad you made it, Ted. Sorry to be late."

The boy turned, snapping erect, and was almost as tall as Brennan. With consternation, his head bobbing, mouth unsmiling, he dumbly accepted his father's short handshake.

"I see you had no trouble finding it," Brennan said. "You're looking great, Ted. You've really grown up since I last saw you."

"Thanks," said Ted. Swallowing, he added, "You're looking good, too."

"Well, Venice—" Brennan said vaguely. He gripped his son's arm. "Let's sit down."

He guided Ted toward the swinging doors, pushed one open, and followed his son into Harry's Bar.

Brennan surveyed the room. Except for the bar beside them—the ten stools occupied by Italian, English, and American customers thirstily imbibing gin fizzes and dry martinis and nibbling at the hot toasted prosciutto sandwiches—the ground floor of the restaurant was relatively empty. At a later hour the place would be a smoke-filled madhouse of wealthy tourists, celebrated actors and actresses, authors, Italian aristocrats, and fading contessas with their eager, natty, effeminate young male escorts. But now, except for a few couples scattered about the room, most of the tables were unoccupied, and Brennan was grateful. He would have some degree of privacy with his son.

He nudged Ted and pointed to the left, to a framed photograph on the wall, near the bar's cash register. "That's a signed picture of Ernest

Hemingway with Giuseppe Cipriani, the Italian who opened this place, taken around 1931, I think. They were great friends, Hemingway and Cipriani."

Ted was peering at the photograph with genuine awe, and Brennan was pleased.

"Do you know why Giuseppe Cipriani named this place Harry's Bar?"

"No."

"Cipriani was a plain bartender, and a rich American from Boston, Harry Pickering, took a liking to Cipriani and lent him the money to start a restaurant and bar of his own. So Cipriani showed his appreciation by naming his place after his patron. Celebrities of every stripe have come here. I'm told that once, in the good old days, four different monarchs ate here at the same time in a single evening, each at a different table. There were other regulars like Winston Churchill and—wait, they're signaling us. We'd better claim our table."

As they made their way past the bar, the bartender and his assistant waved cordially to Brennan, and he waved cheerfully back. Then the proprietor materialized, beaming, pumping Brennan's hand, and displayed his pleasure at being introduced to Brennan's son. At the corner table, two effusive Italian waiters greeted Brennan with familiarity, and were also pleased to meet his son.

Sitting, watching his son out of the corner of an eye, Brennan sensed that their reception could not have been more effective had he staged it. Bewilderment was clearly evident in Ted's face, and Brennan guessed at the source of the boy's confusion. Ted had arrived here, driven by the guilts of duty, to meet reluctantly with a parent who had been branded a latter-day Benedict Arnold. He had expected, perhaps, to find a disgraced, cringing, ostracized traitor; yet in this public place, a stunned Ted had found his parent enthusiastically welcomed, highly respected, openly admired.

The waiter, toothlessly grinning down at father and son, said, "You celebrate tonight?"

Brennan nodded. "Do you drink, Ted?"

"Not legally. But—I wouldn't mind something."

"Well, I don't want to corrupt you entirely. I'd suggest a Bellini. Specialty of the house. Peach juice and champagne. Okay?"

"Sure."

"One Bellini," Brennan said to the waiter. "And I'll have the usual. After that, we'll eat. My son's got to make a date."

They discussed the menu, or rather Brennan did, with Ted responding in monosyllables, and when the drinks were served, Brennan was prepared to order their dinner. Having convinced Ted that Harry's open-faced hamburger, served on round slices of toasted bread, was the best in the world, he ordered this for his son but took the calf's liver and onions for himself, with two servings of cannelloni from the list of *Farinacei* to start them off.

They were alone, at last. Ted sampled his peach juice and champagne without interest, then stared down at it uncomfortably. Brennan had finished his Scotch-and-water in three swallows, praying alcohol would help him, and, to be certain, he called out for a refill.

Looking at the top of his son's head, he braced himself. There had to be communication, somehow. "How's your mother?" he inquired.

Ted brought his head up, but avoided his father's eyes. "She's—well, she's okay, I guess. She's been seeing some specialists. They think it's bronchitis. Uh—right now she's in—in Hawaii, for a rest. She took Tracy with her."

"And Tracy? How is she?"

"As usual. Noisy. She wasn't doing well in geography, so Mother got her a tutor. Oh, yeah—I almost forgot—she said for me to thank you for that birthday present."

"Yes, I had a cute note from her. She writes well for a twelve-year-old."

"I guess so. I get letters from her at every American Express. She keeps bitching about being in Hawaii."

"Why?"

"She wanted to come to Europe with me."

"Well, you remember to kiss her for me when you're back home. Don't forget, Ted."

"I won't."

"Now, you. I've been waiting for this—for our meeting—for a long time. I want to hear all about you."

Ted glanced at him suspiciously, then averted his eyes. "Well, I don't know if there's much worth hearing about. There's nothing special, not really."

Brennan had emptied his highball glass and motioned to the waiter for a third drink. He returned his attention to his son. "I only meant that I'd like to know what you've been up to. It's hard to learn much from letters. I'm curious about what interests you these days, in school, out of school, your sports, hobbies, the kind of friends you have, the girls you see. And Yale—I'd like to know what you're going to major in, that kind of thing. And this trip. Exactly where have you been, what have you seen, and how about the rest of your itinerary?"

"Well, I don't know. Let me see . . ." His voice had faded out, and he seemed reluctant to speak.

"Where did the trip start?"

"We came across on the S.S. *France*—second-class."

"How was that?"

"It swings."

"Then where?"

"London. We picked up the car, a Peugeot, in Amsterdam, then we began driving . . ."

He went on, haltingly, sparingly, colorlessly, as if not wishing to share his summer's vacation with his father. In a few minutes, Brennan had both his third drink and the end of his son's grudging recital. To their mutual relief, the cannelloni materialized. Desperately, Ted gave himself to the *pasta,* while Brennan ignored his own, and devoted himself to the Scotch and a persistent observation of his troubled child.

When the cannelloni dishes were removed, Brennan had a fourth drink and a renewed determination to make some meaningful contact with this boy. He resumed with specific questions about Ted's schooling and social life back home, and Ted continued to respond with his laconic replies. The hamburger sandwich and the calf's liver appeared, and rapidly disappeared in the expanding silence, and still the chasm that separated them had not been bridged.

With despair, after ordering a chocolate mousse for his son and another Scotch for himself, Brennan decided to make one last effort. Perhaps candor would shock the boy out of his determined withdrawal.

After they had not exchanged a word for a full minute, Brennan suddenly sat up straight and said, "Ted, let me ask you something, quite frankly. You seem to be here under some kind of duress. You don't seem to be interested in me the least bit, and you seem even less interested in letting me know a damn thing about yourself. That's an odd condition for a father and son. So, okay, tell me—why in the devil did you bother to come to Venice and see me at all?"

Taken aback, Ted blinked at him across the table. "Why I came?" he asked, confused.

"Yes. Why are you here? Did your mother tell you to stop in Venice to see me?"

"Mother?" This was emphatic. "She doesn't even know I'm here."

"Does Tracy know?"

"Not exactly." He thought about it. "Well, I guess maybe she does. It came up between us. She wanted to know if I was going to see you, because if I was, she wanted to, too."

Tracy had wanted to see him. Ah, Brennan thought, little girls and their fathers, the surest faith and love of all. But Tracy was a digression. The primary subject here was Ted, and Ted had not yet answered the question. Brennan decided to ask it once more. "All right, Ted, but you still haven't told me why you are here. Why?"

Ted's confusion had given way to discomfort. He shifted in his seat, and began to ball up his napkin. "I guess I felt that—that I should—" Brennan interrupted. "You mean, you felt it was your duty?"

"I wanted to see you."

"Wanted to," Brennan repeated. He wondered if the expression of desire had been spontaneous or was an effort to appease, to mouth what was expected of him. Brennan felt sorry for the boy, was ready to relent, yet, somehow, it was important to solve this mystery. "You wanted to see me. But you don't know why. Was it nostalgia for remembrances of a father? Was it naked curiosity? That is, Can my father be the ogre everyone says he is? Or was it the need to see for yourself that your father is exactly what you've been led, by others, to think that he is—and after confirming this, you could leave here with no more guilts, free at last to relegate me to the skeleton in the closet, and transfer any filial relationship to your stepfather?" He paused, unhappily watching his son twist the napkin. Brennan frowned. "Does any of that make sense?"

"I—I don't know." Ted glanced up. "I really don't."

"Okay. Let's forget it." He clutched his highball glass. "Is there anything else you'd like to order?"

"I'd like to go to the bathroom."

Brennan pointed toward the cloakroom alcove. "That way."

Ted bumped the table, sliding out of his place. He went quickly, gawkily, out of the room.

Brennan surveyed the restaurant. It was becoming filled, and the bar, as ever, was crowded. Beyond the bar, above the swinging doors, he could see that the day was graying, readying for darkness. He looked at his wristwatch. The dial showed him ten minutes after seven. There was little time left for anything more, if, indeed, there was anything more to be said. He had tried for his moments of truth, and learned nothing of the boy, although his son might have learned something of him. As for small talk, there was no more of that left. But truth still remained the uncharted area. Perhaps he should make a final desperate attempt to give truth some definition, or else make his peace with the loss of a son forever.

He drank slowly, and the taste and fumes of the Scotch were behind his eyes and in his brain, only mildly dizzying, yet liberating him from inhibition and clarifying his feelings. He wanted Ted as son. He wanted his son's esteem. Perhaps it was too late to win either, but, win or lose, he wanted his truth in the open, this once.

Impatiently he waited, wondering why Ted was taking so long, what Ted was thinking, how Ted would react after returning, if he did return.

He saw Ted edging sideways between the tables. When he looked up, Ted was standing, making no effort to resume his seat.

"I—I just looked at—at the clock," Ted stammered. "I guess maybe I sh-should take off."

"In a few minutes," said Brennan firmly. "Sit down."

Surprised, the boy resumed his place on the other side of the table, slowly lowering himself into his chair, where he sat tentatively, his pimply features apprehensive.

Brennan pushed aside his glass and folded his hands, one over the other, on the table. He looked directly at his son. "I'll let you go shortly, Ted, but I won't let you go without the truth."

"What do you mean?"

"The truth about your father, whatever it's worth to you, but the truth, take it or leave it."

Ted blinked, but remained silent.

"When the crisis happened, you were too young to understand it," Brennan said. "You were—what?—not yet fourteen. Now you're going on eighteen. Now I can speak to you as one adult to another."

Ted squirmed. "You don't have to. I know—"

"You know nothing." Brennan had raised his voice and several persons at a nearby table looked up. Brennan sought control and, finding it, resumed in an urgent, low-pitched tone. "All you think you know comes from questionable sources—your mother, whose judgment was prejudiced by personal considerations, or from your friends, whose opinions come from parents who had no access to the evidence, or from your reading of rehashes in the press and history books. All your knowledge, from those sources, adds up to a belief that you are the son of a traitor, a turncoat, a spy, a man who betrayed his country. All you know, from your sources, is that your father is, at worst, Klaus Fuchs or the Rosenbergs, at best Alger Hiss. That's it, isn't it?"

"I—I never said—"

"But that's it, isn't it?"

"I didn't—"

"Dammit, quit being slippery with me. Try to be honest with me once tonight." He regarded his son drunkenly. "That's what you think of me, isn't it?"

Ted's features had colored, and he began to tremble. "If you're so innocent," Ted blurted, "why didn't you ever try to prove it? Why didn't you? Why did you run away?"

At last, at last, Brennan thought, and he felt eased. Resentment and shame were no longer invisible. They were there, recognizable, to be fought.

"Now," said Brennan quietly, "we can talk."

Yet it would not be easy. There was too much, far too much, for this time and place. His son had posed a single question, and maybe answering that would be enough. At least, it would be the truth, the only bulwark he could provide his son against the onslaught of distortions and lies.

He stared across the table. Ted sat frozen into an attitude of expectation and dread.

Brennan spoke quickly. "If I was innocent, you asked, why wasn't I able to prove it? That's a fair question. I *was* innocent, Ted, completely innocent—not because I wasn't found guilty, but because I had done nothing wrong, absolutely nothing, and three persons on earth knew it, and I knew it, but I couldn't prove it or produce those three persons to prove it. A political scandal had occurred. A political scapegoat was needed. I was the chosen victim, and not of evidence or justice, but of character assassination. To paraphrase Rousseau, if there had not been a Senator Joe McCarthy in his time, society would have invented one. There were McCarthys—as well as their victims—before McCarthy himself, and there will be more in years to come. There were such men three years ago, seeking victims, and I happened to be a vulnerable target."

He paused, having heard himself as he spoke the last words, and now he sensed that to his son, even to his son, this was merely special pleading, his self-protective words against the august and unanimous pronouncement of his peers. He was giving Ted too little, he knew, if he did not give him the facts.

"Four years ago," Brennan said, "after we'd had hundreds of discussions with the Red Chinese representatives in Warsaw, the Chinese agreed to join with the United States, Soviet Russia, Great Britain, and France in a preliminary foreign ministers' parley in Zurich—a preliminary to the final high-level talk at which a permanent disarmament treaty would be signed. At that point China was an extremely muscular member of the world's nuclear club, but still somewhat behind us in the production of thermonuclear bombs of advanced design, and she still lacked a long-range delivery system. Nevertheless, we recognized that the Chinese must be dealt with as a military equal, and the sooner the better. Also, in China, the climate seemed about right. Chairman Kuo was proving more realistic than his predecessors, more concerned with the fact that another domestic Leap

Forward economic program had turned out to be only a stumble, and Kuo was less concerned with military aggression. The Chairman was demoting Maoists from key positions, and quoting Mao's old Yenan lecture that China's policy must be 'to avoid a decisive engagement in every campaign or battle when victory is uncertain, and to avoid absolutely a strategic decisive engagement which stakes the destiny of the nation.' This was a China we could talk to. But before proceeding to a Summit meeting, we decided that there were certain areas of disagreement that must be thrashed out first, disagreements involving geographical conflicts of interest—in Japan, India, Southeast Asia, Siberian frontiers—as well as problems involving prisoners of war, trade, and so on.

"Equally important, before attempting a Summit conference, was the ironing out of many differences on nuclear disarmament. For example, if every one of us agreed to reduce our conventional warfare capabilities, well, how could we do so equitably? We were an air power. China was a land power. Who would give up how much of what? Or the problem of concealment. If we each reduced our armaments in stages over six or eight years, how could we be positive some country wasn't violating the treaty by hiding a few nuclear bombs? Or the problem of the members of the neutral on-site inspection teams. How would we know their reports were truthful, that they were not secret anti-Communist or Communist agents, or fanatics, or deranged, or unstable? You see, Ted. Such details had to be ironed out, also, before we could go ahead with a meaningful Summit conference. In short, an important preliminary parley was indicated. And so, this confrontation in Switzerland, at Zurich, was arranged.

"When our delegates to Zurich were selected, Simon Madlock, President Earnshaw's right-hand man—actually everyone considered Madlock the unofficial President—well, Madlock called me in and appointed me a delegate because of my experience in the field of disarmament and because he felt that my dedication to the cause of world peace would be attractive to the Chinese. Then, almost at the last minute, Madlock assigned Professor Varney of Caltech as part of my team. Madlock felt that Varney's presence would impress the suspicious Chinese—first, because of Varney's prestige as the so-called father of the neutron bomb, a weapon China did not yet possess; second, because, unlike many of his more belligerent colleagues, Varney had made many conciliatory statements about friendship with Red China and had been active in numerous Ban-the-Bomb schemes, perhaps in expiation for his own guilts over helping produce the ultimate Bomb. Well, I did a little poking around on my own, even had a glimpse of a CIA report on Varney, and I began to feel uneasy about the professor. I got up the courage to go to Simon Madlock, and—face to face, just the two of us alone—I told him I would be more comfortable without Varney on our team. I couldn't tell him that I'd seen a classified CIA report that graded Varney as a security risk. But I could and did tell Madlock that Varney's notions about peace were, well, emotional, amateurish, impractical, and that his presence might inhibit our realistic approach, which had been formulated by the U.S. Arms Control and Disarmament Agency. Madlock simply would not listen to me. Amateurs such as Professor Varney, he insisted, were often more effective than professionals like myself. Moreover, *Hung Chi,* the journal of China's Central Committee, had several times praised Varney as 'a flower in the reactionaries' garden of poisonous weeds.' In short, Varney must accompany us. And my assignment, in addition to my regular duties, was to keep Varney on a practical course as much as possible, since he was politically immature, employ him to the best effect, and keep an eye on him in general. Because Varney was highly individualistic, Madlock did not want him making statements contrary to our official policy. And so, reluctantly, we went to Zurich with Varney. . . . You've heard none of this before, have you, Ted?"

"No, not exactly."

"It's true, and important for you to know considering what happened next. I won't go into the details of the conference itself. That's all been written. But let me tell you about another person who was there. At the time, Russia felt that Red China was as much a threat to them as to us. The Russians were on our side, working with the West to bring China into line. Understand that. Well, my counterpart on the Russian delegation was a youngish man, perhaps two or three years younger than I, named Nikolai Rostov. An attractive, dynamic fellow. Picture a clean-shaven Gorki in his youth. Rostov, with his shaggy eyebrows, Neanderthal forehead, ill-fitting clothes, rough manner, looked like a descendant of muzhiks. Actually, this was only half true. On his mother's side, he came from a family of scholars. His father, a laborer, was the anti-intellectual, a weak drunk who was at odds with his wife and son. Rostov adored his mother but despised his father, and yet, I suspect, he was something of both of them. For all his tough posturing, Rostov was full of erudition, could quote Pushkin at the drop of a hat. He spoke a clear, although not idiomatic, English. And while he was a dedicated Communist, he was not a parroting one, mouthing the litany of party-line dogma. We became good friends, very good friends, or so I thought. Anyway, Professor Varney, with his airy idealism, was as difficult as I'd expected, and Rostov became as worried about him as I was. We used to get into constant arguments with Varney. I would argue with him over his impractical ideas for peace, and Rostov would argue with him over his unrealistic interpretation of modern China.

"Then, Ted, it all went wrong, everything came apart, and it happened in a single day, the day the conference was to adjourn. I was making notes around lunchtime in my room at the Carlton-Elite, and Rostov broke in on me, extremely upset. He'd got a tip from the KGB that twice Professor Varney had secretly visited Red Chinese delegates, at night in their rooms at the Dolder Grand Hotel. This kind of private unilateral business was strictly against security regulations, and it unnerved me. Both Rostov and I rushed to the Baur au Lac, where Varney had insisted upon staying because he liked the view of the lake. We found him, and confronted him with our knowledge of his activities, but the old man waved us off as if we were children. He admitted that he'd seen the Chinese a couple of times on his own, especially their well-known physicist, Dr. Ho Ta-peng. Varney felt that scientists had a common tongue. He also felt that he could accomplish more with the Chinese this way than we could at the formal meetings in the Kongresshaus. He was trying to prove to them that our intentions were honorable and peaceful, and they were obviously beginning to trust him, because they had already informally invited him to visit Peking.

"Well, Rostov and I pleaded with Varney not to continue on his own like this, not to visit another Chinese without one of us present. After an exhausting hour, we convinced him. He promised to behave. But once we were outside his hotel again, our uneasiness revived. Rostov decided to speak to his superiors, and I determined to call Simon Madlock directly at the White House. I went to our headquarters and placed my call on the scrambler, only to be told that Madlock was unavailable. When I spoke of the urgency of my message, I was advised to try again several hours later.

"I returned to my hotel, and as I walked into my room, the telephone rang. It was Nikolai Rostov. He had horrifying news. He had just learned that Professor Varney had defected to Red China. An hour before, in company with a group of Chinese delegates, nuclear physicists like himself, he had boarded a Pakistan International Airlines plane and taken off. I was thunderstruck, speechless, not only by the act of defection but by its implications. But Rostov had more to say. We would not be blamed, he assured me. A note had been delivered to him, addressed to both of us, written in Varney's hand. Rostov read it to me twice, and the second time I wrote it all down, every word of it. It read: 'Dear Nikolai and Matthew. After much soul-searching, I have decided to go over to the Chinese and do a missionary's work in converting them to peace. I know how earnestly you both have labored to stop me from seeing our Chinese brothers, but I am convinced that your path is wrong and mine is right. Only by giving China every equality with the West will we gain their trust, as well as force the militarists in our own countries to put an end to their Catonian strategy, their echoing of Cato's cry, "Carthage must be destroyed," and to cease their aggressive acts. We shall force them to treat seriously with the New China for an enduring peace. I shall now devote the remainder of my life to achieving this peace. Forgive my sudden departure. It is your work I do. This note will absolve both of you of any responsibility for my act, an act made entirely on my own good conscience. Varney.'

"The note was a major consolation, since I sensed that my personal situation was a precarious one. Varney had been assigned to my charge, although over my protests, and now he had defected to America's enemy with America's secrets. There would have to be explanations. I had no doubt that my explanations would be satisfactory, for I had been only a minor instrument in Madlock's peace offensive on behalf of President Earnshaw. Still, instinctively, I knew that I must reinforce my personal position.

"After recovering from the initial shock, I demanded to know whether Rostov still possessed Varney's farewell note, which exonerated both Rostov and me. Rostov assured me that he was holding the precious note in his hand. I said it was of great importance to me to have either the original note or a photocopy of it. Rostov understood, and instantly promised to make a copy for himself and to deliver the original to me personally at the Carlton-Elite within the hour. He told me to stand by, and he hung up.

"I waited. Rostov did not appear within the hour or within the next two hours. I became frantic and began to make telephone calls, trying to reach him at his hotel, his delegation headquarters, his office in the Zurich Kongresshaus. Everywhere, I was told that he was not in but should be back shortly. I was too distraught to rely on the telephone any longer. I rushed over to Rostov's hotel and asked for him. I was told that he was no longer registered. He had checked out two hours earlier. I insisted that he must have left either a message or an envelope for Mr. Matthew Brennan. There was no message, no envelope. In short, no copy of the life-and-death Varney note absolving me. Much later I learned that after Rostov telephoned me, agents of the KGB had entered his room and forced him to return to Moscow with them for questioning.

"That was the last of Rostov for me. I never saw him again, or heard of the Varney note again.

"Well, Ted, I suspect you know much of what happened next. Varney's defection to Red China made headlines throughout the world. It caused an uproar in the United States. And even before I could leave Zurich, the word was out that Professor Varney had safely arrived in Peking. He had held a press conference in the Hsin Hsiao Hotel, and had been quoted in the official government journal, *Hung Chi,* as stating that he was on a mission to give China's nuclear scientists the neutron bomb, and that this would give China the strength to force the Western powers to abandon belligerence for realistic peace talks. I remember Marshal Chen, Vice-Chairman of China's Communist Party Central Committee, saying at the time, 'Peace grows from the barrel of the gun.' But most of us had not forgotten the original quotation, made by Mao Tse-tung years before, which was, '*Power* grows from the barrel of the gun.'

"Overnight, editorials began appearing in the American press demanding to know who was responsible for this horrendous security lapse. I was deeply troubled, but I was still confident of my own position. While I did not have either Varney or Rostov to vouch for my innocence, I had someone more important. I had the President's right-hand man, Simon Madlock himself, to testify that he alone had appointed Varney to our delegation. I knew he would admit that in a private meeting I had opposed Varney's appointment, warning him that Varney was a risk; he would admit that subsequent events had proved me a prophet. As for Madlock, whatever his shortcomings, he was an honest man. This he was. And under oath he would, I knew, clear me and assume full responsibility for the fiasco himself. I was one of several delegates detained in Zurich for three or four days to undergo questioning by the CIA and various other intelligence agencies. Then we were returned home.

"Moments after I descended from our jetliner at Kennedy Airport, I learned the latest, and for me the most stunning, news. Two hours earlier, in Walter Reed Hospital, Simon Madlock had died as the result of a sudden and massive coronary.

"You know how I felt, Ted? I'll tell you. Like being in one of those thrillers you always read where a newspaperman pretends to have committed a crime in order to ferret out the real murderer, and only the District Attorney knows his stunt, and is in on his game, and then, suddenly, the District Attorney dies, and the newspaperman has no witnesses left on earth to prove his innocence. You've read that one a hundred times. Ridiculous fiction, we've all said. But here it was, happening to me.

"The rest came fast. Dexter's Joint Committee on Internal Security had its public inquisition. Vainly, frantically, I had Madlock's secretary try to locate Madlock's notes on our private meeting. They did not exist. I tried to get an affidavit from Professor Varney in Peking. There was no reply. I tried, through both our Embassy in Moscow and our correspondents in Russia, to reach Nikolai Rostov, begging him for a copy of the Varney note. Rostov had disappeared from sight. During the weeks of the hearings, and for a year after, I directed appeals to Rostov. There was no answer from Rostov, from anyone, only a rumor that Rostov had been disciplined for his own laxity and demoted to a minor post in Siberia.

"Prove my innocence, Ted? You bet I tried, and I did not stop trying until lately. But as far as I know, Varney is as dead as Madlock and Rostov has been quietly purged. And I am left, the only living witness to my own innocence.

"I ran away, you said. You wondered why I ran away. I'll tell you why. Because, with all of that guilt by implication, I had to resign from the Disarmament Agency. There were no jobs or positions open to me. Then, well, your mother—I suppose she had no choice—she left me, and took you and Tracy. There just wasn't enough reason to remain in a community where I was a pariah, to stay on in a homeland that wanted me evicted. Maybe it was weak of me to leave finally, but by that time, I'll confess, I *was* weak. So I went abroad, I sentenced myself to this island city, where I would be accepted for what I was and not what I was supposed to be."

Brennan halted, breathless, emotionally spent, throat and lungs dry.

"There is your Judas parent, young man," Brennan said with a thin smile. "I'm sorry to have gone on at this length. But in a sense, you asked for it, coming here, and I had to answer—not perhaps because it was important to you, but because it was important to me." He smiled fully now. "Okay, Ted?"

The boy nodded, dumbly. He tried to find his voice, and he did. "Okay," he said, almost inaudibly, and averted his worried eyes.

Brennan pitied him. Ted had sat rigidly, phlegmatically, throughout the recital, like a young Spartan trained to endure and survive any test of manhood. Yet it was evident that he had been deeply moved. He appeared like a grown adolescent who wanted to retreat into childhood, but was willing himself to resist the urge. His composure had been shattered, and what remained were pieces: the downcast, blinking eyes, the unsteady lips, the locking, unlocking hands.

Brennan ached to be beside him, arm around him, as once in the long ago, and address Ted not as a defense counsel but as a loving parent. It was no use. Ted could give him nothing back, at least not now. Ted had come to this meeting with one mind. His mind had been invaded, torn asunder, and now, possibly, he was of two minds, and it was strange to him and it was unsettling.

In his son's mind, Brennan perceived, there was recorded his father's brief. But that same mind was already filled with another brief, an accusing prosecutor's case built large over four years, the years of stern Mother, whispering friends, vicious newspaper stories, the years of regarding Father as a troublemaker not a protector, seeing Father as a threat not a shelter offering security. Could this impromptu brief in Harry's Bar in Venice overturn all that the boy had heard and suffered during the recent years in America?

Brennan did not know. And now he did not want to know.

He could see Ted shifting restlessly in his place. He could see that the boy wanted to be free of the half-guilts and total confusion his father represented.

Brennan said, "It's getting late, Ted. You'd better be off. I don't want you to miss your one night on the town in Venice."

Ted hesitated. "I—I suppose I should. They're expecting me."

Brennan pushed back his chair and rose, to make it easier for his son, who quickly and gratefully stood up. "You're leaving in the morning?" Brennan asked.

"Yes. Like I said, real early. We're heading down to Florence, and on to Rome."

"You'll enjoy both. If you want any suggestions on offbeat things to see—?"

"Thanks, I appreciate it, but we're only spending a couple of days, and my friends marked the guidebooks."

"Well, then—" Brennan offered his hand, formally. "Good luck. I'll write you at Yale." Ted took his hand stiffly, then released it, and Brennan added, "Try to write when you have spare time. I'll be at the same old stand."

For seconds they were a few feet apart, and his son looked directly at him, eyes moistening, Adam's apple going up and down, and in those seconds it was as if Ted wanted to say something, offer something, perhaps something akin to love. But he could say nothing, after all, except "I'll write," except "Thanks for everything," and Brennan would never know.

Brennan turned to watch his son pass quickly through the room, through the swinging doors, into Venice and out of his life, and he wished that the boy had at least once, just once, called him Dad.

Brennan settled himself in the chair, trying to understand, and after thinking about it a few minutes, he understood fully: Ted had hurried off like this, unable to speak, because he had not wanted to be a traitor to his mother, the only one in life upon whom he could still depend.

In his utter aloneness, morosely contemplating his empty highball glass, Brennan considered the companionship of one more drink. The accompanying dirge was ready: *A rivederci, Ted, a rivederci, Lisa, a rivederci, Everything*. But he remembered that Lisa had not yet gone, and that he had promised to see her off if it was possible.

After weighing the pain of another emotional parting against the pleasure of one more glimpse of Lisa's loving face, he knew that he had to see her one last time, no matter how painful the encounter. It was twenty minutes to eight. He could still make it.

He reached inside his jacket for his wallet, and immediately, as always, his sense of alienation was heightened by the feel of the over-sized wallet for foreign currency and the ever-present passport bulging in his pocket. This night, of all nights, he did not wish to be Philip Nolan, the Man Without a Country. Determined not to dwell on his role, he paid his bill, hurried to the telephone inside the cloakroom hall and called the Gritti Palace hotel. Not unexpectedly, he learned from the reception desk that Miss Elizabeth Collins had checked out ten minutes before. He would catch her at the depot.

Hastily leaving Harry's Bar, Brennan made his way to the busy San Marco station. Ignoring the gondoliers, he sought a motorboat for hire, and soon found one. Stepping down into it, he asked the pilot to take him to the railway depot as speedily as possible. He received the usual complaints in Italian about the traffic regulations, nodded patiently, and ducked into the dimly lighted cabin. Once the boat was under way, rocking through the Basin, wheeling into the wide opening of the Grand Canal, Brennan felt claustrophobic. Crouching, he went back to the open rear of the craft and settled on the low bench, offering his face to the rushing air and the Venice night.

For a while, Brennan gave his attention to the Gothic and Renaissance façades of the *palazzos* flashing by on either side of the Canal. After passing the dining terrace of the Gritti Palace hotel, he could make out the imposing design of Sansovino's Corner della Ca' Grande, the mammoth Rezzonico Palace, the Mocenigo Palaces, where Lord Byron lived in the period when he had met and taken for mistress the Countess Guiccioli, and then the two palaces of the Municipio which Ruskin had praised, and at last Brennan closed his eyes to the sights so often seen and visited. Without Lisa beside him, they were of no interest.

Once, when the motorboat churned to a stop, Brennan opened his eyes, hoping that they had reached the station. He was irritated to discover they had only stopped for a traffic signal, an overhead red light (it had always amused him, a traffic light above a canal, but tonight it irritated him). The light changed, and their progress resumed. And shortly, when he heard the craft bumping against the cement quay, he opened his eyes, and sat up to find himself before the railway depot.

Rapidly coming to his feet, he paid the pilot the 3,000 lire, leaped ashore, and dug out a tip for the ganzer who was waving his outstretched palm and hooked pole. Speedily Brennan started across the sweeping square that led to the interior of the railway station. He had always enjoyed this walk, and he enjoyed it now, the white stretch of it from the water and up the steps to the depot and the sounds of mellow Italian voices upon which were superimposed the musical strains of "Ciao, Venezia."

As Brennan attained the top of the stairs, he saw a beaming, swarthy young Italian in military-type service cap and immaculate white uniform break off from a cluster of hotel greeters and solicitors and start toward him.

The young Italian touched his fingers to the brim of his cap beneath the band reading ROYAL DANIELI EXCELSIOR, and inquired solicitously, "Good evening, Mr. Brennan. Anything I can do for you?"

"Nothing at all, Alfredo, thanks. I'm seeing a friend off for Paris."

Inside the station, Brennan sought the clock. He still had ten minutes before Lisa's departure, and now he was ashamed of having come empty-handed. He swerved toward the brightly lit shops, paused before the kiosk, hastily scanned the latest periodicals and settled on two glossy Italian fashion magazines and a copy of the day's Rome *Daily American* for Lisa's train reading.

Ready to start for the train shed in the terminal, he involuntarily glanced at the front page of the Rome *Daily American* for news of a world that was no longer of interest to him. The headline, the leading stories, concerned the convening of the representatives of the earth's five major powers in Paris for the Summit. A large three-column-wide photograph in the center of the front page held Brennan's attention. Above the picture was the heading: RUSSIAN LEADERS PREPARE TO LEAVE MOSCOW FOR CRUCIAL PARIS CONFERENCE.

Automatically, he dropped his gaze to the figures lined up in the official Tass photograph. These were the different faces of a new USSR, the benign countenances of a younger generation of Russian Communists who had come to understand that their future interests were as one with America's interests, and that the common obstacle to their prosperity as well as to world peace was the People's Republic of China.

Brennan recognized the face in the center of the picture at once, the chubby visage of Premier Alexander Talansky. The sterner face next to the Premier's, Brennan guessed, belonged to a military hero of the Soviet Union, the First Deputy Premier, Marshal Zabbin. The other faces, so reasonable and benevolent-looking (until you met them at the bargaining table, Brennan remembered), were those of persons unfamiliar to him, members of the Presidium or physicists or specialists, no doubt. And then, as his gaze reached the end of the row, his eyes narrowed upon the last face—fixed on it, staring—and instantly he felt the skin from his temples to his cheeks tighten and prickle. It was uncanny, the resemblance, but he knew it could not be, that it was simply impossible.

Quickly he brought the picture close to his eyes. The newspaper was grainy, the face of the one at the end of the row now clear enough to be better identified. Yet there it was, so like the youthful Gorki's, the primitive Cro-Magnon face, the rough muzhik face with its hidden intelligence and erudition, the Zurich face, the Varney-scandal face, the face that had disappeared from the earth's face and his own life four years ago. Was it possible? Or was it a twin?

Brennan's eyes darted down to the caption and across it. This was the USSR delegation to the Summit, expected to arrive in Paris tomorrow morning. "Front row, L to R: Asst. Minister for Far Eastern Affairs N. Rostov—"

Rostov.

Confirmed. True. Rostov, no other. He was restored to public power. He was en route to Paris. He was alive, he was available, he was hope incarnate.

Rostov!

Brennan could feel his heart pounding wildly. He tried to control himself. He tried to think clearly, but all the past, the present, the future—now the future, too—rushed to his head, buffeting his brain, until his mind was out of joint.

Dazed, he sought the depot clock. Four minutes remained.

That instant, it was as if he had been charged by a loose electric wire. Galvanized, he spun toward the railway-station entrance, and trying not to run, striding swiftly, he hastened to the top of the outdoor steps.

"Alfredo!" he shouted.

From nowhere, it seemed, the Danieli representative materialized, puffing as he doffed his service cap. "Mr. Brennan, sì—"

"Alfredo, listen to me—" He grasped the Italian's shoulder tightly with his free hand and pulled him closer—"and don't forget a thing I say. There's an emergency, and I've got to leave for Paris at once. I haven't had time to pack, or notify the hotel, or do anything. Now you get on that phone over there and call the manager and tell him I had to take off for Paris like this, and tell him to hold on to my rooms. Then speak to the concierge. Tell him to send a couple of his boys up to Suite 116, take out my two largest suitcases, the brown leather ones, and pack three suits—no, four—two evening ones, two for afternoon—and shirts, shorts, shoes, pajamas, my toilet articles—and get those suitcases over here and on the first train that leaves for Paris tonight. Address them to me at the—the—California Hotel, 16 Rue de Berri. Got that?"

"*Sì—sì!*" Alfredo was already scribbling notes on the back of a hotel rate card.

"Tell the concierge I'll phone him tomorrow from Paris, and—" He fumbled in his coat pocket, and handed Alfredo a key. "My safe-deposit box in the hotel. Tell him I authorize him to open it and airmail me the lire, checkbook, travelers checks, and—"

He was interrupted by the public address system. Brennan halted, listening to the other-worldly voice chant, "The Simplon Orient Express now departing from Track 14 for Milano, Lyon, Dijon, Paris!"

Brennan released Alfredo's shoulder. "I've got to hurry. Do you understand it all? I'll take care of you when I come back." He started to go, then asked anxiously, "Can I get on without a ticket?"

"*Sì—sì—*you pay the conductor after—"

Brennan wheeled and ran, dodging between passengers and vendors, through the depot to the track shed, and then, searching up ahead, he cut his stride.

He saw her on the platform, almost the only one left on the platform, four cars down, still waiting, still peering off but about to give up. He resumed running as fast as he could, waving one arm, calling, "Lisa! Lisa!"

She saw him, and her face brightened with relief, and then he had her, grabbing her up in his arms, kissing her, gasping, panting, trying to tell her. "Lisa, I'm going with you—Paris—something happened—I have a chance—I'll explain—"

But her mouth was pressed against his, and her vibrantly alive body was against his, and there was no more need to speak. He felt the Wagons-Lits conductor prying them apart, pushing at them, and Brennan hurried her to the car, bodily lifted her onto the steep step-up, and he followed her onto the train and into the corridor as the Simplon Orient Express jolted forward and began to move.

Only later, after he had explained, was he able to sit back, one hand covering hers, and gaze out the window, and realize that the last yellow lights of the causeway were in the distance, and the icons and buildings of Mestre were receding, and that they were on terra firma once more. The isolated fairyland was behind them. This was the real mainland, solid ground, and his feet were on it, and he was in the open, exposed, revealed, engaged.

For a split second he felt a doubt, and the premonition that, having abandoned Venice, he might never be so safe again or know the euphoria of its illusory protectiveness again. Briefly he mourned the loss, and the last of a canto from *Childe Harold* entered his head, and being of a single voice with Byron, he recited it to himself:

> *And of the happiest moments which were wrought*
> *Within the web of my existence, some*
> *From thee, fair Venice, have their colours caught:*
> *There are some feelings Time cannot benumb,*
> *Nor Torture shake, or mine would now be cold and dumb.*

Yes, whatever tomorrow would bring, there was this. But there was more. In Venice hope had been dead, and without hope he had been no better than a corpse. But now hope was alive, and he was alive.

He brought Lisa's fingers to his lips and kissed them gently, and he thought of her, and he thought of his son, and he thought of Rostov, and then he sat back to wait for Paris. . . .

II

ON SUNDAY MORNING, the fifteenth of June, the weather in Paris was 21 degrees centigrade, and the early morning mist had been penetrated by the high, full ball of the sun, and the day would be warm and lovely.

During the morning, between nine-thirty and eleven-thirty, the four of them arrived.

At Orly Airport, Jay Thomas Doyle, after a two-and-a-half-hour flight from Vienna, and despite his lack of sleep and his obesity, bounced cheerfully down the ramp of the Austrian Airlines jet plane. The pageantry that met his eyes stopped him in his tracks. Above the airport, French flags rippled in the breeze. At his feet, a long red carpet ran to the *salon d'honneur,* and the blue-smocked women who had been sweeping it now made way for the passengers. Ahead, members of the Garde Républicaine, in red-plumed gold helmets and black boots, swords still sheathed, were assembling. Beyond the roped-off sections, the crowds were gathering, the blue-uniformed agents of the CRS were circulating. Then Doyle remembered. These preparations were for Premier Talansky, who would be arriving shortly from Moscow for the Summit conference. Hugging the attaché case containing his precious manuscript, Doyle proceeded inside the air terminal, took a diet pill at the first water cooler, cleared his luggage through customs, and, once outside again, directed the driver of a Renault taxi to take him to the Hotel George-V.

At the Gare du Nord, Emmett A. Earnshaw, after the six-hour train and channel-steamer trip from London's Victoria Station, waited in the green armchair in his compartment while his niece Carol, after rubbing the sleep out of her eyes, carefully combed her hair. There had been little rest the night before, once Sir Austin's call had awakened

Earnshaw to tell him there were now two Golden Arrows, and that one left at five in the morning and the other at eleven in the morning. Earnshaw, preferring to arrive in Paris in the late morning rather than the late afternoon, had awakened Carol, and both had dressed immediately and departed from London. Now, leading Carol out of the train to the platform, Earnshaw stood uncertainly before the legends on the sleeper, which read GOLDEN ARROW and FLÈCHE D'OR. Almost immediately the United States Embassy foreign service officer, introducing himself as Callahan, appeared, followed by another Embassy official and a Secret Service agent. Bemused, Earnshaw hardly heard Callahan's apologies on behalf of the absent Ambassador, who was tied up with the recently arrived President and the Secretary of State. However, the Ambassador's personal car was outside, waiting in readiness, and entirely at Earnshaw's disposal during his stay in Paris. Before the Gare du Nord, a saluting chauffeur held open the rear door of the Cadillac limousine bearing a miniature Stars and Stripes, and Earnshaw got inside. When he inquired where they would be staying, Callahan replied that the Embassy had been fortunate enough to obtain exactly what Earnshaw had requested, an excellent suite at the Lancaster Hotel, which was handy to everything.

At the Porte d'Italie, Medora Hart, after almost sixteen hours on the road, braked her Mercedes sports car to a halt beside a stoplight, lifted her sunglasses to her dust-caked forehead and consulted the Michelin Guide, with its map labeled *"Sorties de Paris."* She had her bearings by the time the light changed, and she shifted gear and headed for the Place d'Italie, trying to remember that she must turn right there to reach the Quai d'Austerlitz, and then follow the avenues along the left bank of the Seine until she reached the Concorde bridge. Only now did she realize how far she had come and how fast she had driven since leaving Nardeau, making her phone calls, and checking out of the Provençal hotel. She had followed Route Nationale 7 all the way, with just the briefest of stopovers to eat and rest at Montélimar and Dijon. Her speedometer registered over 900 additional kilometers. And only now, stopping and starting the car in Paris traffic, did she realize that the calf of her right leg was cramped and her right foot was numb. She could not wait to reach her hotel, and shower and nap, and she was grateful that the proprietor of the Club Lautrec had been influential enough to reserve for her a choice room in the Hotel San Régis.

At the Gare de Lyon, Matt Brennan and Lisa Collins, at the end of their fourteen-hour journey from Venice on the Simplon Orient Express, refreshed after sleeping in one another's arms most of the night, climbed down into the vast station. Since Brennan had wired the California Hotel from Milan requesting rooms and someone to meet them, they waited alongside the blue Wagons-Lits sleeping car to see if anyone would come for them. Then Brennan noticed a uniformed hotel porter advancing, searching among the exiting passengers, and when the porter came closer, the woven lettering HOTEL CALIFORNIA was clearly visible above the breast pocket of his jacket. Brennan hailed him, and the relieved porter explained that he had held the taxi that had brought him here. After locating Lisa's luggage, the hotel porter guided them through the milling passengers, past the ticket cubicles, to the taxi, a shining new Citroën, waiting before the Gare de Lyon. The porter helped Lisa and Brennan into the rear, and himself got into the front seat next to the driver. He ordered the elderly driver, in French, to take them to the California Hotel in the Rue de Berri, and the driver grunted, and complained in French that Paris was too crowded for this time of the year, especially with all those foreign Communists arriving who wanted everyone else to give up their nuclear stockpiles so that they could later take theirs out of hiding and conquer the world, meaning conquer France.

This was Paris, this June morning, history's City of Light, but tomorrow's City of Hope or Despair. . . .

B RENNAN HAD WANTED Lisa to see Paris her first time as he had seen it his first time, and as he always liked to see it on each new arrival. He had asked the taxi driver not to bother with the shortcut up the Avenue Gabriel and the Rue Ponthieu that would take them directly to the hotel, but to take, instead, the slightly longer approach up the Avenue des Champs-Élysées. The driver, conscious of his ticking meter, had grunted approval.

Holding Lisa's hand in his lap, Brennan watched through the rolled-down window as they swung past the Obelisk of Luxor and through the Place de la Concorde, where the traffic was light because it was early and it was Sunday.

The hotel porter's arm had swept out toward the Concorde as he expounded in heavily accented English that this had been the site, during the Revolution, where the guillotine had stood and where King Louis XVI and Marie Antoinette had lost their heads. Neither Lisa nor Brennan was listening, for they had entered into the broad rising slope of the Champs-Élysées, with the majestic Arc de Triomphe, a gigantic tricolor floating from its center, in the distance. And figuratively, they had lost their heads, too.

Lisa, wide dark eyes scanning what lay before them and what passed beyond their windows, wanted no guide's instruction, but only a chance to assimilate these sensory pleasures, and so she was silent. A true Frenchman, the hotel porter became respectfully silent, too. And Matt Brennan was free to bring the city into the privacy of himself, at last.

Slumping back in the taxi seat, Brennan found it amusing the way he constantly permitted the city to surprise him. In recent years, since the time of his trouble, he had always approached Paris with dread, fearing the place where he had once been accepted with honor and where he would now be reminded of disgrace. He had always come with dread, and every time, upon entering the Champs-Élysées, he had been seduced into helpless love.

It had happened to him again, as always, these moments of this Sunday morning.

He savored the sight of the chestnut trees, at attention along the grandest of the grand boulevards, and behind them he could see French children at play on swings and romping beside the goat carts. There was the familiar Théâtre Marigny beyond the trees, and the Rond-Point des Champs-Élysées, with its clumps of evergreen foliage and public fountain, and a short distance off, the busy open-air gathering of philatelists, selling and trading their stamps this Sunday morning.

They were passing the corner edifice that housed the staff and presses of Le Figaro, and then the two huge outdoor terraces of the Café du Colisée, with middle-aged Frenchmen absorbed in their newspapers as they enjoyed their brioches and coffee at yellow formica-topped tables, and with petite Parisiennes, the urchin-faced girls in sweaters and skirts gossiping beneath the fringed umbrellas, and then there was a bus with the sign PONT DE NEUILLY, and a Loterie Nationale ticket booth.

He could see, peering up the intersecting Rue la Boëtie, the lofty neon sign reading Club Lautrec and the mammoth cardboard cutout of a nude chanteuse with a streamer across her thighs reading: PREMIÈRE DEMAIN—LA SCANDALEUSE BEAUTÉ ANGLAISE—EN PERSONNE. There were, on the broad sidewalks, large French families in their Sunday best, boys walking their bicycles, pigeons strutting, and window-shoppers hiding the fronts of the luxurious stores. They were rolling past No. 76, the maw of Les Arcades that led into the underground Lido, and suddenly, they were at the corner of the Avenue des Champs-Élysées and the Rue de Berri, where two bearded Left Bank art students were squatting as they sketched a holy picture on the pavement while tourists gathered, and where a vendor nearby was selling foreign magazines from his improvised plank counters, and now they were turning to the right and entering the Rue de Berri.

Leaving the Champs-Élysées, he thought: Paris. It was all he had just seen, and it was more. It was *mille-feuille* and *le scotch*. It was *feux d'artifice* from the Pont Neuf on Bastille Day. It was *les grands magasins* closed Mondays and *épiceries* open Sundays. It was a *carnet de tickets* for the Métro. It was *garçon* and *service compris*. It was *pissoirs* and *les Immortels de l'Académie Française*. It was *vin ordinaire* and *citron pressé*. It was *géraniums en pots* and *porcelaine de Limoges*. It was *pneumatique* and *zones bleues*. It was *le bistro* and *le bidet*. It was Prisunic and Cartier. It was Simcas and truffles and Flaminaires and Opéra-Comique and Venus de Milo and the Sorbonne and girls named Gisèle. It was *Noël* in June. It was *bien*. It was *très jolie*. It was Paris, his Paris, unchanged, and he felt extraordinarily alive. He did not know if the sorcery was Paris alone, or Lisa in Paris, or Rostov in Paris, and he did not care. He felt wonderful.

His excitement, he realized, had been crystallized in a fleeting moment, for they had only just entered into the Rue de Berri.

"We get out in the next block," he said.

"You think it'll be all right?" Lisa asked.

He smiled. "Of course it will. This is Paris."

"I love Paris, it's so beautiful," she said, kissing his cheek, "and I love you, Mr. Brennan." She looked ahead. "Very well, sir, I'm prepared to live in flagrant sin."

It had not been until they were nearing Milan last night that Brennan finally persuaded Lisa to move into the California Hotel with him and occupy an adjoining bedroom, or, if necessary, share his own room. As for the suite her company had reserved for her in the Plaza-Athénée, she could retain it and pretend to be living there to satisfy her fashion associates, but she would use it merely as working quarters.

Brennan had told Lisa that they would enjoy more privacy at the quiet California than at the bustling Plaza-Athénée. What he had not told her was that the Athénée was the hotel where he and Stefani used to stay, and that he did not wish to relive painful memories or meet those who might remember. Since the divorce and his expatriation, he had broken from the past and taken to staying at the California Hotel whenever he was in Paris. He had done this not only because the hotel was new to him, inexpensive, casual, accessible to restaurants and shops, but because, despite the newspapermen in the New York Herald Tribune Building across the street (who were fellow expatriates and friendly), the California was not a prestige hotel attracting the famous, and therefore he could remain relatively unrecognized.

217

"Here we are, Lisa," he announced. "Number 16 Rue de Berri, the California."

"I can't get used to that name for a French hotel."

"Well, we crossed the Avenue Franklin-D.-Roosevelt coming here, and the next block down is the Rue Washington, and one night I'll take you to the Crazy Horse Saloon, and that's not Las Vegas, that's Paris, too."

The porter had the taxi door open, but Brennan felt Lisa's restraining hand on his arm. "Matt," she said softly, "I'm glad you came here. I know you won't be sorry."

He gave her a tentative smile. "If you're even half as much of a prophetess as you are a woman—well, maybe something will work out. Let's pray to God and Comrade Rostov."

The moment that they entered the lobby, the beefy concierge, M. Dupont, red-cheeked and reeking of red wine as usual, rushed out from behind his counter to pump Brennan's hand, and to acknowledge jovially his friend's friend, Miss Collins, and to welcome her. At the reception desk, running another line of greetings and introductions, Brennan was pleased to learn that the management had transferred several Chinese journalists from the first floor to the seventh to accommodate an old customer. Brennan signed the registry card for his bedroom and parlor, and Lisa signed for the single bedroom next to Brennan's own.

They took the confining elevator to the first floor. Brennan led Lisa up a dim corridor to Room 110. Inside, two porters were already setting Lisa's suitcases on luggage stands. Then, after pulling open the heavy drapes, they lingered briefly for the tip and were gone.

Happily Lisa examined the bathroom, with its deep tub, bidet, washstand, and the narrow toilet next to it with a pull chain dangling from its archaic overhead watertank. Then she went into the green bedroom, studying the mirrored armoire and large brass double bed. She followed Brennan to the French windows, which he had opened, and she hung over the rail of the tiny balcony, looking down into the serene inner court with its splashing fountain.

She turned back and hugged Brennan. "It's charming, quaint and charming, and best of all, it has my favorite decor—you. Brennan XIV baroque. That's what I adore . . . Matt, where are you going to be?"

"Wait," he said. He indicated the door between the windows and bed. "Unlock and open that, Lisa, and then wait."

He left Room 110, hurried around the corner past 111, and entered 112. The stiff old-fashioned parlor held a velour-covered divan, maroon plush chairs, leather-inset desk, and marble-top commode. He continued on into his bedroom, unlocked the second of the two doors between their rooms and pulled it back—and there was Lisa, waiting. "Lo, we're one," he announced, bowing her into his larger bedroom. She entered slowly. "Maybe you should carry me over the threshold," she said. She glanced about. "It doesn't feel like sin. It feels like light housekeeping. I'm so glad you made me come here with you."

"Only one thing, Lisa. The amenities. When we're together, alone, we can keep our two connecting doors open, have our three rooms. But whenever one of us leaves, we probably should play the game for the maids and any visitors, by shutting and locking the connecting doors. Pretend we have separate rooms."

"I never knew you were really a prude, Mr. Brennan."

"I'm really a gallant gentleman, protecting my fair lady's honor."

"Of course, Matt." She walked into his sitting room, then gayly returned to him. "Oh, I adore this. . . . Well, here we are—you—me—Paris. It's bewildering. What do we do next?"

Sitting on his bed, smoking cigarettes, they discussed what she should do this first day here, and what he must do. She would take a lazy bath, she decided, then unpack, separate her work materials and a few unneeded articles of clothing, and repack them and check them into the Plaza-Athénée. There she would read her mail, go over her schedules of the fashion showings, and confer with her colleagues. As for himself, Brennan decided that he, too, would freshen up before seeking a means of locating Nikolai Rostov.

When she turned her back to him so that he could unbutton her blouse, she said, "I may be tied up for dinner tonight, with my confreres."

"I rather expect you will be."

She pulled off her loose blouse. "What will you be doing, Matt?"

"Maybe I'll get lucky and connect with Rostov right away. More likely—well, I have a few friends around—"

"Any of them pretty girls?"

"They all have mustaches."

"No, seriously—"

"I'll probably be too bushed to go out tonight. Maybe I'll take a walk on the Champs, grab a snack somewhere, and be back here early to plan the next few days, catch up on my reading, and wait for you."

"Will you? I don't want to sleep alone my first night in Paris."

"You won't, Lisa."

"Mmm, good. . . . Can I walk to the Plaza-Athénée?"

"Yes, but don't, not with a piece of luggage. Ask the doorman to get you a taxi."

"What do I tip the taxi driver?"

He dug into his pocket for a handful of coins and sorted through them. "If you want to be a rich American and spoil it for everyone else, and make it simple for yourself, tip either one of these coins." He handed her two silver coins. "The one with the female head and torch is a 100-franc piece, old style—do you see?—and the other with the full figure of the woman is one franc, new style—100 old francs, one new franc, and they both have exactly the same value. They're worth twenty cents American each. Got it?"

She nodded. "You see how much I need you?"

He kissed the back of her neck and rubbed his cheek against her soft dark lustrous hair, and unfastening her brassiere, he whispered, "I need you more, darling."

As her brassiere fell away, and his arms encircled her, she said unsteadily, "Shouldn't we wait until tonight?"

"No," he said, and then withdrew his hands and said, "but we will." He lifted her from the bed to her feet. "Have a good time, darling. And lock that door behind you."

She went quickly into her room, closed the door, and turned the latch. Reluctantly Brennan shut and locked his door. He went into his sitting room and phoned down to have the concierge send out for shaving and toilet articles and four bottles of Scotch and cognac. He explained about the luggage that was following him and requested M. Dupont to check customs for it. Then he asked that a long-distance call be put through to the Hotel Danieli in Venice.

Waiting for his call, Brennan removed his drip-dry shirt, washed it thoroughly, and hung it near his window in the sun. He ran his tub. As he finished, the connection with Venice was made. He learned that his suitcases were on their way to Paris and would arrive that evening. He discussed the holding of his rooms at the Danieli and the forwarding of his money, and he left messages for several Italian friends, especially the Armenian fathers at San Lazzaro, who might worry about him. He promised that he would be back in Venice in two weeks, if not sooner.

Once undressed and immersed in the tepid water of the tub, he tried to concentrate on his mission. Since learning in the Rome *Daily American* last night of Nikolai Rostov's resurrection, and telling Lisa about it on the train, he had not had time to think clearly about his next move. Now, rubbing himself with a soapy washrag, he considered the immediate future. He must locate Rostov. He must arrange to see Rostov. He must know what to say to Rostov. But first, he must locate him. The latest newspapers had offered no information. Yet, Brennan believed, discovering this would not be difficult, despite the fact that Rostov was a Russian and Russians were usually secretive, because

Rostov was also a public delegate to a public international conference. By the time Brennan had dried and dressed—except for his shirt, which was still damp—he knew what his first step would be. Actually, he had known from the moment of his arrival in Paris. He would telephone the United States Information Service at the American Embassy and ask for Herb Neely, the press attaché. Of the handful of Brennan's friends from the past who had remained steadfast after the Congressional hearing, Herb Neely had been the most trustworthy and the most loyal. Brennan and Neely had been roommates at Georgetown long ago, and they had worked together as recently as Zurich four years before. Afterward, the new President had appointed a new Ambassador to France, and this Ambassador had selected Neely as his press attaché. Whenever Brennan had passed through Paris, coming from or returning to Venice, he had always looked forward to the ritual dinner and evening with Neely and his wife Frances and their three adopted children. With Neely, there was no need for apology or pretense. With Neely, Brennan could be himself.

Going to the telephone, Brennan suddenly realized that it was Sunday and Neely might not be available. Yet, as he sank into the deep feathery divan, he knew that the entire American Embassy staff would be on the job, since the five-power disarmament conference would open at the Palais Rose in the morning.

Brennan lifted the receiver and asked for Anjou 74-60, Extension 7549. When a woman in the American Embassy press section answered, he asked for Herb Neely. After giving his name, he sat expectantly, and to his relief he heard Neely's mellifluous, faintly Southern, faintly weary voice.

"Hallo. That you, Matt?"

"None other," said Brennan. "How are you, Herb? How's the family?"

"Fine, fine. It's sure good to hear your voice again, old man. Frances and I, we've discussed you a hundred times. Worried maybe you fell into a canal. Not a peep since last Christmas."

"Well, there's really been nothing to write about, I guess. You know—"

"Dammit, I don't know, Matt. Next time write about nothing. That would mean more to us than most people who write about something. So—no changes?"

"Well, I saw Ted in Venice last night."

"No kidding? How was it? Sticky?"

"Not easy, but I may have reached him. Then—" Brennan hesitated, weighing the next and deciding that he could be honest with

Neely. "Well, one more thing. I'm not here alone. I brought a young lady."

"Now I reckon that's the best news I've heard in years. The old man's rejuvenated, and about time. An Italian babe?"

"American. Here to cover the fashion shows. It embarrasses me a little, she's so young."

"Lucky dog."

"I'm serious about her, Herb, but I don't know . . . there are so many other considerations."

"I hope I get a chance to meet her."

"You will. . . . Look, Herb, I don't want to eat up your time like this. I know how busy you must be right now. I do remember. Actually, I'm calling you about something specific. Let me tell you, quickly, why I came to Paris."

"I already know."

Taken aback, Brennan said, "You do?"

"Sure, I know. His initials are Nikolai Rostov. He's out of hiding, or whatever, and he arrived here this morning. If you hadn't showed up by tomorrow, I aimed to call you in Venice."

"Thanks, Herb. That was certainly a jolt, seeing his name again."

"All of us in the Embassy were just as surprised, believe me."

"Well, now you know why I'm busting in on you like this. I've got a question—"

"And I'll try to get you the answer as soon as possible," said Neely. "Where can you find him? Is that it?"

"That's it. Do you think he'd be staying at the Soviet Embassy?"

"Doubt it, Matt. Rostov's a big fish all right, but the Russians have plenty of whales here, and the whales get first call on the prime space. He's probably at some hotel. Let me find out and phone you. No, hold it, I'll tell you what—I've got to be in your vicinity anyway—I've been ordered to take some of the American press on a dry run of the Summit headquarters, the Palais Rose, at one o'clock. Have to show them where it's taking place, give them a briefing. But I'll have time for a drink and a quick sandwich round noon, and I reckon by then maybe I'll have what you want. Unless"—he paused—"would you prefer to come over here, join me in the Crillon bar?"

Brennan felt his frown. "That might be a little rough for both of us, Herb. If the Crillon is what it used to be, we'd probably run into your Embassy crowd, and some of my old State Department colleagues, and well, you know—"

"Still carrying the Scarlet Letter, eh?" Neely snorted. But he quickly softened. "Oh, hell, I understand, Matt. It was a lousy suggestion anyway. I guess I was trying to force you out into the open again. Therapy of defiance. Don't pay it any mind. Okay, back to your bailiwick—it's the same arrondissement anyway. Let's say the joint on the corner of the Champs-Élysées and Rue Marbeuf—Café Le Longchamp, twelve noon."

"Twelve noon."

"If I have anything to say about it, you're going to pin down Rostov once and for all, and go home as pure and shining as Galahad."

"I hope so. Thanks for everything, Herb. See you at noon."

After hanging up, feeling that the plan for his exoneration had been set in motion, Brennan accepted delivery of his toilet articles. He shaved leisurely, visualizing what life could be like after Rostov's support had cleared him, life with Lisa, life with Ted and Tracy, life in Washington, D.C., once more. Completing his dressing, he saw that it was a quarter to twelve, and he left immediately for the Champs-Élysées.

When he arrived at the Café Le Longchamp, the sidewalk tables beneath the awning were only half occupied. He could not find Herb Neely. Moving in to stake claim on an isolated shaded table, he heard his name called and spun around, to find Neely waving as he hurried toward him in long straight-legged strides. For an instant Brennan saw his friend as Chad Newsome walking out of the pages of Henry James's *The Ambassadors,* because Brennan had expected Neely to look so American and harried and, instead, he appeared so French and at home. He has found his place, Brennan thought, and envied him.

They shook hands, and took the café table beneath the front of the awning.

"We'd better order before it fills up," said Neely, twisting around to find a waiter.

Brennan observed his friend with affection. The blond hair had thinned, and as a result the sideburns had lengthened and the tuft of beard on his chin ("my authentic imperial," he liked to say) had thickened, and his hair was combed sideways to cover a patch of bald pate. The rimless spectacles perched on the beaky nose, the high, pointed collar of the shirt, the short jacket and tight trousers of the striped mohair summer suit were French. Yet, the businesslike haste of his speech, with the contradictory roll of a Kentucky accent acquired in childhood, remained American.

A waiter took their order and hurriedly left them.

"Well, Matt, old man, I've got it," Neely announced at once. *"Voilà!"* He extracted a slip of paper from his shirt pocket and handed it to Brennan. "Hotel Palais d'Orsay. There's the address, 9 Quai Anatole-France. That's just across the river from the Tuileries. You go over the bridge, the Pont Royal, and turn right to where the Gare d'Orsay used to be."

"Yes, I remember."

"The Russians keep most of their overflow in that hotel. They always did and they still do."

"I've never been there."

"I have, several times," said Neely. "It's a surprisingly drab hotel for them to patronize. Shabby yellow walls in the lobby, uncleaned columns, a faded Oriental rug. But maybe not so surprising, since our Russian friends, despite their drift toward a capitalist economy, like to cling to the myth of pure Marxist proletarianism. Anyway, Nikolai Rostov, Assistant Minister for Far Eastern Affairs, sleeps there."

"I can't tell you how grateful I am, Herb."

"Nonsense. My part was routine," said Neely. "You're the one with the big job, Matt. What do you intend to do?"

"See him," said Brennan wryly. "Just go there and ask for him, or camp in the lobby until he passes through. The minute we've finished here, I'll go straight to the Hotel Palais d'Orsay."

Neely was shaking his head. "No, not today. Forget it. Rostov went right on from the airport to the five-power Ministers' confab in the Quai d'Orsay, where they're laying out the agenda for the plenary sessions, and determining the protocol and rules—you know, chairmanship, the order in which to give the floor to each delegation and its proposals—all touchy and complicated, with Red China here. I'm afraid Rostov'll be burning oil until midnight. You could leave a message at his hotel."

"Maybe. I think I'd prefer to make it person to person. I read somewhere that tomorrow morning's opening session begins at ten. I'll be in his hotel by seven or seven-thirty."

Neely began to eat the omelet the waiter had placed in front of him. "Think you'll have any trouble seeing him?"

"Could be. What I'm up against is the fact that Rostov made a promise to me four years ago, and walked out on it, or maybe was blocked from seeing me or anyone else. Against me, also, is the fact that Rostov could not or would not respond to any appeals from me directly or through my intermediaries. Against me is the other obvious fact that he was in trouble as a result of Zurich, was *persona non grata,* and now that he's been restored to government, he may want no part of me or of anyone connected with a damaging episode in his past." Carefully Brennan applied more mustard to his ham sandwich, then looked up. "What I have going for me is the fact that Rostov really appeared to like me personally, to enjoy our friendship, short though it was, and he may have wanted to help me and been prevented from doing so. Also going for me—well, now that he's active again, important again, Rostov may feel secure and powerful enough to give me a hand, may even want to, and, as I recall, he was a gutsy person, tough, independent—"

"Yes, I remember."

"—and he may still be like that, and not let anyone prevent him from doing what, in good conscience, he feels obligated to do. I don't know, Herb, except it'll be so very little I'm asking of him, a copy of the old Varney letter, or an affidavit swearing that I tried to restrain Varney and that I was innocent of complicity in his defection or of any security lapse. It's such a small thing for him to do, but it's a big thing to me. It can change my whole life."

"Yes," said Neely. He looked at his omelet. "I reckon you've got a good chance," he added, but his voice was uncertain.

Brennan put down his sandwich. "What really puzzles me, Herb, is where Rostov disappeared to these last four years, and what happened that made Premier Talansky restore him to favor. I wish I knew. It might help."

"No one knows for sure," said Neely. "Ever since our alliance with the Soviets, many of us have hoped that they would open their books, so to speak. But I guess it's hard to learn to trust when you've distrusted for so long, and it's equally hard to shake off the old habits of secrecy." He was thoughtful, and then he went on. "As I told you on the phone, the minute I learned that Rostov was back on the Soviet team and coming here, my mind went to you. I began to make casual inquiries, from the Ambassador on down, including a few friends from the President's staff, from State, from the CIA." He looked up. "It's not much, with so much data missing, but conjecturing what the blanks might represent, I can still try to add it up."

"Better than nothing," said Brennan. "What's your sum total?"

"Well, before Zurich, at Zurich, and unswervingly ever since, Soviet Russia has cast its lot with the United States and the Western democracies. Premier Talansky—and I believe this—is not interested in a Leninist-Marxist world revolution if the cost is nuclear obliteration. I reckon that he believes he'll have it, the class revolution, anyway, if the world can survive. His one fear, like ours, is Red China. They've got a nuclear arsenal the match of our own, if not in quantity then in quality, and that's quite enough to plumb blow up the old planet. But China, the new China since Mao has been put away in his mausoleum, is no longer the paranoidal belligerent we knew when we were youngsters. Remember those days, Matt? Remember back when Mao was saying, 'East Wind prevails over West Wind'? Of course, that's when they were still smarting from a century and a half of invasion and oppression by foreigners. I remember Toynbee reminding us, 'In the years between 1840 and 1945 one country or another has taken bites out of China.' Well, once Mao had the Lop Nor explosion under his belt, he was ready to bite back, and in China they dreamed of restoring their country as Chung-kuo, the Middle Kingdom, center of the universe. Adolescent dreams of glory. Because as you know, after Mao, his successors, particularly Chairman Kuo Shu-tung, a rightist, a pragmatist, have considered the realities of the world outside. I think you'll agree he modified the Marxist-Maoist line considerably."

"Perhaps," said Brennan without conviction. "China has hardly been pacifist these last years."

"Of course not, Matt. But somehow, it's been different. Consider what's happened. Taiwan was neutralized. The United Nations admitted Red China. After that, China won back a good deal of the traditionally Chinese territory it had lost in the past—parts of Outer Mongolia, portions of Siberia—and it gained political control of Vietnam, Cambodia, Indonesia, Burma, Thailand, Malaya, Korea—and it did so without igniting a major war, with hardly any need to draw upon the three million men in its People's Liberation Army or the ten million in its militia. All this accomplished with little shooting and nary a nuclear weapon dropped. How? Well, you know how, Matt."

Brennan smiled. "As Confucius never say, 'i i chi i'—'use barbarians to control barbarians.' "

"Exactly. Red China, after organizing and activating its own Cominform, encouraged or provoked, and supported or supplied, all those People's Wars, wars of national liberation, revolutions, fought by Communist parties in every Asian country. And it worked, and they got away with it, because they were doing it in their own backyard. The minute that they began tampering with Japan—well, we intervened fast, and Russia intervened, because we couldn't let Red China take over a tremendously industrialized nation. That would be bigtime, big-power stuff, endangering world peace. So, after all these recent nervous months, Red China has let up on Japan and agreed to come and sit with us at a Summit and thrash things out. But I think that's what they wanted in the first place when they started the Japanese adventure."

"You really think so, Herb?"

"I'm sure of it, and so are the boys in the State Department. And this is the point I've been trying to make. The new Chinese leadership, now that it has established its own sphere of influence and control, now that it has achieved equality with its enemies, is realistically aware that

226

it can't go for world-power status *alone*. No nation can go for the jackpot, today, *alone*. With Russia on its side as an ally, as Russia was until 1960, Red China was set up to dominate the entire world. *But,* with Russia on *our* side, as she is today, China knows it cannot dominate a damn thing more, cannot impose Communism, through aggression, on the world because too many mighty powers are aligned against her. Alone, the most China can do is to do what she has been doing, hold sovereignty over the area around her frontiers, occasionally win back some old real estate, continue to sweat at ending feudalism and improving industrialization at home. The comrades in Peking know that any effort to annihilate others means certain annihilation of themselves. So, at last, China's Chairman and Premier, relative conservatives, I'd say, have fully turned their backs on the Marxist-Maoist expansionist policy, and have decided that survival as an equal power is better, more sensible, than no China at all, no planet at all. Believe me, Matt, China provoked the Japanese unrest and attempted coup as a face-saving device to tell us that she was ready to talk coexistence, rather than to dare coextinction. We understood, and we invited China to come here to Paris and join us in developing, once and forever, a real and workable foolproof system for arms control, disarmament, peace. Now, the Peking contingent is still talking tough, acting tough, and, indeed, they are tough, but most of us suspect that that's a bargaining posture. In the end, I reckon they know, as we know, that the name of the game is hang-together-or-hang-separately. So hail, the gang's all here for the Summit. And eighteen other smaller nations, with nuclear hardware or nuclear capability, are pledged to obey the treaty hammered out by their bigger siblings. Excuse the background briefing, Matt, but I do it so much with the press that it's become a habit. Now then, Nikolai Rostov. Where does he fit into this?"

"Yes," said Brennan, finishing the last of his wine. "Rostov. At the Zurich Parley he and his Russian comrades worked side by side with me and our crowd to bring Red China to its senses—that was four years ago—and make them see they had to be a party to any future disarmament agreement. At that time it seemed we'd have no trouble with them. Their nuclear stockpile wasn't as advanced as our own, and their delivery was inadequate. Then it all went poof. They got Professor Varney and, in effect, complete equality with the top nuclear powers. Varney gave them the neutron bomb, as well as secret data on the anti-missile missiles that can carry the N-bomb. And as a result—"

"You and Rostov were blamed," said Neely, shaking his head. "I reckon I'll never forget it. You both wound up with the Black Spot. Okay. We know what happened to you. But what you want to know is exactly what happened to Rostov. Not easy. As far as I've been able to ascertain, Matt, your friend Rostov was snatched out of Zurich by the Soviet secret police, dropped back in Moscow, kept incommunicado at the KGB headquarters in Dzerzhinski Square, questioned by Chekist officers there, then probably tried for treason before a secret tribunal. Our experts thought that he had been found guilty of conspiracy for giving military secrets to China, and that he'd been shot. But since he's surfaced very much alive, the general feeling currently is that he was acquitted of treason, maybe with the help of Varney's letter, but was found to have been soft on China, and a questionable risk, and therefore he was unofficially punished by being removed from the center of government. There have been a couple of educated guesses on where Rostov has been the last four years. Someone thought he'd been given a minor diplomatic post out in Sverdlovsk, in the Urals. Someone else heard Rostov had been one of the administrators of Vorkuta, a Soviet labor camp in the Arctic. No matter. Here he is."

"But why was he forgiven?" Brennan wondered.

"No one really knows, except that he had always been a Talansky man. He was probably on good behavior these last years. Above all, ever since Russia broke off with China, the Soviets have been deprived of real knowledge about China and I suppose they hated to go into this big meeting with the Chinese lacking sufficient trained, expert advisers. Rostov was an expert, as you know only too well, so presto, they forgave, they forgot, they brought him back."

"It sounds too simple," said Brennan.

Neely laughed, removed his spectacles and began to polish them. "Probably is. But that's the best we can conjure up. It's a pity our Government doesn't forgive and forget in the same way. We sure could use you in this Summit hassle, Matt."

"Thanks, but I'd be useless now. I've stagnated too long, been out of touch. I'd be as helpless as Metternich discussing nuclear disarmament. There have been too many new proposals since I was active."

Neely slipped on his rimless spectacles and pushed them high on the bridge of his nose. "Not really. There are only so many ideas you can have about deterring nuclear suicide. What's changed is not the means of containing the weapons, but the realignment and new ideas of the potential combatants. You remember the old setup? The United States had one set of proposals for disarmament, the Soviet Union had another, the United Nations had a third, and the People's Republic of China had none. Well, tomorrow, when the five countries sit down at the table, the United States, the Soviet Union, and Great Britain have agreed on a single plan for arms control, Red China has an opposing one, the United Nations stands as an observer, and France has decided to play host and side with the majority vote of her guests. But basically, nothing has changed, Matt. The obstacles remain economic, political, military—and China has added two unique obstacles peculiarly its own: the matter of face and the matter of Oriental fatalism. The Chinese have to leave the Summit with a ban treaty that will keep their pride intact. If this is impossible to achieve, they will leave here alone, without signing a disarmament treaty, and to beef up their strength they've threatened to give nuclear bombs to ten other Communist countries under their influence in Asia and Africa. If pushed too hard, they just might walk out, and one day another Government there might set into motion the first strike, even if it cost them several hundred million lives, because they're inured to national disasters and calamities like plagues and floods and famine, and they're used to death on a mammoth scale. We are not. However, that's another problem. But the Western proposals, from what I hear, should be acceptable enough. What's shaping up would be gradual armed forces reduction; gradual destruction of nuclear stockpiles and of conventional, bacteriological and chemical weapons; abolishment of missiles and delivery systems; and cessation of nuclear weapon production; all of this to be accomplished in three stages over a six-year period. Also, there would be strict limitations on the types of vehicles used in outer space, an international control organization under the United Nations that would employ inspection teams and aerial observers, and above all, a peace policing force, conventionally armed, highly paid, composed of soldiers from thirty of the smaller nations. And as a sop to the Chinese economy, there would be a provision whereby every country could maintain nuclear reactors for peaceful purposes, each of these to be under strict international supervision. There will also be proposed, finally, a foolproof means of overcoming the worst obstacle of all."

"The worst obstacle of all? You mean fear of concealment?"

"Exactly," said Neely. "The major defense against fear will be a two-billion-dollar worldwide network of listening posts equipped with the latest Swedish seismographs that register the pounding of the surf a thousand miles away, and that can distinguish between earthquakes and underground nuclear explosions. There will be on-site arms-control inspection teams, and their inspectors themselves will be regularly screened as to their reliability through lie-detector tests and injections of truth serum. There will be orbiting satellites sent aloft by the international control organization, these satellites varying their orbits constantly so that nothing can be hidden from their cosmic eyes.

Daily, hourly, inspection reports from all sources will be funneled into an evaluation center, and processed by computers, and if any report is suspect, the peace policing force will fix to move in swiftly. Well, that's basically the plan we hope and expect the Chinese will accept in the next days. Sounds familiar enough, doesn't it, Matt?"

Listening intently, Brennan, for the first time in months, felt a longing for his old career, his old idealism, his old commitment to striving for a practical peace. It was strange to be aware, again, of emotions that had atrophied, emotions like curiosity and optimism and, somehow, faith. He nodded to his friend. "Yes, it sounds familiar, and it sounds good."

Suddenly Neely sat up. "My God, there's the car coming. That means I've got to run to the press briefing at the Palais Rose." He grabbed the check before Brennan could reach for it, and began to peel off bills. "I'm ashamed," Neely said. "Our first time together in half a year, and I didn't let you open your mouth. . . . Matt, what are you doing right now?"

"Right now?"

"I mean after I leave here. You can't see Rostov yet. You've seen the sights. Why don't we stick together? Come along with me to the Palais Rose."

"I—I'm not sure about that, Herb."

"Why not? Come on. None of the reporters there will even recognize you. They'll think you're someone from the Embassy, and besides, there'll be such a mob, all of them busy making notes, that you'll be ignored. You might enjoy a preview peek of the Summit arena. The Palais Rose is an absolutely fascinating pile of pink marble. Built back around 1905, a duplicate of Marie Antoinette's Petit Trianon out in Versailles. It's on the Avenue Foch. Takes up about two-thirds of a block—7,500 square *yards,* to give you an idea—and I'm fixing to show the press mainly the *grand salon,* where the Big Five start meeting tomorrow morning. After today the *grand salon* will be out of bounds to everyone but the delegates. Then—well—there's a practical reason you should see the inside. For the next ten days your friend Rostov will probably be there daily, sometimes at Premier Talansky's elbow. If you run into any snags trying to catch up with Rostov, you might buttonhole him at the Palais. And you should know your way around there, if I ever have to slip you in. It may be useful, Matt, it should be painless, and I guarantee it'll be over with in an hour."

Although still reluctant, Brennan found that Neely's enthusiasm had persuaded him. Especially the Rostov part.

He stood up. "You win, Herb. Take me to your leader's Palais."

As they walked to the mustard-colored army sedan idling in the *contre-allée,* the narrow, brick second street or lane running between the sidewalk and the strip of grass parallel to the Champs-Élysées, Neely gestured toward the car. "Not one of ours," he said. "We have fifteen in the Embassy pool. But our delegation from Washington has taken most of those, so we borrowed a dozen military vehicles from EUCOM, our base out by St.-Germain, a post-de Gaulle restoration. The cars came furnished with noncom chauffeurs. Not bad."

Once settled in the rear seat, Neely gave directions to the Negro corporal. Then, rolling down the window, he offered Brennan his pack of Gauloises *bleues,* and when Brennan refused, he lit one for himself and relaxed with it.

The car swung around into the Champs-Élysées and headed toward the Arc de Triomphe. "Paris in June," said Neely, exhaling. "My favorite place and time in the world." He pointed out the window. "Look at those girls, Matt, those wonderful hair bobs, urchin faces, so pretty, wistful, fun-promising, and the easy way they dress and walk, and how they look at you, those French kids, straight at you. What a wonderful place to grow up, and be seventeen, and fall in love, right here on a Sunday on the Champs-Élysées." He squinted out the window again. "Well, I'm satisfied with my old girl at home, but those French femmes *are* a welcome diversion, especially when you're so plumb overworked you want to die." He turned to Brennan. "This Summit has made it real mean for a person in my job, Matt. At least fifty more correspondents, besides the regulars, are here now, and it's like trying to organize, direct, satisfy a battalion of anarchistic, spoiled prima donnas and tenors. Absolutely awful."

"Do the delegates give you much trouble?"

"Nothing but. Mostly it's the President's personal staff. They behave like emissaries from the Shah and as if I were their messenger-eunuch, especially the ones who still have fuzz on their chins and are fresh from Poli Sci, like that youngster, Wiggins, who's with the President, so officious and snotty. I reckon what I've forgotten about press relations, he'll never learn. And then unscheduled things happen, like The Ex's arrival—"

Brennan showed his surprise. "You mean Earnshaw?"

"None other. Our generation's answer to Warren G. Harding. Whenever I look at your old friend Earnshaw, I see genial and generous President Harding, and I'm reminded of what Harding's father once said to him: 'If you were a girl, Warren, you'd be in the family way all the time. You can't say no.' "

Brennan chuckled, then was serious again. "What's Earnshaw doing here?"

"That's what I'd like to know," said Neely. "In the middle of last

231

night we received a frantic call from our London Embassy. The Ex is on his way to Paris. The gimmick? He's coming as an accredited correspondent for the Ormsby chain and for ANA—500 syndicated words a day—I didn't know he knew that many words in all. So now we've got the man on Olympus looking down at the Summit. 'Course, I don't know why he's really here, Matt, unless he wants attention. Well, he's getting it. The entire morning reporters have been pounding my door to get me to arrange interviews with Earnshaw. But I couldn't and I can't. I'm representing the President-that-is, not the President-that-was. I've got to keep Earnshaw silent and out of the way. If he opens his mouth, he might embarrass our delegation and our policy at the Summit. So I'm busy trying to get him lost. This morning I arranged for Callahan to take Earnshaw and his niece on an extended sight-seeing tour, followed by lunch at the Quai d'Orsay, and more sight-seeing. I've got to wear him down before his presence wrecks us. . . . Oh boy, Matt, you got an extra cell on that island of San Lazzaro?"

Their military vehicle had made a harrowing half-circuit of the Étoile, and Brennan was able to breathe again as they entered the quiet residential elegance of the Avenue Foch. They proceeded between the stately set-back mansions of French aristocrats and the glossy modern apartments of American and European millionaires, until they slowed at the blue street sign announcing the intersecting Avenue Malakoff. The corporal turned the car sharply, and braked to a halt at the open gates in the high black iron fence before No. 122–124.

Behind the fence, off the large courtyard, Brennan could see a massive, palatial two-story building, although he had heard that there were actually three stories in the wings. The front of the Palais Rose consisted of a series of great vaulted windows set into pink marble. The main entrance, beneath a second-floor grilled balcony, featured three arched doors and was reached by a flight of five wide stone steps leading up from the broad courtyard.

"Drive inside, Corporal," Neely ordered the driver.

Their car backed up, then passed though the gates, and immediately they were surrounded by uniformed French police while a group of plainclothesmen, evidently a mixture of American, Russian, English, and Chinese, watched curiously from beside the entry staircase.

As Neely showed an agent of Services de la Sécurité Présidentielle both his identity card and Embassy Summit credentials, Brennan heard his own name mentioned by Neely and saw the officer nodding. Through the windshield, Brennan observed a husky plainclothesman hurrying toward them. The French security agent was directing their chauffeur toward the line of parked automobiles, when the plain-clothesman reached their car, and walked alongside it as they cruised into a parking slot.

"Hi, Hal," Neely said. "This is a friend of mine—Mr. Brennan." He turned to Brennan. "Hal's Secret Service."

"You've got a real mob in there waitin' for you, Mr. Neely," the Secret Service agent was saying. "Those reporters been streamin' in for half an hour. We got them contained in the big downstairs hall. But glad you're here, 'cause they sure are gettin' mighty restless."

Neely and Brennan left the car hurriedly and walked with the Secret Service agent across the courtyard. Leaving him, they went up the short flight of stone steps, and entered the Palais Rose through the center door.

Although forewarned, Brennan was surprised at the great jam of humanity stretching before them in the immense and soaring hall, with its rectangular green-veined white pillars and vaulted ceiling. The members of the American press, at least sixty in number, covered every foot of the marble floor, obscuring its pink and white squares, and the overflow spilled down several granitelike steps and up another rise of steps to the edge of an elevated marble deck with an inlaid star in its center. From the middle of the landing, across the way, marble staircases rose to the first floor above.

So captivated had Brennan been by the grandeur of the Palais Rose that he had not realized that something was going on. The members of the press, their backs to Neely and Brennan, were giving their attention to a tall, elderly, familiar-looking man who was standing alone on the star pattern of the marble deck, near the staircases.

"Oh, Christ," Neely muttered, and his features showed disgust as his eyes met Brennan's. "It's that damn worrisome thorn, Earnshaw, giving an off-the-cuff press conference. How in the hell did this happen? Where's that stupid Callahan?" He craned his neck, exploring the crowd for his Embassy colleague.

Brennan returned his gaze to the speaker. At this distance Earnshaw's words were inaudible, but his appearance was exactly as Brennan had remembered it from their last meeting before Zurich about four years ago. The same Earnshaw, the bush of white hair, pug nose, seraphic smile, Everybody's Kindly Grandfather. Brennan tried to decide whether he still hated Earnshaw, or whether he had simply no feelings about the man. But then he remembered that he had never really hated Earnshaw—could you hate a marshmallow or a mound of Jello?—that he had only resented him once for weakness and cowardice.

Because of Madlock—and always in Madlock's presence—Brennan had met with the President several times to confer on disarmament. He had found Earnshaw affable and slow-witted, and relatively uninformed. At the time, Brennan had possessed a mild affection for Earnshaw because the President had seemed to respect him. After the Zurich debacle, and Madlock's death, Brennan had expected Earnshaw to come to his aid. He had believed that the President would be loyal to one of his appointees. He had believed that the President knew, from Madlock, of Brennan's private concern about having Varney on the delegation to Switzerland. Yet during the entire Dexter hearings Earnshaw had remained remote and unavailable. Brennan had not allowed for the possibility that the President might not know that his appointee was innocent. Brennan believed that Earnshaw had gauged the mood of Congress and the public—the need for a scapegoat—and had accepted the consensus, subscribed to it, and permitted Brennan to become that scapegoat. In short, Earnshaw had refused to oppose popular opinion, and so had himself emerged from the political fracas unsullied and still pure.

At the time, Brennan had not hated his superior, but he had been embittered by the President's weakness of character and lack of integrity. In the years since, as Earnshaw faded from his memory, as certainty of The Ex's knowledge of his innocence had been replaced by uncertainty, Brennan had ceased to have any strong feelings about the former Chief Executive. And right now, watching Earnshaw's choppy gestures, Brennan felt more sorrow for The Ex than contempt or anger. Briefly he wondered whether or not Earnshaw would recognize him if they should come face to face.

He realized that Neely had located Callahan and brought him back to the immediate area of the entry. Neely was plainly furious, and Callahan was plainly wretched. Brennan tried not to listen, but he could not help hearing their abrasive whispered exchange.

"What in the hell is he doing here, holding a press conference?" Neely was demanding to know.

"Herb, listen, it's not my fault," Callahan was pleading. "I'm as upset as you are."

"Oh, sure, but the President who is President is going to eat my ass out, not yours."

"I couldn't prevent it," Callahan insisted. "You said take Earnshaw on a tour, keep him out of the way, so I tried to. But the first thing, right off, the girl—his niece, Carol—wanted to see where the Summit was being held. So he said okay, and told me to show them through the Palais Rose. What could I do?"

"If we were able to keep Khrushchev out of Disneyland, you could've kept Earnshaw out of the Palais Rose," said Neely with venom. "You knew I was fixing to have the press here at one o'clock."

"Herb, sure I knew, but be reasonable—he's a former President, and he gave me an order. And besides, I figured it was early enough to go through this joint quickly and get out before your gang turned up. But Carol is a Sightseer, capital S. She's got to see everything, know everything, and the tour dragged on and on until I had ants in my pants. I still thought we'd slip out in time. And we would've made it, but your wolf pack assembled early. So I hustled Earnshaw and his niece down the stairs—and smack, bang, right into the fourth estate. Everyone shouted for The Ex to talk, and he hasn't shut up since."

"We better find out what the devil he's saying," said Neely, and he eased his way around the fringe of the crowd, followed closely by the distraught Callahan and by Brennan.

They could hear clearly now, the correspondents' questions and Earnshaw's grandiloquent but muddled answers. Someone had asked him for a comment on the agenda of this Five-Power Summit, and Earnshaw was replying that Summit conferences were usually good things in these tense times, in this age we lived in. Several correspondents tried to interrupt with pointed questions about this particular Summit, but Earnshaw did not hear them, or would not, as he rambled on like a senile New England schoolmaster, discoursing on the evolution of the modern Summit.

"You may or may not know, my old friends, that the entire idea of—uh—a Summit conference attended by powers who are—uh—powerful—that is, powerful and in conflict—is a new idea," Earnshaw was saying, his sentences interspersed with the "uh" pauses that always plagued him when he was under public pressure. "Way back in the horse-and-buggy days, I should say horse-and-coach days, that is, before the Second World War, the heads of state did not meet like this, in this way. They sent off their leading diplomats to Vienna or Rome or St. Leningrad—uh—that is, Petersburg—to confer—moving the knights and bishops out ahead of the kings, as we say—and there was a reason, you see. In the old days, a head of state, an emperor or king, was supposed to be of divine origin, so anything he said, maybe offhand, on the spur of the moment, became the last word, the law, the rule, and it might not be what he really wanted to say at all, if he'd thought it out, so in those days it was considered better to have diplomats, ministers, princes do most of the work, and later let the heads of state meet merely to affirm what had been settled. But the Second World War, mechanization, airplanes, all that, changed diplomacy. Conflict developed too fast, and there was a necessity for faster communication among top men with full authority to make quick decisions. Also, in the Second World War, our ally, Russia, was ruled by one man, one-man rule, Stalin, and only he could make any real decision for Russia. I mean—uh—well, now—there was no second-in-command—I mean, a Molotov had no right to act independently, could make no decision; whatever was said, he would have to go back to Stalin for what should be done, and you know, that took time, and there was no time. So, to get things done fast, the Summit conference as we know it was invented, where a Stalin could meet across a table from a Roosevelt and a Churchill and together they could make decisions speedily and—uh, well now—that explains the Summit here, and answers your questions, I'm sure."

Someone was inquiring if Earnshaw had been requested to come to the Summit as an elder statesman, and Earnshaw was replying good-naturedly that he was only in Paris as an observer, a journalist like the rest of them, and he had taken the job simply because he wanted to find out, once and for all, what it was like to be someone who knew more than the President and his Cabinet and the Department of State thrown together. To this, there was an outburst of pleased laughter from the press, and Earnshaw stood beaming happily.

Neely leaned over closer to Callahan and Brennan and whispered, with a gust of relief, "We're off the hook. He's in his best form, saying nothing, thank the Lord. It's okay, Callahan, we can relax."

But suddenly, from nearby, a shrill, grating female voice called out, "Mr. Pres—Mr. Earnshaw, I have a question!"

Brennan tried to locate the speaker but was unable to do so. He heard Neely whisper, "Hazel Smith, ANA. This could be trouble."

"The question," the high-pitched female voice went on, "concerns your own responsibility for this critical Summit meeting. To what extent, Mr. Earnshaw, do you feel that your Administration contributed to the international crisis that forced this Summit—made this Summit necessary?"

Brennan felt a clutch near his heart, a fear that his own name might be brought up, and he heard Neely whisper to Callahan, "This *is* trouble. I'm going to stop it."

Brennan saw the press attaché push through the crowd; then he directed his attention to Earnshaw once more. He could see that Earnshaw's face had reddened and his lips had compressed. "Young lady," The Ex said tartly, "except for the work of my Administration, there might not be this Summit. There might be war and devastation. We—Mr. Madlock and myself—tried to inculcate in our foreign counterparts abroad the idea that only reason and reasoning can maintain peace, and I think we succeeded—uh—succeeded admirably. As a matter of record—"

Earnshaw droned on and on, discussing his Administration as one child embellishes a fairy tale for another, half believing it, casting himself and Madlock as the twin good princes, and casting Red China as the fiery dragon they had tamed and caged. Then he capped it off with one inaccurate quotation from Luke, which he attributed to Mark.

As Earnshaw paused, before resuming, Neely burst through the front platoon of correspondents, climbing toward him, greeting him, thanking him, pumping his hand. While Earnshaw muttered in bewilderment, Neely pivoted toward the press gathering, telling them that Earnshaw's submission to this inquisition had indeed been generous, but that the former President was here to ask questions about the Summit, not be questioned about it, and that he deserved a Sunday of rest. It had all been handled swiftly and adroitly, and Brennan observed Neely with admiration, wishing that he himself possessed the same talent for applying authority.

Still holding Earnshaw firmly by the arm, Neely announced to the throng, "A two-minute break while I escort our former President to his car! Smoking is permitted down here, but not upstairs! I'll be right back, and then we'll go upstairs for a look at the conference room!"

The correspondents fell back as Neely opened a path for Earnshaw, who had now been joined by his niece. Progress was slow. Earnshaw, obviously reveling in the attention, waved to old acquaintances and paused here and there to shake hands with journalists he had known in his White House days.

They emerged a few feet from where Brennan and Callahan were standing, and Brennan, feeling uncomfortable at Earnshaw's nearness, tried to slide away but was wedged in against a pillar. In the open at last, Earnshaw halted to mop his brow. He glanced around, smiling aimlessly, to be sure that he was not overlooking or neglecting anyone. His eyes lighted on Brennan, and his smile broadened, although his eyes were vague.

Earnshaw offered Brennan a friendly nod. "Hello," he said. "I seem to remember you." He hesitated. "We have met before?"

Brennan swallowed, stood straight, and said tightly, "Yes, Mr. Earnshaw. We met when you were in the White House. I'm Matthew Brennan."

"Brennan, yes—" Earnshaw's brow had furrowed ever so slightly, and suddenly it creased into a hard frown, and the smile disappeared as full recognition came. "Yes, of course," he said coldly. "I remember. I guess I'm surprised to see you here."

"No more surprised than I am to see you here," said Brennan.

237

About to say something more, Earnshaw checked himself. Nodding quickly at Brennan, turning his back on him, he took his niece by the elbow, and accompanied by Neely, they marched out the door that Callahan was holding open.

In seconds Neely returned. "Sorry, Matt," he said. "One of those things."

"It was nothing," Brennan reassured his friend. And, indeed, he told himself, it *was* nothing, for once more he felt vindicated and anyone's equal, anticipating the clearance that he would soon have, after leaving Rostov.

"I've got to show the demoniac hordes the upstairs," Neely said. "Sure you don't mind? I mean, you can take off if you still feel uneasy."

"I feel fine," said Brennan defiantly.

"Good. I'll lead the charge. I suggest you bring up the rear."

Brennan waited as his friend began to lead the way up one of the marble staircases with the chattering, unruly correspondents trooping after him. Brennan hung behind until the last contingent started the climb to the first floor, and then he climbed after them.

At the top, the journalists formed into an irregular column, wending their way around a corner and into a long spacious gallery. They crossed the parquet floor, between tall windows and beneath a white, gilt-rimmed arched ceiling. From far up ahead, Brennan could hear the reverberation of Neely's voice.

"You're passing through the Salle des Glaces, the Hall of Mirrors, a miniature copy of the gallery in the Palace of Versailles," the press attaché announced. "We're heading straight into the *grand salon* of the Palais Rose, where the heads of the five powers will be sitting in conference tomorrow. This Palais was built by an American, Anna Gould, daughter of the famous railroad magnate, Jay Gould. She and her husband, the Marquis Boniface de Castellane, entertained 4,000 guests on the day that they moved in here. Anna Gould abandoned the Palais in 1939, and not long after, when the Nazis occupied Paris, the German military governor of France, General Karl Heinrich von Stuelpnagel, made this his residence. But I understand that to play it safe, he had a huge bomb shelter dug beneath the Palais. It's not open now. . . . Well, here we are. This mirrored door leads into the *grand salon*. When we're all inside, sort of form a circle around the walls, and I'll be fast with my spiel because French security is giving us only five minutes in there."

More attentive and orderly now, the correspondents filed into the *grand salon*. Brennan was among the last to squeeze inside. He

238

propped himself against the mantel of a fireplace while the American journalists jostled and elbowed to form their double circle around the perimeter of the Salon. While his friend Neely chatted with various more prominent members of the press corps, Brennan surveyed the room itself.

With an ache of nostalgia, Brennan found himself peopling this magnificent room with delegations, and their memorable meetings, of his career past. There had been so many of these conference rooms up until Zurich—awesome palace rooms in London, Bonn, Geneva, Rome —when he had been a participant, sitting beside an American Ambassador or Secretary of State, listening, making notes, often being called to advise upon or reinforce a policy statement with facts, or to clarify and expand upon a line in the Department of State's black-bound Position Book. It had given him not only pride but deep satisfaction to collaborate with the movers and shakers of men, to be one of the representatives of humanity trying to eradicate the madness of war and killing. He had known that his brother Elia, a good lamb sacrificed to this madness, would have been proud of him. But now, at this site in Paris, he realized that nostalgia had led him down a mean path. It was hurtful to be an outsider, helpless, useless, no part of this, when so much work desperately needed to be done. Inner rage and inner self-pity lay immediately ahead, his private Scylla and Charybdis, and with determination he avoided them and devoted himself to the superficialities of his surroundings.

There had been other rooms in other royal manors, yes, but none ever quite as impressive as this one. Dominating the *grand salon* of the Palais Rose, occupying most of its center, was the largest round table that Brennan had ever laid eyes upon. A thick felt tablecloth, of a tobacco color, had been laid over it like a tarpaulin over a gaming field, and surrounding the huge circular table were—he counted them —twenty chairs. Fifteen of the chairs, he could see, were gilded, straight-backed, armless. And five were velvet-seated, cane-backed, armed thrones, *fauteuils* for the mighty, the quintet of extraordinary men selected by millions of their fellows to determine man's destiny on earth.

Since Neely was moving toward this table, and a hush was falling over the room, Brennan hastily scanned what was left to be seen—four crystal chandeliers hanging heavily from the ceiling, six doors decorated with carved, gilded moldings marking the gray-pink marble walls, four mammoth white plaster medallions high on the walls engraved with representations of the four arts, three great French doors opening out on what appeared to be a garden.

A bizarre atmosphere, thought Brennan, for three democrats and two communists who were to debate about nuclear explosives.

Neely was holding up one hand for attention as he adjusted his rimless spectacles with the other. Correspondents were readying their pencils, pens, and note pads.

"Since this will be your only opportunity to visit this room, where the stories you will write in the next ten days will originate, I know you will want to observe carefully what is here and learn what you can about it, to give your stories color and background," Neely began. "We haven't much time—the Russian press will be arriving here shortly, and after them, the British—so why don't I proceed? This *grand salon* was used only once before as an international conference room. In 1949, the French Government asked Anna Gould if it could rent the Palais Rose for a four-power Ministers' conference. She offered its use for free. In 1949, the United States, Great Britain, France, Soviet Russia, represented by Acheson, Bevin, Schuman, Vishinsky, held meetings here. In the several decades since, the Palais Rose has lain empty. Now, once again, the French Government has borrowed it, and for this Summit meeting has furnished it with chairs, tables, desks moved in from the Élysée palace in the city and from the Petit Trianon in Versailles."

Neely paused, offering a needed interval while the reporters jotted their notes, once catching Brennan's eye as he surveyed his audience. At last, he resumed.

"In case you are interested, outside the three French doors there is a formal garden, very beautiful, the stone urns decorated with cupids and filled with flowers, and the main statue out there is a nude Venus. Make what you want of that. There are benches in the garden. Hopefully, all of this beauty will have a salutary effect, a calming one, on the heads of state."

There was mild laughter, and Neely acknowledged it with a crisp smile and went on.

"I might add, the garden is on the Avenue Foch side, just to orient you. All right, I reckon we'd better proceed to the main business, the conference table. It's made of a rare soft wood, and was especially designed and constructed for this historic Summit. Each of the five leaders will sit in one of these Louis XIV *fauteuils*—you can see the armchairs are upholstered in red velvet and the wood is gilded—and each leader will have three members of his team in three of the side chairs—two interpreters and his leading Minister or assistant. Then, tonight, five small tables will be placed, one behind each leader's armchair, and at each table a secretary will sit making a record of the

240

talks in shorthand or on a stenotyper. Of course, there will be place cards directing each group to its proper chairs—"

"Mr. Neely," a shrill and insistent female voice broke in, "where are all the other delegates to be?"

Neely seemed startled. "I was coming to that," he said, adding parenthetically, "Of course, it was understood, there wouldn't be time for me to answer any questions during our tour. If you have questions, you can call me or see me at the press attaché's office in the United States Embassy. But as for the other delegates and negotiators, yes, they'll be spread throughout this upper floor—you can see the telephones and cables all around so they can be summoned from adjacent rooms or from anywhere in Paris. I mean, if Premier Talansky needs information to reply to a question raised by the Chairman of Red China, Kuo Shu-tung, why, he can summon his Far Eastern experts for a quick consultation by phone or by sending a *huissier* with a message. Of course, most of that kind of thing goes on privately inside each embassy at night. The daily meetings themselves tend to be rather cut-and-dried and formal. As the Ambassador told me, when you have more than two or three at a conference table, each delegate tends to make speeches, orate, rather than participate in a give-and-take conversation. The main progress is made during informal meetings between the various leaders, discussing matters over drinks, in their embassies or ambassadors' residences or in hotel suites."

Using his finger as a pointer, Neely indicated the six doors.

"Those doors lead to other rooms of the Palais Rose which have been converted into offices for the Summit delegations. The American delegates will take over a green bedroom once used by a duke. The Chinese will have, for their headquarters, appropriately, a red-brocaded bedroom, now a red-brocaded workroom. The Russians will have a white-and-gold bedroom in—again, appropriately—in the left wing of the Palais. And so on. As we leave, I'll walk you through those rooms. You'll see that the French Government has not neglected the fourth estate. A dining room and a smoking room, furnished with desks, telephones, teletypes, snack and drink bars, have been converted into press rooms for the few of you, and a select number from the other four nations, who are actually accredited to cover the Palais Rose part of the Summit.

"The first plenary session of the Summit is scheduled to open in this Salon at ten o'clock tomorrow morning. Diplomatic protocol will follow the form codified in 1815 at the Congress of Vienna. The first meeting is expected to adjourn round about noon. Then, in the afternoon, at three o'clock, the foreign ministers from each delegation will convene at the Quai d'Orsay, while the heads of state take part in special ceremonies at the Mayor's Hôtel de Ville and observe the usual wreath-laying formality beneath the Arc de Triomphe. I suggest that all correspondents accredited to cover the Palais Rose be in the press rooms here no later than nine-thirty tomorrow morning, for last-minute briefings and handouts. I think that does it. I'll show you the delegates' individual workrooms as we leave, and after that, at least for today, we stand adjourned. Thank you, and when you write, find time for a prayer—for yourself, for all of us, for the whole worrying world."

Someone shouted, "Amen!" and Neely began leading a serpentine of journalists out of the *grand salon,* and again Brennan hung back and was among the last to follow.

Twenty minutes later the tour was completed, and Neely herded the corps of correspondents downstairs into the chilly main hall. Most of the journalists departed immediately, but a handful lingered to chat with their colleagues and rivals before going, and Brennan tried to find an inconspicuous place by the front doors to wait for Neely.

Eager to escape unnoticed, Brennan nervously sought his friend. At last, he saw Neely removing his spectacles to rub his eyes as he listened to five journalists, two women and three men, who had detained him. Suddenly Neely said something, offered a gesture of farewell, and broke away from the ambush. He had seen Brennan and was hastening toward him, but he was not alone. An energetic redheaded lady, with an overstuffed handbag slung by its strap over the shoulder of a brown suit, was pursuing him, striding alongside him, jabbering away. Plainly distressed, obviously determined to escape, Neely kept walking as he made some curt reply.

When they were almost upon him, Brennan could near Neely say, with a trace of sharpness, "That's absolutely all I can tell you now, Miss Smith. If I hear anything more about the President's wife, I'll leave word for you at ANA."

They had come to a halt before Brennan, and Brennan recognized her at once because he had seen her likeness in the newspapers in recent days. In fact, Lisa had once pointed at the woman's photograph and said that she wished she could have been a foreign correspondent like Hazel Smith, who had such a romantic and adventurous career. This was Hazel Smith, no doubt about it, Brennan concluded.

Despite the piercing quality of her strident voice, the obviously dyed red hair, the facial features as jagged as a cubist's drawing, the severely tailored suit, Hazel Smith was, inexplicably, more feminine than Brennan had expected. Perhaps, he thought, it was the wariness of her quick eyes, or the smallness of her desperately painted mouth, or maybe the flare of her broad hips, that contradicted all else and made her seem, finally, a woman.

The quick, curious eyes had gone toward Brennan, held on him, wondering, and then dismissing him, they had turned themselves on Neely again. "I'll take your word, Mr. Neely. I'll expect to hear from you. I'm doing a series on the big shots' wives, and I've got to include our First Lady. Now remember—"

"I gave you my word, Miss Smith," Neely said impatiently. Abruptly, he turned away and gripped Brennan's arm. "Okay, Matt, let's get going. We have—"

Before they could start for the exit, Hazel Smith intercepted them, planting herself almost between them. "Did you say Matt?" she demanded of Neely, as she stared directly at Brennan. Suddenly she snapped her fingers. "Old photographic-memory me," she said to Neely, her gaze still relentlessly fixed on Brennan. "I thought he looked like someone I'd seen, but I wasn't—"

"We're late, we've got to leave," Neely said urgently, trying to push Brennan past her, but Hazel Smith held her ground as firmly as a concrete roadblock.

Ignoring the press attaché, Hazel Smith said, "Matt is for Matthew and in my time Matthew was not from the Gospels, it was from the Dexter hearings. You're Matthew Brennan, aren't you?"

Brennan tried to remain contained. "Yes," he said quietly, "I'm Matt Brennan."

"I mean, *the* Matthew Brennan."

She had released the last like an arrow from a bow, shafting him as she might impale *the* Julius Rosenberg or *the* Klaus Fuchs, and Brennan gave a resigned smile. "None other," he said. Neely was anxiously worrying his arm, trying to push him to freedom, until Brennan said from the corner of his mouth, "It's okay, Herb."

"I'm Hazel Smith of ANA," she was saying, "and I—"

"I know who you are," Brennan said.

"Good. Then you know I'm here doing feature stories about the unusual people who've been sent to Paris or been drawn here by the Summit." She was fishing excitedly in her cluttered handbag for a pen, which she found, and notepaper, which she could not find. "What a wonderful break," she continued. "You'll make a marvelous story. It'll be great." She looked up from her purse briefly. "You know the sort of angle, the ghost of a famous diplomat revisits scenes of his old triumphs—the self-exiled unofficial delegate rises from the bog of the long ago—oh, don't look like that, Mr. Brennan, you don't have to be scared of Hazel Smith. This'll be useful for you, too. Give you a

243

chance to speak out on your own behalf to millions of readers. Matter of fact, to give you an idea of what I think of this, I have an appointment to do another interview in an hour, an interview with that little English chippy they're headlining over at the Club Lautrec—you know, Medora Hart—but I'll put that off. Her tired old-hat scandal doesn't have half the human interest this does." She resumed searching in her handbag. "Why don't we just walk over to a café and—"

"Don't bother," said Brennan.

She paused, and looked up surprised. "What?"

"Don't bother looking for notepaper," said Brennan. "I can't give you anything to put on it. I'm not here to engage in interviews."

"Are you refusing me? Because if you are, it's a mistake. I told you a sympathetic story right now could be useful to you. And if you cooperated, well, it would only be natural for me to be appreciative, feel more kindly disposed toward you. I'm sure my story would generate considerable goodwill. And God knows, you need it, Mr. Brennan."

"No, thank you, Miss Smith. I'm sorry."

Hazel Smith shrugged, deliberately held her pen high before dropping it into the handbag, then fastened the purse clasp shut. "Your funeral, Mr. Brennan." She looked at him pityingly, and she shook her head. "Very unwise, your behaving like this. Everyone knows your responsibility for the present world crisis. You'd be smart to have the press on your side. Go on behaving like this, and—well—you may really be sorry, I mean really."

"Miss Smith, I appreciate your concern," Brennan said steadily, praying his demeanor hid the ague he suffered inside. "Your so-called press used me for target practice four years ago. There is no future in being a target, I have learned. So now, when I see an archer, I keep moving."

With that, Brennan started past her, once more filled with the urgent need to confront Nikolai Rostov and, through him, bring an end to this punishment.

As Brennan went out the center door of the Palais Rose with Neely, he could hear Hazel Smith's last comment trilling after him.

"Well, at least that chippy singer at the Club Lautrec has enough good sense *not* to be self-destructive."

And hearing this, as he left, Brennan thought: Good luck, poor chippy singer, wherever you are. For while he was still sorry for himself, he somehow did not envy Hazel Smith's chippy singer, whoever she was.

Paris had held no surprises for her so far. It was exactly as it had been the other times, and as she had anticipated it would be this time. In the short walk from the Hotel San Régis in the Rue Jean-Goujon to the Avenue Montaigne, and then to the Rond-Point des Champs-Élysées, Medora Hart had been approached on four different corners, by four different Frenchmen, who had flirted with her or propositioned her in undertones, each hoping for much but expecting little and undismayed by her haughty shrugs of dismissal.

One would think, she had thought, that they would have been surfeited by the readily available fashion mannequins in the neighborhood, or be put off by her unprovocative city attire (this was not the Riviera, after all), but she knew better. In Paris, the husband or lover of France's most beautiful actress might flirt with a waitress, and everyone would understand. And so Medora Hart, a veteran of male overtures, understood, and was neither annoyed nor flattered.

Having attained the Champs-Élysées, and being closer to her destination, Medora slowed before several shopwindows to appraise herself. The ravages of the long drive from Juan-les-Pins and the sleepless night had been repaired by a sound two-hour nap in her quiet, darkened, Louis XVI inside room above the inner San Régis court. Refreshed by her rest, and a cold shower, Medora had returned Alphonse Michaud's call, promising to be present for a brief rehearsal to ready her for the next night's show. She had disposed of her rented Mercedes, and at last she had dressed.

She had intended to do her flaxen hair in pigtails, and wear a middy blouse and skirt, all childish innocence, but she had discarded the notion as too cute and too much of a blow for Michaud, who was awaiting a sex symbol. In the end, she had decided upon a compromise, the tousled fun look, and dressed herself in a teal-blue light-weight-wool dress with a yellow stand-away collar that matched her soft yellow boots. She had swept her blond hair up, pinning it into place, and set a teal tam-o'-shanter on her head. Finally, with her makeup kit, leotards, and dance slippers in a yellow straw handbag, she had been ready.

Glimpses of her reflection in the display windows along the Champs-Élysées, and the swiveling heads of male passersby, reassured her that she would make a satisfactory first impression on Michaud.

Actually, the Club Lautrec engagement occupied the lesser part of her mind. It was no more to her than a means of keeping herself occupied until she had humbled Sir Austin Ormsby, and a final effort to make a bundle of money to pay for her beautician's course once she was happily back with her mother and sister in her beloved London. Yet the fussing about her appearance, the eagerness to attend the rehearsal and to do well at the cabaret, were vaguely tied in with her determination to bring about Sir Austin's surrender. If she were well reviewed, well publicized, her appearance in Paris could not help but come to Sir Austin's attention. Her audacity might unsettle him, make him more receptive to compromising with her so that he might be permanently rid of her. She had not yet had the opportunity to learn where she might reach Sir Austin or Fleur. She assumed this information would be mentioned in the evening papers, and if it was not, she would find out anyway. All that mattered was that she possessed Nardeau's blatant nude of the hitherto unassailable Lady Ormsby, and that the nude, discreetly wrapped, was resting in the safety of the hotel vault.

Medora had arrived at the Rue la Boëtie. As she turned right off the Champs-Élysées, she saw the massive neon sign proclaiming the location of the Club Lautrec and, below it, the giant cardboard cutout of a nude female. Suspicious, she hastened toward the cabaret entrance, but even before she had planted herself in front of the grotesque nude, her suspicions had been confirmed. The painted cardboard face in no way resembled her own, and the mammoth moon breasts and six-inch navel could be claimed by no woman alive. The sparkling silver fig leaf between the legs, disproportionately small compared to the size of the nude cardboard body and the reach of the legs, was offensive. There was no doubt that this Amazon was meant to represent Medora herself, for there it was in oversize black letters on the streamer across the thighs: PREMIÈRE DEMAIN—LA SCANDALEUSE BEAUTÉ ANGLAISE—EN PERSONNE—DANS SON FAMEUX NUMÉRO DE STRIP-TEASE—ELLE CHANTE, ELLE DANSE—C'EST MEDORA HART.

Not only the indecent size of the figure angered Medora, but also its total lack of feminine appeal, which she was sure would repel any questing male. Turning away, she realized that several Frenchmen were standing nearby, staring up at the cutout with smirking approval.

Well, maybe, Medora decided. Perhaps Michaud did know what he was about, but at least, at the very least, he could use more delicacy when publicizing her. This kind of promotion would only confirm in Sir Austin's mind that he was treating with some four-bob chippy instead of a top-flight entertainer who was admired by celebrities like Nardeau.

She hurried into the tunnellike lobby of the Club Lautrec and walked by the tastefully framed original Toulouse-Lautrec *affiches* hanging on the walls, until she arrived at the high desk where a skinny bespectacled Frenchman in a blue serge suit was taking a dinner reservation over the telephone. When he was through, she introduced herself, and his wizened countenance came alive. In a torrent of French, he told her that M. Michaud was expecting her and that this moment he was directing the rehearsal inside.

Abandoning the desk, the receptionist preceded Medora down a short flight of green-carpeted steps and opened heavy velvet curtains to allow her to pass through a doorway. In a dim cavern to her left, she made out an elegant padded horseshoe bar, and turning to her right, she was overwhelmed by the vastness of the cabaret. Now, it was erratically lighted except for the glaring brightness on the distant stage, a highly polished wooden platform that extended out into the dining area and was surrounded by empty tables.

While the receptionist raced ahead to inform the proprietor of her arrival, Medora, who had never been inside the Club Lautrec before, advanced slowly and unobtrusively between the tables. Below the stage, several young Frenchmen were gathered, and a broad-shouldered, well-dressed gentleman sat tilted backward in a beige chair smoking lazily. Nearby, a stoutish, shapeless elderly woman, with short shingled purple hair, an empty cigarette holder clenched between her teeth, hands militantly on her hips, surveyed the stage, then addressed herself to the sound engineer at her elbow. The engineer, a curly-haired Algerian in a checked sport shirt, sat behind an intricate metal tape recorder and player, busily going through reels of tape.

On the stage, a dozen, closer to a dozen and a half, tall young girls, magnificently limber and flawlessly beautiful, stood around, at ease and with apparent disinterest. These were, Medora guessed, the highly publicized girls of The Troupe. There appeared to be no standard for rehearsal dress except that it be comfortable and scanty. Several bare-legged dancers wore black tights cut high at the sides. Others wore blouses knotted behind or in front, and skin-hugging bikini bottoms, their navels exposed. Still others wore form-fitting jersey sweaters, and pastel shorts or long dancers' body stockings.

Off to the right, below the platform, a half-dozen other leggy girls lounged at the tables in various states of rehearsal undress, sipping coffee or Cokes from paper cups, or smoking as they read French, German, English newspapers. Behind the girls, chattering and flirting among themselves, Medora could make out six or eight willowy young male dancers, probably French judging from their haircuts, most of them in T-shirts or thin sweaters, blue jeans or shorts, all of them in tennis shoes.

Suddenly the elderly woman clapped her hands together. "Troupers, *attendez!*" In rapid-fire English she loudly commanded, "Let us try 'The Lady Is a Tramp' from the beginning. Remember, remember, to kick out sharply, kick out, turn, look above the heads, but kick, don't behave as if you have sticks in your backs." She was gesticulating like an orchestra leader. "One, two, kick—three, four, turn—five, six, kick—fluttering your hands—and forget your old ballet lessons, don't lay your heads back—heads straight—then weave forward, plop, down you go, up fast, get your derrières off the floor fast, spin and start the march to the rear. Now, let's have it perfect this time. You, Christine, what's the matter? Why that frown? You've been a swing long enough to manage right off, and if you become rattled, just do as Denise does. Ready? To your places!"

The elderly lady said something to the engineer, who had finished adjusting a tape, and suddenly "The Lady Is a Tramp" blared from loudspeakers above, and the elderly lady was clapping her hands to mark the tempo, and the stockinged legs and bare legs were kicking high together. And then Medora realized that the broad-shouldered, handsome Frenchman was coming briskly toward her.

She recognized him from the layout that she had seen in *Paris Match,* the pictures of him beside his Karmann-Ghia convertible, on his yacht outside Biarritz, in his luxurious bachelor's apartment on the Île St.-Louis, in his *régence* office above the Club Lautrec (chatting with his Troupe girls as he indolently fed his Yorkshire terrier). Yes, he was well-made, virile-looking, jaunty, she could see, slicked hair, broad tanned features, athletic body in a blue alpaca suit, diamond tiepin and heavy gold cuff links.

"I am Michaud," he said, lifting up Medora's hand gracefully and brushing the back of it with his lips. "Welcome to Paris, Miss Hart. This is a distinct honor."

She nodded uncertainly, instantly disliking the arrogance of his eyes and manner, the surface glibness that would too thinly mask lies. But this was bread and butter, and perhaps the trap for Sir Austin, and so she said, as coolly remote as possible, "I am pleased to be here, Monsieur Michaud. I hope that I can work into the show satisfactorily despite so little preparation."

"No difficulty about that, my dear." The din of the taped music became louder, and Michaud wrinkled his nose, peering off at the stage. "We can put you on in fifteen minutes. My apologies for that long a wait. My assistant, Countess Ribault, she is entirely in charge of The Troupe, and she has her endless problems. Her ancestry is half English, half Norman, thank goodness. It takes one of such sturdy forebears to cope with our little United Nations of eighteen girls and the two substitutes—swings, as we call them. Unfortunately, there has been a minor disaster. One of the swings has had her eye blackened, and one of the regulars ran off with a customer to Majorca, and a third announced this morning that she is pregnant, so we must contend with three new girls in the line." He shook his head. "Someone is always becoming pregnant. Understand, I do not mind our girls having a love life"—he winked at Medora, and then studied her—"for I am certain, Miss Hart, that you agree that every young lady must have a satisfying love life. It is a necessity for well-being, no? I only resent, among my charges, carelessness. I cannot imagine you, if I may venture to say so, Miss Hart, being careless when making love?"

It was the first slippery feeler, and with its inevitable appearance, Medora felt easier. This was familiar home ground, and here she had confidence. In her mind she turned the key, locked the door. Ignoring his question, she said, "I don't mind waiting my turn to go on. I can use the time to change."

He smiled a handsome false smile. "How rude of me to keep you standing. Let me show you your dressing room, Medora."

The first feeler had been made, and now the intimacy of the first name, but Medora refused to waver. "Thank you, Monsieur Michaud."

He took her arm possessively, although she stiffened the muscles beneath his grip, but then he paused to hold her off, examining her from the teal tam-o'-shanter to the yellow boots. "What a cunning outfit," he said. "Very clever. You are as winning as one of Colette's cats. However, I'm afraid our clientele might not appreciate the ensemble, since it does not accent your best features."

"I dress as I please on my own time," she said.

"I spoke for our clientele, not for myself," he said. "I, for one, admire individuality. Come now, my dear."

The music had ceased, and on the way to the cabaret dressing rooms Michaud paused to introduce Medora to the Countess Ribault, who was formal but friendly. Passing the girls on stage and off, who watched her with interest and envy (no doubt having heard rumors of her salary), Medora followed Michaud through a door at one side of the stage and entered the backstage area, which resembled a warehouse. Halting between the control booth and the resin box, she was introduced to an amusing Australian named Lewis, who was the chief of the control booth and who directed all cues from lighting to revolving stage sets.

Preceding Michaud up a steep, winding circular staircase, conscious of his eyes on her calves and thighs, Medora hurried to reach the corridor above. Michaud stepped ahead to open the second door, and he bowed her inside. What she beheld was the replica of dozens of dressing rooms she had known throughout Europe, a cramped, utilitarian cubicle, with flat, dirty whitewashed plaster walls, tiny yellow bulbs arranged in a halo around the dressing table mirror, a lumpy cot, a chest of drawers, and a torn Japanese screen folded against one wall.

"My profound apologies for the accommodations," Michaud was saying. "They are not commensurate with your salary or billing, but since you were booked at the last minute, the more commodious rooms had already been taken by the other specialty acts. However, if you find this depressing, I might say that my own office suite is just above, and there is a magnificent dressing room which I would be only too pleased to—"

"Thank you," she interrupted. "This will do nicely."

"*Je suis enchanté*. It is good you are so easy to satisfy."

"Not always," she said pointedly.

He shot his cuffs. "Very well. If there is anything more I can do to accommodate you, Medora, do not hesitate to ask. Always *à votre service*."

Then she remembered. "As a matter of fact, there is one thing. I am concerned as to how you—you present me to the public. That frightful poster of a woman, outside the entrance. It's too obvious. And it doesn't look like me at all."

"Ah, my dear, perhaps it does not do you full justice—what reproduction could?—but I suggest it does accurately convey your fine points, your voluptuousness."

Medora turned her bosom away from his gaze and began to open her straw handbag. "Well, maybe it's not that so much as the words referring to the scandal. I don't see any sense in dredging that up. It's old history, and not very refined."

"My dear, we must be practical. This is a business. I am paying you an enormous fee. To make it worth my while, on top of the other salaries and overhead, you must attract customers we might otherwise not have. The Folies and the Lido have feature attractions who can sing well, dance well, offer nudity, but you alone can offer that little something more. The city is filled with foreigners, and the Jameson case is a part of their lives, and, in a sense, so are you."

She felt irritated. "At least play it down, and if you have to refer to it, please use good taste."

"Mademoiselle," he said mockingly, "I have no desire but to present you exactly as you are, not as less than you are. I promise you that future advertising and publicity will be most discreet."

"That's all I ask," she said, dismissing him. "Thank you, Monsieur Michaud." She had turned her back fully to him, and begun to remove her leotards, slippers, and makeup kit from her bag. When she did not hear the door close, she looked over her shoulder. He was still there, arms crossed over his chest, gazing down at her with an insolent smile. "I thought you'd gone," she said.

"No."

"What do you want?"

"I thought I should see what I bought."

"You'll see it when I'm ready to show you," she said sharply. "Please allow me to change."

Arms still crossed, he shrugged. "Of course, my dear." He opened the door. "I'll be waiting downstairs."

After he had gone, she tried to secure the door latch, but it was broken. Exhausted by these never-ending male games, she undressed slowly. Then she stepped into her all-white one-piece leotard and pulled it on until it covered her as snugly as another thin layer of skin. After sticking her feet into her dance slippers, she unpinned her hair before the mirror, and regretted that she had not selected the black leotard. This white one, which revealed the deep cleft between her breasts, which failed to hide the outlines of her nipples, and which, she could see on half turning, exposed half of her buttocks, was too inciting for a playboy like Michaud.

But what bothered her even more was that this routine rehearsal costume was relatively chaste, and that what she would be wearing (or not wearing) later would be far more provocative. How would the satyr Michaud behave after he saw her in the show itself? How impossible would he be when, having finished her striptease, she came off the stage nude except for that minute triangle of fabric held in place only by spirit gum? Well, she had been through this tiresome business before, and mostly she had survived the passes, the attempted seductions, the insults. She would find the strength to endure the unpleasantness one last time before finally accepting Sir Austin's capitulation and her safe passage to England.

Quickly she fixed her false eyelashes, did her lips, powdered, made one last satisfying pirouette before the mirror, and then she hurried downstairs.

Upon entering the cabaret, she found to her surprise that the stage was empty and the music stilled. Off to the left, most members of The Troupe were seated in an irregular circle around Countess Ribault, as she paced and lectured at them. Straight ahead, Michaud, who had divested himself of his suit coat, was deep in conversation with the

Algerian engineer. Boldly she started toward Michaud, but not until she was almost upon him did he glance up, and instantly straighten to his full height.

She halted. Impersonally he inspected her up and down, took a few steps sideways to view her in profile, and at last he nodded.

"Satisfied with what you bought?"

He did not smile. He was all business. *"Bon,"* he said. "The customers will not be displeased."

"Merci bien," she said with a trace of sarcasm.

"Sit down," he ordered. "The countess will join us in a moment. Here is what we have in mind for you. You will make four appearances in each show. Our show is divided into two acts, with a fifteen-minute intermission between. You will do one solo song with a striptease early in the first act, and a very brief song and dance in front of The Troupe at the close of the act. In the second part you will do another solo, and then merely appear, marching and singing in chorus with the entire company, at the grand finale. You understand?"

"Yes," she said, liking him more this way and hoping that he had decided to keep their relationship strictly that of *le directeur* and *la chanteuse.*

They sat down at a table removed from the others, and when the countess had appeared with a pad and pen, and pulled up a chair, Michaud resumed. "Now, Medora, we want your entire repertory of numbers. We'll select two numbers out of your repertory, those most in keeping with the show, for your solos. These we will note for the *chef d'orchestre,* and tomorrow morning you can work with the musicians. We will try to agree upon a third number for you to do with The Troupe, something they are doing or have recently done. That should not be difficult to decide. They are very quick and adaptable, perhaps the equal of the fine Bluebell Girls over at the Lido. Now, Medora, you tell the countess and me what you can do."

Medora asked for a cigarette, then crossed her bare legs, pleased that Michaud was ignoring them, and after several puffs she began to recite the title of every song she had done or worked up in the last six months. Once the countess had listed these, there was a long discussion about which could or should be done and which were consistent with the theme of the Club Lautrec show. After a half hour it was unanimously agreed that for her solo striptease numbers Medora would do "That Old Black Magic" and "Souvenir de Montmartre," and for her brief appearance with The Troupe she would do "Sing, You Sinners," a number most of the girls had done in last year's show.

Next, Medora was requested to do a run-through of her two solo numbers. She ascended to the stage, while Michaud and the countess remained at their table directly beneath. The Algerian had already gone over to an upright piano and begun thumping the keys. Off to her left, Medora could see the girls of The Troupe giving her their attention, and to her right, in the shadows behind the Algerian, three white-clad cooks had emerged from the kitchen to watch.

At first, explaining her costume and her entrance, Medora was discomfited, but when she heard the opening bars of "That Old Black Magic," and started to sing it, as she had done so many times before, she began to feel easier and finally confident. On the reprise, she explained, instead of singing she would do her striptease. As the piano cued her, she half walked, half danced through her movements about the perimeter of the stage, pretending that she was not in a leotard but fully clothed, and making the motions of shedding her garments, until she was center stage and completely disrobed, except for the triangular patch, at the blackout.

When this was done, Michaud bobbed his head but said nothing. The countess came to the apron of the stage to discuss the lighting. With that settled, the countess asked Medora if she wanted to rest before the second solo, but Medora said that she was ready to continue. The Algerian began to play the bouncy "Souvenir de Mont-martre," and Medora sang the song, and, after calling for a slower tempo on the reprise, she once again simulated a striptease. This time her pantomime indicated that a lover was trying to undress her, and she was resisting, until, unable to resist any longer, she found herself breathlessly helping him disrobe her.

When she finished, she saw the countess beaming appreciatively.

Michaud sat up. "Very good, Miss Hart. Why don't you and the girls take a ten-minute break, and then we'll work on your short number with The Troupe." He slumped moodily back into the chair, chin on his touching fingertips. As Medora crossed the platform, she was aware of Michaud's eyes following her. Climbing down from the stage, she decided to challenge his gaze as coldly as possible. But when she looked over her shoulder, he was accepting a tumbler of red wine from a porter as he spoke to the countess.

For a moment Medora stood there, uncertain of where to turn, where to sit, what to do. The girls of The Troupe had devoted themselves to their own occupations, eating, drinking, reading, gossiping, one sewing, another writing a letter, and Medora felt quite apart from them, an alien in a foreign place once more.

Then she became aware of a milky arm raised, a long hand

fluttering, and she realized that a generously endowed French-appearing girl in a jade-green bikini was beckoning to her. Eager as a homing pigeon, Medora hastily made her way to the table at which the girl sat alone, isolated from the others.

The French girl, raven hair in a short gamin cut, great orbs of eyes heavily shadowed, tremendous helicoid breasts straining against her bikini top, offered her hand in a clasp of welcome and gestured with a glass toward her plates of bread, Italian cheese, slices of Bayonne ham, bottle of Vittel, and the empty chair across from her.

"I'm Denise Averil, and I'm drinking a Fernet Branca because I've got a hangover, and I don't know which is worse," she said, "but I do know it is awful the first day, not knowing a soul. Sit down, Medora, if you don't mind. You can have the Vittel water, all of it."

"Thank you," said Medora, hesitantly, "I mean, if it's not imposing on you?"

"Cut it out," said Denise Averil. "I say only what I think." As Medora settled down gingerly, Denise poured some mineral water into a paper cup for her, and went on. "Besides, I like to keep up on my English. I was born in Marseille, but only my mother was French. My father, I guess he was my father, was a Czech who'd been an American GI. My parents didn't speak each other's language, but they both knew English, my mother from school, my old man from living ten years in Detroit, so I was raised on some kind of bastard Anglo-American speech. I've had occasion to improve it since. My name really isn't Denise Averil. I mean, it is Denise, but my father's last name—well, you had to shake well before pronouncing—so when I got into the club here, they insisted I take Averil for my last name because some chick named Jane Avril had been one of the babes Lautrec painted for a poster. Is your name really Medora Hart?"

"My father changed Horth-something-or-other—something longer —to Hart when he moved to England. Yes, I was christened Medora Hart. Unfortunately."

"Oh, come off it. It's a beautiful name. Besides, it's making you ten times what the rest of us earn in a week."

"Yes, I suppose I shouldn't complain. But it gets overwhelming— always being the—"

"The Jameson girl," said Denise. "Honey, I can guess what that means. Like your track record's in the open for every stud, and the second they lay eyes on you, they see an invitation for an advance."

"Something like that."

With her forefinger under her nostrils, Denise tried to prevent a sneeze, and then she sneezed and apologized. "This filthy Fernet Branca, or maybe the Vittel, does it to me every time. Not champagne, just medicinal potions and charged water." She touched the corners of her eyes with a napkin. "Michaud made his pass at you yet?"

Startled, Medora was at a loss for words. "I—I don't think so. I mean, not directly."

Denise winked broadly and grinned. "He will, my pet. Expect it." She leaned forward confidentially, her overflowing spiral breasts almost slipping out. "That was another reason I wanted to speak to you. I took a liking to you when you were up there. You looked like a waif. Listen to *me,* saying that to *you*—you could probably tell me a thing or two—"

"No."

"But you seemed nice, so I wanted to warn you to slip into your chastity belt offstage—that is, unless you don't give a damn—or maybe you even like it—except, if you do, you can do better than Michaud. He's a sort of mechanical monster. You get the prerecorded words, the windup motions, the Moët et Chandon and caviar and silk-canopy bed, the feeling of being first, but before you get used to the floral-decorated bidet, you get the boot, and the mechanized contraption moves on to another victim. I mean, it's nothing terrible, except that it is nothing, it's zero. You realize you've been used, all one-way, you've got nothing back emotionally, not even one warm feeling, and you're just a little sicker of yourself, that's all. Denise *knows.*"

"You do know?"

"Three months' worth, two years ago."

"But why—?"

"The job, honey. I wanted to step up in class. And I'm not all that classy. So what the hell, you do what you have to. I figured it's no worse than a cramp. And well, it paid off. Here I am, the youngest old retainer." She grinned. "And you're next. I can spot the Michaud look. The nostrils flaring. Means he's turned on. The dragon is breathing hot passion. He's preparing to envelop you."

"Not a chance," said Medora. "I'm not exactly an innocent, as you know. I can't be bothered by small dragons."

Denise was plainly skeptical. "This one usually gets what he wants. He saw you to your dressing room and wouldn't leave. Right? His speech became more informal and provocative. Right? You were armed and resistant. Right? You came down here to rehearsal, and to your surprise the passionate ogre was all disinterest and business. Right? You are now disarmed. Right?"

Medora laughed. "Well—"

"Well, next, sweetie pie, the rehearsal is over. He will tell you not to leave right away. He will say he wants to discuss your act further." She paused, grinning. "You doubt me?"

"I don't think he'll try anything, Denise. He knows where I stand. I made it clear. . . . I don't have time for any Michauds. I'm in Paris for something else."

"Good luck," said Denise. She nodded off. "The countess stirs. That means we're on."

Denise and the seventeen other girls clambered onto the stage. Medora took one more sip of her mineral water and joined them on the platform. While Michaud remained in his chair below lazily studying Medora and The Troupe, the countess ascended the stage. For fifteen minutes she walked the veteran dancers through her choreography of the old "Sing, You Sinners" number, then gave the newcomers in the line and Medora more detailed individual directions, creakingly pantomiming entrances, the steps, the exits.

After that, the Algerian hooked up the tape, and the loudspeakers blared forth. Under Michaud's noncommittal gaze, and following Countess Ribault's stomping and shouting directions, The Troupe pranced, kicked, split, leaped, gyrated. Medora, weaving and undulating before them, portable microphone in hand, sang out the lyrics, finally merging with the chorus line for their arm-shaking march off the stage.

The first time through, the number was alive but woefully ragged, and Medora knew it and was ready for more. By the third time through, the number had begun to smooth out as timing and coordination improved. By the fifth rehearsal, when the small of her back and the calves of her legs were beginning to ache, Medora sensed that it was finally right and prayed that the session was over. With a grateful gasp she heard the countess applaud and congratulate them.

Michaud was rising. "Thank you, girls. That is enough for today. See you tonight."

The line of The Troupe broke formation, and there was chatter and laughter as the tall chorines began to leave the platform for their dressing rooms. Wearily Medora started to follow them.

"Oh, Miss Hart!" It was Michaud's voice, and Medora stopped and turned as he approached the apron of the stage. "I thought you did remarkably well, all things considered."

"Merci," she said warily.

"Just one other thing," he said. "I'd like to see you briefly for a little private talk before you go. I want to discuss a few points about your act. And then there is some business."

Medora hesitated. "If it's important—"

"It is important."

With a sigh Medora descended from the platform and entered the backstage area. Several members of The Troupe, Denise Averil among them, were gathered about the soft-drink vending machine, conversing. Immediately, Denise saw her, and her eyebrows went up questioningly. Medora could not help but smile. "Thanks," she called out. "Your radar was right." Denise nodded seriously, and held up her fingers to form a V-for-Victory sign. Medora shrugged in a gesture of helplessness, and hastened up the staircase.

Once enclosed in her austere dressing room, Medora pushed off her dancing slippers, and rolled off her adhesive white leotard. She felt the dryness across every inch of her naked body that always followed a perspiring rehearsal or performance, and she wished that she could shower or bathe, but there would be time enough for that at the hotel, after she had made short shrift of *le directeur* and his so-called business meeting. She took up her white nylon panties, stepped into them, and straightened the elastic waistband as she returned to the mirror to find some facial tissue and wipe off her makeup.

Suddenly she heard a quick sound behind her, the door opening and closing, and she whirled around to see what had happened. Inside her room, leaning back against the shut door, was Alphonse Michaud, his unblinking eyes judging and approving of her semi-nude body.

Her first automatic impulse was to scream, but the audacity of his entrance had struck her dumb.

"Forgive me, Medora," he said contritely, "but—"

She groped for a garment to cover herself, but realized her clothes were on the chair beside Michaud and on the door hook behind him. Desperately her hands went up to shield her breasts. "What in the hell are you doing here?" she demanded angrily.

"I became impatient. I could not resist. I had to speak to you alone."

"You've got your bloody nerve, busting in like this. Can't you even let a lady dress in privacy?"

For the first time, he smiled. "Come, my dear, be sensible. It is not as if you are a Floradora or cancan girl. Your condition right now is more respectable than it will be on the stage tomorrow. There is less for me to see than any customer will see in the next few weeks."

Her hands spread wider across her bust, and she was conscious of her transparent panties. She had never felt more naked. "I just don't like the idea of anyone intruding on my privacy. And I don't like your insolence. Who in the hell do you think you are?"

"I am your employer," he said softly. "I am also the director of the club."

"That doesn't mean you can behave as you like with me. That's not in your damn contract."

"You are most pretty when you are angry," he said. "I am one more

257

person besides your employer, Medora. I am a man who is madly in love with you. It was instantaneous, the moment that I laid eyes on you. The girls come and go here. They are my trade, my stock in trade, and I am hardly conscious of them as women. You are different. You have had a profound effect on me. Your beauty, your youth, your personality—I am shaken—I feel weakness. Medora, I could be your slave. I am wealthy and a member of the best circles, but I am alone, truly, and in you I sense a compassionate, compatible soul. I ask that we be friends."

"I ask that you get your arse right out of here," said Medora with mounting fury, "and save your oily insincerity for those scared little wretches who are afraid of you."

Michaud had straightened during the last, his features bunching unpleasantly into a scowl. "Medora, I suggest you calm down and reconsider your position and my own. You want a career. I could make it possible for you to have one at the top level. I could make life very comfortable for you—if you were sensible and considerate."

She dropped her hands from her breasts, knotting them into fists. "I don't want a lousy career, and above all I don't want or need you. I'm not in the habit of crawling into bed with just any old lecher, so—"

"Medora," he interrupted firmly, "your paean to virtue seems hardly in character. We both know you are anything but a lily-white virgin." His features had set in a look of superior disdain. "Let us stop this fencing. Let us be open. Now I think we shall get somewhere. You know and I know that you have little talent. You cannot sing. You cannot dance. You cannot act. All that you have to offer is a remarkable body. Even that would not be enough—there are so many—but your attractiveness is enhanced by your reputation for looseness with many men, from the filthy Jameson up to that young brother of the British Cabinet Minister. I make no criticism. I am a Frenchman and a man of the world. We are what we are, no? Let it be. Let us understand and enjoy ourselves. So why this pretense with me? Why this act? I can do more for you than anyone has—"

He had taken one step forward, and she went rigid. "Get out of here!"

He stopped and squinted at her.

"If you don't get out this instant," she said, "then I'm getting out, walking right out of your bloody show."

He rocked uncertainly, taking measure of her. At last he heaved his shoulders upward, and then let them drop downward, signifying defeat. "You win, Medora," he said, "although I think you lose. Of course, I shall not come to you again. You will have to come to me."

"For that you can wait until hell freezes over."

"*C'est la guerre,*" he said with a smile, reluctantly lifting his gaze from her breasts. "But one thing I do not retract. You *are* beautiful." As he turned away, trying to hold on to dignity, he paused to pick up her brassiere and toss it to her. Hand on doorknob, he came around once more, and watched impersonally as she settled her breasts into her brassiere and fastened it. The tone of his voice was changed. The lasciviousness had gone out of it.

"There was actually real business, you know, and I had better speak of it now, Medora. There are two clauses in our contract, ambiguous in the wording, but important, and clauses with which I expect you to comply."

"Please give me my dress," said Medora.

Now the Frenchman of commerce, not amour, Michaud absently took her teal-blue woolen dress off the hanger and handed it to her as he continued to speak. "First, I should want you, as well as the other performers, to be friendly with our clientele. It is of the best. With the Summit conference here, our tables will be filled with many important figures. If some foreign official sends you a card, or invites you to share a bottle of champagne between shows, or after your own act, it would be advantageous to accept."

Medora held the dress before her, smoothing it. "Advantageous to whom?"

"To the Club Lautrec, of course. Not the extra champagne that we might sell. That is minor. Rather, the goodwill your friendliness could engender. And advantageous to you, too. I have the impression that you have never been averse to meeting politicians and diplomats. Perhaps you will still find them of interest."

"I'm not soliciting for any pimp," she said angrily, "and I never have."

He flushed, but contained his temper. "I never asked you to solicit. I asked you to be cooperative."

She thought, at once, of the British delegates who might visit the show, and who might help her contact Sir Austin, if that became necessary. She said, "All right. I'll be cooperative."

"Thank you. Next, the second point, of greater importance. Our contract states that you will also be cooperative about participating in any promotion and publicity that the staff of the Club Lautrec arranges. This is extremely important at this time, Medora. Usually, when we contract for a feature act, we have many weeks to build public interest in that act. But you were hired overnight. Aside from posters, advertisements, a few newspaper squibs, an article in *Une*

Semaine de Paris, we have had no time to sell your attraction to the public. However, there is one bit of good fortune. The Summit has brought to Paris more than a thousand newspaper reporters, many with local outlets for their stories. My staff has been in touch with the press, making an effort to arrange appointments for interviews. With these, I would expect your fullest cooperation."

"Very well. You have it. Now will you permit me to dress?"

"I have your cooperation, you say? *Bon!* Then I must advise you that your first interview has been arranged."

"Well, you let me know when and where, and I'll—"

"Right now and right here," he said. "She'll be here in—in fifteen minutes."

Medora glowered at him. "Oh, how clever. Aren't you the crafty one, sneaking it in like that! Couldn't you have told me first off? Well, I'm not so sure. I think it's inconsiderate of you. In fact, downright unfair. I'm absolutely a wreck—driving all night, rehearsing half the afternoon, and you say that I must see some horrible reporter person now. If you're halfway decent, you'll give me a chance to get my bearings. I'm sure you can postpone it."

Michaud's features were pained. "Medora," he implored, "this interview is the most vital to us of any. It was difficult to make this appointment. A postponement might antagonize her and lose us the story. Surely you have heard of Miss Hazel Smith?"

"I don't know, I don't remember," said Medora petulantly. "I only know I'm tired and want to be left alone."

"Miss Smith is the most renowned American correspondent in Europe," Michaud pleaded. "Her Atlas syndicate will publish the interview with you everywhere in the world. But to us, the importance is that the interview will appear in the European edition of the New York *Herald Tribune,* in *France-Soir,* even in *Die Welt* and *Il Messaggero* and others which are sold in every Paris kiosk. The story will attract—"

"You win," said Medora suddenly, weary of combating him. "Only tell her no more than a half hour, and—"

He had opened the door, singing out gayly, *"Merci bien,* Mademoiselle Medora."

"—and you be sure to tell her this interview is strictly about my career, understand? One word about Jameson and the interview is *fini.* You tell her that."

"I promise. I vow. It is done."

He went quickly, and when the door closed and she was rid of him, Medora collapsed on the bench with relief. After five minutes and one cigarette, she had regained her strength. She finished cleaning off the last of her stage makeup, then she used the eyebrow pencil, powder puff, lipstick lightly, to ready her for the woman reporter and the street. Finally, her dressing completed, she took up her straw handbag and started downstairs.

Entering the cabaret, she found it unexpectedly dismal and forlorn, like an uninhabited coral reef devoid of all that was animate and alive. Empty nightclubs in empty afternoons had always made Medora melancholy, as if she were wandering through a necropolis. But going past the stage, she could see that the hall was not entirely empty of people. In the distance, near the entrance, three men and a woman, wearing something that resembled drab prison garb, were laying cloths on the tables. And now she was aware of more human activity in the foreground, in front of the stage.

Michaud, exuding charm, was addressing a woman who was taking notes. This was probably the reporter woman, Medora decided, and approaching the pair, Medora guessed that the reporter woman, an American, was formidable. The woman carried a terrible mussiness of brick-red hair that somehow went with her pinched nose but seemed unreal when contrasted against her cream complexion. She was too broad-beamed for the cut of the brown suit she wore, and as a consequence the skirt had wrinkled. She held her writing pad close to her face, and Medora supposed that she was nearsighted but too vain to wear spectacles. Well, at least she was American, which was more promising than the British journalists, whose savaging Medora had so long endured. She prayed that the interview would be bland and brief.

"Ah, and here comes my star of stars!" Michaud exclaimed. He rushed forward to take Medora's forearm, and gallantly led her to his journalist. "Miss Medora Hart, Miss Hazel Smith, the celebrated Miss Smith of ANA."

Medora greeted her interviewer with constrained warmth, and Hazel Smith acknowledged this with a lipless one-second smile that came on, went off. Then Hazel Smith cocked her head and examined Medora as she might if evaluating a new piece of statuary that had received mixed reviews.

"Well, the two of you have met," Michaud announced with exuberance. "I am sure you would prefer to be left alone to have your conversation."

"We won't need you anymore, Mr. Michaud," said Hazel Smith.

"*Bon!* Nevertheless, I shall be in my office upstairs, always available, should there be a question," said Michaud. "I've ordered coffee and cakes. They will be here any moment. If you will forgive, I go."

"So go already," said Hazel Smith.

For an instant Michaud lost his poise, but recovering, he chuckled and said, "I know you will always write a good story, Miss Smith." He winked broadly at Medora and added, "But do not tell her *everything, my pet.*"

At last he was gone, and Hazel Smith plopped down into the chair and shook her head. "What an ass he is," she said.

Trying to restrain herself from agreeing, or in any way showing her delight, Medora placed her handbag on the table and sat down, more relaxed than before. After fussing with her yellow collar and her hair, Medora looked up to find the American reporter staring intently at her. Wriggling uncomfortably, Medora pulled herself erect and drew down the hem of her wool dress.

"You're quite a dish, Miss Hart," said Hazel Smith. "Now I can understand all that brouhaha in England a couple of years ago."

Disconcerted, Medora was not certain what her reaction should be. "Well, I don't know—I—but, thank you, anyway."

Hazel Smith crossed her legs, opened the pad on her knee, and scratched her pen on the paper to see if her pen was working. "I'm ready, you're set, let's go," she said. "What are you doing here, Miss Hart?"

"What am I doing here?"

"You know what I mean. Why did you come to Paris at this time?"

"To—to work in the Club Lautrec. Isn't it obvious?"

Hazel Smith impatiently rapped her pen against the edge of the wooden table. "Come on, now, come off it. We're the two of us together. No one around. You can level with me. It'll write better that way, and be better for you."

"I haven't the slightest idea of what you are speaking about, Miss Smith."

Hazel Smith pushed herself against the table, head projecting like a pecking hen. "Here's what I'm speaking about. I looked you up in our morgue at ANA. For the last few years you've batted about the Continent playing honky-tonks. Not much fun, I'm sure. Suddenly, overnight, you're the star of a big Paris nightclub. You're in Paris, in fact, for the first time in God knows when. So I ask myself—how come?"

Medora stiffened. "I'm here because Monsieur Michaud needed a name attraction known to most of the international delegations. I suppose he decided that I had the name by now."

"That figures. In short, he wanted the Jameson girl."

The woman was thoroughly disagreeable, and Medora began to hate her. "Put it any way you wish," she said icily.

"Oh, I will, I will, I assure you," murmured Hazel Smith as she wrote. "That still leaves my other question unanswered. Why Paris now?"

"I *told* you."

"You told me nothing, Miss Hart. But I don't mind telling you what I suspect. I suspect that you came to Paris because Sir Austin Ormsby is here for the Summit and his brother is here, and you wanted to take up with them again. I assume you were as well acquainted with Sir Austin as his—as that brother—Sydney."

Medora felt her entire body shaking at the outrageous behavior of this offensive woman. "Miss—Miss Smith, that's not fair, that's bitchy of you. Michaud promised to tell you I'd—I would only discuss my work, my work, that's all."

Hazel Smith was pointing the pen at her. "I *am* discussing your work, Miss Hart."

"Oh, you—how can you—?"

"Easy, Miss Hart. Level with Hazel and you won't be sorry. Now, I don't know if you came running here to have a reunion with Sir Austin or with Sydney Ormsby. I believe this is the first time you've been in the same city with the Ormsbys since the Jameson scandal. No matter. What I *am* asking is—did *you* come to see *them*—for auld lang syne, you know—or did *they* send for *you?*"

"How horrid!" Medora cried. She wanted to go on, but she could not. She began choking, suffered a spasm of coughing, then she grabbed at her straw handbag and jumped to her feet. Standing unsteadily, eyes brimming, she looked down at her tormentor. "You're a dreadful bitch, and I won't talk to you!" Crazily, the tears began to roll down Medora's cheeks, and she sobbed uncontrollably. "How—how can you—bring, bring all that—bring that up? How can you, after the hell—the rotten hell I—I've been through?"

Starting to choke again, Medora wiped a fist against her flow of tears. Seeing the inhuman redhead coming toward her, Medora backed away, shouting brokenly, "Leave me alone!"

She wheeled, stumbled, caught herself by grabbing a table edge, then ran up the aisle, past the alarmed Club Lautrec waiters. Continuing to sob, continuing to run, she went through the lobby and burst into the Rue la Boëtie.

Outside at last, freed of the hateful presence of her past, she tried to control the wretched sobbing that had already attracted the attention of pedestrians. Fumbling for a lace handkerchief, she dabbed at her eyes and streaked face, and blew her nose, and blindly made her way up the street.

When she reached the corner of the Champs-Élysées, she stopped to catch her breath and compose herself. Seeking her compact mirror, she tried to understand her hysterical outburst. The American reporter's revival of Medora's past had been blunt and offensive, but everywhere in Europe, these last years, sooner or later she had undergone similar reminders, yet she had never dissolved in tears before. Of course, Hazel Smith's coarse insinuations about why Medora was here, and what she was up to, had been unexpected and hurting, perhaps summarizing too rudely the world's frank opinion of her and the hopelessness of her ever becoming anything more than the Jameson girl. Yet even the insinuations had not been provocative enough to explain her wildly emotional reaction.

Trying to steady her hand, she held up the compact mirror and powdered over the unattractive tear streaks on her face. She looked a hag for twenty-one, for any age, she saw, an utter mess, but it was understandable, for she was a mess. She had overreacted to the reporter, probably, because the accumulated years of enforced exile and frustration had caught up with her. Too, she was a bundle of tensions, every quivering nerve exposed, because she was banking so much on using the Nardeau oil painting of Fleur to bend Sir Austin to her just demands. This centering of her entire hopes on one chance, the uncertainty of how to proceed, this, combined with her lack of rest, the exertion of the rehearsal, the ugly scene with Michaud, had brought her to the brink of disintegration. The American reporter's cruel questions had merely pushed her over.

Closing her compact, putting it away, she felt her sanity somewhat restored although she did not feel better.

A hand was on her elbow, and she started. She heard someone say "Miss Hart." She spun around.

Hazel Smith was standing before her, and at first Medora hardly recognized her. Except for the pile of red hair and the wrinkled brown suit, she did not seem to be the same person. Her metallic inquisitor's eyes had softened, the nostrils of her pinched nose were quivering, her lipless mouth had become feminine, her frightening pad and pen were missing. It was as if Mrs. Hyde had swallowed from the vial and become, incredibly, Mrs. Jekyll.

Medora's mechanism of automatic response—anger, flight—remained unactivated. She waited with dumb wonderment.

Hazel Smith, pale and concerned, ducked her head abjectly, and when she spoke, her tone was contrite. "I—I'm glad I caught you, Miss Hart. I want to apologize." She raised her head, embarrassed. "I want to tell you as quickly as possible I'm ashamed. I guess I haven't said that to anyone in years. You're right, you know. I did behave like an awful bitch. It comes naturally. Maybe for a reason you might understand." She paused. "Anyway, when you've devoted yourself to your work for years, to keep busy, to escape thinking, to avoid being a vulnerable person, you sort of get in the habit of treating your interview subjects like—well, like bloodless Names, not like real human beings. You forget they have feelings, because you want to forget you, yourself, once had feelings. It's easier that way, going at it like a relentless automaton, and believing the subjects across from you are automatons. Also, I suppose, it's the best way to get good stories, by hitting hard at people, refusing to consider their sensitivity, just being brutally frank and ruthless. I mean, if you stopped for a second to think how your subjects really felt, as people, why, you couldn't do it, and then you wouldn't get the stories and have a big career. And having a big career is everything, when there is nothing else. . . . I do hope you will understand, Medora, and forgive me."

During this recital, spoken so sincerely and directly, Medora's emotions had been utterly upended, and altered to such an extent that she had found herself too incredulous to interrupt. Ten minutes ago she had despised this middle-aged woman. Now, standing in the sun of the Champs-Élysées, listening to her, and finally believing her, she found herself sorry not for herself but for Hazel Smith.

"I suppose, maybe, you shouldn't be the one to apologize," said Medora hesitantly. "Maybe I should, for dissolving like I did, making such a scene over routine questions that I—I've heard many times before."

"No, Medora, it was me, myself, and I who were to blame. Your breaking up that way was like a healthy slap, bringing me to my senses, making me see the reality of what I've become. When you ran off, I realized what I had been asking you, and I realized that you weren't just a brainless little tart who had used her body to exploit men and be exploited by them. I sensed that you were someone who had been victimized, forced to grovel and suffer, and in you, well, I sort of saw something of myself—that'll surprise you, but I did see that—and then I realized you weren't a headline only, just as I'm not a by-line only, but a person with a heart, just as I am, and—well, it's not like me, but I suppose this is something of me, too, but I decided to hell with the damn story. All I wanted was for you to know I was sorry. So now you know."

"Thank you, Miss Smith. I just—"

"Hazel—I'm Hazel in my off hours."

Medora assented gratefully. "Thank you, Hazel, but I have to say again that I blew up because I guess the pressure had been building a long time and it had to be released. It's not that I mind talking about the Ormsbys—Sir Austin, really—or the whole Jameson affair; it's just that there's no one to talk to about it, as a friend—you have no idea, but there's no one—because if I want to confide, I can't trust anyone, because they want to use me or use what I tell them, and so the best I can do is have miserable little talks with myself, and that's not healthy."

Hazel Smith offered a sympathetic smile. "You can talk to me, Medora. Maybe I can help you more than I've ever been able to help myself." She waited, then went on. "I mean it. You might be surprised to find that you're not alone. I'll tell you what. Unless you've got something better to do—because I haven't, and even if I had I wouldn't right now, anyway—why don't we sit somewhere with a cup of coffee or a drink and let down our hair? I mean, strictly off the record. No interview. Just an old bag and a pretty young girl who both want comforting. Oh, of course I'll write a story, to make your boss happy and give you some publicity, which maybe would be helpful. But it would be strictly about you as an accomplished young lady who's come out of the lower depths to carve a big career for herself and finally attain the summit of show business in Paris. I'd refer to the Jameson case only in a passing line."

"I shouldn't mind that."

"But right now, no paper and pencil. My bunions are killing me. And you don't look exactly like a tower of strength. There's a café over there. Let's sit down."

Medora did not resist. She permitted Hazel Smith to steer her away from the corner. They walked up the Champs-Élysées until they arrived at the Café Français, a modest sidewalk oasis between a dry-goods store bearing a sign reading SOLDE, and a shop with the sign TABAC, and located near the large open entrance of the Lido Arcade.

One small table, in the second row of the Café Français, was relatively isolated from the lazing customers enjoying their coffee, croissants, and newspapers en plein air this Sunday afternoon. They took their places at this table beneath the shade of a spreading umbrella, and they ordered sandwiches and tea. Hazel Smith lit Medora's cigarette and her own, and after an interval of silence they looked at one another.

"Medora," said Hazel Smith, "I'm not prying, and turn me off if you think I am, but I gather from you that there's more to your whole involvement in the Paddy Jameson affair than anyone knows. Do you want to talk about it? I mean, look." She opened her palms to Medora. "No pen, no paper. In fact, as the kids say in America when they ride a bike, no-hands. It's up to you."

"If you're sure it wouldn't bore you?"

"Bore me? Get off it. As long as it isn't too painful for you."

266

"Oh, it's not all that painful. It might even be good for me, telling someone the whole truth and nothing but. If we're to be friends, I should be thankful for some advice or guidance."

"When were you last home, Medora?"

"Not since before the trial. Better than three years ago."

"You mean you've been rattling around Europe all that time? Why? For a career?"

"Crikey, no. I detest what I'm doing. I'm here because that bloody bastard, Sir Austin Ormsby, talked me into leaving England. Now he won't let me back."

Hazel Smith's eyes were round with astonishment. "Sir Austin?"

"None other."

"But how could he?"

"Well," said Medora, "I'll be glad to tell you."

And in the next half hour, in a voice flat and worn by the unpleasant familiarity of the events so long past, she related what had happened to her.

Hazel Smith was incredulous. "I've never heard anything like this. Not even in Moscow. He really framed you."

"That's right," said Medora, and feeling cleansed, she drank her cold tea.

"But you should have done something about this," Hazel Smith insisted. "It's an outrage. You should have told the whole world, everybody you could get to."

Medora made a bitter sound. "I tried, Hazel, I assure you that I tried. Nobody would believe me. They had their views of me. I'm unstable. I'm immoral. My word is suspect. I tried to get the press to print it. They all refused. No proof."

"I'll print it," said Hazel Smith grimly.

"Without proof beyond my word? I don't think your press association would let you."

"Well, you must have *some* evidence?"

"Not an iota in writing. No, I haven't."

"I see," said Hazel Smith. "You're right. It would be tough to get the full story into print, especially with your antagonist being such a big shot."

"It was always his spotless word against my tarnished word. So there's never been a chance, and I've had to stew and make my own way—"

"How have you lived, Medora? What's it been like these last years?"

Willingly, without restraint, almost as a catharsis, Medora confessed it all to her, the endless circle of cheap and smoky clubs in France, Germany, Italy, the countless rows of frightful male audiences with leering eyes and busy hands, the never-ending queue of men offering to barter their assistance for her body (and after possessing her goods, delivering nothing in exchange but promises, after all).

Finishing, Medora slumped back in her chair, spent. "That's most of it," she said wearily. "I don't know if anyone who hasn't been through it can possibly understand what it has been like."

"I understand," said Hazel Smith firmly.

With curiosity, Medora looked at the American. "You sound as if you do. Do you mean you've been through something like this?"

Hazel Smith stared off. "Not exactly. But in a way, yes. I know the feeling." She seemed to search for the exact words to convey her feeling, and then she said, "In a sense, I've been as alone as you, and as alienated from, well, from a normal woman's life. All because of one man, one fat-headed slob, a real son of a bitch—you wouldn't recognize his name, you're too young—but in his day he was as well-known as Sir Austin, and nobody, at least nobody like me, was good enough for him, and I blame him for everything—well, most of everything—that's happened to me since." She stopped, and smiled wanly at Medora. "So, you see, I do understand, and if there is anything on earth I can do to help—"

"Thank you, but I think I can manage now," said Medora. "I can't tell you how much I appreciate your offer, Hazel. It's a good feeling to know that there is one person in the world who wants to help, although . . ." She was thoughtful a moment. "When we met, you asked why I was in Paris. You were almost right when you guessed. I *am* here to see Sir Austin Ormsby. He doesn't know it yet. But that's why I'm here." She had come alive again, and she drew her chair closer to Hazel's. "I said it was good to know there's one person in the world ready to help me. Meaning you. But actually, there is one other. He's done a wonderful thing for me. He's given me my chance." She paused. "Have you ever heard of the painter, Nardeau? You have? Well, I'll tell you why I'm really in Paris. . . ."

I'M LOOKING for Hazel Smith," he said. "I'm an old friend. I've just flown into Paris to see her. Is she around?"

The French secretary licked the down on her upper lip and appeared puzzled. *"Je ne comprends pas,"* she said worriedly. *"Répétez, s'il vous plaît."*

268

Spacing his words, speaking slowly, he repeated his inquiry. "I am looking for Miss Hazel Smith, one of your journalists. I am an old friend."

The French secretary's squeezed visage suddenly opened up brightly. "Ah, Ay-zell Smith!" She held up a finger. "*Excusez-moi, monsieur! Attendez!*"

She dashed off between the cluttered desks of the main editorial office of the Atlas News Association's Paris Bureau, halted to consult another French girl who was typing, and then dashed off into an adjacent office.

After she disappeared, Jay Thomas Doyle nervously waited to see if she would reappear with Hazel Smith. When she did not emerge immediately. Doyle wondered if Hazel was instructing the girl to say that she was not in and to dismiss him. After unpacking his luggage at the Hotel George-V, Doyle had considered telephoning Hazel to announce his arrival and beg for a reunion. He had rejected the telephone approach as one less likely to be effective than surprising her in person. On the telephone, she could hang up. But confronted by his bulk, she could only give him the cold shoulder, and he could still overwhelm her with his eagerness, his desire, his need to be reunited with an old love.

Finding that he was still puffing from the exertion of his four-block walk from the Hotel George-V to the New York Herald Tribune Building in the Rue de Berri, he began to inhale deeply in a desperate effort to regain his equilibrium. Part of his short breath, he knew, came not from the walk or his considerable avoirdupois but from his eagerness about the reunion. Even within the confines of the creeping elevator that had brought him up to the ANA offices on the sixth floor, Doyle had been unable to alleviate his difficulty in breathing. No, it was neither excessive exertion nor excessive weight, Doyle knew. It was fear. It was Hazel Smith.

Despite all this gasping, this outer manifestation of the anxiety that triggered it, Jay Thomas Doyle felt that his inner confidence was rocklike. Whether it was truly rocklike, or merely papier-mâché, did not matter. That is, whether his confidence was solidly based on his good cause, or whether it was an artificial self-assurance developed by the appetite-depressant pill (a yellow, fifteen-grain mighty mite that made even the thought of food nauseating, and that compensated for his lack of protein by offering in its place doses of pep, energy, well-being), was of no consequence. All that mattered was that he felt strong, strong enough for Hazel, strong enough to obliterate their darker moments of the past and revive their best days of love. She would give him the final chapter for *The Conspirators Who Killed Kennedy*. Then at last, together, they would own the world.

But now, as his sight roved across the editorial office, he realized that his arithmetic was faulty. Together they would own the world meant that the two of them would own it. The fact remained that one of them already owned it, Hazel owned it, was on top of it, and finally, his fantasy of fulfillment was only for himself.

Observing the activity in the editorial room, he suffered a deep pang of yearning for the past. There were the cigarette-scarred, booze-spotted desks, each with its spindle laden with news reports, memorandums, cablegrams. There were the girls typing feverishly, the intent French legmen hastening in and out, the American foreign editors and correspondents in the next office, conferring on the news that was and the news that would be, and determining assignments and strategy, and deciding who would be on the night shift, and who would cover the Palais Rose, and who would have the next turn at the pretty *Herald Tribune* file clerk imported last week from Sarah Lawrence College.

A wonderful world, this, more alive than any other, to be so committed to the times, to have one foot in today and another in tomorrow. It was so much better than fame or money or power, if those involved only appreciated their unique good fortune. Remembering his own newspaper experience, Doyle appreciated it now, longed for it now as one longs for youth, and the memory painfully reminded him of his present situation. He was an outsider. And the shameful cookbook made him feel even more an outsider. Only the Kennedy assassination book could lead him back inside. But that book was not born yet, and until it was, he would have to suffer being one of those outside whose pitiful noses were pressed against the shopwindow.

Hearing the sudden clatter of a teletype, he was drawn to it. Standing over the miniature window, mesmerized by the automatic keys hitting the roll of paper (BULLETIN MATTER . . . FIRST LEAD HONG KONG . . . LONDON, FIRST ADD FIRST LEAD . . . XXX . . . MORE), was like peeking into a seer's globe that reflected all of the activities of the human race in a single day. The keys hammered ceaselessly. The teletyped news cascaded from the squat machine. A fire. A flood. A tennis score. A murder trial. A press conference. A financial report. A death. A birth. Then, ring-a-ling, an announcement from the Élysée palace. Chinese Chairman Kuo Shu-tung safely landed at Orly, all leaders of the five powers now gathered in Paris.

Miserably, Jay Thomas Doyle pulled his belly away from the teletype. It was unendurable, being a reader of the news instead of a purveyor of the news.

When he turned around, he saw that the French secretary had come out of the inner office, accompanied not by Hazel Smith but by a gangling young American with a crew cut and in shirt-sleeves, holding a sheet of yellow copy paper. The secretary had pointed out Doyle, and the young reporter came swiftly through the maze of desks to where Doyle stood.

"Sorry to keep you, sir," the young man said. "I was on the phone with Orly. They're sure crowding us today. I'm Fowler, on rewrite temporarily, but usually I'm on the outside, so I don't know the office too well. But maybe I can be of some help?"

"I told the girl I wanted to see Miss Hazel Smith," said Doyle.

"I thought that was it. You never know. Those French secretaries, their English is atrocious, like their typing, although their legs are fine. But I guess our girl got it right. You told her you had an appointment with Miss Smith? Because if that's—"

"No," Doyle interrupted. "I flew in from Vienna this a.m. to see Miss Smith on a personal matter. We're old, old friends. I wanted to surprise her. So I came straight over."

"I get it," said Fowler. "I saw her for half a second when I came on, but she went out. I think she's been out all morning. Let me have a look. We've set up a temporary desk for her, and she usually leaves a note on her appointments in case we have to contact her."

He hurried to a small oak desk in the center of the room, and rummaged through the papers. Victoriously waving a piece of note paper, he returned. "Here it is. Let me see." He read aloud from the sheet. " 'Eleven-thirty to twelve forty-five, lunch interview with Legrande at Méditerranée, Place de l'Odéon. One o'clock, Embassy tour of Palais Rose. Two-thirty, interview with Mlle. Hart at Club Lautrec.' " He looked up. "That's it. You might still catch her at the Club Lautrec."

"Off the Champs-Élysées, isn't it?"

"Rue la Boëtie. You can't miss it. There's a giant poster of Medora Hart on the sidewalk in front. Wish I had that assignment, seeing that Hart babe. I'd sure like to make time with her." He shook himself from this momentary reverie. "Anyway, if you miss Hazel there, she's certain to show up here later. You can leave a message."

"I think I'd better," said Doyle.

"One sec." Fowler found a pencil, and turned over Hazel Smith's schedule in order to scribble on the back of it. "Okay."

"Tell her I came by to see her, and I'll call again. Tell her I'm at the George-V."

"Who should I say?"

"Oh, sorry. Tell her Jay Thomas Doyle wants to see her."

The young correspondent had begun to write when his pencil seemed to freeze to the paper. He looked up alertly, his face transformed into cub awe, as if Doyle were a Presence like Richard Harding Davis or Floyd Gibbons or Ernie Pyle. "You—you said Jay Thomas Doyle? Are you *the* Doyle, the 'Inside and Straight' Doyle?"

"None other," said Doyle, childishly pleased.

"Holy mackerel! I'm sure honored to meet you," said Fowler, his breeziness having given way to formal reverence. "I grew up on you in high school and college. We used to study your columns in Journalism and in Social Science. My old man used to quote you more than the Bible."

"Thank you," said Doyle loftily, now the Prince being benign to the Pauper.

"Half of us are in this racket because you made it so glamorous. When I first started working, I used to wonder what had happened to your column. I thought you'd retired, but—"

Doyle's ego, which had been ballooning, suddenly deflated. "No. As a matter of fact, I've been more active than ever. I decided that I'd had enough of journalism and I should give my time to creative writing. Several publishers were after me. I've been on a secret book project for some time."

"Boy, I can't wait for that one," said Fowler. "I bet it'll be a dilly. When's it coming out?"

"Oh, in the near future, when I'm satisfied with it." He decided to exit while his stature was still intact. "Well, I'd better try to catch Hazel at the Club Lautrec. Be sure to give her that message anyway, young man."

"I positively will. Gosh, this was certainly a pleasure, Mr. Doyle. Wait'll I write my old man. It'll make his day, knowing you're still active."

Masking his shudder at the last remark with a weak smile, eager to escape the young man and his Old Folks' Home, Doyle bade him goodbye and made an active but measured monarchial exit.

Leaving the Herald Tribune Building, starting up the Rue de Berri, Doyle found himself wheezing asthmatically and blamed it on the psychosomatic encounter upstairs. He hoped fervently that while his energy was still at its peak he would be in time to trap Hazel in the Club Lautrec. He tried to rehearse his opening lines to her, was momentarily diverted by the framed photographs of semi-nude dancers in the forecourt of an unprepossessing nightclub he was passing, then he resumed experimenting with his Hazel lines once more.

Approaching the glass entrance doors of the Hotel Lancaster, he could see a Cadillac limousine with United States Embassy plates parked before them, and a chauffeur opening the rear door of the car. Two men and a young girl, plain and plainly American, came out of the hotel. Doyle was almost upon them when a lanky, elderly gentleman, for whom they were obviously waiting, hurried out of the hotel, and Doyle saw the bush of white hair, pug nose, cleft chin, and identified him immediately. This was unmistakably Emmett A. Earnshaw himself.

Earnshaw had slowed to call back to someone inside the hotel, and in doing so he swerved. Doyle jumped sideways to avoid him, averting a collision only by holding a protective hand out against the former President's back.

Startled, Earnshaw maintained his balance and came around to offer his apologies. "I'm sorry—" he began, then swallowed his next words, thrusting his head forward to squint at Doyle, and instantly his blue eyes lit up with recognition. "Sa-ay now, aren't you—why, I'll be darned, you're Doyle, Jay Doyle, that's right."

"That's right, Mr. President," said Doyle, beaming over the former President's remembrance of him. "Good to see you after so long."

Doyle accepted the former President's hearty handshake and started to move on, but Earnshaw remained planted in front of him. "Uh—well, now—this is unexpected," said Earnshaw. "Almost didn't recognize you."

"It's been a number of years, sir."

"No, it's your weight. You've put on some poundage since I saw you last. Too much good living, eh?"

Doyle tried to smile. "You might say so, sir. You look trimmer than ever."

"You eat half of what you order, that's the secret, Doyle, that and early to bed, early to rise. . . . Have you met my entourage? Carol! Callahan! Secret Agent X!" The three came quickly, and Earnshaw introduced them—his niece, his Embassy guide, his Secret Service protector—to Jay Thomas Doyle, giving them an elaborate and impressive briefing on Doyle's fame. "Now all of you get in your cars. Be with you in a minute. . . . Well, Doyle, we—uh—those were some good times we had in the White House."

"I wish you were still there, sir," said Doyle politely. "Are you here as a delegate?"

"Golly Moses, no. You couldn't drag me or my blood pressure into that tangle with a team of mules. Nope, let the young men do the shouting. It's their world now. But I'm taking advantage of all the courtesies and freeloading, of course. This is Carol's first visit here, and I want her to see what she can while our Embassy and the French still feel they owe me some attention. Uh—we're off to the Quai d'Orsay for one of those overspiced lunches that give me heartburn, and after that, maybe an hour of sight-seeing around town. What about you, Doyle? Here to cover the conference?"

"No, no," said Doyle quickly, embarrassed. "I'm taking it fairly easy this time. I'm doing some research on a book, and—well—loafing a little."

"Good, and good to see you again. Maybe we can have a drink sometime. Well, good luck, Doyle."

Earnshaw ducked into the limousine, and the chauffeur slammed the door. Up ahead, the Secret Service agent had joined a colleague, who waited behind the wheel of a small sedan. With a vague smile at the occupants of the limousine, Doyle started away. He heard the motor purr behind him, abruptly die, and he heard his name.

Bewildered, he turned to hear Earnshaw, who was being helped out of the limousine, calling to him. "Doyle! Wait—hold on!"

Doyle began to return to the car, still puzzled, but Earnshaw met him halfway. Placing a paternal arm around his shoulders, the former President drew him over to the curb. "Uh, Doyle, the second I set myself inside the car, something occurred to me. Uh, that book you're researching—can't take all your time, can it?"

"Well—no," said Doyle cautiously.

"That's what occurred to me. You see, to be truthful, there's a little business here I could use some help on, uh, something more in your own line of work, and it struck me that maybe it could be of interest to you."

"It depends—"

"I'll tell you what it is," said Earnshaw. "Uh, I need a writing collaborator to work with me from tomorrow, the sixteenth, to the last day of the Summit, which is the twenty-fifth." He grinned shyly at Doyle. "Uh, the old adage holds—what fools we mortals be. In a moment of weakness I agreed to spend some of my time in Paris as an observer of the Five-Power Conference, strictly as an ordinary citizen, and to produce a 500-word daily commentary for the Ormsby Press Enterprises—they're in London—and just now our own national syndicate, ANA, has contracted for my daily columns, too. Uh—now what the devil, Doyle—I've never made any great pretensions about being a writer fellow. You know that. So what would be real useful for me, I just realized, is to have a professional kind of assistant to attend the Summit meetings every day, report to me what's been going on, and I'd interpret it for him and let him write it up under my name and put it on the wires, and I'd let him keep most of the money I get. Well, seeing you made me realize how perfectly you'd fit the bill. I can't imagine that it would be much of a sweat for you, and you'd get a press pass on my behalf, entrée into everything, lots of free meals and sport, a chance to see everyone and everything, and maybe, oh, to make it worthwhile, maybe I'd see fit to pay you $300 a day for the ten days. I'm sure that's chicken feed to you, but it would provide you with tip money. And the work involved is little enough. You'd have plenty of time to carry on with your own book research." He watched Doyle's face. "How does it strike you, my friend?"

Doyle had already been thinking hard, balancing the pros and cons of the offer. On the con side, all that he could find objectionable was that the ghost-writing chore might cut into the free time he required to pursue Hazel and the big breakthrough on his book. Weighed against this were numerous pros. For one, Hazel would be busy most of the day with her own work and would be difficult to see, so very likely he'd have plenty of time on his hands. Besides, and more important, with Earnshaw's prestigious press credentials in his possession, credentials underwritten by Hazel's very own syndicate, ANA, Doyle would have legitimate access to wherever Hazel might be, both around the city and in the ANA offices. Finally, the money was nothing to sniff at, and, indeed, might be sorely needed if Hazel demanded a payoff for her secret information on the Kennedy assassination.

"Did you say ANA?" Doyle asked.

"ANA and the Ormsby chain."

"And I'd get full press credentials?"

"Absolutely. I could arrange it before the end of the day."

Doyle's porker face wreathed into a smile. He stuck out his hand. "Mr. Earnshaw, you've got a deal."

Earnshaw wrung the extended hand enthusiastically. "I'm so pleased. This is a load off my mind. . . . Okay, Doyle, why don't you drop by my suite in the Lancaster around five o'clock? We can iron out the details, and by that time I'll have squared you away for credentials from our press section. Five o'clock, then?"

"I'll be there. And make it bourbon."

Cheered by his decision, and by the opportunity the job offered him of constant and natural contact with Hazel, Doyle resumed his walk to the Club Lautrec. Reaching the Champs-Élysées, he turned his back on the Arc de Triomphe and pointed his steps toward his destination. Preoccupied with what might await him at the cabaret, he was oblivious of the French couples and families lazily promenading on this mild Sunday afternoon. His overburdened legs carried his shimmying belly swiftly through the mass of strollers as he wended his way nearer to the Rue la Boëtie.

Approaching the Café Français, Doyle involuntarily succumbed to the Parisian practice of scanning the habitués of every outdoor terrace. His eyes passed over those in the rear, moved across those in the center, and began to glimpse those in the front rows—and suddenly he stopped walking.

From a distance of thirty feet, he stared at her. Except that her hair was redder, her figure fuller, her dress smarter, the erosion of more than a decade had left little mark upon her. There could be no mistake about it. Sitting at the café table ahead, deep in conversation with a pretty young girl, was Hazel Smith, at last, at long, long last.

Doyle's throat constricted, and he tried to swallow. For the life of him, he could not remember his lines. He could only remember his goal. Nervously he smoothed back his sparse hair, brushed at his lapels, hitched up his belt to pull his pants over his stomach, regretting the million extra calories that had been his only companions in the gluttonous years since Hazel. Resolutely he started toward her.

As his shadow fell across her, he bellowed effusively, "My God, it can't be! Hazel—how are you, Hazel?"

Alarmed, she jerked her body convulsively and twisted her head around. Before she could react further, Doyle bent low, rocking the table and knocking over an empty cup as he tried to kiss her. Hazel's face congealed in horror, and when his puckered lips were almost upon her, she pulled her face away to avoid them, and his kiss landed wetly on an ear lobe.

With a grunt, he straightened. "What luck, running into you like this. I'd read you were in Paris, and when I had to come here, my first thought was to try to find you." He was conscious of the perspiration growing on his brow. "You look younger than ever, Hazel. Wonderful. You've hardly changed at all!"

She examined him with cold distaste. "That's more than I can say for you."

"Very funny, ha-ha." He patted his belly. "It's an old wives' tale that you waste away when you pine for someone. Sometimes it has the opposite effect. Anyhoo, I was just up at ANA asking for Hazel Smith. First order of business. I wanted you to know I've been following your stories from Moscow, from everywhere, and they are tops, absolutely tops." He had been reaching behind him for a chair, and now grasped one and dragged it forward. "Mind if I join you for a minute? Unless you two are in the middle of something earthshaking?"

Hazel tried to ignore him. Nevertheless, Doyle sat down firmly, beaming foolishly at Hazel, then at her pretty young friend. There was an awkward strained silence until finally Doyle swallowed, nodded at the confused pretty young girl, and said, "I don't believe we've been introduced. I'm—"

Sourly Hazel's voice buried his own. "Miss Medora Hart, Mr. Jay Doyle. I'm sorry, Medora, but—"

"Miss Hart?" said Doyle. "Of course. The famous dancer."

"Singer," said Medora weakly.

Hazel glowered at Doyle and cast an apologetic glance at Medora. "I'm sorry, Medora. You were in the middle of a sentence."

Medora looked helplessly from Hazel to Doyle, and, vaguely uncomfortable, she addressed Hazel. "Well, I—I guess I've told you almost everything. I appreciate your being so kind. Well, I suppose all that is left is for me to locate Sir Austin Ormsby and—and convince him of—"

Doyle, poised to pounce on any conversational cue, leaped on this one, even though it had no meaning to him. "You want to locate Sir Austin Ormsby?" he said quickly. "I can help you. I just flew in from Vienna to go to work with former President Earnshaw, writing a daily column on what goes on at the Summit, and you know who I'll be writing my column for? Miss Smith's American wire service, ANA, and Sir Austin's own press chain. So if you want to know how to get hold of Sir Austin, I'm sure I—"

"Nobody asked you, so please stay out of this," said Hazel frigidly to Doyle. "It's a private matter." She returned her attention to Medora, who was clutching her handbag. "Medora dear, I'll have the information for you tonight. I'll call you. Then you can get hold of Sir Austin in the morning."

"I deeply appreciate that, Hazel."

Hazel Smith was already signaling off. "Waiter!" she called. "*Garçon!*" She located the check, lodged beneath the water carafe, and tried to reach it, but Doyle was already dislodging it and he held it up triumphantly. "The pleasure is mine, ladies."

In a flashing movement Hazel's hand zoomed upward, tearing the check from Doyle's grasp. "You don't owe us anything," she said angrily. As she began to fish through her change purse, ladling out francs, Medora quickly pushed her chair back from the table.

"Glad to meet you," she said uncertainly to Doyle. She touched Hazel's arm. "I'd better run. I don't know how I can ever thank you for being so decent."

Hazel glanced up. "It wasn't just conversation, Medora. I'm on your

277

side all the way. As I said, I'll phone you tonight." Then, obviously for Doyle's ears, she added, "I want to talk to you some more when we can be alone. We'll make a lunch date. Okay?"

Medora nodded vigorously, and before Doyle could bring himself fully to his feet she was out of the chair and gone up the Champs-Élysées.

Dropping back into his seat, still wearing his jocular Dionysian mask in a desperate attempt to hide his anxiety, Doyle watched Hazel pay the waiter and determined not to allow her to escape him.

The instant that the waiter left, and Hazel had snapped her purse shut, Doyle wrenched his chair closer to her. "Hazel, my dear, I can't tell you what a sight you are for these sore eyes. When I last saw you, you were a callow youngster. Now I see a sophisticated and handsome woman."

"Some people have reason to grow up overnight."

He pretended not to hear her. "I'm proud of your achievements, Hazel. I still remember our long talks, about writing, your future, when we were together. It pleases me that the student outdid the master."

"It pleases me, too."

Doyle gave a soulful sigh. "It's been a long time, hasn't it?"

The serrated teeth on Hazel's bridges (too white and inexpertly done in Moscow) were clenched. "Not long enough for me," she said.

Absorbing this punishment, which he acknowledged to himself might be deserved, Doyle fought to carry on. "It's been ages since we last sat like this, yet, in all honesty, it seems like yesterday. I have so much to tell you, Hazel. And there's so much I want to hear about you. I'm sure you know that. You must've got all those letters I wrote you these last years."

"Really?" she said. "I didn't know you could still write."

Deflecting her sarcasm, he persisted. "Aw, come on, Hazel, I wrote you maybe fifty times telling you how much I wanted to see you."

"You did?" she said. "How surprising. I'd have thought you were too busy with your society sluts after Vienna, like the Countess Ester-ass, or whatever her name was."

"I—I don't know what you're talking about."

"You don't? Let me refresh your conveniently failing memory," she said scornfully. "Let me see. The last time. Your suite, wasn't it? Hotel Imperial. Vienna. There we were, big-shot you and nobody me, and you said something like this. You said, 'I've had about enough, so why don't we call it quits, Hazel, and thanks for the memory, and you take off and go back to your fairy-tale Russian and leave me alone, because I've got to change for the opera, because I've got somebody coming by, the Countess Ester-ass, and your being here could be embarrassing.

Okay, baby? I think we understand each other now.' And I said, 'You're a goddam son of a bitch, and I never want to see you again in my life.' " Hazel stood up, rigid. "How long ago was that, *baby?* Thirteen, fourteen years ago? Okay. No rewrites. I still don't want to see you again, now or ever."

He had trembled to his feet, mask shattered, all his chins and layers of fat quivering. His voice sniveled and groveled. "Hazel, listen, no—you got it wrong—you got it mixed up—I was busy in those days, sure, lots of pressure—but one thing sure, I loved you, and I've never been interested in any other woman since, because you're the only one I ever loved." He tried to smile, failed, and said, "You're kidding, aren't you? Sure you are. That was one of your best points, always, your sense of humor. Aw, come on, Hazel, what's done is over with, and we all live and learn, and that's all that counts, because there's so much ahead. If there were faults I had once, well, lots has gone under the bridge, and like I said, you live and learn, and I've learned, I've changed. Be reasonable. This is a reunion. We've meant too much to each other to—to not pick it up now. Give us a chance, Hazel. Let's start with dinner tonight. I've missed you." He halted because her thin face was pale and pinched tight and her lips were one lip and her eyes were working him over like cleavers.

"You've missed me," she said with contempt. "I can see you've been pining away, wasting away, all three of you. Well, all I can say to you is that you always were an insensitive bastard, and now you're not only an insensitive bastard but an insensitive slob as well. Dinner, you say? What'll the menu be—pick my brains and eat my heart out? You can go to hell, Jay Doyle. But go it alone. I wouldn't be seen with you in public, anywhere!"

She went past him so fast, he was unable to move. Horrified by his loss, he turned and called after her, "Hazel! I'm at the George-V if you—" His voice trailed off behind her swiftly receding figure—"if you change your mind. . . ."

He stood wavering, feeling like one riddled by a firing squad, and at last he slumped into his chair. He gazed blankly down at the table until the aproned waiter came over to mop it with a wet cloth. "Anything for you, monsieur?" the waiter asked.

"Arsenic on the rocks," he started to say, but a frog caught it in his throat. He had expected her to be difficult, but not impossible. He had expected her to be angry, but not vindictive. He had expected a scene, but not one like this. His bright hope had become a black cloud of despair. Still, she was here and he was here, and they were both ANA, and there must be some means by which he could bring her down to what she had once been, his own, his entire Trilby. He had to devise some kind of stratagem, but he could not think because his mind and stomach were weak from starvation. His hunger had finally overrun and obliterated the diet pill, and now it attacked him, so that he could not concentrate on anything else, certainly not on Hazel or himself. Appeasement was necessary, survival was necessary, before he could possibly devote himself to thoughts of a triumphant comeback.

"What've you got?" he demanded of the waiter.

"At this hour, monsieur, only the sandwiches—sandwiches jambon, rosbif, poulet, saucisse, fromage—"

"I'll have the sandwiches," said Doyle.

"A sandwich? *Oui, monsieur.* Which one shall it be?"

"All of them, you idiot!" Doyle exploded angrily. "One of each. And *un verre de bière*—no, make it *une bouteille de bière.* And make it fast!"

"Tout de suite, monsieur!"

You're damn right, *tout de suite,* Doyle thought, grimly staring out at a young French couple, hugging and kissing, as they went past the café. He'd better think of something at once, *tout de suite,* or otherwise blow his brains out.

WITH THE SINGLE-MINDEDNESS of a fugitive who had successfully escaped his prison walls, Emmett A. Earnshaw left the grand vestibule of the French Ministry of Foreign Affairs, and strode swiftly, looking neither right nor left, through the courtyard toward the Embassy limousine. The chauffeur was at attention, and Earnshaw smiled absently at him, paused to note that the two Secret Service agents were entering the sedan pulled up behind, and then he got inside.

Once safe in the cushioned rear seat, Earnshaw unbuttoned his suit coat, loosened his belt, and peered back at the formidable Quai d'Orsay. The others—Carol, their guide Callahan, and the French President's head of protocol, Pierre Urbain, a narrowly intellectual museum piece with a monocle—had emerged from the vestibule and were still huddled in the court. Earnshaw saw Urbain gesturing toward the Italian-style roof, the balconies, the columns of the Quai d'Orsay, and Earnshaw was relieved to be out of earshot.

He was bored with Urbain's minute descriptions of the Ministry's mixed Louis XIV and Renaissance interior, with the French protocol chief's endless monologues on each precious console, mantel clock, chandelier, most borrowed from the Louvre. For Earnshaw it was tedious because he had been here before, actually slept here with

Isabel, dear Isabel (the King's Chamber, the Queen's Chamber, the Beauvais Salon in their private royal apartment), in better days, when he had been President and his host had been the President of France and not some lowly academician recently transformed into a government receptionist.

Yet what he had suffered from the most in the last two hours, Earnshaw knew, was not so much the boredom of rehashed history as a kind of insult—well, that was too harsh—rather a degradation or humiliation of having been invited to a second-rate and late-starting official luncheon.

Brooding about it, and how it had accentuated his awareness of his unhappy fall from popular favor, Earnshaw now regretted that he had accepted the invitation. Of course, he had done so for his niece, because of her understandable excitement over an opportunity to see the restricted *inside* of the Quai d'Orsay. But still, it had not been worth it. Pierre Urbain had begun apologizing to him from the moment that they started for the Great Dining Room. The French President, Urbain had said, sent profound apologies for not being able to attend. He was occupied receiving the recently arrived Premier of Russia and the Chairman of the People's Republic of China. The President expected to receive Earnshaw formally later.

Of course, it was all logical, Earnshaw knew, since the French President's duty was to attend to active world leaders, not retired ones, not has-beens. Moreover, Earnshaw's sudden appearance in Paris *had* been unexpected. Still, from the moment that Earnshaw had settled himself at one of the two magnificently decorated tables, no amount of rationalizing could alleviate his hurt. The caliber of the other state guests made it clear that he was receiving the B treatment, not the A treatment to which he had so long been accustomed. Among the two dozen guests present, there was not a single important current or past head of state. There was a throneless Bourbon monarch, an inactive British general, a Pakistan minister, a small African nation's ambassador, a UNESCO secretary, an Italian Nobel Prize winner, a Greek shipping magnate. And there was the former President of the United States, Emmett A. Earnshaw.

He could not remember the meal, except that it had been underdone and overspiced, at least for his country palate, and the overwhelming smell of cut flowers and perfume had nauseated him. He could not remember the small talk, except that it had been uninteresting, steered safely past the political shoals by M. Urbain into the safer soundings of art, books, music. When the ordeal had ended, Earnshaw had popped out of the Foreign Ministry like a cork out of a champagne bottle.

Once more peering through the rear door of the limousine, now opened, Earnshaw could see Carol approaching, freckled face and hands animated, as she addressed Urbain and Callahan. Her glow of pleasure momentarily lightened Earnshaw's dark displeasure, even made him ashamed of his irritability. To see her like this was compensation enough. Besides, in all fairness to the French President, both he and Simon Madlock had several times, during their term in Washington, treated out-of-office foreign guests in this same manner, especially when there had been more useful foreign leaders staying in Blair House. He must not, he knew, expect anything better.

The others had reached the limousine door. Embarrassed, trying to repress a giggle, Carol allowed the French protocol chief to kiss her hand. She was effusive in her thanks, and Earnshaw added his own. Finally Carol and Callahan were in the seat beside him, and the limousine was on its way.

An hour and a half of sight-seeing had been scheduled for the remainder of the afternoon. Earnshaw had meant to suggest that this be postponed until tomorrow because of what might be waiting for him at the hotel, but before he could speak, Callahan was informing Carol that Les Invalides was nearby and that the sight of the red granite tomb that held the corpse of Napoleon Bonaparte, a tomb set deep in a circular well, was a memorable sight.

"Oh, I'd love to see it!" Carol exclaimed. She covered Earnshaw's hand with her own. "Wouldn't that be fascinating, Uncle Emmett?" With a weary smile, Earnshaw surrendered.

They left the Quai d'Orsay and the Seine behind them, turned up the Rue de Constantine, moved past the green trees in the spacious Esplanade des Invalides, circled around the seventeenth-century Invalides' complex of buildings, dominated by the towering gold-leafed dome.

When they parked in the Avenue de Tourville, Earnshaw felt his niece tugging at his arm. "Here we are, Uncle Emmett," she said.

He remained seated. "You run along with—uh—run along with Mr. Callahan, my dear. I've visited the Invalides before. I'd prefer to stay put and finish my cigar." Conscious of her concern, he added, "I'll be happy right here. You have a good time."

"If you don't mind," she said slowly. Then she brightened. "I know what. You're just jealous at the idea of my going inside to see another great man."

Earnshaw chuckled. "I'm jealous of nobody in his position. Just give Napoleon a bon joor from your Uncle Emmett."

After they had gone, and the chauffeur had received permission to step outside and stretch his legs, Earnshaw glanced behind him. He was relieved that the pesky Secret Servant agents were keeping their distance. Luxuriously he sank back, welcoming this interlude of privacy. Relighting his cigar, he remembered what he had said to Carol: he was jealous of no man in Napoleon's position. He knew this for certain, because often he himself felt entombed. The difference was that he could do something about premature burial, especially a burial without honor, and immediately his mind went to Dr. Dietrich von Goerlitz and to an assessment of what had been accomplished, so far, this first day in Paris.

Except for his luck in stumbling upon Doyle, it had been a frustrating and profitless day. Once he had settled in the Hotel Lancaster, early this morning, his first order of business had been to get hold of Dr. Dietrich von Goerlitz. Filled with trepidation, but somehow confident that his name would bring the voice of the gruff old industrialist to the other end of the line immediately, he had telephoned the Goerlitz suite in the Hotel Ritz. He had been mistaken.

Someone who had identified himself as Herr Schlager, Goerlitz's general director—speaking in an incongruous blend of the Teutonic with American colloquial, yet businesslike—had taken the call. Earnshaw had given his name, even spelled it out, and it had unnerved him that Schlager gave no indication of recognizing it. Desperately in those moments, Earnshaw had wished for Simon Madlock alive, beside him, briskly and efficiently overriding the German general director, who was either dumb or insulting. But alas, there had been no Simon Madlock, only himself. Irritated, Earnshaw had explained that he was an old friend of Dr. von Goerlitz, and that he must speak to the industrialist at once.

Schlager had gone off to inquire as to the whereabouts of his employer, and Earnshaw had waited uneasily at the silent telephone. Schlager had returned shortly and breezily explained that Dr. von Goerlitz was in a meeting and would be tied up for hours, perhaps the entire day. Possibly, Schlager suggested, he could handle whatever Mr. Earnshaw had wished to discuss. Earnshaw had restrained himself from saying that he was not used to dealing with subordinates. What he had said, finally, was that he was calling on a purely personal matter, that he could speak only to Dr. von Goerlitz, and that he would like to leave a message.

"Tell Dr. von Goerlitz that Emmett A. Earnshaw telephoned. I have an urgent matter to discuss with him as soon as possible. I'm at the Hotel Lancaster—do you have that?—Lancaster. I'd appreciate it if he'd leave word at my hotel exactly when I can see him. The appointment can be entirely at his convenience. Is all of that clear?"

Apparently all of that was clear, and Herr Schlager had written down the message, for he had repeated it aloud and had promised to put it in Dr. von Goerlitz's hands sometime during the afternoon.

While returning to the hotel from the Palais Rose to dress for the lunch at the Quai d'Orsay, Earnshaw hoped he'd find some message from Goerlitz. For even though—as he had confessed to Sir Austin—he anticipated resistance from Goerlitz in removing the offending material from his memoir, Earnshaw had come to believe that the German would nevertheless be ready to meet with him in person. But when he had returned to the hotel in the early afternoon, there had been no message from Goerlitz in his mail slot behind the concierge's desk and no message in the paper bag hanging from the doorknob of his suite.

While the silence had not necessarily meant that Goerlitz was avoiding him—after all, he might have still been occupied with his meeting—the lack of response did give Earnshaw minutes of anxiety. After changing for lunch, he had decided that the best strategy would be to present his request for an appointment more directly. Sending a telephone message through Schlager might prove less persuasive than a personal handwritten note. And so, on the hotel stationery, he had addressed himself to "My dear Dietrich." He had invoked their old friendship, the warm memories of dinners together in the capitals of Europe when they had had corporate dealings, of their social evenings in the Villa Morgen outside Frankfurt-am-Main. He had gone on to recollect Simon Madlock's glowing report to him of Goerlitz's comeback and good health four or five years ago. Earnshaw had then written that he prayed his friend's health was still as good today, and that he hoped all went well with his children. As for himself, Earnshaw had added, life had become lonely since the loss of both his wife and his trusted adviser and aide. His only consolations now were the devotion of a niece, Carol, who was vacationing with him on the Continent, and his continuing interest in doing what could be done to keep America as well as Europe, and especially Goerlitz's West Germany, democratic, strong, and free of outside domination. While visiting London the other day, Earnshaw had gone on, he had learned that Dr. von Goerlitz was in Paris. At once he had determined to see his old friend again, not only to renew a long friendship but to discuss a private matter of concern to both of them. He hoped that Dr. von Goerlitz could receive him as soon as possible. "As ever, most cordially yours, Emmett A. Earnshaw."

That had been two or three hours ago. He was certain that Goerlitz, no matter what mistaken bitterness he felt toward Earnshaw, would reply immediately. Goerlitz possessed many shortcomings, but while frequently ruthless and occasionally brusque, he was still an aristocrat and a gentleman of the old school. Doubtless he would respond to Earnshaw's appeal and would receive him. When the confrontation became a reality, Earnshaw felt assured, the battle would be more than half won. For Earnshaw persisted in trusting his greatest asset, a geniality as powerful as an amulet. His charm, he had read, could bring down the Walls of Jericho. It would also, he was positive, melt Goerlitz's steely anger. He needed only the chance to exercise this natural talent.

To his surprise, Earnshaw realized that Carol and Callahan had returned and were entering the limousine. Although impatient to be done with sight-seeing and to get back to the hotel and Goerlitz's reply, he checked himself, and despite his preoccupation he tried to be attentive to his niece's enthusiasm over the Invalides. Enraptured, she bubbled on. Wasn't the sight of Napoleon's tomb deep in its majestic well, seen from the circular balcony above, terrific? Did Uncle Emmett know that it had taken the French seven years to persuade the British to allow the Emperor's body to be exhumed from St. Helena and returned to Paris? Did he know that six layers of coffins, one of metal, one of acajou, two of lead, one of ebony, one of oak, encased Napoleon's remains? Did he know that the French had hunted everywhere for six years to find the red stone for Napoleon's sepulchre, and found it at last (irony) in Russia, and they spent three additional years quarrying and carving it?

"Oh, I've never been more thrilled, Uncle Emmett," she was saying. "Wait'll the kids back at school hear about this. . . . What do we see next?" Then, a worried pause. "Maybe you're too tired, Uncle Emmett?"

The last, from Carol, brought Earnshaw back to the present. Instantly, he was ashamed of his self-absorption. Carol had been so much to him, meant so much now, and he had given her so little of himself. She was his blood, in effect the daughter that he had never had, and she deserved his paternal devotion.

"I think I'd like to see a little more," he said reassuringly. Callahan was rattling off the possibilities, the Eiffel Tower, Sacré-Coeur, the Place des Vosges, but Earnshaw ignored him. "Why don't we continue driving around the Left Bank a bit, and then we can decide?"

They had gone past the Eiffel Tower and swung into the Quai Branly on the river, when Earnshaw saw the massive rise of the Palais de Chaillot on the Place du Trocadéro across the water. Something was illuminated in his memory, and with more excitement than he had evinced on the entire ride, he leaned forward and said to the driver, "I think that's the—uh—Pont d'Iéna—however you pronounce it—the bridge there. Take it to the other side. When you get on that Kléber street, I'll tell you where to stop." He sat back and winked at Carol. "There's something I've got to show you. I think you'll get a kick out of it."

The limousine went around the Place du Trocadéro, and finally eased into the Avenue Kléber.

Earnshaw, squinting across the pair beside him and through the car window, called out to the chauffeur, "Go slow now—slow—mmm, yes, just one block down—that's right, good!" He sat up. "Park anywhere around here."

There was a problem finding a place to park, and when the chauffeur, out of exasperation, at last drew up in an illegal zone, a blue-coated *agent de police* materialized immediately. Callahan slid out of the car with his Embassy credentials and delivered a torrent of French interspersed with Earnshaw's name and former rank, and finally it was the *agent de police,* apologizing, deferential, who opened their rear door and signaled the Secret Service sedan into a spot behind them.

On the sidewalk, Earnshaw insisted that Callahan stay with the limousine, and if the Secret Service men had to come along, that they keep their distance. "This is something special I want to show my niece. It's strictly between Carol and myself."

"I can't imagine what this is."

"Really not that important," said Earnshaw.

"But I love mysteries. Should I bring my camera?"

"We-ll, that might be fun."

She took her Kodak from Callahan, entwined her arm in Earnshaw's, and they walked to the Rue de Longchamp and turned into it.

Earnshaw strode purposefully up the street, and Carol had to skip every few steps to keep up with him. At last he slowed his pace, and she said breathlessly, "Now that we're practically alone, can you tell me?"

"Sure can. It's just a little thing that I thought would amuse you. Well, you've seen where they keep Napoleon, haven't you? So I thought you'd like to see where they keep your old uncle. I'm taking you to the Avenue President Earnshaw."

Carol stopped short, her eyes saucers. *"Avenue President Earnshaw!* Ohh, no. Oh, that's fantastic!"

He grinned with deep pleasure. "Yup. The French named the street after me—well, about five, six years ago. Isabel and I saw it on our next trip, not long after. Not much of a street, but there it was, and I must say, I was impressed."

"So am I!" She fumbled at her camera case. "Let me get this ready.

I want to take you standing right under the street sign, so I can put the picture on my wall, and I'll make a copy for the Library. Are we far from it?"

Earnshaw looked up toward the street plaque at the intersection. "Next one," he said. "Let's go."

Together they hurried down the short block, and when they reached the corner, Earnshaw motioned toward the narrow bricked thoroughfare that ran into the Rue de Longchamp. "Here it is. And the sign—"

He went sideways around the corner of the granite office building and pointed upward, and his voice died.

The high square metal street sign, blue with white lettering, read: RUE CATHAY.

Earnshaw's face, tilted backward, remained pointed at the street sign, but he could feel the crimson creeping to his cheeks. "Well, now—" he said.

Carol was aghast, and frantic. "You must have the wrong street, Uncle Emmett."

Slowly, he lowered his gaze and stared thoughtfully into space. Finally he shook his head. "I'm afraid it is the right street, Carol. I recognize the small café and that old-fashioned pharmacy. Yup, this is—was—the Avenue President Earnshaw." He pulled out a handkerchief, honked into it, stuffed it back in his pocket. He grimaced foolishly at Carol, and shrugged. "As someone said—here today, gone tomorrow."

He could see that Carol was desperately trying to cover his embarrassment and her own. "You know the French," she said quickly. "Somebody was telling me how they're like chameleons, always changing their looks and attitudes, absolutely mercurial—like—like they change street names as if they were newspaper headlines. Why, you know what, just before, I asked the concierge about an antique shop in the Rue de Trieste, and he looked it up, couldn't find it, and then he asked what year my guidebook was published, and when I told him, he said that it was outdated, because in the latest guidebook the Rue de Trieste has been renamed the Rue Mohammed. I thought it was funny, but now I see it's insane sick of them, that's what." She glared up at the sign, and suddenly thumbed her nose at it. "So much for you, Rue Cathay."

Earnshaw was forced to laugh. "I wouldn't carry on that way, Carol. It's not all that darn important."

Her anger had not subsided. "Well, it is to me. Only it makes no sense. Why get rid of Avenue President Earnshaw for something silly like Rue Cathay?"

"French logic," he said quietly. "Cathay was the ancient name for

China. De Gaulle recognized Red China, and France has been their ally during the years since. Today, China is in, and Earnshaw is out. Today, China is important, and Earnshaw is nothing."

"That's not true!"

"No matter, my dear. It is their logic." He took her elbow. "Let's go." He considered the street sign once more, then sighed. "I'm sorry you didn't get your picture."

Walking slowly, without exchanging another word, they returned to the limousine. Settled inside, Earnshaw had no more heart for sightseeing. Yet he was reluctant to give voice to his feeling because he did not wish to spoil his niece's day further. But then he heard Carol addressing the chauffeur and Callahan.

"Ouch, my poor aching feet," she complained. "I think I've had it for today." She turned her head. "Do you mind terribly if we go back to the hotel, Uncle Emmett?"

"Whatever you say, my dear."

In the wake of ignominy, at least one good thing, Earnshaw thought. At least there was Carol, his brother's child once and his own for the rest of his time, and she was faithful and constant. It was something. Maybe it was everything. Again, with greater urgency than earlier, he wanted to return to the hotel and learn what the future held in store for him—and for his child.

The limousine had hardly halted before the Lancaster when Earnshaw leaped out of it, waved a thanks to his retinue, and hurried into the hotel. At the concierge's desk an assistant manager was already waiting with his key and messages. There were formal invitations to government functions and there were advertisements, delivered by hand, but there were no telephone messages, and nothing from the Hotel Ritz or from Dr. Dietrich von Goerlitz.

Disheartened, he started for the birdcage of an elevator, and Carol hurried to join him in it.

After they reached the sixth floor and had climbed up the flight of stairs to their seventh-floor suite, Carol said, "Is anything wrong, Uncle Emmett?"

"Wrong? Uh—no, nothing. I'd expected to hear from someone on a business matter, that's all."

In the foyer of their suite, after putting down her camera and purse, Carol asked if she could make him a drink. Earnshaw nodded tiredly.

He followed her up the short flight of carpeted steps into the large sitting room. As she went to the antique mahogany tambour desk, where the tray of bottles, glasses, and ice stood, he moved restlessly within the luxurious rectangle of overstuffed furniture. At the tall

French windows, he paused and looked out upon the irregular roofs of Paris, streaked by the orange rays of the day's last sun, and he studied the far-off misty white Byzantine domes of the Church of Sacré-Coeur that rose out of Montmartre like giant magical mushrooms crowning some wizard's aerie. The beauty of the scene deepened his sense of loss and isolation.

Moodily he turned to accept the bourbon from Carol, as the telephone rang.

"I'll take it," she said, and ran to pick up the receiver.

He sipped the drink and waited while Carol listened. She cupped her hand over the mouthpiece. "Uncle Emmett, it's the desk. There's someone downstairs in the lobby to see you. I think the name is Goerlitz."

He came erect so fast that it was like a man, clinging to a rope, suddenly being yanked up from a deep pit by rescuing hands. Spilling part of his drink, he shouted, "Send him right up—have him come right up!"

Repeating this instruction, Carol dropped the receiver back in its cradle and moved forward, puzzled. "Goerlitz. Sounds familiar. Is he—isn't that the German munitions man, the one who was in jail?"

"One of the richest and most powerful men in the world," said Earnshaw quickly. After glancing around the sitting room, he hastened to look at himself in a mirror. "Is everything in order, do you think?"

"Why, I don't know what you mean. Why, yes—"

Earnshaw gulped at his drink. "He's important, Carol, *very* important."

"You mean—do you mean important to you?"

"What? Yes. Do we have enough liquor? No, not liquor—soft drinks? Cigarettes? Turn up the lamps. You'd better change before—no, I guess you're all right. You can be here when he comes in. He's—uh—rather old, maybe in his seventies, kind of Prussian-formal, and he'll seem grumpy, but actually he's not half bad. We've known each other a long time. Yes, I've been waiting for his call. I expected a call for an appointment. He's the one I wrote the note to. But he's come all the way across town to see me. A good sign, that's a good sign."

Still puzzled, Carol asked, "Is this a private meeting? Should I stay or go?"

"Stay or go? By all means stay for a while. Yes. I—uh—I wrote him about you. I think it would be nice for him to meet you. Then—uh—when you see we're settling down to a real talk, you—uh—make a sort of polite, well, excuse yourself, you can go to your bedroom."

"I'll go out and do some shopping."

"Anything you want," Earnshaw said abruptly. "The lamps—turn up the lamps."

Putting his drink down on an end table, Earnshaw hastened into the foyer to await his guest. Every nerve fiber within him had been roused and quickened, and he felt ready for the old man. He had expected his note might touch Dr. Dietrich von Goerlitz. He had not expected his note to bring Dr. von Goerlitz to him. Yes, a good omen, and he was heady with anticipation.

The buzzer sounded.

Earnshaw charged at the front door, taking no notice of the creaking protests of his aged legs. Holding the knob, his greeting already framed, he drew himself up, and then he pulled the door open.

What met Earnshaw's eyes was so confounding that his jaw dropped, while the rest of him stood rooted and dumb.

He had expected to find in the doorway the gnarled, hunched, severe Teuton, and what he found before him instead was a slender boy in his twenties, a boy with dark blond hair, light blue eyes, a boy with the keen whippet face of a Swiss skier, a boy standing straight in his navy blue sport jacket with its metal buttons and Heidelberg insignia sewn on one pocket, an ascot, and gray flannel slacks.

"You—you must have the wrong room," was all that Earnshaw could say.

The boy was not flustered. "You are President Earnshaw?" he inquired.

"Why, yes, that's—"

"I had them telephone from the lobby. I am Willi von Goerlitz, sir. Dr. Dietrich von Goerlitz is my father. He has sent me to you with a communication, sir."

Recovering from his first shock of surprise, Earnshaw understood. The heir had been dispatched with tidings. That old Goerlitz had selected none other than his only son to bring word was heartening. "I see, I see, your father's made you his courier. Very good. Forgive my first reaction. When I heard from the desk that Goerlitz was here, I—I expected your father. I couldn't—" Suddenly Earnshaw remembered his manners. "Good heavens, I mustn't keep you standing in the hall. Come in, come in."

The young man bowed formally from the waist. "Thank you, sir." He stepped through the doorway. "Forgive me if I intrude. I will only be a minute."

"Nonsense! You come inside now—have a seat, have a drink."

"Thank you, sir, but . . ."

Earnshaw guided Goerlitz's son across the foyer and led him up into the sitting room. "Besides, I'd like you to meet my niece." Carol was standing, looking very ladylike, in front of the fireplace, and the first sight of their visitor surprised her as much as it had Earnshaw. "Carol," Earnshaw said, beckoning. As she advanced, still bewildered, now diffident, Earnshaw said, "This is Dr. von Goerlitz's son, Willi. . . . Willi, my niece, Carol Earnshaw." She extended her hand, boarding-school manners for Europe, expecting to shake Willi's hand, but instead he took it lightly and bent low over it.

"I am pleased to make your acquaintance, Miss Earnshaw," said Willi, looking directly at her.

She avoided his gaze. "I'm pleased to meet you, too."

"Well, now, you know each other," said Earnshaw jovially. He addressed himself to his guest. "How old are you, young man? Carol here is nineteen."

"I have just had my twenty-sixth birthday, sir."

Earnshaw was thoughtful. "Yes, that adds up. I knew you when you were about—let me see—you must have been no more than fifteen. Well, now, you've grown into quite a young man. . . . Sit down, will you? Let's sit down here."

Earnshaw lowered himself into the plump folds of the richly textured sofa, and Willi, trying to sit stiffly on the edge, fell backwards with a thump, feet in the air. As he made an effort to regain his balance and his dignity, Carol covered her mouth to suppress a giggle. Willi's waxen poise broke, and he grinned. "It was like sitting on edelweiss," he said to Carol.

"Or dandelions," she said, laughing. Feeling easier, she added, "I'm still kind of stunned by you. I expected someone much older to walk in, your father, that is, and there you were, and it sort of threw me, like as if your father had just come from getting de-aging animal-cell shots from one of those miracle doctors in Switzerland."

"But he has taken those shots," Willi said seriously. Their eyes met again, and both burst into laughter.

Earnshaw coughed. "Well, young man, as I remember, you were going to some sort of private school in Switzerland."

"Yes, sir," said Willi von Goerlitz. "After that I studied in Paris and attended the University of Heidelberg." He looked up at Carol. "But no scars, you see. Everyone was most pacifistic. I had my diploma in Engineering."

"What do you do now, Willi?" Earnshaw inquired.

"I am in the Industry, as my father refers to his firms. I am under Mr. Schlager, the general director, who is instructing me in management."

"That must be literally fascinating," said Carol.

Willi von Goerlitz nodded vigorously. "Yes, it is like learning to rule a country. It is extremely trying. My father sometimes thinks I am too impractical and poetic for it, my head in the clouds above, and perhaps he is right."

"Uh—your father," said Earnshaw. "How is your father?"

"His health? He is better, sir. He has been often unwell in recent years, but I believe he is stronger now, but not with his old strength. He travels infrequently. However, he felt it imperative to visit Paris, although his physicians considered it too strenuous. He will be only one week here."

"Ummm, I see," Earnshaw muttered. He had brought his drink to his lips when he realized that he had been deficient as a host. "Uh, Willi, I'm sorry—I forgot to get you that drink I offered you. What would you like Carol to mix?"

Willi squirmed forward on the sofa. "Thank you, sir, but nothing right now." His narrow Nordic features had become grave. "I must deliver my father's communication to you, and take my leave."

"Of course. Business before pleasure." Earnshaw stood up restlessly, then moved to a hard-winged armchair. He looked at the young man. "You have a message to give me from your father?"

"Yes, sir. It is not in writing, but oral."

"I see, I see. Very well. Go ahead, Willi."

"My father requested that I relay the following." He began to recite in a monotone. "He has received your letter. He is surprised to hear from you after so long. He is able to remain in Paris no more than six or seven days. He is here to confer on several vitally important business ventures. Since he has so much to do, and since the time to do everything is limited by his impaired health, he is unable to see anyone or meet anyone outside of his scheduled business meetings. He has not one minute to spare." Willi caught his breath, and finished weakly, "He is sorry that he cannot see you. He sends his regrets."

Willi had come to a full stop and now stared down at the pattern woven in the carpet. While Earnshaw knew that there was no more to the message, he could not accept its finality. "Uh, Willi—that is all of it? You are sure?"

Willi swallowed hard. "I have left nothing out, sir. That is my father's entire communication precisely." He came hastily to his feet, avoiding Carol's eyes. "I had better go."

Frowning, Earnshaw rose. As Willi ducked an apologetic nod to Carol and started to turn away, Earnshaw suddenly said, "One minute, Willi." The young man halted hopefully. Earnshaw went on. "I don't think your father really understands how vital it is for him to see me. It might be best if I responded to his message with one more of my own. Do you think you could repeat to your father, accurately, what I tell you? Or should I write my message?"

"I can repeat it, sir."

"Good. Uh—you'd better give me a few moments to think it out. You just keep yourself busy—uh—talk to Carol, yes, you and Carol can talk. Tell her about Paris. I'll be back in a jiffy."

Earnshaw went down the steps into the hallway and entered the darkening master bedroom. He switched on a lamp, and noticing that the door to the breakfast terrace was still open, he moved thoughtfully out upon the terrace. The air was wondrously mild, and the largest dome of Sacré-Coeur was still visible in the distance, yet Earnshaw's inner turmoil was not soothed. Dr. Dietrich von Goerlitz had sent word that he was too busy to see him. No man was ever *that* busy. Since Goerlitz could not know that Earnshaw knew of the contents of the memoirs, the rebuff was for other reasons. Plainly, Goerlitz remembered that Earnshaw, as President, had not stood by him when he had been indicted as a war criminal. The German still nursed the old grievance and would not forgive. Earnshaw could see that there was only one hope: to be more explicit, to jolt Goerlitz by revealing his own knowledge of the memoirs. This might have no effect, but it was the only course left.

After giving the matter more thought, Earnshaw returned to the sitting room. As he silently entered the room, he became aware of his niece and Willi seated together comfortably on the sofa, too absorbed in conversation to notice him. Carol had just finished saying that she wished she had been to Paris at least once before, as Willi had been, so that she might know how to use her time to the best advantage. And now Willi was saying that he had studied in Paris for two years, after going to boarding school in Switzerland. Definitely, he was saying, Carol must visit the old Les Halles district one dawn, and try the grilled pork with garlic at Le Cochon d'Or, a marvelous bistro with sawdust on the floor, in the Rue du Jour. Carol had begun an animated reply when Earnshaw cleared his throat and interrupted them.

"Uh—Willi," he said.

Willi leaped to his feet, standing ramrod-straight, as if called to attention by a drillmaster. "Yes, sir."

"Give your father this message," said Earnshaw. "Inform him that I appreciate hearing from him, and that I can also understand how he might be too busy for what he regarded as purely a social meeting. But tell him that the meeting I should like to have would involve more than a social exchange. Tell him it concerns a subject of—uh—well, of vital importance to both our interests." He paused, exhaled, then plunged. "Tell him that I have heard that he has written a—a memoir or autobiography." He paused again. "He *has* written such a manuscript, hasn't he, Willi?"

"Yes, sir."

"Well, all right, you tell him that I've learned from an unimpeachable source that he has devoted an entire chapter to discussing my administration as President, and, in fact, my own activities as President." He considered Goerlitz's son. "I assume that you've read this material, Willi?"

Willi shook his head vigorously. "No, sir. I have not read the book. However, I do know it exists, sir."

"Well, forgive me. That should be no concern of yours. Anyway, tell your father that I know, in a limited way, the contents of his chapter on me. I wish to see him in order to give him fuller information for that chapter, firsthand information that only I can provide, information he cannot possibly possess. I can help him be more—well, more accurate—and thereby help him avert much trouble."

Carol was standing. "What did Dr. von Goerlitz write about you, Uncle Emmett?"

Earnshaw dispatched his niece's question with a wave of his hand. "Never mind." His gaze remained fixed on Willi von Goerlitz. "That's the sum of my message. Do you think you have it straight?"

"I have, sir."

"Then you deliver it, and I'll await his reply."

"Yes, sir. I will not see my father until dinner, but I shall present the communication to him at that time." He hesitated. "Well, I had better go."

Carol had come forward. "Do you mind if I leave for a little while, too, Uncle Emmett? There's some shopping I absolutely must do."

"Whatever you wish," Earnshaw said absently. "I doubt if you'll find anything open on Sunday."

"Mr. von Goerlitz mentioned that there's a drugstore near the Arc de Triomphe—"

"Le Drug Store," amended Willi hastily. "It is always open. It has everything on earth for sale. I should be pleased to show you where it is."

"How very nice of you," said Carol to Willi. "But if it's a bother—"

"No bother at all, Miss Earnshaw. I would be honored."

"Fine. Thanks." She looked at Earnshaw. "I'll be back soon."

"You needn't hurry," said Earnshaw, hunting for a cigar.

"And I shall deliver your message, sir!" called Willi von Goerlitz with more enthusiasm.

"Very good, young man."

After they had gone, Earnshaw unwrapped his cigar, placed a match to it, and wandered restlessly through the big, lonely sitting room. He tried to recollect his conversation with Sir Austin in London last night, and exactly what the abstract said Goerlitz had put into his manuscript. He could not remember exactly. He could only recall that it had been bad, very, very bad, and he hoped that the young man would somehow convey the depth of his personal disturbance.

The telephone was ringing. Earnshaw went to it, stood over it, and finally picked it up. The concierge's desk was announcing that a Mr. Jay Thomas Doyle was downstairs, and that he claimed to have an appointment. Belatedly, Earnshaw remembered what he had forgotten, the invitation to his newly hired ghost-writer to discuss the daily column that must begin tomorrow.

Earnshaw hesitated. He was in no mood for diversions and subterfuges. He wondered if he should postpone seeing Doyle until the morning. But then something else occurred to him. Doyle was a famous correspondent, with a keen reporter's instinct for news and with countless connections. As Earnshaw's collaborator, carrying the influential press pass that Earnshaw was obtaining for him, Doyle could be out in the city serving as Earnshaw's brain, eyes, legs. Doyle could be made to keep track of Dr. Dietrich von Goerlitz's daily activities in the busy city, and report on them. Thus, if this last message through Willi failed to elicit a favorable response, there would still be Doyle to advise him where Goerlitz might be from day to day and where he might be confronted by "chance." It would be another iron in the fire, and always better two irons than one, as Simon Madlock used to say.

"Yes, I'm expecting Mr. Doyle," Earnshaw said into the telephone. "Send him up."

ON THE SHEET of yellow foolscap, still curled in her portable typewriter, she had written two paragraphs and begun a third:

PARIS, June 15 (ANA)—Night has fallen on Paris, and Paris sleeps, while a tense and anxious world awaits the coming of daylight, when its leaders awaken to join together in the hazardous ascent to the Summit.

With morning, the sharply etched faults and craggy pitfalls that stand between the international leaders and the highest goal on earth, the goal of peace, will be starkly revealed. At 10 o'clock in the morning, the common attempt to surmount what man has never before surmounted will be under way at last.

Yet, in this fretful night, not quite all of Paris sleeps . . .

Hazel Smith had written that much a half hour earlier, and since then she had written no more. First, she had been taken away from the typewriter by young Fowler's brief visit, delivering to her both an advance edition of tomorrow morning's international edition of the New York *Herald Tribune,* and the warning from ANA's night editor that her copy had better be ready for the messenger who would call for it in an hour and a half. Second, there had been the distraction of the apartment itself.

Once having left her typewriter on the enamel kitchen table and wandered into the elaborately decorated sitting room, she had been loath to return to work. She had found the atmosphere of the sitting room seductive, the magnificent commode stamped with the mark of Jacob, the Baccarat astral lamps, the Louis XV *bergère,* the sofa upholstered in damask, and most of all the inviting *vitrines* lovingly filled with pieces of Limoges and Meissen, with Portuguese ceramics, Japanese ivories, and English snuffboxes. It had been so much more pleasant than sitting in any kitchen, where the functionalism would remind her of her dingy apartment in Moscow, with its loose floorboards, uncovered radiators, and exposed water pipes and electric wiring. Enjoying the sitting room, she had knocked wood at her luck in having become its tenant.

The two-level apartment—the bedrooms and dressing rooms were on the floor above and reached by a winding staircase—was located in the Rue de Téhéran, a half block off the Boulevard Haussmann, which was a choice location for Hazel. The apartment was owned by a successful French actress who, when considerably less successful and trying to make her way at a Moscow Film Festival, had been befriended by Hazel. The actress, leaving for Athens to make a film, and and learning that Hazel would be staying in Paris, had insisted that Hazel enjoy the comforts of the seven-room apartment and not waste money on a hotel. While she had taken her maid to Greece, the actress had left Hazel a ring of keys, a well-stocked larder, and a dozen bottles of fine champagne. Now the unaccustomed luxury of her surroundings interfered with Hazel's work.

After Fowler's departure, determined to enjoy the sitting room a few minutes more, Hazel had sat down on a fragile divan and opened the next morning's *Herald Tribune* to see how her story was placed, and to count the typographical errors. When she came upon her story, she realized it was the one she had pounded out after leaving that poor Medora Hart, and then she remembered that she had promised to call Medora about where that bastard, Sir Austin Ormsby, could be reached.

Rightly, Hazel knew that she should finish what was in her typewriter before getting on the telephone. But then, Medora would be waiting by the telephone, and Hazel had a vivid memory of what *that* was like.

She had called Medora and told her to be sure to see the next day's *Herald Tribune*. But since Medora could not wait, Hazel had read her the interview over the phone. The interview—no mention of the Jameson case, no mention of the beastly Ormsbys—had recounted the exciting life of an English girl abroad, her adventures and triumphs, culminating in her star appearance at the Club Lautrec. Medora had been embarrassingly grateful.

"Do you think," Medora had asked, "that Sir Austin will see it?"

"You bet your life he'll see it, honey. Not only will he see it, but his wife will, and so will Sydney. Did you know Sydney's in town?"

"I couldn't care less, Hazel. I'm only interested in Sir Austin's knowing where I am."

"Well, he *knows*. Now, step two—"

Step two had been to ferret out Sir Austin's whereabouts. It had not been easy, but Hazel's British sources were of the best. With pleasure she had been able to tell Medora that since the Prime Minister and his staff were occupying the British Ambassador's residence, his Ministers had been located in the Paris hostel most favored by the English. This was, Hazel had explained, the smart Hotel Bristol in the Rue du Faubourg-St.-Honoré, near the Place Beauvau. Sir Austin and his wife Fleur, as well as their own servants, shared a double suite on the third floor. Then, wishing Medora the best of luck, and asking her to phone tomorrow and report how she made out, Hazel Smith had hung up.

Now, rising from the divan, determined to force herself to finish her story before the deadline, Hazel knew that she had no intention of going back to the kitchen immediately, and she knew the reason. What was blocking her from her work—unusual in itself, for she was an uncomplicated and fast reporter—was not the interruption of young Fowler, nor the *Herald Tribune,* nor the comfort of the borrowed living room, nor the need to speak to Medora Hart. The major distraction was not one of these, or all of these, but the hateful fact that Jay Thomas Doyle had lodged in her mind and she was unable to kick him out.

Her present dreary situation had been glaringly irradiated by her accidental encounter with that accursed bastard, Doyle, and by a reminder of what might have been and what was. She had not been writing well tonight, any amateur psychologist could tell her, because she had not wished to finish what she was writing. If she finished too soon and gave her story over to be filed, she would be left with nothing to do. She would be left in these beautiful rooms to scrounge up a supper for herself, to eat the meal alone, to wash the dishes alone, to read the newspapers or watch television alone, to sleep alone—*in Paris, festive Paris,* with life teeming in the streets and bistros, and herself alone, without normal male companionship, condemned to perpetual intellectual onanism.

Of course, she did not have to be alone tonight. On some pretext, as always, she might have telephoned her friend (even after all these years it unnerved her to conjure up his name) and possibly he might have dropped by for a while, a little while, but her demand would have been unfair, especially at this time. Jay Doyle had invited her to dinner, and that would have been another way out—but a worse alternative than the first, kowtowing to the bastard who had put her in this horrible situation, submitting to him because of her need. The loss of self-respect would not be worth it. And so here she was, an embittered thirty-four-year-old spinster, if not quite a virgin, all dressed up with love and no one around to take it.

The return of Doyle into her otherwise orderly existence was upsetting. Several years before, after obsessively reliving their old life together, she had made up her mind that he could have no more reality for her than her dead grandfather. Yet persistently, in those lapses of time when she was unable to see her friend, Doyle would reappear in her memories and imaginings to disconcert her. And now he was here and she was here, and it was disturbing.

He'd had his chance once, the bastard, and treated her swinishly. The shameless effrontery of the fiend, at the café, pretending to forget all he had done to her, begging to take up with her again, as if nothing had happened between them a dozen years ago. And even worse, in the last years, harassing her with letters and long-distance calls simply so that he might use her for that idiotic book of his. Now again, this afternoon, pestering her. How dare he, the pitiful slob!

She thought of their encounter at the café this afternoon, and how he had looked. He looked awful! He looked like—like Falstaff—like a gross, self-indulgent, misshapen and repulsive cretin child. What had she ever seen in him?

And then, nervously pacing the sitting room, she gradually began to recall the good times, the year and a half, the two years, in New York, in his Park Avenue apartment, his attractiveness, his cleverness, their fun, their passion. It had been perfect, that first part of it, and there had never been anything like it since, with anyone, the feeling of belonging, the feeling of possessive pride in another. What had that Frenchman once written? La Bruyère, yes, she had underlined it. "You are only really in love once in your life, and that is the first time."

But maybe, Hazel reflected, she was romanticizing the past, because it was so long ago and because it was all she'd ever had that was entirely her own. Maybe his behavior before Vienna, and in Vienna, could be understood in the light of his eventual fall from popularity. Under pressure, trying to grasp everything from life while he was still exalted, he had sacrificed her in order to squeeze something more out of a precarious and receding success, but he had already been on the verge of a nervous breakdown or some kind of decline. The years since corroborated that view of him. He had slipped. She had heard the gossip in newspaper circles. He was down.

Suddenly she did not hate him. How could you hate a person who deserved your sorrow and pity? Doyle had always needed someone like her, someone solid, someone who cared. With her beside him to steady him, he would not have fallen, the poor self-destructive child. He was proof that everyone on earth needed someone, some close human relationship that would serve as insurance against growing old alone. Nor was she, herself, any different from anyone else. She needed someone. She had her friend, of course, and that was a little, but it was not enough for what she had to give. Doyle had once been enough, if only he had appreciated it. Perhaps he knew it now, at last, after all the harsh years. Perhaps he had been tempered into manhood by those mean years. Perhaps. Because if he had, if he had . . .

She ceased her pacing and considered the telephone, and suddenly, her heart told her, to hell with it, to hell with pride.

She dialed the Hotel George-V. She told the operator that she wanted to speak to Mr. Jay Thomas Doyle. She waited in suspense through all the ringing of his room, but there was no answer. Still waiting (maybe he was in the shower), she thought: The damn fool is out eating himself to death somewhere, but maybe he wouldn't be if he had someone to talk to, if he wasn't lonely.

When the operator confirmed that Mr. Doyle was not in his room, Hazel said that she would like to leave a message. "Tell Mr. Doyle that Miss Hazel Smith called. Tell him I'll have dinner with him—do you have that?—I will have dinner with him tomorrow night. Tell him to pick me up at 27C Rue de Téhéran at eight o'clock in the evening. Eight o'clock sharp . . . got it? Thank you."

It was done. While she felt better for having done it, she did not feel exactly happy. Yet somehow, she did feel less alone, and free to resume work on her story.

She returned to the kitchen table, stood bending over the portable typewriter, rereading the last line that she had written: "Yet, in this fretful night, not quite all of Paris sleeps."

Quickly she sat down and resumed typing:

The five great world leaders, those of the United States, Great Britain, France, Russia, China—they sleep. The members of their teams—they also sleep. But elsewhere, in hidden recesses of the French capital, hundreds of lesser-known persons, the Sherpas of the Summit—they are the ones who remain wide awake. These are the persons who, without fanfare, and often in secrecy, are engaged in tasks that will make tomorrow's crucial and arduous climb to the Summit possible.

Among these little-known persons who are sleepless tonight, who will be burning midnight oil until the gray hours of dawn, none is more important, yet more unobtrusive, than Maurice Quarolli, a Divisional Superintendent of a security branch of the Prefecture of Police which is known as Direction de la Sécurité du Président de la République et des Hautes Personnalités. On the shoulders of Quarolli and the crack force of 150 agents falls the responsibility of protecting visiting heads of state as well as their ministers and other eminent officials staying in Paris.

Superintendent Quarolli's branch of the Prefecture of Police is rarely heard, seldom seen. Late this afternoon, by a stroke of good fortune, I was granted a one-hour interview with Maurice Quarolli. At the designated time, I appeared at an unnamed, unmarked, rather ordinary administrative building in the Quai de Gesvres . . .

Hazel Smith ceased typing, picked up the note pad lying open beside her typewriter, and slowly began riffling through the scribbled pages to refresh her memory about what had occurred during the remarkable interview and what she was permitted to report of it.

Soon lost in deciphering her cryptic notes, she sat back to summon up what had been an unexpected audience and a truly amazing hour.

Being granted the interview had been sheer luck. Her contacts with certain officials in the Élysée palace had lent weight to her application. To her surprise, Quarolli had agreed to see her, with the understanding that their talk would be largely off the record. High-placed friends had told her that purely by an accident of politics, her application had been perfectly timed. The French Government, under constant criticism for its refusal to align itself outright with the United States, Great Britain, and Russia in the disarmament conference with China, for refusing to do more than walk the fence and play host, had been stung by the poor press it was receiving throughout much of the world. Now eager to win the favor of the press, to propagandize its active role in the forthcoming Summit talks, the command in the Élysée palace had sent down the order: Be cooperative with influential journalists, within the bounds of security. Obviously, Superintendent Quarolli had been apprised of the order. With reluctance, he had complied with it.

Hazel Smith replayed the interview from the beginning. In the beginning, she had breathlessly followed a uniformed *agent de police* up the staircase. Then, with him, she entered an elevator, in which the push-button panel was masked by a small cloth drape. The policeman's hand snaked beneath the cloth, and the elevator rose swiftly, releasing them on an unnumbered upper floor. The corridor through which they hurried was ostentatiously drab.

In a starkly furnished reception room she was turned over to an unsmiling plainclothesman, who in turn escorted her into a spacious office of restrained elegance. There she was left sitting in an oval-backed black leather armchair before a six-foot-long veneered desk, which held a rectangular gray blotter, a blank sheet of paper, a pencil, three telephones, and a miniature television set.

From a side door, a Frenchman entered quietly. He was slightly less than five feet nine. His thick hair, black and gray and wavy, was combed back in a high pompadour. His blunt face, with elongated nose and jaw, was tan, masculine, preoccupied. His thickset frame, which seemed vulcanized, filled his double-breasted conservative suit. He wore a red ribbon in his buttonhole. This was Maurice Quarolli.

There were no social ceremonies, no amenities. His demeanor was that of a public servant who had more pressing things to do; yet, once seated behind his desk, he was eager to please. Without waiting for Hazel's questions, he began to speak, his voice low and authoritative. She must not quote him directly, he said, unless she received permission for each quotation she wished to use. She could summarize their conversation, no more.

The French police system, stemming out of the Prefecture of Police and the Prefect's Cabinet, was too complex a network to be explained in a short time, he said. Their interview would be confined to those services which were in charge of safeguarding participants in the Summit.

When foreign leaders and delegates arrived in France, but were still technically outside Paris—such as at Orly Airport, or the new Paris-Nord Airport, or when they traveled outside the city limits of Paris to

Chantilly or Versailles—their protection devolved mainly upon the agents of the Compagnie Républicaine de Sécurité, known as the CRS, and the ordinary police (incorrectly known as gendarmes, colloquially known as *flics,* properly known as *agents de police*), and the armed Garde Républicaine de Paris, he said. Also, whenever foreign leaders or delegates traveled outside Paris, a considerable burden of responsibility for their safety fell upon the plainclothesmen of the Service des Voyages Officiels and the detectives of the Sûreté Nationale.

As Hazel concentrated on her note-taking, Quarolli went on without pause. Once the foreign President, Prime Minister, Chairman, Premier, their Ministers, and their key advisers, were inside Paris, the responsibility for protection widened to include other branches of the French judiciary. His own highly trained agents of the Direction de la Sécurité —"How many? I suggest you name your own figure, Miss Smith. Let us say 150, yes?"—were the ones principally accountable for guarding Summit personnel. But many, many other branches collaborated with them. There were the agents of the Service de Documentation et de Contre-Espionnage, known as SDEC ("Like your CIA, Miss Smith"); there were the agents of the Direction de la Surveillance du Territoire, known as DST; there were the agents of seven specialist squads and six investigating units under the senior Commissaire de Police; there were the agents of Renseignements généraux et jeux, who were intelligence officers and who investigated, as did Quarolli's own department, all aliens visiting or resident in Paris.

Impatient with generalities, Hazel sought specific answers to specific questions. Cagily, Quarolli deflected some questions, replied to others. He explained that at any official meeting involving Summit guests, or even at an official reception, there might be a dozen members of the Garde Républicaine placed before all entrances, and twenty or more plainclothes agents of various French security branches scattered inside the buildings. Each foreign embassy would be surrounded by French agents. Every hotel in Paris which lodged foreign delegates would have two to six agents circulating inside and a number of agents stationed on the roof. When delegates rode from their embassies or hotels to the Palais Rose, or elsewhere, a *motard*—a motorcycle escort —would make an effort to precede or follow them.

"What do you mean—'make an effort' to follow them?" asked Hazel Smith.

Superintendent Quarolli offered the smallest shrug. "We *try* to attend our distinguished guests, for their own safety. Many do not wish to be followed. Many do not wish us to know their destinations. Perhaps they are off to a secret diplomatic meeting. Perhaps they have a private rendezvous. As a consequence, dangerous as it is, they escape our many eyes, and are gone. But only briefly, I promise you." He sat back, and a glimmer of self-satisfaction shone in his eyes. "Not much escapes our security, Madame Smith, this you must believe. We know of *every* foreigner in Paris at this time. We know about all of them. We know what they look like. We know where they stay. We know where they go. We know whom they see. We are in the business of *knowing,* knowing and watching *every* visitor, night and day, to guarantee security for those who may possibly guarantee us peace on earth. We are not infallible, by any means. But we try to be infallible, you see, and we are close to it, very close. . . . Any more questions, Madame Smith?"

His self-complacency, his claims to near perfection for his section, had nettled Hazel. Since the interview was almost ended, she decided that she could risk challenging him.

"Monsieur Quarolli. When you say you know about *every*—you emphasized *every*—foreigner in Paris right now, or almost every one, I assume that you mean visitors other than the heads of state and their families, and the many delegates?"

"Yes, Madame, that is precisely what I mean."

"Well, now, I don't want to be skeptical or anything like that—I have great admiration for French police efficiency and ingenuity—but I don't see how what you claim is really possible."

He sat forward, superciliously amused. "No?"

"I'm convinced, absolutely convinced, that your famous intelligence and police services know everything necessary to know about the delegates from the five powers, and that you are really doing a remarkable job in providing security for those directly involved in the Summit. But when you speak of knowing at least something about *every* foreign visitor—well, I'll be perfectly honest with you, monsieur —I am a doubter and unbeliever. How can you possibly know about *every* visitor? You don't have the necessary personnel, the number of agents—"

Quarolli stared at Hazel with less amusement. "We have thousands of security agents right here in Paris."

"But there are many more thousands of visitors, from ordinary American and European tourists to journalists to entertainers to business people to fashion editors. My God, how could you conceivably—?"

"Madame Smith," Quarolli said with asperity, "I have spoken of our official agents. But there are many others, the unofficial ones. I cannot go into details now, for obvious reasons. Let me simply say that every apartment concierge, hotel clerk or waiter or chambermaid, garage attendant, bartender, Place Pigalle streetwalker, shopgirl, taxi driver, could be a valuable source of information. Do you understand? Now, perhaps you are less skeptical?"

Hazel, like a tigress out to protect her offspring, in this case her story, waved her pad airily. "I understand more, yes I do, but I'm afraid I still have my doubts. At the risk of annoying you, I can't see how your informers can supply you with facts about everyone, about every inconsequential person, nondelegates, nonentities, pouring in. When I just think of the people, the variety of visitors, who have no connection with the Summit, whom I run into in a single day, I can't imagine that you even know of their existence. I mean, especially the unimportant ones."

She had got to him at last, she could see. Superintendent Maurice Quarolli's features, beneath his tan, had taken on the hues of the tricolor. "Forgive me, but I see that you are quite the intractable and stubborn young lady, Madame Smith. Perhaps I can only convince you with a demonstration."

"Demonstration?"

"We once had a great detective in France. I refer to Alphonse Bertillon, Director of the Sûreté's Identity Department. There were many journalists who were skeptical of his methods of keeping records of criminals through photographs and measurements. When these critics could not be convinced by other means, Bertillon would convert them by demonstration. There was a journalist here in Paris named Sarcey, who frequently ridiculed Bertillon's methods, insisting that no criminal could be photographed in a natural way if he did not wish to be. Bertillon invited this skeptic, Sarcey, to the Sûreté headquarters, and guided the heretic through the laboratories to show how painstaking and foolproof were his methods. At the end of the tour Sarcey remained unconvinced, until Bertillon handed him an envelope containing ten true and candid photographs of Sarcey, taken automatically minutes before, by hidden cameras that snapped pictures of the journalist whenever he passed through a doorway. These pictures converted Sarcey. They were worth a thousand words. Perhaps I would be wise to emulate my predecessor."

Hazel, who had been noting the anecdote with delight, looked up. "What do you mean?"

"I mean to offer a similar demonstration to a doubter, madame. We have discussed security surrounding the Summit, yes? I have stated that we not only keep eyes on the official delegates, as best we can, but on every foreign visitor to Paris in this critical time, yes? You have severely questioned whether that is possible."

"I did more than question, monsieur. I was flatly dubious."

"Très bien, madame, nous allons voir si nous sommes en mesure de dissiper vos doutes," said Quarolli, flattening his palms on the desk top. "You spoke of the variety of people you meet in a single day. You said that you cannot imagine that we in the Direction de la Sécurité would know of their existence, of the existence of these casual tourists who have no connection with the Summit. Is that what you said?"

"Yes."

"Very well, madame. Who are the foreigners you have met in Paris today, this very day, the ones not connected with the Summit?"

This was a surprise, and Hazel was momentarily flustered. "Well, I don't know—do you mean *everyone* I met today?"

"Anyone you can recollect meeting, or wish to mention, that you had a confrontation with today. Visitors. Foreigners who have nothing to do with the Summit." He took up his pencil, and his challenging eyes fixed upon her, as he waited.

"Well—" She tried to remember, going back to this morning, moving herself through the long day, then remembering. "You might possibly recognize one or two, but for the rest, it's ridiculous, they're simply too—"

"Proceed, madame," said Superintendent Quarolli sternly.

She rapidly screened the names, fearful of committing any indiscretion, but finally she felt reassured that they would be, with one exception, maybe two, absolute strangers to this overbearing police director. "Okay," she said. She had determined to play the game. She would give him the names, no rank, no serial number, nothing but the cold names. "Okay. You're going to write them down?"

"If you please."

She recited slowly, allowing time for Quarolli to jot down each name. "Emmett A. Earnshaw . . . Matthew Brennan . . . Medora Hart . . . Jay Thomas Doyle." She paused. "Well, there are more, but—"

"As many as you wish."

"No, that's enough. Now, what are you going to do?"

"Demonstrate," he said. He reached behind the telephone and punched a buzzer.

Almost immediately a side door opened and a pallid-faced young Frenchman in a plaid suit materialized and came quickly, silently, across the carpeted room to the desk. Quarolli handed him the sheet of paper. *"Cherchez-moi les dossiers de ces gens-là, André. Et dépêchez-vous."*

The civil servant named André gave a short knowing nod and hastened out of the room. Quarolli offered Hazel his first full smile of the interview, then fished inside his coat, extracted a sterling cigarette case, and snapped it open.

"Nous allons nous ditendre un moment. Have a Royale, French, filtered," he said pleasantly. "And I shall, too." She accepted the cigarette and the light, unaccountably nervous, and he lit his own cigarette and said, "It will be no more than three minutes."

She pretended to review and amend her scrawled notes, and she smoked steadily. She waited with growing suspense, feeling that he had overreached and that she would embarrass him, yet not fully certain of it, not positive.

They smoked in silence, and in less than three minutes the side door swung open, and the civil servant named André strode briskly into the office carrying four manila folders. These he handed to Quarolli, who elaborately thanked and dismissed him.

Grinding out his cigarette, Quarolli said with mock innocence, *"Maintenant, madame, nous allons voir ce que nous avons ici*—let us see what we have here."

Quarolli drew the top folder from the stack, placed it neatly before him, and opened it.

"The first dossier. The first name you spoke of. *Voilà,* Mr. Emmett A. Earnshaw." He held up a sheet of blue paper and scanned it. Then he read aloud, "Earnshaw, age 66. Arrived 11:01 morning 15 June Gare du Nord. Accompanied by niece Carol, age 19. Met by American Embassy officer Callahan (See dossier Callahan, R. L.). Suite number 712 Hotel Lancaster. Visited Palais Rose, held impromptu press conference. Brief meeting, exchange with Matthew Brennan, once disarmament specialist and negotiator in Earnshaw's Administration. Lunched 2:30 Quai d'Orsay. Two-hour sight-seeing tour. Returned Lancaster at hour 16:30. Received visitor Willi von Goerlitz, age 26, son of Dr. Dietrich von Goerlitz, German industrialist, Frankfurt, suite at Hotel Ritz. Goerlitz with Earnshaw 37 minutes. Goerlitz and Carol Earnshaw left to shop on Champs-Élysées. 5:15 Earnshaw received Jay Thomas Doyle, former American journalist."

Quarolli looked up and returned the blue sheet to the folder. "There is more, of course, but it would be indiscreet to read it aloud."

Hazel nodded. "Very impressive, *very.* But, of course, Earnshaw is well-known."

Quarolli sniffed. "Everyone is well-known, madame, to *someone.* However, whom would you consider less well-known?"

"Right now? Well, take that journalist, Doyle."

"A pleasure." Quarolli pulled out a second manila folder, opened it, lifted out another blue sheet, and read aloud. "Jay Thomas Doyle, age

306

45. United States citizen. Arrived Paris, Orly, via Austrian Airlines 10:44 morning 15 June. Checked into Suite 323 Hotel George-V. Attended barber, manicurist in hotel. Visited editorial offices of Atlas News Association afternoon. Met E. A. Earnshaw in Rue de Berri, talked approximately ten minutes. Walked to Café Français. Met American correspondent from Moscow, Hazel Smith, and her companion, Medora Hart, English entertainer Club Lautrec (See Ormsby, Sir Austin, Ormsby, Sydney dossiers). Brief altercation. Shortly after, Doyle—"

Hazel had felt the chill creep up her arms as she listened, and she held up a hand to interrupt the superintendent. He paused in his reading, and waited.

"I surrender," said Hazel weakly. "I'm convinced."

Quarolli grimaced. "Come now, surcly you wish to hear of your other acquaintances, too?"

"Don't rub it in. I said I'm convinced. You are all-knowing, you are all-seeing, you are frightening, and the Summit is safe."

Quarolli smiled. *"Merci, madame."*

"Just one last thing. Tell me that and I'll go. Why *everyone?* Why do you go to the trouble? Why bother about so many inconsequential, ineffectual people? Most of them are harmless, and many of them are simpletons and fools, weaklings and fools and nothing more."

Quarolli was nice now, and he was thoughtful. He considered what Hazel had said, and after thirty seconds he stood up and roamed about the office. "Madame, I grew up in the small port of Paimpol in Brittany, and we lived as a closely knit Catholic family in my grandfather's house. My grandfather was never without his Holy Bible, and every night he would read to us from it. Why do I bother about simpletons and fools? Because I remember one line he read us from his Bible. The line was 'Every fool will be meddling.'" Quarolli smiled again. "The days ahead are too crucial for even minor distractions."

"May I quote you?"

"You may quote me, madame."

Now, hours later, in the kitchen of the apartment in the Rue de Téhéran, Hazel Smith had finished reliving the interview recorded in her note pad. Placing it beside her typewriter, she touched her fingers to the keys, then rapidly resumed writing down what she had learned in her interview with the officer of the Direction de la Sécurité. In a page and a half she summarized the workings and methods of the French security agents. She wrote of their thoroughness in investigating *every-one*—"adequately demonstrated to me by M. Quarolli"—but she did not write the details of the actual chilling demonstration.

She used no direct quotations until her very last paragraph, and then she wrote:

So the masters of the Summit sleep easier tonight, and Paris sleeps easier, and the world may, too, aware that little-known men like Maurice Quarolli guard them, and by guarding them, protect the world's last hope for peace. If Quarolli has his way, no outsider will interfere with the progress to the Summit. For, to men like Quarolli, no visitor to Paris tonight is too small, too unimportant, in fact, too stupid, to be overlooked.

As M. Quarolli said when bidding me farewell, "Why does our security even bother about simpletons and fools? Because of a line I remember my grandfather reading me from the Holy Bible. That line was 'Every fool will be meddling.' The days ahead are too crucial for even minor distractions."

She typed "-30-" at the bottom of her story, yanked the last page from her typewriter, and with a glance at the kitchen clock, she hastily began proofreading it.

Suddenly, the nagging thing that had chilled her from the first struck her with forceful impact, and she sat back and closed her eyes tightly. For suddenly it had occurred to her, the full realization of it occurred to her, that "they" must have a complete dossier on *her,* too, and if they did, she wondered if they knew the *truth,* and then she was horrified and finally she was afraid.

III

"*A rrêtez ici, monsieur,*" Matt Brennan commanded the taxi driver. "*Je veux descendre.*"

The driver, whose rattling old Citroën had been inching up the Avenue Malakoff in the heavy traffic, stamped hard on the brake. The taxi shuddered and stalled.

Peering over the driver's shoulder through the windshield, Brennan could see that it was no use going farther in the taxi. He had wanted to reach the Summit headquarters as early as possible, hoping to be at the entrance or in the courtyard by nine-thirty, when Nikolai Rostov passed through, coming or going. But the traffic had conspired against him. First, the Avenue Foch had been made inaccessible to public vehicles by wooden barricades and a cordon of police. Next, trying the Avenue Malakoff approach to the Palais Rose, his taxi had gone no more than a half block before it had been caught up in a tumultuous clog of cars. Now, ahead, there were more barricades, and policemen detouring traffic away from the Palais Rose into a side street. And the time was not nine-thirty but nine-fifty. He would, he decided, make better progress on foot.

In defiance of the law, angry horns were honking in unison from the rear. Quickly Brennan paid the driver and hurried to the sidewalk. Immediately he found himself in a maelstrom of bustling pedestrians, jostling, pushing, as they tried to reach the Palais Rose for the last of the opening day ceremonies.

Briefly he made forward progress, but there was an interminable wait at the corner of the Avenue Alphand, into which the traffic was being diverted. Finally, risking his neck to dodge across the intersection, Brennan suddenly was brought to a standstill, trapped tightly in a heaving mass of bodies, as thick and squirming as hundreds of worms in a container. While some of the mob broke off to join the rows of spectators at the curb, who were craning for a sight of the motorcades that would bring the last of the world leaders to the Summit site, the rest of the spectators continued to alternate between maddening immobility and creeping movement toward the Palais Rose.

At last, Brennan abandoned his efforts at accelerating his progress. He submitted to control by the mob. When it moved, he moved. When it stopped, he stopped. An old and familiar fatalistic attitude, shaded by pessimism, suffused him and calmed his frustration.

This was simply not his day, he decided.

Hours earlier he had hoped for more. A Monday morning always held promise. He had begun the morning early, full of purpose and confidence. Awakening at daybreak, he had slipped out of Lisa's bed without disturbing her, since they had been up so late the night before discussing their dreams of the future and then making love. After fastening the lock on his door, to preserve their masquerade of virtue before the chambermaids, he had dressed hurriedly and gone down to the hotel breakfast room. A cup of acrid French coffee had dispelled his drowsiness, and at last, fully aroused, he had hurried into the telephone operator's alcove behind the concierge's desk.

"Please get me the Hotel Palais d'Orsay," he had told the operator.

Inside the booth across from the switchboard, he had soon begun to feel like Kafka's hero, K, in *The Castle*. Like K with his elusive Count West-west, Brennan soon realized that he was confronted with the task of seeking an equally elusive Nikolai Rostov. The annoying operator at the Hotel Palais d'Orsay had flatly stated that there was no Rostov listed. When Brennan had insisted that she was mistaken, she had angrily transferred him to the reception desk.

The reception clerk had listened, then said, "A Mr. Rostov here, you say? . . . May I inquire who is speaking, sir?" After an instant's hesitation, Brennan had told him. The clerk had said, "A moment, please. Let me see our registration cards." There had been a silence, and then the clerk's voice alert and firm. "Sorry to keep you, Mr. Brennan. I have checked our guest list. We have no Nikolai Rostov registered on the premises. I am sorry." Before Brennan had been able to retort, the receiver at the other end had banged in his ear.

After that incident, Brennan had wondered briefly whether Neely's information had been wrong or if Rostov had moved to another hotel. At the same time, Brennan's knowledge of Russian diplomats, their instinctive adherence to seclusion, convinced him that not only Rostov, but the other Soviet delegates as well, had been ordered to keep their places of residence and their movements concealed. The hotel had probably been instructed not to acknowledge the presence of any Russian delegates, except to a restricted list of callers. Brennan had not been sure of this, but had realized that there was only one thing left to do—to verify it for himself.

He had gone hastily into the Rue de Berri and caught a taxi to the Left Bank. The traffic, extraordinary for this hour, had delayed him, and it was not until twenty minutes after eight that Brennan arrived in front of the iron awning and yellow entrance doors of the Hotel Palais d'Orsay on the Quai Anatole-France.

Entering the lobby cautiously, hoping to be as inconspicuous as possible, Brennan had been surprised by the lack of activity inside. Except for a bellboy on the run, the lobby had appeared empty. To his left, Brennan had become aware of a rheumy-eyed, bloated old man behind the concierge's desk, slowly sorting the mail.

Brennan had confronted the old man and had quietly inquired for Nikolai Rostov. The old man had examined the guest file and shaken his head. "No Rostov here." Brennan had winked understandingly and shoved a crisp 100-franc note across the counter. The bribe had inspired nothing but fright in the old man. In a furry undertone he had explained that the head concierge was ill, that he himself was merely a humble *portier* filling in until the concierge's replacement, a new concierge just arrived from Biarritz, came on duty at nine o'clock. But even the new concierge might be of little help, the *portier* had explained, for he was not part of the hotel's regular staff, only a substitute for these few busy weeks, after which he would go back to Biarritz.

"But he comes on at nine o'clock?" Brennan had asked. "You're sure of that?"

"Yes, yes—"

"I'll wait," Brennan had said, pocketing the 100-franc note.

To consume time, and work off his nervous energy, he had gone outside, ambled past the long-abandoned railroad station, purchased a London newspaper at a kiosk, visited the modern bar of a café called Le Rapide, and finally he had returned to Rostov's hotel.

The lobby had come to life and was teeming with guests and bellboys. The bloated old *portier* had still been alone behind the concierge's desk. Brennan had made his way to the far end of the lobby, settled in an imitation-leather chair beside a stone column, and pretended to read his newspaper. Once, he had noticed that two bulky men in brown suits, the first with a chalky face, the other with a pitted face, had ceased their circling of the lobby to cast sidelong glances at him, and then, conversing in undertones, they had climbed the central staircase. Worriedly Brennan had watched them, pondered upon their

311

identity—hotel detectives, or French DST, or Russian KGB? He had speculated on the possibility that the old *portier* had informed them of a stranger's interest in Rostov, of his attempted bribe, and that they had looked him over for this reason and were now reporting his presence to someone upstairs.

Nine o'clock had come and gone, and the *portier* continued to work alone behind the desk. Nine-fifteen, and still there had been no change. By nine twenty-five Brennan had become extremely uneasy and apprehensive. Suddenly he had realized that there were two behind the desk. The second one, to whom the *portier* was whispering, was a shriveled Frenchman with wisps of mouse-colored hair and abnormally thick-lensed spectacles, busily fastening the brass buttons of his long concierge's jacket.

At once Brennan had crossed the lobby to face the new concierge.

"Good morning, monsieur," the concierge had said gently, showing his gold teeth. "I am advised that you have been waiting for me. You think I can be of assistance to you?"

"I hope you can," said Brennan.

"You have made inquiries with the regular hotel personnel at the reception?"

"No."

"Ummm. Well, you see, I am not part of their permanent staff, so I am not burdened by the same obligations—you understand?"

"I understand."

The concierge's gold teeth had flashed. "Good. This—this guest you have inquired about—I am not certain if one with such a name is here—it does not come easily to the mind."

"Perhaps you will remember it in due time," Brennan had said. His hand had gone across the counter. "In any event, I wish to thank you." They had shaken hands, and now the 100-franc note was no longer in Brennan's palm.

The concierge's hand had dropped to his pocket, and after a moment returned to massage his brow. His gray eyes, distorted by the convex lenses of his glasses, had considered Brennan with an affection that heretofore they had not possessed. "Now that I have thought about it longer, I do remember. How remarkable. Yes, we do have a Nikolai Rostov registered in this hotel. But because of security, we must be discreet about visitors. Otherwise, anyone might go to"—his voice dropped—"to Rooms 214 and 215."

Brennan had restrained a smile. "Thank you. I wonder if he is in right now?"

"Excuse me. I must use the telephone in the bar."

He had left his desk, and Brennan had made a pretense of reading his newspaper once more. By the time that he had turned to page eight and the cricket scores, the concierge had returned. After casting a glance at the reception desk, he had taken up a pencil and a directory of Paris entertainment, and leaned over the counter confidentially. "I have had a ten-franc conversation with the floor valet. Mrs. Rostov is still in the suite, dressing. Mr. Rostov has departed. He was seen to leave the hotel before eight o'clock, and heard to remark to his wife that he was on his way to the Soviet Embassy, but that he expected to be at the Palais Rose by ten." The enlarged pupils behind the thick lenses had appeared to expand. "Perhaps what I relay is useful. I can say no more. Good morning, monsieur, and the best of luck."

Leaving the Hotel Palais d'Orsay, Brennan had realized that although he had missed Rostov, a disappointment, the early visit had not been a complete loss. At least he had learned where Rostov would be at ten o'clock. Brennan's next step had been clear to him.

He had hastened to the Rue de Lille, gone into the café Le Rapide, and put through a call to Herb Neely at the United States Embassy. To Brennan's intense relief, Neely had still been in his office. Quickly Brennan had summarized his morning, his plan, and his problem.

"No problem," Neely had assured him. "We have a number of extra press passes prepared for correspondents from nonexistent newspapers or syndicates. We give them to the CIA, FBI, and several Embassy people we like to have in the Palais Rose. Ingenious, eh, old man? Okay, here's what. I'll have one of these phony press passes dropped off at your hotel. Your name will be on it, also your fictional affiliation, and it'll be signed by me and countersigned by the Ambassador. All you have to do is paste one of your passport pictures in it. Then, just flash it at the gate and march inside like you belong. If you want to intercept Rostov in the courtyard, well, hang around with the photographers. If you can't grab him there, go up to the press section, have something at the snack bar and read my releases. When the Russians announce their press briefing, after the first session breaks, why, you attend it. I reckon you're most likely to run into Rostov there. And, Matt, listen, if you run into anyone who recognizes you, like that Hazel Smith bitch, except she's not covering the Palais Rose itself, well, play it cool. You have your credentials. You're accredited. You're a writer. Sue me. Savvy? Okay now—sic 'em."

Those had been the earlier events of the frustrating morning, Brennan now recalled, as French bodies bumped his body and French elbows jammed his ribs, and he allowed himself to be carried along with the pushing crowd down the Avenue Malakoff. Still, he was not disheartened. The ornate press pass, bearing his likeness, was secure in his inner coat pocket.

Unexpectedly, like a giant breaker smashing against a granite wall and being rolled back, the surging crowd had been stopped by a solid *revêtement* of French police, and then fallen back. As Brennan struggled to keep his balance, he saw police officers opening a path through the mass of sightseers, shoving some against the black iron fence and others across the thoroughfare.

Momentarily freed, Brennan yanked the press pass from inside his coat and stepped up to a policeman, waving it. The policeman glanced at it and gestured down the open path. Brennan went swiftly, holding his pass before him like a white flag of truce, until he reached the iron gates of the Palais Rose. A French *commissaire* snatched up the pass, examined it carefully, and pointed him into the courtyard filled with photographers, security agents, government officials, and chauffeurs standing beside their variety of limousines.

Hearing the sounds of motorcycles growing louder, and scattered cheers from the spectators lined up outside the gates, Brennan joined the group of photographers racing for positions on the stone steps before the Palais Rose entrance doors. The motorcycles were deafening, and all at once an escort of helmeted French mobile police burst through the opened gates, some leading and some following a custom-built Red Flag sedan, with curtains drawn across the rear windows, and the banner of the People's Republic of China fluttering from a front fender. Until now, Brennan had not seen China's first luxury automobile, except for photographs of it in periodicals, where he had read it was manufactured near Peking, at a cost of 30,000 yuan or $12,000, and was equipped with three forward speeds and a speedometer that recorded 100 miles per hour.

The motorcycles idled noisily. The doors of the Red Flag opened like wings, and a half-dozen Chinese stepped out into the courtyard. All of them wore immaculate gray uniforms, and all were of indeterminate years except one, the eldest, whom Brennan recognized immediately as Chairman Kuo Shu-tung.

The head of the Chinese Communist Party and Politburo resembled a patriarchal Tao philosopher more than the leader of a progressive, rapidly industrializing nuclear-armed nation. Kuo Shu-tung traversed the yards of carpeting with surprising energy for one of his years and consumptive appearance. He alone of the delegation appeared to be enjoying himself. As he marched into the semicircle of raised cameras, their shutters clicking steadily, Kuo Shu-tung's lively, darting eyes, which seemed fastened to a face possessing the texture of brown rice paper, were alert and amused. Once, perhaps for the cameras, he dropped a gnarled hand from his goatee and patted the three medals on

314

his otherwise unadorned uniform, then apparently made a joke over his shoulder, for his taller, younger aides reacted promptly with a restrained tittering in unison.

As the Chinese Chairman mounted the stairs, he was engulfed by French protocol officers and French and Chinese security agents, and the whole band disappeared inside the building. An American photographer near Brennan came out of his crouch to shout to a colleague, "That's the last of them, isn't it, Al?" Across the way, another photographer, pure Brooklyn, bellowed back, "Yeah! They're all inside now playin' catch with the N-bomb!"

The news that they were all inside dismayed Brennan. He had guessed that he was once more too late to intercept Rostov, but yet, he had hoped. Now not only Rostov, but everyone who was anyone at the Summit, was inaccessible within the Palais Rose. In minutes the leaders would be convening in the *grand salon*. For Brennan, there was nothing more to do except follow Neely's advice. Turning toward the entrance doors, his press pass in hand, he trailed several security agents into the mammoth inner hall.

Ten minutes later, after being halted three times to have his credentials examined, after ascending one of the marble staircases, Brennan followed the signs—on which all directions were given in four languages—to the palace's upstairs dining room and smoking room, which had been converted into the Summit's press quarters.

Incredibly, there were angels over the doors, but even these did not prepare Brennan for the bewildering incongruity of the pressroom's interior. The domed ceiling painted with pink clouds, the milky window, the Louis XIV consoles, and the green-and-gold Ionic columns were the only reminders of the pre-Summit Palais Rose. Everything else was jarring to the eye, for the vast room was furnished with rows of wooden tables holding typewriters and telephones, and nearby were teletype machines. Along the far wall two portable bars had been placed, one for dispensing drinks, the other for sandwiches and light snacks. Beside the bars there were two more doors, a decorative fake one and a real one topped by an arched niche from which the statuary had been removed.

Standing inside the entrance, Brennan guessed that there were at least three dozen correspondents posted in the reconverted dining room. Several were at their typewriters, several were at the bars, and the rest were scattered throughout the room in conversational groups. Most of these seemed American, English, or French, although Brennan moved aside for one party of journalists that was mostly French but included some Chinese and possibly a few Russians, who continued on through the room and out the door under the niche that led into the reconverted smoking room.

Uncomfortable as he was in this strange environment, densely occupied by members of an estate so hostile to him, Brennan determined to look as if he belonged here. Busily he made his way to a felt-draped counter heaped with mimeographed press releases and schedules, each of which was available in English, French, Russian, and Chinese. Gathering up a variety of releases written in English, pretending to be absorbed in their contents, he wove his way across the room to the liquor bar.

Ordering a Scotch-and-water, he wondered how long the first plenary session of the leaders would take, and whether the Russians would hold their press briefing afterward (as Neely had predicted), and whether Nikolai Rostov would be present. Lost in thought, he gradually became aware of a familiar American voice ordering three ham-and-cheese sandwiches.

Brennan looked up. At the adjacent snack bar an elephantine correspondent, his face not entirely visible, was leaning against the counter and pointing across it. "No, *garçon,* not three plates," he was saying. "Put all the sandwiches on one plate. They're just for me. Got to keep my figure, you know."

The full face was visible at last, and even though the cheeks were puffier, the chins more numerous, Brennan still recognized it. Instantly computing whether this had been friend or foe, he knew this had been friend. Taking his drink, he moved toward him. "Hello, Jay Doyle," he said.

Doyle separated the half-consumed sandwich from his mouth and, still chewing, came around warily. His features widened into recognition and surprise. "Matt! Of all people! What in the devil are you doing here? This is great! You don't look a day older. You look terrific."

"So do you, Jay."

"Sure, sure, I'm two for the price of one these days. My God, when was the last time? I know. Don't tell me. Zurich. The Zurich Parley. That was—what?—three, four, five years."

"Four years, Jay."

Doyle put down the remnant of his sandwich. "Shouldn't be eating anyway," he said. He nodded at Brennan. "Four years, yes. I—I guess you have good reason to remember, Matt. I—I was damn sorry about the whole mess. It was unfair."

"Forget it," said Brennan. "What have you been up to since? Same old stand?"

"Well, no—not—not exactly. I'll tell you—"

With a curious compulsiveness and candor, Doyle began to relate everything, his fall from favor in recent years, his obsession with the theory that an international conspiracy had been responsible for President Kennedy's death, his earlier relationship with Hazel Smith (which astonished Brennan completely), his unsuccessful efforts to obtain her help, and the reason for his presence in Paris.

Then, as if he were in the confessional admitting a sin, desiring forgiveness, Doyle suddenly said, "Matt, I wouldn't be bending your ear like this, except I'm trying to get to something that involves you, to get it off my chest."

"Something that involves me? I can't imagine—"

"Just hear me out another minute. By the time I got to Zurich, I was near hitting bottom. I'd lost my column. I'd latched on to some small syndicate that didn't count for much or pay much. I went to Zurich supposedly to cover the Parley. Actually, my outlets couldn't support and didn't rate that kind of coverage. But I went, I was really there, because I expected to run into Hazel. I was sure she'd be covering the Russians. But she wasn't there. Then I figured, well, maybe some of our delegation could fill in my leads or clues on the Dallas assassination, but I couldn't get anywhere with anyone. Back in Washington, President Earnshaw and Madlock had always been good to me—leads, leaks of information—when I was on top, and Earnshaw was still friendly, but Madlock knew I wasn't top-level anymore and didn't rate top-level tips. In Zurich, the guys from the State Department, some of the others, knew I wasn't important to them anymore. So they avoided me. And the ones I got to, when they heard what I was after—they treated me like a crackpot and a nuisance. You were the only one, Matt, who took me seriously and bothered to help. You introduced me to Herb Neely, a few others, and because of you they were nice to me. They treated me seriously, even though they had nothing to offer on my conspiracy angle. I simply wanted you to—to know how much I've always appreciated it."

Listening, Brennan sipped his drink and tried to remember. Professor Varney and Nikolai Rostov had absorbed so much of his time in Zurich, and still dominated his memory of that time so completely, that he found it difficult to recollect his relationship with Doyle there. "Jay, I'm sure you're greatly overvaluing anything I was able to do for you."

"I'm not," said Doyle, shaking his ponderous head. "I know what I'm saying. I—" He faltered. "I owe you an apology for how I acted afterward."

"I don't know what you mean."

Doyle sucked in his breath, and his chins quivered. "After Varney defected, and the vigilantes pulled the rug out from under you, I was furious. You needed friends, and I was a friend, believe me, but"—he shrugged, and finished lamely—"I couldn't help you." He stared down at his belly. "Matt, when Senator Dexter and the Joint Committee on Internal Security were crucifying you without an iota of evidence, all innuendo, I should've been in the press box covering it, exposing them, defending you, but I wasn't." He raised his head slowly. "I was down pretty low, and like I was saying, my last important pipelines for news, left over from the old days, were President Earnshaw and the ghost of Madlock. I sensed that any defense of you would have been construed as an attack on them. I needed them, so though I owed you so much, I chickened out. What I did was solve my dilemma by going somewhere else—Chicago, I think—covering something else when the heat was on you. I didn't cover the Congressional hearings. I suppose you might say I ran out on you in Washington—the way I ran out on Hazel before that—and, well, no week has passed since that it hasn't come into my mind and that I haven't felt guilty or ashamed." He paused. "It's too bad, because I felt I was a sort of friend and that we could have continued to be good friends. So—"

Touched by the correspondent's abject apology, Brennan said firmly, "Jay, whether you had stayed in Washington or not wouldn't have made a damn bit of difference. No one on earth could have helped me except Madlock or Varney or Rostov, and Madlock was dead, and Varney was gone and so was Rostov. You can put it out of your mind. We were friends, and we are friends still."

"I appreciate that, Matt." Relieved, Doyle grabbed one of the sandwiches and began to munch on it. "Hey, what in the devil are you doing *here?* Have you turned reporter?"

Brennan chuckled. "Never. I can't even spell my name. No, it's a subterfuge." He glanced around. Then he said in an undertone, "Neely got me in. I told you Rostov was one of the persons who could fully vindicate me. Well, he's in Paris—"

"I didn't know that. I thought he was dead."

"A lot of people thought so, dead or in Siberia. But he's here all right. I guess he was pardoned for good behavior. Premier Talansky needed experts on China, and so Rostov is in the Palais Rose right now as Assistant Minister for Far Eastern Affairs, no less. Quite a promotion. Anyway, I'm having trouble connecting with him. Neely thought that I might bump into Rostov at the Russians' first-day press briefing. I hope so. Americans can attend, can't they?"

"Absolutely. The Russians are going to stage their daily briefings in one of their offices on this floor, in what used to be the white-and-gold

318

bedroom in the left wing. There's a big U.R.S.S. sign over it." He cocked his head sideways. "Look, Matt, I'm Earnshaw's alter ego here and that packs a little weight. If there's anything I can do——?"

"Thanks, Jay, but no. If Earnshaw found out you were doing anything for me, he'd fire you. No, I'll manage."

"He wouldn't fire me, but if he did, so what? I don't need the job. Really, Matt, I mean it. I'd like to help you. Information, even. Anything."

Brennan considered the offer more seriously. "We-ll, to be truthful, I've got to find out the places where I might accidentally-on-purpose come across Rostov. For example, this press briefing. I'd like to know if Rostov will be there. Of course, that's something no one——"

Doyle snapped his fingers. "I can find out. Of course, I can. I've got a pretty good friend in the Russian press crowd. I don't know if you've heard of him. Igor Novik of *Pravda*. We've crossed paths at these conferences for years. The minute we first set eyes on each other, rapport was established. He calls me Henry VIII and I call him Balzac. Except he's really fatter than I am. Nothing so effectively dissolves the Iron Curtain as having a Chateaubriand with sauce Béarnaise in common. In fact—you've heard of the great French gourmand, Claude Goupil, haven't you?—well, he's invited both Igor and me to be honored guests at the next dinner of the Société des Gastronomes— we're always invited when we're in Paris. Igor and I were talking about it just before I saw you. He's in the other room. Let me ask him if Rostov'll be at the Russian briefing."

Brennan watched Doyle go through the door. Then he finished his drink and he began to read the press releases. Other correspondents, mostly British, were gathering at the snack bar, and Brennan sidled away, waiting near the entrance to the smoking room, trying to absorb himself in the releases but praying that Doyle would bring some favorable news.

He had finished reading the first release when Doyle loomed massively before him.

"Apparently nothing here for you today, Matt," he said, shaking his head. "According to Igor, the Russians won't have any press briefing until tomorrow. There'll only be a canned statement from Premier Talansky. But I did ask if Rostov was around. Made up I wanted some background stuff for Earnshaw. No go. None of the Russian delegates will be available for formal interviews this week. As for Rostov, he's not even here. He wound up his preliminary work and took off for the Russian Embassy. Know where that is? A couple of blocks off the Boulevard St.-Germain—79 Rue de Grenelle."

"I doubt if they'd let me in. I suppose I could try to phone Rostov there. Maybe set up an appointment."

"No harm trying." Doyle was thoughtful. "Something else occurred to me. I'm having dinner with the—the lady I told you about—Hazel Smith."

"Good luck."

Doyle returned a sickly smile. "I'll need it in spades. Anyway, it's a step. But what occurred to me is that she's been covering the Moscow beat for years. She must know most of the Russian delegates. I could explain your problem and find out if she knows where you might—"

Brennan silenced him with a gesture. "Don't bother, Jay. I'm a four-letter word to your Miss Smith."

"I don't have to mention your name."

"Forget it. You have enough to talk to her about already."

"There must be something I can do," Doyle pleaded. He seemed to think of something. "Wait. Let me see if I've got it right. What you really want to know about is places in Paris where you might run into Rostov. Is that it?"

Brennan nodded. "That would be useful. Yes."

"When I leave here, I'll be going to ANA to do some research on Premier Talansky and Chairman Kuo. While I'm at it, I'll look up the latest clips on Nikolai Rostov. There might be material about his schedule of activities. Then I'll ask some of the smart young Paris hands in the office what they know. If I come up with any good leads, I'll drop them at—the Hotel California, isn't it?"

"Across the street from your office." Brennan offered his hand and Doyle took it warmly. Brennan smiled. "Thanks, Jay."

"Let's have dinner one night this week. We can exchange progress reports. I'll phone you."

Doyle's promise to phone him reminded Brennan that he himself had a telephone call to make. When he had stopped briefly at the hotel for his press pass, there had been a hastily scrawled note from Lisa asking him to be sure to check the hotel in the next few hours for further messages from her. Now he wondered about her cryptic note and wondered what possible messages she could have for him.

Leaving the Palais Rose, he felt discouraged by his inability to contact Nikolai Rostov. Making his way through the courtyard, Brennan realized that he had expected too much of his visit to Paris. Somehow, the very discovery of Rostov alive, of Rostov in Paris, had made success seem a foregone conclusion. Despite a natural cynicism that usually deflated all quick hopes, Brennan had secretly assumed that the mere existence of Rostov within reach would automatically solve his problem and change his life. Until now he had not completely faced the fact that Rostov, because of his high post, because of his busy schedule, because of his commitment to Russian security, might be unavailable or elusive. Above all, Brennan had not fully faced one more fact—that Nikolai Rostov might not want to see him.

On the Avenue Malakoff, he surveyed the neighborhood in search of a public phone. Before deciding how he could best approach Rostov through the Russian Embassy, he must comply with Lisa's wish.

At last he came upon a restaurant, Le Berlioz, which he recalled having frequented in better days. He entered it, found the telephone, and reached the Hotel California. What surprised him was not that the concierge, M. Dupont, had a message from Miss Collins, but that the message was an urgent one.

Through the static on the line he listened closely to M. Dupont's careful reading of Lisa's message:

" 'Matt, if you possibly can, try to meet me at Maison Legrande by noon. It is the fashion house in the Avenue Montaigne. I'll leave word for them to let you in. I will be waiting at the boutique counter. If you're late, I will be in the showroom and be watching for you. This could be important. It has to do with you-know-who. Lisa.' "

Brennan heard his heartbeat quicken as he hung up the receiver. Her message had said that she wanted to see him about you-know-who, and that could only mean Rostov. Yet it made no sense. Rostov and Legrande were incongruous. Puzzled, he hurried out of the restaurant to find a taxi.

Fifteen minutes later, Brennan stood before the turbaned and sashed African doorman guarding the towering pale green entrance to Maison Legrande. On either side of the doorway, a glass showcase displayed a kneaded and elongated sculpture of a bronze Giacometti nude, which had been draped across the bosom with a swath of silk.

Giving his name, hastening inside, Brennan was assailed by a dazzling hall of glass prisms and brocade drapes, and then, beyond a cluster of shrill women surrounding a bean pole of a man, he saw Lisa waiting at the boutique. Approaching her across the thick flower-patterned carpet, he again enjoyed her glossy dark hair and Grecian profile, and the symmetry of her figure in the simple short sheath, and the long perfect legs, and again he marveled at his luck.

She moved toward him and quickly offered her white-gloved hand, drawing him away from the chattering cluster of women.

"I'm so glad you made it, darling," she whispered. "Listen, this is a long shot, but it could be a break. I mean, about getting to you-know-who." She paused, and met his eyes with sudden hope. "Unless you've seen him already. Have you?"

"I called his hotel. They'd never heard of him. I went there. For 100 francs they'd heard of him. But he'd left already. I got into the Palais Rose. He was gone. He's supposed to be in his Embassy now. That's like trying to get to see the Kaaba in Mecca. Only harder. There you are. Zero minus for today."

She squeezed his hand sympathetically. "Then maybe this'll add up, or maybe it's foolish. A little while ago I found out that Premier Talansky's wife Tania and—guess who?—Rostov's wife Natasha— Natasha Rostov—are attending Legrande's showing. They should be here any minute. And I arranged to get you a spare ticket to go inside. I'm not sure if that can be helpful, but—"

"It's interesting," Brennan said slowly. "Let me think."

"I'll tell you what came to my mind. Maybe at the intermission I could get Legrande to introduce you to Natasha Rostov as—as an old, old friend of her husband. Then you could tell her you'd like to meet her husband. Maybe that can work better than anything else."

"Yes. Maybe it can, Lisa."

She began to pull him toward the center of the room. "I think it's important that you meet Legrande first. I've known him since his last trip to New York. We're quite friendly. Come on."

She led him to the border of the circle that still enclosed Legrande. As the renowned designer addressed the women—members of the fashion press and several buyers—airy and flowing gestures accompanied his extravagant, rococo, sometimes chiding, sometimes calculatedly shocking monologue. His listeners, even the veterans from *Vogue, Harper's Bazaar, Women's Wear Daily,* clung to every lilting word, enchanted.

Observing him, Brennan saw a reincarnation of Aubrey Beardsley, illustrator of Oscar Wilde's *Salome* and fey genius of *The Yellow Book.* Yet, for all Legrande's matchstick thinness, his effeminate grace, he appeared as supple and muscular as a young Nijinsky. Beneath the bangs and long hair, the boyish visage was shrewd and clever. Neither the bracelet on one wrist nor the loose-fitting silk shirt deceived Brennan. The young French designer was tough at the core.

Fragments of what Brennan had read about Legrande, or had heard about him from Lisa in Venice, floated back. Legrande had been an apprentice, first under Balmain, then under Balenciaga, until a great perfume corporation offered to put him into business for himself. With the opening of his *maison,* from the showing of his first collection at a cost of $300,000, his daring, his instinct for reminding all women that as long as they were women they were young, had made him the darling of the press and his couture house the favorite of American buyers and wealthy international customers alike. And now this man,

322

the symbol of modern luxury and decadence, would be the host to the mate of the leader of proletarian Russia, and her companion, Rostov's wife. Incredible.

Brennan edged forward to hear what Legrande was saying. He was saying, "Yes, my dears, I'm accenting the bust this year, because it is the staunchest stronghold of feminine beauty. The face, the torso, the limbs may show their years, but the breast preserves youth and attractiveness the longest. You remember the exquisite paean from sweet Keats? 'Breasts of beauty that plucked out mine eye.' Concepts of beauty vary from age to age. Note the varying ideals of the Flemish painter, the Italian Renaissance painter, the French expressionist painter—and then note that the one object they've worshiped in common, in all times, has been the female bosom. They are my masters. Today Legrande returns femininity to all females."

Amused, Brennan watched Legrande adjust his soft shirt cuffs, revealing miniature gold scissors as cuff links, and then he heard Legrande resume.

"Now to answer your question, my dears. Why have Madame Tania Talansky and Madame Natasha Rostov—actually Rostova, in the Russian feminine, if one is a purist, which I am not, so no matter— why have these estimable ladies decided to honor my collection? Perhaps there are two reasons. For one, their motherland has emerged from behind the steppes to join hands with those of us in the West, and the Russian woman's femininity and fashion have emerged apace. For another, I took a modest collection to Moscow two years ago, and showed it in the auditorium of GUM, the mammoth department store in Red Square. Madame Talansky was there, and we had a charming conversation afterward. She was quite taken by my fashion designs. And impressed by my utter honesty. I had attended several Russian designer collections at the Dom Modeley—the House of Fashion— there are three dozen of them about Russia—and I told Madame, well, my dears, quite frankly, I told her that Russian fashion and design were abominable. I mean, dears, Communism is absolutely Christlike, despite everyone breathing on everyone else, but Presidiums and Politburos and workers' committees simply cannot design dresses. I told Madame that you simply couldn't design properly for women if you pretended that they were still in coveralls steering cranes or pitching wheat or directing traffic. I warned her that the birthrate of the Soviet Union would simply crumble unless their women were dressed as women for dinner and parties and bed. And I added that those stout matrons they use as mannequins, along with younger slender girls, were perfectly all right, but it was wrong—and I was fierce about this—it was wrong to dress them in gunnysacks and babushkas. I hadn't seen the slightest hint of female breasts during my entire stay in Moscow. Udders, yes, but enticing breasts, not at all. Today, I hope to change that sorry state of Bolshevik affairs. We shall see, we shall see! But I do believe Madame Talansky is coming here to be convinced. And after today, my dears, romance in Mother Russia shall be revived and the birthrate shall soar!"

The circle of women giggled and twittered, and quickly Legrande dispersed them. "To the salon, my dears, hurry. The showing begins in mere minutes. I must linger to receive my special guests."

As the others left, Lisa brought Brennan forward to introduce him to Legrande and the stern middle-aged woman in dark glasses beside him, who was handing the designer a lace-trimmed handkerchief. Legrande dabbed at his forehead, suddenly recognized Lisa, beamed, quickly brought her hand to his lips, then stood back appreciatively.

"Lisa, my dear!" he exclaimed. "More divine than ever. So they've allowed you to fly on your own, at last."

"Yes, Legrande—"

His fingers nipped at a seam of her dress. "Fine. A fine Legrande copy. But it is not for the new season." He traced a long V from her shoulder blades to her waist. "We remove this. No more will your magnificent breasts be hidden. Henceforth, we shall have all of Lisa Collins." He grinned crookedly. "An ungallant Italian journalist once said that an undressed woman is like a plucked chicken. I believe the opposite. I believe, as Courrèges would often say, that a woman is never more beautiful than when she is naked. The task of the couturier is to make a woman *decently* naked. So that is why we must have all of Lisa Collins."

"I'll try to cooperate," said Lisa. She had Brennan by the arm. "Legrande, I want you to meet my friend, Mr. Matthew Brennan. And Mr. Brennan, Legrande's *directrice,* Madame Demaillot." As the three acknowledged the introductions, Lisa added, "Legrande, I insisted that Mr. Brennan accompany me to the show. He's an old friend of Madame Natasha Rostov's husband, the—"

The *directrice* had tugged at Legrande's sleeve, and he looked off at a *vendeuse* who was signaling from across the room. Quickly he said to Lisa, "Inside you go. The show begins."

Desperately Lisa said, "I thought it would be fun if you could introduce Mr. Brennan to Madame Rostov."

Legrande was entirely distracted now. "Yes, yes, Lisa. See you later."

Hurrying after the beckoning *vendeuse,* Lisa and Brennan entered Legrande's main salon. Brennan had expected a showroom and audience orderly and staid, but instead he found himself in a stifling, churning hall crammed with humanity. Everywhere, the *vendeuses* in their black smocks were settling fashion writers, department store buyers, celebrated private customers in small gold chairs around an elevated carpeted runway.

Dazed and shaken by the sudden transition from the grim aura of the meetings at the Palais Rose to the frivolity of this fashion carnival, Brennan groped after Lisa toward their reserved seats five rows back from the runway. Suddenly the hoarse masculine voice of the *directrice*, Mme. Demaillot, announced the beginning of the Legrande collection, and instantly the babble ceased and the showroom was blanketed by a hushed silence.

Now, from behind the brocade curtains, Mme. Demaillot's voice announced, first in French, then in English, the number and name of the initial dress. A haughty blond mannequin, Oriental eyes, hollow cheeks, parted pale lips, swished out from behind the curtains. She slithered down the runway in a low-cut tight afternoon dress, all bright yellow except for the half-moon insets of lighter yellow circling beneath her breasts. She halted above Brennan, thrust one shapely leg forward, arched her body backward, straightened, pirouetted, and strode disdainfully off, trailed by a burst of applause. Already another mannequin had appeared. The Legrande collection was under way.

While Lisa devoted herself to making coded notes—it had cost her firm $2,000 for the buyer's *caution* that had admitted her to this show—Brennan, in a state of euphoria, watched the skeletal mannequins come and go above him. They glided forth with provocative shadowed eyes and moist half-open mouths, they posed, they twisted, they removed suit jackets, they preened in strapless or one-shouldered décolleté sequined silk-crepe gowns. They trailed sables after them. They were acclaimed. And after fifteen minutes the never-ending parade of beauties, of dazzling fabrics, was a soporific to Brennan.

His mind had returned to Rostov, and to Rostov's wife, and constantly he kept an eye on the doors through which he and Lisa had entered the salon. But, after a half hour, there was no sign of the special guests. Once more discouraged, he ignored the doors and the runway, and lapsed into a spell of moodiness. He did not know how long a time he had detached himself from his immediate surroundings. He was certain that he had not dozed. Yet the flurry of whispering all about him seemed to awaken him, and he felt Lisa's hand press into his arm.

She was close to his ear. "Matt, behind you, Madame Talansky and Madame Rostov! Legrande just brought them in."

He spun about in his chair in time to see the group as it entered the rear of the showroom. Legrande was pointing toward several empty front-row seats, and the older and larger of the two women was persistently shaking her head, declining, indicating that she preferred a seat in the back. Behind these three were gathered at least a dozen hefty plainclothesmen, and from the superior cut of their suits Brennan guessed that four of them were probably Russian KGB agents.

Unhappily, but still valiantly exuding charm, Legrande was ushering the party to chairs in the last row. The first of the two women, sixtyish, dumpy in a formless mustard-colored dress, led the way, and from the attention that she was receiving, Brennan surmised that this was Mme. Tania Talansky, wife of the Premier. The other, a wraithlike mite of a woman, no more than forty, in a checked suit and matching checked pillbox hat, nervously followed, and Brennan guessed that this one was Natasha Rostov. Observing her, Brennan remembered a dinner with Rostov in Zurich. When Rostov was in his cups, he had complained that robust men should never marry tiny, frail women—"like trying to pour a liter of vodka into a wine glass," Rostov had said, "you cannot get enough to be satisfied." Brennan was positive that the wispy woman was Rostov's wife.

He turned back to Lisa. "How can I get to her?"

"There'll be an intermission in ten minutes."

"Good." Suddenly he said, "Lisa, give me a piece of your note-paper." She handed him the paper, looking at him inquiringly as he took out his pen. "When I meet Madame Rostov," he explained, "I'm sure she won't remember a damn thing I say. Too much confusion. Too many people and names. I'm going to write a note and ask her to give it to her husband."

"That's a wonderful idea."

"The best one I've had." He put pen to paper. "This may do it."

While Lisa gave her attention to the parading mannequins once more, Brennan constructed his note in his head, and then he wrote it out as quickly as possible. He addressed it directly to Nikolai, stating that he was in Paris to see Nikolai on private business, that their reunion need be only a brief one, and that he hoped his old friend would phone him. He signed his name clearly, adding his Paris hotel and telephone number.

By the time he had finished, there were no more mannequins on the runway and the lighting had brightened. He slipped the folded note into his pocket and jumped to his feet. "Come on, Lisa. Let's get to Legrande and have him introduce me."

While many of the spectators were already standing, mostly gathering in groups and mostly repeating the superlative *divine,* the majority remained seated, some finishing their notations, others accepting glasses filled with champagne or fruit juice, or selecting pastries from the trays being offered by green-jacketed waiters.

Brennan, with Lisa right behind him, pushed his way past the rows of people, down the irregular aisle, to the rear. Then his heart fell. Legrande and his Russian guests, only partially protected by the formation of security agents, were the center of a thick mass of fashion writers, all vying for introductions or shouting questions to Mme. Talansky. The crowd around Legrande and his guests was already ten deep in every direction.

Brennan glanced helplessly at Lisa, whose own face reflected disappointment. "It would take two days to see even the color of their eyes," Brennan said. "It's no use, Lisa."

Lisa was on tiptoes. "Wait—I think maybe—take another look, Matt."

He raised himself to peer over the heads of the others, and he saw what she had seen. Mme. Talansky, the Russian Premier's wife, was the celebrity. Mme. Rostov, to all but Brennan, was a nonentity. The clamoring fashion press wanted the Premier's wife, wanted the number-one guest and the number-one designer, and no one else. The crush of reporters had broken between the two Russian women, separating them, had engulfed Mme. Talansky, had isolated Mme. Rostov and rudely pushed her toward the rear. Now the wraithlike visitor, after a losing effort to hold her place, had given up and was retreating toward the outside of the vortex, attempting to stagger free.

Brennan did not wait for Lisa. As fast as possible, he ran around the circle of gesticulating females, then skidded to a stop. He could see Mme. Rostov, pillbox hat askew, breathless and afraid, trapped among the outermost members of the horde.

Yanking two aggressive female fashion writers aside, Brennan opened a hole, an escape hatch for Rostov's wife, and she darted through it. In the clear, she wavered, gasping, and then she saw Brennan staring down at her, blocking her path, preparing to address her, and she covered her mouth and backed away.

"Madame Rostov," Brennan was saying, "I'm a friend of your husband and I'd like you to—"

His hand had gone swiftly into his jacket pocket for the note that he had prepared. Mme. Rostov's eyes widened at his bulging pocket, and she squealed, *"Nyet! Nyet! Kto ty?"*

He had extracted the folded slip of paper, trying to explain, "I am *gospodin—gospodin—tovarich—"*

But she was casting about in desperation, forearm raised protectively before her, as she cried out for help in Russian. Brennan snatched at her lifted palm, trying to shove the note into it, but she knotted her fingers into a fist, batting and lashing out at him.

"Madame, listen, I only—"

That instant, heavy hands, like steel clamps, smashed down on his shoulders. Buckling, Brennan tried to turn, to explain, but the hands were scooping him under his armpits, closing in like vises. Protesting, Brennan found himself half lifted from his feet, swung around like a stuffed dummy, and hastily dragged from the main salon through the door and into the vacant entry hall.

Pummeled toward the boutique counter, and suddenly released and dropped weak-kneed and wobbly on his feet, Brennan choked as he stood trying to catch his breath. Three glowering, angry, stocky, plain-clothesmen, as muscular as weight lifters, one cursing in Russian, stood over him. He could see several French DST security officers approaching on the run. One of the officers, older and more authoritative, less volatile, than the others, brushed past the KGB agents, flinging back a question to them in Russian and receiving a torrent of Russian in reply.

Nodding, the Frenchman moved to within inches of Brennan, fixing him with an autopsic glare. *"Je suis l'inspecteur Gorin, de la Sécurité Présidentielle,"* he said. *"Quelle est votre nationalité?"*

Panting, Brennan gasped, "American."

Immediately the inspector switched to impeccable English. "Your passport." Brennan produced it, and the inspector examined it, then looked up. "What was in your hand when you confronted the Soviet Minister's wife?"

"This." Brennan produced the note. Inspector Gorin accepted it in one hand as his other patted Brennan's pockets for weapons. Reassured, he slowly read the note. Again he looked up. "Minister Rostov is a friend of yours?"

"He was. We were both delegates to the Zurich Parley."

"You can prove this?"

"Call Rostov. I wish you would. Or better yet, call the United States Embassy."

The inspector ignored this. "Where are you staying?"

"Hotel California."

The inspector spoke rapidly to a French agent behind him. *"Voilà, son passeport. Allez voir ce que nous avons sur lui, et revenez immédiatement."*

"À vos ordres, monsieur," replied the agent, and he disappeared around the corner.

Brennan could see a frightened Lisa watching from the door. He tried to wave her away. But the inspector, noticing his gesture, walked over to Lisa and began to question her. Unable to hear a word, Brennan nervously observed them in conversation. As the inspector finally doffed his flat-topped cap to Lisa and started back, his aide returned and intercepted him. There was another indistinct exchange. Nodding once more, the inspector summoned the KGB men and addressed them rapidly in Russian. After the exchange they appeared only partially satisfied, but with a last backward glance at Brennan they left for the salon.

Brennan came forward. "Well?"

Inspector Gorin made an aimless gesture. *"J'ai des bonnes nouvelles pour vous. On vous a innocenté.* You are free to go. But with one word of advice, monsieur. Do not ever again attempt to approach any minister's wife or any minister, during our Paris conference, in such an abrupt and suspicious manner. Next time there may be gunshots first and questions later. If you want to see Minister Rostov, see him personally. I always suggest the direct approach. Good day, Monsieur Brennan."

Alone with Lisa at last, Brennan convinced her that he was perfectly all right. While he had no more interest in Legrande's collection, he insisted that she return to her seat and finish her work. As for himself, he promised that he would not pursue Rostov any further this day. There would be no more spur-of-the-moment attempts to get to Rostov, he pledged. He would return to the hotel and rest, and give careful thought to how best to resume his hunt tomorrow.

With reluctance Lisa finally went back into Legrande's main salon. Once she was inside, Brennan walked thoughtfully out of the fashion house and slowly started for his hotel on foot. Sauntering up the Avenue Montaigne, he found that he was more amused than embittered by his rashness as well as by his rough manhandling. But what amused him most was his recollection of Inspector Gorin's advice: "If you want to see Minister Rostov, see him personally. I always suggest the direct approach."

The direct approach.

It was like advising a tourist, who was eager to get down from the Eiffel Tower in a hurry, to jump. That would be the direct approach. Jump. It would get him where he wanted to be fast—even if feet first.

No, he could not jump, not after this brief experience with the KGB. There must be a safer and surer, if more circuitous, route to Rostov. All that was wanted was a sense of direction. Right now he had been deprived of such sense. He was lost, and less confident than ever that he would find his way.

Aᴌᴛʜᴏᴜɢʜ ɴᴏᴛ ᴏɴᴇ ᴏꜰ ᴛʜᴇᴍ was French, the waiter pointed out, the three of them made a perfect tricolor.

They laughed agreeably as they sat squeezed together in the semi-private booth that was separated from the other booths by tasteful curtains above the glass-and-wood dividers. As Hazel Smith and Carol Earnshaw finished the last of their interview, Medora Hart fiddled with the dessert spoon and checked to see if they were, indeed, a tricolor. And, indeed, they were. Hazel wore red, as if to flaunt her rebellious daring, Carol was in white, as if to announce her purity, and Medora was in blue, as if to—well, complement her mood, which was blue.

Medora was not sorry that she had accepted Hazel's last-minute invitation to lunch. It had been pleasant, the lunch, and it had rescued her from the claustrophobia of her hotel room and the maddening dumb telephone. But, unhappily, the escape, the companionship, had not altered her despairing mood.

When the telephone had rung two hours ago, she had leaped at it, certain that it was Sir Austin Ormsby. It had only been Hazel Smith, calling from ANA, to find out whether Medora had had any luck. The futility of her efforts to reach Sir Austin had made her pour out her heart to Hazel, who, although obviously busy, had been sympathetic and kind enough to listen.

After learning last night that Sir Austin was staying at the Hotel Bristol, Medora had been unable to restrain herself, she had admitted to Hazel. She had called the hotel at once, and been connected with his suite. Someone with the supercilious tone of an old family retainer had answered. Medora had given her name and asked to speak to Sir Austin himself about an extremely personal matter. On the other end the mouthpiece of the telephone had been muffled, and at last the servant had reported that Sir Austin was out, might return by midnight, and would call her back. Medora had left her telephone and room number.

There had been no response before midnight, or after, Medora had reported to Hazel Smith. This morning, early, Medora had tried Sir Austin's suite again, and someone who sounded like a servant had told her again that Sir Austin was out, and it was not known when he was expected to return. Medora had insisted upon leaving her name and number once more. By midmorning, thoroughly frenzied, she had telephoned a third time, and this time the hotel operator had curtly informed her that Sir Austin's suite was taking no calls. It had begun to be familiar, a repetition of the occasion, three years ago after the Jameson trial, when she had tried to reach Sir Austin in London, from Paris, and had failed to get through to him.

Spurred and emboldened by desperation, Medora had composed an ominous telegram to Sir Austin: I AM IN POSSESSION OF CERTAIN INFORMATION ABOUT YOUR FAMILY THAT YOU SHOULD SEE. IT WOULD BE ADVISABLE FOR YOU TO CONTACT ME IMMEDIATELY AT THE HOTEL SAN REGIS. She had made a duplicate copy of the telegram, sending one to Sir Austin at the Hotel Bristol and the other to him at the British Embassy. To neither had she received a response.

"I'm sorry to trouble you with all this," she had apologized to Hazel. "Next time you'll know better than to ask me how I am. But I admit it—I'm utterly despondent. What use is Nardeau's painting of Fleur Ormsby if I can't even get to His Majesty to tell him about it, let alone show it to him? I'm at my wits' end."

"I suppose you might leak word of it to the press," Hazel had said. "That might bring him on the run."

"I've even considered that. But Nardeau gave me permission to use his name only privately, that is, to pretend that he would support me in proving the nude is Fleur herself. He said that it would be unethical for him to reveal publicly that it was Fleur. Besides, if I had the picture published, well, there it is, it's out, and there's nothing left to hold over Sir Austin's head. My ace in the hole is my promise that I shan't put it in the press if he simply arranges my re-entry into England."

"You're right, Medora. It's a tough problem."

"Too tough for my bird brain. I really could kill myself."

"Now, you stop that kind of nonsense," Hazel had said sharply. "There must be some way of letting Sir Austin know about what you have. It takes concentration. We'll discuss it later. I've got to take off for an interview with—" Her speech had skidded to a halt. "Medora, what are you doing right now?"

"Nothing at all between now and tonight when I open at the Club Lautrec. Nothing but waiting to hear from Sir Austin, which is like counting on hearing you've won a football pool."

"Look, Medora, I've got a lunch interview with Carol Earnshaw. She's in Paris with her uncle—you know, Emmett Earnshaw—he's the former President of the United States."

"Oh, yes."

"Carol sounds like a perfectly sweet, unspoiled kid. About your age. Maybe younger. I thought she might make a good feature story. Well, something just occurred to me. I was getting some background from her on the phone, in order to help me line up questions. I asked her if she'd met many famous people on this trip, and she named a few, and one of them was Sir Austin Ormsby. She said her uncle and Sir Austin were friends, and they'd got together in London a few days ago and expected to see each other again here. Now it just hit me. If Carol and her uncle know Sir Austin, then maybe it wouldn't hurt for you to know Carol. We could feel her out. Maybe she'd want to help."

Medora had been doubtful. "Why should she want to get mixed up with me? I've met some of those snooty rich American girls around Europe. You'd think they were born with built-in chastity belts, the way they look at me. As if I were dirty and unclean, and it might be catching."

"No, Medora, I don't think Carol's that kind at all. I trust my instincts. And I want you to. Why don't you get out of that miserable room and join us? If no gain comes of it, okay, you've had a free meal on ANA, got your mind off the enemy for an hour, and nothing lost."

"I—I'm really not sure—"

"Come on, Medora. Take Auntie Hazel's advice. Go on brooding like this and you'll wind up in the nut house. I want to help you. But you've got to be ready to help yourself first. What do you say to joining us in an hour?"

Medora had been shamed, and was now hesitant. "You really wouldn't mind?"

"I've no time for insincerity. I want you there with Carol Earnshaw and me. Joseph's restaurant. A block off the Champs-Élysées. Make it in an hour and a half. I'll be expecting you."

"Hazel, you are a dear. You're too considerate of me. One day, if ever I'm home, I shall put you in for the Victoria Cross. Heroism against the common enemy, you know. . . . Very well, I'll be there. Look forward to it. I'm sure your Carol will be a doll."

Now, in Joseph's, Medora Hart knew that her journalist friend's instincts had been correct. Carol Earnshaw *was* a doll. From the moment that Hazel had introduced them, almost an hour ago, they had hit it off.

Medora considered Carol's profile as the American girl lengthily and enthusiastically answered the final question put to her by Hazel Smith. She considered Carol's adolescent bob, little nose, spattering of freckles, fresh and untroubled oval face, and chaste, unsophisticated white dress (like a Communion dress), and she guessed that Carol was a virgin and she envied her. How wonderful, Medora thought, to be nineteen and unused, so excited about the present, so optimistic about the future. How wonderful, Medora thought, to have such advantages, to be brand-new and prepared to offer all of love and all of self to the right man when he came along.

Medora felt her eyes welling with tears of self-pity, and to prevent her mascara from running, she stopped envying Carol and forced herself to trace the restaurant wallpaper—a fabric decorated with roses—visually, and then she allowed her gaze to roam over the dining room of Joseph's until it held on a great abundant green plant that was the room's centerpiece.

She must not equate her life with others' lives, Medora reminded herself. Where there is life there is hope, she told herself, and despite the past, her disillusionments, she could still feel renewed and cleansed inside when she met the right man, if ever. She remembered an American play she had once seen in London, where the mature heroine, who'd had a "chequered" past, finally met her true love, who knew of her past and suffered for the knowledge of it. And the heroine said to the hero that in her life she'd had no way of knowing she would ever meet him, meet the one she would love, and so she'd had no one to save herself for. But now that she had finally met the man she wished to live with forever, the past had no existence or meaning, for there had been no love in it, and only the present had existence and meaning, for she was in love for the first time and therefore was a virgin in love. Medora had always cherished those lines. But suddenly, this moment, in her situation, they sounded stage-contrived and false.

"*Garçon!*" she heard Hazel call out, and guiltily Medora brought herself back to the booth.

Hazel was counting out francs for the bill, grouchily muttering about the way French restaurants included the fifteen-per cent service charge and yet expected customers to tip on top of that. "And when you realize the word *tip* is derived from the initials of the phrase 'to insure promptness,' it slays you." But once the waiter was gone with the money, she grinned. "Like to keep them on their toes," she said, adjusting her hat and picking up her purse. "Got to skip the dessert. I'm late for another interview. You girls stay put. Get your money's worth. Besides, I've done all the talking. I'm sure you'll both have a lot to say to one another." She edged out of the booth and straightened her wrinkled tweed skirt. "Carol, thanks for the interview. It'll please your uncle, I promise you. . . . Medora dear, don't fret. Let me set my mind on your problem. In fact, tonight I'm seeing someone—you know, the man who interrupted us in the café yesterday—and I'll put it to him. He's got a fat-head enough to have maybe one idea. Anyway, I'll be in touch."

They watched her leave in a rush, and when she was gone, their eyes met and they smiled awkwardly.

"I wish I had Miss Smith's energy," said Carol. "She must love her work."

"I suppose she does," said Medora, but then she recalled Hazel's confession about having been ill-treated by some man, and she added, "Of course, one never truly knows about another person."

"No," said Carol quickly, "one doesn't." She seemed anxious to say more, but the waiter appeared with the profiteroles glacées au chocolat and they both felt rescued. There had been a breach left by Hazel's departure that had momentarily left them strangers. Somehow, the profiteroles in common closed the breach between them.

When Medora finished and raised her head, she saw that Carol was already done and waiting to speak to her.

"Medora, I want to make a silly apology about something you don't even know about," Carol began. "When I met Miss Smith, and she told me you would be joining us, I was as excited as I used to be when I was a kid and my uncle had some movie star to dinner in the White House. I told Miss Smith I couldn't wait to set eyes upon you. I told her all of us at school used to discuss you constantly, like you were the glamorous woman that all of us dreamed of being, except you didn't dream like us, you lived it. I told Miss Smith I'd be a big wheel when I got back to school, because I could say I'd met you. I carried on just like that when I heard you were lunching with us."

Surprised, Medora said, "I'm flattered, Carol, but I'm nothing at all like you've imagined, you know." She paused. "Perhaps Hazel told you?"

Carol gulped and nodded vigorously. "She did. I hope you don't mind. She was very frank about everything you've been through."

"I don't mind. It's not much of a secret."

"I guess she spilled it all out because she didn't want me to behave starry-eyed and foolish in front of you, like a silly *fan*. I guess she thought it would embarrass you. But honestly, I'm glad she told me. Not only so I wouldn't behave stupidly, but because it made me realize how immature and lacking in understanding I was. I can't tell you how ashamed I was of myself after I heard what you'd been through. I guess, without ever thinking deeply, all of us, the friends I know, myself, we thought of you as a grand courtesan, with men at your beck and call, that kind of silliness, never realizing what a horror it must've been for you and how badly you were treated. Suddenly, after Miss Smith was done, I saw the whole Jameson case in a new light, and I saw you as a human being, like—like myself, going through all that when you were my age, and I was so ashamed of my childishness. And—well—I thought I'd tell you."

Medora wanted to reach out and hug this girl, but she refrained. "You're very nice to have told me that, Carol, you really are. I appreciate it."

334

Embarrassed, Carol said quickly, "When you're young and kind of cloistered, and brought up strictly, as I was, all you know is what you're taught or what you read in books. Not until you've broken away and been on your own do you find out that most of what you've learned is a glossed-over version and maybe one-half true. I remember reading about Madame de Pompadour in several history textbooks. All you learned was that she was gifted and beautiful, and as the mistress of King Louis XV she ruled over Versailles for twenty years and had everything a woman could want. Well, you read that and you have to tell yourself, ah, that's the life, that's glamour, that's being a woman. But a few months ago I read an honest biography of Madame de Pompadour, and my eyes almost popped out. There it was, the real truth in black and white. King Louis XV was obsessed about—about sex. All he wanted to do was to make love. And Madame de Pompadour, poor woman, she was really frigid—she couldn't help it but she was cold—and the King wore her out—isn't that wild?—and she was always trying to avoid sex and yet she was forced to cooperate because she wanted to stay his mistress. So she went on special diets and took special drugs to make her more passionate, and she begged Dr. Quesnay, the court physician, to help her, and he prescribed more exercise. But nothing helped. Her private life was literally a terror. Only most girls today don't know that. They sigh and envy her, the way they envy you, Medora. I'm glad Miss Smith told me the truth."

Listening to this naïve, engaging American girl, knowing that she could be trusted as a friend, Medora suddenly said, "How much of the truth did Hazel tell you? Did she tell you why I'm in Paris?"

"Why, yes. To see Sir Austin. In fact, she said you were expecting to see him soon, to persuade him to let you go home again."

"Did Hazel tell you how I intended to persuade him to let me go home?"

"No," Carol said uncertainly. "No, she didn't."

"Well, you know he's the one who got me banished from England on an immigration technicality, although it really amounts to a morals charge. And you know he's the one who's keeping me in exile. You know all that?"

"Yes. I think it's awful, it's sinful. I didn't like him when I met him in London. There's something so selfish and insincere about him. But I couldn't tell my uncle. My uncle trusts everyone—you should know how people use him. He trusts everyone except people in the opposite political party. When Miss Smith was telling me about you, my first thought was to have Uncle Emmett go to Sir Austin and make a plea for you. But then—well, I had second thoughts—you see, I know you'll understand, but Uncle Emmett is a little old-fashioned, and—"

Medora stopped her. "I do understand. And I appreciate your even thinking of it, Carol. But you're right. It wouldn't work. Anyway, I don't mind confessing to you what Hazel was too discreet to mention. I'm not in Paris to talk Sir Austin into letting me return home. I couldn't do that in a million years. I'm here to *blackmail* him into letting me return home."

Medora had expected her companion to react with shock. It surprised and pleased her to see that Carol's single visible response was one of being totally intrigued. "Blackmail?" Carol whispered.

"Just that," said Medora. "I've thought about it, and it's absolutely as right as Robin Hood taking money from the evil rich to help the oppressed poor. Sir Austin used his power to warp the law, in order to exile me. Now I've got the means to ruin his name unless he revokes what he's done and behaves decently."

"How?" Carol asked breathlessly.

Medora launched into the entire story of her friendship with Nardeau and the nude of Fleur Ormsby that Nardeau had once painted. She had come to Paris, Medora explained, for the sole purpose of arranging a barter with Sir Austin—his guarantee of a re-entry permit to England in exchange for the scandalous nude of his wife.

"Sounds a perfect scheme, doesn't it?" said Medora. "It would be, except for one flaw that I hadn't anticipated. To make it work, I have to see Sir Austin. Well, I haven't been able to see him. I've telephoned, I've telegraphed. No luck. The invisible man. You can't dicker with someone you can't reach. So I'm up against a blank wall."

"But it shouldn't be that hard," Carol said. "Why don't you send him a letter telling him right out what you have? And enclose a photograph of the painting?"

"I've thought of that very thing, Carol. I don't believe he'd pay attention. He'd think it more fiction from a hysterical girl. He'd simply tear up my letter and the photograph and ignore me. Besides, my intuition tells me that if this is to be successful, it should be handled quietly and privately between Sir Austin and myself. If others in his entourage should see my letter and photograph, Sir Austin would be inclined to ridicule it or demand absolute proof from me. I can pretend I have Nardeau behind me, but I really don't, I mean not in supporting my blackmail publicly."

"Why not write Sir Austin a frank letter and threaten to make this public unless he sees you?"

"It amounts to the same thing, Carol. Maybe worse. As Nardeau reminded me, Sir Austin is not an ordinary person. He's a Cabinet Minister, a guest of the French Government. He could show my threat to the police, and they might run me out of France. I don't dare risk it." She sighed. "Oh, I've tried to think of every possibility, all kinds of improbable schemes. There *is* one other I've been considering." She thought about it and looked at Carol. "I've considered having a go at Lady Ormsby," she said. "Fleur herself. She's the principal. Her stake in keeping the nude a secret is as great as her husband's. And she might be easier to get to. If she knew I had the painting, she might do anything on earth to get her hands on it and destroy it. To acquire it, she might prevail upon her husband to drop the immigration edict against me."

Carol's enthusiasm was instantaneous. "I think that's the best idea yet! You must try it, Medora. There must be a way for you to get to Fleur."

"There must be," said Medora, "but I can't figure out how to manage it. If I call or write her, I'll receive the same treatment I've been getting from her husband. Silence. She knows about me, and how I've been swept under the family rug. Well, I'm sure she wants to keep me there, too, because now she's part of the family. I did have one notion, but . . ." Medora's voice had drifted off as she reviewed the notion in her own mind.

"What was it?" Carol inquired eagerly.

"Oh, a bit fanciful, I'm afraid. You see, there's a big Retrospective Exhibit of Nardeau's work to be shown here, at the Nouvelle Galerie d'Art, in celebration of his sixtieth birthday. This evening there's a special-preview grand opening, admission by invitation only, for the press and celebrities and that sort. I had a brief letter this morning from the Riviera, from Signe Andersson—she's Nardeau's present model—oh, it's no secret, his mistress, too—we're friends—and Signe wrote that she was arriving in Paris this morning, bringing along a few more oils Nardeau wanted hung. She invited me to drop by the Galerie tonight for champagne. Said she'd see that I got in. Well, I can't do that, of course. I'll be working, anyway. But then I had the notion that I might ask Signe to get Monsieur Michel Callet—everyone calls him Michel, he's the proprietor of the Galerie and Nardeau's dealer—to hang my picture, my nude Fleur, in the Galerie as part of the exhibit. My notion was that Fleur, priding herself on being such a publicized art collector and being interested in Nardeau, would sooner or later have to look in on the Retrospective Exhibit. Well, she'd see the nude of herself—how could she miss it?—and she'd recognize it and become terribly anxious and distraught and try to find out who owned it. And Monsieur Michel would tell her who. And then she'd *have* to look me up to try to acquire the nude. And then I'd tell her my price."

If a person could dance while sitting, Carol Earnshaw was dancing.

"Medora," she said excitedly, "that's it! It's a tremendous idea! Why haven't you done it?"

Medora made a face. "Because it won't work," she said. "I mean, it won't work unless Fleur Ormsby visits the exhibit. And the odds are she hasn't the time for any exhibits here. Haven't you read the papers? She's the social hit of the Summit. Giving parties, going to parties, meeting celebrities, traveling everywhere. So there my picture is, hanging there, and here I am, waiting, waiting, and no Fleur to see it. And before I know it, the Summit is over, and she's gone back to London, and I've lost my chance."

Medora looked to Carol for agreement, and was disconcerted to find that her companion had hardly been listening. Carol sat as if in a trance, eyes squeezed shut, nose wrinkled, entirely removed into a world of her own.

Suddenly, like a delighted jack-in-the-box springing free, Carol's features sprang open, eyes opening, mouth opening, and her expression was one of ecstatic delirium. "I've solved it, Medora! I know what to do!"

Taken aback, Medora murmured, "To do about what?"

"About getting Lady Fleur Ormsby to positively see the nude of herself in the Galerie Whatever-it-is." She gripped Medora's arm. "Medora, listen, I can swing it, I know I can. My uncle is real close to the Ormsbys, you know that. We're supposed to go to dinner with them one night here. I don't think it's been set up yet, but we're supposed to. Uncle Emmett's the key, and he'll do anything to make me happy. So what if I go back to the hotel and tell him I'm dying to see the Nardeau exhibit, and tell him there's a grand opening tonight, and it would be great fun if we invited the Ormsbys along for it, since Fleur is such a Nardeau expert, and she might like it and could explain the pictures to us. That would do it. Uncle Emmett would call Fleur, invite them to the exhibit opening tonight and to dinner afterward, and there we'd be. Of course, if Sir Austin is busy with diplomacy tonight, well, we could go to the exhibit tomorrow or the next night. But Fleur is a big one for social openings, and I'm sure she'd want to go tonight. She might even cancel anything else for that, because she'd want to please Uncle Emmett, anyway." Carol released Medora's arm and beamed at her. "What do you think of that?"

Medora could not control her blinking. "Do you—do you think it's possible, Carol?"

"Of course, it is! You just arrange for that nude of Fleur to be hung in the show—"

"But I will, immediately."

338

"—and I'll guarantee to produce Fleur in front of it, in the flesh!"

After that, both of them, caught up in their collaborative intrigue, reviewed it and reviewed it again as they left Joseph's restaurant. At the Champs-Élysées they parted, Carol to go back to the Hotel Lancaster and try to wheedle her Uncle Emmett into fixing an immediate date with the Ormsbys, and Medora to return to the Hotel San Régis and transport the painting from the hotel vault to the exhibit building.

For Medora, the hour that followed had the unreality of a dream. Her telephone call caught Signe Andersson as she was about to leave for the Nouvelle Galerie d'Art for the third time that afternoon, to oversee M. Michel's supervision of final preparations for the evening's grand opening. Medora begged Signe to come by the San Régis on the way to the Galerie, for a few minutes only, for a few private minutes, about something personal concerning the exhibit.

When Signe appeared, little had to be explained to her. Nardeau had already recounted to her the discovery of the nude of Fleur Ormsby, and Medora's plan to use it. Rapidly, then, Medora apprised Signe of the scheme she had devised with Carol Earnshaw's help. The Swedish model abandoned all Nordic reserve in her delight with the complex ruse. She rushed off, the wrapped painting under her arm, to bully M. Michel into making last-minute changes, in order to give a prominent place to Nardeau's *Nude in the Garden*.

Signe had promised to call Medora after the arrangement had been made. Medora, fortified by a ten-grain tranquilizer—enough to keep her calm, not too much to keep her from being at her best at the Club Lautrec that night—paced the hotel bedroom, watching the cradled telephone as if it were a judge readying to announce a verdict.

When the telephone sounded at last, Medora pounced upon it.

She heard Signe's cheerful voice. "It is on the wall. It is beautiful and very naked."

Medora sagged with relief. "Oh, Signe, thanks, thanks, thanks ever so much."

"Medora, a moment. Michel is calling to me." Medora could hear a muted conversation, and Signe was on the line again. "Medora? Ah, that was Michel. He wishes to know if he may reveal the name and address of the owner of the nude, should a visitor inquire about it." Signe laughed and said gayly, "I told him the owner welcomes all who inquire. . . . Now we cross our fingers and wait. We have dangled the bait. We are ready for the lioness."

After that, Medora's tranquilizer did not work. There was no drug on earth, she knew, that could restrain the excitement of her high hopes.

339

The bait was placed.

The trap was set.

The lioness need only be lured.

Medora's mind had gone to Carol, and desperately she wanted to pray, but for the life of her she could not remember a single prayer. It was a sin, not knowing a prayer.

Well, God will forgive me, she thought, it is His business.

She had never heard of Heinrich Heine.

SLUMPED DEEP in the sitting room sofa of his suite, the telephone receiver caught between his ear and shoulder, Emmett A. Earnshaw rattled the ice cubes in his highball glass and listened, trying to understand Fleur Ormsby's quick speech and unclear Mayfair accents. Aware of his niece hovering nearby and of her anxiety, he listened more closely and finally understood.

"Of course, Fleur, that's all right," he said into the mouthpiece. "Fine. I know how it is, but that's fine. Good-bye."

No sooner had he completed the call than Carol was over him. "What did she say, Uncle Emmett? You mean, they can't make it?"

"Can't make it?" He swallowed the last of the drink and set aside the empty glass. "Of course they can make it."

Carol gave a whoop of joy, and quickly bent to plant a kiss on the bridge of his nose.

"Well, now," Earnshaw said, pleased, "someone would think I'd gotten a maharaja to take us to dinner. No, there was no problem. Fleur had planned to stay in tonight, to get some rest for the festivities ahead. She'd intended to skip the—well, that painter's show altogether, because she's busy, but she said the combination of having us as well as seeing a preview of the show was too much to resist. Apparently, that man is one of her favorite painters."

"Nardeau. Yes. She collects him."

"No matter. All that bothered Fleur was that Sir Austin is going to be tied up at the Embassy early in the evening. She said he'd have to miss the exhibit, and did we mind if she came by here, picked us up, and the three of us went to the Nar—uh—Nardeau show together. Then later—well, she'll reserve a restaurant table—and she said she'll arrange for Sir Austin to meet us there, at the restaurant. Oh, yes, and she'll get invitations for the art thing. Are you satisfied?"

Carol did a little mincing two-step, singing out over her shoulder. "I'm thrilled, Uncle Emmett. *Merci beaucoup.*"

He scratched an eyebrow and contemplated her. "I never knew you were so interested in art."

She stopped her solitary polka. "This isn't just art, Uncle Emmett. This is Nardeau. I mean, it's like getting into the first night of a Gauguin exhibit when he was still alive. Now, don't grump, Uncle Emmett. I promise you that you'll enjoy it. Fleur'll explain anything we don't understand. And that's another thing. Won't it be fun to be with the Ormsbys, hearing all the intimate lowdown on the Summit?"

"Yes, I suppose so," Earnshaw said without conviction. He was emotionally exhausted, although he had done little that was tiring this day. He had confined himself to the suite these many hours, waiting to hear Goerlitz's reaction to the explicit message communicated through Willi yesterday. As yet there had been no reply, and the long vigil had drained his strength. Still, he'd been unable to deny Carol's request to visit the art show with the Ormsbys. Perhaps, he decided, he would nap later in the afternoon.

"I'd better pick out what I'm going to wear tonight," Carol was saying.

As she started for her bedroom, Earnshaw wondered if he should order a corsage for her, and this reminded him of something else. "Carol! I almost forgot. A box of flowers came in for you a little while ago. On the chair next to the desk."

Carol rushed to the long pink box, tearing off the ribbons and lid as if expecting to find the Koh-i-noor inside. "Roses!" she exclaimed. "Gorgeous long-stemmed red roses!" She had found the card, opened it, and then dropped to her knees, dreamily enjoying the roses.

Piqued by curiosity, Earnshaw came off the sofa. "Who are they from?"

Without looking up Carol said, "From Willi von Goerlitz."

Confused, since Earnshaw related the Goerlitz family only to himself and his problem, he wondered what any Goerlitz could have to do with his niece. "Why on earth would he send you flowers?"

Carol scrambled to her feet and scooped the dozen roses out of the box. "To thank me for having dinner with him last night."

"You had dinner with young Goerlitz last night? I thought—" He remembered that he had been too tired to take Carol out, and after having a sandwich in the room, he had retired at eight. "I thought you were going to have a bite in the hotel dining room downstairs."

"I was. But after you went to bed, Willi von Goerlitz called up from the lobby to find out if I was in. He said he was free, and if I was, also, he'd like to take me to the old Les Halles district."

Earnshaw's feelings were mixed. He tried to sort them out. His niece going out on a date with a Goerlitz was like one of his political cronies

341

consorting with members of the opposition party. On the other hand, it was also like an ambassador treating with a potential ally. "I'm surprised you didn't tell me about it."

"Uncle Emmett, you were asleep. And today I've been out until now. Last night it was just dinner. Actually, very nice of him."

Earnshaw tried to define his paternal role and wished for Isabel's advice once more, but there was only himself. "I hope—uh—I trust he behaved himself."

Carol flushed. "Really, Uncle Emmett. You're sounding just like some stern Victorian papa—like, I mean, in Wimpole Street or something." She hesitated, then added with sincerity, "Willi was a perfect gentleman. We had onion soup and steaks at Au Chien Qui Fume, and talked, and danced to an accordionist, and then drove out to the new Les Halles, called Rungis, and walked through the markets watching the *forts* and *clochards*—that means porters and bums—literally unbelievable. And I was back here at midnight."

Earnshaw's personal problem had begun to intrude upon his parental role. Since they had talked and danced, he wondered if Willi had discussed his father and his father's reaction to the message. Apparently not, Earnshaw decided, or Carol would have mentioned it. He settled back into the role of his brother's child's keeper. "What about today? You've been out for hours. Were you with Willi again?"

"I was not. I had a long lunch with a newspaperwoman who interviewed me. And I was very careful about what I said. I mean, no politics. Oh, yes. And Medora Hart was at the lunch, too. The Ormsbys' *bête noire*—the one who was involved with Sydney, remember?"

Earnshaw suddenly and distinctly remembered. "The prostitute," he said. "That doesn't show good sense, Carol." He frowned. "I don't want to be harsh, but I must say I am somewhat concerned about you, Carol. I feel I have a great responsibility for your guidance and behavior. Here you are in Paris only two days, and the minute you're out of my sight, you go off gossiping with one of the most shameful young ladies alive. And before that, you're out half the night with some wild boy, whom we know nothing about except that his father was a Nazi war criminal. Carol, what's got into you?"

Her cheeks matched the roses in her arms. "I—I think you're being unfair, Uncle Emmett, terribly unfair. Willi's perfectly nice, like I told you. Why, even you were impressed with him when he was up here. Whatever his father was or is has nothing to do with him. As for Medora Hart, she's suffered more than you can imagine, and meeting her was a lesson to me not to believe everything I read in the scandal newspapers. She—" Carol caught herself abruptly. "I'm not blaming the Ormsbys, you understand. If I did, I wouldn't have wanted to see them tonight. I—I don't know all the facts. No one does. I'm only saying I happened to meet Medora, and it was interesting. That's all. Is that so awful of me? I haven't done anything wrong. I'm surprised you're so—so—oh, I don't know—how did we get into this squabble anyway?"

Earnshaw was about to embark on a detailed explanation of his duties as her father substitute when he checked himself. He and Carol had an honest relationship, a close one. She was a decent child, and she could be trusted, although possibly she was a bit unsophisticated for the kind of people she was being thrown together with in a dangerous city like Paris. Considering the evidence, he was probably being unduly exercised. Nevertheless, in this setting immorality was rampant, and there would be temptations. He made up his mind that once his business was concluded—and the sooner that was done the better—he would remove Carol from this place, revive their excursion to Scandinavia, and return to California as soon as possible.

For the moment he would relent and withdraw disapproval, lest he lose her confidence. "I didn't mean to criticize you so severely, Carol, even if it came out sounding that way. I have complete faith in you. I was only trying to warn you of how easy it is to fall in with questionable company. That can lead to trouble. So let's—"

The telephone on the mahogany rolltop desk rang out loudly, and Earnshaw was grateful for the interruption. He was satisfied to have the discussion terminated, just as he used to be relieved when a minor emergency brought to a close those interminable and never happy meetings with his Cabinet in the West Wing of the White House.

Carol had answered the telephone. He could see her features light up and he heard her saying, "Oh, hello, Willi. . . . Yes, I enjoyed it, too. Les Halles was just what you promised, the living end. And the flowers, thank you ever so much. You shouldn't have. How did you know roses were my very favorite? What? . . . Ummm, that might be fun. Why don't you call me? . . . All right. . . . What? . . . Oh, yes, he's right here beside me. . . . No, he's free. I'll put him on." She cupped a hand over the mouthpiece and beckoned to her uncle with the other hand. "It's Willi von Goerlitz, Uncle Emmett. He was really phoning for you. He says it's urgent. Here."

She held out the receiver, and Earnshaw eagerly took it. Seeing her sweet girl's face, conscious of how openly she had spoken to Willi in his presence, he regretted the unnecessary scene that he had provoked.

343

He, too, covered the mouthpiece with his palm. "Carol, I'm sorry if I upset you by being old-fogyish. I'm sure you understand."

Her smile was instantaneous and forgiving. "I've forgotten it," she said. "I hope you'll do the same. I'd better look over my dresses. I want something low-low-cut for tonight." She winked. "Evil Paris." She nodded at the telephone. "Hope it's good news."

She hurried off to her bedroom, and Earnshaw realized that he was alone with the telephone. He was reluctant to remove his hand from the mouthpiece. He hated moments of irrevocable decision. If Willi had reached his father, he would have a definite answer. This time it would be yes or no, and if yes, his future would remain suspended, and if no, his future would be a ruin.

He brought the bare mouthpiece closer. "Hello, Willi? Good to speak to you again. How are you?"

"Very well, sir. I hope you are, too." The voice at the other end was clipped and formal. "I am sorry I was unable to report to you earlier. My father was occupied with his business colleagues. I have right now spoken to him. I have delivered your message."

There was the briefest interval of silence, like the blank space preceding the indentation of a new paragraph. "My father has requested that I convey to you his reply. He has carefully considered your statement that you are informed as to certain of the contents of his memoirs, that you feel some of his information is misleading, and that you are prepared to offer fuller information. He says that while he would not have the time to receive you for merely a social visit, he will make the time to receive you for a short business appointment, inasmuch as you feel it is important. He is prepared to confer with you one hour from now in his suite at the Hotel Ritz if this is satisfactory to you, sir."

Earnshaw waited for Willi to say more, but Willi had nothing more to say and was awaiting his reply.

"That's certainly satisfactory, Willi," said Earnshaw. "Tell your father I'll be there in exactly one hour."

After hanging up, he realized that he was more wrought up than elated. The hour ahead would be longer than the years of his life. The ordeal of confronting Dr. Dietrich von Goerlitz after that would be nerve-racking. Yet it must be done. It was the meeting that he had so desperately wanted, and had despaired of ever obtaining, but now it was arranged at last.

Slowly Earnshaw started down to the master bedroom to change his clothes and to organize his approach toward the old German.

He saw Carol emerge from her bedroom with a dress on her arm.

She held the dress up. "I've got to have it pressed." Then she studied him questioningly. "Is everything working out?"

"Working out? Yes—oh, yes. Willi was reporting on his talk with his father. Dr. Dietrich von Goerlitz is seeing me in an hour." Earnshaw shook his head. "That took some doing."

"I'm glad."

Earnshaw stared at her with sudden suspicion. She was glad. But she was not surprised. It was as if she had expected this all along. A dark suspicion crossed his mind. "Carol," he said slowly, "did you have anything to do with this?"

He observed her closely. She feigned bewilderment, or was bewildered. "I don't understand," she said.

"You were out with the Goerlitz boy last night. Maybe you spoke about me. Maybe you even told him how important it was for me to see his father. Did that happen?"

"Of course not! Well maybe the subject came up in passing—we talked so much—and maybe, well, I might have said it was too bad you and his father weren't able to get together, since the two of you were such old, old friends, and all that—but there was nothing else, literally nothing."

"Good enough." Earnshaw still remained unconvinced and troubled. "Well, whether you did try to help me or you didn't—and I accept your word that you didn't—I still don't like the idea of your spending too much time with the Goerlitz boy. Maybe I was unfair to him before. But the whole thing bothers me. You come from different worlds. His background and yours are complete opposites. I'm sure your father would have agreed with me that you must be prudent. I don't want to dictate to you. I merely want you to promise me you'll give some thought to what I'm saying."

"I promise," said Carol gravely.

"Uh, and one more thing. It would distress me to know that you were discussing me, or my affairs, whatever you know of them, with anyone else. I don't want you involved in grown-up matters. You'll have time enough for that later."

"Yes, Uncle Emmett."

"Well, I'd better get ready. I like to be on time. Not that seeing Goerlitz is all that vital, actually. It's been blown up way out of proportion, no matter what you think. It's a minor irritant, nothing more. But I like to keep my house in order. Well, I—uh—I should be back with plenty of time to spare before Fleur Ormsby comes around. I think I can dispose of the Goerlitz nonsense rather quickly. In fact, I'm sure of it. Now, you take care."

He had left the Secret Service agent at the far end of the corridor, and now he stood alone before the double doors to the Goerlitz suite on the first floor of the Hotel Ritz.

Earnshaw pushed the button and shifted his weight from one leg to the other uneasily. Dimly, a memory of his last visit to the Ritz, when he had been the occupant of its best suite as President of the United States, came to mind. During that visit what had impressed him was the history of this hotel, where King Edward VII had stayed, where a countess had been asked to move out because her pet lion had grown too big, where an opera singer had inspired the invention of Melba toast. In those days, Earnshaw recalled, he had been received with pomp and ceremony. Unhappily, he contrasted the past with his present unostentatious, almost furtive, reception and appearance.

The doors were opening, and he braced himself.

A butler with a white thatch of hair much like his own and an elongated, phlegmatic face, attired in a livery of silver-satin waistcoat and green breeches, was ushering him inside. *"Guten Tag, Herr Präsident,"* the butler said, taking his hat.

"Good day," Earnshaw replied. Standing in the entry hall, he found the surroundings were familiar. Off this hall, if memory did not fail him, there should be three rooms for servants. Yes, and in the master bedroom there would be buttons to summon the hotel's own valet or chambermaid or waiter, but there would also be a fourth button marked *Service Privé,* which a guest pushed to summon one of his personal retinue of servants from one of these hidden rooms off the entry hall. Yes, he had not forgotten the opulence of it, and he had kept his White House valet, his press secretary and secretary's assistant, in those quarters.

Not until he was led into the vast first salon of the suite was Earnshaw positive that he had been here before. It was the very suite that he had used as President in what seemed another era. It was the suite Hermann Goering had commandeered for his headquarters when the Nazis had occupied Paris in the Second World War. This was the suite Dr. Dietrich von Goerlitz, one of the world's half-dozen wealthiest industrialists, was using today.

He realized that he was once more alone. Goerlitz was not here to greet him. The liveried butler had vanished. Earnshaw examined the salon with full recognition—the stucco murals showing Napoleon in Egypt, the wood-burning fireplace with the decorative gold sphinxes, the magnificent Empire furnishings. Then he remembered how he and Isabel, accompanied by Simon Madlock, had wandered through the incredible complex of rooms attached to the suite which included another salon like this one, six bedrooms, four baths, and those elaborate servants' quarters. Involuntarily Earnshaw shook his head in wonderment, as he had done in the past: that certain people lived like this. It made him feel as uncomfortable now as it had then, to realize how uncompromisingly he had defended a society in which capitalism took care of its own, and how persistently he had attacked Big Government, the welfare state, and all forms of socialism as wicked.

The grandeur of this Hotel Ritz suite reminded him of Goerlitz's power—how do you bargain with a man who has everything?—as contrasted with his own dubious position, which was supported only by past honors and no present strength.

Restlessly he thrust his hands into his trouser pockets and moved to the windows. Below, he could see the European compact cars, mechanical bugs, spinning around the octagon of the Place Vendôme. He studied the imposing column in the center, topped by a statue of Napoleon wearing a laurel wreath and Roman toga, and somehow Napoleon was transformed into Goerlitz, and Earnshaw forced his gaze from this to the parked cars beyond and the de luxe shops lining the shadowed rim of the square.

He heard no one enter the salon. There was only the instinctive feeling—as if someone was staring at your back, as if your ears were reddening because someone was discussing you—that he was no longer alone. He spun around. An elderly man, hunched over a Malacca cane, was in the room with him. For a moment Earnshaw was speechless at how so few years had so enormously aged, and apparently enfeebled, Dr. Dietrich von Goerlitz.

"Good day, Emmett," the elderly German rasped. "So you are here."

"How are you, Dietrich? It's been a long time, too long."

Mentally alert and as prepared as an actor about to emerge from the wings to center stage, Earnshaw summoned up all of his social charm and warm amiability. He had started forward, as one who was wanted and welcomed, intending to take the German's hand, but before he could do so, Goerlitz's cane pointed him to a stately Empire chair between the carved coffee table and divan. "Sit there, Emmett," he ordered.

Off balance, and somewhat abashed, Earnshaw veered in the direction of the chair and sat down. He saw Goerlitz hobbling to another antique armchair, decorated by gold sphinxes and resembling a throne, opposite him, across the low table.

Settling with a grunt, Goerlitz muttered, "Damn gout." He hooked the cane on the back of the chair, asking, "Drink? Champagne? Sherry?"

Recalling a dinner at Villa Morgen, the *Stammhaus* in the suburbs of Frankfurt, Earnshaw remembered in time that his host was a teetotaler. "No, thank you, Dietrich."

Goerlitz blew his nose and fixed his unblinking agate eyes on Earnshaw. "You have not changed," he said grumpily. "You are the same healthy pumpkin."

Earnshaw wished that he could return the compliment with sincerity. In truth, although the German was less enfeebled than he had first thought, Goerlitz's physique had deteriorated. Strands of blue-gray hair were still combed neatly across his head, but his forehead resembled the ribs of an accordion, his eyes surmounted large bloodhound bags, his bulbous nose was a crisscrossing of reddish veins, his cheeks and jowls were age-spotted loose folds, his suit coat and the vest with its gold chain were too large for his wasted, concave chest.

"You're looking trim, Dietrich," Earnshaw managed to say. "You've lost weight. It befits you."

"If you want my diet, I suggest you apply to the International Military Tribunal," Goerlitz growled. "It is a four-year diet served only in Spandau Prison in Berlin."

Earnshaw squirmed, and worked at the knot of his tie. It was evident that even if Goerlitz had weakened physically, he had not weakened in any other way. He had always been brusque, vainglorious, arrogant, cunning, taunting, and to these qualities, now exaggerated, there had been added a certain dismaying spitefulness and venom. He was still the heir to a dynasty that had first gained power under Chancellor Otto von Bismarck, and although Goerlitz had suffered, he could mock his tormentors, for his family dynasty had not only survived World War II but had grown ever more invincible.

"Well, I'm glad you think I look all that healthy, Dietrich," said Earnshaw, seeking some small portion of sympathy, "but actually I haven't been in tip-top shape. I was unable to run for another term, you know, because of some kind of cardiac insufficiency. And then, after Madlock passed away, and then Isabel—you remember my wife?—well, I just haven't had the strength I used to have."

"But you are still strong enough to insist to come to Paris to see me."

Earnshaw hoped that he was not perspiring. "Yes, as I've made clear, I wanted to see you. I was very pleased when your boy called me to say we could get together. He's a nice boy, your Willi. You must be very proud."

348

It was as if Goerlitz had not heard the last. He reached behind him for the cane, clutched the handle, and brought it in an arc before him. He brushed it with a wrinkled hand, then, as if addressing the cane instead of Earnshaw, he said, "You have insisted we must confer because you have heard—from an unimpeachable source, as you put it—that I am about to publish my memoirs and that I have devoted a chapter to your activities as the President of the United States. You know the contents of this chapter—"

"Only to a limited degree," Earnshaw interrupted.

"—and from what you know, you believe you can provide me with more information than I possess—"

"More *accurate* information, Dietrich."

"—and by this meeting you can help me avert certain legal difficulties. Is that correct?"

Earnshaw shifted in the chair. "I didn't say legal difficulties, exactly. I said, well, I suppose I meant I might save you embarrassment, and unnecessary controversy that would result if you made any mistakes."

"So now we know why you are here. *You* want to save *me.*" His wrinkled face shrunk into a cruel semblance of a smile. "How decent of you, Emmett. How extremely thoughtful."

Earnshaw felt the dampness inside his shirt collar. With a finger he pried loose the collar that had pasted itself to his neck. "Naturally, Dietrich, I have a stake in this, too."

"Naturally," agreed Goerlitz with thick sarcasm. "Yes, naturally." He weighed his cane in one hand, then laid it across his lap. "How did you hear of this chapter in my memoirs?"

"Well," said Earnshaw nervously, "well—uh—a—an English friend who—uh—who is in publishing—"

"Of course," said Goerlitz shortly. "Actually, I am not truly interested in your sources. What I have recorded in my memoirs is no secret. It has been a secret only from the press, so that a distorted version of my comments does not get out to the world before the entire volume is published. I am here, among other reasons, to make contracts for the publication of my story. Soon it will appear everywhere, and everyone will know what I have chosen to speak about. No, Emmett, I have no secrets. We can speak openly."

"I'd hoped we could."

Goerlitz had tugged a large old-fashioned watch from his vest pocket, glanced at it, returned it to the pocket. "In a busy day I have set aside thirty minutes for you. There are but twenty minutes that remain. I suggest you tell me exactly what you have to say."

Earnshaw could feel his breathing quicken and become irregular,

349

and he wondered if he had brought his pillbox. He reached down into his pocket. It was not there. But then he realized he could not afford to waste time worrying about a temporary physical discomfort. Minutes were precious. He had been putting off the showdown. He must come to grips with it, now or never.

"Yes, if you don't mind, I will speak bluntly, Dietrich. We are—are—uh—old friends, old, old friends, and old men, and we have seen much in our days, and for both of us there is little time left. I think we can be honest in a—in a special way—I think so—uh—within the confines of these four walls, can't we?"

"You are wasting time, your time and mine," said Goerlitz. "Speak your mind."

Earnshaw nodded nervously. He had pulled a cigar from his pocket, but he did not unwrap it.

"As I understand it, Dietrich," he said, "you have written that I was—uh—I was an indecisive Chief Executive. You have said I had no interest in my office. You have said I delegated decisions to my subordinates, mainly to Simon—Simon Madlock. Correct me if I am mistaken in what you wrote."

"You are not mistaken. That is what I wrote. Except you are too kind to me and to yourself. I phrased those judgments in much more severe language."

"All right. Be that as it may. In any case, you've blamed me for hastening Red China's emergence as a nuclear power. You've blamed me and you've blamed Madlock for China's getting possession of the neutron bomb, a rocket arsenal—"

Goerlitz raised his cane to interrupt Earnshaw. "I have not *blamed* you for China's ultimate power," he said. "To blame means to censure or condemn someone for his acts. I do not censure or condemn you for helping China build the neutron bomb. I am not like you Americans, Emmett. I do not pick heroes and villains. I am as pleased for China to have the bomb as I am for your country to have it. I am in business with both sides. In my memoirs I have only *stated* that you, first, and Madlock, second, are responsible for China's new power."

"You know very well what that means," Earnshaw said in an uncontrolled flash of anger. "In my country, in my world, that so-called statement puts blame on me, accuses me of nothing less than treason."

"Not treason, Emmett," said Goerlitz. "Culpability. Irresponsible weakness. Disinterest. All of these are crimes, too, for a leader. No, Emmett, I have not charged you with premeditated murder, to use a term from your law. I have charged you with potential manslaughter through inexcusable negligence."

' "And I reply that you are misinformed and on the verge of fostering a dangerous lie," said Earnshaw heatedly.

"If that is a lie," said Goerlitz, "what is truth, Emmett, what is truth?"

"The truth is in the record," snapped Earnshaw. "You can read it just as easily as anyone else can. Everyone knows my stand, and my Administration's stand, on the People's Republic of China and on that Mr. Kuo Shu-tung. I would not deal with them unless they were ready to stop all aggression and join us in nuclear disarmament. That was my unswerving policy."

"Apparently your memory is failing you, Emmett. According to the complete record, you did deal with the People's Republic of Red China. You dealt with them extensively."

Earnshaw tried to comprehend what the German was saying. When he thought he understood, he was partially relieved. "Oh, you mean those preliminary lower-level conferences we had with them in Warsaw, The Hague, Calcutta? Yes, of course, we had to communicate, keep those lines open, if we were ever to bring them to the peace table. And the Zurich Parley? Yes, I agreed with Simon Madlock that this was as far as we could go in our attempt to reason with them. But I wouldn't call that dealing with the Chinese. No, not a—"

"Emmett," Goerlitz interrupted harshly, "I am not speaking about those public-relations and propaganda conferences. I am referring to what really happened. I am referring to your underhanded, secret dealings."

Earnshaw straightened. "What in the devil does that mean? Secret dealings? What secret dealings?"

"Come now, come now, I am in possession of the documents, the letters bearing your signature, which authorized my firm in Germany to supply certain materials, on behalf of the American Government, to the Chinese Reds through intermediary nations like Albania. It is something German firms have done occasionally before, as in 1966, when they sold Luftwaffe Sabre jets to Pakistan through Iran, to overcome your arms embargo. It had been done for others, and it was done for you."

Instantly Earnshaw remembered the night in the Dorchester Hotel when Sir Austin had shown him actual photocopies of such documents and letters, typed over his own signatures. He had forgotten, and now the reminder of this evidence shook him. He heard Goerlitz speaking again.

"You don't deny the existence of such papers, do you?"

Earnshaw felt confused. "I—uh—no—well, Dietrich, I did see some photostats of these—uh—papers in your possession—yes—some orders for you to fill, to be paid for out of our special defense funds, yes. Now I remember."

Goerlitz toyed with the cane. "You signed them or you did not. One or the other."

"I signed them. But you know, Dietrich, I have no recollection of actually signing them. I simply haven't. I was signing so many things. I mean, on most I was fairly well informed, but many papers were relatively unimportant. Simon Madlock would simply pile them on my desk and explain the important ones as I endorsed them. Possibly some of these materials that went to China, the authorizations for such, were among the papers I signed. But what we gave them couldn't have been important or Madlock would have briefed me first."

Earnshaw could see his host considering him with open contempt. Goerlitz's head slowly went up and down as he said, "They *were* important, in terms of evaluating China's growth to its present position of power." He had edged himself forward, bending toward the end table near the divan to open a drawer. He extracted a sheaf of papers, held together with a large clip, and tossed them across the coffee table toward Earnshaw. "There is the complete file. The photostats are of documents that are reproduced in my book. Have a look for yourself."

With trepidation Earnshaw picked up the sheaf of correspondence. After a minute, he knew that every one was on the stationery of the White House. A few were signed by him, and many by Simon Madlock. He had peeled them back slowly. Document after document, letter after letter, authorizing the purchase of materials—defined only by reference numbers—from Goerlitz Industriebau in Frankfurt-am-Main to be shipped, by them, via Albania, for ultimate delivery in Shanghai. Other correspondence authorized Goerlitz to arrange unpublicized economic meetings in Frankfurt and in other European and Southeast Asian cities, between representatives of the United States and those of the People's Republic of China.

Not one page of the correspondence was familiar to Emmett Earnshaw.

He looked up, heartsick.

Goerlitz had been observing him. "Emmett," he said, "are those signatures of yours and Madlock's authentic?"

"Yes."

Goerlitz hit the carpet gently with his cane tip. "Then, there is your record."

Earnshaw dropped the papers on the table. He felt hot and feverish. He stared at the German, and finally he began to shake his head and then kept on shaking it. "No, Dietrich, that is not my record. Maybe it makes no sense to you, but I know nothing about any of this."

"Exactly!" exclaimed Goerlitz, now thumping his cane hard. "That is the whole point of my chapter. It is not Madlock I expose. It is you. It is you, Emmett. Because of your weakness, you abdicated your Presidency to Simon Madlock. You were not interested in these vital matters. He was. You would not act, so he acted in your stead. He performed in your name."

Deeply shaken, Earnshaw tried to find words. "I refuse to believe it. There's something missing. I knew Simon like a brother. He was incapable of performing behind my back in such a way."

Goerlitz snorted. "You would do well to read Nietzsche. 'Wherever I found a living creature, there I found the will to power.'" The German paused. "Perhaps I knew your friend and aide better than you did. He was loyal, it is true. He would not usurp your power. He would only try to fill the vacuum left by your disinterest in power, and naturally would attempt to fill it with his own policies, performing in your best interests, he thought."

"It still makes no sense. Why would he want to help those Reds in China this way? He didn't want a future war—"

"No, he did not," Goerlitz interrupted. "He was a man of peace—in my opinion a foolish one, an impractical one—so he acted this way only for peace. Was he right or wrong? Perhaps the Summit will answer this question. No matter. The fact remains that the world condition that exists today is largely due to your dereliction of duty, to Madlock's experiments on your behalf; and since I was in the midst of all this, I believe I have every reason to publish this little private episode in our recent history."

The unassailable revelation of his beloved and trusted aide's hidden role in his own affairs had stunned Earnshaw beyond protest or denial. He sat as hunched over as his host, as old and gray, twisting his cigar. He lifted his head. "I—I'm trying to—to—uh—digest it, Dietrich. I'm trying to make heads or tails of your charges."

"I shall summarize it for you quickly, and then we can be done," said Goerlitz. "Be attentive, please. I am not your Madlock, remember. . . . While you were in the White House cutting paper dolls and playing cards and occasionally prattling about lower taxation, your ship of state was without a strong hand at the helm, and floundered deep in foreign waters with no charted destination. So, in effect, Simon Madlock took over at the helm. He thought he had a foreign policy that would make you a great man of history. He was a well-intentioned person, your Madlock, but a stupid one, muddy-minded, overidealistic, evangelistic, determined to bring peace in our time in his own way. He saw that your country's future would forever be interlocked with China's. He saw, also, that China had to be reasoned with, but could not be reasoned with so long as it was distrustful of American capitalistic imperialism and American goals. He set out, silently and behind the scenes, to woo China out of Russia's orbit and into America's orbit by proving, with tangible gifts, that America was friendly and wished only peace. He needed a discreet means by which to contact China. He could not depend on another nation. He needed an individual. He knew that I was trading with China, so he sought me out for the role of unofficial intermediary. His idea was to create a Marshall Plan for China, no strings attached. He would give me orders for materials, and I would pass these along under many guises, but with the donor always clearly known. These orders represented economic aid, even to new materials for nuclear power plants. Using mainly your signature or approval, but sometimes entirely on his own, employing any funds authorized by Congress that did not have to be accounted for, Madlock implemented his policy. The Chinese were suspicious, but receptive. Perhaps, in time, they might have come around, and you would have had an enormous diplomatic victory. But Madlock went too far. He personally handpicked Professor Varney to go to the Zurich Parley, because Varney was a dreamer like himself. Madlock was positive that Varney would be the last seduction needed to bring China over to your side. This was a major risk, and Madlock knew it, but he deliberately took it—in your name. He loaded Varney down with assorted classified information, feeling sure that these bits and pieces would impress the Chinese and disarm them long enough to get them to the peace table. However, Madlock miscalculated. Varney went a step further than Madlock had foreseen. Varney defected. And China, momentarily lulled by your peace offensive, awoke and could not believe its good fortune. Overnight, peace on Madlock's terms went out the window. Overnight, China had the means to achieve nuclear equality and would no longer discuss future peace on America's terms but only on its own terms. If anyone dared to risk war in those times, China was probably the best prepared to take that risk and knew it. In my opinion, if Soviet Russia had not made an alliance with your country, it is conceivable that we might this moment be living in a world full of rice paddies, so to speak. But today, with Soviet Russia on your side, the balance of power is once more aligned against China. Yet perhaps the arrangement is tenuous and temporary. International tension remains. Is one man entirely responsible for this dangerous situation? I doubt it. But should one man bear the major portion of the responsibility? I believe so. Who, then, is this culprit? Simon Madlock? No. Emmett Earnshaw? Yes. It is you, Emmett, who must bear the responsibility before the bar of history, because you were inattentive and disinterested and derelict in your duty during a critical period of our epoch. This failure of yours I have witnessed firsthand. This I have written. This I shall publish."

Puffing, Dr. Dietrich von Goerlitz leaned forward on his cane as if to rise, but seeing that Earnshaw had made no move to leave, Goerlitz restrained himself and waited.

Earnshaw had absorbed the original shock of learning fully of Simon Madlock's independent activity. Even if the German industrialist had overdramatized it, the activity could not be denied. There was the sheaf of documentation lying on the coffee table. And what this represented was not an aide's disloyalty but Earnshaw's own bankruptcy as a leader.

What must come next would be difficult, but there was no other choice.

"Dietrich," Earnshaw said quietly, "I came here to request that you drop that chapter about me from your book. In the light of—uh—of what you've said, perhaps I cannot ask that much. Instead, I shall make another request. In all fairness, I think you should modify some of your judgments. I cannot be convinced that what you have written will tell the public the whole truth. You and I know there is much more to it, much more to my Administration and—uh—leadership that you are omitting. You have said that Simon was a man of good intentions. Well, so was I. Yes, Dietrich, I was a man of peace and honor, and in my Administration I sought only peace on earth for all men and honor for my people's cause. You know that is true, and I suggest that it deserves to be said."

The wrinkled folds on Goerlitz's face shook, but his agate eyes stayed hard. "Nothing deserves to be said except what is fact. Your regrets and good intentions and soft sentiments are not facts. They are apologies. They distort existing truth. The only facts are in those documents. Let the world see them and interpret them as it wishes. If you desire changes in my chapter, I will gladly make them. But the changes must be facts, nothing less. If you have other documents I have not seen, documents to contradict or modify these facts, I shall include them in my book. Do you have such papers?"

"You know I do not."

"*Verzeihung!* But then you must be judged now, as I was judged in the recent past, solely by available evidence. You must be judged by me as I was judged by your International Military Tribunal in Germany. I was judged not on my word but on cold documents that involved me with Hitler, that indicated I had used 80,000 Nazi captives as slave laborers in my factories during the Second World War. The fact that I resisted using such workers, that they were forced upon me, was not a fact to your Tribunal, because I could not prove it. All that existed for them was the fact that those slave laborers worked in my plants. I appealed to those in authority, I appealed to you, to support my word, to modify the cold documents. I was ignored. So I paid for what had been written over my name. I paid, Emmett. And now you must pay, too."

"But our cases differ," Earnshaw protested. "I did not judge you. An international court judged you. But you, alone, are taking it in your hands to judge me." He caught his breath, and then said quickly, "What I cannot understand is your motive, Dietrich. What have you to gain by unfairly crucifying me? If you had a political motive, I would understand. If you were anti-Chinese, and felt I had betrayed your cause by helping China, it would make sense. But you are not anti-Chinese. You trade with them every day. So why punish me?" He hesitated. "Unless—you have secret feelings?"

"I have no secret feelings," said Goerlitz brusquely. "I am neutral. Business is neutral. I serve those who pay their bills. Today I have no interest in causes." He glared across the table. "My motive, you want to know? I am not interested in crucifying and punishing you, as you put it, as a personal matter. I am interested only in truth, because only truth will eliminate those who are not fit to survive, those whose weakness destroys not only themselves but even the strong around them. What did our philosopher say? 'I teach you the superman. Man is something to be surpassed.' But Man can be surpassed only if the weak are revealed and cast aside."

Earnshaw had heard the words, but they were beyond his comprehension. He knew only that they sounded strangely sinister. "Dietrich —" he began, seeking to bring them both back to simplicity and understanding.

Goerlitz held up his hand. "Allow me to finish. I am trying to say—and now I will be more blunt—that you were not fit to be a leader. Vanity made you pretend to leadership, and your weakness enmeshed us all in potential catastrophe. Like my father, like his father before him, I have been taught to abhor and oppose weakness. Now, weakness has many disguises. One is indifference. Another is stupidity. Yet another is cowardice. You have worn every face, even cowardice, as when I appealed to you to speak out on my behalf during my trial, and again when I petitioned you to have my sentence mitigated. Your

356

weakness made you afraid. You put your own political safety before integrity and honesty. You allowed me to go to Spandau Prison, to remain entombed behind those thick walls and electric barbed wires. You permitted me, a Goerlitz, one you once called friend, to suffer confinement with lowly, disgusting Nazi war criminals, to live like an animal in a hole, shorn of dignity and freedom, feeding off scraps like a pig, with no human companionship except from that shrieking, howling, heiling madman, Rudolf Hess. Four years of that I suffered, when your strength instead of your cowardice might have influenced the Americans to save me from that hell. In the end it was the Russians, their leader Talansky, who was strong enough to release me, because he needed my factories. But you—where were you, my good friend? You were occupied only with your comforts and your vanity, and just as you ignored me, you ignored your holy duties and abdicated policy-making to Madlock, and you were thus instrumental in allowing Varney to defect."

In the silence that followed, Earnshaw stared back at the German. Voice trembling, Earnshaw finally spoke. "Now I know why you are doing this to me, Dietrich. It is not truth you are after. It is personal revenge."

"No, you fool!" Goerlitz shouted. "I wouldn't demean myself for personal revenge. Emmett, you are a simpleton. You cannot understand, not in your lifetime. But try, try. I read you a last time from my primer." He spoke in measured sentences, enunciating clearly as if explaining to a child. "There are those of us who believe that the world must not be run by men who are smiling, charming, incompetent reflections of the nincompoop masses. There are those of us who believe that the affairs of the world can be conducted peacefully and efficiently only by authorities who are not experts alone but who are also men of decisiveness. We respect and support the Movers, the ones who Do, the ones who Act. There are many such men, in many nations, and among these are the leaders of China. They Do, they Act, and in so Doing and Acting, they deserve to survive, for they will make the world better for most of us by forcing the West to choose men who are their equals. I repeat, I have no politics. I have coal mines, I have blast furnaces, I have the goods of the world, and among those goods, weapons. I offer all I possess to each and every nation on earth, to use as it pleases, in the safe knowledge that the fittest will survive and bring peace."

"You spoke of everything except human friendship," said Earnshaw. "Doesn't that count for something?"

"That counts for much, if the friends are held together by strength.

At one time, when you represented the American elite, I thought you were one of us. After you succumbed to the euphoria of popularity, I saw that I was mistaken. You chose to serve no one but yourself. You abandoned us, and now you must suffer the consequences." Goerlitz's agate eyes remained fixed on Earnshaw. "Do you understand me now?"

At last Earnshaw felt that he understood. Inside himself there was an emotional comprehension that he found difficult to define intellectually. *You abandoned us,* Goerlitz had said, and the *us* was the same as the shadowy *they* that people used to indicate that super-club, super-cult, super-government that was not exactly a club or cult or government. It was—what? It was *they*—no roll call, no membership, but an elite that influenced and directed the affairs of the planet, an elite that observed no boundaries of nationality but ruled by an unspoken yet mutual understanding of the uses of power in every area. In short, *they* ran the world, and only *they* could save it. And according to Goerlitz, for a time Earnshaw had qualified to be one of them. But then, because he lacked the toughness required for leadership, he had failed to help a blood brother, he had committed the unpardonable crime. He had betrayed them. *And now you must suffer the consequences,* Goerlitz had concluded.

Earnshaw understood at last.

He had been sentenced. There could be no appeal.

Yet one minor puzzle nagged him. "Dietrich," he said, "I know my time is up. One final question. Why did you bother to see me today?"

"Because I promised I would, so I did."

"Promised? Whom did you promise?"

"I—" Goerlitz stopped, considered his cane, and said, "I promised myself. I decided you deserved one hearing. If you had spoken to me clearly and directly of your failures, if you had recognized them and repented them, if you had shown some strength of character, I might have reconsidered publishing that chapter. But, Emmett, you have not changed, you have not changed at all." Slowly, with effort, Goerlitz pushed himself to his feet. "I shall publish the book as it stands."

Earnshaw had risen. "Do whatever you wish."

Goerlitz hobbled to a cord beside the window. He tugged at it. "My butler will show you out."

Earnshaw started for the hall. He heard Goerlitz call his name. He halted and turned.

"I see your face," Goerlitz said. "I see you still do not understand. . . . You have not read Nietzsche? You should. It is made clear in Nietzsche." Then, in a croaking voice, he went on. " 'What is good?

358

All that increases the feeling of power, the will to power, power itself, in man. What is bad? All that comes from weakness.' " He paused, and then he said, " 'Thus spake Zarathustra.' "

Not until some minutes later, when he had emerged from the Hotel Ritz into the Place Vendôme, did the enormity of his defeat and loss completely engulf Earnshaw. His mind had teemed with a hundred hurts and angers. His mind had ranged from sadness over Madlock's misdirected idealism to anger over Goerlitz's fanatical cynicism. Now, in the fresh air, his mind was left with only himself and his baffling weakness of character.

The limousine door was opened, but Earnshaw was loath to enter it. The limousine resembled a hearse.

Standing there, he wished himself dead and did not care if the wish was blasphemous. But he knew that his wish would too soon be granted, and it was out of his hands anyway. Within twelve days, before the Summit's end, a member of *they,* whom he had abandoned, would perform the brotherhood's ritual of liquidating Emmett A. Earnshaw from the living. His disgrace would affect Carol, his card-playing cronies, his Presidential Library visitors, his political party's faithful. His disgrace would obliterate poor Isabel and poor Simon, whose good names depended upon the survival of his own good name. His disgrace would blot his name from the earth's honor roll for all eternity.

He would vanish, and all that would remain of him would be a gravestone bearing two chiseled words: RUE CATHAY.

THE LEFT BANK was as congested with traffic this late afternoon as the Right Bank had been early in the morning, and Matt Brennan wondered what he was doing here. Cringing as his insane taxi driver swerved in front of another car to gain the inside lane, Brennan sat up in time to watch his driver turn safely into the Rue de Seine.

Although he knew that it was a wild goose chase—one too ridiculous to mention even to Lisa—Brennan consoled himself with the virtuous feeling that came from doing at least Something.

Yet, perhaps, there was a small degree of sense in pursuing the lead. Jay Thomas Doyle had thought so, and Doyle, despite his aberration concerning the Kennedy assassination, was an otherwise sensible person.

Brennan had bumped into Doyle after the fiasco at the Maison

Legrande. He had taken a long walk, ruminating over his situation as he window-shopped, and it had been quite late in the afternoon when he returned to the Hotel California. He had entered the lobby at the very moment Jay Doyle was about to leave a manila envelope for him at the desk.

"Research for you," Doyle had explained, handing him the envelope. "I promised I'd look up Rostov in the ANA files. Well, after I finished my work for Earnshaw, I poked through the morgue. Sure enough, there was a fresh folder on Rostov. Not much in it, really. A few pages dated a day or two back. Apparently the staff has been getting up background data on every delegate. I'd guess Hazel Smith supplied what little there is of this. Russia's her backyard. Anyway, Matt, there's mostly statistical and biographical information on Rostov. And a paragraph on his avocations. Maybe you'll see something there. I admit, I don't."

They had strolled across the lobby while Brennan opened the envelope, took out Doyle's notes, and hastily scanned them.

Doyle, looking over Brennan's shoulder, had pointed to the last paragraph. "There's the best stuff. Rostov when he relaxes. He likes Hungarian food. Okay, there are several good Hungarian restaurants in Paris. You might run into him in one of them. Then there are his favorite recreations. Horses and chess. Maybe that means he might take an hour off to watch the races at Longchamp or Neuilly, or look in on a chess club—there are almost a dozen in Paris, like the Caisse Brasserie des Templiers—though he probably wouldn't have time for that. And his hobby is collecting rare books and manuscripts. Well, if he's a serious collector, he won't be able to resist the shops on the Left Bank. They're great." Doyle had been apologetic. "That's all, Matt. Sorry. Guess it's too general to be useful. But I thought you should see it."

A dead memory had been sparked alive in Brennan's mind. "You were right to show it to me," he had said. "I'm grateful, Jay. There just might be something here."

"No kidding? I can't imagine what."

"I'll have to give it some thought. See what I can remember. When Rostov and I were in Zurich, we got along famously because we had several common interests. One was that we were mutually fascinated by certain historical figures. I'm a reader. I liked to read about those personages. Rostov is—well, was—a collector, and he liked to collect first editions and autographed letters by and about them. Actually, he was a serious collector, and you're right, he might find the Paris antiquarian bookshops irresistible. The trouble is—it's like hunting for a needle in a haystack, to coin an expression. If he browsed at all, where would he browse? And when? And—well, hell, none of this is your concern. I'll have to sort it out."

"I think it's worth a try," Doyle had said.

"Jay, in my present state, anything's worth a try. I'm genuinely grateful to you."

After Doyle had left, Brennan had gone into the dim California bar and settled at a table. Drinking his Scotch-and-water, nibbling his popcorn, he had reread the last paragraph of the research material.

With little effort, he had sent himself backward through four years, to the evenings when Rostov and he had sat in the Cabaret Voltaire or Kropf's in Zurich, discussing politics and personal pleasures. Brennan had picked through his remembrance of the many conversations and had gradually narrowed memory down to what he sought. There were two subjects on which Rostov had collected material avidly. One was Lord Byron. The other was Sir Richard Burton, explorer and archeologist, the Burton who had visited Mecca in disguise, had discovered Lake Tanganyika, had called upon Brigham Young in Salt Lake City, and had either written or translated at least fifty books, among them the classic *Arabian Nights*. Brennan had guessed there might have been other great men that Rostov collected, but Byron and Burton were the names most vivid in his memory, and especially the name of the eccentric, headstrong Burton.

The next had been more difficult for Brennan to remember. The sources of Rostov's collection. This had been discussed, too, Brennan was sure, but the exact sources teased just beyond his memory. Brennan had thought and thought, and finally the name of a rare-book store in London had come to mind, and then another in Berlin, both of which Rostov had dealt with by mail. There had been some in Paris, too, of course, one shop for certain, one from which Rostov had regularly received catalogues, and Brennan remembered that the name of the shop was somehow connected with a famous French personality. He had begun to review French names. But that had been an appalling game. There had been too many. And suddenly, a clue had come to him. Rosetta stone. He had begun to associate names involved with the Rosetta stone. The man who had deciphered the hieroglyphics? Champollion! That—but no, that had not been it, either. Then who? Who had found the basalt slab? Napoleon? No. A soldier of Napoleon's, a French officer, an engineer, Boussard. Yes, but that wasn't it, either. Where the devil had that slab been found? The town of Rosetta in Egypt—yes, but no, actually an excavation near a military—a military installation—a fort—a fort—Fort St. Julien. Yes! Julien!

Hastily paying his bar bill, Brennan had rushed through the lobby to the telephone switchboard. There, with the help of an operator, he had leafed through the formidable Paris telephone books. Five minutes later, with a triumphant smile, he had written on a torn strip of paper, "Librairie Julien—Livres et Autographes—Rue de Seine."

A wild goose chase, but nevertheless, here he was in the Rue de Seine.

Outside the taxi window he could see the quaint and cranky little art shops, book stores, grocers' cubicles, bistros, as they flashed by, and then he saw a cracked sign, JULIEN, blurring past his vision. He gripped the taxi driver's shoulder. "Here—*ici*—let me out right here," he ordered.

Leaving the taxi, he walked back to the dilapidated shop. In one window, handsomely displayed against a velvet-draped stand, was a framed letter dated 1766 and signed "Jean Jacques Rousseau." In the other window, arranged in a semicircle, were rich leather-bound first editions of Marcel Proust's works.

Opening the door and entering, Brennan heard a bell tinkle above. He found himself in a small anteroom furnished with three ladderback chairs and a low commode inlaid with tortoiseshell, on which rested a bronze ashtray and a stack of the shop's latest catalogues. Ahead, a pair of four-shelf bookcases, neatly filled with rare volumes, served as dividers, separating the anteroom from a recess for an office beyond.

A cherubic head, with incongruous mussed gray hair and gold-rimmed spectacles, popped up from behind one of the bookcase dividers. The proprietor nodded his greeting, called out, *"Tout de suite,"* and lowered his head from view.

Brennan drew a chair up to the commode, sat, and found the most recent Julien catalogue, which was devoted to "Documents et Livres Historiques." The numbered book items for sale were listed alphabetically by author, then title, and each was followed by a description in French of its contents and condition, as well as an explanatory line stating whether it was a first issue or only an early edition, an autographed presentation copy or a private press volume. Brennan turned to the authors listed under "B," and immediately he found "Burton, Sir Richard Francis." Two first editions were for sale: *Falconry in the Valley of the Indus,* London, J. Van Voorst, 1852; *The Highlands of Brazil,* 2 vols., London, Tinsley Bros., 1869. Next, Brennan searched for a listing for "Byron, George Gordon, 6th Baron Byron." There was "Butler, Samuel." There was "Byrd, William." There was no Byron.

The availability of Burton, the lack of Byron, immediately determined Brennan's strategy. He would ask to see the Burton items. He would ask whether there were others for sale that had not been listed. Casually he would inquire whether there were many Burton collectors who purchased through this shop, and if there were, and Rostov's name was not mentioned, he would mention it himself. He would state that Rostov and he were old friends, that Rostov had recommended this place to him, and that they frequently corresponded about their Burton acquisitions. He would try to learn whether Rostov had been in touch with the shop, and whether he was expected in, and if so, exactly when—for Brennan would like to surprise his old friend and fellow bibliophile. It was a long shot, but, again, it was Something.

He heard a voice say, *"Bonjour,"* and he looked up to find the individual with the cherub head, body attired in a gray smock, standing between the dividers.

Brennan came to his feet. "Monsieur Julien?"

"Oui . . . Américain?"

"Yes. I just—"

"Welcome," the proprietor said in English. "What can I do for you?"

"As a matter of fact, I collect Sir Richard Burton. I—"

"Of course, of course," said M. Julien. "Right this way."

Brennan passed between the bookcase dividers into the office. To his immediate left there was a desk holding an open issue of *France Nouvelle,* and a book-covered refectory table draped with green felt stood in the center of the room. The walls on all sides of the room were lined with shelves of either old books or elaborate slipcases that contained holograph manuscripts as well as private press publications.

The proprietor was bustling toward his desk. "I was expecting you," he was saying. "I was expecting you a half hour ago. I have the Burton books all wrapped, Mr. Peet."

Mystified, Brennan was about to speak when suddenly the proprietor, about to reach beneath his desk, straightened and said, "I almost forgot. First, the list, Mr. Peet."

"I'm afraid you've mistaken me for someone else, monsieur," Brennan said. "I'm not Peet. My name is Matthew Brennan."

M. Julien appeared startled, then unsettled, but quickly he recovered his poise and bustled back to the felt-covered table. *"Excusez-moi,* forgive me please for my error," he said apologetically. "I was, you see, expecting another American. A collector of Sir Richard Burton, too. He had ordered the books and was to have picked them up more than thirty minutes ago. So I thought—" He shrugged.

"It is understandable," Brennan said.

"Now what can I do for you, monsieur?"

"Well, as I said, I am a Burton collector. I'd like to have a look at the two firsts you've listed in your catalogue."

"They are sold."

"Oh, that's too bad. Well, perhaps you have some lesser items that you didn't list?"

"Only the ones your fellow countryman purchased through the mail in advance," said M. Julien. "There is nothing else. I am cleaned out, I am sorry to say." His hand waved toward the shelves. "Of course, we have many other rare and interesting—"

"No, just Burton," said Brennan. "I'm surprised you sold those items so quickly. I thought there wasn't much interest in Burton. What's happened? Are you getting a rush of business from visitors to the Summit conference?"

"Summit?" The proprietor snorted. "Those delegates are not here for books. They are here to kill Chinese. And when they are finished, they will go to the Folies and the Club Lautrec." He had become impatient. "Well, if there is nothing else—"

M. Julien's contempt for those who would "kill Chinese" piqued Brennan. He wondered if the proprietor was simply a Frenchman sympathetic to the Chinese or a member of the French Communist Party. While his quest had been a failure, he was reluctant to leave. He sought for a reason to stay on. Then he remembered Rostov's interest in Byron. "As a matter of fact, there might be something else. Have you—?"

The bell over the door tinkled, and Brennan stopped. M. Julien looked toward the door, absently murmured an excuse, and hastened between the dividers into the anteroom. Brennan had turned his back to the entrance, meaning to peruse the titles on the shelves, when he heard a reedy American voice with a flat Midwestern accent inquire with forced aggressiveness, "You Mr. Jewel-yan? I'm Joe Peet. I called you before, remember?"

"Of course, Monsieur Peet, I was expecting you to come earlier," the proprietor was saying in a forgiving, silky, customer-pleasing voice.

"Yeah, I know. Sorry I'm late. I couldn't help it. Flew in from Chicago in the wee hours. I slept like a log, then I got tied up in business. Everything's running behind. Anyway, you got those Burton books I ordered?"

"I have them ready for you, Monsieur Peet." There was a pause. "First, so I have made no mistake, your order list, monsieur? You have the list?"

"Sure."

Listening to the dialogue floating across the dividers, Brennan was suddenly curious. What intrigued him was the sound of the American customer, Joe Peet, a person for whom he himself had been mistaken. To Brennan's sensitive ear, Peet's accent did not suggest a collector of anything literary except possibly *True Detective* magazine or *Popular Mechanics* magazine.

Brennan edged toward the center of the room and peered around one of the dividers. He got a brief glimpse of the customer just before the proprietor moved closer to his visitor and blocked him from sight. In that moment Joe Peet had reached inside his striped sport jacket for a letter and had begun to unfold it. Peet's chestnut hair was plastered flat with some pomade. His thin sallow face, faintly pimpled, was ordinary and expressionless, like that of a thousand male carhops and gas-station attendants across the United States. He was short, perhaps no more than five feet five or six inches, but he was wiry. He had held the letter open before him, high, and it was then that the proprietor's body had inadvertently blocked him from Brennan's view.

Brennan pulled back behind the bookcase divider and listened to Peet's shrill voice as it read off his list of desired acquisitions.

"I have ordered the first editions, in a mint and if possible uncut condition, of three of Sir Richard F. Burton's published books, which are translations by Burton," Peet read aloud. "They are the following: *The Book of the Thousand Nights and a Night,* volume one, published in Benares, 1885; *Wit and Wisdom from West Africa,* published in London, 1865; *The Scented Garden,* the first printing of the revised edition, published pos—posthumously in London, 1890."

Listening, Brennan recognized each of the titles despite Peet's halting and uncertain reading, because they had been a part of Brennan's most exhaustive college term paper so long ago. Listening again, he could hear the proprietor speak.

"Excellent, exactly what you have ordered and paid for," M. Julien said enthusiastically. "I have the three books in the office, wrapped and prepared for you."

Suddenly the proprietor dashed between the dividers as Brennan turned back toward the shelves. Preoccupied with his task, M. Julien seemed to have forgotten the presence of another in the office. He stooped, dragged a heavy package from beneath his desk, and cradling it in his arms, he hurried back into the anteroom.

His professional proprietor's voice could be clearly heard. "Here you are, Monsieur Peet, here you are. *The Book of the Thousand Nights, Wit and Wisdom from West Africa, The Scented Garden.* All three first editions, uncut, pristine, as they were published. I hope you will find them satisfactory."

"I'm sure they're okay," said Peet. "Well, so long. Be seeing you."

"Thank you, Monsieur Peet. Good day, and thank you."

The bell over the door tinkled, but Brennan hardly heard it. A strange thought had crossed his mind, and his memory had gone back to that college term paper.

He looked up to find the proprietor, wide-eyed, staring up at him. "I had almost forgotten you were here, monsieur. Forgive me, please. So—*à votre service.* You were saying, before we were interrupted, you were saying you might be interested in some other items?"

"No, nothing else," Brennan replied abruptly. "I've been studying your shelves. There is nothing for me except what your other customer has already taken away. He's got all that would interest me."

"Ah, monsieur, it is a lesson, then—to have foresight, always to act in advance and decisively. That is of primary importance."

"I'm sure it is," said Brennan. "Well, anyway, thanks for your time. Good day."

The moment that he was outside, he looked up and down the Rue de Seine for another glimpse of Joe Peet. But Peet was not to be seen anywhere.

Slowly Brennan walked to the modest corner café, took a wicker chair at the rear, and absently ordered a *demi* of Evian water.

Alone at last, free from distraction, Matt Brennan reviewed the curious exchange between M. Julien and Joe Peet. As best he could reconstruct what he had overheard in the rare-book store, Peet had ordered three printed first editions by Sir Richard Burton. He had ordered and paid for *The Book of the Thousand Nights and a Night,* and he had received it. He had ordered and paid for *Wit and Wisdom from West Africa,* and he had received it. He had ordered and paid for *The Scented Garden,* and he had received it.

Immediately Brennan revived a paragraph in the second to last page of his college paper which had been devoted to Sir Richard Burton.

Five years before his death, Burton had begun a new translation of a manuscript of Arabian erotology that he expected would be his most successful and scandalous book. He had sent a brief extract to a friend, and had written this friend, "Enclosed will show you what my present work is. More than half already done. It will be a marvellous repertory of Eastern wisdom; how Eunuchs are made and are married; what they do in marriage; female circumcision, the Fellahs copulating with crocodiles, etc. Mrs. Grundy will howl till she almost bursts and will read every word with immense enjoyment."

Burton had completed the manuscript of this book in Trieste, and there, on October 20, 1890, he died. Shortly afterward, Burton's

366

prudish widow, Isabel, had received a vision of her husband in the night. She had consulted an Italian peasant priest about the vision. The priest had agreed that Isabel Burton must follow the dictates of this vision. So Isabel Burton rejected a publisher's offer of £6,000 for her husband's last book. And then, because she believed that the contents of that last manuscript were foul and would tarnish her husband's memory, and because the vision of him had commanded her to destroy it, Isabel Burton fed every single page of the only existing manuscript of that last book into the flames of a fire.

And thus, Brennan remembered, the single draft of Sir Richard Burton's last book vanished from the earth, never to be published, never to be read.

And this book, Brennan remembered, had been entitled *The Scented Garden.*

Yet minutes ago, in an obscure rare-book shop on the Left Bank of Paris, a bookshop patronized by a Russian Minister named Nikolai Rostov, who collected the works of Burton, an American stranger named Peet had requested of a French dealer named Julien three published books by Sir Richard Burton, and had received them and taken them away, and one of these had been *The Scented Garden.*

Incredible.

Someone had sold a book, and someone had bought a book, a book that did not exist anywhere on earth.

Why?

Brennan had no answer. But he felt surer of one thing—that perhaps this had not been a wild goose chase after all.

THE ENGRAVED INVITATIONS to the first night of the long-awaited Retrospective Exhibit celebrating Nardeau's sixtieth birthday, and showing forty years of his evolution, from impressionism to fauvism and then to a style of his own (if faintly reminiscent of Vuillard), had attracted a record and enthusiastic gathering of art critics and celebrities to the Nouvelle Galerie d'Art in the Avenue de Friedland.

The art editors of *La Croix* and *Paris Arts* and *Le Monde* and *Figaro Littéraire* and *Paris Match* and *Réalités* were present. Correspondents of the foreign press, representing newspapers and periodicals as diverse as *The New York Times* and *Der Spiegel* and the *Manchester Guardian* and the Montevideo *Marcha,* and even Igor Novik of *Pravda,* were present. And there were others, a Rothschild, a mayor of Nice or Marseille, a relative of Stavisky, a pretender to the throne of Romania just arrived from Lisbon, three ambassadors, eleven delegates playing truant from a night session at the Summit, numerous millionaire collectors, numerous dealers who had represented Braque, Chagall, Valtat, Picasso, Giacometti, and who were still wooing Nardeau—all of these were present. And Hazel Smith, of ANA, in her chic iridescent beaded cocktail dress and matching stole, was present.

Precariously, in the movement and crush of the guests occupying the oblong gallery, Hazel Smith clung to her long-stemmed glass of champagne, obtained from the sideboard set up behind the white pedestal holding Nardeau's bronze sculpture of a female torso.

She had been watching the wall clock above Michel's office window, and the constantly opening and closing front door. Her eye caught the clock again. It was exactly eight thirty-five, a moment when she was beginning to worry about keeping Jay Doyle waiting too long, a moment when she was beginning to wonder whether Carol's scheme had failed and whether they would appear at all, when she saw the door open and the three of them enter the Nouvelle Galerie d'Art.

Instantly relieved, immediately excited, Hazel Smith pushed through two groups of champagne-swilling guests to attain a point of vantage. She had planted herself six feet from *the* painting.

With glee Hazel studied Nardeau's *Nude in the Garden,* the challenging haughty adolescent face sensuously offering the naked body, small breasts rigid, one long leg brought up, the other flat, the cut of navel, the brazen vaginal mound, all vivid in oil. From this abandoned and canvas Fleur Grearson, Hazel's eyes traveled toward the gallery entrance. Rising on her toes, stretching, she was able to make out the mature and living Lady Ormsby, blondly cool and aristocratic, glittering in a diamond tiara and bare-shouldered white satin evening gown from which she had removed her white sable stole. The impending drama was too, too much, and Hazel could not repress a vicious grin of anticipation.

She could make out the gallery dealer, Michel Callet, welcoming Her Ladyship, Earnshaw, and Carol, and then finding them catalogues, before leading them to the first picture.

Calculating, Hazel decided it would be five minutes before they arrived in front of her to observe *Nude in the Garden.*

More at ease now, Hazel swallowed her champagne and waited for the victim to reach the trap. No longer was Hazel sorry that she had come to the exhibit. It had been a wearying afternoon, and near the end of it she had hoped to rest before the tension of her reunion with Jay Doyle. But Medora had telephoned to thank her for bringing Carol to her aid. With little encouragement, Medora had outlined what had occurred in Joseph's after the lunch and after Hazel had left them. Then she had outlined the scheme. When Medora had regretted that she could not personally be on hand to observe the drama unfold, Hazel had blurted out that she would represent Medora by proxy. Prodded by an old instinct to be where news was being made, even if it was news that could not be printed, Hazel had volunteered her attendance.

After making her promise, Hazel had felt conscience-stricken about treating Jay Doyle so rudely. He had been due to pick her up for dinner at eight. But now she had offered to be at the Nardeau Retrospective Exhibit at eight. She had considered taking Doyle with her to the showing before dinner, but had finally vetoed the notion. Their reunion deserved the absence of public distractions. Instead, she had telephoned the Hotel George-V to leave a message, but had found Doyle in his room. They had spoken briefly. She had explained that she had promised to attend the art exhibit in order to help a friend, and would tell Doyle about it later. The delay would be of brief duration. Could he make the dinner for nine?

After the call, she had been even sorrier about the interference of the exhibit. She had wanted to be with Doyle as soon as possible, to overcome the awkwardness of reunion after so many bitter years of separation, and to find out if there was a possible future for them, which she had seriously begun to doubt. But once inside the teeming Nouvelle Galerie d'Art, she had been caught up in suspense, and had forgotten Doyle until these reflective moments.

She glanced off again, and with a start she realized that the three of them, led by the springy, voluble French dealer, were almost upon her.

Lady Ormsby, regal, unmussed, above the crowd really, glided toward her, an open catalogue in her gloved hand. Accompanying her, but a step behind, was former President Earnshaw, appearing older, grayer, than at yesterday's impromptu press conference, and seeming strangely tormented. Hazel's reporter mind wondered why: Was he suffering some political slight from the incumbent President, or merely suffering from hurting corns? Then came Carol, solemn, plainly nervous about the success or failure of her stratagem. Hazel caught Carol's eye. Except for an acknowledging blink, there was no recognition.

They were passing between Hazel and *the* painting, and Fleur Ormsby, reading her catalogue, seemed not to see it. Suddenly Carol dashed forward between Fleur Ormsby and her uncle and gripped each by an arm, bringing them to an abrupt halt and forcing them to give attention to *Nude in the Garden*.

Pressing forward, Hazel could hear Carol's voice clearly above the noise in the room. "Oh, Fleur, wait—look at this one—how beautiful! Have you ever seen anything like it?"

As bystander, able to observe Lady Ormsby only in profile, Hazel waited breathlessly, automatically pushing closer for a better view.

Beneath her penciled, highly arched brows, Fleur Ormsby's eyes had narrowed. In silence she examined the oil.

"Nude in the Garden," announced Carol, reading from the printed placard beside the oil. "Nardeau did it ten years ago."

Earnshaw had directed himself to the object of his niece's ecstatic praise. He scowled. "What's so good about it? Some shameless girl with her clothes off. That's not art. That's just fancy—uh—pornography. I'm sure there are better things to look at."

"Oh, Uncle Emmett, really, there's so much more to it. You've got to understand Nardeau. I'm sure Fleur could tell you all it symbolizes." She had turned to Fleur Ormsby. "It's magnificent. Don't you agree?"

Behind them, Hazel continued to stare at Lady Ormsby's profile. It offered no sign of comprehension, no reaction, no comment. But Hazel could see the growing rigidity of muscles along her chin line.

"Rather interesting," conceded Fleur Ormsby, turning away, "although rather obvious, as your uncle suggests, Carol. It was not one of Nardeau's better periods. It was obviously transitional. Still, his craftsmanship is always evident." She looked indolently at Carol. "It's not really quite Nardeau at his best. The nuances are not so subtle as in his later period."

"Oh, I didn't mean the painting was that great," Carol said quickly. "I meant the model in the picture. I think she's the most attractive woman I've ever seen. You just know every man on earth would desire her, and she looks as if she wouldn't mind." Carol turned back to the painting. "Lucky girl. What I'd give to be so attractive."

Earnshaw frowned at his niece, but Fleur Ormsby was examining the nude once more.

"I see what you mean," Fleur Ormsby said almost to herself.

"In fact," said Carol, looking from Fleur to the painting and back to Fleur again, "you know what—I mean, if you don't mind, Fleur—there's a sort of resemblance between you and the girl in the painting. I mean, look—"

"Carol!" Earnshaw interrupted angrily. "What's got into you? You've got better manners—"

Fleur Ormsby's patronizing smile and gesture were airy. "I'm really flattered, Emmett. I'm sure Carol means well."

"I meant it as a compliment," Carol explained with urgency, "a big compliment, that's all, Fleur. I'm not talking about the nude body part, really I'm not. It's the face. It's exquisite, just like yours."

"Well, thank you, Carol."

"I'd like to see a picture of you when you were that age. I bet you looked almost the same."

Fleur Ormsby forced a laugh. "I was a ghastly fat Lilliputian." She nodded at the painting. "If I'd looked anything like that, I wouldn't have shed so many tears of self-pity in boarding school."

"I don't believe you," insisted Carol. "You're just being modest. I'm going to look up some pictures of you in magazines—"

Fleur Ormsby's features had tightened. "I wouldn't bother, Carol. Take my word, it would simply be a waste of time."

"Well," said Carol, staring longingly at the oil, "if I looked like that, I'd want to own the picture, just so I could remember when I was old and gray."

"How fanciful," said Fleur Ormsby with a short laugh, but to Hazel's ear she did not sound at all amused.

"If I had the money, I'd buy it for you as a present," Carol said, "I really would. I'd hate to have anyone else own my double and not— not appreciate it."

"Well, you are generous, Carol, but she's just not quite my double, you know," she said with a trace of peevishness.

"I'd still hate to have anyone *else* own it."

Fleur Ormsby's gaze had gone from Carol back to the painting once more. She considered it in silence. "Yes, it has a rather blatant charm," she said at last. "It *is* a Nardeau, and it might enliven some dark corner of our country house. Nothing Austin would want the P.M. to see, I'm certain, but at any rate, it's surely not for sale."

Carol was pointing to the placard. "It's 'On loan. Donor anonymous.' What does that mean?"

Fleur Ormsby continued staring at the painting. "I really can't say."

"Let's move on," Earnshaw grumbled. "Half the press is coming this way."

"Are they?" said Fleur Ormsby, looking around nervously, then back at the painting. "Yes, we'd better push along."

As they resumed their round of the exhibit, Hazel could see that where Earnshaw had become more impatient, Lady Ormsby had become completely lost in thought. With surprise Hazel realized that Carol, who had hung behind, had drifted close to her. "What do you think?" Carol whispered. "I did my best, but I don't know."

"I don't know either," said Hazel.

"She's veddy, veddy cool," said Carol. "Maybe she didn't even recognize herself."

"I have a hunch she did."

"Oh, I hope so. We'll see. You going to be here a little longer?"

"Well, I've—"

Carol looked off, then said quickly, "Fingers crossed."

"Good luck," said Hazel, but Carol was already gone.

The end of the scene had been disappointing, flat and inconclusive as the champagne she was finishing, Hazel decided. Yet she was certain that Fleur Ormsby had recognized Fleur Grearson.

Making her way past the Nardeau sculpture, past two Riviera landscapes, Hazel meant to return her empty glass to the sideboard and leave. But the thought of Jay Doyle waiting for her made her edgy, and she held out the glass to the waiter for one last pouring of the yellow, sparkling champagne. Drinking it too quickly, she searched the far end of the gallery for another glimpse of the drama's cast of characters. She finally saw them, Fleur Ormsby addressing herself to the gallery owner, Michel, with Carol nearby, attentive to them, while Earnshaw stood somewhat apart, tearing at the wrapping on a cigar.

The refilled champagne glass was empty, and Hazel felt better, if not about Medora's future, then at least over her own prospect of a conceivably nice and nostalgic evening with Doyle. Firmly putting aside the glass, she opened the compact from her evening bag, glanced at her makeup, and started for the door. She had got no more than halfway when she heard Carol call, in a whisper filled with repressed excitement, "Miss Smith—Hazel—I'm right behind you, but make like I'm not."

The child is a lover of games, Hazel thought, but all right, she would play. "Okay, Carol."

As they progressed single file through the crowd, Carol said, "It's utterly fantastic. You won't believe it. Listen. When we got to the other end, Fleur kept looking around for the guy who runs the gallery—you know—"

"Michel."

"Right. She finally brought him over. Then—"

They had reached the door, and Hazel halted, and came around to face Carol and hear the rest.

"Can you see them over my shoulder?" Carol asked anxiously.

Hazel peered off. "No."

"They think I went to the powder room. . . . Oh, this'll kill you, Hazel, but literally. Fleur got hold of this Michel, the proprietor, and she wanted to know if any of Nardeau's paintings were for sale. Michel told her none were officially, but he had reason to believe some were unofficially. Of course, he said, he had no prices, and wasn't acting as agent for any of the owners who had been generous enough to loan their stuff for the exhibit. But if Her Ladyship was interested in inquiring about the availability of any specific painting, he would be only too pleased to give her the name and telephone number of the owner. He went on to say she'd have to negotiate and transact any business on her own. And, hear this, Hazel. Fleur said, 'Well, there are several oils about which I should like to inquire. May I have the names of the owners?' And he said, 'Do you have the names of the paintings?' And Fleur said, 'Yes, I believe I've jotted them down somewhere,' and then she said, 'May we go to your office? Dreadfully noisy here.' And she excused herself to us, and off she trotted with him." Carol patted herself on the chest proudly. "I bet it's working. I bet this minute she's asking who owns *Nude in the Garden.*"

"If she is, it's a helluva story," said Hazel, "and I wish I could write it. Especially if your plan does work out."

Carol's face fell. "You mean—you think there's some doubt?"

"If you were dealing with anyone else, some coming-apart wife who's quick to get the vapors, I'd say you're in. But as you said, our Fleur is a cool customer. She doesn't panic easily. She's on top of everything."

"But she's got to think of her position, and there's that shocking nude out in the open. What if someone recognized her as the one in her birthday suit? She's got to worry about that."

"She doesn't have to worry about anything, Carol. But she might. In fact, she should and probably will."

"Well, after we get back and Uncle's safe in bed, and after Medora is finished with her show, I'm going to call her and try to see her. And I'm going to tell her exactly what I'm telling you right now."

Hazel smiled at the young girl's eagerness to make Wish into Fact. "What are you telling me right now, Carol?"

"That one'll get you ten that Medora Hart receives a phone call from Lady Fleur Ormsby tomorrow morning. Want to bet?"

"Honey, I won't bet on anyone I'm for," said Hazel, "because I'm a born jinx. If I bet on Medora's chances, it's a cinch that her phone will be out of order tomorrow morning. So I'll stay out of it. But, Carol, you go to Notre-Dame Cathedral and light a candle for Medora Hart tonight. Because she'll need everything possible going for her, *everything,* believe me."

Nᴏᴛ ᴏɴᴄᴇ but several times during the two and a half hours that they had been sitting at the corner table of La Tour d'Argent's sixth-floor penthouse dining room had Hazel Smith remembered her parting advice to Carol Earnshaw and wished that someone had been kind enough to light a candle for her. Because she now felt, watching the second of Jay Doyle's empty main-course dishes being removed, that she needed everything going for her, too.

Thus far, it had been, at least for her, and perhaps for reasons subtle and highly personal, an absolutely excruciating evening.

During the first moments following her tardy arrival on the sixth floor, after emerging from the small elevator, she had thought it would all work out very well. Her companion, and the background of their meeting, had made the reunion a promising one. Jay Doyle, despite two unaccustomed drinks of whisky and his considerable bulk, had been spruce-looking, freshly cologned, neatly dressed, friendly, even sweet, if a trifle too eager. The setting that he had chosen was perfect, the lovely room of one of the oldest restaurants in Paris. In this restaurant, in other times, a clientele that included Cardinal Richelieu, Alexandre Dumas, Napoleon III, Edward VII, Sarah Bernhardt, had been surrounded by the same Gobelin hangings and Aubusson rugs that surrounded her, and had enjoyed the same ambience that she and Doyle were enjoying.

They had been placed at the table where the two large picture windows met, and this, if nothing else, should have been enough to make their evening a success. Always before, when she had dined at La Tour d'Argent, Hazel had been mellowed into romanticism by the illuminated Gothic towers of Notre-Dame visible outside, by the beautiful night silhouettes of the Panthéon's dome, the Sacré-Coeur's cupolas, the Place de la Bastille's golden statue of the God of Liberty, as some of these shadowy outlines were swept by light from the circling beacon on the Eiffel Tower.

Yet tonight, for the first time, once seated and engaged in conversation with Jay Doyle, she had not attempted to enjoy what was beyond the windows; she had become entirely oblivious to the charm of the dining room because she had been forced to revise her first hopeful impression of the mighty person she had once loved so truly and had later hated so persistently in her bittersweet love-hate fantasies.

What had made the evening excruciating for her, after the strain and testing of their small talk, had been the spectacle of Jay Thomas Doyle, Fallen.

Over the years, she had heard all the latest rumors about him from the visiting press in Moscow and from other correspondents met in her travels, but she had never quite believed what she had heard. Competitors in the fraternity of the fourth estate were as merciless in their rending of one another as competitors in any other fraternity on earth, be it one of entertainers or politicians or housewives. Her only sure picture of Doyle had been her memory of a powerful figure, invincible, kingly, self-sufficient, and not even his begging letters in recent years (clever, crafty Trojan horses, she had surmised) had altered her old image of him.

Tonight had been a shock.

In their first minutes the man across from her, despite his unnatural bloat (which, like the Germans, she equated with good living and continuing success), had seemed a fair representation of the one she had known as dominant, authoritative, superior, and therefore the same one she had once invested with her love. But as the evening had worn on, a transformation had taken place before her eyes. She had come to see that this was not the Doyle she remembered. This man did not match the memory she had so masochistically clung to, but was only a reasonable physical facsimile. The character of the inner man had been replaced by that of another, one who was a stranger to her, a usurper who was anything but kingly, or kingly only if one regarded the drooling, sniveling buffoon, Emperor Claudius, as Caesar. For the Doyle revealed was obsequious, uncertain, unsuccessful (without so much as the grace or strength of pretending). With silent grief she had conceded to the veracity of the press rumors, to the obvious meaning of those begging letters, to the simple truth that, divested of his syndicated column and his reading public, Doyle was as helpless, as ineffectual, as pitiful, as Samson shorn of his locks.

Loneliness had brought Hazel to this reunion. Rashly, defying all reason, she had wanted to regain the past, or the best of it, but she had learned to her dismay that the past was inevitably gone and there was only the unpromising present.

There was Doyle, across from her, lumpy and sodden from his gorging, asthmatically wheezing at the open menu, fat-larded eyes still glittering over La Tour d'Argent's delights.

"Now for the dessert," he said.

"I'll skip it," she said angrily.

He peered over the menu. "Skip it? Aw, come on, Hazel. Have something."

"I said no."

"Oh, you must. Crêpes Suzette? Or at least petits fours?"

"No. That's spelled n-o-t-h-i-n-g."

"Well, all right. You don't mind if I have a nibble." He offered a boyish smile. "Chronic sweet tooth, you know. Needs a filling." He looked up at the waiter. "Well, let's make it a soufflé Valtesse for one. And you might as well bring a plate of petits fours. And, oh yes, first a refill on the bread and rolls, and some more butter."

Watching him now, listening to him now, Hazel was more sad than angry. The menu had been another of the earlier deceptions. Two hours ago when he had first taken it in hand, he had discoursed on the red legend imprinted upon it—*"La grande cuisine demande beaucoup de temps"*—and heeding its advice, he had taken considerable time to discuss the cuisine with her. When he ordered dinner, he had been alive, certain, assured, turning aside suggestions that they must have caneton Tour d'Argent—two of the numbered pressed roast ducks—to insist, instead, on poularde en papillote.

As Doyle went on, Hazel's hopes had soared, but then, as he went on and on and on, her hopes had been dampened. To order the chicken baked with white wine sauce, in paper, for both of them, had been one thing. But to order yet another main course for himself—actually two more, filets of sole with aurora sauce, then a sirloin steak with port wine sauce, and potatoes—all that besides the chicken ("You know chicken, Hazel," he had said. "It leaves you, like Chinese food, hungry")—had been a major disenchantment for Hazel. For the authority he had exerted in ordering dinner had not been authority at all, only insatiable gluttony. After this she had seen him clearly for what he was: not a man, as he had once been a man (in his fashion), but a sickeningly compulsive, helplessly weak, voraciously stuffing male mammal of the family Mustelidae.

Throughout most of the dinner she had driven herself to dominate the conversation. There had been reasons for this. Before the meal he had done most of the talking, and it had not pleased her, for his accounting of his recent years had been too self-denigrating, his pride in her achievements had been too servile. Among all the characters in literature that she remembered, she had detested Uriah Heep, with his cringing humility, the most. So she had forced herself to speak, to drown him out. During the dinner itself his mouth had always been full, and so she had continued to talk, if only to overcome the sounds of his constant chomping. Finally, with the meal almost finished, she had not ceased her chatter because she had feared testing him.

She had invented the testing of Doyle, in her head, before their evening. She had told herself that Doyle had rudely discarded her in New York, rudely rejected her and insulted her in Vienna long ago. Only after Kennedy's assassination had Doyle tried to resume their relationship through long-distance calls and voluminous letters. She had hoped against hope that he had grown up and had had second thoughts about her, that he had come to need her as a woman. Yet she had suspected—actually had *known,* but anything that was known was too final—he had tried to reach her again only because she might have the solution to his lousy book. But, at least, in those days and months before, she had never been absolutely sure of his motive. When readying herself to meet him again in person, she knew she would now learn the truth of his feelings, and the decisiveness of the confrontation had frightened her.

Yet, she had told herself, she must know the truth. And so she had invented her test. She would let him talk. She would listen. If he made no mention of his damn book or of the conspiracy information he had wanted from her for the book, if he confined his talk to the two of them and other matters, he would pass with flying colors. She would see him again. She might even trust him soon. There would be solid hope. But if he started in on her about the book, or made any direct references to the fact that she could save the book, he would fail the test, fail abysmally for trying to use and exploit her. Then she would never see him again. Yet she had not possessed the courage to learn, once and for all, whether he would pass or fail. And so for this reason she would not let him speak. Instead, she had entered into a lone verbal marathon, a kind of lonelyhearts filibuster, and only now, with the arrival of his desserts, was she giving up the floor.

Sorrowfully she watched him liquidating his soufflé. There was no point in postponing the test further. She took a cigarette, lit it, and fell silent. It was his turn now.

He finished the soufflé with satisfaction, then seemed to become aware that he was not alone. "Well, now—well—" He wiped his mouth with the napkin, and reached for the plate of petits fours. "Well, it's certainly wonderful, all those people you've been interviewing, and the ones you've got lined up. That's great for a change of pace."

"Change of pace?"

"Well, seeing a variety of people like that fashion designer or old man Earnshaw's niece or the stripper over at the Club Lautrec. Something different, after years of nothing but Russians and more Russians."

"I see. Yes, it's a welcome change."

"Although your Russian stuff is awfully good, Hazel." He was chewing two petits fours. "Sa-ay, that reminds me. I was poking through the ANA files up in the bureau this afternoon. Had to get up some background material for my Earnshaw stint." He grabbed for the wine, to hold down a belch, then, breathing heavily, he resumed. "Anyway, I came across some unsigned background material someone just got up on each member of the delegation. Was that yours, Hazel?"

"Yes, what there was of it. I didn't have much time. But the chief wanted something on file about each delegate."

"Well, thanks from Matt Brennan."

"What?"

"You remember Matt Brennan. He—"

"Of course, I do. I ran into that snooty bastard yesterday."

"He's not snooty, Hazel. He's shy, and besides, he's taken an awful beating. Anyway, Brennan's a friend of mine from way back. He's here to try to contact someone in the Russian delegation who can clear him. Brennan's always insisted that he was innocent. I believe he was. Anyway, there was only one man who could prove it. A Russian delegate that Brennan had worked with at Zurich before Varney defected."

"Yes?"

"Well, I found the Russian delegate's file—his name is Rostov—and your notes on him, and I gave a copy to Brennan. He helped me once, and I owed him a favor. Hope you don't mind."

She continued to look at Doyle. "Why should I mind? Though I can't imagine why on earth that Brennan of yours would want those notes."

Doyle's eyes rolled glassily, and he lost to the belch after all. "Sorry." Absently he began to open his belt buckle. "Brennan and those notes? Well, he's been trying to meet up with this Rostov, and he's failed. So he wanted information on Rostov's habits, hoping maybe that would suggest a way to run into him. I think there was something about that Russian collecting rare books, and maybe buying some while in Paris, and Brennan was trying to find the store."

"Absolute juvenile idiocy," said Hazel with more sharpness than she had intended. "What I can't understand, Jay, is how you let yourself get mixed up with such losers. It just looks bad. Earnshaw, fine. I can understand that. Your working for him, I mean, although that must be like working in a molasses factory. But Brennan? That mush-headed pinko. Even as a traitor he was second-rate. No guttiness like the Rosenbergs' or dignity like Hiss's."

Doyle washed the last of the petits fours down with wine. "I don't think Hiss was a traitor. And I don't think Brennan was, either.

Unfortunately, those two can't prove their innocence, and neither can I prove it for them." He shook his head. "There's too much injustice in the world because of emotions, circumstantial evidence, the need for victims so everything will be tidy. It's like Lee Harvey Os——"

Hazel saw him make the effort to hold his tongue. He had bitten off the surname so as not to speak it. Hazel sat, heart thumping, because the truth was near, just as Vienna was near, and the conspiracy clue she had given him there was near, and the subject of her help on his damn book was near.

The test. She waited to grade him F for Failure.

He sat brooding, a Buddha who had overeaten at dinner, trying to sort wisdom out of the calories.

"What the hell," he said suddenly. "Who wants to talk about victims on a nice night like this?"

Hazel almost whistled her relief. Still, it had been close, and she was not yet satisfied. She brought forth the test again, aggressively.

"You still haven't told me why you're in Paris, Jay. Surely not just to work for Earnshaw?"

"No."

"Why, then?"

He hesitated, then he said, "Okay. You want to know? All right. I'm writing a book. Maybe I can wind it up here."

Damn the test. "A book?" she echoed hollowly.

"Yup. It embarrasses me to bring it up in front of you, but we know too much about each other to start hiding things now." He paused. "It's a cookbook, a gourmet's cookbook."

Hazel's elbows almost slipped off the table in the sudden grateful release of her tension. "A cookbook!" she exclaimed out of hysterical relief. "Why, that's nothing to be ashamed of, Jay. I think it's wonderful. I can't wait to see it."

"Well, it's not really what I'm interested in doing," he said unhappily, drawing the refilled basket of bread and rolls toward him. "I'd still like to have the old column back. Politics and action. That's the game." He began to slap and smear butter on the crusty French bread. "Then—well—there's another reason I came to Paris, Hazel. As I told you at the café, I read you were here, in a place where I could see you easily, and so I came here to see you. I've missed you and I—I wanted to see you."

"Don't give me that. Save it for your other girls."

He waited to swallow the bread before protesting. "There are no other girls, Hazel. I've had that. Maybe it was good I had it, because it made me realize what a horse's ass I was, letting you slip through my fingers. Je-sus, I was a horse's ass. I don't blame you if you never forgive me. But you know, it takes some people longer to grow up than others. It does, Hazel. And now I think I've about grown up." He shoved another half roll into his mouth. "I wish we could have those good times over again."

He had passed, he had passed the test, and she glowed.

"Jay—"

About to shove the other half of the roll into his open mouth, he waited.

"Stop eating, will you?"

He lowered his chubby hand to the table and released the half roll. "I'm sorry, Hazel."

"I appreciate everything you've been saying. I'd like to talk about those good old times again, too. Let's get out of here."

"Whatever you say."

"Let's get some fresh air. It's late and I've got an early interview in the morning. But—if you like—you can come up to the apartment for one nightcap—maybe a little talk—one part reminiscing, two parts nostalgia—then I'd better get to bed. How's that?"

"Great."

"Where's the little girls' room? You pay up and I'll be ready in a jiffy."

Fifteen minutes later, when they had emerged onto the Quai de la Tournelle, Hazel thought of suggesting a walk along the Seine in the cool night. But the three main courses, on top of countless other courses, appeared to have immobilized Doyle. He stood with his legs wide apart, trying to support his massive belly, while gasping for air like a vanquished Sumo wrestler.

Hazel forgot about the walk along the Seine and summoned her rented Volkswagen. She allowed Doyle to help her in behind the wheel, and she suffered seeing him double over and try to fold and squeeze himself into the seat beside her in the miniature car. Worrying that it would require a derrick to get him out again, she drove the Volkswagen across the bridge and toward the Boulevard Haussmann.

Presently they were parked in the Rue de Téhéran, and Hazel waited in suspense for Doyle to extricate himself from his seat. After he had succeeded, he waddled around the automobile, made a gallant effort to help her out, and this done, he groggily accompanied her into the building and up to the apartment.

In the sitting room, Hazel insisted that he remove his suit coat and loosen his collar, and when he had done so, she steered him away from the fragile divan to the softer, deeper sofa across from it. After he had settled back among the pillows, muttering his thanks, she busied herself around the room, turning down all the light except that from the astral lamps, then turning on the shortwave radio to a music station, although leaving the volume low. At last she went into the kitchen to mix the drinks, and to find some cocktail tidbits.

He was watching her every move as she re-entered the sitting room with her tray. He was breathing heavily, she could hear, as she placed the tray on the low shallow table. She wondered whether his breathing was passion—or overeating.

She gave him his highball, took her own, and curled up on the sofa beside him.

"To the good days past," she said, toasting.

He touched his glass to hers, too hard, so that some of her vodka spilled. "To the good days present," he said hoarsely.

They drank in silence. She determined to be forthright. "Jay, did you really mean what you said before?"

"What I said?"

"About missing me?"

"Every word of it," he said thickly. "Every word. No night since, all the years since, no night I haven't thought about you, kind of remembered something, like the first time we met, and the first time we—"

"Jay," she said softly, "tell me about it."

From the recess of the sofa, from behind the multiplicity of chins resting on his chest, he recollected vignettes of their old affair: a night, a morning, a walk, a ride, a kitchenette, a supper club, a rondelet, a dance, a frankfurter, a steak, a soft drink, a hard drink, a tear, a fight, a kiss, a floor, a bed. His speech was cottony, his words slurring, but for Hazel, close to him, they were as the music of a bard.

"You were the only one I ever loved," he murmured, "only I didn't know it until now."

"You know it now?"

"Hazel," he pleaded, "I want to see you again and again."

Impulsively she leaned across him and touched his lips with her own. "You will," she said, and she drew away, her mind made up. "Let me get into something comfortable. I'll be right back, darling. Don't you move."

Aroused, she hastened up the circular staircase to her bedroom. Even as she entered it, she was unfastening her beaded dress, freeing herself from it. Quickly she disrobed, perfumed herself, combed out her red hair, and pulled on her sheerest, shortest pink nightgown. Then, wearing her matching negligee, loosely belted, she started out of the bedroom.

She had once been a young fool. She would now be an old fool. But at least she would be something.

Slowly and seductively, she descended the stairs. Slowly and seductively, she crossed the room toward the sofa.

"Jay, darling," she whispered out of the shadows.

There was no reply. The vast lump did not stir.

Perplexed, she was approaching him, advancing closer and closer, when suddenly, like the bursting rattle of machine-gun fire, Doyle's snoring shattered the stillness of the room. Frightened, Hazel recoiled. At last, steadying herself, she returned to examine the heap on the sofa. His head was slumped to one side, his eyes shut tight in sleep, his nose snorting as he inhaled, his mouth wheezing as he exhaled.

Incredulously she took in the coffee table at his knees. The two highball glasses had been emptied of drink. The two dishes had been emptied of peanuts and cheese tidbits. Not a drop, not a crumb, remained. All that was left was the ruin on the sofa.

She stood over him, not knowing for how long, not knowing whether to laugh or to cry.

How could she possibly fall in love again with *this?* But then, it was not love that finally moved her. It was pity. He needed someone, he needed someone desperately. It was pity, and it was deeper and more binding than love.

Efficiently, but gently, she removed his necktie, opened another button of his shirt, undid his belt, and worked off his shoes. Carefully, she buttressed him about and behind with the soft throw pillows. She dragged an ottoman across the room and propped his feet upon it. After that, she located a blanket in the maid's room, and she covered him with it. Then she wrote the note and placed it on the coffee table. She wound the clock, set the alarm, and placed the clock upon the note on the coffee table.

She looked at him once more—fat baby, poor darling—then she kissed his forehead lightly, and then she went upstairs to bed.

Sleep was not easy.

She lay in bed, and her mind was full.

This reunion was dangerous, she knew, extremely dangerous. She could destroy what little there was to her life by having Doyle here this night. She could destroy everything, everything that was sure and certain, should the key unexpectedly turn in the lock of the front door.

It was madness, this risk; still, she was chancing it, so maybe it was worth it, this risk. For if Doyle really needed her for herself, and not as a means of leading him to the finger that had pulled the trigger in the

Texas School Book Depository, then the gamble was worthwhile. If he honestly loved her, she would undertake greater risks than this one to see him, to be with him, to be absolutely certain of their future.

Perhaps, she reflected, the Summit would be a turning point in her own private world, which could become a world of wondrous peace or, conversely, one of total devastation.

She and Doyle required time. There might be time, if there was not first the key in the lock of her door.

She shuddered, and she drew her blanket higher, and finally she was calm. Everyone, she told herself, must live with risk. As she had written in a story this afternoon, quoting Napoleon's Minister of Police: "The air is full of poniards."

Hazel turned in bed, burying her head in the pillow, deep, deep into the pillow, hiding from poniards, and hoping for the best in this best of all possible worlds.

IV

T HE SHRILL scream of air-raid and missile warnings had been part
of his life for so long that his reflexes were attuned to immediate response.

The instant that the shrieking alert drilled into his subconscious, Jay
Thomas Doyle awakened, eyes opened wide in terror, confused only as
to whether he was in Seoul, Saigon, Calcutta, Damascus, or Leopold-
ville, and frantic to remember where the shelter was located.

With astonishment, he slowly became aware of the exquisite sitting
room around him, the gold silk wallpaper, the curio cabinets filled with
glassware and ivory, the fancy furniture, and gradually he realized that
he was nested in a quilted couch, legs stretched upon a footstool, and
that he was attired in a wrinkled suit and not in fatigues, and that the
persisting alarm was being issued by a ridiculous clock on a coffee
table at his feet.

Even as he sat up to muffle the clock, he recollected where he was
and who had brought him here. Groping forward, he knocked over the
clock and pressed down the alarm button, and suddenly the apartment
room was still.

Casting the blanket aside, he slipped down to the ottoman and sat
on it, wide-awake but dazed. Running his fingers through his sparse
hair, he tried to recall what had happened the night before. Hazel.
Tour d'Argent. Swilling food like a hog. Her Volkswagen. This apartment. Her softness, her forgiveness, her kiss. Her whisper, "Let me get
into something comfortable. I'll be right back, darling. Don't you
move." The drinks. The bowls of nibbles. The lying back, so weary, so
optimistic. The wondering what she would change into, and what it
would mean, and if it could really mean a resumption of the past. The
expectant waiting for her. The nothingness.

He could recall no more, nor did he wish to imagine what she had found when she returned to him. Hot shame suffused him. A repulsive glutton, surfeited by food, he had gone to sleep on her. To a woman, the ultimate insult.

His gaze fell on the clock, flat on its face. The alarm. He wondered why she had set it. Perhaps she was upstairs, expecting to be awakened by him. But no, she had mentioned something about an early interview. He picked up the clock and turned it over. It was nine forty-two. Too late for Hazel. She would be gone.

About to set the clock back on the table, Doyle noticed for the first time the sheet of paper with its large scrawled salutation, "Good morning, Jay!" He snatched up the note and hastily read it:

Hope you slept well. I'm setting the alarm because I have to be out by 8, and so won't be able to wake you later. Jay, try to leave by 10, since I may be returning with guests and your presence would be hard to explain. Thanks for dinner. Let me treat next time.

Always,
Hazel

P.S.   Tear up this note and flush it.
P.P.S.   Put blanket out of sight.

He reread the note, and reread it, as if it were a reprieve. His despair had dissipated. Despite a sour dryness in his mouth, a stiff neck, an itchiness from having slept in his clothes, he felt renewed and invigorated. She would see him again. She was a dream. Good, good Hazel. The day would be beautiful. He would phone and tell her so. He would phone her the minute that he had left her apartment, and apologize, and insist upon seeing her this evening.

Staggering to his feet—God, he must have put on at least another three pounds last night—well, no more of that from now on, he pledged himself—he decided to comply first with Hazel's instructions. He tore up her note and stuffed the scraps in his shirt pocket. He folded the blanket, sought a closet, and laid it on the upper shelf. Returning to the sofa, he pounded and kneaded it back into shape, puffed up the throw pillows and arranged them neatly.

Putting on his shoes, he inspected the coffee table. It had been cleaned. Taking his tie and the clock, he found the downstairs bathroom, quickly flushed away the shreds of Hazel's note, combed his hair, knotted his tie, and did what he could to smooth out his rumpled suit. There was one act that remained to be performed, and it was the most distasteful one of all. He opened his pillbox, constructed from two tarnished United States silver dollars, and he found the yellow tablet. With the enthusiasm of a house guest accepting a drink from Lucrezia Borgia, he washed the diet pill down his gullet. A fat man, a Welsh friend had once told him, has a thin soul. Well, Hazel deserved better of him, at least a thinner man with a fatter soul.

At exactly four minutes before ten o'clock, pleased to have conformed to Hazel's deadline, Jay Thomas Doyle left the apartment, confident but not positive that he would see it again.

Coming out into the morning brightness of the Rue de Téhéran, intent on telephoning Hazel at the ANA bureau, he saw a neighborhood café about thirty yards off, just before the corner of the Boulevard Haussmann. As he approached the café, it occurred to him that any call to Hazel would be useless. She would not be in the office. She would either be out somewhere on a story or be on her way back to the apartment. In her note she had stated that she would be returning "with guests" sometime after ten. The next step, then, was clear. He would sit at a table inside the café, next to the glass window, and from there have a perfect view of Hazel's entrance. After she went upstairs with her guests, he would telephone her briefly to apologize and make a date and a new beginning. Yes, this made sense and the café made sense because, as yet, the diet pill had not taken effect and he was famished without his breakfast.

Luckily, there was an empty table in the row of tables flush against the glass siding that extended onto the sidewalk. It furnished him with an unobstructed sight of the entrance to Hazel's building, and, at the same time, it kept him partially concealed. After snapping his fingers for the waiter, he tried to confine his breakfast order to a cup of tea, but his quarrelsome stomach (not yet quieted by the tardy pill) demanded more, and so he ordered one croissant, then made it two, then added a request for bacon and eggs (since a hearty breakfast would, after all, enable him to skip lunch).

For a while, marking time until the *déjeuner à la fourchette* arrived, he kept glancing through the window for a glimpse of Hazel and her guests. By ten-fifteen she had not appeared, nor had his morning meal, and so he began to reflect on his opening performance at dinner last night.

He had done rather well, he thought, considering how many opportunities there had been to bring up the subject of *The Conspirators Who Killed Kennedy*. Several times he had almost succumbed to the temptation to discuss the book, but each time some intuitive signal had prevented him from plunging. Now hindsight told him that his strategy had been right. Hazel was no longer the unsophisticated, pliable cub of years ago. She was hardened, experienced, and suspicious of all men, especially of him since receiving his countless letters. Surely she must have wondered whether he was pursuing her with an ulterior motive. If he had evinced such a motive at the outset, Doyle guessed, her feminine pride would have been affronted, and she would have stormed out and avoided him thereafter. But instead, cleverly drawing upon his knowledge of the opposite sex in general, and of Hazel in particular, he had treated her as an object of love rather than as a source of information. By so behaving, he had succeeded in denting her defenses. Once her defenses had been entirely brought down, he would not have to petition for her help. She would eagerly volunteer it.

With self-congratulations, Doyle gave himself to the bacon and eggs and heated croissants that had been set before him. He had consumed no more than half his bacon and eggs, and but a single croissant, when he heard the humming charge of an automobile speeding into the Rue de Téhéran.

Immediately his head swiveled. Through the café's window he could see a medium-sized black sedan with a shining silver radiator grille slide up before Hazel's apartment building and jar to a halt. His fork poised in midair, Doyle kept his attention riveted upon the car.

On the driver's side the door had opened, and a stocky man in a dark fedora and dark topcoat had begun to emerge. Almost simultaneously the opposite door had opened, and a woman was stepping out. Doyle's attention swung from the male driver to the female passenger, and then held on her, for the female passenger was Hazel Smith.

She stood on the sidewalk, waiting for her companion, and what was unusual was her behavior. She was clutching her purse nervously, searching the street, looking furtive and worried, as if afraid to be seen. The stocky man with the springy step had come up beside her, his back to Doyle, momentarily obscuring her from view. The two exchanged words, and then he took her arm intimately and walked her the few strides to the building entrance. He stopped, she stopped. He dropped his hand from her arm to her hand, and held her hand as he said something. She nodded. Suddenly he kissed her quickly, very quickly, and she smiled and disappeared into the building.

Doyle's eyes went wide and his jaws clenched on his croissant, as he waited for the man to turn around.

The man turned around. His brow, narrowed by the hat, his broad countenance, his square jaw, made him appear forbidding. Hands thrust into his topcoat pockets, he looked down the street in the direction of the café, pivoted casually on a heel to look behind him, and jauntily started back around the car to the driver's seat. Opening the door slowly, he paused and threw his head back to squint up toward the sun. The pose was that of a peasant in the field before harvesting, a peasant enjoying his acres of sky above. His face was plainly visible now, and the moment before he ducked in behind the wheel, Doyle was convinced that he had seen that face before.

The black sedan had started, jumped forward, made a sudden reckless U-turn, and was gone.

The instant that the car was out of sight, the identity of the driver hit Doyle. The belated realization of who the man was struck him with redoubled force. He sat stunned, trying to overcome disbelief. Dropping his croissant to the plate, he twisted in his chair and stared back at the spot where, seconds before, Nikolai Rostov had stood.

Nikolai Rostov.

There was no mistaking it. Doyle had seen the Russian Minister's grim kulak features in the newspapers. He had seen the face more than once yesterday, while examining the clippings on Rostov in the ANA files, when he had sought information for Matt Brennan. There could be absolutely no doubt about it. He had seen Nikolai Rostov. And then, in the afterwave of shock, he pinpointed precisely what had shocked him. It was not seeing Nikolai Rostov. It was seeing the unexpected pairing. It was seeing Nikolai Rostov *and* Hazel Smith together.

Doyle's mind reeled backward, ransacking through the past, stumbled forward into the present, ranged ahead, and suddenly he had no interest in any food except for thought.

Hazel and Rostov.

But of course. Initial surprise was now modified by the logic of it. Hazel and Rostov. But naturally. How obvious this discovery made the events of the past, and how clear it made the present. Instantly, he saw the enormity and value of his discovery. At last he had found the one who could supply the missing piece to the puzzle in his book. He need only reach the one, the one through the other, to obtain the missing piece, complete the puzzle of the Kennedy assassination, and his great work would be done and his comeback assured.

He felt supreme, like a puppeteer controlling the strings. He knew everything about his marionettes now. There had been Hazel, in Vienna, so many years ago, speaking of her new friend, her "gentleman friend," a Soviet diplomat, a "lesser" Soviet delegate assigned to assist Premier Khrushchev's press secretary. This Russian friend had dated Hazel, danced with her, drunk with her, and babbled to her of being carefully approached by a former classmate, on the staff of a Russian newspaper, about joining with "a group of unnamed international Communist officials" who believed that "Kennedy must be

388

liquidated." When Hazel had come to Doyle with her "scoop," she had adamantly refused to disclose the name of her new Russian friend and informant. Doyle had ridiculed her at the time, and not until Dallas had he believed her Russian friend even existed. The assassination had convinced Doyle that Hazel's Russian friend had been very real indeed. And this morning, in Paris, Doyle finally knew who this Russian friend had been all along.

His mind raced past Vienna. Hazel had moved on to Moscow, been stationed in Moscow, off and on, for years, and she had made her reputation with "inside" stories no other foreign correspondents were able to obtain. How had this been possible? Well, anything was possible for a round-heeled American girl who had a Russian diplomat for her lover. That bitch in heat, Doyle thought, thinking of her. That dirty bastard, Doyle thought, thinking of him. But determined not to be sidetracked by personal emotions, Doyle relentlessly turned his mind again to its tracking of the pair.

Rostov had been riding high until the Zurich Parley. That conference had been a debacle for him, as it had been for Doyle's friend, Matthew Brennan. After Zurich, Rostov had disappeared from the Moscow scene, presumably sent off to Siberia, and Hazel—Doyle tried to recollect the period—had also left Moscow around that time to become ANA's correspondent in Budapest and Prague, as well as various cities of the Middle East. How coincidental, if his memory was exact. How very coincidental. And then—oh, he was almost sure of this—Hazel had suddenly been reassigned to Moscow last year, probably at her own request, probably because Rostov had been returned to the good graces of the Government in Moscow. The lovers reunited once more. The American trollop and her Russian friend. How nice. And now, just now, minutes ago, Hazel and her Rostov again, conveniently together in Paris, conveniently in front of her borrowed apartment. How very nice.

Once more Doyle tried to repress personal emotion, which could only lead to anger and would get him nowhere. In a world of untrustworthy, two-timing bitches, a man must look out for himself, just as Hazel had looked out for herself. Oh, she had, she had. Absolutely. She had used Doyle to learn her trade and become a correspondent. She had used Rostov to further her career and become a famous correspondent. Yet he could not be certain of the last, any more than he was sure of the first. After all, he had thrown Hazel over; she had not thrown him over. And, after all, if Rostov had been her Russian "friend" from the start, and had the same relationship with her today, she would hardly have remained attached to one man so long without loving him.

There was a doubt rising now in Doyle's mind. Maybe Rostov had not been the other man all along. Maybe there had been someone else, a different Russian friend back in Vienna. Or maybe she had not traded herself to any Russian in Moscow to obtain her beats but had merely been a crack reporter. Maybe she had not actually been in Moscow when Rostov had been there, and had not been away when he had been away, and had not returned when he had returned. Maybe she and Rostov were no more than acquaintances, girl reporter and Russian subject, and she had interviewed him at his Embassy today and he had graciously dropped her off at her apartment on his way to the Palais Rose.

But then, replaying the scene he had just witnessed in the Rue de Téhéran, he doubted his doubt and felt confident of his original deduction. Rostov had been Hazel's Russian friend from the start in Vienna, until this day in Paris. Minutes ago there had been nothing casual or platonic about their behavior. Rostov had taken her hand familiarly. Hazel had shown that she was worried about their being seen (Ah yes—Rostov was married). They had conversed intimately. He had kissed her good-bye. And before that, before all that, her note to Doyle instructing him to make her apartment chaste, and to be off the premises by ten o'clock. Why this, if she had not been expecting to return with Rostov, jealous lover?

Doyle was more sure than ever. Rostov had been the one all along. He had been the one to know of the murder conspiracy against President Kennedy when it had first been formed. He possessed the truth, and Hazel possessed him, and for the moment he, Doyle, possessed—or almost possessed—Hazel. Three was the number for the countdown. Three-two-one—and wham—he'd explode his story, and he'd be King of the Hill again.

Disconcertingly, his elation was not satisfying. He wondered why. He had come here to charm old Hazel, use her, and go on his destined way. He had hunted her down not because he was interested in her but because he was interested in his book. And last night his hunt had begun successfully. And Hazel had proved a sweetheart. So, why was he exasperated with her now?

Well, somehow she seemed to have cheated on their old pure love. Perhaps he had expected that anyone who had deeply cared for him could never care for another man. It surprised him how possessive he felt about her. She really was his girl, despite their spats and long separation. And he knew her inside out, he really did, and she was really a decent girl. It was wrong of her to submit to some uncouth foreign barbarian, not her kind at all, a Russian, a Communist, a married man even. It was no good for her. As for Rostov, he was an unscrupulous son of a bitch for taking advantage of Hazel's innocence, although Doyle could not fault his rival's good taste. At least Rostov's good taste confirmed what Doyle had always known: that a plain and intelligent girl like Hazel—and she really wasn't half bad-looking and she really was darn bright—was worth any number of beautiful and shallow young Muscovite ballet dancers. Well, to hell with all that mushy thinking. If he became sentimental and jealous, he'd never get where he was going. And right now, he was on his way.

Leaving the café, he felt secure once more—the supreme puppeteer holding the strings—finally possessed of the knowledge needed to manipulate his marionettes at will.

Starting for the Boulevard Haussmann, Doyle remembered that he had meant to telephone Hazel to apologize for his dozing off last night and to make a new dinner date with her. He decided that could wait until later. For now something more important was on his mind. He wanted absolute and final confirmation of the relationship between Hazel and Rostov. Once positive, meaning absolutely positive, that it had been Rostov from the beginning in Vienna, he would have the sensational ending to his book about the assassination in Dallas.

Walking along the street, Doyle decided that the files of the Paris bureau of ANA were too skimpy for his final research. The most complete files of newspaper clippings and back copies, and the most accessible, were those in *Le Figaro's* morgue, which he had used several times. That was where he would go to find the dates of Rostov's stay in Moscow, his disappearance from Moscow, his return to Moscow, and these dates he would place side by side with the datelines of Hazel's stories from Moscow, away from Moscow, from Moscow again. If the two series of dates coincided, he no longer need have even a lingering doubt; if they did not coincide, he would have to move more warily. After visiting *Le Figaro,* he would try to locate Matt Brennan. In exchange for confidential news about his morning's discovery, Doyle should learn every bit of information Brennan could dredge up of his personal friendship with Rostov in the Zurich days.

Doyle enjoyed his own smile.

Once ready, he would pull the strings and his puppets would dance for him willingly.

Standing on the curbing of the Boulevard Haussmann, he knew that he could reach the Rond-Point and the offices of *Le Figaro* on foot, but he had no patience for playing pedestrian right now. He was rich. He would indulge in a taxi.

He stepped down into the street and began to wave energetically at each passing taxi, and when he saw an unoccupied one approaching, he waved even more frantically. It slowed down.

As he began to waddle toward it, a flashy young blond girl suddenly darted in front of him and grabbed the taxi door to open it.

"Hey, wait a minute, ma'am," Doyle protested. "It's my cab."

"I was waving, too," she insisted, straightening to defend her rights.

As he regarded her with hazy recognition—she was too pretty to forget—she suddenly said, "Why, you're Mr. Doyle, aren't you? Don't you remember? Hazel Smith introduced us in that café a couple days ago. I'm Medora Hart."

"Of course, I certainly do remember," said Doyle gallantly.

"I *was* flagging for a cabbie, on my honor, Mr. Doyle. Do you mind awfully? I'm in a mad rush for an appointment. Terribly important. Matter of life or death, I swear."

"I insist you take it," said Doyle, now the compleat gentleman.

He watched her leave in his taxi, saw her raise her arm gratefully, and he waved back and philosophically prepared to find another taxi.

Matter of life or death, she had said. The thought made Doyle snort. If people only knew what went on with other people, with himself for instance, then maybe they'd really know what was meant by a matter of life or death.

IN HER TAXI, approaching their point of rendezvous in St.-Germain-des-Prés, Medora Hart had never felt gayer or more self-assured.

Ever since last night, the world had become a wonderful place. Her debut in the Club Lautrec, before an absolutely packed house, had been smashing. Not only had the show gone smoothly, not even one missed cue, but her every number had been cheered. Afterward she had received either flowers or invitations to champagne suppers from at least a half-dozen male customers—two of them, Denise Averil had told her, extremely wealthy—but she had ignored them all to hasten back to her room at the San Régis and await Carol's telephone call.

The call had come, and she had hurried out to meet Carol and her date at the Lido Bar. The report on the events at the Nardeau exhibit had exceeded her highest expectations. She had awakened early this morning to suffer the suspense of listening for a more important call, but she had not suffered long. The telephone had rung as she stepped out of the bathtub, and she had answered it with theatrical calm. She had made the rendezvous on the Left Bank, for a pre-lunch drink, for a brief business talk. Marvelous.

There had been several hours of the morning to pass. She had written her mother, during breakfast, that there might be good news shortly, and that she expected to be home within at the most a fortnight. She had selected her outfit for the rendezvous with care. Something rather offhand yet unflashy was wanted. She had settled on a Verona brown slacks suit, cute bolero jacket and not too tight slacks. She had combed her flaxen hair straight down, no fuss, rather Left Bank studentish. With time still left to spare, she had taken a long stroll to the Avenue de Friedland to see, as unobtrusively as possible, what the Nouvelle Galerie d'Art looked like and how the dealer had placed *Nude in the Garden*. Then, pre-empting the taxi of that fat-man friend of Hazel Smith's, she had sped to the critical meeting.

Now, as the taxi brought her to the corner, she could see the lettering on the awning: CAFÉ DE FLORE. Once out of the vehicle and on the narrow strip of open sidewalk—the rest of the sidewalk taken up by tables and chairs—she remembered the café from her first bad time in Paris. It was an intellectual hangout for Camus and Sartre (she had tried reading them in paperback, but no luck), and for all sorts of unshaved, seedy, Soho types, brainy young men in corduroy motorcar coats and liberated young women with dirty fingernails and revolting boy haircuts. A date had once told her in those days that he had read in some French book that the Café de Flore was "a stone which the devil threw one night into the sixth arrondissement." This moment, she could think of something else the devil had thrown this morning into the sixth arrondissement.

She scanned the tables of the sidewalk terrace. Most would not be occupied until an hour from now, when the real Flore habitués awakened for noon breakfast. There were fewer than a dozen shabby tourists or students or writers sitting around, and only two of them possibly female, both happily wearing short hair and chain-smoking Celtiques, probably the very ones who passed a hat for francs while their boyfriends crayoned fifth-rate Chagalls on the Right Bank sidewalks.

Either she was early, Medora decided, or her caller of the morning was waiting discreetly inside. Medora went past the tables, through an open doorway, into the café. Except for the gossiping waiters at the bar, a wizened patriarch rustling a newspaper, and two buxom French ladies with shopping bags chatting over Alsatian beers, the place was quiet. Momentarily Medora wondered if she had got the rendezvous spot right.

Revolving toward the staircase beside the bar, she became aware of a young woman, definitely English, seated at a table and holding a cigarette, lost in thought. At first Medora was not sure. She had looked for the high-fashion golden blonde of the Sunday supplements, and here was someone with platinum hair drawn back severely in a chignon, and sporting a tweed suit, with an unbecoming square-cut jacket and straight skirt, the color of Medora's own slacks outfit, but not really, because it was actually more brown and more drab.

Suddenly the young woman saw Medora, too, and removed her sunglasses, pulling herself up, erect and formal. Without the glasses, and seen full face, the woman—the high cheekbones, the upturned nose and delicate nostrils, the small round mouth, the slender pre-Raphaelite neck—was at once familiar. There was no mistaking *Nude in the Garden,* slightly aged.

For one hanging second, Medora's self-composure faltered. With effort she gathered up her nerve and the accumulation of three years' indignation, and she went determinedly on stage.

"Fleur Ormsby," she said flatly, not asking, and pleased that she had courageously adhered to her vow not to ennoble the kin of the enemy with "Lady." She had made the first warning thrust. To it she added unsmilingly, "I'm Medora Hart."

Fleur Ormsby's eyebrows arched in a pretense of surprise, and she extended a limp hand. "Miss Hart. How good of you to come. Do sit down."

Medora took the cool hand, released it quickly, mildly annoyed by the other's superior hostess manner. Casually she dropped herself in the wooden chair across the table.

"Perhaps we had better have something," Fleur said. "I know it's a ghastly hour, unless you haven't had your breakfast yet—"

"I've had my breakfast," said Medora.

"Well, I rather think I can manage a glass of sherry. What will it be for you, Miss Hart?"

"Wine," said Medora sullenly. "Tavel."

Fleur Ormsby summoned one of the platoon of waiters to take their order. Meanwhile, Medora tried to assess the enemy's delegate. Fleur's well-bred face was almost devoid of makeup. She wore some kind of clever new shade of lipstick, more beigy than red, and, while chic, it made her lips appear cracked and dry. Medora found the lack of makeup, and the fact that Fleur had dressed herself down for this meeting, somewhat insulting. Perhaps she had done this in order to appear inconspicuous, to avoid calling attention to the fact that a Cabinet Minister's wife was out with a notorious striptease artist. More likely, she had done this because she had no respect for her lessers and felt she could best remind Medora that they were not equals by presenting herself in the guise of an equal. The Queen at the servants' annual ball. Her manner, so far, was composed and social, as if they were not met here on an ugly matter, as if her mere presence would make the silly child abandon fantasy and turn tail and flee.

Medora considered playing along against simply resorting to unlady-like candor, showing her trump card at once, taking her trick, and having the mean barter over with. Before she could decide, she realized Fleur Ormsby had dismissed the waiter and was studying her with interest from behind the tinted glasses she had put back on.

"Have you been long in Paris, Miss Hart?"

"What's today? Tuesday? I drove in from the Riviera three days ago. I saw Nardeau before I left. We're old friends, you know. And he gave me a farewell gift. The nude you inquired about at his exhibit."

"How fortunate you were. Well, that explains it." Fleur Ormsby waited while the drinks were served, then continued. "I looked in on the exhibit last night. Nardeau has always been one of my favorites among contemporary artists. I thought the study of the adolescent in the garden rather a charmer. Not exactly from Nardeau's best period, but there was a naturalness, a *joie de vivre* about it, that attracted me. I thought, when I saw it, that the oil might make a rather nice decorative balance with a Sisley my husband and I possess. Out of curiosity, I asked the dealer to tell me who owned it. He gave me your name. I must say that I was a bit puzzled. Most of the names of those loaning pieces to the exhibit were familiar to me. They are, almost all, well-known art collectors. I had never seen your name among them before. But now you've explained it." She lifted her glass of sherry. "Well, cheers."

"Cheers," said Medora, sipping her Tavel.

"Mmm. Delicious," murmured Fleur Ormsby. She set the glass down. "Well, now, where were we? Oh, yes, Nardeau. How sweet of him to give you so valuable a gift. He must think a good deal of you."

"If he does, it's mutual."

"A lovely farewell gift, I must say," said Fleur Ormsby. "I assume you came to Paris to appear in that cabaret show? It took me a while to place your name, after I'd heard it at the Galerie. I should have known at once. I've been seeing your name everywhere, on every kiosk."

Medora had tired of the fencing. She wanted an opening, and here it was. "I didn't come to Paris to appear in the show, Mrs. Ormsby. That was merely an afterthought and a convenience."

"Oh? Well, then—"

"I came to Paris to see your husband."

"My husband? Really?" For the first time Fleur Ormsby's brow had furrowed. "For whatever reason?"

"I thought that he might be interested in acquiring *Nude in the Garden.*"

"What could possibly have given you such an idea?" She offered a short mirthless laugh. "Sir Austin's a perfect idiot when it comes to art. He merely pampers my interest." She paused. "Perhaps you read of my interest in Nardeau and thought that he shared it?"

"I had an idea he might be particularly interested in this particular painting."

Fleur Ormsby offered her mirthless laugh once more. "My dear, you couldn't be more mistaken. He is interested in no art at all." She smiled. "But as you seem to know, I am. No doubt you've guessed that I suggested this meeting for no other purpose than the faint hope that I might persuade you to part with the painting. But you've just made it clear that you came to Paris prepared to sell it, anyway."

"Yes."

"Then we should have no problem, my dear. Suppose we discuss terms?"

"Certainly."

"Of course, the question of authentication is always a factor. But you *have* said you acquired the oil directly from Nardeau. I presume that he would acknowledge it and certify it as his own."

"No problem at all," said Medora. "He's sent me a document not only certifying *Nude in the Garden* as his work but explaining when he painted it, where, even the name of the model, all from his records. I think possessing that should be of great interest to any buyer, don't you?"

Fleur Ormsby stared across the table. "Very well. I'm quite satisfied. Since I'm in rather a hurry, I see no reason why we cannot settle the terms of the transaction right here and now."

Medora was briefly tempted to prolong the game. She had never before played the role of cat in cat-and-mouse. "It's a costly painting," she said. "Wouldn't you prefer to have your husband see it first?"

"Not necessary," said Fleur Ormsby curtly. "I have my own drawing account. Not to waste time, I'll proceed on the assumption that you are fully aware that Nardeaus are rather dear today. His oils, similar to your own in size and subject, occasionally go for as high as £5,000 at Sotheby's. Of course, selling without an intermediary, you won't have to be out a commission. I'm prepared to write you a check for £5,000 in return for your bill of sale and the document covering the picture's provenance."

"I'm sorry," said Medora, shaking her head slowly, "it's not quite what I wanted."

Fleur Ormsby frowned. "I'm surprised at you, Miss Hart. That's a great deal of money for anyone, but I should think especially for—well, someone in so unstable a field as entertainment."

Fleur peered at Medora, waiting, but Medora sat silently, a complacent smile on her face, also waiting.

"Oh, very well," Fleur Ormsby said suddenly. "I detest haggling. I'm sure you do, too. Let's have it done with. When I want something, I want it. I'll give you my top offer. I'll give you £6,500. Shall we call it a deal?"

Medora's complacent smile remained. "No," she said, "it's not a deal."

"My dear child—"

"I'm not interested in selling it for money," said Medora.

"Not interested in selling for money? What on earth do you think you can sell it for?"

"A re-entry visa to England," said Medora. "That's my price."

"I haven't the faintest notion what you're speaking about."

"Of course you have, Mrs. Ormsby. You know who I am. You know about Sydney and me and the Jameson mess. You know what your husband did to me. If you wish to own the painting, all you need do is go to your husband, ask him to cancel the immigration ruling against me and get me a safe passage, and you shall have your painting."

"My dear, what are you going on about? Of course, I know your record, your past—I was trying to save you the embarrassment of having it brought up—and I know how Sir Austin saved you by sending you abroad. That the Government discovered you were quite possibly not a British citizen, as well as determining you were morally undesirable, surely is no concern of mine or Sir Austin's. And now you want me to put pressure on Sir Austin, to make him controvert the law, as the price of a mere dab of oil? Really, my dear. I can tell you, there are a thousand paintings for sale in this city—"

"But there is only one," Medora interrupted, "*only one* of Lady Ormsby, wife of the Foreign Minister, posing naked as a chippy. There is only one such—and, *my dear*, I have it."

Fleur Ormsby sat unmoving, and even Medora had to admire her poise. Fleur's eyes had become flinty. "You're rather sure of yourself."

"I am. I have the painting. I have Nardeau's statement, in his own hand, that you posed for it. Two wonderful art pieces, I should think, for the world press assembled here this week."

"You know the penalties for blackmail, I presume."

Medora was all innocence. "Blackmail? Mrs. Ormsby, how can you ever imagine that? I mean, isn't it correct to show appreciation for a favor by sending over a gift? If Sir Austin is so kind as to straighten out for me a clerical error made by our immigration department, I would surely be remiss not to thank him in some way. With a painting of his wife, perhaps." Suddenly Medora had sickened of this, and she said bitterly, "You're bloody right it's blackmail or whatever you want to call it, but whatever it is, I tell you it's a damn sight less vicious than what your goddam Sir Austin is doing to me. He's kept me away from my home for three years. And now I'm going back, because if I'm not, I've a hunch you won't have any home to go back to, either. There you have it, Mrs. Ormsby. There's the price for an authentic Fleur Grearson."

Fleur puckered her lips thoughtfully. Her eyes did not leave Medora's face. At last she reached beside her chair and picked up her handbag. She shook her head. "Miss Hart, you are a sick young lady," she said. "My husband and I are not interested in your terms."

"The world press will be, I assure you of that! If I don't have the re-entry visa in forty-eight hours, every newspaper in the world is going to be filling its front page with my picture of the perfect British Cabinet Minister's wife. Quite an eyeful, I must say. I wager a bob you'll get more attention out of this bloody scandal than I got out of the Jameson affair."

Fleur slid from behind the table. She stood up and calmly secured a button of her jacket. "Miss Hart, you are inviting serious trouble for yourself." Her smile was chilling and her voice contained. "No one will take the word of a senile old painter and a vindictive little whore against that of—"

"They'll believe the little whore once they have a good look at the picture of the big whore lying there waiting for it in the grass!" Medora screamed. "You'll find out in forty-eight hours, if you don't—"

But Lady Fleur Ormsby had turned on her heel and departed from the Café de Flore.

And then, alone, ignoring the stares of the customers and waiters, Medora realized that her bluff had been called and she had lost.

There was so little left that she wanted to cry. And then, finally, not giving a damn, she covered her face with her hands and wept.

HE HAD BEEN forty minutes on the road, driving leisurely southwest of Paris through rolling green countryside, and now the rectangular sign ahead, giving the route number and the department of France in small lettering, announced to him in large lettering: SACLAY.

Matt Brennan slowed the dusty new Chevrolet coupé he had rented in Paris (at thirty cents per kilometer) into the main thoroughfare of Saclay. It would be, his friend and concierge, M. Dupont, had warned him, an ordinary and undistinguished small French town. Yet, guiding his car slowly through it, Brennan was captivated by the quaint shops and church and atmosphere of unhurried rural peacefulness. It gave him a start to realize that this lazy village near the winding Seine was the center of France's atomic research program.

He had been told by the concierge that Saclay was thirty-two kilometers from Paris—and his speedometer now confirmed this—and also that his actual destination was eight kilometers beyond the town. Steering with one hand, he hung out the open coupé window, searching for some marker that would lead him to where he was going. At last he saw one, and with more assurance but some reluctance, he left Saclay and accelerated, heading for the château and buildings at Gif-sur-Yvette that contained the Centre National de Recherches Scientifiques, where Professor Maurice Isenberg awaited him.

Beyond the village, the countryside presented sights that were strange and contradictory. There could be seen houses, well set back from the road, as modern and new as those in any California suburb. Between these structures and the road stretched a vista of green fields that was definitely French provincial. Then, startlingly, between the edge of the fields and the highway were barbed-wire fences. And at once you remembered where you were in history and what was going on in Paris these minutes, and that, depending upon the decisions of five men, this might not be here tomorrow or, again, it might be here for centuries to come. Coexistence or nonexistence, Herb Neely had said last night.

The dashboard clock, presuming it was accurate, promised Matt Brennan plenty of time. He lightened the weight of his foot on the gas pedal and permitted his mind to wander back to the previous night, remembering the conversation in which Herb Neely had encouraged him to make this trip.

Last night Brennan and Lisa had been invited to an informal dinner at the Neelys'. Despite his assurances that she would feel comfortable and at home, Lisa had been anxious about the impression that she might make on his friends. But from the moment that Herb and his wife Frances had enthusiastically welcomed them to their sparsely furnished apartment in Neuilly, on the far side of the Bois, the evening had gone as well as or even better than Brennan had predicted it would. Perhaps it was because Brennan had brought along someone who was good-humored and friendly, someone eager to like and be liked, rather than his former wife, Stefani, who had been sour and sarcastic, condescendingly superior toward the Neelys, whom she had considered Kentucky hillbillies.

Brennan had meant to keep the evening purely social, determined not to intrude his personal business upon a night of serious fun talk. Only until dinner, and through dinner, had he succeeded.

After dinner, when the four of them had settled down around the liqueur tray in the living room, it was Frances Neely who, with the support of her husband and Lisa, had coerced Brennan into discussing the progress of his hunt. Frances was, she had said, simply intrigued, and she wanted to hear everything.

Beginning reluctantly, then talking with growing enthusiasm to his captive and fascinated audience, Brennan had paraded his dreary failures. He had, he admitted to his host and hostess, reached an impasse. He had no idea what his next step should be. At once his listeners had been full of ideas. Unanimously they had agreed it would be difficult for him to reach Rostov without getting an important intermediary to arrange the confrontation. The talk had then centered on names of qualified intermediaries, at first loosely, then practically, so that at the end it had become as challenging as the solution to a super-acrostics puzzle.

Finally Neely had summarized the best possibilities. Someone on the staff of the President of the United States could be helpful, a person who had the President's ear, so that the President might be persuaded to speak to the Russian Premier, who in turn might order his Assistant Minister, Nikolai Rostov, to receive Brennan. Such a person, Neely thought, might be Thomas T. Wiggins, one of the President's youngest and most faithful White House aides, a man whom the President often listened to, and who was now staying at the American Ambassador's residence in Paris.

Next, Neely had suggested that Brennan must find someone, no matter what his nationality or vocation, who was officially connected with the Summit, was sympathetic toward Brennan, and had ready access to Rostov so that he could intercede. Try as he might, Brennan had been unable to think of one such person. In the end, it was Neely who had thought of a perfect go-between.

"Matt, during the Congressional hearings, when you were being condemned, wasn't there a well-known French nuclear scientist who gave a feisty interview blasting Senator Dexter's joint committee and defending you?"

Instantly Brennan had remembered. "Isenberg. Professor Maurice Isenberg."

Neely had exclaimed, "That's the one! He's with the French nuclear advisory group at the Summit. His lab is at the CNRS headquarters—Centre National de Recherches Scientifiques—near Saclay. He's Mr. Big. If anyone can get you to Rostov, I reckon he can. You've got to try him."

Brennan had agreed that Professor Isenberg was a possibility. Then Neely had gone on looking for other likely intermediaries, especially someone who had some sort of stake in wishing to have Brennan's name cleared, a person who might wield influence over other Summit delegates. Someone like Earnshaw. After all, in the past year the Administration of Earnshaw and Madlock had been under a barrage of fire from the press, and perhaps by now The Ex had come to realize that the present crisis was mostly the result of his own defection from responsibility, rather than due to any dereliction of duty on Brennan's part. "He just might be more responsive to you at a time like this," Neely had suggested. "He could get to the people who'd get you to Rostov. He might pitch in, Matt."

And Brennan had replied, "I doubt it, but I'll see how desperate I've become by tomorrow."

Last night had ended on an affirmative note. Neely had promised to arrange, first thing in the morning, for Brennan to meet young Wiggins, the President's aide. Brennan would, on his own, telephone Professor Isenberg for an appointment. As to Earnshaw, Brennan had preferred to avoid him if possible. But all in all, the evening had been a success. It had charged both Brennan and Lisa with fresh hope.

Early this morning Neely had telephoned with good news. Wiggins had been agreeable to seeing Brennan briefly. He would expect Brennan at the United States Ambassador's residence, 2 Avenue d'Iéna, by a quarter to eleven.

Inspired, Brennan had determined to compound his good luck by locating Professor Maurice Isenberg. After several local calls, Brennan had learned that Isenberg would be, the entire day, in his office at Gif-sur-Yvette. Brennan had hesitated before putting through this last call. He had never met Isenberg personally. Four years ago there had been that interview in *Le Monde*, picked up by the wire services, in which Isenberg had publicly doubted Brennan's traitorous intent, had minimized the importance of Varney's defection to China, and had flatly stated that Brennan was being used as a political scapegoat. Moved to have anyone in the public eye, especially a famous scientist whom he did not know, proclaim his innocence, Brennan had written a grateful thank-you letter to the Frenchman. And Isenberg, in a short but kindly note, had replied that he had been quoted correctly and that he wished Brennan well.

That had been the extent of their exchange. After four busy years

Isenberg would probably not remember him, and even if he did, Brennan somehow felt that any effort to trade on this man's long-ago impersonal championing of him was presumptuous. Nevertheless, Brennan had placed the long-distance call. A lively voice, ageless and nonpedantic, had identified the speaker as Professor Maurice Isenberg. Brennan had no sooner given his name than the Frenchman recognized it. Of course he would be pleased to see Brennan! When? Why, this very day; perhaps after lunch would be best. What had pleased Brennan most was that Isenberg's invitation had been made without curiosity, only with hospitality.

Driving the Chevrolet that he had rented for the day, Brennan had gone first to the American Ambassador's residence, a dignified three-story stone mansion hidden behind black gates in the Avenue d'Iéna. Once Brennan had entered through the doors beneath the enameled oval seal of the United States, he had been led to a sitting room, where he waited beside the fireplace and tall mirror above it for the United States President's youngest and most influential adviser.

From the moment that Thomas T. Wiggins strode into the room, announcing that he had only five minutes to spare and suggesting Brennan get right to the point, Brennan had known it would go poorly. Wiggins, callow, runty, officious, too recently out of Harvard Law School, too successful too soon to understand either failure or charity, had been disagreeably impatient from the outset.

When Brennan, before posing his request, had attempted to outline the truth about the Varney defection and his own role in it at Zurich, the young Presidential aide had cut him short. Wiggins had studied the affair while taking graduate work in political science. He had been satisfied by the objectivity of the scholars who had written the textbooks. The Standard Version would do. He would not require Brennan's Revised Version.

Annoyed, Brennan had persisted briefly with the Revised Version, explaining that if the Varney defection had helped China gain nuclear power, the fault had been far less his own than that of Earnshaw's Presidential aide, Simon Madlock. In any event, if Wiggins or his chief, the incumbent President, could try to bring Brennan together with Rostov, it would be an act of decency, and history would be served by this truth-seeking.

"Sorry, Mr. Brennan," Wiggins had said, "but neither the President nor I have time for ancient history, when we are in the midst of making new and more important history."

"But the strength of our history is in its truth," Brennan had said. "If a lie has crept in that you can now rectify—"

"Like our helping prove you a saint and Simon Madlock a devil? No, thank you. If there is one thing I cannot abide, it is the disloyalty of a subordinate to his superior. I'm sorry, Mr. Brennan. Good day."

Departing, more angry than defeated, Brennan had wondered why the supercilious boy had bothered to see him at all. And then Brennan had perceived why the meeting had come about. Wiggins had wanted to see him for the same reasons people want to see a freak show, to reinforce their own superiority and to collect a conversation piece. Successful young men, Brennan had thought, so far from death, so invincible and immortal, possessed of too few years on earth to have experienced the disenchantment all men must endure before they come to human understanding. He had been sorry for young Wiggins, for how far he would have to fall, and only finally had he been sorrier for himself, whose history could not be revised.

Brennan's mood of self-pity, and the familiar despondency he had known in the Venice years, lay heavily on him the remainder of the morning and through lunch. But once he had driven beyond the city limits of Paris into the countryside, toward the appointment with a relative stranger who had displayed adult consideration for him, his depression had lifted. Perhaps the old English proverb—he who lives on hope will die fasting—was the correct view of things. But in the drive to Saclay, and beyond, his hope for a solution had revived again.

The eight kilometers had gone by, and he was in Gif-sur-Yvette.

Shouting out to a cyclist, he learned that the château and woods of the atomic research center were directly ahead.

At once there were the hoary trees of the park, partially obscured by old but sturdy stone walls. The huge iron gate was wide open. Brennan drove through it and followed a winding road between the trees, catching only an occasional glimpse of the château, until he emerged into a clearing, a quiet compound surrounded by squat and intensely modern buildings that appeared to hold offices and laboratories.

A concierge with a writing board under one arm flagged him down and approached his car window. Brennan stated his name, mentioned Professor Isenberg, and gave the time of their appointment. The concierge consulted a sheet on his writing board and was satisfied. He gestured Brennan to a parking spot and indicated the one-story building sprawling out before it.

Leaving the car, Brennan stretched, then hurriedly caught up with the concierge, who was already hobbling into the building. Brennan passed through a large scrubbed entrance hall, walked up an empty corridor with freshly whitewashed walls, then abruptly came upon a laboratory filled with counters on which complex miniaturized machinery hummed, as white-coated male and female technicians checked the readings on dials and made calculations.

On the opposite side of the laboratory there was a door, set so flush in the wall it seemed camouflaged. The concierge rapped twice, tentatively tried the door, peered inside. He opened the door wider, beckoning Brennan to follow him. Once in the spacious, austere office, the concierge announced, "Isenberg *est ici,*" and he backed respectfully out.

The severity of the white-walled square office surprised Brennan, until he observed in the far wall a sizable window looking out on the woods, which made the room seem warmer and more serene. The oak desk had a jar of sharp yellow pencils, several writing pads, two opaque Lalique ashtrays on the dark gray blotter. To one side of the desk were four light gray metal file cabinets, each locked with a vertical security bar. On the other side stood a portable blackboard, its slate face pocked with countless incomprehensible formulas. Except for a telephone on a carved *faux-marbre* console, with a heavy *bergère* upholstered in velour beside it, and a bookcase with five shelves tightly packed with worn scientific books and journals, there was little in the room that gave a clue to its occupant's personality.

Then Brennan noticed a large framed display of photographs hanging from a wall beside another door. Lighting a cigarette, he moved toward it. The dominant portrait was that of Albert Einstein, taken in his younger days, and signed by him. There were photographs of Marie Curie, Max Planck, Enrico Fermi, all autographed to Professor Maurice Isenberg. The last picture, the smallest, was a snapshot of Isenberg and J. Robert Oppenheimer, both in sweaters and slacks, each with an arm around the other's shoulder, both smiling with mutual affection. And immediately, Brennan knew. He would get on with Maurice Isenberg.

Suddenly the door beside Brennan was wrenched open. A tall, ungainly man, with the burning eyes and craggy gaunt face of a Jewish prophet of the Book, someone El Greco might have put onto canvas, burst into the office, slamming the door behind him.

Brennan had stepped back, but Professor Isenberg was upon him at once, slapping his back, shaking his hand, pouring out a torrent of words, English words but French-accented. "Brennan? You are Brennan? Forgive me, forgive me, my dear sir. *Mon Dieu,* fool that I was, I agreed to dine with a group of visiting students from the Polytechnique and take them on a guided tour of our establishment. But I do not blame them for my lateness. It is I who am at fault. Once I begin to speak, and I have those who listen, I cannot cease. Yet how could I resist my Polytechnique? It was the university from which I graduated as a specialist in thermonuclear physics, and whenever they summon, it is like the summons of one's father, and I am honored and respond. I am apologetic for not having been here to receive you. Forgive me, forgive me—" Forcibly he began to lead Brennan toward the desk.

"There's nothing to forgive, Professor Isenberg," Brennan said. "It is I who should apologize for breaking in on your day."

"No, no, definitely no. Here, sit, please sit."

He pushed Brennan into the armchair, hastened to the desk, removing his baggy sport jacket but leaving on his sleeveless blue sweater. He began to roll up his shirt-sleeves as he pulled his swivel chair into place. "A cigar, my dear sir? Ah, no. I see you prefer cigarettes. A drink? Something to drink?"

"Nothing, Professor, thank you."

Isenberg had opened a desk drawer, rummaged through it, while carrying on an inaudible dialogue with himself, until at last he found a pair of bifocals and set them high above the bump of his nose. Next he produced a well-burned, smelly meerschaum pipe and a half-pound can of Dutch Cavendish Amphora pipe tobacco. Sloppily, he filled the pipe.

Now, with the spectacles tilted on his prominent nose, the ornate pipe clenched between his discolored teeth, his bony fingers massaging his protruding jaw, his entire appearance seemed to undergo a metamorphosis in Brennan's eyes. The fervent look of the Jewish Old Testament prophet was gone, and in its place sat hunched the wise man of science, one resembling a thoughtful Nuclear Age Sherlock Holmes.

"We will talk," said Isenberg, contentedly puffing. "You are in Paris on business or pleasure?"

"On business which, if I can resolve it, will provide pleasure," said Brennan. "You remember my trouble in America four years ago? Well, without complaining at length, life has been somewhat altered for me since that time. I've been a recluse in Venice most of these years."

"Banishment," said Isenberg. "It can make an ordinary man a great man or it can destroy him. Garibaldi, Sun Yat-sen, Lenin, Victor Hugo—they all grew to greatness in exile. But poor Kościuszko and Stefan Zweig—they were ruined."

Brennan smiled thinly. "I'm afraid I've not found exile an inspiring condition. It's made me something of a paranoiac. Not a happy state, as you can imagine. But you mentioned Paris. I came to Paris because I saw a possibility that I might be able to clear my name."

"Your name—*Mon Dieu,* that was a crime," said Isenberg, glowering. "That was a filthy crime to force one with your intelligence and talent to waste energies clearing a name that needed no clearing to begin with." He shook his head. "No, my friend, you are not a paranoiac, because you are not suffering from delusions of persecution. You have, in fact, been persecuted." He leaned forward through the smoke, placing his sharp elbows on the desk. "I volunteered that old interview of mine because, from afar, I could dispassionately observe the deceit reflected in those Congressional hearings in your country. I could see you were being as victimized as my old, dear friend, Oppenheimer, had been earlier. I could see that if you were sacrificed to ferocious political tyrannosaurs, to sate their electorate, then all of us, the remaining thinkers, were vulnerable, too. So I spoke out. I wish my words could have had more effect. I am afraid they fell on deaf ears, because your prosecutors would hear only what they wanted to hear. But you heard my protest, and I was touched by your letter." He wagged his head again. "I have not altered my opinion since. I would repeat the interview today, were I not a delegate to the Summit and hence restricted by security from speaking. If a mistake was made, it was not made at your level in Zurich but at a higher level in Washington. Professor Varney's confused political idealism was no secret. I knew his work. Brilliant man. But his political sense I had always questioned, as I always questioned Bertrand Russell's behavior whenever he tried to save mankind instead of individual man. If there must be blame for Varney's not surprising defection, it should have been placed on those who appointed him. Once appointed, once sent abroad to deal with the Chinese, he obviously was entirely free to behave as he wished, unless he had been sent manacled or in chains. But all of that, my dear Brennan, is begging the real issue. For the real issue was, and remains, the simple truth that—in fact—your Varney's defection was a matter of little importance. I hinted at that in my original interview, if you recall. Varney's going—or not going—to China could not have changed or deterred by one iota the course of Chinese evolution or world history. Varney did not give the People's Republic of China the neutron bomb. He did not give them the means of delivering the bomb. They already possessed the knowledge for constructing both. He could do no more than confirm designs for, or speed along, what was already being accomplished in China. In short, my dear sir, you could not be charged with being an accomplice to a crime when there was no crime. You see?"

Brennan, listening attentively, enjoyed a feeling of exhilaration. He had been waiting to hear Isenberg deliver a verdict on his guilt or innocence, or on the degree of his culpability, and instead Brennan had learned that there had been no transgression against public good because there had been no homicide. It was as if the iron weight of unfair guilt, crushing and trapping him, had been made of papier-mâché and was no more.

"You're really sure that Varney gave them nothing they didn't already possess?" Brennan asked with wonder. "Everyone says that because Varney got away from us, went over to them, China was able to become the power and threat that she is, and bring on the present crisis, even forcing a Summit meeting whose entire agenda concerns only one subject—human survival. Yet you really think that's not all Varney's doing?"

Professor Isenberg plucked the meerschaum from his mouth and shook his head, laughing. "Brennan, Brennan, I give you my sacred word it is not so." Sobering, he wagged his pipe at Brennan, spilling ashes, tobacco, live sparks over his desk. As one hand put out the sparks on his blotter, Isenberg said, "Listen to me, my fine fellow. Red China exploded her first atomic bomb back in October, 1964, near Lake Lop Nor in the Chinese Takla Makan Desert. It was a real bomb and a strong one, as powerful as your Hiroshima bomb. How was China, so backward and industrially underdeveloped, able to create that first atomic bomb? I will answer. The Chinese have always had a genius for science. Before Christ they constructed the colossal Great Wall that was 2,500 miles long, the only man-made object on earth, I am told, that might be seen from the planet Mars. Over a thousand years ago the Chinese invented printing. Then, and hear me, as many years ago they invented gunpowder, and they invented the rocket, filling a bamboo stalk with powder, lighting this fire missile and sending it off against enemies.

"Today, my dear Brennan, the same pool of native genius continues to exist in China. In our time, China has developed a corps of the finest nuclear scientists on earth. I speak of Dr. Chien San-chiang, who graduated from the University of Paris and was trained by Madame Curie in our Paris Laboratoire Curie. I speak of Wang Kan-chang, who studied in Germany and Russia and was deputy director of the Russian atomic research center, Dubna Institute, in 1959. I speak of the many Chinese nuclear physicists trained by 10,000 Russian scientists and technicians who visited China between 1950 and 1960. I speak of the 60,000 Chinese who were trained in the Chinese Academy of Sciences and similar schools. I speak of a new Chinese nation, one with great uranium resources that were mined at Tachang, in Sinkiang Province. I speak of a nation able to build gaseous diffusion plants at Sanchow and plutonium-producing reactors at Paotow. I speak of a nation so ambitious and determined, that it was prepared to sacrifice the welfare of its population—the average man still earns only 500 francs, or less than $100 a year—in order to devote one and a half billion dollars to develop its first atomic bomb in an effort to win the respect and fear of a world that had so long despised and exploited it."

"Then you think the Chinese developed their first atomic bomb entirely on their own?" asked Brennan.

"No, no, not quite. Eventually they would have developed one, but they did so as quickly as they did because Russia and the United States helped them along. When Stalin thought of using Mao Tse-tung as a Communist puppet heading a Russian Communist satellite, he started China along the nuclear road. He gave the Chinese a heavy-water nuclear reactor and accelerators—intending these for peaceful uses—but China developed its first chain reaction in that reactor in 1958. In 1951 Stalin almost gave the Chinese a sample atomic bomb, but changed his mind. Still, Russia went on sending nuclear scientists and raw materials into China, even giving the Chinese jets and super-sonic bombers until that day when the Soviets realized that China was determined to become Russia's equal as a military power. But your own United States, Brennan, also contributed to China's first bomb, long, long before the Varney incident."

"You mentioned that before," said Brennan. "Do you really mean it?"

"I do. At Los Alamos, where the United States developed history's first atomic bomb, one of the members of your trusted team of scientists was Dr. Klaus Fuchs. Later it was learned Dr. Fuchs was a traitor who had passed your secrets on to Russia, who in turn filtered many of these secrets down to Red China. Another traitor, Bruno Pontecorvo, worked in England with your nuclear secrets, and in 1950 he defected to Russia, and your secrets again became known to Communists in Moscow and Peking. You see, Brennan?"

"Yes."

"The rest was easy. I put it this way. Once an aggressive man has seduced a virgin, she, the mademoiselle, has no more mystery or secret to keep from him. He can go on and on in his conquest of her, in developing her love in many ways. But it is the original penetration of secrecy that is the important one. So it was with China and the bomb. Once the Chinese had solved the first mystery, their further wooing and seduction of more complex nuclear secrets came easier. Your Nobel Prize winner, Dr. Urey, predicted at that time that Communist China would quickly 'produce hydrogen bombs by a comparatively secret process.' He was correct, of course. With experience and growing confidence, with vital information pieced together from the reports of a network of embassy spies, from defectors, from studies of your tests and Russia's tests, and, again from the genius of their own scientists, China easily produced the H-bomb. The necessary next step was the N-bomb."

"Did Chairman Kuo Shu-tung really need the neutron bomb? I've never been sure—"

"To become a respected member of the Nuclear Club, yes, indeed yes. Consider the strategy. If China had the hydrogen bomb alone, they could devastate an enemy country but would have nothing left afterward to go in and occupy. Destruction, but not real victory. But to possess the neutron bomb would be to possess the most sophisticated and sensible annihilation weapon in history. Consider this weapon. The neutron bomb is a pure-fission clean device that is triggered by electromagnetic means instead of by fission detonators. It is a lightweight bomb capable of wiping out every human being in a target area, yet capable of leaving buildings and terrain untouched, intact, habitable. So, due to the many diverse factors that I have mentioned, China was already well on its way to the final development of this N-bomb when your nuclear savant, Varney, defected and moved over to Peking. You have my word, dear Brennan, that Varney could do little more than confirm for his hosts that they were on the right track. To believe that Varney handed China the entire N-bomb, and accuse you of complicity in this act, is absolutely ridiculous."

Brennan felt as he had once felt in his boyhood, when he thought that he had gravely sinned and his father had absolved him, and he had looked upon his father as the reincarnation of St. Peter rescuing him from Hades. "You're extremely kind to tell me all that, Professor Isenberg," he said.

Isenberg seemed surprised. "I tell you only facts. These are the facts. And there are more. Varney was also blamed for helping China complete a delivery system for its nuclear warheads. Thus you were condemned, secondarily, for letting him do this. That is another ridiculous fiction. China's delivery system, crude as it is, was developed by Chinese. To begin with, the Chinese had samples of early Russian rockets to analyze. Then China was able to purchase precision-made electronic parts from manufacturers in countries like Germany and Sweden, from friends in Czechoslovakia and Japan, and from nations who recognized them like France. But China's most valuable rocketry gift came from the United States. This gift was in the person of a Chinese named Tsien Hsue-shen. He went from China to your country

409

to study. He obtained a master's degree from the Massachusetts Institute of Technology and a doctorate from the California Institute of Technology. Dr. Tsien became professor of jet propulsion at Caltech. He contributed greatly to America's nuclear rocket program. He even worked as a consultant to your Navy. But overnight, Dr. Tsien was accused of being a Communist and although he denied this charge, your country deported him in 1965—and presented Red China with one of the world's foremost rocket experts. Not long after, the Chinese were testing missiles on their 700-mile range at Chiuchan. Going from these medium-range missiles to long-range intercontinental ballistic missiles was a shorter step than you imagine. As Dr. Cheng, an authority on Communist China who had been at the University of Michigan, once told us, Chinese leaders always compensate for material scarcity by employing a greater use of intelligence and by inspiring in their people a determination to work harder. He said that powerful rockets could be produced without a big industrial base. He said, as I recall his words, 'If one uses the Western standard to measure the Chinese capacity for producing bombs and rockets, one easily commits the error of underestimation.' Personally, I have never underestimated the Chinese. I have always known they did not need your Varney to develop their ICBM's. And so now they have their missiles that can cross an ocean, they have enlarged their submarine fleet from thirty to ninety underwater craft in a decade, they have their imitations of the token Soviet TU-4 bombers that were once loaned to them, and they have the delivery system for their nuclear warheads. And, as a result, we have been forced to bring them to the Summit."

"Do you think we can convince them to disarm along with us?" Brennan wondered.

"That is the problem. If America and Russia insist on a nuclear ban, with freezing of present-day stockpiles, with policing by an international army of neutrals, I think China will refuse to accept the conditions and the Summit will fail. Because, first, our stockpiles are greater than theirs and they would remain inferior, and because, second, they do not trust us, especially an America who has so long contested them in Southeast Asia and who still rings them with bases having nuclear-armed aircraft and missiles and Polaris submarines. But if America and Soviet Russia and the other powers will agree to total nuclear disarmament, including not only destruction of every nuclear weapon stockpiled, but destruction of every facility for producing such weapons, then I suspect that China will go along. Because nations will be left to face each other with conventional weapons and ground soldiers, and China will emerge slightly superior, with its three million armed men in its People's Liberation Army."

"But would they really compromise in working out disarmament agreements?" asked Brennan.

"Perhaps. I am not certain." Professor Isenberg had emptied the gray ashes from his meerschaum pipe, and thoughtfully he packed it with fresh tobacco. After lighting it, he said, "There are two Chinas, as there are two Russias, and it will all depend on which China is speaking in the Palais Rose. You saw how Red China modified its aggressive ambitions after Mao and the angry and vengeful men had gone, and the moderates led by Chairman Kuo Shu-tung took over. Under Mao and the old leaders, one way or another, China finally won back or regained control over their ancient imperial territories in Tibet, Burma, Indochina, and they managed to control most of Southeast Asia and to neutralize Taiwan. Having won such controls as those the Russians exercised in Eastern Europe and the Americans exercised in its own offshore islands and in Central and South America, China's feeling of pride and security was somewhat restored. And their present Chairman could afford to adopt a milder attitude toward the West and agree to treat with us at the Summit."

"Milder attitude?" said Brennan, remembering that he had made this same protest to Neely. He was curious to see if Isenberg would have a different reaction. "It was that dangerous incident in India, and the exposure of the fact that the left-wing attempt at a *coup d'état* in Japan had been financed and directed by China that really brought on the Summit."

Professor Isenberg smiled. "Yes. But that is pertinent to the point I am making. Chairman Kuo Shu-tung is really a man of peace, I believe, but he is also shrewd. He may have staged those recent crises in India and Japan to gain him more respect at the bargaining table, to make us prepared to compromise. On the other hand, those crises may have represented something else. I told you there were two Chinas, and the second China is composed of the sons of the Maoists, the hotheads, the diehards, the ones who pay homage to Lenin and the world revolution, the ones who are eager to show their muscle, or even to use it, in order to continue spreading Marxism and make Communism the dominant ideology on earth. If they are running China, and merely using the moderates like Chairman Kuo Shu-tung as figureheads, then we must expect trouble. But I doubt it. I think the Maoists are only a relatively small dissident group. I think Chairman Kuo Shu-tung's program to go along with us in ending nuclear competition and the threat of war, and to join us in creating a peaceful world, in diverting military expenditures into bolstering domestic economies, is the real China that prevails in the Palais Rose. At least, that was the impression I took away from Peking two years ago, and this feeling has been reinforced by my meetings the last few days with my Chinese counterparts in the Palais Rose."

Brennan uncrossed his legs, and sat up. "You were in Peking two years ago?"

"Yes, yes. There was a convention of nuclear scientists. We were treated in grand style. I had a wonderful room in the Hsin Hsiao Hotel. Our Chinese hosts took us on a tour. They can be the most gracious and charming of hosts, especially when they are not trying to propagandize, and that's my point. They weren't. I heard hardly a word about American imperialism, or about Russian revisionists becoming a capitalistic pawn of the democracies. My Chinese hosts were confident, proud, and really quite friendly."

"Did you hear anything about Professor Varney?"

"I was coming to that," said Isenberg. "I wondered whether the West's most famous defector was still around, whether he was alive or dead. I was curious to chat with him and learn his opinion of his adopted homeland after two years there. Also, quite honestly, I remembered your hearings and wanted to ask Varney about you and, if he was agreeable, see if I could get an affidavit from him that would clear your name, Brennan."

"That was thoughtful of you, and I'm thankful."

"Nothing to thank me for, because nothing happened. When I asked to see Varney, my Chinese hosts said that he was too senile and ill to receive any visitors. But from other things I heard, I doubted that Varney was *that* senile or *that* ill."

"What things did you hear?"

"Oh, there was considerable talk about a new Nuclear Peace City—reactor-powered factories with their own community—that China is having private industry from West Germany come over to build for them. And since this new nuclear project involves advanced fission techniques that the Chinese scientists are not yet trained to handle, it was evident to me that they would need a foreigner capable of directing or managing the project. They can't use a German for the single top job, because he has to be someone who is a Communist or is sympathetic to Communism. They can't use a Russian, because they have fallen out with Russia. Although, to my surprise, there were a number of Russian scientists at our convention in Peking. Well, I suppose that was understandable, since scientists like to think their world is one without national frontiers. Anyway, I had the feeling when I was over there that if Varney was actually alive and healthy, he might head up the project. I wish I'd—"

"Those Russians you met in Peking," Brennan interrupted. "Was one of them named Nikolai Rostov? He's the—"

Isenberg held up his pipe. "I know, Brennan. He's the other one who was mixed up in Varney's defection. No. Rostov was not in Peking."

"He is in Paris now, you know."

Isenberg nodded. "Yes, I've heard."

"That's why I came to Paris, Professor Isenberg. To see Rostov."

Isenberg removed the pipe from his mouth, stared at Brennan, but remained silent.

"Only two men alive can prove my innocence," said Brennan. "One is Varney. Even you couldn't get to him. The other is Rostov. And he's right here."

"Have you seen him?"

"I've tried." Brennan shook his head. "No luck. He's inaccessible to me."

"Ummm. Well. I suppose I am not surprised."

"I *must* see him," said Brennan with passion. "My entire future depends on my seeing him. But I realize that I'll be able to get to him only through an intermediary. That's the real reason I came to you, Professor Isenberg. You believe in me. You're a delegate to the Summit. So is Rostov. He would know and respect you. He might listen to you. I rather hoped you could try to—to arrange for the two of us to get together."

Isenberg laid his pipe carefully in the ashtray, not looking at Brennan. Slowly he settled backward in his swivel chair, eyes closed, fingertips meeting before his lips, as he thought about the request. After almost half a minute he opened his eyes, dropped his hands to the arms of the swivel chair, and rocked forward in it.

"Brennan," he said, "I would do anything for you that is possible. What you request, I fear, is impossible. My official position at the Summit, a delicate one, limits my activities. I am under surveillance, as are all of us connected with nuclear research, and if I treated with a Russian delegate without a directive to do so, I might be questioned or even arrested. I have not met Rostov, and it is unlikely I ever shall during this conference. He is a diplomat and politician from a secretive country. I am a scientist and adviser pledged to a certain secrecy by my country. Rostov and I have no common ground. We are assigned to different areas and different levels of activity. If I were to have the opportunity to speak to him officially, I would not forget to speak on your behalf at the same time. But such an opportunity is not likely to arise. My friend, I *am* sorry."

Brennan was embarrassed. "It was improper of me to bring it up—"

"Not at all, not at all. In your place I should have done the same."

"—but, well, desperation drives men to behave as they would not normally behave. My request was unfair to you. I understand the restrictions surrounding you. I should have remembered from my own past."

Brennan stopped, aware that Isenberg had hardly been listening to him. The scientist had tilted back in his swivel chair once more, and he seemed to be concentrating on a light fixture in the ceiling. Suddenly his features were those of a man who had been blessed by a revelation or had made a discovery. He slowly sat up. "Varney," he mused. He yanked open a desk drawer, pulled out a leather appointment book, and thumbed through the pages. Holding one page, he nodded, slapped the book shut, and returned it to the drawer. "Yes," he said to himself. He smiled apologetically at Brennan. "I'd almost forgotten, and it just came into my mind. The appointment—"

Brennan started to rise. "I'm sorry. I know you're busy. I've taken enough of your—"

"No, no, it's tomorrow, not now. Sit down. It concerns you. I was trying to think of people who might help you, and suddenly it came to me. One name. He can't be of any assistance in regard to Rostov. But he might get you some firsthand information on Professor Varney."

"I appreciate that," said Brennan. He shrugged. "But Varney, I doubt if Varney could ever—"

"One never knows," said Isenberg. "Always wise to have one more rabbit in the hat. If you should fail utterly to contact Rostov in Paris, it is quite possible that Ma Ming might intercede on your behalf with Varney one day, after he returns to Peking."

Brennan was not sure that he had heard the name correctly. "Ma Ming?"

"Sorry, sorry, the way I skip along. Ma Ming, that's right. Wonderful fellow. He came to interview me when I was in China, and we hit it off. Most friendly, and extremely well-informed and articulate. A fellow brimming with marvels. It was he who introduced me to the Hung Society. Ever hear of it?"

"I don't think so."

"It's a secret fraternal organization, harmless, rather like your Masons, with four or five million members throughout China. If a person belongs to the Hung Society, he converses with his brother members only through pantomime outsiders cannot notice, a language made up of hand movements, body postures, other actions, such as the way a cigarette is smoked, a cup of tea held, a package carried. Fascinating, and quite unheathen, the Chinese. I'm an honorary member of Hung, thanks to Ma Ming. Anyway"—Isenberg paused—"yes, I am almost certain Mr. Ma was the Chinese I first broached the subject

414

of Varney to when I was over there. And he was the one who told me Varney was ill and incommunicado. Now, maybe all Chinese journalists were supposed to say that. Or maybe it was the truth. If it was, Ma Ming might know where Varney was being kept in China. If Mr. Ma liked you, and I think he would, and if he became interested in your plight, he just might look in on Varney and try to get you some sort of clearance, the sort of thing you want from Rostov. I don't know. It would also depend on Varney's being alive, being in his right mind, being willing or allowed to cooperate."

Brennan could not hide his skepticism. "Do you think a mere journalist could possibly—?"

Isenberg shook a bony finger at Brennan. "No *mere* journalists in China, dear Brennan. No, sir. Ma Ming is the foremost correspondent with Hsinhua, that is the New China News Agency, the official bureau that one of their propaganda ministers once called the tongue and eyes of the Chinese Communist party. I recall being told that Mr. Ma was very close to Chairman Kuo Shu-tung. At any rate, Mr. Ma was gracious to me in Peking, and I'm trying to repay him in kind while he's here, although he is busy enough. I'm having him out to Gif-sur-Yvette tomorrow, and I'm giving him a little lunch. I'd like nothing better than to speak to him about you."

"I hate to have you bother. You've done more than enough already."

"If you don't mind, I shall insist on this. I shall speak to Ma Ming of your case. If he is cooperative, would you see him?"

"See him? I'll embrace him. I'll see anyone who—"

"Very well. Do not forget the name, should he call upon you. Ma Ming."

Brennan smiled. "It's not likely I'll forget that name." He stood up. "Professor, I'm deeply grateful for your—well, I'll say it—for your friendship."

"You deserve more," said Isenberg, troubled, as he rose to his feet. "I know it is Rostov, not Varney, who is your best hope. I wish I could suggest someone for you to enlist in my place. It should be someone who is an important diplomat or politician, really, someone above petty restrictions. Surely you must know such a person. I hope so, and I wish you luck. Meanwhile, if there is anything else I can do—?"

Ten minutes later, driving his dusty car out of Gif-sur-Yvette, heading back to Paris, Matthew Brennan still felt deeply discouraged. Yet Isenberg's last advice had not left his mind. To speak to Rostov on Brennan's behalf, the French scientist had suggested an "important diplomat or politician," a person "above petty restrictions."

And now Brennan admitted to himself that there was such a one in Paris, someone who knew him, who was a politician, who was unhampered by security. This was a person, Brennan reflected, who surely could get him to Rostov. This was also a person who, Brennan remembered, would just as soon see him dead.

But if you *were* practically dead, Brennan decided, the other person might feel less threatened and more sympathetic.

Besides, he and the one he was now determined to see, to call upon without an appointment, had one thing in common. They were both forgotten creatures of the same past. Each of them in his own way, one as a leader, the other as a human being, might honestly be called The Ex.

As BRENNAN PLACED the thick binder of transcripts on the coffee table in the sitting room of Earnshaw's Hotel Lancaster suite, and settled into the downy sofa, he could hear the former President saying, "I—I'm sorry I can't give you any more than—uh—a few minutes, Mr. Brennan, but after all, your visit was unexpected. I—uh—it's a busy day—Mr. Doyle is coming up shortly, so that I can dictate my column—then, uh, other matters. If you had called for an appointment first—"

"If I'd called first," said Brennan, trying to keep his tone light, "you might not have seen me at all."

Earnshaw scratched at a pointed eyebrow, and protested. "Come now, Mr. Brennan. If you had good cause to see me—"

"I don't know if I have good cause," said Brennan. "I only know I have a problem, one that involves you, and you're the remaining person who might help me solve it."

"Well, in that case . . . " Earnshaw's voice had trailed off, and he gripped a wing chair near him for support and eased himself down into it.

Observing him, Brennan was surprised at how gray, aged, enfeebled the former President appeared. Only three days before, when they had encountered one another in the main hall of the Palais Rose, Brennan had thought Earnshaw remarkably well-preserved and energetic. This afternoon, he was an old man, as frail and brittle as the hundred-year-old Civil War veteran and GAR survivor whom Brennan used to see in his youth, a dribbling relic in a rocking chair on a wooden front porch that the gang always passed on the way to the ice-cream shop. Brennan wondered what could possibly have happened to Earnshaw in three days to inflict this transformation, and then he ceased to speculate on geriatrics, since it might soften his approach.

"I know my walking in on you like this, unannounced, is rude," said Brennan, "and that my being here probably makes you uncomfortable. I wouldn't have done it, believe me, if it weren't necessary."

Earnshaw's fingers drummed nervously on the arm of his chair. "You are mistaken, Mr. Brennan. I've nothing against you personally."

"Well, perhaps you still feel that I failed you in that whole Varney business, and that the sight of me symbolizes the one bad mark against your Administration. So be it. You needn't answer. Let me put it this way. Whatever happened in the past, whatever you've felt about me or I've felt about you, there is one judgment I've had about you that has remained unchanged. I've always felt you were a man of goodwill and decency. I still feel that way. Otherwise I wouldn't dare to be here right now."

Earnshaw's grave blue eyes wavered. Slowly he rubbed his cleft chin. He waited for what was next.

"As you probably recall," said Brennan, "when I testified under oath before Senator Dexter's Joint Committee on Internal Security, I explained that you and Simon Madlock had insisted that Professor Varney accompany those of us who were going to the Zurich Parley. Then I testified about a private meeting I'd had with Madlock. I had learned Varney was a poor security risk, and I felt his presence at Zurich might be dangerous to us. I asked that Varney be left behind. Madlock insisted I take him along. Do you recall my saying that in my testimony four years ago?"

"Uh—I think so. Yes."

"Then I told the congressmen that the worst that I had feared did finally happen. Varney defected. The responsibility for this defection was Madlock's. But when I returned to Washington, Madlock was dead. He was not around to accept the blame, which I am convinced he would have done. So I was blamed in his stead. I said all of that under oath. Do you remember?"

"Vaguely. I'm not sure."

Brennan laid the flat of his palm on the thick binder of transcripts. "It's in here, Mr. Earnshaw. This is the transcript of my days of testimony before the Congressional Joint Committee on Internal Security. Have you ever read it?"

"No, no, I don't think I have. A President rarely has time for that amount of reading. Besides, as I remember, I was too upset, in grief, over Simon's passing. And there were numerous executive matters that had piled up and that required my full attention. However, I was briefed on the hearings, on the testimony of the various—various—uh—witnesses. I can't say at this late date whether or not I recollect all of your testimony."

Brennan kept his hand on the binder. "I wish you'd read some of this, especially the part where I tell of the private meeting Madlock and I had, when he forced me to take Varney to Zurich over my protests."

"I don't know if I'll have the time, Mr. Brennan."

"Well, if you can, sir, I'd appreciate it. The fact is, there was that meeting, and I've always wondered why you didn't come forward in Madlock's place to back me up, after he was no longer alive to corroborate my statements. Certainly Madlock must have told you of our talk." Brennan paused. "He did, didn't he?"

"I'm not sure he did. I have no recollection of it."

"But he *must* have told you."

Earnshaw wriggled in his seat. "Not necessarily," he said. "He was extremely busy—uh—devoted to his job—working to relieve me of many burdens—and he didn't always have the time to speak to me of all his multiple activities."

Brennan overlooked this and went on. "If you weren't a party to the advance warning I gave Madlock, you couldn't have defended me. I understand that. And we know Madlock died before he could speak out for me. But if and when you read this testimony, you'll learn that there was one other person who could have cleared me. Do you remember the name Nikolai Rostov?"

"The Russian at Zurich. Yes. Yes, indeed."

"Rostov could have proved that while Varney duped us both, he left an apologetic note clearing us. Rostov had the note and disappeared with it. I tried to locate him, get the evidence from him, but I never could." Brennan paused, then he said, "Do you know this same Rostov is in Paris right now?"

"I may have heard."

"He's on Premier Talansky's staff. I've tried to reach him and I've failed. Yet one word from him would not only clear me, but erase the single black mark against your Administration as President. I have the greater stake in getting to Rostov, but I'm suggesting you have a stake in this also. You are the only person left I can appeal to, the only person I know who can go to the incumbent President of the United States or our Secretary of State, and prevail upon him to speak to Rostov on my behalf, our behalf. Under such pressure, I'm sure Rostov would comply. We'd have the truth at last."

Brennan looked at Earnshaw, waiting, and what he saw embarrassed him. The former President was scratching and squirming, uncomfortable and worried. "Uh—yes, I see what you are after, Mr. Brennan—and while I wish for truth as much as you, I'm not all that certain I'm in any position to help you. If I intervened—uh—approached the President, that is, at a time like this, it would be regarded as highly improper. It wouldn't be correct form, you see."

Earnshaw seemed to expect some understanding and relenting on his visitor's part, but Brennan refused to offer him any such solace. Brennan sat stolid and uncooperative.

Staring up at the ceiling unhappily, Earnshaw resumed. "Uh—there are many difficulties for one in my—uh—situation that you cannot possibly appreciate. Certain things are—uh—easier said than done, you know. It's like, well—"

Earnshaw rambled on and on, and Brennan listened to The Ex's familiar circumlocutions, ambiguities, digressions, generalities, indecisiveness. With mounting disgust, Brennan realized that Earnshaw at sixty-six was no different from Earnshaw at sixty-three, or at any earlier age, and that trying to expect a molehill to have grown into a mountain was being unrealistic.

"Mr. Earnshaw," Brennan interrupted, "I do appreciate your situation. I hope you will refresh your memory with this transcript, and then try to appreciate my situation. Look at me, sir. I am one last bit of unfinished business from your Administration. I am unfinished business that you and Madlock never resolved. If you are a man of good faith, you will try to resolve it, not only for me but for your own and Madlock's places in history."

Earnshaw was twitching again, eyes rolling, avoiding Brennan. "Uh—well, now—I don't know. I can't promise anything, because, as I've said—still, one never knows—perhaps if the opportunity arises, let me see, let me keep my eyes open, ears open, and if anything can be done, at the appropriate time, well—"

Brennan's disgust was complete. He stood up. "Thank you anyway, sir. I know you'll do what you can. Thank you for giving me your time."

Once he had left the suite and gone down the flight of stairs to the elevator, Brennan realized to what extent the meeting with Earnshaw had sickened him.

The person he had just left was the very person who, only short years ago, had held the fate of America and the free world in his hands. The thought made Brennan shudder. If ordinary people only knew the frailties, susceptibilities, weaknesses of their revered leaders,

419

if they could see the slack real faces hidden behind the confident public masks, not one of them would ever sleep easy again. Relating this thought to the leaders and Ministers at the Summit, Brennan shuddered again.

From cradle to the grave, he thought, no man dared depend wholly on other men, for all men were vulnerable and flawed. And it was that way from the first breath of life, he thought. If helpless infants, looking up at their godly parents through the tiny eyes of childhood, entrusting their innocent lives to the infallible wisdom of these parents, could only know how troubled was the mother, how complex the father, how insecure were both their guardians, each of the little ones would swiftly crawl back into the womb for eternity.

But then, as he stepped inside the elevator, another thought came to Brennan, surmounting his disillusionment. Perhaps each of us demands too much of our elders, he thought. Earnshaw had been a disappointment to him. Yet he himself had been a disappointment to his son Ted. Still, Brennan knew, he was more than his son believed him to be. And so, perhaps, Earnshaw was more than Brennan believed him to be.

He wondered about this, and then he wondered why Earnshaw had suddenly seemed so old, so old and lost. . . .

For an hour Earnshaw had been sitting by himself in the unlit room, steadily reading. Now he closed the binder covers that held the transcript of Brennan's testimony before the Congressional Joint Committee on Internal Security, lifted it from his lap, and returned it to the coffee table.

What he had read in such detail was, for the most part, new to him. And in the light of what Dr. Dietrich von Goerlitz had told him yesterday, it was deeply disturbing.

Earnshaw sat back to reflect morbidly on these revelations and to consider his present lot. It was as if his orderly world, which had begun to disintegrate, but which he had thought could still be shored up and repaired, had finally overcome all of his efforts and tumbled down into a hopeless rubble heap around him.

He had always, he supposed, lent credence to the innuendos, hints, rumors reported by those close to him, because for him it was a truism that whenever there was smoke there must be fire. When Senator Dexter had publicly implied—not charged, but implied—that Professor Varney's defection had been due not merely to a public official who had been derelict in his duty, but had been due to a public official with highly suspect left-wing affiliations (who had deliberately encouraged Varney's plan to strengthen China in a warped scheme to assure peace), Earnshaw as President had accepted the implication as fact. And when the traitor, Brennan, had tried to shift the responsibility for Varney's defection onto poor, dead Simon Madlock, Earnshaw had considered Brennan's evasion cowardly and despicable. And had he reviewed Brennan's formal testimony any time before today, Earnshaw realized that he might have still felt the same way.

But yesterday's disclosures had shaken Earnshaw. In his meeting with Goerlitz he had seen actual evidence of Madlock's activities, undercover activities unknown to Earnshaw. He had learned, with sorrow, that his once beloved aide, like a misguided missionary, had employed shameful means to attain a desirable end, an end to war. No matter what his motives, Simon Madlock had been perfidious, had been disloyal, had committed a kind of political forgery for which Earnshaw must now pay.

Having this knowledge, he found it more than possible to believe that Brennan's original testimony had been honest. Yes, it was possible that Brennan *had* gone to Madlock and warned him about Varney, and that Madlock, in his Messianic zeal, had ignored warnings in his determination to have America's foremost scientist-pacifist in Zurich to disarm the Chinese. Yes, it was possible that Madlock, not Brennan, had been the well-intentioned traitor to his country. If this were so, then Brennan had suffered unfairly. Also, if this were so—and Goerlitz's memoirs had made it clear that most of it was so—Earnshaw would be the ultimate victim of his aide's monumental stupidity.

Earnshaw felt ill. It was too late, too late for retribution. There was nothing to be done for Brennan, assuming Brennan had been truly guiltless. There was even less than nothing that Earnshaw might do for himself, for he was truly guilty, guilty of abdicating his responsibility for a public trust to a willful and deluded crony.

He had mourned Madlock's death. He had mourned Isabel. And now, in this shadowy hotel room, he once more mourned his own death, the worst of the three, because it was a living death.

In his self-flagellation and self-pity, he had not been aware that he was no longer alone. He looked up, startled, to find Carol standing over him, studying him, her young face crossed with concern.

"Carol," he gasped. "When did you come in?"

"Uncle Emmett, I've never seen you like this. You look positively ill. What is the matter?"

He tried to sit up, and failed, and slumping back, he tried to smile, and failed. "Oh, I'll be all right," he said. "Don't you worry your pretty head. Merely a passing mood. Everyone has a right to be depressed once in a while."

"Not you, Uncle Emmett. I know you too well. Something must have happened."

"Just one or two business setbacks. I came to Paris on a couple of personal matters and, well—well, I guess they didn't work out as I had hoped. People—people can be difficult."

"Why do some people behave like ghouls?" she demanded angrily. "I don't know how you can stand them, Uncle Emmett, the reporters back home, the rival politicians on the other side, and here, even here, that horrible Goerlitz with his spiteful, vicious, dirty book."

Instantly Earnshaw was alert. He held her last word in the air between them. "Book," he said.

He could see that her expression had changed from one of concern over him to one of frightened self-concern. It was as if she wanted to snatch back her last spoken word and hastily bring it inside her.

"Book," Earnshaw repeated, pushing himself to his feet. "What do you know about it?"

"About what?" she said, stalling desperately.

He circled the coffee table to confront her directly. "What do you know about Goerlitz's memoirs?"

"Why, I—I heard you mention it—you mentioned it to Willi the time he was up here—when you were giving him the message."

"No good, Carol," Earnshaw said. "I mentioned the book, I mentioned that I wanted to see Goerlitz to straighten out some information in the memoirs, but I never said a word, not a word, about its being a vicious—what did you say?—vicious, spiteful, dirty book directed against me. I made it a point never to discuss the contents of those memoirs with you or anyone else. Now, apparently, you know the contents. I think you'd better tell me how you found them out."

"I—I just assumed, I mean from your tone with Willi—and your being so anxious to see his father—and even changing our itinerary to come to Paris first—"

"Carol," he said, "don't lie to me."

"I—Uncle Emmett, really, I—"

"Carol, I *demand* the truth. You read that book."

"No, I didn't! Willi did. He—"

"Willi von Goerlitz read it. I see. Then he lied to me, too. He told me he hadn't."

"He didn't lie," Carol protested. "He hadn't read it. But after the last time he saw you, he became curious and he read it, and he told me about it last night. He was all mixed up. He just couldn't match what was in his father's memoirs to the way you seemed when he met you. So he told me what was in the memoirs, and I got real sore and told him most of it wasn't true at all, and I told him what you were really like. I mean that's what happened, literally. It came up, and I had a chance to tell your side of everything last night."

Earnshaw had fastened on to something else. "Last night," he said. "How could you see Willi last night? You spent the whole evening with the Ormsbys and me."

"Well, I mean, we weren't out late, and after you went to sleep, I remembered that I'd promised to meet Miss Hart after her show, at the Lido Bar for a hot dog. When I got down in the lobby, the night concierge said there was a call for me. It was from Willi. He wanted to see me. I guess he'd just finished his father's book, and sort of wanted to discuss it. So he met Medora and me, and the three of us went to Pub Renault, and we just sat around talking, and after Medora left, he and I kept on talking, and the book came up naturally."

"What time did he bring you back last night?"

"I don't know. Maybe two or three o'clock."

Earnshaw mocked her. "Maybe two or three o'clock." His contained anger had turned to rage. "Who do you think you are, staying out all night against my express wishes? And rousting about with that Goerlitz kid when I've forbidden it? I ordered you not to see him again. You pledged not to see him. But there you were, doing it behind my back, carrying on with someone whose father is out to kill me." He gasped, and he blurted savagely, "How dare you!"

Carol had gone white. "Uncle Emmett, what—what's got into you? I told you last time that Willi has nothing to do with his father. I mean, Willi is one person and his father's another. I know what his father is, but Willi's another generation, and he's better educated and smarter and nicer."

"You're prattling like a child."

"I am not! You're just angry because you're having trouble with his father. But that has nothing to do with Willi and me—"

"Willi and you, is it? That's cozy. That's darn cozy."

"Uncle Emmett," she pleaded, and her voice broke. "What's happening? I don't understand. I—"

"What's happening is that you've lost your head. You're behaving in a foolish and disreputable manner. If your father and mother were alive, they'd never permit such—such indecent behavior. And I won't either. I have a responsibility to them and to you for your welfare. You can't see it now, what you've been letting yourself in for, but you'll thank me one day."

"Uncle Emmett, you've never, never been more wrong. You're sore at old Goerlitz, so you're trying to take it out on his son, and—"

"You hold your tongue, young lady!"

"You simply have no right to push me around. It's not fair. If I want to see Willi, I'll see him."

"Do that, and I'll pull you out of here and drag you straight home!" he shouted. "I've been as lenient as possible with you always. But not this time, young lady, not this time. This is once my mind's made up. And it's an order. You're not to see that Goerlitz boy again."

She looked fixedly at him, and began to tremble. "I—I'm glad your mind's made up for once," she said, teeth chattering. "I didn't know you were capable of that. It's the first time someone has seen you make a decision!"

Earnshaw stood immobilized, stricken, as if hit by a bullet fired from a revolver in the hand of his child. He stared at her, deeply hurt, irreparably wounded, dumbly watching the tears of remorse welling in her eyes.

The tears were rolling down now, and she was stumbling toward him, throwing her arms around him, hugging him tightly, head on his chest, as she sobbed, "I didn't mean it—honest to God, I swear—I swear on Mom and Pop—I didn't—"

For a while he held her, patted her, until her tears had ceased. Then he found his big handkerchief and gave it to her.

"That's enough now, Carol. That's enough of that. Want to ruin my best suit? . . . You said nothing that was so wrong. We all say things we don't mean under stress."

"But I didn't mean it," she begged.

"I know you didn't, my dear. I blame myself. You wanted to help me, and I was ashamed and—and unreasonable. I had to strike at someone, and you happened to be at hand. This is all bad. It's been— it's been a bad time here, and we mustn't let it go on. Maybe it would be smartest if both of us cleared out, just turned around and went back home where we belong, and got away from where I can be hurt, and from where I can hurt you."

"Whatever you want to do, Uncle Emmett."

"Yes, I think that will be best. I'll make arrangements tomorrow. Uh—now, if you don't mind, I think I'd better lie down for a while before dinner. And you'd better wash your face. It needs it. See you later."

Vacant-eyed, he went into the entry hall, and he turned into his bedroom just as the bedside telephone began ringing. Undoing his tie, he picked up the receiver.

"Hello?"

"Mr. Earnshaw? Jay Doyle in the lobby, ready to come up and raring to get to work."

"I'm not up to it today, Jay," he heard himself say. "You go off and write whatever you want."

"But don't you want to—?"

"No, Jay. Do it on your own today. I don't care what you write. Say whatever you think is right—I trust you—and sign my name."

He hung up.

No, he did not care what he said about the Summit. Or what was said about it for him. He didn't give a damn whether anyone saved the world or not, since it was a hostile world in which he no longer wished to live.

He drew off his coat, and unlaced his shoes before slipping them off, and then lay down on top of the bedspread.

To hell with everyone and everything, he thought, and then his mind went to the many pulpits of his past.

And there were voices, and thunders, and lightnings; and there was a great earthquake . . . so mighty an earthquake, and so great. And . . . the cities of the nations fell.

Come, Armageddon.

That was his mood.

Confused by Earnshaw's refusal to see him, Jay Thomas Doyle picked up his bulging briefcase, thanked the telephone operator, retreated through the lobby, and stopped on the sidewalk in front of the Hotel Lancaster.

Earnshaw's refusal was unexpected and his short temper was unusual. Doyle wondered what was eating him. He wondered, also, what column he should write today under the former President's name. Not that Earnshaw had shown himself to be a useful collaborator in their few meetings. To date their procedure had been simplicity itself. Doyle would dig up what information he could on the proceedings, official, and the progress, unofficial, of the five-power conferences at the Palais Rose. He would research background facts. He would report his findings to Earnshaw, who, in turn, would fumble helplessly for a topic to discuss in his next column. Doyle would discreetly guide him toward

425

a subject, write the column, obtain Earnshaw's approval, then file the story for syndication. There was little enough that Earnshaw did, but to do absolutely nothing, as he now intended to do, was an utter abdication of responsibility.

Yet Doyle did not mind. It would be easy to find a noncontroversial subject concerning the latest disarmament talk and write it up in the noncommittal style that so accurately reflected Earnshaw's image. Best of all, for Doyle, was the fact that, not having to visit with Earnshaw, he had gained an hour to concentrate on what was in his briefcase and uppermost in his mind.

He had spent a long time in the third-floor reference room of *Le Figaro,* peeling through cardboard-bound copies of the newspaper, stacked behind shuttered shelves. He had located almost every available story of the last decade and a half that mentioned Nikolai Rostov, and he had arranged to have these stories photocopied. He had spent an even longer time in the Paris bureau of ANA, digging out stories bearing Hazel Smith's by-line over many years, and he had had these copied also. Then, after routinely finding the background material he might need for the Earnshaw column, Doyle had filled a spare office briefcase with his combined findings, meaning to use some of the material when he met with Earnshaw, and examine the more important papers with greater care before and after he saw Hazel Smith tonight. He had reached her by telephone only an hour ago, and she had readily agreed to another dinner date. He had been elated, but eager to study his research material one more time before seeing her. Now with the Earnshaw appointment canceled, he would have that opportunity.

Standing on the sidewalk, he had almost decided to go to his hotel room when he saw the attractive, informal café-restaurant, Val d'Isère, across the street. He realized with surprise that he had put nothing in his stomach since his late breakfast, nothing except three or four soft drinks. The diet pill had worked. He would be trimmer, as well as more alert, for Hazel tonight. Still, he must not starve himself to the point of weakness. At Val d'Isère he could have coffee and a roll, and sufficient solitude to study the contents of his briefcase with care.

Crossing the Rue de Berri in a step less ponderous than any taken in the last days and weeks—he had lost three or four pounds since morning, he was certain—he reached the Val d'Isère, moved between the flowers and green plants shielding the outer terrace from foot traffic, and entered a dining room which seemed cooler for the framed scenic photographs of white ski slopes on the walls.

About to take the first empty place, Doyle saw Matt Brennan at a table in a corner, engaged in conversation with a waiter. Doyle made his way past the other diners, most of them relaxing over their apéritifs.

"Matt, good to see you. I was intending to look you up later."

"Well, here I am. Rest your feet. I need company."

"Thanks." Doyle placed his briefcase against a table leg, and sat with a grunt. "What did you order?"

"Hemlock."

"So that's the way it is," said Doyle. "Maybe I can make you change your order."

"Okay. Make it a Danish beer, *garçon*. . . . What's for you, Jay?"

Doyle started to count calories, and then he stopped. "The same."

When the waiter had left, Brennan said, "Aren't you supposed to be up there with Earnshaw right now? That's what he told me."

"That's what he told me, too," Doyle said. "Amazing thing. I rang him from the lobby, and he wouldn't see me. Ordered me to go off and write whatever I damn pleased. I never heard him in a more despondent mood. Kind of surprising. He's a pretty smooth-tempered guy, even when things are rough. . . . Hey, what do you mean, Earnshaw told you I was coming up? Did you see him?"

"I probably contributed to his bad mood. Yes, I saw him. I walked in on him without being invited."

Doyle was impressed. "All things considered, that took a lot of guts."

"Guts is all I've got left, Jay. And they've been going, going, and I think they're almost gone." He offered a cigarette to Doyle, who refused it, and then he picked one out of the package for himself. "Trying to get to Rostov has been like trying to find Judge Crater on the continent of Atlantis. Only harder, as you know. Matters haven't improved since yesterday. Well, I was despairing enough to be foolhardy. I walked in unannounced on Earnshaw, hoping he would help me. I've got news for you, Jay. Foolhardy is still foolhardy."

Doyle was interested in knowing more. "Do you mind telling me what happened?"

"Between Earnshaw and me? I'd relish it. Reinforces my natural masochism."

Brennan waited for the beer to be served, and for the waiter to leave, and after that he recounted his entire experience with Earnshaw.

Doyle had been nodding throughout the recital, and when it was finished, he said, "That explains it."

"Explains what?"

"His miserable mood. Refusal to see me. Now that I think of it, he sounded absolutely suicidal."

"Because I laid it on the line for him about Madlock? And laid the

427

whole responsibility for the Varney mess in their laps? Hell, despite his phony vagueness, he heard all of that when I testified at the Congressional hearings."

"No, that's not it alone," said Doyle slowly, still trying to think. "It was a matter of timing, Matt. You see, I know something very few people know. I don't mind sharing it with you. I've been up in Earnshaw's suite quite frequently, and books or no books, I guess I'm still a journalist at heart. I've always had big ears, and I still have. I can also read letters, notes, telephone pads upside down. I see what I'm not supposed to see. I know how to go out, use what I have, to learn more. Once you have the acorn, it's not hard to find the tree. Maybe one time only God could make that tree. Not anymore. Not in these days of super-gardening. Anyway, from what I've learned, put together, what I've guessed, here's what I know about Earnshaw. You got time?"

"Nothing but," said Brennan. "I'm listening."

"He wasn't supposed to be in Paris at all. He was supposed to leave London for a tour of Scandinavia. Suddenly he changed his mind and came to Paris. Why? Because his old pal—I checked this out—Dr. Dietrich von Goerlitz is in town. If you've heard of Zaharoff, Krupp, Wenner-Gren, you've heard of Goerlitz."

"I've heard of Goerlitz," said Brennan.

"Why is Goerlitz in Paris? Officially, to meet with the Chinese about something called a Nuclear Peace City he's contracted to build and run for them, using his German scientists and technicians."

"Yes. I heard about that from a French scientist today."

"Well, that's why Goerlitz is really here. That's his big official business. But he's also here on some other business, and that's unofficial. He's here to sell his memoirs. His memoirs touch lightly—like a sledgehammer—on his former friends. One of them was Earnshaw."

Doyle went on to relate what he had learned of the earlier relationship between Earnshaw and Goerlitz, of the German's vengeful chapter on the former United States President, and of Earnshaw's determination to persuade Goerlitz to omit or revise that chapter before publication.

"Yesterday I found out that Earnshaw went to see Goerlitz at the Hotel Ritz," said Doyle. "How'd I find out? Through Earnshaw's chauffeur, who's trying to convince me that I should write his autobiography. All right. Yesterday Earnshaw saw Goerlitz. Today Earnshaw is suicidal. It doesn't take a computer to figure out what happened."

"No, it doesn't," agreed Brennan.

"And just now you barge in on Earnshaw and heap more coals on the fire. So first Earnshaw sees what a bum he's been from the German, and now he gets more of the same from you. For the first time he has to face the truth about himself. No wonder he wasn't in a mood to see me."

"And no wonder he wouldn't help me," said Brennan. "I guess he's got other problems on his mind besides helping me get to Rostov."

"Rostov!" Doyle sputtered from his beer, sending foam dribbling down his chin. "The devil with Earnshaw. It's Rostov I really wanted to talk to you about."

"Have you found out anything?" Brennan asked quickly.

Doyle wiped the foam from his face with a napkin. "Found out anything? Bro-ther!" He pushed his chair back so that he could bend forward despite his belly. "Matt, I *saw* Nikolai Rostov in person this morning. Saw him with my own two eyes."

Savoring every moment, Doyle began to narrate the events of the night before—how he had had a date with Hazel Smith, how Hazel Smith had delayed their date in order to participate in the scheme to help Medora Hart, how he had accompanied Hazel to her apartment after La Tour d'Argent, how he had fallen asleep, how he had awakened to find her note, how he had gone downstairs for breakfast, how he had seen a man drive up with Hazel and walk her to the entrance, how he had recognized the man to be Nikolai Rostov himself, and how he had figured it out afterward and how it all made sense.

Brennan had been listening intently. "So it turned out you were the one to see Rostov," he said.

"Mind you, this is confidential, Matt."

"Of course."

"Do you realize what this means to me, if Hazel and Rostov have always been a twosome? It means he's the one who accidently spilled to her, back in Vienna, the news of the conspiracy to assassinate Kennedy. It means at last I know her source, and I'm in with the girl who can bring me together with that source. It means I almost have the final proof of my story, and it means, if I play my cards right, I'll have the biggest exposé book in history."

"Yes," Brennan agreed. "It's just difficult for me to think of Rostov as Lothario. Your whole hope is predicated on the fact that they really have been intimate for years."

"That's right. And I had to be sure. So look what I've done." He yanked the briefcase to his lap, and opened it. "See these photocopics from *Figaro?* Rostov's movements. These from ANA? Hazel's movements. I've matched them hastily. I'll double-check them later, but from what I've seen so far, it's open and shut. Nine times out of ten, when Rostov was in Moscow, Hazel was also there. When Rostov left Moscow, or was forced to leave, Hazel left, too. When Rostov returned, Hazel returned." He looked up. "Conclusive or not?"

"Conclusive as circumstantial evidence can be. I think there's no question. You've got them paired. You're on the right track." He smiled faintly. "I only wish I were as close."

"Look, Matt, I haven't forgotten you, by God. Now we're both after the same man. I'm positive that even as I try to help myself, I can be helping you. I may get stuff on Rostov from Hazel. Or I may get to meet him personally. In either event, I can be watching for something useful to you, or even make a pitch for you, when the time comes."

"I'll appreciate that, Jay."

"You deserve it. There's not enough I can do for you." He pushed aside his beer mug and laid the bulky briefcase on the table. "I gather, from what you said before, you've had no luck on your own."

"Still zero," said Brennan. "Earnshaw, well, you know. Before that—" He went on to report the results of his meetings with Wiggins and with Professor Isenberg. "Yesterday was no better."

Doyle recalled their exchange in the lobby of the Hotel California the day before. "What about that rare-book shop that Rostov patronized in Paris? Were you able to come up with it?"

"Oh, yes, I remembered it, all right. That is something I wanted to discuss with you. I haven't told a soul about it except the girl I'm here with, Lisa, but I thought maybe you could figure it out. I went there yesterday. Absolutely improbable. I'm a little embarrassed about telling you what happened."

Doyle's curiosity was now fully aroused. "What do you mean? Was it the shop Rostov buys from?"

"I'm sure of that. But listen—"

Quickly Brennan related the details of his visit with M. Julien, the rare book and autograph dealer. Then he described the appearance of the American, Joe Peet, and of Peet's acquisitions.

"And there you have it, Jay. First, the proprietor mistakes me for Mr. Peet. Next, Mr. Peet comes in to pick up his three rare books by Sir Richard Burton, one of them so rare it doesn't even exist. Who'd believe that? But it happened. I can't make any sense out of it, yet that's exactly what I heard and saw."

"I believe you," Doyle muttered, but already his reporter's mind had sent him poking into his briefcase. "You said the name was Joe Peet?"

"Yes. . . . What are you doing? Does the name mean anything to you?"

"It might," said Doyle cautiously. "I think so." He had removed the clipped photocopies of Hazel's by-line stories from Moscow, and he was turning them back hastily. "Peet is not an easy name to forget. Anyway, it rang a bell."

As Brennan watched anxiously, Doyle continued to scan the contents of Hazel's by-line stories.

"About a year or so ago," said Doyle, still concentrating on the clippings, "there was an American kid who went to Russia on an Intourist sight-seeing trip. Along the way he got himself involved with a young Russian girl—a ballet dancer, a garage mechanic, I forget what she was—and he fell for her. When the tour was ended, the American kid didn't want to leave her. He tried to get his visa extended, but the Russians refused. Then this romantic nut called a foreign press conference in Moscow and proclaimed that he was ready to renounce his American citizenship and become a full-fledged Soviet citizen if the Russians would let him stay on and marry his girl. The Russians said no again, and threw him out. And then—hey, lookee here." He held up a photostat triumphantly. "Here it is, Matt. By good old Hazel herself, reporting from Moscow early last year." He handed it across the table. "Meet Mr. Peet."

Brennan read the interview rapidly, reread it carefully, and put it down.

"Crazy," he said. "Hazel Smith quotes Peet as saying he was raised in Chicago, dropped out of Roosevelt High School after two years, was drafted and sent to Vietnam where he drove a supply truck. All kinds of jobs after that. Was working as a sort of errand boy backstage at Lincoln Center in New York when the Bolshoi Ballet was there. The Russians were nice to him, and he fell in love with them. He'd always thought his parents were Lithuanian, but after that he decided they'd emigrated from Russia. Then—"

Brennan picked up the clipping again and scanned it. "He told Hazel Smith he became obsessed with Russia. He saved money, went on this short trip, met a twenty-three-year-old Russian girl named Ludmilla in Moscow. She was working in an automobile factory. He'd known some American girls, almost married one, but this Ludmilla was the most wonderful girl he'd ever met—she treated him differently from the way American girls did—she made him feel like a man—" Brennan looked up. "Whatever that's supposed to mean? Anyway, Ludmilla wasn't permitted to leave Russia with Peet, so he decided to stay and marry her. But because his motives for becoming a Russian citizen were decadently romantic, instead of healthily ideological, the Soviets refused to let him stay." Brennan stared at the clipping. "Peet's last words to Hazel Smith were 'I'm going to devote the rest of my life to getting back to Moscow and marrying my Ludmilla. I'm going to keep after my Government and the Russian Government until I make it.' That's it, Jay."

He started to hand the clipping back, but Doyle said, "Keep it. . . . Well, what does it tell you?"

"I don't know," said Brennan. "Maybe Peet's Ludmilla is working for the Soviet delegation and he came here to see her."

"A factory worker with the Soviet delegation?"

"No, I suppose not," said Brennan.

"More likely he's flown over here because some important Russians are in Paris, and he wants to persuade them to let him be readmitted to Russia."

"That sounds more logical," said Brennan. "But what isn't logical is this, Jay—I go to Rostov's favorite rare-book shop in Paris to find out whether Rostov has been there, or whether any other Russian has been there, to buy up first editions of Sir Richard Burton, and instead of Rostov, I run into an unlettered American buying up rare Burton editions."

Doyle had an idea. "Maybe he heard Rostov was a Burton addict, and he bought some of Burton's books to bribe Rostov, or someone on Rostov's staff, so he'd be more kindly disposed to Peet's application for Russian citizenship?"

"Possibly," said Brennan. "At least, that theory ties Peet in with Rostov. Gives his action some meaning. Yet why would he buy a book that doesn't exist—and *get* it?"

Doyle was fascinated. "Maybe he asked for that nonexistent book and went away with something else in place of the book. Maybe the title was a password, and maybe that rare-book store is a Communist drop."

"Espionage drop—yes, that was what I was thinking, but it seemed so fanciful, I was afraid to mention it. Julien could be a French Communist. They're not uncommon. I remember seeing a copy of *France Nouvelle* in his back room. That's the official Communist weekly, isn't it? But picturing him running an espionage drop—I don't know."

"Those things happen," said Doyle.

"Yes, they do," Brennan agreed. "But in a way, that notion makes no sense either. It doesn't go anywhere."

"Only because you don't know enough about it," said Doyle. "Why don't you look into Peet a little more?"

"And come up with what? No, I don't think I want to play boy-detective. I came here to meet with Rostov, and it's becoming quite apparent I'm not going to meet him. If Earnshaw had pitched in, well, there might have been a chance. But obviously, he can't help himself, so how's he going to help me, and why should he? No, Jay, I've just about had it. I don't want to be a pigeon for false hopes, at least not here. I belong back in the Piazza San Marco along with the real pigeons, who know there's nothing more to life than sleeping, eating, and eventually dying. I'm afraid that's what I'm going to have to tell my young lady tonight. But you've been swell, Jay. Thanks for the old college try. And good luck. At least one of us should make it to Rostov."

H E HAD TURNED IN his rented car before dark, and at a quarter to eight in the evening they had taken a taxi to the Left Bank, to have dinner at the restaurant that Doyle had recommended.

Now the taxi came to a halt at the intersection of the Quai de la Tournelle and the Rue Maître-Albert, hard on the closed wooden bookstalls that ran along a wall of the Seine, and just south of the massive Cathedral of Notre-Dame. The driver, grateful for the generous tip, pointed down the narrow, dimly lighted side street. *"Atelier Maître Albert, monsieur,"* he said.

Assisting Lisa Collins from the taxi, Brennan was pained to see how beautiful and buoyant she was this night. Elaborate gold earrings accented the Grecian face, and the chartreuse chiffon cocktail dress dramatized her classic figure. She was vivacious because she was in love and she was twenty-two and she was in Paris. And his pain came from knowing that emotionally he could not afford her, that he must lose her and lose with her his second chance at life, and that tonight would be their farewell dinner. He had meant to tell her at once, but her gaiety and expectancy of a wondrous evening had been too great and he had not had the heart to spoil it so early. He would try to hide his melancholy, he had decided, and let the evening have its life before he destroyed it and the eternity of evenings she dreamed about.

Taking her arm, Brennan escorted her into the side street. "Doyle insisted we come here," Brennan said. "He said it's positively unique. I suppose he should know. He's a rabid restaurant collector, specializing in offbeat issues in mint condition."

"I can't wait, darling."

"Here we are." They stood beneath a long rectangular sign reading:

ATELIER MAÎTRE ALBERT . . . BAR./ROTISSERIE/GALERIE. Brennan opened the door, and they went inside.

It *was* unique.

There was a barroom, but instead of bar stools to sit upon, there were children's swings, actual swings suspended by ropes from the ceiling. The maître d' was attentive, checking and confirming M. Brennan's reservation, but perhaps madame and monsieur would enjoy a drink in the bar swings first?

Wide-eyed, Lisa watched several patrons swinging and laughing as they tried to balance their spilling glasses of whisky. "Oh, let's!" Lisa said cheerfully.

He was too sober, and in no mood for fun. "Next time," he said, guiding her toward the main dining room.

She cast him a sidelong glance. "All right, Matt. . . . I'm sorry you're not happy."

"I'm sorry I'm too old for what you enjoy."

"Oh, Christus. Must you?"

They passed through the dining room. To their left, on a huge open hearth, a fire crackled and blazed. Before the fire, dinner guests circled a heavy wooden block of a table upon which were heaped platters and bowls of appetizers, and some guests were slicing pieces of salami from the rolls hung from the rafters, dangling over the table. To their right was a steep staircase that climbed to the art gallery upstairs.

It was a perfect room for lovers, Brennan thought bitterly, resenting the waste of it. Rough wood beams crossed beneath the roof. The stone walls were covered with deep red cloth hangings, and here and there a crazy swishing of abstract art grinned down at them.

Their table was intimate, illuminated by candles thrust into two empty Ballantine bottles that were streaked with white wax.

"Yes, I think I will have something to drink," Lisa was saying. "Lots and lots of champagne."

Brennan tried to smile. "We'll start with one bottle." He considered the menu. "We'll live it up." He nodded at the red-jacketed waiter. "Clicquot Rose 1955."

Lisa was hidden behind her menu. "Why the most expensive, Matt? That's twice the cost of the entire dinner." She peered over the menu. "You feeling guilty or something? Found another girl?"

"Found three. And they speak French."

"I speak French, too. Listen." She devoted herself to the listing of the fixed dinner, reading aloud, *"La table de hors-d'oeuvres et charcuterie. La grillade au feu de bois. Salade de saison. Plateau de fromages. Dessert, Glace noisette au chocolat chaud. . . .* How's that? Do I qualify?"

434

"Now I've got four girls."

"Nobody loves you more than I do, Matt." She put aside the menu. "What made you so depressed?"

"I'm not really."

"You are *really,* my boy. I know you."

"Here's the champagne." They waited, and then they had it before them, and he said, "And here's to you."

"Not on your life," she said. "Revision. Ready?" She lifted the glass. "Here's to *us.*"

Falsely, he acknowledged the toast, and they drank.

"It *does* get bubbles in your nose," she said with delight, and then she seemed to remember. "All right, Matt, out with it. Bad day?"

He gave a short nod. "Bad."

"Tell me."

He told her. Wiggins, Isenberg, Earnshaw.

"I don't blame you for not swinging at the bar," she said. "But tomorrow's another day, as the saying goes."

"Yes, it is. I'll be better tomorrow. In fact, I feel better already. More champagne?"

The first drinks had begun to relieve his head of self-pity. He wanted her forever, but he loved her enough to want her to be happier than that. He wished her a bright, handsome, ambitious young man—and already hated that young man—a young man nearer her age, who would have youth's funnel vision that saw only victories and success ahead and could not see or know of the Waterloos lurking.

But tonight, this last night, he was her young man, and she deserved better than his complaints and recital of defeats. "Let's forget Rostov until tomorrow," he said. "Let's enjoy tonight. Make believe we're on the swings. Well, the first thing I'd want to know is all about you, and about your day, everything, every move you made, everyone you met, everything you heard, every thought you had."

"I missed you. That's the main thing. I wasn't cut out to be a career girl going places. I was cut out to have your babies."

It wrenched him, this, their babies, but he was determined on a mindless amusing evening for her. "Okay. Babies in the works. But where were you today? Tell me about those fashion shows you covered, everything."

"Are you really interested, Matt?"

He drained his glass and poured them both more champagne. "If you were involved, I'm interested. Come on, Lisa."

She was hesitant. "Well, you asked for it." She seemed eager to divert him as she began to recount her activities from her early waking until they had come together in his rooms to dress for dinner.

435

She had gone to a *Harper's Bazaar* luncheon and stopped by to look in on a *Vogue* cocktail party, and at the latter she had run into Legrande, who had invited her to an informal dinner party toward the end of the week at his château in Vaucresson. Legrande had remembered her friend—"meaning you, Matt"—and had heard about her friend's trouble with the police at his showing. The designer had been most apologetic and hoped that she would bring Brennan to his party. "So remember, you've got to take me, Matt. His parties are supposed to be fabulous."

Before she had gone to the cocktail gathering, she had covered three collections, one at Saint Laurent, one at Balenciaga, one at Givenchy. The collections were exhausting, a strain, and the best parts were the intermissions, during which everyone gathered around to gossip. Tons and tons of gossip. The buyers and fashion press were always insiders, and they were truly an international crowd, and the whisperings were beyond belief. If she were only a newspaperwoman like Hazel Smith, or a columnist, Lisa said, she could write a million stories.

"And have a million lawsuits for libel," said Brennan to the two Lisas created by four glasses of Clicquot Rose 1955. "Hold out your glass and let me fill it."

Holding out her empty glass, she went on with her chatter. No, she did not think there'd be many libel suits about what she'd have to report, not actually, because most of what one heard could be proved true. The sources were the best. Top people. Like hearing a *directrice* telling today how one of her mannequins had been propositioned by Sir Austin Ormsby's brother, Sydney Ormsby, the fellow who was involved in the Jameson case, and the model had rejected Ormsby because he was an overbearing and horrible person. "Which reminds me of what you told me a little while ago about that Medora Hart and how she was being persecuted," said Lisa, "and now I believe it."

But the wealthy customers were still the best sources of gossip, Lisa went on, and many of them were the wives or mistresses of Summit delegates, and they probably knew more about the latest activities in the Palais Rose than the leaders and Ministers themselves.

"One wife of a French minister was pointed out to me at the Balenciaga collection," Lisa said, "and she was there to buy a décolleté dress, the latest, the most, because she was seducing an English delegate to get hold of information for her husband. How do you like that?"

"I like that," said Brennan, feeling slightly drunk. "That's love and devotion. If you loved and devotioned me, you'd pick up some gossip about Rostov."

"I wish I could, Matt," she said seriously, "but so far, no luck. Now, if you were to ask me something else about politics, maybe I could help. The things you hear. Even Chinese stuff. The inscrutable Chinese, ha. Take the two Chinese wives of Red Chinese delegates I overheard this afternoon at—I forget—either at Givenchy or Saint-Laurent—babbling away a mile a minute in pretty fair English about how Germany was building some kind of nuclear city in China, and is supposed to run it, but when it's done, Russia is going to run it instead. Now, wouldn't that be news to Germany? . . . What's the matter, darling? Oh, I've lost you. I bet I'm boring you."

Brennan had been only half attentive, but the last of what Lisa had said had suddenly penetrated through the vapors of champagne anesthetizing his brain. An alert signal had reached and aroused a gray mass of shallow memory. He appeared momentarily distant to Lisa, because he was distant, off listening to Professor Isenberg, off listening to Jay Doyle.

Brennan's brain replayed the Isenberg recording: ". . . a new Nuclear Peace City, reactor-powered factories with their own community, that China is having private industry from West Germany come over to build for them . . . involves advanced fission techniques that Chinese scientists are not yet trained to handle. . . . They can't use a Russian, although to my surprise, there were a number of Russian scientists at our convention in Peking."

Brennan's brain replayed the Jay Doyle recording: "Why is Goerlitz in Paris? Officially, to meet with the Chinese about something called a Nuclear Peace City he's contracted to build and run for them, using his German scientists and technicians."

Brennan's brain replayed the Lisa Collins recording: ". . . two Chinese wives of Red Chinese delegates I overheard this afternoon . . . babbling away a mile a minute in pretty fair English about how Germany was building some kind of nuclear city in China, and is supposed to run it, but when it's done, Russia is going to run it instead. Now, wouldn't that be news to Germany?"

News to Germany? And how, Lisa!

Brennan's mind leaped ahead. News to Dr. Dietrich von Goerlitz also, Goerlitz who was investing a fortune in China. News to Emmett A. Earnshaw also, Earnshaw who was trying to win over Goerlitz. News to the leaders of the United States and Great Britain and France also, who trusted that Soviet Russia had made a clean break with Red China and was now completely on the side of the Western democracies.

News. The initials of North, East, West, South spelled N-E-W-S.

But did gossip, overheard by a twenty-two-year-old New York fashion designer at the intermission of a Givenchy or Saint Laurent fashion collection, a frivolous fashion showing—did that also spell N-E-W-S?

"Lisa," Brennan said slowly, "what did you just say?"

"Well, welcome back to the earth people, astronaut Brennan. . . . What did I just say? I said I bet I'm boring you."

"No, dammit. Before that. I was listening, all right. What did you say before that? The wives of two Chinese delegates babbling on about the nuclear city Germany is building in China, and the Russians—"

"Oh, *that*," said Lisa. "I was just trying to tell you the sort of—"

"Tell me the whole thing, everything you saw and heard, everything you heard, every word of it."

"Every word? I don't know if I remember—"

"You've got to remember," Brennan interrupted sharply.

She was instantly contrite and concerned. "I—I didn't think it meant anything. Is it terribly important, Matt?"

"Maybe. Maybe not. It could be. Yes."

She swallowed. "Okay. Well, these two Chinese women were talking, as I said—"

"Who, why, what, when, where? Every detail you can recall. Don't gloss over it." He pushed his champagne glass aside. "Where were you when you heard this? Go ahead. Do your best, Lisa."

"I feel awfully dumb suddenly. But I'll try, although I don't understand." She tugged at one earring, trying to remember. "It was at one of those fashion houses about two o'clock—no, later—about two-thirty this afternoon, almost at the intermission. I slipped out of the collection to go to the ladies' lounge before the big rush. I locked myself in—this is embarrassing, Matt—I went inside the lounge and locked myself in where all little girls go, and there I was when I heard these three women come in—"

"Three? I thought you said two."

"No, three. I forgot to tell you. There was also a very genteel aristocratic French woman—I'll call her the countess, because I think she sounded like one—and she was sort of the hostess for the two doll-like, rather young and pretty Chinese wives, who seemed to be her guests."

"How could you see them? I thought you were locked in?"

"I *was*," Lisa said with exasperation. "Really, Matt, don't be so mortifying. Haven't you ever been inside a public toilet? You can see through the crack in the door. The women were at the washbasins and mirrors, fixing their hair, freshening up, and I had glimpses of them. But mostly, I heard them conversing. The French countess had brought them in, minutes after me, also to beat the intermission rush. Apparently the French countess spoke no Chinese, and apparently the two Chinese wives spoke no French. But I gathered that they had a knowledge of English in common, fairly fluent English but rather stilted, the kind foreigners learn in a British colony school."

"Fine," said Brennan, "there they were talking, and there you were, out of sight, listening. What next?"

"The Chinese wives were discussing their social engagements for the week, and one of them said that she expected the most lavish dinner would be the one that the German industrialist, Dr. Dietrich von Goerlitz, was giving for the Chinese delegation at the Ritz this coming weekend. Then one Chinese wife said to the French countess, 'My husband considers this dinner terribly important because our Government is concluding negotiations with Goerlitz for a Nuclear Peace City that the Germans are going to build for us in Honan Province—' " Lisa hesitated. "Yes, I'm sure she said Honan Province, and in a section of it, a county, called Lankao. I've loved Chinese names ever since I first saw *The Mikado*. Or was that Japanese? Anyway, she said something to the effect that this new nuclear center would be bigger than the ones the Chinese already had at—at—oh, I can't remember."

"Lanchow and Paotow?"

"I guess something like that, and something about this city the Germans were constructing being China's real Leap Forward."

"What else did *she* say, in her words, if you can remember them?" Brennan persisted.

"Let me think." Lisa finished her champagne. "Yes. This Chinese wife went on in this way. 'Marshal Chen appointed my husband to help conclude the negotiations and sign the contracts with the Germans in two or three days, and Goerlitz is giving the dinner party to celebrate. It is a great honor for my husband, and he was eager that I appear at my best for the Goerlitz dinner. So he ordered me to go out today to find a new gown. He wants me in Western dress. I don't mind that, except it is so frightfully costly.' Then the French countess said, rather nastily I thought, 'I wouldn't condescend to wear something especially to please Goerlitz or any German Nazi. I detested them before the war, and I despise them even more now. They were murderers before, and they're economic bloodsuckers now.' That's almost exactly what she said, Matt, and immediately both Chinese wives were defensive. The second Chinese woman said, 'Oh, we don't care for the Germans any more than you do. We're only using them. Our country's welfare comes before a profiteer's piece of paper. We'll let them build for us, but we won't let them stay on and manage things.' Then the first

Chinese wife said, 'That is true. I've heard my husband say that once he's rid of the Germans, we can bring in our Russian friends to direct the nuclear center with us.' The French countess continued to be rather testy. She said something like 'I'm not sure the Russians will be much better. The Germans are arrogant, and the Russians are savages who can't be trusted.' Both Chinese wives began protesting excitedly. One of them was saying, 'No, you are mistaken. We know the Russians well. Their scientists are intelligent, dependable, and sympathetic to our cause. We have had our differences with them, it is true. I don't understand enough politics to know the reasons, but I have heard my husband say that we will soon be comrades again.' Then she began powdering, and worrying whether she could find the right gown in time, and after that they left. I don't know why I listened so closely, but I guess I did so because I'd never seen or heard a native Chinese up that close, and I was fascinated and hung on every word. I guess I'm lucky I did, if this is so important to you, Matt. Is it, now that you've heard the whole thing?"

Brennan nodded vigorously and summoned the waiter. He requested a piece of scratch paper, and the waiter tore a blank page out of his order book. Brennan thanked him, found his pen, and turned back to Lisa.

"It could be very important," he said.

She pointed to his pen and paper. "What are you doing with that?"

"I'm going to make notes on what you've been telling me. I want you to start all over again. I want you to repeat every word you've spoken to me. Do you mind?"

"Matt, must I? I'll faint from nervousness, trying to remember everything again."

"Lisa, please try. I think I have most of it in my head. But I just want to be sure."

"Well . . . all right, I need some more champagne."

Brennan poured, and then he waited, his pen ready. "Go ahead, dear. Make believe you haven't told me a word. You were in the powder room, and the Frenchwoman and the two Chinese wives came in. And one of the Chinese ladies began speaking of Goerlitz."

With a sigh, Lisa put down her champagne glass and began reciting her entire story once more, sometimes altering or enlarging upon what she had already told him, and as she spoke, Brennan wrote steadily until he had filled both sides of the notepaper in a crabbed hand.

"That's it," said Lisa, "the whole thing, and now promise you won't make me tell it *again*."

"No. You've done wonderfully." He studied what he had written. "Drink your champagne. Let me think a moment."

It had the ring of truth, all of it, Brennan felt. The gossipy casualness of the entire dialogue that Lisa had overheard, the very setting, the sounds of wifely chatter, the way it fitted in so logically with what Brennan had already heard from Professor Isenberg, gave it the sound of veracity.

Goerlitz, like Krupp before him, was actually constructing factory complexes, and entire prefabricated cities along with them to house the workmen. Years ago, Brennan recalled, Krupp had built similar factories and cities, like the city of Djerba in Tunisia and the city of Rourkela in India. Krupp had actually advertised this Instant City service for sale in his annual catalogues. In India, several hundred miles west of Calcutta, he had taken an underdeveloped area—plains, rice paddies, hills, primitive villages—and converted that area into prospering Rourkela, a steelworks that produced one million tons of raw steel a year, and a modern city that now held a population of 100,000 persons. It had been an unbelievable undertaking and achievement. Thereafter, Krupp's competitor, Goerlitz, had tried to emulate him in a smaller way, and with the Chinese Nuclear Peace City he was attempting to exceed Krupp.

Brennan continued to reflect upon this. Goerlitz headed a mammoth private industry. He was in it for the profit. He was building the Chinese city not only for the immediate money he would make from its construction, but for the money that he would make by having hundreds of his German scientists and technicians move in to operate the plants on a permanent basis. From a long-term point of view, Goerlitz's greatest profits would come from having his experts and laborers run the plants, and from the monopoly Goerlitz would possess in supplying both new and replacement equipment to the factories and installations in the prefabricated city. For one of the world's most powerful industrialists, it was a brilliant investment—providing his contracts were honored. If they were not honored—it could be a financial disaster.

But here, from Lisa, was startling information, hitherto unknown to Goerlitz or to any Westerners: that Red China secretly planned to abrogate its contract. Once the Chinese had their nuclear city, they would confiscate the factories, nationalize them, discontinue payments, and throw Goerlitz and his Germans out. Then, because they needed assistance in running these advanced-design nuclear reactors, the Chinese planned to revive their friendship with the Soviet Union and bring their old Russian comrades in to replace the Germans.

The implications were stunning.

Brennan heard Lisa speaking. He looked up. She was pointing to his notes. "Matt, what's all that for?"

441

He folded the scratch paper carefully and placed it in his pocket. "It's for Emmett A. Earnshaw," he said.

"What's that got to do with you?"

"It's got a lot to do with *us*," said Brennan. "It could mean everything or nothing."

"I'm in a fog."

"I'll help you out of it, a little. I've got to think this through. But as of now, Lisa, Goerlitz is about to destroy Earnshaw, and Earnshaw is helpless unless he has some leverage to move Goerlitz out of his hardened position, make Goerlitz amenable, make Goerlitz grateful and indebted to him. If Earnshaw can use this information of yours to give the German a warning, well, he should be able to get anything he wants from Goerlitz."

She squeezed her eyes. "I think I see. Maybe I do. But you—us—what's in it for you?"

"Just as Goerlitz'll be in Earnshaw's debt for this information, so Earnshaw will be in my debt for helping him. Earnshaw will owe me something."

"What?"

"A ticket to Rostov, dear. Do you understand?"

Lisa looked at him blankly. "No," she said. "Champagne doesn't understand." Then she said, "But all this mystery and trading, it's good for us?"

Brennan reached for her hand. "It's very good for us," he said. He was happy now, and glad that he had not told her earlier that this was their farewell dinner. For now it wasn't. Now it had the makings of a celebration.

"You hungry?" he asked.

"No. Do you love me?"

"I love you. Want to try those swings in the bar?"

"Anytime."

"Now," he said.

For HAZEL SMITH, thus far, it had been a divine evening, one of the best in several years of memory.

A glass panel in the dome-shaped, bubbletop roof of the *bateau-mouche,* their luxurious Seine excursion boat, had been slid back, and a balmy breeze curled through the dining room, teasing the candle on each red-clothed table and caressing Hazel's cheeks and shoulders. She sliced the last of her pintadeau régence, and ate it, and the portion of baby guinea hen melted in her mouth. Lifting her eyes, she could see Jay Doyle, so neat and quiet and smelling of cologne, eating sparingly of his Chateaubriand, ignoring all sauces, and she was as proud of him as if he had been her husband.

She supposed the enchanting river ride would be over soon—they had been talking and drinking and dining on the *bateau-mouche* for nearly two hours—and she hated to have it end. Sipping her wine, she listened to the organist playing a selection from Massenet's *Manon*— and then recognized it as *"Adieu, notre petite table,"* Manon Lescaut's plaintive farewell to the little table where she and the Chevalier des Grieux had dined—and suddenly Hazel realized that it was more than this trip on the Seine that she did not want to come to an end.

She looked off through the side of the transparent dome, and she could make out the vines cascading down ancient walls and the quays of the Right Bank into the river. She could see, on the weathered stone steps leading up from the bank of the Seine toward the city, a French boy and girl locked in an embrace, and overhead, above and beyond the green treetops, she beheld the spires of Notre-Dame shining against the darkened Paris sky.

The *bateau-mouche* moved on through the water, and Notre-Dame was gone, and only the stars remained. They were passing the Quai d'Orleans on the Île St.-Louis, and in a moment they were under the Pont de Sully, and the illuminated white boat was making a wide sweeping turn, to return and pass the point where the evening had begun.

She watched the weeping willows touching the water, and as they glided beneath the iron bridge connecting the Île St.-Louis and the Île de la Cité, she studied the islands she had always enjoyed.

"Jay," she said, still looking off, "there's a statue on the Île de la Cité, at the tip. It's King Henri IV on horseback. Have you ever seen it?"

"I don't think so."

"I love the statue, because I've loved Henri IV ever since a guide told me the last time I was here that Henri changed his religion from Protestant to Catholic, to become King, explaining, 'Paris is well worth a Mass!' Don't you love that? But you know what really made him popular? Henri IV, I mean. He once announced that he wanted every Frenchman to have a *poule* every Sunday. A *poule* means a hen, but in French slang it also means a chick, a whore. They adored him after that."

Doyle laughed, his chins shaking. "Great, Hazel, absolutely great."

"Jay, I'm so glad you took me out here for dinner."

"I am, too, but the credit is yours, Hazel. You were the one who suggested the *bateau-mouche*."

"Did I?" This was disappointing, but she refused to allow it to detract from her cavalier's romantic judgment. "Well, I'd never taken the night ride on one of these boats, and I thought it was the kind of thing you'd want us to share."

"That's right." He was busy with his omelette norvégienne. Conscious that she was watching him, he suddenly ceased eating the soufflé-and-ice-cream dessert, and firmly pushed it aside.

Observing his new Spartanism, pleased with his strength of character, Hazel said, "I've never even had dinner on the *bateau-mouche* before, have you?"

"No. But it was a great idea."

"Now I remember where I got the idea. I've been interviewing some of the delegates on their favorite eating places in Paris. This was one. So I thought I'd check into it for a possible feature. The publicity director met me at the top of the stairs, on the Place de l'Alma, and took me on a guided tour of one of the boats that were anchored. Colorful material, very good."

"What kind of thing?"

"Like Paris was always a big boat city. But when the underground Métro was built, that was practically the finish of the passenger boats, except for a few beat-up excursion craft left over from the Paris Exposition of 1860. Anyway, in 1930 or so, a Sorbonne student named Bruel used one of these old river hulks to sleep in. He loved the Seine, felt it was the center of Paris, and later, when he became affluent, he created his flotilla of *bateaux-mouches*. He named his first vessel after Jean-Sebastien Mouche, and even commissioned a statue of Mouche."

"Mouche? Who was he?"

"The little man who wasn't there," said Hazel with delight. "He was an imaginary person—just right for an unbelievable boat to be named after. But you ask anyone in Paris today, and they'll probably tell you Monsieur Mouche founded the French Navy." She took up her wine glass. "Anyway, I thank Monsieur Mouche and I thank Monsieur Doyle for a marvelous dinner."

Doyle picked up his glass of Evian water. "And I thank you for being you—and I thank you, again, for seeing me after last night."

"I was just as sleepy as you, with all that food we'd put away," she said. "Jay, I appreciated the way you tidied up my apartment. It was pristine when I returned this morning with those fashion editors I was interviewing."

444

"Whenever you need a day worker, call on me. I hope you had a good morning."

"Oh, yes," she said quickly, guiltily, praying he would not ask her about the interviews.

He did not pursue the matter. He seemed lost in thought as he gazed out the window, and she was relieved. Lighting a cigarette, Hazel considered his porcine profile. He was nice, nicer even than on their last date. He had dressed with pathetic care, like a high school junior going to his first prom. He had dominated his appetite, controlled it, eaten normally and sensibly, perhaps for her rather than for himself. He had been a gentleman throughout the excursion, and he had been a gentleman last night, too. She wondered about last night, whatever weakness and madness had induced her to go upstairs and change. She had not wanted him then, any more than she wanted him now. Perhaps she had been betrayed by the past, by a nostalgia for what had been but likely could never be again.

Surreptitiously, she continued to scrutinize him. Well-groomed he was, well-behaved he was, but he was not the monument of a man she had once imagined him to be. He was a ruin, ravaged by gluttony, brought down by many failures and one obsession. There was not enough of him left for a woman to lean on, depend on; there was not enough strength to support another's love. She had returned too late to preserve the monument.

She mourned her loss, then fiercely she resented it, hating to give up hope. Certainly, she told herself, there was more to him. There had to be a force beneath the flabby layers of flesh, else how could he have passed her test a second night? For not once had he brought up his assassination book or indicated that he was here to use her. Apparently he possessed remarkable willpower, a virtue—or possibly, better yet, he possessed a matured affection for her, an endearment.

Once more she studied him, now with more kindly eyes. There he was, fat face at the window, silently absorbed, but she could not determine whether he was absorbed in self or in what lay outside. She gave her attention to the window, to see what he was seeing.

There were houseboats docked along the banks of the Seine, and now their own boat was traveling under the Pont de Bir-Hakeim. It was turning in the river, and the small replica of the Statue of Liberty and the illuminated brown girders of the Eiffel Tower passed in review. They were heading back to the point of their original departure.

She and Doyle came away from the window simultaneously. The music had stopped. The candle between them had burned out. And the fat face above the candle holder—definitely it had been absorbed in self.

She felt the faintest flush of shame. So determined had she been that he pass her test tonight, that she had purposely avoided asking him about himself or encouraging him to speak of his activities. And now the excursion was almost over. She had, because of her fears, been grossly unfair to him.

"Jay," she said, "you haven't told me a thing about yourself. What have you been up to today?"

He stared at her. "I—I've—well, I hate to say it, but there's been nothing very much."

"Have you been working on your cookbook?"

"I've been doing some research."

"What are you going to do after—well, after you leave Paris?"

"I don't know."

He had spoken the last so despairingly, so helplessly, that Hazel found herself shaken. No longer did she see before her the fat face of self-indulgence and weakness, but instead the lean and macerated face of the lonely and the haunted. It was a trick of the darkness, perhaps—all the candles were out, the lights of the landing dimmed—or perhaps her yearning heart now saw him more clearly than her colder eyes. He was lost, he was lonely and this was the hidden language behind words that she understood, for so was she as lost, as lonely, as he. At once, all rationale was discarded, all reservations were shed. She felt empathy for him, because she felt pity for herself. She wanted to hold him, all of him, warm in her arms, and suffocate their loneliness forever.

He was pushing back his chair. "We'd better go, Hazel."

Dazed, she joined him, following the line of people to the gangplank, barely aware of the passengers remaining behind to continue their drinking. On the narrow rim of deck she waited for him to tip the effusively grateful headwaiter, and then they were on the landing below the Place de l'Alma.

For a moment, bewildered, she tried to remember where she had parked her car, and recalled that she had not brought her car, because it had seemed unromantic for her to drive on a dinner date. She had been tired of her strident independence, her career-dominated self-sufficiency, and she had wondered if she was still capable of allowing someone else to look out for her. She had wanted to be a woman wanted, not a redheaded journalist terror. Even in Moscow, so many years, so very many, this yearning part of her had not been satisfied. She had not been alone in those years, but she had been lonely. She had been made to feel female, but she had never felt feminine. Doyle was offering her an opportunity to learn whether any soft and pliable

446

dependence was left in her. Perhaps this was why she had so rashly changed into her lingerie the previous night. Perhaps this was why she had not taken her own car earlier this evening. Perhaps she was testing not Doyle but herself.

Self-consciously she held his arm as her free hand clutched the silly white, red-trimmed handkerchief imprinted with the menu of the *bateau-mouche* on one side and the emblem of the river cruise boats— a Zouave in blue jacket and red pantaloons, and bearing a rifle—on the other side. It was the first souvenir she had saved since she had been a schoolgirl in Wisconsin. Retarded femininity, she thought. But femininity, none the less.

Doyle led her between the iron barriers guarding the benches, chairs, rows of flowerpots on the Seine side, and the rows of parked automobiles on the other side, toward the stairs leading from the quay to the Place de l'Alma above.

"Jay," she said, "did you really mean you don't know what you're going to do after you leave Paris?"

"That's true."

"But you must have something in mind."

"I'm not sure. It depends. It depends on what happens here."

Desperately, as they walked, she tried to interpret this. Upon what did his future depend? On making a success of the cookbook here? On doing a good job for Earnshaw here? Or on—on Hazel Smith—on winning her back, to give his life motivation and purpose?

They reached the steps and ascended them in silence. At the top, they were confronted by the wild traffic spinning around the circles and triangles and illuminated corner posts of the Place de l'Alma.

Still puffing from their climb, Doyle glanced about. "I'd better find a taxi. It's eleven-thirty. I guess you'll want to get some sleep."

"I'm not sleepy. What were you going to do?"

"Well, I—I was just going back to my hotel. But if—"

"I'll go with you," she said. He looked bewildered, and she added quickly, "You can treat me to a brandy, can't you? Brandy makes me sleepy."

"Why, I'd love to, Hazel."

They survived the crossing of the Place de l'Alma and walked a half block until they found a taxi, and five minutes later they arrived at the Hotel George-V.

Hazel preceded Doyle through the revolving door, and they entered the vast lobby, with its black lacquered Louis XV desks and tables, its arrangements of brown velvet-covered chairs clustered together on the areas of marble floor not covered by the great central Oriental rug.

Doyle pointed ahead. "The bar's through that corridor."

Hazel did not move. "I don't want to go to the bar," she said. "I'd prefer to go to your room. I'd rather have privacy. Do you mind, Jay?"

"Mind?" His hangdog expression was gone. "It's what I'd like most. I can send for drinks, and we can kick off our shoes and talk. That is, if you're not too tired."

"I'm not too tired."

She hung back while he asked for his key at the desk and received with it a telephone message slip from the concierge. In the elevator he opened the message, read it, and looked puzzled. Stuffing the message in his pocket, he became aware of her concern. "Nothing, Hazel. Matt Brennan phoned an hour ago. Asked if I could manage to arrange for him to see Earnshaw sometime tomorrow. Urgent. Said he'd explain in the morning." He shrugged. "I can't imagine what that's about."

"Brennan and Earnshaw," said Hazel. "Now, there's a combination."

"I know. I'll try to explain it someday." The elevator had stopped. "Here we are. Fifth floor. Be it ever so humble—"

When she passed before him into his room, she was surprised to find herself in a suite. She had quite forgotten that Jay Doyle had always lived beyond his means.

He caught up with her and waddled ahead of her into the salon. Expansively, he gestured toward the window overlooking the marble courtyard, the sofa covered in rich brocade, the crystal chandelier gleaming above. He patted his portable typewriter resting on the table next to the green lamp.

"My office," he said.

"For heaven's sake, how many rooms are there, Jay?"

"Only this and"—he indicated an open door—"the bedroom and bath in there."

She walked slowly past him into the bedroom. Tasteful, with a pink ceiling, light gray walls, a large bed, the headboard pearl-gray leather, the bedspread ivory-colored velvet, already turned back for the night. Next to the sumptuous bed, next to the silver candlestick lamp that held a smart white shade, stood Doyle's own clock. It was a cheap and dented traveling clock. It was incongruous.

He was across the room. "A million built-ins," he said, expansively. "Even a built-in safe. How do you like that?"

She joined him. "What's in the safe?"

"Nothing," he said sheepishly. "Except my passport."

"Passport," she repeated hollowly.

She pulled out a drawer beneath the safe. There were several shirts in it. The collar of the top one was frayed. She moved to the wardrobe that doubled as a closet, and opened it. It was empty except for two suits, shiny, oversized suits, the kind she had seen on struggling Russian laborers when they wore their Sunday best while strolling down Karl Marx Prospekt or munching hot pirozhki along Gorki Street.

She had turned to speak to him, but he was leaving the bedroom and she was alone. Sadly she surveyed the room, and for the first time she noticed the messy suitcase, the piles of notes and blank notepaper pads, the misshapen night slippers, the open telephone book, the heap of foreign coins, the half-filled bottle of Evian, the discarded tie hanging over the back of a chair. Suddenly the bedroom was not luxurious at all but merely the prideful fan of a peacock's tail. Suddenly the bedroom was like any one of a hundred rooms belonging to those who were dispossessed, those who had no roots, those who belonged nowhere. Suddenly the bedroom was another way station for those running, always running, destinations unknown. It was Doyle's countless rooms and it was her countless rooms, and it was their lives, and she wanted to weep for him and for herself, for both of them.

Her mind was made up. Resolutely she went into the salon. He was on the telephone.

"What are you doing?" she wanted to know.

"Ordering brandy," he said. "Haven't gotten through yet."

"Hang up," she said.

Taken aback, he dropped the receiver into its cradle.

"I hate brandy," she said. "I didn't come up here for brandy."

He looked at her incredulously as she walked directly to him and stood straight before him.

"But, Hazel—"

"Jay, you damn fool, can't you see? I want you."

"Hazel—my god, Hazel—"

His bearish arms and bulk smothered her in a fervent embrace, and through all his layers of fat she could hear his heart and feel his trembling.

It took willpower to restrain her tears. But then, pressed against him, she wanted no willpower, which was unfeminine, she wanted to be what she was, which was feminine, feminine, feminine. She tasted the salt of her tears and she did not care. She desired only to be a woman, a woman who was no longer alone.

"Jay—" she whispered brokenly. "Love me."

IT WAS THE FIRST LIGHT of the new day shining through the drapes that forced her to open her eyes. The bedside clock was ticking loudly, and she reached for it, grasped it, brought it in front of her. The hour was six-thirty in the morning.

She could hear him snoring and exhaling, and she dropped the clock on the bed between them, turned her head sideways on the pillow. In the half-light between the last of the darkness and the first of dawn, she could make out the mound beside her.

He lay on his back like a beached Moby Dick, eyes tight, nostrils distended, mouth open, exhaling and whistling. She shouldn't be looking at him, she knew, when he was helpless like this. It was unfair to observe and judge another person while he was sleeping or eating, when he was unaware he was being watched, when he had not slipped on the public mask. Yet she was pleased to see how relaxed and content was his puffy countenance. It was something, something good.

She turned her gaze upward at the pink squares of the ceiling, and she felt luxurious enough to belong in these luxurious surroundings, because she owned so much, so suddenly.

In retrospect, what she clung to of their lovemaking six hours ago was the snugness and safety of being in his arms, naked, wanted for herself and not her by-line, wanted for her total femininity and not her sex alone. It had not been like the past, when he was younger, harder, stronger. It had been like now, when he was older, flabbier, weaker. His love had not been arrogant, as once, but more anxious and needing. And his panting—the panting had been of age, not passion. Or maybe some passion. But the rest, short-windedness. He must reduce. He must exercise. He must learn to obey her.

It had not been perfect, but then, she remembered, it never had been, not really. Younger, successful, he had sometimes made love alone, it had often seemed, using her for his pleasure and feeling that she should be sufficiently satisfied by just her knowledge of his satisfaction. Last night he had made love not alone, not with her, but almost for her, to please so that he could be pleased. But in the end it had been for himself, too, she guessed, except much differently from long ago. For finally, he had made love needing her too much, needing the security of her approval, like an infant suckling at a mother's breast.

No, in the honesty of dawn, it had not been physically stimulating, nothing like the wild animal love, the almost helpless and therefore

450

guiltless rapings, that had aroused her in the nights of the years after the young Doyle and before the present Doyle. No, last night had not been like those other nights, the Russian nights, when her nakedness had resisted yet begged for the sunderings and wrenchings that had so often torn body free from mind. No, last night's engagement, soft and timid and apologetic, had not served to arouse her sexuality, but it had touched and moved something deeper, and she supposed that to be her total femininity.

Yes, last night had been better than any other night she had known. She and Jay, stretched on their sides, holding one another, needing each other, joining—this had been sweet, delicious, this had been familiar, comfortable, mutual; this had been belonging with one of your own, not being serviced by an alien bull.

Yes, this had been sweet love, if not good sex, and she had shown her appreciation, she had helped, she had given all of herself to make more of him, and then gloried in his pleasure because it had come from her. Yet that had not been quite enough, for after his fulfillment she had whispered of her own need, and he had helped her, and she had become his slave until her release, and it had been wonderful.

He had slept first. She had remained awake, drowsy behind closed eyes, projecting his future. And finally, before sleep, she had come to her decision. He needed her in many ways: this way, but in many more ways. She had satisfied one part of him. Now she would fulfill the rest of him. For himself, so that he would be made whole. For them, so that they could go on together. She had yawned and thought how little there was left of life. It was worth any emotional gamble to make the most of what was left, to use it well. It had been her final thought, she supposed, before sleep.

Now, with dawn, she was wide-awake, and her final thought had become her foremost morning thought.

Quietly she left the bed, determined not to disturb him, for there was much to be done before he awakened.

She would bathe and dress, and search through his belongings, and then do what she had promised herself she would do. After that, she would know what was possible.

Methodically, and with zest, Hazel followed her plan, and it seemed that two hours could hardly have passed when she heard Doyle awakening. At the sounds of his getting out of bed, she looked up from the sofa of the salon where, stockinged feet curled beneath her, she had been absorbed in her reading.

Through the slight opening of the bedroom door she could hear him thumping about.

Cupping one hand to her mouth, she called out, "Jay? . . . Are you up?"

His hoarse morning voice came back. "About time, I'd say. Why'd you let me oversleep?"

"Because you're a darling, and you needed it. Should I order breakfast for us?"

"And how. Eggs and coffee. Let me wash. I'll be right out."

She waited to hear his bathroom door close, and then she ordered breakfast for both of them. After that, she telephoned ANA to find out if there were any messages for her. There had been several, and one was from Medora Hart.

Promptly, she called Medora at the San Régis. She told Medora that she could speak only briefly to her, since she was phoning from a booth, but she would talk to her at greater length sometime during the day. Remembering the Nardeau exhibit the night before last and suspecting why Medora had called her, Hazel asked if the nude painting had flushed out Lady Fleur Ormsby. It had, indeed, and that was the reason Medora had telephoned. Quickly Medora recited the details of her scene with Fleur Ormsby. Then, Medora unfolded her newest scheme. If Hazel would be willing to write a feature story on Nardeau's Retrospective Exhibit, pretending to have interviewed the dealer of the Galerie, as well as Nardeau by telephone, and pointing out that the sensation of the opening had been *Nude in the Garden,* which Nardeau had confirmed was a painting for which the present Lady Ormsby had once been the model, this might be enough to break Fleur down. Hazel's story, of course, would not be intended for publication, but Fleur would not know that. It would be written as if it were ready to be put on the wires. Medora would send a copy of it to Fleur through Carol, and Medora would promise Fleur to have it killed if Fleur met her terms. Was this too much of an imposition upon Hazel?

"Imposition? Nonsense! It's a sensational idea, Medora. And it'll work. This'll do it. Absolutely a cinch. Okay, honey, here's what. Soon's I get back to the office, I'll bat it out. I'll send a flimsy of it over to your hotel by special messenger. Then you two carry on from there. Honey, you're in, you're home free. Accept my advance congratulations."

Hanging up, Hazel was delighted that she could contribute to Medora's final triumph. She would help save Medora. Now all that remained was to help save her beloved Jay—and herself.

There was a knock at the door, and she opened it and waited while the Room Service waiter rolled in the breakfast cart and set the places. After he had gone, she plopped down on the sofa, picked up the manuscript and became engrossed in the remaining pages. Five minutes later she had finished her reading. Sitting back, stimulated and excited, she reviewed the contents of the book and deliberated on her own role.

Suddenly she was aware of Jay in the room, advancing toward her. He was clean-shaved, freshly groomed, neatly dressed. He came toward her, a cow-eyed pudgy Romeo, sank down on the sofa beside her, took her in his arms and kissed her.

"Thanks, Hazel," he said at last.

Somehow, his anxiety to be grateful irritated her. This morning she wanted not obsequiousness but authority. "Jay, you don't thank someone for love. It's mutual."

"I only meant—how happy you've made me."

"I'm happy, too."

"It was like old times," he said. "Only better."

"Yes," she said.

"Well—breakfast." He drew the cart closer to them, and as he did so, his eyes fell on the manuscript resting on the low table before Hazel.

He blinked at it, puzzled, and then he looked at Hazel. "Honey, what's that?"

She smiled at the discovery of her surprise. "Your book," she said. *"The Conspirators Who Killed Kennedy."*

"But, Hazel—" Still confused, he said, "Did you—did you read it?"

She continued to smile. "Every word of it. The first chapter. The entire outline."

At once he was troubled. "Hazel, I didn't bring you up here for that. I—"

"Jay, you didn't bring me up here, period. I brought myself up here. And this morning I hunted for the book, found it, and read it, because I wanted to."

"But I didn't want to bother you."

"Jay, listen. I *wanted* to read it. I'm glad I did." She gripped his arm. "Jay, it's a masterpiece, the best work you've ever written. The research, the writing, the suspense, an absolute cliff-hanger. How did you do it? I gave you so little to begin with in Vienna, and look what you've done with it. Why, Jay, it's not just a book. It's a historic document. It'll be a world sensation, the greatest best seller in best-seller history."

He had been listening open-mouthed, and now his eyes had filled. "My God, darling, my God, you really mean it?" He grabbed her in his big arms, clutching her to his chest. "Hazel, you really mean it?"

She freed herself and smoothed her hair back into place. "I've meant everything I've said, Jay. You know how tough a critic I am. But I couldn't put it down. It's a winner." She shook her head. "After Dallas, after they got Oswald, even I began to have my doubts about what I'd heard in Vienna, about the conspiracy. Yet here you've gone out and demolished all the arguments pointing to Oswald as the killer and built up the case for conspiracy with your incredible challenges and questions, questions that are as shattering as facts."

"That's right, Hazel, that's right."

Suddenly she straightened, and all at once she was no longer Hazel Smith, soft-hearted bedmate, but Hazel Smith, hardheaded journalist. "Now let's have our coffee, Jay, and let's be practical." She watched his quivering hand as he gave her a cup and saucer, and she observed the unsteadiness increase as he brought his own coffee to his lips, eyeing her expectantly.

She sipped the coffee, no longer hot, but she did not mind. She drank down half of it and set her cup and saucer back on the tray. "Okay, Jay," she said, "you've got everything there but the final proof. I suppose you've heard that before."

"Yes, Hazel."

"Okay, I've made up my mind. Your book deserves it. You deserve it. Jay, I can't guarantee anything, but I've decided to help you. I'm going to help you get the final proof."

"Hazel, I—I can't tell you what that means to me," he said emotionally.

"I know what that means," she said. "It means you'll be on top again."

"We'll be on top," he corrected her quickly.

Good boy, she wanted to say. Good, good boy. Instead she said, "Very nice." Briskly she resumed in her practical tone. "I've been in Moscow forever, as you know. I've seen everyone, got to know everyone who is anyone. It's part of my job. I know many Russians in Government, some big ones, and a lot of them are my friends." She paused. "And the Russian in Vienna, the one who hinted at the conspiracy—he's still around, he's more important than ever, and luckily he's still my friend."

She could see that Jay Doyle was beginning to perspire. She could see, also, he was becoming too abject. "Hazel, I—I can't tell you how I—"

"You don't have to tell me a thing," she said crisply. "You just listen. . . . This old friend of mine from Vienna—I told you he's more important than ever. Well, he is. He's important enough to be in

454

the Russian delegation to the Summit. In other words, he's right here in Paris this minute." She went more slowly now, attempting to think before she spoke. "I'll try to see him, and if I can, I'll try to bring this matter up. Naturally, it's a touchy subject. It was never clear to me, in Vienna or since, whether he meant that he was approached to join a Russian-directed conspiracy to assassinate President Kennedy or whether he was approached to join an international Communist—what might be called a new Comintern—conspiracy, I mean, one inspired by the worldwide Communist hierarchy in general, by the party, or simply by one Communist government specifically. Also, it was never clear to me from the little I heard in 1961 whether the conspiracy was official or a completely unofficial intrigue concocted by a handful of fanatical Red extremists. I don't know. That's what makes it touchy. If I bluntly bring up the subject, or even find a tactful way to work it into conversation, and the conspiracy happened to have been Russian and was official, well, I'm not going to get anywhere, except into hot water. My Soviet informant will clam up, and that'll be that. The last door'll be slammed shut, Jay, and you'll have to give up and forget it."

Doyle nodded in assent.

"Just so you understand," Hazel continued. "And on the other hand, if the assassination was not an act that involved Soviet Russia, if it was something committed by Communist party hotheads without official sanction, that might be another thing altogether. Then my Russian friend, my informant, might be willing to talk, spin out a little more information, once he recalls that I know this much from him. He wouldn't have to talk much, just a few facts, or hints of facts, or maybe clues or leads to the real killers. Even a single name of some Communist, living or dead, in Hungary or Albania or Italy or Cuba."

"That's all I'd need, Hazel, that's all."

"Yes," she said, reflecting upon it, "but even that much, even at best, won't be easy. The only thing I've got going for me—for us—is my old friendship with—with this informant. I've done him many small favors over the years. This'll be a chance for him—if it's not dangerous for him, if it's humanly possible for him—to do a favor for me in return."

She had become lost in the recent past these moments, remembering nights in Moscow and afternoons in the countryside—their enjoyment of the garlic-flavored chicken tabaka at the Aragvy restaurant; their shopping in GUM for a karakul cap for him and black lace underwear for her; their *dacha* hideout with the outdoor privy; their compliance to *"do dna!"* when they drank bottoms up; their serious hours of *dusha-dushi,* those soul-to-soul talks. She was remembering, remembering favors given and favors received, uncertain how the balance sheet stood right now, uncertain how she would go about it and what would happen once she did, knowing only she must make the effort.

She had come out of the Rabbit Hole, and there was Jay Doyle. "All right," she said, "that's it. I'll get right on it. What's today? Tuesday. No, that was yesterday. I'm all mixed up. This is Wednesday. Okay. I should have something definite for you this week. Consider it in the works."

"I—I don't know what to say to you, Hazel. I don't know why you're doing this for me."

She made a snorting sound and reached for a piece of toast. "Because I'm in love with you, you fathead. Now, eat your breakfast before it all gets cold."

V

HAVING LEFT Doyle's suite reluctantly, and the Hotel George-V lobby willingly (embarrassed by the covert glances from tourists and bellboys, who had stared at her dressy evening attire), Hazel Smith returned to her apartment a few minutes before ten o'clock in the morning. After changing into her work uniform, a black-and-white-checked linen suit and low-heeled shoes, she settled down to make two telephone calls.

Her future with Jay Doyle was still uppermost in her mind. And so her first call was to the Russian Embassy in Paris.

Once again, as she had done a hundred times before in Moscow and in other European capitals, Hazel followed the procedure that she and Nikolai Rostov had long ago agreed upon. She represented herself as the secretary of an employer who had assigned her the task of leaving a message for Minister Rostov. There was always one secretary, herself, but there were always many mythical employers she had invented, naming them to suit the city in which she made her call.

This morning she was M. Gérard's secretary. *Oui, madame,* Monsieur Gérard would like to leave word for Minister Rostov to telephone him. It concerns the business matter about which they have corresponded. Minister Rostov might best reach Monsieur Gérard between the hours of noon and two o'clock. *Non, madame,* not necessary, for Minister Rostov is already in possession of Monsieur Gérard's private telephone number. *Merci.*

Next, Medora Hart's future was on Hazel's mind. And so her second call was to the Hotel San Régis.

Medora, who was in her room, admitted she had hoped Hazel would call back, and was pathetically pleased that she had done so. Still elated over Hazel's approval of the new scheme directed against

457

Fleur Ormsby, Medora was further thrilled by Hazel's promise of cooperation. The two discussed the Ormsbys at length, and Hazel outlined the contents of her fake ANA story. She would, she promised, write her feature story as if it were a breathtaking front-page beat—Nardeau had confessed, under questioning by this reporter, that the hit of his Retrospective Exhibit, *Nude in the Garden,* had been painted from a living model, and that the naked girl who had posed for the painting while still a wild young debutante was none other than Lady Ormsby, recently become the wife of the British Foreign Minister, Sir Austin Ormsby. Furthermore, M. Michel Callet, the proprietor of the Nouvelle Galerie d'Art, where the astonishing painting dominated center stage, admitted that it was creating greater controversy than had Édouard Manet's nude *Olympia* when it had been exhibited in Paris in 1865, and the disgusted Empress Eugénie had slapped it with her fan.

Listening, Medora squealed her appreciation. It sounded so *authentic.* "Thanks, Medora, but it had better *look* authentic when Fleur, and maybe her husband, read the advance flimsy," Hazel said. "After all, they're in the newspaper business, too. In fact, I'm beginning to think I'd better not goof it up in any way. I'll tell you what—I was just going to sit down and knock out the story, but I really haven't anything special to do until late afternoon. So I think I'll just walk over to the Avenue de Friedland, pop in on Monsieur Michel and the Galerie, have myself another peek at our precious Lady Ormsby bare-ass, maybe ask Michel a few questions without letting him know what we're up to, you know, just to get the real ring of truth in the quotes I'm inventing, and then I'll have notes and can dash it off."

Promising Medora that she would have the story in her hands before nightfall, Hazel checked her purse for pad and pencil as she left the apartment and started toward the Nouvelle Galerie d'Art.

It was not a long distance, no more than eight or nine blocks, and she covered most of it at a leisurely pace, enjoying the early warmth of the summer's morning and fantasying the new promise that life held for her.

The landmarks were familiar, and she guessed that she was in the neighborhood of the Galerie. Squinting ahead, she could discern the poster of the exhibit a half block away, and she crossed the street and headed for it. Nearing a small café, her attention was distracted by an American family of four, the twin children noisily complaining about the lateness of their breakfast. The rawboned father of the family, a Stetson pushed far back on his head, glowered at his shrill wife and his brawling brats, and lay back in his wicker chair to read his Paris edition of the New York *Herald Tribune.* He opened the paper wide to screen off his troublesome family as he sought the latest sports results.

As he buried himself in the newspaper, Hazel automatically glanced at the boldest of the front-page headlines. Suddenly she stopped dead in her tracks.

Her vision had tricked her, she was sure, but she darted toward the newspaper being held aloft in the tourist's hands. The headline was distinct now, and there was no mistaking what it trumpeted:

DARING PARIS ART THEFT
FIVE NARDEAU PAINTINGS STOLEN FROM GALLERY EXHIBIT
POLICE MYSTIFIED

Chilled by apprehension, Hazel tried to make out the lead. The front page buckled, and the head of the Texan, obviously Texan, appeared glaring above it.

"I—I'm sorry," Hazel said quickly. "I hadn't got my paper today, and there was something on the front page—"

"You American?" the Texan drawled, instantly companionable. "Hey now, sure. Already finished that part." He separated the front section and handed it to her. "Have a free look on the house."

Hazel snatched at the paper and began to scan the lead story, one sensational enough to have nudged the Summit news over to the next column. In seconds her trained eye had picked up the gist of the fragmentary news report, the flash slugged in on the final night run of the newspaper. A charwoman had been cleaning in the Nouvelle Galerie d'Art after midnight. She had finished her labors around two in the morning and had taken out her keys to secure the rear door after her when she left. Then she remembered she had forgotten to put away her broom. Returning with her broom to the utility room, she was surprised to find that two large windows had been left open. Going to close them, she saw that the iron shutters had been pried apart. Fearful and frantic, she had at once telephoned M. Michel, and he had notified the Commissariat de Police of the arrondissement. And then the proprietor and the authorities had converged upon the Galerie to find blank spaces on the walls. At press time, all that had been ascertained was that five valuable Nardeaus were missing—the art dealer had not yet seen fit to announce precisely which paintings had been stolen—and the police were still carefully combing the premises for clues.

Hazel shoved the newspaper back at the Texan. "Thanks a million," she called out.

459

"We Americans gotta stick together," he bellowed after her.

Hazel walked no more. She ran, arriving breathless at the Nouvelle Galerie d'Art, and rushed inside. In contrast to the opening night, when the main exhibit hall had been swarming with festive celebrities carrying glasses of champagne, the main room was occupied by grim-faced uniformed police sent by the arrondissement's Commissariat and with intent plainclothes detectives from the brigade de voie publique. Some officers were in hushed conference. Others were searching for fingerprints.

Hazel saw the distraught dealer, Michel, emerge from a side door. She hurried to intercept him. "Monsieur Michel, which paintings were stolen?"

He considered her suspiciously. "Who are you, madame?"

"I'm Hazel Smith from ANA, the American newspaper—"

"I have nothing to comment," he interrupted rudely. "I cannot speak to journalists as yet."

He turned on his heel and started toward a group of busy police. Hazel took several steps in pursuit of him. "But, monsieur, I'm a friend of Medora Hart, and she's—"

"Medora Hart?" someone behind her repeated.

Hazel wheeled to find herself facing a tall, ash-blond, magnificent Scandinavian girl attired in blouse and slacks. "Yes," Hazel said, "I'm a friend of Miss Hart's. I'm Hazel Smith."

The Scandinavian girl's solemn features softened. "Ah, Miss Smith, I know of you. Medora, she has spoken to me of your kindness."

"I was just on the phone with Medora," Hazel continued. "I came here to help her on something when I heard about the robbery. What's going on?"

"It is terrible, very terrible," said the Scandinavian girl. "I too have been on the telephone, to locate Nardeau—I am Signe Andersson, his model, also Medora's friend. All morning I have been trying, but Nardeau is not in the villa, not in St.-Paul. He is off somewhere in the hills and will not be back until later. But the *commissaire division-naire* himself—the bald one over there with Monsieur Michel—he has taken over personally, because he is a friend and admirer of Nardeau and it is his belief—mine, too—this has been the theft of a French national treasure."

"Signe, just tell me one thing," Hazel said. "Is Medora's painting still here? *Nude in the Garden.* Is that still here?"

Signe Andersson did not reply. She raised her arm and pointed past Hazel's shoulder to the center of the main exhibition wall.

The center of the wall was blank.

There were Nardeau oils hanging to either side, but in the center, where *Nude in the Garden* had previously been, there was only a metal hook and an empty wall.

Hazel stood very still, feeling rage against Medora's persecutors rising within her. She wanted to shout out to everyone in the room, to the judiciary police, the brigade of detectives, the dealer, the model beside her, that she knew the thieves. She wanted to cry out that the culprit was Lady Ormsby, or Fleur and her big-shot husband, who were not above any act of crime that would protect the Ormsby name. Tempting as it was to do so, Hazel contained her venom.

She heard Signe addressing her once more. "Such a pity. I grieve for Medora. Himself, Nardeau, presented it to her, his farewell gift, because he thought it would take her back to her home."

"You know about Medora and the Ormsbys?" said Hazel.

Signe nodded. "I know."

Hazel's hand swept toward the French police. "Tell them, then. Maybe they can do something about it."

"Tell them what, Miss Smith? What can be proved against the Ormsbys? That they have harmed Medora? That they have put her in exile? That they committed this theft? I have thought of it, but no, there is not one evidence to show. The French police, I know them, they will think us lunatics. Besides, Miss Smith, maybe it was not the Ormsbys. It was maybe ordinary thieves, who could have taken that picture by a coincidence or because it was hanging in the important place."

"You know as well as I do that's not true," said Hazel fiercely. "Fleur met with Medora yesterday. Fleur was scared and she had to do something. She has money. She has connections. She could have hired a professional who has done this sort of thing, several of them, to pull it off. Now she has the painting and she's safe. And Medora, poor Medora, she has nothing."

Signe was thoughtful a moment. "I think you are maybe right, Miss Smith. Because it is strange. The thieves, they took the nude of Lady Ormsby and four others—they took five paintings worth one and a half million francs—but they left behind others much, much more valuable. There is one across the room, one alone, borrowed from the Jeu de Paume, that is worth two million francs by itself, and another over there on loan from the Musée National d'Art Moderne worth as much. But no, those they do not touch, but Medora's one and the four other not costly ones they take. Why? This I ask myself."

"You just ask me," said Hazel. "Fleur's paid crooks stole Medora's oil painting, because that's what they were paid to steal, paid plenty, you can be sure, without any headaches about being chased for well-known museum pieces. And they took the four others, just anything at all, to make it look like a routine theft. I'm still tempted to tell the police about Fleur Ormsby—"

"Please, I would not," said Signe hastily. "It cannot help Medora. And maybe it could cause her trouble. The police will not side with her, an English scandal girl who is undesirable in her own homeland, such a one against a famous British Cabinet Minister who is here as a guest of France to the Summit. It is impossible. And maybe it would make Medora undesirable here, too."

The Scandinavian girl's common sense blunted Hazel's fury. Signe was right, and Hazel knew it. "But, Signe, we must do something. We can't let that poor helpless girl—" She paused. "Does Medora know about this?"

"No one has called her. I have not the heart to, yet. After I speak with Nardeau, I shall have courage to call her. Of course, maybe she has read the papers. But there is nothing of her painting in there at this hour. The names of the paintings will not be given out until later." She looked off, troubled. "I do not know what progress they make. They have taken the wax castings of the marks on the shutters, where the shutters were forced open. They still take fingerprints. The *commissaire* has ordered all former art criminals, now free in Paris, to be brought in for the questioning, and he has called the Sûreté Nationale in Nice to make an interrogation with those on the Riviera who have police records. Perhaps it will lead to something, but—"

She halted abruptly as M. Michel appeared between them, ignoring Hazel to speak rapidly to the Scandinavian model. "Signe, if you reach Nardeau before I do, you must inform him of the latest developments. So far, the police say it was an outside job. A motorcar jack was used to rip the shutters. In the rear there are tire markings of a light Citroën truck. The police are definite in the feeling this is the work of a specialist who has done the same before, who has done it now for immediate cash, but one too clever to take the most costly works which are difficult to be rid of. You tell Nardeau that the *commissaire divisionnaire* himself has the plan to deal with certain informers, and they may lead us to the thief and the paintings. . . . *Mon Dieu,* every newspaper is calling to the office. You would think this is the biggest art crime since the—since when?—since more than a half century ago when the little Italian house painter stole the *Mona Lisa* from the Louvre. . . . But this has its importance. It is shameful. We must recover the paintings. I go now. If there is more news, I will give it to you, Signe, before you speak to Nardeau."

The moment that the dealer left them, Hazel took Signe's hand. "Thank you. I'll keep my fingers crossed. I'm going to call Medora. Someone's got to tell her before she reads it. And, Signe, I do want to be kept up on this. Well, I'm sure you'll be in constant touch with Medora, so I'll learn any new developments from her." She hesitated. "Signe, we've got to get that painting back. We've got everything solved if we have the painting. That girl's life depends on it."

"We will try, Miss Smith. Nardeau will turn Paris upside down, if it is necessary."

At the door Hazel looked back at the darting, jumping, kneeling police, and the Galerie seemed to be exhibiting not a collection of Nardeau paintings but a collection of Gaboriau characters. She opened the door and went outside. She needed cool, clean air to clear her head, but the day was hot and muggy.

She would go back to the apartment, she decided, and telephone Medora Hart from there. She would tell her what had happened and give her hope that the painting would be recovered, but promise her that even if it were not, Hazel herself would find someone, somehow, to intervene with the Ormsbys on Medora's behalf.

And then Hazel vowed that she would go even further. She would telephone Jay Doyle at ANA or at Earnshaw's suite, wherever he was, and try to meet with him before noon, so she could put this whole problem to him and find out what he thought could be done. This was important, suddenly as important as her own problem. No one on earth had the right to treat anyone else as less than human. Everyone on earth had the right to dignity and freedom and the pursuit of happiness. Meaning not only herself but Medora too. Dammit, something must be done and would be done. Meaning not only for Medora but for herself as well.

Satisfied, Hazel started back to her apartment and the telephone.

Accepting the instrument from Earnshaw, Doyle said apologetically to Earnshaw and Brennan, "Sorry, it'll just be a minute." He brought the telephone receiver closer to him. "Hello, Hazel. How are you?" He waited, listening, then said, "Yes, I've just come in. I don't think there'll be much work. I should be through soon. Why?"

From his chair across the coffee table, Matt Brennan watched

Earnshaw watching Doyle, knowing that the former President was puzzled and made uncomfortable by Brennan's presence in the Hotel Lancaster suite.

Brennan had enjoyed a wonderful and drunken celebration with Lisa last night, and he had overslept this morning, awakening with only the slightest hangover. Something about a hangover always anchored high hopes to reality. In the sober light of midmorning, last night's celebration seemed premature. Still, after objectively reviewing what Lisa had related to him twelve or thirteen hours earlier, there was enough to justify making a move.

Brennan had telephoned the Hotel George-V and been relieved to find Jay Doyle in his room. Without going into detail, he had informed Doyle that he had stumbled upon certain information which might be highly useful to Earnshaw in his relationship with Dr. Dietrich von Goerlitz. Doyle, in a gay mood, almost manic, had been eager to cooperate. He had to speak to Earnshaw anyway, he had said, to learn whether The Ex wanted to resume collaborating on his daily commentary about the Summit or whether he preferred to have Doyle continue to ghostwrite it entirely on his own. He would be pleased to pass on to Earnshaw what Brennan had been telling him. Five minutes later, Doyle had called back to report that while Earnshaw, listless and unconcerned, was not interested in working on the column, he was interested in hearing any word Brennan possessed about Goerlitz.

Within a half hour, Brennan had met Doyle in the Hotel Lancaster lobby, and together they had gone up to Earnshaw's suite. Even as Earnshaw and Doyle had settled into the overstuffed sofa, Brennan had perceived that The Ex had become dubious about the meeting. It was as if Earnshaw, on second thought, had decided that Brennan was merely leading him on with what would prove to be another disappointment, as if he had decided Brennan was employing any means to see him again, in a persistent effort to use him. Brennan wondered how Earnshaw would react to the information Lisa had inadvertently acquired for them. The answer to this had been briefly postponed by Doyle's phone call from Hazel Smith.

Doyle was speaking into the telephone. "All right, Hazel, of course. Any friend of yours is a friend of mine. I don't know, but maybe I can help. Let's say—I'd say in forty-five minutes, maybe less. How's that? . . . Okay, dear, Fouquet's. Perfect. I'll find you."

He hung up, once more apologizing as he gave the telephone back to Earnshaw, who was slouched in the corner of the sofa. After returning the telephone to the end table, Earnshaw busied himself with a cigar, slowly unpeeling the wrapping, seemingly reluctant to begin the meeting.

"I'm glad you were able to see me again, sir," Brennan said to the former President. "I have a hunch you won't regret it."

Earnshaw finished lighting the cigar. For a moment his troubled blue eyes were friendly and his countenance was benign. "On the contrary, Mr. Brennan. It is I who should be grateful to you, since Jay here tells me you know something of my difficulties and you have a notion you can help me. I want you to know I'm appreciative. I truly am."

"Well, I've had my share of problems, as you know," Brennan said, "so I'm highly sympathetic toward other people's problems. Not that a person in your position needs my help. Still—" He shrugged.

"No man can walk alone all the time," said Earnshaw. "I have often, in my public speeches, referred to the parable—uh—the parable of the good Samaritan. One of my favorites. Now then—" He took one more puff of his cigar, laid it in an ashtray, and cleared his throat. "I suppose we can be perfectly frank, Mr. Brennan. My good friend, Jay Doyle here, tells me that somehow you've found out about Dr. Dietrich von Goerlitz's memoirs and—uh—about the unfortunate chapter in those memoirs concerning my Administration. Well, I'm sorry all of that leaked out, but I can't say I'm surprised. In any case, I don't suppose it matters too much since Goerlitz intends to make his misrepresentations public soon enough." He considered Brennan through the haze of smoke. "You may or may not know that I met with Goerlitz personally, to try to knock some sense of decency into his Teutonic head. I didn't have much luck. He's determined not to listen to me. He's bent on—uh—on doing me harm."

"Well, I guessed as much," said Brennan. "It's my hope that what I have to say will make Goerlitz listen to you."

Earnshaw smiled wanly. "I doubt if anything will make him listen to reason. Forgive me. I know my man." He contemplated his cigar, and finally looked up. "Well, now, enough of that. Let's find out. Jay says you've stumbled upon something—just exactly what wasn't clear to me—but something that you felt would be helpful in giving me some bargaining power with Goerlitz. Naturally, I was immediately curious. Although for the life of me, Mr. Brennan, I can't imagine what you have in mind."

"I'll tell you." The moment had come, and Brennan locked his hands tensely and leaned forward. "But understand, I can't reveal the source of my information. You'll have to take my word for it that my source is trustworthy. It was told to me by someone very close to me, told to me quite innocently by someone who had overheard it and had not the faintest idea of its implications." Both Earnshaw and Doyle were eager and receptive. With confidence revived, Brennan posed a question. "Besides peddling his memoirs, do you know why Dr. Dietrich von Goerlitz is in Paris?"

"Yes," said Earnshaw, "some big business deal—I remember— he's here to sign contracts with representatives of the People's Republic of China about—he's building a nuclear plant and one of those prefab communities to go with it. Isn't that it?"

Jay Doyle, silent until now, interjected, "A Chinese Nuclear Peace City. The Germans are supposed to construct it, maintain it, manage it."

"Right," said Brennan. He looked at Earnshaw. "But what if I were to tell you a piece of information that Goerlitz himself does not know? Simply this—that the Chinese Reds intend to sign the contract but not honor it, intend to use Goerlitz to build the multi-million-dollar plant and adjacent city but later nationalize it, confiscate it, and throw Goerlitz's German crews out. What would you think of that?"

Momentarily perplexed, Earnshaw tried to absorb and digest the information. At last he succeeded, for his blue eyes widened with astonishment. "I'd say that would be a remarkably useful piece of information, if true. I'd also say it's incredible that you could know this, Mr. Brennan, when Dr. von Goerlitz himself does not know it."

"But it is possible?" persisted Brennan.

"Oh, certainly, anything's possible. Complicity exists. Bad faith exists. Yet—"

"And if this were true," said Brennan, "and you knew it, but Goerlitz did not, don't you think this rather shocking information would enable you to see Goerlitz again and make him indebted to you?"

Earnshaw nodded vigorously. "If it were true, he'd want to see me. He'd want to listen to me. But is it true?"

"Here's the story. Decide for yourself. The wives of two Chinese delegates, unaware that they were being overheard, revealed the following—" began Brennan.

Consulting the notes taken from his questioning of Lisa, and without embroidering upon them, Brennan repeated the essence of what he had learned. For five minutes Brennan spoke without interruption, conscious of Earnshaw hanging on his every word. At last he was done, concluding, "There is all that I know. The Chinese in charge of the Nuclear Peace City intend to take it over entirely, get rid of the Germans, replace them with Russian scientists and technicians, and together with the Russians continue to operate the plant or plants. It could cost Goerlitz millions and millions of marks. It might ruin him, because he'd have no recourse in any court of law."

He watched Earnshaw, and it was almost as if he could observe, through a transparent plastic skull, the slow workings of The Ex's brain. When Earnshaw lifted his head, it was obvious that he was excited but instinctively cautious. "And you don't think Goerlitz knows or even suspects this?"

"If he knew, would he still be in Paris treating with the Chinese? He *is* here. He is giving a celebration dinner for his Chinese customers at the Ritz this weekend. I don't think he can have any idea of this, Mr. Earnshaw."

Earnshaw had come full circle, to unqualified acceptance of the story. His eyes shone. He slapped his knee enthusiastically. "Yes, it must be true!" he exclaimed. "Golly Moses, isn't this a piece of news? It's tremendous, Mr. Brennan, absolutely tremendous."

"The minute I heard it, I saw what it could mean to you," said Brennan. "If you could go to Goerlitz with this, you could forewarn him. You could save him. He'd have to consider you with new eyes. He'd be indebted to you, deeply indebted. I shouldn't think you'd even have to ask, to get that disagreeable chapter on you dropped from his memoirs."

"You're right, you're right," said Earnshaw. As he came to his feet, he appeared to shed twenty years. "Heavens to Betsy, this can be it, the miracle I've been praying for." He paced the sitting room, talking to himself in a low tone, as if preparing the future dialogue between Goerlitz and himself.

From the sofa, Doyle, as cheerful as Santa Claus, caught Brennan's eye and winked broadly. Brennan acknowledged this with his half-smile, then twisted in his chair to address Earnshaw once more. "Of course, there's more to all this than its value to Goerlitz and yourself. Perhaps you've overlooked it, but the implications are far greater."

Earnshaw ceased his pacing. "What do you mean?"

"Ever since I've arrived in Paris, I've been picking up little hints, disturbing little hints, about the Chinese and Russians," said Brennan. "When Khrushchev had his falling out with Mao Tse-tung in 1960, Soviet Russia and Red China became antagonists, and in the years since they have drifted farther and farther apart. Today China considers itself the keeper of Marx's flame, the heartland of international Communism, the capital for the new Cominform, and continues to chide Russia for having become corrupted by the imperialistic and capitalistic Western powers. Today China and Russia are enemies, and at the Palais Rose the Premier of Russia sits with the

467

Prime Minister of Great Britain and the President of the United States, and the President of France sits in the middle, and the Chairman of China sits alone. But, I repeat, China and Russia are, publicly, enemies. Correct?"

Earnshaw nodded in agreement, and Doyle said, "Correct, Matt."

"Very well," said Brennan. "Enemies. Yet, in the last few days, I keep picking up stray hints suggesting that China and Russia may be more friendly than we realize. Yesterday I was having a conversation with a French nuclear scientist. He had been in Peking fairly recently. To his surprise, he ran into a party of Russian scientists there. Last night I received this new piece of information I've passed on to you. Not only is China going to double-cross Goerlitz, but China is going to replace his German experts with Russian experts. I repeat, *Russian* experts. I think that's significant and disturbing. It suggests that the Chinese may be treating their Summit partners as they'll treat Goerlitz. Publicly they'll agree to disarm, and then privately they'll double-cross their Summit partners also. They'll pretend that without Russia as an ally they must submit to arms controls, yet leave the Palais Rose to intrigue secretly with the Russians, to torpedo any pact made here. And one day soon, together with the Soviets, they will resume international Communist expansion. In short, sir, there seem to be fragments of evidence to indicate that even as China and Russia publicly berate one another, publicly pretend to be in opposition, they are secret allies. This implies that any peace attained at the Summit will be a paper peace, nothing more, and that while we are being lulled onstage, contradictory activities are going on backstage." He paused. "I tell you, frankly, I'm worried."

Earnshaw had drawn nearer to Brennan, and now he smiled down upon him benevolently. "You've got quite a brief there, Mr. Brennan, and, I must confess, for a moment or two you had me shaken. But you know, if you can be objective, it is unlikely that this secret alliance— uh—this alliance between China and Russia, of which you speak, has any real existence. After all, whatever their political differences, China would have every right to invite scientists from Moscow to Peking, and to hire individual Russians to replace individual Germans in that Honan Province plant. That's not necessarily a political coalition."

"I think it may be, sir," insisted Brennan. "I can see Goerlitz's German scientists and technicians in Honan Province. They are individuals. Private enterprise. But Russia has no private enterprise, no individual scientific specialists for hire. Their experts could only be sent with Government approval, from Government research facilities."

"I don't know about that, Mr. Brennan. Things have slackened up a good deal in Russia. Oh, you've made an interesting case, but I must say this—when I was in the White House, I read all sorts of cases being concocted in the world press, based on my activities or speeches or off-the-cuff remarks. I mean, outsiders would take this little clue, and that one, and paste together some nefarious new foreign policy or activity which they'd suggest was what my Cabinet and I were really up to behind the scenes. And you know what? The speculators and second-guessers were always wrong. I've seen it happen too often. That's why I say, Mr. Brennan, your suspicions have a certain logic, based on this and that, but if you had the true facts, I think you'd find that your ideas are farfetched and the situation is not as alarming as you think."

Brennan's faith in his theory, while not destroyed, was under-mined. He would have to give it more thought. "Perhaps you're right, sir," he said uncertainly. Then, seeing Doyle bring himself erect, Brennan came out of the chair. He stood facing Earnshaw. "Anyway, I'm sure you won't find the information I've given you for Goerlitz farfetched."

He hesitated, wondering how he should say what had to be said next. He had not come here out of love for the former President. He had come here as one would come to a marketplace, to barter. He had provided Earnshaw with valuable goods to use when he bartered with Goerlitz, and Brennan expected something of equal value in exchange.

Before he could speak, he saw that Earnshaw was wearing a smile at once contrite and friendly. He felt Earnshaw's hand on his arm, and, to his surprise, he heard Earnshaw address him as Matt for the first time.

"Matt," Earnshaw was saying, "I'm ashamed of my behavior toward you yesterday, but, you see, I had been misled. I had no idea of the kind of man you were, and, more than that, I was selfishly self-absorbed, I was—uh—concerned with my own problems, no one else's. But even before you came here this morning, I had reasons, from some things Goerlitz told me, and from reading the marked transcript of the Congressional hearing you'd left for me, to—uh—to revise some of my evaluations of you. Now—well, Matt—I apolo-gize, sincerely, and I trust you will be charitable enough to accept my apology."

Moved almost to a feeling of affection for Earnshaw, Brennan said, "That's not necessary, really—"

"You've graciously volunteered assistance that may save me," Earnshaw went on. "Now, though you haven't requested it, I'd like to help you in turn—give you the help today that I was reluctant to offer you yesterday. Today you have my promise that I'll do everything possible, within my power—my curtailed power—to help clear you, Matt. I don't know if I can get anyone to speak to Nikolai Rostov on your behalf or help you get together with Rostov. I don't know if I can manage that. But I pledge you this: I'll try." He smiled broadly. "You can count on this much. You have my word that I'll speak to the President of the United States about you this week. There it is. Now we both have something to look forward to."

"Thank you," said Brennan.

"Thank *you*, Matt," said Emmett A. Earnshaw.

A FTER THEY HAD LEFT Earnshaw, Brennan was too elated to return to his hotel room. Buoyed by hope, he wanted human companionship, and automatically he accompanied Jay Doyle to the Champs-Élysées.

But once they had crossed the broad thoroughfare, he saw Doyle peering off toward the awning and cane chairs of Fouquet's fashionable outdoor café. Brennan remembered that Doyle had an appointment with Hazel Smith.

He halted. "I'll leave you here, Jay. I'm going to take a walk."

"What do you mean—leave me here? I'm treating you to a drink. With The Ex on your side, we've got something to celebrate."

"But I thought you were meeting Hazel Smith."

"I am. Only you're going to join us."

Brennan shook his head. "I don't think so. I'm sure she expects this to be a private meeting."

"Nonsense. Nothing's private between us." He faltered. "Except, of course, if she wants to speak to me alone about my book. If that's it, she'll let us know right away. And if that happens, you can take off. But now, she seemed to indicate it was something else, and she mentioned Medora Hart. Come along."

Brennan hung back. "Look, Jay, I'm not her favorite American. She—"

"That's why I want you along," said Doyle. "I want to do some lobbying for you, and this is the time to start. Matt, I've known this woman most of my adult life. Her first judgments of people are always filtered through old headlines cluttering her mind. When she met you at the Palais Rose, she saw you through those old treason banner-heads. That was all she had to go by. I know if she could meet you socially, come to know you as I do, her attitude would

470

change. I guarantee it. Hazel's not at all as fierce as she seems. That crustiness outside is self-protective, her survival tortoiseshell. Inside, she's a frightened, lonely dame, all putty, wanting to love and be loved."

"I don't know," said Brennan, unconvinced.

"I do," replied Doyle, grabbing his arm. He began to propel Brennan toward Fouquet's. "Besides"—he lowered his voice meaningfully—"she's a useful friend to have, considering her contacts, if you know what I mean. She's giving me a hand with Rostov. Eventually she might give you a hand, too."

"Okay," said Brennan. "You've sold me."

As they approached the café, Doyle quickly whispered, "One caution. No mention of Rostov. She has no idea that I've seen them together, and she has no idea I've figured out Rostov's her—her boyfriend."

"My lips are zipped."

"Good. Let me cue you in when I see an opening."

They stood in the sun before the rows of yellow and red chairs. A third of the places were occupied, and, as ever, Brennan enjoyed the diversity of the occupants. A pretty French girl, *beaux yeux,* in a blue silk blouse and pleated white skirt, had set a long bread loaf on her table and opened her copy of *L'Express.* Behind her, two tall Africans in tight gray suits were arguing over their sandwiches. Near them, a pudgy Frenchman, wearing pince-nez and goatee, directed the shoeshine man kneeling over his pointed Oxford shoe planted on the small portable box. A few seats away, a comely Indian woman, her hair braided and her sari purple, was purchasing a copy of the London *Evening Standard* from a vendor. In the aisle, a blue-coated policeman, absently swinging his white club, chatted with an elderly waiter in black bow tie and white jacket. And Brennan knew for a certainty that these two were discussing either the races at Chantilly or the lottery, and he knew this was Paris and this was Fouquet's and life could be worthwhile.

"There she is," he heard Doyle say.

Following the direction of Doyle's finger to the shaded table in the rear, before the café-restaurant wall, Brennan made out the mass of hennaed hair. Hazel Smith was busily powdering her jutting chin. Doyle had started up the nearest aisle, and with misgivings Brennan fell in behind him.

Hazel looked up from her compact and smiled. "I'm so glad you could make it, Jay."

"Sorry to be late," Doyle said. He stepped aside to reveal Brennan, and as Hazel recognized him, her smile vanished. "We were working together with Earnshaw," Doyle went on hastily, "and I insisted that Matt accompany me so you two could become better acquainted. You should, you know. You have a lot in common—including me." He laughed nervously.

Hazel did not reply. She returned her compact to her purse.

Brennan was in no mood to chill his own warm happiness by trying to embrace a glacier. "Sorry to barge in on you like this, Miss Smith," he said. "Blame Jay's overenthusiasm. He's still working for One World." Hazel looked up sharply, eyes bringing Brennan into focus. Brennan smiled, and said, "Anyway, three's a crowd when you have personal matters to discuss. Nice to have seen you again, Miss Smith."

He had started to turn away when Hazel said, "Don't be silly, Brennan. I simply have no patience with politeness. This isn't the Ivy League. Sit down, will you?"

Doyle beamed, and shoved a chair behind Brennan, who lowered himself into it as Doyle squeezed into a place beside Hazel. "Great, Hazel—" he started to say.

Hazel's attention was still on Brennan. "I didn't ask Jay to come here on personal business. In fact, what I have to tell him is anything but private. The truth is, I'd like the whole world to know about it. Since you and Jay are buddy-buddy, I don't mind your sitting in." She turned to Doyle. "Have you seen today's headlines?"

"No, not yet."

"Help yourself." She gestured toward the three afternoon newspapers piled on the table between her purse and the silver-metal soda siphon.

Doyle took a newspaper. Brennan lit a cigarette as he watched Doyle unfold the paper, read the headline, and scan the story below it with a frown. Finished, Doyle handed the newspaper to Brennan and turned toward Hazel.

Listening while he, too, read the story of the art robbery, Brennan heard Doyle ask, "You mean one of those five paintings stolen from the Nouvelle Galerie d'Art was Medora's Nardeau?"

"Medora's Fleur Ormsby," Hazel corrected him. "You're damn right hers was one of the five. The one called *Nude in the Garden.* Does that tell you anything, Jay?"

"It could've been a coincidence."

"Come on, Jay, I thought we were on the same wavelength."

"You mean you detect Lady Ormsby's fine artistic hand."

"I mean I'm positive."

472

Having read the story, Brennan tossed the paper on the table, bewildered. Doyle had recently told him something about the stripper at the Club Lautrec—Medora—Medora Hart—and about the Ormsbys' persecution of her, and something about a Nardeau painting, but he could not recollect the details.

He found Hazel staring at him. "Did Jay tell you what this is all about?"

"I think so. I sort of remember that—"

"I'll give you a quick recap, friend, just so's you can belong to this table," said Hazel. She stopped, irked by the appearance of the waiter, and she said to Doyle, "I'll have a Coca-Cola without the lemon peel." Impatiently she waited for Doyle to give their order, and once it was taken, she addressed Brennan again. "You remember the notorious Jameson affair in England about three years ago?"

"How could anyone forget it?" said Brennan.

"Okay," said Hazel. "Medora Hart was one of Jameson's girls. Her last lover was Sir Austin Ormsby's younger brother, Sydney Ormsby, a real aberration. Sir Austin—protector of family name, home, hearth—railroaded Medora out of England, and then double-crossed her by having her barred from re-entry as an alien, actually on some trumped-up technicality."

With indignation Hazel revealed the tawdry details of Medora's enforced existence abroad, and of her helplessness in combating the Ormsby clan—until she had remembered a certain painting of a nude that Nardeau had done.

"There it was," said Hazel, "the sublime, impeccable Lady Ormsby as Lady Horizontal herself, garbed only in a smile. With that, Medora had her big bargaining instrument. But lo, this morning, no more painting. It is pilfered in the night. In summary—yesterday Fleur tries to buy the scandalous painting from Medora, fails; today Medora has no painting, gone, snatched. Okay, jurors, what say you as to the culprit? Fleur guilty or not guilty?"

"Guilty as charged," declared Brennan.

"Whatever you did once, you still have all your marbles, Brennan," said Hazel. "Then you're on Medora's side?"

"I'm on the side of all losers." Brennan smiled wryly. "They're my kind of people."

Hazel turned to Doyle. "And what say you, Jay?"

"Fleur? Guilty beyond a doubt."

Hazel leaned over and kissed his cheek. "I adore *all* of you, Jay. . . . Okay, the verdict is unanimous. Even if it weren't, I'd still want your advice, Jay. Medora needs a Brain Trust."

"You know I'd do anything I could for her," said Doyle.

"But please, not for my sake, Jay. For hers. I'm not being sentimental over an unhappy whore. I'm aching for every young kid on earth who gets taken by her so-called betters. This is a *nice* girl, pure at heart, still more decent than dozens of virgins who get theirs in movie houses or in dreams. Medora's helpless, lost—no friends. What she needs is muscle on her side. The enemy's got muscles. She needs equal heft."

Hazel, seeking a cigarette, accepted one from Brennan and gave her attention to Doyle again. "I had to break the news of the art theft to her this morning. Rough, I tell you. The poor thing got hysterical, and I can't say I'd have behaved differently if I'd had my last hope stolen. Jay, I didn't like the way she sounded on the phone. I'm afraid of what this might do to her. I simply won't have it. I promised her anything, just to settle her down. I promised her that if the police didn't get her painting back, I'd find another way to force Sir Austin to run up the white flag. Well, the pabulum worked. She's clinging to that. But now I've got to deliver. I can't have her life on my conscience. And I won't see it wasted, either. I've got to do something. So I did something. I called you. I know this isn't fair, Jay. I don't want to pressure you into backing my pet charities, but you've got to help me find a means of salvaging Medora's life. I mean, I come strictly from the steppes. You know more people than I do in the Big City. What about it, Jay?"

Doyle massaged his moon face thoughtfully. "Of course, I'll do what I can, Hazel. The question is—what?" He was silent for some moments before speaking again. "I suppose the smart thing to do would be to investigate Ormsby's circle. Who are Sir Austin's friends and enemies here? There may be numerous newspapermen and diplomats who might know of a skeleton in his closet. And maybe we could look into Fleur's circle, too."

"And what about that pinhead Sydney Ormsby? I hear he's in town."

"Sydney, too. Yes, I ran into that little snot in Vienna. He's here all right. They're all here. . . . Honey, let me give this a little thought. We can talk about it more in the next few days. I'll try to come up with an idea. Then we'll do something for Medora."

"But soon," implored Hazel.

"Very soon," Doyle promised.

Hazel slumped back in the wicker chair, exhausted. And Brennan, who had listened carefully to her plea and the subsequent exchange, suddenly found that he was viewing Hazel Smith with complete

474

affection. The change in his attitude was dizzying. He had come to Fouquet's prepared to tolerate a heartless bitch. He had found instead that the bitch was a warm and eloquent Madonna. The very notion of Hazel Smith as Madonna made him smile to himself, but the fact remained that she had just performed selflessly for another soul, one who could be little more than a stranger to her and one who was considered undeserving of sympathy in the eyes of the world.

Still, Brennan reminded himself, he had better keep his new affection tentative, and to himself. Hazel Smith seemed the type of person who saw other people in a simple spectrum that consisted of only black and white. To Hazel, Medora had become Joan of Arc-white. To Hazel, Brennan was still Benedict Arnold-black. Now, with his new affection for her, with his new affection for life itself, Brennan wanted this affection returned, desired at least Hazel's understanding and good opinion, wished her to see that if black he must be, let that black be not the smut of villainy but only the darkness of undeserved martyrdom.

It surprised him, with a small jolt, to find that he cared at all. It was like emerging from the unfeeling numbness of anesthesia into the pain of life. But care he did.

He saw that Hazel was busily removing her purse and the newspapers from the table, to give the waiter room for the Coca-Cola and the two cups of coffee.

She placed her straw in the soft drink, swore softly at the lemon peel obstructing her straw, picked the peel out, then drew on her straw steadily. Afterward, when she sat straight, she appeared as revived as if she had partaken of ambrosia. "I feel better," she said. "I was drying up inside. I don't know if it's the weather or my aggravation about Medora. Anyway, so much for immediate business. . . . Jay, did you say you and Brennan were both up talking with Earnshaw?"

"Yes."

"Why?" She did not wait for Doyle's reply. Her gaze had shifted to Brennan. "You, of all people. What were you doing with The Ex? I thought he was your Mortal Enemy Number One."

"Well," said Brennan uncomfortably, "he's not half bad, when you get to—"

"He signed your execution papers," said Hazel.

Hastily Doyle intervened. "That was four years ago, dear. People change."

Hazel kept her eyes on Brennan. "But their deeds remain. Brennan and Earnshaw closeted together. Wouldn't that make a fine story?"

"Hazel, you wouldn't—?" Doyle began with alarm.

"I'm kidding, Jay. Can't you tell? I just don't figure what those two would have to talk about at this late date."

"Nothing to do with their old differences," said Doyle hastily. "Earnshaw happened to need some information and advice on a certain pending matter. I happened to mention to him that Matt could probably be helpful. So Earnshaw invited him over. Actually, Hazel, Earnshaw was passive during Matt's Congressional hearing. As in all such decisions, he would have allowed Simon Madlock to think for him. But Madlock was dead, so Earnshaw didn't turn thumbs up or thumbs down. Instead, he abdicated judgment to Senator Dexter, and Dexter fed Matt to the lions."

Hazel heard this out with undisguised skepticism. She made no comment. She studied the foot traffic on the Champs-Élysées. "Look at that girl," she said. "The one in the loose white jersey blouse and blue skirt. I bet she's not wearing a stitch underneath. I think it's unbecoming. What do you men see in those French girls?"

"No brassieres, for one thing," said Brennan with a grin.

Hazel scowled at him. "I'm trying to remember. You still married?"

"No."

"Now I remember. Well, I was wondering, but I guess I know why you're in Paris."

"A man doesn't have to come to Paris for that, Miss Smith."

"I suppose not. . . . What does he have to come to Paris for, then? What are you doing here?"

"Well—" This was dangerous ground, and Brennan hesitated. He was tempted to utter the name of the one that he and Hazel knew in common. But he had promised Doyle that he would not. He considered some fiction he might offer her. But before he could invent a plausible excuse involving general business, Doyle came to his rescue.

"Matt's always coming up to Paris, Hazel," Doyle was saying. "He's tied up with an import-export firm in Italy. And—and while he's here, he's seeing his old State Department friends who happen to have checked in for the Summit."

Hazel looked at Brennan. "You mean they're still your friends?"

"Not many, Miss Smith. But a few. There are still a few who believe in me. I like to see them. And, of course, I'm still trying to clear myself."

"Well, if you're still trying, why didn't you give me that interview last Sunday?" demanded Hazel. "The first thing you need is a sympathetic press."

"How could I know that it would be sympathetic, Miss Smith?"

"You couldn't know. But you've still got some remnants of that State Department charm. Besides, most of us reporters are usually for the underdog. However, treating us like beasts of prey isn't going to help you much."

"Miss Smith," said Brennan earnestly, "sob stories aren't news. Facts—real facts, *new* facts—are news. If I ever find factual evidence to support my claim of innocence, something beyond my own word, I'll have news, and you'll be the first one I'll come to with it."

"Maybe I'll appreciate that, Brennan. Right now—thanks for nothing."

"Because I have nothing, Miss Smith." From the corner of his eye, Brennan could see Jay Doyle sweating like a nervous press agent seated between a hostile reporter and an intractable client.

Doyle lurched forward heavily, determined to prevent an utter calamity. "Matter of fact, Matt, you do have something, something that might interest a really astute foreign correspondent like Hazel." Doyle now addressed himself to Hazel. "Honey, seeing Matt in action here tells me one thing. You can take a man out of diplomacy, but you can't take diplomacy out of a man. In renewing his acquaintance with some of the delegates, inside people, Matt picked up a little backstairs gossip that you or I, without his trained ear, would have thought unimportant."

"Oh, yeah?" said Hazel. "Like what?"

Puzzled, Brennan wondered what his press agent was up to, and he waited, allowing the perspiring Doyle to go on. "Well, Matt's heard a lot of strange things, and privately he's come to the conclusion that there might be something fishy going on behind the scenes of the Summit."

At once Brennan detected what his ally was trying to do, and he attempted to head it off, to avoid embarrassment. "Wait a second, Jay. I don't have any concrete evidence yet, only some provocative clues. Maybe we'd better not go into it until—"

Hazel ingnored Brennan. She gave Doyle her inquisitor's glare. "What's fishy behind the Summit?"

Holding up a hand to reassure Brennan, Doyle continued to engage Hazel. "Hazel, you're the pro on Soviet Russia, but I think you'll agree that in recent years Premier Talansky has been inclined to align his country with the democracies as the best means of containing Red China and maintaining world peace. As a result, China has denounced Russia as antiparty and antisocialist, and has been treating Russia like an unfaithful mate or a traitorous friend. China and Russia are on the outs, and China, forced to go it alone, has also been forced to compromise face and pride by coming to the Summit. All because of the ideological falling out with Russia. Is that an accurate estimate?"

"Accurate enough," said Hazel.

"Well, now, Matt Brennan finds himself with evidence, based on hearsay and deduction, that entirely contradicts what the world sees and believes. According to Matt, while the Russians and Chinese pretend to be enemies in public, they are secretly palsy in private. In other words, they're paying lip service to a concord of nations, a world community dedicated to peace, but planning a Communist alliance to be maintained *sub rosa* after the Summit. If this is true, if Matt's findings and deductions are true, it means the Summit makes no sense. It means the Summit is only a Potemkin façade erected to deceive the democracies about the realities of Communist ambitions. And if it's true, it'll give you the biggest beat of the year, Hazel. I think it's worth looking into. I'm sure Matt won't mind. In fact, I'm sure he'd be delighted and would encourage you to do it."

Hazel had been listening, stony-faced. She continued to ignore Brennan as she said to Doyle, "On what does your friend base his deductions?"

Momentarily, Doyle was at a loss. "Well—" He glanced at Brennan.

Brennan roused himself. "I'd rather not cite my sources or evidence yet."

"You can understand that, Hazel," Doyle said in quick concurrence. "You know how many times we've had to refuse to divulge our sources. Ethics of the profession."

"Brennan has no profession," Hazel said flatly.

"But he has friends, honey. Look, he's given you a lead. That's all you require to start with. If I were in your shoes, I'd at least look into it. You have the connections." He paused. "What do you think, honey?"

Slowly she turned to Brennan. "I think your friend is nuts," she said to Doyle.

Doyle protested. "That's being a bit harsh, Hazel, but—" Eager to placate her now, he said to Brennan, "Of course, in somewhat different language, that's what Earnshaw thought, too."

"Well, for once that nincompoop was right about something," said Hazel. "Brennan, I don't care what gossip you've heard. Political delegates carry unsubstantiated rumors the way Typhoid Mary carried the bacillus, and if you're weak-headed, it becomes catching —because one thing I do know, and this is fact. I do know the Russians. I've been in and out of the Kremlin dozens of times. I've

478

interviewed the whole Politburo. I've been to dinners at which Premier Talansky spoke off the record. And this I know. The Russian leaders believe going along with China means splitting the world and continued arms escalation and inevitable war and total catastrophe. The Russian leaders believe that by ostracizing China, by joining the Western democracies, they can force China to join with the rest of us and guarantee peace. There isn't a chance in the world Premier Talansky will renege on this avowed policy. If you've heard rumors to the contrary, I remind you they are only rumors. But even if any of them have validity, you've misinterpreted their meaning. If the Russians and Chinese are talking of an alliance after the Five-Power Summit, you can be sure it will be no more than a trade or economic agreement. After all, once the Summit is over, there'll be total disarmament and peace on earth, and there's no reason why Russia and everyone else shouldn't be on friendly terms with China. We'll all be weaponless then, in the same boat, devoted to the same cause, survival, meaning we sink or swim together." She took a sip of Coke. "Sorry, Brennan. If you're going to make something of your theory, you'd better get hard facts, which I doubt that you can find. You said you wouldn't discuss your own innocence until you had facts. Well, don't discuss the guilt of other parties either, until you have facts. Take it from me—and this means you, too, Jay—don't go broadcasting this irresponsible kind of talk. Listen to me, Brennan. If you don't, you'll only make your reputation considerably worse, if that's possible."

Brennan picked up his pack of cigarettes, his lighter, and dropped them in a pocket. Hazel had made some sense, yet she had irritated him. "Thank you for your advice," he said stiffly. "You're probably right, but you don't know what I know. I have sound reasons for my suspicions. There have been other inexplicable activities going on here, also. But—"

Suddenly Doyle came to life. "Matt, maybe you should tell Hazel about the bookstore on the Rue de Seine that you investigated—the one we thought was a Communist drop—"

"What's that?" Hazel interrupted.

Brennan shook his head firmly. "No, Jay. At the moment, Miss Smith suspects me of being a lunatic. If I tell her any more of my adventures, she'll be sure I'm batty. Let's put the lid on it, Jay, for now." He came to his feet. "Thanks for the coffee, Jay. And again thanks for your advice, Miss Smith. But I'm not giving up. I like the smell of political intrigue. I guess it's good to be back in harness, even unofficially. The next time I discuss my ideas with you, I'll

479

discuss them only if they are facts, not theories. Either that or I'll bow to your wisdom and manfully concede I was, as you put it, nuts. Well, I'll leave you two."

"See you later," said Doyle.

About to leave, Brennan hesitated. "Just one more thing, Miss Smith. I was going to say it before, when you were discussing Medora Hart. I haven't met her, but I want you to know I'm with you. I don't like helpless people being ganged up on. I've had some experience in that area, and it's rotten. So for whatever it's worth, I'd like to enlist on Medora's side, too. If you and Jay fail to get anywhere, please let me know. When you two were talking about her, something struck me. A notion. A possibility. A long shot, but at least an idea. If you can't get her home again, maybe I can try. Anyway, do let me know."

For the first time, Hazel Smith offered him a friendly smile. And then she offered him her hand. He leaned over the table to shake it.

"Okay, Brennan," she said, "let's call this an option on each other's friendship. Maybe you're not the heel everybody, myself included, thought you were. Maybe I could come to like you. Right now, Brennan, you've got two pluses going for you: first, Jay likes you; second, Medora moves you. So you can't be all bad. Let's watch it and see if we both want to pick up the option."

"It's a deal," Brennan said.

As he turned to leave Fouquet's, he heard Hazel exclaim to Doyle, "My God, look at the time! Someone's expecting me for an interview. I *can't* be late for this one."

And Brennan, departing, wondered who would be the next lucky one to have to endure Hazel Smith's serpent tongue and grudging goodwill. . . .

Breathlessly, Hazel Smith left the taxi that had brought her to the Porte Maillot at the northeast corner of the densely wooded Bois de Boulogne, which was the entrance to the combination children's playground, fun fair, and zoo known to Parisians as the Jardin d'Acclimatation.

Joining the line before the ticket booth, Hazel felt certain that the acceleration of her heartbeat came not from physical exertion or fear of being tardy (for she was on time), but from anxiety over her new dual role. Moving forward with the line, she had sympathy for Gertrud Margarete Zelle, who had become both Mata Hari and

Agent H.21 at one and the same time. Here she was, to a certain American a woman named Hazel Smith, and to a certain Russian a woman who was the nonexistent secretary of a nonexistent M. Gérard. This would be her first trial as a person of divided allegiance, and she was not sure she could carry it off. Once more, the muggy French air felt full of poniards.

She had arrived at the cage of the booth, and she purchased her ticket for the miniature railway. There was a quicker entrance into the Jardin d'Acclimatation, one made on foot, but Hazel had chosen this way because it was slower and more picturesque. She wanted the extra minutes to calm her nerves and regain her poise. She wanted, also, the most soothing and nostalgic entrance into the fun fair.

Since earliest childhood, when her father had introduced her to American Legion carnivals on the Milwaukee beach front and the honky-tonk streets and dizzy rides of White City in Chicago, Hazel Smith had become a connoisseur of these retreats to happier, simpler years. As a grown woman, she had allowed no artificial playground to escape her presence. She had reveled in Anaheim's Disneyland, in Brooklyn's Coney Island, in Copenhagen's Tivoli Gardens, in Vienna's Prater, in Moscow's Gorki Park and Sokolniki Park. But her favorite of them all was this little section of the Bois outside Paris given over to the Jardin d'Acclimatation. Whenever she was in Paris, Hazel let others dutifully visit the Louvre, the Sacré-Coeur, the Luxembourg Gardens. For herself, time and again, she preferred the diminutive train that whisked her through the enchanted forest into her favorite fairyland.

She had never been able to discern why she enjoyed a visit to the Jardin more than the world's more magnificent playgrounds. Certainly it possessed none of the grand attractions of its lavish competitors—offered nothing comparable to the giant ferris wheel in Vienna's Prater or the pavilions in Moscow's Gorki Park—yet it had always proved infinitely more satisfying. On second thought, she supposed that other amusement parks, like so many children's toys, were designed primarily to attract the eye and pocketbook of the adult. Their pretense was an offer of juvenile pleasure, but their lure was for the adult sophisticate. The Jardin d'Acclimatation, on the other hand, made no concessions to jaded maturity. It made no claim to being more than it was, a modest outdoor playroom with ordinary rides, inexpensive game booths, unpretentious snack stands, a limited zoo, just enough diversion and no more than might be absorbed in a few feverish hours by the dancing mind of an eight-year-old. Hazel liked it because in this easy haven of the French working-class family she could be young again and enjoy the dreams of childhood, and still believe in the illusion that some part of life was meant to be carefree and pleasurable.

Passing through the gate, she took a wooden seat in the last open passenger car of the miniature train. As the stationmaster blew his whistle and the tiny locomotive began to pull the sparsely occupied cars through the scenic forest, she remembered why she had come to the Jardin d'Acclimatation this early afternoon. It was not her need for a pink juvenile palliative or for an even stronger sedative that would settle the turmoil in her mind. It was the need for a safe place, one unlikely to be visited by delegate tourists, especially on a Wednesday lunch hour, yet a site public enough and distracting enough to remove the pressures that an intimate, private rendezvous would hold. The intimate rendezvous would come soon. But first she must be ready for it. She must understand her new dual role. And she must understand where her allegiance lay. She must be *positive*.

It surprised her that the miniature train had pulled to a stop on the circle of tracks that was the end of the line. Never before had she made the short trip without any awareness of the funny train and green woods along the route. Leaving the coach, she knew why. Today she was not escaping into childhood. Today she was facing up to adulthood, and what remained of it. With regret, she surrendered her ticket, and her youth, to the gateman. Never again, she knew, would the Jardin be the same.

She went swiftly up the main entrance street, thinly populated at this hour of a midweek day. At her left, she passed the artificial river, where oarless boats floated magically around miniature islands, all propelled by a single churning water wheel, and she saw again the stunted replica of the Eiffel Tower. To her right was the riotously colored banked garden with a floral clock in its center, and after that the stage and entrance of a sideshow.

She had reached the heart of the Jardin, a semicircle of snack bars and game stalls that looked out upon an enclosed diminutive French highway, where youngsters drove small cars at fifteen miles an hour, guided by French traffic-safety police. Here and there, at the stalls, she could see parents watching their offspring engage in rifle games and ball-rolling games. She could see a nursemaid and her three charges, all nibbling away at barbe à papa, papa's beard in French, cotton candy in English. But she could not see the one she was to meet.

Then, searching the last curve of the semicircle of booths, she saw Nikolai Rostov.

482

From this distance he appeared much smaller in stature than he had yesterday during their brief reunion, or in Moscow during their long years together. Starting toward him, she realized that it was not the distance that made him seem smaller, but the measuring of him, in her mind's eye, against the enormous bulk of Jay Thomas Doyle.

As she closed in, Nikolai Rostov grew in size. He was of medium height, chunky, brawny, and though his charcoal suit was too dark for the time of day and too heavy for the weather, it had a better fit than the suits on most Russian men. The broad and deceptively peasant face was partially hidden behind some kind of paper-wrapped food. The shrewd penetrating eyes looked up and off, and a free hand brushed back an untidy forelock of gray-flecked black hair. Suddenly the hand rose high and waved, as he saw her approaching.

She reached him. "Hi, Niki."

Quickly, one thick arm encircled her, almost lifting her from her feet, and then, still chewing his food, Rostov kissed her cheek. *"Milochka,* sweetheart, my precious." In the day she was always *milochka,* his sweetheart, his darling. In the night she was usually *lyubov,* his love. Rarely was she Hazel, which he found awkward on his tongue. "You are well?" he asked.

"Fix your tie," she said. "What *are* you eating?"

"A crêpe au confiture with jelly inside," he said, holding up the crêpe folded within a paper wrapping. "Come, you will have one. You are starved." Arm around her, he began to lead her to the food stand.

She touched the fingers grasping her ribs. "Niki, aren't you being a little reckless? What if your wife should see you here like this?"

He laughed throatily, refusing to release her. "My wife—what is your song?—is going to the country, hooray, hooray—is that what you taught me? Natasha is already on her trip to the châteaux with Tania Talansky and maybe a hundred French guards. They will be busy."

At the food stand Rostov ordered two more crêpes au confiture. Hazel stood close to him as, with childish delight, he watched the old French lady spill the batter on the sizzling griddle.

"When is Natasha coming back to Paris?" Hazel asked.

"Not today, not tomorrow, the day after tomorrow, on Friday."

He observed the brown crêpes being filled with jelly, folded in two, and wrapped in paper. Quickly he brought out a fistful of coins, sorting among the kopeks and rubles for francs, and then he paid. Handing Hazel her crêpe, he began munching his own as he led the way along the row of game booths, each with its shelves of cheap prizes. "Hungry," he said, biting off another mouthful. "This is true passion, *milochka*, to give up one's proper lunch to meet one's love." He was a rough bear who'd been tamed, she thought, or no, better yet, a nice bull, sometimes. "You're sweet today," she said. "You can be sweet."

"Because I think ahead to tomorrow. You telephoned a message to me, but even before I received it I planned to telephone you. When I knew Natasha was going, I could only think of my *milochka*. I was going to invite myself to come to you tonight. But—*nyet*. Today with the meetings is very much work. I could only use the lunch time to come to here." His eyes prospected their surroundings. "Fun place. Good place. The French know how to make pleasure." He stared into her eyes. "Sometimes some Americans, too. But tonight, no, I cannot see you. I am crazed with desire, but the Premier, he is crazed with the debates in the Rose Palace. So tonight, many of us, we must work."

Hazel's disappointment was genuine. "That's awful, Niki."

Now he wore a wide grin. "But tomorrow night it is different. I am free. I will come to the apartment. Maybe nine o'clock. We will have the night together."

"Oh, Niki, that's wonderful." She clutched his hand, massaging the furry hairs on his knuckles. "That's really why I called you. That's the only reason. We had fifteen minutes yesterday, and it made me so lonely for you. I wanted to see you again, right away, to find out when we could really be together. It'll be such fun. We can talk and—"

He drew her to him. "We can do better than talk." He kissed her on the lips.

She tried to pull away, and finally succeeded. Despite the crêpe, his breath still bore the faintly acrid smell of pickled herring. She glanced about nervously. "Really, Niki, even if your wife is gone, someone might see you. How could you explain this?"

He cackled. "The same as I would explain if they saw us on Kirova Street. I am a cossack. I always kiss pretty women, especially the one who makes a press interview with me."

"Very neat, Niki. I'm beginning not to trust you. I bet you're not doing a bit of work at the Palais Rose. I bet you're in Paris to size up the French girls. That's it, isn't it? French girls. That's why I'm not seeing you nights."

Rostov snorted as he wheeled her around and started her in the opposite direction. "French girls, you keep. Matchsticks. They are matchsticks only, fancy hair, fancy clothes, wigs, pads, stinking perfume instead of water, buttons not breasts, no normal love only decadence, either harlots with wide-open legs or priss Catholics with tight-crossed legs, but no strong honest women. No women like Russian women. You are a Russian woman, *milochka,* your family blood is from Moskva Matushka. I have always told you. It is true. You are a true woman for a man."

Somewhat taken aback by his fiery outburst, then dismayed, and finally feeling guilty over her disloyalty, Hazel walked silently beside Rostov. At last she murmured, "I appreciate all that, Niki. *Spasibo.* I thank you. I appreciate your coming here."

She cast a sidelong glance at him. He could excite her. He was no Adonis. The thick eyebrows, the Mongolian aspect of his features, the rough face of one who had shaved with a blowtorch, the sloping shoulders, the burly body. No Adonis. Not even the appearance of a *bolshaya shiska*—a big pinecone, a big shot. Physically he was unprepossessing. Physically he was coarse, primitive. Physically he evoked the image of *virilia.* She felt weak and hot inside, and ashamed, and once more suffused with guilt.

"I only wish I could stay more time," Rostov was saying. He dug the battered brass watch he had inherited from his father out of his vest pocket. "Almost the hour to return to save the world." He wrinkled his nose to show he was joking, slipped the watch back in the vest pocket, and said, "Maybe ten minutes more. I do not know where I go, but I think there was a zoo I could see."

"There is one straight ahead."

"It is good to look at animals after looking at people," Rostov said.

"Niki, what does that mean?"

"People of five countries meet in one room. People of five backgrounds, five feelings, five ideas. People who look at one world globe, and each sees it a different shape. But it can be only one shape. People become ugly, very ugly."

"Yes, I can understand that. I—I was teasing before about French girls. Poor dear, I know you've been working hard."

"Hard days, hard nights."

They paused before a toy house enclosed by a wire fence, which contained a little kingdom of hamsters, some dozing, some cavorting in play. "Aren't those hamsters cute?" said Hazel. "Look how nicely they play."

"Put a cat in their cage and they will not play," said Rostov.

She looked at him. "Are you alluding to China?"

Rostov shrugged. "I name no names." He took her arm and they resumed their promenade. "Sometimes, in a nation of hamsters, there are some who think all others outside are hamsters, too. They do not believe in cats. Who knows who is right?" He released her arm. "But the work—yes, it is difficult."

She questioned him softly, not as a journalist but as a woman who had shared so many nights of his life, and gradually but guardedly he discussed his activities at the Palais Rose, and at the ministerial meetings that followed daily at the Quai d'Orsay. Mostly he spoke of the conflicting disarmament proposals and the problems standing in the way of achieving compromises, and finally of the suspicions that the leaders and delegates had of each other, and of the clash of their personalities.

At the peanut stand he purchased two small bags, one for each of them. He cracked several shells, for her and for himself. "Enough of politics," he said firmly. "That I have the whole day. You are the only one who gives me pleasure. I cannot waste you with politics. What have you been doing yesterday and today?"

"Politics," she said with a teasing smile.

Rostov grimaced. "Naturally," he said. He glanced across at the pit of bears. "We have enough of them at home. For now, I prefer the monkeys. They amuse. It is good to laugh at yourself."

They strolled to the enclosure of monkeys, who were swarming across an artificial hill ringed by a moat. The monkeys were captivating as they begged for food, and gayly Hazel and Rostov began to toss them peanuts.

Leaning on the rail, feeding the monkeys, Rostov said, "You have not told me how you spend your time."

"Like you, Niki, mostly work, as I explained yesterday. What crazy people a Summit conference attracts." She pitched a peanut high, and an agile baboon caught it and did a somersault. "Most of my interview subjects are more peculiar than those animals."

"Yes? I have no hours to read your stories. One I saw. Of President Earnshaw's niece. She sounded nice to have so stupid a relative. Both Premier Talansky and Marshal Zabbin wondered why he is here."

"I haven't the faintest idea."

"But I have found out. It shows you I should be the journalist, not you."

"If ever you're out of work again, I'll hire you."

"I shall never be out of work again," he said seriously.

"Why is Earnshaw here, Niki?"

"Because Dr. von Goerlitz is here. Goerlitz is seeing our—our difficult Chinese delegation. He is building for them a peace nuclear reactor. It is a good sign. He is also to make contracts for his memoirs. There he is warlike against Earnshaw's past idiocies. Earnshaw is trying to stop him. . . . *Milochka,* look at that ape down there. He hoards his peanuts like a capitalist, even when his children starve. . . . So, what other monkeys fill your hours?"

"Oh, anyone and everyone, mostly people not directly concerned with the Summit. You know, lighter stories to balance the heavy political stuff the wires are carrying." She tried to divert and interest him with anecdotes about her interviews with Legrande, the fashion designer, Claude Goupil, king of the gourmets, Maurice Quarolli, French special security officer.

When she had finished, he was silent, continuing to feed the monkeys until his bag was empty. He threw the bag away. "And pleasure, *milochka.* Whom do you see for dinner when I am so busy?"

His last question disconcerted her. She tried to determine whether it had been asked casually, conversationally and without motive, or whether he was toying with her, hinting that he knew about Jay Doyle, since the Russian Embassy was composed of a thousand eyes and ears. Yet, his kulak face was open, only mildly curious, and his behavior since they had met this afternoon had revealed no suspicion.

Quickly she evoked the names of several old journalist friends in Paris, all female. She remembered Medora Hart, and briefly told Rostov of Medora's tribulations.

He listened attentively, taking the last of the peanuts from her bag, breaking and eating them. When she was through, he said, "But only women you see? You do not mention one man?"

Fear stabbed through her chest. In her desperate anxiety not to mention Doyle, she had blundered. She had spoken only of evenings spent with women, and it was unnatural. She must conjure up a male name quickly, a name not involved in her work.

Matt Brennan. She had just left Matt Brennan at Fouquet's.

"I don't care to see any men, Niki, not when I have you to wait for every evening," she said. "I've had a few casual dates, that's true, because it's uncomfortable for a woman to go out anywhere decent to dine alone. Let me see. Oh, yes. Someone at our Embassy introduced me to an American who's here from Italy on business. We got to talking about Paris, and I mentioned I'd never been on a *bateau-mouche,* so this fellow insisted we have dinner on one of the boats. In fact, last night. God, it was dull. This fellow used to be a diplomat, and even though he's in business now, he still likes to think he's a hot-shot international expert. Full of crackpot theories. Like one he's worked out since coming here and listening to gossip—he's one of those guys who pick up more dirt than a vacuum cleaner—and he's obsessed with the notion that your delegation and the Chinese are only pretending to be enemies, that you're secretly friends, and that neither Russia nor China intends to honor the Summit treaty. Isn't that a laugh? Now you know what a poor working girl goes through to have a date."

Rostov was amused, but interested. "That is the wildest nonsense I have heard yet, and, believe me, I hear the wild ones." He paused. "Your businessman friend, the one who stuck that in your ear—what is his name?"

"Brennan, I think. Yes, Brennan."

Rostov appeared surprised. "Matthew Brennan?"

That instant, when Rostov uttered the full name with such familiarity, Hazel had total recall. She had been going on compulsively, her mind devoted to camouflaging her relationship with Doyle, quite forgetful of Rostov's past and her own, but now came total recall. Rostov after Zurich and before Siberia, mentioning the name in anger.

She felt sickened by regret over her stupidity. If only she had thought of another name. But merely two had come to mind—Doyle, who was tabu, and Brennan, whom she had also just seen and whom she had considered inconsequential. It had been a mistake to speak of him, a minor mistake, and she was determined to turn it to her advantage by demolishing Brennan completely.

"That's right, Matthew Brennan," she repeated innocently. "He got into some political trouble—" she stopped, touched his sleeve. "Niki, didn't you meet him once?"

Rostov made a face. "Unfortunately, to my bad luck, yes. It was not for much time, but in the Switzerland conference. I think I spoke to you of it, but that was long ago. Brennan was the American in charge of the other demented one, Professor Varney. Brennan was a bad baby-sitter, as you call them. That was when Varney ran away, and this naïve Brennan got in trouble and got us all in hot water. . . . So he is here and you have seen him?"

"A thundering bore. But one never knows beforehand. A single girl has to take pot luck."

"My tragic *milochka*. It is my fault that I cannot give you more time. . . . So Brennan, the philosopher, the capitalist provocateur, he says we are intriguing with the Chinese and will not honor the Summit? Where did he become inspired by such a fanciful idea?"

"Rumor, Niki. People with time on their hands collect rumors."

"What did you say when he told you?"

"I told him he was nuts. Just like that."

Rostov threw back his head and laughed uproariously. "Good girl, good girl, just like my little *milochka*. . . . I am surprised such a one would show his face when his fellow Americans are here now."

"I think his behavior is routine for exiles. They brood about persecution until they become complete paranoids. Their only hobby is trying to envision how they can right the wrongs of humanity. I had the impression he's come here to lobby for himself. Since everyone refuses to listen, he's trying to play diplomat without portfolio, to show how patriotic and valuable he is. He's a sad nut, but harmless. America is full of them. We once had a man, in San Francisco, I think, who declared himself the Emperor of the United States and Mexico. He was pathetic. So everyone humored him."

Rostov nodded with understanding. "Lunacy is universal. We have our share in Russia. Empress Anna Ivanovna married one of her Ministers to the most ugly woman in the kingdom, and built a bedroom of ice for their honeymoon. Ivan the Terrible with his personal bodyguard of German war prisoners dressed in monks' robes. Queen Catherine who always kept her hairdresser in a cell so he would not gossip about her wigs. Catherine who paid her physician fifty thousand dollars for one smallpox inoculation and had fifteen thousand dresses in her closets. This I call lunacy, too. But any nation can afford a little lunacy in its leaders. After all, it is possible sometimes they have method in their madness. They pretend lunacy to attract lunatics for their purposes. Your President, for example—" Rostov was thoughtful now. "It is not unknown in America, or other nations, to create traitors falsely, and banish them, so they will be accepted by the enemy and become useful undercover agents. Perhaps Brennan is an instrument of your CIA?"

"Oh, Niki, my God, are you serious? Brennan? He's weak-kneed, a lightweight. Above all, he's a fool."

Even as she uttered the last word, she recalled her interview with Superintendent Quarolli, of the French Sécurité Présidentielle, and the quotation his grandfather had given him from the Holy Bible. She remembered exactly: "Every fool will be meddling."

Momentarily she sobered, but then she recollected something else, an exchange between Doyle and Brennan at Fouquet's before they had broken up.

"Yes, I had thought him foolish and childish from the first," Rostov was saying. "You are right about Brennan. *Kakoy durak*—a fool."

"I'm positive of it," Hazel said. "No government agency would employ anyone who goes around blabbing such crazy things in public. He's on his own, trying to give himself importance. Something else just came to mind that proves it. Niki, not only is he, alone, trying to prove

489

that he knows more about Russia and China than delegates who really know, but he's running around Paris looking for spies."

"Spies?" said Rostov incredulously.

"Sure. Brennan said something about having investigated a bookstore in the Rue de Seine which he thought was a Communist drop, a place for Communist spies to drop off or pick up their precious secrets. He didn't go into it, and I didn't have the patience to listen to him, even if he'd wanted to. But that should convince you, Niki, that he's no more than a kid playing cops and robbers. He has no man's work to do, so he does this. Anyway, so much for my marvelous dates."

Rostov placed an arm around her, and they began to move away from the monkey pit.

"My poor heart," he said. "You will forgive me?"

"I always forgive you," she said. "I know your life, and I know mine. I settled for that long ago, didn't I? I'm not complaining." She considered his rugged features, and she smiled. "No more dates with any more men. Just you. I'll wait for you tomorrow night. Don't disappoint me, dearest."

"I will not disappoint you." He was studying his watch. "And now I had better not disappoint the Premier. It is almost two o'clock. I must not be late. I must go to help save the world."

"Well, leave some of yourself to help save Hazel," she said. Hazel Doyle, she had almost said.

They parted at the miniature Eiffel Tower.

"Tomorrow night, *milochka*," he said.

"Yes," she said.

She watched him stride hurriedly past the train entrance toward the outer gate of the Jardin d'Acclimatation.

After a while she walked slowly to the little train. She knew that she would never ride it into the past again. After tomorrow, there would be only the future. She wondered why she was not happier.

WHEN MATT BRENNAN rushed out of the Hotel California, it was already sixteen minutes to five o'clock. Since he had only sixteen minutes before the five o'clock appointment in the Bois de Boulogne, he did not want to risk being late by waiting to catch a taxicab cruising through the Rue de Berri. It was a one-way street, and the taxi would be forced to carry him the long route around. It would be faster to hasten directly to the Champs-Élysées and commandeer a vehicle there.

All but running, he reached the Champs-Élysées. Two taxis were parked behind the light post in the center, both pointed toward the Arc de Triomphe and the Bois de Boulogne beyond. Without waiting for the signal to change, Brennan dodged through the traffic. He arrived at the first taxi just as a Chinese couple were entering it. Dismay turning into agitation, he looked toward the second taxi. No one was near it, and the LIBRE flag was still up.

Hastily he commandeered the remaining vehicle. "Bois de Boulogne," he ordered. He opened the rear door of the ancient Renault and stepped inside. As the sleepy, mustached driver sat up, Brennan enunciated carefully but with urgency, "Route de la Muette and Chemin de Ceinture du Lac on the eastern side. Near the *boule* courts on the lake. Almost across from the Châlet des Îles. That's the restaurant on one of the islands in the lake. Do you understand?"

"*Oui*," grunted the driver, turning the ignition key.

The moment that the taxi edged into the traffic of the Champs-Élysées and shook forward into second gear, Matt Brennan sat back in his seat, still winded but exulting in the imminent fulfillment of his desperate search.

This was his most exciting time in Paris, the most alive time he had known in four dead years.

The ride to his destination would take ten to fifteen minutes at the most. At the end of it waited Nikolai Rostov.

As the taxi rattled forward, speeding, slowing, speeding again, Brennan extracted the English briar pipe from the pocket of his sport jacket, then found his tinted sunglasses, opened them, and slipped them on. Behind the glasses, eyes closed, he tried to recapture the electrifying experience of the telephone call.

He had been resting, fully clothed, on the brass bed in his hotel suite. He had been exhausted by the meeting with Earnshaw, the session with Hazel Smith in Fouquet's, the long walk afterward. Since Lisa was still out, he had wanted a short nap in order to be in peak condition for the dinner to which Herb Neely had invited Lisa and him this evening.

He had been lying there, stretched out on the bed, thinking of his success with Earnshaw, speculating on the chances of Earnshaw's success with the President or whomever else he might see. He had tried to imagine what it would be like to come face to face with Nikolai Rostov at last. He had felt wonderfully, tiredly optimistic, and had twice begun to doze off, and had begun to doze off once more when the piercing sound of the telephone had almost split his eardrums.

Sitting up, eyes heavy, fumbling for the receiver, he had made out the hour and minute hands of his traveling clock. It had been twenty-five minutes after four.

The caller would be Lisa, he had thought, or maybe Neely, or possibly, possibly Earnshaw with some news.

The voice on the other end had been female but it was not Lisa's voice or the voice of anyone he knew. The voice had been softly modulated, slightly British in accent, and its owner was extremely terse.

"Mr. Matthew Brennan, if you please."

"This is Mr. Brennan."

"Mr. Brennan. I suggest you listen carefully. Do not interrupt. Do not make inquiries. Merely note what I am about to say. I am calling on the instruction of Minister Nikolai Rostov. Do you have a pencil and paper? You may reply. Do you have a pencil and paper?"

"Yes—yes—"

"Minister Rostov is aware that you have been attempting to make contact with him for several days. He did not feel it beneficial to either of you to respond to your messages. However, no more than an hour ago, an important American interceded on your behalf. Minister Rostov was convinced that it would not be improper to meet with you briefly. I have been advised to inform you that Minister Rostov has agreed to see you, on the terms and conditions he finds it necessary to impose."

"Of course. Anything—"

"Minister Rostov cannot see you publicly or officially. He will be pleased to meet you for a discussion in privacy. Mr. Brennan, make note of these directions. You will wear a sport jacket and slacks. You will wear dark sunglasses. You will smoke your pipe. You will take a public conveyance to the Bois de Boulogne. There is an artificial lake, Lac Inférieur, with two small islands in its center. You will take the thoroughfare along that lake, the eastern side of the Chemin de Ceinture du Lac, to the intersection of the Route de la Muette. There you will leave your vehicle, cross over to the wooded park along the lake, and make your way to the *boule* courts opposite the restaurant Châlet des Îles, which is located upon the island in the lake. You will arrive there no later than five o'clock. You will stand among the trees beside the *boule* courts, and watch any game then in progress. A gentleman holding two *boule* balls, one in each hand, will approach you, and he will say, 'Would you like to join us in the game?' You will nod, follow him to a parked motorcar, enter the rear of it. There Minister Rostov will be waiting to speak to you. Is that understood, Mr. Brennan?"

"Yes, but—"

"Five o'clock, Mr. Brennan. Good day."

There had been a metallic click. There had been a humming silence. There had been the ceaseless thumping of his heart.

He had hung up, still in the aftermath of shock, and at last he had stared down at his scribbled notes. The Bois. Five o'clock. Minister Rostov. It was real.

Before coming off the bed, he had considered the possibility that this was a practical joke. All of the obvious trademarks derivative of thriller and espionage fiction had just occurred—the anonymous call from a female, the complex instructions for reaching a rendezvous point, the orders that he dress and deport himself after a given fashion, the immediacy and secrecy of the meeting. Sifting this through his pragmatical mind, Brennan had been uncertain.

But then, swinging off the bed, Brennan had arrived at another view of the call. He had recollected his years of treating with Russians throughout the world, before Zurich, at Zurich, and had remembered specific encounters with Communist diplomats and the Russian KGB, and had recalled how often he had thought that the inventions of storytellers were pallid compared to the potential of suspenseful intrigue he had detected in the real thing. The behavior of Soviet Russian Government representatives, at least as he had experienced it, had always been melodramatic, devious, stealthy, the complexity of it forever exceeding the alarms of fiction. In dealing with the Soviets, it was not that Life imitated Art, but that Life was an exaggeration of Art. Because of this knowledge, Brennan had been able to accept the telephone call from one of Rostov's secretaries as perfectly normal.

Changing into sport jacket and slacks, he had decided the possibility of its being a practical joke was remote. Only a handful of persons, this week, had known the purpose of his visit to Paris. He had tried to enumerate, to himself, the exact number of persons aware of his quest for Rostov: Lisa Collins, the Neelys, Doyle, a nameless concierge and members of the staff of the Hotel Quai d'Orsay, Earnshaw, Wiggins, Isenberg, perhaps a few others, perhaps even a Chinese journalist named Ma Ming (although this would have been about Varney). Brennan had been unable to imagine any one of these as concerned enough, or sadistic enough, to stage so elaborate a practical joke. The possibility of a joke made no sense, and so he had put it from his mind.

It was real, that phone call, the promise of a clandestine confrontation with Rostov. He had felt it in his bones, and that had more reason than logic.

493

Having completed his dressing, he had remembered the disembodied feminine voice explaining to him that an "important American interceded" on his behalf, persuading Rostov to see him finally. He had tried to imagine who this American might have been. Neely or Wiggins? Unlikely, unless they had spoken of his problem to the Secretary of State, who had then been moved to act. Isenberg might have mentioned Brennan to some American delegate who, in turn, had gone to Rostov. Or perhaps there had been no important American at all, and Rostov had invented one merely to explain his sudden change of heart after so much elusiveness. Or maybe Doyle had somehow— but then, thinking of Doyle, Brennan remembered former President Earnshaw and his promise of this morning. Suddenly it had been clear to him. Earnshaw had acted on his behalf.

Although time was running short, Brennan had been sufficiently consumed by curiosity to telephone Earnshaw. Instead of Earnshaw, it had been Carol who answered the phone. No, she had said, her uncle was not in. If it was urgent—well, she was not sure where he could be reached, but he had gone off at noon for a luncheon at the United States Ambassador's residence. "Nothing at all that urgent," Brennan had said. "When your uncle returns, just give him this message from me. Tell him, 'Brennan says thanks.' He'll understand." Hanging up, he had felt reassured. If Earnshaw had been with the Ambassador since noon, he had undoubtedly made a successful plea for Brennan during that time.

About to leave his rooms, Brennan had realized that he was without his sunglasses and pipe. He had found the glasses on the bedroom table, and then he had gone through his larger suitcase to find the worn briar pipe. Thus equipped, he had hastily sought a taxi that would bring him to the fateful reunion with Rostov.

Now the taxi jarred to a halt, pitching Brennan forward. Regaining his balance, he looked out the windows of the Renault and was dismayed. His vehicle was in the center of a sea of automobiles, and high to his left loomed one section of the arch of the Arc de Triomphe. Ahead, blocking the way from the Avenue des Champs-Élysées to the Avenue de la Grande Armée, were three cars grotesquely accordioned. Tow trucks and police were arriving, but the collision had brought all traffic to a complete standstill.

Frantically, Brennan checked the time. It was eight minutes before five o'clock. And in the Bois de Boulogne, at five o'clock sharp, Nikolai Rostov would be waiting.

"Driver, can't you back up and take me some other way?"

"Non, c'est impossible. Vous n'êtes pas capable de vous en rendre compte vous-même?"

Brennan glanced out the windows, and he saw that it was impossible. They were hemmed in by stalled automobiles in every direction. At this rate he wouldn't reach the Bois by six o'clock, let alone by five. He considered paying off the driver, making his way on foot through the jam to the other side, and finding another taxi headed north. But he decided that there would be no vehicles available on the other side, for few cars were getting through the bottleneck.

The madness of the frustration was almost amusing. After the years of waiting to meet with Rostov, the recent days of intensive searching for a means to see him, he was being kept from achieving his goal by a ridiculous and typical Gallic smashup at the Étoile. To lose his opportunity to achieve vindication, a vindication that could restore him to life, because three French drivers had been belligerent or drunk or reckless was too fantastic to accept.

But now his own driver was poking his stubby finger ahead of them. *"Regardez, ça a l'air de s'arranger. Ça ne va pas durer longtemps."*

Brennan squinted through the windshield, across the tops of the cars in front, and he could see that the three crushed vehicles were being slowly pried apart with the aid of a repair-truck winch and police muscle. Shortly the traffic would move. He would not be very late after all. He was certain that Rostov would give him ten to fifteen minutes' grace.

Feeling better, he sat back in the taxi seat and reviewed the instructions given him.

He knew the Bois de Boulogne very well. In another time, when his wife Stefani had not yet been hateful, when Ted had been a child and Tracy an infant, Brennan had often visited the Bois. Since Stefani had mocked the Bois as a bourgeois picnic ground, detesting the outdoors (unless it was the fashionable St. Moritz), Brennan had usually gone to the Bois with the children, showing them the windmill, the cascades, the polo field, letting little Tracy ride a camel and teaching young Ted the simple rules of *boule*. More often he had gone to the Bois alone, to tramp the narrow paths into the woods, picking up leaves with his Basque walking stick or enjoying a cheese sandwich or merely reflecting on how much closer he was to the simplicity of this world than the sophistications of Stefani's world.

Yes, he knew the Bois de Boulogne, and he knew where he would be headed in not many minutes. They would enter the Bois at the Route de Suresnes, and ride between the thick forest to the left, the woods partially hiding the Lac Inférieur to the right. Here and there, on rented benches along the water, lazing elderly Frenchmen and their wives, or romantic young couples, would be feeding the ducks and swans. There would be the pier, and the motorboat that for thirty centimes each, would take both natives and foreign tourists to the triangular-roofed, open-terraced Châlet des Îles, situated on one of the artificial islands, where one could enjoy a bottle of Beaujolais or Bordeaux rouge.

But today he would not visit the Châlet des Îles or travel on the lake. Today he would not go as far as the water. He would hang back, beneath the dense foliage of the trees, observing the several *boule* games in progress and waiting for Rostov's emissary, carrying two *boule* balls, to lead him to the privacy of an automobile parked nearby.

Reflecting upon his instructions, he was surprised that Rostov's girl had ordered him to wait near the *boule* area. While Rostov, as best as Brennan could recall, was worldly, there had been no evidence in Zurich that Rostov had known the slightest thing about sports, and especially about a sport as typically French as *jeu de boules*. On the other hand, *boule* was probably spreading in popularity. Brennan himself, after first being introduced to the game in the Bois, had been charmed by the ease and pleasure of playing it. No regulation court was required. You simply needed any small surface of land that was solid lawn or hard dirt, and you used only four of the heavy two-pound metal *boule* balls and one small (no larger than a large marble) wooden *cochonnet* or jack, the target ball. You played one against one, or two against two, and someone tossed the wooden target ball up ahead, and your opponents took turns to see which of their heavy steel balls, pitched or thrown overhand or underhand, could land nearest the wooden target ball. The players throwing their *boule* balls closest to the target ball won points. But it was the refinements of the game that made for sport. If an opponent had his *boule* ball closest to the little target ball, you had the right to try to hit his *boule* ball and knock it away, or to hit the wooden target ball and send it flying away. After his introduction to the game in the Bois, Brennan had gone to the sports department in Au Printemps and purchased two *boule* sets to be sent to his home in Washington. But once home, except for an occasional Sunday game with young Ted, he had had little opportunity to play. Stefani had thought the game common and uninteresting, and had much preferred the same time be given over to tennis or riding. Perhaps he was being harsh in his memory of her. But that was the way it had been.

His mind had wandered too great a distance backward, and now he had to search to remember what had sent him on the journey. Then he recalled it. Rostov's girl ordering him to wait near the *boule* area in the Bois. Still, this was not unusual either. He himself had taken *boule* to America. Other Government visitors had, too. In Italy, when in the

496

mood, he had sometimes joined in the game of *boccie,* which was similar to *boule.* And he supposed that the Russians, who had been to France so frequently in recent years, had taken *boule* back to their *dachas* outside Moscow and adapted it to their own purposes, by now probably claiming to have invented it. Brennan was reminded never to underestimate the breadth of interests exhibited by the Russians and the Chinese—and above all, by Nikolai Rostov.

He felt the taxi moving once more.

Ahead, he could see that the impacted cars had disappeared and the way was clear. They drove around the Étoile, jerking and swaying to avoid the oncoming traffic pouring out of twelve converging thoroughfares, and finally they were speedily bumping up the vast stretch of the Avenue de la Grande Armée. They made their turn at the Porte Maillot and rode along the sudden border of greenery that was a boundary of the Bois de Boulogne. He would reach his rendezvous point at a quarter after five. He prayed Rostov had been generous enough to allow him the tardiness of fifteen minutes. If he had, they would be shaking hands in less than a minute or two.

Approaching the tree-laden banks that encircled the lake, Brennan became conscious of the steady honk of French police klaxons. Then from out of nowhere, it seemed, a louder honking from their rear merged with the disconcerting sounds ahead, and his taxi wheeled to the side of the road as a boxy ambulance bearing the Red Cross insignia roared past them.

His driver had slowed, hunching over the wheel, peering ahead, and Brennan saw what the driver was seeing. The ambulance, and a police wagon that had approached from the opposite direction, were drawn up before the very intersection where Brennan was expecting to be dropped off. Dozens of people, men in shirt-sleeves, women in cottons, the users of the Bois, were running toward the scene of the disturbance.

"Better pull up here," Brennan commanded. "I don't think you'll get much closer."

Paying his driver, Brennan left the taxi and strode quickly to the Route de la Muette. Ignoring the tumult caused by hurrying people and police, Brennan hesitated at the intersection and reviewed his orders. *Cross over to the wooded park along the lake, and make your way to the boule courts opposite the restaurant Châlet des Îles, located upon the island in the lake . . . stand among the trees beside the boule courts . . . watch any game in progress. A gentleman holding two boule balls, one in each hand, will approach you . . .*

Like a robot, dutifully obeying electronic commands in the midst of human chaos, Brennan traversed the street known as the Chemin de Ceinture du Lac until he attained the cool shade of the trees that guarded the shore of the lake. Penetrating the grove of trees, he finally emerged into the open, and off to his right, on one of the artificial islands in the center of the lake, he could plainly make out the larger of two buildings, the triangular roof and brick-red walls of the Châlet des Îles. By walking along the lawn that followed the edge of the woods, he would arrive at the *boule* courts. There he would hang back among the trees until approached.

Because he was late, he went fast. He kept looking for the habitual players, but none could be seen. He watched for the courts—which he knew were not courts at all but merely worn areas used for the games—and at last he came upon these. To his astonishment, they were abandoned. He stood there, lost in confusion. He had been told there would be *boule* games to observe from the trees. But there were no games. All that he could do was stand back among the trees and wait.

He turned toward the woods, and for a second time he was astonished. So single-minded had been his devotion to his orders that he had completely forgotten about the accident, about the people and police on the run, and he had ignored the sights and sounds of emergency. But now the sights and sounds assailed him, for there, through the trees, beyond the area where he was to have waited, were at least a hundred noisy spectators, craning their necks, chattering, with police coming and going, and a team of stretcher-bearers being allowed through the crowd.

Brennan surveyed the appalling mob. Fifteen minutes earlier he would have shared that area with very few persons, perhaps even owned it for himself. He would have been easily found and identified by Rostov's man. But now there was considerably less chance that this would happen. He had been told to wear sunglasses and sport jacket, and to smoke his pipe. But there were dozens of male onlookers who seemed to be wearing sunglasses, many men in sport jackets, and several with pipes, all attracted here from adjacent sections of the Bois to revel in some kind of accident.

Discouraged, Brennan knew that he still must make an effort to stand where he was supposed to stand. After all, quite possibly no other person in the crowd possessed all three props—the sunglasses, sport jacket, pipe. It was also unlikely that anyone else in the crowd resembled Brennan closely, and surely Rostov's emissary would have been given some kind of description.

Holding his pipe, Brennan walked across the lawn to the edge of the woods, and then to the circle of spectators among the trees. As he arrived, the circle split open, spectators falling raggedly back to make way for a solemn *médecin de la police* and an unhappy police *commissaire,* who were conversing almost inaudibly.

As they passed Brennan, he could make out the *commissaire's* question, *"C'est la boule qui l'a tué?"*

Only a portion of the police physician's fading reply was distinct: *"Sans aucun doute . . . en cognant la tête . . . fracture du crâne . . . commotion cérébrale . . . il est mort sur le coup . . . quel malheureux accident par une aussi belle journée. . . . . Allons, continuez, je vous verrai au poste, Monsieur le Commissaire."*

Brennan attempted to piece the conversational fragments together. Apparently, someone had died while playing *boule,* had suffered a fractured skull, a brain concussion. Interest aroused, Brennan pivoted slowly, searching up the narrow lane through the crowd to the wide patch of ground upon which all eyes had been concentrated.

In the center of the grassy clearing, sprawled face down, lay the twisted body of a slender young man.

For Brennan, cultural victim of countless television programs, motion pictures, stage plays, the dead victim of this accident, as he lay motionless in the clearing, appeared as unreal as an actor. Brennan waited for the corpse to stir and rise. It did not.

Suddenly Brennan realized that the *commissaire,* returning to his duty, was going briskly past once more. Spurred by some unreasoning impulse, Brennan quickly fell in behind the police officer, staying at the officer's heels as the awed spectators closed up the aisle behind them. When Brennan reached the inner hub of the large circle, he halted. He watched the *commissaire* speak briefly to the ambulance attendants, waiting with their stretcher. Next, the *commissaire* moved toward two uniformed *agents de police* and a plainclothesman, who were inspecting the area and were gingerly picking up minute objects and carefully placing them in little bags. After observing their routine and bobbing his head in approval, the *commissaire* moved back toward the corpse in the center, where a police photographer tirelessly snapped photographs of the inert body.

Watching this sad spectacle, Brennan involuntarily dropped his gaze to the figure of the sprawled corpse. The back of the victim's head, partially shattered from a crushing blow, was a gruesome sight, and the shock of dark hair was matted with clotting blood. The shoulders of the victim's gray sport jacket were also spotted with blood, still crimson, not yet turned black. The *commissaire* knelt while remaining in Brennan's line of vision. Whipping out a handkerchief, he reached down beside the victim's face to retrieve what appeared to be a pair of glasses, and placed them carefully in the handkerchief. Then he lifted a dead arm and removed another object, and nested it in his handkerchief also.

The *commissaire* rose, signaling to the ambulance attendants. They responded swiftly, one carrying a folded stretcher, the other a blanket. With practiced hands they turned the corpse over on his back. There was no reverence in their actions. They were not handling a human being. They were handling a slab of meat. Brennan shuddered.

In brief seconds, while the *commissaire* addressed the two attendants and the photographer continued to take his obscene pictures, Brennan had a glimpse of the victim's face. It was a visage both bony and angular, with lifeless eyes, a thin long nose smudged with dirt, a mouth at once pained and surprised and now slack in death. It was not a French face, but British or German or possibly American. And then it was no more, for the blanket had been drawn across it.

The victim's face had had an eerie familiarity for Brennan, and he averted his head while the corpse was being lifted to the open stretcher.

The spectators around Brennan were dispersing, to go back to their benches, their strolling in the late sun, their picnics, their games.

Brennan felt someone rudely bump against him, and he whirled around, annoyed, to find an eager young American college type, complete with crew cut, apologizing to him. "Sorry, sir," the young man said. He was tugging a pad from his pocket. "Geez, but I'm late."

He hurried directly toward the *commissaire,* calling out, "Monsieur, I'm Fowler of ANA. Remember me? We—"

Apparently, the *commissaire* did remember him, for he shook the American reporter's hand and appeared cordial. "Yes, Mr. Fowler. How are you?"

"We just got the tip from the Préfecture. But we couldn't get it straight. Was it homicide?"

"An accident, ordinary accident, but unique because of its infrequency."

They drifted out of Brennan's hearing, walking slowly around the clearing, Fowler obviously probing, the *commissaire* obviously cooperative. Then they approached Brennan once more.

"That is the story, Mr. Fowler," the police official was concluding.

"But you don't know who was playing *boule* with him? Any clues at all? Anything special in that handkerchief?"

"Nothing, nothing," replied the *commissaire.* He unfolded the handkerchief in his palm and held up a pair of shattered bent sunglasses. "Just personal effects. This, too." He indicated an object still in the handkerchief so that Brennan could not see it, an object in which the reporter showed no interest. "Check the Préfecture, if you wish, for further information. Good day, Mr. Fowler."

The *commissaire* hastened off, and Fowler, crew cut bent over his pad, remained in his place, busily scribbling notes.

In the last minutes Brennan had nearly forgotten the reason for his presence in the Bois. Something else had seemed more vital. Slowly he started toward the occupied reporter.

"Mr. Fowler?"

The reporter looked up with surprise.

"I couldn't help hearing you were from ANA," said Brennan. "I happen to have two good friends attached to the bureau—Jay Thomas Doyle and Hazel Smith. My name's Brennan."

Fowler was instantly respectful and attentive. "How do you do, Mr. Brennan."

"I won't take up your time. I know you're in a hurry. But I am curious. What happened here?"

Fowler tucked his notes and pencil into his pocket. "We thought it was an American, that's why I was sent out. Actually, it's nothing much for us. The guy that got killed is a Britisher, name of George Simmons, thirty-five, an engineer from Liverpool. An ordinary tourist, nothing to do with the Summit, unfortunately. Just a plain gawker, here on a holiday."

"What happened?" Brennan repeated.

"A freak accident, maybe worth two paragraphs. As far as I can learn, he was wandering about the Bois, sight-seeing. He came on the *boule* games here, and he paused to watch them. Then, according to a couple of witnesses, some guy carrying a couple of *boule* balls came up to him, looking for a fourth to set up a new game. Apparently, Simmons, this Englishman, was interested. They went off back through the trees—to this *boule* area—and the next thing, maybe five minutes later, a couple of French kids went scrounging back in the brush, and they stumbled on Simmons' body right here, in this clearing, and when they saw the blood, they began to yell. As far as the police can make out, Simmons joined this pickup game, but not being experienced at *boule,* at waiting for turns, he must have darted out to see the lie of his ball just as one of the others pitched another ball hard and high. It smashed Simmons on the back of the skull. Killed him instantly. Well, I guess he just dropped down to the ground, and when his partners saw he was dead and nothing could be done, they scrammed out of here. Just got scared and didn't want to get involved in the accident. That's not right, but it's human nature. Can't say I'd have behaved differently."

"What time did this happen?" Brennan asked tightly.

"Exactly, I don't know. Witnesses think he disappeared into the woods, to join the game, around five o'clock. Maybe a little after." The reporter paused. "Well, I'd better get back to the office."

"Mr. Fowler, one more thing."

"Yeah?"

"I watched you and the *commissaire*. What was he showing you in the handkerchief?"

"Handkerchief? Oh, yes. Nothing much. He'd just picked up a couple of the victim's personal effects. A pair of sunglasses he'd been wearing."

"I saw that."

"And the poor guy's pipe. That was in the handkerchief, too. . . . I'm driving back to town. Want a lift?"

"No, thanks," said Brennan. "I'll hang around awhile."

"Can't say's I blame you. I love it here. Most peaceful spot on earth. Well, glad to have met you. So long."

"Thanks again," said Brennan.

Briefly he stood alone in the clearing, and then he turned and walked through the trees to the edge of the woods. He stopped before the regular *boule* courts. They were still abandoned. On the lake beyond, there were swans and several boats.

He held up his wristwatch. It was twenty minutes to six. He considered waiting. But he knew that no one would come. He knew no one would come, because he knew that someone had already been here.

It seemed inconceivable, what was in his mind, yet he had conceived it and he had begun to believe it. His brief glimpse of the victim's face was vivid in his memory. There had been the strange familiarity about the face. He understood the familiarity. It had been a face not quite like his own, not one that might be mistaken for his own by anyone who knew him, but it had been a face that, in its gauntness and thinness, was generally similar to his own. It had been a face that vaguely resembled the way he, Brennan, had looked some years ago. And it occurred to him now that if someone had been shown a photograph of him, it would have been a photograph taken no more recently than four years ago, during the Congressional hearings, when he had appeared younger, more like that poor Englishman. For no recent photograph of him existed. He had not permitted his picture to be taken again in four years.

He had seen the bloodstains on the victim's gray jacket. It had been a sport jacket. He had seen the smashed sunglasses. He had been told of the victim's pipe. And more—more—the Englishman, here watching a *boule* game, had been approached by someone carrying

502

boule balls, someone inviting him to join a new game. That had been five o'clock. Or shortly after. And he—no, not himself, but the Englishman mistaken for him—had gone into the woods, and been found dead minutes later, an accident.

All at once Brennan was unsure of himself. His recent flights of fancy, his recent tendency to overdramatize everything, had been doubted and ridiculed by Earnshaw and Hazel Smith. Perhaps the French police were right. An accident. Perhaps all that he was conjuring up now was explained by coincidence. There were countless foreigners like him who came to the Bois, who wore sport jackets, slacks, invariably used sunglasses and often smoked pipes, and who watched *boule* games and were invited to participate in them. Perhaps Simmons had been one of these, and *had* been killed by a freak accident. And as for himself, no one had come for him because he had not kept his appointment on time. He had been dreadfully late. Perhaps he was wrong and unduly alarmed.

But he doubted it.

He could not endure the Bois a moment longer. Hastily he retraced his steps to find a taxi.

Later, riding back to his hotel, Brennan realized that he was shivering in the mild air. It was, he supposed, the after reaction to the potential of danger. A passage from a popular book he had read and reread in prep school entered his head: "He was not, as he knew well from experience, one of those persons who love danger for its own sake. There was an aspect of it which he sometimes enjoyed, an excitement, a purgative effect upon sluggish emotions, but he was far from fond of risking his life . . . and since the war, whenever there had been danger again, he had faced it with an increasing lack of relish unless it promised extravagant dividends in thrills." That had been Glory Conway, a fictional hero of his youth, the hero of James Hilton's *Lost Horizon*. That had also been Brennan as a man.

He was, essentially, an intellectual, an observer, a bystander of life. He had taken risks, especially when he had attended international conferences in distant places for the Department of State, and he had taken blows and fallen into traps and been afraid of his daring, but those had been the risks and dangers of a purely cerebral combat. Physical danger had always been foreign to him. Not since prep school—when he had got into an argument with a rival shot-putter during a track tryout, and they had lashed out at one another with bare fists, bloodying each other until the coach had come between them— had he been a party to actual physical violence. It was not fear of loss, or of hurt or impairment to his body, that had made him avoid violence, but his belief that man abdicated his role as man for that of animal if he stooped to settle differences physically rather than through the power of reason. It was because of this opposition to senseless violence that he had abhorred the sacrifice of his brother Elia on the battlefield. It was why he fought against wars, and why he had so long devoted himself to the cause of an effective disarmament that would guarantee peace.

He had simply no understanding of premeditated murder.

Yet today, in the Bois, he had been violently struck at. He had been missed, by wild chance, but he had been struck at, and there was no enemy to be seen, no enemy with whom to reason or compromise. Nor, oddly, did he wish to reason or compromise with such an enemy. Some sudden inner anger made him wish only to strike back, exact an eye for an eye. Passionately—for the real victim, Simmons, for the intended victim, himself—he wanted to strike back, to punish, to dispense justice on his own terms, and to hell with rationality.

But there was no one to hit. Who was the enemy?

He could think of no person on earth who would risk murder to be rid of him. Nor could he think of a solitary motive for any individual or group, in Paris, in the world, to wish him liquidated by violence. Not Rostov, certainly. The voice on the telephone had merely used Rostov as the lure to bring Brennan to the ambush. Not any Russian, or any Chinese, or any American, Frenchman, Englishman, or German. There simply was no identifiable enemy. There was only the brush of death. And now, unknown danger.

Not until Brennan entered his hotel did one aspect of the game of *boule* come to his mind. In *boule*, when you were closer to your target than was your opponent, but your opponent still had a chance, he would try to smash at your ball with his own, try to knock you aside, deflect you from the target and put you out of play, so that the target could be safely his own. And the opponent who did this was called, by the French, *"l'assassin."*

The assassin.

And not until Brennan entered his hotel suite, hardly aware of Lisa's humming as she dressed for dinner in her room next door, did something else, more chilling, occur to him. Shaken by what had transpired, he had become conscious of the empty pipe clenched between his teeth. He had wanted a smoke, and so he began to cast about for his tobacco pouch, and then he realized that there was no tobacco pouch and there was no tobacco. Nor had there been either for almost four years. The last time he had smoked a pipe had been in Zurich. At the time of his return to America, for his unjust trial, he had lost patience with the

504

pipe, with its slow mellowness, and had forsworn its use, taking up cigarettes in its place. He had always carried a pipe in his luggage, meaning to go back to it and recapture the repose of better times, but he had never used it, only used cigarettes, until four-thirty this afternoon, when a soft girl's voice on the telephone had sent him to the Bois with the reminder and order, "You will smoke your pipe."

It hit him now, these moments, with the force of an assassin's blow. *Your pipe.*

The voice on the telephone had believed that he still smoked a pipe, as he had until after Zurich. Someone was totally unaware that he had given it up soon after Zurich, four years ago.

Who would have known of the pipe in Zurich and in the years before, and who among those who had known him then was in Paris this very day?

He read off to himself the roster of possibilities. Earnshaw. Doyle. Neely. They might have known, could have known, but they had all seen him without a pipe since. They formed a roster of impossibilities.

He read off one more name, and his mind trembled over the possibility of it. One more had known of his pipe-smoking habit in Zurich, and that one was now in Paris but had not seen him lately and could not know of his change of habit. There was one who might think that he was today as he had been four years ago. To himself, he mouthed the name.

Nikolai Rostov.

Logical.

Also, illogical.

Nothing made sense except one fact. Somewhere in this vast city there were hunters. And he, Matt Brennan, by the grace of Simmons, was still the quarry.

Absently he rotated the nicked old briar pipe in his hand. Perhaps the day hadn't been lost at all. True, he had not seen Rostov. But he had seen death. Until he learned whether they were one and the same, or were a person and a specter quite apart, he would not quit Paris.

J UST ONE MORE number before the intermission," said Jay Doyle, putting down his program. " 'Sing, You Sinners,' featuring Medora Hart and The Troupe." He turned his head toward Hazel Smith, who was drinking champagne beside him, and his expansive features were contracted with concern. "Wonder what's keeping Matt Brennan and his lady friend. It's not like him to be this late. Neely says he invited everyone for eight o'clock sharp. Now it's—let me see—almost nine-thirty. Dinner nearly finished. The first act practically over. I wonder what's happened."

"Easy," said Hazel, finishing her champagne. "Your brilliant friend's probably locked up with Premier Talansky and Chairman Kuo Shu-tung, warning them that he knows the truth, and they'd better stay enemies, or else."

"Aw, come on, Hazel, he means well. Even Neely's worried. He just went to call Matt's hotel. He could be sick or something."

"Jay, quit hogging the champagne." She held out her glass, and eagerly Doyle refilled it. Thus reinforced, she shifted in her chair, half turning her back on Doyle's concern. She had no patience with any petty concerns tonight, and she gave her attention to her surroundings.

She was enjoying the Club Lautrec enormously, especially after the tensions of the last few days. Coming here had been like entering a gaudy cavern of hedonism. Surrendering your ticket at the entrance, you surrendered also your cares and intellect, and submitted yourself to the mindless pleasures of food and drink and silly talk and naked, acrobatic entertainers. Before her, jammed elbow to elbow at crowded tables, were at least a thousand convivial celebrators of life, who could be heard above the music but could not be seen through the hazy screen of smoke and dim lighting.

She was glad Herb Neely and his wife had invited them for this festive evening. There were two other tables of Neely guests besides their own—all three tables beautifully situated below the runway of the stage—but the other two tables were occupied exclusively by American correspondents here for the Summit. Hazel guessed that Neely was performing as personal host rather than as United States Embassy press attaché. She was pleased to be at Neely's own table. She supposed she was at this table because Doyle was Brennan's friend, and Brennan was Neely's friend. Anyway, friends, and as a result the atmosphere was cozy and warm rather than freeloading-professional and public-relations cold. It was a good evening because it was like playing house, playing married. It was as if she were truly Doyle's wife and they were out on the town with his business cronies and his cronies' wives. It was fun belonging.

Suddenly the cavern darkened completely. Only the blaze of floodlights on the stage and runway remained. From overhead, from every side, came the sound of the raucous orchestra playing the raucous "Sing, You Sinners." Expectantly, Hazel turned back toward the stage, staring up over Frances Neely's head.

The long-legged girls of The Troupe had burst onto the stage, half from one wing, half from the other, until they were linked arm in arm in a long single line. Attired in buttoned raccoon coats, exaggeratedly short, they were a French version of the American flapper girls of the twenties. They swayed. They undulated. They did a modified Charleston and broke into high kicks, and then the line of The Troupe parted, as did the curtain behind them. Down a center staircase, resembling an American football stadium staircase, came Medora Hart, wearing a short fur coat cut in the style of those worn by the members of The Troupe, except Medora's coat was mink, not raccoon.

Grinding and bumping at each step, Medora descended to the stage and The Troupe closed ranks behind her. All of them came prancing forward, frenziedly shaking, like possessed participants in a religious revival meeting. They were whirling dervishes now, and as they spun round and round, the bright white illumination gave way to varicolored spotlights, catching and distorting the dancers in red, in green, in purple. Abruptly the colored spotlights were gone, the flat white illumination returned, and there they were, Medora and The Troupe, divested of their furs, wearing straight-cut, spangled flapper dresses of America's Roaring Twenties, but with the hemlines not merely above the knees but six inches above the knees.

Holding a hand microphone, Medora came swinging forward as The Troupe fell into a short-kicking, V-formation behind her. Head shaking from side to side, her loose flaxen hair flying, her shoulders and hips rolling with abandon, Medora began to shout forth the lyrics of "Sing, You Sinners."

From her seat below, Hazel sat hypnotized by the performance. She tried to see Medora through the two thousand other eyes in the nightclub. If one thousand of the other eyes were those of males, believing only what they saw, wanting to know nothing but what could be seen, investing the hallelujahing girl, her head thrown back, her pelvis thrust forward, with their own desires and fantasies, then Hazel could imagine that to them Medora Hart was the sexiest bitch alive.

Quickly Hazel abandoned this second sight, and allowed her own eyes to view Medora plainly. And suddenly what she was seeing was not only Medora's hoax but every woman's hoax. Medora as Everywoman, only Medora more so than others, offered every man fake promises. There was the outer woman, with her wild or sleek hair, her shy or frank eye, her parted mouth and painted red lips, her teasing bosom and flashing silken leg. There was the outer woman with her artificial fragrance, her studied smile, her practiced mode of speech. There was the outer woman with her hundred movements of eyelids, mouth, hands, hips, legs. There was her façade, there were the hints to her secret, there were the reassurances of an offering of unimaginable transport and rapture, of a giving single-purposed, devoted, concentrated.

This, thought Hazel, was the Big Lie, the Lie that hid the inner woman, the real woman, with her inhibitions, her fears, her timidity, her illnesses, her problems, her selfishness, her confusion, her recurrent hostility, her mother, her father, her flawed human-beingness.

Let the buyer beware, thought Hazel. He bought, on the basis of the wrappings, sex and love. He opened the package, and to his amazement, sex was the smallest part of the contents, love was not quite the right size, and the rest of the contents had not been bargained for and could not be disposed of.

Perhaps, thought Hazel, her view of her own half of the human race was prejudiced by her own years of frustration, by her disenchantments, by her cynicism. Yet, no, because her Exhibit A was up on the stage, performing vertically what women ordinarily perform horizontally, disrupting the libido of every male in the club (even Doyle, she was sure, pitiful fool), as the blue smoke rose to the ceiling ever more thickly.

There was Medora of the stage, of the night, the perfect package, being bought without question by every male dreamer in the audience. Yet there was the same Medora of the lonely rooms, of the empty days, the Medora that Hazel knew intimately, who had never once spoken of love, who obviously hated men and hated sex, who was obsessed with insecurity, with revenge, with Mum and Sis, with returning to the womb of home. The Big, Big Lie. Poor Medora, Hazel thought, and poor Everyman everywhere. Only truth can set you free, she thought, but you shall remain slaves to the Lie for all eternity. Else civilized Christian life on earth should cease to exist.

Hazel's attention was returned to the stage by another change of lighting. Medora's song had finished, and now she and the girls of The Troupe were caught up and lost in the changing colors from the spotlights, revolving like so many bright bits and pieces of glass in an ornate kaleidoscope. Again the changing colors stopped, the stage was bathed in white, and the audience emitted a united gasp.

For Medora and the girls of The Troupe had shed their spangled flapper dresses and stood revealed in a semi-nudity more naked than total nudity. Except for abbreviated copies of flapper step-ins, the chorines of The Troupe wore nothing. And Medora, their star, wore less. Like the others, her naked breasts were exposed, but unlike the others, her breasts were perfectly formed, and unlike the others, she wore a flesh-colored, sequined G-string in place of step-ins.

Fascinated, Hazel watched the frenzied finish of the first act. The orchestra screamed, and the girls screamed their final reprise. There was female flesh everywhere, Medora, her dancers, all wriggling their arms to the heavens, shaking their unconfined breasts, arcing their torsos round and round. Sing, Sing, Sing, You Sinners!

And then there was momentary darkness before the lights came up and the music went down, and the waiters were on the run, and the Club Lautrec was a Tower of Babel once more.

Hazel sank back. She looked at Doyle. He was sitting as straight as a pasha counting his harem, glassy eyes still fixed on the empty stage. He felt her gaze, for he turned, grinning sheepishly. "Guess it's okay if you like girls," he said. "I happen to like just one. She goes by the name of Hazel Smith."

She had never felt lumpier or more unattractive. "Oh, sure," she said. But it was nice of him to be so nice. "What do you think of our Medora?"

"Same as I said the first time around, Hazel. Seeing her up there, you'd never imagine in a million years what she's really like or what she's going through."

Hazel was pleased. "That's exactly what I was thinking, Jay." Her affection for him continued to increase. She felt fewer guilts about her afternoon meeting in the Jardin, and she felt better about the following night, now that she had a Cause.

"Some of these kid performers are remarkable," Doyle was saying. "If I owned a Nardeau painting, and my whole life depended on it, and then someone stole it away, I don't think anything on earth could make me go out in public and pretend nothing had happened."

"It's her job, Jay. As a matter of fact, she is feeling better. I spoke to her on the phone just before you picked me up. Didn't I tell you? She had a little bit of good news."

"Really?"

"I called her to tell about how you, Brennan, and I put our heads together at Fouquet's today, and had agreed we'd find some means of helping her. Well, meanwhile, the Sûreté located Nardeau on the Riviera and informed him of the robbery. He was incensed, more about Medora's loss than his own, and he's been on the phone to Paris all day. The upshot of it was that by the time Nardeau called Medora, he was able to cheer her up a little. He said that the Paris police were trying to get in touch with some underworld figure—you know, a paid informer—who might finger the art thief or thieves for them and help them recover the paintings."

"Wouldn't that be great?"

"Anyway, Medora was a little higher tonight. Nardeau's arriving in

Paris in the morning, on the Train Bleu, and he wanted Medora to meet him. . . . By the way, I asked Medora if she'd like to join us after the show for a drink. She grabbed at it. She's been so alone, poor kid. We'll wait for her in the Lido Bar, and we can have something there or maybe all go over to my apartment. I hope you don't mind, Jay?"

"Suits me fine. I only hope Matt—" He saw Frances Neely returning from a visit to her other two tables of guests. About to address her, he waited, since she was waving to someone at the other side of the stage runway.

She came back to their table. "Just bringing Herb in," she said. "He's on his way with Mr. Brennan and Miss Collins in tow. We were so worried. Herb sneaked out to call the California Hotel, but I guess he ran into Matt in the lobby." She waved past Hazel again. "Well, thank God they're here, safe and sound."

Hazel turned in her seat, and Doyle puffed to his feet as Neely arrived victoriously with Matt Brennan and Lisa Collins.

"Sorry, sorry, sorry," Neely apologized. "They would have been here half an hour earlier, but all my fault. I caught them coming in, and when I heard why they were late, I kept them in the lobby where we could talk without interruption. Let me see, now—" He brought Brennan and Lisa forward. "You two know everyone?" Quickly he introduced Lisa Collins to Hazel and Doyle.

Hazel studied Brennan carefully. His features were drawn, unsmiling, harassed. He was carrying two rolled French newspapers, and his fists kept working them tighter and tighter. The Collins girl, dark, tall, lovely, wearing her pink brocade dinner gown with the aplomb of a mannequin, also appeared disturbed. She had poise, but her graciousness seemed forced as she constantly, anxiously, looked at Brennan. A marvelous body, Hazel decided, nothing as blatant as Medora's figure or the figures of The Troupe girls, but subtler, slender and cool. Probably a great bed partner, Hazel decided, and then wondered what ever these young girls saw in older men.

"Before you sit down," Neely was saying to Lisa and Brennan, "let me have you meet my guests at the other two tables."

As Neely herded them ahead of him, Doyle, still standing, called after him, "What kept them, Herb?"

"Murder," replied Neely over his shoulder. "A slight case of murder."

Hazel looked at Doyle as he sat down next to her. "Now, what in the hell does that mean?"

"I don't know," said Doyle slowly. "Except he didn't seem to be joking."

Hazel drank in silence, and when she finally turned around, she found Brennan settling Lisa into a chair, then seating himself next to her, with Hazel on his other side.

Neely had secured a freshly opened bottle of champagne. "This is what you need, Matt."

"To the brim," said Brennan, holding out Lisa's glass before offering his own.

Pouring, Neely said, "I'd better drum up two dinners."

"No, thanks," said Brennan. "No appetite."

"Me neither," said Lisa.

Hazel felt Doyle lean across her. "For Chrissakes, Matt, what's been going on? Herb said something about murder. Is he kidding?"

"I wish he were," said Brennan. "I'll tell you, but first—" He picked up the newspapers beside his plate, unrolled one, and handed it to Doyle. He unrolled the second, flattened it, and gave it to Hazel. "Lisa and I were up in ANA waiting for the late editions and hanging around while Fowler was telephoning the Préfecture for us." He pointed. "Turn them over. Story is on the bottom of the front page. The one about the Englishman killed in the Bois. Read that first. Then I'll tell you what happened."

Puzzled, Hazel slowly translated the three-paragraph French news story. George Simmons, thirty-five-year-old engineer and British citizen. Found dead in the Bois de Boulogne. Playing in a game of *boules*. Stepped in front of a flying ball. His skull crushed by ball. Died instantly of compound skull fracture. Death officially attributed to accidental causes. His fellow players, frightened, fled. Police still investigating in an attempt to discover their identity. No other witnesses. The victim, Simmons, a resident of Liverpool, England. Came to Paris two days ago for a three-week holiday. Registered at Hotel Scribe. British Embassy has notified next of kin, brother in Liverpool, three sisters in Manchester.

More confused than ever, Hazel looked up to find Brennan staring at her. "A freak accident, but otherwise not extraordinary," Hazel said. "What's it got to do with you?"

"First of all, I have every reason to believe that it was not an accident," said Brennan evenly. "Simmons was murdered, and the murder was premeditated. In the second place, I have every reason to believe that I was the intended victim." He touched the newspaper. "The only accident that occurred was that someone got Simmons by mistake instead of me."

"Come on now, Matt," protested Doyle quickly.

"Well—" said Brennan, and he hesitated. The unconcealed skepticism on Hazel's face gave him pause.

"Go on, Matt, tell them exactly what you told me," Neely called from across the table. "I've just been catching Frances up on what happened to you."

"I can't believe it," said Frances Neely with emotion.

Hazel had made up her mind. He *was* a nut. But she didn't want to disrupt the party. "Yes, Brennan," she said in a flat, challenging voice, "go on, tell us."

"All right," Brennan said defiantly. "It started around four-thirty this afternoon. I was in my hotel room, trying to sleep. The telephone rang. A girl—no idea who—a girl with a slight British accent wanted to speak to Matthew Brennan. I said I was Matthew Brennan. She said—" He stopped. His eyes shifted from Hazel to Doyle, and then back to Hazel. "I'd better explain something, Miss Smith. It hasn't been exactly a secret, but it hasn't been highly advertised, either. People who know me casually think I'm in Paris on business. I am, but not the kind of business they think. I'm here because I learned that a certain Russian diplomat is also here for the Summit. He's a fellow I once knew quite well. He was with me when Professor Varney defected at Zurich. As you know, I was blamed for that, and bore the disgrace of the whole affair. But this Russian friend of mine was there in Zurich with me, and could still help me clear my name. So when I found out he was in Paris, I came here, hoping to see him." Involuntarily his gaze strayed past Hazel, then quickly returned to her. "You've been working in Moscow. Maybe you'd recognize his name."

Hazel sat phlegmatic and contained, hands folded before her. "Maybe," she said.

"He's Talansky's Assistant Minister for Far Eastern Affairs. His name is Nikolai Rostov. Do you know him?"

For Hazel it was strange, hearing her Niki's name spoken openly among these Americans, her new friends, and in front of Doyle, her past and her future lover. It was strange and it was unsettling, for suddenly she felt half of this place and half of another. She must betray nothing, especially in front of Doyle. Brennan had asked her a question. What was it? She remembered.

"Do I know Rostov?" Hazel repeated. "Only slightly. I've met him several times, in the line of work, the way I've met most of the Russian Government officials."

Brennan nodded understandingly. "Well, he's the fellow I've been trying to see. But for some reason he hasn't wanted to see me. So I've approached several important people who I felt might intervene on my behalf, help bring Rostov and me together. I'd been anticipating that I'd have some luck, but I had none until that telephone call at four-thirty this afternoon. This anonymous female said someone had approached Rostov for me, and Rostov had agreed to see me. I was instructed, carefully instructed, to be at a certain place in the Bois."

Now all of Hazel's senses had been aroused. She desperately wanted to hear every word Brennan spoke and she was afraid that she showed it. "Sounds dramatic," she said lightly. "Don't skip a thing."

"Did you get to see him?" Doyle called out.

Brennan shook his head. "No. I don't think I was ever meant to see him. In fact, I'm almost sure he wasn't there. But let me go back to the phone call—"

While Brennan related the events of his late afternoon, Hazel absently fiddled with her newspaper, but she gave him her full attention. Toward the end of his recital, she began to lose interest in his obvious delusion of persecution. Her mind wandered, until she realized that there was silence. Brennan had finished. He was inspecting the others at the table for their reactions.

Frances Neely had covered her mouth with her hands. "It's perfectly horrifying."

"I'm frightened for Matt," Lisa Collins blurted out. "To think that—"

Herb Neely interrupted. "Matt, why don't you let me put you in touch with the FBI and CIA?"

"No, Herb, absolutely not," Brennan said. "They wouldn't believe me. I can't even prove I received that telephone call. It would be my word against that of the French police. And the police say accident."

"Matt?" It was Doyle now. "It could have been an accident, you know. The laws of chance, coincidence. Maybe that was a crank call you received. There are plenty of people, delegates, journalists, who still think you're a traitor. Some of them may have heard of your need to find Rostov. Perhaps Wiggins spread it. There might be some sadist who wants to tease you, see you run around, suffer disappointments, because he thinks you hurt your country and deserve harassment. There are people who get big charges out of that."

"And the murder in the Bois?" asked Brennan.

"Maybe not murder. Repeat. A unique accident. Plenty of people are accidentally killed every year because they've been clunked on the head by hard objects, balls, baseballs, shot-put balls. And *boule* balls, too."

Brennan thought about it. "Well, possibly, Jay. Yet, somehow, I doubt the crank call and accident theory. If you'd been through it, you'd feel the same way. I believe someone was after me. I really believe someone meant to murder me. The only thing I can't figure out is why If I knew why, I might know who. But why on earth should anyone want to get rid of me? I'm harmless. I'm nobody."

Hazel had been listening to Brennan with renewed skepticism, more and more sure that he was paranoidal, when she felt the weight of Doyle against her as he addressed Brennan.

"Matt, some people might not think you as harmless as all that," Doyle was saying. "Set aside what I've said for a moment. Let's give credence to your own version of what was behind that anonymous phone call. We'll agree someone wanted you out of the way. But you can't figure out why. Right?"

"Right," echoed Brennan.

"Well, Matt, remember at noon today, when you, Hazel, and I were in Fouquet's? When I got you to divulge to Hazel some of your grab bag of hints and suspicions about the Summit? Well, any one of a hundred people, had they been sitting with us and heard you, might have had good cause to consider you a serious troublemaker, or worse, as someone whose political prying was dangerous."

"You mean—do you mean—?"

"Matt, you've told me you have suspicions about the way the Russians and Chinese are behaving at the Summit, because you think there's some hanky-panky behind the scenes. You have as much as accused the Soviets and Chinese of perfidy. You told me so, and I got you to tell Hazel, and you told her, and I don't know how many others you've told. But Hazel warned you not to go around prattling that stuff because it was nonsense."

Hazel found her voice. "Only because I was afraid you'd make a fool of yourself, Brennan."

Doyle patted Hazel's shoulder. "That's right, honey, that's what you said." He addressed Brennan once more. "But, Matt, suppose it wasn't nonsense. Suppose you've stumbled on some genuine political treachery. And suppose some foreigner, a Russian, a Chinese, a Commie of any stripe, overheard you. Especially suppose they overheard you announce, as you did, that you were going to continue searching until you'd tracked the whole thing down. What would they want to do?"

"They'd want to shut me up," said Brennan.

Doyle clapped his pudgy hands. "Exactissimo. And can you name a better way of shutting up a person than making him extinct?"

Brennan bit his lip. "No."

"I'm not saying that's what happened, Matt. Maybe you're a mile wide of the truth about a secret, fishy friendship between Russia and China. But even if you are wrong, the very fact of your talking around like that, being so provocative, might touch on other open sores among certain people. There are plenty of people in Paris right now who would kill for less, real pros, trained for the job. Security is their only concern. To preserve security, they'd stamp out a human the way you'd stamp out an ant." He looked up. "Herb, isn't that so?"

Neely nodded gravely, and said to Brennan, "That's no exaggeration. You should know from experience, Matt."

Lisa had slipped her hand over Brennan's. He looked down at her hand a moment, and finally he raised his head, first facing Neely, then Doyle.

"Very well," he said. "Let's say I've been a provocateur. I can see the danger inherent in that. But one thing you've got to believe. I haven't discussed my ideas with anyone outside our tight little circle. I can name my confidants on my fingers." He held up a hand, fingers widely spread, and slowly, bending down one finger at a time, he announced the names of those who had heard of his suspicions. "Lisa knew. Herb—no, I never discussed this with Herb until now. All right. Lisa. Jay Doyle. Let me see. Earnshaw this morning. That's three. I think that's it."

"And Hazel," said Doyle.

"Forgive me. I forgot. And Hazel Smith. That's four. And that's all. Not a Chinese or Russian or Communist of any kind among you. So whom have I provoked?"

Doyle threw up his hands. "Beats me."

The overhead lights had begun to dim, and as darkness enveloped the Club Lautrec, the white spotlights crisscrossed above the stage. The sound of customers' voices gave way to a blaring medley of French cancan music.

Matt Brennan smiled and shrugged. "Beats us all," he said. "Another of life's lesser unsolved mysteries. You may be right, Jay. I'm gradually leaning toward your crank call and accident theory. That's the only interpretation that seems to make sense. . . . Well, the devil with it. Sorry to have bored you, friends. You're free to go back to your Agatha Christie. At least, she provides answers. Better yet, let's enjoy the show."

"Let's, darling," Lisa said, sliding her chair closer to his and curling into his extended arm.

The Troupe, clad in feathers and bare bosoms, was on the stage.

All the occupants of the Neely table were concentrating on the spectacle above them—all, that is, save one.

Hazel Smith stared down at the rolled newspaper in her lap and was not surprised to find that she had shredded it. Unobtrusively, she slid the tattered newspaper beneath her chair and brushed the torn pieces of paper from her dress.

She sat silent and alone, staring down at her dessert knife.

Minutes ago, when Brennan had enumerated those who knew of his findings, of his suspicion of a Chinese-Russian intrigue, he had counted out the names of Lisa Collins, Jay Doyle, Emmett A. Earnshaw, and herself. *That's four, and that's all,* he had said. *Not a Chinese or Russian or Communist of any kind among you,* he had said.

In those moments Hazel had felt the goose pimples spreading across her back and down her arms, and now she felt sickly cold and weakened.

Because now she knew that Brennan was wrong about one thing. There were not merely four persons who knew of his suspicions. There were five.

The fifth was Nikolai Rostov. The fifth was Nikolai Rostov in the Jardin d'Acclimatation.

My tragic milochka. . . . So Brennan the philosopher, the capitalist provocateur, he says we are intriguing with the Chinese and will not honor the Summit? Where did he become inspired by such a fanciful idea?

Niki, not only is he, alone, trying to prove he knows more about Russia and China than delegates who really know, but he's running around Paris looking for spies . . . investigated a bookstore in the Rue de Seine . . . Communist drop. . . .

She heard no music now, only the ridiculing reverberation of her idle gossip and the hearty boom of Rostov's laughter.

But she was not reassured.

At two o'clock this afternoon she and Rostov had parted company. At four-thirty Brennan had received a call that Rostov would see him. At five minutes after five o'clock a man who had been where Brennan was supposed to have been, who wore sports attire and sunglasses and carried a pipe, as Brennan was supposed to have done, lay dead of a skull fracture. The police had said accident. Brennan had said intentional murder. *But why on earth should anyone want to get rid of me? I'm harmless.* That from Brennan. *Matt, some people might not think you as harmless as all that.* That from Doyle.

Automatically, Hazel massaged her arms to warm them, to rid them of the ghastly goose pimples.

And automatically she was possessed of a new view of two men.

One was Brennan. She could see him now as anything but a paranoidal fool. She could see him as someone solid, clever, perceptive, attuned to detect any word off key. She could see him as someone she had better begin to take seriously.

The other was Rostov. She could see him as more than friend, patron, lover, more than a man who was only solicitous, amusing, sentimental. She could see him as a savage (as often this potential had been revealed in bed), a Communist party savage, manipulated by those above, manipulating those below, capable of any act to preserve Mother Russia.

These were the possibilities Hazel saw now. Maybe they were distorted by her upset and fear, and maybe her original view of both men—Brennan as the paranoidal fool, Rostov as the constant friend and lover—was the correct one. But if it wasn't, if the new view of the two—especially of Niki—was the correct one, then what lay ahead for her, the decision she must soon make, would be easier and reconcilable.

But first she would have to know the truth, the truth Doyle wanted and then the truth Brennan wanted, and yet both truths had merged into one. For if men were capable of assassinating President Kennedy in Dallas, these same men were capable of attempting the murder of Matthew Brennan in the Bois de Boulogne.

While her future actions were clearer now, it did not make her feel better.

She shivered, and then she understood.

She had caught the disease of fear. How her tough colleagues would laugh if they only knew. Good ol' Hazel Smith, intrepid, dauntless ol' Hazel Smith, *afraid*. Well, dammit, why not? It wasn't any ordinary story she was after. It was her own story. Only scared people won medals for valor, an army psychiatrist had once told her. Only people who wanted to live had to be brave. Hazel had never been afraid, because she had never cared about the next day. Now, for the first time, she cared.

Tomorrow night there would be Rostov. And herself. No other. And, somehow, there might be truth. For herself, feeling as she felt now, there would be terror. And if Rostov was truly an animal, he would smell her fear. She refused to imagine what might follow.

"Isn't it wonderful?" Doyle whispered against her ear.

"What?"

"The show, Hazel. Isn't it wonderful?"

"Wonderful," she said. "Everything's wonderful."

A FTER THE SHOW, they thanked the Neelys and bade them good night, and fell in step with the customers who were leaving the Club Lautrec. They walked from the Rue la Boëtie to the Champs-Élysées, and there turned right.

Allowing Matt Brennan and Lisa Collins, who were deep in conversation, to stroll ahead of them, Hazel tugged at Doyle's coat sleeve. "Jay, I don't know if I'm up to a nightcap at my apartment or anywhere else," she said. "I'm afraid I've got a little headache."

He was all sympathy. "I've got some aspirin in my pillbox."

"When we get to the Lido Bar."

"Can't I take you straight home?"

"I promised Medora we'd be waiting. She'll be right along. We can have coffee with her and afterward I'll make my excuses. I do want her to meet Brennan, since she may need him yet."

"If you're up to it. Okay. What do you think of Brennan's little adventure?"

"I don't know. Sounds fanciful. What do you think?"

"I don't know, either. When in doubt, I always go with Billy boy, the Bard. 'There are more things in heaven and earth, Horatio, than are dreamt of in your philosophy.' Anything's possible."

"I suppose."

"I hope you're feeling better tomorrow, Hazel. Maybe we can spend a quiet evening alone."

Hazel had been waiting for this opportunity. "Tomorrow? Oh, dear, I'd almost forgotten to tell you. I'm sorry, Jay, but I'm tied up for tomorrow night. I—the—some of the Russian delegation are giving a private dinner, and I've been invited. I wish I could have asked you to come, but I couldn't. I'm accepted by them. But you're an outsider."

His disappointment was evident to her. "Of course, Hazel," he said.

"But you'll be with me in spirit, Jay," she added quickly. "I may have a chance to—to make some discreet inquiries to help your book."

"Don't take any chances, darling."

"You are sweet. You needn't worry. I'll be among friends. Can I have a rain check for the night after?"

"For all the nights after, Hazel."

Matt Brennan and Lisa Collins were waiting for them at the entrance to the Lido Arcade. They went inside, between the jazzy record shop and the lines of tourists preparing to descend into the Lido Club for the late show, which was part of most tourists' "Paris by Night" sight-seeing schedules.

The main section of the Arcade, running from the Champs-Élysées the depth of the block to the Rue de Ponthieu (where the service entry to the Hotel California was located), consisted of expensive shops on either side, with a pastry cafeteria, a restaurant, and a modern bookstore in the center. Immediately to the right of the main section was the open door of a narrow snack stand, furnished with a long counter and stools. Since it served until four o'clock in the morning, the stand was much frequented by people from the entertainment world, including the girls of both the Lido Club and the Club Lautrec. This was the Lido Bar, and the menu signs on the wall promised a Gallic version of the American hot dog and hamburger stand.

There were three vacant stools near the cash register, and Brennan insisted that Lisa, Hazel, and Doyle take them. As they perched themselves at the counter, Doyle said to Brennan, "I'm afraid Hazel and I aren't quite up to going on from here. Do you mind if we make it another night, when we can get an earlier start?"

Brennan, behind Lisa and Hazel, was packing tobacco into his pipe bowl. "I'm glad you said it, Jay. I wanted to. I've about had it for today."

"I should think so," said Lisa from above her compact. "Matt, I've never seen you with a pipe. I must say, it fits you. Complements your soulful eyes. Most men don't look good with a pipe. One usually sees only the pipe."

Brennan's match flared over the bowl. "I'd almost forgotten how steadying it is. Once I had it out, I got myself some tobacco and—"

"But, Matt, maybe it's not wise."

"The mood is defiance, honey. From now on my uniform is sunglasses, sport jacket, slacks, and the pipe."

"You're asking for it, Matt," said Doyle.

"For what?"

"I don't know," said Doyle lamely. "Well, we'd better have something to justify occupying this counter space. I recommend the hot dogs *américains*. What'll you have, Hazel?"

"Those aspirins," said Hazel. "And a Perrier."

After she had got both, and while the others waited for their hot dogs, she said to Lisa, "Sorry to poop out on you. I wouldn't keep you here any longer, except I wanted you and Matt to meet Medora. If you think *you've* got problems, Lisa—do you mind first-naming? I've finally converted Brennan to Matt—formality is so tiresome—anyway, has Matt told you about Medora Hart?"

Lisa nodded. "Yes. I'm so sorry for her. I'm always surprised when awful things happen to beautiful people or rich people."

"They do, they do," said Brennan. "Scott Fitzgerald was wrong. The very rich are no different from you or me. But on the other hand, he did name a book *The Beautiful and Damned*."

Hazel said, "Our Medora is beautiful and she is certainly damned, and if Nardeau can't change that last part, we should."

"We shall," Brennan promised.

Hazel spun sideways on her stool and looked off. "She should be here any second. Once the show is over, those girls go over the side fast. She said she'd be here ten minutes after us. We can have a bite with her—and, Jay, then we can take her home."

The hot dog sandwiches and soft drinks were served, and Hazel moodily watched the other three eat, only half listening to their inconsequential conversation. Once, she noted that not ten minutes had passed but twenty minutes. She lost herself in thoughts of Brennan's adventure, and of her first meeting with Rostov in Vienna in another age, and of some of the times in Moscow, and before she would permit herself to consider the next night, her headache had gone. She noticed that the hot dogs of the others had disappeared, and they were reordering drinks to hold on to their seats. She realized that fifty minutes had passed, and still Medora was missing. She wondered if there had been a misunderstanding about their meeting place, but no, she was certain it was Medora who had suggested the Lido Bar right after the show.

Restless, and about to wander out into the Champs-Élysées to watch for Medora, she heard a voice behind her say, "I'm terribly sorry, Hazel."

She jumped off the stool to greet Medora Hart.

Without stage makeup and spangles and spotlight, sloppily dressed in a dark turtleneck sweater and slacks and sandals, Medora resembled a lonely adolescent more than a nightclub star. Hazel took Medora's hand as the English girl, with her free hand, frantically pushed back her flaxen hair.

"It's so good to see you, Medora," said Hazel. "I want you to meet our friends, and, from tonight on, your partners."

Breathlessly Medora said hello to Doyle and warmly acknowledged the introductions to Lisa Collins and Matt Brennan. Everyone congratulated her on her performance.

"Thank you, thank you ever so much," Medora said, still trying to catch her breath. "It went off well enough. It's not the show that gets me in a state, it's what one has to endure afterwards. . . . And look at the filthy mess I am because of it. But when I saw how late I was, I just couldn't bother. I'm sorry to have held you up this long. I ran practically all the way here."

"Nonsense, Medora," said Hazel. "As long as there was nothing upsetting. I suppose it was your boss again—"

"No, this time it was a customer."

"Oh, *that,*" said Hazel. "Well, by now you must be used to that."

"I'm used to it," agreed Medora. "If it had been only myself who was involved, I'd have been on time. Unfortunately, this was a bit different, because what happened involved my only real girl friend at the Club, and I had to do her a favor. Some bumptious little American tourist fellow has had the hots over my girl friend, and was kicking up a frightful row, and she begged me to get rid of him. What could I do? I had to pacify him before I could send him packing, so I had to sit there with him, knowing all of you were waiting, and listen to the little bugger's miseries. Why has everyone got miseries? At least this one was a bit more original. Trying to get to Russia to marry some girl he's in love with. Now, who'd want to go to Russia for anything? Anyway, I beg your forgiveness—"

"And I beg you to get off your feet," insisted Hazel. "You've been on them all evening. Here, sit down and have something—"

Doyle had come off his stool. "Sit here, Medora."

"I'm not really hungry," said Medora hesitantly. "But if—"

Hazel was conscious of Brennan, of how oddly he was looking at Medora. "Miss Hart—" said Brennan.

"First names, remember?" said Hazel.

Brennan ignored her as he advanced toward Medora. "Did he happen to give his name?"

Medora seemed bewildered. "Whose name?"

"The man who detained you in the Club just now," said Brennan. "The fellow who wants to marry some girl in Russia. Do you know his name?"

"Sure thing," said Medora with surprise. "It's—" She tried to remember. "Silly name. But I know it." Suddenly she said, "I've seen them, those brown bogs in Ireland that they cut up for fuel. When I heard his name, I thought of them."

"The bogs are called peat," said Brennan softly.

"Peet!" Medora exclaimed with delight. "That's it. His name was Joe Peet."

"That's what I thought," said Brennan.

Medora looked up at him incredulously. "You know him?"

"Not really," said Brennan, "but I'd like to."

Hazel had stepped back to let Doyle join Medora and Brennan. "Medora, where is Peet now?" Doyle asked. "Is he still in the Club Lautrec?"

Medora shook her head. "Afraid not. By now I daresay he's been tucked away in his trundle bed by his friend. That was another thing that was eerie. I was listening to the poor little blighter's life story, meanwhile expiring from my anxiety to escape, when in like Father Christmas came Peet's friend and told him in so many words to cut along. So away went Peet trotting after his friend, and at last I was free and I just charged out of there to meet you."

Hazel saw Brennan and Doyle exchange meaningful looks, and she

521

wondered what was going on. "If this Peet's the same person I'm thinking of," said Hazel, "I met him once in Moscow."

"I know you did," said Brennan.

Bewildered, Hazel asked, "What's he got to do with what?"

"That's what we want to find out," said Brennan.

"I'll explain it later, Hazel," said Doyle.

Brennan was addressing Medora. "Would it be an imposition if I asked you to tell me exactly what Peet was doing in the Club Lautrec and what you two talked about?"

"I don't mind at all," said Medora, "except it doesn't mean anything."

"It could," said Brennan. He glanced around him. "Close quarters here. I think it would be better if we went outside."

Annoyed, Hazel stepped firmly between them, "Wait a minute, Matt. I don't know what this idiocy is about, but give the poor kid a break. Let her have a sandwich or something. She—"

"No, I'm fine, Hazel," Medora interrupted. "I don't want a crumb. I was just going to see you and get to bed. I have to be up early for Nardeau. . . . Yes, Mr. Brennan—Matt—I don't mind telling what little there is if you really can endure listening. This is fun. Let's go outside."

The others followed Brennan and Medora out of the Lido Bar, and through the Arcade entrance to the sidewalk of the Champs-Élysées, which was still thronged with pedestrians even at midnight.

"Would you like to go to a café?" Brennan inquired.

"I'll forget what happened by then," said Medora. "No, this is perfect. Here's what happened—"

Hazel, Doyle, and Lisa closed into a tight circle with Medora and Brennan.

"The minute the show was over," said Medora, "I raced up to my dressing room. Denise was there ahead of me, waiting, and very distraught."

"Who is Denise?" Brennan wanted to know.

"Denise Averil. One of the very best girls in The Troupe. The most attractive, by far. She's got more of everything, wherever it matters. She's from Marseille, half French, half Czech. Speaks beautiful English. She's been at the Club Lautrec two or three years. Remember the number when The Troupe comes from behind the fountain? Well, Denise was the nymph who came up out of the water."

"Who could forget?" said Hazel sourly. "I thought gas balloons were bringing her to the surface."

"She's forty inches," said Medora matter-of-factly, and returned her attention to Brennan. "Anyway, Denise was waiting for me in my

522

cubbyhole, all upset, and she begged me to help her. There was a young man in the Club, a real creep she'd dated a few nights before, who was pestering her for another date. The first time he came to the Club, I guess three or four nights ago, he was attracted to Denise and sent her a note with—well, if you don't mind—with considerable money inside. Denise is rather a playgirl, likes to go out every night, and this lavishness titillated her. So she went out with this gentleman."

"Joe Peet?" asked Brennan.

"Yes," said Medora. "I don't know if it's proper to tell you the details—I don't suppose I'd truly be betraying any confidences, since Denise is rather frank with everyone—well, she admitted to me she went to his hotel room for the night—he was waving around all sorts of large-denomination bills—and anyway, what followed was perfectly unutterably ghastly. I mean there are certain types who can't make out, like in those books, like Krafft-Ebing, I'm sure you're grown up enough to know about that—"

"Go on," said Brennan.

"Peet couldn't make out normal, or wouldn't, I don't recall which, so he kept wanting poor Denise to engage with him in all sorts of—well—abnormal kinds of acts—perversions—and Denise is the sort who's solid female and frightfully lusty, but conservative, and she loathed what Peet was after. So at dawn she simply walked out. You'd think the little beast would let well enough alone, but never. Turns out, according to Denise, he'd picked her from all the girls in The Troupe because she reminds him of his true love, some Russian girl in Moscow he's trying to get back to see and marry. Anyway, in his mind, Denise was this Russian girl. So the next night Denise found herself bombarded with millions of flowers, and cards begging her forgiveness, and all kinds of gifts from Galeries Lafayette and Michel Swiss. Well, this attention seduced her again, and besides she was sorry for the vain hopeless little punk, so she gave in and saw him a second time. I shan't go into it. Simply a rotten replay of the first time."

"You mean, she walked out again?" asked Brennan.

"Exactly. Well, Peet didn't show up the next night, and Denise decided that was that, and was grateful to be free of it. But tonight, during the last act, the flowers and trinkets began to pour into her dressing room, and then a half-coherent note arrived to the effect that he must see her or die, that he missed her like he missed his Ludmilla —that was the Russian girl—and that he would not leave the Club until he could see her. Ordinarily Denise wouldn't have been too worried. She's a cool sort. And there's a rear exit from backstage. But tonight, of all nights, Philippe Feron was in the audience. You know, the French cinema producer. And he took rather a fancy to Denise, and sent her a formal note inviting her to his table after the show. He had a party of cinema people with him, and he wanted to meet Denise and have her join them. Well, she had stars in her eyes. So suddenly there was the great Feron holding a place for her, and all that stood between Feron and herself was this maniac, Joe Peet. She didn't dare send Feron a note explaining her predicament, or ask to meet him elsewhere. She had to go to his table. But how, with Peet out there ready to create a frightful scene? So here she was with me, pleading for a favor. Would I go and tell Peet she'd not felt well and had left by the rear exit? Would I get rid of Peet and let her know when the way was clear? What could I do? Friendship. She described Peet to me, and where he was sitting, and then she went to change and await the all-clear signal from me. So I had no time to throw on anything but this outfit. Then I went out to do battle with Mr. Peet."

"Did you recognize him?" asked Brennan.

"As easily as spotting a ferret or a weasel let loose among people," said Medora. "Only he wasn't at his table. He was trying to force his way backstage by the second of the two doors, and a couple of Michaud's pugilistic waiters had him by the collar, arms pinned behind him, and were giving him a bad time. They were about to—how do you Americans say—the bum's rush, give it to him, when I intervened. I asked the waiters to let go of him, leave him to me, and they did, of course. Well, he was so grateful for my rescuing him from such an indignity that I almost felt sorry for the lad. I passed on Denise's message, and he accepted it calmly, though I'm afraid skeptically. But he was so shaken up, I doubt if he'd have pursued Denise further tonight anyway. He told me that he wanted only a few minutes to settle down, and insisted I join him for a drink so he could show his appreciation for my helping him. If I did this, he promised to give no more trouble and leave afterward. I kept thinking of poor Denise cowering upstairs, waiting for the all-clear, so I agreed to have just one for the road with this pathetic little Mr. Peet. I went to his table with him—littered with Coke bottles—can you imagine?—and we had a spot of whisky each, and he told me about this girl friend in Moscow, how he was going to marry her, all that, and how mean everyone had been to him, and he was feeling sadder and sadder about what he'd been through, and warming to me because I'd been sympathetic. And then he ordered more whisky, determined to continue talking, and I was wildly desperate, thinking of Denise gnashing her teeth upstairs, and of you waiting at the Lido Bar, but I simply couldn't get rid of the little beast."

"Did he tell you why he was in Paris?" asked Brennan.

"Only that he was trying to get back to Russia to marry his girl."

"Did he mention books at all?" said Brennan.

"Books?" Medora's face had gone blank.

"Reading them, collecting them."

"Him?" Medora burst into laughter. "I'd wager he signs his name with an X. Anyway, the second whiskies came round, and he resumed talking and I was ready to scream, but suddenly a very big man in a sort of raincoat came up to the table. Didn't even give me the time of day. Simply put his hairy hand on Peet's shoulder. He said in sort of a gravelly voice something like 'My friend Joe, girls yes, but no drink, no drink.' Something like that. Then he said, much as I could make out, 'I have been waiting. Come, Joe, it is late. We go.' Like that. Peet started to get surly and protest, but he seemed to think better of it and merely thanked me, left money for the drinks, sent regards to Denise, said he had another appointment he'd forgotten, and away he went with the behemoth who was my salvation. I dashed off to sound the all-clear for Denise, and then came dashing to meet you."

"Very good, Medora," said Brennan slowly. His eyes met Doyle's. "What do you make of it, Jay?"

"Interesting. The keeper, that is."

"Yes," said Brennan. He smiled down at Medora. "I wish I'd known Peet was in the Club when we were there. But your account was thorough enough. By the way, Medora, that friend who came to pick up Joe Peet—did he speak with an accent?"

"Oh, he was a foreigner for sure."

"Any idea of his nationality?"

"Not the faintest," said Medora. "I'm not very clever at telling that."

"One more thing," said Brennan. "Do you know where this Joe Peet is staying?"

"His hotel? Oh, I know. Denise mentioned it several times." She snapped her fingers. "Plaza-Athénée."

"You're sure?"

"Positive."

"Okay," said Brennan. "Thanks for everything, Medora. . . . Jay, would you mind seeing Lisa back to the California?"

"Where are you going?" Lisa wanted to know.

"I thought I'd pay Mr. Peet a visit."

Lisa clutched his arm. "Not alone, you won't."

"She's right," said Doyle. "Why don't we come along?"

Brennan frowned. "It'll be tough enough trying to see Peet alone, without—" He shrugged. "Okay. You can wait for me down in the Plaza-Athénée bar."

"I have my car here," Hazel volunteered. Then she remembered. "I forgot. It'll only hold three—Jay and myself."

"Funny, funny," said Doyle.

"I'll get a cab," said Brennan. "Want to come with us, Medora? . . . See you in the lobby of the hotel, Jay. Incidentally, no more secrets. You can tell Hazel how I first ran into Joe Peet."

Hazel watched Brennan lead the two girls into the middle of the Champs-Élysées toward the row of taxis. Then, taking Doyle's arm, she walked with him to her car parked in the Rue de Berri. Her headache had not returned. Instead, her dependable journalist's inquisitiveness was alive within her.

Not until she was behind the wheel of the Volkswagen, and heading for the Avenue Montaigne, did Hazel voice her curiosity. "All right, Jay, no more games. What's with Brennan and his fix on Joe Peet?"

Doyle began to recount the story of Brennan's adventure at Julien's rare book and autograph shop in the Rue de Seine, concluding with Joe Peet's purchase of a nonexistent 1890 edition by Sir Richard Burton.

"I get it now," said Hazel when he was finished. "That's the place you and Brennan considered a possible Communist drop."

"That's it."

With dismay, she remembered having told Rostov something of this, too. "And what does Brennan think?" she asked. "That Peet's maybe a Communist spy?"

"Or errand boy. We're not sure. But we're fascinated."

She looked out the window. "I'll park over there." She maneuvered the Volkswagen into the empty space near the Canadian Embassy. Leaving the car, she joined Doyle on the curb, and they started for the Hotel Plaza-Athénée.

"Whatever you're thinking about Peet, forget it," she said flatly. "I can't explain that Rue de Seine episode. But I can tell you this about Peet. After his press conference in Moscow, I took him to my apartment to find out if there was more to his story. I filled him full of booze and got him talking, and all he had to talk about was that Russian broad of his. You want the truth? You must have suspected it from what Medora's girl friend had to say about Peet. He's nothing but an impotent half-pint who took a vacation and it happened to be to Russia, where he found a girl who didn't scare him the way American girls did. With this Russian girl, Ludmilla, he was Somebody. And so he got it up. Got laid straight for the first time in his life. Well, that was it. Like that girl was a gift of manhood to him. It's happened before, to

526

some mighty important people, including even a king in our time. Know what I mean, Jay?"

"I sure do."

"That's all little Joe Peet is interested in. Connecting with that girl again and being a man permanently. Otherwise he's nobody and nothing. Spy? The Communist apparatus, our own CIA, the Chinese—they wouldn't take him on even as dogcatcher." She smiled at Doyle. "Maybe your friend Brennan is on the beam with some of his other notions. But with this one, he's wasting his time and ours."

"I guess you're right," said Doyle unhappily. He pointed ahead. "There they are outside."

Under the shell-shaped glass awning of the entrance to the Hotel Plaza-Athénée, Brennan and the girls were waiting. Doyle tried to hurry Hazel along, but Brennan had seen them, and with Lisa on one arm and Medora on the other he came toward them.

As they approached one another, Hazel could see the excitement in Brennan's features.

"Peet was registered at the Plaza-Athénée all right," Brennan said quickly. "But he checked out a half hour ago."

Doyle whistled. "No kidding?"

"I told the concierge I was a lodge brother of Peet's, and we got quite chummy," said Brennan. "Joe Peet had a reservation at the Plaza-Athénée for a week and a half. Then suddenly, an hour ago, he came in with his big friend—the concierge has seen them together before—and a few minutes later he phoned from his room and announced he had to leave Paris immediately. The hotel was a trifle upset, but they brought his bags down, and away he went, he and his friend, a half hour ago."

"Any forwarding address?" asked Hazel, impressed.

"None," said Brennan. "You'd think he'd have been expecting mail here if he was planning to stay on, and would leave some sort of address. He left nothing behind. Just took off into thin air. Whatever any of you have to say, I say it's queer."

Silently Hazel agreed. It *was* queer. Forgetting what she had just been saying to Doyle, she now reminded herself of her new respect for Brennan. "Yes, it's odd," she said to Brennan. Something else had crossed her mind. She considered Medora, and suddenly she found herself saying, "Medora dear, that friend of Peet's, the big man who came into the Club and convinced Peet to leave with him—"

"My savior, you mean?"

"Your savior. Do you think you could recognize him if you saw him again?"

527

"Why, of course. He looked like one of Paddy's—like—like someone I once met socially in London. I mean not exactly, but rather the same type."

"Can you describe Peet's friend?"

"Big, like I told you," said Medora, "maybe upwards of six feet and husky. Hardly any forehead, chin, neck. A kind of pushed-down-sideways nose. Lots of eyebrow. Sooty complexion, and one cheek—one cheek sort of mottled, pockmarked. And foreign, definitely foreign."

Hazel glanced at Brennan. "You're probably thinking what I'm thinking, Matt."

"What are you thinking?"

"This." Hazel stared at Medora. "Do you think you could meet Matt and me at the automobile gate of the Palais Rose tomorrow morning by a quarter of ten? That's when the delegates begin arriving."

"I believe I can," said Medora. "Yes, definitely. I'm meeting Nardeau's train earlier, but I'll have time enough for both. I'll be there. Palais Rose. You can count on it." Her smooth brow furrowed briefly. "Why do you want me there?"

"Why do we want you there?" Hazel nodded with deference to Brennan. "Tell her, Matt. Tell her why we want her there."

Brennan looked at Medora. "To help us find out who Joe Peet really is," he said. "It could be of great consequence."

VI

THE CHAUFFEURED Citroën that had called for Medora Hart early
that morning, and had taken her to the Gare de Lyon to meet
Nardeau's train from the Riviera, was now parked across from the building
of the Préfecture de Police, in the Boulevard du Palais on the Île de
la Cité in the middle of the Seine.

In the rear seat, Medora Hart crossed her legs, adjusting the short
skirt of her comfortable Italian wool suit, and she leaned contentedly
on the armrest. Despite her lack of sleep after the late excitement of
last night and her early awakening, she felt refreshed and renewed.

From the moment that Nardeau had emerged from the train, seen
her, and lifted her off her feet with his lovely shout of "Maydor!" her
spirits had soared. He had ordered the chauffeur to drive them directly
to the Préfecture de Police. He had been indignant about the theft of
his paintings, above all about the theft of *Nude in the Garden,* and he
was going straight to the top about the matter. No mere police inspector, not even the *commissaire divisionnaire* of the quartier where
the robbery had occurred, would do. *Non!* Only a personal interview
with the Secretary-General, the chief executive under the *Préfect de
Police,* would satisfy him. And the interview had been arranged. He
had arranged it by telephone from Nice.

Arriving at the Préfecture he had decided it would be best to meet
with the Secretary-General by himself. He had hoped that Medora did
not mind waiting, and that she had no other plans. She had told him
then about her new friends, Hazel Smith, Doyle, Brennan, Lisa Collins,
and of her appointment with Hazel and Brennan at the Palais Rose
by a quarter to ten. Nardeau had said that he would be finished with the
Secretary-General well before that time, and would report to her what
news he had learned, and would then drop her off at the Palais Rose.

That had been a half hour ago. It was now nine-thirty. Medora speculated as to whether the length of Nardeau's stay in the Préfecture meant good news or bad.

Medora pressed the electric button beside her to lower the window for some air. At once she realized how nippy it was this gray and cloudy morning. She was watching the chauffeur gossiping with two *agents de police* when suddenly, since the group blocked her view of the Préfecture entrance, she saw Nardeau walking around them. The beret that he was clapping on his bald pate, the string tie he wore, the unpressed trousers of his blue suit, did not deceive her. He looked more than a bohemian artist. He looked like France incarnate, just as Napoleon Bonaparte had. Following his passage across the street, Medora thought that Nardeau was probably the tallest short man alive. The *agents de police* doffed their caps, the chauffeur leaped to open the rear door, and Medora sat up, intently studying Nardeau's expression to see if it contained optimism or pessimism.

"Palais Rose," Nardeau commanded the chauffeur. He turned to Medora. "You see, as I promised, you shall be on time."

"I wasn't worried a bit," she said, still searching his face.

As the Citroën began to move, Nardeau brought his fists down hard on his thighs and said, "Well, Maydor, there is now reason to be confident."

Medora sagged with relief. "There really is?"

"Absolutely. I gave the Secretary-General a proper tongue-lashing. This theft, I let him know, was not a mere theft of private property. It was a rape of France's honor. When a bandit steals a Nardeau, he does not steal the goods of an individual but the treasure of France. The responsibility, I told him, belongs to the Government, the Republic's protectors. If a president or premier were kidnaped from the Summit, I told him, would the concern be a private family's or all of France's?" Nardeau uttered a short hoarse mischievous laugh. "That is the way one must handle officialdom. Disarm them quickly, before they can bind one in red tape. I had the Secretary-General jumping. You'd have thought Louis XIV or de Gaulle was standing over him. I think he personally telephoned, on the emergency line, every branch and department of the police in Paris. He even, sad fellow, suffered a nosebleed. But results, Maydor, I have some results."

Awed, Medora asked in a small voice, "You think they can recover the painting? I mean, is there the slightest hope?"

"More than hope," boomed Nardeau. "The police will now do what they were reluctant to do before. They have a lead to a criminal of the Paris underworld, a much wanted mastermind of robbery, a specialist in directing thefts of *objets d'art,* but until now they have not desired to compromise with him. They have wanted to catch him—this Savary, his name—and incarcerate him for life, not negotiate with him. But after my tirade the police have reconsidered. Through several intermediaries they are contacting this Savary. They are offering him complete pardon and amnesty for past offenses, as well as a sizable cash reward from the Government and myself, if he will lead them to my five missing paintings. The Secretary-General of the Préfecture felt certain that Savary would be cooperative, and if he was, the police would have no trouble in locating and returning the art, including, my dear Maydor, your *Nude in the Garden.* Are you satisfied, kitten?"

"I love you, Nardeau!" Impulsively she bent over and kissed his chapped lips.

Nardeau pushed her off. "Save your thanks for the one called Savary," he growled. "He is the one we must depend on."

"Oh, Nardeau, I can't tell you what this means. You see, once I have that nude of Fleur back, I can go ahead with the scheme that Hazel Smith—you know, the American journalist I spoke of—she's been such a marvelous friend—the scheme she's worked out with me." Quickly Medora explained the entire plan of showing Fleur Ormsby a fake wire story, written by Hazel, which would guarantee Her Ladyship's unconditional surrender.

"Clever," Nardeau agreed when she had finished, "but such subterfuges and playacting are no longer necessary. I have made my mind up to enter personally into the Ormsby contest. We shall bring this business to a successful conclusion by direct action."

"What do you mean?"

"Today is what? Thurday? So. Friday or Saturday, if all goes as the police expect, you shall once more be in possession of *Nude in the Garden.* We will allow Sunday for the sensational news of the recovery of the paintings to appear in print. Fleur Ormsby will read it, and know her reputation is truly in danger. On Monday morning I will telephone her myself, and inform her that I, Nardeau, am representing you. I will warn her that unless, by nightfall, she has prevailed upon her husband to lift the banishment order on you and give you documents guaranteeing safe passage back to England, I shall call a press conference that will lead to her exposure and damage to her husband. I shall summon the press to the Galerie, and there, with you beside me, I shall hold up *Nude in the Garden* and identify the naked woman as Lady Ormsby, who so posed for me as the model not many years ago. This will be my warning. Do you think our Ladyship will capitulate?"

"She'll have to!" Medora exclaimed. "This is so generous of you,

Nardeau. Only—I hate to see you become involved over me—I mean, publicly—"

"It is not for you alone," said Nardeau shortly. "It is for everyone who is not treated with the dignity of human respect."

He cast his gaze out the window, and Medora, deeply moved by the one who was the father and husband she'd never had, wanted to thank him again and again. But knowing Nardeau as she knew him, she understood that his last declaration had been his punctuation, his period, to end the discussion of the subject. He loathed not only bathos but the slightest hint of sentimentality.

She could see they were passing through the Avenue Foch. "The Palais Rose is somewhere near here," she said.

"Two blocks ahead." He came around in the seat to study her again. "You are not permitting your American friends to get you into any trouble?"

"Oh, no, nothing like that. They've been trying to help me, and there was a chance for me to help them in a little way, and I was eager to do anything I could. They're nice people, Nardeau, extremely nice."

"I am pleased. . . . What is the rest of your day?"

"Well, after I leave them, I want to have my hair done, and then, well, nothing planned until show time."

"I am going to the Galerie to see Michel. The stupid idiot is worried about me, but secretly happy. The exhibit is now attended by thousands, not hundreds, but for the wrong reasons. Now they come to stare at the blank spaces on the walls. It is not art that interests them but crime. Such people—*merde!* So. After, I will have lunch with Signe and maybe go with her to buy clothes at Henri à la Pensée and Chanel's boutique—yes, I will indulge the Swedish slut—she suffers much from me, yet loves me—but after that I am free. Do you eat before your show?"

"A sandwich."

"You will have the sandwich and drinks with Signe and me. At five. I am staying at Picasso's old studio at 7 Rue des Grands-Augustins. You remember? I will expect you." The Citroën had slowed, and Nardeau squinted ahead. "The side street to the Palais gate is full of police."

"You've had enough of police. Tell him to drop me here, Nardeau. It's a half-minute's walk." The car had stopped. Quickly, she kissed Nardeau's unshaved cheek, and descended to the curbing.

She waited until the Citroën had gone, and once it had, she started quickly toward the Palais Rose.

Approaching the intersection of the Avenues Foch and Malakoff,

Medora could see a woman on the corner waving in her direction. A few yards more, and she clearly recognized the woman as Hazel Smith, and Matt Brennan was with her. Waving back, Medora quickened her step as the pair, in turn, hurried toward her.

The moment they met, Hazel took her arm warmly. "Just in time, Medora, right on time. The American and British delegates are already inside, and also the French. The Chinese are just arriving. That means the Russians should be here any minute."

"What am I supposed to do?" Medora asked nervously.

Brennan, striding alongside, said reassuringly, "We'll brief you when we get to the little vantage point we've staked out."

As the three of them turned the corner into the Avenue Malakoff, Hazel said to Medora, "My, but don't you look cheerful? Have you—"

"I was with Nardeau," Medora announced happily.

"Nardeau," repeated Hazel. "Of course. I almost forgot. Did he have good news?"

"I think so," said Medora. "He was at the Préfecture de Police. They have someone who's supposed to recover all five paintings, mine included, by tomorrow or the next day."

"That's glorious, Medora," said Hazel with delight. "I can't wait for you to clobber those Ormsbys."

"Great," said Brennan. He pointed toward the open gate and high iron fence protecting the crowded courtyard of the two-story pink-marble palace. "Let's cross over."

They scurried to the opposite curb. On either side of the open motorcar gate, both Frenchmen and foreign tourists lined the protective iron fence, every one of them observing with wonder the dignitaries and their ceremonious greetings as they met in the courtyard.

Brennan led the two women away from the gate, along the fence lined with spectators. "We'll get a good view of every arrival through the fence," said Brennan.

"How?" asked Medora. "All those people. I can't see over their heads."

"Just wait," said Brennan. He halted behind three college-age French boys, one bearded, one in corduroys, the third in a black turtleneck sweater, who were slouching against the iron fence. Brennan tapped the bearded one on the shoulder. The young man swung around sullenly, but recognizing Brennan, he was instantly cordial. His companions had turned around now, acknowledging Brennan but mesmerized by Medora.

Medora thought: One of them will whistle.

The boy in the turtleneck whistled softly, and suggested in French to

Brennan that he'd take Medora instead of the money. Brennan, removing franc notes from his wallet, replied gravely that he appreciated the compliment to his taste, since Medora was his wife. The three boys were immediately apologetic and abject. As they backed off from the fence, giving way to Brennan, Medora, and Hazel, one of them muttered something to himself in French about rich and lucky Americans.

The boys were leaving now. Medora, grasping a paling, knew that all three would be looking at her legs. Half turning, to confirm her guess, she realized she was wrong. Only the bearded one was considering her legs. The other two were staring boldly at the outline of her bosom, which even the light wool suit could not conceal. The turtle-necked one blew her a kiss, and Medora threw her head back to laugh, and then, because it was June, and because it was Paris, and because soon she would be snugly home again with Mum, she gayly blew a farewell kiss back to all of them.

Clinging to the fence, she saw that Brennan and Hazel, one on either side of her, were concentrating upon the activity in the courtyard. She addressed herself to Brennan. "How clever of you to arrange for orchestra seats."

Brennan dismissed it with a gesture. "Stand-ins come cheap this summer," he said. "Fifteen francs a head. Can you see the people in the courtyard clearly, Medora?"

"Even the warts on their noses," said Medora. "I have twenty-twenty vision."

"There's the last of the Chinese delegation spilling out of that car," said Brennan. "Look at them. Aren't they incredible?"

"Why incredible?" asked Hazel Smith. "They're Chinese and they look like Chinese."

"That's not what I meant," said Brennan. "The other day a French nuclear physicist was discussing the Chinese with me, and he reminded me that they were far advanced in the sciences long ago, using gunpowder when Europeans were still using bows and arrows. But whenever I look at Chinese, I always see something else. I see men of an ancient culture, wise, fragile, other-worldly. I see the men of the Golden Mean, Confucius, Mandarin scrolls, the Ch'in dynasty, the patient people of Tang with their silks and porcelain and poetry, even the quiet, the silent coolies in the rice paddies. So when I look at them over there, I find it hard to believe that they are suddenly the people of Marx, the new Cominform, the neutron bomb, the intercontinental ballistics missile."

"You sound like some kind of colonialist," said Hazel grouchily.

"People change with the times. They have to or they become extinct."

"Of course they do and they must," said Brennan with a trace of annoyance. "It is only the incongruity of its happening to the Chinese that rattles my brain. I deplore it esthetically. I'm sure what's happened to the Chinese should have happened, had to happen, considering how many unprincipled foreign barbarians have violated China for centuries. There they go into the Palais Rose, the people of the Golden Mean, wearing nuclear chips on their shoulders. That's what's sad—that they have to behave that way because of us, of all of us in the Western world."

Medora had listened, fascinated but bewildered. Hazel appeared less entertained. Grimacing at Brennan, Hazel said crossly, "Confucius say amateur sociologist nuttier than fruitcake. Come off it, Brennan. We're taking a risk being here—I'd sure hate to be seen by certain people—while you—"

Brennan searched down the row of spectators standing between them and the gate. "We won't be noticed," he said. Then he added, "But you're right. We'd better brief Medora."

Hazel took Medora by the arm. "In a second you'll have to be on the ball. Six limousines filled with Russians are going to pile into that courtyard. Thirty or forty Russians will be pouring out of the cars. Now, I know most of them, who they are, what they do. All you've got to know is one of them. Understand? One of them. Take a good look at every man you see, and tell us if any one of them resembles the big fellow who came into the Club Lautrec last night and took Joe Peet off your hands. Think you can do that?"

Momentarily unsure, Medora said, "I'll try. Only I never said Mr. Peet's friend was Russian. I only said he was foreign."

"I know, honey," Hazel reassured her. "Just do as I say. Okay?"

"I'll try," Medora repeated. "I—it's—it's all so mysterious."

"What we're doing may come to nothing, Medora," Brennan said. "We're only playing a hunch." There was the sound of rubber tires skidding on pavement, and Brennan glanced off. "Here they come."

The three of them peered through the iron bars of the fence as a French motorcycle escort preceded the two Zil limousines, a Chaika limousine, and a smaller Pobeda into the courtyard. French security police were leaving both the gate and steps of the Palais Rose to surround the cars.

"That's Premier Talansky in the old Zil III limousine up front," whispered Hazel. "They fly it in ahead of him whenever he travels. I wrote a story about it once. Formidable. Bulletproof windows. Custom-built bar, Oriental rug, and a portable armory. . . . Dammit, only four cars." She sounded disturbed, but she looked relieved. "That means we missed the first two with the Ministers and advisers. They must have arrived earlier. Well, let's see—"

From the corner of his mouth, Brennan said, "Eyes open, Medora."

Her eyes were alert and straining, but it was all so confusing. Men, mostly big men, wearing dark suits, were spilling out of the four motorcars at the same time. She had thought it would be easy, but suddenly there were so many men, so many faces, people mingling, standing in front of each other. She began to feel distracted.

One party had broken away from the main group, and the members of it were starting for the entrance to the Palais Rose. "There goes Premier Talansky," Hazel said quickly.

Medora's eyes followed the lead group. Three or four faces could be seen clearly. Two or three others offered her only a fleeting side view. "No," she whispered back.

Again she concentrated on the two dozen or more Russians who remained in the courtyard. She recognized none of the faces that were visible. Her attention shifted to the second Zil limousine, where three burly Russians were attending the rear door which one of them, back to her, held open. A slight, bespectacled Russian ducked out of the Zil, followed by a heavyset officer attired in a Red Army uniform flashing with medals.

"Marshal Zabbin," said Hazel in an undertone. "The Premier's First Deputy. The one with the glasses is Dr. Tushin. A famous nuclear physicist."

"No," said Medora weakly.

Most of the new group began to fall in behind Marshal Zabbin as he strutted toward the steps of the Palais Rose.

Suddenly Medora's eyes widened. She grabbed Hazel's wrist, and in a strangled voice she cried out, "There he is!"

"Shhh," Hazel hissed. Quickly she brought her head next to Medora's head, trying to parallel Medora's line of vision. "Which one?" she asked urgently.

Medora was poking her finger through the opening between the bars. "The car the Marshal just came out of—he turned from it and I saw his face—he's shutting the door now."

They all saw him as he finished closing the rear door of the Zil and turned slowly around, hands on his hips, to observe Marshal Zabbin's progress into the Palais Rose. He was a big man, an Atlas of a man in excess of six feet, and solid as a soccer goalie. He was briefly full face now, flat black hair, beetle brow, broad misshapen Tartar nose, pocked left cheek, head set deeply between massive shoulders.

"That's the one," said Medora excitedly. "Mr. Peet's friend."

Hazel Smith did not respond as she continued to stare straight ahead.

Brennan had turned from the scene to look at Medora. "You're sure, Medora?"

"I'm absolutely certain."

In the courtyard, the big Russian had once more turned his back toward them as he went to have a smoke with the Zil's chauffeur and a French officer.

Medora and Brennan were waiting for Hazel to speak as she pushed herself away from the fence with finality. Hazel eased her spine, kneading it with both hands behind her. At last, lost in thought, she walked from the fence to the curb. Brennan went after her, and curious as ever, Medora did the same.

Medora heard Brennan say, "Well, Hazel?"

Hazel Smith gave an affirmative nod. "Yes," she said, "I know that one. I recognized him immediately. I've seen him around Moscow, and on Government trips away from Moscow. I've seen him, and some of his friends, a hundred times. I don't know his name. But I know who he is."

Brennan remained silent, tensely waiting.

For long seconds Hazel stared down at the curbstone. Finally she lifted her head and met Brennan's questioning eyes.

"He's a KGB agent," Hazel said. "He's a veteran Soviet security police agent."

Utterly lost, Medora shifted her gaze from Hazel to Brennan. Now it was Brennan who was silent, thinking.

"KGB," he said at last, to no one in particular. "Joe Peet and a Soviet security agent." Brennan's forehead wrinkled. He looked at Hazel a moment, then he said, "Why?"

Hazel straightened, and she was her old brisk self again. "That's for you to find out, my friend." She offered Medora a smile. "Thanks, my dear. I'm not sure for what. But thanks. Now let's get out of here."

ONCE AGAIN, as he had done three days ago, Emmett A. Earnshaw was marching along the first-floor corridor of the Hotel Ritz. Once again, the young fellow from Secret Service was dutifully tagging after him. Once again, Earnshaw was on his way to see Dr. Dietrich von Goerlitz.

Usually, Earnshaw reflected, when one revisited the site of a debacle, especially a recent disaster where the stench of defeat still hung in the air, one was cowed and humbled and devoid of hope. Understandable, thought Earnshaw, if one returned to a site of slaughter and rout as the vanquished, alone, stripped of arms and army.

But Earnshaw felt neither humbled nor hopeless this midafternoon. If he had been briefly routed by Dr. Dietrich von Goerlitz last Monday, he had not surrendered. Perhaps there had been a black period, yet an unexpected cohort had supplied him with the arsenal needed to fight again, and this time Earnshaw felt invincible. He expected nothing less than total victory.

Striding vigorously, he reached the end of the corridor. He ordered the Secret Service fellow to wait for him. Now, on his own, he started optimistically toward the Goerlitz suite.

Part of his buoyancy, Earnshaw knew, came from the knowledge that his visit was perfectly timed. Ever since yesterday, when that decent young Matt Brennan had so kindly passed on to him the information about Red China's secret plan to use Goerlitz and then double-cross Goerlitz, Earnshaw had been considering different approaches to the bitter old German industrialist. Although confident of his strength, Earnshaw had not been ready to rush in where angels fear to tread, as Madlock used to say. He had considered a telephone call or a letter, but had finally decided that a personal visit would be the most effective and decisive means of bringing Goerlitz to his knees in abject gratefulness.

Earnshaw was glad he had not hurried the meeting, had postponed it until after the United States Ambassador's lunch this noon. It had been an intimate, relatively informal lunch that the Ambassador has hosted in the official residency, the comfortable mansion on the Avenue d'Iéna that Myron Herrick had bought for the United States in the 1920's. There had been a dozen guests, mostly from State or Foreign Service, many of them holdovers from Earnshaw's incumbency (and all of them friendly to him), just as the Ambassador himself had been an Earnshaw appointee (to Italy, then after resigning, reappointed to France by the new President). The food had been mouth-watering, too. None of those fancy French dishes with all that sickening oil gook and wine. It had been a down-to-earth American meal, the kind Isabel used to cook for him, the crisp green salad with Thousand Island dressing first, and fried chicken and mashed potatoes and string beans, and a huge slice of deep-dish apple pie.

In this natural and convivial atmosphere Earnshaw had flourished. He had been the center of interest, congratulated for his British award, questioned about rumors that he might take a seat on the Supreme

538

Court bench. He had purposely avoided being entrapped in any political discussions. Instead he had regaled the Ambassador and his onetime assistants with jokes and anecdotes about fishing and poker and foreign customs. Because he had been among friends, it had been an easy matter to let drop the name of Dr. Dietrich von Goerlitz. He had cast his line perfectly, for in minutes he had reeled in an excellent catch—the information that Goerlitz was meeting with Marshal Chen, of the People's Republic of China, the next morning to formalize a business agreement with the signing of contracts to build a Nuclear Peace City in the heart of China.

After that, the others had discussed international politics, and Earnshaw had withdrawn into himself to relish his delicious morsel of information. This, too, he had known, added to his bargaining power with Goerlitz. It was as if the German economic acrobat was about to make his greatest and most daring leap from on high in the morning, and Earnshaw was grabbing him in the nick of time to tell him there would be no net below.

Over the dessert, Earnshaw had remembered his indebtedness to Matt Brennan. He had pledged himself to speak to the President on Brennan's behalf. Mindful of this, he had told the Ambassador he rather hoped to run into the President during the Summit. "Why, you'll be seeing him tomorrow night, Emmett," the Ambassador had said. "You'll be at the same party, the reception the French are giving at the Hôtel de Lauzun. I know, I saw your name high on the list." Earnshaw had forgotten, but at that moment recalled, the invitation. It had pleased him that he would be able to speak to the President about Brennan. Earnshaw hated unpaid debts. He knew also that, in this one respect, Goerlitz was like himself. And he had felt even better.

As he paused before the Goerlitz suite in the Hotel Ritz, the feeling of well-being and confidence remained. He need only push the button, and the offending chapter in the German's memoirs would go up in smoke forever, and his own reputation would survive unsullied.

Earnshaw pushed the button.

One second, two, three, four, five, and slowly the double doors opened.

To his surprise, it was not the liveried butler who stood before him, but the boy, Willi von Goerlitz, in shirt-sleeves, hair disheveled, eyes bloodshot, in want of a shave, and holding a filled highball glass.

Taken aback by the young man's appearance, Earnshaw sought to maintain his composure. "Hello, Willi."

Willi did not acknowledge Earnshaw's greeting. He simply said, "Yes?"

Annoyed by the young man's unusual disrespect, and even more irritated by the fact that the young man was keeping him standing in the corridor, Earnshaw said, "Do you mind if I come in for a moment?"

Willi hesitated. "I—I'm not sure—" He swallowed, and stepped aside. "Please."

With determination, Earnshaw walked through the doorway into the spacious entry hall. He waited for Willi to take his hat and topcoat, but the young man did neither. He merely rolled his drink in one hand and considered his guest owlishly.

"I know I'm here unannounced, and perhaps it's improper," Earnshaw said, "but there are times when formalities should be dispensed with, and this is one of them. I've learned something that could be of vital importance to your father, something he'll want to know. I came right over to tell him about it."

Earnshaw pointedly looked at the salon beyond the hall, waiting for Willi to invite him into it, but Willi made no such move. Instead he gulped his drink.

Watching him, Earnshaw decided that the boy must be exceedingly intoxicated. There could be no other explanation for his rudeness. Earnshaw remembered that he had warned Carol about the boy. But that warning had been motivated, as Carol had rightly guessed, by his own pique with the boy's father. Actually he had been favorably impressed by Willi. But now, having caught the boy unprepared, Earnshaw decided that Willi was probably his father's son after all, as spoiled and as churlish.

"I *must* see your father, Willi," said Earnshaw with all the sternness at his command.

"You—you can't—"

Earnshaw could feel his blood pressure rising. "Of course I can. See here, young man, when you're older, you'll realize there are times when we can't stand on formality. Something's come up involving your father, and he must hear about it immediately, certainly before he meets with the Chinese tomorrow morning. Now, will you tell him I'm—"

Willi waved his drink, to interrupt Earnshaw. "No—no—it is impossible, Mr. Earnshaw. My father is not here. He was called out of the city a few hours ago. He is in Frankfurt."

"In Frankfurt? Well, why didn't you say so? Well—uh—that makes it a little difficult. Perhaps I can phone him there, even go to see him there tonight, if I must."

"He cannot be reached," said Willi laconically. "I—I do not know where he has gone for his conference."

"What about tomorrow?" Earnshaw persisted. "I know he has this business meeting and contract signing with Marshal Chen in the morning. He'll be back in Paris for that, won't he?"

"Maybe," said Willi. "I do not know." He began to drink again, adding, "If he is not returned in time, the meeting with Marshal Chen will have to be delayed."

Earnshaw was at a loss. It was as if he were addressing the wall. "Willi, will you be in touch with your father?"

"Yes—yes—later."

"Okay. Can I depend upon you to tell him I was here?"

"Yes, of course—"

"Impress upon him that it is absolutely imperative that he hear what I have to say before—do you understand me?—*before* he meets with the Chinese Reds to sign the Nuclear Peace City contracts. Tell him I've learned something about the Chinese that he'll have to know before he does any further negotiating with them. Is that clear?"

"Yes, it is clear. I am not a dumbbell as you think. I do not forget." Willi was plainly distraught. "Next time, please telephone before coming."

Earnshaw glared at the young man. Willi was not only befuddled from his excessive drinking, but he was being deliberately impudent. For an instant Earnshaw was tempted to put him in his place, but he thought better of it. He still needed Willi to pass on the message to Dr. Dietrich von Goerlitz. Also, there could be good reason for Willi's behavior. Possibly Carol, in her naïveté, had repeated something about Earnshaw's disapproval of the boy and his desire that she not keep company with him. That was probably the explanation.

From somewhere in the salon, a voice shouted, "Willi!"

Willi gravitated toward the summons. *"Ja, Herr Schlager?"*

"Kommen Sie—" Schlager, a small, well-fed middle-aged man, managing director of all the Goerlitz industries, appeared in the salon archway. Upon seeing Earnshaw, he changed over to English. "Sorry, Willi, I did not know you had company, but—"

"Mr. Earnshaw is leaving," said Willi hastily. He looked hopefully at Earnshaw. "Good-bye, sir."

"Don't forget to tell your father what I told you," said Earnshaw.

Willi von Goerlitz did not reply. He had already gone to Schlager, who had taken him by the arm and begun to lead him into the salon.

Disconcerted, Earnshaw edged toward the open doors. He could hear Schlager's resounding voice, still speaking in English. "Come, come, Willi, do not waste time. We must see your father immediately. It will take us another twenty minutes, and we are late already. The car

541

is waiting downstairs in front." Willi's voice responded in German this time, and Schlager's receding voice interrupted in German.

Overhearing them from the doorway, Earnshaw had been unable to understand the last. But now he understood something else. The pair were hastening off to meet Dr. Dietrich von Goerlitz somewhere nearby. Willi had lied. His father was not in Frankfurt. He was right here in Paris.

Wondering about the strangeness of it, about the reason behind Willi's behavior and his lies, wondering if Dr. Dietrich von Goerlitz would know that he had called with urgent information, then wondering how he would be able to see Goerlitz before the industrialist met with the Chinese, Earnshaw left the hall of the suite for the corridor.

It surprised him not at all that the acrid smell of defeat once more hung in the air.

B Y SIX-THIRTY in the evening, Matt Brennan had almost finished shaving. Studying his jaw line and neck in the bathroom mirror, he could see that he had made a poor job of it. He always did when he had other matters on his mind. Still, he wanted to look well-groomed this evening. For the first time, he was going to meet some of Lisa's associates and friends, people who also represented her Manhattan fashion house.

Lisa had planned the evening carefully. There would be eight of them, and even though her expense account did not cover a personal night on the town, she had made reservations at Le Grand Véfour, where the cuisine was of the best and most expensive in Paris. After dinner, if there were time, she had thought that they could visit Montmartre and look in on Le Lapin Agile, which Brennan had so often praised, and have fun joining with the other customers in singing French ballads. Or, if it were too late, since her colleagues had to rise and go to work early, she might bring everyone to the hotel bar for coffee and cognac.

Because the unveiling of Brennan to her circle was so important to Lisa, he was determined to be at his best and most youthful.

He started the electric razor once more, and resumed shaving.

As always, the solitary act of shaving inspired introspection. Running the razor over his chin, Brennan realized that all this preening and preparation might be futile. The odds were still heavy that he would never see Lisa's friends, or indeed Lisa herself, after they took their leave of Paris. He had not succeeded in accomplishing that which had brought him here. He had not cleared his name. Unless this was done, it would be useless to continue the charade with Lisa. He would remain an outcast, and he would have no choice but to return to the stones and tombs of Venice.

Brennan had little patience for self-deception. He was an ex-romantic turned realist. As realist, he could see that his future was as unpromising as it had been a week ago. Only one hope had any substance. Emmett A. Earnshaw. But even this lone hope was iffy, too dependent on the vagaries of other people. The rest of the tumult, and there had been plenty, represented counterfeit hope. You came upon a man named Joe Peet buying a nonexistent volume in a rare-book shop that Rostov had done business with, and you deluded yourself into thinking this had something to do with Rostov. You received tantalizing hints from Isenberg and Lisa that Russia and China had a nefarious alliance, and because Russia was involved, and Rostov was Russian, you thought you had discovered something useful, when in fact you had gained nothing. You went to a meeting in the Bois, and because another who had been there before you had been killed, you were convinced you were an intended victim, despite the contrary opinion of the French police. You learned that the improbable bibliophile, Joe Peet, American, had a Russian KGB agent for a friend, and you thought it meant something to you, but there was no proof it had a damn thing to do with you.

Off and on throughout the day he had thought of Joe Peet and his KGB friend. Why would a Russian security agent have anything to do with an American nonentity like Peet, unless the agent had been assigned to keep an eye on Peet because Peet was a small cog in the Soviet spy apparatus, an errand boy possibly, or unless the Russians regarded Peet as a troublemaker because he had so long pestered them about getting back to Russia and his true love? At the same time, simpler explanations had occurred to Brennan, and he supposed they made as much sense. Perhaps Peet, on his tour of Russia, had actually made a friend of this Russian, who just happened to be a security agent. Perhaps the KGB man was a relative or acquaintance of Peet's girl friend in Moscow. There were a hundred explanations, all as illogical as linking Peet to espionage.

But the point was, and Brennan saw it distinctly now, his interest and involvement in these findings and happenings were purely diversionary, as time-wasting as an author's pencil sharpener. Frustrated by his inability to reach his real goal, namely Rostov, he had occupied himself chasing after spurious articles, pretending they were part of his mission. He had deluded himself into believing that the various clues would lead him to where he was going, when, in fact, they were leading him nowhere—except back to the life of a broken recluse in Venice.

Enough, he told himself. No more diversions, he pledged himself.

He heard his bedroom telephone ringing. Quickly he rubbed the last of the after-shave lotion into his face, and hurried to catch the call on the third ring.

"Matt Brennan?" inquired the feminine voice with an English accent.

Cautiously, he said, "Yes, this is Brennan."

"Medora Hart. I'm at the Club, backstage. Are you still interested in finding out where Joe Peet is staying since he left the Plaza-Athénée?"

Brennan's heart leaped, and he hated his excitement. Nevertheless, he broke his pledge, consoling himself that vows were intended to be altered by changed circumstances. "Am I interested? You bet I am, Medora."

"I rather thought you might be," she went on. Her voice dropped perceptibly. "My girl friend here, you know, Denise Averil, the one Peet's been after—"

"Sure, I remember."

"Well, she knows where Peet is staying. She just heard from him."

"Do you know the place?" he asked eagerly.

"No, but I think I can help you find out. It's difficult for me to talk from here, Matt. Why don't you come right down to the Club before the show starts? Meet you in the lobby."

"In ten minutes," said Brennan.

Hastily he slipped on a fresh shirt and knotted his tie. There was no time to change into the freshly pressed suit he was to wear to dinner. Then he remembered the dinner, Lisa's dinner, at Le Grand Véfour.

Snatching up his sport jacket, he hurried through the open double doors into Lisa's bedroom. He heard her in the bathroom, humming, still splashing in the tub.

He went to the door and called through it. "Lisa?"

"I'll be right out, Matt. I know I'm running behind."

"Honey, listen, something terribly important has just come up. I've got to run over to the Club Lautrec for a little while. Can you make it to the restaurant alone? It won't be for long. I'll catch up with you by the time you start eating."

There was a momentary silence. "Must you, Matt?" She sounded distressed. "Can't you put off your business until tomorrow?"

"I hate to do this to you, honey, but this is important, or could be."

"Does it have to do with *him?*"

He knew that she meant Rostov, the real thing. He couldn't tell her he was off again after a spurious article. "I don't know," he said. "That's what I have to find out."

"Well, all right, of course. If you've got to go, you've got to go. But don't be too late, Matt. I'd hate to look like the bride left standing at the altar. . . . Oh, forgive me. You go. But hurry. And, Matt—good luck!"

Rushing out of Lisa's bedroom into his own, he closed and latched the door on his side as usual, for the night maids who were probably never deceived, and quickly he left his rooms. Downstairs, as had become his habit, he told M. Dupont where he might be found if someone wanted to see him. With that, he hurried out of the hotel.

Turning off on the Rue de Ponthieu, to avoid the crowded Champs-Élysées ahead, Brennan walked rapidly and made good time. In little more than ten minutes he entered the long lobby of the Club Lautrec. A few late arrivals were still passing into the nightclub. The lobby was virtually deserted, and he was able to find Medora Hart at once. She was waiting beneath the framed Toulouse-Lautrec *affiche* of May Belfort. Both Medora and May Belfort were posed in red and black. Pretty poster, Brennan thought, but prettier girl.

"Here I am, Medora," Brennan called out.

"Whew, in the nick of time," she said. "Show's beginning in a few minutes. I bullied Michaud into releasing one of the up-front tables for us."

He started into the din and smoke of the nightclub after her. "Aren't you in the show tonight, Medora?"

"Oh, yes, but not till the middle of the first act. So I have a bit of time before changing. Denise is in the opening number. I'll point her out to you."

The lights were dimming and the music coming on as she merrily led him down the crooked aisles, between crowded tables, until they arrived at the tiny reserved table in the second row before the end of the stage runway.

When both were seated, Medora said, "You don't have to have dinner, but I'm afraid you'll have to order a bucket of champagne. Sorry."

Brennan smiled. "Nobody has to twist my arm when it comes to champagne." The waiter had appeared, and Brennan placed his order. He saw Medora turning her glass upside down. "Aren't you going to have a drink with me?"

"Never before I go on," said Medora. "Established foreign policy. It's bad enough that I had a couple with Nardeau late this afternoon."

"Any news about the painting?"

"Not yet." She listened to the music a moment, then said, "I'd better

545

tell you what this is about. When Denise came in tonight, she found a bouquet of flowers at her dressing table and an envelope. There was a note from Joe Peet inside. He wanted her to know that he'd moved from the Plaza-Athénée to another hotel. He said he regretted he wasn't able to attend the show tonight, but he'd be in his hotel room before midnight. Since he couldn't go to Denise, he begged her to come to him. Apparently he offered her some fantastic sum of money to spend the night with him. She didn't seem too inclined to accept his proposition. The money enchanted her, but another Krafft-Ebing encore with Peet repelled her."

"I think you said you didn't know Peet's new hotel?"

"No. I thought of you, and I inquired, but Denise played it coy. She may be frightfully munificent with her sexual favors, but when it comes to her purse, she's as niggardly as any Provence housewife. I know that while she's rejecting Peet's offer, she's still regarding Peet rather as money in the bank against a rainy day. And I suppose if he raises his offer higher, she'll find herself reluctantly in bed with him once more, wherever he operates. So she's loath to tell me, close as I am to her, or to tell any of the girls in The Troupe, where she has Peet and his money cached. She's afraid, and rightly, that some poacher might move in on a good thing."

"Well, Medora, if you can't find out the name of Peet's new hotel, then who can?"

"You can," said Medora brightly. "I told Denise, as an incidental, that I'd just happened to run into a handsome and wealthy and very lonely American diplomat whom I'd once met in London and who'd just flown in for the Summit. And I told her that by crazy coincidence this American diplomat was a close friend of Joe Peet's millionaire father in Chicago, and the diplomat had been asked by Peet's family to look Joe up in Paris. I asked Denise if she wouldn't, as a favor to me, let this nice and attractive American diplomat know where he might find Joe Peet."

"What did she say to that?"

"She said, 'It depends on how nice and attractive he is.' "

"Meaning?"

"Denise wants to look you over. She's in the opening number, and I promised her I'd be sitting right here with you. If she approves, she's agreed to meet you after the show for a drink."

Worriedly, Brennan thought of Lisa Collins and her friends waiting for him, expecting him, at Le Grand Véfour. "After the show? That's an awfully late start, Medora."

"Oh, you won't have to give her much time. Denise is usually as

546

washed out as the rest of us at the end of the performance. Merely stand her a drink around the corner, and meanwhile a little flattery will go a long way. Maybe talk about making a real night of it one evening soon. That'll be enough. You'll get the name of Peet's hotel, I promise you." She glanced toward the stage. "Here they come. I purposely sat us at this table because part of the spotlights will pick us up. Otherwise it's difficult to see anyone in the audience from the stage."

The girls of The Troupe had formed two lines at the head of the runway. They were supposed to represent ladies of a harem, Brennan thought. They wore saucy turbans, and their faces were half veiled, and from low on their hips hung diaphanous short skirts, revealing their narrow tights and full thighs and long legs. All were naked from waist to neck.

The music from above was suddenly singsong Oriental, and to its cue, the girls of The Troupe came snaking and shimmying forward along the polished wooden runway.

As they advanced closer and closer, Brennan found himself drumming his fingers on the table in rhythm with the exotic beat, involuntarily submitting to the seduction of the number. He wondered which of these pseudo-Turkish delights was the bountiful Denise Averil, Keeper of the Peet. Then he wondered what she would see when she lowered her eyes to pass judgment on him. Would she see a world-weary, tired, prematurely aged American expatriate who gave promise of nothing beyond boredom? Or would she see a sophisticated, charming, mature American diplomat whose aspect suggested romance and riches? Or would she see a composite of both, or neither? Or would she see what Lisa Collins saw in him, whatever that was?

Self-conscious about the impending inspection, he considered how best he might pose himself. Should he sit straight, cool, dignified, the unattainable millionaire? Should he sit slouched, half amused, sated, the errant King waiting to pluck a chorus girl or the Sultan waiting to choose one mate from the harem? Or should he lean forward, elbows on the table, chin cupped in his hands, eyes hooded, lips sensuous, body taut, the irresistible and legendary playboy and sexual acrobat, seeking to receive and to give one more memorable experience? Or should he simply be himself, whoever in the hell he was?

He had no opportunity to answer these questions, for directly above, the two rows of fleshy show girls had converged, regrouped, and were now in lines of four.

"There's Denise," said Medora, "second from the left, front line."

Brennan gaped upward. From afar, all of the tall beauties in The Troupe had seemed as one, but suddenly they had individuality, their good points, their bad. Anatomically, each differed from the next, and as for Denise Averil, she was the most awesome physical specimen of sheer female sexuality he had seen in years. To Brennan, Lisa Collins, half remembered, was exciting because of a more acceptable conventional beauty, and because of her love, her giving. Medora Hart, beside him, was more compactly and perfectly exquisite, with her dramatic and theatrical countenance and figure. But to create a Denise Averil, the Lord could not have rested on the seventh day.

Brennan kept his eyes fastened on Denise, writhing above him. He examined her urchin hair below the turban, her teasing almond-shaped eyes, the flagrant swell of her naked breasts trembling to the gyrations of her generously curved hips. This was an animal-lazy, generous-natured Messalina, if such there could be.

Denise was kneeling now, and so were the other girls of The Troupe, to the belling of great musical gongs. Their heads touched the runway floor. Then, gradually, they lifted their heads, and as Denise's came up, Brennan found her staring directly at him. He squirmed uncomfortably, holding his fixed grin, when he felt Medora's forefinger jabbing at him as she identified him for Denise.

The show girls leaped to their feet, tossing aside their veils, and Denise was smiling at Medora. As Denise spun to leave the runway with the others, she gave Medora a quick nod of approval. In fleeting seconds The Troupe was gone, the number ended, and the lights were changing.

Medora gave a squeal of elation. "Did you see that, Matt? She said yes. She's pleased. That means she'll meet you after the show. You've practically got the name of Peet's hotel in your pocket."

"Thanks to you," said Brennan uncertainly.

Medora was rising. "I've got to dash and change. I hope you don't mind waiting until the finale. It'll be over with before long, and when it is, and we've dressed, I'll bring Denise out and introduce you to her properly. See you soon. Cheers."

A specialty number, by a team of three humorous ventriloquists, was already performing on the stage, and Medora bent low so as not to obstruct anyone's view as she departed. Brennan found himself with two hours on his hands. He reached for the champagne, pondering how he could speed the next two hours and how he would fare with the formidable Denise Averil.

He sat through two more numbers, and when The Troupe came on again, once more elegantly costumed, once more bare-breasted, he realized that they were impersonating the models that Henri de Toulouse-Lautrec had made famous in his expressionist lithographs.

There were the delightful Club Lautrec's girls as Toulouse-Lautrec's originals, as Yvette Guilbert, La Goulue, Marcelle Lender, Loie Fuller, May Belfort, Ida Heath, May Milton, Mlle. Eglantine's cancan troupe, and Jane Avril, the last represented, naturally, by her namesake, Denise Averil.

Brennan watched Denise, in her smart wide-brimmed hat and parasol and ankle-length skirt, vast mounds of exposed breasts bobbing, slink toward him in measured tread. She had reached the end of the runway, haughty, eyes glazed as they looked off through the smoke and darkness toward nothing, when suddenly her eyes dropped to hold on Brennan. Instinctively he lifted a hand in a half salute. Denise's visage remained expressionless except for one eye. She winked. She paraded off.

As the number ended to a thunder of applause, Brennan found himself clapping with enthusiasm. He felt foolishly pleased that this magnificent female had singled him out for attention. Then, almost simultaneously, he felt childish and guilty. For he had remembered Lisa.

Quickly he came to his feet. The lights were still up but now slowly dimming. He wended his way past several tables, but was hemmed in by a jam of waiters.

Impatiently biding his time, he heard two young voices in a tense exchange directly before him. He looked at the table's occupants, and instantly he recognized the girl, whom he'd met just yesterday in Earnshaw's suite and whom he'd heard something about from Doyle. She was a slip of a straw blonde, unadorned, with a freckled but otherwise commonplace face. She was holding her brown coat and small suede purse on her lap, and addressing her male companion intently. Earnshaw's niece Carol, definitely.

Brennan's attention shifted to Carol's companion, expecting to find a typical young American, but instead he found a rather attractive German lad, the lean Nordic and Almanach de Gotha type that used to frequent international tennis tournaments at Forest Hills and Wimbledon before the Second World War. He might have been handsome, were he not so wretched this minute, Brennan decided. Carol was speaking insistently in an undertone, and the German boy was shaking his head as he took up his tumbler of liquor.

Carol's voice rose, and was momentarily audible. "Well, whatever you say, Willi, my Uncle Emmett is absolutely positive you were lying to him. He knows your father is in Paris and not in Frankfurt."

Carol had addressed her companion as Willi. The name registered in Brennan's mind, and he recalled some of Doyle's gossip, so that he was now able to identify the boy. This was the son of Dr. Dietrich von Goerlitz. Willi, yes. The one Carol had been seeing despite Earnshaw's disapproval.

Brennan took note of Willi again. He was muttering something incoherent to himself. He was spilling part of his whisky. He was not only wretched, Brennan could see, he was also drunk.

Embarrassed to be witness to a private disagreement, Brennan sought an escape route. There was none. He was trapped, two waiters ahead of him, the sommelier behind him. Helpless, he submitted to overhearing another snatch of conversation.

Carol Earnshaw was desperately trying to control the emotion in her voice. "Willi, why did you lie? Uncle Emmett was only trying to help your father. Why wouldn't you let him?"

Willi's eyes rolled. His words were thick and mournful. "Carol, I could not do any other way. Maybe someday you will understand."

"There won't be a someday," she said with a flash of anger. "Uncle Emmett's not going to try to see your father again. He has his pride, too. You want to help someone, and that someone's son kicks you in the face. I—I can't believe you behaved the way you did. I thought you were so different."

"Please, Carol, in a few days, in a week, maybe you will understand."

"There's not going to be any few days or a week. Uncle Emmett told me he's getting out of here, leaving Paris the day after tomorrow. And, Willi, I'm going with him. I don't—"

Willi fumbled for her wrist. "Please—please—I am not responsible—"

"I don't want to hear any more."

She tried to free her wrist, but Willi gripped it more tightly. "Carol, do not leave—"

Brennan had no desire to find out whether Carol Earnshaw was leaving or staying. He wished only to flee the scene, and in the darkness he saw that the waiters had parted and were moving away. With relief Brennan located a free aisle through the tables, and speedily he put the earsplitting music, the new number on the stage, and the lovers' quarrel behind him. He had problems of his own, including another lovers' quarrel ahead of him.

The lobby was an oasis of peace and quiet. Brennan purchased several *jeton* telephone tokens and folded himself into an empty telephone booth. From information he obtained the number of Le Grand Véfour. He dialed, asked to speak to Mlle. Collins, and girded himself for the explosion.

She was on the phone, and she was cheerful. "Oh, I'm so happy you called, Matt. I was terribly worried about you. I kept thinking this might be another Bois episode. Are you all right?"

"I'm suffering from nothing more than boredom," he said. "Look, Lisa, I'm still in the Club Lautrec. I'm stuck. I've got to hang around until the whole damn show is over before I can see my—the person I'm supposed to see. I'm afraid I won't be able to make dinner."

He did not know what he would hear, but what he heard was what he least expected. "Darling, don't fret about it for one second," Lisa was saying. "I miss you so much, and everyone did want to meet you, but they can another time, and I—well, I'll see you soon anyway."

"Yes, you will," he said without conviction. "How's the evening going?"

"The restaurant's a marvel. I've put on ten pounds. Foie gras with grapes, can you imagine? And the wine, Montrachet 1962, or something like that. Anyway, it beats LSD. The rest is rather tiresome. If you were here, at least I could look at you. But this way I have to listen to endless chatter about underpinnings and bodices and hemlines. I can't wait until you take me away from all this. Let's make babies, darling, and let's take a long, long time to make each one."

"Lisa, I love you."

"I want you, Matt. Will you come to me tonight?"

"What do you think?"

"I think I can't wait. But come to me intact. I keep worrying about you. Who do you have to see tonight?"

He was about to tell her, but he hesitated. He was serious about Lisa. He would have to treat her seriously. "Some decrepit old Frenchman somebody feels I should meet."

"Can he help us?"

"I don't know, Lisa, but I can't afford to pass up a bet."

"No, you mustn't. But don't be too late."

"I won't. Now you'd better get back to your table."

"Yes, I'd better, if I can navigate," said Lisa. She paused, and then she said, "Matt—"

"I'm here, darling."

"—tell that decrepit old Frenchman, when you see him—tell him about how I want to make babies, so maybe he'll help out a little more. Until later, darling."

She hung up, and he felt like a bastard.

Crossing the lobby, he slowed before the reservation counter, considering whether or not he should go through with the evening. If Denise were able to lead him to Rostov, that would be another matter.

551

But the best she could give him was the means of reaching a nobody named Peet. Yet there was one link between Peet and Rostov: an English scholar-adventurer named Sir Richard Burton. Tenuous link. To learn if it really existed, he must locate Peet. What troubled him was the test that he must pass even to get to Peet. Had anyone ever spent an evening talking only business with Messalina?

Reluctantly Brennan went back inside the nightclub. Unsteadily he groped his way toward the stage until his eyes had become accustomed to the darkness.

When he found his table and sat down, he realized that the first act was ending. In a chorus of song, and a flurry of feathery fans, and a seeming acre of pink flesh, it ended. The overhead lights glared down.

Brennan searched for a waiter. His eyes fell on a nearby table. Where there had been two, there was now one. Carol Earnshaw's chair was empty. Only young Willi von Goerlitz remained. He appeared badly drunk, blond hair tangled, necktie loosened, stains on his lapel. He was trying to refill his tumbler from a depleted bottle of Scotch. A portion of the liquor overshot the glass. After that, he wasn't drinking Scotch. He was inhaling it.

Brennan tried to remember what the quarrel had been about. Willi and Carol had not been fighting about themselves but about the grown-ups, his father, her uncle. Apparently Earnshaw had tried to see Goerlitz and had seen Willi instead, and Willi had lied to The Ex by saying his father was not in Paris. Then Brennan realized his own contribution to the quarrel. He had been responsible for Earnshaw's having a reason to see Goerlitz. Earnshaw had failed to see Goerlitz. Briefly Brennan wondered if the failure would invalidate Earnshaw's debt to him. Unlikely. Yet it might, if Earnshaw planned to quit Paris the day after tomorrow.

Again Brennan felt Rostov slipping from reach, and again he worried.

He squinted off at Willi once more. The morose young man was imbibing steadily. At this rate, he would have to be carried out feet first before the show was over. Brennan decided that this was none of his business. His business was—and he felt himself smile sheepishly—a decrepit old Frenchman named Denise Averil.

Once more he turned to find a waiter, and found instead, to his amazement, a Chinese punchinello at his elbow, a roly-poly little man who stood grinning down at him.

"You are Mr. Matthew Brennan, sir?"

"Yes?"

"I am Ma Ming, of Hsinhua, Government of China press agency."

For a moment Brennan was confused. Then he remembered the unusual name that he had jokingly told Professor Isenberg he could not possibly forget, and as he quickly came to his feet, both he and Ma Ming said simultaneously, "Professor Isenberg."

"Professor Isenberg," Brennan repeated. "Of course, he spoke to me of you."

"Professor Isenberg, yesterday at our lunch, he spoke to me of you," said Ma Ming, still grinning. "I promised him to see you."

"You're very kind, Mr.—Mr. Ma." Brennan glanced past his Chinese visitor at the crowded nightclub, and once more he was bewildered. "Forgive my behavior, but I just didn't expect anyone here. I hadn't expected to be here myself. How did you find me?"

"Concierge," said Ma Ming.

"Of course. I must thank Monsieur Dupont. It *is* kind of you to take this trouble. Please do sit down. Will you join me in a drink?"

"I have now only a few minutes," said Ma Ming. "I must go to do my work. But since Professor Isenberg spoke to me, I have meant to call upon you, yesterday, today, yet always there is work. But tonight, driving to the Embassy, I was ashamed to be so remiss, so I thought I would make the courtesy call, and perhaps, if it is possible, answer any question." He started for a chair across the table from Brennan. "A few minutes."

Brennan watched him. Curious punchinello. His head looked like a small yellow beach ball balanced atop the slightly larger medicine ball that was his body. His gray suit was floppy, and the sleeves were down over his thumbs. As he sat, the grin remained unchanged, and since his eyes were deep-set pinholes and his flat nose was flush with his cheeks, the grin seemed his only prominent feature. Brennan wondered if it was a deformity.

"I am not disturbing you?" said Ma Ming.

"No, no. Quite the contrary. I've wanted to meet you. As for the show, I've seen it before. I'm only here waiting to meet one of the performers afterward."

Ma Ming appeared unconscious of his surroundings, and very serious, although the grin remained. "Professor Isenberg spoke most affectionately of you. As a parent might."

"He's too kind. I'm sure I don't deserve it."

"You were treated badly in your country."

Instantly Brennan was on guard. Ma Ming's jester appearance, supported by credentials from Isenberg, had been disarming. Now Brennan was reminded that his guest was a product of the People's Republic of China, a correspondent from a Communist nation so long

553

in conflict with the United States. What was it he had just said? *You were treated badly in your country.* What would he say next? You were treated badly because your country has a capitalistic, imperialistic, aggressive, avaricious, heartless Government?

What he did say next was, "I sympathize with you. It has been that way in my country, too." He nodded and went on. "My father suffered as you did, Mr. Brennan. My blessed father was an instructor in Peking Teachers College. As a youngster, he had followed Mao Tse-tung on the Long March. It was an epic flight that preserved and saved China. It began in Kiangsi Province in 1934. Chiang Kai-shek and his German General and his Kuomintang army surrounded Mao's Communist band. Mao's own wife was murdered by Chiang's troopers. But Mao and his small band broke free, and made their exodus. For twelve months they marched sometimes twenty-four miles a day. In rags, on bare feet, they marched, always fighting rearguard actions, and they covered 6,000 miles, until they reached the safety of the caves of Yenan. My father was among them, and in that time his admiration for Mao was boundless. It was only later, long after Mao had driven Chiang and his corrupt landowners out of China, and established a government of the proletariat, that my father had misgivings. My father believed that Mao, in his zeal to establish China as a self-sufficient power, had become too tyrannical, and the lack of freedom was oppressive. My father publicly protested that the Central Committee had made the nation a mute, and would soon suffocate it. Shortly after that, Mao instigated the period of the 'Hundred Flowers.' You know of that? A period when Mao permitted intellectuals to criticize the regime openly. The period was named after the legend, in red letters, above the Peking Teachers College. 'Let a hundred flowers bloom, let a hundred ideas compete.' But the intellectuals spoke too critically of the regime, and Mao revoked the 'Hundred Flowers' and commanded silence once more. My father refused to remain silent. As teacher and philosopher, my father continued to make his lectures and speeches that were critical of the Government. Finally he was arrested, charged with counterrevolutionary activities, and sentenced to life in prison. He died in his prison cell."

With growing astonishment Brennan had listened to this frank and tragic account from his grinning visitor. Brennan found that he was moved. His instinct told him that he could trust Mr. Ma Ming, whom Isenberg also trusted.

"What made your father risk speaking out as he did?"

"The efforts of Maoists to suppress the private beliefs of individuals. My father revered the teachings of Confucius. From 478 B.C. until

554

1949, generation after generation of Chinese lived and died by the moral principles set down in the Confucian *Analects*. Confucius was not, to us, a religious leader. He believed in no personal God. Confucius was a spiritual leader, a philosopher. He taught the five virtues—kindliness, truthfulness, politeness, integrity, sagacity—and he stressed worship of ancestors and obedience to parents. He taught subordination of one's self to one's parents and relatives, and this gave one immortality because it made one's life merely a link in an infinite chain of lives. My father subscribed to this belief. But Mao Tse-tung felt the Confucian system was the opium of our people. In its time, he felt, it had been useful, promoting authority through its family system in days when there was no other authority. But in modern times, he felt, it was a feudal superstition that hampered China's progress, favoring the old, burdening the young, impoverishing the peasantry, obstructing change, promoting selfishness, and opposing the central authority of the Communist party. My father understood Mao's feelings, and would not have objected if the Maoists had proceeded to oppose Confucianism slowly, through education, yet allowing every man the freedom to determine his faith. My father's objection was to the overnight dictatorial suppression of individual freedom."

"And today?" asked Brennan.

"Today? Today we have a new and better China, perhaps as a result of Mao's ruthless activities. In that, my father may have been wrong. But today we not only possess the precious end products of Mao's regime—adequate food, clothing, dwellings, hygiene, education, strength, pride—but we also have, at least by past standards, relative freedom. In desiring that, my father was right."

Brennan found himself fascinated. "I've read and heard that Chairman Kuo Shu-tung is more liberal than his predecessors, but I had no idea he could be as liberal as you say."

Mr. Ma's pinpoint eyes were serious, but the grin was permanent. "Oh, make no mistake, Mr. Brennan. The bourgeoisie and exploiting classes are gone forever, and we are still Mao's children, all of us, only we rebel a little and go our own way. Chairman Kuo has never repudiated Mao entirely. He has merely modified Mao and made use of Mao, to make it possible for us to be part of the world community. For example, in 1946, Mao stated that reactionaries were paper tigers who appeared frightening but were really not to be feared, since the proletariat was stronger and would prevail. Later Mao stated that the atom bombs of China's enemies were paper tigers, too, since they could not be used. But in 1957, while still insisting the reactionaries and their bombs were paper tigers if the long view were taken, he admitted that from a short view 'they are also living tigers, iron tigers, real tigers, which can eat people.' Chairman Kuo Shu-tung seized on this recently to tell our people that China was a real tiger itself now, living in a world of real tigers, and unless we tigers learned to live together in harmony, we would devour one another and none of us would survive. And when Chairman Kuo undertook to restore some freedom of speech in China, he shrewdly drew upon a remark Mao had once made in a different context, to the effect that 'He who does not allow himself to be criticized during his life will be criticized after his death.' "

"Very good."

If anything, Ma Ming's grin had deepened. "The difference between Mao's China and our own China of today can be put simply. Mao had told Nehru, in 1957, that he did not fear a nuclear war, since it would wipe out only half of mankind, and the half that survived would be predominately Communist, and so Communism would finally prevail. In short, because population distribution favored China's survival, Mao felt that a nuclear war would completely eradicate imperialism, and that the sacrifice of 300 million Chinese lives, almost a third of our population, would be worth 'the victory of the socialist world revolution.' But our Chairman Kuo saw that with the neutron bomb, with the buildup of stockpiles and delivery systems everywhere, a nuclear war would wipe out not half the world's population but all of it. And so he set China on its present course, and so he is treating today at the Summit for disarmament and the end of war."

Brennan had savored every word he had heard, yet he felt no safer. His bewilderment had returned. A respectable, decent, candid, apparently sincere Chinese journalist, one close to Chairman Kuo Shu-tung, had projected the firsthand picture of a respectable, decent, candid, sincere People's Republic of China. Yet elsewhere, throughout the week, Brennan had been led to believe quite the opposite. He stared at the roly-poly Chinese across the table from him. Either the man was a monumental liar, or else all the rumors and alarms that Brennan had been collecting were a tissue of lies. Brennan's confusion was total.

"Now, as to Varney," Ma Ming was saying. "You wished to ask me about Professor Varney, did you not? Forgive my earlier digression. It is unlike me. I was carried away. But you would like to know of Varney?"

"Yes, Mr. Ma, I would. You know my story. It would be important to me if he were alive and I could—"

"He is alive, Mr. Brennan. But being alive is a relative matter.

Varney is alive and he is not alive. He is suffering from an advanced hardening of the arteries of the brain. It is often a disease of the elderly. His mind is ravaged and his memory is no more. For all human purposes, Varney remains a living vegetable. I called upon him last year, hoping for an interview. I was too late. He lives out his days in the village of Nan Liu, in a modern convalescent sanitorium, where he is well cared for and venerated by those who come to see him as they would come to visit a Marxist monument. I am sorry, Mr. Brennan."

"I am sorry, too."

"Perhaps you will find other means." Ma Ming was suddenly on his feet. Before Brennan could rise, Ma Ming had come around the table and with one plump hand had forced Brennan to remain in his chair. "No formalities. It was a pleasure to meet you, Mr. Brennan. Perhaps we shall meet once more on another occasion."

"You were very gracious to come here to see me."

Ma Ming's grin suddenly vanished. "I came because I did not wish you to waste further time seeking what does not exist. Good night, Mr. Brennan."

Brennan stared after the Chinese journalist, who was finding his way hastily between the tables. Mr. Ma's last words still rang curiously in Brennan's ears. Mr. Ma had come here, he had said, because he did not wish Brennan to waste time seeking what did not exist. There had been an odd double edge to his words, and there had been no smile to accompany them. Had Mr. Ma meant that Varney did not exist? Or had he meant that China's intrigue with Soviet Russia did not exist?

The overhead lights in the cabaret were blinking on and off. With a start, Brennan realized where he was and why he was here. Nearby, at another table in the Club Lautrec, Willi von Goerlitz was drinking still. Everywhere the customers were settling back for the second half of the show. And soon there would be Denise Averil. The lights were lowered. Already Ma Ming was receding from Brennan's memory, an improbable phantom who had come and gone and left nothing behind. Brennan was impatient for his talk with Denise and the more probable Joe Peet.

He signaled a passing waiter. He wanted something that contracted time. Champagne was too slow. Willi von Goerlitz had the right idea. Brennan ordered a double Scotch on the rocks. And then, finding his pipe, he settled back for the last of the show to start and end, so that his evening could begin.

A N HOUR LATER the final curtain had closed on the Club Lautrec's gaudy spectacle, and most of the customers had streamed out of the cabaret. The mammoth room was empty except for the diehard drinkers here and there about the room, sitting individually or in groups, still tippling steadily.

Brennan had limited himself to three Scotches, enough to make him relax, not enough to make him foolish. Now, having paid his bill—an amount sufficient to pay up both Russia's and China's United Nations assessments for a year, he was certain—he waited for the appearance of Medora Hart and Denise Averil.

Although a miniature pinwheel seemed to spin behind his eyes, he felt it must be a hangover from the dazzling colors and intricate movements of the show and not intoxication from his several drinks. His head was clear enough. Yet he was not sure that he would recognize Medora or Denise with their clothes on. He had seen them so constantly and intimately in the naked flesh these past hours, by now able to place every birthmark and scar (Medora's birthmark, a strawberry, graced her left buttock; Denise's scar, a mystery, was inside her right thigh), that he was fearful they would be strangers to him when fully robed.

Forcing himself out of his chair to stretch, and to keep an eye on both backstage doors, Brennan was distracted by a small commotion off to his right. He saw that the altercation was taking place at Willi von Goerlitz's table. A chunky red-faced waiter, brandishing a bill, kept trying to shove it under Willi's nose, and Willi drunkenly kept pushing the waiter away. Cursing in German, Willi swung his arm against the waiter's chest and sent him reeling backward. Satisfied, Willi laid his arms heavily on the table, knocking over a lamp, dropped his head wearily into his arms and prepared to sleep.

The furious waiter was searching for assistance, and finding none, he charged at Willi again. He laid his hands on Willi's shoulders, and began to shake him violently.

Brennan decided that he had seen enough. Hurrying forward, he grabbed one of the waiter's arms.

"Leave him alone," Brennan said. "He is a friend, *comprenez-vous?*"

"Friend? *Ça me fait une belle jambe!*" Indignantly the waiter yanked the crumpled bill out of his pocket. "Three hundred francs, monsieur! He will not pay!"

"Because he's unable to," said Brennan, bringing out his wallet. "I repeat, he's a friend of mine. I'll take care of it." He counted out the francs. "There, that should do it." He added one more large note. "And that's for your tip and a big pot of black coffee."

The red-faced waiter was all sweet benevolence now. *"Excusez-moi. Merci beaucoup.* Of course, monsieur. I am sorry. The coffee at once. Thank you!"

Brennan turned back to the table to find Willi's head slightly raised above his arms, eyes blearily contemplating his rescuer. "Whoyou are?" he mumbled, words slurring. "Youfrom Switz—Switz—St. Bernard Hospice? Wheresyourbrandy—brandy keg?"

Brennan knelt close to him. "I'm Matt Brennan. I saw you earlier with Carol Earnshaw. I know Carol."

*"Guten—*good—*danke sehr—*I'm friend of Carol, too, also." Willi's eyes began to close.

Brennan shook him gently. "You'd better get back to your hotel, Willi. Let me call a taxi."

One of Willi's eyes opened. "Lancaster, get me Lancaster."

"Is that your hotel?"

"Carol. Carol in Lancaster. Gotta see Carol. Important see Carol."

His head had fallen into his arms once more.

Crouching, wondering what to do next, feeling some vague responsibility to Carol Earnshaw, Brennan became aware of a pair of shapely female legs circling the table. He heard his name, looked up, and came to his feet.

Medora Hart, hands on hips, was waiting. "What ever are you up to?"

"Well, this poor fellow passed out, and I was trying—"

"Drunks," she said. "Every club I've ever been in has at least a half dozen every night. If you bothered about every one, you'd never get out of here. Michaud's staff'll take care of him."

Brennan realized that Medora, identifiable despite her sweater and skirt, was quite alone. "Where's Denise?"

"She'll be right along. Still primping herself. A good sign, Matt. She's frightfully impressed by you."

Brennan swallowed. "That's nice."

Medora laughed. "Don't look so stricken. It's not as if you're married and sneaking off somewhere. You're not, are you? Married, I mean?"

"Well, no—but—"

"It doesn't matter. Despite the appearance she makes up there, Denise is quite tame. No trouble."

559

"Medora, I'm not sure what she expects tonight. Will she want to go on the town?"

"After all that prancing on the stage? Are you mad? Crikey, never. Take her to some quiet side-street bar. One or two drinks. One or two jokes. She's a sporting type. Exert a little charm. You've plenty. And then see her home. You'll come away with what you want. . . . Just listen to me, old Mother Hart, giving *you* advice. I'm sure you've been around."

The table rocked, and Willi lifted his head and groaned as he tried to open his eyes.

Brennan was instantly solicitous. "Don't you feel well, Willi?"

"Willi?" repeated Medora. "You know him?"

"Not exactly. But I saw him with Carol Earnshaw before, and I know her."

"Carol Earnshaw? She's a friend of mine. You mean—" She stared down at Willi. "Is this—? This must be Willi—that's right, Willi von Whatever."

"Goerlitz," said Brennan. "I gather he and Carol have been going out together."

"Yes, they have. I was with them briefly a couple of nights ago." Immediately Medora pulled a chair over next to Willi and sat down, massaging the back of his neck. "I must say, I hardly recognized him. Good Lord, if Carol had any idea of the condition he's in. Utterly crocked. I wonder what's troubling him."

The waiter had arrived with the coffeepot and service, and began setting them on the table.

"Don't you think somebody should get him back to his hotel, Medora?" Brennan asked.

"I will," said Medora firmly. "Safely back to his hotel. I owe Carol that much." She shook Willi. "Come on there, wake up. I'm taking you back for some beddy."

Willi squinted at her as she separated him from his folded arms and forcibly shoved him upright against the chair. "Now snap out of it, Willi boy. I'm a friend of Carol Earnshaw, and—"

"Gotta see Carol, gotta see Carol," Willi mumbled.

"Not in the shape you are in, you're not seeing anyone," said Medora. "Come on, now, you're going to drink down this coffee, and then you're going to sleep in a right proper place. You'll have plenty of time for Carol tomorrow."

"Too late tomorrow," Willi mumbled.

Watching, Brennan felt the slow movement of a hand down his arm. "Good evening, Mr. Brennan," he heard a faintly French feminine voice say.

He wheeled, and almost bumped into Denise Averil. She wore a teasing smile, and blouse and skirt, yet she looked more undressed than ever. The silk blouse, clinging as tightly as her brassiere cups, was slit deeply, yet revealed only the merest parts of the lacy brassiere webbing. The short skirt was also silk, draped to accent the contours of her hips and thighs.

"Hel-lo, Miss Averil," said Brennan.

"Oh, cut it, you two," called out Medora as she began to feed the slumping Willi his black coffee. "Denise, meet Matt. Now you're properly introduced, and off you go, both of you, and I'll sober up this poor wreck."

Brennan hung back a moment. "Are you sure you can manage him, Medora?"

Medora looked up once more. "I've managed men when they weren't drunk, Matt, so I daresay I can handle this one."

"Well, if there's any trouble, leave a message for me at the California," said Brennan.

"Don't worry. Now off you go, both of you."

Brennan found Denise Averil still smiling at him. He smiled back awkwardly. "Anything you'd particularly like tonight?" he asked.

Her smile remained. "You," she said. She slipped her arm through his possessively. "Take me to You."

On leaden legs, he started her toward the lobby. Once outside the Club Lautrec, he said, "You must be exhausted after that show. Would you prefer some place nearby?"

"I've never felt livelier. I really don't care where we go, as long as it's cozy and quiet."

"Cozy and quiet?" He tried to think, and wished that he had his Michelin, or better yet, that he'd never got into this.

She studied him. "You're cute."

"Well, so are you." He determined to keep their conversation on an uncute plane. "I'm trying to remember some good bistro—"

"Where was it you told Medora you're staying?"

"California Hotel."

"Around the corner," she said. "There's a nice bar there."

"That's it, then," he said.

For a moment he suffered indecision about the most sensible way to reach the hotel. It was too close for a taxi. If they had to walk, there was the Champs-Élysées or the Rue de Ponthieu. On foot, the Champs-Élysées had its advantages and its perils. The busy main thoroughfare would be filled with night people, and this was anti-intimacy and therefore offered safety in numbers. At the same time, Denise Averil's flashy attire and blatant physical attractions would draw attention, possibly from someone who knew him. The Rue de Ponthieu, on the other hand, had in its favor fewer pedestrians and subdued street lighting, but its isolation might invite too much provocative talk.

Teetering with indecision, Brennan damned himself for being one of those persons who became neurotically immobilized by small dilemmas. Suddenly, to his relief, Denise made up his mind for him.

"I'm thirsty," she said, and she turned him toward the Rue de Ponthieu.

It was two and a half blocks, mostly along a darkened street only occasionally illuminated by dull streetlamps. Except for complimenting her on her performance in the show, which pleased her, and intimating that Medora might have exaggerated his status as a millionaire diplomat, which she would not believe, he kept his conversation to a minimum. But soon he sensed that she had misinterpreted his withdrawn and relatively mute behavior. To Denise, he had become the strong and silent type, a welcome change from the whispering seducers, and therefore more interesting.

As they walked along, her hand went down his arm and her fingers entwined themselves in his and squeezed them playfully. She began to lean more intimately against him, so that once, to give way to an approaching pedestrian, he was forced to put his arm around her waist and draw her toward him. Appreciative, she refused to unsnuggle afterward.

Passing between the rear of the Lido Arcade on the one side and his favorite small restaurant, Le Tangage, on the other, he realized that they were nearing the brighter, more traveled Rue de Berri up ahead, and he firmly separated himself from Denise.

"Around the corner," he said.

"I know," she said. Her green eyes were fixed on his mouth. "I can't see you and Joe Peet together."

Warily, he asked, "Why not?"

"You behave perfectly normal. You act like a gentleman. Joe Peet could hardly be called either."

"I'd never quite thought of that."

"It takes a woman to find out," she said. "But even then, I don't see what you and Joe can have in common. Medora told me you're old friends."

"Not exactly," he said in haste. "Joe Peet's father and I are friends. His father is extremely wealthy. He's a meat-packer. We became acquainted in Washington years ago, and whenever I'm in Chicago I see him. That's how I got to know Joe. He's an odd, lonely young man, always seeking affection—"

"If that's what you call affection," said Denise tartly.

"—and I suppose he found something in Russia he could never find anywhere else."

"His *femme à passion*," she said coarsely.

They had arrived at the entrance to the Hotel California. Brennan had intended to lead Denise to the bar entrance down the block, but she had already turned into the lobby. Nervously, he followed her. It comforted him that neither M. Dupont nor the night man, Le Clerc, was behind the concierge's desk. One of the uniformed grooms was in their place, sorting keys.

Quickly Brennan caught Denise by the elbow, guiding her through the abandoned sitting area of the lobby toward the arch that led to the bar on one side and the dining room on the other. With familiarity, Denise turned toward the bar, but suddenly halted.

"It's closed," she said.

Brennan refused to believe it. He stepped inside the dim, empty room. There was no one in sight. He recalled that several times Jules, the affable and well-read bartender, had told him with the pride that came from independence that he closed the bar any hour he wished after ten, especially when business was slow.

Disconcerted, Brennan turned to face Denise. "You're right," he said. "Well, I guess we'll have to go somewhere else, Denise."

She had finished dabbing at her eye shadow with a Kleenex. "Why?" she asked. "Haven't you got your rooms here?"

"Of course—"

"My feet are too tired to walk anymore. Let's have some drinks in your room." Abruptly she raised one shapely leg and pulled off a high-heeled pump. Then balancing against him, she lifted her other foot and removed the second pump. In her stocking feet, holding aloft her spike-heeled shoes, she was happier. "I'm ready," she said.

He knew that he was sentenced to quarters. There were two fifths of Scotch upstairs. If he gave her a couple of strong drinks, he'd probably manage to learn Peet's hideout quickly enough, and then have no trouble hustling her out to a taxi.

He simulated good cheer. "Swell, I'll get the key. Meet you at the elevator."

Before she could accompany him, he strode back into the lobby to the concierge's desk.

"Key to 112," he commanded the groom. Taking the key, he added, "Have Room Service send up two highball glasses, a bottle of Evian, and a bucket of ice. *Tout de suite.*"

"*Oui,* Monsieur Brennan."

He hurried straight through the lobby to the two elevators. Both were in use. He could see Denise Averil, swinging her pumps and her

563

lips, crossing languidly toward him. He peered up the elevator shaft. One cage was slowly descending.

From behind him he could hear the chatter of guests entering the lobby from outside. A single voice was clearer than the rest. "Concierge, any messages for Miss Collins? I'm expecting one."

Brennan stood petrified. Lisa's voice and his heartbeat were deafening in his ear.

Her voice drifted across the lobby again. "Well, if anyone calls, you can get me in the bar."

"Apologies, madame. No bar tonight. Closed early."

"Darn it! . . . Sorry, folks. I'd ask you up to my room here, but it's only for work, a hole in the wall. We can go back to my suite in the Plaza-Athénée, or the bar there, and . . ."

Her voice trailed off, and Brennan turned his numb face to look over his shoulder, praying that Lisa and her party were leaving. Instead, he saw her, still at the concierge's desk, staring past the group of four women and two men in her party, her gaze settled on him. For Brennan it was like looking up the barrel of a machine gun.

Shrinking, he half expected her to call out his name, but suddenly he understood the reason why she did not, for he felt Denise Averil's arm slip cozily inside his own. He stared helplessly at Denise, who was rhythmically snapping the nimble fingers of her free hand, undulating sexily as she did a little dance shuffle in her stocking feet. "Elevator's waiting, big boy," she teased. "What's keeping us?"

Brennan wanted the lobby floor to open up, swallow him, deposit him deep in the bowels of the earth for all eternity, but it was only the metallic creaking elevator gate that was opening. Denise danced into the elevator.

Madly desperate, Brennan cast another glance at Lisa. His instinct was to rush to her, explain, but with her friends around her, this would be impossible. Lisa was continuing to glower at him. From the distance across the lobby, he could not make out whether her face was really as white as it seemed.

He held out his hands, a dumb supplication for temporary understanding, a pantomime promise of explanations later. He did not know whether Lisa saw this begging. She had swung angrily toward her friends and said something, and she stalked out of the hotel as they straggled after her.

Cursing Joe Peet under his breath, cursing his own juvenile excursion into mystery and adventure, Brennan entered the elevator, which now reeked with the scent of Carnet de Bal—or possibly—could it be?—La Vierge Folle.

564

Four shots of Scotch and one hour later, Matt Brennan felt no pain.

Denise Averil lay back on the velour divan, deep among the puffs of pillows, light-headedly studying the reflections in her half-filled glass. Brennan was still sitting upright, a few feet from her, draining the last of his drink.

On first entering the sitting room of his suite with Denise, he had been suffering the aftermath of the encounter with Lisa in the downstairs lobby. He had ruined Lisa's evening and disrupted her dinner party by bowing out of it at the last minute. He had betrayed her confidence in him by telling her that he was meeting with "some decrepit old Frenchman somebody feels I should meet." She had caught him taking a shoeless and sexy young Marseille show girl up to his room. He had doubted that he would ever be able to talk his way out of it, and he had felt heartsick over his stupid white lie. Life had never seemed bleaker than when he had poured the first drinks for Denise and himself.

But with each drink his anguish had been alleviated a little more, until soon an alcoholic mist protected him from remorse. From the start, as self-protection, he had encouraged Denise to speak about herself, her earliest past, her growing up, her entry into show business, her life in Paris and at the Club Lautrec. Willingly she had succumbed to the reminiscent mood. Twice he had tried to bring her around to the subject of Joe Peet. She had not been interested. She had preferred to discuss, if not herself, then her fascinating escort. Brennan, after a brief and unsuccessful attempt to undermine Medora's fiction about him, had at last decided to play out his assigned role, and had therefore remained a potential substitute for the affluent and generous Mr. Peet.

Now, before they both became too drunk and before he took her in a taxi to her apartment, he felt that he must revive the name of Joe Peet. He sat contemplating his empty glass, wondering how to begin.

"Matthew," she said.

She had startled him. "Yes, Denise?"

"Pour your baby one more short one." She held out her glass.

He set down his own glass, took hers, and went unsteadily to the tray on the leather-inset desk next to the closed and draped windows. He opened the second bottle of Scotch.

"You married, big boy?" Denise asked.

"No."

"Funny. I thought you might be."

He poured her drink on a cube of ice. "I used to be, once. But not now. Not for a long time."

"I thought you were."

He dropped another cube into her glass. "Why?"

"I dunno. What's the difference? You going to be around Paris a while?"

"For a while. I come and go. I've got some business to finish here." He paused. The moment seemed propitious. "Then I promised Joe Peet's father I'd see Joe. I've got to find him."

"How come old man Peet didn't give you his son's hotel address?"

"He did. Plaza-Athénée. But when I got there—I had something important to pass along from his father—well, Joe wasn't there. He checked out and forgot to leave his forwarding address. He could be in any one of a hundred hotels or boarding houses or apartments—"

"A hotel," said Denise.

"That's right. Medora did say you knew where he moved." Brennan returned to the divan and handed Denise the drink.

"I know all right." She sipped the Scotch tentatively, and then she took a big swallow.

He remained standing over her. "I'd appreciate it if you'd give me the name of his hotel. I should see him tomorrow and get it over with."

She took another swallow, and savored it. "Oh, I'll tell you, in due time." She handed up the drink. "Here. I've had enough. Finish it."

Brennan brought the glass to his mouth and tipped it. The Scotch went down warmly.

She watched him. "Now maybe you feel the way I feel."

"How do you feel?"

"Sexy," said Denise.

He refrained from replying. He gave much attention to finishing the last of the drink.

"Put the glass down," she said. As he did so, she patted the divan beside her. "Sit here."

Dutifully he obeyed. He felt the fullness of her large thigh against his own, and the nearness of her flesh and scent of her perfume overwhelmed him.

"What's wrong, big boy?" she pouted. "You've been a million kilometers away all evening. You're still too far." She reached out with both her hands. "Come on back here to baby."

He hesitated. "Look, Denise, I'm not sure this is the time for— for—"

"For what, big boy? For a little loving? It's always time for loving. Maybe you've had too much business on your mind. Let baby take care of that. What else can there be? Joe Peet and his papa? Didn't I promise to help you before I left—in the morning?"

He had been avoiding her mocking eyes, but now he looked up. She had stated her conditions without stating them. He could have the name of Peet's hotel in the morning. If he would not let her stay the night, there would be no morning and no information on Peet.

His conscience sought Lisa, but Lisa had fled. There was nothing, no one, to be found by his conscience. There was only, behind his eyes, a wondrous intoxication and feeling of irresponsibility.

He sat blinking at Denise, her tangle of short black hair against the pillows, her beckoning green eyes and long white arms, one bulge of the lacy white brassiere entirely exposed by the fully opened front of her silk blouse, her thin short skirt caught on the edge of the divan drawn high to reveal the curve of her ample thighs. It was breathlessly wanton, and he wanted it. Senselessness rejecting sense, he wanted it now and completely.

He turned, reaching for tantalizing arms, and fell backward beside her in the pillows, embracing her, as her arms slid around him, drawing him against her, pressing him into her wriggling body.

"Denise," he whispered, "we shouldn't," but his hand did not stop at her buttocks but moved around to the skirt drawn even higher until he touched the flesh of her thigh.

Her tongue kissed his ear. "Foolish big boy. Your talk is *américain,* but your hands are French." She groaned, and her head fell back, and she groaned again. He put his lips to her throat, and her back arched and her breasts swelled against him. "Good, good, good," she cried.

Suddenly her hand groped for his below, gripped it, and pulled it away. She tried to sit up, and finally she succeeded. She sat, eyes tightly shut, breathing hard.

Brennan was beside her, arm around her. "What is it, darling?"

"It is all right, everything is fine. We will make beautiful love. But not here. Only in bed. Your baby makes love only in bed. First I must go to the bathroom to put in the—" She offered him her back. "Help me undress, big boy."

Drunkenly Brennan sought for buttons. There were none. There was a knot at the waistline of the blouse. He picked at the knot and undid it, and the blouse fell apart in front. She began squirming out of it, and he pulled it off.

"The brassiere," she said.

Enjoying the sight of her broad shoulders and smooth back, he unhooked the brassiere. It dropped to her lap, and she tossed it aside.

567

She leaped to her feet and whirled about to face him, boldly cupping the undersides of her great naked breasts in her hands. "You will love me all night?"

"Denise—"

He reached to caress her breasts, but quickly she covered the hardened brown nipples. "Not yet, not so fast, big boy, unless you have—" She cocked her head. "You have *les préservatifs?*"

"*Les pré*—oh—no, I don't, I don't have any."

"Then I must be the one to take care. My purse. Hand me the purse."

The liquor was high in his head now, and his blurring eyes searched for the purse. He yanked it off the end table beside the divan, and she took it from him. Quickly she opened it, removed the white plastic case inside, then returned the open purse to him.

"Where is the bathroom?" she inquired.

Brennan stumbled to his feet and signaled her to follow. They went into the bedroom, and he pointed to the vestibule and bathroom beyond it. Gravely she thanked him, laughingly evaded his effort to kiss her, and started for the vestibule.

About to enter it, she turned and indicated her purse, which Brennan still held in his hand. "It's in there," she said.

"What?"

"Your friend Peet's hotel," she said. "Tonight he sent me a letter with also his spare hotel room key to use when I would come to him. The hotel name is on the disk. You can keep the key. Give it back to Peet when you see him. After tonight I will not want to see him again, will I?" She smiled. "I will have you, won't I?"

"Yes," he said drunkenly.

She began to unbutton her skirt. "In five minutes, big boy."

As she disappeared into the vestibule, he stared at the open leather purse. When he heard the bathroom door close, he sank down on the bed, ignoring its tremulous squeak, and clumsily riffled through the contents of the purse. He found the iron key and took it out, hypnotized by what was on the dangling key ring. He held the disk in his hand. It read: HOTEL CONTINENTAL, 3, RUE CASTIGLIONE, CHAMBRE 55, ETAGE I.

Joe Peet, at last.

Another door was opened distantly, and then it slammed shut hard. Brennan sat upright. It was the corridor door to Lisa's room. He could hear her tread, and he realized that he was facing the two doors that connected their adjoining bedrooms. He leaped off his brass bed, wincing at its second prolonged squeak, and staggered forward to see if

568

his side of the door was locked. He found it exactly as he had left it earlier for the maids, bolted fast. Pressing his ear against the double partition, he listened. The muffled noises were more eloquent than an outraged wife's temper: Lisa was banging angrily about her bedroom.

At once, all sexual desire for Denise Averil evaporated.

Yet he was trapped. Any minute, Denise would appear, nude and passionate. He would have to undress. There would be the duet, Denise's moaning endearments and the bedstead's shuddering complaints, and this entire spectacle before a stadium of Lisa's. There was no way to avoid the obligatory performance. He weighed the key to Joe Peet in his hand. He had been paid in advance. He had never broken a contract yet.

Brennan tried to console himself with fatalism. What is to be, will be. Besides, he had lost Lisa already. One could not lose something one did not possess.

Dreading what lay immediately ahead, not only because of Lisa on the other side of the doors but because of his own temporary impotence, he determined to deaden his fear with more liquor.

As he started for the sitting room, he heard the telephone beside the divan ring loudly. He rushed to it, wishing only to muffle its shrill intrusion, but the instant his hand touched the receiver, he hesitated. It was probably Lisa calling from the next room. He could not suffer her fury and hurt. Yet never could he leave a telephone ring unanswered.

He picked up the receiver, acknowledged his name, and then realized that the feminine voice on the line did not belong to Lisa Collins. It belonged to Medora Hart, and it was frantic.

"Matt, I'm in a terrible stew. I need help desperately."

Brennan was instantly alert. "What's the trouble, Medora?"

"Willi von Goerlitz," she gasped through the telephone receiver. "Thank the Lord you're already there. I poured a gallon of black coffee into Willi, got him on his feet, walked him up and down the Champs-Élysées for some air. But when I tried to get him into a taxi, he refused to go. He absolutely insisted he wouldn't sleep without seeing Carol first. I kept arguing that he was in no condition to see anyone, least of all Carol. I warned him that if Carol saw him this way, certainly if President Earnshaw saw him, he could expect to be cut by them forever. But you know how impossibly stubborn a drunk can be. So, to pacify him, I began to lead him toward the Lancaster, then I decided I'd better sober him a bit more. Finally, when we reached the Val d'Isère—you know, the outdoorsy restaurant across from Carol's hotel—I managed to sweet-talk Willi into it for more black coffee. He didn't resist, and I daresay he was beginning to be grateful. Well, Matt, when Willi started sobering ever so slightly, he began blabbing about his father, spilled the whole frightful thing, and I must say I can hardly blame him for becoming stoned. It's a bloody business, poor fellow."

"What are you talking about, Medora?" demanded Brennan. "What about Willi's father?"

"He's had a stroke," said Medora, voice quavering. "Old Goerlitz keeled over in the Ritz late this morning. Worst part, it had to be kept secret. The company director—Schlager, I think he's called—clapped secrecy on the whole thing and ordered Willi not to speak a word of it. Something to do with not affecting the international market and needing time to reorganize management at the plant while they waited to see how seriously ill Dr. von Goerlitz was. So poor Willi and this Schlager, they got the management of the Hotel Ritz to co-operate. Arranged for a private ambulance, some sort of little-used exit, and whisked old Goerlitz out and off to the American Hospital in Neuilly, where he's registered under another name."

"What shape is Goerlitz in?" Brennan asked.

"Critical, I'm afraid. In a coma, and according to Willi, it's nip and tuck tonight. Willi's been at the hospital two or three times, but Schlager won't let him stay, afraid that in his upset he might let out who the old man really is, what with the press checking there all the time for celebrated patients."

"I see. That's awful. And now Willi wants to get to Carol Earnshaw?"

"Yes. To explain why he was so rude and had to lie to Carol's uncle this afternoon. He's frenzied about helping his father, but he doesn't have much of anyone here, so he's rather set about explaining things and holding on to Carol."

Trying to think, Brennan realized that he was nodding to himself. "Yes, I can understand," he said into the telephone. "Have you still got Willi with you?"

"In the Val d'Isère, yes, down the block from you. I've got my eye on him right now. He's still taking coffee, but he's only half sober, and I don't know what to do, Matt. We've just had a frightful row. I want him to go back to his hotel to sleep it off. There's enough time for Carol Earnshaw later. But no, he won't budge. He's absolutely determined to go up to the Earnshaw suite under his own power and clear the misunderstanding up. But, crikey, how can I let him break in on a—a former President? And especially at this hour?"

"The time doesn't matter nor does it matter who Earnshaw is or was," said Brennan quickly. "Willi's right, Medora. Earnshaw should be informed of this development. Carol is secondary. But Earnshaw—you don't know the complete facts, Medora, but there might be more ramifications to this than meet the eye. Quite definitely, Willi should be allowed to see Earnshaw."

"I'm sorry to have disturbed you. But I had no idea what to—"

"No, no, you did the right thing."

"Well, I'll just continue nannying Willi until he's perfectly sober, and then—"

"You can't wait for that," said Brennan with impatience. "Earnshaw should know about this immediately. He's one of the few people who might be able to do something for Goerlitz. Does Goerlitz have his own physician with him?"

"No. That's another problem. Willi was in a frenzy because his father's doctor—in fact, his father's three doctors—are off in China somewhere on some kind of official inspection tour. They can't be reached until tomorrow. And that may be too late. And Schlager's afraid of calling in any French specialist, because the case history would have to be sent for and Goerlitz's identity would leak out. Oh, they have doctors, but they need—"

"Medora, that makes it more imperative than ever that Willi see Earnshaw about this at once."

"Right now?" Medora sounded distressed. "Matt, I can't manage him. I'm afraid I'll need your help. Can you—"

The creak of the bathroom door diverted Brennan's concentration from the telephone. He heard footsteps, and suddenly he remembered his guest and bed partner.

"—come right over?" Medora was pleading. "I can't manage without you. Will you?"

"Of course—of course I will—there's only one problem. I—" He had no idea how to explain it.

"What's the matter, Matt? Are you in the middle of something?"

He lowered his voice as the footsteps came nearer. "Denise is with me," he said desperately.

"Denise?" exclaimed Medora. She seemed to understand. "Jesus, I'm sorry, Matt."

A purring sound brought Brennan's attention from the telephone to the bedroom doorway. Holding the receiver, he came fully around. Denise Averil was leaning lazily against the door frame, whispering, "Naughty boy, look at me, and look at you."

He could not help but stare at her with amazement. Except for the narrowest strip of white lace panties, Denise was stark naked, and as easy and reposeful as only one more used to nudity than to clothes can be. He had never seen, so intimately, so infinite an expanse of bare feminine flesh. Denise's long arms reached out over the milky mounds of her deep cone-shaped breasts, and her fingers wiggled, silently beckoning him.

With his free ear Brennan thought that he could hear Lisa kicking over a piece of furniture in her locked bedroom. With his telephone ear Brennan could hear Medora saying, "You really mean Denise is there?"

"She's not only here," Brennan gasped into the telephone, "she is *all* here. Look, Medora, you'd better speak to her—explain for me—and—I'll be right over to help you." He leaped up, proffering the telephone receiver to Denise. "Medora wants a word with you. Absolutely urgent."

Puzzled, Denise left the doorway and advanced in her feline walk. Nervously Brennan waited, holding the phone as far from him as possible, as if it were some device that would ward off the temptation of mortal sin. Waiting, he could not help but marvel at her naked poise. He shoved the instrument into her hand and hurried to the wardrobe.

Observing him with bewilderment, Denise brought the mouthpiece to her lips. "Hello, Medora, what's all the—?" She stopped short. Brennan had snatched down his coat and tie, and was heading for the corridor door. "Hey, wait a minute, big boy!" Denise shouted across the mouthpiece. "Where in the hell do you think you're going?"

Hand safely on the door handle, he called over his shoulder, "Medora will explain. Forgive me. I've got to run. It's an emergency."

Before slamming the door behind him, Brennan could hear Denise's shrill epithet for him after the ignominious episode. It was directed to the telephone. "Dammit, Medora, what in the hell kind of friends do you send me? Another *femmelette!* Spelled *fag,* to you!"

STANDING THERE in a shadowed corner of Earnshaw's suite in the Hotel Lancaster, Matt Brennan could sense the air of tension in the room.

Medora Hart was at the windows, less confused, smoking cigarettes ceaselessly, not peering outside at the darkened roofs of Paris but gazing steadily across the sitting room at Earnshaw. On the sofa, Carol, in shirt and jeans, her hair still in curlers, sat beside Willi von Goerlitz, still pale but now cold sober, as both of them anxiously stared at Earnshaw.

Now Brennan looked at Earnshaw, too.

The former President, wide-awake, jaw set, remained on his feet, rigidly keeping the telephone receiver to his ear.

Not twenty minutes ago, Brennan and Medora had half carried, half dragged Willi von Goerlitz to the door of this seventh-floor suite, had brought Carol on the run from her hair dryer, roused a sleep-dazed Earnshaw from his bed, and had explained their mission. First Brennan had spoken, next Medora, but finally it had been Willi who had found the sobriety and strength to take over.

When Willi had finished, he had lamely added his apologetic postscript. "Perhaps you can understand, Mr. Earnshaw, my behavior to you this afternoon. I am sorry to have offended you."

"You just forget about me," Earnshaw had retorted crisply. "Your father's our only concern. . . . It's a doctor we want, a cardiovascular surgeon. Well, with any luck, we might be able to borrow one of the best ones in the world. He's right here in Paris with the United States delegation. Admiral Oates, the White House physician, was a vascular specialist at Bethesda Naval Hospital. He's served four Presidents, including the incumbent and me. I'm going to try to locate him. I can't promise anything after I do, but let's find out."

And then Earnshaw had gone to the telephone and made two calls, and this was his third, to the United States Ambassador's residence, where not only the President was staying but his physician as well.

Suddenly Earnshaw pressed the telephone to his ear. "Yes, I'm still on." He listened, frowning, and he barked back, "Well now, young fellow, I don't care if he has just gone to sleep. You go right in there and you wake Admiral Oates and you tell him Emmett A. Earnshaw is on the phone waiting to talk to him. You tell the Admiral it's mighty important."

Snorting, he changed the receiver to his other ear and stood tapping one slippered foot on the carpet impatiently.

"Uncle Emmett," Carol called from the sofa, "let me get you a brandy."

"I don't want brandy," Earnshaw growled. "I want the Admiral."

He glared down at the mouthpiece, and paced in a tight circle. Abruptly he halted.

"Admiral Oates? Earnshaw here. Sorry to shake you out of bed at this ungodly hour. You know I wouldn't bother you if it wasn't important. . . . No, no, Admiral, I'm perfectly fine. Just darn irritated by all the snarl of red tape. Now listen to me. You remember Dr. Dietrich von Goerlitz, don't you? You were there with me in Frankfurt when—" He paused. "That's the man, Admiral, that's the one. Well,

I'm right here in the Lancaster Hotel where I'm staying, and I've got Goerlitz's son here beside me. I've been doing some business with Goerlitz, but he had a stroke this morning. . . . Yes, you heard me, a stroke, a cerebro-vascular accident. It's all been kept hushed up, for various reasons, but they've got him over to Neuilly, the American Hospital, registered under some phony name—name of—uh—" He looked off. "What was it again, Willi?"

"Goessler, sir. Hans Goessler."

Earnshaw was back at the phone. "You hear that, Admiral? He's registered as Hans Goessler. His own physicians are off somewhere in the Far East. Haven't been reached yet. His plant director, fellow named Schlager, is getting his medical history and treatment record down from Frankfurt, but he won't show it to the French doctors. They need somebody in on the case they can trust, the best man available, and I thought of you. . . . What? What do you mean—what's this got to do with us, our Government? It could have plenty to do, and you're going to have to take my word for it. No need to go into that, just take my word for it, Admiral. . . . Okay, okay, I knew you'd go along. When you've played poker with a man, you get to know what he will do and won't do, right? . . . No, I don't have any information about that. Hold on a second." Earnshaw consulted Willi von Goerlitz once more. "Willi, the Admiral wants to know if the French doctors mentioned how serious it was and if they talked about surgery."

"They said it is extremely critical, sir. They do not know if he will survive tonight. My father is half paralyzed, has suffered a loss of speech—and the last few hours he has been in a coma—from an obstruction in the innominate and left common carotid artery. I believe they said the clot has been located between the artery and the heart. They must operate, but they are afraid because of my father's weak heart. The hospital says they have heart pumps, but not one that can be implanted in a patient's chest. One or two of the new types are available in Europe but they do not possess one here. I must give permission for surgery tonight, but I cannot with so little hope."

Earnshaw had been holding the receiver out toward Willi. Now he brought it back to his mouth. "You hear that, Admiral? . . . Yes, yes . . . yes, I guess you'd better. I sure appreciate it. I'll be right here waiting."

He hung up, glanced at the others, and finally addressed Willi. "Admiral Oates is phoning the American Hospital. He'll speak to their staff and learn exactly what your father's condition is. If it's necessary, he'll act. In any event, Willi, you've got your father a doctor, the very best, the President's own."

574

Willi von Goerlitz was close to tears. "I cannot tell you what this means to me. I thank you, sir, with deepest sincerity."

Moved, Earnshaw said gruffly, "Don't go thanking anyone yet, least of all me. I've got my own selfish reasons for pitching in. Not what you think. But your father and I, we were friends once. When he got in trouble, I let him down. That's still on my conscience. I don't intend to let him down a second time." He looked around. "Anyone want a drink?"

Brennan considered holding up his hand. But he thought better of it.

Earnshaw roamed the room restlessly. "Where're those darn cigars?"

Carol started to rise. "I'll get you one."

"Just tell me," Earnshaw insisted.

"The new humidor I bought you, remember? On the dresser in the bedroom."

"I forgot," said Earnshaw. He stared at the telephone. "What's keeping the Navy? He said he'd call right back."

Brennan watched Earnshaw leave the sitting room. He saw Carol pouring a soft drink for Willi. His mouth felt dry, and he said, "Carol, if you have enough, I could stand a sip."

He accepted his soft drink as Earnshaw returned, smoking a cigar. Brennan had just brought the sparkling glass to his lips when the telephone rang out. In three long strides Earnshaw was beside it.

"Hello," he said into the mouthpiece. "Well, what is it, Admiral? . . . Yes, yes, go on." He listened, for what seemed to Brennan an interminable time. Once he interrupted. "What was that, Admiral? Did you say a bypass graft operation? Is that the surgical technique?" He was listening at length again. At last he spoke. "Yes, I think it's clear, Admiral. Chest incision between the ribs. Artery graft to bypass the extensive obstruction. Is that right? . . . Yes, but if it's that routine, then what are you worried about? . . . Oh, I see, I see. . . . Yes, I understand. The regular heart pumps on hand won't do. But what about that implantable device you always had flown around after me? The Garrett-Farelli artificial heart. Don't you have one of those with you? . . . You do? And a newer one, you say? Well, wouldn't that pull him through? . . . Okay. At least those are reasonable odds. All right, then, go ahead, use it."

He listened, and gradually his face began to knot with anger. "Wait a minute, Oates!" he interrupted. "What in the devil you saying—you can't use it? The hell with the President's permission. We're not waiting until morning, Admiral. I've given you plenty of orders when I was your Commander in Chief, and I'm giving you one more right now. I want you to call Orly and get that Garrett-Farelli device over to Neuilly on the double. I want it there for Goerlitz immediately. That's my decision, and I'm taking full responsibility for it. What do you say to that?" He listened, and suddenly his face broke into a broad boyish grin. "Thanks, Admiral. I knew it. When all's lost, you can count on the Navy. . . . Okay, friend, see you there in an hour."

Brennan came forward, as did Willi, Carol, and Medora, when Earnshaw turned away from the telephone.

Earnshaw smiled at them. "Admiral Oates is on his way to the American Hospital. So is that new heart contraption." Earnshaw brushed past the others to Willi von Goerlitz and placed a hand on his shoulder. "Willi, your father goes into emergency surgery in an hour. At his age, it's going to be rough, and you've got to face that. But maybe this'll comfort you. A little while ago, the odds were ten to one against his surviving. Right now, with Admiral Oates and that latest cardiac pump, the odds are down to two to one against him. He's got a solid outside chance."

"Whatever happens, I will never forget what you have done," said Willi.

Earnshaw snorted. "What have I done? Played President again for a few minutes back there? Well, I tell you, I only did what comes"—he paused and grinned—"unnaturally. And you know what? It felt good, felt darn good for a change. . . . Now give me a jiffy to dress, and we'll get out to that hospital."

With a determined step, Earnshaw left the room.

Seeing him thus, Brennan wanted to rub his eyes. To himself he made a silent vow to think twice before ever again referring to Emmett A. Earnshaw as The Ex.

LONG AFTER MIDNIGHT they still kept the death watch.

There was no sound in the spacious, rectangular waiting room of the American Hospital in Neuilly except the regular ticking of the tall grandfather clock in the far corner.

Slumped in a green leather *fauteuil,* Matt Brennan puffed steadily at his pipe, hypnotized by the hands of the grandfather clock, knowing that the surgery must be in its crucial phase and almost finished. At last he inspected the others in the waiting room, to judge whether they knew that the operation had probably reached its climactic point and to judge also their degrees of anxiety.

Medora Hart, legs crossed, was seated on the maroon leather sofa between the clock and the television set, leafing through the pages of

Paris Match. While she had been the catalyst of the death watch, she now appeared the bewildered interloper, the distant relative who had arrived in town to meet the family at an unexpected moment of grave crisis. In the very center of the room, holding on to the arms of his chair, waited the heir, Willi von Goerlitz, staring down at the asparagus fern set on the long, glass-sheeted table. At a small desk nearby, Carol Earnshaw, resembling a youthful Dutch girl in her bulky coat, huddled nervously, continually casting glances at Willi. She rose as if to go to him, but seeming to think better of it, she turned to the prominent marble bust atop a column with the lettering JOHN H. HARJES, FOUNDER AND FIRST PRESIDENT OF THE AMERICAN HOSPITAL.

There were the four of them, and only the fifth and sixth members of their party were missing. Emmett A. Earnshaw had drifted out into the corridor to join Herr Schlager, and with him find someone connected with the surgery who could provide an interim report on the progress of the operation and the condition of Dr. Dietrich von Goerlitz.

Reaching toward the ashtray before him, Brennan knocked the bowl of his pipe against the heel of his hand, emptying it of ashes. Filling the pipe once more, he looked off through the wall composed entirely of French doors that revealed a terrace. It was too dark to see beyond the terrace, but Brennan was reminded that in another time, when he and Stefani had brought young Ted here for diagnosis of a persistent fever, he had stood by in this very room and from the doors had seen, below the terrace, a lovely garden. It reminded him that tonight he could not see the garden, and that while his son had survived the fever, the boy had not survived for his father. Nor had Stefani. The loss of the boy had been, for himself, a true bereavement, even if the second loss had not. And now there was a third. There was the fresh loss of Lisa Collins over the evening's drunken nonsense, but then he rationalized that the loss would have occurred anyway.

Life had become mathematical, a game of subtraction. Without Lisa, there could be no reborn Brennan. Without Rostov, there could be no Lisa. Without Earnshaw, there could be no Rostov. Without Goerlitz, there could be no Earnshaw. Without Admiral Oates, and a miracle, there could be no Goerlitz, and—full circle—no Brennan.

He had not allowed his mind to contemplate his own immediate future if Goerlitz did not survive the surgery. Such selfish concern seemed indecent, like worrying about tomorrow's dental appointment while attending a friend's funeral. Nevertheless, the concern hovered gloomily behind his frontal lobes. If Goerlitz died, the lever that Brennan had given Earnshaw would be useless, and if it were useless,

Earnshaw would probably have no more interest in lingering about Paris merely to intervene with the President on Brennan's behalf.

The waiting-room door opened, and he saw everyone's face turn toward it, and he turned, too.

A bemused Earnshaw had come back to the waiting room, closely followed by Herr Schlager, who resembled a bantam Hindenburg trying to make sense out of the Reichstag fire.

Earnshaw had gone to Willi, who had leaped to his feet. "Well, young man, we couldn't find out much, of course. There's a whole team in there working with Oates, the best people available, we were told. We managed to lay our hands on a French intern who was leaving the surgery, and Mr. Schlager here spoke to him in French, and as I gather it, the operation is going as well as can be expected."

Willi looked inquiringly at Schlager. *"Herr Direktor,* is there hope?"

"Hope, of course, always hope," said Schlager with a show of his old ebullience as he patted Willi on the back. "Your father is a strong man always. The carotid, one of Dr. Dietrich's arteries, has an extensive clot formation. But they have reached the obstructions. They have made an incision between the chest ribs, and because the troubled area is long, they are now inserting an artery graft to bypass the bad area. It is my understanding this is not unusual."

"Then it is successful so far?"

"Yes—" said Schlager, but he could not disguise his uncertainty.

Willi swung toward Earnshaw. "Is it, Mr. Earnshaw? I want the truth. I am no child."

"Uh—yes, yes, Willi, we have nothing to keep from you," said Earnshaw. "Apparently the operation is going along smoothly. The only problem—well, now—uh—I know you are aware of your father's cardiac condition—there is some, well, concern whether his heart can hold up—"

"But the pump, the special machine, is it not here?"

Earnshaw exhaled loudly. "Yes, but not every patient reacts to its implantation in the same way." He shrugged. "There is nothing to do but put our complete faith in the Admiral's hands and in God's will."

The young man nodded. "Yes, Mr. Earnshaw."

"It won't be much longer," Earnshaw promised. "Ten or fifteen, maybe twenty minutes. I have the Admiral's word he'll report to us directly the second it's over. Okay?"

"Yes, Mr. Earnshaw, thank you."

The former President glanced absently around the waiting room, smiled at Carol, and found a cigar in his breast pocket. "I think the best thing for all of us is to keep ourselves distracted until we have the result. Simon Madlock used to—well, matter of fact, I've always said—speculation is as senseless as trying to locate Heaven or Hell, since you're going to find out for yourself soon enough anyway. Let's wait for results." He clamped his cigar between his teeth, permitted Schlager to light it, nodded his thanks, and looked about aimlessly. He became aware of Brennan. "Oh, Matt, by the way—"

Brennan advanced to join Earnshaw, Willi, and Schlager.

"—I wanted to tell you," Earnshaw continued, "I had a little talk with Herr Schlager while we were tramping around the corridors. I thought I'd better inform him of what I was going to tell Dietrich when I dropped by the Ritz this afternoon. I must say, Herr Schlager was pretty stunned."

"Unbelievable," Schlager muttered. "It is impossible to imagine the dishonoring of such a contract. The People's Republic of China has always been one of our best customers. They have always been trustworthy. I cannot see why they would—how do your television gangsters say?—double-cross—why they would double-cross Goerlitz Industriebau now. They have needed us before. They will need us in the future."

"Not necessarily, Mr. Schlager," said Brennan, "not if they have Russians to replace you."

"Russians!" the German director exclaimed. "Impossible. For years the Russians and Chinese are not friends—"

"Friends who have fallen out have been known to make up again," Brennan reminded him.

"In business, yes—" admitted Schlager.

"In politics, too," said Brennan. "For you, the Nuclear Peace City may be purely business. For your customers, it may also be politics."

Earnshaw intervened. "Matt, I've told Herr Schlager you were the source of this secret piece of information. Maybe he'd find it more acceptable if he got it directly from you. Also—" Earnshaw reached back, took Willi by the arm, and brought him closer into the group. "Also, come what may, I think Willi here should know what's going on. Have you got a mind for this right now, Willi?"

"I—I do not know."

"Your father was in Paris to sign contracts with the Chinese Government to build that nuclear complex for them. Now Matt Brennan has learned a little secret, that the Chinese were going to let your father spend all those millions of dollars or marks constructing the nuclear reactors and the workers' community. Then, when the time was right for them, the Chinese intended to default on payments, nationalize the plants and city, confiscate the equipment, throw your personnel out, and bring in Russian engineers and physicists to help manage it with them. Your father knew nothing of this. That's what I was coming in to tell him today—or yesterday—whatever time it was—because once warned, he could've been fully prepared for anything." Earnshaw gestured at Brennan. "Run through it, Matt. Let them hear it from the horse's mouth."

Urgently Brennan began to recount the story of Lisa's adventure. His audience hung on every word until the very end. As he concluded, Brennan tried to assess their reactions. But suddenly he was aware that all eyes were focused on the entrance to the waiting room. He glanced over his shoulder.

An elderly physician, wearing green surgical cap and gown, and with the aspect of a dour Scot, stood inside the door.

"Admiral Oates," Earnshaw called out.

Oates limped forward, washing dry hands. His wrinkled countenance showed neither victory nor defeat.

"Which one is the young man?" rasped Admiral Oates.

"This is Willi von Goerlitz," said Earnshaw, pulling Willi toward the White House physician.

Admiral Oates bothered about no formalities. "The surgery was a success," he announced curtly. "We performed an end-to-side bypass graft. We used a synthetic arterial graft, diverted blood around the obstructed passage, and completely restored brain circulation. I won't deny there was one bad moment, as we implanted the Garrett-Farelli artificial heart at the beginning. But the patient's heart action soon stabilized, and remained constant and strong to the completion of the surgery. Dr. von Goerlitz has just been wheeled into the intensive care ward." Admiral Oates put out his bony hand. "I am pleased to bring you this news, young fellow."

Willi gripped the physician's hand fervently. "I thank you. I thank you more than I can explain with words. I would do anything on earth to repay you."

"Never mind about that," said Oates sourly. "Just send a case of good German bock over to the Ambassador's residence and we'll call it square."

"Done!" exclaimed Schlager, elatedly pounding Willi's back. "Willi, your father made it! I knew he would make it!"

"Admiral Oates," Willi was saying, "when can I see him?"

"In due time, in due time," said Oates. "Perhaps later in the morning. More likely, in the afternoon. Where can I reach you? The Ritz? I'll be in touch with you there."

Carol had edged into the circle. "Willi, I—I'm so happy for you."

He nodded dumbly, but was smiling.

"Admiral." It was Schlager holding up a chubby hand. "How long do you anticipate Dr. von Goerlitz must be hospitalized?"

Oates pursed his lips. "Ah, yes, I was about to get to that. He will have to be kept in the intensive care ward for at least a week. After that, well, I hesitate to predict. I am certain you understand the variability in the postoperative conditions of patients who have suffered a CVA or stroke. A stroke can take a great toll, especially in a man Dr. von Goerlitz's age. Right now, of course, once he regains consciousness he might find either side partially paralyzed, his speech impaired, his vision blurred. Under these particular conditions, rehabilitation would be lengthy. As soon as feasible, Dr. von Goerlitz would be moved to his home or a rehabilitation center, and be provided with physical therapy to prevent the atrophy of the affected muscles, to restore his speech as much as possible, to put him on his feet, so to speak."

"How long before he can communicate with us?" inquired Schlager anxiously.

"It could take time."

"You mean even months?" asked Schlager.

"Sometimes years, but again progress may be surprisingly rapid," said Admiral Oates. "In any event, barring complications, he should be on the road to recovery soon. He certainly needn't be a paralytic. At the same time, I won't promise that you can depend upon his being the active businessman again. Well, if you'll excuse me, I'd better return to my patient."

As Oates turned to go, Earnshaw caught his arm. He handed the physician a cigar. "On me, Admiral."

"I was waiting for you to offer me one," Oates growled, and with that he limped hastily from the waiting room.

The death watch was ended, and yet, Brennan sensed, the business of the evening was not.

Willi had gone off to one side with Carol when Schlager summoned him back.

"Willi," the director of Goerlitz industries said, "tomorrow morning at ten o'clock is the long-prepared-for meeting at the Chinese Embassy to sign the contracts with Marshal Chen and Economics Minister Liang for the Nuclear Peace City. With your father disabled, you are now in charge of the industries. You must attend in his place."

Willi recoiled. "How can I? What do I know of this complicated matter?"

"Almost enough," said Schlager sternly. "You will know enough. Besides, I shall be there with you, and the attorneys will be in from Frankfurt to join with us."

Willi gestured at Earnshaw and Brennan as he spoke to Schlager. "You heard what they said about the real intentions of Marshal Chen. Don't you believe it?"

"It may be true," Schlager conceded, "quite possibly true. We can proceed with caution, feel them out. But if this rumor is untrue, if we believe the Chinese act in good faith as always, we dare not miss the opportunity. We have too many competitors eager to replace us. We must try, and you must be with us, Willi, available to sign."

Willi shook his head adamantly. "No, I do not like it. I'd rather cancel or postpone the meeting for a while—"

Earnshaw interrupted, "May I have a word? Willi, as I see it, Herr Schlager is right about one thing. It would be a mistake not to meet with the Red Chinese while they are here in Paris at the same time you are here. This is no time for evasions and indecisions. This is a time to act, an opportunity that comes only once. You must meet with them, Willi, but I would suggest for a reason different from the one Herr Schlager gives you. Not merely to take advantage of a big deal, if it's really there. No. The real reason you should go ahead is because for once you can confront the Chinese with truth—assuming this is the truth, and I believe it is—rock them with it, throw them off balance by exposing to them your knowledge of their secret intentions. In fact, this may serve to thwart inflammatory political activities in the future."

"A risky business," said Schlager.

"Life is a risky business," said Earnshaw. "Listen, Willi, you level with them, and they'll respect you more for it. You can't afford a deal that's one-sided, their-sided. At the same time, you want them for a customer, if they can be trusted. Okay. You lay it on the line with them, and either they get mad and throw you out—which is just as well, because it proves they meant to cheat—or they decide it's worth their while to be honest, and you find a compromise, a way of keeping the deal alive without your being hurt. Whatever happens, you should be there to let it happen, my son."

Willi had been listening with respect. "Mr. Earnshaw, maybe you are right, but I am not capable of handling such a situation. My father could do it brilliantly. But I have no such experience. Perhaps the business part, with our *Herr Direktor,* with the attorneys—I could manage that. But the other part—accusing them yet not accusing them so they suffer no loss of face, the diplomatic and political part—that I cannot do and Herr Schlager cannot do. It needs someone like my father, with his tactical skill."

Throughout the exchange Brennan had been listening carefully, studying the three speakers, studying Earnshaw most of all. His mind was made up. "Willi," he said, "allow me to make a suggestion."

They turned to Brennan, waiting.

"You're worried that neither you nor Mr. Schlager can treat diplomatically with the Red Chinese. Am I correct? You require someone with the skill your father possesses in this area." Brennan paused. "You have such a person who, I am sure, would be pleased to assist you. I'm referring to our former United States President, Mr. Earnshaw."

Willi blinked at Brennan, glanced at Earnshaw, then looked back at Brennan. He seemed hesitant and uncomfortable. "Why—maybe—I—I don't know," he stammered.

An understanding smile had crossed Earnshaw's face. In a kindly tone he said to Willi, "Of course you don't know, young man. Matt is right in two respects. I'd be glad to pitch in. I'd feel confident of my experience. But you don't know about me, and—let's be frank tonight —you have every reason not to be sure about me. You've read what your father has written about me in his memoirs, and you have cause to doubt my value to—"

"No, no, Mr. Earnshaw," Willi interrupted. "I have no such—"

"Let me finish, Willi. In part, your father's low opinion of my record is justified. I can see that now. But once something is made clear to a person, well, if he has any intelligence, he's better off for it." Earnshaw's smile disappeared. "I assure you, young man, I'm ready to make up for a good deal of lost ground. In fact, I'm eager to do so. I didn't do too well with our Chinese friends when I had the chance, some years ago. I suspect I might do better with them today. I'd like nothing more than to try, not only for you but for myself. Anyway, I won't blame you for saying no—"

"But yes, Mr. Earnshaw!" Willi exclaimed with excitement. "I want you with me. We will only have the meeting if you are there to counsel us. It is the only way."

Earnshaw grinned. "Thank you, Willi." He turned to Schlager. "Here's what you'd better do. Call Marshal Chen, advise him about Dr. von Goerlitz, but tell him you're going ahead with the meeting anyway. Don't mention me. But get Chen to change the time of the meeting from ten in the morning until—let's say—three in the afternoon. That'll give you plenty of time to brief me, and give us time to map out our battle plan. As a matter of fact, I just had a notion—"

583

The three of them were deep in strategy as Brennan moved away and finally gravitated toward Carol and Medora Hart, who were drowsily sitting on the leather sofa. Informing them that he was going back to Paris for some needed sleep, Brennan added that he would be delighted to drop both or either of them off at their hotels. Carol chose to remain. But Medora tiredly accepted his offer.

After making their farewells, and receiving Willi's deep thanks, Brennan and Medora left the American Hospital. They strolled in silence down the steep incline of the driveway that led from the hospital entrance to the stone arch that would bring them into the cobbled Boulevard Victor-Hugo.

As they continued in the darkness, Medora sighed. "What a long peculiar night it's been. I'm pleased it came off so successfully."

Brennan screwed up his face. "Not all of it came off so well, Medora. You win a little, you lose a little. I'm afraid this evening cost me my girl friend."

"What ever do you mean?"

Briefly Brennan explained his relationship with Lisa Collins, and related details of the awful moment when Lisa had seen him going up to his rooms with Denise Averil.

"But, Matt, surely Lisa trusts you. I mean, you only have to tell her what really happened."

"I'd tell her if she'd listen. But I doubt if she will. And if she did, it's unlikely she'll believe me."

"But she will listen to me," said Medora simply, "and she'll believe me. She has to. I got you mixed up with Denise. Now it's only proper I get you unmixed. I'll get hold of your Lisa tomorrow."

"Will you?"

"The very first thing. I *owe* it to you. That wretched Denise. Behaving the way she did."

They had arrived at the street at the bottom of the hospital driveway, and a taxi was parked at the nearby stand.

Brennan had opened the rear door for Medora when suddenly she turned to him. "I almost forgot how it all began. Did Denise at least give you the name of Joe Peet's hotel?"

Brennan took the metal disk with its attached key from his pocket and swung it victoriously. "Hotel Continental," he said.

"Are you going to see Peet?"

"If he'll see me."

"And if he won't?"

He flipped the key into the air and caught it. "Maybe I'll see him anyway."

584

He followed Medora into the taxi, and as he pocketed the key, it occurred to him that it might unlock a door to something that would provide him with the necessary bribe to bring Nikolai Rostov, in haste, to him.

In the upstairs bedroom of the apartment in the Rue de Téhéran, unlighted except for one small lamp, Hazel Smith threw aside her negligee, lifted the flimsy special-occasion nightgown over her head and discarded it, and quickly crawled into bed, pulling the blanket up to her shoulders.

At this hour between midnight and dawn, when it was pitch-black outside the window, the stillness was eerie. It was a time when she usually fled from the loneliness of night into the canyon of sleep, which was populated only by unreal dreams. But now, lying beneath the covers, on her back, she was wide-awake.

The sound of water splashing in the basin beyond the bathroom door unnerved her. Rostov was bringing life to his vodka-numbed face before undressing.

Hazel shifted uneasily beneath the blanket, trying to find comfort in the bed. But she knew that there could be no comfort. Every muscle of her naked body was taut with dread. Yet the quality of dread that all but paralyzed her in these suspenseful minutes before revelation was markedly different from the panic that she had felt before Nikolai Rostov's arrival.

Yesterday, at the Jardin, he had promised to come to her around nine o'clock for a relaxed evening and night of pleasure, one such as they had known in and about Moscow for so many years. She had done her hair, put on her most enticing dress, arranged the plate of his favorite caviar and crackers, filled the ice bucket, opened the vodka bottle, and waited. Twice he had telephoned, hurriedly, cryptically, the first time to say that he would be a little late, the second time to say that he was still tied up at the Russian Embassy but would definitely be with her before midnight.

For Hazel, the delay had made the evening hours endless. She had wanted him here and wanted it over with, but when at last she had heard his approach, the unmistakable clump of his thick square shoes, she had wished that he had not been able to come at all. And she had agonized in her first cramp of dread.

As she went to greet him, at twenty minutes to twelve, the fear she had felt was the unutterable fear of receiving a longtime friend who you'd secretly learned might be a long-sought murderer. This possibility, which had tortured her mind, was brought on by the knowledge that someone had tried to do violence to Matt Brennan, and that she alone had—unwittingly—given someone the motive for killing, and that the someone was Rostov. The potentiality of real danger was what had now frightened her. This first dread had been that of the sudden unknown.

Yet the moment that Nikolai Rostov had come into the apartment, secured the door, and taken her up in his arms, tenderly, lovingly, whispering his apologies and desires, most of her apprehensions had vanished. He was still her friend and lover, companion of a hundred trysts, and he was no different here and now than he had ever been in Moscow and the past.

At first, Rostov had been keyed up and restless. Overworked, he had grumbled. Not only those constant conferences at the ministers' meetings, not only those high-strung confrontations at the Summit, but the maddening stretches of after-hours discussions, wrangling, compromise-seeking at the Russian Embassy with Premier Talansky and Marshal Zabbin and dozens of other Soviet delegates. Tonight the policy debates had frayed his nerves, and he had not been able to escape soon enough. And even then, he had not been sure that he was free. Marshal Zabbin had wanted to know if he could be reached, at any hour, at the Hotel Palais d'Orsay, and Rostov had said no, that he would be visiting an old friend. Marshal Zabbin, who had met Hazel several times in Moscow, had understood, and requested only the telephone number of the place where Rostov might be found. But, Rostov had added to Hazel, it was unlikely that the Marshal would bother him tonight, for he probably would want sleep for himself.

Gradually, in the hours that had followed, Rostov had begun to unwind and unbend. One arm around Hazel, he had consumed spoonfuls of caviar on crackers, and he had gulped down straight vodka unceasingly. While Hazel had known his capacity for alcohol to be enormous, she had speculated to herself, after his sixth drink, on whether or not she might succeed in making him completely intoxicated. She had been able to see the advantages. She might be able to make him talk about the past in general, about Vienna specifically, in a natural way. She might be able to make him remember, and recall more fully, his confession to her of so long ago about the conspiracy against President Kennedy, and she might manage this without incurring his slightest suspicion.

586

Handing him his seventh drink, she had tried to lead him backward, but his interest had been fixed only on what lay immediately ahead.

Examining this glass of vodka, he had said, "Vodka is the enemy of love, after a point." Then he had taken a swallow of it, adding cheerfully, "But I have not reached that point yet."

After the seventh drink, he had set down the empty glass unsteadily. He had brought her into both arms and begun to kiss her and caress her ardently. He had spoken, under his breath, of their future. Listening, Hazel realized that the few drinks she had taken, one for each of his two or three, had not been enough to repress her guilts. He had been saying, "My *milochka*, we will have more nights like tonight, I promise you, more very soon, after we are back in Moscow. I will have my vacation, and you, *milochka*, will share it with me."

"But your wife, Niki—?"

"Not this time. She does not return to Moscow with me. After the conference, she goes off to Bombay with Marshal Zabbin's wife, three other delegates' wives, and she will not return soon. Natasha will be at least three weeks in China."

"I thought you said Bombay."

His eyes had become glazed, and he had looked at her with momentary confusion. "Did I? Bombay? Ah yes, but only to deceive the inquisitive ones. Bombay to change planes for Peking. Three weeks we will have together, *milochka*."

"Where will it be?"

"The Black Sea again. Odessa. Or Batumi. Or better, Yevpatoriya. The beach. Remember?"

"I'd love that."

"Settled." He had released her from his arms. "I cannot wait."

"I can't, either. But it's only another week or two."

"I do not mean I cannot wait for the vacation—I mean I cannot wait now, to possess my little *milochka*. Let us go to bed."

She had stood up. "I'll use the bathroom first."

"But not too long. . . . *Milochka*, before you go, one more, one small drop of vodka."

Now, fifteen minutes later, she reclined between the sheets, waiting for him. She listened for the bathroom faucet. It had been turned off. He was undressing. Her feeling of dread intensified.

Yes, the quality of dread was very different from what she had suffered earlier. For upon his arrival tonight, it had been fright of the unknown. These minutes, it was fright of the known.

The known was Rostov and herself, Doyle and herself, and the terrible secret all three held in common. The known was giving herself to Rostov, for the first time in years, without love. The known was embracing him for another, yet pretending to him it was for himself. The known was Vienna and the long-unmentioned conspiracy that would soon be mentioned again. This spelled danger. Rostov's peasant façade hid a brain that was quick, perceptive, clever. Should he detect, in her false response to love or in her probings into his past, any sign of emotional espionage, her future would be dead, not necessarily her person but her future. There were only two men in her life, and since she did not yet have the one, she did not dare to let go of the other. But to win one, she must gamble with the other. This, she supposed, was her real dread—a mistake, and the inevitable sentence to eternal loneliness.

There was a shaft of light from the bathroom. Then the bedroom was enclosed in semidarkness once more, and suddenly his powerful, chunky, hairy naked frame materialized out of the shadows. The bed sank toward him, the blanket was torn off her body, and her trembling flesh and limbs were dragged into him and engulfed by him.

She could smell his breath against her face, and feel the hardness of his limbs, and she tried not to recoil.

"Milochka—milochka—my lyubov—my roza—"

"Niki, mine."

She endured his rough caresses, then feared that he would suspect she was enduring, not participating, and so she touched him with her hands, remembering how he liked to be teased when entering into love.

"How good, Niki," she whispered. "You excite me. Do I excite you? How can I, after so many years? What do you see in me, Niki, with all those younger, more beautiful Tanyas at your beck and call?"

His hand stroked her breasts, her belly, and his lips kissed her throat. "You see how I love you," he said at last.

"Yes, but why?"

"You are you, milochka, and you are different from any other. You are my American spinster Puritan, and you challenge me. Your body is always closed up so tight, like your face and lips, and when I play like this, it is always a surprise and excitement to see you open and bloom." He chuckled. "You have so little self-love, you are able to give everything to another. I am the lucky one."

The analytical part of her brain had heard him out, and now, clinging to him, she thought about it. She was, she guessed, always an experiment to him and, each time he shook her in an invisible tube and when she fizzed in response, he exulted in the renewed discovery of his male prowess and virility.

Tonight the knowledge of his prowess was somehow degrading, and she wished that she could remain tight beneath his advance, not open up, certain that this rejection was possible but knowing that tonight she did not dare it. She was used to his frankness, and knew he had meant no insult, not really, and she should not resent what he had said, but still, it would have been good to show him her own strength and independence. But what the hell. . . .

She had been offering him only her body, secretly keeping her mind chaste for Doyle, but the passion in his lips, his fingers, was unfairly digging into her mind, tearing it from Doyle, oh Jay, hold on, don't let me be taken, Jay, help me, help me. But too late. Her mind, all senses, had defected from the one who was not here. Her mind had joined her treacherous naked body in surrendering.

She groaned, she wriggled, she clung to him, her torso heaving, wanting her Niki, not wanting her Niki, loving him, hating herself, needing him. Blindly she saw the primitive face above her own, and then she shut her eyes and opened herself to him.

She wanted no finesse, no delicacy, and she received none. She was filled with him, and on fire, and she writhed with him in the consuming flames. The heat inside her womb, licking beneath her skin, was unbearable but sheer ecstasy, and her thighs shook and her arms flailed and she cried out to be freed. And when he would not let her escape, she screamed and cursed, and her curses turned him into a raging animal, and suddenly she felt him surrendering to her and at once she gave up to him, and together they were released and free.

He had fallen away from her, panting, trying to whisper endearments despite his complete exhaustion, but unable to do so for his lack of breath.

She lay back on her pillow, dropping her weary arms at her sides, and her weak legs flat on the bed. She lay satiated and happy, but only half happy in the clarity that followed love. From the navel down, she knew pleasure. From the navel up, she knew shame. Yet she resented the knowledge that Doyle would inevitably condemn her behavior, and she resented it doubly because after all she had sacrificed herself for him.

She wanted to argue with Doyle. She hated all his sanctimonious guilt-making. Who in the hell did he think he was anyway? She wanted to humiliate him for labeling her a whore. She wanted to tell him a woman needed real masculine love sometimes, real love, not just a lifetime of his flabby, soggy, pipsqueak passion. But she couldn't humiliate him, she couldn't, because she loved him so dearly, so maternally, poor lost baby, and she wanted to tell him his love was better in the end because it was so considerate, sweet, unhurting, and it was the best in the end because she loved him and wanted the security of him and of his name.

Her inner dialogue reminded Hazel that she was carrying Doyle's shrouded shield, and that it was for his cause, and their cause, that she had undergone the pain of an alien love. The time for risk had come at last.

She felt confident. Rostov's head was sufficiently befuddled by drink to make him unwary. Rostov's body was satisfied by her loving and it was beholden to her. After alcohol and orgasm, he was always pliable. After love, before sleep, he always liked a brief interlude of pillow talk.

She turned on her side. Rostov's panting had abated. He was breathing almost regularly now. But his eyes were heavy-lidded, and he stifled a yawn. His head moved. He saluted her with a tired smile. "Very good, my *milochka*. If I sleep too soundly, do not forget the telephone."

She slid over and nestled against him. "Ummm." She ran a finger along the line of his jaw. "You're not going to leave me alone already?"

"It is your fault for making me feel so peaceful."

"Let's talk a little."

"About what?"

"Us. I like to talk about us."

She kissed his lips, and he returned her kiss. "All right," he said, "but first make me one more drink."

"Gladly."

She left the bed for the dresser, where the tray of bottles, glasses, and ice now stood. She covered two cubes with vodka, and mimicked the mincing steps and servility of a Japanese geisha as she brought him the drink. Laughing, he pushed himself up to a sitting position against the headboard and accepted the glass of vodka. She considered going into the bathroom to use the bidet, but was afraid that by the time she finished he would have fallen into a deep slumber. Instead, she returned to the bed, climbed over him feeling as fleshy as a Rubens nude, and snuggled against him, legs drawn up, head pillowed amid her loose red hair upon his chest.

He had swallowed a considerable quantity of vodka, and she could hear the alcohol go down his gullet. "So, now we will talk about us," he said, his voice slurred from drink and sleepiness. "Make it a lullaby."

"I remember it like a lullaby," said Hazel. "Do you, Niki?"

"Yes, everything."

"Do you remember so long ago when we met?" said Hazel. "That week is as alive to me as the present. I was thinking about it before, when I was waiting for you. I'll never forget Vienna. Do you ever think about it, Niki?"

He yawned. "Many times. How could I forget?"

"We were so much younger then. The wonderful thing is that it doesn't seem we've changed much. At least, I don't think you have."

"You haven't either, *milochka*. Maybe prettier now."

"See, you still are kind. That's one of the things I found in you that attracted me in Vienna. I remember you when we were introduced in the Bristol bar. I was so impressed. A mysterious Soviet diplomat. I used to believe they wore horns."

He chuckled. "Maybe they do. . . . I was nobody then. Adviser to Premier Khrushchev's press secretary."

"Well, you were somebody to me. I was barely more than a cub reporter on my first foreign assignment. It was crazy that night, tearing around with you in Vienna, in that small gray Moskvich. I felt like a princess in a chariot. There was that place called the Flaker-Bar. I think we danced half the night. I was afraid you'd never want to see me again. I was drunk, and such a miserable dancer."

"Not to me, *milochka*."

"I'm glad you didn't give up on me. Look what we'd have missed. Remember that place we registered as man and wife?"

He nodded sleepily. "Vienna Woods." He finished his vodka and with an unsteady hand set the empty glass down. "Vienna Woods," he repeated.

"The Tulbinger Kogel Berghotel. Women don't forget those moments. I know men have other things on their minds."

"No, I remember, too."

She buried her head deeper into her hair and his chest. Here we go, Jay, she thought, the death-defying leap.

"Well, I don't mind your not remembering everything," she said. "We were drinking a lot, and you had every right to, because you had so much on your mind. I even remember—was it that night or one of the next?—when you were so upset, poor dear, because some friend you'd gone to school with—he was representing one of the *Pravdas* in Vienna—tried to get you to join in with him on that plot. It was so

591

hard for you, with all the other things you had on your mind." She lifted her eyes. "Remember, Niki?"

His glazed eyes met hers blankly. "Plot?"

"Oh, you remember, Niki," she said lightly, "that sort of rattle-brained plan to assassinate our leader, and they, whoever they were, wanted you in it."

"Assassinate?" He squeezed his eyes to focus them. "What are you talking about?"

Very dangerous ground, she thought. "Well, maybe you don't remember it," she said quickly. "Just as I was saying, you had so much on your mind organizing the Kennedy-Khrushchev meetings, and this was just one of those other things that came up, and I was so sorry for you, poor dear. I suppose, also, the fact that it was an old school friend who tried to suck you into it made it worse. I don't blame you for the way you drank that night, and even though you passed out on me, Niki, I loved you more than ever. I felt I was sharing your problems."

His face was troubled, and when he spoke, his voice was thick. "No, I recall nothing of that," he said, rubbing his forehead. "Perhaps, as you say, I was too drunk. There are times—" His voice drifted off, and then he looked down at Hazel. "What kind of plot in Vienna?"

She came off his chest and propped herself on an elbow. "You never really went into it, but I won't forget that night, the very idea—it made you seem so exciting and adventurous in my little-girl eyes."

"What kind of plot in Vienna?" he repeated.

"You told me this old school chum approached you about joining in with some dissident group of international Communists who felt our boss stood in Russia's way, and that he'd be more dangerous to your aspirations in the future, and that he must be liquidated right there in Vienna, or if that was impossible, someplace else soon afterward. You told them flatly you were against the whole project because you saw nothing to gain by it. You refused to participate. I was so proud of you. But anyway, the whole experience upset you."

Rostov looked off, past Hazel, his eyes narrowing to snare memory, and then flickering. "Yes?" he said, but it was not really a question.

"Oh, well, it was one of those things," she said, "and you've had worse times since. I've seen it, but I've learned to understand your life, Niki, and learned to treat your problems and confidences as if I were your real wife. And I have tried, as you know. I really have. But you also know how my imagination runs riot, and once or twice I've wondered to myself—I've wondered why those conspirators, the ones you rejected, why they didn't really kill him in Vienna as they had planned. It would have been so easy there. Why did they wait—I mean, assuming they were the same ones—why did they wait for Dallas? I always—"

"Dallas?" Rostov echoed incredulously. He came forward from the headboard. "*Milochka,* what in the devil are you talking about?"

Worriedly, she hesitated. Then she said, "That group, if it was the same, I've sometimes wondered why they didn't just kill President Kennedy in Vienna instead of waiting until two years later to get him in Dallas. That's all I—"

"Kennedy!" Rostov burst out. "Kennedy?" Suddenly he was totally awake, his broad visage broken by a wide grin, and he threw back his head and gave out a roar of laughter, and continued to laugh, his shoulders shaking with delight, as he looked down at Hazel, wagging his head, his eyes tearing with amusement.

Frightened and confused, she drew back and tried to sit up on the bed, but his hand caught her behind her head, and he brought her face close. Still convulsed with laughter, he kissed her forehead.

With indignation, she pulled away. "What's so damn funny, Niki?"

"You, my little *milochka,*" he said, trying to control his amusement. "You, my little American innocent abroad."

"Maybe you'll let me in on the joke," she said coldly.

"Oh, come now, come now," teased Rostov, tickling her under the chin. "I do not mean to hurt your vanity. Do not be so serious. But it is funny to me that you have thought this long time that any Russians or Communists from anywhere would even dream of assassinating Kennedy or any American President. Why should they? You get rid of one, you have another. They are of the same stripe and color. It is silly—"

Hazel sat up straight, covering her nakedness with her pillow. "Niki, are you trying to make me out some kind of scatterbrain? Next thing, you'll be denying you ever told me there was a plot in Vienna."

"I am not denying it—it is all brought back to my mind—"

"Or you'll be telling me there was no intention to assassinate Kennedy?"

Rostov's smile remained. He cocked his head indulgently, regarding Hazel as he might some overimaginative child. "If you will be calm, and carefully think back to that night in Vienna, I will ask you to remember exactly, the precise words, I spoke to you. Do you believe you can recall them?"

"I can," said Hazel with pique. "Can you? You were plenty drunk—"

"You were drunk, too," he said nicely.

"But I remember clearly."

"Let us see. Tell me exactly what you remember about what the—the so-called conspirators planned to do."

"I'll tell you what you told me."

"Yes?"

"We were sitting on a bed in some hotel, like here, except we were dressed, and you told me how you'd been approached—"

"Go on, *milochka*."

"—and you said, you said, 'Those madmen, they want to get rid of K, they want to liquidate him because they think him an enemy of Russia.' That's what you said."

"Exactly. 'To get rid of K.' " He shook his finger at her, treating her as if she were a child. "Think, *milochka*. In Vienna, in 1961, there were two who were K, not one but two. To your mind, naturally, your American mind, there was only one K, your Kennedy. But to Russians, there was another K, the only one with such an initial, and this was Khrushchev, Premier Khrushchev."

Hazel's head spun. "But you said they were getting rid of the one who was an enemy of Russia, the one who stood in Russia's way, who would be dangerous to them in the future. That could only mean the American President, not your own."

"It meant our own, it *was* our own," said Rostov flatly. "There were always those who fanatically believed that Khrushchev was the enemy of Russia, one who stood in the way of Russia's future well-being and progress. They were concerned with Russia's leadership, not yours, which your capitalists pretend to change every four or eight years anyway. There were those who opposed Khrushchev's anti-China course, his desire to divorce Russia from China's then secret Cominform, and his efforts to bring Russia closer to the Western democracies. Those were the ones who felt he was his own country's worst enemy, leading us down the road to disaster. I refused to enlist with them, because I believed they were wrong and our Premier K was right. In fact, I don't mind confessing, I was one of those who tried to hint to our K of the opposition within his Government. My loyalty, as you know, was well rewarded. I was promoted. I was sent to Zurich to rap the knuckles of the Chinese. But when that soft-headed Brennan let Varney defect to China and strengthen China's hand against us, I was made to suffer for Brennan's stupidity. You remember how I was suspected of playing both sides, of having been intimate with the pro-China conspirators in Vienna and exposing some of them merely to advance myself further in the Government until I could sabotage the Government in Zurich. You and I both knew that was untrue, but I had to suffer much before the Government would trust me and bring me back into its good graces." Rostov shrugged. "But that is all by the way. I digress. To get back to your simple, but perhaps understandable, assumption that it was your J.F.K., your K, that the Vienna group was after. No. They wanted only to get rid of Khrushchev—*get rid of,* not assassinate—and as you know, ultimately, they succeeded. They did dispose of him, remove him from office. But actually, in the long run, they failed, too, for they have never supplanted him with a Premier who agreed with them to bring Russia away from the democracies and back to an alliance with China. Every Premier since, our present Talansky also, has sided with your country against China, to bring China into line. This remains our policy at the Summit." He paused, and offered Hazel a kindly smile. "I am sorry to spoil your little melodrama, *milochka.* But see the good side. It has given you much pleasure of speculation through the years. That is something, is it not?"

"Yes," she said dully.

He reached down and began to pull the blanket over them. "But we have talked enough about fantasies. In the end, what is real is best. What we had in Vienna, and since, and tonight—yes, tonight—that is real and that is what matters." He slid under the blanket and lowered his head to the pillow. "I am dizzy with fatigue. Sleep, *milochka,* let us sleep."

"Yes," she said, but she remained inert, seated beside him in a state of shock.

Because of a fragment of bed talk in Vienna long ago, Jay Thomas Doyle had given years of his life to building a mosaic that would earn him immortality. And here, now, in Paris, another bed talk had shattered her loved one's magnificent mosaic, and with it his dreams, and perhaps her own dreams, too.

She sat there, sickened by the realization of how the truth would not only shatter the mosaic of Doyle's great work, rendering it worthless rubbish, but would also break his heart. She wanted to weep for him and for herself.

She heard Rostov's fuzzy voice from his pillow. *"Milochka,* the light, put out the light and sleep."

"I will, Niki."

With effort she crawled off the bed, picked up her nightgown, and started for the lamp. She had taken no more than two steps when the telephone's ring brought her to a frightened halt.

"Answer," she heard Rostov command.

She dashed around the bed, clutching her nightgown in front of her, and grabbed up the receiver on the fourth ring.

"Hello?"

"Miss Smith?" The accent was Russian. "Marshal Zabbin. Is the Minister still there?"

"Yes—" She turned. Rostov had swung to the edge of the bed and was reaching for the telephone. She gave it to him.

Shakily, she pushed her head and arms into the nightgown as she heard Rostov say, "Yes, Marshal. . . . Of course, sir. . . . I shall be there in twenty minutes."

He hung up, massaged his closed eyes, and stood up, stretching. Opening his eyes, he saw her and considered her affectionately.

"I am sorry, Hazel. I must dress and leave at once."

"I—I'm sorry, too."

She allowed herself to be embraced by him. Pinned against his hard frame by his muscular arms, she went limp and laid her head against his naked chest. She so desperately wanted Doyle to have his book, his manhood, that she was like a young war bride crying inside herself to have her mutilated soldier-husband's limbs, his masculinity, restored. She wanted Doyle not to give up, not to destroy himself through self-grief and self-pity.

"I will try to see you again before we are at last together," he was saying.

She heard his distant words only faintly.

"Oh, please—please—please—" she whispered to Doyle, pleading for him to survive what she must tell him, so that they might both survive.

She was surprised that it was Rostov's voice replying. "Have no fears, *milochka*. Your Niki will look after you. Forever."

She had heard him, and she shivered. For the words had sounded like a sentence to purgatory.

VII

I T HAD RAINED briefly before daybreak, a thin, steady shower, but by the middle of Friday morning the city of Paris was dry and clean and bright.

It was the kind of French morning that Matt Brennan had always enjoyed, when the warming air was fresh and the green trees along the *grands boulevards* were crisp and when even the sidewalks of the Champs-Élysées sparkled back at the sun.

Yet now, striding toward the Arc de Triomphe and the breakfast date at Le Drug Store, Matt Brennan derived little pleasure from the attractiveness of the new day.

For one thing, he had slept poorly, his head teeming with the unfinished handiwork of tiny demons—the Denise fiasco that had so provoked Lisa Collins, the personal meaning of the long vigil at the American Hospital, the continuing mystery of Joe Peet, as well as the maddening vacuum left by one phantom, the elusive Nikolai Rostov.

For another thing, Brennan had been awakened too early. To his surprise, it had been a telephone call from Hazel Smith that had roused him from fitful slumber. With agitation, she had summarized the results of an interview held last night with the Russian who had first hinted to her, in Vienna, of the conspiracy against President Kennedy's life. It had all been a grievous error, the conclusions that she and Doyle, mainly Doyle, had drawn from the sketchy allusions the Russian official had let fall so long ago. The disastrous truth must be passed on to Doyle at once, Hazel had felt, so as not to allow him to add another wasted day to so many squandered years. She had already made a breakfast engagement with Doyle, but suddenly Hazel the Strong had been reduced to weakness. She had found herself unable to face Doyle, with her black news, alone. She had thought of Brennan, Jay's best friend here, and she had wanted Brennan's presence and moral support. And Brennan, reluctantly because of all that was on his own mind and his aversion to funerals, had consented to attend. With uncharacteristic gratefulness, Hazel had told him that she and Doyle would be waiting for him at Le Drug Store around ten o'clock.

After trying to gain admission to Lisa's adjoining bedroom, and failing, Brennan had learned from a chambermaid who was sweeping the corridor that Lisa had left the hotel early. Wondering how Medora would ever reach her to present his defense, Brennan had washed, dressed, and remembered to stick the key to Joe Peet's room in his pocket, and then he had hastened down to the Champs-Élysées.

Now, at last, beneath the shadow of the Arc de Triomphe, he had reached that exotic and improbable modern hangout of the young French set—and of older tourists, who preferred it to the zoo—known as Le Drug Store.

Brennan opened the first heavy glass door, then the second, and he was transported into the tumultuous and raucous world of Le Drug Store. He went between the counter dispensing Dior stockings and the gaudy booth selling Chinese dolls, past the showcase displaying wristwatches imported from Leningrad, and he halted before the glassed-in pharmacy section. He looked about for Hazel and Doyle. There were four Germans, seeking succor for their hangovers, lined up before the coin-operated oxygen machine. Off to the left, dozens of morning customers were browsing at the semicircular international newsstand. Off to the right, a Frenchman was buying a bottle of Rémy-Martin cognac, an Italian couple was considering a Fath necktie, a beautiful Spanish girl was selecting several Jacqueline François phonograph records. Neither Hazel nor Doyle was to be seen.

Brennan proceeded into the snack bar and restaurant. As ever, despite the early hour, it was overcrowded. The black leather-upholstered booths and the tables, enclosed by cedar-paneled walls hung with California Gold Rush posters and formal Currier and Ives prints, were filled with customers, while unseated newcomers hovered over the soon-to-be-vacated places. Noisy waiters balancing trays of hamburger sandwiches, chocolate malted milks, Burgundy wine, and vanilla mousse pushed through the crowd. As always, the room was a bedlam of conversation and amplified French recordings of New Orleans Jazz.

Distressed by the swarm of humanity, the clamor, the lack of privacy, Brennan wondered why Hazel Smith had selected Le Drug Store as the background for the dirge she must sing to Doyle. But then, seeing both Hazel's and Doyle's upraised arms beckoning to him, Brennan thought that he understood. She had wanted a public arena, with the atmosphere of a boisterous and racketing Irish wake, as a counterpoint to alleviate Doyle's mourning.

As he joined them, Brennan could see Hazel's visible relief at his appearance. Doyle, on the other hand, gave Brennan only the briefest acknowledgment. Doyle was eager to hear out the report that Hazel had apparently already begun. But Hazel seemed to have no heart to hurry Doyle's agony. Stalling, she devoted herself to Brennan.

"I figured you'd be famished," she said to Brennan. "That's your orange juice. Fresh. And I ordered you bacon and eggs."

"Excellent, Hazel."

"I didn't know what you drink," she went on, "but you can have Jay's coffeepot and toast. He had only a sip of coffee and one slice of—"

"I'm dieting," interjected Doyle, adding with pride, "and without an appetite-depressant pill today. I think I've got it made." He took the coffeepot and poured for Brennan. "Hope this is what you want."

"It'll do fine," said Brennan.

"Excuse me, Matt," he said, "but I'm all on edge. Hazel was just beginning to tell me that she got to see her Russian friend last night, the one who first tipped her off on the conspiracy to get Kennedy, and she got him to talk." He turned back to Hazel, eyes glittering and chins jiggling with anticipation. "Well, Hazel, this is it. I can't take the suspense. What's the big word?"

Brennan averted his gaze, giving himself to the orange juice. As a youngster, after reading Gandhi and Dr. Schweitzer, he had never killed a fly or purposely stepped on an ant. Later he had never been able to bear the sufferings of any living creature, be the pain physical or mental. He had found the resilience to endure his own degradation and loss these last four years, but he hated seeing another similarly shorn of hope, since he, more than most, understood the soundings of the depths of despair and knew that they descended almost endlessly to the very brink of hell.

The platter of bacon and eggs was set before him, and no dish had ever received such undivided attention. But now and then he could hear Hazel Smith's melancholy voice and snatches of her recital. She was telling Doyle that she had reminded her "Russian friend" of his confidence in Vienna back in June of 1961. The Russian had remembered. He had confirmed that a conspiracy had been in the making— during this part, Doyle's ecstatic wheezing became more pronounced

—but the intrigue had in reality been directed against Premier Khrushchev, not against President Kennedy.

Doyle's happy exhalations suddenly became a single strangled groan.

There followed a gap of silence. Quickly Hazel tried to close it with puny words of explanation. To Brennan, it seemed as futile as a postmortem. The victim could not be brought back to life. With pain that dulled his taste, Brennan continued to consume the eggs, half listening to Hazel repeat how first she, then Doyle—she in Vienna, he after the assassination in Dallas—had misinterpreted the conspiracy information that the Russian had leaked out. It had been only natural for them to assume, from the first, that when the Communist conspirators had spoken of getting rid of the Head of State who obstructed the Soviet Union, they had meant the American leader, not their own Communist Premier. The assassination at Dallas, slightly more than two years later, had appeared to confirm this view of the conspiracy. But now it could all be seen in a new light. The Communists had conspired to get rid of their own leader. And shortly after, they had succeeded.

"I'm sorry, Jay, I can't tell you how sorry," Hazel was concluding, "but there's the final truth and we have to live with it."

For Brennan there was no place to hide. The eggs and toast were gone, the juice glass and coffee cup empty, and he had to accompany Hazel to the graveside.

He looked up. Doyle, who had not once spoken during Hazel's recital or since, still did not speak. After his initial groan of disbelief, his massive head remained high, immobile, the features still held firmly in some semblance of dignity. Yet Brennan suspected, from the draining of color, the twitching around the eyes and mouth, there was awful defeat. Earlier, at the beginning, Doyle's profile had reminded Brennan of a self-indulgent and eminently victorious Caesar engraved on an ancient Roman coin. The profile was still Caesarly, but in it could be read portents of the decline and fall of the Roman Emperor.

Waiting for Doyle's first verbal reaction, Brennan worried at his unnatural silence and wondered if his friend was in shock. He hoped for a normal outcry of grief, the realistic acknowledgment of ruin that alone could lead to survival and rebuilding. Brennan's mind had gone back to another Caesar, the Emperor Augustus, who, upon hearing of the annihilation of his greatest Roman army under Publius Quintilius Varus at the hands of the German barbarians, had screamed out his lament, *"Vare, redde mihi legiones!"* And now Brennan waited for Doyle, hope slain, to shout tearfully, "O Varus, give me back my legions!"

Instead, it was Hazel whose voice broke the silence as she repeated, "I'm sorry, Jay, but good or bad, I know you wanted the truth."

Doyle's jowls trembled. His dry lips began to move. For the first time he spoke, and the words were ones that neither Hazel nor Brennan had expected.

"It's not the truth," said Doyle defiantly. "I don't believe it!"

Astonished, Brennan stared at the fat correspondent, the Caesar who insisted he still had his legions. Although the words were brave, even admirable, promising undying persistence, Doyle's face gave lie to the words. Something alive had gone out of Doyle's face, and it was empty, hollowed of hope, and suddenly the brave false words it had uttered were like all the brave false whistlings through the cemeteries of childhood.

"But, Jay, you heard—" Hazel pleaded.

"No, dammit, I don't believe one word your Russian pal told you last night. If I'd heard it before Dallas, I might have. Maybe I'd have believed it and not undertaken the book. But I've found out too much on my own since Kennedy was shot. You've read the stuff in my book. You said it's great. It is. It's irrefutable. It's the facts from a hundred sources that the Warren Commission and your Commie pal want to evade. What did you expect from that Russian friend of yours? That he'd confess that the members of his gang were the ones who killed Kennedy? How could he? Of course, he has to deny it to you. When he first told you, nothing had happened. It was only another plan. But now it's not a plan. It's outright murder, and he's not going to admit his gang did it. If he did that, he'd be putting his life in your hands. Of course, he couldn't tell you the truth about Kennedy. It would be too dangerous for him."

"But Jay darling, listen. He did admit to the conspiracy against Khrushchev—and that was just as dangerous for him. Jay, listen. I know this man. He didn't have the faintest notion I was interrogating him for you. He thought it was for me, confidentially, and he had no reason to lie or be dishonest. Jay, really, you've got to see we blundered, we were fanciful, and we've got to put all that behind us."

"What have you got to put behind you?" Doyle demanded angrily. "If I believed what you just said, I'd be the chump, not you. All those years of research, correspondence, phone calls, interviews, working it out, writing, knowing what it could lead to—and now you want me to throw all that overboard because a drunken bum who was once indiscreet wants to take it all back to save his own neck? Now suddenly it's Khrushchev, not Kennedy? Ha! A likely story, after all I've found to prove there were a couple of guys in Dallas who got

Kennedy. No, Hazel, not on your life, nope, no fast-talking Russki who's conned you is going to pull the wool over my eyes. He's using you to stop me—he's probably heard what I'm up to and he's trying to stop me—but nothing's stopping me, Hazel, nothing and no one, until I get what I want and let blast with the biggest story in history."

Weakly, shaking her head, Hazel said, "Okay, Jay, do what you want. But where else are you going to obtain the final proof of your theory?"

"Never mind about that. Paris is full of Russians right now. I'll start moving in on them. I'll find someone."

"Jay, I don't think you'll find them very cooperative. I mean, I want to help you. I'm ready to keep on trying, too. It's just that I don't know to whom to turn anymore."

"You might try your Russian friend again," said Doyle pointedly. "Maybe a few extra drinks will act as a truth serum, the way it did in Vienna."

"Well, maybe, although he wasn't exactly sober last night. I don't know when he can give me time again during the Summit. He's a busy man."

"There's no rush," said Doyle. "You can see him in Moscow. We can work out some new questions together—"

Hazel shook a cigarette from the pack. When she brought it to her lips, her hand trembled. Accepting Doyle's light, she said quietly, "Jay, I was rather thinking of not going back to the Moscow bureau. I was thinking of asking for a transfer to New York, and sort of—of settling down."

Doyle's face fell. "You think that's wise? Don't get me wrong. I'd like you in New York, where we could see each other. But Moscow's your career—" He stopped, and then said, "No, I'd rather have you in New York, to be selfish. Only, maybe you could go back to Moscow for maybe a few months, until you've had another crack at your Russian friend. It would mean a lot to—to both of us, Hazel."

"Yes, I suppose I could do that. I mean, if you're right and he was bluffing me, well, it could mean a lot." She was thoughtful a moment. "As a matter of fact, he did tell me last night he'll have plenty of free time once the Summit is over and he's back in Moscow, because his wife and Marshal Zabbin's wife and a few others are leaving here to go on a tour of China. Yes, Jay, I might have another try at him, although I'm still not too optimistic. We'll discuss it further."

Brennan, listening to the exchange between the pair, sensitive to the personal undercurrents, had been as detached as a playgoer in the balcony observing a scene on the stage far below. Now, something he had just heard brought Brennan down from the audience and right onto the stage.

"Hazel—" he said quietly.

She jerked toward him, seeming surprised to find that he was still present.

"Hazel," repeated Brennan, "did I just hear you say that the wife of this friend of yours, this Russian friend of yours, is going to China with a party of other Russian delegates' wives?"

"Why, yes."

"It must be an official tour, since Marshal Zabbin's wife will be along."

"I think it is."

"Doesn't that strike you as odd?" asked Brennan. "Here we have the Russians and Chinese publicly at swords' points. And here you are telling me what has not been announced, that the Chinese will be hosts to a party of important Russian women in a few weeks. Sounds rather strange."

"I—I hadn't thought of it that way, Matt."

Brennan smiled. "Seems to me I've been thinking of little else these days. It's like all the other tidbits I've been picking up about the Chinese and Russians really being friends in private. You remember—"

"Yes," said Hazel. "But of course, if the Summit works out, everybody should be friends right after."

"On paper," said Brennan mildly, "paper friends. But I haven't heard of parties of American or English technicians or delegates' wives going to China after the Summit. No, only Russians, who've made such an elaborate hullabaloo about being on the outs with China." He considered Doyle. "I don't know, Jay, but if your assassination conspiracy book has come to a dead end, you might find that there's a bigger story in the making. Perhaps you should look into it."

Doyle, who had paused in summoning a waiter to listen, now signaled for the waiter once more and said to Brennan, "Thanks, Matt, but that's your baby. You look after it. I'm satisfied with my own."

The waiter appeared. Doyle ordered oysters, a filet mignon with fried potatoes, a basket of bread, a hot fudge sundae. He glared at Hazel and Brennan defensively. "I'm starved. Anyone care to join me?"

Both Hazel and Brennan shook their heads.

Doyle unfolded his napkin. "I'm going to need a lot of energy."

Hazel regarded him with sorrow. "Jay, I know it's been a bitter blow, what I had to tell you."

"Well, you're going to go back to the same guy, you agreed, so let's hold off on discussing that."

"I can't hold off," said Hazel. "I'll speak to the man if I must, but I've got to be perfectly honest with you. Jay, I don't think there is going to be any new information that'll change matters, support the theory in your book—"

"Let me be the judge of that," said Doyle with an edge to his voice.

Hazel sighed. "Jay, I don't want to fight with you in public, or anytime. Why don't you come over to the apartment tonight for dinner? We can give your future some thought and—"

"Sorry, Hazel, I'm tied up tonight," said Doyle. "I'm attending the gourmet club dinner I was invited to by Monsieur Goupil."

Distressed, Hazel said, "I thought you told me you weren't going."

"I did," said Doyle. "I've just changed my mind. I am going."

"Oh, Jay, why do you do things like that? You were on the wagon. Now off you go. Must you be so self-destructive? You're punishing no one but yourself. There are a million calories there tonight."

"There's also a book," said Doyle angrily, "one book you haven't torpedoed yet. You've already tried to bury my assassination book. Now you're ready to discuss my future. Great. But this moment my future is in that cookbook I'd better finish. And the way to write it is to start eating like a human being again."

"Jay—Jay—you're behaving like a petulant child. Please be reasonable."

"Like what? Like shooting myself over the great news you've brought me this morning? Well, if I've got to go, I'll go my way, counting all those big soft calories all the way down."

Brennan decided that he'd had enough. He pushed himself from the table, thanked them for asking him to join them for breakfast, and excused himself. He was late for a business appointment, he explained. He promised to see them soon.

Outside Le Drug Store, in the sun once more, he was relieved to be free of those two unhappy people, even though he himself was neither happy nor free. It was as if he had been fettered by unknown hands, to keep him from pursuing many mysteries, or perhaps only one. Yet, standing in the Champs-Élysées, renewed by the heat of the sun, he determined to liberate himself from his shackles and continue his hunt. Thrusting one hand in his trouser pocket, he touched the cool metal of the key. The possibility of what it might open filled him less with reassurance than with trepidation. Nevertheless, his mind was made up. Even if he came to Doyle's sad failure, he must try.

He started to the curb to find a taxi that would take him to the Hotel Continental.

I T TOOK MATT BRENNAN ten minutes to reach his destination.

Leaving his taxi in the Rue de Rivoli, he turned his back on the Tuileries, crossed under the arcade, and entered the Rue de Castiglione. Walking along the mammoth pile that was the Hotel Continental, he could see the rising shaft of Napoleon's column in the Place Vendôme up ahead. A few more strides and he had reached the iron gates and garden courtyard that led into the Continental.

Going through the court, past the beds of roses, the towering Corinthian columns, the pink-draped tables with their cane and bamboo chairs, Brennan arrived at the revolving door, went through it, and entered the long, narrow, busy lobby.

From the crystal chandeliers above to the Oriental rug covering the mosaic marble floor, Brennan found the Hotel Continental unchanged despite the passage of so many years. As a young diplomat, he had once been ordered to stop in Paris for a week and consult with members of the United States delegation to NATO, who were using the Continental for their headquarters. He was glad the lobby was not unfamiliar.

Quickly Brennan started toward the reception counters, and he waited his turn behind a swarm of American tourists. At last he moved up to the bronze-trimmed wooden counter. One of the harassed concierges greeted him wearily. "Yes, monsieur?"

"Mr. Joe Peet, please. He's registered here."

"Peet? Peet?" The concierge checked the guest list, found the room number, and glanced at the key and mail slot. "His key is in, so I am afraid he is gone out for the day."

"Can you check his room just to make sure?"

The concierge placed his hand on the phone. "If he is in, who shall I say is calling?"

About to give his name, Brennan hesitated. An appropriate pseudonym came to mind, the name of the one who had sold Peet the nonexistent book. "Tell him Mr. Julien is in the lobby."

The concierge did not blink, but as he phoned upstairs, he regarded his visitor with interest, as if to let Brennan know that he was perfectly aware "Julien" was not in accord with an American face or accent.

After a moment he put down the receiver. "Sorry, sir, no answer.

I'm afraid Mr. Peet is definitely out. Would you care to leave a message?"

"No message," said Brennan. "I'll be by later. Thank you."

He withdrew from the counter, and two tourists jostled each other for his place.

Retreating toward the entrance, Brennan felt no disappointment. From the start, he had rather hoped that Joe Peet would not be in his room. For, even if he had been able to visit with Peet, he had devised no sound approach to a personal conversation. He had toyed with several possibilities, that he was an emissary from Denise Averil, that he was a colleague of Hazel Smith's who hoped for an interview, that he was a fellow book collector who had been directed to Peet by M. Julien. But to Brennan, all of these introductory devices had seemed implausible, and he had feared that Peet would see through them.

Coming here to the Hotel Continental, he had secretly wished that he could see the effects and luggage in Joe Peet's room rather than Joe Peet. Now, suddenly, he had the opportunity to do so, and now, suddenly, he was uneasy and uncertain about taking advantage of his chance. Brennan knew that he was the civilized product of a culture that believed every man's home was his castle and that invasion of privacy was a criminal offense. But, Brennan also suspected, every man was a shameless Arsène Lupin at heart. Since he could not satisfy this instinct in life, he satisfied it by identifying with the fearless heroes of stories and films who were always slipping into unoccupied rooms, defying countless dangers, to search for or examine the effects of someone under suspicion. It was marvelous to behold, but it was make-believe. In real life it was unthinkable, unless one was outside the law, or ignored propriety, as a thief or a spy or a detective did. Despite his public reputation, Brennan thought of himself as none of these but as merely an ordinary citizen. The idea of breaking into Peet's room went against the grain, and momentarily it stopped him.

He stood in the lobby, immobilized by the restraints of guilt, until another feeling overcame these restraints. He was not, this morning, an ordinary citizen. Circumstances had cast him in the role of private investigator—for what?—one wanted moral approval—well, for good, for Good.

Matt Brennan turned toward the elevator.

Starting to pass the busy concierge's desk, he heard a rasping voice with an unmistakable Russian accent, and cautiously he turned his head around. He saw the big browless man, pomaded flat hair and misshapen nose and mottled cheek, leaning against the counter. Brennan recognized the Tartar giant at once, for he had seen him yesterday morning in the auto court of the Palais Rose, and here he was again—Medora's discovery, Joe Peet's friend, Hazel's Soviet KGB agent.

Brennan's instinct was to duck out of sight, but curiosity subverted caution. He slowed, and hung back.

The big man waited, elbows on the counter, until the concierge returned to him with an envelope.

"You are Mr. Boris Dogel?" the concierge asked.

"I am."

"He left this for you, Mr. Dogel."

The big Russian took the envelope, tore it open, removed a slip of paper, read it, snorted, and stuffed both the paper and the envelope into his suit-coat pocket.

As the one named Boris Dogel began to turn from the concierge's desk, Brennan turned away from him. He waited several seconds, then glanced over his shoulder toward the interior of the hotel. The KGB agent was not to be seen. Carefully, Brennan glanced over his other shoulder. He caught a last glimpse of Dogel as the Russian, light-footed for one so heavy, started to leave through the revolving door.

Brennan relaxed his compressed lips and exhaled.

For the time being, he felt safer. Without losing another moment, he hurried past the reception desk and gift shop to the elevator, which was half filled.

"Deuxième étage, s'il vous plaît," he directed the boy at the control lever.

At the second floor, Brennan stepped out, quickly cut back to the staircase near the front of the hotel, then ran down the stairs to the first floor. From the ground floor and the lobby below, he could hear continuing sounds of activity. He left the sounds behind and proceeded up the corridor, removing the key from his pocket and casually twirling it as if he were a guest going to his room.

He counted off the room numbers. Soon he was nearing number 55. His step faltered, but he forced himself ahead. His thoughts had gone to the Bois, to the demise of the man who might have been he, to his reflections on danger after leaving the Bois. For a solid citizen, he reminded himself one last time, he was committing himself to a foolhardy endeavor. He had no idea of where Peet was or when he would return. He had no idea whether Peet's KGB friend, Boris Dogel, had left the hotel for an hour or a minute. He had no guarantee of safe espionage. He might be cornered by Peet, or Peet and Dogel, or surprised by a maid or valet, while inside the room. He had provided himself with only one explanation if he should be caught. The key—by mistake, the concierge had given him the wrong key. But then, those who came upon him could verify that he was not a guest of the hotel. Then who was he? He had no answer, and now there was no time to invent one.

He stood before number 55. He looked up and down the corridor. Not a soul in sight. He shoved the key into the keyhole and tried it. A click. The door unlocked. He opened it, entered, closed it behind him. He was committed.

He was in the center of a confining entry hall, surrounded by doors. The one he had closed behind him. One on either side of him. Two straight ahead.

Brennan tried the door to his left. It revealed a shallow closet. Only an inexpensive trench coat with epaulets hung inside. He tried the door to his right. It opened into a small bathroom, a curtainless shower over the bathtub, a washbasin with bottles of deodorant and after-shave lotion on the glass shelf above it, and a bidet folded beneath the sink. Nearby, hanging next to the toilet, was a blue terry-cloth bath-robe monogrammed with the hotel's initials.

Softly Brennan shut the bathroom door and advanced to the two doors ahead. He turned the knob of the first. It was locked. He guessed it opened by option of the hotel should a guest wish to add a sitting room to his quarters. Brennan moved to the last door, twisting the knob, and he entered into Joe Peet's single room.

Brennan's gaze explored the room. There were twin beds separated by a telephone stand. The twin beds were already made up for the day, and for this Brennan was grateful. The drapes drawn across the large window were of pale green brocade to match the upholstery of the three chairs placed about the room. Near the window stood a modern reproduction of a Louis XVI writing desk with a white-enameled top. Next the *coiffeuse,* and finally the armoire.

It was a comfortable room, Brennan thought, one that might be taken by a lone traveler of means. Yet it was an oddly impersonal room, as if it were being used only for its bed and bath and was otherwise left abandoned. There was no stamp of its occupant upon it.

Slowly Brennan crossed the oblong rug to the telephone stand between the beds. He picked up the scratch pad. On the upper half, in ink, were doodles of something resembling a bird or an airplane surrounded by linked circles. Beside that was scrawled "Club Lautrec" and then "D" and beneath the "D" were two larger circles with dots in the middle of them. On the lower half of the pad, written in soft pencil, were the words, "Novik—Pra—noon." Instantly Brennan recognized the name "Novik." He had heard it from Jay Doyle several times.

There was a renowned Soviet correspondent, Igor Novik, connected with the Moscow *Pravda,* who was Doyle's gourmet friend. But any reason for a relationship between Peet and Novik was difficult to establish, unless Peet had been interviewed by the Russian journalist in Moscow and was now being interviewed again. Or, possibly, Peet had sought out Novik to intervene on his behalf in an effort to obtain a Russian visa or citizenship. The name did not seem significant, except that just as the Julien bookshop episode and the friendship with the KGB man had tied Peet in with the Russians, this did, too.

Brennan dropped the pad and walked to the desk. On one side, propped against the marble base of the lamp, was a frayed snapshot. Brennan bent low. The picture was out of focus, but still Joe Peet and the girl could be made out. Peet had an arm around the girl's waist. His hair was a slick pompadour, his expression solemn, and he was attired in a buttoned sweater and khaki trousers. The girl was plump, making Peet seem slighter. She had braided hair and Slavic features, and wore a forced smile and a cotton dress. At the bottom of the snapshot, written in a stilted hand, was *For My Joe, For Always, Yr Ludmilla, Moscow.*

Thoughtfully Brennan considered the snapshot. Strange pair, the errand boy from Chicago and the factory girl from Moscow, and yet not so strange. Ludmilla looked earthy female and sensible, and for some men home was where they found affection and safety, and often the haven was not a place but a person.

Brennan directed his attention to the opposite end of the desk. He became aware of what he had not noticed before. Several books were neatly stacked on top of a dozen magazines. He moved to study Peet's portable library. He began to remove the books, one by one, considering the titles. There were seven in all: *Michelin's Paris and Principal Sights Near By, English Edition; French Phrase Book; The Female Form, Studies in the Photographing of Women; Plan de Paris; Versailles and the Trianons; Paris by Night; 101 Ways to Play Solitaire.*

There was, Brennan observed without surprise, no title by Sir Richard Burton.

He began to go through the periodicals. Except for the weekly hotel pamphlets—*Allo Paris* and *Une Semaine de Paris,* guides to the city's entertainment—every magazine appeared to be devoted to a single subject. That subject was the unclad female. There were three different issues of *Lui, le Magasin de l'Homme Modern.* The other magazines bore such names as *Continental Nudist, Paris Tabou, Régal, American Sunbather,* and *Eden.*

The diversions of a lonely man, Brennan thought, and poor substitutes for faraway Ludmilla.

Putting down the magazines, stacking the books atop them again, Brennan felt more charitable toward the tenant of this room. And because his brief search had been so ludicrously unproductive, Brennan began to feel more ashamed of his invasion of another's privacy.

As he turned from the desk, his shoe hit the wastebasket and knocked it over. He stooped to right it and became aware of the discarded trash inside. Reminding himself that a Sam Spade or a Philip Marlowe would not overlook such a potential treasure trove, Brennan took up the wastebasket and emptied its contents on the desktop. Besides the wrappers from two empty gum packages and the blunted stub of a pencil, there were four crumpled balls of paper and the fragments of a card kneaded into a spitball. He opened the three smaller balls of paper, flattening the creases out of each by pulling it tightly down across the edge of the desk. Now he began to examine the Burton collector's ephemera.

The first two sheets he had flattened—one a laundry bill, the other a receipt for the Michelin guidebook from Librairie Galignani, located in the neighborhood—were of no interest. The third piece of paper, although also a receipt, struck him as unusual. It acknowledged advance payment for the rental of full-dress evening attire "to be delivered." The contents of the future delivery were itemized: white shirt, bow tie, shirt studs, cuff links, trousers, tailcoat.

As before, when confronted by Peet's dealings, Brennan was perplexed. He tried to translate the wrinkled paper in his hand into a picture of Joe Peet in formal dinner tails. The picture was as incongruous as the other of Peet poring over his rare Sir Richard Burton books. Had this receipt been for a mere tuxedo, Brennan would have been less surprised. In Paris one was required to wear black tie on special nights to certain places open to the general public, the Opéra, Maxim's, or to a private dinner. But tails were required most often for more stately, less plebeian occasions. For Brennan, it was impossible to envision Joe Peet, reader of girlie magazines and the *French Phrase Book* at any such affair.

Mystified, Brennan turned his attention back to the desk. The spitball and one larger crumpled paper remained. Carefully Brennan began to peel apart the spitball. When he had the six shreds free, he pieced them together on the desk. The tiny jigsaw represented an embossed calling card. The lettering read:

610

```
┌─────────────────────────────────────────┐
│                                         │
│              MA MING                    │
│                                         │
│    Foreign              Hsinhua         │
│    Representative       Peking          │
│                                         │
└─────────────────────────────────────────┘
```

At once Brennan could picture the owner of the calling card. The
yellow beach-ball head. The almost perpetual grin. The New China
News Agency correspondent and friend of Chairman Kuo and Professor Isenberg. Ma Ming's calling card in Joe Peet's trash. This was the
most incongruous and puzzling find so far.

Peet and the Russians—that at least made some sense because of
Ludmilla. But the thought of Peet and a Chinese—that was impossible.
Yet here it was, Ma Ming's card. Obviously the card had been no
treasure to Peet. He had ripped it six times, molded the fragments into
a spitball, and cast it into the wastebasket.

And then another puzzle offered itself to Brennan. Overnight, Peet
had departed from his reserved rooms at the Plaza-Athénée, leaving no
forwarding address, and had settled into a different hotel. Brennan
had undergone a great trial to obtain information of Peet's whereabouts. Yet, suddenly, a small parade of people knew Peet's seeming
hideout. There was Boris Dogel. But that was understandable. There
was Igor Novik. Less understandable. And now, Ma Ming. And that
was incomprehensible. What conceivable interest could a Red Chinese
journalist have in a nonentity of an American? Certainly not for a
press interview. How many among China's 850 million would care to
read about the frivolous romantic quest of a lovesick Chicago errand
boy for a Russian girl mechanic?

This was no time for speculation. One larger crumpled paper
remained. Brennan opened it, flattened it, and found himself looking at a single page of the Paris edition of the New York *Herald
Tribune*. It was the third page, dated the day before yesterday, and its
only point of interest was a jagged hole near the top where something
Peet had wanted to keep, a news story or a photograph, had been torn
out. Because what was missing was still unknown, and therefore not
yet disappointing, Brennan enjoyed his first moment of optimism since
his search had begun.

He glanced at his wristwatch. More than ten minutes had passed
since he had entered Peet's hotel room. So far he had had everything
his way, and mentally he crossed himself and knocked wood. Return-

ing the debris to the wastebasket, he wondered how much more time he could afford. He listened for the verdict of his second sense. It told him: make haste.

In haste, yet without creating disorder, he searched the desk drawers, the wardrobe drawers, every nook and cranny of the room. They offered him nothing new about Joe Peet beyond the fact that Peet liked his shirt collars starched. Brennan opened the closet. Except for two suits (pockets empty) and a folded luggage rack, it contained nothing providing the remotest clue to Peet's presence and activities in Paris.

As he left the closet, one thing nagged after Brennan, until he was able to define it. There was one odd omission, one that might be likened to the incident that had piqued Sherlock Holmes in "Silver Blaze." Colonel Ross had inquired, "Is there any point to which you wish to draw my attention?" Sherlock Holmes had replied, "To the curious incident of the dog in the night-time." Colonel Ross had said, "The dog did nothing in the night-time." And Holmes had said, "That was the curious incident." True. It was not unusual when a dog barked at the approach of a nighttime visitor. It was only unusual when the dog did not bark. Similarly, it was strange to find a luggage rack folded and unused in a transient's closet, especially when there was no other rack to be seen in the room.

Peet's luggage. Brennan realized that this was the one possibility he had completely overlooked.

He tried to survey his surroundings with keener eyes. There had been no suitcase in this closet or the hall closet, none in the bathroom, and nothing even resembling a valise was apparent from where he stood. He studied the room. He had covered every inch of it. His eyes fell on the two beds, and he dashed toward them.

Dropping to his knees, Brennan lifted the fringe of one white bedspread and peered beneath the bed. No suitcase. He crawled to the second bed, and peered beneath. Suitcase! He had found the last of Joe Peet.

Taking the handle, Brennan pulled the lone piece of luggage out into the open. It was a new rawhide-colored valise, plastic, lightweight, meant for air travel and for a man in a hurry. Praying that it was not locked, Brennan pressed the brass buttons on either side with his thumbs. The lid of the suitcase sprang free from the bottom, and eagerly Brennan lifted the lid off his last hope.

As he reached down to dig under this second cache of starched shirts and shorts, some still bearing price tags, his arm stiffened, and his spine arched and froze. Faintly, from the hotel corridor, came the voices of two persons engaged in conversation. The voices grew louder, until they were at the outer door. He waited for the voices to recede. They did not. The dialogue continued at the door.

I'm dead, he thought, and it was interesting, the trivia that passed through the mind before death, the inconsequential that superseded intellect. For his intellect, which might organize the means to fend off death and seek survival, was paralyzed. He thought what a pity it was that no one knew where he was at this moment, and there would be no one to identify his dismembered remains when they were fished from the Seine, and he would be buried in some French potter's field, instead of in the handsome family mausoleum outside Philadelphia. He thought of the ten thousand lire he had forgotten to pay back to the monk on San Lazzaro. He thought of Robinson Crusoe: "It happened one day about noon, going towards my boat, I was exceedingly surprised with the print of a man's naked foot on the shore, which was very plain to be seen in the sand. I stood like one thunderstruck, or as if I had seen an apparition; I listened, I looked round me, I could hear nothing, nor see anything . . . terrified . . . looking behind me . . . mistaking every bush and tree, and fancying every stump . . . to be a man . . ."

Brennan measured his fright. Crusoe had at least been able to fortify himself. But Brennan, kneeling on the floor at another's open suitcase, was helpless. He crouched, waiting for Joe Peet and Boris Dogel to fall upon him.

He heard the key being inserted in the outer door. He heard the door creak open. He heard a man's voice speak in French: "Well, see you later. I've got this room to do." He heard another man's voice speak in French: "That room's done, all done, Gabrielle and I did it early this morning." The first voice: "My thanks. Then I'll join you for a glass of wine."

The outer door was pulled closed again. A ring of keys jangled and the jangling faded, and the conversation of the two *valets de chambre* receded, and there was silence.

Brennan looked down. The footprint in the sand was no longer there. It had been a mirage. But the very illusion of threat had been enough to bring perspiration to his forehead and to quicken his pulse. Time was running out. His shaking hands burrowed back into Joe Peet's suitcase.

From beneath the newly purchased clothes he removed whatever his fingers touched, and hastily he piled the trove on the rug beside him. When the traveling bag was emptied of all but the apparel, Brennan considered the mute witnesses to Joe Peet's daily existence and hoped that one would communicate to him enough to dispel or solve the mystery of the owner.

Carefully Brennan examined each of Peet's personal effects before returning it to the suitcase. There was a cellophane-wrapped box of condoms, to tell Brennan of Peet's concern about personal hygiene. There was a maroon imitation-leather medicine kit, and once unzipped, it revealed a neat row of patent medicines and one small bottle of sedative. There was the very latest Polaroid camera, a subminiature version of the camera that not only takes but also automatically develops colored photographs. There were two envelopes packed with the pictures Peet had already taken in Paris.

Brennan extracted the photographs from the first envelope. Six of them were nude shots of Denise Averil, sprawled and wakeful on a double bed in the Plaza-Athénée. Twelve more of the pictures were also female nudes, some taken in the room at the Plaza-Athénée, some taken in this very room, all utilizing two other female subjects, probably French hotel maids who had agreed to strip and pose for a rich and generous American. This art, Brennan conceded wryly, represented Joe Peet as a person of fine taste and sensibilities, an esthete of the natural, a connoisseur of *Montes Veneris*.

Brennan wondered if the second envelope contained more of the same. Here the contents deceived him. The two dozen color photographs had not a single nude female among them. Here, instead, were pictures of landmarks, taken in Paris and its environs. Actually, only a third were taken inside Paris, and these were unimaginative shots of the Arc de Triomphe and the exteriors of the Palais de l'Élysée, the Opéra, the Palais de Chaillot, the Louvre. The remaining two-thirds of the colored photographs were routine shots of the château at Fontainebleau, the outside of Malmaison, the esplanade and gardens and exterior of the wings of the main palace at Versailles. In only one of these photographs had Joe Peet intruded his own person, perhaps as a keepsake for Ludmilla one day, should that day ever come. Someone had captured Peet on film as he stood before the statue of the Sun King on horseback in the middle of the courtyard leading to the entrance of the Versailles palace. Whoever it was who had taken this picture had left his own shadow on the cobblestones between the camera and Peet himself. The shadow, although distorted, was that of a big man, a bulky man. Perhaps an official guide that Peet had hired. Or perhaps a friend from the KGB named Dogel.

Well, Brennan conceded silently, this was the other side of a dual personality. For here was Peet the classicist, the appreciative lover of Fontainebleau, Malmaison, Versailles. The very one who hoarded the scholarly translations of that rough diamond of the nineteenth century, Sir Richard Burton.

With care, Brennan settled the camera and envelopes back into the suitcase. So much for Joe Peet the hobbyist.

There were more magazines waiting. Brennan leafed through them rapidly. Another archive of ungarmented girls. Brennan returned these to the suitcase, also.

The pile of effects had been reduced to one bundle of pamphlets held together by a rubber band. Slipping off the rubber band, Brennan fanned out the rectangular glossy travel-bureau folders. Again, Peet the classicist, the student of France's glory. Two tour folders of the wonders of Fontainebleau, one of Chantilly, two featuring a visit to Malmaison, and one, two, three—seven—seven advertising the historic beauties of Versailles, its grand palace and the two Trianons.

In his mind Brennan tried to marry Joe Peet to these magnificent monuments to France's past. The pairing simply did not take—unless, of course, he did not know this other side of Peet, unless he had been misinformed and had underestimated him. While this was unlikely, it was possible. After all, he had had only one brief glimpse of Peet. His only real knowledge of the young man had come from a clipping carrying Hazel Smith's by-line, and from some offhand remarks and judgments imparted by Hazel and Doyle, these and Peet's lewd behavior with Denise and the nude photographs and cheap magazines in this room. Yet Brennan had read of great scholars whose avocations had been pornography, and he had read of uneducated men who had become lettered through self-discipline. Perhaps his own sketchy view of Joe Peet was the false one. Brennan promised himself to find out more, the moment that he left this room, *if* he left this room.

About to close the fan of sight-seeing leaflets and secure them with the rubber band, Brennan found his attention arrested by one of them. The sight-seeing leaflets had seemed unused, or well-preserved, but now he noticed one that was well used and had a dog-eared page. Brennan separated this leaflet from the others.

The worn leaflet bore the title: *Visit the Splendours of Versailles.* A reproduction of Louis XIV's palace graced the front cover, and on the back page was a montage of photographs of the Marble Courtyard, the exterior of the palace, the Queen's Staircase, the King's Council Room, the Hall of Mirrors, the Grand Canal and Gardens, the Grand Trianon, the Petit Trianon. Imprinted at the bottom were the name, address, and telephone number of the tourist agency that had issued the pamphlet, as well as their tariff for a day's visit, including limousine and driver and lunch at Le Londres restaurant.

Brennan opened the leaflet. The two inside pages were given over to a three-dimensional map of the main building and two wings of Versailles Palace. Apparently the map had been consulted by Peet, for there were coffee stains on the Salon of Hercules. Then something else caught Brennan's eye. The inner courtyard had been marked in pencil. There were three lightly crossed *X's,* one outside the Queen's Staircase, another below the King's Council Room, a third beneath the King's apartments. Brennan scrutinized the map for other markings. An *X* had been made and erased before the Versailles museum section of the Palace.

Brennan raised his head from the leaflet and stared into space. It was difficult to invest any of Peet's effects with significance. Yet these markings gave Brennan pause. They were probably meaningless, scratched on the map while taking coffee at Le Londres to remind Peet where he had made his photographs or to indicate a fascinating site he wished to remember. Yet Peet, the classic-minded tourist gathering folders on Versailles, Fontainebleau, Chantilly, Malmaison, was one thing. But Peet as historian annotating a map in his collection was another thing, a rarity worth further consideration.

Quickly Brennan began scanning the other tourist leaflets, looking for more *X's.* There were no more. The leaflets were immaculate. Even the two duplicates of the marked Versailles advertisement were in mint condition.

Brennan became aware of the sound of his wristwatch ticking. He looked at the watch dial. He had been an interloper in this room for twenty-five minutes. He sat back on his haunches. There was no sense in pushing his luck further. About to bind the leaflets together with their rubber band, he hesitated. Some instinct in him, unsatisfied, wished to retain the stained and marked Versailles tourist map for further study. Yet another instinct in him warned not to take it, for it might be missed. He remembered the duplicates. He separated one from the pack, opened it to its map, and laid it side by side with the one bearing Joe Peet's markings. Finding his pen, Brennan brought it down to the unmarked duplicate, and with as much accuracy as possible he copied the placement of Peet's penciled *X's* by inking in similar *X's* on the clean map.

Finished, he folded the duplicate of *Visit the Splendours of Versailles,* and stuck it in his inside jacket pocket. The original leaflet he returned to the pack, bound the pack with the rubber band, and shoved the leaflets into the suitcase. He took one last look at the bag. Everything was in order. He closed it and pushed it back under the twin bed.

Jumping to his feet, he dusted the knees of his slacks. He surveyed the hotel room one final time. Nothing appeared amiss. Joe Peet would return to it and find it as seemingly uninvaded as when he had left it early this morning.

Swiftly Brennan moved to the outer door. A decision. Should he open it gingerly, peek outside to see whether the corridor was clear, before slipping out? Or should he boldly open it and make his exit? Of the two, the first was the greater risk. If he peeked out and was seen, he invited suspicion and detention. If he simply walked out naturally, as if leaving his own room, he was safer, even if a maid saw him and remembered too late that he was not the room's present occupant.

Brennan yanked open the door, stepped into the corridor, looking neither left nor right, pulled the door shut, took out his key, unhurriedly locked the door, and turned away from Room 55. Only then did he covertly glance to his left and his right. Not another person was in sight.

Exhilarated by his successful foray, he started briskly away. Not until he reached the stairs was he able to evaluate the degree of his success. At what had he actually succeeded? At surviving a dangerous mission. That part was true, but it was merely negative. For what had his mission accomplished? He had not obtained a single concrete piece of evidence, not even a clue, that linked Joe Peet, American, to Nikolai Rostov, Russian. Brennan had learned only that Joe Peet might be more than merely a post-adolescent lecher. If he was, if this could be confirmed, then there would be no reason for Peet not to have been collecting Sir Richard Burton (despite the nonexistent edition of a book whose title might have been overheard incorrectly) or not to be interested in Versailles and the other landmarks of French history. If there was clear evidence of his having a self-educated second side, there was no reason to link him to Rostov, or to expect to catch Rostov through him. In that event, Brennan knew, the sole alternate avenue to vindication would be shut down to him, and only Earnshaw would remain to clear the path to Rostov.

But first, he must make sure whether the time he had given to Joe Peet had been a waste.

He started down the steps to the Hotel Continental lobby to do what he had overlooked doing before: to telephone Herb Neely about Joe Peet. The call was mandatory before he went on to the United States Embassy to hear in full what Neely had been able to learn, presuming anything more could be learned, or even should be learned, about the schizoid Mr. Peet.

A FTER SPEAKING BRIEFLY to Herb Neely on the telephone, Matt Brennan had paused at the zinc bar of a bistro to order a small bottle of Perrier and watch two French laborers in berets play the pinball machine. Refreshed by the mineral water, Brennan went outside into the Rue de Rivoli, and at a leisurely pace he walked toward the United States Embassy.

Only after he had covered six blocks, and was passing the Hotel Crillon and entering the Avenue Gabriel, did he feel perturbed about what lay immediately ahead. Although Neely, a friend, would be waiting to welcome him, Brennan considered the Embassy itself a bastion of the enemy. Since his country had, in effect, disinherited him, he had come to look upon its embassies as hostile fortresses peopled by belligerent men who were openly scornful of him. Perhaps his attitude was unreasonable, even paranoid, but it existed. Reality was not always what you felt, he reminded himself, but was often how you felt.

He passed through the open gates, nodded sadly at the familiar statue of wise old Ben Franklin in the cobblestone court, and marched straight to the double doors that stood beneath the legend chiseled into stone: UNITED STATES OF AMERICA.

Once he was inside, an irony brought a crooked smile to his lips. He was here on Joe Peet business. Joe Peet wanted to abdicate allegiance to this country and was not allowed to do so. Brennan wanted to pledge allegiance to this country and was not allowed to do so.

Brennan crossed the black-and-white marble floor to the high reception desk situated between two mammoth Ionic columns. He told the gray-haired lady that Mr. Neely, the press attaché, was expecting him, and before she could inquire, he gave his own name and waited tautly for those arching eyebrows. If she recognized his name, she showed no sign of it. She telephoned upstairs. Hanging up, she said, "Yes, Mr. Neely is expecting you." She pointed off. "You'll find the elevators over there. Tell the operator M-1. The press attaché has his office across from the elevator."

Brennan thanked her—for more than assisting him, actually—and he headed toward the elevators. Moments later he emerged into the mezzanine corridor and walked in the direction of the teletypes hammering steadily outside the press offices. Entering the large room that always reminded him of the city room of a metropolitan newspaper, he saw that three of the four desks were occupied by Government press personnel at work. Not one looked up.

Through the doorway to his left, Brennan could see Herb Neely in his tiny book-lined private office, hunched low over an ancient Underwood standard typewriter, pecking away on the keys with two fingers.

As Brennan approached him, Neely raised his head, bemused, squinting from behind rimless glasses, and then he grinned warmly. "Hi, Matt." He jerked a thumb toward the lone chair in the crowded office. "Be with you in a minute. On the last line of an official release."

Neely returned to his typing, and Brennan remained standing, examining the titles of the reference books inside the press attaché's bookcases. The typing had ceased. Brennan turned back to find Neely yanking the sheet out of the machine and handing it to him.

"Have a look, Matt. Good news for a change."

Brennan took the sheet of paper. The letterhead read: "AMBASSADE DES ETATS-UNIS, *Service de Presse, Information pour la Presse, Paris, le 20 juin.*" Neely's two-paragraph release contained an optimistic quotation from the President of the United States, stating that he was satisfied with the progress the leaders of the five powers had made in their disarmament discussions, that complete accord had been reached on the reduction of conventional armed forces, on the reduction of non-nuclear armaments, on a timetable for achieving both, and that now the more difficult areas of nuclear weapon and delivery system prohibitions, as well as international control and policing measures, were being explored. The President foresaw an agreement on these crucial points that would be satisfactory to all nations represented at the Summit.

"Very good news," agreed Brennan, handing back the release. "Maybe the species *Homo sapiens* will not become extinct after all."

"And maybe you'll get a chance to join the species again, Matt."

"What do you mean?"

Neely held up the release. "The President's in an excellent mood. Didn't you tell me Earnshaw has agreed to see him on your behalf? Well, the President ought to be mellowed and receptive."

"I hope so. I'm afraid to depend upon it. That's why I keep looking for other baskets to put some of my eggs in. I guess that's why I'm here this minute." Brennan moved to Neely's door and firmly closed it.

Neely watched him. "So it's that way, Matt."

"I've been involved in some research that I'm afraid should be strictly between us," said Brennan. He sat down across the desk from Neely. "But first, Herb, did you have any luck on Joe Peet?"

"No problem," said Neely. He ran a hand over his thinning blond hair, removed the rimless spectacles from his nose, and bent forward to open a legal-sized manila folder. "As I suspected, we had a little on him. When Peet was unable to get his visa extended in Moscow, he stopped off in Paris and made a nuisance of himself around the Embassy. He treated us like a lonelyhearts agency. He wanted us to intervene with the Russian Embassy here. But I reckon you understand, Matt, we couldn't promote the cause of an American trying to give up his American citizenship, even if his motivations were not political, only romantic."

Brennan smiled. "I can understand that."

"Nevertheless, to get Peet out of our hair, we occupied him with filling out every sort of form, mostly those asking for autobiographical information. I have those forms here. Also, after Peet got back to the States, he bombarded us with letters appealing for our help. I've got those, too." He fingered the contents of the file. "Of course, Matt, according to security regulations, I can't show you what is in the file. Restricted, you know." He put on his glasses again, and his eyes twinkled. "But I happen to have read it all, and I don't remember anything in the regulations that prevents me from discussing Joe Peet. What I mean is, if someone I trusted happened to ask me, 'What do you know about a fellow named Joe Peet?'—well, I might be inclined to tell him."

"What do you know about a fellow named Joe Peet?" asked Brennan with solemnity.

"Funny thing, your bringing him up," replied Neely with equal gravity. "I was just thinking about this Peet fellow. No, I don't mind telling you the little I know." Silently he turned the pages of a form in front of him and then studied several letters before he looked up. "Joseph Peet, no middle name. Born thirty-two years ago in Chicago. His parents were of Lithuanian extraction. His mother died in childbirth. Joe was the child. No brothers, no sisters. And no known relatives, either. When Joe was five or six months old, his father had to go to Milwaukee for a job interview. His father left infant Joe with the landlady overnight. His father never came back. Joe wound up in an orphanage on the North Side."

"Tough," said Brennan.

"Yup. . . . Anyway, I guess he wasn't a very attractive kid, because in one of his letters he says he was the longest resident that orphanage ever had. He was at least thirteen before the city finally farmed him out to foster parents, who I gather were somewhat unlovely. They didn't want a child. They wanted someone around the house to do the dirty work and they wanted the city's support check.

Well, the first chance Joe Peet had, he cleared out. Ten minutes after he was finished with the sixth grade, he hit the road."

"Are you sure? Hazel Smith interviewed him, and Peet told her he'd had two years of high school in Chicago."

"Public relations," said Neely. "Once a man gets up in the world, he wants to appear educated. I know a publisher who had two semesters of night classes at Columbia University, nothing more, but you read *Who's Who* and you'd think he was a Columbia grad. People aren't afraid of making up things for the press, but they're afraid to lie to the Government. And these forms on my desk are Government, and Joe filled in that his education stopped at the sixth grade."

"Okay," said Brennan. "What else?"

"Peet knocked around the country, hitchhiking, riding the rails, odd jobs, scrounging out a living, until he was drafted. He was in Army Ordnance. They sent him over to Vietnam. He was a truck driver. He claims to have won a medal. It turned out to be a Good Conduct ribbon." Neely shook his head. "Sad."

"Well, all things considered, he might have behaved worse. I guess he considered the ribbon an achievement."

"Oh, I'm not denying that. It's just sad, the whole thing, that's all. Anyway, after his discharge, Peet took his army savings and went straight to New York. He was a dishwasher or something for Schrafft's, then a bellhop at the St. Moritz Hotel, and because he did some favors for some out-of-town actor staying at the hotel—favors—you can guess the kind—the actor helped Peet get a job as a sort of messenger and errand boy at Lincoln Center. And then came the Bolshoi Ballet, and he was assigned to bring them food and cigarettes, backstage, and the Russian dancers apparently treated him with kindness and respect —'like a proletarian,' Peet wrote in one letter—and I suppose this was the first warmth the kid had ever received, and so he became fascinated with Russia. Well, you know the rest, Matt. He saved up for a short tour of Russia, met this young Russian broad—she was twenty-three— and fell head over heels in love."

"It was more than that, from what I hear," said Brennan. "The Russian girl was the first female he'd ever met who made him feel virile and normal sexually."

"So that was it? I didn't know." Neely shook his head. "No wonder he tried to move heaven and earth to get back to her."

"Did he let you know he was coming to Paris again?" Brennan asked.

"No. I—"

"Has he been by?"

"Not so far as I know I was going to say I can't blame him for not getting in touch with us. I guess he got the message before. We don't intend to help him become a Russian citizen, true love or no true love. Only the Russians themselves can help him. I reckon that's why he's here now. To pester them some more, the way he's been pestering us."

"I suppose so," said Brennan without conviction. "Herb, in that form he filled out, does Peet mention anywhere anything about his interests and hobbies?"

Neely consulted the file. "He took a correspondence course in the Russian language. Does that qualify?"

"Did he finish the course?"

"He doesn't say."

"If he did, he'd have said so. . . . Herb, does he make any mention of collecting rare books or any books of any kind?"

"Oh, you're on that kick again." Neely laughed. "Of course not. No books."

"Or hobbies? Photography?"

"Not a word."

"France. Is there anything to indicate some interest in France or the French?"

"Nothing." Neely wrinkled his brow. "What are you up to, Matt?"

"I'll tell you what I have been up to in the last hour."

Lowering his voice, Brennan related how he had obtained a key to Joe Peet's room in the Hotel Continental, how he had used it, and what he had found there.

"Does any of that make sense to you?" Brennan finally asked. "The nude girls, okay. That's in character. But the avid interest in châteaux, palaces, Fontainebleau, Malmaison, Versailles. What do you make of it?"

Neely shrugged. "All tourists are interested in those places."

"But not obsessively so. Photographs, books, all the pamphlets. From what you've told me, I'm not even sure he can read."

"Well, from what this file reveals, he certainly can't write. You should see his letters. Hardly literate. My seven-year-old does better."

Brennan remembered something that had slipped his mind when he was recounting his investigation of Peet's hotel room, the contents of the wastebasket. "Another thing, Herb. When I was in his room, I found evidence he's rented a formal suit—tails. Now, what would he want with tails?"

"Maybe he's our new ambassador from Chicago? But seriously, half the men in Paris are wearing tails."

"Who are the ones who really require tails?"

"Well, the delegates, of course. For various state or diplomatic receptions."

"Name some."

"Receptions?" Neely reached behind him for an ornate booklet. "Let's have a look at our host's *Ordre du jour officiel de la Conférence du Sommet des cinq puissances.* Last night the British had a dinner in their Ambassador's residence. Tonight the French Foreign Minister is tossing a big soirée in the Hôtel de Lauzun. Tomorrow night the French Premier is sponsoring a dinner dance for delegates at Fontainebleau. Sunday night it is the President of France's turn, the traditional banquet in the Hall of Mirrors at Versailles. Next week, more. A dinner dance at Malmaison, a dinner at the Soviet Embassy. Then we're doing a reception of our own in the Embassy annex. Well, that gives you an idea."

"All white tie?"

"All."

"Well, I can't see Peet being invited to any of those functions, can you?"

"Hardly." Neely dropped the program booklet on the table behind him. "Look, I suppose there *are* some private parties where tails are required. And anyone who collects rare books might be invited to one of these."

"Oh, sure," said Brennan. "Dammit, it's still a dead end."

"And you still think this Peet might somehow lead you to Rostov?"

"I'm not as convinced anymore. . . . Herb, if Peet did come to Paris to wheedle the Russians into letting him enter their country, become one of their citizens, do you think they'd give him any consideration? They refused to two years ago in Moscow."

"That was two years ago, but they might be cooperative now. Two years ago Peet seemed to be acting on a romantic impulse. His desire to defect looked like a frivolous flip-flop to the Russians. But now, after so much time, if he's still persisting, they might take him seriously."

"Why would they even bother?"

"Why not? True, he's small potatoes, not much of a catch. But they like to have tried and tested American citizens go over the Iron Curtain to be on their side. A Chicagoan. A laborer. An army veteran. They can make propaganda hay out of that. It's not much, but every little bit helps."

Brennan nodded. "That must be it. I guess that's why they have a KGB agent keeping an eye on him."

"Well, you can bet I'd have a CIA man on a possible Russian

defector, if he was a good enough story. It all comes down to propaganda value, Matt. When they're sure of our boy, they'll take him in. It's got a natural press angle, you know."

That moment, Brennan conjured up Novik's name on Peet's scratch pad, and that moment, it seemed logical. If Peet had propaganda value for the Russians, they would want one of their writers to see him. Then Brennan wondered whether Peet had propaganda value for the Red Chinese as well. He was tempted to ask Neely about Ma Ming. But this was too much of a diversion. Instead, Brennan said, "You say there's a natural press angle in Peet?"

"Definitely. Clean young American lad, embittered by lack of opportunity in American capitalistic society, surrenders his passport, passes through the Curtain, accepts the ennobling Soviet citizenship, and—happy proletarian ending—finds true opportunity, true equality, true love."

Brennan could not help but smile. "Yes, I see. For an ex-newspaperman like you, that could be the angle." He paused. "But for an ex-diplomat like me, there might be other possibilities."

"Name one other."

Brennan threw up his hands. "I can't, you so-and-so, and you know it. Ask me a couple of years from now, and maybe I'll have the answer. Right now I can tell you only two things—first, if you have it, I'd like to see the day before yesterday's Paris edition of the New York *Herald Tribune,* and second, I'd like to use your telephone."

Neely swiveled around to the table behind him, and then made the full circuit back, handing Brennan the newspaper. "There you are. Looking for a new job?"

"Looking to see if Peet cuts out paper dolls." He opened the paper to page three, and whistled. "By God, he does."

At the top of page three, where the page in Peet's wastebasket had had a portion torn out, was a three-column photograph of a Legrande mannequin modeling the latest in bikinis, a sequined one for formal beach parties. "Another gem for Peet's girlie collection," murmured Brennan.

Automatically, he turned the page over to see what was on the opposite side. Behind the photograph of the leggy mannequin in the bikini, almost back to back with it, was a candid news picture showing a half-dozen Russian delegates to the Summit climbing the steps to the Palais Rose. In the foreground of the photograph, Brennan recognized Premier Talansky and Marshal Zabbin. The next three delegates were unfamiliar to him. Then he clearly recognized the one bringing up the rear. This one was none other than Minister Nikolai Rostov.

Staring at the photograph, Brennan could feel himself sinking deeper and deeper into a morass of confusion. Here was a newspaper published three mornings ago. Joe Peet had torn a picture from it. But which? The one on page three or the one on page four? Had he wanted to preserve another semi-nude for his growing collection, or a memento of a new-found friend named Nikolai Rostov?

Baffled, Brennan folded the newspaper.

"What is it, Matt?" Neely was asking.

"Another mystery," Brennan answered, and then he added firmly, "to be continued. . . . Okay, Herb, now give me your telephone. I want to check the hotel and find out if anything good has been happening behind my back."

AFTER LEAVING the Embassy, Brennan decided that there was time enough to stroll the length of the Rue de Rivoli and that at least one good thing had happened behind his back. Lisa Collins, it seemed, was ready to see him one more time.

The single message waiting for him at the Hotel California had, indeed, been from Lisa. The concierge, M. Dupont, had obligingly read it to him twice, enunciating each word carefully. A half hour ago Lisa had called in the message for Brennan. She had to see him briefly on an urgent matter. She would be outside the entrance to the Jeu de Paume, on the Place de la Concorde side of the Tuileries, at exactly one o'clock. While she could not be reached directly, she would phone the California once more before leaving for the Impressionist museum, in case Brennan called in and said he could not make it at that time.

Since he had almost an hour to spare before his meeting with Lisa, he sauntered between the shops and concrete pillars of the Rue de Rivoli, appreciating the shade of the continuous arcade roof and the awnings lowered toward the Tuileries, which offered relief from the blazing noon sun. Passing Smith's bookstore, Sulka and Company's glittering display window, the Angelina patisserie, he tried to analyze Lisa's message.

The only thing that the message told him was that, despite last night's episode with Denise, Lisa was prepared to see him again. The message implied that Medora Hart had finally got hold of Lisa, explained away the whole misunderstanding about Denise, and now Lisa was ready to forgive and forget. One fact prevented his having hopes of a permanent reconciliation. Lisa's message had baldly stated that she wanted to see him about "an urgent matter" and then only "briefly." The implication here was that their meeting would be anything but a timeless lovers' reunion, and that she had something other than their misunderstanding to discuss. Actually, if she had not seen Medora, or even if she had seen her but had refused to accept her story, Lisa might have impulsively made the appointment to tell him off brusquely and bid him good-bye.

By the time that he arrived at the Place des Pyramides, Brennan found he had worked himself into a mild state of agitation. He did not know why the loss of Lisa, under these circumstances, should differ in some way from the growing likelihood of losing her shortly, inevitably, because of his inability to clear his name and his determination not to spend his life with her under a cloud. But somehow, with Peet drawn nearer, with Earnshaw on his side, there was a flicker of hope for their future. On the other hand, if Lisa were female-foolish enough to distrust him because of last night, regarding him as a restless middle-aged roué who was poor mate material, there would be no reasoning with her, and therefore no hope. And therefore he was agitated.

He teetered on the curb, with no more heart for walking. Exposed to the sun, he was now hot, as well as hungry and thirsty. His hunger he would control, and he would try to persuade Lisa to lunch with him. But he had to slake his thirst. He turned into the corner café-restaurant, Le Carrousel, and sat and ordered a *citron pressé*. Soon, with the fresh lemonade in his hand, the cool tile at his feet, he felt better. He contemplated the Place des Pyramides, the gilded statue of Joan of Arc, upraised flag in her hand, astride her golden steed, and he watched the incongruous sport cars and trucks wheeling around her, and gradually his anxiety was allayed. Feeling restored, he decided to go to the Jeu de Paume and wait for Lisa.

Walking more briskly, he retraced his steps along the Rue de Rivoli, at the Rue de Mondovi chanced the traffic to dodge across the street toward the path and trees fringing the Tuileries Garden. He strode around the edge of the park facing the Place de la Concorde and climbed the steps to the modest nineteenth-century museum named after a tennis court whose site it occupied and which was now the popular stepchild of the gigantic Louvre, situated some distance into the gardens behind it.

Lisa was not yet present. Brennan's watch read twelve minutes to one o'clock. He was twelve minutes early and once more too restless and hot to stand in the sun waiting for her. It would be cooler inside, and the brilliant Impressionists would keep him occupied. Moreover, he had not been inside the museum in a half-dozen years, and he

626

wondered if it would offer him as much delight and stimulation as it had done when he was younger.

Going to the counter, he bought his one franc and fifty centime ticket, handed it to the uniformed doorman, and went into the Jeu de Paume, where the thick walls and protection from the sun offset the dazzling and varied brightness of the Impressionist oil paintings surrounding him.

He wandered from room to room, at first detached but soon caught up by and lost in the personalized and daring world those late-nineteenth-century innovators and masters had hewed out of an older world, a world where conservatism and conformity of style were making of beauty an art on a candy box top. From painting to painting he went—Toulouse-Lautrec's *The Woman Clown,* Manet's *Picnic on the Grass,* Sisley's *Flood Landscape,* Van Gogh's *Room at Arles,* Seurat's *The Circus*—constantly awed by both their courageous rebellion and their consistent genius. For one who wanted courage, Brennan thought, it was moving and inspiring.

Leaving the crude wooden door upon which Gauguin had painted a picture in Tahiti, Brennan returned to the Degas exhibit for another examination of his horse-racing series.

"Marvelous, aren't they, Matt?"

He did an about-face, and there was Lisa, tall, unsmiling, wearing a wide-brimmed floppy hat that matched her white purse, and a light silk print dress that curved softly down her young, shapely body.

He bent to kiss her, but absently she offered him her cheek. Her full lips remained compressed and her face was troubled. He wondered whether her concern was over their relationship or over something else.

"I was outside, but I was early," he apologized, "so I came in to look around and I guess I lost track of time."

"It doesn't matter," she said. "When you weren't there, I knew you'd be in here." She glanced about. "It's wonderful. I wish I had more time. I came through here with some of the girls the other day between collections. It was the only place in the neighborhood I could think of when I left the message for you to meet me. I'm glad I caught you. Are you all right?"

"Are *you?*" he countered, still worried by her unrelieved seriousness. "Did you see Medora Hart?"

"Yes—"

"Then she told you what happened. You're not sore at me anymore, Lisa, are you?"

She seemed bewildered. "Sore at you? What do you—?" She

627

remembered, and her reaction was one of exasperation. "Oh, *that,* you and that French chorus-girl bitch. Don't be a fool. Last night, sure, I was angry as hell, the effrontery—but you know me well enough, I wouldn't let you get away from me that easily—no, I heard all about it just now, from Medora, and I thought it was funny, about the only funny thing that's happened this morning."

Brennan's relief was crossed by a flash of annoyance: He did not ever want to be ridiculous in Lisa's eyes. But the annoyance passed instantly. He loved her, and he had not lost her. "Well, I'm glad, Lisa," he said. He paused. "What's been happening to you this morning? Your message—you wanted to discuss something urgent."

"Yes." She looked at the other sightseers in the museum. "Not here, Matt."

"Why don't we go to lunch? I know a—"

"I can't. I promised to meet some fashion editors at Taillevent in twenty minutes. After that, I have to attend another damn collection. Anyway, we'll be dining together tonight. You haven't forgotten, have you? Legrande's big dinner bash at his villa outside Paris, town called Vaucresson. Everyone tells me it's going to be wild, the event of the season." She looked at him. "You're taking me, aren't you?"

He had forgotten, and he would have preferred to be with her alone, but he said, "I've been looking forward to taking you for days. I even turned down another invitation from Denise."

"You bastard." She took his arm and said, "Don't tease me, Matt. I'm not in the mood. There is something urgent. Let's go outside."

They left the Jeu de Paume, circled the outer terrace to the side stairs leading down into the one-mile expanse of the Tuileries Garden. Descending the stairway between the massive stone statues of *The Tiber* and *The Rhône,* they walked in step, arms linked, toward the octagonal fountain.

Beside the splashing water Lisa halted. She appeared to be looking off at the tree-lined lawns and at the statue that Maillol had sculptured to honor Cézanne and that was known as *Reclining Woman.* But then Brennan realized that Lisa's pained eyes were looking at nothing, seeing nothing, except perhaps some fresh and hurting memory.

"It's Medora," Lisa said suddenly. "It's awful." She turned her frightened dark eyes to Brennan. "Medora tried to kill herself this morning."

"What?"

"Yes, she did, Matt. She tried to commit suicide. It's a God-blessed miracle I—I was able to save her."

All pleasure had gone out of him. He brought Lisa toward him, squarely in front of him. "What happened?" he demanded. "What happened to her?"

Lisa went on rapidly. "When I was leaving the hotel this morning, early, I found a telephone message in my box from Medora. She asked if I could come by this morning to see her. She had something to tell me about you. Well, I was tied up the first part of the morning. But when I was coming out of Dior, I realized I was only a few blocks from the Hotel San Régis. I ran over there, buzzed upstairs to Medora's room. No reply. I started to ask the concierge to tell Medora I'd been around, when he said that he was positive she was in her room. No one had seen her leave, and she'd just taken a phone call from Monsieur Nardeau a half hour before. So I thought maybe she was in the bathroom when I rang, so I went upstairs. I rapped. No reply. I was about to go again when, I don't know why, I tried her doorknob, and the door gave. It was unlocked. And there she was, Matt. What a sight."

"Unconscious?"

"In her nightie, face down on the bed. I rushed in and shook her. She was limp as a rag doll. Her heart was still beating, but her pulse was irregular. I went into the bathroom to look for salts, something, anything, and there it was—an uncapped bottle on the sink, absolutely empty. Nembutals. I had no idea how many she'd taken, only that she'd purposely swallowed an overdose of sleeping pills. Well, I settled down. I was very level-headed. You'd have been proud of me, Matt. I remembered that silly first-aid course we had to take in school—how I used to hate it—and some of the antidotes came back to me. So I went back to Medora. I figured if she'd been on the phone with Nardeau little more than a half hour ago, she must have done this right after, so maybe I'd caught it early enough. I turned her around, began to rub and pinch her, and finally sat her up. I brought her to, but she was incoherent and she kept passing out. I was desperate."

"You should have called for a doctor."

"I thought of it, but vetoed it. No, Matt. If a doctor came, she'd have been all over the front pages again. Another scandal. Even if she survived this, she'd never survive that. Oh, I figured if I couldn't bring her around, I would call for an ambulance. But not right away. I got her to her feet, half dragged her to the bathroom, and gave her the basic antidote. Warm water made soapy. I spilled it into her. It worked instantly. What a mess. She kept throwing up. When she'd had it—and she was plenty conscious by then—I led her back to the bed. Then I ordered tea and burnt toast and milk of magnesia. While I was waiting, I telephoned Carol Earnshaw. Then, when the tray came, I

629

poured some magnesia into the tea, shaved some of the burnt toast into it, and forced her to drink up. Antidote number two. In an hour she was better. Terribly weak, but safe and recovering, and both grateful and resentful that I'd saved her."

Brennan gazed past Lisa at the bursting life of the green trees, bushes, grass, and the bright flowers, and the wretchedness of Medora's effort to court death seemed more gruesome than ever to him. "Why did she try it, Lisa?" he asked.

"Well, you know how much hope she had that some police informer who'd been paid off by the police and Nardeau would recover her painting? It was all she lived for, to get that painting back and, with Nardeau's help, get Fleur Ormsby or her husband to capitulate. Well, there was the great expectation of that, and there she was waiting for me to drop around when Nardeau called—and wham-bam, the whole dream blew sky-high."

"You mean the informer didn't come through?" Brennan asked.

"Worse, Matt. He did." She paused. "He learned where the stolen paintings were supposed to be hidden. He tipped off the authorities. The police and Nardeau went there at dawn, some abandoned mill off the road to Chartres. Sure enough, there were the pictures, every one of them, a heap of charred ashes, with just enough fragments to make it clear that the ashes represented *Nude in the Garden* and the rest of the oils. Well, there they were, incinerated, gone forever. And there was nothing to be done, except for Nardeau to tell Medora. I gather he did it nicely on the phone, but how could anything be done nicely enough for poor Medora, once she knew she'd lost her last chance to go home? I gather she was too stunned to say anything much on the phone. But once Nardeau had hung up and she was alone with the disaster, she had a convulsive fit of hysteria, absolutely wild with grief, and she just sort of groped into the bathroom and began feeding those Nembutals into herself."

"Is she all right now, Lisa?"

"Depends on what you mean. She won't be able to work for a few days. Otherwise she's recovering, physically. I wanted to get a nurse, but she wouldn't have it. Finally, when Carol Earnshaw arrived, Medora agreed to let Carol stay with her today and tonight. But what happens when she's alone again, Matt? She'll try it again, and if she's saved, she'll keep trying suicide until she makes it. You should have heard her. She kept mumbling about what's the use of staying alive, what's the use of going on and on in this crummy, bloody way. And I kept trying to soothe her, putting all kinds of pies up there in the sky. But she wouldn't have it. Everyone, she said, has tried to help her and failed. And she saw no more reason to expect any more help. All she wanted was to be allowed to shut her eyes and sleep forever. Then, as I was about to leave her with Carol, despite what she'd been through she remembered the nonsense about you and Denise, and actually found the strength to tell me the truth about it, just because she wanted someone to be happy and because she felt you and I deserved it."

Brennan stared at the scenery of the Tuileries, no longer sure if all this celebration of life wasn't what was unreal, all this and not Medora's wretched wish for the final comfort of extinction.

"She's a good kid, Lisa," he said at last. "She also deserves better."

"She's entitled to everyone's help, because she has a right to live," said Lisa intensely.

He nodded, his mind off on a journey. "Yes," he said.

"She can't fight those Ormsbys alone. She needs all of us, and the two of us specifically. She needs devoted allies. That's the reason I wanted to see you, Matt. I remembered hearing you say once, about Medora, that if nothing else worked out, well, you might have a way of helping her. Were you just talking? Or did you mean it?"

He took out his pipe, and thoughtfully he filled it. He looked at Lisa. "Yes, I meant it."

Lisa reached out and clutched his arm. "You really mean there is something you can do for Medora?"

"There is something I can try to do."

"Do you want to talk about it?"

"Not yet, Lisa. First I've got to speak to Emmett Earnshaw. It would involve his help, too."

"Earnshaw," Lisa said derisively. "He's too self-centered to help anyone. After all those promises, what has he done for you?"

"Never mind me," said Brennan. "Whatever Earnshaw is, I think he is a man who does honor his debts. I'm not the only one to whom he's indebted. He owes Medora a lot, too, for bringing Willi von Goerlitz to him when she did. I'm simply going to present him with her bill for payment."

"When?"

"When? Today, Lisa. This afternoon." He held up his wristwatch. "In twenty-five minutes Earnshaw and Willi von Goerlitz are going into the Red Chinese Embassy to settle something mighty important. I guess he should be out of there, win or lose, after a couple of hours. Okay, at four o'clock I'll be at the Lancaster Hotel to see Earnshaw. If he'll help me help Medora, we've got an outside chance of saving her."

"But a chance?"

Brennan smiled. "A real one, Lisa."

Impulsively her arms went around him and she kissed his lips. When she released him, she said breathlessly, "There. Even if you keep cheating on me, you immoral baboon, I'll always love you. Always. . . . Now I've got to run. See you for dinner. And I only hope Earnshaw, after he sees the Chinese, is in as good a mood as I am right now. I'll be praying, Matt."

T HEY WERE RIDING to their two o'clock appointment in the Goerlitz family's Sedanca model Rolls-Royce, while the Goerlitz family's deluxe Mercedes-Benz 600 followed closely behind them carrying Earnshaw's Secret Service agent and the German stenotypist who had come down from Frankfurt with the legal staff at daybreak.

They had left the Arc de Triomphe behind several minutes before, and now, peering out past the chauffeur in the open-air front seat and across the silver hood and "Silver Lady" on the radiator cap, Emmett A. Earnshaw could see that the Avenue de la Grande Armée had become the Avenue de Neuilly, and that the Embassy of the People's Republic of China would not be far away.

Earnshaw glanced at Willi von Goerlitz next to him and at *Herr Direktor* Fred Schlager at the opposite window seat. Willi had just returned from seeing his paralyzed father in the American Hospital. Admiral Oates had been there, too. Dr. Dietrich von Goerlitz had been conscious, but was still too disoriented to recognize Willi. He had been in the intensive care ward, but Oates had reassured Willi that the old man had been making normal progress toward recovery. Somehow, Willi had not been reassured, for his father's improvement by no means guaranteed recovery of his former powers. From the start of this ride, Willi had been sober and taut. Observing the boy's hard profile now, like the bas relief of a Teutonic prince on a Prussian monument, Earnshaw could not detect whether Willi was disturbed about his father or about his new responsibility as the acting head of the Goerlitz Industriebau and chief negotiator with the Chinese of a 300-million-dollar deal.

Herr Direktor Schlager, on the other hand, appeared unperturbed by the crucial meeting that lay immediately ahead. At the start he had opened the walnut desk of the custom-made Rolls-Royce, emptied his briefcase upon it, and was tranquilizing himself by reviewing columns and columns of figures that represented German marks and Chinese yuan.

"Well, now, I guess we should be on time," said Earnshaw to no one in particular.

"On the minute," said Schlager with satisfaction.

"I was reflecting that it's been—uh—well, a number of years since I had anything to do with any of the Chinese Communists," said Earnshaw. He realized that Willi had cast him a worried look, and he hastily added, "But I always found that I could talk to them. I must say, and I'm not one to hold on to the clichés of the Fu Manchu legend, that while they were always courteous and clever, they were also inscrutable, yes, inscrutable. Of course, that was Premier Kuo Shu-tung. I had him to the White House, after his United Nations speech, and he was rather a gentleman, no Maoist—"

"The Chairman will not be present, of course," interrupted Schlager. "The Vice-Chairman of the Central Committee, Marshal Chen, has headed the negotiations until now, with Mr. Liang, the Minister of Economics, always at his elbow. There will also be, I would think, Dr. Ho Ta-peng, one of their foremost physicists, who will be the Operations Superintendent of the Nuclear Peace City under our Operations Manager."

"Well, I don't know them," said Earnshaw. "That's the new breed since China became a big voice in the United Nations and has been shaking its neutron bomb at us. But if they are like their predecessors, I don't anticipate the meeting will be too abrasive. When they hear our proposal, I can't imagine them raving or ranting."

"They will be polite," said Schlager, and then he added without humor, "politely angry . . . I do not know what will happen after that."

"Leave it to me," said Earnshaw, more for Willi than for Schlager.

He fell back into the silk-upholstered rear seat of the Rolls-Royce, lowered the electric window slightly for the breeze, and lapsed into silence.

Earnshaw knew that his personal confidence was real, not mere dressing for the others who depended upon him. Of course, he had always been confident in his White House days. But in that period it had not been unalloyed self-confidence, but also the conviction that Simon Madlock was doing well for him. He had dwelt, as Dr. von Goerlitz's memoirs made clear, in a fool's paradise. Now his self-confidence was based solidly on his own capabilities, which he had permitted to atrophy too long. He knew what was right and what was wrong, he knew how to handle people, and he was well briefed for the forthcoming encounter.

He had arrived at the Hotel Ritz suite before nine o'clock this morning, just as the Goerlitz legal staff, down from Frankfurt, had concluded their preliminary talks with Schlager and Willi. The three attorneys, led by their senior member, the respected Walther Jaspers, unaware that Earnshaw would be a member of their team, had gone off immediately to the Chinese Embassy, where Economics Minister Liang had been waiting for them to review last-minute modifications in the 300-million-dollar contract. At the Chinese Embassy, the past hour, four design engineers representing the Goerlitz industries had been going over the small-scale mock-up of the Nuclear Peace City with Dr. Ho Ta-peng and his Chinese engineers.

Alone with Schlager and Willi von Goerlitz, Earnshaw had spent almost five hours listening to the *Herr Direktor's* briefing on the project, having his own questions answered, and debating alternative proposals that might protect Goerlitz Industriebau from Chinese deception and yet allow the project to be undertaken. There had seemed no compromise solution that might be acceptable to both the Goerlitz interests and the Chinese until Earnshaw had struck upon one, and it had been by far the best, entirely acceptable to Willi and Schlager, and possibly acceptable, at least possibly, to the Chinese.

Earnshaw realized that Schlager had stuffed his papers back into the briefcase and was closing the walnut desk of the Rolls-Royce.

"Boulevard d'Inkermann," Schlager announced. "The Chinese Embassy is on the far corner. It is Boulevard Bineau 104. Are we ready? How are you, Willi?"

Willi von Goerlitz stirred. "I am rehearsing my lines. I will not hide it—I am nervous."

Earnshaw laid his hand on Willi's coat sleeve. "Nothing to be nervous about, my son. Just be natural and easy. It'll be very civilized. As I always used to tell myself before I went into a conference with foreigners, 'No need to worry, Emmett, when you've got truth and right on your side. Those are the best allies you can have, along with a little faith in the Maker.' "

Willi looked doubtful. "I—I am depending mostly on you, Mr. Earnshaw."

"Then you know I'll do my darnedest, try to handle it as your father might have if he were going in there."

The Rolls-Royce came to the stoplight at the intersection as it turned green, and the chauffeur started to steer the car from the Boulevard d'Inkermann into the Boulevard Bineau, but braked to allow two oncoming cars to pass. Earnshaw had a brief glimpse of the thoroughfare they were about to enter. The Boulevard Bineau was wide, almost majestic, with rows of trees seeming to rise out of the sidewalks, and attractive houses from another century set behind iron fences attached to stone foundations.

They were moving once more, and turning again, and Earnshaw had his first view of the Chinese Embassy. It was, if not an eyesore, an incongruity in this old and gracious neighborhood of Neuilly. For one thing, it was unattractively modern. For another, it looked cheaply constructed. It seemed to be all windows with gray stone and metal slabs in between, with its great bay windows opening onto glass-shielded terraces instead of the usual French wrought-iron balconies.

As they passed through the entrance gate, a uniformed French policeman stepped out of the entry cubicle to wave them along. Riding into the parking area of the courtyard, Earnshaw could see the yellow stars against a red field that was the flag of the People's Republic of China. The main building climbed to six stories, and from close up, the numerous windows were more attractive, the wooden shutters folded back to reveal soft lacy curtains. As the Rolls-Royce came to a halt, Earnshaw noticed a small, pretty garden surrounded by diminutive lawn-level light fixtures with colorful red mushroom tops. It was homier now, more California now, and Earnshaw approved.

Their chauffeur, as well as the Secret Service agent from the Mercedes-Benz idling beside them, leaped out to open the rear doors of the limousine. Earnshaw stepped into the courtyard, followed by Willi von Goerlitz and Fred Schlager.

As he stretched his legs, Earnshaw's attention was caught by the emblem above the double doors and the sign beside it. The sign, a copper plate, read: EMBASSY OF CHINA IN FRANCE. The emblem over the doors was a gold-edged red shield on which were engraved a large gold star, four lesser ones, and a gold representation of T'ai Ho Tien, the ancient Imperial Palace in Peking.

Suddenly the double doors of the Embassy were swung open by a young man in a dark blue fatigue uniform and a stout middle-aged lady in white blouse and navy blue skirt, and between them appeared a scraggy unicorn of a man with an abnormally small head. His pointed cranium was shaved; his crinkling smile revealed prominent cuspids; and his attire was a natty lightweight gray suit. He seemed to be in his middle thirties.

Bouncing out of the doorway, he came in ungainly loping strides toward Schlager, hand outstretched. "Mr. Schlager, how good to see you, sir."

Schlager shook his hand, then took his reedy arm. "Minister Liang, I should like to present Mr. Willi von Goerlitz."

"Yes, yes," said Liang enthusiastically. "I believe we met briefly at the Hotel Ritz shortly after your arrival." He dropped his smile and lowered his voice. "We commiserate with you on your father's illness. I understand he is improved. A magnificent constitution. Give him our respects and best wishes for health."

"Thank you, I shall," said Willi. "Minister Liang, in my father's absence, knowing what his desire would be in this matter, we have invited his old friend and frequent adviser in business affairs, the Honorable Emmett A. Earnshaw, former President of the United States, to join us in this meeting. Minister Liang, Mr. Earnshaw."

As they shook hands, Liang's sallow features were devoid of any sign of emotion. "We are honored, Mr. Earnshaw."

"My pleasure," replied Earnshaw. He revived in his mind his earlier descriptive word, *inscrutable,* and was pleased.

Liang had started to direct Willi von Goerlitz toward the open doors. "Marshal Chen has joined Dr. Ho Ta-peng and your engineer staff upstairs to have the pleasure of seeing your magnificent model of the city. Shall we look in on them before settling down to conclude our business?"

"Whatever is preferable to you," said Willi.

Earnshaw fell in beside Schlager, following the other two into the Chinese Embassy. They went into a small hall, one wall made of marble, the other plastic-covered, where a Frenchman was filling out a form at the reception desk. Liang rattled off something in Chinese to the female receptionist, and quickly she reached for the telephone.

Liang led them toward an elevator. Beyond, Earnshaw could make out a narrow staircase, the steps carpeted in maroon-colored grass cloth.

They crowded into the cramped elevator and were carried up to the first floor, Liang apologizing profusely to Willi for the discomfort of the elevator. Spilling out of the elevator, they were in a constricted gray corridor decorated with modern light fixtures.

Liang leaped ahead. "First room," he called back. Excusing himself, he opened the door and preceded them inside.

The room was low-ceilinged, spacious, bright, cheerful, despite the thick cerise drapes and dark carpeting. In the middle of the room a dozen men, Chinese and German, several of the latter in shirt-sleeves, were gathered around a large rectangular table upon which had been built a toy city including futuristic models of industrial plants. A placard attached at one side of the table read in Chinese, in German, in

English: NUCLEAR PEACE CITY—LANKAO, HONAN PROVINCE—MODEL DESIGNED BY GOERLITZ INDUSTRIEBAU, FRANKFURT-AM-MAIN—SCALE: 1 CENTIMETER EQUALS 20 METERS.

From the moment of their entrance every occupant of the room except one had frozen into a posture of respectful attention. The one exception had turned to regard them with lazy curiosity, and then, stubbing out the cigarette he held in his left hand, he had started toward them.

This, Earnshaw suspected, was the redoubtable Marshal Chen, the Vice-Chairman and youngest member of the Chinese Communist Party Central Committee. He looked more formidable than his height, which Earnshaw guessed to be five feet eight or nine. His wiry black hair was combed straight back. His rigid, unsmiling visage was handsome except for a walleye and definitely reflected his Mongolian origin. His body was slender and athletic. Alone among the Chinese in the workroom, he did not affect Western dress. To Earnshaw his attire was unusual yet not unfamiliar. It was neither civilian suit nor uniform. It consisted of a loose gray tunic with a soft high collar and baggy trousers of the same color and material, and glossy brown military boots. And then Earnshaw remembered where he had seen a similar outfit, long ago. It was the one that Mao Tse-tung had always worn.

Liang had jumped ahead to intercept the man in the gray tunic, whispering to him as he brought him forward.

Now Liang pivoted to address them. "Gentlemen, I have the pleasure of introducing you to Marshal Chen. . . . Marshal, this is Mr. Willi von Goerlitz, the son of Dr. Dietrich von Goerlitz, who is for the present the head of the firm."

Marshal Chen nodded solemnly. "I am pleased to meet you. I offer you my country's sympathies."

"And *Herr Direktor* Schlager, whom you have met before," Liang continued.

"Yes, of course, *Herr Direktor,*" said Marshal Chen. "This is a day we have long awaited."

"And, Marshal," Liang went on hastily, "I would like to present the Honorable Emmett A. Earnshaw. Mr. Earnshaw formerly served as—"

"I know how Mr. Earnshaw formerly served," said Marshal Chen sharply to Liang. He faced Earnshaw. "A pleasant surprise, Mr. Earnshaw. How do you do?"

Nervously, Liang intervened. "We owe the unexpected pleasure of former President Earnshaw's presence to Mr. von Goerlitz, who wished to have a friend of his father's beside him during our final talks and the signing."

Only half of Marshal Chen's walleyed gaze remained fixed on Earnshaw. "Understandable," he said slowly. "Again, it is our pleasure to have you in our Embassy to witness the signing. I fear you will find little else to occupy you. Certainly there is no more to talk about."

Marshal Chen turned toward Willi. "I am happy to say, Mr. von Goerlitz, that your legal representatives and our own are in full agreement on the several minor changes and deletions we have suggested. These pages are now being typed and will be prepared for our signatures in fifteen minutes." He gestured over his shoulder. "I had not seen the entire model assembled before. Most impressive. In two years, I trust, we will meet in my country to see it a reality."

Willi swallowed. "It can—can be a reality, if we both work together to—to fulfill the contract."

Schlager had a fit of coughing, and once having controlled it, he bustled forward. "Marshal Chen, have our experts explained to you all of the innovations in the complex?"

"I believe so. I have no ear for scientific jargon. But since our Dr. Ho Ta-peng approves, I am satisfied."

"It will be a wonder," said Schlager with a salesman's heartiness. "If you can spare me five minutes, I should enjoy clarifying several of the operations."

"Five minutes," agreed Marshal Chen with a curt nod. "After that, I should think we can sit down to conclude our agreement."

They started for the model of the Nuclear Peace City, with Liang, Willi, and Earnshaw trailing behind them. The Chinese and Germans at the table parted, greeting them with deference. Marshal Chen indicated a paunchy, rumpled hunchback, a bemused Chinese with an ageless countenance, as the notable Dr. Ho Ta-peng. Next Marshal Chen introduced a plump, beaming little man as Mr. Ma Ming, of the official Hsinhua news agency, who would prepare the official press release of the deal at an appropriate time. After the introductions, Marshal Chen gestured for Schlager to take over.

Picking up a rubber-tipped pointer, Schlager, his enthusiastic drummer's voice booming, swept his wand over what resembled a wealthy child's miniature play city.

"Our village for the workers and technicians and scientists is the most advanced yet most economically constructed prefabricated community on earth," Schlager announced. "It exceeds, in every respect, the prefabricated towns our competitor Krupp developed in Tunisia and India. It is an improvement even on the atomic-powered town of

Farsta, in Sweden, which cheaply produces electricity and pumps its water supply for 35,000 citizens by means of a nuclear power station. But your Lankaoville, as we have been calling it, will be provided with electricity from the nuclear power plant for next to nothing, so that your Chinese workmen and our own specialists will live here with their families amid the highest standards and at a minimum cost."

Earnshaw watched with fascination as Schlager's pointer lifted the tiny roof off a miniature model house.

"This is the typical residence for your average worker and his family," Schlager continued. "The Goerlitz-Fertighaus Number 225-B. Consider it. Living room, dining room, *Küche*—that is, kitchen—two bedrooms, one for *Eltern,* the other for *Kinder*—five beautiful rooms and a work shed, all taking up no more than 120 square meters of ground. Each of these houses preconstructed in Frankfurt, erected overnight in Honan Province, and not one costing your Government more than 8,000 yuan Chinese or 16,000 marks German or 4,000 dollars American. A bargain?"

Marshal Chen grunted. "A temptation to the luxury-minded and softheaded who might think of themselves as capitalists."

There was some tittering around the table, but Schlager seemed to ignore it as he answered seriously, "But you must have the best for the best products of your technical schools."

"Yes, yes," said Marshal Chen, "Go on, please."

Schlager moved along the table. His pointer tapped a larger miniature building that, to Earnshaw's eyes, bore some resemblance in design to an elongated armory.

"Here," said Schlager, preening, "the most remarkable steel plant on earth. Here are the oxygen furnaces that replace the old open-hearth technique, and here are the most advanced hot-strip mills. And our continuous casting operation is entirely computer-controlled. The production capacity will be two million tons of steel a year, at a cost of half that in a conventionally powered steel mill. I remind you, Marshal, there are only three nuclear-powered steel factories on earth, and this is the fourth and by far the largest. I am sure you understand the operation. Rapidly produced, inexpensively produced finished steel for China's 850 million. Our Goerlitz metallurgists, many owing their training to Professor Ivan Bardin, who first conceived this Leap Forward, will efficiently and expertly oversee your plant."

"Very good," said Marshal Chen.

Schlager had gone to the end of the table and was lovingly admiring a group of minute buildings encircling an oversized sphere. His pointer touched the ball-like structure.

"The heart of the entire complex," announced Schlager theatrically. "The huge containment sphere that harbors the nuclear reactor vessel. Centering about it are the atomic furnace, the neutron shield, the coolant tank, the heavy water, the control devices and so forth. Within this cylinder, uranium conversion provides the nuclear energy for the city, for the steel plant, and above all gives China its radioactive by-products. There is almost no limit to what this nuclear reactor, and others you will add later, can provide. As by-products you will have radioactive isotopes of chemical elements for your medical laboratories. You will use them to make drugs and fertilizers and genetically altered agricultural foods and plastics, all these marvels at practically no cost. Once this Goerlitz reactor and the others are operational, China's standard of living will drastically improve." He paused, out of breath, and looked at Marshal Chen. "I hope that I have clarified—"

"You have," Marshal Chen interrupted. "Most impressive, as we have known for a year. Now it is time to execute the documents that will make this miniature our servant." He beckoned to Willi von Goerlitz, to Liang, and finally to Earnshaw. "Follow me."

As they went into the corridor, Earnshaw once more tried to understand why Schlager had gone to all this trouble to sell the miracles of the Nuclear Peace City when he knew that it had already been bought and when he secretly knew that it could not be sold as had originally been agreed. At first, to Earnshaw, Schlager's propaganda had seemed irrational, for it made Willi's immediate task and his own more embarrassing and difficult.

But as they all filed into another corridor, Earnshaw had a glimmer of understanding. Schlager was not feebleminded. In the world of international cartels, his shrewdness was legend. And now Earnshaw began to perceive his strategy. With his pitchman's spiel, Schlager had sought to dramatize through his exhibit how necessary this project was to China. When the truth was out, when the nuclear project was withdrawn, was no longer for sale at the old price, he wanted Marshal Chen's desire for it so whetted that he would pay any price rather than forgo its purchase. Brilliant, Earnshaw admitted to himself, brilliant of Goerlitz to have hired and delegated authority to one so crafty as Schlager, and brilliant of Schlager to have so perfectly maneuvered Marshal Chen before the kill. With a silent prayer, Earnshaw beseeched the Maker to endow him with the gift of brilliance, too, if only for the next half hour.

They had entered a conference room of modest dimensions. Along the wall inside the entry door sat the German male stenotypist, his machine perched on his knees, and beside him the senior Goerlitz attorney, Walther Jaspers, an attaché case at his feet, and then two Chinese with contracts on their laps, the pair presumably the legal representatives of the People's Republic of China.

On an end wall, in solitary splendor, hung a carved frame holding a patriarchal photograph of Premier Kuo Shu-tung. Across the way were shuttered windows, with two benches upholstered in a beige material beneath the windowsill. On the remaining short wall were three gilded frames containing collages of graceful Chinese designs made up of bird feathers and synthetic grass.

"You may be seated here, gentlemen," Marshal Chen announced.

He stood in the center of the room, behind a magnificent long table with a glistening rich black-lacquered top adorned by a bowl of goldfish and a variety of ashtrays. The effect of the table, somewhat lower than the ordinary conference table, was to invite sociability rather than business conversation. There were five straight teakwood chairs on either side of the table. Marshal Chen directed the Germans and Earnshaw to the chairs on one side, and he himself took the middle chair opposite, between Economics Minister Liang and Dr. Ho Ta-peng, with the cherubic journalist, Ma Ming, sitting next to the physicist.

Earnshaw saw that Willi had taken the chair directly across from Marshal Chen, and was gesturing for Earnshaw to occupy the seat at his right, while Schlager was already at Willi's left.

The atmosphere of formal sociability continued. A young Chinese male retainer, with extremely slanted eyes, dressed in white quilted jacket and black trousers, was carrying a tray holding a steaming pot of aromatic tea and pink-and-white cups without handles. He glided around the table, serving. At once he was followed by another menial offering cigarettes from a red-lacquered metal box.

Although desperate for one of his own cigars, Earnshaw, conscious of his host's eyes upon him, accepted a Chinese cigarette. When the box reached Willi, he, too, took a cigarette, and then he pointed to the gold engraving on the red box. "The old Imperial Palace in the Forbidden City, is it not?" inquired Willi of Marshal Chen.

The Chinese Vice-Chairman stared at Willi, impressed. "You are correct. Except the Imperial Palace *was* in the Forbidden City. Peking no longer has forbidden areas for anyone who is a friend. The Palace and our capital are open to all who come to us in peace."

After that, Marshal Chen lapsed into silence, sipping his tea, watching the goldfish, listening as Liang cheerfully discussed the sights and inhabitants of Paris with Willi and Schlager. Ten minutes of this inconsequential conversation went on, and just as Earnshaw was

641

beginning to wonder how long the polite exchange could continue, he saw the Marshal crook a finger toward his attorneys, who were standing off chatting with Walther Jaspers.

Instantly the social prelude to the business meeting was ended. A Chinese attorney busily began to distribute copies of the bulky contract for the Nuclear Peace City, one to each of those around the table. From somewhere, Earnshaw realized, note pads and sharpened pencils had materialized on the black-lacquered conference table. And he also noticed that a stand of gold pens had been set before Marshal Chen.

"I think that we are ready to conclude the business at hand, are we not?" said Marshal Chen. He held up the contract. "Mr. von Goerlitz, your father read and approved the contract in this version the day before his illness. However, he dictated a few minor revisions, and we ourselves suggested a few minor revisions, and orally we agreed on these. I believe your Mr. Jaspers will confirm what I am saying."

Willi and Earnshaw glanced at Jaspers—who had moved to a seat at the end of the table—and he bobbed his head in assent.

"All that your father personally was not able to approve was the exact language of these last revisions," Marshal Chen went on. "This morning Mr. Jaspers and his colleagues studied this language on your behalf and gave their final approval to the completed contract. . . . Is that not so, Mr. Jaspers?"

"It is," said Walther Jaspers. He leaned toward Willi. "The contract is as your father wished, Mr. von Goerlitz."

Marshal Chen gripped the edge of the table. He addressed himself to Willi. "Unless you wish to review the minor revisions—each such page is marked with a paper clip—then I believe that we can agree every clause is in perfect order. In that case, I would suggest that we are both ready to climax our protracted negotiations by affixing our signatures to the contract. Are you so prepared to proceed, Mr. von Goerlitz?"

Earnshaw's gaze was fixed on Willi von Goerlitz's profile. The ridges of Willi's jaw muscles were visible. Suddenly his lips moved. "No," he said. "I am not prepared to proceed."

A flick of surprise touched Marshal Chen's face, and his walleye seemed to take in the entrance door while the other eye disconcertingly held on Willi. "You are not? . . . Ah, *hun how,* I see. You do wish a moment to check the contractual changes?"

"No," said Willi.

Marshal Chen's brow wrinkled. "No?" Then, half to himself, he said, *"Wor bu ming ba?"*

642

"The Vice-Chairman says he does not understand," Liang interpreted quickly.

"I cannot sign this contract for Goerlitz Industriebau until one clause is entirely removed and a new one added," said Willi. "Before we go ahead, I should like paragraph A, including subsections I, II, and III, on page eight, eliminated in its entirety." He paused. "Once this is done, we will submit the new clause to replace it."

Across the way, Marshal Chen's head was bent low as he leafed through the contract. Beside him, Liang and a Chinese attorney were also turning pages. They found page eight, and they began reading silently.

Marshal Chen was the first to look up. "I am afraid, Mr. von Goerlitz, you have confused me. I have reread the clause to which you seem to object. It merely states that the Nuclear Peace City you agree to build is specified to be in the area of Lankao, in the Province of Honan, in the People's Republic of China. Is this the clause to which you refer?"

"Yes, sir."

"But to what can you object? It was the site surveyed and selected by our Government as most suitable for a project of this kind. Your own engineers agreed a year ago that it was suitable and qualified for your construction. Beyond that, our choice of location can be no concern of yours."

Willi's jaw muscles quivered. "I am sorry, sir, but the location must be our primary concern and shall continue to be. The site we mutually agreed upon a year ago was based on mutual trust. However, lately, certain intelligence has reached us that undermines our trust in this transaction, and because of this new information, I feel we must protect the future of our investment by changing the location of the Nuclear Peace City."

Marshal Chen's face offered no more emotion than that on a wax statue. "What are you talking about, Mr. von Goerlitz?"

"I am speaking of our investment, Marshal Chen. We are a private company financing a more-than-one-billion-mark industrial complex and city for a foreign Government. We have reason to believe that a customer—such as the Government in question—could see fit not to honor this contract, this agreement, in a year or two. We would be helpless, and we would be nearly bankrupt, in that case."

Liang had half come out of his seat. "But that is absurd, if I may say so. Whatever gave you such a fantastic suspicion? The People's Republic of China trades with private industry throughout the world, and pays its bills, and honors its agreements. No nation has a better record, and you know it, Mr. von Goerlitz."

"You are speaking of the past," said Willi, "and I am speaking of the future."

Marshal Chen had pushed Liang back into his chair. Now he faced Willi. "You, sir, are also speaking insultingly of our honor. Unless, of course, you are joking in a manner I do not understand?"

"I have never been more serious," said Willi doggedly. "We are eager to construct and maintain the Nuclear Peace City for you, but not in Honan and not anywhere else in China. We will proceed to deal with you, but only if the site is so located as to give us better control of our share of the investment."

Marshal Chen's face had hardened. "Your behavior, Mr. von Goerlitz, is unbelievable."

"My behavior," said Willi, "is as believable as certain facts that have just been brought to my attention about China's future plans concerning foreign investors."

"What plans?" demanded Marshal Chen. "And brought to your attention by whom?" His eyes darted to Earnshaw, then returned to Willi. "By capitalistic imperialists who conspire to destroy the People's Government of China?"

Willi looked helplessly at Earnshaw, but Earnshaw was sitting erect now, knowing the time had come, and he addressed himself to Marshal Chen. "The information was brought to our attention by your own people. The evidence was irrefutable that it is you, in concert with other Communist aggressors, who are the conspirators, conspiring to destroy, ultimately, foreign investors from abroad who have dealt with you in good faith."

"I was not speaking to you, Mr. Earnshaw," said Marshal Chen harshly. "We know your record. I was speaking to Mr. von Goerlitz."

"And I was speaking *for* Mr. von Goerlitz," said Earnshaw.

Marshal Chen disregarded him. He turned to Willi once more. "I can forgive you, with your inexperience, for allowing yourself to be manipulated by others who are our enemies," said Marshal Chen. "But I cannot forgive your disloyalty to your parent. Your father, before his stroke, had complete faith in our honor as we had faith in his honor."

"My father had no opportunity to become acquainted with the facts," interrupted Willi.

"*Ch'i yo tsi li!*" Marshal Chen exploded. Then, regretting his oath, he recovered his poise. "What facts?" he demanded.

Willi began to reply, faltered, and paused.

"I—I prefer that Mr. Earnshaw speak for me now," he said.

644

Marshal Chen's gaze shifted to Earnshaw. "What facts?" he repeated.

"I'll be only too pleased to tell you, if you'll permit me," said Earnshaw calmly. "According to our information, you planned to have the Goerlitz Industriebau construct this nuclear factory complex and city, and to have them staff it, as per contract, with their German Operations Manager and his expert maintenance crew of engineers and physicists. But, according to our information, once the nuclear power plant was started up, you planned to nationalize the plant and factories, confiscate them, cancel your debt, throw out the German staff and replace it with equally experienced Soviet Russian scientists and—"

"A lie!" Liang shouted.

Marshal Chen remained imperturbable. "More than a lie, comrade," he said quietly to Liang. "A typical American Wall Street slander and smear of truth."

"If it is a slander," said Earnshaw evenly, "it is not American, but your own. The sources for this truth were the wives of two of your Chinese delegates, who happened to be indiscreet in a public place."

"Wives? Where are these wives? I do not believe your fable from such a source," said Marshal Chen. "You are troublemakers, you Americans. You are warmongers breeding dissension among friends and allies for your own greedy ends. You are also fools. Surely you could have been more clever, concocted a more logical fable. To what end would we ever dream of such a dishonorable plan?"

Earnshaw remained unflustered. "Simple. You get a rare and costly nuclear reactor for nothing. Then you convert it from peace production to plutonium production to increase your nuclear arsenal."

Marshal Chen's head swiveled toward Willi von Goerlitz. "I cannot listen to your friend further," he said. "He speaks like a child. Mr. von Goerlitz, you have read the contract. You have obtained the approval of the International Atomic Energy Agency in Vienna to sell us the uranium fuel with the condition that we permit regular on-site inspections by IAEA representatives. They would see that our facilities are not converted to military use. Your father was satisfied with that protection."

"Well—" said Willi, bewildered.

Earnshaw touched Willi's shoulder. "Let me answer, my son." He stared across the table. "I'm afraid you'll have to listen to me, Marshal. Your agreement to on-site inspections doesn't mean a damn thing, nor does the paper it is printed on, if you and your Russian col-

645

laborators gang up and refuse to admit the inspectors into China or Honan."

"You are not only fanciful, Mr. Earnshaw, but you insult the intelligence of every person in this room," said Marshal Chen. "Why are we treating for world disarmament and peace at the Summit? To convince Goerlitz Industriebau to build us a plant so that we can nationalize it and make more bombs? To wage war with these bombs in partnership with the Russians, to whom we have not spoken in years, not since Khrushchev followed Tito in betraying Marxist ideals, to whom we speak now in Paris only to prevent imperialists from leading us all into a suicidal global war?"

Earnshaw removed a cigar from his breast pocket, considered it, and suddenly pointed it at Marshal Chen. "Very well, Marshal," he said. "If we are misinformed, if your intentions are indeed honorable, then you won't mind making the change in the contract that Mr. von Goerlitz has advocated."

"What change? *T'ien ah!* What is this change?"

"Revision of the clause stating that the Nuclear Peace City must be built inside China. We are proposing a substitute clause that will safeguard the Goerlitz investment. We are prepared to hand you a list of cooperative neutral nations outside the Communist orbit, nations like Sweden, Switzerland, Bolivia, possibly even Hunza, Chile, Kenya, and we will ask you to select one such neutral nation as the site for your Nuclear Peace City. We will arrange with that neutral nation to accept your Government and Goerlitz Industriebau as foreign investors in their country. This is done, in many forms, throughout the world. You will have your nuclear reactor, your steel mills, your city peopled by your nationals, and you will receive the peaceful products of this industrial complex. Goerlitz Industriebau, in turn, will have its safeguard. This is complicated, but it can be worked out. Those are Mr. von Goerlitz's terms. If your intentions are good, as I have said, you will accept these terms. If you refuse the compromise, then we are forced to regard the disturbing information we have received as entirely credible."

Marshal Chen tilted back in his chair, staring with hatred at Earnshaw. At last his chair banged down and he sat straight. "I apologize to you for one miscalculation I have made, Mr. Earnshaw. You are not stupid. You are diabolically clever. You are an agent provocateur, an inciter, a pawn of the CIA sent to foment ill-feeling among allies in business and political affairs. You are one of the fanatical anti-Communist breed who would eradicate those who threaten capitalist

646

wealth and those who desire bread and peace for the underprivileged. You are one of the racists who despise all those who are colored, be they black or yellow. You are one of the white devils who have spread their poison far and wide. You have infected many, temporarily, and many of these are in high places. You have managed to lead even the Russian Premier by the nose, coming between the Russians and ourselves, encouraging our disagreements. But I promise you, Mr. Earnshaw, you and your bankers shall not win. The Russian Premier and his people will see through your machinations one day, and know who their real friends are, and who their real enemies are, too. And now, now you have captured the ear of young Mr. von Goerlitz, your Faust, but I promise you that in the end he, also, shall know who his real friends are, and in the end he will turn away from you."

There was a silence as Willi von Goerlitz helped Schlager gather together their papers and return them to the briefcase.

Marshal Chen watched, and then he spoke again. "This is your last word, Mr. von Goerlitz? The word your American collaborator has given us?"

"Yes," said Willi. "Mr. Earnshaw has spoken for my father and myself. I think our proposal is eminently fair. It cannot hamper you, and it can protect us from harm. I do hope you will permit reason to overcome passion, and that you will accept the contract with the one clause revised. If you agree to do so, we shall make immediate arrangements to go ahead together. It is up to you."

Marshal Chen came to his feet. "If it were up to me," he said angrily, "you would have my reply this instant. Unfortunately, it is not up to me. The final decision is up to Chairman Kuo Shu-tung. You shall have his verdict to cancel or not to cancel by next week."

"We shall await his reply," said Willi von Goerlitz.

"*How ma*—good day, gentlemen," Marshal Chen snapped, and with that he turned on his heel and left the room.

Five minutes later Earnshaw, Willi von Goerlitz and Schlager had departed from the Chinese Embassy and settled themselves in the security of the waiting Rolls-Royce.

Not until the car rolled out of the Chinese Embassy courtyard did they abandon dignity to boisterous self-congratulations.

"We've won!" Schlager chortled. "The minute he didn't give us a flat no, mentioned going to Chairman Kuo, I knew we'd won. There will be a lot of shilly-shallying back and forth, but in the end we shall have our contract, I predict, and on our safe terms—your terms, Mr. Earnshaw—yours. You were brilliant, the way you handled Marshal Chen with such outspoken authority."

Willi enthusiastically nodded his agreement. "We would have been lost without you, Mr. Earnshaw. Whether we obtain the contract or not, you have saved us from a catastrophe, and, as well, you have let the Chinese know whom they are dealing with. Best of all, you have afforded them a face-saving device to let them revive our negotiations. We owe it to you. If it were in my hands, I would know how to thank you, but the attorneys have taken away the memoirs. According to my father's old instructions, they are not truly in my hands, or anyone's hands, until my father recovers sufficiently to communicate his wishes. The moment he does recover, I promise you, he will know what you have done for him, and for our family. When he is able to comprehend what you have done, I honestly feel he will repay you in the best way he can."

Earnshaw smiled, and sank wearily back in the car seat.

Until this moment of the afternoon, he had entirely forgotten that his reputation lay in old Goerlitz's hands and in the final disposition of the chapter about him in the ailing German's memoirs. He had forgotten, in his single-minded dedication to besting the Chinese; but now (indirectly) Willi had reminded him of the literary sword over his head.

What had Willi just said? Yes. *The attorneys have taken away the memoirs. According to my father's old instructions, they are not truly in my hands or anyone's hands until my father recovers sufficiently to communicate his wishes.* The feeble promise offered small consolation. The wait might be a long and discouraging one. And when Dr. Dietrich von Goerlitz did recover, the stroke might leave him in such a condition that he would be indifferent to the debt he owed Earnshaw and interested only in releasing his memoirs, his last testament, as originally written. Or worse, the attorneys might insist on proceeding with publication of the memoirs immediately and as they had been written.

Yet, somehow, right now, assessing his own position, Earnshaw relegated what old Goerlitz owed him to petty debts. It seemed of little consequence, this radiant afternoon, considering the enormous gain he had reaped this important day.

Pleased, he brought a light to his cigar and puffed contentedly. For suddenly he realized that what pleased him most was not the way he had handled Marshal Chen, but that, during the crucial meeting and exchange, he had not once wished for Simon Madlock's help. How proud Isabel would have been to know this, he thought.

He enjoyed the sweet cigar. The new brand was an improvement, he decided, and he would have to try more of the same.

J UST AS HE HAD PROMISED Lisa and himself hours earlier, Matt Brennan had gone to the Hotel Lancaster to call upon Earnshaw and seek his assistance in trying to save Medora Hart. He had waited in the lobby for Earnshaw and there had been joined by Jay Doyle, who had to see the former President about the next day's column. After a short time Earnshaw had returned, and together the three had gone up to his suite.

During the entire past week Brennan had not seen Earnshaw so exuberant and confident. This transformation of a tentative and tired old bovine into a self-assured and lively lion had been remarkable. Like the ancient institutions of Paris, he seemed to have undergone a *ravalement de façade,* and as a result his real character had begun to show forth.

Before Brennan had been able to bring up the matter of Medora, and before Doyle had been able to remind his employer of the daily column yet to be written, Earnshaw had launched into a detailed recounting of the engagement with Marshal Chen at the Chinese Embassy. Pacing tirelessly, waving his cold cigar to emphasize points, Earnshaw had gone on without a stop for ten or fifteen minutes.

After Earnshaw had finished, and while Doyle and Brennan were still profusely congratulating him, Brennan's mind was puzzling over both the mention of the presence of Ma Ming at the meeting and one other remark that the former President had made. Brennan thought about it as Earnshaw poured marc de Savoie in the liqueur glasses for the three of them. Brennan came forward in his chair.

"One thing, Mr. Earnshaw—" Brennan began.

"Emmett's my name, Matt," the former President called back cheerfully. "We've been too close these last few days to stand on formality." Handing out the sliver-thin glasses of liqueur, he added, "We're friends."

"Thank you, Emmett," Brennan said. "There was one thing you mentioned when telling us about the conversation with Marshal Chen. I wonder if I heard you correctly."

"What's that?"

"The part where Marshal Chen accused you and all Americans of propagandizing Communist nations, trying to generate ill-feeling among Communist allies so that you could split them and weaken them."

"Just what he said." Earnshaw sat down with his drink. "Called us white devils."

"Right. I believe you then quoted him as saying something to the effect that the democracies had even corrupted certain Communist leaders with their propaganda, leaders like Russian Premier Talansky; that you were partially responsible for promoting the ill-feeling that has existed between China and Russia."

"His words," said Earnshaw.

"And if I remember correctly, you quoted Marshal Chen as saying China would overcome our propaganda yet, that—"

Earnshaw raised his hand. "Here's just what Chen said, Matt. He said that the Russian people and their leader would see through us yet and come to know who were their real friends and their real enemies."

"Exactly what I thought I heard," said Brennan. He looked inquiringly at Earnshaw and Doyle. "Don't you see the significance of what Marshal Chen was saying? I'm sure it's something he'd never have let slip if he hadn't been so damn angry."

"The significance?" Earnshaw repeated blankly.

"Yes," persisted Brennan. "You know how steadily I've been telling both of you about the little hints and rumors I keep picking up. By now, my ear is attuned to them. And inadvertently Marshal Chen added one more to back up my theory that while Red China and Soviet Russia continue to air their feud in public, they are privately performing as friends and allies. Hell, Emmett, you went into the Chinese Embassy to tell them you know China intends to kick out their German staff one day and take in the Russians. Now you come out of the Embassy with the information that Chen himself warned you, in a moment of fury, that the Russians would soon know, or do already know, who their real friends are—not us, not the democracies, but the Chinese Communists."

Earnshaw slapped his knee. "By God, you're right!"

Pulling up his belt, Doyle said, "Of course, Chen's remark or threat or whatever it was meant to be, may have just been wishful thinking, not to be taken literally."

"No," said Earnshaw quickly. "Not the way he said it. I believe Matt has something there, although I'm not sure where it leads us to."

"Maybe right up to the Summit," Brennan said. He could see that Doyle was restless, and he quickly added, "Well, there's nothing we can do about it, at least for now. But anyway, I'm beholden to you, Emmett, for another piece of research."

Earnshaw stood up. "You're beholden to me for nothing, young man." He went to the tray of drinks to fill a goblet with Evian water.

"I'm the one who's beholden. No matter what happens with old Goerlitz, and it looks like nothing much will, I owe you a good deal, Matt. And I mean to make it up to you, possibly tonight. There's a big soirée, or whatever you call it, a big one this evening at some kind of Paris hotel—"

"It's not really a hotel, even though it's called Hôtel de Lauzun," said Doyle. "It's a tremendous seventeenth-century mansion on the Île St.-Louis. The French use it as a sort of town house, for formal receptions the city of Paris gives for important visitors."

"Glad you told me," said Earnshaw. "Save me making any conversational blunders. Well, now"—he had turned back to Brennan— "anyway, I'm invited, and I understand our President is, too, and also the Secretary of State. The first opportunity I have, Matt, I'm going to take one of them aside and discuss Rostov and you."

"I'm grateful," said Brennan.

"You thank me when I come back with good news," said Earnshaw. "I have a hunch I'll get somebody to bring you and that Russian together."

From the sofa, Doyle was again grunting impatiently. "Emmett, I want to remind you we've both got a column to get out, and we'll both have to be dressing for dinner fairly soon. You've got the Hôtel de Lauzun. And I've got the Société des Gastronomes affair at Lasserre."

"Jay," said Brennan, as kindly as possible, conscious of the shock that his friend had endured that morning and of the depression he must be suffering. "Jay, there's just one more matter I must discuss with Mr. Earnshaw—with Emmett. It's really quite pressing and the reason I came up to see him. It'll interest Hazel and you as well. I promise you, I'll make it as quick as possible, and then beat it and leave you to your work. Do you mind?"

Doyle fell back into the sofa cushion with sulky indifference. "Okay. Go ahead."

Brennan swung back to Earnshaw. "I'll tell you why I came up here. It's to request a special favor that may help a friend of ours who's, well, in a desperate situation right now. I'm speaking of the English girl, Medora Hart, the—"

"Medora," said Earnshaw. "Sure, of course. She's the youngster who brought Willi up, and came out to the hospital with us."

"That's right," said Brennan. "I feel we all owe her something, and even if we didn't—anyway, she tried to commit suicide today—"

Brennan saw that not only Earnshaw but Doyle, as well, was surprised and disturbed.

"—but luckily, she was saved."

651

Earnshaw tapped his goblet. "So that's it. I thought something was going on. Carol, my niece, got a call this morning, and she was as upset as I've ever seen her. She told me that girl, Medora, was sick over at some hotel near here and needed someone to take care of her, at least until tomorrow." He paused. "But it was actually a suicide try, was it?"

"Did Carol tell you why?" asked Brennan.

"Why? Let me—" With difficulty he seemed to ransack his memory, and thoughtfully he tapped his glass again. "I remember. Carol told me the whole sordid business—well, that was some days ago—about poor Medora Hart and the Ormsbys, and I must say, knowing Sir Austin as long as I have, I refused to believe it. But yes, before leaving this morning, Carol did tell me the rest, about the Nardeau painting of Fleur and what it meant to that young kid, and how it was stolen—and yes, that it was destroyed, found burned last night—and when our Medora heard, she just collapsed." He stared at Brennan. "But she actually tried to kill herself? That was it?"

"Yes," said Brennan. "And she'll likely try again, and succeed, unless somebody does something for her. She hasn't a chance against Sir Austin and Fleur by herself."

Earnshaw frowned, and kept shaking his head. "I finally had to believe all Carol told me about Sir Austin. It was hard to swallow. He was such a gentleman, fine young fellow, when I first came to know him. Of course, that was years ago. I haven't kept up much with him lately. I always disliked Sydney—that's his younger brother, a black sheep, in and out of trouble all the time. But Sir Austin—still, thinking back, I can remember certain qualities he had that were unattractive. I mean, he was always decent to me—but maybe that's because I was somebody—but he could be abrupt, even cutting, and especially ruthless with—with servants or people under him. I guess that's the way some people get to the top. And once at the top, well, it's not only power that corrupts, it's also vanity. Sir Austin has plenty of that, not only for himself but for his family name. It has even occurred to me, it's conceivable, that his urging that I quash that chapter in the Goerlitz memoirs was as much motivated by the fact of his name being in it as my own being smeared. I don't know." Earnshaw shook his head unhappily. "I guess it could be true, all that about destroying the painting to preserve himself."

"It's true," said Brennan.

"All right, Matt. Now, Medora Hart, I want to do what I can for her. You said there was something I could do."

"A little thing. . . . Some days ago, when I first heard of Medora's predicament, I was struck by a farfetched idea, a means of helping her. I've thought about it since. It's somewhat theatrical and sinister, my notion, but after all—and I'm convinced of this—in the Ormsbys we are dealing with theatrical and sinister people. What I'd like to undertake is actually a plan that might be put in the form of a two-act playlet. The first act would be in your hands. The last act would be in mine."

"I'm listening," said Earnshaw.

"I'll tell you what inspired my plan. Something I heard about Sydney Ormsby, who is here in Paris on publishing business. And then, something about Jay's book, a book he is writing—"

Doyle stirred. "A book he *was* writing," he interrupted bitterly.

"I'm sorry, Jay," said Brennan. He looked at Earnshaw once more. "At any rate, by crossing Jay's book, dealing with communist conspiracy, with my knowledge of Sydney Ormsby's proximity, I evolved my plan. If we can pull it off, we can save Medora, make Sir Austin wave a white flag and permit her to return to England. If we can't make it work, well—I'm afraid there's nothing else we can do for the girl. Now, the springboard for my Medora plan is not Sydney but rather Sir Austin Ormsby himself. You're still on good terms with him, aren't you, Emmett?"

"Yes, I am, although I'm not sure I want to be any longer."

"Nevertheless, you are on good terms. Do you expect Sir Austin to be attending the Hôtel de Lauzun dinner party tonight?"

"I should think he'd be there. I'm sure the Prime Minister and all the topflight British delegates have been invited. Yes, I'm almost certain Sir Austin will be on hand."

Brennan left his chair for a place on the sofa beside Doyle and across from Earnshaw. "Okay," he said, "then tonight at the Hôtel de Lauzun is when and where the plan to save Medora gets under way. Now, here is what I have in mind for your role in the opening act. The first chance you have, I want you to engage Sir Austin in conversation. Then this is what I'd like you to say to him—"

As he rapidly went on, it did not surprise Brennan that not only Earnshaw, but Doyle, too, was hanging on his every word.

Because his spirits were so low, it had taken Jay Thomas Doyle longer than ever before to complete his writing of Earnshaw's daily column. And because, from the moment that Hazel had shattered his world with her Rostov bombshell at Le Drug Store, he had eaten compulsively, gluttonously, self-destructively through the entire day, it had taken Doyle longer than he had anticipated to cover the short walk from the Avenue George-V to the restaurant Lasserre in the Avenue Franklin-D.-Roosevelt. As a result, Doyle was the last of the members of the Société des Gastronomes to arrive at the reserved table in the upstairs dining room.

The founder and self-elected lifetime presiding officer of the Société, seventy-year-old Claude Goupil, whose face looked like that of a grouchy Egyptian mummy and whose general aspect closely resembled Cruikshank's drawings of Ebenezer Scrooge, greeted Doyle as he always greeted tardy guests, with a dyspeptic snarl and a line plagiarized from Anthelme Brillat-Savarin. "So, at last, Monsieur Doyle, and alas, for you seem to have forgotten that the most indispensable qualification of a cook is punctuality, and the same must be said of guests."

"I was too weak to dress," retorted Doyle lightly, "because I'd been starving myself all day for tonight."

Offering a vague wave of his plump hand to the other members, all of whom he had met in Paris at one time or another, Doyle waddled to the one empty place at the table and moored himself to the cut-velvet chair.

Since the guests on either side of him were deep in conversation, Doyle had a respite, an interval in which to determine his mood and take his bearings. Despite his genial demeanor upon entering, his mood was one of unrelieved irritation, irritation with Hazel for accepting Rostov's version of the Vienna conspiracy over his own, irritation with Earnshaw for forcing him to write the inane column every day, irritation with his publishers for having bound him to a contract to write the hack cookbook for his personal survival, and now irritation with that supercilious and blithering imbecile Goupil.

Doyle surveyed the dining room of Lasserre, one of his favorites, seeking relief from his dark mood. Briefly, all that galled him was alleviated. The crystal chandeliers sparkled. The fashionable diners appeared handsome and well-bred. The waiters were impeccable and their stately progress across deep-piled carpets was silent. The canard à l'orange, decorated with an orange from which stemmed a flickering candle, was mouth-watering and attractive as it was served at an adjacent table. The melody from a piano nearby was soothing. Before him, the vermeil-handled knives and forks, the gold-rimmed plates, were exquisite.

Attracted by a sound from above, Doyle raised his eyes in time to see Lasserre's famous ceiling slide apart, opening wide, revealing to the diners a starry cloudless sky above for their roof.

An earthly honking brought Doyle's head down from the heavens and disclosed to him Claude Goupil, blowing his nose in his handkerchief before he resumed his instructions to the proprietor. Again Doyle's mood darkened as he considered his repulsive host.

He had been introduced to Claude Goupil many years ago, in the better days, the best, when he was the king of columnists and Goupil only the prince of gourmets. Goupil had already founded his private club of epicures and was eager to include a renowned journalist as a member. Doyle had become aware, early, of the dues. There existed a tacit understanding that if Goupil knighted you, the price of admission to the round table was only to speak well (and often) of the founder. Word of mouth would do, but newsprint was better. Doyle had understood, and a month later had devoted the first of what were to be many columns to Claude Goupil. For the founder had ambitions. In that time, the king of French gourmets, which meant all gourmets, was Maurice Curnonsky, who was known to partake of a considerable lunch daily, allowing only a boiled egg for his dinner, but who, in his later years, skipped lunch altogether and devoted himself to only one meal a day, and that dinner rarely without its foie gras truffé. That was Curnonsky, the king; and all other gourmets, Goupil among them, were merely princes, although one day one must become the heir. It was this throne to which Goupil aspired, and it was this throne, after Curnonsky's passing, that Goupil achieved. And his throne, as he had known from the start, was built of paper.

In the beginning Doyle had been proud to be a member of Goupil's court, no matter how he was being used, but later he had come to tire of Goupil's dictatorial tactics concerning meals and his overindulged and unchallenged egocentricity. And lately, as tonight, Doyle had come to detest Goupil because the Frenchman was phony, parasitical, and boring. Yet still, as tonight, Doyle had been unable to decline an invitation to a gathering of the Société des Gastronomes. Helplessly he obeyed Goupil's call, not because he was a gourmet writing about gastronomy but because he was, at last, a defenseless glutton.

Tonight, he saw, would not differ from the Société's other nights. Four times annually, Goupil notified twelve out of the membership to attend a dinner he personally supervised in a Paris restaurant that had been crowned by two stars or three in the pages of the *Guide Michelin*. The restaurants were always receptive to having Goupil in their kitchens and at their tables, because of the resultant publicity. Goupil, it appeared, had caught up with his legend. Two thirds of the diners were regular members, residents of Paris, and the other third was composed of floating members, international travelers who came through Paris once or twice a year, industrialists, playboys, journalists, professional men, but all of them wealthy or celebrated (or once-celebrated) self-styled epicures, and all of them prepared to tolerate Goupil's eccentricities and ego in order to partake of a memorable feast and share an occasion that not only gave them a conversation piece but made them feel like social arbiters.

Glaring at Goupil with mounting distaste, Doyle had a sudden insight into his detestation of the celebrated gourmet. He hated Goupil, he suspected, because he had come to hate himself. For Doyle, in these enlightening moments, Goupil represented a specter of what he himself would inevitably become in the years immediately ahead. A parasite. A tiresome raconteur. A rootless, scrounging old man without a *raison d'être,* reliving diminishing glories of the past.

He continued to glare at Goupil: the skeleton head, the mean eyes jealously searching for attention, the dry masticating of food not yet served, the dribbling Don Quixote with only pepper mills to joust against. There he sat at the head of the table, hunched like one of Shakespeare's spider kings, cranky and imperious, attired in one of his renowned vulgar neckties and purple shirts, readying to release his dogma on wines and viands, to revive thrice-told anecdotes whose punch lines he garbled or had forgotten, to dispense a largess of Brillat-Savarin's wisdom and pretend (perhaps even believe) that each aphorism was his own.

Chrissakes, Doyle thought, it's going to be one hell of a night, after one rotten hell of a day.

Doyle felt a ponderous hand on his shoulder, a hand that shook him from his musings. He turned quickly to find that the partner at his right was none other than his long-time acquaintance, Igor Novik, the political feature writer for Moscow's *Pravda.*

Novik rubbed his own corpulent stomach, and between his matted toupee and wisp of goatee his inflated face beamed down at Doyle's swollen belly.

"Aha, hallo again, Mr. Henry VIII," croaked Novik.

Despite his mood, Doyle joined in on their old game. "Hello, yourself, Mr. Honoré de Balzac."

"I have not see you since the first day at the Palais Rose," said Igor Novik. "What have you been doing, comrade?"

"Eating," said Doyle glumly. But he felt somewhat better, for at least Novik, a mixture of buffoon and astute political analyst, was a glutton like himself and would make the tedious evening more companionable.

"Why do we not eat now?" the Russian muttered under his breath.

With a pang Doyle realized that despite his own constant gorging the entire day, he was starved, absolutely ravenously hungry. "Because we have to await our monarch's pleasure," Doyle whispered back. "I think he's going to start his damn ceremony now. What an hors d'oeuvre to start with."

Indeed, the king of gourmets had wobbled to his feet, making grating little nasal and guttural sounds to attract the attention of the members of the Société. Annoyed that all conversations had not ended, that all eyes were not yet upon him, Claude Goupil rapped his glass with a knife several times, disregarding the startled looks of other diners in the restaurant Lasserre.

"Ah, *bon*. So. Fellow gastronomes," Goupil announced in his shrill piercing voice, "welcome to the forty-seventh gathering of our exclusive Société. As ever, through the delicious years, we begin with our credo."

Covertly, Doyle grimaced at Novik. Doyle hated Goupil's ritual, especially tonight, when he was so famished.

"Let the number of guests not exceed twelve," Goupil intoned to the twelve. "Let the guests be so chosen that their occupations are varied, their tastes similar. Let the dining room be brilliantly lighted, the cloth pure white, the temperature between eighteen and twenty degrees centigrade. Let the men be witty and not pedantic. Let the dishes be exquisite but few, the wines vintage. Let the eating be unhurried, this dinner being the final business of the day."

Goupil inclined his head to the light patter of applause.

Once more irritated, Doyle leaned back and whispered to Novik, "Well, he left out only one thing—the name of the author of those words."

Novik grinned. "Brillat-Savarin?"

"Who else? Except that was the King's own digested—or rather, indigested—account for the Constant Eater."

Goupil was holding up Lasserre's large menu. "Tonight," he continued, "I have commanded the chef to serve us the following." He dribbled, wiped his chin, and read aloud. "Casserolettes de filets de sole, Caille confite sur foie gras, and for the *pièce de résistance,* Gourmandise Brillat-Savarin—to be followed by les salades de Goupil and pêche meringuée. For the wines I have selected from the *bourgognes blancs* a Beaune Clos des Mouches '61, and from the *bourgognes rouges* a magnificent Grands Échézeaux '55."

He looked up, not for approval but for humble gratitude, and received a louder round of handclapping. With a satisfied nasal snort, he sat down, lifted a hand, and gestured imperiously.

The waiters descended upon them, and the elegant serving carts—carrying the patty shells filled with filets of sole, and truffles and numerous other ingredients—came rolling up, and the forty-seventh indulgence of Goupil's Société des Gastronomes was under way.

Doyle wolfed his food down, hastening to bribe and glut his tyrannical stomach. Once, Goupil admonished him to savor each morsel, reminding him, "Animals feed; man eats. Only the man of intellect and judgment knows how to eat." But even though this was criticism, and Goupil again did not give credit to Brillat-Savarin for it, Doyle was too drunk and sated with food to resent chastisement.

Midway through the main course, silently and steadily shoveling the veal-filled pancake into his mouth, Doyle began to feel at ease and expansive, even somewhat sanguine about the possibilities of his immediate future.

Throughout the endless afternoon of mourning, left to himself, Doyle had become more and more discouraged—not over his deep belief that an international conspiracy had been responsible for President Kennedy's death, but because of the hopelessness of finding support of his belief through Hazel's Russian "friend." He had slowly realized that Hazel had done her best to help him, and failed, and that she could probably not learn anything different from the same source. If the proof was to be found, it would require fresh sources. But Doyle had no fresh sources. His dream had dissolved, and he had been thoroughly disheartened.

But now, gorging himself on the veal, it was as if his confidence was being tangibly restored. Perhaps his book, declaring Lee Harvey Oswald a dupe, a fall guy for foreign assassins, deserved one more effort at immediate authentication. There still existed the single known source that might prove or again disprove his historic beat, and this source remained Hazel's so-called Russian "friend," whom Doyle knew to be none other than Nikolai Rostov. The blinding thought came to him: If Hazel would not speak to Rostov again, then he, Doyle, might personally seek out Rostov and provoke him into admitting the truth.

He realized that Matt Brennan had tried the entire week to see Rostov and had been rebuffed at every turn. But that was another matter. To Rostov, it was likely that Brennan was a sprig of poison ivy, to be avoided. But to Rostov, the name of Jay Thomas Doyle might stand for something else, something less troublesome, something even useful for propaganda purposes.

The conviction grew in Doyle that if he applied to Rostov for an ANA interview (after all, ANA was also the faithless Hazel's outlet and one that had always been fair to the Soviet Union) or even for an Earnshaw interview to be ghosted by himself, his request for the interview might be immediately approved. Once having managed to confront Rostov, he would cleverly squeeze out the remaining facts about the old conspiracy.

A lone obstacle remained. He must find the conductor that would lead him to Rostov. He dared not attempt to use Hazel for this. He wanted someone else. Preferably a Russian, someone he knew and who knew Rostov. Someone like Igor Novik.

He turned toward Novik, sensing that the presence of the knowledgeable Russian journalist beside him had probably unconsciously inspired his whole train of thinking. He must find out if Novik knew Rostov well, or even knew the Minister at all.

He realized that Novik, who was looking past him at Goupil, was engaged in some kind of conversation with the founder.

Impatiently, Doyle waited.

"The French wine here is excellent, excellent, fine bouquet," Novik was saying with amiability. "I meant only that a foreigner, raised on his native drink, can rarely adopt the drink of another country as a substitute for his own. We are conditioned by our environment. That is why I confess that even in Paris I miss my vodka."

"Vodka!" Goupil snorted disagreeably. "Vodka is nothing. Vodka is the aunt of wine."

Novik grinned teasingly. "Those words, Comrade Goupil, are from a Russian proverb."

"Then your Monsieur Proverbe stole them from me," snarled Goupil, and instantly he turned his attention elsewhere.

Igor Novik shrugged and met Doyle's eyes, and they both laughed.

The moment that they had recovered, Doyle sought to take advantage of their mutual pleasure over this harassment of the insufferable gourmet and the warmth that had been generated between them.

"Igor, earlier you asked me what I'd been up to all week, and I told you I'd spent it eating," Doyle began. "Of course, I was pulling your leg."

Wiping his mouth with his napkin as he prepared for the dessert, Novik said, "I knew that, for I know you to be the most industrious American of my acquaintance. I supposed you had no wish to discuss your work."

"Nothing like that, nothing secret," said Doyle. "It's simply that I was a little ashamed, because the stuff I've been writing for ex-President Earnshaw has been fairly routine and dull. Actually, to keep myself busy, keep my hand in more serious politics, and pick up a few extra rubles, I've been helping a friend of mine write a book about Russia."

"At last you have come to Russia, *tovarich.*"

Doyle made a self-deprecating gesture. "I'm not contributing much to it, Igor. My friend researched and wrote this book, but he's not a writer, he's a—well—a former diplomat. He needed someone to sort of polish it for him, so I've undertaken the job. But along the way, I've found some holes in his material, and I told him I'd try to fill them in. There are a couple of your Russian government people I'll have to try to interview while they're still here in Paris. One in particular. I'd like to see him, ask him some questions. I wonder if you know him. He's Assistant Minister for Far Eastern Affairs."

"Nikolai Rostov?" said Novik immediately.

"That's the one."

Igor Novik laughed. "Know him? Of all people. Certainly I know Rostov. I have known him ever since we went to school together."

"You went to school with him?"

The Russian journalist nodded, stuffed some peach meringue in his mouth, and said as he chewed, "But we went our separate ways. I worked for *Izvestia,* and then became foreign editor and correspondent for the Central Committee's *Pravda* in Moscow. Rostov went off to the Far East, and then into the diplomatic corps. But we had reunions at international conferences where he was sent and which I was assigned to cover. When I am in Moscow, I sometimes see him—three, four times a year. We both like"—Novik shot a look at Goupil, and grinned at Doyle—"the aunt of wine, and to make talk about life."

"Have you seen him here in Paris?"

"Once, twice, maybe. He is too busy. I tried to lure him out to one of my favorite restaurants, but it is no use. He has no taste for food." Novik swallowed some red wine, then winked. "His taste is for women. I've heard he has for many years a mistress in Moscow, English or American, I think."

"American," said Doyle quietly.

"You have heard, too? Of course, in this day nothing is private. Well, I do not blame Rostov. If my wife cooked as abominably as his wife, I would also look outside for my pleasure. . . . Try the pêche meringuée, comrade, excellent. . . . Where was I? Yes. Food.

Natasha Rostov, nice old woman, terrible cook. I remember once I was in Moscow, six months ago maybe, Rostov invited me to his apartment for dinner. It was an important dinner party, Marshal Zabbin, some—some foreign guests—so I could not refuse. I told myself this time Rostov will not permit his wife to cook, will bring in a cook, for such guests. But no, Natasha insisted to cook. She outdid herself. Who in the world can make a bad borscht? No good kasha? And spoil the chebureki? You guessed, comrade. Natasha. Awful meal. Anyway, I say this, even Rostov understood and was ashamed. So to repair the evening, the very next night in Moscow, Rostov took the same guests, Zabbin and the Chinese, too, to the Peking restaurant in Ulitza Bolshaya Sadovaya, and while the dishes were not of the best, they were an improvement on Natasha's."

Doyle had heard every word, but he had to be sure he'd heard them correctly. He tried to speak casually. "Igor, were you along when Rostov took his Chinese guests out to dinner?"

"Was I—?" Igor Novik's expression suddenly changed from one offering gossipy reminiscence to one surprised and immediately protective. "What did you ask?"

"If you were along when Rostov took his Chinese guests out in Moscow."

Novik frowned. "Chinese guests? What do you mean? Did I say that? No, no. The guests were from Yugoslavia. My poor memory, when I eat so much, it leaves me. Chinese in Moscow?" He gave a short laugh. "Can you imagine such a thing these days? Anyway, enough of that, enough of Rostov."

"I asked if you knew him, Igor, only because I thought you might help me get an interview with him."

"With Rostov here? No, no, I think he is too busy for the press."

Doyle observed that Novik's manner had quite obviously changed. He was guarded. Doyle persisted. "I don't want to see him as a journalist trying to get an interview for publication," said Doyle. "Remember, I told you I'm helping a friend, a former diplomat who's written a book about Russia. I want to assist him in getting his facts right. Rostov happens to be one of the few men who were in Vienna back in 1961 when President Kennedy and Premier Khrushchev met there. Rostov could tell me what's wrong in that section of the book and what's right. He wouldn't be quoted by name in the book."

"This book," said Novik warily. "Exactly what is it about?"

At the moment of engaging Novik in this conversation Doyle had remembered something of Brennan's scheme to save Medora, and he

661

had decided to adapt one small part of that scheme to his own purposes. He did not dare mention his real conspiracy book, so he had chosen to use another book written by another author, hoping to hold Novik's attention by it, knowing full well that Novik might then run to Rostov with the news and Rostov, in turn, would be sufficiently curious to receive Doyle. "What's it about? Well, just between us, Igor, meaning strictly us only, my friend had written a documentary account of the whole conspiracy that started in Vienna in 1961 to get rid of—of Premier Khrushchev and all other Russian revisionist leaders opposing a grand alliance of Russia with Communist China."

Igor Novik's chubby countenance was a portrait of innocence. "What an amusing story. Where did your friend ever hear it? I have never heard of such a story, in Vienna or anywhere."

"I assure you, my friend heard it," said Doyle.

Novik threw up his hands. "Ah, well, comrade, everyone hears everything these days, and most often not one syllable of it is truth." He reached for his wine. "I will speak to Minister Rostov about your interview request if I have the opportunity. But I can advise you now, there is no likelihood he will find the time to see you. If I were you, I would forget it."

"Too bad," said Doyle.

But by that time Igor Novik was already speaking to someone else.

After that, Doyle could not wait to leave Lasserre. He made a show of listening to Goupil, to other members of the Société, but all that he could hear was Novik's words: *The very next night in Moscow, Rostov took the same guests, Zabbin and the Chinese, too, to the Peking restaurant.* Hours ago, in the Hotel Lancaster, Doyle had heard Earnshaw relate how a Chinese leader had angrily implied that Russia was China's ally. Now, minutes ago, Doyle had heard—with his own ears he had heard—a Russian inadvertently let slip that Chinese had been in Moscow in recent months, dining with Soviet officials like Zabbin and Rostov.

For the first time, Doyle believed that there might be some truth to Brennan's theory of a secret international Communist union that would supersede what was going on at the Summit. In the Palais Rose the doves were meeting. But in Moscow and Peking the hawks were working.

For the first time, too, Doyle began to take Brennan's suggestion, made this morning, seriously. When Hazel's news had seemed to demolish Doyle's book on the conspiracy against Kennedy, Brennan had suggested that there might be an equally important book, one as sensational, in his clues to a secret partnership between two of the earth's three greatest powers. Now Doyle's excitement about the possibility of developing such a project began to match, even momentarily overshadow, his interest in fully resuscitating a project that he was having difficulty in keeping alive.

And there was something else, something else nagging. What had Igor Novik said? That he and Rostov had been schoolmates before he had gone into journalism. Novik had joined *Pravda,* and Rostov had gone into government. Well, now. What had been Hazel's story in Vienna so long ago? Her "friend"—of course, Rostov—had been approached by an old classmate who now wrote for one of the *Pravdas* and who wanted Rostov to enlist in a conspiracy against K.

Doyle weighed it coolly. Vienna. Igor Novik representing the conspirators and going to his old friend Nikolai Rostov to draw him into an intrigue. Possible. Even probable. Lending credence to Novik's slip about the Chinese in Russia, but offering little more, because from now on Novik would be as talkative as a Vladivostok clam.

Doyle felt real excitement. He wanted only to leave, so that he could call Brennan and repeat to him every word he had heard in Lasserre tonight. He wanted to hedge his bets, have two hopes instead of one. To possess a second hope, he had to be on Brennan's team, to contribute, so that he could be the historian of what might come of this.

Nor did Doyle feel any disloyalty to his precious main hope. He would be no traitor to truth. In his heart of hearts, he *knew* that not Oswald but two or more conspirators had assassinated Kennedy. No matter what Rostov had told Hazel, no matter what the majority of Americans believed, Doyle remained convinced from other evidence that the death in Dallas was still an unsolved murder. As long as he lived, for what was left of his life, Doyle silently vowed, he would ceaselessly pursue that mystery until he had resolved it. Meanwhile, he must survive, find new hopes, fresh dreams, easier and surer ones. In Brennan's findings there was the best chance for an overnight success. Suddenly the future was brighter.

He heard old Goupil saying to the others, "If the parents of the human race ruined themselves for an apple, what might they not have done for a truffled turkey?"

Doyle heard himself laughing with all the others. What difference if Brillat-Savarin had said it first? All that mattered was that Claude Goupil had said it now and said it better. Good old Goupil. Witty old Goupil. Thank you for a lifesaving dinner, O Wise and Generous King of Gastronomes.

STANDING THERE, trying to balance his long-stemmed glass of vintage champagne in the midst of the crush of notable people crowding the Salle des Gardes, the first-floor reception room of the Hôtel de Lauzun, Emmett A. Earnshaw felt thoroughly uncomfortable.

There were, he was perfectly aware, valid reasons for feeling as fretful as he did. For one thing, he disliked wearing this monkey suit, white bow tie, starched shirt, white waistcoat, tailcoat, pinching patent leather shoes. For another, in this mass of celebrity—at least two hundred persons, he guessed—he was one of the few who were outsiders, he was actually an interloper, since he had nothing to do with the five-power disarmament conference.

From the moment that he had been driven, so resplendent in his aged inaugural top hat, toward the Île St.-Louis and into the Quai d'Anjou, passing all those peacocky police of the Garde Mobile at the bridgeheads, the swarming spectators, the jumping photographers, he had felt a fake and had wanted to turn back. But he had gone on under the loggia, through the courtyard, and up the white stone staircase to this room, because he had known that it was his duty to see the evening through. And it was duty that was the final reason for his uneasiness.

Earnshaw had come to the French Foreign Minister's reception, he had kept reminding himself, not as an official representative of the United States who had to engage in diplomacy, not as a distinguished private citizen who wished to enjoy the social hospitality of the host nation, but as a debtor determined to balance his ledger by performing two difficult missions.

He missed Carol, whose understanding and natural verve were always supportive on these stiff state occasions. And, too, he was sorry Carol was missing this. The colorful guests would have excited her— over there, the British Prime Minister and his wife deep in conversation with the American Ambassador; near them, in front of an immense tapestry, the Russian and French Premiers toasting; and a stone's throw away, a cluster of Chinese wives gathered about the Chinese Chairman and the President of the French National Assembly.

The palace or mansion, or whatever it was, would also have thrilled Carol—all those fancy mirrors, and crystal chandeliers, and gilded candelabra, and oak tables (Louis XIII, someone had said), and Brazilian-rosewood commodes, and most of all, the green silk brocade

664

hanging on the walls. Nobody, but nobody, could dress up a place like the French. And Carol, why, she'd have had enough material to write a dozen papers for her English and history classes when she got back to school in California.

At once, in his old man's ruminations, Earnshaw remembered the reason why his niece was not here to give him a hand, to help him enjoy this reception. She was nursing Medora Hart. Carol had telephoned just as Earnshaw had been about to depart for the reception. She had said that Medora had made a nice recovery, but was still weak and again asleep. Carol's only concern had been Medora's state of mind when she would completely awaken. Without going into the details on the telephone, Earnshaw had assured her that he and Brennan had worked out a wonderful plan. If it came off—he could not be sure it would, but if it did—well, Medora might be saved.

With a start, Earnshaw realized that this plan to liberate Medora was only half of the mission that had brought him to the Hôtel de Lauzun. He had better get going before the entire mob was summoned upstairs to the formal dinner in the Music Room.

He had begun to search for Sir Austin Ormsby when he saw a lady waving at him as she pushed in his direction. He wished he'd worn his glasses, but then he made out that the woman was Fleur Ormsby with a monocled Frenchman in tow.

Gaily swishing her long gown, to straighten it, Fleur demanded, "Emmett, what are you doing here so frightfully alone? I won't have you behaving like a wallflower—oh, dear me, have you met the Foreign Ministry's chief of protocol? This is Monsieur Pierre Urbain—"

"I think so," said Earnshaw, accepting the Frenchman's handshake.

"We have met several times," said Urbain. "At our recent lunch in the Quai d'Orsay. And twice before, I was so honored when you were President, Mr. Earnshaw. I hope that you are having a good time? Perhaps I can introduce you to several—"

"No, not necessary," said Earnshaw. "I've already met a large number of your guests."

Fleur Ormsby pouted. "Well, Emmett, I'm simply not going to let you play hermit. Monsieur Urbain was about to take me, and several other ladies, on a quickie tour of the Hôtel de Lauzun. You mustn't miss it, really." Her delicate hand swept toward the beamed ceiling. "Utterly fabulous place, Emmett, despite its wretched history. Monsieur Urbain was telling me it was built by some dreadful son of an innkeeper—whatever was the boy's name?"

"Charles Gruyn," said Urbain.

"Gruyn. That's right. Well, Emmett, I tell you—he became a

wheeler and dealer in armaments, made a load under Louis XIV, and built himself this cozy manse. He used the same architect who helped build the Louvre and Versailles palaces. It took him two years and a fortune to get this place finished, but it was worth it. Then—what was it you told me, Monsieur Urbain?—oh yes, Gruyn got into trouble misappropriating public funds—embezzlement circa seventeenth century, and wound up in the Bastille. Later his son sold this place to a handsome blond playboy named the Comte de Lauzun, who had rather a sporting time of it with several of King Louis XIV's mistresses. This lad was also condemned to imprisonment in some château—for trespassing—but wound up marrying the King's first cousin. What happened next, Monsieur Urbain?"

"In 1899, the City of Paris acquired the Hôtel de Lauzun for a museum," said the protocol head, "but in 1945 decided to use it for Government receptions. In earlier times, Théophile Gautier had a club of hashish smokers here, and once Baudelaire rented a heart-shaped room here." He smiled formally. "More recently, the clientele has improved. We have received here a queen of England, a queen of Holland, a king of Denmark, and tonight, of course, the Summit."

Fleur Ormsby had taken hold of Earnshaw's arm. "Oh, do come along with us on the tour, Emmett. We must see Baudelaire's heart-shaped room."

"Thanks, Fleur, but I must decline," said Earnshaw. "I'm afraid my ancient legs aren't up to it tonight."

"I'm sorry," said Fleur. "Can't be blamed for trying." She glanced around. "By the way, where is your darling niece?"

Earnshaw opened his mouth to tell her, and suddenly, remembering, clamped it shut. It was difficult to remember that Fleur Ormsby was the enemy. He swallowed Medora's name and said, "Carol? She's off on some date."

"Delightful," said Fleur. "Can't say I blame her. What would she want with all these doddering fogies?"

"I haven't seen Sir Austin yet," said Earnshaw. "Any idea where—?"

Fleur aimed her beaded evening bag toward the high windows overlooking a quay of the Seine. "There, where you'd expect, where the champagne is being served. Should I take you to my master?"

"Fogy I may be, but I'm not doddering, Fleur. I can make it." Feeling traitorous to Medora and Carol, Earnshaw gave the enemy a warm smile. "Thanks for your invitation. Enjoy the tour."

Sipping his champagne, which had gone flat, Earnshaw wove his way through the packed reception room. He approached Sir Austin

Ormsby just as the Englishman was turning away from the champagne tray with a fresh glass in hand.

"Make it two," Earnshaw called out.

"Ah, there you are, Emmett. Two it is." Sir Austin accepted Earnshaw's half-filled glass and traded it for a brimming one. "Was about to set out on a safari after you, despite the dense and impenetrable jungle, rather like Stanley on the hunt for Dr. Livingstone. Smashing party, don't you think?"

"I'm afraid I'm out of shape for this sort of thing," said Earnshaw.

He could see that Sir Austin was devoting himself to the champagne. He could also see that Sir Austin's features—hooded eyes, thin aristocratic nose, tight lips beneath the small mustache—no longer gave the impression of affected fatigue but reflected genuine fatigue. For an instant Earnshaw wondered whether it was Sir Austin's participation in the Summit that had tired him so, or his underhanded efforts to protect the family name by assisting Fleur to obtain and destroy the scandalous painting of her. Earnshaw observed that the Englishman's face was flushed, and suspected that he had been drinking excessively. Earnshaw decided that this was not in celebration of progress made at the Palais Rose but in celebration of a cruel victory over a helpless showgirl. For the first time in his long relationship with Sir Austin Ormsby, he could see his friend—his former friend—as Carol and Medora saw him.

Earnshaw wondered how he should begin, but before he could decide, Sir Austin had already begun. "Emmett, I wanted to say—"

Other guests, pressing about them, had pushed them closer together, and Sir Austin was momentarily annoyed with someone who had backed against him.

"Shockingly overcrowded," he muttered to Earnshaw, and then, making an effort to recover his poise and display some affability, he lifted his champagne glass higher. "Cheers, Emmett, and our gratefulness for the fine column of commentary you've been producing daily. Our subscriber response has been ecstatic. What I wished to say was— thank you ever so much."

"Well, that column wouldn't have come about if you hadn't tipped me off about the Goerlitz memoirs," said Earnshaw.

"I've been meaning to ring you up about that. Forgive me. The last I heard—the beginning of the week, wasn't it?—you weren't too optimistic. Did you finally get to Dr. von Goerlitz?"

"You mean did he see me? Yes, he saw me. It was as I predicted to you in London. I tried, I tried very hard, but he was intractable. He wouldn't change a word of the chapter against me, let alone pulling it out of his book."

"Damnation," said Sir Austin. "I was sure you'd win him over."

"No."

"Well, Emmett, I do hope you're not discouraged. You've got to prevent that offensive chapter from seeing the light of day. Are you keeping after the wicked Prussian?"

Earnshaw was tempted to reveal what Sir Austin apparently did not know, that Dr. Dietrich von Goerlitz had been incapacitated by a stroke and was this minute lying mute in the American Hospital at Neuilly. But since it was still a secret, he decided to refrain from making Goerlitz's condition public. "I haven't given up, but I'm afraid there's no chance of swaying him, Austin. I'll simply have to gird myself and take it. I've suffered worse blows in my life, although not much worse." He halted, trying to determine how to proceed. "By the way, Austin, have you heard anything more about the publication of those memoirs?"

"I wish I could tell you something, but that's really Sydney's department," said Sir Austin. "I do think that I heard him mention, just the other evening, that there had been bidding from various publishers. Of course, Sydney isn't following the fortunes of the Goerlitz memoirs too closely, since we have no interest in publishing them. As I advised you before, Emmett, I wouldn't associate our firm with anything that might be detrimental to a friend."

"I can only repeat, Austin, that I have nothing but admiration for your decency," said Earnshaw with a trace of irony that he was certain the Englishman would not detect.

"If a man doesn't have moral standards," said Sir Austin piously, "he has nothing. I have always held with Lord Chesterfield that to do as you would be done by, is the plain, sure, and undisputed rule of morality and justice."

"I'm with you all the way," Earnshaw acquiesced, but he could bear no more of Sir Austin's sanctimonious cant. "Incidentally, how is your brother making out otherwise?"

"With the foreign publishers? Poorly. We'd rather hoped to latch onto a potential best seller or two here, before the Frankfurt Book Fair. But aside from the Goerlitz memoirs, there is nothing salable being offered, worse luck. Sydney's quite depressed about the whole situation. I wish I could invent a best seller for him, just to give him a pickup, and bolster our next list, but I'm afraid there is little that anyone can do."

668

Earnshaw had been biding his time. Now he blurted, "Maybe there's something I can do."

Surprised, Sir Austin Ormsby blinked down the hook of his nose. "How's that, Emmett?"

"Help Sydney get a best seller, I mean." He went on hurriedly. "I've really felt bad that you and your brother had to miss out on the Goerlitz memoirs because of your friendship with me. I was praying for some way to make it up to you. Well, don't sell the Lord short. Yesterday my prayers were answered. And quite by accident. I was going to telephone you or Sydney immediately, but I decided I'd better read the manuscript first. I finished it a couple of hours ago. It was so remarkable, the impact of it so great, I was tempted to run straight to your hotel. But I figured I'd see you here and tip you off."

Sir Austin's eyes were shining as brightly as avarice. The languor of the gentleman had been supplanted by the restless lust of the tradesman. "What is this manuscript, Emmett? You say you've read it?"

"Every word," said Earnshaw, trying to maintain a pitch of controlled enthusiasm. "I'm no literary judge, but just from the contents, I'd say it could be a tremendous find. Let me tell you quickly how it came about. When I was in the White House, one of our most promising young diplomats was a fellow named Matthew Brennan. Maybe you recall the name? He ran afoul of our security people because one of our physicists, who was his responsibility, slipped away at the Zurich Parley and defected—"

"Of course, I remember," Sir Austin interrupted.

"Okay. This Brennan was forced to quit government, and he's been living in Europe ever since. Well, when I arrived in Paris, I happened to bump into him. I'd really never known him. We got to talking, and I got a new view of him, and we agreed to let bygones be bygones, and we patched things up. Well, yesterday, rather diffidently, this Brennan asked to see me about a personal matter, and so I invited him over. He came into the suite lugging an impressively bulky manuscript. He explained that he'd been quietly researching and writing it for the last three years. He asked if I would read it and tell him what I thought, insisted he'd shown it to no one before, and said if I liked it, perhaps I'd write a foreword. Well, Austin, as you know, I'm not much of a reading person, but I couldn't say no to this fellow, so I promised to have a look. I intended simply to scan and skip and be done with it." Earnshaw paused for effect. Then he shook his head with wonderment. "Austin, from the first page on I couldn't stop, couldn't put the darn thing down. I kept reading it all of yesterday, half into the night, and picked right up at breakfast and just finished it hours ago. It is dynamite. As far as I know, the best political exposé that's been written in a decade. The research is incredible, almost too incredible, and every page of it documented. Well, I called this Matthew Brennan right up and I told him I'd pay him to be allowed to write the foreword. Then I thought about you and Sydney, and so I asked Brennan if he had a publisher. No, he said, he had none, and wasn't sure how to go about getting one. I told him I'd get him one. He was delighted."

Sir Austin Ormsby's face twitched with cupidity. He gave up his empty glass to a passing waiter, took another one filled with champagne, and almost spilled it. "Emmett, I can't tell you how appreciative I am. Knowing how conservative you are, I'm absolutely impressed by this—this manuscript—absolutely dying of curiosity. What's it about? You haven't told me what's inside it."

Earnshaw felt the calm that precedes victory. The fish had been snagged. He needed only to reel it in. "Brennan calls his book *The Secret Civil War Inside Russia Today*. The point is, and he dramatizes it, proves it, there are two separate governments in Moscow right now. The public one, in the Kremlin, in the Palais Rose, is pro-West, pro-coexistence, pro-One World, anti-International Communism. The second government, working underground in Moscow, outside the Kremlin, too powerful to be eliminated but not yet strong enough to take over, is anti-West, anti-One World, pro-Cominform, in support of acting jointly with Red China against the democracies. As a result, according to Brennan, the Summit conference is a sham, and whatever the outcome, it will prove meaningless. The future of the world, of mankind, will depend entirely upon which of the two Russian governments wins the struggle inside Moscow."

Sir Austin appeared shaken. "Good heavens, can that possibly be? I've never heard of such a thing. How could he document it? You say he has?"

"Every sentence, every paragraph. Understand this, Austin—" Earnshaw lowered his voice. "Brennan was accused of leftist sympathies and driven out of the United States. I'm ashamed of that, but there's the fact of it. Naturally, he was attractive to Communists and Commie agents in Europe. When they beckoned, he responded, because he felt bitter toward his homeland. So he got himself involved with—with certain people around Europe, behind the Curtain, and he began to find out that there was a hard core of Russians who opposed the present government and were organizing to overthrow it. Well, Brennan's an American, after all, and he couldn't go on watching this happening, this subversion of future peace, and so he broke away, began writing it down, and came to Paris to see certain people meeting at the Summit to dig out the final material he used in his exposé."

"And you read it, Emmett? You believe it?"

"There's no question about its veracity. Here and there, perhaps, he stretches a point for effect, or overdoes it, or conjectures, but overall I'd vouch for the accuracy of the manuscript. Can you understand what this adds up to, Austin? This isn't merely a literary document. It's a gospel for our survival on earth."

Sir Austin had taken a strong grip on Earnshaw's arm. "Emmett, you *did* say this chap doesn't have a publisher, and you'd recommended us?"

"I said that, and Brennan is agreeable to letting you have first look."

"If it is half of what you claim it to be, Emmett, and Sydney concurs, this can be a worldwide sensation—not only as a book, but by its immediate serialization in the press—good Lord, Emmett, I'm not merely speaking of profits. I'm also thinking of how this could alter the political picture, our attitudes toward the Summit and the near future."

"Exactly."

"Did you tell Brennan you were going to speak to me?"

"Yes, Austin, we discussed that part of it at great length. The author, understandably, is suspicious and wary, and I think he has a fair idea of what his findings are worth. So you'll have to handle him with kid gloves. I told him I was sure you'd be interested, and I explained it was your brother Sydney who was in charge of your book division, and you'd want Sydney to call upon him."

"You're darn right Sydney will call upon him. What's the soonest Brennan can be seen?"

"I should think sometime tomorrow afternoon, if Brennan isn't too busy," Earnshaw said, "In fact, I'm sure Sydney will be able to see him tomorrow. I might add that Brennan has only one finished draft of the book, and I doubt if he'll let it out of his hands for even a minute. I think Sydney will be expected to skim through the manuscript right there in Brennan's presence."

"No problem, no problem," said Sir Austin anxiously. "What should I do? Have Sydney phone Brennan?"

"Yes. He's at the Hotel California. And I'll tell Brennan to expect the call and set aside plenty of time tomorrow."

"I promise you Sydney will be there promptly, wearing his reading spectacles and carrying a contract in one hand."

Earnshaw grinned. "Better have him carry a quart of J & B whisky in the other hand. Brennan likes a convivial drink. I hope your brother does."

"Sydney? You know Sydney. The prototype for Wine, Women and Song. But tomorrow I shan't mind, if he comes away with this winner." Sir Austin snatched up Earnshaw's hand and pumped it. "I'm truly grateful to you, Emmett. I'm absolutely blithering with excitement. Do you mind if I dash off this instant and phone Sydney? I want to prepare him. And you remember to keep the Brennan chap under wraps until Sydney pops in on him. Thanks, Emmett. See you up at the festive table."

As Sir Austin whirled around to rush for the telephone before dinner, he bumped into the heavyset man immediately behind him. The other guest staggered off balance, and Earnshaw was about to assist in keeping the guest on his feet when he saw that Sir Austin had managed to do so. Satisfied, Earnshaw turned his back to them and began to move away, although still able to hear Sir Austin's mortified apologies, "Sorry, sir, dreadfully sorry, but I—oh, it's you—well, now, instead of sending your cleaning bill to the British Embassy, send it over to the Quai d'Orsay. That'll teach our overenthusiastic hosts not to shovel guests into a room as if it were some sort of Black Hole of Calcutta."

Still marveling at Sir Austin's unfailing social aplomb, Earnshaw felt doubly pleased with himself for having so smoothly manipulated a crafty British Foreign Secretary. The first step in Brennan's plan had been successfully taken. Earnshaw suffered no twinge of disloyalty toward a former friend. Certain persons should, when the opportunity presented itself, be taught compassion for others. This had been such an opportunity. As one who had recently been ill-used by others, Earnshaw had transferred his sympathies to his niece's friend, Medora Hart.

But now, with the first half of his mission in the Hôtel de Lauzun concluded, Earnshaw knew that the second half must be discharged before the call to dinner. It was to Matthew Brennan that he owed his major debt. However, it was more than the mere repayment of a debt that motivated Earnshaw at this time. Brennan had gained not only his sympathy but his compassion. Brennan's stigma was similar to the one that Earnshaw himself would soon have to bear. Both would be unfair. If Earnshaw could do nothing more for himself, at least he could try to remove the burden of disgrace that was destroying Brennan.

Earnshaw halted in the center of the Salle des Gardes and sought the President of the United States.

There were too many gay, effusive people in the room to make identification of any one of them easy. Yet Earnshaw thought that it should be easy. In contrast to the others in the room, the President would be remote and aloof, the handsome soulless human computer, the political executive of science designed for a nuclear age.

Seeking his successor, Earnshaw found him at last, standing before a window with his overattentive aide, young Wiggins, both peering out at the Seine below, as the French Foreign Minister described some sight or other to the pair.

Earnshaw hesitated. The task ahead, the second part of his pledged mission tonight, was not only more difficult than the first, but also more disagreeable. While Earnshaw was charitable to almost every fellow being on earth, he could find little that was attractive or praiseworthy in his successor. His dislike for the Chief Executive stemmed not alone from his personal dislike of cold, calculating people. It did not even stem from political differences or from the means by which the President had encouraged, or permitted, his staff, his press, to denigrate Earnshaw's record in office. Earnshaw's resentment had a more primitive basis: It was against human nature (anyway, Earnshaw's nature) to feel any warmth toward an equal who obviously regarded you with condescension and disrespect.

For a moment, recollecting his last confrontation with the President less than a month ago, Earnshaw could feel his hackles rise. The humiliation remained hot within him. He recalled how he had been summoned by his successor to his old stamping grounds, the Oval Office of the White House, and with good reason had expected to be offered the highest judicial seat on the highest judiciary bench in the country, the post of the Chief Justice of the Supreme Court. But even more certainly, he had expected to be notified of his appointment as an official delegate to the Summit conference, to sit beside his successor and advise him in treating with the leaders of the world. Yet, in his meeting with the President, he had been tendered neither appointment, but had been used as a dumb political prop, briefly brought into the White House for press propaganda, to enhance his successor's image. This had rankled when he had returned to his home in Rancho Santa Fe, and it rankled still in Paris.

With firmness, Earnshaw reminded himself that he must subordinate selfish pride if he were to seek help for another who deserved it. The next step would be onerous, but it was necessary to take it. There might be no second chance. Moreover, if he must engage his successor, this was the best time for himself, while he was still fresh from his victories over Marshal Chen and Sir Austin Ormsby and while he was still sparked by confidence.

Earnshaw swallowed. Lumpily, pride started down. Handing his empty champagne glass to a waiter, Earnshaw pushed forward, elbow-

673

ing through the mass of guests, returning a greeting here and there, until he arrived at the window.

The French Foreign Minister and young Wiggins had just turned away from the view of the Seine when Earnshaw reached them. His French host welcomed him with friendly graciousness. Wiggins acknowledged his arrival with nervous concern. Their mentions of his name brought the President of the United States from the window.

"Emmett, good to see you," said the President in his indifferent tone of voice. "I wondered if you'd be here."

The handshake was brief. "Couldn't resist," said Earnshaw. "I hoped to catch up with a few old friends again. I also wanted to thank you for loaning me the services of Admiral Oates last night."

"Yes. Oates reported to me."

"I would have asked your permission, but it was late and there was no time to wait."

"No problem," said the President. "I'm pleased that he was of some use." His gaze had strayed to other guests nearby as he added absently, "If at any time there is anything more we can do to make your vacation more comfortable—"

Earnshaw fiddled with his white tie, then gulped hard. Pride went down all the way. "As a matter of fact, there is something you can do for me."

The President appeared surprised, even faintly distressed, as if he had rhetorically inquired how-are-you only to discover that he was about to be told at length. "Why, yes, Emmett, what is it?"

Earnshaw glanced pointedly at the French Foreign Minister and at Wiggins. "Well, now, I don't want to break into any tête-à-tête, but as soon as you are through with these gentlemen, I'd appreciate a minute of your time, no more than a minute of it, before dinner."

"Of course. We can talk now."

"Well—uh—it's a little personal matter I'd—I'd prefer to discuss in privacy."

"In privacy?" The President surveyed the room. "I doubt if that's—"

The French Foreign Minister came to their aid. "It can be arranged, Mr. President, and I am certain that you have had enough of my discoursing on the beauties of the Île St.-Louis. Actually, we have a number of small salons throughout this floor for guests who wish their privacy. Allow me to show you to the petit salon just alongside you."

"Thank you," said the President.

Earnshaw thought that he detected a trace of disappointment in his successor's voice, disappointment that a means had been found to bring himself and Earnshaw together alone.

About to follow the French Foreign Minister, the President said to his aide, but obviously meaning the words for Earnshaw, "We'll be no more than a minute, Wiggins. Stand by."

The French Foreign Minister had opened a door of the east wall, a door masked by green brocade like that on the wall itself, and he gestured inside. "Right in there, Mr. President, Mr. Earnshaw. You will have complete privacy."

The President of the United States went through the doorway, and Earnshaw followed him. Earnshaw listened for the door to close behind them. The babble of voices had suddenly been shut off. The silence in the salon, like that of a decompression chamber, made Earnshaw's ears ring.

He could see the President wandering about the small salon. Except for a window and a fireplace with a mirror above it, the walls of the salon were covered with murals, portraits, and landscapes, each one bordered by a gold frame built into the wall. The assault of all this bright gilt made Earnshaw suffer a slight imbalance. The President, he saw, was squinting up at the ceiling. It was also covered by a mural, an enormous one, depicting a bare-bosomed young woman seated on a cloud, with some kind of pagan god holding on to the cloud, a naked young man kneeling before her, and numerous winged cupids carrying garlands ringed around her.

"Magnificent," said the President.

Earnshaw had been about to remark that it was atrocious, and was now relieved that he had held his tongue.

"People could do things in those days," said the President, "before deficit spending and Internal Revenue."

"And union labor," Earnshaw said, he thought rather wittily, but his successor did not appear to have heard him.

The President made his way to a green-and-gold Louis XIV sofa no larger than a love seat, lifted the tails of his coat, and sat down in the middle of it, leaving no room for Earnshaw to sit beside him. Biting his lip, Earnshaw took hold of a rebuilt sedan chair, pushed it to a position directly across a table from his successor, and lowered himself into it.

The President was balancing a glass ashtray in his hand. "Heavy," he said to himself. "Baccarat crystal. Look good in the Cabinet Room. Perhaps I'll drop a hint."

Earnshaw had taken out a cigar to occupy his hands, and he made it ready and lighted it.

675

The President shoved the crystal ashtray across the walnut table toward him. "Well, Emmett, we have our privacy. What's on your mind?"

Earnshaw had been observing that until now the President had seemed less energetic, more worn out, than usual. His tan had recently faded, giving way to an indoor pallor. His face was puffier, and even the bags under his eyes had grown. But now his natural resilience appeared to restore his lost vigor, and he became more animated. Certainly his impatience with small talk, his blunt approach, indicated that he had no liking for this face-to-face meeting and was eager to have it concluded.

"I want to ask a small favor of you," said Earnshaw.

"Go ahead."

"Do you remember a young man named Matthew Brennan in my Administration? He was one of our key people in the Arms Control and Disarmament Agency when it was connected with State."

"Brennan? Certainly. The left-winger. The one that Senator Dexter raked over the coals. Four years ago, wasn't it? He was branded a dangerous security risk, and you forced his resignation."

"I approved his resignation," Earnshaw corrected. He hesitated. "I was mistaken, Mr. President."

One of the President's eyebrows lifted. "Meaning what?"

"Brennan's been an expatriate ever since," said Earnshaw. "He's here in Paris right now. I've met with him. I've reread the testimony he gave to Dexter's Joint Committee on Internal Security. I now have every reason to believe that Brennan was unfairly treated. I'm convinced of his innocence and I'd—"

"There is evidence of his guilt in the record," said the President. "Does he have proof of his innocence?"

"Not yet," said Earnshaw, disconcerted. "First of all, and I won't be long, let me review the background of Brennan's case before and after Professor Varney's defection to the Chinese—"

The President made a distinctly negative gesture with one hand. "Not necessary, Emmett, not necessary. I had the whole business reviewed for me the other night, after Brennan had dropped in to see Tom Wiggins. I trust Tom. Astute young man. One of the best on my staff. At any rate, Tom got a poor impression of Brennan. Felt he was trying to lay the blame for Varney's defection on your friend Simon Madlock. That didn't sit well with me, either, when Tom told me about it. As much as I may have disagreed with Madlock's policies, or your policies, I never questioned Madlock's integrity, or your own. You know that, Emmett. So I find it quite surprising to hear you champion-

676

ing Brennan, a left-wing sympathizer who's going around damning Madlock."

Earnshaw found his next words difficult to speak, but he spoke them. "Perhaps Madlock deserves to be damned for his—uh—his role in Varney's defection."

"Oh?" said the President.

"I've seen some new evidence that would indicate all of us in my Administration should share the blame. In any event, if Brennan is blameless, as I suspect him to be, I think he deserves our help in restoring his good name and being permitted to serve again in government."

"Laudable on your part, Emmett, but impractical," said the President, "unless Brennan can submit concrete proof of his innocence."

"Well, it's about that, the proof, that I wanted to see you. Only one man can back up Brennan's claim of innocence and make it acceptable—"

The President's hand made a negative gesture again. "I know all about that. Tom Wiggins advised me. Brennan requires the backing of Nikolai Rostov. I gather he has been unable to reach Rostov. He wishes someone in our Government to speak to someone on the Russian delegation and arrange the reunion with Rostov. Is that it, Emmett? Is that the favor you're here to ask of me?"

It was the incumbent President's favorite tactic, Earnshaw knew, to anticipate what people wished to say to him, to guess it and voice it beforehand, in order to take the wind out of their sails and leave them becalmed and helpless.

The President had done it again, and while it had rattled Earnshaw, he was more determined than ever to persist in his request. "Mr. President, the favor I want is for you to give an innocent man a chance to prove his innocence to the entire world. It would be a simple matter for you or the Secretary of State to mention this to Premier Talansky before you sit down to the conference table tomorrow. One word from Talansky, and Rostov would come on the trot to see Brennan, give him a signed and witnessed affidavit admitting that he had possessed a note from Varney which clearly indicated Brennan's innocence. Then either you or I could release this to the press, and we would have honorably rectified an executive error that Madlock and I participated in and a mistake that the Joint Committee committed. Doing this would make us all look better, and it would restore Brennan to public usefulness and trust. That's the favor I'd like. I hope you'll do it for me."

The President stared at Earnshaw with cold, unblinking eyes.

Earnshaw gripped his cigar tightly. He waited.

677

The President sniffed, sat up, straightened his back. "No," he said. "No, thank you. Quite impossible."

Earnshaw had expected, at worst, at very least, a promise of co-operation, a promise of some effort to grant the favor. Now the President's absolute refusal, offering no chance for appeal, left Earnshaw temporarily speechless. He fought to repress his personal resentment of his successor, sought a means to touch the President's sense of decency.

"Mr. President, perhaps you misunderstood. I'm not asking you to absolve Brennan. I'm merely requesting that you intervene with the Soviets so that Brennan will have a chance to clear himself, if that can be done."

"I understood you very well, Emmett. The answer is still no."

"But why?"

"I'm in no position to risk the good relations I've built up with our allies, the Russians, to endanger the good work I've done in coddling the Chinese, in order to make you happy and to satisfy the selfish paranoia of one branded traitor. If Brennan is not a traitor, let him prove it on his own. There is probably good reason why Rostov does not want to see your man, and it is probably the same reason I don't want to involve myself and my Administration. Neither of us wants to stir stagnating scummy waters and be splattered by them. We're clean. Why dirty ourselves? And why disturb all the goodwill the Summit has engendered by going out of our way to remind the others of espionage and security and defectors, especially one shameful case that is dead history and not relevant here? We're dealing cards for millions of lives, Emmett. We can't worry because one individual was dealt, or dealt himself, a bad hand."

"Mr. President, this has to do with more than one man," Earnshaw said urgently. "It has to do with the whole image of democracy you're representing in the Palais Rose. The Chinese have always charged us with being a capitalistic dictatorship, and here is an opportunity to show them dramatically that it is untrue. We made a mistake. Now we're the first to admit it in public, and rectify it. That's democracy as it truly is. I assure you, Mr. President, such an act would absolve our America—"

"It would absolve *your* America, Emmett," interrupted the President, "your America, not mine. What you are really asking me to do is to help you wipe out one of the worst blots on your Administration."

"That's not so," said Earnshaw angrily.

"All right, then. Whatever your motives for this sales pitch, I'll tell you once more, I'm not buying. At another time, under different

678

circumstances, I might be more charitable. I know, Emmett, that you don't believe me capable of charity. But I am. But not at a critical period like this. I can't waste time airing and cleaning your dirty laundry, when your Administration left me so much else to try to repair and save. And now that we've finally got China coming along with all of us on disarmament, now that we're in accord and the Summit is going smoothly, I don't see—"

Still simmering, Earnshaw said, "I'm not so sure that Summit of yours is going half as smoothly as you believe or make out."

The President glowered at Earnshaw. "Are *you* trying to tell *me* what's going on at the Palais Rose?"

"I'm trying to tell you what's going on *outside* the Palais Rose, outside and behind the scenes of your conference."

Earnshaw could feel the President's eyes upon him, probing to evaluate whether he was daft or simply lapsing into senile alarms. The President spoke at last. "I haven't the faintest idea of what you are implying, if anything."

"If you'll listen to me, and not sell Brennan short, I won't mind telling you what I've heard. To do it, I've got to go back to the subject of Brennan. In trying to arrange his meeting with Rostov, he's stumbled upon considerable information, from a variety of sources, that indicates that while the Soviet Union and the People's Republic of China are pretending to participate in a community of nations, disarm forever, at the Summit, their real intentions are less honorable. Brennan's information indicates that the Russians and Chinese have also been having secret dealings, and many of them point to a continuing nuclear buildup *after* the Summit accord is reached. I can't give you documentation. But I trust Brennan, and I can only repeat what he's heard. I would suggest to you, Mr. President, that despite Premier Talansky's public friendship for us, you might be wise not to take him entirely at his word but to be tougher and more uncompromising on the international policing and inspection clauses of the disarmament treaty—"

"Hogwash!" the President exclaimed. "If I wasn't positive before, I am now, I'm more positive than ever that your boy Brennan is a crackpot, an inveterate troublemaker, and that he's played on your weaknesses to convert you to his side. What kind of rot are you passing on to me from Brennan? What does he know? Does he know more than all our intelligence branches and the CIA and the FBI? He's passing on that nonsense to you to convince you he's patriotic and deserves your help, when all he's really doing is performing a disservice to every one of us. How could you let yourself be taken in twice by the same leftist crackpot, Emmett?"

"I haven't been taken in by anyone," Earnshaw replied evenly. "I thought some of Brennan's information, which could easily have escaped our intelligence services, had merit, at least enough to make it worthy of consideration. Also, I've been in politics long enough to be alert always to the possibilities of—of—uh—a certain degree of duplicity among our neighbors."

The President rose, came around the table and drew himself to his full height. His face seemed to be sculptured from a block of ice. His tone was no longer one of anger, but was now one of contempt.

"Emmett," the President said, "before I leave you, let me straighten you out about a matter of geography. The Summit conference is taking place in the Palais Rose, and not in Brennan's hotel room or your hotel room. Furthermore, let me straighten you out about America's representation at this disarmament conference. The interests of the American people are being safeguarded by me, their President, and by my staff, the choicest of the best minds in the fifty states, and not by some self-serving, deluded traitor whom you and Madlock created, and not by a former President who has suddenly become interested in his nation's welfare."

Earnshaw came quickly to his feet. "That's hitting below the belt."

"Where have you been hitting, Emmett, trying to foist your problem bad boy on us? And then trying to tell me that I don't know what's going on, and trying to tell me how to conduct my foreign affairs?" He caught his breath. "You want to whitewash Brennan and your Administration? Do it yourself. See Rostov for yourself. He's right in the next room. You want to see Rostov? I'll have Tom Wiggins introduce you. Clean your own linen. Just don't get my White Housekeeping mixed up with your own."

He started for the door, stopped, and turned back.

"One more thing, Emmett, and I'll put it to you simply. You want a job, something to do, I'll find something in Washington for you. The Supreme Court—that I'm not sure about. I don't know if you have the nerve for it. Anything else, though, and I'll play along. But, Emmett, when you want another term in the Oval Office, my Oval Office, without earning it, then I've got to say no, absolutely no, Emmett. You had your chance in the White House. You messed it up. You can't have it again. Sorry, Emmett. That's life. Good luck."

Without another word, the President walked out of the salon.

Earnshaw remained where he had been standing for long minutes. He felt no more anger toward the President, because gradually his anger had been redirected against himself, against wasted years and neglected opportunities and the small shock of realization that most of his life had been lived and that none of it could be lived over again and that he was an old man in retirement when almost all of the world was young and active.

The cigar between his fingers had gone out. He flicked off its long gray ash, applied a match to it, took several puffs, and finally dropped the tasteless cigar into the crystal tray. He had failed to help Brennan, and he had just remembered the President's having told him that Nikolai Rostov was in the next room. Earnshaw did not know Rostov, but he did know what he owed Brennan. Certainly he owed him one last try.

He returned to the Salle des Gardes.

He was searching for Wiggins when he saw the President's youthful aide advancing toward him.

"The President asked me to introduce you to Mr. Rostov," said Wiggins.

"Yes, I'd like to speak to him."

"I thought you had before. When you and Sir Austin Ormsby were together, the man standing behind Sir Austin was Mr. Rostov, and I thought you both spoke to him."

"I didn't," said Earnshaw.

"Now I'm afraid you've missed him, sir," Wiggins said. "I've just been looking for Rostov, but one of his colleagues tells me that some kind of emergency matter came up fifteen or twenty minutes ago, and Rostov had to leave in a hurry. I'm afraid he's not expected back tonight. Perhaps you can see him another time."

"Another time," said Earnshaw dully. "Thank you."

Wiggins looked off cheerfully. "There's the call for dinner. I'm famished. Sorry about Rostov."

Earnshaw stood alone before the brocade-covered door. He observed the guests leaving for dinner. He had no desire to face the guests again, or himself. He would plead illness and depart at once, to seek refuge in the easy oblivion of sleep. Or more likely, this night, suffer the uneasy oblivion of sleep. For his debt to Brennan remained unpaid, and this weighed heavily on his conscience.

Still, as someone used to tell him, there was nothing as futile as regret. It was Simon Madlock who used to tell him, and now he tried to blame Madlock for his lot. But it was no use.

He could feel the airy confidence, gained in overcoming Marshal Chen, slowly seeping out of him. Soon his deflation would be complete. Not a foreigner but an American President had undone him. He had been reminded of what he had almost forgotten for a day. That he was now, and would be for all time hereafter, The Ex.

To celebrate the approach of midnight, the five-piece orchestra in the Petit Château de Legrande had at last given up its boisterous head-spinning, hip-swiveling yé-yé music to launch into a medley of sweet and slow vintage French melodies. The girl singer on the bandstand, with the hoydenish haircut and figure, cuddled the microphone seductively and swayed to the rhythm so that her shimmering rhinestones caught the lights and sprayed their reflection across the living room. Now the singer, as if a reincarnation of Édith Piaf, began to sing hauntingly and sadly, soft and low, of love sought and love lost.

Outside, at the stone rail of the balustraded terrace, Matt Brennan felt the music and the song drift over him, and his hand touched Lisa Collins' hand. Both continued to gaze out over the illuminated rear garden of Legrande's château. First came the wide moat with its silver carp flashing and its white swans gliding among the water-lily pads. Beyond the ancient bridge were the narrow gravel walks, the center one leading through towering cypresses toward a grotto that was now the haven of a reclining sculptured Venus, once the possession of a Renaissance cardinal. Another path curved between columnar junipers into the exquisitely landscaped flower beds bursting with geraniums and roses and surrounded by rhododendrons. The third path disappeared into a century-old orchard of lime and lemon trees that screened the modern heated swimming pool.

The music from inside blended with the vista ahead, and for Matt Brennan it was the first mellow and romantic interval of the evening.

He had escorted Lisa to the dinner party with reluctance. He had endured a long and emotionally charged day. By eight o'clock this evening he had been exhausted. Yet, knowing that he had let Lisa down once, he could not disappoint her a second time. Her enthusiasm for the Legrande dinner party surpassed and overcame all his other considerations. Lisa had heard that the fashion designer gave this party once a year, at the height of the collections, not only for the elite among the fashion press and store buyers but for a most fabulous cast of characters who flew in from every corner of the Continent to attend it. Lisa had been told that the party would be "lavish and wild and unforgettable"—her words—and since she was twenty-two, and still in the process of gathering experiences to paste in memory's scrapbook, Brennan hadn't the heart to deny her this special night.

Brennan had arranged for the rental of a chauffeured limousine for the evening. They had been driven outside Paris, on the route to Versailles, and taken the turnoff into the small French village of Vaucresson. While Lisa had been excited by the prospect of the new night, Brennan's weary mind had still been mired deeply in the events of the old day. Even in the moments preceding their arrival at Legrande's party, Brennan's mind had lingered behind in Earnshaw's suite, reviving Earnshaw's promise and wondering if Earnshaw had succeeded in seeing the President and had managed to gain Brennan entrée to Rostov at last.

But from the moment that their limousine had drawn up in front of the Petit Château de Legrande, Brennan had been forced—at the outset unwillingly, but soon quite willingly—to relinquish introspection and the day past for extroversion and the evening present. With wonderment he had led Lisa beneath the entry arch and stood with her in the graveled courtyard of Legrande's château.

Behind the hump of bridge that crossed the moat, the restored seventeenth-century château had been an enchanting sight. Wistaria and roses climbed the weathered yellow stone of the mansion to the height of the carved dormer windows set in the slate-covered mansard roof. At both corners were ancient round towers illuminated by glowing lanterns. Despite the scurrying parking attendants, the village police, the curious neighborhood children, the unending stream of arriving guests, the first view of the storybook Petit Château de Legrande had been magical.

After that, Brennan and Lisa had gone inside, and once inside, they had found the magical serenity rent by a bedlam of unremitting madness. No sooner had they left the frescoed central hall to enter the largest of the three living rooms, and been introduced by the bacchanals to the bacchanalia, than Lisa had surrendered her hesitation to gaiety and Brennan had surrendered his sobriety to light-headedness.

Legrande himself, sporting an open-throat silk shirt and velvet slacks, carrying a bottle of champagne in one hand and his favorite fluffy white Angora cat with its diamond-studded collar in the other, had shrilly welcomed them. Immediately they had been thrown into a maelstrom of several hundred guests. They had wandered from room to room, and in every room there was a buffet table laden with drinks and exotic foods, and Lisa had taken champagne punch at each buffet and Brennan had taken whisky straight. The music had blared steadily.

The raucous conversations and shouts and quartets had been pitched higher. And the alcohol had risen mistlike to invade their heads.

The dancing in every room had been frenzied, primitive, uninhibitedly sexual. Beautiful young men and women had seemed glued together, gyrating, making love with their clothes on, and here and there wildly drunk young actresses and mannequins twirled in reckless abandon, holding their skirts above their waists, revealing animated flesh and pantie briefs, while their male partners discarded their shirts and shoes to join in the revels. Behind a statue of Neptune a middle-aged Frenchman had been locked in embrace with someone else's wife, her arms around his neck, his hands clasped beneath her buttocks. On an eighteenth-century Savonnerie rug, eight drunken women and men, in various states of undress and a common state of hilarity, had been kneeling and playing strip poker. Nearby, two guests had removed Legrande's Italian mandolins from the wall and were strumming them, while a third guest had pulled down a Japanese mask and was trying to mimic the antics of a Kabuki dancer.

Aside from Legrande, flitting from group to group, Brennan and Lisa had known almost no one. They had eaten a little standing up, they had drunk a lot sitting down, they had joined in the singing and in the appreciation of each glimpse of low comedy.

Once Lisa had recognized a fashion buyer from New York, a stout female who was intent on loosening her girdle, and had asked her who all the guests were. The stout buyer had been only too eager to parade her knowledge of the celebrities and the gossip about them.

Backed against the pink wall decorated with *trompe-l'oeil,* the buyer had hoarsely identified various guests on the marble dance floor, at the heaping buffet, in the conversational groups among the *régence* furniture. There was the pipe-smoking female French literary agent, renowned for her lesbianism and an ancestor named George Sand. There was the Yugoslavian actress who'd gone water skiing in the nude at the last Cannes Film Festival. There was the English dentist with an office in Paris whose staff included two valets. There was the son of an Iranian shipping magnate who had invested two million dollars in racing cars and philately. There was the Lyon banker who kept his wife and mistress, and the children of each, conveniently under one roof. There was the homosexual American author whose creativity had been diverted to seducing adolescents in Naples and pontificating upon the death of the novel over television. There was the Deauville surgeon thought to have a secret vice (probably LSD) because his public behavior was perfectly normal. There was the mousy Marseille housewife whose only claim to fame was that she had once taken her traveling-salesman husband to court for having encased his better half in a medieval chastity belt. There was a Luxembourg journalist who . . . a Legrande mannequin who . . . a deposed Balkan king who . . .

And finally there had been Brennan and Lisa, who by this time had wanted only a respite. Lisa had wanted to escape the music, the noise, the rocking instability of the revelers. Brennan had wanted fresh air to counteract the effects of his heavy drinking.

They had fled the room for the terrace and gone down to the grounds, traversing the moat's bridge, making their way along the gravel path that led into the orchard. They had been enjoying their peaceful walk for ten minutes when they had heard the sounds of laughter and splashing. Coming out of the trees, they had reached the decking of the modern swimming pool, and they had halted with amazement.

A stark-naked French girl had stood poised on the diving board, arms above her, and then she had jackknifed into the water, where two older men and another girl, also naked, left the sides of the pool to swim toward her. Off to one side, before an open cabana door, a French girl, extremely tall, had been yanking her cocktail dress over her head and throwing it into the cabana.

Lisa had been dumbfounded. "Well, at least I can say that I've seen it," she had whispered, and then, clasping Brennan's arm, she had added, "Let's go back to the château, Matt."

When they had climbed back to the terrace, they had lingered there and given themselves over to the less disconcerting and less threatening beauties of the gardens, and to their own musings.

And now the music behind them had become softer, sweeter, the accompanying sounds of revelry had become more sporadic and distant, and sanity appeared a possibility.

Brennan still felt high and good, and mellowing. All that had gone on this evening, he supposed, had nothing to do with the real world beyond the château. It had little to do even with Legrande's own day-to-day world, where creativity and competition and advancement were his reality. For Legrande and most of his guests, Brennan supposed, a night such as this was an annual safety valve, releasing repressions, so each could act out year-long dreams without the punishments of law or of guilt. At the same time, Brennan guessed, there were those in the château tonight who behaved like this, lived like this, reckless and mindless, every day of their existence. He did not envy them. At the same time, he had to admit to himself, it had been fun, a change and therefore fun, and an exaggerated symbolic reminder of what life could

685

be like if you were free and Lisa's husband. Life could become what he thought no longer attainable for himself—not a continuous wild party, but a continuous source of experience and pleasure shared.

The melody of "La Vie en Rose" engulfed him. He looked at Lisa. "How are you feeling, darling?"

"Good. Sort of floaty and fine. But I think I've had enough, Matt. It's been too rich. I want to get back into our snug little bed and feel safe with you and belong to you."

He kissed her cheek. "All right. I was about to say the party seems to have settled down and they're playing the first music tonight that a normal human being can dance to."

"Would you like to dance? I'd like to."

He took her arm. "Just one for the road. Then off to our chaste little bundling bed in our own little château in the Rue de Berri."

"Ummm."

He led her inside. The crystal chandelier had been extinguished, and except for flickering lights from the candelabra and a beam from a ceiling spot that fell on a Fragonard painting, the large classic room was shadowy. Guests still stood or sat along the walls, conversing or petting, but the atmosphere was one of midnight calm. On the area used for the dance floor a dozen couples moved easily, lazily, to the music.

Brennan turned, extended his arms, and Lisa came into them. With the palm of one hand caressing her back, the fingers of his other hand entwined in hers at her side, with her lithe young body pressed against his own, Brennan slowly began to dance.

He had not danced often in recent years, and now he felt graceless. But soon, as he moved slowly around the marble floor with her, the music welded their two beings into one, and they moved with rhythm and grace. There was one number, and as it segued into another, Lisa seemed to come closer to him. He was conscious of every contour of her body, every movement of it, and he held her tightly, his lips to her cheek, his body responding to her own.

The second number had ended, and they separated, observing the musicians putting down their instruments for an intermission.

Lisa held both his hands. "It was lovely, Matt."

"You still want to go?"

"Yes."

They had started off the floor when a shrill voice called out Lisa's name. They stopped and turned to see their host, Legrande, hurrying toward them with mincing steps.

686

"Lisa, dear child, my pet," cried Legrande, "wherever are you going?"

"Home, to the hotel," said Lisa. "It's been a marvelous party, Legrande, but tomorrow's another workday."

"But the night's not ended, and you must spare me one last minute," begged Legrande. "Your friend—" He looked at Brennan. "You *are* Matthew Brennan, are you not?"

"The same," said Brennan.

"I knew it, I simply knew it!" exclaimed the designer. "Dr. Fisher had seen you dancing and thought he recognized you, and he asked me your name—and I'm so forgetful—but I told him I thought it was Matthew Brennan—I simply thought so—I remembered it from when dear Lisa introduced us at my showing—and Dr. Fisher insisted I find you and verify it—and I have. I'm absolutely pleased with myself."

"I'm pleased for you," said Brennan with amusement. "You tell Dr. Whoever-he-is that your memory is intact. Thanks for an enjoyable evening, Monsieur Legrande. Good night."

"Mr. Brennan, wait!" cried Legrande frantically, snatching for Brennan's arm. "I promised Dr. Fisher that if I was right, I'd bring you back and introduce you. Oh, really, both of you, do allow me this pleasure. Only a minute. And a most, *most* remarkable man, Dr. Karle Fisher." He paused, searching their faces. "You don't know of him?"

"The creator of the bra-less bra?" asked Lisa hopefully.

The name Karle Fisher teased Brennan, but he could not place it.

"Really, dear Lisa, for shame, for shame," sang Legrande. He edged in between his two guests and linked arms with them. "The universe's foremost psychoanalyst, and you've not heard of him? His famous clinic in Berne? My dears, he's Freud and Jung, he's Merlin and Nostradamus, and a dash of Charcot, all rolled into one."

Legrande was propelling them across the dance floor. "He's the one who made the musty old Vienna couch passé, remember? He makes you recline in this deep, deep chair, and he administers his own psychedelic drug—a hallucinogen—that exceeds lysergic acid and peyote and mushrooms and Zen. The verbal dam opens majestically, and in mere minutes you are on an archeological expedition into your past with Dr. Fisher as your guide. No more grubby years on the doilies and sticky leather of some ridiculous couch, transferring to some Freudian wretch who insists you give up half your present life to understand the other half long gone. Now, with Dr. Fisher, with mind-expanding drugs and the disciplines of analysis, you can take the trip backward, then forward, in a dozen days. I promise you, my dears, Dr. Fisher is no quack. He's read more medical papers to more medical conventions than I have shown original designs in my life. If Grand-papa Freud was the Galileo of the mind, then Karle Fisher is its Einstein. . . . He's in the next room. Much quieter that room, strictly reserved for talk, not fornication."

Brennan remained puzzled. "What does Dr. Fisher want with me?"

"I haven't the faintest idea," said Legrande.

They had entered a smaller, more rustic room. In a corner someone was picking a guitar, and three others were humming softly to it. Here and there the sophisticated young and middle-aged were gathered, exchanging attitudes or philosophies. On a sofa upholstered in pale green velour, a short darkish gentleman who appeared to be in his middle fifties was holding Legrande's Angora cat in his lap as he expounded on some point to a fascinated French couple beside him.

Releasing their arms, Legrande broke forward to interrupt the short darkish gentleman. As Legrande pointed behind him at Brennan and Lisa, the gentleman let go of the cat and struggled to his feet.

"Dr. Karle Fisher of Switzerland," chirped Legrande, "it is an honor to introduce you to Miss Lisa Collins and Mr. Matthew Brennan of America."

Gravely Dr. Fisher took Lisa's hand, performed the formality of kissing it, quickly straightened and shook Brennan's hand.

"A real pleasure, this opportunity," said Dr. Fisher in his low resonant bass. A pulpit voice, Brennan thought immediately.

Legrande, impishly eager to see the introduction consummated, prepared to play catalyst by dipping into his grab bag of small shocks. "You recognized Mr. Brennan," cried Legrande to the psychoanalyst, "but he did not recognize you, my dear guru. You see, Doctor, it is as I always told you, you must not hide your light beneath a bushel of drugs. You must appear in the world of men and announce your Second Coming."

Dr. Fisher's blue hyperthyroid eyes, veiled by steel-rimmed, amber-tinted spectacles, continued to be fixed on Brennan as he said to Legrande, "I have no need for self-praise so long as I have you for my propagandist, Monsieur Legrande."

Embarrassed, Brennan said, "Despite our host's little joke, Dr. Fisher, I did recognize your name, although I'm afraid I didn't know too much about your work or you."

Dr. Fisher's platy mouth offered a pinch of a smile. "I have the advantage over you then, Mr. Brennan. You see, I happen to know a good deal about you." He waved to the pair of velour armchairs across from him. "Please do sit down."

Brennan exchanged a glance with Lisa. She shrugged.

688

"Well, only for a minute, Dr. Fisher. We were on our way back to the city."

As Brennan drew a chair closer for Lisa, and then sat down himself, he heard Dr. Fisher say, "I appreciate this, Mr. Brennan."

Observing the Swiss psychoanalyst again settling on the sofa beside the French couple, Brennan was suddenly curious about the other's unexpected knowledge of him. "You mentioned that you happen to know a good deal about me, Dr. Fisher. How so?"

"My interest? Purely professional." Dr. Fisher cleared his throat before proceeding. "Lately I have been researching and preparing a paper to be read before various learned psychoanalytical societies. My study I have entitled 'The Judas Instinct: An Examination of the Necessity for Treason.' To put it quite simply, the paper amounts to a review and analysis of case histories of Western-educated men and women of our time who were self-confessed or publicly accused traitors, renegades, betrayers. A fascinating project, I have found."

"Fascinating," echoed Legrande enthusiastically as he hovered near Brennan's chair.

Brennan found himself less fascinated. The analyst's explanation possessed the same potential of threat that Brennan had often felt in Venice when, sitting in Quadri's, he had seen an American tourist looking back at him a second time, or when he had opened the latest issue of a newsmagazine to find a heading that indicated that another article was about to survey the contemporary history of nuclear security. There was always, in those times, the constricting fear that his name would be linked with the names of known traitors. More often than not his fear was justified. Dr. Fisher's prologue promised the same danger. Yet Brennan could not conceive that the Swiss specialist, in this background of revelry and shallow pleasure, would go into a subject so serious and personal. Warily, he waited.

Dr. Fisher was continuing. "For my paper, I have investigated, through the reading of official reports, letters, journals, confessions, and through numerous interviews, a wide range of personalities. I have made studies of William Joyce, Dr. Alan Nunn May, Alger Hiss, Harry Gold, Dr. Klaus Fuchs, Donald Maclean, Guy Burgess, Julius and Ethel Rosenberg, Bruno Pontecorvo, Colonel Abel, William Vassall, and numerous others who committed treason or were accused of lesser indiscretions against their countries."

Dr. Fisher paused, inclined his head as if to catch a word from Jehovah seated beside him, and then he resumed speaking in his measured magisterial bass. "My purpose in this study has been to find the unconscious motivations that compel an individual to betray his

689

closest lifelong ties, to reject one authority, be it parent, employer, church or state, and transfer his allegiance and trust to another, bartering a gift of secrets to acquire the love of the new and alien authority. I cannot believe that Judas deceived Our Lord, and delivered him into the hands of an enemy, for thirty pieces of silver alone. No, there were deeper unconscious needs that were temporarily satisfied by this treacherous act, for had it been avarice alone, Judas would not have hung himself, as legend has it, in that place aptly called the Field of Blood. And so, Mr. Brennan, I have gathered my case histories and probed them to learn if the need for treason, sublimated and repressed in the psyche of most men, but acted upon by a handful of men charged as traitors, has any common denominator, any single root."

"Magnificent!" exclaimed Legrande, quickly beckoning for others in the room to join in the sport.

Brennan, ignoring Legrande, sat grimly staring at the Swiss psychoanalyst and waiting for the swordsman's *coup de fond*.

Dr. Fisher also ignored his host as he went on pedantically. "It is not surprising, therefore, in a research so far-flung yet so detailed, that I came upon your name repeatedly, Mr. Brennan. At no time did I equate your case with the major case histories of proven disloyalty, yet I found your circumstance had a pertinence to my study and contributed to an understanding of my analysis. Naturally, since I had met you only among the papers littering my office desk in Berne, it was a pleasure to find myself at the same social affair with you and to have an opportunity to meet you and inform you of my project. I honestly believe that you will find my paper not only interesting but also sympathetic in its approach. I have no pretensions to being a judge of men's deeds, Mr. Brennan, but am merely a humble student of their motivations. I should be most delighted to mail you a copy of an early draft for your comments, which might add to the authenticity and worth of my work. But in any event, I repeat, you may find it interesting and even useful."

The *coup de fond*, at last. The thrust had been a long time in coming. Now it had been struck, and Brennan bled inside.

He sat quietly, determined to maintain reserve and dignity before the eyes of this insensitive and heartless and quite foolish surgeon of men's psyches. For the first time he examined the all-knowing one across from him with care. Dr. Karle Fisher, of Berne, was possessed of a bulging forehead and bulging eyes and a weak chin. His little body was swollen with self-importance, superiority, and self-indulgence. His smug aspect was that of one used to being listened to and obeyed, of one who expected gratefulness when he parceled out capsules of wisdom. In all, a formidable picador.

For a moment Brennan wondered whether he should bother. From the corner of his eye he was conscious of Lisa, watching him with anxiety. She would probably prefer that they rise and leave. Had this happened in Venice, when he had been utterly lost and defeated, he would have done so. But in the past weeks he had rediscovered his ego, its value, and in the past week he had revived his old feelings about justice and injustice, and suddenly this seemed an evening when survival was an issue worth bothering about.

Emerging from introspection, Brennan could see that Dr. Fisher waited expectantly for a response. This, too, irked Brennan, supporting a feeling within him that the psychoanalyst's discussion of his report had not been merely to deliver facts but calculated to goad one possessed of the Judas instinct into angry self-revelation. Brennan was tempted to debate in his own defense, but this would only provide more gray matter for Dr. Fisher's dissecting table. Brennan determined to be as secretive about himself as humanly possible while still attempting to contend with his opponent.

"You think I will find your paper interesting and even useful," said Brennan at last. "Tell me Dr. Fisher, why do you feel it would be of either interest or use to me?"

"Well, only because of your—"

"Dr. Fisher, do you believe that I committed treason four years ago?"

The psychoanalyst's tongue circled and wetted the rim of his round mouth. "No, not exactly, Mr. Brennan. Certainly not in the political sense that Dr. Fuchs and Dr. May committed treason. But I would suggest that your case history offers some indication that in a purely psychoanalytical sense you were unconsciously involved in a fantasy of treason that you were unable to act out. I have gone by the record alone. According to the record, your guilt was not proved, but your innocence was not proved either. You were suspect, and you were cast aside as untrustworthy. But the very fact that you were given a top security assignment, the safeguarding of Professor Varney, and that you failed in your assignment, might indicate certain unconscious problems that would be pertinent to any study on the need of certain men to—shall we say, flirt?—to flirt with treason, premeditated or accidental, although very little of any human being's behavior is ever accidental. At any rate, your act of omission—I only cite the *official* record—contributed to giving the Chinese Communists your Professor

Varney and the neutron bomb, and disturbed the balance of power and coexistence in the world."

Remembering the certainty with which Isenberg had cleared him of this responsibility, Brennan said, "Dr. Fisher, did you find anything in the *official* record that named me, specifically, or Professor Varney, specifically, or any other Westerner, specifically, as being responsible for China's neutron bomb?"

Dr. Fisher was thoughtful. "Well, it was discussed, and generally believed—"

"Was it known, proved? Were we so accused by our Governments?"

Dr. Fisher squirmed, reached for his highball glass, and saw that it was empty. "You are quibbling, Mr. Brennan. In your Government's brief against you, as I have noted, your guilt was only implied, as were the results of Professor Varney's defection. Often, in the matter of the consequence of treason, deduction suffices. I can refer you to an official report made by the United States Joint Congressional Committee on Atomic Energy in 1951. I can recite it to you. With your forebearance, I shall, to wit: 'The conclusion seems reasonable that the combined activities of Fuchs, Pontecorvo, Greenglass, and May had advanced the Soviet atomic energy program by 18 months as a minimum. In other words, if war should come, Russia's ability to mount an atomic offensive against the West will be greatly increased by reason of these four men.' That seems fair enough to me. It also seems fair enough, reasonable enough, to assume that Varney's defection advanced China's nuclear strength by a half-dozen years or more."

"And you imply that I must share the guilt for that, assuming it were true," said Brennan.

"I imply nothing more than the possibility that you may have been coerced into aiding an act of treason, performed by another, because of your unconscious personal needs to be cast in that role."

Brennan tried to remain calm, but it was becoming difficult. "All of this, Dr. Fisher, when you have already admitted there is not one shred of proof, in the official record, that I was a traitor?"

"Mr. Brennan," said the psychoanalyst with a shade of impatience, "I am not interested in political games. I am not interested in legal definitions of proof. I am only interested in why men behave as they do, and how they become involved in impossible situations because they are victimized by their own neurotic conflicts and needs. Mr. Brennan, I remind you again, I am not a judge, I am a psychoanalyst."

"Hear, hear, well spoken, Doctor," called out Legrande with a clap of his hands. Other guests smiled their approval at Dr. Fisher, as did the French couple on the sofa beside him. Dr. Fisher glanced about, accepting the mass approval with feigned modesty.

Brennan, who had been watching the others, looked at Lisa. She was flushed with anger, and she made a quick movement of her head to indicate that they should get up and leave. Brennan held up a finger to her, and turned back to his tormentor.

"Dr. Fisher, if I may contradict you—and it is apparent to me that you are not used to being contradicted—I should like to suggest that you are behaving less like a psychoanalyst than as the Christ. I look at you, hoping to see the physician-scientist, the cool objective healer, and what I see instead is a vainglorious and self-satisfied little man, with the weaknesses of all mere mortals, playing to the gallery for attention and congratulations."

Dr. Fisher smiled, but the smile was wicked. "Really, Mr. Brennan, I would have expected more from you than mere insolence—"

"And I would have expected more from a man of medicine than cheap sleight-of-hand. When it suits your purposes, you climb atop your medical degrees, and from that exalted and unassailable position you analyze and then expound your dogmas. You are above prejudices, above inferences and gossip, above politics, above passing unsupported judgments. Yet from your invulnerable citadel the wise edicts you hand down are counterfeit, composed of prejudices, inferences, politics, highly personal judgments, none of them based on facts. Your performance may amuse the others, Doctor, but I find it disappointing."

Dr. Fisher was no longer smiling. "One moment, sir. . . . Setting aside, if you can, your understandable displeasure, do you still insist that my analysis—or unsupported judgment, as you prefer to consider it—is not based on facts? Mr. Brennan, tell me, was it a fact that you were charged by your Government with looking after Professor Varney four years ago? Yes or no?"

"Against my wishes—"

"I am not interested in your wishes, Mr. Brennan, only in your Government's wishes. Were you so charged? I repeat, yes or no?"

"Have your fun. . . . Yes."

"Did Varney defect to the Reds from under your nose in Zurich?"

"Yes, of course."

"And you were investigated by your Government for complicity? Is that a fact?"

"Right or wrong, yes."

"And your security clearance was revoked, and you were forced to resign from your post?"

"Yes."

Dr. Fisher smiled, and opened his palms to his audience. *"Facts."*

Brennan came forward in his chair. "You were clever enough to omit one question, Dr. Fisher, because it might play havoc with your learned paper and your childish parlor game. You failed to ask me if I was innocent."

The psychoanalyst dismissed this with a disdainful gesture. "There was no need to ask. I have done my homework. You are innocent, all of you are innocent, now and forever, because you must maintain this delusion to assuage your guilts. Are you satisfied, Mr. Brennan?"

Brennan nodded slowly. "I am satisfied, Dr. Fisher, that if Sigmund Freud had heard your performance he would have sentenced you to the couch for life."

There was a burst of laughter, applause, and even a giggling Legrande clapped Brennan on the back as Brennan stood up to join Lisa.

About to depart, Brennan found that Dr. Karle Fisher was also on his feet. The short analyst came strutting toward Brennan, his countenance a study in controlled fury.

Dr. Fisher planted himself in front of Brennan. His voice shook. "Since you have chosen to exceed the boundaries of fair play and decency, Mr. Brennan, going out of your way not once but twice to launch a personal attack against me, to disparage me professionally in the company of my friends, I do believe I deserve one last word."

Lisa tugged at Brennan's arm. "Come on, Matt."

"You have accused me of unprofessional behavior and you have announced that I am seriously disturbed," continued Dr. Fisher. "You made one mistake. You tried to analyze me without any knowledge of me. I, on the other hand, attempted to analyze you in my paper only after I had considerable knowledge of you. Your regrettable tirade just now has convinced me that you need individual help, as well as the benefit of my written findings on you and my other case histories. Since you have chosen to be personal, I should like equal time to reply. The difference between us will be that out of your own hurt you sought to hurt me, whereas my own motives are more charitable. I hate to see an obviously disturbed man leave my presence without his accepting some modicum of the help I can offer him."

"I appreciate your solicitude, Doctor," said Brennan. "I'm always interested in pain-killers. But I always remember that Dr. Guillotine prescribed a pain-killer, too."

"Matt," Lisa urged, "don't listen to him. Let's go."

Brennan resisted her, not because he had been dared by Dr. Fisher but because he was always curious to learn about himself.

"All right, Dr. Guillotine," said Brennan, "give me a sixty-second diagnosis of the anatomy of a traitor."

Holding one silver-rimmed lens of his spectacles, Dr. Fisher spoke in a low churlish tone, rapping out his words of reason viciously at Brennan.

"Your dictionaries will tell you that a traitor is one who betrays a confidence or trust, one who performs perfidiously or treacherously, one who even violates his allegiance and betrays his country," said Dr. Fisher. "As a definition of what we discuss, that is correct; yet for our purposes, it is inadequate. It was Shakespeare who came closer. 'Though those that are betray'd do feel the treason sharply, yet the traitor stands in worse case of woe.' It is this woe that interests the analyst."

"You've got forty-five seconds more, Doctor," said Brennan.

"I will give you a miniature portrait of a traitor, based on my studies. Like all other men, he is possessed of three basic needs: the first, to be secure, dependent on someone who can keep him safe; the second, to advance, to achieve mastery, to satisfy his aggressions; the third, to perform normally and cooperatively with other human beings, to fulfill his urge to give and receive love. But the potential traitor is unlike most men in that his basic needs, impulses, urges are unfulfilled, inhibited, and eventually warped. Most often he will have suffered disapproval or rejection or lack of love from a parent or parents. As a child, he will have yearned for safety, protection, and been deprived. Usually he will grow to adulthood longing for someone to depend upon, hating a parent who has failed him yet filled with anxieties over his repressed hostilities. His normal aggressions toward his parent, controlled by his need for love, would ideally be redirected in adulthood into healthy defenses against new dangers that arise. But because of his abnormal upbringing, he cannot sublimate his aggressions. He finally turns them against the authority of a parent or parents. Yet he still has a need for dependence on a protective authority, as well as a need for approval. In such an unhappy situation, some men will seek the authority of the church, and subordinate themselves to a power all-encompassing and too lofty to be resented, and others in their helpless anxiety might seek to find comfort in the authority of their fatherland. But suppose their fatherland is a flaccid democracy of individuals, as are America and Great Britain, unable to give these men a dependable image to cling to, offering them no channel through which to alleviate their hate or satisfy their need for love? Supposing also the fatherland's values are cynical and materialistic in their eyes? Such men may

695

become desolate, unsuccessful, despairing neurotic clods. But our man, the one determined man, finds a way out. He will be attracted, in America, or in Russia, or in China, by a political sect, let us say the Communist party, with rigid rules and complex dialectics. Here is the parent with authority, granting approval he has never before known. Here is a totalitarian symbol upon which he can depend, through which he can find an outlet for hostility and aggressions, from which he will receive the reward of love. And here, too, as has been remarked, is 'a vision of the Kingdom of God on earth.' And so, our man resolves his neurotic conflicts. He turns to a new and higher authority than his remiss parent or disinterested fatherland. He offers his allegiance to Communism, but since he wishes adoption, he must prove himself, and so he betrays his present authority to his future one, stealing secrets from his fatherland—his father, who had rejected him—and passing them on as gifts to the new authority that has adopted him. Oversimplification or not, this is the portrait of a conscious or unconscious traitor. And this, Mr. Brennan, I offer you with my compliments, as also a picture of you yourself."

Brennan had listened closely. He considered Dr. Fisher's analysis in silence. No longer was he in a mood for sarcasm or argument.

Lisa had stepped forward angrily. "I've never heard more inane drivel," she said to Dr. Fisher. "How can you analyze a person you don't know personally? It's impossible."

Dr. Fisher gave Lisa his condescending smile. "It was possible for Freud. He analyzed da Vinci. It was possible for Marie Bonaparte. She analyzed Edgar Allan Poe. It was possible for a hundred other modern-day psychiatrists of the present who have analyzed figures of the past whom they had never met."

"How do you know they were right?" flared Lisa. "Da Vinci and Poe aren't here to prove that their analysts were clever but wrong."

Dr. Fisher's smile remained fixed. "You are correct, young lady. The patients are not here. They are dead. But you would be surprised how much information can be obtained from dissecting a cadaver."

"But Matt's alive, and you can't—"

"In terms of normal usefulness, I would suggest he is dead, too, more dead than alive," said Dr. Fisher.

Legrande was hoisting and spilling his glass of champagne. "*Olé*—to the Doctor of the Dead!"

Dr. Fisher, his superiority restored, had turned back to Brennan. "I hope you understand I was only trying to be helpful. If you have any further comment—"

"Only two comments, two judgments from the analysand to the analyst," said Brennan. "You are, consciously or unconsciously, arrogant and exhibitionistic. I deduce this from two bits of evidence." He paused, and then he said, "You have bad breath, Dr. Fisher, and your fly is open."

Before the roar of laughter had subsided, Brennan had taken Lisa by the arm and led her out of the Petit Château de Legrande.

After that, driving back to Paris from Vaucresson, he and Lisa had only one conversational exchange.

Staring glumly out of the limousine window into the darkness, Brennan said, more to himself than to Lisa, "He was a sadistic bastard, but I behaved badly, too. I behaved like an immature and petulant child. I don't understand, because I usually don't let myself be baited into name-calling bouts."

She took his hand. "My God, Matt, don't castigate yourself. What were you supposed to do, let him run all over you? You had to say something. He's got the fancy lingo. You said what you could." She squeezed his arm. "Darling, it was a wonderful evening. Don't let a ridiculous incident like that spoil it."

"I won't," said Brennan.

But both of them knew that it had.

Not until almost an hour later, after they had returned to their suite in the Hotel California, did they speak to one another again.

He had been sitting for some time, tieless, shoeless, slumped deep in the pillows of the drawing room sofa, reflecting in solitude upon every word that he could remember of Dr. Fisher's analysis of a traitor.

He was still deeply lost in thought, but filled with growing wonderment, when Lisa emerged from the bedroom in her nightgown and stood over him.

Brennan came to his feet, and Lisa ran her arm around him and kissed him. "I'm sorry we went," she said. "I've just been thinking. I hate all those noisy fake parties, loaded with sadists and smart-aleck games. Matt, I hope you're not still angry. Dr. Fisher isn't worth it."

"I'm not angry anymore," he said. "But you know, I've been thinking, too."

"About what, darling?"

"About Dr. Fisher's analysis of the psyche of a traitor, a real traitor or a potential one."

"Oh, come on now, you're not taking any of that quack's junk seriously."

"I am," said Brennan, "because I'm afraid he was not a quack and every word of his analysis was valid."

Lisa stepped back and studied Brennan with astonishment. "What ever do you mean?"

"I mean he was accurate . . . only not about me. None of it fits me or my background or personality. He was way off there, but then, of course, I'm not a traitor, potential or actual. No, I mean he was right about Nikolai Rostov. It's uncanny how absolutely his analysis fits Rostov. I've been examining it all this while, remembering things Rostov told me or revealed of himself in Zurich, and other things I've heard since. All the bits and pieces, his parents, his upbringing— they're a perfect fit for Dr. Fisher's portrait of a traitor."

"Rostov as a traitor?" said Lisa incredulously. "When? How? Why?"

"I wish I had the answers, Lisa. I don't have them yet. I only know the whole thing goes together." His arm encircled her waist, and he began to walk her slowly toward the bedroom. "As a matter of fact, so does something else, Lisa. I've got a hunch—no, more than a hunch— it's a definite feeling based on certain facts—a feeling that I'm getting close—much closer now."

"To what?" she asked with bewilderment. "To Rostov?"

He looked at her blankly. "Rostov? . . . No, not Rostov."

"Closer to what?" she insisted on knowing.

"To the plot," he said. And with that he led her into the bedroom.

VIII

MATT?"

"Yes?"

"Jay Doyle. I didn't wake you, did I?"

"Hi, Jay. No, of course not. I've been up for hours."

"I'm in the Palais Rose, phoning from the press room, so I'll have to make it quick."

"Sounds like something's going on."

"Maybe. Maybe not. You're still interested in chasing down Rostov, aren't you?"

"You bet I am. More than ever, Jay."

"Good. Well, I've just got a hot tip. Some of the top Russian delegates are going out to Maisons-Laffitte today. The racetrack. You know where that is?"

"Maisons-Laffitte? Sure. I was there a couple of years ago with Herb Neely. That's out near the Forest of St. Germain, isn't it? About ten or fifteen miles from here?"

"Right. As far as I can learn, the third or fourth race, the *Prix du Sommet,* is being staged to honor the Summit. The Russians have a horse in it named Prince Yuri, and at least a dozen of the Soviet big shots are going to be on hand to cheer the nag in. I know that the Premier and Marshal Zabbin are going to be there. I don't know what other Russians, but I'm guessing that if Talansky and Zabbin are there, then our friend Rostov can't be far away. I thought of you immediately. I think it's worth a try, unless you're tied up this afternoon."

"You're darn right I'll be there. You know I have no other business besides Rostov—wait, hold it a minute. Dammit, I almost forgot— Medora. Earnshaw called earlier. He pulled off his part of the plan. Then Sydney Ormsby called. I made an appointment to see him here at the hotel for cocktails at four o'clock. Well, in case I'm late coming back, I can always have the concierge tell him to wait. When's the race?"

"I don't know exactly. I'd guess early enough. But you'd better leave by one o'clock. It's Saturday. It could be crowded all the way."

"I remember."

"Matt, I'll be meeting you there."

"That's great."

"I was at that gourmet dinner last night. I picked up something that might be useful to you, to both of us. And minutes ago, in the Palais Rose—well, I can't talk now—but the way it's going—well, let's see how it develops. I'll explain when I see you. Do you know any special place we can be sure to find each other?"

"Let me think. . . . I know. There's a big snack bar right under the grandstand. Where the W.C. is, also. We won't miss each other there."

"Okay, Matt. That's it, then. Maisons-Laffitte at—let's say no later than one-thirty."

"I'll be waiting. . . . Oh, by the way, Jay, before hanging up, if you have the time, there's another little favor you can do for me in the Palais Rose."

"You name it."

Brennan told him and hung up, and all of that conversation had taken place three and a half hours ago.

Now, having parked the smart compact Peugeot he had managed to rent for the entire weekend, having walked past row upon row of automobiles in the dusty lot, reviewing the phone call from Doyle and the promise it held, Brennan hastened toward one of the ticket windows.

Waiting impatiently in line—the bumper-to-bumper traffic and the crush of people outside the racecourse had been intolerable and had made him late—he was surprised at how fresh and invigorated he felt.

Last night, after the insane party at Legrande's château, both he and Lisa had been too exhausted to make love. In bed they had talked drowsily from their pillows a little while until both had fallen soundly asleep. Yet, despite his weariness and the short rest, he had awakened strangely exhilarated.

Over breakfast his mind had been recharged by the odd and appealing possibility that while the Swiss psychoanalyst's description of a potential traitor or a real one had not fitted him, it did seem tailored to fit Nikolai Rostov. Brennan had not been sure whether this might be a

Fact or merely a Wish, but the possibility had opened new avenues of exciting speculation in his mind. After breakfast only Earnshaw's depressing call had dampened Brennan's spirits. But that low point had been of brief duration. For the phone had rung again with Doyle, fat and faithful friend, offering him new hope.

Cheerfully now he purchased his ticket at the booth, hurried through the turnstile, and entered Maisons-Laffitte to find Jay Thomas Doyle and, after him, perhaps at last, Nikolai Rostov.

Viewed from the side, the gigantic grandstand seemed planted with an acre of animated heads, and between the stand and the track railing a thousand more bettors milled about in the sun, touting long shots or dark horses to one another. After adjusting himself to the scene, Brennan took out his sunglasses, put them on, and started toward the rear of the stand.

Jay Doyle, belly hanging over his loosened belt, was waiting inside the snack bar, beneath the stadium, as agreed. He was at the counter, munching a sandwich and guzzling a stein of beer, when Brennan came upon him.

"Sorry to be late, Jay," Brennan apologized.

"Doesn't matter. They're not here yet." He pushed a plate holding a sandwich roll wrapped in wax paper toward Brennan. "But you've come in the nick of time to save me. I've had five of these *jambon* sandwiches already. Do a good deed. Save me from the sixth and Hazel's disdain. Danish ham. Delicious. Try it, please."

Brennan wasn't hungry, but he had skipped lunch and he did want to do a friend a favor. He called out for a Coca-Cola and uncovered the last sandwich. "Call me Pythias, good Damon," he said, and took a bite. "I really appreciated your call, Jay. It came just at the right time, pulled me back from the brink of the dumps. This morning Earnshaw telephoned just before you did. Bad news. For ivy-covered Brennan U.—poison-ivy-covered, I guess—he gave it the old college try last night. The reception at the Hôtel de Lauzun. Our President was there. Earnshaw got him off alone. It must have been tough for him, but he did it. He made a big spiel for me, and asked the President to help me see Rostov. The President refused. Earnshaw was still upset this morning, and he kept promising to try to do something else. But there's nothing he can do. Then you phoned, and hope sprang eternal."

Doyle finished wiping his mouth with a paper napkin.

"As long as you haven't forgotten your rabbit's foot."

"Jay, I've turned myself into a rabbit's foot. Did I hear you say the Russians haven't arrived?"

"Not yet," said Doyle. "I went up to what we call the press box

701

trying to find one of the French correspondents who might fill me in. I ran into that kid Fowler, of ANA. He said the foreign press was not notified of this little Soviet outing until an hour ago. I happened to know about it as early as I did because—between us, Matt—I happened to take a peek at the schedules on the spindle of the *Pravda* desk, Igor Novik's desk, in the Palais." He stared hungrily at Brennan's disappearing ham sandwich, sighed, and went on. "According to Fowler, an entourage of a dozen Russian leaders and their bodyguards is heading this way. They're scheduled to arrive before the third race. I'll show you the one."

Doyle pulled a single sheet of paper from his pocket, and unfolded it for Brennan. It read: PROGRAMME OFFICIEL, SOCIÉTÉ SPORTIVE D'ENCOURAGEMENT, COURSES À MAISONS-LAFFITTE. His finger went down the page and pointed at the line: 3ᵉ COURSE, À 15 HEURES, PRIX DU SOMMET.

"That's the one they're coming to see," said Doyle. "Three o'clock sharp. Right now we're between the first and second races, so there's still plenty of time. The Russians—there's a reserved section for them near the entrance of the first mezzanine upstairs." He patted his other pocket. "Brought my trusty Osaka mini-binoculars. From the field you'll be able to make out whether Rostov is with the others. If he is"—Doyle shrugged—"you'll have to figure out how to get to him."

"Oh, I'll get to him."

"It won't be easy in public, Matt. They'll be ringed round by KGB security guards."

"If he's there, I'll reach him," insisted Brennan. "Come hell or high water, I'm not missing this time. . . . Well, we've got a wait. What should we do? Place some bets? Get some sun? Whatever you say."

"I want to talk. I've got to talk to you, Matt."

Brennan detected an air of urgency in Doyle's speech and manner. "I'd like nothing better."

"I'm full up and bursting with material for you. And, well, there's something personal I want to discuss."

"Let's go, then. Let me see. Not here. What about the lower part of the grandstand? At least we can get off our feet. There's always plenty of room between races."

They stepped outside into the rear area of Maisons-Laffitte. Hundreds of French spectators were congregated between the trees. Off to the left, a wide circle of bettors had gathered to watch the thoroughbreds entered in the second race being walked and shown before being mounted by their elfin jockeys. To the immediate right, blocking one open-air passageway to the track, a thickening cluster of additional bettors peered upward at the broad slate tote board where, since the old-fashioned flat track still resisted automation, the odds next to each listed horse were being written in with white chalk. All about them were small structures, like so many islands, with grilled windows for wagers to be placed. The lines in front of the two-franc and ten-franc windows were no longer than those strung out before the 100-franc windows.

Pushing hard, Brennan cleared a path for Doyle and himself. At last they broke out of the horde of gamblers, and left the shade for the less crowded and unshaded dirt area between the front of the grandstand and the white metal railing protecting the length of the grassy homestretch.

"I told you there'd be plenty of seats," said Brennan. He preceded Doyle to the half-filled bottom row of the grandstand, and they found places together on the cement tier.

Doyle pointed over his shoulder and upward. "That block of empty seats with half the Sûreté around them—that's where the Russians will be sitting."

Brennan turned and lifted his gaze above the occupied tiers of grandstand seats toward the level above. He made out the square of vacant reserved chairs. His gaze shifted, seeking the means of access.

Guessing his intent, Doyle said, "There's a wide flight of wooden steps, back where we came from, next to the snack bar. It takes you right upstairs. But I don't know if they'd let you in."

"Jay, space age or no, whatever goes up has to come down. If Rostov goes up there, he'll have to come down. And when he does, guess who'll be waiting for him."

Brennan turned back to study the configuration of the almost oval grass track, and realized that half a hundred people were running and fighting for choice points of vantage at the railing. He heard the loudspeakers blaring, and he saw the prancing and wheeling colts and fillies moving out to parade on the track.

"I'm not interested in this race," he said to Doyle. "I'm interested in what you have to tell me."

Doyle was perspiring profusely in the direct heat of the afternoon sun. Beads of sweat formed and trickled down his puffed cheeks. "I'll get sunstroke," he muttered, searching for a vendor to sell him a head covering of any kind. There were no vendors, but then Doyle sighted something, excused himself, moved crabwise along the row, and stooped to pick up a newspaper. Triumphantly he returned to his place, waving a folded copy of *Paris-Turf*, which he opened and set on his head.

Protected at last, Doyle was all business. "It's about your theory, Matt. The Russians and Chinese using the Summit as a Trojan Horse, to put us off guard while they play secret hanky-panky unknown and unseen inside the horse. I've picked up some juicy evidence for you, Matt. There's so much, I hardly know where to begin."

"Why not at the beginning?"

"Okay. Last night. Like I told you on the phone, I attended one of the dinners of the Société des Gastronomes at Lasserre. I found myself sitting next to my old friend—well, not exactly friend, but a nice guy I've been bumping into around the world for years—Igor Novik, the one who does foreign stuff for *Pravda*. His only other claim to fame is that he outweighs me by twenty pounds. Anyway, there we were, and I was still shaken up by the bomb Hazel had put under me earlier in the day. And I got to thinking, maybe Hazel couldn't get the truth out of Rostov about the Kennedy conspiracy, but maybe I could, because I used to be better at that sort of thing. Besides, what's to lose, making one more effort? Then I told myself another thing, that even if Matt Brennan couldn't get to Rostov, maybe I, as an American journalist under the auspices of someone like Novik, could pull it off."

"A good idea," admitted Brennan.

"But not good enough, really. Because right away, last night, I had a better one."

He had pretended to Novik that he was helping a friend finish an exposé about a political schism that existed in the Soviet Union because of differences over Red China. Since Rostov's name had come up in this exposé, Doyle hoped to verify the book's accuracy with Rostov personally. He had wondered if Novik knew Rostov well enough to be of assistance.

"This opened the can of peas," said Doyle excitedly, "but you know what was inside? Beans. And inadvertently, Novik spilled the beans. He'd grown up with Rostov, it turned out. He still saw him socially—"

As Doyle continued with his recital, Brennan was hardly aware of his surroundings, of the clang of the starter's bell or the clamor from the racing fanatics all about them. With complete absorption, and without interruption, he listened to the very end.

The moment that Doyle had concluded, Brennan said, "You mean Rostov and Marshal Zabbin entertained some top-level Chinese in Moscow only six months ago?"

"I don't know if they were top-level, although they probably were if

Zabbin was also a dinner guest. But it was about six months ago, yes."

"Unusual. From all I've read and heard, there hasn't been a ranking Chinese inside Russia in several years. Premier Talansky stated time and again that he would not treat with China separately as a Communist brother, but only as a member of a family of nations."

"Precisely, Matt."

"And you trust Novik's word?"

"I might question it except for the circumstances. He'd been eating and drinking last night, and felt expansive. He was just rattling on, and he mentioned the Chinese in Moscow, and suddenly when I called him on it, he tried to backtrack."

Brennan considered the information. "Strange, and possibly significant."

"I thought so," said Doyle, pleased. "Now I'll tell you something more that happened just this morning, that might be equally significant." He adjusted the newspaper covering his head. "I was hanging around the press room of the Palais Rose, trying to dredge up something for Earnshaw's column. You know, it's awfully difficult to pick up anything new. You get the press attaché's handouts. Or you hang around until the leaders break up their meeting, and you go to one or all of the press briefings, and they're always about the same on the points debated that day, on the progress made. One is no different from the other, except for the language they deliver it in. And the song is always familiar and always in harmony: 'Satisfactory progress was made.' But once in a while, if you know someone, you get an inkling of what's truly going on. I remember one time, in Geneva, when I was still up there on top and I was covering an important eight-nation conference. All I could get from the daily press briefings was sweetness and light. But one day, just after a meeting adjourned, I saw the Secretary of State coming down the hall. We were on fairly familiar terms. So I went up to him and asked, 'Mr. Secretary, how are the talks really going?' And he looked at me and he said, 'Jay, it's piss-poor.' So I nodded gravely, and then rushed back to the typewriter and wrote, 'Inside sources at the Ministers' conference reported today that the atmosphere was unusually tense.' " Doyle looked at Brennan. "That actually happened."

Brennan laughed. "I believe you, Jay. I've done that sort of thing, too."

"Well, it happened to me again. It happened in the Palais Rose," said Doyle quickly. "Just as the Big Five adjourned this morning's session, I caught one of the officials I'd known for years, and he said something similar, cryptic but negative. So for the first time this week I gathered that there was trouble behind the closed doors of the Summit. I decided to do what most of the correspondents have no patience or need to do, and that is cover each and every one of the press briefings. As I said, the work is usually unproductive because they have an agreement to say the same thing in different languages. You remember how those briefings are conducted, don't you, Matt? There are five short ones every noon, a few minutes apart, staggered, in different rooms of the Palais Rose. A spokesman representing each power briefs the press in his own tongue, with interpreters next to him translating everything he says into French and English."

"Are they employing headphones here?"

"Yes. Like at the United Nations. And each spokesman reads off a prepared progress report, rarely more than 500 words. Anyway, I started out by attending the briefing held by the spokesman for Great Britain. Then I raced down the corridor to catch the French one, then back to catch the press briefing Neely gave for the United States. These three were absolutely the same, as if cranked out of the identical machine. As usual, satisfactory progress had been made. General accord was being achieved. 'However, on one point—disarmament control measures—the representatives of the People's Republic of China unexpectedly submitted a new proposal for consideration. As a result, it was agreed that the leaders of the Five Powers would have to convene for a special session tomorrow morning, Sunday, 22 June.' Now, that is what I heard, exactly that, in the British, French, and American briefings. Then I rushed over to the Chinese briefing. Again the wording was the same, except for the very last announcement. The Chinese press officer said, 'However, on one point—the vital matter of policing and inspection of nuclear disarmament—the delegates of the People's Republic of China, Chairman Kuo Shu-tung and Marshal Chen, put forward a broader and more elastic new proposal for immediate consideration.' Okay, that said the same thing but the wording was considerably altered. I was a little tired of all the droning announcements by then, and worried about being late to meet you, so I almost skipped the Russian briefing. But finally I decided to look in on it. I made it just as it got under way. And again more of the same, word for word with the others, until the last, when the Russian press officer concluded, 'However, on one point—the vital matter of policing and inspection of nuclear disarmament—the delegates of the People's Republic of China, Chairman Kuo Shu-tung and Marshal Chen, put forward a broader and more elastic new proposal for immediate consideration.' When I heard that from the Russian press officer, well,

Matt, I tell you, I sat up. I could feel the goose pimples on my flesh. All I wanted was to get to you with it." He searched Brennan's face excitedly. "Did you hear everything I said? Did you get the significance of *that?*"

Brennan strove to shut out the increasing clamor in the grandstand behind them and digest what Doyle had reported. It was becoming difficult to concentrate. "It doesn't seem too—" He stopped. "By God, I think I see it, Jay. There was something—"

"You're goddam right there was!" Doyle exclaimed. "The British, French, American, Chinese, Russian press spokesmen all parroted one another on all points of the press announcement except the last. On the last, the new proposal, the British, French, American press officers took the same line in almost the very same words. But on that point, the Chinese, since the new controls proposal was their own and concerned them, reworded it and expanded it. And the Russians, who would normally use the same line and language as the others, this time repeated that point of the announcement *exactly* as the Chinese had rewritten and expanded it. A small difference, but *vive la différence,* Matt. I'm sure no other reporters covered all the briefings, or if any did, they overlooked this. But you've got me alert for those oddities, and there it was. You see what it adds up to?"

Brennan's excitement matched Doyle's own. "It adds up to collaboration."

"On the side, between the Chinese and Russian press officers, who don't even recognize each other in public. How do you like that?"

"I like it very much," murmured Brennan.

"There you have it, my hard-won booty."

"I appreciate it very much, Jay. I wish I could repay you in kind, but I'm afraid I can't offer anything to support your Kennedy conspiracy theory."

"To hell with that," said Doyle, yanking the newspaper off his head and balling it up. "You can offer me something better, much better and more practical."

"I can?"

"And how. You remember, on the phone, I said there was a personal matter I wanted to discuss with you also."

"Yes, I remember."

"This is it," said Doyle. Perspiration was again ringing his forehead, and his eager expression was now giving way to anxiety. "Matt, I'm going to be frank with you. From the start, I was like Hazel. I didn't believe that the things you were hearing about the Russians and Chinese meant anything. I thought your theory was way out, and I attributed your taking it seriously to the fact that you'd been off alone too long, out of touch, brooding, so that you had become susceptible to seeing phantoms where there were none. But recently all of your incessant suspicions put me on my toes, even against my will. I began to see things the way you've been seeing them. And I realized that everything that had happened to you in exile had not had a detrimental effect, but rather had sharpened your senses, made them keener than other people's, like the way dogs are equipped by nature to hear higher decibels of sound in the air than the duller human ear can pick up. Your perceptions and awareness simply had become more acute than my own or Hazel's. Last night I saw it all in a blinding flash of light. You were way ahead of us, above us, the prophet—"

"Maybe a false prophet, Jay."

"No, the real thing, the McCoy of prophets, the True Prophet, and now I've got religion, I'm the True Believer. And here's what I honestly wanted to say to you, Matt. Even if I'm a Johnny-come-lately, I'm with you, and I'd give a good deal of myself for a piece of the action." Doyle hesitated, embarrassed, and finally resumed. "In the cause of your theory, I'd give you not only my allegiance and loyalty but my services, based on years of know-how. All I ask is—well, let me put it this way—yesterday, when you, Hazel and I were in Le Drug Store and my Kennedy project was torpedoed, you suggested I undertake a book about the material you've been uncovering. I was too upset to consider it. But now I've settled down. I don't know if you made the offer because you were sorry for me or if you—"

"I meant it, Jay. It was a sincere offer."

Doyle beamed. "I accept it. *The Conspirators Who Killed Kennedy* is dead. Long live *The Secret Civil War Inside Russia Today*—or whatever that title was you invented for the make-believe book that Earnshaw was to bait the Ormsbys with. Only now I'm as determined as you are to make both the book and title real."

"I appreciate that, Jay." Brennan hesitated. "You mean you're finally giving up the Kennedy assassination book?"

Doyle stared back at Brennan for several seconds. Slowly he shook his head. "No, I'm not giving it up, Matt. I'll never give it up. When I said it was dead, I meant that only as a figure of speech. Inside me, it's alive. It'll always be alive, as long as I am. Oswald didn't do it, you know. There *were* others. And I'll prove it someday." He began to smile again. "The same way I now intend to help you prove your theory is a fact. You're onto something, Matt, and I'm with you all the way. I repeat, we're going to make your book and title real."

"Depending, Jay, on whether what we've found out to date is real.

Like your Kennedy theory, this hypothesis of ours means nothing unless we can prove it."

"I'm willing to gamble," said Doyle fervently. "From now on I hear evil, see evil, speak in search of evil." Momentarily distracted, he grabbed at Brennan's arm. "Matt, the third race!"

Startled, Brennan looked up. On the track, sleek horses, their jockeys mounted, were parading from left to right past the grandstand. "Is this the one?"

Doyle had his program open. "This is it. The *Prix du Sommet*. And here's the Russian hope—Prince Yuri—Number 7."

Simultaneously Brennan and Doyle twisted around and stared up at the reserved section of the mezzanine. All of the seats except three were occupied. "I can't make out their faces," said Brennan.

"Here, use these." Doyle handed him the miniature binoculars.

Brennan removed his sunglasses and brought the binoculars to his eyes. The reserved section above was fuzzy. Brennan rolled his finger across the control knob, and suddenly the Russians sharpened into focus. Moving the magnifying lens across the Slavic faces, each almost as large and clear as Doyle's face beside him, he sought the familiar visage of Nikolai Rostov. His lens passed across the three rows above, once, then twice. He counted nine Russians, and not one did he recognize.

Slowly Brennan lowered the glasses.

Doyle looked at him inquiringly. "Well?"

"Nope." He handed the binoculars back to Doyle. "Rostov didn't come."

"What about Premier Talansky and Zabbin?"

"Not up there. They didn't come either."

Doyle was crestfallen. "I'm sorry, Matt."

Brennan shrugged. "It's disappointing, but there's nothing to be sorry about. There was no guarantee he'd come."

"No. But I figured if the Premier and Marshal were coming, Rostov would tag along." He thought about it. "The Premier and Zabbin *were* coming. They were on Novik's list. I wonder why they didn't." With a wheeze, he stood up. "I'm going to see if I can find out. The kid with ANA, Fowler, he may have heard. Maybe they're just late. Want to come along?"

"No," said Brennan, once more dispirited. "I'll just stay for the race and get back to the hotel."

Doyle edged past Brennan's knees and waited in the aisle. "If you're going to watch the race, you might as well put down a bet." He glanced at the program and handed it to Brennan. "Which do you like? Prince Yuri? Unbeaten at Moscow's Hippodrome."

"No, thanks. I'm through betting on Russians." He scanned the list of nine horses and the early odds that Doyle had penciled in alongside each name. Then he took a 100-franc note from his wallet and handed it and the program up to Doyle. "Even though he's five to one, I'll play a hunch for old time's sake. Lay it all on the nose. Number 2. Diplomatique. It says, *'Couleur blanche, étoiles bleu-clair.'* "

"I'll take the Portuguese filly," said Doyle, "I guess because I knew one once, and she was mighty fast. All right. You've got Diplomatique. Number 2. I've got the one called Iberian. She's Number 5. *Couleurs rouge et violette.* I'll try to get back before the bell. Right now, I want to see Fowler." He shaded his eyes and looked up toward the Russians again. "I wonder why they didn't show."

He stepped down and waddled off to the rear of the grandstand.

After a few minutes Brennan rose and glanced up at the mezzanine. Nothing had changed. He wandered to the white railing, leaned against it, and stared gloomily down at the bright green grass of the home-stretch. Presently, realizing that the railing to either side of him was becoming crowded with spectators, mostly French families, he looked across the way. The opposite railing was lined with spectators, too, and the throng was especially heavy before the infield clubhouse with the pagodalike roof. Brennan guessed that was probably the finish pole. Beyond the clubhouse, in the distance, he could make out the thoroughbreds parading irregularly around the curve toward what appeared to be three strands of white webbing.

It was a beautiful sight and afternoon, here at Maisons-Laffitte, and he wished he could enjoy it more.

"Matt?" he heard Doyle call out loudly.

He glanced back and raised his arm. Doyle came toward him and shoved in beside him against the rail, flourishing two pasteboard tickets. "Placed the bets. And saw Fowler. Mystery solved."

"What happened?"

"From the little that Fowler could find out, that unexpected Chinese proposal today was not merely a new piece of machinery to be considered in the disarmament design. It was actually a big monkey wrench tossed into the existing machinery. A real stiff ultimatum from the Peking gang. The whole Summit is shaken. I gather when Premier Talansky understood the full import of it, he blew his top at the Chinese afterward. Anyway, he canceled everything today—including Maisons-Laffitte, which he'd looked forward to—and gathered his main advisers around him at the Russian Embassy—Zabbin, I suppose Rostov, the rest of them—for an emergency huddle. So that's it."

"I don't believe that's all of it," said Brennan. "I don't believe the Russians got sore at the Chinese. But we'll know soon enough."

"The fact is, Matt, the top Russians aren't here."

"No, they're not."

As Brennan stared across the track, he saw a flag go up in the distance, a gong resounded, and the white webbing that restrained the nine entries disappeared. A deafening shout, from thousands of throats in unison, tore through the air.

"They're off!" Doyle yelled. "Come on, baby, come on, Iberian!"

To Brennan, the galloping steeds, so far away, resembled diminutive toy animals wound up and released en masse. They were bunched together, jamming toward the rail, fighting for position. They came pounding at the farthest turn, larger and more real now, more defined, glossy bodies on perpetually hammering legs. They were stringing out, rushing along the inner rail, driving hard toward the last turn.

Although captivated by the fluidity of this perpetual motion, Brennan again was struck by the most unusual aspect of French horse-racing for an American. The horses, he realized with renewed incredulity, were running in the reverse direction, coming from the right to the left, clockwise, while races in the United States ran from left to right.

All nine thoroughbreds were swinging around the last turn and straightening into the homestretch, and Doyle, binoculars pressed to his eyes, was groaning, "Where's Iberian? I can't even see her number!"

They were looming large now, the jockeys hunched over their mounts, going to their whips, the big colts, geldings, fillies thundering toward the finish line. While Brennan could make out that two horses were clearly in the lead, from his angle he could not make out which one of the two was in front.

The bedlam, the steady roar of the crowd, had reached an ear-shattering crescendo, and above it, Doyle, binoculars still pinned to his eyes, was bellowing, "It's Number 7 and Number 2, Matt! Theirs and yours! Prince Yuri and Diplomatique! Here they come, neck and neck—look at them!"

Brennan could see them plainly now, charging hard, and suddenly, when they were twenty meters from the finish, he could see one falter, and the other go flying ahead, passing under the wire a full length in front. His eyes followed the winner as it flashed past him. Number 2.

Doyle was pounding his back. "You won, you lucky bastard, you won!"

Brennan nodded dumbly, and turned away from the rail. "Well, coming here wasn't a total loss."

"Your diplomat took the Russian by over a length. . . . Maybe that's prophetic."

"I wouldn't bet on *that*," said Brennan wryly.

"You going to stay for the next race?" asked Doyle.

"I'd like to, but I can't," said Brennan. "The spider's receiving the fly in his parlor, remember? I'm seeing Sydney Ormsby at four. Operation Medora, for better or for worse. No, I'll just collect and take off. What about you? Want a lift?"

Doyle considered the invitation only briefly. "I think I'll hang around and try my luck on the fourth race, Matt. Maybe see you later for a prayer meeting."

"We could both use one."

"Dammit, I just remembered. I've got an appointment with the proprietor of one of my favorite restaurants tonight. Got to sample the cuisine for my cookbook. I'd better follow through until I have something more important to write about. See you tomorrow anyway." He shoved his binoculars in his pocket, felt something, and called out to Brennan, "One second, Matt." He brought out a folded sheet of paper. "You wanted me to pick up the program of the banquet that the President of France is giving for the other four leaders at Versailles tomorrow night, didn't you? I got hold of a copy. Here it is. Formidable heading. PROGRAMME POUR LE DINER OFFICIEL OFFERT PAR LE PRÉSIDENT DE LA RÉPUBLIQUE FRANÇAISE AU PALAIS DE VERSAILLES. It gives the evening's schedule of events, the times, so forth. Is that what you wanted?"

Brennan accepted the schedule and stuffed it into his pocket. "Exactly. Thanks, Jay. I'd better cash in and run."

Leaving, Brennan saw a crush of people at the rear grandstand stairway. The spectators were pressing against two rows of police who, arms linked, were holding them back to leave a passageway. Brennan hurried forward to catch a glimpse of the departing Russian visitors. As onlookers applauded sympathetically, to make up for Prince Yuri's defeat, the Russian delegates descended the stairs, smiling, waving appreciatively. Brennan went up on his toes, trying to inspect each one. He counted off nine of them, and as before, every one was a stranger to him.

He watched them continue toward the exits and their limousines, and at last he turned to find the nearest cashier's window. Clutching his ticket, he saw a line of winning bettors forming, and he fell in behind the others.

The line moved forward at a snail's pace, and Brennan consoled himself with the thought that the 500 francs he had won would buy Lisa a deserved gift. He speculated on what he might purchase for her, and tiring of that, he thought of his forthcoming appointment with Sydney Ormsby, and finally he put that out of his mind, too.

Idly, he looked off. The rear compound was teeming with horse-players, marvelous French types and some not so French, and then, far across the compound, Brennan made out two husky men walking rapidly toward the exit, and they were definitely not French, and one of them, the one he could see clearly, seemed familiar.

Brennan squinted, and that instant he identified the one who seemed familiar. The Tartar giant with the misshapen nose and mottled cheek. Boris Dogel. The KGB security guard. His shorter, stockier companion had slowed to light a cigarette, and for a moment, before Dogel blocked him from view, a portion of his face was revealed. Nikolai Rostov.

Brennan gasped. Rostov! Rostov here, after all. Their backs were to him now, and he couldn't be sure, couldn't be absolutely positive, but the man had resembled Rostov, was undoubtedly Rostov, with Dogel serving as his KGB protector.

The Russian pair was moving toward the exit once more, and Brennan found himself moving, too. He had left his place in line and was striding quickly across the rear of the compound. He shoved people aside, attempting to keep the two Russians in sight. They were nearing the exit. Brennan began to run, but other visitors were running before him, running across his path toward the circle where the horses for the next race were being walked and mounted.

Desperately Brennan tried to battle through the unruly crowd. Pushing free, he had started to run again when suddenly a young Frenchman, sprinting, loomed up before him, and they collided.

Jolted off balance, Brennan stumbled and fell heavily to his knees. Stunned and bruised, he remained on one knee, shaking his head, trying to get rid of the dizzying specks of color swarming across his eyeballs. He closed his eyes tightly, opened them, and although one leg pained him, his vision was almost restored but his dizziness remained.

He felt friendly hands reaching under his armpits. He looked up. Several Frenchmen, including the one who had bumped into him, and an Oriental gentleman, all of them filled with concern, swam before his eyes. They were trying to assist him to his feet. He stood up groggily, tottering, thanking them, thanking them again, insisting that he was fine now.

As the Frenchmen melted away, Brennan realized that the Oriental

713

gentleman had stayed behind. The Oriental gentleman was rotund and grinning. Brennan stared at him.

"Ma Ming?" Brennan said.

The Chinese nodded. "Bad fall for you. Are you all right? Dangerous to run in a crowded place. They stumble that run fast. Wisely, and slow, that is best. From your Shakespeare."

All at once, Brennan remembered the reason he had been running fast.

Rostov and the KGB guard. Rostov and Dogel.

Ignoring Ma Ming, he frantically examined the area around the exit. They were no longer there. He searched beyond the exit. They were not there, either.

Filled with self-anger and self-recrimination at his missed opportunity, Brennan said curtly, "Sorry, excuse me, but I've got to catch up with someone."

"I know," said Ma Ming pleasantly.

But already Brennan had resumed his pursuit on wobbly legs, hastening across the remainder of the compound. He reached the exit gate breathless. He scanned the special parking zone. The last of the limousines had gone. His gaze moved to the taxis as they inched up to take on passengers for Paris.

A large Renault had cruised into position, and two passengers leaped forward to claim it. Brennan's eyes narrowed.

The first of the two passengers, yanking open the rear door of the taxi, was Boris Dogel. He held the door, impatiently waving his companion inside. Brennan's eyes shifted to the companion. And, to Brennan's amazement the companion was no longer Rostov or anyone who resembled Rostov. The companion entering the taxi was pimply, sallow, slight, and his name was Joe Peet.

Rooted to where he stood, bewildered, Brennan watched the KGB man follow Peet into the taxi, slam the door behind him, and then Brennan watched the taxi grind forward, slide past him, and spin away toward the Forest of St. Germain and Paris.

He had wanted to shout after them, but it was useless. He had wanted to chase them in his car, but that was hopeless, too, and besides, his Peugeot was parked at least ten minutes away in a crowded lot.

Immediately he remembered Ma Ming, back in the compound, Ma Ming who had also tried to call upon Joe Peet. And he again heard Ma Ming's last words, uttered minutes ago, after he had told the Chinese that he had to catch up with someone. Ma Ming had said, *I know.* What did Ma Ming know?

Brennan turned around, his eyes roving over the area behind the grandstand, trying to seek out the Chinese.

Like Rostov, like Peet and Dogel, Ma Ming had vanished.

For a moment Brennan considered retracing his steps and hunting for the Chinese journalist. But his sure instinct told him that his effort would be a waste and would only serve to make him late for his appointment in Paris.

Limping on his bruised leg, trying to make some sense out of several acts of legerdemain that made no sense at all, Matt Brennan left the premises of Maisons-Laffitte.

Not until a half hour later, when he guided his car into the Champs-Élysées, did he remember that he had forgotten to cash in his win ticket on Diplomatique, conquerer of Prince Yuri.

WITH HIS BACK to the English publisher, Matt Brennan stood over the tray of depleted bottles resting on his desk in the sitting room of his Hotel California suite, and once more he mixed a round of drinks. For himself, one inch of Scotch and the rest water. For Sydney Ormsby, three inches of Scotch and a dash of water.

Brennan considered his handiwork. Then, on second thought, he added another fourth inch of Scotch to Sydney Ormsby's whisky. Comparing the color of the drinks, he could see that Ormsby's was deep amber, his own pale yellow. It had been his formula throughout the meeting, but Sydney Ormsby had been too eager to please a potential best-selling author to note the difference, and now he would be too intoxicated to be aware of such refinements.

In the two hours that had passed since Sydney Ormsby had introduced himself at the door and entered Room 112, Matt Brennan had worked with Machiavellian care to bring the young Englishman to the moment of decision. That moment was swiftly approaching, the critical moment, and the one on which the entire scheme balanced. This drink, Brennan prayed, would make what was to follow possible.

Taking up the drinks, Brennan turned from the tray and started toward Sydney Ormsby, who was lolling on the velour-upholstered divan, eyes closed, whistling to himself.

Brennan was conscious again of how singularly unattractive the young English publisher was, and how difficult it had been to wear the guise of friendly hospitality in his presence. Of course, Brennan knew, his dislike of Ormsby had been predetermined by the awareness of the

715

English playboy's unsavory role in Medora Hart's life. But from the outset, Ormsby's appearance and manner had served to prejudice Brennan even further.

Sydney Ormsby had arrived wearing the attire of a dandy, and affecting an ascot and umbrella cane. No matter how winning he had tried to be, how eager to impress a potential asset to the book publishing division of Ormsby Press Enterprises, Ltd., what came through of him to Brennan was a spoiled, supercilious, nasty young boy who had no respect for his elders and was used to having his own way.

But Ormsby had tried to be charming, no doubt about that. He was on special assignment from his brother, sent after big game, and his instructions obviously were to come home with the trophy at any cost. In his adenoidal high-pitched voice he had tried to play masseur to Brennan's ego. How he had envied Brennan's Bohemian life, and wished he himself possessed the gift of writing that would enable him to be a free soul and nonconformist. How he had admired Brennan's experience of the Continent, and regretted his own insularity and his inability to adapt himself to the plumbing and varied tongues across the Channel. How he had always desired an afternoon such as Brennan had just enjoyed at Maisons-Laffitte, but alas, how inhibited his own visits to Ascot had always been since he had been expected to devote himself to representing his brother whenever the family silks were entered in the steeplechases. How he had craved the pleasures of Paris that a person like Brennan could know, and which he could not, hampered as he was by his relentless duties and Sir Austin's exalted position. How wonderful, he had said, to be an American unrestrained by tradition, to be a traveler with an experience of politics, to be a researcher and crusader courageous enough to pierce secrets behind the Iron Curtain.

To Sydney Ormsby, for two hours, Brennan had been a potentate among mere mortals and altogether admirable.

To Matt Brennan, for two hours, Ormsby had been a detestable little fake.

Now the time had come for Brennan to re-examine "the pleasures of Paris" that Ormsby had earlier insisted had been denied him. The fact that these pleasures had actually not been overlooked by Ormsby, as Brennan knew from the gossip of Lisa and others, was the very fact that had inspired Brennan to undertake this action on Medora's behalf. In battle, one scouted and probed for the weakness of a foe, and when the weakness was revealed, one struck fast and without mercy. Brennan suspected the publisher's weakness, and the moment to strike at the vulnerable heel had arrived.

"Your whisky-and-water, Sydney." They had swum to a first-name basis after the second round of drinks, and this was the fourth.

Sydney Ormsby stirred himself, came to life, and sat up, still projecting eagerness. "Thank you, thank you, Matt," he said through his nose. Immediately he downed a quarter of the whisky and smacked his lips. "Best yet." Nervously, his ferret eyes followed Brennan to the chair, and then he said, "To get back to the book—"

"Yes, the book, good ol' book," muttered Brennan, remembering to simulate a thickness of speech.

"S'great book."

"An' great title," said Brennan proudly. He savored it aloud. *The Secret Civil War Inside Russia Today.*

"If book's all Mr. Earnshaw says, it can make you a bloody fortune."

"Like what?"

"Generous advance, royalties, subs-iary, maybe one hun'ert, two hun'ert thousan' pounds sterling."

"Not bad," said Brennan.

"Maybe more," said Ormsby craftily.

"Ummm," said Brennan.

"Depen's on book. Earnshaw tol' my brother your manuscript's all finish—finished."

"Practically."

"Anyone see it yet?"

"Earnshaw."

"Oh, yes, yes. I mean anyone in book fiel—field?"

"Not really, Syd. 'Cept I'm here to sell it, an' several—"

The telephone rang. Brennan jumped to his feet and hoped that it was the prearranged call. If it was, the timing could not have been better.

He answered the telephone.

"Mr. Brennan?" It was what he had hoped for, Carol Earnshaw's voice.

"Yes. Brennan here."

"Is that horrible beast still there?" she whispered.

"Ah, yes, Mrs. Winkler. I meant to call you, but I've been terribly tied up. I received the offer you sent over by messenger. The advance against royalties seems fair enough. Especially since you were kind enough to make it sight unseen, based only on our conversation. But I'm entertaining several offers, and I'll need the weekend—"

He went on in this vein for a minute, watching Sydney Ormsby from the corner of his eye, pleased that Ormsby was imbibing steadily and becoming increasingly nervous.

Hanging up, Brennan returned to his chair, saying, "American publishing female. Openhan'ed enough to make an offer without reading the manuscript. It shows trust—"

"Well, actually we—we're not pushing to make our decision on a reading, either, Matt—only want a glance to know how far, how far we can go—"

"I don' mind at all, Syd, ol' boy, not at all. Matter of fact, that's not what's upper-foremost in my mind. No, sirree. I prob'ly going to turn Mrs. Winkler down, 'cause she's a bit of a bore, if you know what I mean?"

"Of course!" said Ormsby, happily baring his tiny yellow teeth.

"I mean that I mean this book's so important to whole world—so serious—like what's in it—" Brennan launched into five minutes of sensational, if fictional, anecdotes about a Russian underground government inside the Soviet Union and its incredible and little-known activities. He could see Sydney Ormsby's tongue lapping at his mustache and the glass trembling in his hand, and when he knew that he had him, Brennan abruptly concluded his summary of the contents.

"Most important book I ever heard about!" exclaimed Sydney Ormsby.

"Glad you see that," said Brennan. "An' that's the point. Book's so serious, so important, I've got to work closely, hand in hand, with my publisher from editing to publishing it. Got to work together closely. But can't work together with that Winkler woman, 'cause even though she's a good-looker, maybe thirtyish, could be a good roll in hay, she's type who's fuddy-duddy business and straitlaced and wears girdles to bed, I bet."

"Ha-ha."

"Glad you understand, Syd, my frien'. I can't work months with publisher who's all business—an' book so serious important—got to have some diversion, too, some kicks, laughs—got to have someone, publisher, who likes to loosen up after hours—little relief—what we alive for, 'cept to have some fun—got to have fun publisher who likes fun. Like here—like drinking—"

Ormsby held up his glass. "Drinking, absolutely, Matt."

"An' laughs."

Ormsby laughed nervously. "An' laughs. Right you are, Matt."

"An' women."

For the first time, Sydney Ormsby's enthusiasm was genuine. "An' women. Righto, women, God bless 'em."

"Knew it. Knew it!" Brennan exulted. He leaned over and hit Sydney's knee. "Knew you were my type, Syd, ol' boy. So you like the broads, too, eh, Syd?"

"Love 'em, love 'em all."

"Knew you were my boy, Syd. Yes, sir, got a solid feelin' we're going to make a deal on my book." He paused, and considered Sydney Ormsby through slit eyes. "You're not jus' being agreeable, about havin' fun?"

"You know me, Matt, love drinking an' lotta laughs an' fun."

"You didn't mention dames," said Brennan suspiciously. "What about dames?"

"Love 'em more than anything else."

"Wasn't sure, 'cause you look too gentlemanly."

"Not gen'lemanly, not a bit," Ormsby protested. "Just on good behavior to impress you, 'cause we wanna have you with us, Matt." He preened. "Fact is, Matt, I got somewhat a reputation for being bit of a ladies' man, you know. Assure you, you won'—won't be disappointed."

"You like fun, you mean?"

"Fun first, business secon', s'my motto."

"You're my boy, yes sir," said Brennan. He halted, stared at Sydney Ormsby, and then he asked, "How's about some fun right now, Syd?"

Ormsby looked startled. "Now?"

"Can you name a better time? Now, sure. Matter of fact, I have—" He squinted at his wristwatch. "I got me a hooker coming up here in less than an hour. An American kid. Art student studies on Left Bank, lives 'round corner. Does it on the side to pick up some easy change. Been havin' her up here regular—great kid—an' she's got a roommate girl friend who I hear's even better—gorgeous dancer who does some acrobatics on side. What do you think? Doesn't that sound like fun?"

Ormsby's expression of concern belied his enthusiastic response. "Sounds great fun, Matt. Maybe we can do it next time. Right now, I'm rather anxious to have a glance, jus' a glance, at your manuscript before—"

"Thought you said pleasure before business," said Brennan peevishly.

"I meant it, I meant it," said Ormsby hastily, trying to mollify him. "Only I thought—"

"Either you like dames or you don't," insisted Brennan with belligerence.

"I do, I like nothing better!"

"That's more like it," said Brennan, slapping Sydney Ormsby's leg again. "Knew you were right for my book. Tell you what, Syd, let's

719

have our little roll, an' after we get rid of the broads, I'll drag out the manuscript, an' we can have some dinner relaxed an' you can read." He studied the publisher. "What do you say, ol' Syd?"

Ormsby worried his mustache with his fingers. "Well—" Suddenly he sat up and grinned, decision made. "Sounds like a perfect program, an' beginning of a long relationship."

"You said it, kid." Brennan came to his feet. "One call, an' I can get them here from 'round the corner in five minutes. Sit tight."

Brennan hurried into the bedroom, pleased that he had carried the plan this far. The earlier events of the day at Maisons-Laffitte had been pushed to the back of his mind by the immediacy of the need to bully through the project that might help Medora. Only one step, the most precarious and unpredictable, remained.

Brennan took up the telephone and gave the number of the Berri Bar across the street. When the waitress brought her to the phone, Brennan spoke only two words. "Come over."

After that, he went into the bathroom, splashed cold water on his face, combed his hair, and then, satisfied, he went quietly across his bedroom into Lisa's vacant one. He surveyed the room. It was in order. He returned to the sitting room.

Sydney Ormsby was standing at the liquor tray, sloshing more Scotch into his glass. On Brennan's approach, he turned, staggered slightly, and looked at Brennan inquiringly.

"All set, Syd. Her roommate was available. They started over here couple minutes ago. If her friend's anything like what that broad of mine tells me, this is your lucky day." He placed a comradely arm around Sydney's shoulder. "You're a good sport, Syd, good sport, my kind. We're going to do mighty big things together."

Ormsby took a swallow of his whisky, and his lips curled with anticipation. "Sorry if I appeared a bit of a stick-in-the-mud earlier, but I'd better explain confidentially, since we're gonna be friends. I've been 'round the ladies in my time, an' once I got myself in a little trouble with a prosty, an' my brother, who's always upholding the family honor, took a dim view of the affair. Ever since, Austin's kept me on a tight leash, so to speak, 'specially here in Paris, where he's had me under restraint and behavin' like a eunuch." He grinned. "Got my new author to thank for ending my frightful fast. 'Bout time. This is safe enough, and to the devil with abstinence. I got my brother a book—right, Matt? Now I deserve a reward, rather doin' what comes naturally. Don't mind having a last laugh on Austin once in a while. That brother's-keeper routine is a bit outmoded, anyway, eh Matt?"

"Now you're talking, Syd."

"Better go to the bathroom," said Ormsby.

"Straight ahead."

Ormsby started for Brennan's bedroom, calling back over his shoulder, "I hope she's a bloody bitch of a whore. I like 'em dirty, dirtier the better, eh, Matt?"

Brennan watched him go with distaste. Alone, he made a hasty check of the sitting room. When he heard the toilet flush, he moved back to where he had been, and when he heard the faucet start and stop, he poured himself a drink but did not touch it.

Ormsby strutted back, stroking his mustache. "Ready for action. What's the pillow arrangement?"

"I've got my bedroom, and the adjoining one for another lady friend—"

Ormsby clucked appreciatively. "You're going to be my favorite author."

"—so I'll take my American hooker into that one, the extra one, and lock the door, and you can have this bedroom here. I'm payin' for the chippies, so don' bother."

"What about after I've had the tart?"

"Send her off an' buzz me. Room 110."

"Good show. Well, I'm—"

There was a discreet series of raps on the door. They both looked up.

"Here they are," said Brennan. "Well, let's see—"

He hastened to the vestibule, and opened the door to the last act of his playlet.

He embraced Lisa, who was chewing gum loudly. "How are you, honey? And welcome to your friend. Aren't you going to introduce us?"

"Maggie, this is Matt."

"Hi, Matt, heard plenty about you," said Medora Hart.

"Come on in, girls. . . . You Australian or English, Maggie?"

"English."

"Great. Want you to meet a countryman of yours, good guy, so be good to him."

Brennan brought the young ladies into the room. As he did so, he could see the transformation in Sydney Ormsby's expression. Never in memory had he seen a person so quickly drained of blood and so instantly sobered.

"Girls, you gotta meet the greatest little lord—well, anyway, brother of a lord—British Empire ever produced. Girls, this is Mr. Sydney Ormsby, and you can call him Syd. . . . An', Syd, we got here my little friend I was tellin' you 'bout." He placed a proprietary arm around Lisa so there would be no mistake. "This is my Alicia." He reached over to draw Medora forward. "An' here's her roommate, who's all she's been cracked up to be, namely—what was the name again, honey?"

Medora's face was a tight mask of hatred as her smoldering eyes fixed on Ormsby. "Maggie, my name's Maggie."

"Okay, Maggie, meet Syd."

Neither Medora nor Ormsby spoke. They stood silently glaring at one another, like two cats, a tom and a female, backs arched rigidly before hissing.

Brennan looked from one to the other. "Hey, what's with you two now?"

Ignoring him, Medora said to Ormsby, "Haven't we met before?"

"If we have," said Ormsby with restrained ferocity, "I wouldn't remember."

"Whoa, Syd, whoa. What's got into you?" demanded Brennan. "Why you bein' so standoffish suddenly? This is Alicia's friend Maggie, who's done some good shows in good clubs, and she's here like the rest of us for a few kicks. Come on, Syd, admit you're lucky. Where else could you ever meet a gorgeous girl like this on a blind date? Truth is, you got the best of the bargain." He nudged Lisa. "Or don't you agree, Alicia honey?"

"Oh, shut up," said Lisa, chomping her gum.

Brennan turned back to the publisher. "Well, Syd," he said darkly, "what do you say about our Maggie?"

Plainly worried about having incurred Brennan's displeasure, Sydney Ormsby came stiffly forward. "She's very lovely," he said. "What threw me off was that Maggie resembles a girl I once knew who was dreadfully unpleasant to me. For a second, my mind went back to that." He bowed to Medora. "Forgive my rude behavior—Maggie. Can I get you a drink?"

"As you please," said Medora with a shrug.

Ormsby went to the tray and busied himself with the bottles.

"What about you, Alicia honey?" asked Brennan. "Want some booze?"

Lisa shifted her wad of chewing gum to the opposite cheek. "I want less talk and more action," she grumbled. "I haven't got all day, you know. There's three more tricks waiting after dinner."

"Commercialism demeans love, baby, or so they say," said Brennan. He patted Lisa's behind. "Anyway, come along, Alicia, let's find out if

722

it does." From the doorway to his bedroom he called back, "Have a good time, you two."

Sydney Ormsby looked up from the drinks he was mixing and forced a smile. "We certainly shall, I promise you. See you later."

Brennan led Lisa through his bedroom and entered her bedroom, closing first his door, then latching her door shut. He turned and went quickly to Lisa, who was waiting worriedly at the foot of the bed.

"Beautifully done, Lisa," he whispered, embracing and kissing her.

"Do you think it'll work?"

"I don't know, but we'll soon find out." He guided her toward her corridor door. "Now off with you. You go back to your collections, and let me concentrate on mine."

Throwing him a kiss, she departed on tiptoe. The instant that she was gone, Brennan strode to her bed, sat down on it, reached for the FM receiver on the nightstand, and then, hesitating, he finally pulled up the indoor antenna.

SILENCE.

Ice cubes against glass.

Medora: "No, thanks, I wouldn't take anything from you, not even a drink, you bloody bastard."

Glass against metal tray.

Sydney: "Commendable, but it's frightfully late to try to regain your amateur standing, don't you think?"

Medora: "I see you haven't changed a whit, not even in three years."

Sydney: "Nor have you advanced in your chosen career. So now it's Medora in public, for the come-on, and Maggie in private, for the payoff. How's the payoff these days, without Paddy at the cash register?"

Silence.

Medora: "I couldn't imagine I'd ever be capable of hating any one else as much as I hate your filthy brother. But you've just made it possible. You're bloody well right I have to Maggie it, since you and your filthy brother sent me off into exile to protect your bloody names and then left me destitute here."

Sydney: "It's no use your going 'round blaming the whole world for your lot. You chose your profession. Now you're practicing it. Simple."

Medora: "I don't have to stand here and listen to your foul tongue.

I've been up to my ears in Ormsby muck long enough, and I see no reason to endure another minute of it. Go back to your paid chippies. Why do you have to pick on me again?"

Sydney: "What? Wait a minute, there. Who's picking on whom? Are you implying I arranged this reunion?"

Medora: "I'm not implying. I'm saying you did, because you're a goddam sadist."

Sydney: "Now see here! You shut up and listen. Why in the devil would I ever want to see you again? I don't need secondhand goods and I don't need trouble, and you're nothing but trouble. You want the truth? When you walked through that door, the first thing that crossed my mind was that this was some sort of—of—well, put-up thing— something *you'd* fixed to put me on the spot."

Medora: "Something *I'd* fixed? Are you insane? How could I? I've never laid eyes on this stinker, Brennan, before. I knew he was banging my girl friend, that's all, and that he was supposed to be a nice fellow, that's all. But the second I came in this room and saw that his friend was you, that he could make friends with a dirty little rat like you, he dropped clunk to the bottom in my regard. And that he'd pimp for you, that dropped him even lower."

Sydney: "I hadn't ever set eyes on Brennan until a few hours ago. I was seeing him on business."

Medora: "Typical Ormsby business as usual."

Sydney: "Very well. This was an accident, so—"

Purse rubbing upholstery, purse clicking shut.

Medora: "So I'm leaving the scene of the accident, that's what. I wouldn't give you the satisfaction of spitting on you, let alone being in the same room with you. You're a dirty wretched beast, like your brother, no better, and all I want to do is get out of here and cleanse myself."

Leather soles on the carpet.

Sydney: "Hold on, Medora—"

Medora: *"Let go of me!"*

Sydney: "Listen, Medora, be reasonable, will you? Your walking out like this—it'd upset Brennan terribly. I mean, the whole thing would come out and upset him. And, Medora, listen. I'm in no position to upset him. We're negotiating a contract, very delicate, and any little thing like this could throw it off. Look, be practical. You walk out and you give me a pack of trouble, and you have yourself an empty handbag. But if we just sit here and have a drink, nothing more—I'll mess up the bed a bit, but you can simply sit here—and after fifteen or twenty minutes—"

724

Female laugh.

Medora: "Be realistic, Sydney. After two minutes, right?"

Sydney: "Savage me all you wish, but be sensible. Sit here a bit, and then let me pay you off double your price."

Medora: "Sydney, drop dead."

Swish of a skirt.

Sydney: "Medora, don't go—"

Medora: "Ouch. Let go, you're hurting my shoulder, you—"

Blouse ripping.

Medora: "You bastard, now look what you've done, torn off half my best silk—"

Sydney: "I'll buy you three new ones. I'll—"

Silence.

Medora: "Now you're hurting both my arms. Where do you get off with that? Will you or will you not let me go? I'll scream. I'll—"

Silence.

Medora: "What are you staring at like that?"

Sydney: "I can't help it. I—I'm sorry I tore your blouse, but I'm not sorry, either. You—you still don't wear—wear brassieres, do you?"

Medora: "It's none of your business what I choose to wear or not wear."

Sydney: "I know, but I couldn't help remembering the past, those times in my flat. You know, Medora, I thought then—I've never changed about that—I thought you were the loveliest and most attractive young girl on all the earth. I was truly serious about you. If that stupid Paddy Jameson hadn't made a botch of things—"

Medora: "Never you mind him. Just you leave Paddy out of this."

Sydney: "I was only thinking of what could have been for us. With all the trouble, I'd—I tried to put you out of my mind—and God knows there have been many girls since—but right now, Medora, seeing you again like this—why, you're a young woman now, not a child—I realize you've always been on my mind. There's never been any other girl like you, no one half as desirable. I realize, I honestly realize, I don't want to lose you, and more than anything in the world, I don't want you hating me."

Silence.

Medora: "Pretty speech, very pretty, only why didn't you think of making it three years ago, when you meant something to me still, when I was in the soup and needed somebody to help me out, somebody who loved me enough to care? That was the time to think of it, Sydney, when you could've been a real man, behaving properly, independently like a man and not like the slavey robot your stinking filthy brother has turned you into."

Silence.

Medora: "You had your chance, Sydney, you sure did."

Sydney: "Give me another, that's all I ask. Forget the past. I'll make up for it by ten. I'll do anything you say, get you the best apartment in Paris, an allowance, a motorcar, and you'll be free of this miserable Maggie-magging about and of all those dreadful stripteasings about. You can have your self-respect again, and—and your mother—I'll provide for her, too. Please, Medora."

Silence.

Medora: "I—I don't know."

Sydney: "Please, dearest, please—"

Medora: "I wish I could believe you, trust you. But you're too weak to do anything on your own. Your brother winds you up, sends you off, and you go in his direction. We'd end up like the last time, with your brother throwing me out, defaming me, and sending you to your room. And you, you'd be afraid to lift a finger. I can't risk it again, Sydney. If you knew what real love was, you might find strength, but this way—"

Sydney: "I know what love is, Medora. I know this minute. I've got to have you. Let me love you now, and I'll prove—please, Medora, let me—"

Kiss, moan.

Medora: "No, Sydney, don't."

Moan.

Medora: "No, really—no—"

Sydney: "I've got to—ah, your softness—"

Medora: "Don't unbutton me. I won't have it. Once was enough. I won't have you leaving me again."

Sydney: "Dearest, dearest, I won't leave you, I never left you the first time. It was Austin who was to blame, just as you said. He forced me to stay away from you, against my will. It was Austin who made you leave London for Paris before the Jameson trial. It was his scheme to protect the Ormsby name and his own reputation. All that matters to him, all that ever matters, is Sir Austin Ormsby and his bloody ambitions. He's the one who drove you out of England and has kept you out all these years. He's a Minister. He can do anything. He's the one who went to his colleagues and rigged the naturalization charge against your father and the morals act against you, even though they were not justified. I had no part in any of that. But, Medora—you must believe me—I wasn't as passive as you think. I fought him tooth

726

and nail. It was no use. He controlled the family purse strings. But it's different now, Medora. I've come into money of my own. I don't have to listen to him anymore. I can take care of you—"

Medora: "Sydney—"

Sydney: "What?"

Medora: "Maybe you have changed, if you're finally man enough to admit your brother used his power to have me illegally banished from England all these years."

Sydney: "That's what I said. I don't mind telling you, 'cause what's right is right and what's wrong is wrong, and my brother behaved wrongly, and I intend to make it up to you. . . . Now come on, Medora, let's go to bed. After that we can discuss some arrangement."

Medora: "Some arrangement. What kind, Sydney?"

Sydney: "I told you. I'll put you up comfortably on an allowance in a flat—"

Medora: "Where, Sydney?"

Sydney: "Where? Why, as I said, here in Paris."

Medora: "Why not in London?"

Sydney: "London?"

Silence.

Sydney: "Well, perhaps one day—might be a bit sticky at the moment—but I promise you, one day—"

Medora: "Right now. What about setting me up in London right now?"

Sydney: "Well, there's that bloody immigration ruling against your entry, but—"

Medora: "You've admitted it's illegal."

Sydney: "Of course, Medora, but some of that we have to live with. I couldn't impose upon my brother at this time, but one day, at the right time—oh, look, Medora, London isn't half as good as Paris, and I can cross over in an hour's flight. It'd be the same."

Silence.

Sydney: "Medora, what in the devil are you doing?"

Medora: "I am buttoning my blouse, Sydney."

Sydney: "But I thought—"

Medora: *"You* thought. I had no such thought, my friend. I have no intention of hopping into bed with you. I haven't the slightest interest in you, not the slightest. Now I shall take my sweater, my handbag, and I shall bid you farewell."

Light footsteps.

Sydney: "Hey, now—"

Heavy footsteps.

Medora: "Stop where you are, Sydney. If you come one inch closer, I'll shout the rafters down. That'd be a pretty pickle for you, wouldn't it?"

Sydney: "What's got into you? Why were you leading me on? You can't—"

Medora: "I can do whatever I please, my friend. Unlike you, I need dance to no one's tune. Today it pleased me to hear the truth from an Ormsby. Just once, the truth. I heard it. That's my only interest in you, my puny friend."

Sydney: "You're talking like a bitch."

Medora: "How else does one address a bastard? Sydney, I wouldn't sleep with you for all the gold on earth, not only because you're a mole, a worm, a squirmy slug and a lousy lover, but because you're as rotten and corrupt as your beloved Sir Austin."

Sydney: "You goddam chippy!"

Medora: "That's my only qualification for becoming an Ormsby, just like your sister-in-law Fleur. Ta-ta, Syd, my sweet."

Sydney: "Medora, damn you, listen—"

Medora: "Pass my best wishes on to your brother. My best wishes for both of you are that you go straight to hell."

Door opening, door slamming.

Silence.

Heavy footsteps.

Cork pulled. Whisky splashing.

Silence.

Telephone ringing.

Sydney: "Hello, Mr. Brennan's suite. . . . Oh, you, Matt? Ha-ha. Quite forgot. Where the devil are you? . . . Next door? That's right . . . Maggie? Who's—oh, Maggie, yes. Frightfully exciting, Matt, marvelous little whore, must see her again when the red corpuscles have had a rest. Just packed her off. . . . What's that you say, Matt? . . . I see. You're having another go-'round? Well good luck to you, 'cept wouldn't want you to overdo it, have a heart thing or any such before you've signed our contract, ha-ha. Well, I'll just wait about here till you've . . . Oh, I see. You'd really prefer Monday? I mean, I'd hate to let that book get away from us. . . . Fair enough. I have your word. The manuscript under lock and key until Monday. And you'll call me at the Bristol? . . . Good, good, I'll be there waiting. What's that? . . . Oh, I *did* enjoy her. Not every man can say he's had a tigress by the tail, ha-ha!"

THEY HAD AGREED beforehand that she would be waiting for him after it was over, and twenty minutes later, when Matt Brennan reached Le Colisée café, she was seated under the red umbrella, waving to attract his attention.

Medora Hart's anxious eyes never left him as he went up the aisle to her table. She had been poking at a tarte aux fraises, but now, as he dropped into the wicker chair, she put down her fork and automatically covered the shoulder tear in her silk blouse.

"Congratulations, Medora," he said instantly. "You pulled it off."

"I did, didn't I?"

"You certainly did." He observed her hands clenched bloodless. "Are you all right?"

"It was depleting. But I'll survive." She paused. "I hated it, Matt."

"So did I," he said. "But remember, they didn't observe the Marquis of Queensberry rules, and we couldn't either. They set up the game. When it was our turn, we had to play it their way."

"I know." She paused, and stared at Brennan. "Sydney confessed the whole bloody thing. He damned Sir Austin. I remember every word. There was no mistaking it for me. The only question is, did you—?"

Brennan smiled reassuringly. "Yes, Medora."

He took the cartridge of magnetic recording tape from his pocket and held it in his hand, showing it to her.

She blinked at the cartridge. "You mean it's all there, everything Sydney and I said?"

"All there. I played some of it back. It's all there, 600 glorious feet of it. Take a good look, Medora. The odds are it's your re-entry visa to England, your guarantee of English citizenship and permanent residence in your homeland again."

She slumped back in the chair and closed her eyes. Her fingers unclenched and her hands went to her eyes. "I want to cry, Matt," she said. "I just want to cry."

"I wouldn't blame you," he said.

He tried to offer her his handkerchief, but she refused it. She lowered her hands to her lap and opened her eyes. They were brimming, but no tears escaped. "I'll save it for Mum and Sis," she said. She was staring at the magnetic tape once more, and suddenly, worriedly, she lifted her gaze to Brennan. "Is that enough evidence?" she asked, anxiety returning.

729

"Depends where it's presented," said Brennan. "If it was presented at the Old Bailey, I'd say it might not be enough. But if it's presented in Sir Austin Ormsby's suite in the Hotel Bristol here, I'd say it's almost too much. Of course, everything depends on what Sir Austin says. If he wants to keep the family respectable, he'll buy, and you're on your way home. If he doesn't give a damn, if he's bullheaded about it, then I'm afraid that's that and you'll have to dream up something else. My guess is he'll buy, and if *he* does, *you* can, too—you can buy a one-way ticket home, Medora."

"What's the next step, Matt? How'll you manage it?"

"I'll have a copy of the tape made this evening. That'll give us two recordings of Sydney's confession. One I'll place in a bank vault. The other I'll turn over to Earnshaw, and he'll probably get Doyle or Willi or someone else to make the proper diplomatic negotiations with Big Brother. I imagine the tone will be, 'Sir Austin, would you prefer to acquire this rare taping for your personal library or prefer that it be played for the London press? Oh, certainly you may own it. Much more desirable to possess than a Nardeau. But the price is the same, you know. A scratch of your pen, permanently lifting the ban on Miss Hart and permitting her return to London.' What do you think Sir Austin will say to that?"

Medora smiled broadly, and then, watching Brennan pocket the cartridge, she shook her head and asked, "How did you do it, Matt? I still don't understand."

Brennan winked. "We are living in the Age of the Ear." He slipped his hand inside his jacket, dug into his shirt pocket, and carefully placed two tiny objects on the formica top of the café table. "What do you see, Medora?"

She bent her head, glanced up blankly. "Two paper clips."

"Two ultrasensitive subminiature microphones, powerful enough to pick up any sound in a room, a whisper, even the scuff of a shoe on the carpet. I borrowed these mini-microphones and the recording devices from a friend in the United States Embassy who shall be nameless, who borrowed them from a friend in the CIA who shall also be nameless." Brennan brushed the two metal paper clips into the palm of his hand. "One of these was attached to some notepaper lying on the desk of my sitting room suite, next to the tray of drinks. The other was clipped to a travel folder in my bedroom, in case Sydney ever got you into there."

"Fat chance."

"When you and Sydney were having it out, the paper-clip microphone in the sitting room transmitted every word into the bedroom

730

adjoining mine. I picked it all up through headphones I was wearing. The headphones were attached to an FM receiver. Also, hooked up to the FM receiver was a patch cable leading to a voice-activated automatic tape recorder next to me." He patted his coat pocket. "And lo, the electronic re-entry visa was won and Operation Medora ended successfully."

"Thanks to you," said Medora. "Thanks to you forever."

"Let's shelve expressions of gratefulness for the duration. We owe one another a great deal. If you're in the hotel tonight, I'll call to tell you whether Earnshaw carried the word to Sir Austin successfully. Or are you back at the Club?"

"Oh no, I couldn't. That overdose has still got me groggy. I told Michaud I needed rest until Monday. But I might be out for dinner tonight. I hate being alone on Saturday night. Carol Earnshaw and Willi von Goerlitz were nice enough to invite me to join them for the show at the Crazy Horse Saloon. I might take them up."

A café waitress, pink apron wrapped around her blue dress, loomed over them. She was carrying a tray of cakes, and affixed to the tray was a sign reading: "TARTE AUX FRAISES, PÂTISSERIE, BRIOCHE, TARTE."

"*Monsieur?*" she inquired.

"No, thanks," said Brennan.

Medora touched his arm. "Do have something, Matt. My treat to celebrate."

"Thanks, Medora, but not before dinner. I've—" He held up his wristwatch. "My God, I'm five minutes late already. I promised to meet Lisa for an early dinner at Le Tangage. She's got to eat early this evening to catch some fashion conference, and I've got some home-work to do."

"Oh, I hope I haven't kept you too long. Is it far—that place?"

"Le Tangage? A couple of blocks. I can cut through the Lido Arcade. You come out the rear and the restaurant's right across the street in the Rue de Ponthieu, alongside the Hotel California. You must try it with us sometime. My treat though, to celebrate the liberation of Medora Hart." He came hastily to his feet. "I'd better run. Lisa'll be waiting out in front."

"Kiss her for me, and tell her that Medora says she's lucky to have the greatest guy in the world."

About to leave, Brennan hesitated. Medora's eyes had filled again, and her cheerfulness had evaporated, as she took up her fork and glumly and listlessly cut into her pastry.

"Medora—"

She looked up, surprised. "I thought you'd gone."

"Medora, is there anything else I can do for you? I mean—"

"You mean because of the way you caught me just now? Don't worry about me, Matt, really. I'm a born manic-depressive. And besides, you know, good news is often harder to take than bad. When you've been sent to Coventry for so long, it's frightening to know you're free again. Takes getting used to."

"Yes, it does, Medora."

"And then, well, that whole give and take with Sydney Ormsby—it must've played havoc with my nervous system. I'm suffering a belated reaction, that's all." She paused. "Matt, our Sydney—he is a son of a bitch, isn't he?"

"He is, Medora. Don't give him a second thought."

"You're right, of course, only—you know, I can't help it, but right now I'm sorry for the poor bastard. Those brothers—who killed who? Cain or Abel?"

"Cain murdered Abel."

"Poor Abel. . . . Off you go, Matt, or your Lisa'll never forgive me."

Brennan left Le Colisée, and entered into the heavy after-work foot traffic on the Champs-Élysées.

The traffic signal was with him at the Rue du Colisée, but after that, proceeding in the direction of the Étoile, he was slowed by the crush of pedestrians and delayed by the light at the intersection of the Rue la Boëtie. Once he was on the other side, going rapidly past the Hotel Claridge and the Café Français, his worry about keeping Lisa waiting in front of Le Tangage too long began to recede. He would be not more than ten or twelve minutes late. He considered stopping at the shop with the TABAC sign over it, for another package of pipe tobacco, but thought better of it.

Quickly he turned off into the glittering tunnel of the Lido Arcade.

By now, the interlude devoted to helping Medora had all but dissolved from his mind. Memory had leapfrogged backward to the earlier part of the afternoon, to the new information with which Jay Doyle had provided him, obtained from the journalist Novik and from the contradictory statements at the press conferences in the Palais Rose. With wry amusement he noted that his theory of secret Russian-Chinese rapport had already gained the status of an unpublished book, promoted last night by Earnshaw at the Hôtel de Lauzun and by Doyle at Lasserre restaurant. It was a book, he realized, that would never see the light of day, under either Doyle's name or any other, unless he himself were to give the theory substance by obtaining more proof. Instantly his mind developed one additional mental photograph, unblurred, distinct, the one taken at the exit of Maisons-Laffitte when a KGB guard had opened a taxi door for Joe Peet.

He would try out this new information on Lisa, over dinner, and in so doing, attempt to make some sense of it for himself.

The Lido Arcade, too, was crowded. He glanced into the Lido Bar. Every counter stool was filled. Inside the Arcade proper, stretching the depth of a block, late shoppers were gathering at various window displays to study suits, dresses, shoes, dishware, antiques. In the middle of the Arcade dozens of laborers and white-collar workers were having their hasty sandwiches at stand-up counters, while other Frenchmen, more affluent, sought the relative comfort of tables within the confines of an indoor restaurant walled around with showcases.

Continuing through the enclosed Arcade, Brennan found himself inexplicably oppressed. It was as if every noise was too loud, every glass window too shiny, every strange face too hostile, every shadow of every passerby too grotesque. The air was dispiriting, stifling, and he felt claustrophobic, eager only to escape into the open air and then to the intimacy of a quiet haven like Le Tangage.

It was unreasonable, he knew, and he attributed his feeling of anxiety to his obsession, lately complicated by so many enigmas. The week of tension was taking its toll, and his nerves were ragged. He would have a drink and light dinner with Lisa, later a tranquilizer and his first evening of rest, and by morning he would be restored.

Near the exit of the Lido Arcade, the pedestrian traffic thinned out and Brennan came to the open doors with no further delay. With relief he went through the nearest of the doors and outside into the narrow one-way Rue de Ponthieu.

Stopping on the sidewalk, he looked across the street and off to the right. Lisa, in something attractive and yellow, was standing before the entrance to Le Tangage, examining her face in her compact mirror.

"Hi, Lisa!" he shouted, and raised his arm.

She looked up, smiled, and waved back.

As he started for the curb to cross the street, he saw a huge black-and-gray delivery truck rushing upon him from the right, careening down the Rue de Ponthieu at a reckless speed toward the intersection at the Rue de Berri.

In the nick of time, Brennan caught himself, not daring to chance it, and he teetered on the edge of the curb, waiting for the vehicle to pass.

The truck closed in with a roar, and then, a split second before it came between Lisa on the far side and Brennan on the curb, a split second before it obstructed her from his view, he saw something

733

strange. Lisa's arms had gone up, both of them, not waving to him, but wildly gesturing, and her lips moved frantically but no sounds reached him.

That instant, the speeding truck blotted this vision of a frenzied Lisa from sight.

That instant, simultaneously, from beyond the truck, over the rumble and reverberation of its engine, he heard Lisa's scream of terror.

"Look out, Matt—look out—he's going to—!"

The warning caught him like the wail of a shrapnel. Instinctively he recoiled, crouching low to escape from he knew not what. As his hands and knees hit the cement, he heard an explosion of breath behind him and a giant shadow was thrown, like the silhouette of a midnight beast, upon the street before him. An open-palmed hand and an arm zoomed past his shoulder, and like twin crowbars two legs smashed into him from behind, and the body of a man went hurtling over Brennan's head, upended, somersaulting from its own momentum onto the paving and directly into the path of the charging truck.

There was a grinding, a terrible thud, Lisa's screaming, and Brennan, flattened against the curb, raised his head in time to see the smashed body catapulted into the air from the force of the truck's iron bumper and grille, and flung high against a side wall across the way.

Brennan closed his eyes tightly, lying there, panting, and when he opened them, he could see that the truck had screeched to a halt, shielding the body from his sight. The truck driver and his assistant had leaped down from their cab, and were stumbling around the truck, bellowing in French, *"Nom de Dieu! Andouille!"* From the Rue de Berri ahead, pedestrians were racing in to help the victim of the accident, and then there were two policemen, one blowing a whistle, coming fast, their capes flying.

Someone was trying to help Brennan to his feet, and he realized it was Lisa. "Thank God it wasn't you," she sobbed. "I was sure it was you."

Brennan rose to his knees, still seeking breath, and with effort he pushed himself to his feet and stood swaying, allowing Lisa to dust him off.

"What happened?" he gasped.

"Whoever it was, he tried to kill you, Matt!" she cried out, voice choked. "I saw him come out of the Arcade right behind you, and he kind of stood there a second, waiting for the truck, and just as it came by, he started edging toward you, sneaking up behind. I—I couldn't believe my eyes at first, Matt—but when I saw him suddenly stick his arms out in front of him and run toward you, I tried to scream—and I guess I did, I don't know—because he was trying to push you in front of the truck and kill you. You *did* hear me?"

"The second I heard you, it was like the times I visited battle zones, instinctive reflex in response to danger, unseen danger, usually from behind or above. I just went down to my knees and this, this person—"

"Murderer, Matt, murderer."

"—he came at me with such force that when I went down, he missed me completely, kept right on going, and his legs must've hit my back or side, and he went over me in a somersault and landed in front of the truck, and was hit." Brennan reached out and brought Lisa closer. She was trembling. "Lisa, did you recognize him?"

"No. How could I?"

"Maybe I can," said Brennan. "Let's see."

He led her across the street, around the truck, to the widening circle of onlookers gathering about the victim of the accident. Signaling for Lisa to remain behind, Brennan shoved through the crowd, listening to the excited French voices, and finally listening to the police kneeling on either side of the body and speaking rapidly in French.

Brennan waited for one clear view of the victim, and at last he had it.

His brief glimpse of the crumpled body on the pavement, the body a sightless remnant of a human being, bloodied, crushed, misshapen, was nauseating. But when Brennan turned away, there was one emotion rising within him that overrode all others. What he had just seen had filled him with terror.

Blindly he pushed back through the noisy crowd, grabbed Lisa roughly by the elbow, and led her, stumbling from his haste, between the truck and the traffic jammed up behind it. Her eyes never left his face as she followed him to the opposite side of the street.

There he stopped, trying desperately to think. "Lisa, give me a cigarette."

Hurriedly she gave him one, and hurriedly she lit it for him. "Matt, I've never seen you like this before. Are you ill? If you are, I don't blame you—"

"I'll be all right."

"Did you see the man, the one who tried—?"

"Yes, I saw him."

"Well? Did you recognize him? Was he anyone—?"

"I recognized him, what's left of him," Brennan said. "It was Boris Dogel."

"Boris who?"

735

"The Soviet KGB agent."

Her hands had gone to her mouth. "Oh, no—"

They heard the distant sound of an approaching ambulance. Then they saw a French police officer, notebook in hand, emerge from the thick circle of onlookers. The police officer moved slowly from spectator to spectator down the street, questioning each in his hunt for witnesses.

"The police don't know who the victim is," said Brennan quietly, "and I doubt if they'll find out from anyone here. I overheard them talking. There wasn't a shred of identification on the body. Absolutely nothing." He inhaled. "The KGB plays it safe when they send out their killers."

"Matt, you can tell the police right now." She looked at him anxiously. "You will, won't you?"

His grip tightened on her arm, alerting her, as the police officer crossed the street and came toward them.

The policeman touched the brim of his cap. "Monsieur, this accident, perhaps you were a witness to it?"

Brennan shook his head regretfully. "No. We have just arrived to see what the trouble was. I am sorry."

The officer nodded. "*Merci.*" He moved away to others.

The second the policeman was out of earshot, Lisa turned on Brennan. "Matt, you should have told him."

"No, Lisa," he said firmly. He started her toward the corner of the Rue de Berri. "Men sometimes have intuition, too, and my intuition tells me to keep my mouth shut. Our KGB agent is back there dead. The police report will set him down as an unidentified pedestrian, a vagrant, accidentally killed by a truck while jaywalking in the middle of the Rue de Ponthieu. That'll be the official story. I'd prefer to leave it that way, for now."

"And leave yourself unprotected," protested Lisa. "It's foolish, Matt. When they tried to murder you in the Bois and killed that young Englishman by mistake, you let that be written off as an accident, too—but at least, there was some question there—but this time, this was an obvious attempt to murder you. Matt, I saw that monster try to push you in front of the truck."

"I know. This was overt and premeditated. And don't think I'm being brave about it. I'm not. I'm scared stiff. My knees are jelly. But going to the police won't help me. If I told them, what would happen? There'd be the most sensational headlines. My background would be dredged up. Our—our relationship would be plastered across the front pages. The Russian Embassy would deny that the corpse was one of their agents, and it would be my word against theirs, and whom do you think the police and public would believe? The publicity would end any chance I have of catching up with Rostov or getting to the bottom of what's going on with the Russians. But this way, I've got a better chance than ever."

"What do you mean?"

"I've gained myself a day. Someone in the Russian Embassy will be waiting for the results of Dogel's assignment. Even though he doesn't report back to them, they'll be searching tomorrow's obituaries for my name. Not until they fail to find it, not until they read or hear of an unidentified corpse, not until they send someone to join dozens of others in the morgue trying to identify the unknown victim, will they discover their murder attempt did not succeed. In other words, not until tomorrow will they know their killer is dead and his victim is alive."

"Why does that matter?"

"I need time, time until tomorrow."

"For what? Oh, Matt, don't be so reckless with your life. You mean too much to me. You weren't like this when I met you."

"Because then I was half dead and didn't care. But now—"

"Now you'll be all dead," insisted Lisa. "They missed once, they missed twice, but tomorrow, when they find out, they'll try again."

"Maybe. But maybe by that time I'll be ready for them, and be able to beat them to the punch."

"I could be stupid, Matt, but you're making no sense."

"Honey, I've never made more sense." They stopped before the revolving door of the Hotel California. "Do you realize what just happened back there?"

"Someone tried to kill you."

"Someone? Not someone. A Russian agent tried to kill me. Why?"

"Why? I—I don't know."

"But *I* know. For the first time, I really *know*. It's because all of my stumbling up blind alleys in Paris—after Rostov, after Peet, after faceless Russians and Chinese intriguing in secrecy—had brought me too close to some hidden truth. And the KGB has been ordered to prevent me from going further. That means I'm on the right track, and what happened in the Rue de Ponthieu confirms it at last." He realized that he had been speaking more to himself than to Lisa. He said to her, "Let me see it through, darling—my way."

"I don't know how I can stop you."

"Thanks, darling. . . . Still interested in dinner?"

"Oh, God, no. My insides are upside down."

"I'm afraid mine, too. Okay, let's go upstairs. Our menu will be one tranquilizer and one drink, well done."

They went into the lobby, where Brennan gave the concierge, M. Dupont, the cartridge of tape containing Medora's and Sydney's conversation, to be copied. Dupont said that he had already made the arrangements, and that Brennan would have the original tape and the copy back by eight o'clock. Dupont was prepared to describe the terrible accident in the Rue de Ponthieu, putting the blame on irresponsible truck drivers who filled themselves up with wine all day and then sped around Paris like maniacs, but Brennan cut him short, explaining that he and Miss Collins had just come from the scene of the accident and had already heard about it.

They took the elevator to the first floor and went to their suite. There Brennan found a tranquilizer for Lisa, and made her wash it down with straight Scotch. For himself he mixed a light drink. When she felt calmer, he suggested that she go ahead to her evening's fashion seminar.

"I'm afraid to leave you here by yourself, Matt."

He took a scratch pad and pencil from the desk. "I won't be here most of the evening, Lisa, and I won't be by myself."

"I wish you wouldn't constantly speak in riddles, Matt. Now, what does that mean, you won't be here or by yourself?"

He sat on the sofa, and placed pad and pencil on the end table beside his drink. "Lisa, I'm going to be very busy until quite late, and if I'm lucky, I'll be with allies. I'm going to sit in this room for the next few hours and do some homework in preparation for a final exam, so to speak. I'm going to put down some facts that I figure to be of vital importance. I'm going to add them up. When I have the solution, and I think I'll have it—"

"What solution? Are you talking about your future?"

"My future, yours, the future of our friends, perhaps everyone here in Paris now, and back home, and perhaps all over the world. If the words seem pompous, bear with me. Because it may add up to that. Anyway, when I have the solution, I'm going to act. But I can't act alone. I need the support of allies."

"Whom do you consider your allies?"

"I've been thinking. There are four of us. We're very different, but we have one thing in common. We've all in some way contributed to reaching the solution I hope to come up with. There's Emmett A. Earnshaw, for one. There's Jay Thomas Doyle. Then there's Medora Hart. And, of course, myself. We're all involved in this. I think the

738

time has come for the four of us to get together and have a serious conference."

"It sounds like the Summit."

Brennan smiled. "Something like that. Let's call it the Little Summit, convened by interested outsiders who have as much of a stake in peace as the insiders in the Palais Rose. I don't want to sound pretentious, Lisa, but I have a strong suspicion that in some respects our Little Summit tonight may produce results more meaningful to peace than what's going on at the Big Summit. I could be wrong, but if I'm right—heaven help us all if the Big Five don't listen to the Little Four."

B Y TEN O'CLOCK in the evening, Matt Brennan had finished writing, was done reflecting on what he had written, and he was ready to convene the unofficial delegates to the unofficial Little Summit that he would chair.

Ripping ten pages of notes off his pad, he folded them and stuffed them into his trouser pocket. It was time to set about locating his delegates. Medora Hart, he remembered, had mentioned that she might accompany Carol and Willi to the Crazy Horse Saloon. Jay Doyle had spoken of researching at some restaurant or other for his cookbook. As to the whereabouts of Emmett Earnshaw, he had no clue.

Brennan began by trying to trace Doyle. He telephoned the concierge at the Hotel George-V, but the concierge had no idea where Doyle had gone to dinner. Deciding that Hazel Smith might know where Doyle could be found, Brennan rang her apartment. There was no reply. Then Brennan called the Paris bureau of ANA, and here he had luck. The correspondent on the night desk reported that Hazel had left word she could be reached at En Plein Ciel, the larger restaurant in the Eiffel Tower, where she would be conducting an interview. Next Brennan called the concierge at the Hotel Lancaster, and learned that Earnshaw had gone to a ballet performance at the Opéra with the United States Ambassador and his wife. Finally, Brennan called the Hotel San Régis. As he anticipated, Medora was not in her room. Most likely, he guessed, she would have gone to the Crazy Horse Saloon after all.

Briefly Brennan considered trying to make contact with each of his unofficial delegates by telephone. After a moment's consideration, he vetoed the notion. To impress upon each of his allies the importance of the meeting, he should see them personally.

Slipping on his coat, he hurried down to the lobby, picked up the extra tape, then went out into the Rue de Berri and started for his car. Passing the Rue de Ponthieu, he was amazed at how deceitfully peaceful and innocent of violence it appeared by night. He hastened on to the Garage Berri, sent for his car, and drove the Peugeot down the ramp and into the street.

He would start after Jay Doyle first.

He headed for the Eiffel Tower. In fifteen minutes he was parked near the École Militaire and making his way on foot toward de Maupassant's "assemblage of iron ladders," Verlaine's "cheapjack's Notre Dame," Dumas *fils's* "loathsome tin construction." Once there, he climbed the twisting staircase up through the girders to the first floor, and entered En Plein Ciel. He sent for Hazel Smith, and she responded quickly. He told her that he had to speak to Jay Doyle tonight, and hoped that she knew where he was dining. "Le Roy Gourmet," she said at once. "It's a delicious restaurant in the Place des Victoires, near the Bourse. Jay loves the chitterling sausages. I wish I knew what that dish has that I don't have. What's up, Matt?" Promising to tell her tomorrow, he thanked her and was off.

It was almost a half hour before Brennan found Doyle, and stood with him inside the entrance of the quiet, old-fashioned family restaurant.

"Something happened to me after I left you, Jay, and I think it's given me the answer to all the mysterious political goings-on. I need your help, and Medora's help, and Earnshaw's. It's imperative we meet together tonight. There's no time to lose."

"What happened?" Doyle asked excitedly.

"I don't want to go into that now. I'll explain when we're together."

"You know I enlisted in your cause," said Doyle, removing the napkin from under his chins. "I'll be there." He looked blank. "Where?"

"Where? Why, I hadn't thought. We could go to one of our hotels or any public place that stays open late."

"Got it," said Doyle. "La Calavados. It's perfect. A little Spanish-type restaurant-bar across from the Hotel Princess Elizabeth in the Avenue Pierre-Ier-de-Serbie. Easy to find. Central for everyone. It's— why it's just off the Avenue George-V, about two, three blocks from the Champs-Élysées. When the other places close, La Calavados is still open. Strictly French clientele, so we wouldn't have the wrong people eavesdropping. But best of all, the proprietor's an old pal of mine. I'll ring him immediately and tell him to hold a table for four. Something real private. What time?"

"What do you think?"

"Well, if you've got to make a time for four different people, I'd say—oh, right after midnight, maybe one o'clock."

"Agreed. One o'clock the Little Summit comes to order."

Doyle's eyebrows lifted. "Little Summit? It's like that?"

"Like that, Jay. So be on time."

Taking leave of Doyle, Brennan got back into his Peugeot and set out to see Earnshaw.

The drive to the Opéra was short, but parking was difficult, and by the time Brennan had found a place for his car near the American Express, walked to the baroque front entrance of the opera house, used his bogus Embassy press credentials to get inside for a moment, and convinced a minor Opéra executive to carry a message from him to former President Earnshaw, three quarters of an hour had passed.

Feeling unkempt and rumpled and out of place amid this elegance, Brennan paced restlessly in the Italian loggia under the stony stares of the busts of classical composers and the suspicious surveillance of the ticket takers. From the theater inside, he could hear the strains of music accompanying the ballet, *Giselle,* and it made him feel uneasy to be breaking in on Earnshaw like this, especially if his errand should prove to be a waste of everyone's time.

Yet when he saw Earnshaw, so dignified in his formal attire, descending the white marble staircase and coming worriedly toward him, Brennan felt relieved and reassured as to his purpose. At once Earnshaw dismissed Brennan's apologies, even thanked Brennan for an interval of escape since he neither understood nor appreciated the ballet.

Brennan handed over the cartridge of tape, which Earnshaw promised to pass on to Sir Austin. Then quickly, but cryptically, as he had done with Doyle, Brennan explained the imperative necessity of a conference tonight. Not hiding his curiosity, Earnshaw promised to appear at La Calavados by one o'clock.

Returning to his car, Brennan was satisfied that now they were three. Doyle, Earnshaw, himself. One more was needed. He hoped that he would find Medora Hart at the Crazy Horse Saloon, and prayed that she would be well enough to attend his meeting.

After turning his car back to the attendant in the Garage Berri, Brennan crossed the Champs-Élysées and walked to the Crazy Horse Saloon in the Avenue George-V. He entered through the tunnel and descended into the overcrowded, darkened cabaret—decorated to suggest a saloon in America's old Wild West—where he slipped the captain fifteen francs.

Immediately Brennan was assigned a shirt-sleeved waiter as his guide. In the blackness, with only the brightly lit stage and the beam of the waiter's miniature flashlight to guide him, Brennan squeezed down among the jammed tables. On the stage a tawny nude German girl, wearing nothing but a G-string, was rising from her couch and beginning a languid and titillating striptease in reverse. She was rolling the first sheer black stocking up her fleshy thigh when Brennan bumped into the motionless waiter and realized they had arrived at Willi von Goerlitz's table.

In an undertone he greeted Willi and Carol, and bending low, he made his way to Medora and crouched beside her. He had, he said, already given the copy of the tape recording to Earnshaw, who had promised to present it to Sir Austin Ormsby in the morning. But right now, he whispered, he needed Medora's assistance on another matter. Flushed by a feeling of celebration, she was agreeable to anything. Brennan explained the meeting that he had called, reeling off the participants, the time, the place. "You know I'd do anything for you," Medora whispered back to Brennan, and she planted a soft kiss on his forehead.

Outside again, Brennan found there remained forty minutes before they were to meet. He was impatient, but he was also hungry. He strolled back to the Champs-Élysées. The waiters at Fouquet's were beginning to put chairs up on the tables, but Brennan caught the eye of one waiter whom he had known for years. He ordered a cheese sandwich and tea, and the waiter hurried inside as Brennan sat at a table several rows behind those occupied by the evening's last customers.

A grizzled Algerian came hawking the next morning's Paris edition of the New York *Herald Tribune,* and Brennan bought a copy. Nervously he scanned each page for an item about the accident in the Rue de Ponthieu. There was no reference to the death in any column. Brennan tossed the paper aside, realizing that a routine traffic fatality involving one who was apparently an unknown vagrant was hardly news for an expatriate American newspaper. He felt safer, although he suspected that tomorrow's French press would carry some kind of story. But for tonight, the KGB agent's death was a secret belonging only to Lisa and Brennan, at least until one o'clock.

Thinking of the notes in his pocket, Brennan ate his sandwich without relish, finished his tea absently, and glanced at his wristwatch once more. He found his check under the sugar bowl, paid it, and hastened up the Avenue George-V toward the intersection which would bring him to La Calavados and his fellow delegates.

They were already gathered together at the farthest and most isolated table along the wall, ordering drinks, when Brennan arrived. From inside the doorway, from the bar to his right, from the full distance of the long, narrow, oblong café-restaurant, Brennan studied them.

There were three—Jay Doyle, in a wrinkled gray business suit, loosening his belt as usual; Emmett Earnshaw, in a white tie and tails, unwrapping a cigar; Medora Hart, in a low-cut clinging cocktail gown, smoothing her coiffured hair with one hand as she read from the drink list held in the other. There they were, his allies. Tonight he desperately needed their reassurance, as well as their pledge of assistance (should he need their help in the hours ahead). And tomorrow, perhaps, many, many more than he would need them, need them and himself.

He started forward. Except for a half-dozen late customers at the bar, and two tables occupied by other latecomers—one group being serenaded softly by the three Spanish guitarists—Brennan and his fellow delegates would have La Calavados to themselves.

Doyle struggled to his feet to shake Brennan's hand, eager to begin. Earnshaw was no less eager. Medora, still flushed, was only confused and desirous of pleasing.

"What'll you have, Matt?" Doyle wanted to know. "Medora's having some Spanish sherry, Emmett's having a cognac. I've ordered Grand Marnier."

"Cinzano," said Brennan. He sat down in the empty chair beside Doyle, and across from Earnshaw and Medora, who were against the wall. He glanced around him. "Not exactly the Palais Rose, but more comfortable."

"I spoke to the proprietor," said Doyle. "Nobody'll disturb us."

Brennan nodded. "I'm grateful you could all make it. What I have to say, I think, affects not only me but every one of us."

"When do we begin?" asked Doyle.

"Now," said Brennan.

"You've got the gavel, Matt," said Earnshaw gravely.

"Very well," said Brennan. "The first and final meeting of the delegates to the Little Summit is herewith called to order."

A waiter came with the drinks, quickly set them down, and as quickly disappeared.

"As each of you knows," resumed Brennan, "one week ago I came to Paris to speak to Nikolai Rostov. While I was unable to reach him

743

personally, my quest for Rostov continually confronted me with persons and names that seemed suspiciously and inexplicably connected with him. I need only refer to Joe Peet, Marshal Zabbin, Igor Novik, Boris Dogel, Ma Ming. My quest also provided me with information I had not, from the start, been seeking. I began to learn that while the Union of Soviet Socialist Republics was aligned with the United States, Great Britain, and France in public and at the conference table in the Palais Rose, and was openly opposed to the policies and aggressions of the People's Republic of China, there appeared to be a wholly contradictory Russian behavior toward China behind the scenes. I continually acquired information—some of it by myself, most of it through my friends and your friends, or from each of you—that the two greatest Communist powers on earth, while paying lip service to peace and disarmament at the Summit, were quietly making mutual plans out of sight of the Summit. By siding with the West instead of with its onetime Communist partner, Russia had made the Summit possible and future disarmament and peace a possibility. Yet, disturbingly, there were continuing clues that Russia and China were also preparing a long-range partnership in private, a secret partnership of these two old international Cominform members with policies that would supersede those agreed upon at the Summit. These isolated clues, each meaningless in itself, began to mount, until tonight they have assumed, at least for me, a grand design that is alarming because it is threatening to the future of all mankind."

"You've been insisting on that, Matt," said Earnshaw, "but I must say, never so definitely or emphatically. I gather something happened today to—"

"Something did happen today," said Brennan. "Six hours ago, for the second time, an attempt was made on my life. Only today there was no subterfuge and there could be no doubts. The attack on me was direct and it was public. The attack was clearly witnessed. The attack was made with the object of murdering me. And the attacker was a Russian KGB agent from Moscow."

Brennan's announcement created an immediate sensation among the other three. Doyle's rotund face was bathed in perspiration. Earnshaw's mouth became a study in alarm. Medora's eyes blinked.

Doyle's voice cracked as he spoke. "A Soviet agent tried to murder you?"

"Yes. The one Medora first brought to our attention. The one Hazel Smith identified as a KGB man. The one I found out was named Boris Dogel. He made an attempt on my life outside the Lido Arcade. Lisa Collins witnessed the entire incident."

Hastily, without wasting words, Brennan recounted the terrifying experience in the Rue de Ponthieu that had sent Boris Dogel to his own death. As he related the story, Brennan could see that the shocked reactions of his listeners were devoid of any disbelief.

By the time Brennan finished, Earnshaw had become grimly thoughtful and Doyle had become the quivering journalist on the scent of an international newsbeat. Only Medora, apolitical and less involved, reacted like a playgoer at the suspenseful second-act curtain of a matinee.

"But *why* Matt?" she blurted out. "Why would anyone want to do you in?"

"I asked myself that after the first attempt, and I've asked myself the same question again," said Brennan. "The first time, I'm still convinced, I was the intended target for murder instead of that young Englishman in the Bois de Boulogne. But I'll never be positive. Six hours ago there was no mistaking who was the intended victim and who was the killer. But as you asked, Medora, why me? What was the Soviet motive? I think I can answer that now. It's obvious to me that all the clues I've been gathering were valid and the conclusion they were leading me to was a true one—or close to a true one—and therefore seriously threatening to the Russian delegation. If that weren't so, the Soviets wouldn't have bothered about me. They'd have merely written me off as a crackpot. But if there was an actual secret conspiracy, and I had stumbled upon it, I would be considered extremely dangerous. To prevent my exposing their scheme, I would have to be eliminated. So, six hours ago, the Russians did try to eliminate me. And six hours ago, I knew that I was in the possession of facts."

Earnshaw gravely nodded. "There can no longer be any doubt, Matt, that you're onto something very serious."

"Only one point continues to mystify me," said Brennan. "It did the first time they came after me. It does again. How on earth did the Russians come to know I had all this damning information about their secret designs? Only a handful of you know." He paused, and looked around the table. "Unless one of you, inadvertently, spoke of this to some Russian?"

Earnshaw sat erect. "But of course we did, Matt, or at least I did, at your own instigation."

Brennan was puzzled. "I don't understand."

"In order to help Medora, you invented the title of a book and requested me to use it on Sir Austin Ormsby at the Hôtel de Lauzun dinner," said Earnshaw. "You told me to tell Sir Austin you were preparing something called *The Secret Civil War Inside Russia Today.*

745

So I did it, I repeated it, as a come-on to bring Sydney Ormsby to—"

Brennan clapped his hand against his forehead. "My God, I forgot all that nonsense."

"When I was speaking to Sir Austin, the room was crowded, and there were Russians and Chinese around us. And—now I'm recalling something else, no, two things—when Sir Austin and I parted, he bumped into someone behind him, and apologized, and apparently the one he bumped into was Rostov—because later, when the President told Wiggins to introduce me to Rostov—yes, I'm sure of this— Wiggins said he thought I'd already met Rostov, because Rostov was standing beside Sir Austin and me."

Doyle poked a finger at Brennan. "And you forgot something else, Matt. Don't you recall what I told you at Maisons-Laffitte? How I attended the gourmet dinner at Lasserre last night, and got to talking to Igor Novik of *Pravda,* and tried to get him to bring me together with his old pal Rostov? I told him I was helping a friend, a former diplomat, finish a book about—well, exactly the one you had Emmett describe to Sir Austin. That makes what happened doubly clear. Igor must have trotted straight back to the Russian Embassy to tell Rostov, or the KGB, or someone, that a former American diplomat was onto them. And at the same time, Rostov, fresh from the Hôtel de Lauzun, already knew that you were that former diplomat. Motive? Oh boy, they sure had it by then."

Brennan nodded. "That's it, no question."

"The thing that concerns me now," said Earnshaw, putting down his cigar, "is simply this—if the Russians tried to get you out of the way because you knew too much, precisely what did you know too much about? Until now, you've generalized about clues that indicated something fishy was going on behind the Summit. But that's not enough. What I mean is, knowing the Russians as well as I do, it's not enough to drive them to committing murder. They're decent people, most of them, despite their atheism and authoritarian state. They're not ruthless or violent unless seriously provoked. So I keep wondering—what is it of the material you've amassed, exactly what is it that they feared, that drove them to attempt an act of murder?"

Brennan sipped his Cinzano, allowing Earnshaw's inquiry to dance in his mind to the soft strumming of the Spanish guitars behind him. Finally he set his glass on the table.

"It is because we must find the answer to the question you've posed, Emmett, that I called this meeting." Brennan locked his fingers together on the table, contemplated them, and at last looked up. "I've given considerable thought to the answer. I believe I have it. But first, before giving you my conclusion, I thought that I should check my clues once more with the three of you, to be certain these clues are facts. I want to review them for you, briefly as possible—I know how late it is—but I want your comments when you have any to make. And when I'm through, I want your conclusions, whether they concur with mine or not. I have more than a sneaking suspicion that one way or another tomorrow, Sunday, may not be a day of rest. Shall I proceed?"

"By all means, at once, Matt," said Earnshaw.

"The faster the better," said Doyle.

"I—I'm not sure I'll understand," said Medora.

Brennan smiled at her. "I think you will. In any case, you can be helpful." He reached into his pocket, extracted his folded notes, and flattened them out on the tablecloth. "These jottings—I haven't organized them to make points. I've put them down as simply as possible, but whenever possible, in chronological order."

"Good enough," said Doyle, trying to look over his shoulder. "Go on, Matt."

Half reading, half improvising, Matt Brennan began the case of the Little Summit against the validity of the Big Summit.

"Clue one. I arrived in Paris seven days ago. I met with Herb Neely in a café. We discussed Nikolai Rostov. Now, in Zurich, when I knew Rostov, he was perfectly representative of the Soviets' line. Rostov was, one might say, anti-Chinese. When Varney escaped us and defected to Peking with the neutron bomb secrets, both Rostov and I were accused of being pro-Chinese and traitors to our Governments. Rostov was punished by being sent to some obscure post in Siberia. Yet four years later, Rostov, who'd been accused of being treasonably sympathetic to China, was recalled by the anti-Chinese Soviet Government and rewarded by Premier Talansky and Marshal Zabbin with a key appointment to a sensitive post, a post involving negotiations with China at the Summit. It made no sense. I thought it strange when I first heard about it. I still do."

Brennan looked up. The others were silent, waiting.

"Clue two," said Brennan. "Jay got me some clippings on Rostov. I was reminded that Rostov collected rare books, among them those written by Sir Richard Burton. I remembered Rostov's favorite rare-book store on the Left Bank. I went there. All the Burton items in their latest catalogue had been sold. They were being picked up by a young American of dubious literacy named Joe Peet. Among the three Burton titles that Peet had requested and paid for, and eventually took away with him, was an 1890 edition that had never been published, because Burton's wife had considered Burton's enlarged translation of this volume salacious and she burned the manuscript immediately after his death. This was odd, this American of questionable intellect acquiring a nonexistent book authored by one of Rostov's favorite writers, and acquiring it from Rostov's favorite French book store." Brennan glanced up at Medora. "Hardly the type to collect rare editions, wouldn't you agree, Medora?"

"Nudie magazines—that was his speed, according to Denise," said Medora.

"Which I confirmed later," said Brennan. "All right. Clue three. I drove out to Gif-sur-Yvette, near Saclay, the French nuclear research center. I had a long talk with the French physicist, Professor Isenberg. I learned that the reactor in the Nuclear Peace City that Goerlitz Industries were to build for the Chinese in Honan Province was capable of being easily converted to producing ingredients for nuclear bombs. I also learned Professor Isenberg had visited Peking recently and had come upon Russian scientists there. That, too, was odd, I thought."

Earnshaw nodded his agreement.

"Next clue, number four," said Brennan. "Jay Doyle accidentally turned up information on Joe Peet, and someone else, a friend, Herb Neely, gave me more. I learned that Peet had a Russian girl behind the Iron Curtain whom he wished to marry. He had persistently appealed to the Soviet Union to let him become a Russian citizen so he could be reunited with his love. But he had been denied this citizenship. I thought it unusual of the Russians to reject an American who wanted to defect to them."

"I still think it's unusual," said Doyle.

"Neely thought Peet was probably here to appeal to the Russian delegation for citizenship, and that they might soften and take him in, especially at a moment when they might make propaganda hay of it," said Brennan. "Anyway, clue five, and a big one you all know about. My fiancée, Lisa Collins, deserves the credit. She overheard two wives of Chinese delegates speaking of throwing Goerlitz's German personnel out of the Nuclear Peace City in Honan, nationalizing it, and taking in Russian engineers to help them run it. That was a jolt, the strongest evidence that the two Communist powers, hostile to each other in public, were holding hands behind everyone's back." He looked at Earnshaw. "You still consider that to be credible, Emmett?"

"Absolutely," said Earnshaw. "If you could have seen Marshal

748

Chen's face when I accused him of that kind of bad faith, you'd never question Miss Collins' information again. We're lucky to have got out of the Chinese Embassy with our necks intact."

"Clue six," said Brennan. "An anonymous phone call advised me to come to the Bois de Boulogne if I wished to meet Rostov. I was to wear dark glasses, carry a pipe. I got to the rendezvous late. Someone else, resembling me, was already dead there. He'd worn dark glasses, carried a pipe. Incidentally, the last time I'd smoked a pipe was when I was with Rostov in Zurich." He paused. "The only thing about that whole damn incident that troubles me is how, at that time, the Russians even knew I was collecting these clues. Well, anyway—"

"I'm sure they were after you in the Bois, Matt," said Doyle.

"Well, I wish I could be certain, absolutely certain," said Brennan. "Now, where was I? Yes. Clue seven next. To help her friend Denise, our Medora met Joe Peet in the Club Lautrec. When Peet began to drink, a Russian, whom Hazel later identified at the Palais Rose as a veteran KGB agent, whisked Peet away. Shortly after, when we tried to see Peet at his hotel, he had suddenly been moved to another hotel. There you have two mysteries. An American nonentity befriended by or guarded by a Soviet police agent. An American made to change his residence to another hotel. Odd. Any comments?"

There were none.

"Okay," said Brennan. "Those were the first seven clues that got me started. But others followed, and there are exactly double that number by this time. I'll give you clues eight to fourteen, the most recent ones, in a lump. Thanks to Hazel, I learned a secret that she learned from Rostov, that a group of wives of Russian leaders, including Zabbin's wife and Rostov's wife, will tour China right after the Summit. Then, thanks to Medora's friend Denise, I found the new hotel where Peet was, in effect, hiding out. I'll confess to a misdemeanor. I entered Peet's room uninvited. Nothing much there, at first look. As Medora said, lots of nude girlie magazines. A scratch pad with the name of the Soviet journalist, Igor Novik, scribbled on it. An order for a tail coat, which is usually worn at state functions. A torn calling card belonging to Ma Ming, correspondent for the New China News Agency. A newspaper clipping with a girl in a bikini on one side and the leaders of the Soviet delegation on the other. I don't know which of these pictures interested Peet, or if both did. And then, in Peet's room, another side of his personality, an avid interest in the châteaux and palaces and splendors of Paris and environs, with a special interest in Versailles. Curiouser and curiouser, and one clue following another after that. There was Emmett's visit to the Chinese Embassy, and Chen's undiplomatic revelation that implied that Summit or no Summit, One World or no One World, Russia and China would find one another again and join against their common enemies. Emmett, is that substantially correct?"

"It is entirely correct," said Earnshaw.

"More clues," resumed Brennan. "Last night, at Lasserre, Jay learned from the Soviet journalist, Novik, that six months ago Rostov entertained Marshal Zabbin and a party of visiting Chinese at his Moscow residence. Nearby, in the Kremlin, the Premier was thundering against the Chinese, but in Rostov's home a minister and a marshal hosted the Chinese as friends. Last night, also, at a dinner given by a fashion designer, I met a Swiss psychoanalyst who purported to be an expert on the psychology of traitors, real traitors and potential ones. He described the background and characteristics of a traitor to me, intending it to be my portrait. When he was done, I realized it was not I he had described, but more accurately Nikolai Rostov."

"I didn't know that," said Doyle. "Very interesting."

"Very," said Brennan. "And so we come to today—well, it's long after midnight, so by now today is yesterday, but let's call it today. Anyway, today Jay covered all five press conferences at the Palais Rose. The words in the Chinese and Russian press announcements were identical, but different from the others, which indicated a secret collaboration. Today, at Maisons-Laffitte, at the races, I thought I saw Rostov, which is not significant, but I did see Joe Peet with Boris Dogel, his KGB friend or guard, which might be significant, but which offered me no immediate clue. Also at the races I saw Ma Ming, which brings the Chinese into it, and Mr. Ma's knowledge of Peet and Dogel is another mystery." Brennan halted, and then he said slowly, "And today, after the Russians again heard about my researches, my amassing of these facts, they sent their veteran KGB agent, Dogel, to track me down and kill me. There is the evidence to date. Do you have any comment?"

Medora shook her head. Earnshaw and Doyle shook their heads.

"But I do have a question," said Earnshaw. "What are you leading up to?"

"I'm leading up to one conclusion," said Brennan. "Let me—well, let me be frank and put it to you this way. Each of us sitting here, and perhaps many other persons we don't even know—certainly each of us was drawn to Paris because of the Summit, because someone else brought here by the Summit might be useful in helping us resolve what was still unresolved in our personal lives. I hope you don't mind this, any of you?"

"We're listening," said Earnshaw.

"Consider the four of us. Jay Doyle came to see someone who could give him the final evidence for an exposé which might restore his professional standing. Forgive me, Jay, but I think that's it. Former President Earnshaw came here to persuade a German industrialist to remove material from a memoir that might damage Mr. Earnshaw's reputation beyond repair. Medora Hart came to exert pressure on the English delegate who is responsible for having kept her in exile for three years, and to force him to allow her to return home. As for me, I came here because the one person on earth who could possibly erase the word traitor from after my name was here. Each one of us, one way or another, came to Paris on a mission of personal salvation. Each one of us was, and with good reason, pursuing a selfish end. Each of us had his story and each of us was determined to resolve his little plot. And I am suggesting that in our searches in pursuit of resolutions to our little individual plots, the four of us unwittingly stumbled upon a bigger plot, involving not only each of us but the whole world and the immediate future of man. Right now, our personal plots and their resolutions are minor compared to the major plot we've come upon, and it is this big plot which must be exposed immediately if our personal lives are to have any meaning."

"A big plot that must be exposed immediately?" echoed Doyle. "Do you mean something is going on that we might be able to stop? Exactly what are you talking about?"

"I'm trying to say that every clue we've unearthed indicates that while the fate of the world may hang on the success of the five-power Summit, there are those who are using the Summit as a fraud and a sham because they intend to ignore its result. But—beyond that— every clue I've presented so far leads me to believe that there is a more specific conspiracy going on, in this place and at this time."

"Be explicit, Matt," demanded Earnshaw. "What actual conspiracy do you think is going on?"

"Yes, what conspiracy, Matt?" asked Doyle. "What's the climax to the big plot you say we've stumbled on? What does all you've been saying add up to?"

Brennan looked at Doyle, at Earnshaw, at Medora, then he stared down at his empty glass.

"I'll tell you what I think," he said slowly. "I think it all adds up to one terrible moment, perhaps the last terrible moment in modern history—an assassination in the Palace of Versailles tomorrow night— an assassination, a slaying, a single act of violence that will wipe out the Summit, shatter the world as we know it, and destroy free men on earth forever. That's what I think it adds up to for tomorrow night. That, fellow delegates, is the plot."

IX

I T WAS SUNDAY MORNING in Paris, and the full circle of the week
had been closed.

From the parted drapes and curtains of his hotel room, Matt
Brennan could see the soft cerulean sky above and the misty green
water splashing in the courtyard fountain below.

He could picture the Champs-Élysées on an early Sunday morning
like this one. It would be as placid and lovely as it had been in the time
of Louis XV, when handsome and fashionable Parisians strolled
beneath its stately trees and arbors and gossiped lazily in sunny garden
cafés and magnificent coaches rolled up the thoroughfare toward the
Palace at Versailles. Now the same sun and trees would still be there,
with French couples, French families, in their Sunday best, promenading on the broad walks emptied of vehicles, pausing at each special
periodical stand, watching the cafés coming to life, enjoying their city,
their capital of civilization.

It would be Sunday in Paris, mankind's caress, smile, laughter,
tranquillity, contentment, Eden.

To imagine violence seemed a blasphemy, and suddenly last night,
before and after midnight, seemed less real and more improbable.

Brennan turned away from the windows.

He stared across the sitting room at the telephone, and there it stood,
like a cocked pistol, not yet friend, not yet foe, but in twenty minutes it
would announce itself, and that was reality. And then he knew that this
was not Sunday but an extraordinary and supernormal eighth day of the
week where time was suspended until men decided whether it should
resume or end for all eternity.

He continued to stare at the telephone. When it spoke, he would know if his Little Summit, adjourned only five hours earlier, had been a success or a failure. He told himself that he had better be ready for either.

Unbuttoning his pajama top, Brennan went quietly back into the bedroom. Lisa had moved with the peal of his eight-o'clock alarm, but he suspected that she had fallen asleep again. In the shaded room he could see her curled on her side, still hugging his pillow.

As he continued noiselessly to the bathroom, her muffled voice caught him. "Matt, did you make it for two?"

"What?"

"Breakfast."

"Yes, darling, but try to sleep."

"Are you all right?"

"Never better."

"Good."

In the bathroom he removed his pajamas, started the tub shower, and stepped under it. He tried to remember the dialogue that had followed his sensational announcement in La Calavados.

They had all been in agreement that Brennan had developed a sound argument indicating concealed political activity between the Soviet Union and Red China that might sabotage any Summit accord. Even Earnshaw, conservative and ingenuous, had concurred on that point, swayed by an apparently government-authorized attack on Brennan's life. But what Earnshaw had maintained serious reservations about was Brennan's conclusion that a plot to commit a political assassination at Versailles or anywhere else was in the making. Earnshaw had been reasonable, yet stubborn, in his belief that if there was trouble, the nations would work it out after the Summit, behind their own frontiers and in their own ways. He had been unable to see any clear motive for anyone at the Summit to try to get rid of anyone else in a public act of violence. Brennan had speculated on a variety of possibilities, but they had been so contradictory and so hypothetical that he had been unable to lessen Earnshaw's skepticism in any way. As for the others, Medora had long been out of her depth and too sleepy to care, and Doyle had been ready to accept anything that Brennan stated if only it would provide him with a major newsbeat or a book.

Recalling all of that as he left the bathtub to dry himself, Brennan also recalled that Earnshaw had put his finger on the one weakness of Brennan's conclusions. Preparing to leave the restaurant, Earnshaw had said, "It comes down to this, Matt. If you think our CIA or the French DST would believe your conclusions and act on them, then I

754

think you've got a case. Are you prepared to go to them with your warning?" Brennan had said that he was not prepared to go to the authorities, because he doubted that they would believe him. "That's right, they wouldn't," Earnshaw had said, "because while you have evidence of potential political shenanigans, you don't have a single piece of concrete evidence that points to violence. Until you obtain that, I'm afraid there is nothing that either you or I or any of us can do."

Apparently Brennan had expected, and unconsciously prepared himself for, this one unanswerable challenge. For no sooner had Earnshaw flung it at him than Brennan had turned to Doyle and made the one request that might lead him to the concrete evidence that would prove his case. Doyle had promised to do what could be done. And what was left was the telephone call that would come at eight-thirty.

Hurriedly Brennan finished dressing.

When he returned to the sitting room, Lisa was already at the breakfast table that Room Service had set up. She was scrubbed and pretty in her negligee, and she was completely awake.

He kissed her, and she kissed him back, and then she pushed him away. "We'd better not start that, or we won't have breakfast." She began to pour his tea. "Now, sit down before it all gets cold. Doesn't it look delicious? Let me practice my French. *Omelette aux fines herbes. Brioche* and *croissant* for you, and ditto for me. *Beurre. Confitures.* How's that?"

He chuckled. "Send the food back to Berlitz." He glanced at the telephone behind her and began to eat his eggs.

He ate in silence, and then, looking up, he realized she was not eating but was watching him worriedly.

"What's the matter, honey?"

"I was thinking of last night, the things you told me in bed. I must have been knocked out, but now they're beginning to come back to me. It frightens me, Matt. The whole thing does."

"The plot I've been uncovering? It frightens me, too."

"Not the plot, you dumbhead. It's you. I'm half ill with fear about what might happen to you. Yesterday the Russians tried to kill you before my very eyes. So what do you do about it? Now you accuse them of planning another assassination."

"I'm not accusing them or anyone specifically."

"Well, you did say somebody's going to assassinate somebody else."

"To me, that's what everything seems to be adding up to."

"To me, what it's adding up to is that, if you go on this way, you're liable to be the one assassinated. Matt, listen to me. I don't want to be a widow before I've been a wife. Can't you find yourself some other hobby, something harmless, like free-fall parachuting or swallowing swords?"

Brennan was about to make a joke when the telephone rang.

He leaped from his chair and snatched up the receiver. To his surprise, it was Jay Doyle and not Hazel Smith who greeted him from the other end.

"You did see Hazel?" Brennan asked anxiously.

"I went straight to her apartment after I left you."

"Did you tell her what this is about? I mean, why I want to meet her?"

"Only that it concerns our Little Summit. I told her all I could about that. And I told her you wanted to speak to her this morning, that you needed a favor, and if she would help you, well, you would return the favor by granting Hazel and me exclusive rights to the story if you happened to be right, but you could promise nothing else if you were wrong."

"How did Hazel react?"

"She wasn't interested in any payoffs. She just didn't know if she could see you, or even should."

"She didn't think I was crazy, or anything like that, or did she?"

"I don't know, Matt. She didn't say. She only made it clear that she wasn't too happy about becoming involved in whatever you might be up to. We left it that she'd think about it and make up her mind by morning. Well, she's just made up her mind. She had to run off somewhere now, so she asked me to call you. She said, 'Tell Matt I'll meet him at the Pont de la Tournelle on the Île St.-Louis side at nine-thirty sharp.' She said that the Île St.-Louis is quieter than the Île de la Cité and it's a better place to walk and talk. She'll be there, Matt, so now it's up to you. Be sure to let me know what happens."

Brennan thanked Doyle profusely and came back to the breakfast table filled with anticipation.

Lisa had assumed an air of resignation. "More of the plot?"

He buttered his brioche. "I hope so. If Hazel can help, I'm still in business. If she refuses—" He shrugged.

"In the business of what? Hunting assassins?"

"Could be."

"Matt, you still haven't told me. Who is killing whom?"

"Lisa, I wish I knew. I have a few ideas, but I don't know if they make sense yet. The only thing I do feel I know, and do believe might be true, is that there is some kind of terrible struggle for power inside the Russian delegation, and that there may be Outs who want to be In, so that they can blow up the Summit and have a partnership with Red China and revive the Comintern, and escalate nuclear armament and a cold or hot war against the democracies. I just suspect there's rebellion brewing. But where and when, I'm not sure. My guess is Versailles and tonight. As to who's involved, I truly can't say. In fact, I can't say anything for sure yet."

"Matt, if you're even half right, that would be horrifying."

"Catastrophic is the word."

"And you think it will happen?"

"I think someone wants it to happen—starting tonight."

"Matt, can you prove any of this?"

"That's exactly what Earnshaw asked me last night."

"But can you?"

"I intend to prove it—by the time the state dinner starts in the Palace of Versailles tonight."

"How, Matt? How can you possibly prove there's a plot?"

"By doing one thing."

"What?"

"By seeing Nikolai Rostov, at last."

THE PLACE WAS so calm and quiet, so isolated, that she felt as if she had been dropped on an uninhabited planet.

Hazel Smith had traversed the classical arch of the Pont de la Tournelle from the Left Bank, and now, at twenty minutes after nine of this Sunday morning, she stood at the dip of the bridge, on the stones of the Quai d'Orléans at the southern embankment of the Île St.-Louis and she regretted the meeting that was soon to take place.

She was mellowed by her surroundings and unable to face harsh decisions, if indeed any were expected of her.

Everything in sight moved her this morning. In the distance were the spiritual towers of the Cathedral of Notre-Dame. Along the Quai d'Orléans the sun shimmered through the poplar leaves, and the reflections danced in the rippling waters of the Seine below. Nearby rose the statue of Ste. Geneviève, whose prayer to God once stayed Attila the Hun and saved Paris, and who was immortalized in stone, virginal, and eternally warm and comforting. Behind her, still hidden in the seventeenth century, were the mansions, gardens, high walls, narrow streets

757

of the Île, and the rock ramp sloping down to the river (where fishermen dozed), and somewhere the Sunday bird market.

Hazel's gaze held on a barge creeping down the Seine, and then her attention shifted to a French family—father, mother, three youngsters all fishing from the Paris side—and at once her frame of mind was transformed from calm into fear. She could not define exactly how this peculiar change in feeling came about. Perhaps from envy of that family across the water. Or perhaps it was the isolation of the Île St.-Louis itself that had finally betrayed her. The island, Balzac once wrote, affected its visitors with *tristesse nerveuse,* a malady suffered when one was separated from life and was suddenly lonely and insecure.

It was both, Hazel decided, both the sight of that tightly knit French family on the riverbank and the realization of her own isolated position that had altered her mood.

It was also brought on, this graying mood, by a sudden remembrance of last night, when she had seen all that there was left of hope in her life, and it now seemed so pitifully little. For last night, before the business of the interview in the Eiffel Tower restaurant, she had seen Nikolai Rostov, fleetingly, and after the interview, hours after, she had seen Jay Doyle, unsatisfactorily.

From the first, she had meant to avoid the cocktail party—not cocktail party, since that was an American custom the Russians had never adopted, but reception, really—for the Soviet and foreign press given at the Russian Embassy. She had not wanted to go because she had been afraid that Rostov might be there, but she had finally gone because she hoped that he would be there.

It was a bad period for her, this time in Paris, a period of racking and painful indecision. She had wanted to look at Niki again. Just look at him. Just to see what reassurance her past would give her, in order to divine whether it deserved her future as well.

It had been an early evening reception, and she had arrived promptly, leaving her car off the Boulevard St.-Germain and walking to the Russian Embassy at 79 Rue de Grenelle, a street which, after the first burst of shops, had become haughty and forbidding. But the Embassy itself, a whitewashed three-story mansion constructed in 1713 by the French architect who had designed the building that now housed the Banque de France, was friendlier than its surroundings. Displaying her invitation to French police and Russian plainclothesmen, Hazel had been met in the unfurnished entry hall by a young Russian press officer she had known in Moscow. She had been shown up a staircase, and been impressed by the waxed wooden railing on the wrought-iron balustrade and the antique sconces bracketed to the wall.

Upstairs, the three dozen journalists who had already arrived—more than half of them foreign and many of whom she had met before—were mingling with Russian press personnel and minor Soviet delegates. On a buffet, caviar, smoked salmon, fruit, and sweets had attracted a pack of correspondents. From a portable bar the champagne and vodka had seemed to flow continuously. She had ordered champagne, and had pretended great interest in the room. She had examined the heavy brocade curtains and the red-covered Regency-style chairs, and she had admired the marble fireplace with its display of Russian dolls, and the rich Armenian rug. And all the while, she had watched for Nikolai Rostov and had not seen him.

After a half hour of drink and gossip, when the reception had swelled to fifty or sixty correspondents, and when Hazel had been about to leave, the side door to an adjacent salon had swung open. Premier Talansky and Marshal Zabbin had entered to pay their respects, and they had been followed by a half-dozen advisers, and one of these had been Rostov.

As the Russian leaders had crossed the room, and members of the press began gathering around them, Hazel had hung back, and she noticed that Rostov had hung back, too. He had nodded to her and indicated the room behind him and sidled into it. Unobtrusively as possible, she had followed him. When she entered what turned out to be a conference room—red brocade covering the wall panels, a maroon felt cloth shrouding an oval table, red upholstered Louis XIV chairs lined up in classroom rows before the table—Rostov had come up beside her. He had kissed her fully, quickly, on the lips, hugged her, and whispered in her ear, "*Milochka* mine, I have missed you. I am busy, very, very busy, important work, and I have no more than this second now. And next week, busier, but the week after, Moscow—and we are together. Our vacation, remember? You remember?" She had nodded dumbly. He had kissed her again. "My wife will be gone, and we will have our time. Now go to your friends."

She had returned to the busy public room, and she had not looked back. She had simply kept going, until she had left the Russian Embassy.

After that, she had not permitted herself to think of Rostov, of Rostov and herself, of their future. She had hurried to her appointment in the Eiffel Tower restaurant for her interview. But then, in the midst of the interview, Matt Brennan had appeared from nowhere to inquire where he might locate Jay Doyle. He had been mysterious, and she had been troubled through the rest of the dinner.

Later, in her apartment, as midnight had come and gone without

Doyle, she had begun to worry seriously about him and wonder whether Matt Brennan had got him into some kind of trouble. She had invited Doyle to stay the night with her. She had wanted to comfort him and to know that he was close to her, so she could in some way reassure herself that what remained of her life belonged to him. She had almost dozed off when, at some ungodly hour, he thumped in.

Their night, what was left of it, had been a disappointment. She had wanted to speak of love and of their tomorrows. Doyle, maniacally, could speak only of Brennan's Little Summit and Brennan's unsettling prediction. Only once had Doyle referred to Hazel and himself. Just before dawn, just after they had got into bed, he had mentioned that Brennan wanted to see her in the morning about something terribly important. Doyle had hoped that she would agree to meet Brennan, try to assist him in any way possible. For if Brennan should be proved right, even partially right, it would mean everything to Doyle. "It would mean I'd be back up there on top, Hazel, alongside you, and this time, sweetie, I wouldn't be a fool. I wouldn't let you get away from me, not if I could help it."

It hadn't been much, that, a crumb, a morsel. But still, the promise of marriage had been implied. The promise of a full life with someone who meant something had been suggested, and for Hazel that meant very much.

She had slept on this, slept fast, hard, deep in a vacuum of insensibility. And when she had awakened this morning to all of her partner's eagerness, she had reluctantly agreed to see Brennan only so that she might have Doyle.

But now, as she waited for Brennan at the foot of the Pont de la Tournelle on the Île St.-Louis, it suddenly seemed a bad bargain.

She had committed herself to a meeting that might deplete her pitiful savings in return for—for what?—for dross.

In the distance, the bourgeois French family, people with people, people belonging, continued to upset her. And behind, the gaping silence of the isolated island, foreshadowing the cemetery for the worst dead of all, the alienated, the rootless, the lonely who were the living dead.

Hazel thought of Rostov, his goodness proved but his offering limited. Rostov could never give her the normal background of a family, the security of a home, the position of a wife, because his own family, his legal home, his official status in the puritan party, were too important to endanger merely for love. Niki could give her everything, except that which she desired most.

And she thought of Doyle, who had once had the opportunity to fulfill her needs and had refused to do so. Doyle was still free to give her his name, their family, their home. Yet even if he did, she doubted its rewards. Doyle was, in defeat, so self-centered and self-obsessed that he could be no more than their only child.

This morning, she was frightened by her situation. She had created a patched-up, rickety, precarious shelter for her life, a shelter made up of two-thirds career and one-third lover on loan, and she could occupy this to the end. Once you had this much, you thought twice, a hundred times twice, about trading it for the flimsy blueprints of an unbuilt shelter of unproved design and quality.

She suspected why Doyle and Brennan had collaborated to bring her to this meeting. She anticipated what Brennan would require of her. She found it frightening. Her instinct was to avoid this meeting, to flee, to run as far as possible from it.

Her wristwatch told her that Brennan was ten minutes late. They had agreed on nine-thirty sharp, and the hands of her timepiece were at nine-forty. Now she had an acceptable explanation for Doyle as to why she had not kept the appointment. She looked up the rise of the bridge, her safe escape route, and she saw Matt Brennan striding down it toward her, and flight was no longer possible.

"Good morning, Hazel," he called out. "Sorry to be late. I drove my car and completely forgot they don't allow cars on the quays. So I had to find a place to leave it."

She nodded.

Brennan glanced around him. "Where can we talk?"

Hazel stared at him. He had the look of the attractive fanatic. One amenity, and time for no more. This was business.

"Well," she said, "if you prefer, there are a half-dozen bars and restaurants. Quasimodo, on the other side, might be open for breakfast. Or the Franc Pinot, if you like caves. Or if it's a café you'd like, then the Brasserie le Lutetia—"

"I don't care where we talk. What do you prefer?"

"I'd be satisfied just to walk along the river."

"That's fine," said Brennan.

They started up the Quai d'Orléans toward the Passerelle St.-Louis, the footbridge made up of cagelike steel girders and wooden planks that connected this island to the Île de la Cité next to it.

Hazel fished nervously for a cigarette. The moment that she had it, Brennan had his lighter ready.

Brennan watched her inhale. "Jay says he told you all about the Little Summit I called together last night. Did he tell you about it in detail?"

"I think so. He stayed over, you know. He kept me up half the night."

"Then you're briefed on my whole case, my conclusion about what it adds up to? Do you have any questions, Hazel?"

"None. I'm sure Jay covered your case completely. He has a blotter instead of a brain, I sometimes think. Yes, he reviewed your clues, pro and con, but mostly pro. He's all for you now. He's convinced you are the Messiah, come down to save us all, but particularly him. He's in a fever about your theory. As far as I can make out, if there is anything to your—to what you believe—you've assigned him the exclusive story rights—"

"Jay *and* you."

"Thank you," she said, not certain if he would detect the irony in her tone. "Anyway, Jay's walking on the ceiling over the possibilities of a beat and his dreams of glory. I'm not sure whether he's excited because he actually believes what you believe, or just because he's insanely eager to believe in something, anything, that might give him a substitute to replace his poor Kennedy book. Anyway, he rattled on and on last night, as rigorous in his rightness, and yours, as Savonarola."

"And you, Hazel—did he convert you?"

They were strolling past the Passerelle St.-Louis, and the flat-bottomed pedestrian bridge was as ugly as the cause to which Doyle had tried to convert her. She took a long pull on her cigarette, watched the smoke she had released drift between them and trail away. "Convert me? To what, Matt? You say it. I want to hear you speak the unspeakable aloud."

"Gladly." He was rubbing a thumb across the bowl of the pipe held in his palm, apparently trying to formulate the unspeakable. "My guess—by now an educated guess—is this. First though, remember I can't speak about the Chinese—only about the Russians. There's a split in the Russian delegation, I truly believe. They've chosen sides, or maybe some have chosen a side. I can't name the players yet. I don't know who is for what. But as I see it, on one side are the revisionists, the ones who believe Russia's future security and prosperity are forever linked with the democracies, if they are to be guaranteed permanent coexistence within a grand alliance of all nations. On the other side are the ones who have rediscovered Marx, Lenin, Stalin, who now feel the Summit, nuclear disarmament, a grand world alliance, may make Russia a secondary power subservient to the democracies, and may weaken Communism and finally allow it to be destroyed. These are the ones who want to revive the international

762

Comintern, turn their backs on the West and on Summitry, develop bilateral agreements with China, and then, with China as partner, continue building nuclear stockpiles and spreading their Idea around the globe. These are the ones who want to keep the world on constant red alert and trembling, who want to impoverish capitalism, recolor the map, redirect the course of history." He paused. "That is what I preached last night. I don't know if you're convinced."

"I don't know, either. Several days ago I thought your suspicions fanciful. Now, well, now I'm less sure. What you are preaching may possibly, just possibly, be true."

"May possibly, you concede." Brennan studied her as they continued their slow walk. "I'm pleased you're even giving my theory serious consideration. May I ask, Hazel, what brought you over this far?"

"Because the Russians have tried to get rid of you twice, after you got too nosy."

"Well, I certainly know they tried to kill me once. Yesterday. I've never been sure about the first time in the Bois. I'm still not sure."

"I am," said Hazel, and she looked at him.

Astonished, Brennan halted beneath the blue street plaque reading QUAI DE BOURBON. "You're sure they tried to kill me the first time, too?"

She nodded. "That's right. That's when I started to take you seriously." She resumed walking, and then she continued. "One day, before we knew each other well, Jay spoke of your findings in front of me. Remember? Later the same day, I happened to be with—with Nikolai Rostov—and he wanted to know how I was spending my time in Paris. I told him of all the zany, mad people I'd been meeting, including you, and—just gossiping, looking for laughs—I told him about some of your findings and suspicions. He was amused, but maybe a little annoyed. A few hours after that, you received your call that Rostov would meet you in the Bois de Boulogne. There was a murder, and I suppose the intended victim was you. I don't say Rostov was personally involved. But most likely, as a dutiful party member, he repeated my gossip about your meddling to the KGB. And they acted on their own."

She took one last puff on her cigarette and flipped the butt over the stone embankment wall. "I'm convinced they tried to put you away twice. I've asked myself why. I've answered myself that there must be some validity to your findings and suspicions. Otherwise they wouldn't be afraid of you. Knowing Russians as I do, I am certain they're never afraid, unless someone is getting in their way or endangering their plans. So, while I'm not Jay's kind of convert, I am taking you seriously. There may be something in the air."

"Something that has to do with the President of France's banquet in the Hall of Mirrors at Versailles tonight. You know, Hazel, that's the sum total of what I believe."

"Yes, I know."

"But you can't accept that part of it?"

She looked past him at a boat on the Seine. She said, "I honestly don't know what I believe about your final conclusion. Don't forget, by now I'm the product of two worlds, theirs and ours, and I'm confused by experience and emotion. Assassination? Versailles? Tonight? It's hard to imagine, Matt. I know the Russians extremely well. I've been part of their life for much of my life. They're decent people. Most of them are like most of us. In fact, like most of the Chinese, too. The Russians have law and order, they have Mom and little children, they have laughter and tears, they celebrate birth and mourn death. They abhor violence. They want to live in peace. Just like you and me, just like every American."

"I know that," said Brennan, "but we've also had Americans who've been named Joseph McCarthy or Lee Harvey Oswald, assassins of character or of fellow human beings."

"Well, yes, Russia has its share of those, also. Only, from what I know of the attitude in Russia today, I can't see them assassinating anyone, except in defense of the motherland or in the national interest."

"Someone might conceive the present situation as one requiring a liquidation in the national interest."

"Of course. But nevertheless—"

Brennan interrupted her. "When I was at the Zurich Parley with Rostov, and the professor defected, Rostov and I were brutally judged and treated. He was packed off to Siberia. National interest. In effect, so was I. National interest. Governments, or rebels inside governments, do what they believe to be holy by their own judgments."

"But Rostov wasn't killed. Nor, in fact, were you."

"In a way, we both were, except Rostov was resurrected. All I'm saying is that when it comes to national interest, anything is possible, anything."

"I suppose so," said Hazel unhappily. She held up a fresh cigarette and waited for Brennan to light it, and to light his pipe. "Okay, let's say I'm converted to your case. Okay, you've got your case. What do you intend to do about it?"

Slouching, he ambled on in brief silence. Finally he shrugged. "There is nothing I can do by myself."

"You can go to the CIA, to the American authorities."

"You forget, Hazel, the mark is on me. I'm a traitor."

"Go to the French police, then."

"To them I'd be not only that foreign traitor but that troublesome crackpot as well. Nope, no chance there, especially when my portfolio contains only circumstantial evidence without proof. As Earnshaw put it last night, I have nothing until I have concrete proof. That's what I need, Hazel, proof, and I need it fast."

They were passing the Pont Marie, entering the Quai d'Anjou, and she knew what was coming next. Once more she wanted to run, escape decision, but there would be no escape from herself. Well, she told herself, let's get it over with.

"Well," she said to Brennan, "what's all that got to do with me?"

"Everything," said Brennan. He looked at her anxiously. "You're my court of last resort, Hazel. You're the only one who can help me obtain the concrete proof I must have." He paused. "You're the only one. I'm sure you know that."

She stopped in her tracks, heart pounding, and she walked to the quay and stared down at the Seine. At last she turned from the retaining wall. "It's Rostov you want, isn't it?"

"Yes."

"I see. That's what I thought." She watched Brennan advance, waited for him to come closer, and when he was directly before her, she bit her lip and said, "You know about us, about Rostov and myself, then."

"A little, but yes, I know."

"Does Jay Doyle know?"

Brennan nodded. "I'm afraid so. I found out through him. One morning he saw Rostov bring you back to your apartment. It was evident to him that you were—the two of you were—close."

She shook her head, and kept shaking it. "Jay. Poor bastard." She sighed, and straightened. "Oh, what the hell, the hell with it."

"Of course, I have no idea how well you know Rostov," said Brennan quickly, "but I assume—"

"Whatever you assume, you can double and redouble in spades," snapped Hazel, but then, briefly lost in thought, she softened. "Matt, he's a swell guy, you know, no matter what you've heard or think. Niki's a gentleman, and he can be very nice. I'm not talking about politics. There I don't know for positive. I'm strictly feature-page, women's-page, not politics. Niki's a good man, the kind of man who

765

can be very good for a shriveled-up, lonely, lost American girl who's got nothing to go home for."

Brennan's half-smile was understanding and kind. "I'm sure that's true, Hazel. The little I knew of him in Zurich, I liked."

Abruptly she turned away and looked up the wide river. After a while she began to speak, as much to herself as to Brennan. "You're a male, a political animal, so you can't possibly understand," said Hazel. "You can't know what it's like. Doyle was the first when I was a nobody kid in New York, and he was riding high with his fat ego and vanity, and he was a son of a bitch. It was awful for me. Then, when I was on the beach, emotionally penniless, Rostov came along, so American in so many ways, so thoughtful and useful, whatever his shortcomings, and he half filled my emptiness and he gave me a career, a big one. It's been going on—when it can, when we're both in the same place—for a good hunk of a good number of years. A lot of years. It's like having a husband." Her thin smile was wry. "A husband who's already got a wife. But still—" She shrugged. "So here we are, Matt. You come to me. You appeal to me, your court of last resort. You ask me to—to turn in my man to you—as material witness against himself."

"For all I know, it may not be against himself. I don't really have any knowledge of his role. But whatever it is, he must be aware of what is going on. If there is a plot, he'd know about it, as he knew of the earlier one when you met him in Vienna. Whatever comes out of this needn't necessarily hurt him."

Hazel's eyes blazed. "Come off it, Matt," she said angrily. "Who do you think you're talking to? Up to now you've leveled."

Brennan held up both hands. "Okay, sorry. Look, Hazel, after all, you have the right to say whatever you want to me, yes or no. You can say no."

"I know what in the hell my rights are, and I'll say whatever I want to say. And I also know what's at stake—either you're a fugitive from a booby hatch or you're a goddam Robin Hood—and either I'm a miserable cretin or a goddam Joan of Arc, and either way, heads or tails, I lose." She glared at him. "What's in it for Hazel, lil' ol' Hazel, I keep asking me."

Brennan chewed his pipe stem uncomfortably. "There's Jay Doyle," he said at last.

"Is there?"

"I believe so. He loves you."

"You're sure of that? You'll underwrite it? Oh, hell, I'm sorry, Matt. I suppose he does, in his fashion. As Wilson Mizener once said, some

766

of the greatest love affairs ever known have involved one actor, un-assisted. There's Doyle, same as an actor, there is he, himself, and—somewhere—I." She stopped and shook her head. "Let's not discuss Doyle. Of course, I love him. But Rostov, well, for whatever it amounts to—Rostov loves me. . . . Let's walk."

She started off, and Brennan fell in beside her as they moved down the Quai d'Anjou.

Brennan emptied his pipe and began to refill it. "There is nothing more I can say, Hazel. You know where I stand. You know what I need. Anything more wouldn't be fair. I won't press you further. From here on in, it is entirely up to you. Whatever you decide, that'll be it."

They strolled slowly ahead against the morning's fresh river breeze.

Hazel had retreated inside her head, where she silently performed as prosecution and defense, as judge and jury and defendant, in this time of trial. She wanted to invoke Important Words—Survival, Peace, Progress, Civilization, Man's Heirs, Man's Hope—but the words came out uncapitalized and sounded false. Her mournful words conjured up not the Summit, not nuclear mushrooms, unimaginable devastation and obliteration, but only pictures of a miniature self, her own self, wandering through the wreckage of her years. She thought of the old past and the recent past. She thought of the Doyle days in New York, and the Rostov years in Moscow, both before and after his Siberian experience. She fastened on Rostov and herself, that time at the Kurskaya Metro station, that time in the State Literary Museum, that time in the Tretyakov Gallery, that time in the Praga restaurant, that time on the overnight train to Leningrad, those times, and the times in her apart-ment, the vodka poured in the curtained kitchen, the card games played for kopecks, the jokes and the naked passion on her broken-down bed.

Her Niki.

Yet if Brennan, madman or prophet, was anywhere near right, if there was a plot, Rostov and her life with him would be altered by it. If there were sides, and he was on the wrong one, she would never see him again. If there were sides, and he was on the right one, he might be elevated to supreme leadership, a position too lofty and too exposed for him to bring her up after him.

And Doyle—allegiance to Doyle offered little more that was promis-ing. If Brennan was promoting a fiction, Doyle would sink lower than he had already sunk, to become, without book or balls, an ineffectual travesty of a man. If Brennan, on the other hand, was promoting a fact, Doyle would rise meteorically to where once he had been, the elite world of celebrity, a world too limited for any love except self-love.

In Hazel's head, the judge that was she charged the jury that was she. Summing up.

To accept Brennan's plea, to vote for Doyle, meant Brennan right or wrong. There could be no more Rostov in her life. All her eggs would be in one new but untrustworthy basket.

To reject Brennan's plea, to vote for Rostov, meant no more Brennan, no more Doyle, meant no harm done, no loss, no gain, but a safe half-life as it had been the week before this week.

And of course—damn judge in her addled head, damn built-in guiltmaker—there were, after all, those Important Words, from Survival to Man's Hope, and if something did happen here tonight, she would know until the final hour of earth that she had been mankind's Miss Judas. Yet if nothing happened tonight, the Summit would save man from himself and she would be relieved not to have sabotaged the machinery.

Jurors, have you arrived at a verdict?

Hazel shaded her eyes and looked beyond the quay and river toward the Right Bank. The world of ordinary people with ordinary dreams was coming alive. She had forever aspired to belong to that world. And even now, at her age, she did not want to give it up.

She halted and faced Brennan.

"My mind's made up," she said. "I'm making believe this is Veracruz."

"Veracruz?"

"When I was a kid in Wisconsin, I read Prescott's *The Conquest of Mexico*. I read about how Cortés landed in Veracruz, and how he knew that ahead lay the unknown New World and the unknown legions of the enemy. And he ordered his fleet of ships burned in the harbor so there could be no retreat. I was never more moved or more deeply impressed. I can still remember Prescott on Cortés addressing his troops: 'To be thus calculating chances and means of escape was unworthy of brave souls. They had set their hands to the work; to look back, as they advanced, would be their ruin.' And Cortés said, 'As for me, I have chosen my part. I will remain here, while there is one to bear me company.' Whenever I've had to face a decision I knew I must make, but shrank from it, I would remember that passage. I'm remembering it now, Matt." She tried to smile, but failed. "As for me, I have chosen my part. I'm burning all my ships. Okay, Matt."

"You're on our side?"

"I'll help you, if I can. You want me to speak to Rostov?"

"I want you to produce him, Hazel."

"Produce him? For whom? For you?"

"For me. I want to see him face to face, in person."

"When?"

"Today. As soon as possible."

She worried. "I don't know whether I can."

"But you're willing to try?"

"I've already said yes."

Brennan took Hazel by the arm and led her to the old wall. "Then listen to me. I've thought about it a good deal, given it hours of thought. I have an idea. I think it can work."

"Shoot," she said. "I know you don't like that word, but I'd suggest you better get used to it. Okay. I know the plot so far. But, Daddy, what happens next, Daddy?"

"I'll tell you—"

He began speaking urgently, and although she listened, she could see behind him, in the water, the safe ships that had brought her this far, now aflame and going under, and she knew they were unreal, and beyond them, on the opposite quay, she could see a man and woman going into one another's arms, embracing, kissing, and she knew they were real. . . .

NOT UNTIL LATE AFTERNOON was Hazel able to act for Brennan and herself.

She had met with Jay Doyle in the Rue du Faubourg-St.-Honoré, as prearranged, and together they had walked to the Place Beauvau discussing their strategy, she speaking nervously, he with unrestrained optimism.

They had both been surprised, even unsettled, by the number of uniformed French police swarming through the area and by the number of majestically attired officers of the Garde Républicaine stationed before the entrance to the Élysée palace up ahead. It had been understandable, this massive security, considering what had been going on this morning and this afternoon inside of what had once been Mme. de Pompadour's town house and what was now the headquarters for the presidents of France. What had been surprising was the incredible bustle of activity on a Sunday. Even the shops in the Faubourg St.-Honoré, one for antiques, another for chinaware, another for jewelry, had been open.

They had crossed the Place Beauvau, and at the corner of the side street called the Rue des Saussaies and the Faubourg St.-Honoré, as earlier agreed, Doyle had parted from Hazel and gone on to the Élysée palace to scout for information in the temporary press section. After he had shown his credentials and disappeared from view between the two guardhouses, Hazel had restlessly moved away from the corner to inspect the immediate neighborhood.

She had continued along the Faubourg St.-Honoré and found no café or restaurant and therefore no public telephone. She had returned to her corner and gone around it into the Rue des Saussaies, and immediately had located two cafés with telephones. In the first, the public telephone was too public and would not do. In the second, across the street, the Santa Maria, the interior was darker, more private, and the telephone had been better situated. Okay, she had told herself then, the Santa Maria it would be—hopefully, to take her into the uncharted future and into a New World.

Returning to her corner, she had been sorry for Brennan, for the delays that had made his morning so long and his afternoon probably unbearable. She had spoken to him an hour ago from her apartment, informing him that at last it was possible for her to act. If he did not hear from her again, she had said, the news was good. If she called once more, it would mean her news was bad.

The delays, of course, had been caused by the new disarmament proposal that Red China had unexpectedly submitted yesterday. This had been the reason for the emergency conferences on a Sunday. She and Doyle had gone to the Palais Rose at eleven-thirty in the morning, but the Summit meeting, at the request of the President of France, had been transferred to his private domain, the Élysée palace, to accent France's desire to act as neutral mediator, and at the same time try to achieve some kind of compromise accord that would put the five-power leaders back on the path to harmony.

Hazel and Doyle had rushed from the Palais Rose to the Élysée, only to learn that the Summit leaders had convened briefly and adjourned, and the talks would be continued by their ministers and advisers at four o'clock in the afternoon. These talks, usually held every afternoon at the Quai d'Orsay, had also been transferred to the Élysée, and for the first time that day Hazel had known definitely where Nikolai Rostov could be reached.

Patrolling her assigned corner, Hazel looked at the time. Doyle had gone into the Élysée at precisely six minutes to five. At this moment the time was twenty-two minutes after five. She had a clear view of the entrance, the arched portal and twin guardhouses that dignitaries passed before they walked across the white-pebbled courtyard and up the flight of steps to the huge transparent doors that opened into the

770

Élysée. Doyle had taken this route to enter, and he would eventually return by the same route.

Impatiently Hazel watched for him, wondering what was keeping him, worrying because the festivities in Versailles were only three hours off.

She gazed unblinking at the Élysée entrance until her eyes ached, but at last she relaxed her vigil and turned away in an effort to divert herself with an examination of the display in the window of the luxurious women's shop behind her.

She surveyed the latest feminine knits, of both rayon and wool, draped around a papier-mâché replica in miniature of the Palais Rose. She wished that she could wear such sexily clinging clothes for—instinctively her mind had entertained Rostov, out of habit, and she forced him to leave to make the considerable room necessary for Doyle—well, for the man who would marry her. Unfortunately, she did not have the necessary figure now, nor had she possessed such a figure when she was younger. The Maker gave every human being one advantage, no more. She would have to settle for brains, which were neither sexy nor the right filling for clinging knits. How odd of God, she thought, in dispensing His favors, not to have made all females feminine. But then, He was a male, and males never understood how women really felt.

She withdrew her attention from the depressing window display and pivoted on a heel to resume her watch of the Élysée. And there was Jay Doyle, like Jumbo except for the lack of a trunk, lumbering toward her.

"Well?" she asked quickly, even before he had reached her.

He wheezed noisily, and after an unnecessarily theatrical glance around to be sure they could not be overheard, he said, "Rostov's in there all right. I didn't see him, of course, but some of the other correspondents saw him arrive at four. The ministers are still locked up in the Murat Salon, in the section called the Foreign Sovereigns' Apartment."

"When do they break?" asked Hazel anxiously.

"No one knew for sure, but the best-informed guesses were that they'd adjourn in about fifteen minutes or a half hour. They have to get back to their residences and hotels to change for the President's dinner at Versailles."

"I'd better get right on it," said Hazel, nervously brushing back strands of her freshly dyed rust hair.

"You'd better."

"By the way. Did you find out what room the Soviet delegates are using for their staff?"

"Oh, yes, sorry. Yes, I did. They're set up in the Silver Salon."

"Okay, I found a little restaurant around the corner. The Santa Maria. That's where I'll be. Where'll you be, Jay?"

He flicked his forefinger toward the Faubourg St.-Honoré. "Down the block. I'll be looking at the exhibit in the Galerie Charpentier. It's open. And there's a perfect view, from there, of the Élysée. We'd better hustle. Good luck, Hazel."

"Yeah," she muttered, "good luck."

They parted once more, and she tucked her purse firmly under her arm, banished introspection from her mind, and in rapid, businesslike strides, she hastened to the Santa Maria restaurant.

Inside, she stood beside the map on the wall bearing the legend PER MARE MARIAM, and tried to orient herself. The attractive restaurant had been decorated to resemble a ship. The small bar opposite where she stood was lighted by bulbs from three glass openings made to resemble portholes in the ceiling above. There was a telephone down here, but its location had slipped her mind. She went to the bartender and inquired. He pointed out the public phone, and added that there was another one near the dining rooms upstairs.

Hurrying across the *moquette*-covered floor, hospitably the color of her own hair, she took hold of the nautical-style rope that substituted for a railing and ascended the steps spiraling toward the story above the ground floor. At the head of the stairs, a waiter directed her to the public telephone, and she was relieved to find that it was relatively private.

Determined not to hesitate, lest she weaken altogether, she deposited her *jeton* and dialed the Élysée.

Hazel heard the French operator answer indistinctly above the sounds of numerous other operators in the background.

"Please connect me with the Silver Salon," Hazel commanded in English.

In heavily accented English, the French operator responded. "That is reserved for the Soviet delegation, madame."

"I know. I must speak to someone there on a pressing matter."

There followed a mechanical jangling like the shifting of toy gears. For a second Hazel thought she had been disconnected, but a female Russian voice came on speaking French.

Hazel inhaled, and blurted, "I must have a word with Minister Nikolai Rostov. It is of importance."

The Russian operator's voice had switched to English. "What is your business?"

"It is personal," said Hazel, "but the Minister is expecting my call. Please inform him—" The pseudonym and password escaped her an instant and returned. "Inform him that Monsieur Gérard's secretary is on the line and must speak to him on a matter of great importance."

"I do not know if it is possible . . ." The Russian operator's voice had drifted away, as if she had turned to search the salon, but now it was back at the mouthpiece: "I do not see Minister Rostov, and I am afraid he may be in the conference."

"Can you find out?" said Hazel. "If he is in the conference room, pass him a note that Monsieur Gérard's secretary is on the telephone and must speak to him at once."

"Monsieur Gérard's secretary. I am writing it."

"If he cannot leave, try to learn at what time I can phone him back in the Élysée, and I shall do so. But it would be better if I might speak to him right now."

"I do not know. I will send someone. It may be several minutes. You will wait?"

"I will wait."

The other end of the telephone went blank, silent except for a mechanical humming, that indicated the Russian operator in the Silver Salon of the Élysée had pressed the "Hold" button.

Hazel timed her wait.

A half minute. One minute. A minute and a half. Two minutes. Two and a half minutes. Three. Four and—

And the Russian operator's voice came loudly through the earphone. "You are there?"

"I have been standing by."

"It is fortunate. The Ministers' conference was adjourned, and Minister Rostov was still in the hall outside, in conversation. Your message was delivered. Minister Rostov said he would come right to the—ah, here he is—coming into the room. One moment, please."

A click.

A new voice, male, deep, rasping, familiar. "Yes? This is Nikolai Rostov. You wish to speak to me?"

Automatically Hazel lowered her voice. "This is Monsieur Gérard's secretary."

"Of course, madame." Rostov's tone had become more subdued and concerned. "Is there anything further on our negotiations?"

"Yes. Something terribly important has come up. I was entrusted to

773

pass it on to you. It is vital that you know of this at once. I am in my apartment."

"Surely this can hold over until tomorrow, madame? I have little time. I must go to the state dinner at Versailles."

"I'm afraid it can't wait until tomorrow."

"No?" Rostov's tone had become more troubled than curious. "You are certain of that?"

"I am certain," said Hazel.

A brief silence. "Is there anything that you can speak of this matter now?"

"Well—" She knew that the Élysée telephones might be tapped or all calls monitored, but she had to chance it. As guardedly as possible, she said, "This involves Monsieur Gérard himself. Since he is so close to you—"

"Yes. Go on, please."

"His wife has just found out about the other woman who is his friend. His wife is wild with rage and trying to verify what she has learned. If she can verify it today, she vows to leave Monsieur Gérard and sue for divorce"—Hazel paused for effect, knowing Russian divorce law and knowing Rostov's greatest love and weakness—"and take his children from him."

Rostov's voice quavered. "Where did you hear this?"

"I cannot speak on the telephone."

"Very well. But you are sure of this?"

"Positive. Monsieur Gérard needs help. If you will come to my apartment, even for five minutes, I will explain, and perhaps you will find the means for Monsieur Gérard to refute the malicious lie and prevent a divorce and preserve his home. There may still be time, you understand?"

"I think so." He sounded stricken.

"I admire Monsieur Gérard too much to see him ruined," Hazel said quickly. "I only want to help him."

"Your apartment, you say?"

"Yes."

"I shall be there as soon as possible, quite soon. Thank you. Good day."

She heard him hang up, and after a few moments, she listlessly hung up, too.

Turning away from the scene and the instrument of shame, she went slowly down the winding staircase to the ground floor of the Santa Maria restaurant.

She headed for the bar, set her purse on the dark wood counter, and

774

stepped up and sat on the first of the half-dozen vacant stools. She ordered a beer, and when it came, she drank deeply from it. The beer was malty and full-flavored, but it did not soothe her. She tried not to think. Once again she kept her eye on the time.

After fifteen minutes Jay Doyle finally loomed in the doorway, sucking for air. As he wiped his forehead with a handkerchief, he saw her and came directly to her.

"Our boy just left the Élysée," he announced in a tremulous whisper, and he reached for Hazel's beer stein and gulped from it.

"He left?" she said dully.

Doyle glanced at the bartender. "Let's find a table, honey." He helped her off the stool, took her stein, and they followed the jovial and matronly lady proprietor to a table near the kitchen door.

The moment they were seated, Hazel asked, "What happened?"

Doyle accepted the menus, but waved off the waitress, before he bent toward Hazel. "I was watching from the Galerie. About five minutes ago Rostov came out of the Élysée on the double, I mean fast. Two men were kind of trotting after him. I think one was a chauffeur and the other probably a security guard. He said something to them—I guess that he wanted to take a short walk and would be right back—and away he went, alone, coming toward the Galerie where I pretended to be engrossed in a Giacometti. Then he turned sharply into the Rue de Duras. I gave him a few seconds, and popped out of the Galerie and up the side street just as he was flagging down a taxi. I watched for him to take off in it, and then I came straight here. Well, you did your job, Hazel. It worked great."

"Did it?" she said bitterly.

Doyle had never appeared more bluff and cheerful. He lifted his eyes to the ceiling and brought his fingertips together in mock piety. "Man, oh man, if I wasn't so damn hungry, I'd spend the next hour praying." His lumpy hands separated and eagerly retrieved the menu. "Well, now, I think we've both earned a good high-calorie dinner." He scanned the menu. "Modest but healthy. Potage portugais. Steak au poivre. Fromage. What do you say, Hazel?"

"I'm not hungry."

"Aw, come on, you've got to have something in your pretty belly. We've both got to be trekking out there to Versailles soon to cover somebody's Last Supper—"

"Don't talk like that," she said.

"Sorry, sorry. I know it was tough, honey. But it's over. Now, what'll you have?"

"Nothing, I told you," she said sullenly. "Get me another—make it a martini—but don't ask for a martini or it'll be vermouth—ask for *un dry*."

She watched him, her gross child, beckoning for the waitress, ordering her drink, then reading from the menu with the passion of a Jesuit reciting from the New Testament. She watched him wearily, her gross and only child, and she bade a silent farewell to M. Gérard's faithless secretary and she bade a silent welcome to Mr. Doyle's faithful wife or mistress or mother or whatever the hell she was going to be. She watched him finish, and smile at her sweetly, and she allowed him to take her hand, remembering how nice he could be when he was happy.

"Why so glum, Hazel?" he was inquiring. "What are you thinking about?"

"No maid today, and I was trying to remember if I cleaned the apartment," she said, and then she knew that it all mattered, somehow, and she held his hand tightly.

MATT BRENNAN no longer bothered to consult his wristwatch. The last time he had looked, the long and short hands had formed a straight vertical line, telling him it was six o'clock. Now he did not know exactly. He only knew that he felt as if he had been here, in this position, an eternity.

Nor did Brennan any longer listen for the ring of the telephone resting on a side table next to the showcase of Limoges and Meissen pieces. For the better part of an hour he had expected it to ring, and worried that it would, and dreaded hearing it. But the telephone had remained mute, and by now Brennan believed that it would not interfere with his last, best hope.

He sat unmoving in the light armchair that he had earlier moved to a position which would be behind the apartment door, when and if that door was opened. He had ceased staring at the sliding partition of the small dining area that opened into the kitchen. He had ceased reviewing, over and over again, what must be said, if the opportunity came. Like a yogi, he had cleansed and emptied his mind of all but a disciplined consciousness of one object and one objective.

He sat in readiness, not marking time as it floated past.

But, gradually, Brennan found himself marking time once more, and the consciousness of suspense began to unnerve him. Time had ceased floating past. Time dragged, and what it dragged was Hope. Worse than despair, worse than the bitterness of death, is Hope. Shelley had known, as he, Brennan, had also known and knew right now.

His every sense was attuned to one sound—the knock on the door beside him—and then he caught himself, remembering it would not be a knock but the metallic scraping of a spare key in the lock. A key. He warned his senses to alert themselves to the sound of a key.

He tried to recall key sounds, and realized the range was wide, from the anger of Stefani's key when she had returned home to Georgetown from the theater to find him still at work, to the eagerness of Lisa's key when she had come to join him in bed in Venice; from the sharpness of the key owned by the CIA agents entering his hotel room in Zurich, to the shaking of the key by which he himself had entered Joe Peet's hotel room here in Paris.

He wondered whether he dared get up and go to the bathroom. He wondered whether the sitting room was getting too dark as it got darker outside. He wondered whether he should turn up more lamps. He wondered whether he should visit the kitchen.

Suddenly he stiffened and edged forward in his chair.

There was a creak, another creak, a steady creaking of the corridor floorboards that led from the elevator to the door.

He listened hard. The creaking had stopped.

Then the expected sound came, swift and terrifying as a bolt of lightning at his feet.

A metal key struck the metal lock of the door, grated against it, sank into the keyhole, revolved in a single turn, and the door gave slightly.

Time hung throttled, and Brennan held his breath.

The key rattled free of the lock, and the door widened in an arc toward him. The cuff of a shirt, the back of a hairy, stubby hand, the length of a sleeve, were visible.

Brennan meant to rise, but he did not. Intellect had overruled instinct. He must have his visitor inside, fully. Brennan gripped the arms of his chair.

And Nikolai Rostov came into the room, shutting the door softly behind him.

Himself unseen, Brennan could see Rostov plain, for an instant petrified in profile, like an animated figure made motionless by the snap of a shutter and trapped in a camera box. It was strange to see the Russian so close and unaware after so many years, months, weeks, days of seeking him, after hundreds of hours of remembering him, evoking him, needing him, after countless unspoken dialogues with him. For Brennan he had become more a myth of the mind than a man, an elusive, vaporous shape that had become more the trick of a dream than a reality. But here he was, Nikolai Rostov, and he was real.

He was very real, the Slavic, Gorki, Cro-Magnon features, the muscular, chunky body. He was familiar, the friend of four years ago, larger, fleshier, grayer, but familiar. And he was human, and therefore vulnerable.

First his profile, now his back, as he crossed the room, anxious, distraught. Near the sofa he stopped, looked toward the dining area, the kitchen, the stairs to the second level.

"Milochka?" he called out.

No response.

"Hazel, I am here," Rostov called out again.

Brennan's heart leaped, and he came quickly out of his chair. The slight stir of movement, the rustle of his rising, was enough. Rostov spun around, fast and nimble as an alerted jungle animal.

Brennan stepped between the door and his visitor, offering the ghost of a smile. "Hello, Nikolai. It's been a long time, hasn't it?"

The shock of the unforeseen mashed Rostov's broad face. His eyes, his mouth, reflected the emotions of total amazement and confusion, as yet unjoined by understanding.

"Brennan—" he said.

Automatically, one hand groped for someone beside him, as if to summon a bodyguard, but there was no one there. His features flattened, widened, with the realization that he had chosen to come here hastily, secretly, to answer the call of his mistress, and now by his own choice he was caught off guard and unprotected.

"I'm sorry to startle you this way," said Brennan. "I know this is the last thing you expected. But I had to see you privately."

Rostov's confusion was beginning to recede. He glanced about him. "Where is Hazel? Is she here?"

"No, she's not here. I have no idea where she is."

"She telephoned for me to come."

"I know," said Brennan.

"You know?" said Rostov incredulously. He looked slowly around the apartment, and when his gaze fixed on Brennan again, he understood. "You and Hazel arranged—this?"

"She didn't want to, but—"

"She called me, knowing you would be here instead?"

"At my request, Hazel loaned me her apartment."

"And agreed to bring me running here to meet you?"

Brennan nodded. "Yes, but don't be too hard on her. There's a reason—"

"How could she?" said Rostov, more to himself than to Brennan. "I've always—" He raised his head, eyes narrowing. "In all these years, she is the only American I have come to trust. Now, this. What is she? One of the ones your CIA has corrupted, like yourself?" He shook his head. "I should have known, from the day we arrived here."

"There was nothing to know, Nikolai. And there's still nothing to know. You've been close enough to Hazel to realize that she hasn't a thing to do with the Government. And you've been close enough to me to know that even if I wanted it, my Government would have no part of me. Don't look at me that way, Nikolai. Why must every mistrust or suspicion a Communist has immediately convert the one suspected into a government agent? Because this is so in your country? You know better. You know people like Hazel and me can act out of our own personal feelings."

"Your own personal feelings," repeated Rostov bitterly. "Hazel deceives me, entraps me to see someone I have no wish to see, and you hound me and finally catch me with a typical American deceit, and you say that it is merely selfish personal whim you satisfy? You expect me to believe that?"

"I hope you'll believe that, because it's absolutely true, Nikolai. I'm a friend of Hazel's. That's the extent of my relationship with her. I came across information that I believed you should be told in private. I convinced Hazel of the importance of my information. She finally agreed to arrange this meeting, because she felt what I have to say may be as meaningful to you as it is to us."

"I see, Brennan, so now it is her concern for me, your concern for me, that motivated this—this reunion. Comrade, you have missed your true calling. You have the mealy mouth, the twisting tongue, that would have made you a prosperous capitalistic clergyman. I have no more time to waste on you."

"Nikolai, I suggest you hear what I have to say first. It may involve your—your life."

Rostov snorted contemptuously. "My life or *yours,* Brennan? Do you think I'm a fool? I know why you are here. You have bothered me for years with your pitiful paper missiles, beseeching me to support you, to save you, to pull you out of the hot water you boiled for yourself. I saw from the moment I met you in Zurich that you were a child with your head in the clouds and your feet off the ground, just like Varney. I saw you for a weakling, politically naïve and inept, and self-destructive, and always ready to drag everyone else down with you. Well, Brennan, you had your one success. You killed yourself, and almost managed to pull me into the grave with you. You gave me years of suffering, but I was strong enough to rise again. I don't intend to have you pull me down a second time."

"You know better than that," said Brennan, trying to control his temper. "You know that I was no more responsible for Varney's defection than you were, and I no more wanted the trouble that resulted from it than you did. You know we both tried to stop Varney. You know we both got a note from him acknowledging our innocence and freeing us of any responsibility. All I've ever wanted from you was that note—"

"Ah, that is all."

"Yes. If it didn't help you with your government, it would have helped me with mine."

Rostov glared at Brennan. "You dare compare our governments. Which of us is today free and respected, you or I?"

"You had Varney's letter to clear you. I didn't."

"Varney's note, eh?" Rostov stared at Brennan, and then he said, "I will speak one final thing to you in this room, and after that, let us be done with it and each other. You wanted a copy of Varney's letter and an affidavit from me to clear you. Do you imagine that either four years ago or today such evidence would clear you? Do you think any testimony from a defector to Red China and from a Communist Party Soviet Minister could clear you? If you think so, you are a fool. You were the victim of your own stupid education and degenerate society that inculcated you with the belief that Communism is your enemy, and that by leaking the N-bomb to China you could neutralize Russia, even have China and Russia destroy one another, so that you could have the world for capitalism. Clever, very clever, if it had worked, but it did not, because too many in China, as well as in Russia, knew that we were not the enemies of each other, that the real enemy, our common enemy, was little golden America."

Brennan had listened with growing disbelief. "Nikolai, what's got into you? You never talked like that before. Our countries were friends, and are supposed to be friends right now. We had a common goal. We both wanted peace. But now, you—"

"Never mind that," interrupted Rostov. "I have no time to discuss politics with you. We speak of Zurich. You came there the product of an unthinking, immoral, avaricious society. You prattled of world survival, but you meant America's survival, not ours, not China's. Only long after did I understand your unconscious wish in Zurich. When you personally helped China by giving Varney full freedom, you probably expected praise from your secret Wall Street leaders, the clique that wanted to arm China against Russia so that Communist

780

comrades would fight one another instead of their common enemy. You were surprised when that clique disowned you, threw you to your mad politicians and your puppet press and your moronic public. You were surprised, but I was not." He paused. "Yes, I had Varney's note that cleared us both of complicity. There it was on paper. We were innocent. Whatever your weaknesses that encouraged the defection, and involved me with you, on the basis of factual evidence, you and I tried to stop Varney and failed, and he went off on his own."

"You admit it then, that I was no traitor," said Brennan slowly. "Why didn't you help me prove it?"

"Because it would not have helped you and it would have hurt me," said Rostov. "No matter what proof of your innocence I gave you, your usefulness in a capitalist society was ended. But mine, thanks to our society, was not. So when the KGB came to question me, I turned Varney's note over to them. I was still suspect because of you, but at least I was given a chance to prove myself worthy of trust. Your ridiculous letters, asking for a copy of the letter, for my support, only embarrassed me, gave me more trouble. I refused to acknowledge them because I wanted no more to do with you."

"But we were friends, Nikolai, and you knew I was innocent."

"Innocent of treason to your country, but guilty of being a pawn used to destroy my country. No, Brennan, I could not help one like you in Zurich or from Moscow, and I will not help you here. Now you have heard, and now we are through with our business."

For years Brennan had pictured a moment of confrontation with Rostov, when Rostov should speak the truth that would vindicate him at last. Seconds ago Rostov had confirmed his innocence, and yet there had been no thrill of pleasure in it for Brennan.

Rostov had started to go past him to the door. Brennan spoke quickly. "We are not through with our business, Nikolai. I did not come here to plead for myself. A week ago that would have been my reason. Today it is the less important one. I came here to speak of more vital business, a political matter that involves you as much as myself."

"A political matter? There is nothing you could say that would interest me."

As Rostov pushed past him, Brennan said softly, "Nikolai, if what I've been saying up to now has no interest for you, then why have you twice tried to murder me?"

Rostov stopped in his tracks, and looked up with genuine surprise. "Murder you? You are accusing me?"

"If not you, then your KGB. It's one and the same."

781

"Who would want to murder you, Brennan? Who are you to waste a single bullet upon? You are nobody. You are nothing. Only an unemployed fanatic with delusions of self-importance and grandeur."

"Wasn't that a description of Lenin once?"

Rostov's face hardened. "You compare yourself to Lenin? You contemptible fool. Lenin had an idea."

"So have I. Only my idea is not to foment revolution but to prevent it. My interest is not in the Finland Station. My interest is in Versailles."

Brennan watched for a reaction. Rostov gave him none. But he had turned back from the door into the room.

"What is that supposed to mean?" said Rostov.

"It means I know about the plot."

"What plot?"

"I have evidence of a conspiracy, fomented within your delegation, to overturn your Government, and with it the work of the Summit and the hopes for international peace. I have evidence of a conspiracy that wishes to bring Russia into an alliance with China against the world. I have evidence of a conspiracy that plans to achieve its ends by violence."

"How interesting, Brennan. What else do you have?"

"I have a notion that what began in Vienna in 1961 may be brought to an end in Versailles tonight. If you are not mixed up in this, I feel that I'm helping you and your Government protect yourselves. If you are mixed up in this, I am giving you fair warning not to go ahead because the plot is known."

Rostov's smile was cold. "You are finished, Brennan?"

"Yes."

"If you are, I shall make one comment."

"Go on."

"You are insane."

Brennan continued to stare unflinchingly at Rostov. "I would suggest that anyone sponsoring such a plot might more appropriately be regarded as insane. If it were your country's internal affair alone, I would not speak of it. But the consequences of such a plot can lead to widespread war and destruction. It concerns not only yourself but every human being on earth. Those are my views. You or your colleagues tried to liquidate me for holding them, but it is not I who should be liquidated but those of you who would risk thermonuclear warfare to achieve your ambitions."

Rostov's cold smile remained. "Ah, so we have come to this. You are now threatening my life."

"I am in no position to threaten anyone's life. But you are in such a position, Nikolai. . . . For God's sake, Nikolai, what's happened to you? You were another man in Zurich, thoughtful, full of ideals and hopes, but now—it's as if you've been changed, the same face, but the inside of the skull different—like someone who's been brainwashed."

"Brainwashed?" said Rostov, enraged. "Your easy tabloid word for every man who finds the truth. The truth I have found is that your American capitalist hyenas are trying to brainwash the entire world to do its bidding, become its slaves, out of fear that if it doesn't, Russian and Chinese Communists will unite to obliterate the decadent, militaristic, exploiting tyrants in your society. Well, you have every right to fear—" He halted. "I've endured enough of your madness. I've let you go far enough with your troublemaking and propagandizing and provocations. I advise you to go no further."

"I thank you for your advice, Nikolai. But I can't stop now."

Rostov shrugged. "Your funeral. An Americanism I picked up from one of your compatriots." He pulled a key from his pocket, studied it, and dropped it at Brennan's feet. "No more contamination from your whoring capitalist women. I give her back to you, with the reminder that you can buy as much for ten dollars on any street corner. In fact, you can buy better, because a whore is honest in her whoredom, but your women are lying, cheating jackals, like their men, like you."

He turned to the door, gripped the knob, and held it for a moment. And then, without looking back, he spoke.

"About Zurich, Brennan. . . . Perhaps *I* had Varney write *me* that letter, before I helped him defect to China. Maybe it was not you, but I, who earned and deserved his letter. Had you ever thought of that? You might examine the possibility, merely as an exercise, since you pretend to know much, and actually know little about anything. It might give you pause to look before you leap—again. . . . Good night, Brennan."

The door opened, closed, and Nikolai Rostov was gone.

Stunned, Brennan did not move.

He listened to the elevator descending. Slowly he tried to recover his balance, to think. At last he walked to the apartment window, unlatched the shutters, and peered down into the street. He watched as Rostov climbed into a taxi, and he waited for the taxi to leave.

Wheeling, he went quickly through the sitting room into the dining area.

"Okay, Emmett, it's safe," he called out. "Rostov has left."

He came back into the sitting room again as Earnshaw caught up with him.

"Did you hear all of it?" Brennan asked dispiritedly.

"Every word!" exclaimed Earnshaw. "Once, I was afraid he'd come into the kitchen—"

"No chance. He was too surprised by me at first, and too embattled after that. Well, I guess I—"

Earnshaw threw an arm around Brennan's shoulders and beamed at him. "Congratulations, Matt! I couldn't wait to congratulate you!"

Brennan looked confused. "About what?"

"Come now, young man, you can't have forgotten? Well, I assure you, I haven't and I won't. Yup, I heard it all. You're simon-pure. Rostov cleared you of treason. He wiped the word traitor out of your life. He proved your innocence."

"Yes, I know—"

"Well, my good man, it's open and shut. I was a witness. I'll dictate an affidavit and sign it, and after the Summit is over I'll see that the press and every Government branch and department gets it. Overnight, your name will be cleared. Your security status will be cleared. You can get back to the United States, where you belong, and back into government. I couldn't be more pleased." He slapped Brennan on the back. "Come on, cheer up. This is a big day."

Brennan shook his head. "I don't feel that way. I wish I could, Emmett, but it's gone sour. I don't know what I expected, but I was after something much more important. A couple of times there, I thought, well, I thought he'd blow up and spill some of the truth. He almost did. You heard him, at the door, teasing me with the possibility that he might have been the one who helped Varney give our secrets to China."

"Bravado, showing off, merely to confuse you. Anyway, neither of us could convince anyone—"

"I was almost sure he'd crack along the way. But he didn't."

"No, he didn't," said Earnshaw, fixing a cigar. "I'm sorry about that, Matt, but facts are facts, we've agreed. You've got nothing for the police, not a shred of proof that there is any plot going on at all. I think you have to face it. Without proof, your hands are tied. Besides, Matt, if you want to be honest with yourself, there may be nothing to prove, no plot, no intrigue—"

"I won't concede that," said Brennan. "I'll only concede I'm helpless, and this was my last chance and I lost. It just troubles me what I've done to Hazel, and that I have nothing to show for it. Yet I'm surer than ever that Rostov is mixed up in whatever's going on, and he knows that I know, and he arrogantly doesn't give a damn, doesn't have to lift a finger against me, because he also knows I'm helpless and no threat to him anymore."

Earnshaw drew on his cigar, blew a ring of smoke, and studied Brennan. At last he spoke. "Matt, I'm older than you, and you listen to me. The world is always hard on theorists. In medicine, a cherished theory can be more harmful than useful, until it is proved out. In law, circumstantial evidence can provide as much injustice as justice, when it substitutes for incontrovertible proof. Now, your theory may be right, and if it is, we will all suffer for not having acted on it. Yet, more likely, it is wrong, and if so, we would provoke grave trouble to peace and stability by interfering. You've tried to obtain proof to support your theory, and you've failed. If Rostov had given you one piece of real evidence, even indicated that he would seriously try to block you from pursuing your investigations, I'd say we had enough to act on. But he gave you nothing, either because he wanted to protect himself or because—well—because there was nothing to give you in the way of proof. Matt, you've accomplished enough in this room. If you've found nothing else, you've found yourself, you've found your vindication. Put the rest out of your mind. Go home with your young lady and start afresh."

"Thanks for your help, Emmett."

"I wish I'd been sensible enough to help you long before. But I'm glad I'm able to make some of it up to you now. I'll get that affidavit prepared, sworn to, and signed by me while my name still means something. . . . Well, I'd better get me back to the hotel and change into my monkey suit. I'm expected at the table of honor in the Hall of Mirrors. Your reputation will soon be restored, but I mustn't forget mine will soon be ruined by those Goerlitz memoirs. So, before it finally is, I've got to enjoy any small pleasures and attentions I'm offered. Still, I'll confess, Matt, I feel that I've gained something here in Paris. I've found something of myself I had forgotten existed. It won't be easy for me to live with what's ahead, but you know, I might give it a try. You try, too. Forget the world for a day and think of yourself. And if you can, come up for a drink tomorrow at five. I'll have the affidavit waiting for you. See you then, Matt."

Earnshaw departed, leaving behind a trail of smoke.

Alone, Brennan wearily surveyed the room. Everything was in order, except poor Hazel's life. He sighed, picked up the key and placed it on the coffee table, and went slowly around turning off the lamps.

This done, he paused before the sofa, and finally sank down into it and laid his head back, alone in the darkness.

He thought of Rostov. He thought of himself. And finally his mind went to King Pyrrhus, and Brennan knew that he himself had also lost more than he had gained in his past hour of triumph, and he understood for the first time the bitter meaning of Pyrrhic victory.

At last he thought of one of his favorite stories. In the early 1800's, in Manchester, England, an unhappy and depressed middle-aged man, a traveling man, visited a physician who had been recommended to him. "What is the nature of your ailment?" the physician inquired. The sad-faced patient replied, "I'm suffering from a hopeless malady. I'm in terror of the world around me. Nothing gives me pleasure anymore, nothing amuses me, nothing gives me reason to live. If you can't help me, I'm afraid I shall kill myself." The physician gave his caller reassurance. "Your illness is not fatal. It can be cured. You need only get out of yourself, find things that will amuse you, cheer you, make you laugh." The patient said, "How do I find such diversion? Tell me exactly what I must do." The physician replied, "Simply go to the circus tonight to see Grimaldi, the clown. Grimaldi is the funniest man alive. He will cure you." And the sad-faced patient said, "Doctor, I am Grimaldi."

Brennan thought: I am Grimaldi.

He needed someone to save him. Yet the only person who could save him, who understood, who believed, who could help, was he, himself. And he was impotent.

It was over. The best he could hope for was that Rostov had been right, after all, and that the events of tonight would prove him not quite insane but completely a fool.

Pʜʏsɪᴄᴀʟʟʏ ᴡᴏʀɴ ᴏᴜᴛ, mentally apathetic, Matt Brennan had left Hazel's apartment in the Rue de Téhéran and on leaden legs had walked from the Boulevard Haussmann to the Rue de Berri.

Indifferent to the hour of the evening, for no longer did it have meaning for him, he approached the glass canopy over the entrance to the Hotel California. He was aware that he had spent a considerable time licking his wounds in Hazel's apartment. After Rostov's departure, then Earnshaw's, Brennan had remained slumped on the sofa in a state of lethargy for a prolonged period. Only the sudden arrival of Hazel, who, accompanied by Doyle, had returned briefly to change her dress, had roused him.

Both of them had known at once, from his demeanor, the result of his confrontation with Rostov. Nevertheless, they had questioned him, and miserably he had reported upon his exchange with Rostov and his failure. He had not bothered to inform them of his personal vindication. Hazel had heard him out stoically, obviously guessing Rostov's reactions to her perfidy (even though Brennan had omitted most of that), and when Brennan was done, she had merely shrugged and murmured, *"C'est la guerre."* Of the pair, Doyle had appeared the more stricken.

In her practical manner Hazel had suggested that they put the past behind them and resume their normal work. If they didn't hurry, she had added, they would be late for Neely's press briefing at Versailles.

Emptying her purse, she had found the schedule of the evening's festivities. The motorcades of the five Summit leaders and their wives and their Ministers were due to arrive at Versailles Palace at seven-thirty. After signing the Palace's Golden Book, the guests would ascend the Queen's Staircase and proceed to the Salon des Nobles de la Reine, where they would be received by the President of France, and, in turn, would join him to welcome each of the 200 honored guests invited to mark the occasion.

At eight o'clock the Chiefs of State and the guests would sit down to dinner in the fantastic 242-foot-long Hall of Mirrors. The banquet would end at nine-thirty. After that the leaders, their wives, and their closest aides would proceed to the Cabinet du Conseil, next to the Hall of Mirrors, have coffee for twenty minutes, and continue on through the palace to the Opéra Royal to join the others who had attended the dinner as well as 400 added guests for a ballet performance. Meanwhile, although the press would not be permitted inside the palace, there would be a tent erected at one side of the entrance court where specially invited correspondents could assemble to obtain information on the progress of the state dinner and receive background briefings from their respective press attachés. Neely's briefing for the American journalists would begin at nine-thirty, just as the dinner finished upstairs, and before the ballet began.

"The dinner's just about under way," Hazel had said to Doyle, "and I think we ought to be there by nine." She had started for the stairs to her bedroom, unbuttoning her blouse, but had hesitated on the first step and glanced at Brennan. "Sorry, Matt, that you couldn't prove it," she had said. "I respect you for giving it a try." She had smiled sadly. "And, Matt, given the chance, I'd do it again. Okay?"

Brennan had appreciated that, but it had not been okay then, and it wasn't okay now, as he trudged into the lobby of the Hotel California. Hazel's review of the night's schedule had heightened his sense of failure.

787

He became aware of M. Dupont, the concierge, waving an envelope at him. "Monsieur Brennan, a letter has just arrived by the Special Delivery."

Brennan accepted the letter stamped ESPRESSO, postmarked from Rome, forwarded from Venice, and about to shove it into his pocket, he thought to turn it over. When he did, he saw that the signature of the sender was scrawled above the imprint of the Albergo Mediterraneo, Roma. The signature was that of Ted Brennan.

He stood holding the envelope, blinking, until the full import of the signature struck him. Ted Shepperd was once more Ted Brennan.

He felt the tears well in his eyes as he stumbled into the inner lobby, and sat on the arm of a chair, ripping the envelope open.

The letter, in his son's hand, an almost indecipherable scrawl, was brief. Throughout the past week in Italy, Ted had thought again and again of the evening with his father in Harry's Bar, and he wanted to tell his father that he was deeply ashamed of himself. He believed in his father, in his father's innocence and decency, and he wanted to say it now, and he hoped he would be forgiven for any wrong impression he had created in Venice. He hoped his father would come home to the United States again so that they could be closer. And his sister Tracy felt exactly the same way. They both believed in their father, and missed him, and hoped that he would be in touch with them. The letter was signed "With my best wishes, and love, your son, Ted."

Brennan felt choked and flushed.

His hands trembled as he returned the page to the envelope and folded it into his pocket.

The real wonder of this, he realized, was not that such a letter had come to him at last, but that it had come to him now, at this moment. For in the eyes of the world Brennan still bore the brand of traitor. A letter of faith now, a letter such as this, was worth a million times what it would have been worth in a week or two, when Earnshaw's public announcement and affidavit would have absolved and cleared Brennan of committing any crime and have restored his honor.

He had never loved his son and daughter more than at this moment.

Somehow, too, this letter had revived his spirits. Brennan had come to Paris for self-vindication, and had allowed himself to be sidetracked by a greater quest, pretending his new goal was a more selfless, more ennobling, more humanitarian work. But now, in better perspective, he could see that his greater quest might have been inspired more by vanity than anything else. He had wanted not merely the victory of citizenship but the laurels of conqueror and hero. Unconsciously, perhaps to compensate for the ugly years of disgrace, he had wanted to come back not only as a man but as a prophet—yes, prophet—even as Doyle had facetiously addressed him. As a result, he had undervalued the achievement of reaching his first goal, because he had overvalued what might be gained for himself by reaching his second and greater goal.

He had told himself he was acting in the name of humanity, when all the while he had been serving only his bruised ego.

Maybe.

At any rate, Ted's miraculous letter had restored his sense of proportion, as Rostov's unwitting confession would soon restore his good name. It could be a world worth living in after all. Or could it, after tonight—after tonight at Versailles?

Maybe.

Brennan stood up and crossed to the small cage of an elevator. The adolescent operator banged the iron grille shut and took him up to the first floor. Brennan emerged, heard the elevator descend noisily, and he turned the corner and started up the dimly lighted hotel corridor to his suite. A step from Lisa's room, at the jog leading around to his rooms, he heard a rustle and a hiss. It seemed to come from the service alcove, behind his left shoulder.

Stopping abruptly, he looked back, and there was Lisa in her bathrobe, pressed against one glass swinging door, desperately beckoning to him.

Surprised, he said, "Lisa, what in the—?"

He never finished. Lisa had bounded toward him and clamped a hand full over his mouth. Her hand was icy, and her eyes were strained with fright, and he felt his heart begin to pound.

Removing her hand from his mouth, she put her lips against his ear. "Don't go near your room, Matt," she whispered. "Get away from here. I'll meet you down in the bar and explain—"

"No you don't," he whispered back. "If anything's wrong, I'm not leaving you."

"Matt, please do as I—"

"No."

She glanced furtively at the corridor corner toward which he had been heading, and suddenly she signaled him to follow her. She started back to the cubicle that the chambermaids and valets used, and she pushed open one frosted glass door and held it until he had followed her inside. Avoiding the pails of sudsy water, the pans and brooms, she drew him quickly into a recess of the alcove beside the table stacked high with fresh towels and bedsheets.

"Matt, someone is in your room," she said in a frightened undertone.

"It's dangerous. I've been waiting for twenty or thirty minutes to intercept you."

"Who's in my room?"

"I'm not sure, but I think there are two of them, and they're turning it upside down."

"When did this start?"

"Right after I first heard them. Maybe a half hour ago. I got in late. I was undressing to take a bath, and I kept worrying about what was holding you up. Then I heard you come into your sitting room, or at least I thought it was you. I was eager to know how you made out with Rostov, so I went to the two doors between our bedrooms. They were both shut but unlocked. I opened my door and was about to open yours when I realized there wasn't one voice in your sitting room but two. I figured you had company, had brought some man back with you. Then I realized the two in your room were speaking French, and I tried to listen from my side, and when the two came into your bedroom, I could hear them clearly. It was perfect French, without the slightest American accent, and the voices—neither one was yours, and then I knew they were strangers."

"What were they saying? Could you understand any of it?"

"You know my French—no, not much, just a little bit."

"What, Lisa?"

"Something about a manuscript that Monsieur Brennan had written —I think they were saying a manuscript that was against or attacked Russia."

"That damn fiction again."

"Anyway, they kept throwing things around, they couldn't find it—"

"It doesn't exist."

"—but then one of them shouted to the other that he'd found something else, and it was enough to satisfy the charges against you. I think that's what he said. I'm not positive."

"Charges against me?"

"That's the instant when I closed my door, threw on my robe and slipped out of my room to wait for you here."

"You did the right thing, Lisa. Are they still in there?"

"I haven't heard anyone leave on this side."

"Good."

He started to go, but she caught his arm. "Matt—?"

"I've got to get into your room and find out what this is all about," he whispered. "I have a feeling—well, let's see if we can find out."

He left the service alcove quickly, Lisa at his heels, and crossed the corridor to Room 110, opened Lisa's door swiftly, pushed her in ahead of him, and followed her inside. He closed her corridor door, directed her to stand near the mirrored wardrobe, and started on tiptoe around the brass bed.

Lisa came up behind him, stopping him while she cupped her mouth to his ear. "Matt, I told you neither of our doors is locked. If you open mine, there'll only be yours. And if one of them should try it, you'll fall right in their laps."

"That's the chance," he said grimly.

He continued toward Lisa's connecting door. He pressed against it. He could detect faint voices, but the actual words were inaudible. He reached down and gripped the handle and turned it slowly. He heard the lock retract. Softly he pulled the door open.

Now there was the thickness of only one door, his own, separating him from the intruders.

Moving in closer, he placed his ear against the remaining door and listened.

The sounds were louder, but still indistinct. There were two of them, no doubting that, and they were in his sitting room, engaged in a muffled conversation.

Suddenly he tightened at the door.

They were walking. Their footsteps were distinct. They were coming into his bedroom, very near. The steps ceased. The springs of his bed groaned. One of them had sat down on it. The receiver was being removed from the cradle of the telephone next to his bed.

"Operator? Put me through to the *Commissaire Controleur Général*. You have the number."

It was the crisp voice of a Frenchman, someone in authority, and the moment that he resumed speaking on the telephone, Brennan resumed automatically translating in his head, converting French into English.

Brennan flattened his ear harder against the door, trying to make out every word.

The deep voice on the other side was addressing the *Commissaire Controleur Général* on the telephone.

"*Monsieur le Commissaire?* . . . This is Superintendent Quarolli, des Services de la Sécurité Présidentielle. I am calling you from Monsieur Matthew Brennan's rooms in the Hotel California, Rue de Berri. . . . Yes, that is correct. It is on the formal charges lodged by the Soviet Russian Embassy about two hours ago. . . . No, I do not recall the exact specifications, but they are in the complaint signed by Marshal Zabbin and attested to by Minister Rostov. . . . Yes, about two hours ago. I am sure it is already on your desk. It is the document charging that Monsieur Brennan has made homicidal theats to a member of the Russian delegation. . . . Yes, I will wait."

Listening, Brennan waited also. Not a muscle of his person moved, but beneath his flesh he could feel his nerve ends tingling.

Superintendent Quarolli's voice penetrated the wooden partition once more.

"That is it, *Monsieur le Commissaire,* and I have the original warrant with me. What is that? . . . No, Monsieur Brennan has been out of his room most of the afternoon, but the concierge believed he would be back sometime this evening to keep a dinner appointment. . . . Yes, Inspector Gorin and I have spent three quarters of an hour making a thorough search of his two rooms. We have gone through all of his personal effects, examined every nook of his rooms. We have been unable to discover the manuscript that the Russian Embassy spoke about. However, we have found some evidence which may be far more incriminating. We have a sheaf of notes made in Monsieur Brennan's own hand, and some of these plainly indicate that Brennan has been threatening the Russians and may be potentially dangerous, as charged. One second, please. . . . *Voilà.* Inspector Gorin reminds me that there is one line in Monsieur Brennan's notes that reads 'Assassinate—Russ delegate—soon.' Gorin and I believe that is sufficient evidence upon which to arrest and hold him, and satisfy the charge of the Russian Embassy. . . . No, *Monsieur le Commissaire,* that would have to take place tomorrow. The Russians explained that they could not enter into this matter tonight, since both Zabbin and Rostov are guests of the President at Versailles this evening, the dinner for the Chiefs of State. What? . . . Exactly. They merely requested that Brennan be picked up this evening and detained, held in custody, until tomorrow when they will appear in person to make formal the charges and confront him. Gorin and I believe we have sufficient evidence to indicate the American is a menace to public safety and to the conference security. . . . Agreed. We shall wait right here in his rooms. The minute he comes in, we shall place him under arrest and shall bring him to the Préfecture for questioning. In this way we can keep him locked up overnight and satisfy our Soviet friends. . . . What is that? . . . Well, whatever you say, sir. If Brennan does not return within one hour, I will call you back, and you can issue the order for a general alarm to have him brought in. . . . Yes, *Monsieur le Commissaire,* you need have no—"

Brennan had heard enough.

Quietly he backed away, and noiselessly he closed Lisa's door and secured the lock.

He swung around to Lisa, his eyes shining and all of his being electrified with restored hope.

"I heard most of—" Lisa began to whisper, but she held her tongue when Brennan brought his forefinger to his lips.

He pulled her across her bedroom, and led her to the corridor door.

"What does it all mean, Matt?" she whispered.

"It means I've got my final piece of evidence at last," he said excitedly, "proof that there is a plot in existence, and the denouement of that plot is going to take place at Versailles tonight. You want to know who gave me the proof? Rostov himself."

"When? At Hazel's?"

"No. Right here. Just now. I saw him at Hazel's exactly as we planned. It was no use. He wouldn't crack an inch, wouldn't admit to anything. I accused him of everything, but he simply denied it, and that was that. Or so I thought. But, now—" He beamed at the door across the room. "Now he tipped his hand. I must have been absolutely accurate about an assassination, about Versailles tonight. Because obviously Rostov ran back to his Embassy, informed his superiors—Zabbin, others—and they got in touch with the French police, drumming up any pretext of a charge to get me picked up and hauled off to jail tonight—tonight, mind you. All they wanted to be sure of was that I was out of the way, out of their hair, tonight, so they could be free to do whatever they want to do at Versailles. But I'm going to fool them." Suddenly he took Lisa in his arms and kissed her, and said, "And when I'm done with this, Lisa, I'm going home with you, and we're going to be married, because Rostov confirmed my innocence in Earnshaw's hearing, and Earnshaw is signing an affidavit to that effect, and he's going to release it publicly and clear me."

Tears filled Lisa's eyes, and she whispered against his chest, "Oh, Matt, Matt, Matt—thank God—"

Firmly he pushed her away. "Tell you about it later. Now I've got to hurry."

"Matt, you're not leaving?"

"You want me to stay, when I've finally got the proof? No, darling, too much is at stake. I'm going to get Earnshaw, and he and I are going to finish our business with Rostov."

"But they're at Versailles."

"And I'm practically at Versailles, too."

He reached for the doorknob, but Lisa tugged at his arm. "Don't, Matt. If you cause trouble, get mixed up in this, and you're wrong, the French police will arrest you. They'll be looking for you in an hour

793

anyway, and you'll be all over the front pages again, another scandal. It'll completely ruin the effect of Earnshaw's release declaring your innocence. If you're wrong here, nobody'll believe, no matter what Earnshaw says, that you weren't wrong four years ago. We've got everything in our favor now, this minute. Why risk it when you don't have to? Matt, you do see the danger?"

He nodded. "Yes, darling, but that's not the only danger I see." He kissed her hastily again. "I'm going out there and down the stairs. And in case there are any DST agents out front, I'm leaving by the back way, the hotel's service exit. I'm going to phone Hazel and Doyle, because I'll need help to get into where I'm going." He grinned. "The French invited 600 guests to Versailles Palace tonight. I don't know how, but I promise you, they're going to have 601."

Lisa released him. She smiled up at him lovingly. "Matt, I—" Suddenly she threw up her hands and said, "Oh, hell—just drive carefully."

IT WAS an unforgettable sight.

Directly ahead, filling his windshield, ablaze with thousands of lights, rose the most dazzling, the most magnificent royal residence in the world, the Palace of Versailles, the Sun King's gift of heaven's eye to man on earth.

As Brennan approached it through the staid city's wide sweeping thoroughfare, his shoe brushed the brake of his steaming Peugeot, and he slowed to have a glimpse at the time. His wristwatch read two minutes after nine o'clock. He was sure, he told himself, he had made a record run from Paris.

He had safely slipped out of the Hotel California and slipped into Le Tangage, and from there he had telephoned Hazel's apartment. There had been no answer. He had remembered then Hazel's remark to Doyle that she hoped to be at Versailles "about nine o'clock" to have plenty of time to look around before the state dinner ended and the ballet in the palace's Opéra Royal began, and before Herb Neely started his briefing of the American press.

Brennan had gone swiftly to the Garage Berri and sent an attendant scurrying to an upper level for his rented Peugeot. He had driven out of Paris cautiously, fearful of being stopped for speeding and having his identity discovered. But after recalling that the Presidential Security Superintendent in his room had agreed to wait an hour for him before sending out a general police alarm, he had felt reassured that the law had not yet been alerted to find him.

Speed was of the essence, since he had wanted to reach Versailles before Hazel and Doyle arrived there. So from the second he had left Paris by Porte St.-Cloud, he had disregarded Lisa's final admonishment, and he had driven at a breakneck clip along Autoroute de l'Ouest. The traffic had been light at this late hour, and he had covered the thirteen miles from Paris to the city of Versailles in fourteen and a half minutes.

And here he was—early, on time, late, he did not know—rescue mission or fool's errand, he did not know—obstacles, impossibilities, hazards of the next minutes, he did not know—but for better or worse, here he was in Versailles.

The high black-and-gold gates and railings, the star-shaped entrance court, the shimmering massive three-hundred-million-dollar edifice loomed larger and larger. Brennan turned his steering wheel and swung right, guiding his compact vehicle across the crunching gravel of the Place d'Armes, where row upon row of gleaming cars stood parked in the night.

Locating a slot, he squeezed the car into it, turned off the ignition, and flipped on the inside light. Finding both the tourist pamphlet on Versailles that he had removed from Peet's suitcase and the schedule of the French President's dinner and entertainment that he had obtained from Doyle, he unfolded them on his lap.

He studied the timing of the long list of events taking place in the palace this evening, to be certain that he had memorized them correctly. Next, he opened the Versailles pamphlet to the map inside, and reviewed the markings that he had made on it when he duplicated the original in Peet's room, and once more he fixed them in his mind.

Satisfied, he folded the pamphlet and schedule, stuffed them into his jacket pocket, wrenched the car door open, and stepped out onto the gravel lot.

Going hurriedly between the parked motorcars, he left the area and started trotting on a diagonal line toward the towering grilled gates that were the main entrance to the front palace grounds. Dozens of French security agents in uniform and plainclothes, as well as numerous saber-carrying members of the Garde Républicaine, flanked the open gates. Great swarms of French officials, some carrying guest lists, others carrying press lists, crowded around the portals. And nearby, a throng of hundreds of onlookers, from the city of Versailles itself, from neighboring villages, from Paris, pressed against police lines to ob-

795

serve every new arrival, especially those who came not on foot but by limousine.

Reaching the entrance, Brennan sought the official with the list of correspondents who had been invited. Worriedly, he inquired if Miss Hazel Smith of ANA had arrived yet.

The bumptious French official sniffed. "Why is it your concern, monsieur?"

"I'm working with Miss Smith. I was supposed to meet her here, but I'm a little late. I hope I haven't missed her."

The Frenchman cleared his sinuses and looked down at the names on the sheet clipped to his board. "Smith—Smith—Smith." He looked up and said brusquely, "Not yet. Not here yet."

Annoyed by the press officer's insolence, Brennan had intended to put him in his place. But now he was too relieved by the Frenchman's news to bother with him. *"Merci, monsieur,"* he said.

Brennan moved away from the cluster of officials and police, scanning the thickets of spectators for Hazel and Doyle, and then looking at the nearby automobile entrance to the inner court of the palace. There was no sign of either of them. For a moment Brennan wondered whether the French press officer could have been mistaken. Peering toward the parking lot, he saw a Volkswagen skid into it and he thought that he recognized Hazel at the wheel.

Starting for the Place d'Armes, Brennan saw Hazel rushing out of the lot with Doyle puffing after her. Brennan accelerated his pace, waving at them, and midway between the main gate and the parking lot he intercepted them.

Hazel showed surprise at Brennan's presence, but Doyle, coming abreast of them, revealed only hope and anxiety.

"Matt, what are you doing here?" Doyle wanted to know. "Is something happening?"

"Plenty," said Brennan. "I've got absolute proof the Russians are up to something here tonight."

Immediately he blurted out what had transpired after he had left Hazel and Doyle at her apartment. He repeated everything that he had overheard of Quarolli's telephone call from his hotel room.

Doyle's response was immediate and unrestrainedly enthusiastic. "Matt, you've discovered gold at last. This is the mother lode. This is it."

Brennan's gaze shifted to Hazel, trying to detect any skepticism on her part. Her brows were knit. She was considering what she had just heard, but there was no skepticism in her sharp features. "You say the Superintendent's name was Quarolli? I was remembering. I met him on an interview a week ago. He's literal. No nonsense. Not the type who plays games. If he said what you've just told us, well—" She hesitated. "Yes, Matt, I'd say the Russians had reason to want you out of the way tonight."

Doyle shook Brennan by the shoulder. "What are you standing here for? Aren't you going to do something?"

"There's not too much I can do," said Brennan. "I went over every possibility while I was driving. Only one makes sense. Emmett Earnshaw is the single person inside the palace who knows what is going on and is on our side. Even after Rostov left me, and Earnshaw was convinced I had no case, he did admit that if Rostov had given me any shred of evidence corroborating my theory, like trying to block me from going further, we'd have proof enough to act. All right. Rostov has tried to block me from coming here. There'll be a general police alarm on me in less than a half hour. The Russians want me picked up and out of the way, and chances are I will be. That's the proof Earnshaw wanted, that's something he can act upon. He'd have no trouble getting everyone's ear up there, getting security doubled and tripled, getting the routes changed, getting it out in the open before the top Russians, so that any potential victim and his aides would be alerted and any plotters would cancel what they're planning or even stand exposed. Earnshaw's the only one who could do it."

"You've got to get to him right away!" exclaimed Doyle.

Hazel turned on Doyle. "Don't be silly, Jay. How can Matt possibly get to The Ex? The entire palace is sealed tight. They wouldn't allow Matt or any of us inside." She looked at Brennan. "Do you know anyone who might get word to him?"

"I thought of that, too. There's only Herb Neely, but I'm not sure even he'd dare—"

Hazel frowned. "If he won't help, well, I can't think of anyone else."

"I can," said Brennan. "As a last resort, there's me. No matter what you've said, it would be worth a try."

Hazel looked doubtful. "Not a chance, Matt, unless you know something about palace-breaking that we don't."

"Maybe I do," said Brennan.

"Then go ahead," Doyle begged him.

Brennan studied Doyle for a moment. "I can't, Jay, without your help."

"Anything!" Doyle pledged.

"You'll have to play Sydney Carton to my Darnay. I wasn't invited.

797

You were. I'd need your special press invitation. Is your photograph on it?"

"No." Doyle hesitated. "But if there's a big story and I'm not there, what'll I have? After all, Matt, you did promise me—well, Hazel and me—an exclusive on the beat. And if there's no story at all, I've still got to have something for my Earnshaw column."

"Jay, you ass, quit wasting time and give him your invitation," Hazel said impatiently. "I'll cover for both of us, no matter what gives out."

Doyle pulled the embossed invitation from his pocket. "And, Matt, you—you won't forget? If anything happens—"

"It's all yours," said Brennan. He took Hazel's arm. "Let's hurry."

"Hey, wait a minute," Doyle called out. "What am I supposed to do?"

"There's a restaurant right across the street from the parking lot," said Brennan. "Le Londres in the Rue Colbert. Wait for us there. Try their filet mignon Henri IV, and their escargots from Burgundy. That'll keep you busy."

Brennan and Hazel hastened toward the main gate. In a matter of seconds Hazel was passed through. Brennan tried to appear at ease while his invitation—Doyle's, rather—was checked. Two gate officials exchanged words in French, and Brennan stood by tautly. Finally one official smiled at Brennan. It turned out that he was an admirer of former President Earnshaw, and honored to meet Earnshaw's writing collaborator. He bowed Brennan toward the gate, and with an effort Brennan kept himself from running.

Catching up with Hazel, Brennan made a face. Together, the two of them strode across the cobblestoned esplanade known as the Avant-cour. They headed toward one of the two enormous jutting wings of the Versailles Palace, which were joined together by a setback central section.

There were photographers and correspondents at the entrance of the press tent erected beneath the columns of the left wing, and French workmen surrounded the caterer's delivery trucks alongside the right wing, as uniformed police officers patrolled the Cour de Marbre below the central building. Apparently everyone who was anyone, and everyone who was to guard or serve anyone personally, was inside the palace.

Nearing the press tent, Brennan caught Hazel's arm. "I'd rather not go in there, Hazel. I don't want to risk being recognized. But I would like to see Herb Neely, without too much company. I'd like to find out if I can get his help. That would solve everything. Do you think you can arrange it?"

Hazel nodded. "Still eighteen minutes before his briefing begins. He should have enough time."

"I wish I had as much. It's also eighteen minutes before they all get up from dinner in the Hall of Mirrors."

"I'd better tell Neely you're here."

"Wait, Hazel. Important. Tell Herb I'd like to say hello. Don't tell him any more. Not a word about the Russian demand that I be arrested or Quarolli and the French security. Not a word. If he's free to come outside, you come along with him, understand? I'll handle the Earnshaw part. But I'd rather you asked some questions I'd like to ask. They'll be less suspect coming from you."

"Like what?"

"Play it casual. You want some added color to beef up your feature. Are all the big shots in attendance upstairs? What's the seating arrangement in the Hall of Mirrors? What are the royal apartments like, the ones right behind the Hall, and what's going on inside them tonight? Who's in those rooms? How's the dinner being served? Above all, is the printed timetable still in effect? Where do the Chiefs go after dinner? Coffee, I know, but their route? And after that to the Opéra? The route? And after that?" He searched her face. "Have you got it?"

Her pointed nose wrinkled. "Brennan, you're really CIA, aren't you?"

"I'm Benedict Arnold who was cleared by your friend Rostov today."

"No kidding? Well, congratulations."

"Or condolences again, because I'll be back to Benedict Arnold if I foul up Russian-American relations tonight."

"Let me find Herb Neely."

Brennan watched her disappear into the press tent; then he turned and walked over the uneven cobblestones to the base of the weathered stone equestrian statue of King Louis XIV that stood in the middle of the Cour Royale. Rummaging through his pockets, he located a scrap of paper and his pencil. Placing the paper against the wide base of the statue, he began writing a note to Emmett Earnshaw. He had barely finished and signed it when he heard Neely bawl his name.

Hastily folding the note and shoving it into a trouser pocket, he turned in time to clasp Neely's hand. "Hi, Herb."

Neely, in his rimless glasses and dark suit, resembled the professorial curator of a small obscure museum. And Hazel, beside him, looked as pleased as if she had delivered the Sun King himself to Brennan.

"I couldn't believe it when Miss Smith told me you were outside," said Neely with delight. "What are you doing here, Matt? How'd you get in?"

"Jay Doyle came down with the flu and couldn't make it. He begged me to take his place. He's got to do Earnshaw's column. I don't know if I'll be much good at this."

Neely beamed. "I'm pleased, Matt. Of course, I'm afraid there's not much to see, probably less than you could see on the regular Sunday tour of the palace. It's a miracle they allowed the press in this far. The French consider an affair like this a *private* party. If the Élysée or the Quai d'Orsay invited you, you're in. Everyone else is out."

"No exceptions, Herb?"

"None. Strictly Presidents and Premiers and Chairmen, Secretaries of State, Ministers, Ambassadors, their wives, a couple of former Presidents—oh, like Earnshaw—and some French table dressing, a Duke of Broglie here, a Bourbon pretender to some throne or other there, a baron maybe, and that's it."

"What if someone had to get a message to one of those people?"

"You mean, like a coded government message that was urgent? I suppose we could get it delivered through Pierre Urbain, the French protocol head. He's available."

"No, Herb. I mean a personal message, strictly personal but also urgent." He paused. "Like—well, say I wanted to see Emmett Earnshaw."

"No chance."

"Herb, I *have* to see him."

Neely's eyes blinked behind his lenses. "Is that why you're here, Matt?"

"Yes."

"Surely whatever it is can wait until later?"

"I'm afraid not."

Neely was plainly distressed. "Matt, you know I'd give my life for you, do anything, but this is one thing I simply can't pull off. I'm an outsider tonight, a lower species. This affair is strictly French all the way, top-level, and it's all according to their protocol manual, probably prepared by Louis XIV. The palace is for royalty tonight. We're commoners."

Brennan nodded. He said, "Let me try it another way, Herb. I have a note in my pocket. One I wrote to Earnshaw. Can you get someone to slip it to him before he leaves the dinner table?"

"Impossible, Matt. I wouldn't even try it. I'm sorry, really sorry."

For an instant Brennan was tempted to reveal what he had un-covered, to convince Neely of the life-and-death importance of his message. But then he thought better of it. To involve a close friend in an international intrigue that he himself supposed existed, but which might not exist at all, would be to endanger his friend's entire career in government. To gamble with his own future was one thing. To ask another to gamble for him, at these stakes, was unfair. If use of friend-ship could be entered against his account—and he thought of Hazel, Medora, Doyle, Earnshaw—then he was already overdrawn.

From this point on, Brennan knew that he would have to go it alone.

He forced himself to smile, and laid an arm around Neely's shoul-ders. "Don't look so upset, old boy." He dropped his arm to his side and assumed a relaxed stance. "You know how I tend to get over-excited about what turn out to be inconsequential matters. This was something that—well, seemed critical to me, but I'm settling down, and I think you're right. I can discuss it with Earnshaw later, after these formalities are over."

Neely exhaled relief. "I'm glad, Matt. Because this is a real locked-up place for the next few hours."

Hazel stepped forward. "Don't leave yet, Mr. Neely. I still need a few minutes of your time. I'll be at your press briefing, but besides the wire story I have to do a long mailer on the whole affair. So I need a little extra." She'd brought pen and pad out of her purse. "Mind?"

Neely had removed a silver watch from his vest pocket. Now he returned it. "You can have five minutes extra."

"Did all the Names show up?" asked Hazel, her pen poised to write.

"Everyone. Not a single cancellation."

"And they're still eating?" asked Hazel.

"They're still at it, and will be for ten more minutes." He pointed to the top of the bright central building. "They're up there, two hundred of them."

"In the Hall of Mirrors? I've never seen it. What's it like?"

"Well, the upstairs floor runs the width of the palace, and it is split in half. On this side, the front, looking down at us, are what used to be the King's three major apartments. These rooms are backed smack up against the Hall of Mirrors. What can I tell you about the Hall? Nothing like it on earth. A sort of gallery that's 242 feet long. It has 306 big mirrors on one wall, and on the opposite side it has seventeen arched windows, and these give a view of 250 acres of gardens and

1,400 fountains. It took seven years and 35,000 laborers to lay out those gardens. And that's what those Chiefs of State are looking out on tonight."

"How are they seated?" asked Hazel.

"Well, there's one tremendous banquet table, with lots and lots of smaller ones on either side. The banquet table is decorated with candelabra and flower vases, and the Big Five are all seated in a row on one side with nobody seated opposite them. They sit on gilded Louis XVI chairs upholstered in a claret-colored brocade. There is the President of France in the center, with the Chinese Chairman and British Prime Minister on one side of him, and our President and the Russian Premier on the other side. Incidentally, Earnshaw's only about four or five seats away."

"And the food—where does the food come from, Mr. Neely?"

"Sa-ay, that's a good question. I ought to use it in the background briefing."

"Not on your life," said Hazel. "I asked it. I get to keep the answer."

"Well," said Neely, turning around and gesturing toward four trucks backed into a semicircle around two ordinary glass-paned doors, "you see those trucks? They brought in the food and the cases of wine, brandy, and so forth. There's another truck rolling in now. Guess they must be running out of drinks. Anyway, all that stuff is moved through a passage into a small enclosed but roofless courtyard called the Cour des Cerfs. A temporary roof has been thrown over it, and a kitchen installed for tonight's affair. Six chefs and two pastry cooks borrowed from the Élysée palace have been preparing the dinner. Then there are two portable staircases leading straight up to the Hall of Mirrors. Actually, the traffic is one-way. Workmen use one staircase to go up, and the other to come down."

"Herb, those stairs don't go right smack into the Hall of Mirrors, do they?" Brennan asked.

"Lord, no. The men carrying the food upstairs pass through several rooms to the King's Bedroom, where there's a big buffet, and all the trays, dishes, glassware. From there the maître d'hôtel directs the waiters out into the Hall of Mirrors."

"What happens after dinner?" Hazel wanted to know.

Neely turned back to her. "It's in your program, Miss Smith. At nine-thirty the toasts are finished, the dinner ended. Everyone waits for the leaders to leave. They just retire to the room behind them, the King's Council Chamber, for coffee, which the waiters are serving from the next-door King's Bedroom. Meanwhile, the rest of the guests go on

802

through the King's apartments, through the lobby of the Chapel, to the Opéra, to wait for the Big Five."

Listening, Brennan knew that he had everything he wanted. From his position in back of Neely, he signaled Hazel frantically, pointing a finger to his wristwatch.

Hazel did not seem to notice as she scribbled her notes for a half minute more, but then she glanced at her wristwatch and looked up innocently. "Mr. Neely, forgive me for interrupting, but do you know what time it is? Dinner is going to be over in eight minutes, and your briefing—"

Neely peered at his own heavy watch again. "By God, you're right." He whirled around. "Matt, I've got to run. What are you going to do now?"

"I think I'll just take off for Paris. I can use some sleep."

"Would you like to hear the briefing?"

"I'm too tired, Herb, but thanks. I'll go."

Neely was reluctant to part from him. "Matt, about the other matter, I'm awfully sorry. I'm sure you understand."

"Don't give it another thought. Talk to you tomorrow."

Neely left hurriedly, striding fast toward the press tent.

Hazel lingered a moment, eyeing Brennan. "Are you going back to Paris?"

"I'm going for broke, Hazel."

"Good luck."

She was gone, and he stood alone in the middle of the vast cobblestone courtyard.

From the other side of the equestrian statue he heard voices speaking in French.

"Continue straight ahead to the Queen's Staircase," a pure French voice was saying. "Show the guards your invitation. One of them will take you straight up to the Hall of Mirrors, Monsieur Novik."

"Thank you," said a Russian-accented voice.

Brennan peered around the base of the statue. The two men were parting. The slender French official was returning to the entrance gate. The corpulent figure of Igor Novik, of *Pravda,* was moving hastily toward the inner court and the doorway that would take him up into the Palace of Versailles.

With incredulity, Brennan watched the receding figure of Novik. A journalist going up to the sacrosanct state dinner, when Neely had insisted that no member of the press would be permitted inside the Hall of Mirrors tonight. Yet, there was Novik. And there was a possible explanation. A simple one, to wit: Novik was not a journalist after all.

Brennan knew that he could tarry no longer. If true explanations were to be found, they might be found only within the palace walls.

Quickly extracting the map of Versailles Palace once more, Brennan reviewed the markings, decided on the most logical one, and gazed past the statue at the delivery trucks backed up to the two service entrances.

He returned the map to his pocket, continuing to stare at the trucks.

The air was warm and humid, and perspiration covered his forehead. He found a handkerchief and mopped his face. It felt better, but it hadn't helped the mounting hammering inside his chest. Through narrow eyes he observed more than a dozen laborers lifting cartons and boxes, hoisting them to their shoulders, and weaving into the nearest service entrance. Then he saw two of them wiping their brows with their sleeves, saying something to one another, before quickly divesting themselves of their blue-gray laborers' jackets and throwing them alongside the end truck.

From where he stood, in the shadow of the King Louis XIV statue, Brennan scouted the immediate area. The closest police were gathered deep in the Marble Court, most of them beside the Queen's Staircase entrance, either swapping stories or listening to the organ music drifting down from above. Brennan doubted that he was clearly visible to them, or that they were any longer attentive to him.

It was a chance. He would have to take it.

He undid his tie, pulled it off, and stuffed it into his suit-coat pocket. He opened his collar. He removed his wallet, purposely dropped it and knelt to retrieve it, digging his knees hard into the cobblestones to soil them, and pushing both hands across the stones and the crevices between them. He smeared his grimy hands across his face and white shirt, picked up his wallet and shoved it into his back pocket. He rose slowly.

In a single motion he had divested himself of his coat. He folded it twice, glanced into the Marble Court once more, and, reassured, dropped his bundle at the base of the statue. He rolled up one shirt-sleeve, then the other.

The time. One final glimpse of the time. Six minutes.

He could hear his heartbeat, and hated its cowardly fear.

Swiftly, purposefully, he started across the cobblestones toward the end truck. The driver's cab was empty. He hastened alongside the large van, stopped at the discarded cotton workmen's jackets on the ground —there was a pile of them by now—and he snatched one up. He held it against him. Too small. He tried another. Too small. But the third one looked right. It was dirty, patched, but looked as if it would fit. He pulled it on. A size too large, but it would do, it would have to do.

He could hear the French workmen behind the truck, grunting, grumbling, coming, going.

The next step was, for Brennan, the longest of all. He must take it, before he lost his nerve, and he must behave as if he belonged here. He took the step.

Boldly he came around the truck, skirting the laborers still unloading it, and hustled into line behind three sweaty sturdy workmen. One bent down, lifted his wooden box, heaved it on his shoulder, and staggered toward the service doorway. The next one followed. And the next one. And it was Brennan's turn. He reached for the carton of cognac, took a good hold, praying for enough muscle and for every disc in his spine, and he lifted. It was heavy, but not as heavy as he had expected. He raised it higher and settled it on his right shoulder as others lined up behind him. He moved unsteadily to the doorway and went on through it.

Weighed down by his burden, Brennan stumbled along a dim passageway, entered a large empty hall, followed those ahead of him until he had crossed it. Another doorway, and he emerged into the covered courtyard, the Cour des Cerfs, a kitchen crowded with chefs and their assistants bustling and gesticulating among their ovens and cooking counters, half hidden by steam vapors.

Brennan's eyes smarted. The workmen who had preceded him were now slogging toward a steep wooden staircase. Balancing his cumbrous box of cognac, he plunged after them.

He began to ascend the staircase. His shoulder ached, his strained spine burned with pain, and his knees threatened to buckle. Higher and higher he climbed, driven upward by one obsession, that of reaching the Council Chamber and getting his scribbled warning to Earnshaw before it was too late.

The top of the staircase came into view, and at the same time, on either side of the landing above, a pair of tall, impassive, uniformed security police came into view, both scrutinizing each laborer and his cargo as he passed between them.

This was unexpected. Brennan tried to swallow, and failed. His mouth was parched and his lungs dry. He wondered if the DST alarm had gone out and if the police were on the lookout for him. He could only hope that they were posted routinely to examine every workman delivering refreshments to the second floor. He wondered if their shrewd eyes would instantly detect that he was not a workman at all.

There was a delay, and he wavered on the fifth step from the top,

805

feeling trapped. His brain sought an excuse, and sorted out one of an earlier fantasy. If he were detained, questioned, his American accent would give him away immediately. He would have to brazen it out. He would laugh, brandish his Embassy press pass, and reveal that he was only an impetuous, enterprising American journalist trying to get a jump on his colleagues by this effort to obtain an eyewitness, firsthand account of the fabulous state dinner from behind the scenes. If the security police had been conditioned by enough American films, they might laugh, too, and send him back downstairs. More likely, they would take a dim view of his alibi, and bully him off for interrogation, at which time his true identity would be revealed. A scandal would be unavoidable, and punishment inevitable. At least, he reminded himself wryly, the Bastille and the dank cells of Devil's Island were no more. But somehow, as he resumed climbing, the rationalization did not make him happier.

He attained the top of the stairs, distorting his features as if rebuking the burden on his shoulder, and he moved under full focus of the eyes of the French security police. They inspected him, their gaze lifted to his carton, their gaze dropped to those behind him climbing up from below.

Perspiring profusely, but breathing easier, Brennan resumed his march. He turned into the temporarily enclosed balcony behind the Cabinet du Conseil, tottered around a jog to the doorway where a fretful mustached Frenchman in dinner jacket impatiently directed him through the Cabinet du Conseil into the Chambre de Louis XIV.

Although Neely had explained that the King's Bedroom had been converted into a serving pantry for tonight, the sight Brennan beheld surprised him.

The last time he had visited this central state bedchamber had been on a tour when Ted was a boy. Its lonely splendor had made a deep impression. There had been an engraved gold balustrade, and in the alcove behind the low railing had stood the royal bed, its crimson canopy embroidered with 130 pounds of gold thread, and above it a vast classic mural. There had been paintings everywhere, and across the room a bust of the Sun King on the mantel over the fireplace.

But now the lonely room was a madhouse of humanity, with workmen streaming in to deposit their boxes, waiters and servants rushing in and out of the open paneled doors to the adjoining Cabinet du Conseil that provided the best entry to the Hall of Mirrors. All that remained of the past was the gold balustrade and the fireplace. The royal bed was gone. The mural was covered by a brocade drape bearing a design of golden columns. The bust of the Sun King had been removed. Throughout the bedroom were tables heaped with cheese trays, coffee makers, pastries, silverware, and china.

Brennan stood uncertainly with a group of other workmen, the carton of bottles still balanced on his right shoulder, waiting for instructions and considering what to do after he was freed of his burden. At once his attention, along with that of the others, was drawn to the squat, quick-tempered maître d'hôtel, who had come storming into the bedroom, coattails flapping furiously.

The maître d'hôtel was elbowing his way to the center of the room. With one hand at his mouth, he bawled out in French, "The champagne—where is the champagne and the cognac? There is only another minute. Who has the champagne and the cognac?" Brennan saw four or five workmen raise their hands, and he lifted his own tentatively.

The maître d'hôtel was advancing, scowling at the laborers. "All of you with the cognac and champagne"—he jerked a thumb over his shoulder—"into the Cabinet du Conseil with you, and make haste. But no noise, you hear? Silently, silently. Set down your boxes behind the screen next to the Treaty desk."

He examined the crew hastily. He poked a finger at the sinewy short Frenchman beside Brennan, then at Brennan himself. "You two, you look half respectable, not like complete pigs. You two stay behind the screen in there and unpack the bottles. Take care. No noise. Unpack the bottles, dust them off, set them on the table next to the stemware. Then leave, come right back in here. But silently. If the Chiefs of State enter the chamber before you are finished, cease work at once, fall back out of sight at once, against the wall, behind the screen, and no sound from you. Now hurry!"

Brennan hastened after his partner and the other three workmen.

As he trudged through the doorway into the Council Chamber, he could hear the maître d'hôtel giving more commands. "You—you waiters—what are you doing here? No dawdling. Only a minute before the President and Chiefs appear for their coffee and drinks. Back into the Cabinet du Conseil. And caution. When the doors from the Galerie des Glaces open fully, you will stand stiffly and respectfully at attention in the rows with the other waiters. Once the President and leaders and their aides are inside, you will attend to your duties as instructed. Off with you. Swiftly!"

Carrying his carton of cognac, Brennan returned to the Cabinet du Conseil. Here there was order and quiet. Before the three windows that looked down on the marble courtyard, two dozen waiters in black ties and tailcoats stood at rigid attention, facing the mirror and rococo clock over the fireplace and the doors to the Hall of Mirrors.

Brennan passed before the waiters toward the long table of brilliant Lalique glassware and gleaming bottles of liqueurs, brandies, champagne. A few feet from it, a lavishly decorated screen partially hid the blue velvet rope that guarded the Versailles Treaty desk, a Louis XV mahogany desk inlaid with brown leather, resting on feet shaped like bronze claws.

Brennan waited nervously while the three workmen ahead lowered their cartons behind the screen and quickly departed. Then, with his shorter companion, Brennan moved behind the screen. While his companion, kneeling, opened the cartons and handed up the bottles, Brennan took a linen cloth and dusted them and placed them carefully on the table. He tried to read his wristwatch, and as best he could make out, it was nine thirty-five.

His eyes hypnotized by the doors across the chamber, he was conscious that more waiters were scrambling into position to his left. He could feel the warning note addressed to Earnshaw in his trouser pocket, and he was confident that he could manage its delivery. The honored guests would soon come in for their after-dinner drinks. They would circulate, talk. And if Earnshaw was among them, Brennan would start to return to the adjacent royal bedroom, bump into Earnshaw, and slip the note into his hand.

The wait was unbearable. Tension gripped him, closed on him like an Iron Maiden. His breathing had become an audible rasp.

Suddenly the opposite doors were flung open, and two bewigged servants, in the costumes of eighteenth-century courtiers, held them back.

Brennan stood stone-still.

A rectangle of the Hall of Mirrors was exposed to his view. The backs of the world's leaders, a Premier, a Prime Minister, a President, a Chairman, a President, their coattails dropping down the sides of their gilt chairs, were visible. The table itself, pyramids of lights, low vases spilling out bright flowers, sparkling dinner service, glass reflecting the grandeur of the painted ceiling. And beyond, niches between the windows bearing antique statues, candelabra with bulbs flickering like candles, distant fountains dancing to light.

The President of France, heir to the Sun King's glory, was rising, nodding to the British Prime Minister and to Chairman Kuo Shu-tung, of China, who were also rising. The American President and Premier Talansky, of the Soviet Union, were coming to their feet, Talansky signaling someone out of sight, beckoning for that person to join him.

Instantly the entrance to the Council Chamber was filled with French security police, followed by the personal bodyguards, Chinese,

British, Russian, American, of the Chiefs of State, all of them blocking their leaders from sight.

Mesmerized by the scene, Brennan felt a tug at his sleeve. The laborer kneeling beside him was trying to give him another bottle. Brennan rejected it with a gesture, pointed off, and brought his finger to his lips. The laborer nodded, and froze.

Brennan jerked his head back toward the entrance, to find the police and bodyguards forming two lines with a center path for their leaders to enter through. And then Brennan gasped and recoiled.

Nikolai Rostov had come quickly past the guards, into the salon, and taken a place at one end of the line.

Immediately Brennan dropped his head low and stepped sideways, so that he was partially shielded by the screen. From under his eyebrows he looked up again.

The President of France, austere, grave, engaged in conversation with Chairman Kuo Shu-tung and the British Prime Minister, was entering the Council Chamber. He gestured toward the fireplace, and led his companions there to continue the conversation.

Suddenly Brennan's eyes widened.

Another familiar figure, dumpy, grinning, a hobgoblin, had entered the room. Ma Ming, one hand thrust in his trouser pocket, was making his way, as unobtrusively as possible, in the direction of the fireplace. Slowly he sidled up behind Chairman Kuo Shu-tung and came to a cautious halt.

Bewildered and suspicious, Brennan shifted his attention from Ma Ming to Nikolai Rostov, who was anxiously staring at the empty doorway, and then to the doorway itself, that moment filled by robust swaggering Premier Talansky, his arms linked through the arms of the American President on one side of him and Emmett Earnshaw on the other side.

The Russian Premier was tipsy and jovial. As he led the American President and Earnshaw across the room, the President half smiling, Earnshaw grinning, Talansky's resonant voice boomed out: "I repeat my toast, my dear friends. From the Summit we shall proclaim our skies open to all, our cities, our countryside open, and together we sentence to death the nuclear Lucifer! Come, tonight we drink to international friendship and peace on this earth forever!"

Premier Talansky released the President and Earnshaw from his hold, continuing with them toward the screen, as his hands beat time to the amplified music dinning into the room.

Premier Talansky slapped his thighs. "We drink to that toast once more!"

From the corner of his eye Brennan saw an arm raised on high. It belonged to the maître d'hôtel, signaling his staff to begin serving. Immediately the rows of waiters broke out of their lines, going in every direction to dispense refreshments. And immediately, as Brennan turned his attention back to Premier Talansky, he became aware of another oscillating arm rising behind Talansky. And that arm, Brennan could see, belonged to Nikolai Rostov.

Brennan went up high on his toes. Rostov was signaling someone near the windows.

Brennan's head spun in that direction.

Waiters in black ties and tailcoats, and suddenly, a waiter shorter, stranger than the others, yet as familiar as an apparition spawned by a half-remembered nightmare. The plastered chestnut hair, the thin, sallow, pimpled face, the tailcoat hanging loose on the small, wiry body.

Joe Peet.

Joe Peet, his face drawn tight as a rubber mask, carrying an empty tray in front of him, was advancing quickly behind Premier Talansky, Earnshaw, and the American President.

Hypnotized, Brennan watched Peet's progress.

Ten feet from the trio, Peet abruptly halted. His left hand dropped the tray down to his side to reveal a black Luger clutched in his right fist.

Slowly Peet lifted the long-barreled automatic pistol, aiming it at Premier Talansky's back—and that instant Brennan slammed wildly at the screen, shouting, "Talansky! Look out!"

Frightened, Peet turned his head toward the outcry and the racket of the toppling screen. As Talansky wheeled around, Peet's shocked face went back to his target, and his trembling fist brought the pistol up fast. Brennan lunged forward, charging, throwing himself at the assassin, smashing into him full force as the Luger exploded once, twice, loud as a cannonade.

Brennan hit the floor hard, eyes blinded, ears deafened by the reverberation from the gunfire. He felt the abrasive rip of a shoe across his cheek and tried to open his eyes. Only Joe Peet was in his vision, Peet weaponless, Peet crawling, Peet trying to scramble to his feet to make his escape toward the door. And then another figure came into Brennan's dazed view. Rostov. Nikolai Rostov, frenzied, screaming, "Stop the assassin! Kill the assassin!"

Peet staggered to his feet, panting, panting, and KGB agents, three of them, and French security police, a half dozen, were beside Rostov. Three guns flashed and thundered, and as they discharged, Peet squealed, "No—no—no!" Then, clutching his stomach, he slowly folded into a courtly bow and pitched forward into a heap, his blood oozing into the carpet.

Sitting up, Brennan saw that Ma Ming, revolver in one pudgy fist, had violently knocked Chairman Shu-tung to the floor. Elsewhere, from every corner, the occupants of the salon, immobilized by the horror of those seconds, were coming to life. They began to race toward Peet, toward Premier Talansky, who was clawing at his shoulder as Earnshaw and others propped him upright.

And then Brennan heard a burbling sound and turned his head, and incredibly the sound had come from Joe Peet. Somehow Peet had rolled over on his back and was trying to lift his head, trying to find someone, his glazed eyes searching the gathering semicircle of faces.

With effort he lifted a feeble hand and pointed to Nikolai Rostov. "Goddam—goddam—goddam you—you an' Zabbin—you promised me—you cheated—you promised—" He spat blood, and tried to go on.

Aghast, Rostov had gone white. He grabbed at a KGB agent and tried to push him forward, commanding, "Get rid of the assassin!"

Obediently, the KGB agent had raised his revolver, and Brennan, leaping to his feet, started to cry out "No" when someone beside him bellowed, *"Nyet!* Wait!" It was Premier Talansky, supported by the President of France and Earnshaw.

"Let him speak!" roared Talansky. The KGB agent lowered and quickly holstered his revolver.

From the floor, Peet groaned and weakly shook his fist at Rostov. "Goddam—damn you—Rostov—Zabbin—promised to help me— promised Ludmilla—if I—I—but you didn't protect me—you murdered, you murderer—" He was sobbing as blood trickled down his chin. He whined, "I don' wanna—don' wanna die." His hand dropped to his reddened shirt, his head fell back, his eyes closed.

Brennan looked at Premier Talansky and saw that Talansky was staring at Rostov.

"Arrest him, arrest Minister Rostov." The Premier's voice was low and harsh. "And Marshal Zabbin—put him under arrest this minute." He glanced up at the French President. "Your police with mine will arrest. I do not know which of ours to trust, but I *will* know, I will know soon enough."

Physicians, followed by a pair of stretcher-bearers, were pushing through the crowd. They came directly to Premier Talansky.

"You must go with them to the Escalier de la Reine," the French President was saying to Talansky. "We have there the first-aid station."

Angrily Premier Talansky brushed the physicians aside. "Later for me. It is my shoulder, nothing more. It is superficial, and I am an ox." He pointed down at Peet's body. "That one. Take him. Make him live. I must know everything, if we all are to live."

As the stretcher-bearers moved speedily toward Peet, Premier Talansky glanced around, and his eyes rested on Earnshaw. "Where is the one who saved me?" he demanded.

Brennan saw that Earnshaw was reaching for him, and he came forward. "Premier Talansky, this is Matthew Brennan," said Earnshaw. "He is an American. He is the one who saved you."

"I thank you, comrade," said Premier Talansky gruffly. Then he offered a crooked grin. "Not for saving my old carcass. But for saving the Summit. Now our children will have children, and for them I will thank you, too."

As he started to stumble away, agreeing at last to visit the first-aid station, Earnshaw stayed behind.

"Better hang around, Matt," he said. "They'll want to interrogate you. You'll have to tell the whole story." He smiled. "Shouldn't be hard, when it was your own story from the start."

Briefly Brennan watched Earnshaw hurry after the Russian Premier and the others, and then he turned back, and his eyes sought the one who had brought him on his long journey and to this place.

But Nikolai Rostov was no more.

The plot was ended. At least, for now.

Paris.

A quarter of an hour before midnight. The City of Light darkening, cooling, resting, before another dawn, a new sun.

Fifteen minutes yet of this Sunday, fifteen minutes of this day still alive.

Hazel Smith.

Hair in disarray, blouse half out of her skirt, she sat hunched over her Underwood standard typewriter, fingers flying over the keyboard.

Around her desk, in the main editorial room of the Paris bureau of Atlas News Association high above the Rue de Berri, members of the nightside staff, reinforced by the day staff, whispered, dictated, discussed the art work, moved silently. Nearby, the teletype machines hammered steadily. And undistracted, Hazel continued to write the big beat for Jay Doyle, the exclusive, the definitive, the inside story, replete with hero, villains, intrigue, suspense, all of it factual. There would be 2,500 words of it, and the hungry teletypes in the next office were waiting to consume it and spew it out in New York, and from there to every major capital of the world as well as to every subscribing newspaper in America.

Coolly, objectively, swiftly, she wrote. Like the machine under her fingers, she too was a machine. This was the big one, for Doyle (for both of them); this was fame, honors, praise, bonuses. Only once had she faltered, two thirds of the way through, when she had typed out Rostov's probable fate. But then she had gone on, again a machine, like the typewriter on the desk, like the clock on the wall, whipping the typewriter, racing the clock.

She hit the period key, punched in the black dot after the second to last paragraph. One more paragraph remained.

She stopped, reached for the glass of water, drank from it, and as she set down the glass, her gaze fell on the pile of wire reports already filed. She peeled them off, one after the other, rereading the bulletins hastily:

ANA A3N FLASH PARIS, JUNE 22 (ANA)--ASSASSIN FIRED TWO SHOTS AT RUSSIAN PREMIER TALANSKY IN VERSAILLES.

ANA A4N FLASH--PREMIER TALANSKY ONLY SUPER-FICIALLY WOUNDED. ASSASSIN YOUNG AMERICAN WAR VETERAN JOSEPH PEET WHO WAS INSTANTLY SHOT DOWN BY KGB ALSO VERSAILLES PALACE SECURITY GUARDS.

ANA A5N FLASH--ASSASSIN PEET'S WOUNDS POSSIBLY FATAL BUT HE IS STILL ALIVE.

ANA A6N BULLETIN--ASSASSIN JOSEPH PEET CONFESSED TO FRENCH SECURITY POLICE AND PREMIER TALANSKY HE WAS EMPLOYED BY RUSSIAN CONSPIRACY GROUP TO KILL PREMIER TALANSKY WHO FAVORED DEMOCRACIES AND BY THIS ACT PAVE WAY FOR MARSHAL ZABBIN AND CONSPIRA-TORS TO TAKE OVER SOVIET GOVERNMENT. ZABBIN'S PLAN WAS TO POSTPONE SUMMIT INDEFINITELY AND GRADUALLY REVIVE INTERNATIONAL COMMUNIST ALLIANCE WITH RED CHINA AS RUSSIA'S MAJOR NUCLEAR ALLY. IN RETURN FOR ASSASSINATION, JOSEPH PEET WAS PROMISED SAFETY THROUGH PRETENDED ARREST BY CONSPIRATORS AND LATER PARDON AND RELEASE INSIDE USSR WHERE HE DESIRED TO BE CITIZEN AND WED A RUSSIAN GIRL FRIEND.

ANA A7N FLASH--ASSASSIN JOSEPH PEET DIED OF GUN-SHOT WOUNDS AT 10:04 PARIS TIME REPEAT PARIS TIME.

ANA A8N BULLETIN--FORMER PRESIDENT EMMETT EARN-SHAW AND PREMIER TALANSKY JOINTLY ANNOUNCED THAT THE ASSASSINATION ATTEMPT WAS THWARTED AND TAL-ANSKY'S LIFE SAVED BY A FORMER AMERICAN DIPLOMAT MATTHEW BRENNAN REPEAT MATTHEW BRENNAN.

ANA A9N BULLETIN ADD--BRENNAN WAS STATE DEPART-MENT DISARMAMENT EXPERT WHO WAS CENTER OF ZURICH PARLEY SCANDAL FOUR YEARS AGO WHEN PROFESSOR ARTHUR VARNEY DEFECTED TO CHINA. DESPITE PROTEST-ING INNOCENCE, BRENNAN WAS CONDEMNED BY DEXTER CONGRESSIONAL COMMITTEE, DECLARED SECURITY RISK, FORCED TO RESIGN. BRENNAN HAS BEEN LIVING ABROAD SINCE, RECENTLY IN VENICE, ITALY. HE CAME TO PARIS WHEN SUMMIT CONVENED HOPING TO CLEAR HIS NAME THROUGH MARSHAL ZABBIN'S PROTEGE, NIKOLAI ROSTOV, ASSISTANT SOVIET MINISTER FOR FAR EASTERN AFFAIRS. ROSTOV WAS SAID TO BE ONE OF THE CONSPIRATORS.

ANA A10N BULLETIN MATTER--PREMIER TALANSKY AN-NOUNCED IN VERSAILLES PALACE THAT MAIN PLOTTERS WERE ZABBIN AND ROSTOV, THE LATTER INDOCTRINATED TO SUPPORT WORLD REVOLUTION DURING EXILE IN SI-BERIA. PREMIER ANNOUNCED THAT ZABBIN, ROSTOV, FOUR OTHER UNNAMED CONSPIRATORS HAVE BEEN ARRESTED AND ARE BEING FLOWN TO MOSCOW TONIGHT TO STAND TRIAL. PREMIER SAID OTHER ARRESTS ARE IMMINENT.

ANA A11N BULLETIN MATTER--CHAIRMAN KUO SHU-TUNG OF PEOPLE'S REPUBLIC OF CHINA TOLD PRESS HE HAS HEARD ROSTOV IS CONFESSING DETAILS OF PLOT THAT MAY IMPLICATE HIGH LEVEL CHINESE WHO WERE INVOLVED IN A SIMILAR CONSPIRACY TO OVERTHROW CHINA'S PEACE LEADERSHIP. CHAIRMAN KUO ADMITTED THAT MARSHAL CHEN IS BEING HELD AND INTERROGATED. CHINESE CHAIRMAN HINTED HE WOULD MAKE A FORMAL STATEMENT TOMORROW.

ANA A12N URGENT--LEAVING THE PALACE OF VER-SAILLES, THE PRESIDENT OF FRANCE TOLD THE AS-SEMBLED PRESS THAT HE HAD CONSULTED WITH THE OTHER FOUR CHIEFS OF STATE AND THEY HAD AGREED THAT THE SUMMIT TALKS WOULD BE RESUMED TOMORROW AND PRESSED TO A SUCCESSFUL CONCLUSION.

ANA A13N BULLETIN FIRST LEAD CONFERENCE ASSASSI-NATION PARIS, JUNE 22 (ANA)--RUSSIAN PREMIER ALEX-ANDER TALANSKY SURVIVED AN ASSASSINATION ATTEMPT BY A DEFECTING AMERICAN WAR VETERAN WHO PERFORMED AS GUNMAN FOR A SECRET GROUP OF MILITANT SOVIET

CONSPIRATORS. AS THE PREMIER LEFT THE STATE DIN-
NER IN THE HALL OF MIRRORS AND ENTERED THE GILDED
ROYAL SALON NEXT TO IT, HE WAS ATTACKED . . .

Conscious of the clock on the wall again, Hazel Smith ceased scanning the wire reports and threw them on the desk. She returned her attention to the sheet of paper in her typewriter, and then she smiled. The abbreviated wire reports were the barest bones of the plot and its hero. What she was writing for Doyle, and would file in minutes, was the pulsating mind and heart and flesh of the conspiracy. No other correspondent on the scene, or anywhere, possessed the information that she had poured into her dramatic news story. Not even the security agencies of the various powers possessed as well-rounded a picture as yet. She was reminded of her interview with Superintendent Quarolli of the French Services de la Sécurité Présidentielle over a week ago, when he had stated, "We know of *every* foreigner in Paris at this time," and he had demonstrated it. Yet tonight's events had proved him wrong, for when Peet materialized in the Palace of Versailles, it had been Brennan and not Quarolli or any DST agent who had thwarted the assassin. Quarolli had not known as much as Brennan, or as much as she herself had known all along and knew this very moment. Generously, she forgave the Frenchman for his arrogance. Undoubtedly he had known of everyone who had arrived in Paris, when they had arrived, but he had been unable to follow through on everyone. He had made choices, and they had not been the correct ones.

No matter. In the morning he would read the complete story. It was on paper now, almost all of it, not a fact missing. From Doyle she had every facet of Matt Brennan's incredible detective job. From Brennan himself she had the eyewitness report of the attempt on Talansky's life, of Peet's confession, of Peet's slaying. From Earnshaw, who had been present, she had summaries of the confessions made by Rostov and Marshal Chen, as yet unannounced. From her own painful memories, she had—well, she had all else that was to be known of Nikolai Rostov.

No exclusive beat in her recollection had ever been more exclusive.

One paragraph would finish it off. She bent over the typewriter, resumed her pecking, completed the final paragraph, typed in the "—30—" and it was done.

She stared at the last page. Jay Thomas Doyle's manhood, by way of Hazel Smith. An engagement present, to him from her.

The minute hand on the wall clock jumped, and she acknowledged it apologetically. There was no more time to lose. She had refused to file her copy in short takes, and she knew that the teletype puncher on the outgoing machine was in a frenzy. She tore the last page from her machine, placed it behind the other pages, and picked up a heavy black pencil. If Doyle, who was still nosing about Versailles, called in with any more material, she would gaily tell him that they had quite enough, that the story was off and winging.

Holding the pencil, she swiveled to the cleared section of her desk, placed the story in front of her, and beamed down at the first line. It was the by-line. It proclaimed: "By Jay Thomas Doyle."

Wielding her sharp pencil, she began to proof the news story. Reading with an expert eye, she made minor changes, a paragraph mark here, a deletion there, a comma here, a more colorful word there.

She reread the sensational scoop as if she had never seen it before. It was all on paper, all of it, angled from Matthew Brennan's point of view as the protagonist. The wire reports had already trumpeted the assassination attempt, but had given sparse information on the incredible story behind it, and that part of the story, the better part, was Brennan's own. What was fascinating to Hazel personally was how closely the facts confirmed Brennan's earlier conjectures. But even more fascinating were the answers to the many questions about seemingly unrelated mysteries that Brennan had posed the entire week.

The plot had had its beginnings, of course, in Vienna during 1961, and the target had indeed been Khrushchev. It had been instigated by Marshal Zabbin who, as a youth, had known Mao Tse-tung after the Long March, and who had grown up to believe that the goal of Lenin and Stalin—world Communism—could be achieved only by a confederation of Communist nations, principally of Russia and China. Such an accord alone, Zabbin thought, could guarantee peace. When Khrushchev had become a revisionist, weakened by the siren songs of the Western imperialists, and had turned Russia away from China and toward the democracies, Zabbin had initiated the plan to liquidate him. This end had been accomplished without violence; but disappointingly, the Premiers who had followed Khrushchev had been no better. Zabbin had determined that the last of these betrayers of the international Communist dream would be Premier Talansky, and Zabbin had continued to build and expand his hard-core underground and develop his conspiracy. Meanwhile, in China itself, Zabbin had found a young man with a large following who was of one mind with him. Marshal Chen had been a secret Maoist, even though pretending to support the moderate Premier Kuo Shu-tung, who had deviated from Mao's ideas and had become conciliatory toward the West, believing that China's domestic prosperity and survival in a nuclear age depended upon membership in a world community of nations and not in a Communist club.

Recently an agreement had been reached. Zabbin would arrange to have Premier Talansky deposed, and would himself take over the leadership of the Soviet Union. And in Peking, Marshal Chen, backed by a friendly Moscow, would gradually ease out Premier Kuo Shu-tung, and take over the government of Communist China.

A plot so grandiose had required not only plotters but performers.

Zabbin had kept his eye on many candidates, and when an accident of history had played into his hands, he had his right-hand man. Although Nikolai Rostov, an intellectual and China specialist, had been in the opposition camp, working against bilateral agreements with China and working for a union with the democracies, the defection of Varney at the Zurich Parley had changed all that. For after Zurich, Rostov had been suspected of being a traitor. Indeed, he had been riddled with guilts about his role. Zabbin had seen him as a ripe possibility. Zabbin had saved Rostov's life, and got him off to exile in Siberia. There Zabbin had arranged for Rostov to live among other political exiles, all of them Zabbin men, all of them part of the long-range conspiracy. And there, feeling guilty and bitter about the events at Zurich, grateful to Zabbin and resentful of Talansky, Rostov had been susceptible when they tried the next step. He had been "politically re-educated."

With the approach of the crucial Five-Power Summit Conference in Paris, Premier Talansky had become concerned that Soviet Russia, long isolated from China, possessed few advisers who understood the Chinese. Zabbin had volunteered Rostov's name, emphasized the fact that the real culprit at Zurich had been Brennan, pointed out Rostov's good record while in exile, and personally vouched for Rostov's loyalty and ability. And so, overnight, Rostov had been returned to the Kremlin and the central government. He had been a China expert still. But with a difference. He had become pro-Chinese, a collaborationist, a conspirator. And in him the Zabbinists had, at last, the architect of the assassination.

Premier Talansky must be dispatched, Zabbin believed and Rostov agreed, by a murderer who was not Russian or Communist, but a foreigner. A hundred names had been screened. Rostov had kept coming back to one, an unknown American, Joseph Peet, who had inundated Soviet Embassies with his pleas to be allowed to defect from the United States and seek asylum and citizenship inside the Soviet Union. Peet's background had been investigated by the KGB, and he had twice been discreetly interviewed by a Russian delegate to the

United Nations. It had been evident that Peet would do anything to be allowed back inside Russia to marry—and sleep with—his Ludmilla. It was Peet's primitive motive that had convinced Rostov that he had his assassin. Sexual desire, Rostov had counseled Zabbin, was a more powerful force than political idealism.

Peet had been quietly brought to Paris. From the beginning, the conspirators had led Peet to believe that it was Premier Talansky alone who opposed Peet's entry into Russia. Constantly the conspirators had inflamed Peet's hatred of Talansky until his passion to eliminate the one obstacle between Ludmilla and himself had become as intense as the conspirators' desire to eliminate the one obstacle preventing an accord between Red China and themselves.

Once in Paris, Peet had picked up his expense money and a list of contacts at the Communist-owned bookshop in the Rue de Seine. To avoid any suspicion of him by the French DST or any other foreign security force, Peet had not been permitted to associate openly with Russians or Chinese. However, when he had proved unstable in his relationship with women, he had finally been assigned a part-time KGB guard.

Rostov's design for the climax of the plot had been simple. The Premier would be assassinated at one of three sites where he had been scheduled to appear—the Hôtel de Lauzun, the Maisons-Laffitte racetrack, or the Hall of Mirrors in Versailles Palace—and Rostov had pledged protection to Peet after the killing, promising him a safe arrest and his release once he was flown to Russia. However, it had been privately agreed by the conspirators that Peet would have to be liquidated moments after the Premier's death.

The post-assassination activities had also been planned with care. Zabbin would go before the delegates at the Palais Rose and accuse the United States of having hired a Chicago gunman to kill Russia's beloved Premier. This, of course, would be for Soviet home consumption, disseminated by a minor player, the journalist Novik, to build acceptance of Zabbin's new policy in the Soviet Union and create distrust of the United States as an ally. When the Americans had refuted Zabbin's charges, had proved that Peet had been a psychotic acting on his own, the Soviets would then insist that the anti-Communist climate in the United States had produced such an assassin. Zabbin would demand a dissolution and postponement of the Summit.

In the year to follow, Zabbin would solidify his leadership of Russia, quietly continue to reinforce the Russian alliance with Red China, although publicly he would pay lip service to nuclear disarmament, to

818

an international community of nations, to another Summit. And during this time, Premier Kuo Shu-tung would fall ill, Marshal Chen would succeed him, while foreign trade and investments would continue to be encouraged. At the right moment China would expel all non-Communist foreigners and nationalize foreign factories, including the Nuclear Peace City, which would be converted into a wartime plant.

And together, Zabbin and Chen would reject future Summits with the imperialist West, stage their own tremendous convention of Communist powers, and create the Fourth Communist International, thus reviving Lenin's Comintern dedicated to resolving the class struggle through world revolution. And thereafter, the world would not know peace again, except when the Comintern had triumphed.

This was the plot, and this was the plan, that a dispossessed and disgraced former American diplomat, Matthew Brennan, had stumbled upon, understood, pursued; and at personal risk (Rostov had confessed that twice the KGB had tried to kill Brennan, and once arranged to have him arrested) this was the plot Brennan had thwarted.

The former American President, Emmett A. Earnshaw, had presented evidence clearing Brennan of earlier treason accusations, and the incumbent President had announced that Brennan would be cited at the White House for his patriotism and bravery.

Premier Talansky had indicated that Zabbin would be put on trial for his life, and that extenuating circumstances—the drills in revolutionary Marxism to which he was forced to submit, the turning state's evidence—would be considered in determining Rostov's sentence, which might be limited to twenty years in a Soviet labor camp.

Chairman Kuo Shu-tung, in private, had revealed to Brennan that the chief of Hai Wai Tiao Cha Pu, China's secret intelligence *apparat,* was none other than the affable Ma Ming, who had used his role of foreign correspondent as a cover. From his Russian counterparts Ma Ming had learned of Brennan's suspicions, and after meetings with a French physicist and Brennan himself, after observing Marshal Chen's behavior during the meeting with Earnshaw and young Goerlitz, Ma Ming had begun to follow some of Brennan's leads and even to shadow Brennan. This afternoon Ma Ming's suspicions had been as grave as Brennan's own. There had been one difference. Ma Ming had anticipated that any attempted assassination would be directed against Chairman Kuo rather than Talansky, and Ma Ming had come to the Hall of Mirrors prepared to cope with that eventuality.

Following this disclosure to Brennan, Chairman Kuo Shu-tung, again in private, had made an impassioned address to the other four Chiefs of State. He had assured them that Marshal Chen would be dealt with mercilessly, that other pro-Maoist conspirators inside Peking, Canton, Nanking, and Shanghai would be arrested and tried. And then he had concluded by saying that the People's Republic of China, led by moderates and men of goodwill, would continue its participation in the Summit and not falter in its determination to be a signatory to a disarmament pact that would guarantee tranquillity within its own frontiers and permanent peace throughout the world.

Hazel Smith had finished her proofreading, and that was the sum of the story she had written, facts as yet unknown to the world.

But in hours, the truth would girdle the globe, be read in newspapers, heard on radios and television sets in every city of the United States from New York and Washington to San Francisco and Los Angeles, and in every city of the world from London to Moscow to Rome to Cairo to Bombay to Peking to Tokyo.

And wherever men read it or heard it, they would know the name of truth's author—Jay Thomas Doyle.

Straightening her pages, Hazel suddenly felt chilled. A satanic thought had entered her mind, and it would not leave.

She examined the by-line on the first page: "By Jay Thomas Doyle."

She remembered what she had tried to repress but had never forgotten. A time in New York, so long ago. Doyle to her: *Hazel, listen, we can't go on like this. It's for your sake, too, believe me.* A time in Vienna, so long ago. Doyle to her: *Well, listen to me, baby—no, thanks, I'm not buying, not that way. So why don't we call it quits, and thanks for the memory.*

The arrogant bastard.

In that long ago, his by-line and fame had been awesome, and he had been bloated by fame not food, a fathead not a fat belly, and she had been a convenience, one small trophy of his success.

Doyle was one of those people who, when they were self-sufficient, when they needed no one, were at their worst. He had loved her here and now, not because he had grown up, gained maturity, but because he desperately needed someone, not as a mere physical convenience but as a permanent crutch-companion to sustain him emotionally. But this story, this by-line, would restore him to fatheadedness and self-sufficiency. And she would be—what? A middle-aged biddy with hennaed hair, my old friend Hazel, friend, not companion and wife. He would be too busy with the young ones, the celebrity collectors, the name-fornicators, and their warm flatteries and hot beds.

She had given up half her life, and Rostov as well, for this.

Impossible. She had wanted insurance. She had paid the premiums. She would not be deprived of the payoff.

She stared at his hateful by-line.

What if she did it? She could blame it on a mistake in the Paris bureau, in the transmission, in the New York office. She could get the Manhattan office to support her. And after that, after a personal talk with the executives in New York, she could wangle a solid job for him, a weekly "Inside and Straight," a gourmet column, something he could do when he traveled with her.

She hated it, hated what it would do to him, yet he would only be once more as he had been all the past week, a little ruined, slightly pitiful, and oh so nice. Above all, he would be her own.

Should she?

Her last doubt had disappeared.

Quickly she separated the first page from the rest and ran it into her typewriter. Quickly she began tapping the X-key, and it sounded like machine-gun fire. One moment there had been:

By Jay Thomas Doyle

The next moment there was:

KXXXXXXTXXXXXXXXXXXXX

And now, above his X'd-out by-line, she typed:

By Hazel Smith

She jumped from her swivel chair before she could have second thoughts. She hurried into the next office. The puncher was waiting impatiently at his outgoing machine. She withheld the story one last moment.

"How are you handling it? Continental wire? London retransmitting to New York?"

"For this one? God, no! New York ordered all systems tied into us for the balance. It's going out on every circuit simultaneously to every machine in existence."

"Great." Hazel looked down at the pages in her hand.

In seconds, the glass windows of ANA machines around the world would reflect the clatter of the Paris puncher's keys.

URGENT NIGHT LEAD CONFERENCE ASSASSINATION BY HAZEL SMITH ANA STAFF CORRESPONDENT.

"Great," she repeated. She handed the teletype puncher her story. "Here it is. You can file now."

And then, picking up her coat, she walked out of the bureau office, not happy, not sad, simply solved. She must get back to the apartment before he returned from Versailles. He would be famished and weary, and he would appreciate a hot meal and a warm bed.

E MMETT A. EARNSHAW.

There had been three consecutive telephone calls in the last half hour, and tired as he was, Earnshaw had welcomed and enjoyed each one. The first had been from Medora Hart, to tell him her entry permit to England had arrived and to thank him. The second had been from *Herr Direktor* Schlager to report that he had already heard from Chairman Kuo Shu-tung that China would go ahead with the Nuclear Peace City on any terms, and that Schlager and Willi had agreed that now it *would* be a Peace City and therefore it could be constructed safely inside China. The third call had been from the President of the United States.

After five minutes, Earnshaw was still listening to the President. Seated on his sofa in the Hotel Lancaster, Earnshaw sipped his brandy, and realizing the President had finished repeating his offer, he set the brandy down and held the telephone closer.

"Thank you, thank you very much for those kind words and your generous offer, Mr. President," Earnshaw said. "But I must stick to my first decision. I must say again, I cannot accept. If I should change my mind in the near future, I'll let you know. Good night, Mr. President."

During the last, he had heard the outside door open and close, and he guessed it was Carol. Some friend had called up from the lobby and asked her to come downstairs, and she had gone. Now she was back, bright and cheerful as ever, and carrying a ream-sized stationery box she had probably acquired from the concierge.

"Another call," he said to Carol. "Guess who. The President himself. All graciousness and fawning. He offered me the Supreme Court appointment. Finally."

"Did you take it?" asked Carol eagerly.

"No, Carol, I did not. I think I'd always intended to accept it, if the appointment was offered, but that was before the Summit. A good deal has happened since. I've made up my mind I've got too many important things to do for the party, the people, that I didn't do when I had the chance. And God willing, I'd like to do them soon. But Goerlitz unwilling, I probably won't get that second chance. Anyway, I'd like to keep a free hand, maybe work behind the scenes a little. In any case, I don't want to be benched by the Opposition."

Carol went to him and kissed his brow. "The way you put it, I'm sure you're right, Uncle Emmett."

"Who was it downstairs for you?"

"Willi von Goerlitz. He brought something. He didn't want to come up. He just asked me to give it to you." She handed the box to Earnshaw. "There's a note on top, under the rubber band, that Willi wrote you."

Earnshaw placed the stationery box on his lap, removed a small folded sheet, opened it, and found a brief handwritten note on the stationery of the Hotel Ritz.

Slowly, he read it aloud: " 'Dear Mr. Earnshaw, My father's attorneys impounded the manuscript of his memoirs from the agent. Their decision was that they must hold it until my father recovers, and if he does not recover from his aphasia within a year, they are duty-bound to publish the memoirs exactly as written. These gentlemen are my father's lawyers, but I am his son, and I know more of what my father is truly like than do they. I know that had my father been able to see what you have done for him and for our firm, and see the wonderful things you have done for the world, he would have revised his limited view of you and his judgment of your place in history. Therefore, on my father's behalf, I have found a means of unimpounding what has been impounded. I enclose in this box the original and the carbon, the only copies in existence of my father's chapter on you. I have removed them from his memoirs, and I deliver them to you. They do not reflect the true Emmett Earnshaw and so they do not deserve publication. Do with them what you wish. I send you my deepest thanks. I am proud to have known you. Perhaps, when I visit America next year, you will allow me to call upon you and your wonderful niece in California. Respectfully yours, Willi von Goerlitz.' "

Earnshaw dropped the note on the sofa, and he stared down at the box, deeply moved. He knew that his eyes were full, and he disliked his niece's seeing him this way.

Without raising his head, he said gruffly, "I wish that young fellow had allowed me to—to tell him how much I appreciate his freeing me to—to have a second chance."

"Oh, he's still down in the lobby, Uncle Emmett. I'll be glad to tell him what you said. He was hoping to take me out for a sandwich."

Earnshaw looked up. "Well, what in the devil are you hanging around for? Don't keep the young man waiting. There aren't many like him around these days." He stood up. "Now get along."

"I won't be late." And she ran for the door and rushed out.

He was glad to be alone. Now he was free to go into the bathroom, to tear each page of the chapter to shreds, and piece by piece, drop his past into the toilet bowl and flush it away forever.

It might take some time. But he possessed nothing but time, time and a reputation. He promised himself, and Isabel, he would use them well.

MEDORA HART.

She had been busy, crazily busy, the entire evening.

From the moment that she had received her re-entry permit by special messenger from the British Embassy, she had been in an ecstatic daze. Not until some time after she had ordered the concierge to book her on the first flight to London tomorrow had she remembered that she had promised to return to appear in the Club Lautrec show the next night. She had realized that she must get out of it.

She had hurried to see Alphonse Michaud backstage, and had explained that she could not go on. She had her freedom to return to her home, and she was determined to return tomorrow. Michaud, charming as ever, had gently reminded her of her contract. In France a contract was a contract. He could not release her, it would cost him too much. If she walked out, he would be forced to sue, and he would hate for her to receive such poor publicity at a time like this. Of course, if she wished to buy up her contract, that was another matter. She had been prepared for this. She had asked what he wanted for the contract. He had told her. She had considered it, and decided it was cheap. She had followed him to his penthouse office, and she had given him what he wanted. An hour later she'd had her release. So easy.

Back at the hotel, she had tried to contact Earnshaw to thank him for the permit, but had failed to reach him. Then she had telephoned her mother long-distance with the fantastic news of her liberation. Her mother had been pleased. It would be wonderful to have Medora home at last. Especially at this time, when her arthritis was acting up, when she needed a new doctor and a daughter's tender care, and someone to help watch over Medora's sister. Above all, she hoped that Medora had learned her lesson, and would concentrate on her beautician's course, and open a respectable shop, and find a nice neighborhood boy. Medora had hoped for skyrockets, and there had been only this.

Hanging up, she knew that this call, to which she had looked forward for three years, had been curiously dismaying.

Because it was growing late, she had turned her attention to emptying the chest of drawers and packing. She had dialed the wireless for music, and got the news instead, and understood why Earnshaw had not been in his rooms. But later, half packed, she had reached him by phone and thanked him profusely.

She had considered one more call before midnight. There had been five message slips today, the last one just before she came back from the Club, each asking her to please return the call, and each from Sydney Ormsby. She had thought about it and thought about it as the night wore on, and at last, on impulse, she had picked up the receiver, requested the Hotel Bristol, requested Mr. Sydney Ormsby—"Yes," she'd told the operator, "I'm quite sure he's awake, I am only returning *his* call"—and she had been put through.

And it was to Sydney Ormsby that she was speaking this minute.

"Well, I didn't answer your calls because, well, it hardly seemed appropriate after the way we ended our little reunion yesterday."

"Oh, that? Bosh, Medora. It was all temper on both sides. You forgive, I forgive, we both forget, what?"

"It's fine with me."

"Look here, Medora, I called for several reasons. First off, wanted to congratulate you on getting back to the old sod. I hear good Austin came right through."

"He did. I thought you'd be in a rage about that, Sydney."

"Not a bit, not at all. Quite the contrary. Deucedly clever of you and Brennan, that playlet. Quite justified. You know how I feel, Medora. My brother treated you shabbily. He deserved tit for tat. Besides, it was worth all the dressing down he gave me, just to see that blotched pink face of his after he heard the tape. It was magnificent of you, Medora."

"I'm afraid Brennan should get all the credit. And I'm so happy you're not angry."

"I'm pleased, I tell you. And Brennan. Remarkable chap. Have you heard what's gone on tonight? He's a bloody hero."

"Yes, I heard. I've had the wireless on for hours."

"Medora, one thing. Does Brennan really have that book?"

"Of course not."

"That's what I thought. . . . Uh, Medora, besides congratulations and all that, there's really another reason why I've been calling you. I mean, it's about your being back in London again. Changes things a bit. Rather exciting for you, I'd imagine."

825

"It—it might be."

"Any special plans?"

"Nothing special."

"After being away so long, I should think you'd want someone to squire you around."

"I might. Any suggestions?"

"I'd highly recommend a dashing and generous young chap with a good allowance and dishonorable intentions who goes by the name of Sydney Ormsby."

"Oh, I've heard of *him.*"

"What does that mean?"

"I'm not sure."

"Whatever you've heard, he's not half bad. You really should give the chap another go. . . . You know, Medora, everything I told you during the playlet—I meant it. I'm not the Nizam of Hyderabad exactly, but I'm prepared to lay London at your feet. West End flat. Bentley. Baubles. Gay times. You write your order. Medora, it's been wretched without you. I'd like us to be friends again."

"That's asking a lot."

"I'm not demanding a lot. It's simply that we do have something to offer each other. Could make life a bit more pleasant on both sides. Know what I mean? I mean, you like your comforts. I like mine. Fair bargain. Good contract. Maybe it can even be more."

"I—I don't know, Sydney."

"Come on, dear girl. As the Americans say, London can be dreadfully lonely on Sundays. Hate to see you spend the Seventh Day resting your feet because you've been on them all the other six days shop-girling it behind some plebeian counter for a few bloody pounds a week. Not for you, not at all. Look at it this way. I'm Moses. You're manna from heaven. We belong together."

"Silly. . . . But, well—putting it that way, it—well, it makes a little sense."

"Really, Medora? Oh, good. Simply marvelous. Then we can be friends again?"

"Maybe it's possible."

"When can I know for certain?"

"You might ring me up in a fortnight. Mum's number."

"Can't I call you sooner?"

"If you like."

"Can't wait! See you in London, honey."

"See you—in London."

M<small>ATTHEW</small> B<small>RENNAN</small>.

He lay back, contented, on the double bed, an island surrounded by his discarded pajama top, the newspaper extras strewn everywhere, the emptied bottle of champagne, the radio muted and the television set darkened at last.

He lay back drowsily, looking up at the ceiling and waiting for Lisa.

When she returned, she was naked. She stood beside the lamp, studying him thoughtfully.

He turned his head on the pillow and smiled. "I've always wanted to possess my own nude," he said.

"You own one now," she said.

"Lisa, what were you thinking just then?"

"How proud I am of you. How lucky I am."

"I'm the lucky one, darling."

"Matt, will we live in Washington?"

"Probably."

"I don't care where I live, as long as it's with you."

"It'll always be with me, darling. Always. Come to bed."

She turned off the light and settled down beside him.

"Matt, what were you thinking?"

"What's the first line of that book Melville wrote?"

" 'Call me Ishmael.' "

"Yes."

"Why did you ask?"

"Nothing."

But it was something, he knew. His long hunt, like Ahab's, had ended. He would have to learn to live again.

He took her soft body in his arms, and he kissed her hair, and eyes, and throat, and he felt her smooth stomach against his own, and thought of the life she would give him, give him who need no longer be ashamed of his name.

He held her close, and he listened to the sounds of distant music drifting up through the bedroom windows. It was a romantic French song, and it was beautiful and evocative of something poetic, a wisp of verse, Rimbaud, he had long cherished and dared not call his own. Until now.

To the music, he whispered the words:

> *Elle est retrouvée.*
> *Quoi? L'Éternité.*

He felt Lisa's lips move against his ear, sleepily wondering. Softly, he whispered:

> It is found again.
> What? Eternity.

In the far away, from the heart of Paris, a church bell was ringing, bidding adieu to the past.

A new day had begun.